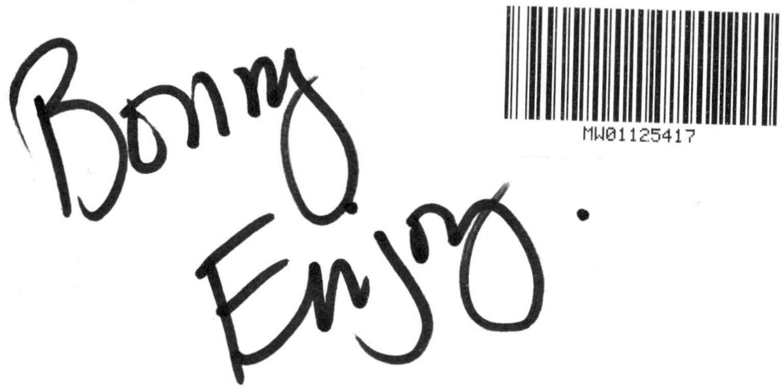

RISE OF THE DEFENDER

AN EPIC THREE-PART MEDIEVAL ROMANCE

BY KATHRYN LE VEQUE

Print Edition

Printed by Dragonblade Publishing in the United States of America

Library of Congress Control Number 2014-031
ISBN 1495340309

Kathryn Le Veque Novels

Medieval Romance:

The de Russe Legacy:
The White Lord of Wellesbourne
The Dark One: Dark Knight
Beast
Lord of War: Black Angel
The Falls of Erith

The de Lohr Dynasty:
While Angels Slept (Lords of East Anglia)
Rise of the Defender
Steelheart
Spectre of the Sword
Archangel
Unending Love
Shadowmoor
Silversword

Great Lords of le Bec:
Great Protector
To the Lady Born (House of de Royans)

Lords of Eire:
The Darkland (Master Knights of Connaught)
Black Sword
Echoes of Ancient Dreams (time travel)

De Wolfe Pack Series:
The Wolfe
Serpent
Scorpion (Saxon Lords of Hage – Also related to The Questing)
Walls of Babylon
The Lion of the North
Dark Destroyer

Ancient Kings of Anglecynn:
The Whispering Night
Netherworld

Battle Lords of de Velt:
The Dark Lord
Devil's Dominion

Reign of the House of de Winter:
Lespada
Swords and Shields (also related to The Questing, While Angels Slept)

De Reyne Domination:
Guardian of Darkness
The Fallen One (part of Dragonblade Series)

Unrelated characters or family groups:
The Gorgon (Also related to Lords of Thunder)
The Warrior Poet (St. John and de Gare)
Tender is the Knight (House of d'Vant)
Lord of Light
The Questing (related to The Dark Lord, Scorpion)
The Legend (House of Summerlin)

The Dragonblade Series: (Great Marcher Lords of de Lara)
Dragonblade
Island of Glass (House of St. Hever)
The Savage Curtain (Lords of Pembury)
The Fallen One (De Reyne Domination)
Fragments of Grace (House of St. Hever)
Lord of the Shadows
Queen of Lost Stars (House of St. Hever)

Lords of Thunder: The de Shera Brotherhood Trilogy
The Thunder Lord
The Thunder Warrior
The Thunder Knight

Time Travel Romance: (Saxon Lords of Hage)
The Crusader
Kingdom Come

Contemporary Romance:

Kathlyn Trent/Marcus Burton Series:
Valley of the Shadow
The Eden Factor
Canyon of the Sphinx

The American Heroes Series:
The Lucius Robe
Fires of Autumn
Evenshade
Sea of Dreams
Purgatory

Other Contemporary Romance:
Lady of Heaven
Darkling, I Listen

Multi-author Collections/Anthologies:
With Dreams Only of You (USA Today bestseller)
Sirens of the Northern Seas (Viking romance)
Ever My Love (sequel to With Dreams Only Of You) July 2016

Note: All Kathryn's novels are designed to be read as stand-alones, although many have cross-over characters or cross-over family groups. Novels that are grouped together have related characters or family groups.

Series are clearly marked. All series contain the same characters or family groups except the American Heroes Series, which is an anthology with unrelated characters.

There is NO particular chronological order for any of the novels because they can all be read as stand-alones, even the series.

For more information, find it in **A Reader's Guide to the Medieval World of Le Veque**.

A Bloody Medieval Soap Opera!

That's what the author thought after she read this novel recently after having not read it in many years. Along the lines of The Dark One: Dark Knight, Rise of the Defender is another million-page epic that narrates the adventures and trials of Christopher de Lohr and his wife, Lady Dustin. It was written a very long time ago when the author believed that bigger – and longer – was better. The same agent who told her to cut down The Dark One: Dark Knight told her to cut this one down as well, but she refused. Now, it is presented to you in its full glory.

It's not only epic, it's mega-epic. It's not only an adventure; it's a bloody soap opera of love, loss, deceit, betrayal, infidelity, politics, passion, and crime. This is "Game of Thrones" drama before there ever was such a thing. Although edited for some content and grammar, the author refrained from any serious re-writing, instead choosing to present it as it was originally written. It is a truly emotional story, the good and the bad of it, that is different from anything you have ever read. You are going to yell at it, laugh, cheer, cry and applaud. It's drama from start to finish.

More to note – you will see several characters you already recognize from other Le Veque novels, most notably, the character of Marcus Burton. Marcus alternates between good and evil in this novel and is an extremely strong presence. However, he is not the "hero" of the novel, but the author liked him so much that she brought him into modern times and made him the hero of the Kathlyn Trent/Marcus Burton action-adventure series. Finally, Marcus was able to shine.

With all of that said, settle in for a good, **long** read (three times the size of a normal four hundred page novel); brought to you in three parts.

Presenting…

RISE OF THE DEFENDER

Part 1: The Lion's Claw

Part 2: Birth of the Legend

Part 3: Long Live the King

TABLE OF CONTENTS

RISE OF THE DEFENDER

THE LION'S CLAW

PART 1

PROLOGUE

Year of Our Lord 1192
The twelfth day of the month of July
Outside of Jerusalem

WAR WAS A terrible thing.

So much death, destruction, and misery; all for a bloody bit of sand in the middle of hell. Yet, 'twas the Holy Land he was thinking such vile thoughts of. God was particularly fond of this strip of hell, this bit of golden grit he had spent three years of his life quarreling over.

Sir Christopher de Lohr stood upon the battlements of the city of Acre, gazing at the carnage below. He shifted his weight on his thick legs, from one to the other, sweating rivers underneath his plate armor. It was always so goddamn hot here and he missed the cold winters of England like a stab to his heart. Thank God that he was finally going home, and going home a new baron, no less. At least there had been some reward to all of this madness.

The siege to the city of Acre had finally come full circle. Today, July the twelfth, Saladin had surrendered the city and her garrisons. Christopher had been beside Richard when Saladin turned over his sword and never had he been more proud of the glory that was England. Years of vicious fighting had finally come to a complete end, and at this very moment the surrender terms were being drawn up and the Muslim rebels were discovering their place in the grand scheme of Christianity.

Yet Richard had had a tough time of it, a fact that didn't surprise Christopher. Although he dearly loved his king, the man was getting old for this kind of thing, even if he was only thirty-five. In fact, several of Richard's knights were older men and far too ancient for this sort of mess when they should have left the fighting to younger knights, stronger knights. But it was the order of the knights that truly bore the spirit of God, muttering that the younger knights were more interested in the booty to be secured than the glory of Christendom.

Which was probably true. Christopher didn't particularly care anymore. True, he had spent a good deal of those first two years collecting anything of value and sending it home via caravans to trusted servants, but his heart wasn't in looting anymore. He simply wanted to go home, and at nearly the very moment Acre was secured Richard granted him his deepest wish.

With Richard indisposed at the moment, Christopher had command of the camp. At his age, some considered him old. He was worth his considerable weight in gold, and Richard had become extremely dependent upon him, his brother, and their tight group of knights. His uncle, Sir Philip de Lohr, was one of Richard's closest advisors and had been with Richard from the inception of the quest. The House of de Lohr was a strong ally of the king.

Richard was known as Lionheart for his fierceness and bravery, yet it was Christopher who actually resembled a lion with his golden mane and massive frame. And the fact that he was Richard's fiercest and most powerful knight had earned him the nickname among ally and foe alike of Lion's Claw because even a lion, or lion heart as it were, was only as powerful as its claws.

Christopher was a well-known sight to his men as well as his enemy. He was exceedingly tall with a glorious crown of golden-blond hair. His body was perfectly formed from the endless hours of fighting and strenuous work, and his strength was unequaled. His face was ruggedly beautiful, his eyes were the deepest sky-blue under a heavy brow, and his jaw was hard and square as granite. But his smile was his most outstanding feature; it was bright and distinctive, and showed nearly every perfect tooth in his head, but it was a rare sight indeed.

He was golden brown from three years under the harsh Middle-Eastern sun, an incredible golden glow that most of the knights had because in this hot climate, they took off their armor and protective clothing at every turn. Christopher in particular would go for days half-naked until called to battle once again. Richard often teased him about forgoing the armor and simply fighting nude, the enemy would think they were up against a Roman statue come-to-life. As superstitious as they were, they'd turn tail and run.

He knew he was damn good on the battlefield, in fact, there were few who could keep up with him. He was, in a manner of speaking, the most arrogant man on the quest and didn't consider his pride a sin, as God did. Had God not meant for him to be so prideful, he would not have made him so perfect.

"Chris!"

A shout roused him from his thoughts. He turned to see his brother, David, and another knight, Edward de Wolfe, jogging towards him. They were both sweating profusely. David was three years younger, several inches shorter, but broad and muscular. His short blond hair was standing straight up with perspiration as his sea-blue eyes sought out his brother.

"Richard has summoned you," he said breathlessly as he came to a halt.

"Why? What's wrong?" Christopher asked.

Edward's dark-gold eyes were serious. " 'Tis old Baron Barringdon, Chris," he replied. "He is dying from that wound to his chest."

Christopher let out a hiss. "Damn," he muttered. Barringdon was one of the most intelligent men in their army, a distant cousin of Richard's. But he was very old, at least 12 years older than Christopher. He was too old to fight and should have never come, but he did for Richard's sake. And Richard, who should now be seeing to terms of surrender, was distracted with a dying cousin.

"And another thing," Edward said in a low voice, "Duke Leopold is demanding that his banners be unfurled when we ride into the city. Richard is in a mood because of it, so take heed and do not mention the duke in Richard's presence."

Christopher grunted in disapproval. "Leopold lost many men when he made his initial attempt to take the garrison but retreated like the coward he is, so in that respect I do not blame Richard in the least," he said, securing his sword. "The man wishes to share in glory that he does not deserve. Well, who's tending to the treaty, then?"

"Philip Augustus and Lusignan," David replied. "The French have their hands all over the vellum, hoping to inject then own wording and stipulations and leave the English out of it."

Christopher raised an intolerant eyebrow at the suggestion, when they all knew it was Richard that brought the city to its knees. "Take the watch for me, then," he said, forcing aside his frustrating thoughts of the politics of the conquest. "Richard and Arthur await."

Leaving his men on watch, Christopher made his way across the burning sand to a large, leaning tent that he knew to be Barringdon's. When he passed through the tent flap, it was like a steambath inside, and smelled rotten and moldy. He controlled his urge to rip off every stitch of clothing as he moved toward the men huddled by the worn and collapsible cot. Richard's weathered face was the first to look up.

King Richard the Lionheart, King of England, looked older than his years. His features were weathered, the dark eyes weary. There was such sorrow on his face, as if the weight of the world had somehow come down to this one man who lay dying on the cot. His human side was seeping through.

"Come here, Chris," he said hoarsely, extending a hand. "Arthur, Christopher has come. Here he is."

Christopher let the king guide him next to the cot where he had to kneel in his heavy armor. Sir Arthur Barringdon lay sweating atop the linens, the wound to the middle-left portion of his chest seeping through the linen bandages. The wound stank something fierce and Christopher resisted the urge to back away.

"Chris?" Arthur's voice was scratchy and faint.

"Here, my lord, next to you," Christopher replied softly.

Arthur coughed violently before turning his head and opening his eyes. His gray eyes focused and he smiled faintly.

"My friend," he murmured, "The greatest warrior in all of England. And you are going home, lad?"

"Aye," Christopher smiled back, taking the old man's offered hand.

"Do you remember I told you of my daughter and my wife?" the baron rambled on.

"Aye, I do," Christopher replied knowingly. "Your wife is Mary, and your daughter is, uh…"

"Dustin," Arthur supplied, "Dustin Mary Catherine. She is nineteen years old now."

"Of course, Dustin, how could I forget?" Christopher chided himself on his forgetfulness. "Nineteen, did you say? She is a woman grown."

"Aye, she is," Arthur coughed again, bringing up blood. "But I will never see her again, Christopher, and I must beg you a favor from the heart of a dying man."

His voice was urgent and Christopher hated to see him like this. Arthur had been a good friend.

"Anything, my lord, simply ask it," he replied soothingly. "I am your loyal vassal."

Arthur's eyes sought out his king, standing over Christopher's shoulder. Christopher should have been suspicious when the king began to bring forth Arthur's request, but it didn't occur to him to be wary. It was his undoing. When the king began to speak, Christopher's guard was down completely.

"Christopher, Arthur is greatly concerned for his daughter's future," Richard said softly. "Since Arthur has been here, with me, for over three years, he has not had the chance to make provisions for Dustin."

"Provisions, my lord?" Christopher turned to look at his king.

"Aye," Richard scratched at his faded red beard. "Dustin is his only child and stands to inherit the baron's fortress, Lioncross Abbey. She is an heiress, lad, and a wealthy one."

Christopher nodded intently. "He wishes for me to find her a husband upon my return," he stated, knowing the request or so he thought. "I will be happy to."

Richard paused a moment, cocking a harsh brow. "Nay, lad," he said slowly. "He wishes for you to *be* her husband upon your return."

Christopher could not help it; his face went slack with shock. "He… he wishes for me to…?"

Arthur grabbed his sleeve. " 'Tis not as bad as it sounds, lad," he said hoarsely. "I simply want to make sure my womenfolk are well-protected, and you are certainly the most capable man I know. I am only asking that you marry my daughter and give her children. The wealth, the fortress, is your reward for the duty."

"You mean my bribe," Christopher snapped, struggling to remain calm. He put his hand over Arthur's, trying to control his outrage. "My lord, when I return home, it will be to Lohrham Forest. I have amassed quite a fortune of my own and…"

Arthur cut him off. "Lioncross has more," he insisted weakly. "Lad, I am not asking that you love my daughter or that you even live with her. I am simply asking that you put my dying mind at ease by consenting to marry her. I know you shall be a fair and considerate husband, and I will go to my grave knowing that Dustin will be well taken care of."

Christopher didn't want to be married. Ever. But Arthur was all but begging him to do it, and he would be lying if he didn't admit the thought of being lord over Lioncross Abbey Castle wasn't appealing. Much bigger and better than Lohrham Forest, his ancestral home. Hell, he wouldn't even inherit Lohrham. It belonged to his uncle and would pass to his cousin, Edward. Even though the boy was twelve years old, it would still be his.

Richard read his hesitation, but what Arthur was offering was quite satisfactory. He pulled Christopher to his feet and took him aside.

"Think on it, Chris," he said quietly. "Lioncross Abbey Castle is quite a prize and it would make Arthur happy to know his family was taken care of. Hell, marry the girl, get her pregnant, and you never have to see her again. Spend your time and your money in London with the whores if you want; I care not. But Lioncross also collects border revenues from Wales and she carries a force of eight hundred men, half of which are here."

Richard's eyebrows lifted encouragingly but Christopher simply stared back indecisively. He didn't want to marry anyone, for any amount of money. His resistance was evident, growing heavier by the moment, and Richard took a hard line. With Christopher, he had to or the man would bowl him right over, king or no.

"I could order it," Richard said after a moment. Even though his tone was steady and even, the statement was ridiculous. It already was an order.

Christopher knew his fate was sealed. It never had been his choice after all; Richard had decided this long ago. Christopher was angry but powerless just the same, seeing an unexpected twist in his future that was unwelcome and frustrating. But it was done, and no amount of arguing would change it. He sighed heavily, looking away from his king so the man would not see his fury.

"You do not have to, my lord," Christopher replied calmly. "I understand."

Richard smiled with satisfaction. "That's fine," he said. "I knew you'd agree."

Christopher rolled his eyes, looking decidedly unhappy, and allowed Richard to lead him back over to the dying baron. Christopher would have liked nothing better than to strangle the old man for suggesting such a thing.

"Arthur," Richard said proudly. "Greet your new son-in-law."

Arthur smiled weakly. He was growing fainter by the moment and Richard was already moving to have his steward draw up the papers.

"Chris," Arthur's voice was no more than a whisper as he extended his hand.

In spite of his anger, Christopher leaned forward and took his fingers once again. He tried not to look as disappointed as he felt.

"I am here, Arthur," he muttered.

The old man was having difficulty breathing. "Dustin is a good girl," he rasped. "She's willful and stubborn, but she's a good girl. Handle her gently. I am afraid that with your quick temper and her quick temper, you will kill each other before the sun sets on your wedding day."

Christopher nodded solemnly but inside he was ranting like a madman. *Stubborn and willful? Quick tempered?* Christ, what kind of shrew was he to be saddled with?

"I will be fair," he assured the dying man.

Arthur's eyes closed, perhaps for the last time now that he knew his daughter would be taken care of. He squeezed Christopher's hand feebly.

"Thank you," he whispered. "You have my deepest… gratitude…."

He faded off and Christopher gazed down at the man, feeling the tug of sorrow over his anger with the forced marriage. He was greatly torn. As he let go of the man's hand, gently, Richard led him away from the cot.

The king walked him to the tent flap. Richard knew exactly what the knight was feeling, but that was of no consequence. He would thank him one day. At least he hoped so. Richard clasped his hands behind his back, facing off against his mightiest warrior.

"Consider Lioncross Abbey Castle and her wealth a gift from the crown to a most deserving knight," he said. "You have served me well, Christopher, and I will not forget it. In fact, I will seek you later, as we have much to discuss concerning my brother, John. Go now. Prepare for your leave."

Christopher bowed deeply and spun on his heel, his mind becoming one angry, muddy bog of thoughts. *A wife.* The word was sand on his tongue, yet he had no choice. Such a bitter way to receive rewards for his years of service. He was coming to wonder if he was somehow being punished instead. He had to go and clear his thoughts; otherwise, he might go against all that he had worked for and, deep down, he knew he could not. He had been ordered to marry, and marry he would.

Later that evening as Arthur Barringdon was prepared for a Christian burial, Christopher, Philip, and King Richard sat in the king's tent around a small war table. Richard had vellum and ink before him, preferring to write his own private missives rather that have his steward do it – especially this missive.

Christopher was grim, his trencher-sized hands folded patiently as Richard scratched away with the quill. Philip, distinguished and fair like his nephew, sat casually opposite his king, pondering the world beyond the tent flap. Not a particularly personable man, but he was brilliant and was Richard's greatest confidante. Finally, Richard seemed to finish his message and he put the quill down, sanding the ink to dry it.

"I apologize for making you sit through this, Chris," he said after a moment. "But I had to put my commands in writing before I spoke to you of them." He looked up at Christopher then, his brown eyes glittering dully in the dim tent. "This is to my brother, John. I have been in the Holy Land a great many years and am well aware of my brother's ambitions for my throne, and I have had enough of the weasel. Christopher, I have bequeathed you a new title this night. From here on you shall be known as Defender of the Realm for my entire empire. My troops, the crown's troops, shall be yours in my absence. The justices will still be the ruling body, but 'twill be you who controls the military might. As loyal as my justices are, 'tis never good to give any one group too much power, especially with my brother panting for my throne. They may not be particularly happy to give up the army, but I must make sure the troops are in experienced and loyal hands. I would hate to return home to find my own army fighting me on the shore."

Christopher was shocked but he didn't show it. He nodded slowly, "As you command, my lord."

Richard knew Christopher well enough to know he had not been expecting the directive. "Lioncross will serve as a fine seat for you, close enough to London to keep an eye on John, yet fairly central to the rest of the country," the king continued. "Read this missive and it will explain everything. Ask me questions when you are finished, should you have any."

Christopher rose and read the missive as it lay on the table, his sky blue eyes studying it intently. After several minutes, he returned to his seat, his face impassive.

Richard watched him expectantly. "Well?"

Christopher, deep in thought, shrugged "You are, in effect, dividing the rule of England three ways, with John, your justices, and me."

"In effect," Richard agreed. "Yet you have no direct powers, other than those over the armed forces. John still continues with his princely powers, and my justices continue to be the ruling body."

"Your brother's limited powers will have decreased substantially." Christopher rubbed his chin, his gaze flicking to Richard. "John will not be pleased in the least."

"That is his misfortune," Richard said sharply, running his hands over his face in a frustrated gesture. "But take heed, de Lohr. John is a wily, cunning, evil little bastard, and you must watch your back at all times. He will not hesitate to take out any threat to his dictator rule, and he has loyalists everywhere. You must beware. My chancellor, William Longchamp, has had a hell of a time with him."

Christopher nodded to what he already knew. "Indeed, my lord."

Richard watched his champion's strong face a moment, confident he had made a sound decision. Christopher was the best of the best, a man with impeccable skills and tactics. He was also the best and strongest barrier between John and the throne of England.

"Christopher," he said in a low voice, "My throne is in jeopardy. In fact, my whole country is bordering on anarchy and disorder. Yet, 'tis my belief that God wants me here in the *Levant* to purge the verminous heathens; therefore, I must trust Him to select people to help me govern England. You are one of the chosen I must, nay, *will* depend on until I return. With Acre captured, my work here is nearly finished and it shan't be long until my soles tread the heady English grass once again. Until that time, I need you."

Christopher gazed back at the king, his friend and liege, feeling the concern and desperation borne of absence. He knew that he was being given an awesome responsibility, a responsibility he took with the utmost importance.

"I shall not fail, my lord, I swear it," he promised with sincerity.

"I know." Richard was suddenly very tired. His years were catching up with him this night. "Yet there is one thing you have not mentioned. I am in essence making you my spy to John's court, and as much as you loathe that duty, yet it is necessary. I must have your eyes and ears. My justices have their hands full simply running my country, which is why I do not expect them to take the time to spy on my brother. I must know vital information if you feel the situation warrants it, and in this I trust your decisions implicitly."

"Situations, my lord? Like what?" Christopher asked.

Richard toyed with his worn chair. "If it appears imminent that John intends to overthrow me," he said. "He will, you know. The only reason he hasn't yet is because the church loves me and is proud of my work here. Yet that will fade, too, in time. And the general populace is an ungrateful, forgetful lot. John will wait for the right moment, and you must be there in my stead to prevent it."

Christopher let out a sigh, the only real show of emotion the entire night. "You ask a great deal, my lord. If the people side with John, it could be a bitter civil war."

"I realize that," Richard said, "Which is why I intend to return before that happens. Yet I need forewarning, and your hand on the pulse of the country."

"You are asking me to anticipate the whim of the ignorant," Christopher returned softly. "I can only tell you that I shall do my best."

" 'Tis all I ask." Richard's voice was dull with fatigue.

Philip cleared his throat, having absorbed the entire exchange of thought. "If anyone can do it, Christopher can, my lord," he said to Richard. "You have made an excellent choice, yet I must admit that I am concerned for his safety. You said yourself John has many loyalists who could strike unexpectedly. And Christopher's brother, David, is in danger as well."

"David and I can take care of ourselves." Christopher glanced at his uncle. "I can assure you that we will be quite safe."

"Beware all the same, Chris," Richard said, rising slowly and stiffly. "Marcus Burton left yesterday for home, under direct orders from me to search out those nobles loyal to the crown and report to you. Expect him and use well the information."

"Aye, my lord." Christopher and Marcus were part of the same group of knights that Richard favored, and were the best of friends. He was as confident in the man's abilities as he was in his own.

Richard sighed and pulled off his mail hood, tossing it to the floor. "Go, now," he said. "I would see you off in the morning."

Christopher and Philip rose and left the tent obediently. They walked together for several minutes in the waning afternoon heat before Philip spoke.

" 'Tis an awesome responsibility you hold, Chris," Philip said softly. "As great as any."

Christopher gazed into the golden sands, wondering if he would ever miss any of it. He didn't think so. "It has been three years since I have been home," he said. "I truly wonder what I will find upon my return."

Philip stopped, as did Christopher, the two men studying each other under the brilliant blue sky. Finally, Philip clapped his nephew on the shoulder.

"God be with you, Chris, and with David," he said. "I shall miss you both, and I shall pray for you."

He left him with that, and Christopher watched him trudge off across the sand. He often saw his father in Philip's actions and movements, remembering Myles de Lohr in faded memories. He wondered what his father would have thought about all of this, of his sons and the directives straight into the heart of England's politics. It was a deadly game they all played. All thoughts of his forced marriage aside, the real issue was John Lackland.

"Pray for the prince, Uncle," he mumbled. "When I return, he will need all of your prayers."

CHAPTER ONE

Year of Our Lord 1192
The Month of September
Lioncross Abbey Castle
The Welsh Marches

LADY DUSTIN BARRINGDON bit at her full lower lip in concentration. Climbing trees were no easy feat, but climbing trees in a skirt was near impossible.

Her target was the nest of baby birds high in the old oak tree. Her cat, Caesar, had killed the mama bird earlier that day and now Dustin was determined to take the babies back to Lioncross and raise them. Her mother, of course, thought she was mad, but she still had to try. After all, if she hadn't spoiled and pampered Caesar then this might never have happened. Caesar had no discipline whatsoever.

She pushed her blond hair back out of her way for the tenth time; her hands kept snagging on it as she clutched the branch. But as soon as she pushed it away, it was back again and hanging all over her. She usually loved her buttock-length hair, reveled in it, but not today. Long and thick and straight, it glistened and shimmered like a banner of gold silk.

Her big, almond-shaped eyes watched the nest intently. But not just any eyes, they were of the most amazing shade of gray, like sunlight behind storm clouds. Surrounded by thick dark-blond lashes, they were stunning. With her full rosy lips set in a heart-shaped face, she was an incredible beauty.

Not that Dustin had any shortage of suitors. The list was long of the young men waiting for a chance to speak with her father upon his return. She truly didn't care one way or the other; men were a nuisance and a bore and she got along very well without them. Nothing was worse than a starry-eyed suitor who mooned over her like a lovesick pup. She had punched many idiots right in the eye in answer to a wink or a suggestive look.

"Can you reach it yet?" Her friend, Rebecca, stood at the base of the tree, apprehensively watching.

"Not yet," Dustin called back, irritated at the distraction. "Almost."

Just another couple of feet and she would have it. Carefully, carefully, she crept along the branch, hoping it wouldn't give way.

"Dustin?" Rebecca called urgently.

Dustin paused in her quest. "What now?"

"Riders," Rebecca said with some panic, "coming this way."

Dustin lay down on the branch, straining to see the object of her friend's fear. Indeed, up on the rise of the road that led directly under the tree she was on, were incoming riders. A lot of them, from what she could see.

Her puzzlement grew. Who would be coming to Lioncross this time of day, this lazy afternoon in a long succession of lazy afternoons? The riders passed through a bank of trees and she could see them better.

She began to catch some of her friend's fear. There were soldiers, hundreds of them.

"Rebecca," she hissed. "Climb the tree. Hurry up."

With a shriek, Rebecca clumsily climbed onto the trunk and began slowly making her way up.

"Who are they?" she gasped.

Dustin shook her head. "I do not know," she replied. "The only time I have ever seen that many soldiers was when my father…." She suddenly sat up on the branch. "My *father!* Rebecca, climb down!"

Rebecca didn't share Dustin's excitement. "Why?" she exclaimed.

Dustin was already scooting back down, crashing into her friend. "It is my father, you ninny. He has returned!"

Rebecca, reluctantly, began to back down the scratchy oak branch. "How do you know that? Are they flying a banner?"

Dustin hadn't even looked. She didn't have to. "Who else would it be?" She was so excited she was beginning to shake.

The army was quickly approaching the ladies' position. Thunder filled the air, blotting out everything else. Now, they were upon them. Rebecca was down from the tree but Dustin was still descending.

Dust from the road swirled about as several large destriers kicked up grit with their massive hooves. They had come up amazingly fast and Dustin found herself paying more attention to the chargers than to what she was doing. As the knights reined their animals to a halt several feet from Rebecca's terrified form, Dustin tried to get a better look at them.

She was trying very hard to single out her father but her distraction cost her as she lost her grip on the branch. With a scream, she plummeted from the tree about ten feet overhead and landed heavily on her right side.

Rebecca gasped and dropped to Dustin's aid. "Dustin! My God, are you all right?"

Dustin rolled to her back, now oblivious to the knights and men who were watching her. All she knew was that she could not catch her breath and her chest was so hot it would soon explode. As Rebecca tried to get a look at her, one of the knights dismounted his steed and knelt beside her.

"Breathe easy," came a deep, soothing voice. "Where do you hurt?"

Dustin could not talk. She could only manage to lay there and gasp for air. The knight removed his gauntlets and flipped up the faceplate on his helmet.

"Take deep breaths," he told her, putting his plate-sized hand on her abdomen, just below her ribs. "Slowly, slowly. Come now, slow down. That's right."

As Dustin's shock wore off, tears of pain and shock began to roll down her temples and, for the first time, she opened her eyes and focused on the man with the kind voice. She was shocked to see how big and frightening he was. He gazed back at her impassively.

"Are you hurt?" he asked.

She shook her head unsteadily. "I do not think so," she choked out. "I can breathe a little better."

He silently extended a hand, carefully pulling her up to sit. The first thing Dustin noticed was how big his hands were as they closed around her own.

The knight continued to crouch next to her, his gaze still unreadable. Shaking the leaves out of her hair, Dustin gave him the once over.

"Who are you?" she demanded softly. "Where is my father?"

"Who is your father?" he returned, ignoring her first question.

Dustin had a bad habit of speaking first and thinking later. If these men were her father's vassals, then they would have known her on sight.

"Why, Lord Barringdon, of course," she said, grabbing the ends of her hair and shaking them hard. "Where is he?"

For the first time the man showed emotion. His sky-blue eyes widened for a brief second and he abruptly stood up. She tried to look up at him, but he was so tall she had to lay her head back completely and she could not do that because her head was killing her. So she cocked her head at an odd angle, still looking up at him, as she struggled to her feet.

The man didn't help her rise, although he probably should have. He just kept staring at her.

"Lady Dustin Barringdon, I presume?" he asked after a moment.

His voice sounded queer. Dustin managed to stand on her own, putting out a hand to steady herself as the earth beneath her rocked. The knight reached out to balance her.

"Aye," she replied, pulling her hand away cautiously and taking a step toward Rebecca, who clutched at her. She eyed the man warily. "Who are you?"

She had no idea why the man's eyes were twinkling. His face held no expression, but she swore his eyes were twinkling.

"I am a friend of you father's," he said. "My name is Christopher de Lohr."

"Where is my father?" Dustin demanded yet again, excited to hear this man was a friend.

The knight hesitated. "Is your mother home, my lady?" he asked. "I bring messages for her."

Dustin's excitement took a turn for the worse. She had asked the same question three times without an answer. She was coming to suspect why and her stomach lurched with anguish. *God, no!*

"*Where* is my father?"

"I will discuss that with your mother."

Dustin stared at him a long, long time. He gazed back at her, studying every inch of that beautiful, sensuous face. The gray orbs that met his blue eyes suddenly went dark and stormy. She closed her eyes and turned away from him, beginning to walk back down the road. Rebecca, puzzled, yet not wanting to be left alone with a company of soldiers, ran after her.

Christopher watched her go, knowing she must suspect at least part of the reason why he had come. When he began to hear soft sobs, fading as she continued down the road, he knew that her fears were confirmed. She knew her father was dead.

He turned to his brother. "Get the men moving," he said, mounting his destrier, but his eyes were still on the lady.

Christ, but he was still reeling with surprise and pleasure at the discovery of Lady Dustin. She was beautiful. Damnation, he hadn't known what to expect. The entire trip home had been filled with dread and foreboding, but he could see his worries were for naught. Even if she were as stupid as a tree and as disagreeable as a mule, she was still beautiful. If he had to marry, she might as well be pleasant to look at. Any other qualities were superfluous.

Slowly, the army followed several paces behind her. Dustin had never known grief before and discovered it to be the most painful thing she had ever experienced. The knight wouldn't tell her where her father was and that in and of itself was confirmation of the worst. She wasn't a fool. Sorrow overwhelmed her and she suddenly could not breathe again. Her sobs grew into raspy puffs of air and the ground began to sway again. Dustin was aware of a blissful, floating feeling as a strange blackness swallowed her up.

Christopher saw her go down on the side of the road and he spurred his destrier forward. The animal came to a halt in a cloud of dust and he dismounted, pulling Lady Dustin's hysterical friend away from the crumpled form in the grass.

"What's the matter with her?" her friend cried. "She's dying. The fall will kill her!"

Christopher knelt down, noting the even breathing, steady pulse, but pale color. Mayhap the fall did contribute to this. He suddenly felt strangely protective, knowing that the woman was to be his wife. Wasn't it right for a husband to feel protective? It was the most peculiar sensation he'd ever experienced.

"What's your name, lass?" he asked the panting redhead.

"Rebecca," she replied, "Rebecca Comlynn."

Christopher nodded, turning back to the woman in the grass. "You will take us back to Lioncross, Mistress Rebecca. I will take care of Lady Dustin."

Rebecca started to protest but David grabbed her and seated her on his destrier before she could put up a fight. Christopher scooped up Dustin and managed to mount his own steed with surprising ease. She was light, this one, and small, too. Standing her full height she barely met his chest. She was little more than a child in his arms.

He stole a glance at her as he gathered his reins. Her lips moistly parted, she looked to be sleeping in his arms. Her hair, so incredibly long and silken, hung all over them both and he had to pull it free from the joints in his armor a couple of times. He could feel lust warming his veins. Spurring his great warhorse, they proceeded on to Lioncross Abbey.

Lioncross Abbey was so named because it was built on the sight of an ancient Roman house of worship and actually incorporated portions of two walls and part of the foundation. Additionally, Arthur Barringdon had christened it Lioncross after Richard and the quest. Prior to Arthur inheriting the keep from his father, it had been named Barringdon Abbey. Some older people in the region still referred to it as such.

The fortress sat atop a ridge overlooking a large lake and the deep purple mountains that marked the Welsh border could be seen in the distance. Thick banks of trees surrounded the fortress and made the region appear lush and fertile, even in the dead of winter.

Christopher took a good look at what was to be his new home, verily pleased. It was a fine fortress, easy to defend, with a small village about a half mile to the north. He found himself growing more and more satisfied with each passing step of his horse. Aye, he was worthy to be lord of this. He already found himself making mental notes about the structure, what needed improvement and reminding himself to ask questions about the revenues. As fine a warrior as he was, he was an equally fine scholar and knew what it would take to make Lioncross a profitable keep.

Dustin stirred in his arms and he was reminded of his burden. He looked down at her just in time to see her lids opening, slowly, as if a curtain rising. Again, he was entranced with the bright gray eyes and noted the thick lashes as she blinked. She was staring up at the sky as if trying to remember where in the world she was when her gaze fell on him. She blinked once, focused on his pale blue eyes, and then sat up so fast he had to throw his arm down on her to keep her from pitching herself right off of his horse.

"Put me down!" she hollered.

"Steady, my lady," he said. "We're almost back to your keep."

Her head snapped to the horizon where Lioncross indeed loomed. She began to struggle against him and he could not understand her panic, but he relented and let her slide to the ground.

She took off like a rabbit, her skirts up around her thighs as she pounded down the road. That incredible mane of hair waved behind her like a banner. Rebecca, not to be left behind, jumped from David's destrier and ran after her.

David reined his steed alongside his brother's, both of them watching the racing figures. "Now, what do you suppose that is all about?" David wondered aloud.

Christopher shook his head. "I have no idea," he replied, then grinned at his brother. "What think you of my new keep?"

David nodded his approval. "Exceptional. As is your new bride."

Christopher cocked a blond eyebrow. "I am surprised as well," he admitted. "Lady Dustin Barringdon looks nothing as I imagined."

"With a name like Dustin, I had no idea what to think," David snorted.

"Nor did I, little brother," Christopher agreed.

They entered the outskirts of the little village, passing an interested eye over the small buildings and tradesman's shacks. It smelled like sewage and livestock, and bits of dust kicked up in the occasional breeze. The road leading to Lioncross was a wide one and peasants scattered to stay clear of the approaching army. Christopher's horse accidentally crushed a chicken and sent a woman wailing, much to his displeasure.

Finally, the jewel of Lioncross loomed before them. The gates of the fortress yawned open before them and he halted the caravan with a raised arm.

"This will cease," he indicated the open gates. "With Wales so close, these people are fools to leave themselves vulnerable."

Beckoning David forward with him, he left the rest of his troops outside the gates. There was one bailey to Lioncross, a huge open thing used for a myriad of purposes. He studied it intently, already noting what needed changing, as he and David rode for the massive double doors of the entry.

Sentries met them at the base of the front steps. Christopher announced himself and his purpose, and waited while one of the guards disappeared inside. He reappeared several minutes later followed by another man dressed in mail and portions of plate armor.

The knight studied Christopher with piercing dark eyes. He was not particularly tall, but Christopher could see the muscles on the man. He was a seasoned warrior. His face was severely angled with a sharp nose and a sharp mouth. Immediately, he sensed hostility.

"What is your business here?" the man demanded in a strong Germanic accent.

"I am Sir Christopher de Lohr," he repeated, matching the man's tone. "I bear a message for Lady Mary Barringdon from King Richard."

The man looked Christopher up and down, taking a step toward him. "Give it to me and I will see that it is delivered."

"I have been instructed by our king to deliver it personally," Christopher said evenly. "I would deliver it now."

The man didn't say anything but continued to glare until Christopher finally had enough of his animosity. Dismounting without permission, he removed two scrolls of parchment from his saddlebags and walked deliberately to the soldier, holding out one of the missives for him to see.

"Richard's seal," he stated in case the soldier was blind. "Twould be unwise of you to go against our king. Now move aside or escort me in; 'tis all the same to me."

The soldier stared at the seal, knowing it for what it was. He tore his eyes away and looked at Christopher again, but this time, with less hostility.

"You scared the devil out of Lady Dustin," he said in a low voice. "For that I should gut you right now, but because you bear the missives from our king, you shall be spared."

Christopher almost laughed. David, in fact, did, drawing the soldier's angry glare. The battle lines were already being drawn.

"What is your name?" Christopher demanded of the warrior.

"Sir Jeffrey Kessler," he replied. "I am captain of Lioncross while Lord Barringdon is away."

Arthur had made no mention of a captain but it was of no matter. Christopher would dismiss the man as soon as he wed the fair Lady Dustin and put David in charge of the men.

"Gain us entrance, Sir Jeffrey," Christopher requested, but it sounded suspiciously like an order.

Jeffrey's gaze lingered on Christopher before complying, just long enough to emphasize he could not be ordered around by a stranger. Christopher followed, somewhat hesitantly, wondering if he shouldn't bring a contingent of men to protect him against any trickery from the Germanic knight.

He kept his hand on the hilt of his sword just in case as he followed the man into the dark and musty keep beyond.

☙

DUSTIN STOOD IN her mother's drawing room, pacing endlessly by the oilcloth-covered windows. Lady Mary, unflappable as always, continued to calmly work on a piece of needlework, ignoring her daughter's sighs and grunts of worry.

"Why don't you change your dress, dear?" her mother said calmly. "We have visitors."

Dustin glanced down at her surcoat. It wasn't even really a surcoat, it was just a dress made from faded brown linen, and a darker brown girdle that would have emphasized the magnificence of her breasts had the white linen blouse not been so over-sized. Dustin never gave any thought to her clothes, mostly concerned with the other aspects of her busy life. As long as they were clean and functional, it was all that mattered.

"Why?" she asked, rather clueless.

Her mother put the sewing down. "Because you look like a peasant waif," she said patiently. "Look at your slippers, they are dirty, as are your hose. Please change into something more appropriate.

"Appropriate for what?" Dustin wanted to know. "Appropriate to hear of father's death?"

"Do not raise your voice, please," her mother said quietly. She was a pale woman with black hair hidden beneath a wimple. She'd never been particularly well and had spent the majority of her life reclining one way or the other. It was a great contrast to Dustin's vigor. "You shame your father dressed as you are. Please go and change."

Dustin grunted in frustration and turned to her mother to argue until she realized the woman's hands were shaking. Her heart sank with despair for her mother's feelings. She knew how much the woman had loved her father. She forgot her own feelings as she focused on what her mother was surely feeling.

"I am sorry, Mother," she said, forcing down her lofty pride as she went to kneel by her chair. "I did not mean it. The truth is that the knight never actually said father was dead. I really do not know why he is here."

Mary stroked her daughter's blond head. "I know," she smiled gently. "Now, please, go change your clothes. That would please me."

"Is there anything else I can do for you? Wine, perhaps?"

"Nay, my dear. Hurry along now and do as you are told."

With a reluctant nod, Dustin rose and moved for the door. She crossed the threshold and turned the corner only to run headlong into a broad, armored body.

It was a strong impact. Dustin shrieked, jumping back as if she'd been burned as her eyes flew up to face her accoster. The same sky-blue eyes that she had seen earlier smoldered back at her, now with something more than mere politeness. Now, there was something appraising there.

"My apologies," Christopher said.

Dustin nodded unsteadily as Jeffrey led Christopher into the drawing room, leaving Dustin standing in the corridor with her hand on her throat, wondering how a mere gaze could make her feel so vulnerable. De Lohr's eyes were piercing and consuming, something she'd never experienced before. It was an odd sensation. Coming back to her senses, she rushed to her bedchamber to do her mother's bidding.

Ready or not, she wanted to hear what the man had to say.

CHAPTER TWO

DRESSED IN A soft blue surcoat that, even with its simplicity, was just about the nicest surcoat she owned, Dustin scurried back down to her mother's drawing room. The full blue skirt was fitted around her slim waist with a black girdle and a snug-fitting white blouse, much more flattering to her figure than the usual sloppy dresses she bound about in. Her cascading hair was pulled back to the nape of her neck and secured, revealing the sweetness of her face. But Dustin truly didn't care how she looked; she'd only cleaned herself up and changed clothes to please her mother.

Eager to get back to the center of action, she took the great stone stairs two at a time and nearly ran across the foyer and into the solar.

What she saw upon her arrival shocked her. Her mother, face in her white hand, was obviously crying. Jeffrey, pale and drawn, stood next to her. Anger flared in her chest and she turned accusingly to the strange knight.

But what confronted her unbalanced her completely. The knight had taken off his helmet, revealing a great crown of dark blond hair slicked back against his skull. His features were rugged and masculine, and a neatly trimmed beard and mustache embraced his square jaw. He was indeed handsome, in her opinion, but she angrily chased those thoughts away. The fact remained that this man had said something terrible to upset her mother.

"What goes on here?" she demanded.

Jeffrey attempted to answer but Mary cut him off. "Come in here, Dustin. Please sit."

Increasingly off balance, Dustin took the indicated chair, which happened to be close to the knight. Mary sniffed daintily and dabbed at her eyes before speaking to her daughter.

"Dustin, I believe you have met Sir Christopher de Lohr. He served with your father and our king, Richard, in the Holy Land," she said softly. "As you suspected, my dear girl, the message he bore concerned your father's demise this past summer."

Dustin's eyes welled but she fought it. She did not want to cry with this knight staring at her.

"Oh, Mother," she sighed. "I am so very sorry."

Mary nodded, wiping her eyes again. "As am I," she replied quietly. " 'Twill not be the same, knowing he will never return."

Christopher watched the two women in their grief. He was sorry for his friend's death, too, but it had been a long time ago. Furthermore, he had only delivered half of his message and he wasn't sure it would be such a good idea for Dustin to be in the room when he delivered the remainder. Yet it was of no consequence what the girl felt; she would do as she was ordered, just as he was.

He revealed the second missive and approached Lady Mary. "My lady, there is more from our king," he said as gently as he could. As shocking as the first missive would be, this one would be explosive. "This message is also from Richard."

Trying to maintain her composure, Mary graciously took the parchment and broke the seal. Christopher stood back, discreetly looking away as she read the contents. From what he had seen of Lady Mary, she was far more in control of her emotions than her daughter and he honestly expected no outbursts.

When Lady Mary finished, she calmly lay the vellum in her lap and stared at it for several long moments. Dustin watched her mother curiously until she could stand the silence no longer.

"What does the king say, Mother?" she asked.

Lady Mary lifted her eyes to her daughter. Christopher did turn and looked at the older woman, then, to see how she was about to handle this delicate subject with her unruly child. Mayhap it would give him insight as to how to handle her once she became his wife.

Mary was surprisingly firm. "It seems your father had a final wish upon his deathbed, Dustin, and that was that you would be married to a man of his choosing."

Dustin stood up, her face suspicious. "Who?" she demanded. "We have been through this subject before. I do not wish to be married at all."

Lady Mary nodded patiently. "I know, dear, but what you want is of no concern to your father or the king," she said frankly. "Your father must do as he sees fit for you and for the future of Lioncross. You will, therefore, be married and your husband will become lord of Lioncross."

Dustin's lovely face darkened. She glared back at her mother a moment before finally averting her gaze.

"Has he selected someone?" she asked reluctantly, hoping beyond hope he had died before it was possible, failing to take into account that the king would have therefore made the choice in his stead.

"He has," Mary replied steadily.

Dustin's head snapped up, her jaw ticking. Hopefully the man was in the Holy Land with the king and it would be years before he returned. Mayhap by then she would be ready for marriage and duty.

Yet she also knew that it was useless to protest anything, her mother had been preparing her for this eventuality ever since her father left. She knew this time would eventually come, as distasteful as the idea was to her.

That was why her mother allowed young men to call on her, young men who came and were as quickly chased off by her quick temper and hard right-cross. Mary hoped that at least one young man would catch Dustin's eye, but alas, that had not happened.

"Who? Do I know him?" she asked after a moment.

Lady Mary turned to look at Christopher. Feeling himself the focus of attention, he straightened, looking from Lady Mary to her daughter as Dustin's gaze fixed on him. It was clear they were all expecting an answer. He actually felt a little nervous.

"You have met him, my lady," he cleared his throat.

She frowned at him. "Then who is it? And why am I asking you this question? Did Richard ask you to inform me?"

"Indirectly," Christopher admitted.

"Then who?" Dustin demanded in frustration.

Christopher slowly cocked a blond eyebrow. "Me."

It took a moment for the revelation to dawn on Dustin. At first she wasn't sure she heard correctly, mulling his words over and over. Then, as realization set in and she understood that her father, as well as the king, expected her to marry this massive, cold man, her mouth fell open.

"You?" she repeated. "I am to marry *you*?"

"Aye," he nodded.

She clamped her pretty mouth shut into a hard line. Lord only knew, she knew her duty well. It had been drilled into her ever since she had been old enough to understand that it was her duty to carry on the Barringdon line. And she was now looking at the man she would marry and breed with.

Dustin's first reaction was to scream and rant, but she knew it would be a waste of energy. Mayhap it would simply be easier all the way around if she gave in to the idea and came to grips with it. The best she could hope for was a quick marriage and then he would go and leave her in peace. Did he really plan to live here, with her? Lord, she knew nothing about the man. What if he intended to force her into a real marriage?

"We will be married immediately," he said decisively. "Today, if possible. Lady Mary, do you have a priest?"

Both Lady Mary and Dustin looked surprised. Jeffrey was positively red. Christopher ignored the soldier, focusing on the older woman and expecting an answer.

"Yes, my lord, we do," Lady Mary replied softly. "Father Jonah."

Christopher looked at Jeffrey then. "Fetch him. Now."

Jeffrey nearly burst a vein but obeyed silently. Christopher watched the man's stiff back, wondering if he were going to have to watch his own until he could kick the man out of the keep. Jeffrey did not like him; that was apparent.

Dustin stared at the knight. Her initial impressions of him had been those of indifferent arrogance. When he looked at her, she saw nothing but ice in those blue eyes and it frightened and angered her at the same time. Yet she knew one thing, she didn't want him and he didn't want her.

Christopher gathered his helmet and gauntlets. "If you ladies will excuse me, I have duties to attend to," he said politely. "I shall return shortly."

Dustin looked away from him as he strode past her and quit the room. As soon as he was clear of the door she whirled to her mother.

"I do not want to marry him," she snapped.

Mary knew this exchange was coming and was prepared. "I know, dear, but as I said, you have no choice. Your father selected the man he felt most capable to provide you your future."

"He is a stranger," Dustin said, snappish and frightened. "You have seen him look at me; he does not want me, either. I do not want anything to do with him!"

Mary opened her mouth when there was a sudden shadow cast into the room from the open doorway. Dustin turned to see Christopher looming in the arch.

His sky-blue eyes were riveted to her and she could feel the coldness. She stared back, wondering why he was looking at her like that.

"You may say whatever you wish about me, Lady Dustin," he said calmly. "But you will not speak to your mother in that manner ever again in my presence."

She stiffened. "It wasn't in your presence. You were out of the room," she pointed out. "And I will speak to my mother however I wish."

He stepped into the room and she fought the urge to step away from him. She wondered crazily if he were going to strike her. But, amazingly, he looked entirely calm.

"Before this day is finished, you will be my wife in the eyes of God and country," he said. "Even as we stand now, you are for all intent and purposes my wife. Therefore, you will obey me, as it is a wife's duty to obey her husband. I say you will speak to your mother respectfully at all times and you will comply. Am I making myself clear?"

Dustin was so angry she was shaking. But she met his gaze, clenching her fists until her nails bit into her palms.

"Perfectly, my lord," was all she could manage to squeeze out.

He nodded shortly, moving once again for the door and leaving the room without another word.

Dustin stared at the empty doorway, outraged and shaken. They were not even officially married yet and already he was giving her orders. She looked at her mother but dared not speak to her, afraid he was lingering in the hallway waiting for her to disobey him.

How could her father have selected this man for her husband? Her father loved her. How in the world could he have sentenced his only child to a life of misery with a man who was such a cold bastard? She shook her head, disoriented with the contents of the entire day. It was all too unbelievable.

"Dustin, dear, mayhap you should go and freshen up a bit before the priest arrives," her mother said softly.

Dustin looked hard at her mother. "And you will just accept this?" she demanded softly.

Mary rose wearily. "There is nothing to reject or accept, Dustin. 'Tis simply the way of things." Her daughter turned away in disgust and Mary sighed. "Think of the positive, dear. Sir Christopher is as fine and tall and strong a man as I have ever seen, and I am sure he will protect Lioncross admirably. The fortress will be in capable hands."

"But what about me?" Dustin whispered, appalled that she was on the verge of angry tears. "What will happen to me?"

Mary put her thin hands on Dustin's shoulders. "Pray treat him well, daughter. Ye shall reap as ye sow."

Dustin rolled her eyes and turned to face her mother. "I do not want to marry anyone. I am only nineteen and I…."

Mary shook her head, "You should have been married two years ago. You know that as well as I." She dropped her hands from her daughter's shoulders. "Now, I am exceedingly weary and wish to rest a bit before attending your wedding."

Dustin gazed at her delicate mother, her heart once again aching for the loss of her father. She could only imagine the pain her mother was feeling. She had loved him so. For the moment, she forgot her own torment. Her mother was right; there was nothing she could do and the sooner she accepted that, the better. But she still could not swallow the thought of being married to that monstrous man.

"I shall come with you, Mother," she said softly.

There was nothing more to say.

CB

OUTSIDE IN THE bailey, Edward and David had everything under control. Edward, his dark hair plastered with perspiration, approached Christopher as the man emerged from the keep.

"Well? How did it go?" he demanded with restrained humor.

Christopher looked at his friend and flashed a brief look of distaste. "I am marrying the lady as soon as the priest arrives."

Edward grinned, deep dimples in each cheek. "Congratulations, old man. And do not look so displeased. She is quite lovely."

Christopher shook his head, not wanting to discuss Lady Dustin further. His mind was already racing ahead, thinking on his return trip to London.

"When we return to London, I wish to leave my own men in charge. I do not trust nor do I like their Germanic captain. I would establish Lioncross as my own from the start."

"Agreed," Edward nodded, but did not volunteer to stay behind.

Christopher eyed him. "One of my own knights, I said."

Edward avoided his gaze. "Understood, my lord. But I wish to accompany you to London. Leave David here."

"David will wish to accompany me as well," Christopher reminded him. "And he is my brother."

Edward let out a heavy sigh and shrugged. "Aye, my lord," he answered grudgingly. "I will stay."

Christopher slapped a heavy hand on Edward's shoulder. "I knew you would see things my way."

Edward nodded in resignation as he followed Christopher across the compound. Christopher studied every inch of his keep critically, seeing things he had not seen in his first sweep. There were sections of the battlements that were missing stone and in spots there were great holes in the bailey. Everything needed to be smoothed out and resurfaced, and the keep needed work. Still, it was worth it. The prize was still mighty.

They met up with David near the squat and sturdy gatehouse, discussing everything from the upcoming wedding to Prince John in London. Christopher knew Edward was terribly disappointed that he would not be able to accompany him to London, but Christopher truly needed his trusted man here. When Edward was called away by one of the men-at-arms, David faced his brother.

"You could use him, Chris," he said softly. "Lioncross will do well with your men-at-arms establishing themselves here. Your presence will be known to all.

"I need no one with me in London, even you," Christopher replied. "Richard asked this task of me and me alone."

"What Richard asked was for you to keep an eye on his brother and report back to him," David hissed. "For all purposes, Christopher, you are a spy, a royal plant. Should John discover this, he will execute you as an enemy of the crown."

Christopher snorted. "He cannot. He has not the authority."

"You saw how he has established himself in London," David persisted, at a loss to understand his brother's attitude. "He has done everything but declare himself king. He rules England, not Richard."

Christopher's eyes flashed at his brother. "Richard is our king," he said slowly. "Whatever I do in London, I do it for our sovereign lord. John has no power over me. My orders come directly from Richard."

David shook his head faintly, not knowing what else to say. "As you say, Lion's Claw. I can only hope that you are not the one to be gored."

Christopher looked at his brother a long moment. Then he smiled. "You worry like an old woman, little brother."

David shrugged. "I do not know why I even bother. You always do what you want to, anyway."

Christopher's jocularity faded. "Not in this case," he glanced at Lioncross. "To obtain this mighty fortress, I must do something I most definitely do not want to do."

"Marry Lady Dustin?" David smiled. "Why not, Chris? Jesus Christ, she's beautiful. Big tits, too."

Christopher cocked an eyebrow. "Does she? I didn't notice. In fact, I can't seem to get past all that hair. She's got enough hair for three women."

David nodded seductively. "Think about it, Chris, all of that hair flowing over you as she mounts you."

Christopher waved his brother off. "I get the picture. She's so damn small that I will probably tear her asunder. Not the most auspicious way to begin a marriage."

David laughed heartily and Christopher joined him for a few moments, chuckling at Dustin's expense.

"On second thought, Chris, maybe I will stay here," David snickered. " 'Twill be a pleasure to watch after my brother's wife, the poor lonely woman."

Christopher's amusement vanished. "You will not touch her. Is that clear?"

David was taken aback by the tone and by the deadly flicker in his brother's eye. He was suddenly very curious about the sudden burst of husbandly protectiveness. The only person Christopher was passionate about was Richard, and himself. Strange that his new bride would provoke that kind of a response.

"Aye, verily," he said. "It was only a jest."

Christopher was embarrassed for his outburst and looked away, wondering why in the hell he had done that. He was a reasonable man and deduced that he was naturally protective of Lady Dustin for obvious reasons. Firstly, she was his chattel. Secondly, she was a weaker female and fell under the category of knightly chivalry. Any other reason disturbed him too much.

"You could always take her to London with you and keep an eye on her yourself," David suggested, goading his brother to see what other responses he could get. "John would go mad for such a lovely woman."

Christopher shook his head. "I'd spend all of my time fighting the prince off her," he said, but in faith, did not think the suggestion to be a bad one. After all, he could keep an eye on her and get to know her better. There was no knowing how long he would be staying in London, and if he left Dustin here, he would be just as much a stranger upon his return.

As he mulled over the possibilities, there was a shout from high atop the wall. Riders had been sighted and were rapidly approaching the village. There were only three, riding fast for Lioncross.

The gates were open and Christopher positioned himself dead center, his huge serrated broadsword in his left hand. David and Edward joined him, a grim welcoming party for the intruders.

As Christopher watched three knights approach, he was aware of his protective feelings towards Lioncross as well. He hadn't been at the fortress for an hour and already he was ready and willing to die for it. It was his, already under his skin. It took him a moment to realize he had finally come home.

The riders reined their great destriers to within several feet of the drawbridge, their horses dancing and kicking up dust. Christopher waited, ready to spring into action and cut off a head should it be so required. He was as coiled as a spring.

The rider in the middle suddenly began to laugh, it was a curiously familiar laugh. Ripping off his helmet, he continued to laugh heartily.

"So the rumors were true, Lion's Claw," he said, dismounting his steed.

Christopher went limp with relief. He knew the face and he knew the man. "Leeton de Shera," he hissed. "How in the hell did you find me?"

Leeton just laughed as he approached, and the other two knights tore off their helmets as well, joining in the laughter.

"Christ on his Mighty Throne," Christopher muttered a curse, gazing at the others. "You brought the devil twins with you. Max and Anthony de Velt."

The de Velt twins were mirror images of each other, of average height but built like the mighty mountains of the north, with long dark hair and brown eyes. Leeton, however, was as blond as Christopher and more so; even his eyelashes and eyebrows were white. He was tall and well-built, and had been Christopher's close friend since they had fostered together in Derby. He had not chosen to crusade with Richard, instead, remaining as captain for the Earl of Derby. Christopher wondered what he was doing so far from his fortress.

"Why aren't you at Derby?" Christopher demanded, taking Leeton's outstretched hand and shaking it.

Leeton shrugged. "I still am, on occasion, but no longer as captain."

Christopher grew serious. Leeton was by far one of the best knights he had ever seen and he was puzzled as well as concerned.

"Why not?" he asked.

Leeton's face grew sad, soft, as he released Christopher's hand. "Do you remember the earl's daughter, Rachel?"

Christopher nodded. "Of course, Leeton I knew her well."

"I married her," Leeton replied quietly, but Christopher could read the tremendous grief in his friend's eyes. "Two years ago. Last year, she bore me a son. She died three hours later."

Christopher was stunned. Aye, he had known the fair Rachel, and he knew Leeton had always been sweet on her. For them to marry was not a surprise, but he was deeply saddened by Rachel's death. He could see that Leeton was still having trouble coming to terms with it.

"Please accept my condolences," he said softly. "But your son was healthy?"

"Aye, Richard is magnificent," Leeton nodded. "He lives with the earl and his wife. I, however, cannot bear to stay at the keep because it was where I met my wife and where she died. So I have spent a great deal of time in Worcester, and in Nottingham, on errands for the earl. I see Richard when I can."

Christopher sighed heavily, feeling the man's anguish. "If I had a son, I would not let him out of my sight," he murmured. "How can you be apart from him?"

Leeton cleared his throat and lowered his gaze. "He is the image of Rachel, Chris," he said softly. "Every time I look at him, I see her, and my grief is fresh."

Christopher understood. With silent sympathy, he clapped his friend on the shoulder and the two of them turned back to the others, now engaged in lively conversation with Edward and David.

"Chris, what's this I hear that you are to be married?" Max asked loudly.

Christopher nodded coolly. "Unfortunately, in order to gain this magnificent keep, I have to marry the heiress," he said. "I have only met her today, and today we will be married. You will all attend the ceremony, of course."

"You are getting married?" Leeton was shocked. "Jesus, Chris, what a hell of a surprise. How on earth did this happen?"

Christopher didn't want to go into that at the moment. He gave Leeton a wry smirk. "By decree of our illustrious Richard," he said, rather grandiose. "He commands and I obey."

Leeton could see the reluctance and the humor, and it was difficult not to tease Christopher because of it.

"Your devotion to our king is indeed limitless," he said dryly. "So what does this woman look like? Twisted and old? Medusa in the flesh?"

Before Christopher could answer, David's gaze suddenly moved to the keep and he found himself following his brother's focus. On a second floor window overlooking the bailey, a small figure in blue silk and flowing blond hair stood watching the knights. When Dustin noticed she had been sighted, she abruptly disappeared back into the castle.

"That," Christopher said, "is her."

None of the knights said a word, looking up at the window as if she were still standing there. The de Velt twins' mouths were hanging open. All jesting faded as the shock of the lady's appearance settled.

"*That* is Medusa in the flesh?" Leeton asked in disbelief. "God, Chris, you failed to mention she was absolutely beautiful. I feel like an arse."

Christopher shrugged noncommittally. "The fact that she is easy on the eyes will only make the marriage a bit more palatable," he said. "But I have come to see that she is exceedingly stubborn and disrespectful."

"Who cares? The two traits can be changed," Leeton insisted. "You cannot do a thing about her looks, but her manners can be molded. She can make you a fine wife."

Christopher shrugged carelessly again, his only answer. The conversation turned back to the king, the prince, and the crusade, and Christopher wholeheartedly joined in. But in the back of his mind, the small woman with the incredible hair kept appearing and try as he might, he could not shake her.

CHAPTER THREE

JEFFREY RETURNED WITH the priest four hours later, Christopher was sure, just to spite him. The big German barely acknowledged him and when he did, it was usually curt and bordering on rude. David and Edward were furious about it but Christopher waved them off. The man was as good as gone, anyway, and he banished him from the castle and from the wedding in a show of complete control, daring the surly bastard to challenge him. Jeffrey retreated without a word, but Christopher didn't trust the man.

It was well after dark when Christopher and the other knights assembled in the great hall of Lioncross. It was a cavernous place with vaulted ceilings and an enormous fireplace with a great lion's head carved into it. The servants had put fresh rushes on the floor and two banks of expensive tallow candles burned brightly. Lady Mary had even insisted that precious frankincense be burned in honor of her daughter's wedding, the pungent scent mingling with the heavy smell of smoke.

Christopher stood in his armor, having not even bothered to bathe or shave. This ceremony was simply a formality and meant nothing to him other than the fact that Lioncross Abbey would legally be his. He was eager to count the wealth in the coffers and get started on improving the structure. He stood, waiting impatiently, for his bride and her mother to appear.

David stood beside him, but Edward and the other knights were hitting the fine French wine pretty hard, beginning to get rather loud and boisterous. Edward was a lively sort and could drink with the best of them, and Christopher enjoyed the man greatly.

Christopher watched him gulping from his goblet, laughing with Leeton. He and Edward had fought with Richard for three years and he had come to think of the man as his second brother. He was tall and dashingly handsome with his dark hair and golden eyes, and he could fight with the best of them. His father, Robert, was the Earl of Wolverhampton and Edward would inherit the title upon the man's death.

Robert de Wolfe was still in the Holy Land with Richard. He and Edward had gone together to fight with Richard, but Edward left with Christopher. Robert and another knight by the name of Royce Culbertson had become the very best of friends, with Royce having been with Richard since the beginning of the crusade and marrying a Saracen woman the very first year. Royce had sent his wife and baby daughter home to England the very next year, and the child was now three years old. Much to Edward's horror, Robert and Royce had drawn up a marriage contract between their two children, and Edward had come home to visit his betrothed, who was exactly twenty-four years younger than him. Edward had protested the ridiculous match but his father insisted.

Christopher could sympathize with him, marrying a girl he had no interest in, but he was jolted from his thoughts by the appearance of the priest. The man politely requested the knights to gather about Christopher, indicating that Lady Dustin and Lady Mary were approaching. Fighting down a resurgence of reluctance, Christopher glanced up and caught a glimpse of the two women on the balcony above the great hall as they made their way to the staircase.

He didn't get a good look at Dustin until she descended the stairs and entered the room, holding her mother's arm. Then, he found he could not take his eyes off her. She was dressed in a creamy yellow silk surcoat, well off her beautiful shoulders and embroidered in gold thread. It was a bit snug, perhaps too snug, and revealed her figure plainly.

Christopher had never gawked at a woman in his life and tore himself away from her lest he make this the first time. But he realized one thing, David had been right. She did have magnificent breasts. In fact, there wasn't one thing about the woman that wasn't magnificent and he was stunned, suddenly feeling self-conscious of his less-than-kempt appearance. He found himself regretting he had not bathed.

"I do apologize for our tardiness," Mary said softly. "Are we ready to begin?"

"Aye," Christopher stepped forward, gazing impassively at Dustin before looking at the priest. "You may begin, Father."

Throughout the quick ceremony, Dustin held onto her mother. The action irritated Christopher and he glared in the direction of the women only to realize that Lady Mary did not look at all well. Instead of Dustin grasping her mother for support, it was the other way around.

But they had to let go of each other when Christopher moved to place a pretty gold band on Dustin's finger. Dustin gazed down at it, puzzled that he had actually taken the trouble to purchase one. She turned her sweet face up to him questioningly.

"I picked it up in London," he told her emotionlessly. " 'Twas a bargain."

Her face washed with a stony expression and she lowered her head. The one thing that might have brought a small amount of pleasantness to an otherwise distressing event was of no worth, either. Dustin didn't know why she had hoped he might have taken some care in choosing a ring, mayhap it was the romantic inside her. After all, weren't weddings supposed to be a happy occasion? Dustin felt as though she might as well be attending a funeral mass… her own.

The priest gave the final blessing and benediction, and Christopher paid him well. Mary kissed her daughter's cheek and, still clutching her arm, moved to Christopher.

"Welcome to Lioncross, my lord," she said. "I pray that you and Dustin will have as much happiness here as Arthur and I did."

Christopher was preparing a harsh retort but he simply could not bring himself to reply to the gentle woman in such a manner. She looked very tired, even more so than earlier in the day, and he attributed it to the fact that the woman had just only learned of her husband's death.

"Thank you, my lady," he said simply.

Lady Mary smiled then turned to her daughter. "Come now, dear. We must help the men with their meal."

Dustin gave Christopher a baleful glare before following her mother into the kitchens. The knights settled themselves around the huge oaken table and Christopher found himself running his hand along the surface. *His* table. He glanced up, looking at the open-beamed ceiling thirty feet above him. His keep. All of it was his. He sighed with satisfaction. His happiness would have been complete had one very large stipulation not come with all of this wealth.

As if she heard his thoughts, Dustin came whisking back into the hall bearing a huge trencher filled to overflowing for her new husband. She set it down heavily before him, slopping over a bit onto the table, and went to retrieve him a goblet of wine.

Her movements were sharp and angry and he found himself watching her with some amusement. When she moved close to him to pour the wine, he smelled roses. He found the scent heady and was undecided as to whether or not it was pleasant.

"Are you to serve me always?" he asked.

She didn't look at him. "My mother said I should tonight as a show of respect for my new husband."

He nodded, studying her more closely than he ever had. David had told him, Leeton had told him, and Edward had told him. They all knew it, as did he. She was indeed beautiful and he was still amazed at his luck.

"I wish for you to serve me at every meal," he said, turning his attention to his food.

"I am not a serving wench," she said stiffly.

"Nay, you are not, you are my wife and I wish for you to serve me at every meal," he repeated calmly, picking up a bit of stringy beef.

Dustin stood back, watching him eat with gusto. Her jaw ticked with outrage at his order. She was not a serving wench and how dare he lower her to that station. But her fury was cut short when she saw her mother, her weak arms shaking, attempting to serve David. The trencher was about to end up in the knight's lap. Discreetly taking the food from her mother, she served her husband's brother herself.

"Thank you, Lady de Lohr," he smiled sweetly at her.

Dustin blinked at the sound of her new title, managing a brief nod before retreating with her mother for the rest of the meal.

David grinned into his food when she had gone. "She hates that name."

"What name?" Christopher asked.

"Lady de Lohr," his brother snickered.

Christopher took a big bite of beef. "That is her misfortune."

The meal was long. Dustin and her mother sat at the end of the table in silence, listening to the strange laughter and conversation. Dustin never looked at her new husband, but she was certainly becoming accustomed to his voice. It was deep and rich, and his laugh was throaty. It could become quite easy to like his voice, for it was masculine and comforting. But she would not allow herself to like any part of him.

She was beginning to recognize the knight's voices as well. David's was higher pitched and gentle, Edward's was loud and exciting. She also learned their names by listening to them address one another, for her husband had not even had the courtesy to introduce them to her. She finished her meal quietly, not having eaten more than a few bites. She didn't even notice her mother had not eaten at all.

The meal concluded very late and Dustin was exhausted. While the serving women cleared the table of trenchers and clutter, Dustin rose.

"My lord," she forced herself to look at Christopher. "I would ask permission to retire."

Christopher's gaze passed between his wife and her mother. He was about to demand Dustin stay and entertain them, but he suspected Lady Mary needed his wife more. He gave a brief nod.

"Good sleep to you, wife," he said, then nodded at Lady Mary. "My lady."

Mary was even paler that she had been earlier. "The steward will show you and your knights to your rooms," she said softly. "I hope the chambers are to your liking."

"I am sure they will be," Christopher replied.

Without another glance, Dustin took her mother by the arm and led her to the stairs. The woman's movements were slow and labored and she seemed to be having some difficulty mounting the steps. The knights watched silently for a moment as Dustin tried to physically lift her mother onto the first stair. Christopher, too, watched until he saw what Dustin was trying to do and then rose swiftly.

"My lady, would you allow me to assist you?" he asked Lady Mary.

"My mother is quite capable of climbing stairs, my lord," Dustin retorted quietly.

He ignored his wife and looked at the older woman. "My lady?"

Mary sighed and cleared her throat very ladylike. "Mayhap I could use a bit of assistance, thank you."

She held out her frail arm to him but he ignored it instead, sweeping her into his arms and mounting the stairs with absolutely no effort at all. In fact, Dustin was still standing at the bottom of the flight gazing up at him with astonishment as he set the older woman down at the top. Recovering, Dustin dashed up the stairs and grasped her mother again.

"Did he hurt you?" she demanded.

"Of course not, dear," her mother replied.

Christopher watched his wife help her mother down the corridor until both women disappeared into a room. Lady Mary was obviously ill and he realized he felt some concern for her. Turning on his heel, descended the stairs in a rush of irritation, disturbed that with this new keep came protective feelings for the occupants. Lady Mary had been nothing less than kind and respectful to him, and he appreciated that. Her daughter could learn lessons in manners from her mother.

He joined his knights, drinking and laughing and reveling deep into the night, pushing thoughts of the Lady Dustin de Lohr to the back of his mind.

☙

DUSTIN WAS AWAKENED from a deep sleep by a hysterical serving woman. She was irritated and groggy until the woman mentioned one word; *mother*.

Dustin bolted up from her bed, clad only in a flowing linen bedcoat, and charged across the corridor into her mother's room. Panic flooded her veins and she heard herself whimpering even as she ran into the room, nearly slipping on the old rushes on the floor. Devastation and horror consumed her to see several female servants hovering over her mother's bed, crying. She knew without even looking that her mother was dead.

Dustin pushed forward, shoving the women out of the way. One look at her mother's pale, wax-like face and her worst nightmare was confirmed. Lady Mary Barringdon was indeed dead.

Her sweet, gentle mother. The woman who had nurtured her through sickness, had tried to teach her to be a dutiful wife and chatelaine, and who tried to impart wisdom into her thick skull. Horrible, agonizing sobs rose in her throat and she threw herself down on her mother's cooling corpse, begging her not to leave her. She didn't want to be alone.

Christopher heard the screaming and flew from the great hall and onto the second floor before the hollering had even stopped. He could hear the other knights behind him, swords unsheathing. He knew instinctively that it was his wife he heard, and his sword flashed wickedly in the firelight as he thundered into the chamber crowded with weeping servants.

It did not take great intellect to see what had happened; it took him all of two seconds to deduce the scene. Lady Mary had died in her sleep, and Dustin was inconsolable.

Christopher slowly sheathed his sword, taking hesitant steps into the room. The servants stood about, sobbing like fools. They certainly weren't doing his wife any good.

"All of you get out," he snapped in a low voice, motioning with his arm. "*Now.*"

Weeping and wailing, the servants quickly cleared the room with rough assistance from David and Edward. When the dim chamber was finally cleared, Christopher stepped to the end of the bed and absorbed the scene.

Dustin was sobbing incoherently, mumbling something into her mother's chest he could not understand. Christopher watched her blond head, feeling a good deal of pity for her. To be married and lose her mother all in the same day had pushed her over the emotional edge and he found himself wanting to comfort her. But he would not, just as she would not allow him to.

Christopher motioned David and the others out, moving for the door himself. With a final glance, he quit the room and closed the door quietly, leaving his wife to deal with her grief alone. But even as the others retreated back to the great hall, he remained behind, standing watch outside Lady Mary's door in case Dustin needed him. He didn't want her to have to go searching.

But Dustin didn't come out and, after an hour, Christopher went back into the room to make sure she hadn't done something horrible to herself in her moment of grief.

The room was nearly pitch black except for the small fire in the hearth. He moved silently for the bed, noticing that Dustin had not moved a muscle. Instead of open sobs, as she had been doing earlier, she was sort of moaning pathetically. Her hands were clutching her mother's bedcoat as if she were to hold on tight enough, she could prevent her mother from slipping into the world beyond.

He realized she was stricken with grief, but she would become ill if he allowed this wallowing to continue. He cleared his throat quietly.

"My lady," he whispered. When he received no reaction, he spoke her name. "Dustin."

She stirred a bit and her eyes flew open. Slowly, she turned her head until her pale gray eyes found him and focused. He gazed back at her, unaware of his gentle expression.

" 'Tis time to return to your own room, my lady," he said softly.

Her head came up. "Nay," she said, her nose stuffed from crying. "I would stay here. My mother needs me."

"Your mother is dead, my lady," he said with gentleness he never believed himself capable of. "Let me take you back to your rooms."

Dustin looked at her mother as if she didn't believe what he was telling her. Her features crumpled. "It is not true," she whispered in a painful burst. "She cannot be dead.

He moved around the side of the bed. Lady Mary was already stiff and the underside of her body was turning deep purple.

"Dustin, she is gone," he said quietly. "You must let the servants take the body away for burial."

Dustin sat bolt upright in bed, her lovely face twisted. "No burial," she snapped. "Not in the ground."

"What do you mean?" he asked with a furrowed brow. "What else is there?"

She looked as if she had an answer but a sob escaped her lips and tears coursed down her cheeks. "The ground is cold and dark," she whispered. "Mother does not like the cold."

His heart went out to her. She sounded so much like a small child, so vulnerable and pathetic. He reached out and grasped her arms.

"Your mother is in paradise, sweetheart," he whispered, feeling her soft flesh in his hands like a painful jolt. "She will not care that her earthly remains have been placed in the earth."

Dustin was amazingly light and he swept her into his arms effortlessly. But she stiffened, twisting and pushing against him.

"Put me down," she cried. "I can't leave her."

He gripped her tightly to his chest. "Relax, my lady. All will be well."

"Nay!" she screamed, beating him with her fists and screaming for her mother.

Christopher took her out into the hall where he was met by several house servants. "Where is Lady Dustin's room?" he barked.

A few women pointed fingers to the room directly across the corridor and he was moving for it, his wife still screaming and thrashing about.

"Remove her mother," he ordered the weeping group. "We bury her come the morn."

He entered Dustin's bedchamber and slammed the door. Then, he went straight to her bed and placed her upon the mattress. Sniffling and weeping, Dustin tried to climb off the bed as Christopher removed his heavy leather vest. The vest hit the floor and he reached out and grabbed her by her leg, dragging her back across the bed and throwing himself on top of her simply to keep her from escaping. He didn't know what else to do.

Surprisingly, she didn't overly resist him. Certainly, she was stiff and unbending, but she wasn't outright fighting. She lay enclosed in his massive arms, her back to his chest as they lay upon their sides. After a while her movements lessened and her crying softened to no more than loud hiccups. He could feel her hands gripping his arms.

She was soft and warm and sweet-smelling against him, igniting his husbandly desire. He didn't want to marry the woman and he wanted little to do with her, but the fact remained that she was beautiful and alluring. He also felt a measure of emotion towards her at the death of her mother, and pity had a way of breaking down one's resistance. When she finally ceased all struggles, he removed one arm from her long enough to pull the coverlet up over them both, realizing he was focused only on her comfort and needs. For the first time in his life, he wasn't thinking only of himself. It was an odd awareness.

It was a long while before her trembling stopped and she went limp against him and he knew she had fallen asleep. Christ, how the scent of roses filled his nostrils. He had never liked roses very much but there was something about the particular scent on his wife that made it different. He thought he could grow to like it.

He smiled into the darkness, laughing at himself. The only time he had ever been in bed with a woman was to satisfy himself, and here he was laying with the most beautiful woman he had ever seen, his legal wife no less, and he wasn't making mad love to her. What in the world was happening to him? Since when did he give a care about anyone other than himself?

He thought of Dustin, how she had been rude to him, how she had been openly hostile. She'd never said a kind word, nor had he even seen her smile. Yet here he was, comforting her. Christ, he was stupid. The sands of the Holy Land must have rotted his brain somehow.

"My lord?" It was Dustin.

"Aye?" he answered, mildly surprised that she was awake.

She took a ragged breath. "When you carried my mother up the stairs earlier, I did not thank you."

" 'Twas my duty, as your husband," he replied.

She paused a moment. "I know. But I will thank you all the same."

He grunted a reply, thinking she sounded quite lucid now and thinking on leaving. In fact, he thought it would be a very good idea considering the warm and yielding thoughts he was having about her. He didn't want to let his guard down for a woman who would only batter him.

"You do not have to stay with me," Dustin said softly, as if she was reading his thoughts. "I am much calmer now."

He unwound his arms and she rolled onto her back, looking up at him with a completely open expression. He was propped up on one elbow, gazing down at her and thinking her face to be wonderful. So much for letting his guard down; he couldn't help it.

"You are beautiful," he said before he could stop himself.

Dustin blinked in surprise at the compliment. She said the first thing that came to mind. "I am too short."

He scowled, showing emotion for the first time. "What does that have to do with your beauty?"

She looked stumped and tired. "I…I do not know. I am just too short, that's all."

He cocked a reproving eyebrow and pushed himself out of bed. "The usual response to a compliment is 'thank you,'" he said.

She sat up wearily, watching his movements. "Were you with my father when he died?"

He paused, looking at her, before collecting his leather vest on the floor. He debated what to tell her but realized he couldn't lie about it. "Aye, my lady."

"How did he die?" she whispered.

He didn't know if he should tell her anything. After all, she had enough grief without hearing about Arthur's nauseating end.

"We will discuss that at a later time," he said after a moment. "As it stands, you will go to sleep and I will see you on the morrow."

She didn't answer him but lay back down, her huge gray eyes still on him. He watched her in return, his movements slowing a bit, not particularly liking the distant look in her eye. He was hesitant, thinking that mayhap he should not leave. Women in grief were known to do all sorts of strange things, and he did not want to be held responsible should his wife decide to hurt herself.

As he wrestled with indecision, something heavy rubbed up against his leg and he took a startled step back, looking down to see a huge orange cat blinking up at him with green cat-eyes. It was the biggest damn cat he had ever seen.

"What's this?" he pointed at the feline.

Dustin tore her eyes from him long enough to follow the direction of his finger. " 'Tis Caesar, my lord. My cat."

The cat was purring loudly and moved over to him, rubbing on his leg once again. "I do not like cats," he said finally.

A flicker of a smile crossed her face. "He likes you," she said. "And he does not take to people easily. Caesar is my very best friend." She clucked to the cat and the beast immediately jumped onto the bed, kneading the mattress to get comfortable.

He watched her pet the cat, a faint smile on her lips. He was becoming enchanted by her faint expression and was seized with the desire to see her smile even larger. He was very curious to see what sort of smile she could display. Was it charming? Twisted? Did she even have all of her teeth?

"That beast is as large as a lamb," he remarked. "What do you feed it? Small children?"

As he had hoped, she smiled wide and he was absolutely captivated. As beautiful as she was, her whole face changed dramatically when she revealed her straight, white teeth and deep dimple in her left cheek.

"Nay, my lord, only chicken and innards," she replied softly, scratching the cat's ears. " 'Tis all he will eat. But he is a fine hunter."

"No doubt," he cocked a dubious brow. "I will have to watch that he does not hunt *me*. I have a feeling that I would become supper."

She gave a small laugh and he found himself smiling in return. But when her eyes moved to him once again, he quickly erased his smile. For some reason, he did not want her to see that she had affected him that way.

"I will leave you and Caesar, then." He moved for the door, strangely feeling better that the cat had made an appearance, as if the animal could watch over her. "Sleep well, my lady."

She watched him close the door, still scratching the cat. Her smile faded and in the darkness of the room, she had never felt more alone in her entire life.

Her husband was a cold man. Even in his kindness, he was a cold barbarian, for his kindness was forced and unreal. When he had held her with those massive, warm arms, he was stiff and not at all comforting. It was obvious he didn't like her, although he had called her beautiful. *Strange*, she thought. Mayhap he just meant her hair and not the whole of her. Or mayhap he liked the color of her eyes. Whatever the reason, he was not sincere.

Sadness swept over her and tears came to her eyes once again. Tears of grief for her mother, tears of pity for herself.

She was entirely alone.

CHAPTER FOUR

DUSTIN BURIED HER mother next to her father's parents in the tiny chapel of Lioncross. She would have liked to have had a nice wake and mass for her mother, but with the oppressive heat, the body simply would not keep, and they buried Mary two hours after dawn.

Christopher stood a few feet away from Dustin, stoically listening to the same priest who had married them, intone the funeral mass. He could hear Dustin's faint sobs, wondering if he should lend her some sort of comfort but not making the effort to try. Deep down, he didn't want to be embarrassed if she refused him. And he knew she would.

His wife was dressed in black, from head to toe, only her porcelain face evident underneath the voluminous wimple. She was so pale that the contrast was striking. She had dark circles under her eyes; evidence that she had disobeyed him last night and had not gone back to sleep.

The mass was over and the priest moved to Dustin, whispering a few words of comfort to her. She nodded but did not reply, instead, continuing to stare at the fresh grave.

Christopher glanced at the other knights, standing several feet away, and dismissed them with a faint jerk of his head. The servants and a few peasants had already left, trekking down the soft green slope and back toward the keep. He waited until everyone was well out of range before attempting to approach Dustin.

"We should return now," he said softly, standing behind her.

She didn't respond and he wasn't sure if she even heard him. He gazed off across the village in the distance and sighed. "My lady, the day grows wa...."

He was cut off when she whirled around in a great gush of black material, her gray eyes dark and her face flushed.

"I hate you," she spit at him. "You caused all of this, you devil's son. 'Twas you who bore the news of my father's death, and you who forced me to marry. You drove her into her grave and I shall hate you forever."

He was taken aback by the accusations but remained quite calm in the face of her raging.

"I forgive you for speaking to me in such a manner, knowing your grief is making you mad," he said. "But as far as I...."

Then she did something so completely unexpected that he was caught entirely off guard. Somewhere from underneath the black cloak, a small balled fist came flying up at him and caught him on the corner of the mouth.

"You arrogant, conceited dolt," she hissed. "I do not care if you forgive me or not, and I am quite sane. But know this; I shall hate you until I die, always, and forever. You may hold the titles and lands of Lioncross, but I am your wife in name only. Never expect my respect or my loyalty or my kindness, for you shall never receive it."

His jaw ticked as he wiped away the bloody trickle from his lips. His anger was apparent.

"Your mother was ill, my lady. I did not kill her," he said, his voice like ice. "As to Lioncross, she is indeed mine. As are you, in name and in body, whether or not it meets with your approval."

"It does not," she spat.

"Nor does it meet with mine," he retorted. "I simply wanted the keep. You are additional baggage."

Stung, she glared up at him, her tears forgotten for the moment. He braced himself for the next barrage as he gazed impassively into the stormy gray eyes.

"For God's sake, de Lohr, if you didn't want me, then why didn't you tell the king? Or my father?" her tone was suddenly pleading. "Why could not you have simply purchased the keep and leave me out of it?"

"Because your father wanted to see you married," he said flatly. "It would seem that mayhap he didn't think you could catch a husband on your own, being as old as you are, so I was offered the keep for the price of marrying you."

She was breathing rapidly but her tears were gone. She lowered her gaze, she understood his words only too well.

"Let me go, then, and you can have Lioncross," she whispered.

"Let you go where?" he asked, puzzled.

"My mother's family lives in Nottingham," she replied. "I would go live with them."

"You are my wife, my lady," he said firmly. "You will stay with me."

"Stop calling me your wife," she flared, then just as quickly relaxed. Her face was pained. "I would not move to annul the marriage, if that is your concern. I would remain your wife and you could keep Lioncross."

He studied her face, his anger abating. "Why do you want to leave so badly?"

She looked at him, then. "Why would you keep me when you plainly do not want me? At least in Nottingham I could find some measure of peace."

"I never said I did not want you," he corrected her.

"You said I was baggage and that our marriage did not meet with your approval," she pointed out.

He cocked an eyebrow; he *had* said that, hadn't he? "But I never said I did not want you," he repeated. "You, however, have hated me from the beginning, that much is clear. Do you find me so horrible that you would flee your lifelong home in order to escape me?"

She thought on that a moment. "I love Lioncross, my lord," she said softly. "But I will not stay where I am not wanted. Lioncross may be my home, but it is your keep now. It is out of Barringdon hands."

"You are no longer a Barringdon," Christopher said. "As of late yester eve, you became a de Lohr. Aye, you belong here."

He saw her face ripple at the mention of her new name and realized that David had been right; she hated it.

"Please allow me to go to Nottingham," she whispered pleadingly. "I would be happy there."

"And you would not be happy here if you remained?" he asked, not really wanting her to go but not wanting her to be miserable if she stayed.

After several long moments she shook her head negatively, her only answer. He could see the tears starting anew as she turned away from him.

Christopher sighed. He found increasingly that he did not want her to go, but he would not order her to remain. It would be better to have no wife at all than a miserable one making his life hell.

"Very well," he replied. "You may depart as soon as you are ready. My men will escort you."

"Thank you, my lord," she whispered, standing over the freshly turned earth of Mary's grave.

With a final, and perhaps sad, glance, he turned and left her in the dimness of the chapel.

ω

CHRISTOPHER DID NOT see his wife the rest of the morning. He knew she had come out of the chapel, according to his sentries, but she did not appear for the nooning meal and he checked with the kitchen to see if she had requested her meal sent to her rooms. She had not, and he grew irritated. He had no time for all of this foolishness; he had a keep to run.

Forcing himself to forget about the woman he had been forced to marry, he delved into assessing his keep and deciding where to begin the renovations. He knew Dustin's dowry was extensive, even though he had yet to know the exact figures, but combined with his own wealth, he knew it to be enough to make Lioncross the jewel of the Marches.

Edward assisted him with his observations. The man had a head for money and building, and was a great help to him. As he talked, Edward listened and offered educated opinions, finally helping him narrow down his priorities.

The sun overhead was warm and but the air was cool toward mid-afternoon. The bailey was virtually void of any activity as the servants stayed within the confines of Lioncross, and the sentries up on the wall were pacing their rounds. At one point, Christopher caught sight of Jeffrey pacing the walls and the two men eyed each other like two cocks.

"What is it about that man that riles you so?" Edward asked, somewhat amused.

Christopher shook his head and turned back to their business. "I do not know. I do not trust him."

"Why? He has done nothing," Edward said.

Christopher shrugged, reading the parchment in front of him that he had been writing on. Edward grinned.

"I have been talking to some of Barringdon's men," he mentioned. "They like him and seem to think he is a strong soldier. They also say he has eyes for your wife."

Christopher looked at Edward and then back up to Jeffrey on the ramparts. "Dustin?" he scratched his neck and refocused on the vellum. "Why am I not surprised? Then mayhap it is a good thing that she is going away."

Edward's mirth faded. "Are you really going to let her go?"

"She wishes it and I will grant it to her," he replied, making another notation.

Edward watched his friend, seeing that the man did not wish to discuss the subject. But Edward was naturally curious and wondered why Christopher could so easily dismiss such a lovely woman. He was shallow, true, but he also knew he was capable of deep feeling.

"When will you dismiss Jeffrey?" Edward asked after a moment.

"Today," Christopher replied.

"And when is Dustin leaving for Nottingham?" his friend asked, peering up at a broken corner on the side of the keep.

"I do not know," Christopher answered. "Whenever she is ready. Mayhap in the next few days. I will want you to ride escort, of course."

"Of course," Edward agreed dryly. "Who else to protect the Lion's Claw's wife? Incidentally, when Jeffrey is dismissed from your command, what is to say he will not show up in Nottingham and serve your wife and her mother's family?"

Christopher stopped what he was doing and looked at him. "He had better not if he values his life."

Edward cocked an eyebrow. "He does not fear you; that is evident. And what better way to seek revenge for his dismissal than to seek out your wife and serve her while you are in London?"

Christopher threw down his quill. "Enough of this, Edward. What are you driving at?"

"Nothing, my lord," Edward turned back to the parchment, confident his point was well taken. Now that Christopher had doubts about his wife going to

Nottingham, hopefully he would conclude that the only logical thing was to keep her at Lioncross or take her with him to London. Of course it was none of Edward's business what Christopher did with Dustin, but somehow, he thought she might need her husband. After all, she had just lost her mother and her father, and Christopher was the closest living relative she had. He just didn't think they should be apart.

Christopher watched his friend's dark head, glancing up at the big man on the wall. He didn't know why the thought of Jeffrey near his wife bothered him so, but it did. Confused and irritated, he turned back to his task, silently cursing Edward for getting him worked up over nothing.

Not an hour later, he heard sentries shouting and immediately mounted the ladder to the wall, jogging in the direction the men were indicating. When he reached the northwest corner of the wall, a worried soldier met him.

"Riders, my lord," he breathed.

Christopher peered in the direction the man was pointing, straining his eyes against the sun. It was a moment before he could make out the little group of riders crossing the distant field, heading toward them. Being that they were on the Welsh Marches, he was alerted.

"Welsh?" he turned to the sentry.

The man nodded. "We get raiding parties on occasion, my lord," he replied. "Just rebels, in faith, but we still must keep them from the village. They like to steal goods and women."

"Christ," Christopher muttered, turning to Edward over his shoulder. "Assemble fifty men and find my brother and the other knights. We ride."

The bailey turned into a hive of activity as soldiers donned their protective gear and the knights began assembling. Christopher dashed to his quarters, quickly acquiring his armor, and then hustled back down to the bailey to find that his steed had already been saddled and was waiting for him.

Leeton, David, Max and Anthony, and Edward were quickly getting the men assembled and moving. Christopher shoved his helmet on and mounted his dancing destrier, glancing in Leeton's direction.

"So it seems that you and I are to ride to service together once again," he remarked.

Leeton nodded. "I have decided to stay here awhile, if it pleases you," he said. "I always did enjoy a good fight with you guarding my rear. Max and Anthony are ready to swear fealty to you as well, as they are bachelor knights. Any objections?"

Underneath his faceplate, Christopher smiled. He was more than pleased. "I will have the best knight stable in all of England," he answered. "Even Richard shall be jealous."

Leeton was preparing to reply when a shout from atop the wall interrupted him.

"Do you know where your wife is, my lord?" Jeffrey called.

Christopher looked up at the man. "You must, or you would not be asking me," he replied loudly, coolly. "Where is she?"

Jeffrey didn't answer for a moment. "In the village," he said. "She left two hours ago and has yet to return. What kind of husband are you that you do not keep track of your wife? You had better get to her before the Welsh do."

"Bastard," Leeton muttered.

Christopher didn't reply. He spurred his horse through the gate, yelling orders to the sergeant in charge to close the gates after the brigade had passed through. As he tore into the village, he was suddenly aware of a curious pounding of his heart. Be it at the excitement or because he was concerned for his wife's safety, he could not be sure. But he knew he had to find her. The thought of Dustin in Welsh hands drove him crazed with anger.

ᘛ

DUSTIN HAD INDEED left Lioncross in the early afternoon to do a bit of shopping in the village. She had been toying with the idea of a few new dresses, purely for appearance sake, but firmly decided that she should now that she would be traveling to Nottingham. All of her dresses were simple peasant clothes, with the exception of the blue surcoat she had worn yesterday. Even her wedding dress had been borrowed from her mother, but it had been far too small in the bustline.

But before she did any haggling with the merchants, she went to Rebecca's small hut near the edge of town. Rebecca's mother was a midwife and her father farmed a small plot of land, which he sold vegetables from. It had been the first time she had seen Rebecca since yesterday, and the young woman's mouth fell open at everything that had transpired in that brief span of time. She was driven to tears by the enormity of it all, yet controlled herself for Dustin's sake. Her friend looked as if she had taken all she could.

Rebecca was glad to go shopping with Dustin, just the thing to get their minds from their troubles. Though Rebecca had little money, she did have an eye for taste and quality, and in no time had three fine bolts of material selected from a nearby merchant.

"Now, just who will sew these dresses, Dustin?" Rebecca asked pointedly as they carried their burden from the shop.

Dustin grinned. "You, of course."

Rebecca rolled her eyes. "I knew it. And what do I get out of it?"

"I shall pay you, Rebecca, have no fear," Dustin replied. "But you will have to have them finished by tomorrow, for that's when I plan to leave."

Rebecca's smile faded. "Nottingham. 'Tis so far away, Dustin. Do you truly have to go?"

Dustin watched the ground as they walked. "Aye, I do. I will not stay here longer than I have to."

"But he did not seem so cruel," Rebecca offered hesitantly. "Mayhap he is a kind man if you will only give him a chance."

"I do not want to give him a chance," Dustin snapped.

"He is your husband for life, Dustin," Rebecca reminded her. "Will you go through your whole life avoiding and hating him?"

"Mayhap," Dustin lifted her chin defiantly. "He does not want me, either, Rebecca. He told me so. He doesn't even know where I am at this moment because he does not care."

"Every man wants you, Dustin," her friend said wryly. "And mayhap he could care if you would just be a bit more...."

"Stop," Dustin told her curtly. "I do not want to speak of this anymore. What kind of dresses are you making me?"

The women chatted and stopped at the bakers for sticky honey bread with currants in it, being careful not to get any on the fabric. The next stop was the cobblers, and before Dustin realized it, the entire afternoon had passed her by.

She felt better than she had earlier. Rebecca always lifted her spirits. She tried hard to forget this was the day she buried her mother. But as the day began to wane, she knew she had to return to Lioncross. She wondered if her husband would expect her to serve him dinner tonight. She would, as a show of thanks for allowing her to travel to Nottingham. But in the deep recesses of her mind she wondered if he would expect more this night.

He was, after all, her husband. It was her duty as a wife to couple with him to produce heirs. It was a frightening thought, for she knew little of coupling, and it was all the more terrifying to think that her husband's cold demeanor would carry over into the bedchamber. She had heard from some of the serving wenches that knights could be most rough in bed, even abusive. She wondered if he was the abusive type.

"Why are you so quiet?" Rebecca broke into her thoughts.

Dustin shrugged, gazing up at Lioncross as it loomed over the village like a huge sentinel. "Just thinking, I suppose. Rebecca, what do you know about coupling?"

Rebecca looked thoughtful. "I know it keeps my mother in business," she laughed. "I know that it can be painful the first time, for the woman, but some say they gain pleasure from it. Why? What was it like?"

"I do not know," Dustin admitted. "He hasn't... that is to say, we slept apart last night. Mayhap I can avoid him until I leave for Nottingham. I do not wish to do *that* with him."

Rebecca nodded. "He is a big brute, the biggest man I have ever seen," she agreed. "I do not blame you for being frightened."

"I am not frightened," Dustin insisted. "I simply do not want him to touch me."

Rebecca shook her head. Dustin had a great amount of dislike for her new husband, yet she could hardly blame her.

The sun was low in the sky but just as intense as the two women made their way back to Rebecca's tidy little hut. Rebecca's mother had a huge pot of lamb stew bubbling over the hearth and the rich smells made Dustin's stomach rumble. Knowing she would most likely lose her appetite tonight when she was forced to serve her husband, she heartily agreed to the older woman's offer of food and ate two bowls of the thick soup.

It was a pleasant meal as they ate and discussed the dresses Rebecca would make. Dustin had purchased dark gold brocade, a lavender silk, and a heavier wine-colored silk. Rebecca had some grand ideas about sleeves and bustlines, and Dustin agreed to everything she suggested. Knowing nothing about fashion or clothes herself, she would agree to anything.

Dustin was comforted by the two familiar women, her grief easing somewhat with the hominess of the hut and the pleasant conversation. She had always liked it here, and Rebecca's mother, Eve, had always been very kind to her. The older woman was most distressed to hear of the events from the previous day and took to brewing Dustin a concoction of chamomile, rosehips and honey to soothe her mind and stomach.

It was just before dusk when Rebecca's father entered the hut, his ruddy face glazed with concern. His fears were doubled when he saw that the mistress of Lioncross sat at his hearth.

"Oh lord, my lady," he exclaimed.

Dustin and the other two women rose swiftly. "What is it, Jacob?" Eve demanded.

"Welsh raiders," the man said. Being on the edge of the village like they were, they were always more vulnerable than anyone else. "We must hide."

Rebecca gave a little shriek and knocked over her stool. "Under the beds!"

"How close, Jacob?" Eve was breathless.

"Close," her husband replied, hustling the women toward the beds. "I barely beat them out of the fields."

Panic rose in Dustin's veins. She had lived here all of her life and had seen what Welsh raiders could do. But never in that time had she been caught outside the protective walls of Lioncross, and she was terrified.

"Are the soldiers riding to meet them?" her voice was shaking.

"I do not know, my lady. I can only assume so," the man replied, practically shoving his wife under the bigger of the two beds.

Of course they were riding to intercept them. Her soldiers were alert, that is to say, her husband's soldiers were alert. And, after all, her husband was a baron and had fought with Richard, hadn't he? Surely he was riding out, too. He would protect them.

Just as Rebecca was sliding under the smaller bed, the door of the hut crashed in with a deafening noise. Dustin shrieked, startled and panicked to see three swarthy Welsh bandits storm into the room, the faces bent on nothing short of murder. She ran cold with terror, she knew what was going to happen to her and there was no way to stop it.

But she bolted away just the same, only to be caught by one of the bastards, who laughed gleefully. At that point Dustin could only think of what was going to happen to her. She was filled with a panic and knew that her only hope was to fight like the devil, and fight she did.

The raider had her around the waist, holding her up against him and babbling in the harsh Welsh native tongue. She was twisting wildly, swinging her fists and putting every ounce of strength she had in her legs to kick him painfully. But he was laughing, spewing Welsh and snorting, and she knew it would not end well for her.

He was carrying her through the main room and back into a smaller all-purpose room. Dustin put her hands out as they passed through the doorway, making it impossible for him to move her through it until he removed her wedged arms. He would succeed in removing one only to have the other grab hold of the jamb and cling for dear life. It took the raider four tries to get her to release her hold so he could move her through the archway.

There was a table in the small room. Dustin threw herself forward and grabbed ahold of it, struggling fiercely enough that the man lost his grip for a moment, and it was enough of a chance for her to grab hold of the leg of the table, winding her arms around it in a death-grip. She could not, would not, let her anchor go, for she knew if she did, then her fight was lost.

The raider was angry now. He grabbed Dustin by the hair and pulled hard, drawing screams from her but she did not release her hold. He tugged and tugged, finally grabbing hold of her arms and pulling with a grunt of effort. He managed to pull Dustin and the table several feet across the floor, but little else.

By now the man was thoroughly frustrated and resorted to smacking Dustin across her head and shoulders, trying to daze her enough to force her to relinquish her hold. She screamed loudly with the shock and pain, but bore down and tried to protect her head as much as she could. But, truth was, she was becoming light-headed and she was scared to death. Mayhap she was to see her mother and father sooner than she had expected.

The man grabbed a big iron spoon and hit Dustin across the temple with it, stunning her. Her grip relaxed and she fell heavily to the floor, her temple bloodied.

Pleased with the result and a bit weary from the effort, the dirty man rolled Dustin over onto her back and tore at her bodice, his filthy hands roving greedily over her breasts. She moaned and made a feeble attempt to claw at him, but he laughed and began to push her skirts up, running his hands along her shapely legs, murmuring in Welsh the entire time. Spittle hung from his lips; he was going to enjoy this one.

But he never had the chance. He heard his cohorts yelling, only to be immediately silenced. Panicked, he rose from his crouch but never made it completely to his feet as a shadow fell across the room. Before he could defend himself, the Welshman's body collapsed on the floor as his head rolled to the opposite wall in a bright spray of blood and flesh.

Christopher's sword was still in his hand and he moved to Dustin. He could see that she was injured and he sheathed his sword with a hissed curse. The strangest feeling welled up in his chest but he chased it off angrily, too busy to deal with it at that moment. All he knew was that he felt a sense of both grief and relief. It was the oddest sensation he had ever known.

He tore off his gauntlets, running his hands gently over her head, probing the gash along her hairline. Her beautiful hair was sticky with blood and he found himself stroking it aside gently. Satisfied her skull wasn't fractured, he proceeded to assess the rest of her body and his concern was lessened to find that she had no broken bones. With his examination complete, he gathered Dustin into his arms and carried her into the greater room.

But his tight chest still plagued him and he was greatly angered by it. *Damn foolish woman.* She was more trouble than she was worth. Christ, how could he let her go to Nottingham when all she ever did was get into trouble? He would not be near to save her if she left. Disgusted with himself for feeling a sense of duty to his wife, he found it easier to deal with if he focused his anger on the foolishness of her actions.

Rebecca and her family were huddling by the hearth, all of them gasping when they saw Dustin, unconscious, with blood coating her head. Christopher passed them a disinterested gaze.

"She suffers no broken bones," he said coolly. "She will live."

"She fought him like a banshee, my lord," Rebecca said bravely, her pale face streaked with tears. "She was very courageous."

He raised a brow. "And very foolish. What was she doing here?"

"We went shopping, my lord," Rebecca said. "She bought material for new dresses. To please you," she added, although it was an out and out lie. The baron looked so angry that she felt she had to say something to ease his fury toward her friend.

A flicker of an expression crossed his face but was quickly gone. He dared a small glance at Dustin's pale face, surprised by her friend's words.

"Be that as it may, you were all lucky I found you in time, or the remains of Lady Dustin would now be coating your floor," he said sternly. "Mistress Rebecca, you and my wife are never to leave the safety of Lioncross unescorted again. Is that clear?"

"Perfectly, my lord," Rebecca replied, seeing his coldness but also noticing just how handsome the man really was. It was an odd combination.

Christopher studied the young woman for a brief second before turning for the door. Two other huge, fierce-looking knights were there waiting for him.

"My lord," Rebecca called out to him, taking a few brave steps forward. "How *did* you find us? There are so many other huts, and you did not know where Dustin had gone."

"Did she tell you that I did not know she was gone?" he asked.

Rebecca nodded. "Aye, my lord, she did and she said you did not care."

He looked back at the young woman with the red hair for a few long moments. He could feel himself relenting somehow, easing. He cared where she went; he forced himself to admit it.

"Her screams," he finally said. "I recognized her screams."

Rebecca's eyebrows furrowed. "I do not understand, my lord."

He sighed sharply and averted his gaze. "You asked me how I found her. It was because I recognized her screams. She carries a distance."

He was gone, leaving Rebecca and her family to clean up a grisly mess in the smaller room but considering it a small price for their lives.

CHAPTER FIVE

DUSTIN'S FIRST COGNIZANT impression was one of pain. Her head hurt, her neck hurt, her shoulders hurt. Everything hurt. She had no idea why she was in so much pain, but she tried to move a bit and was met with sharp jabs and aches everywhere. In a rush, the attack came back to her and she found that she could lift her sore arms, with effort, just enough to put her hand to her spinning head. She only remembered being beat, and then darkness. She could only assume the worst had happened and with that horrible thought, she began to cry.

"Are you in pain?" She recognized Christopher's voice immediately and her eyes flew open, dazed and stunned.

"My lord," she gasped. "What? Where am I?"

"Home, my lady, at Lioncross," he said. "Tell me, do you hurt?"

She stared back at him, her mouth agape. How did she get back here? Lord, she didn't remember a thing.

"Aye," she whispered, letting her arm fall back to her side.

"Tell me where," he instructed.

She noticed that he was dressed in a pair of soft leather breeches and a white tunic that, for the first time, revealed the magnificence of his build to her. His shoulders were extremely broad and his waist was very slender and it made her head hurt to think him pleasantly formed; she didn't want to think him pleasant in any way. Especially in lieu of the tongue-lashing she was about to receive from him. And she deserved it, she had not told anyone where she was going on purpose.

"My head," she whispered, closing her eyes. "And nearly everywhere else."

She felt his hand about her head and was surprised that for the huge size of them, they were as gentle as butterfly wings.

"I cleaned the cut on your temple, but I am afraid I had to put a stitch in it. However, your hair should cover the tiny scar," his hands were moving down her neck to her shoulders. "I didn't feel any broken bones. Do you have any sharp pains?"

"No," her voice was feeble. "Just aches."

He didn't reply and took his hand from her. Dustin had yet to hear him move away from the bed and could only assume he was still standing there, looking at her, waiting for her to open her eyes so he could yell at her.

Then, she heard a joint pop as he turned and walked away, heading across the floor. Secretly, she cracked an eye open to see what he was doing. She saw that he was over near the door, pouring himself a goblet of wine from her pretty pewter decanter.

As he stood there, she began to notice just how well-formed the man was, in spite of the fact that she didn't want to notice. His legs were long and as big around as small trees, and the hand that held the goblet swallowed it up. That had been nearly the first thing she noticed about him, how big his hands were. Yet when he had touched her, he was as gentle as a lamb. It was a confusing paradox, she thought, distressing her all the more. But she would rather die than admit she found her new husband… attractive.

"Would you like some wine?" he was still over by the door, facing away from her.

So he knew she was watching him. No use pretending otherwise. She rolled over onto her side with a great deal of effort, watching him as he turned around to look at her.

"You are grunting like an old man," he commented, coming toward her.

"I feel like an old man," she answered. "I feel like I am dying."

"Nay, my lady, you are very much alive," he said.

Her head suddenly came up. "And Rebecca? Is she…"

"Your companion is well, as is her family," he answered her. "You seemed to have borne the brunt of the assault."

She lay her head back down slowly, relieved. "I was the only one who ran. I suppose they did not want me to escape."

"What they wanted was your soft white flesh," he replied.

She closed her eyes and big, fat tears spilled over, running down onto the pillow beneath her. Her lower lip trembled until she bit it, forcing it still. Christopher watched her struggle with her fear.

"No need for tears, my lady," he said after a moment. "You are safe and will recover."

Her eyes few open and riveted on him. "But I will never recover what that damnable bastard took from me."

"What did he take from you?" Christopher demanded. "Did he steal something?"

She wondered how Christopher fit into all of this, closing her eyes against his angry face. Had Rebecca and her family brought her back to the keep, leaving the explaining up to her? She remembered so little that she was close to admitting she was going to have to ask Christopher how much he knew and what had happened. She was terrified of what he might do to her if he found out she had been raped.

"How did I get back here?" She hoped she could find out what she wanted to know without damaging her pride. She hated admitting she was dependent on him for answers.

"I brought you back here," he said. "Yet you did not answer me. What did he steal?"

"*You* brought me back here?" She lifted her head curiously. "But how did you know? I mean, how did you find me? Did you ride out with the soldiers to intercept the raiders?"

"I did not ride out with my men." He came over to the bed. "Jeffrey told me you had gone into the village and I went looking for you. When the raiders attacked the outskirts, I then moved to defend the village and only by chance heard your screams." He stood at the foot of the bed with a reproving glare. "I found you by pure luck alone, Dustin, nothing more. Had I not been within earshot, that marauder might have taken more than your innocence, he might have taken your life. As it was, you received a nice gash to the scalp for your troubles and you were lucky for only that."

She blinked up at him, his words slowly registering. Then she was not violated? Relief swept through her, making her limp and weak. But along with the same thought she realized that Christopher had saved her life, and the lives of her friend and her family. She was indebted to him whether or not she wanted to be and she found the thought distasteful. She did not want to be obligated to him for any reason.

"You should have let him kill me," she said bitterly, turning away. "Then Lioncross would be yours and you would have no wife to burden you."

He slowly cocked an eyebrow. "I saved your life and this is how you thank me?"

"How would you have me thank you?" she shot back in a rage, thought better of it, and cooled. "I am your wife, my lord. If simple words of thanks do not suffice, you may simply take what pleases you to even the debt."

"Your self-pity grows tiresome," he said, moving around the side of the bed. "I will not take anything from you, wife. You will give it or I will not have it. And simple words will suffice, though I expect none for I was simply doing my duty. You are my wife and I would protect you."

She met his gaze for several long moments. It was an expectant silence, waiting for her reply to determine if this conversation would end as the others had, with anger and bitterness. Surprisingly, her eyes softened just a bit and she licked her rosy lips.

"Thank you for doing your duty, my lord."

She had swallowed her pride, he knew that. He felt no need to rub her nose in it. "You are welcome," he said.

She looked at him for a moment longer before twisting around and trying to arrange her pillows so that she might sit up. The pressure on her shoulders when she lay on her back was painful. Christopher saw what she was trying to accomplish, however weakly, and moved to help her. When the pillows were stacked and she struggled to sit up, he put his hands under her arms and lifted her up, moving her back against the pillows.

"My thanks again, my lord," she said softly. It was becoming easier the more she practiced.

"Are you comfortable now?" he stood back.

She winced as she tried to adjust her sore body. "As much as possible, I suppose. The fiend did do a complete job of beating me."

Christopher's face fell a bit. "He beat you?"

She nodded, glancing up at him and wondering why he looked so disturbed. Surely he knew that.

"Where? Show me," he demanded.

She sat forward a bit, pulling back the collar of her dress. "My shoulders and back," she told him as he pulled the material even further to observe her injuries. "I grabbed hold of a table leg and would not let go, and he took a stick to me."

Her dress had covered up all of this, he thought grimly as he studied the purple and blue bruises. And there were several ugly welts, not enough to bleed through the material, but severe enough to hurt. Certainly he had checked her for broken bones, but he had not seen the bruises she bore.

He stood back and she noticed his jaw was ticking, knowing that he found her repulsive. Absently, she tugged at the collar of her dress, trying to cover her horrible bruises.

"Nay, do not," he told her curtly. "Remove that dress. I will return."

With that, he spun on his heel and quit the room, slamming the door behind him.

Dustin was bewildered. She had no idea what he had in mind, only knowing that the man frightened and confused her. Lord, she was so weary and sore that all she wanted to do was soak her beaten body in a tub of hot water. Tossing off the covers, she stiffly rose from the bed and summoned a serving wench for a bath.

He said he would return. She knew he would, but she didn't care. He would probably be gone hours and she didn't care if he ever returned; only wanting to sit up to her neck in rose-scented water and forget this horrible, horrible day ever happened. She brightened a little to remember that most likely, on the morrow, she would be traveling to Nottingham and there she could start fresh, away from her husband and away from the home that no longer welcomed her.

CHRISTOPHER RE-ENTERED HIS wife's room to discover that she had only partially obeyed him. True, she had taken off the dress, but she had not donned a robe, instead, choosing to take a bath, of all things. She was busy singing away with her back to him, lathering a bar of soap between her hands.

He stood by the door for several minutes, watching her run soapy hands over her arms and legs, the firelight glistening off of her slick skin. He knew she had not heard him enter with all of the noise she was making and wondered if he should announce himself or if he should continue to stand there, stealing glances at the woman he married.

But he was not a voyeur and he cleared his throat loudly, telling her he had returned. Dustin shrieked and covered her nakedness with her arms, sinking up to her mouth in the warm water.

Christopher walked slowly and deliberately around the tub, his hands on his hips as he gazed down at her. She was watching him with huge eyes, obviously quite shocked and outraged at his boldness.

"I do not recall telling you to take a bath," he said.

"The warm water makes my aches feel better, my lord," she replied, water in her mouth.

"I told you I would return," he pointed out.

"But you did not say when," she insisted.

He had to admit she was, technically, correct. He gave her another reproachful glance as to not admit her accuracy and went to put a vial of some kind over on the table. She eyed the container curiously.

"What is that?" she asked suspiciously.

"Get out of that tub," he told her.

She sat a little straighter, eyeing him and the vial. "I would know what that is."

He frowned. "It is not poison, for Christ's sake. Get out of the bath."

"But…but I have not washed my hair," she said, wondering if she was going to have to drink the potion in the glass and absolutely not wanting to.

He looked at her irritably for a moment before beginning to roll up his sleeves. "Very well. I will do it and you will be done with this."

"I am quite capable of washing my own hair," she protested, thinking his hands on her while she was in the tub were entirely too intimate and disturbing.

"Why? Do not you have maids to do it for you?" he was still rolling up his sleeves.

"I bathe alone, my lord," she said stiffly.

He frowned again and moved towards her. "Why in the hell would you do that with a house full of servants to help you?" he asked. " 'Tis most strange that you would."

He had come too close and she suddenly plunged her head underneath the water, as if trying to hide her whole body from him. He fought off a grin, trying to remain severe as he stood over the tub and waited patiently for her to run out of air. She came back up several moments later, sputtering and coughing. He did grin then.

"Are you finished?" he asked, picking up her soap. "Can we get through this, please?"

She started to protest and again attempted to dive under the water but he grabbed her by the hair, rubbing soap into her scalp until it frothed up a rich white. Roses filled the air, permeated the skin of his hands and he knew he would be smelling the scent for the rest of the night. Not an entirely bad prospect, he had had to admit. The scent was growing on him.

Dustin was initially appalled at his actions. She didn't want the man near her, much less helping her to bathe. But the very moment his big, gentle hands started massaging her scalp, she quickly reconsidered. The maids could be rough, which was why she liked to do it herself. But not Christopher; his hands were actually tender as he scrubbed her scalp, lathered her hair, and worked his way down to the very ends.

She felt herself relaxing, closing her eyes at his touch and hating herself for it, yet it was so wonderful she could not help it. There were moments when she would remember that she didn't like him and she would stiffen again, but a mere few seconds later she would go as limp as a wet rag. It was a strange condition that struck in wave after wave until she finally relented completely and allowed herself to enjoy the attention. It was so new to her, so completely foreign, but she knew she liked it very much.

Christopher liked it, too. It was certainly one of the most pleasant experiences he had ever had and he soaped her hair much longer than was necessary simply because he loved the feeling of her hair in his hands and was growing to like the smell of roses. She had stopped fighting him and that pleased him strangely, too.

But the water was growing cool and it would not do for her to take a chill. Taking an empty pitcher left by the side of the tub, he filled it from the bath and poured it over her hair, again and again until the water ran clear.

Neither one of them had said a word the entire time. It was as if both of them were reconsidering their harsh stances, wondering if indeed the other was not as bad as was originally thought. It was a curious time for wondering and reasoning and thinking, trying to sort out insane ideas as to what marriage was truly about. They were married, the holiest and most intimate of unions, yet they were strangers to one another.

Mayhap under different circumstances they might have felt differently toward one another, but their beginning had been so rough that it was difficult to feel any other way.

Christopher twisted her hair, wringing the water from it. Then he moved for the large square of linen and held it up for her.

Dustin looked back at him, stunned at what he was suggesting. Yet his expression was completely devoid of any emotion whatsoever as he held it up patiently; even so, she was extremely hesitant to climb out of the tub. After all, they were strangers. Surely he did not expect her to forget all of her modesty simply because he was labeled her husband.

But the fact was that he *was* her husband. He had every moral and legal right to see his wife unclothed. She could hear her mother's words.

Duty, Dustin, duty!

Swallowing her embarrassment and humility, and knowing she was surely going to die from shame, she rose quickly from the tub as the water coursed off her body. Avoiding his eyes, she jumped over the side and threw herself into the linen towel, pushing herself against him in the process. Much to her surprise, his massive arms went around her and began to dry her briskly.

Dustin was buffeted back and forth by the force of his invigorating drying. She remembered how her mother used to dry her like this when she was young, and it almost made her smile. He was rapid yet thorough, starting at her shoulders and moving all the way down to her feet. As rough as he was, it was actually rather pleasant and she was so relaxed by the time he finished that she almost fell forward onto the floor when he stopped.

He caught her before she could fall and mumbled something she didn't catch, then threw the towel over her head and rubbed her hair vigorously until it was wild and askew and hanging in front of her eyes.

"Do you have a dressing gown?" he asked.

She was standing naked before him and had completely forgotten her state. The way he had bathed her and dried her left her feeling so comfortable and familiar with him that when he asked her the question, she simply pointed to the wardrobe and he retrieved an old robe that her mother had given her.

He held the robe out and she put her arms in the sleeves, tossing her hair out of her eyes as he pulled the sash tight. He pulled it so taut she grunted and he took her hand and led her back over to the bed.

"Now, to take care of your shoulders," he murmured, pulling the top of the robe down to reveal her delicate shoulders and neck.

Truth was, he was so caught up in tending her that he hadn't even stopped to realize that this was the same vicious woman who had slapped him earlier, who had screamed disrespectfully in her rage. The woman before him was calm and obedient and completely, entirely beautiful.

He didn't know why he had held up the towel to her. True, he was intensely curious about her body and was not disappointed with his observations. She was perfectly formed, even for her small size, and her ripe breasts were the most beautiful he had ever seen. Aye, she was damn pleasing and he had been a fool to cover up all of that beauty with the robe.

It was so strange, this relationship they had developed since he had washed her hair. He hadn't spoken but a handful of words to her, and she had yet to utter a sound, yet they moved together and responded to one another with alarming comfort. The male part of him liked it very much, but the rational part did not. To have a wife that was distant and cold was safe for him, someone who could not affect him in any way. But this woman in front of him now, this vulnerable lass, was dangerous. This was a wife who could get under his skin.

"Wait," she put up her hand as he picked up the glass vial. "My hair. I would brush it before it dries into a bird's nest."

"I shall do it."

He said it so fast that he startled himself. Why in the hell should he want to brush her hair? It was a maid's duty. Yet he was brushing it all the same, watching the light from the fire play off of the silver and gold highlights. It began to occur to him that he wanted to do these things because his wife was now an acquired possession and, like most possessions, it was natural to want to inspect what was now his. He had been married to her for nearly an entire day and was not ashamed to admit he was pleased with this fancy piece of property.

Her hair combed out and braided to keep it under control, he once again pushed down the collar of the robe and picked up the vial. He had seen the extent of the damage when he had bathed her, and he rubbed the mint-smelling balm between his hands before massaging it gently into her bruised flesh, unconsciously wincing as he did so.

Dustin gasped as he touched her sore shoulders, trying to squirm away from him.

"Nay, my lady, I promise you that this will help your pains," he said firmly, not letting her escape his touch.

"But it hurts so," she moaned. "And that poison smells fiercely."

He smiled faintly. "It does indeed, but trust me when I tell you that it will help you."

She bravely allowed him to rub more of the stuff into her shoulders, flinching when he hit a particularly sensitive spot. But his hands were expert as they touched her and she gradually relaxed, beginning to trust him somewhat. And as she grew to trust him, she also realized her curiosity about the man was growing, too. She could see no harm in asking him a few simple questions.

"Where do you come from?" she asked softly.

"My home is in Derbyshire," he replied. "The keep where I was born is called Lohrham Forest."

"Is David your only brother?" she asked, her eyes closing drowsily as his warm hands moved over her skin.

"Aye," he replied. "And I have a sister, too, although I have not seen her in some time. She is fostering in Bath."

"How old is she?" Dustin inquired.

"Almost seventeen," he said. "Her name is Deborah."

Dustin's eyes opened. "A biblical name, and very pretty. Is she fair as you and David are?"

"Aye, more so." He put some more ointment on his hands and began to rub between her shoulder blades. "Yet she is not nearly as fair as you are. You have got the whitest skin I have ever seen."

She snorted ironically. "And I am sure it is beautiful shades of purple and green by now. I always did bruise easily."

His lips twitched. "Your back and shoulders are striking shades of blue."

She sighed heavily, hanging her head and he was able to rub the smelly stuff into her neck. "How did you come to acquire your unusual name?" he asked after a few silent moments.

She sighed, feeling contentment and comfort as he rubbed away. "My grandmother's ancestral keep is called Dustinley," she replied. "My mother always swore that she would name her firstborn Dustin, for she was confidant her first child would be a boy. When I was born, she would not go back on her word and named me Dustin after all. Father added Mary Catherine."

"Your father was a level-headed man," Christopher nodded in agreement.

She twisted her head back to look at him, her wide gray eyes latching onto him like a vise. He was mesmerized by the beauty, the color, the emotion he saw in the depths. "How did my father die?" she asked softly.

He lowered his gaze, concentrating on his task. After a pause, he spoke. "An arrow to the chest."

"Did he die immediately?" she asked quietly.

Nay, he did not, he lingered while his body rotted in the heat until it finally killed him. But he would not tell her that. "Aye, he did," he lied.

Under his hands, he felt her sigh. "Well and good," she said. "I should not have wished him to suffer."

It took Christopher a few moments to realize that they had shared an entirely civil, entirely pleasant conversation. The ointment he had applied was well rubbed in, but for some reason he continued massaging her shoulders and back. Her skin was like silk, and God only knew how long it had been since he had tasted female flesh. But if he caressed her any longer he knew there would be trouble, so he removed his hands and she primly pulled the collar of the robe tight about her neck.

"This poison feels warm on my skin," she said.

"Good," he replied, washing his hands in the basin. " 'Twill lessen your aches."

"What is it?" she asked, turning to look at him.

He dried his hands, gazing back at her and noticing the way the firelight played off her hair, turning it the color of downy fluff. "Something I discovered on the quest," he replied. "The Turks used it for nearly every ailment, but we Christians discovered that it works best on aches and strains."

She nodded, wondering what exotic oils were warming her flesh. She knew, at least she hoped, that he would not put anything on her that would harm her, but it was the strange smell reminding her of the alien medicament.

"Now," he put his hands on his hips as he faced her. "You will sleep this night and I do not want to hear from you again until the morning."

"Aye, my lord," she nodded, watching him as he acknowledged her with a sharp nod and turned for the door.

"My lord?" she called.

"Aye, what is it?" he turned with his hand on the latch.

She studied his face, noticing for the first time that it was rather pleasing and masculine, just like the rest of him. "Thank you."

He looked back at her and she felt a peculiar sort of tingle in her arms and chest, wondering if the foreign ointment was beginning to make her sick.

"My pleasure, my lady," he replied, closing the door behind him.

He was gone and she tried to make herself comfortable under the covers, wrinkling her nose at the strong smell about her. She would have to wash the stuff off her come the morrow. Suddenly, something heavy hit the bed and she knew without looking Caesar had decided to come out from his hiding place to join her. She smiled, petting the cat as he got comfortable next to her.

Dustin thought the smell might keep her up, but as soon as her head hit the pillow, she fell into a deep, exhausted sleep with dreams of a handsome blond husband filling her mind.

☙

EVEN AS HIS wife slept the night away, Christopher was wide awake in massive bed that was now his. He could only stare up at the ceiling, his mind a confused jumble of emotions he could not quite grasp.

She had not mentioned leaving for Nottingham on the morrow, which was good. He had reconsidered allowing her to leave and hoped that she might change her mind before he had to order her to stay. After what had happened today, he was reluctant to let her from his sight and the damnable thing was that he didn't have the slightest idea as to why.

He didn't want his chattel damaged. Aye, that was the reason. Should she be hurt or maimed, 'twould be his burden to bear. Should she be killed, he would feel damn guilty for letting her leave in the first place. He could not seem to admit to himself that he was curious about her and she was very pleasant to look at, and in the recesses of his mind he knew if she left, Lioncross would be a colorless place. Besides that, he would have to appoint one of the servant's chatelaine and from what he had seen of them, they were a stupid lot. Nay, he needed someone competent to run his house, and his wife seemed to have her wits about her. Well, sometimes.

Her place was here, at Lioncross, running the castle for him, not dreaming her days away in Nottingham. He only hoped she didn't hit him when he told her that, his lip was still swollen. Besides, if she did that, he might have to put her over his knee.

Something hit the foot of the bed and he jumped, sword in his hand before he drew another breath. Yet his defensive posture was for naught. Caesar was purring madly at the bottom of the bed, kneading at the coverlets as he approached.

He let out a loud hiss of relief and put the sword back down. "Christ, you little maggot," he grunted. "You scared the hell out of me."

Caesar's eyes were half-closed as he bumped up against Christopher's hip, his big claws snagging the coverlet. Christopher sat up and frowned at the animal. "What are you doing here, anyway? Your mistress will be wondering where you are."

The cat's answer was to purr even louder, then yawn a big cat yawn at him. Christopher grinned in spite of himself. "So you want to sleep here, do you? Well, I will not allow it. I do not like cats, especially pushy ones. Go away."

Caesar turned a couple of circles trying to find just the right spot to lay on, and then promptly deposited himself. Christopher scowled. "Nay, beast, not here," he said sternly, reaching to pick up the cat.

Quick as a flash, Caesar rolled onto his stomach and latched onto Christopher's hand, claws digging into him and his big teeth clamping down. Every time Christopher tried to move his hand, Caesar would scratch at his forearm with his huge back claws.

"So you think you have a catch, do you?" Christopher demanded, amused. The cat wasn't hurting him so long as he remained still. "Release me, devil, or I will take my dagger to you."

The cat started to purr again, still clutching his hand with a death-grip. Christopher shook his head. "Let me go and you can stay."

The cat's hind legs scratched at him again and Christopher scowled. "I promise."

He would swear until the day he died that Caesar understood him. The cat immediately released him and rolled into a ball, his green cat-eyes closing contentedly and his purring loud and rhythmic. Christopher had to chuckle, sliding back down under the covers, trying not to disrupt his new friend.

"Damnedest thing I ever saw," he muttered, finally feeling relaxed enough that he might sleep.

CAESAR WAS HALF-LAYING on his neck when he awoke. The sun was just beginning to peer over the eastern horizon and the day looked to be clear. Christopher reached up and carefully removed the animal, lest he find a claw in his neck, and sat up, scratching his head. Finally rising, he ordered hot water so that he might quickly bathe himself.

After a brief wash and shave to trim up his beard, he dressed in most of his armor and gave a quick glance at his bed before quitting the room. Caesar was still fast asleep on his pillows. Christopher shook his head at the beast, he hoped this was not to be a nightly occurrence.

The house was coming alive as he descended the stairs, servants bustling about and the smells of the morning meal floating through the dim great room. David and Edward greeted him as they came indoors from the bailey.

"You overslept," David commented.

"It would seem so," Christopher answered, turning to Edward. "How goes the repair on the north corner of the keep?"

"Done, my lord," Edward replied. "Finished yesterday while you were tending your wife. She looks well enough."

Christopher's brow furrowed. "Is she up already?"

"Aye, up and gone," David said. "She seemed quite distracted, too. Did you two have words again?"

"Gone *where*?" Christopher demanded, ignoring the other questions.

David shrugged. "I do not know, but I sent Leeton to follow her," he said. "Do not worry about her."

Christopher passed a glance at the open front door, noticing the pink hue cast over the stone. He wondered why Dustin was up so early. Where could she possibly go? His inclination was to go after her but he refrained. Leeton would watch over her.

"Well, Edward," he said after a moment, "Let us see what kind of repair job has been done to my wall."

"You will approve, my lord," Edward replied arrogantly. "I, myself, do."

Christopher raised an eyebrow. "Then let us hope that your standards are as high as mine," he said, just to poke at the man's pride.

The repair was indeed well done and Christopher was pleased. There were so many other repair jobs that Edward and David had already put men on them. Even as the sun rose the keep was busy with activity. Christopher would inspect every job, every bit of material, personally.

"Where is Sir Jeffrey?" he finally asked after inspecting the second such repair job.

"On the wall," David replied, glancing up to the ramparts. "He was up there all day yesterday, and was on the parapet before the sun rose. I have yet to say two words to that man."

Christopher stopped and looked up to the top of the wall, his eyes scanning for the big German. It did not take long for him to find the man, standing with his arms crossed near the guard tower, gazing across the distant moor.

Christopher stared at the man for a few long seconds, his face unreadable.

"Send him to me," he said finally. "We would be through with this now."

"You are going to dismiss him?" David asked.

"Hell yes." Christopher turned and went into the castle.

Jeffrey did not keep him waiting this time. Christopher received him in the small solar where he had delivered his missives to Lady Mary, standing by the long, thin windows that opened out onto the bailey. He, however, kept Jeffrey standing in silence for nearly 10 minutes before he acknowledged him.

"How long have you served here at Lioncross?" Christopher asked coolly.

"Six years," Jeffrey answered, then almost as an afterthought, "my lord."

Christopher ignored the potential insult. "Then you served Sir Arthur."

"Yah, my lord," he replied. "I am his captain."

"*Was*," Christopher corrected him as he turned around. "Since the man is dead and the fortress is mine, your position is dissolved."

Jeffrey stiffened slightly. "Lioncross is my home, my lord. I have defended her well, as I have defended Lady Mary and Lady Dustin."

Christopher looked at him then, when he mentioned Dustin, just to see what sort of expression the man held. There was none.

"Then you know of my wife's habits," he said, deliberately using the term 'wife.' "Then, pray, do you know where she went this morning? You seem to keep an eye out for her, as you pointed out to me yesterday."

"I do not know." Jeffrey's voice was colder. "I saw her leave, that is true, but I do not know where she went. Mayhap her watchdog can inform you of her actions upon their return."

"Sir Leeton is an extremely capable knight, far more than a mere watchdog, I assure you." Christopher did not like the man. "In fact, I have so many capable knights here at Lioncross that your services are no longer required. You may gather your personal possessions and be gone by the nooning meal.

He had, in effect, kicked him right out on his arse. Jeffrey, however, was expecting it and did not flinch. Instead, very strangely, he smiled and Christopher went immediately on his guard.

"As you wish, my lord," he said. "In fact, I appreciate the orders. It will allow me the freedom and adventure I have been waiting for."

Christopher didn't answer, still eyeing the man warily. Jeffrey gave a little chuckle and moved for the door, stopping in the archway.

"There is one more thing, baron," he said. "Since I am no longer under your command, then I feel no need to hold my tongue. I know your knights have been pressing the soldiers for information about me, and I can suspect what you have been told, so I will clarify the rumors for you. It is true that I feel more for Lady Dustin than simply friendship and duty. I know that you married her simply to gain the keep and for that, I cannot fault you." His voice suddenly lowered and his smile faded. "Even though I am no longer her protector, have no doubt that I will still be watching over Lady Dustin. If I hear that you have so much as touched a hair on her lovely head in anger or violence, then I will come and I will kill you. Remember that."

Christopher's eyes were glittering at the statement. He had no idea why the words had riled him so, for he had been issued hundreds of challenges and had not so much as batted an eyelash in return. He had no doubt that the man was sincere, and he had no doubt that it would be a hell of a fight from the size of the man. But a peculiar gripping warmth was spreading through him at the confession the man had made for Dustin and he was at a loss as to why, but he knew that the emotion was most overwhelming.

"I will remember if you will also remember one thing. Lady Dustin is now my wife and I do not want you anywhere near her," he said, his voice like cold steel. "If I ever hear that you have so much as speak her name, then I will find you and cut your heart out. Forget what you feel for her, for your emotions will surely be your death."

The two men stared at each other viciously, each trying to read the other, trying to discern any emotion other than hate.

"She is nothing but chattel to you," Jeffrey hissed after a moment. "You would kill me over a piece of property? Are you that possessive?"

"She is my wife," Christopher answered, evading his questions. "That is reason enough to kill for her."

Jeffrey's jaw ticked and his fists clenched. "You are dooming her to a life of unhappiness, you know that," he said. "At least with me, there would have been a chance for joy."

"Then I am curious," Christopher said. "Why did you not marry her before I got here? Surely you could have spoken to Lady Mary."

"I did," he shot back, then quickly regained his control. "She would not consent to anything without Sir Arthur's permission. She said that I would have to wait until he returned from the Holy Land." His gaze turned bitter. "As we know now, he did not return."

Christopher suddenly saw quite a few things clearly and his anger, though not lessened, went no further. The man was in love with his wife and bitterly disappointed that the situation was out of his control. With Arthur's death and the king's decree, there was nothing he could do and he was understandably disappointed.

"Does Dustin know any of this?" Christopher asked after a moment.

"Nay," Jeffrey met his look. "Lady Mary never told her. She knew, as I did, that Lady Dustin had no interest in marriage."

Christopher dropped his gaze thoughtfully. Jeffrey slowly moved toward him, the anger and hatred between them somewhat lessened over the last few moments. After several moments of reflection, Christopher snickered.

"She certainly did not want to marry me," he said ironically. "Nor I, her, for that matter."

"She did not want to marry anyone," Jeffrey said. "The number of suitors Lady Dustin has had over the past three years is staggering. The list of prospects fill an entire drawer in Lady Mary's desk. Knights, barons, a few earls, and even a duke. There was nothing to do but wait until Arthur's return to plead for Lady Dustin's hand."

So Dustin was much pursued? Certainly she was beautiful enough and he was not surprised. He wondered what would happen now when the word got out that Lady Dustin had taken a husband. He wondered if he would be fighting off armies of scorned suitors. *Ah, well, let them come.* He was up to it. He glanced up at Jeffrey.

"Tell me, then," he said. "With all of the suitors, she was not interested in any of them? I find that hard to believe."

Jeffrey smiled, a real one. "You do not know your wife very well," he said. "She would rather tend a garden than recite poetry, or ride a horse rather than sit quietly and embroider. Men are of no interest to her, and I cannot count the times when I have had to pull her off of some hapless fool because he tried to hold her hand or steal a kiss. She is completely unaware of her beauty and her femininity, my lord, I assure you."

Christopher listened to him, absorbing his words. Jeffrey was right; he did not know his wife at all. The big German knight could see the uncertainty in Christopher's eyes.

"Tell me," Jeffrey said softly. "What do you intend to do with her? What I mean is that if you do not want her, and you obviously do not, would you deny her happiness?"

Christopher turned his full attention to the man, studying him. "If you are asking if I would allow her to take a lover simply because you believe I don't want her, the answer is nay. She is my wife and she will not commit adultery."

"But you will give her no affection," Jeffrey said sharply. "The only thing that holds your interest is this damn keep. Your eyes glaze over it as if it were the most beautiful woman in the world and, for that fact, you have already taken a mistress. Lioncross."

Christopher stiffened. "She is my wife, Jeffrey. No amount of pleading and reasoning will change that fact."

Jeffrey's jaw ticked, forcing himself to calm, but there was not the same hatred in his eyes as had been earlier. He was in a no-win situation and he knew it. He was not daft and he knew there was nothing more to say.

"Then I will take my leave, my lord," he said quietly. "But before I go, I would ask a favor of you. Treat Lady Dustin with respect, please. I would be indebted to you for the kindness."

Christopher gazed back at the man, seeing no malice or ulterior motives in the statement. He could see that Jeffrey truly loved his wife, and he suddenly felt a bit of sympathy for the man.

"She is most stubborn and abrasive," Christopher replied grimly. "May I at least spank her on occasion, should she warrant it?"

Jeffrey smiled faintly. "Yah, I have wanted to do the same at times."

Christopher nodded, his gaze impassive. He began to rethink his harsh stance on banishing the man now that he understood why. He felt there was an understanding between them now, and given Jeffrey's experience with Lioncross and the land, he did not want to rid himself so quickly of his valuable knowledge because of a jealous whim. Perhaps it would be better to allow him to remain.

He paused before speaking. "If you wish to stay, I will not oppose you."

Jeffrey s eyes widened. "But you said, I mean, yah, my lord, I would serve you well."

Christopher cocked a stern eyebrow. "Yet there are two conditions. My brother, David, is now captain of the troops."

Jeffrey nodded. "Yah, my lord. He is a fine soldier."

"And you will bank the fever you have for my wife," Christopher finished in a low voice.

Jeffrey cleared his throat, though his gaze never wavered. "With all of my strength, my lord, I swear it."

"You had better," Christopher said, moving past him.

The men proceeded into the great hall, with Christopher confident he had acquired another fine knight and pleased with the turn of events. Now that he understood Jeffrey, his mind was a bit more at ease. Yet that strange feeling of jealousy still filled him every time he thought of the man's admission, but he shrugged it off. He had no idea how to deal with it.

Jeffrey exited the castle with a slight bow, leaving the wide open front doors and crossing the compound to disappear into a wall turret. Christopher stood at the entrance to the castle for a moment, running his fingers through his thick blond hair, his thoughts turning back to Dustin and wondering where she was.

He did not have to wait long. A familiar figure suddenly appeared, walking across the drawbridge and through the front gates. Not far behind was a big man on a destrier, plodding along. Relieved she had returned, he wondered if he should go and greet her or if he should simply go along his way now that he knew she was back, safe. He decided on the latter until he saw Dustin wipe at her eyes, a clear sign that she was crying.

He could not stop himself, he went to her.

"What ails you, my lady?" he asked impassively.

Dustin looked up at him quickly and then immediately lowered her head. Her lovely face was smeared with dirt and tears and Christopher looked up at Leeton in confusion. His friend merely shrugged back.

"Dustin, what is wrong?" he asked again.

She shook her head, quickening her pace for the castle. He followed, catching up with her just as she entered the dim interior. He reached out and gently grasped her arm.

"Tell me what the matter is. Mayhap I can help," he said softly.

She stopped but pulled her arm from his grip. She fully intended to answer him calmly, but when she opened her mouth, she began blubbering again. "Nothing," she bawled.

Concerned, he reached out before he could stop himself and put a comforting arm around her. When he realized what he was doing, he quickly removed his arm and stepped back, putting a hand underneath her chin and forcing her to look at him.

"Stop this now," he ordered gently. "Stop crying and tell me what's wrong."

She sniffled, wiping her eyes and pulling free of his grasp again. "My....my cat," she sniffed and coughed. "Caesar is gone."

"Gone?" Christopher repeated.

She nodded firmly. "He sleeps with me. He has always slept with me, and this morning he was nowhere to be found." She wiped her eyes again. "He has never left before I have woken up, ever since he was a kitten. He always waits for his cream, but this morning I awoke and he was gone. I have looked everywhere for him, in all of his usual places."

She was starting to cry again and he put both hands on her face, gazing down into her beauty. "He is not gone," he insisted quietly, wanting her to stop crying. "I know where he is."

As he hoped, she stopped immediately. "You do?" she gasped. "Where?"

He gave her a little smile and took her hand in his big one. "Come on."

He took her up to his chamber, hoping the cat was still there, and pleased to see the fat animal had not left his comfortable spot. He pointed to the bed. "There."

Dustin's jaw opened as she rushed to the bed. Caesar opened his eyes and stretched contently, purring loudly for his mistress. She gazed at the cat and looked to Christopher, puzzled.

"What is he doing here?" she asked.

Christopher shrugged. "He came to me last night," he said. "I tried to toss him out, but he bit me and refused to leave. So I allowed him to stay, just this once."

Dustin's face suddenly took on a look of utter hurt and jealousy. Then her pretty eyebrows drew together. "Why would he do this? Why would he come to you?"

"I do not know, my lady," he answered.

Caesar stood up and tried to rub against Dustin's hand, but she jumped back and pointed accusingly at the animal.

"Don't you dare try to make up for your disloyalty, Caesar Augustus," she said. "You unfaithful creature. You are hereby banished from my bed, do you hear me? If you want to sleep with the baron, then he can have you. After everything I have done for you, you have the gall to seek him out."

She flew out of the room in a rage, leaving the cat licking his chops. Staring at the open door, Christopher was somewhat amused that she should talk to her cat as if it were a person. Hell, he didn't want the hairy beast. He turned a reproving glance at the cat.

"You have been branded a traitor," he said. " 'Tis only right that you prostrate yourself at your mistress's feet and beg for mercy."

The cat looked at him, blinking lazily and licking his chops again. Christopher went over and picked the cat up. "However, since you have a speech impediment, I will do the talking for you. Come on."

Dustin, laying on her bed and allowing hot, angry tears to drip onto her coverlet, heard the knock at the door.

"Go away," she yelled.

Christopher opened the door and entered. "My lady, I have come to speak on the accused's behalf," he said solemnly.

She ignored him and he came around the side of the bed, looking down at her with Caesar clutched against his chest. She looked so entirely miserable and hurt that he was truly touched. She cared a great deal for this animal and was quite miffed by the rejection. He didn't know why the cat had come to him, but he could certainly think of something, couldn't he?

"I lured him," he said after a moment. "Caesar came to me because I lured him with cheese."

She sniffed, her lower lip stuck out in a pout. "He doesn't like cheese."

"A cat that doesn't like cheese? Well, nonetheless, I lured him, and I apologize," he said. "I do not know why I did it. You had gone to sleep and mayhap I needed someone to talk to."

She eyed him suspiciously. "You have David and Edward and the others to talk to," she said, looking at the cat. "Caesar is all I have left. You would take him, too?"

His amusement was gone and he felt like a heel. "Dustin, I didn't take your cat." He set the animal down next to her. Caesar bumped against her a couple of times before she reached out to stroke him.

Christopher eased himself down on the edge of the bed, watching the two of them, watching Caesar stick his nose against her lips for a kiss. He agreed with the cat, her lips were entirely kissable.

"Do you feel so alone?" he asked after a few moments. "You aren't, you know."

She looked up at him, still petting the cat. "My mother is gone and my father is gone," she said. "I have no family left."

"But I am your husband." Christopher reached up to scratch Caesar's nose as the cat came close to him. "Does that not make me your family also?"

She gazed back at him a moment and he could see the thoughts rolling through the gray eyes. *Arthur's eyes,* he thought.

"Aye, it does," she said softly. "But I do not know you, my lord. You are a stranger to me."

He wasn't looking at her, instead he was watching the cat absently. "Would it be so terrible to know me?"

She sat up, swinging her legs over the side of the bed. He gazed up at her then, noticing the peasant dress she wore, her beautiful hair flowing free. She didn't answer for a while.

"I don't know," she whispered, her head lowered.

He drew in a long breath, rising from the bed and moving to the window. The sun was well up now and the courtyard was busy and alive below.

"I suppose what I am trying to say, my lady, is that I understand how you feel being left alone in the world; at least I had David," he said. " 'Tis a terrible thing to be alone."

Dustin stood up and went over to him, timidly. She was studying him openly, touched at his words and comforted by his tone. His voice had a tremendously soothing quality, and she found it amazing that the same voice could bark orders so harshly that it could chip mortar from stone.

He caught her from the corner of his eye and turned to look down at her. Her expression was so unguarded and guileless that he could not help but match her gaze. Christ, those gray eyes seemed to reach out and touch him. Even when she lowered her gaze, he could not take his eyes from her.

"We are family now, my lord," she said softly. "We are not alone anymore."

He cracked a smile. "That is true," he replied. "I have something now I never thought to have, a wife."

Her head came up and she saw his smile and responded hesitantly. She had a beautiful smile.

"And I hoped I would never have a husband," she said.

He smiled wider. "Is that so? And why not?"

She turned away from him in a coy move. "Because," she replied evasively.

He leaned against the window, crossing his huge arms. "Because why?"

She sat back on the bed and teased the cat. "Because....because husbands are only good for one thing."

"And that is?" he snorted, wondering if she was going to say something rather titillating.

She looked at him, still smiling. "Giving orders."

Relieved her thoughts were as innocent as the rest of her, he snickered and nodded. "I see. And you do not like orders."

"Nay," she replied. "I would rather give them."

His eyes twinkled when he looked at her. "I thought that of you," he said. "See? I am getting to know you better already. Mayhap we shall not be strangers too much longer."

"Mayhap," she shrugged, watching Caesar chase a piece of string.

Christopher watched her play with the cat. "Jeffrey tells me that you had hundreds of suitors," he said. "Is this true?"

She shrugged and made a wry face. "Who can count? Men with honeyed words and soft eyes annoy me to death. I paid them no heed."

"None of them?" he pressed, still amused.

"None." Her chin went up into the air firmly. "Fools that only wish to talk of love and romance, and the color of my hair. Pah." She stuck out her tongue.

He laughed then, a hearty booming laugh that made her heart jump, although she did not know why.

"Good girl," he applauded. "I do not like those fools, either."

She smiled in spite of herself. "There was one man, a baron, who told me my eyes were the color of bruised clouds. I showed him what a bruise was."

He laughed until tears came. "My lady, you are a unique soul. I should like to hear more of your adventures."

She shrugged, somewhat embarrassed by all of the attention. But she liked it, and she liked to hear him laugh. She thought a moment. "There was a viscount, son of the Earl of Leeds. Now, *there* was a slobbery idiot if I ever saw one. He told me I had a spot of dirt on my neck, and when he bent over and pretended to wipe it off, he kissed me." When Christopher feigned disbelief, she nodded vigorously. "Aye, he did. Right on the mouth. And do you know what I did to him?"

"What?" He stretched out his long legs and crossed them at the ankles, thoroughly enjoying her.

She held up her index and middle finger on her right hand. "I put my fingers in his eyes, and when he was blinded, I rammed my fist into his nose." She was animated with her story, mimicking all of her original movements. "Broke it clean through. He had bone chips coming from his skin."

Christopher winced at the thought, though still smiling broadly. "You are a terror," he observed. "Although I must say the man deserved worse for kissing you without your permission."

"Do you think so?" she suddenly went serious. "Do you think I should have broken his….?"

He waved her off quickly. "No, no, my lady, simply a jest," he said. "I believe your punishment fit the crime."

"Oh," she blinked, wondering why she was pleased that he approved of her actions.

He shook his head at her. "I must say I feel most fortunate that I have not spoken honeyed words or tried to steal a kiss from you," he teased. "I would probably find myself missing fingers."

She lowered her lashes with a faint smirk, paying attention to the cat. She should have agreed with him but could not seem to bring herself to do it. "As it was, you still became acquainted with my fist," she looked up at him. "And I do apologize for that. I was tired and not thinking clearly."

He nodded faintly, his smile fading. Would she bring up Nottingham now, he wondered? Their conversation had been so pleasant he was hoping not. Caesar, tired of the game, jumped off the bed and she stood up, opening the door to let him out. Christopher watched her walk, the sway of her hips and the way her hair moved against her back, thinking how graceful she moved. But the peasant dress she wore, although it fit her voluptuous figure perfectly, was sadly out of place on a woman of such beauty. Dustin deserved silks and jewels, not linen and leather.

"Your friend, Mistress Rebecca, told me you went to town yesterday to purchase material for new surcoats," he said. "I will go and retrieve the fabric for you so that you may begin making them."

"Rebecca has the material, as she will sew them for me," Dustin replied.

"I see," he nodded, gazing out over the bailey again.

Dustin eyed him, wondering where that subject came from. Yet it also brought another to mind.

"My lord," she began. "About Nottingham. I had hoped to leave today, but obviously I shall not be. I hope that will not create a problem for you."

He turned back to her. "Why would it?"

She shrugged. "I had told you I would be gone, and if you had made plans for my departure, then I apologize for disturbing them."

"I made no such plans," he told her.

She cleared her throat, nodding, suddenly self-conscious now that the conversation wasn't flowing. Truth was, she wasn't at all sure she wanted to go to Nottingham anymore. She was beginning to feel at ease with her husband and, as they agreed, they were family. After what he had told her about his own history, she almost felt needed. Yet she knew full well he didn't need her.

She cleared her throat again. "To be honest with you, my lord, I am not sure if I wish to go to Nottingham anymore," she said quickly, hoping he would not be mad that she wanted to stay. "Lioncross is my home, after all. And I have only met my mother's family once, so I would be living with strangers anyway. At least if I stay at Lioncross, my surroundings are familiar."

He nodded slowly, greatly relieved she had made the decision herself to stay. "A wise decision, my lady."

She looked at him, studying him. "You are not angry?"

He stood up. "Why should I be? This is your home, too."

"But," she blinked. "But I will be in your way."

"You will?" he asked, puzzled.

"Aye," she said quickly, then stopped herself. "What I mean is, won't I be in your way?"

"Why would you ask me that?" He was moving slowly toward her, his arms still crossed. "I never said that.

"Nay, you didn't, but you called me additional baggage," she reminded him. "I promise I shall make myself scarce. I won't bother you."

He scratched his head, standing in front of her now. He looked down at her, her honest eyes gazing up at him. He found himself responding to her emotionally. "You could not bother me if you tried, my lady. I consider it a pleasure to have you remain."

She smiled with growing happiness. "Truly? You do not mind?"

He shook his head. "No."

She turned away happily, then suddenly stopped and looked at him. "Will you make me serve you dinner every night?" she demanded warily.

He grinned. "Nay, you do not have to serve me dinner," he said. "But I will insist that you sit by my left hand."

She smiled back, biting her lip. "I would sit by your left hand, my lord."

He nodded, satisfied. The day outside was advancing and he had much to do, although he was reluctant to leave Dustin. He was enjoying this time very much.

"I do apologize, my lady, but I have pressing duties that I must attend to," he said.

She nodded quickly. "I understand, my lord."

With a final, perhaps warm, look, he moved for the door. When he opened it, Caesar dashed in and bolted right for the bed. He watched the cat for a moment, noticing that Dustin was cooing to the beast as if it were a baby. Her profile was feminine and lovely, he thought.

"Though you be my wife, it seems strange to call you my lady," he remarked, his hand on the door latch. " 'Tis proper, of course, but every man I ever knew called his wife by her name, or nickname," he gave a sort of shrug and began to close the door. "'My lady' is so formal."

"My lord," she called out after him and he stopped, sticking his head into the room. She was almost smiling. "If….if you were to call me by a nickname, what would it be?"

He looked thoughtful. "Do you have one already?"

"Nay," she replied. "My mother always called me by my name, or dear father always called me Dustin Mary Catherine."

He made a face. "Too long," he said firmly, then looked at her. A small smile played on his lips. "What would you have me call you, should you ever give me permission to do so?"

He swore she blushed when she looked away and lifted her shoulders a little. "I have no preference, my lord," she said.

He smiled and started to close the door again when he heard her make a little sound, and he put his head back into the room again. "What is it?"

She looked at him, her eyes wide and innocent and shook her head. "Nothing, my lord."

The door swung open wide and he filled it with his huge frame, his arms crossed in front of his chest. "I do not believe you. You were going to tell me something."

She blushed to the roots of her hair and sat on the bed, not looking at him. He wasn't going to leave and she was embarrassed, yet at the same time, she felt strangely brave and comfortable with him. "Well," he had asked, after all. Lord, her mouth was threatening to run over with all sorts of crazy thoughts.

"I....the night my mother died, you called me by a name. Do you remember it?" she said very softly.

He came into the room and sat next to her on the bed, their thighs touching. He was so large and warm and she could feel the heat he radiated.

"I confess, I do not," he said softly as well. "What was it?"

She took a deep breath for courage. "You called me 'sweetheart.'"

He smiled vaguely. "Is that what you want me to call you? It fits."

Very embarrassed at her forward nature, she looked away from him. "I wasn't saying that I wanted you to call me that, but I remembered that you called me 'sweetheart' and well, no one had ever called me that. I have never been called anything at all but my name."

He was touched by her honesty, her naiveté. Through all of the screaming and pain that night, she remembered a word of kindness and it had stayed with her.

"Then I will ask you now," he said. "May I have your permission to call you 'sweetheart?'"

She nodded and he grinned wider, thinking her embarrassment to be charming. "And then, may I also have your permission to call you 'Dustin?'"

She nodded and whispered, "Yes." He dipped his head down so he could see the side of her lowered face. "And may I also have your permission to call you 'Lady de Lohr?'"

Her head snapped to him, thinking he was teasing her but seeing he was entirely serious. "That is my name, is it not?"

"Aye, it is, but David said you hated it," he replied. "If you do not want me to call you that, then I will not."

She shrugged, not really giving him an answer and he did not pursue it. Instead, she turned the tables.

"What may I call you?" she asked.

They were sitting quite close together, their faces not far from one another. He could smell her roses, and the faint odor of the mint balm he had applied to her. Her skin was flawless.

"When you feel comfortable enough, you may call me 'Christopher' or 'Chris,'" he said quietly. "Call me whatever you wish, Dustin. I will answer."

He saw color creeping back into her cheeks again and she tore her gaze away from him. "Thank you, my lord."

With a faint chuckle at her restraint, he rose from the bed and went to the door again. "I will see you at the nooning meal, then," he said.

Recovering her badly dissolved composure, she rose as well. "Very well, my lord," she replied. "By the way, I will be going into the village this morning to see how Rebecca is coming along on my dresses."

"Not without an escort, my lady," he said firmly. "Do not leave before seeking out myself or David. Do I have your word on that?"

"Aye," she answered, looking at him. "Will you go with me?"

"If my schedule allows," he answered. "Until then, my lady."

He closed the door and was gone, leaving her standing in the middle of the room with the most peculiar warm sensation she had ever experienced, a wonderful languid feeling she could not have described if she had tried.

CHAPTER SIX

DUSTIN BATHED AND changed her clothing mid-morning. Neither was necessary, yet she did it anyway. She rationalized that taking the bath was essential because she still stank of the poison Christopher had rubbed on her, but the dress was fairly clean. For some reason, she didn't want to wear the dress anymore.

She went across the hall to her mother's room and rummaged through the big wardrobe, inspecting each dress in turn. Her mother had been a slight, frail thing, and Dustin barely fit into her clothes, but they were very nice clothes and she suddenly felt a need to dress a bit nicer than her usual. Strange, because she had never given much thought to her appearance.

Even as she selected her mother's indigo-blue brocade and carried it back across the hall, she didn't know why she was bothering.

She needed help putting the dress on, a rare occurrence indeed. The serving wench who tended her grunted and tugged, but finally managed to get the dress secured. Dustin dismissed her and went back across the hall to look at herself in her mother's mirror; she didn't even have one in her own room.

Much to her surprise, the dress didn't look all that bad. In fact, it accentuated her curves quite nicely and she found herself gazing back at her own reflection, turning back and forth in the light and admiring the fabric. It was a scoop neck, long-sleeved design that flattered her slim waist and full breasts. Her mother used to wear the surcoat with a collar and a wimple, but Dustin always hated to be restricted that way. For her, a corset was about the limit of the severe trappings she would wear, and her mother had even had to plead with her to get her to put it on.

The matching slippers were far too small, she knew that already. Yet she had a pair of durable black leather slippers that went quite nicely, although she thought she might visit the cobbler and see if he could make her a pair to match the surcoat.

Back in her room, she brushed her long, straight, silky hair until it gleamed. She had a natural cowlick on the left side of her forehead, right on the hairline, so she always wore her hair parted on the left. Even as long as it was, she wore it free and pulled it over her right shoulder and let it hang like a waterfall, cascading over her breast and falling to her groin.

Dustin looked down at herself, wondering why on earth she had gone through the trouble to bathe and change and brush and primp. After all, she was simply going into town to see Rebecca, and her friend didn't care how she looked. With a confused shake of her head, she went to find Sir Christopher, as he requested.

The day had dawned clear and in actuality, a bit warm. She squinted under the bright sunlight, looking about for the tall, blond man who was her husband. The first person she ran into was Jeffrey.

"My lady." he greeted her with a smile.

She smiled back. "Hello, Jeffrey."

"You look very lovely," he observed. "The dress looks better on you than it did on your mother."

"Mother had a great many dresses, although I think most of them are far too small," she said. "Mother was terribly tiny."

Jeffrey nodded in agreement. "God rest her soul, my lady. I apologize for not attending her funeral yesterday, but with most all of the knights seeing to her burial, I could not leave the keep."

"I understand," Dustin said, sad anew at the mention of her mother. "You always were terribly loyal, Jeffrey, and mother knew that. In fact...." She suddenly jumped and her hands flew to her back. "*Ouch!*"

"What is it?" Jeffrey asked, concerned.

She was fumbling with something on her back, twisting awkwardly. "Damnation! A stay has snapped."

He turned her around. "Let me see."

Christopher rounded the corner with David just in time to see Jeffrey fumbling with the back of Dustin's dress. Before he realized what he was doing, he charged the big Germanic knight and felled the man with one huge blow to the jaw.

Jeffrey went sprawling, blood spattering on the dust. Dustin yelped, terrified, as David pulled her clear of the fight. Christopher descended on Jeffrey like God's wrath, grabbing the man around the top of his armor and hauling him quite effortlessly to his feet for another round.

"Christopher," Dustin shrieked. "What are you doing?"

He paused a brief second. It was the first time he had ever heard her use his Christian name. When he looked at her, she was shocked at the anger she saw.

"I have a better question," he shot back. "What was *he* doing?"

She was thoroughly perplexed and growing annoyed. "One of my stays broke and he was fixing it. What on earth do you think he was doing?"

Christopher stopped in mid-rage, suddenly realizing with horror what an ass he had just made of himself. He looked at Jeffrey as if to confirm Dustin's answer, and the big man simply stared back at him. Then, Jeffrey's hand came up and he opened his palm, inside was a steel hook.

"It came off," he said, spitting out a tooth.

Christopher let go of him. "Christ," he muttered, turning away from the man. He had never felt so completely foolish in his entire life.

Dustin, still confused and concerned, rushed to Jeffrey's side. "Are you all right?"

"Fine," Jeffrey spit out some more blood, eyeing Christopher.

Dustin whirled on her husband. "Why did you hit him?"

Christopher was standing by David, his hand on his forehead. The hand fell to his side as he faced his wife. "The reason no longer exists. Are you ready to go to town?"

She was angry now. "Then if the reason no longer exists, you will apologize to Jeffrey. 'Twas inexcusable."

Christopher met Jeffrey's eye. "My mistake."

Jeffrey lifted an acknowledging eyebrow but Dustin was livid.

" 'Tis no apology you gave him," she accused.

Christopher gazed down at her evenly. Christ, she looked gorgeous in that dress. "Aye, it is. Now, are you ready to leave? I have time to take you myself."

Her cheeks were flushed with fury. "I shall not go with you," she said. "Jeffrey will take me."

Christopher gave her a slow, reptilian blink, glancing at the German. "I think not," he said quietly. "Come along, my lady."

"No," she exclaimed, moving away from him. "I will not go with a man who strikes for no reason and then refuses to apologize. Stay away from me."

Christopher didn't want to create a scene in the middle of the bailey, but if he forced himself on her, then a scene he would have. She was angry and had every right to be. He took a deep, calming breath and crooked his finger at her.

"Then a word, please," he said politely.

She balked for a moment or so, crossing her arms across her chest defiantly until she felt Jeffrey give her a little shove. Momentarily uncertain as to why Jeffrey should support the man who just clobbered him, she found herself stepping in Christopher's direction.

He pulled her aside privately, looking down at her stormy face. He sighed. "In the first place, my lady, you will never again use that tone with me," he said in a low voice. "Secondly, you would not understand why I struck Jeffrey, but suffice it to say that he understands and we will hear no more of it, especially from you." When she opened her mouth, he put up a warning finger. "And, lastly, I will indeed escort you into the village."

She was so furious that she was grinding her teeth. "Then I am not going into town. I am staying *here,*" she seethed.

"Aye, you are going into town if I have to throw you over my shoulder and carry you," he said with growing irritation.

Her eyes flashed and she stepped back from him, gathering her skirts. "If you touch me, you shall regret it." With that, she spun on her heel and raced into the castle as fast as her legs would take her.

Christopher charged after her, leaving David and Jeffrey standing in his wake. David shifted on his big legs casually, crossing his arms.

"Is she always like this?" he asked.

Jeffrey nodded. "Always. Should we follow?"

"Why? He won't lay a hand on her," David looked at him.

Jeffrey shook his head. "Not to protect her. To protect *him*."

David smiled. Then, he laughed. "Come on, frank. Let's go take care of that mouth."

Jeffrey let David lead him away, not at all annoyed by the fact that he was now missing a tooth. It had been worth it to confirm what he had speculated, that Christopher was indeed concerned for his new wife, as much as he tried to pretend otherwise.

Dustin just beat Christopher into her rooms. She had heard his footfalls close behind her and she was furious and frightened at the same time. But when she entered her rooms and he was right on her heel, she found she was terrified and she ran to the other end of the room, grabbing the first thing she could find. Whirling around, she threw a pretty glass goblet at the doorway just as Christopher entered. He ducked swiftly and the glass shattered on the doorjamb above him.

"Get out!" Dustin screamed, hurling another glass.

The second one shattered on the wall a foot to the left of him and he scowled. "Stop that."

"Go!" she yelled angrily, throwing another goblet and watching it break on the wall above the door.

"Dustin, stop that at once," he said sternly, coming into the room.

She picked up her pewter decanter, half-full of wine, and threw it at him. He turned slightly, catching it in the armor and it exploded, coating him and his mail with wine. He frowned verily.

"Dustin, cease this instant before you do any damage," he ordered.

She was out of ammunition and, with a shriek, ran to the table beside her bed and picked up her hairbrush. The heavy wooden brush went sailing through the air and he deftly dodged it, glaring at her.

"You are going to be sorry," he warned her.

He began to remove his armor, letting it crash to the floor. Dustin, furious and panicked, threw her polished metal hand mirror and ivory clip at him for good measure as he stripped off his hauberk, the mirror catching him in the shoulder.

When he was down to his shin armor, his breeches and his heavy linen tunic, he started advancing on her again. She yelped angrily, jumping up on her bed and grabbing her candleholder for good measure, flinging it at him even as he lunged for her. The metal holder caught him in the cheek, near his ear, and immediately drew blood. His irritation fed, he managed to grab her skirt before she could hop off the end of the bed and tugged hard, pulling her back at him.

Dustin knew he had her and she was as mad as a cat in a snare. When he yanked her back, she balled up her fists and took a good swing at him, but he ducked it, throwing his shoulder into her abdomen and managing to slam her down onto the bed. She twisted and struggled, but it was futile, he had her pinned down with his own massive body and her wrists were captured above her head with both of his hands.

She stopped fighting him, breathing heavily as they glared at each other. Purely symbolic, she twisted a few more times before relenting fully to his superior strength and size.

He scowled down at her, eye to eye, fully aware of her heaving breasts against his sculpted chest. Christ, he had been angry when he had thrown himself on top of her. But now still angry, yet he could feel the long-dormant flames of desire beginning to stir in him, as well. Flushed as she was, she was incredibly beautiful and tempting.

"No more of that," he growled.

She twisted again, her pretty mouth in an angry frown. "Let me go!"

He could match her anger and exceed it. "Not until you regain your senses. I do not appreciate having items thrown at me, lady."

She tensed up underneath him and tried to bring her knee up to his groin. He was fast, moving to cover her completely with his huge frame and trapping her legs against the mattress. He raised a disapproving eyebrow at her attempt.

"That," he said quietly, "would not have been wise. I should like to have a son someday, and I will not have you jeopardizing my bloodlines."

She met his gaze with such fury that he was surprised by it. Unable to look at him any longer because she was completely helpless trapped underneath him, she turned her head away. He continued to study her beautiful face at close range.

"Good," he said. "Now that you are calming, you will hear me. I will not tolerate a disobedient wife, Lady Dustin. I understand that your mother let you run amuck and do whatever you pleased without anyone to answer to, but those days are gone. You will answer to me now, and you will be respectful and compliant at all times, especially in public. Am I making myself clear?"

She was glaring off across the room, trying to ignore him, and his hands tightened on her wrists. "Is that clear?"

She let out a strangled yelp and snapped her head back to look at him. He could not have been more than an inch above her and she suddenly felt her insides quiver strangely. The anger she had felt not a split second before was turning into something so warm and peculiar it was nearly painful in her chest, and her palms began to sweat. The longer she gazed into his sky-blue eyes, the stronger the feeling became.

"I....I understand, my lord," she managed to choke out.

His eyes were riveted to her, her lips, her pert nose, and her wide gray eyes. He almost forgot his line of thought and struggled to retain it, knowing he had to make himself understood or the lesson and the struggle, would be lost.

"Well and good for you," he answered after a moment. "There will be no more yelling and no more displays of temper in front of our vassals. You will never question me, nor will you countermand any order I give. Understood?"

She was losing all feeling in her arms as they gazed steadily at each other. Now that the flash of fire had abated, it was being replaced by something soft and warm and fluid. She had felt it before when he had massaged her shoulders and the sensation was now back again, stronger than before. She kept forgetting to breathe and her mouth went dry, forcing her to lick her lips more than once.

The gesture did not go unnoticed and Christopher was dangerously close to plunging over the erotic abyss. He could not remember ever wanting to kiss a woman as badly, as disobedient and willful and stubborn as she was.

"I told you that I understood, my lord," she replied softly, the fire gone from her tone. "I am not daft."

She was so sweet and soft and warm beneath him that he found himself fighting the urge to run his hands all over her body. Christ, he had to get out of there or he might end up doing something they both regretted. He would not force her, nor would he broach the subject of consummating their marriage. It was a firm vow of his because he knew that if he made any sort of advances, she would most likely respond to him as she had to all of the others and their marriage and relationship would be badly damaged.

She had made it very clear she hated slobbery fools with honeyed words, and he would not act like a stallion to rut even if he did think she was the most desirable woman he had ever met. Nay, he had too much pride to pursue her. If she wanted to establish affection in this marriage, then she would have to initiate it.

Christopher pushed himself off her, leaving her weak and shaken as he moved for the door. Dustin sat up unsteadily, her hair askew as she turned to watch him go.

"And another thing, my lady," he said as he opened the door. "You will cease to wear these ill-fitting dresses. They are too tight and most indecent."

She looked down at the indigo-blue surcoat. "This was my mother's surcoat."

"I do not care whose surcoats they are, you will not wear them anymore," he said sternly. "And that goes for those filthy little peasant dresses you seem to favor, as well."

Dustin's anger rose again as she stood up. "They are perfectly good surcoats. And they are not too tight."

He frowned. "If they are not too tight, then explain the broken stay? I will go and retrieve those dresses from Mistress Rebecca today, and buy material for several more. You will be well-clothed from now on."

Her lip twitched furiously. "My clothes are clean and wearable. I will wear what I please, and I don't need you to dictate to me what is or what is not proper attire."

He sighed heavily, coming out a growl. "I see that you did not, in fact, understand one word I said."

"I did," she spat. "But you said I was to control myself in public. You never said anything about when we were in private. And I will indeed yell at you when you make such ridiculous, insulting statements."

He jaw twitched. "Behave yourself, wife, or you shall find yourself over my knee."

"Ha!" she exclaimed. "You wouldn't dare!" As if to prove that she did not fear him in the least, she collected another candleholder from beside her bed and hurled it at him with all her might. It missed, but barely.

Christopher closed the door and bolted it, crossing the room to his enraged wife, who now realized the foolishness of her actions and decided that running from him might be her only chance to preserve her buttocks.

As fast as she was, he was faster, and she could scarce believe when he actually sat on the bed and threw her over his knees as if she were no more than a small child. She kicked and yelled as he tossed her skirts aside and brought his gigantic palm to bear on her soft, white bottom.

Stunned as she was, it bloody well hurt and her last coherent thought before she began to scream for mercy was that the man was true to his word.

Ƈ

CHRISTOPHER MET DAVID and Edward in the bailey. The two men were on horseback, their arms laden with several packages. Christopher stood with his hands on his hips, watching them hand the bundles down to several waiting serving women.

"Did you have any trouble finding the rest?" he asked his brother.

David raised the visor of his helmet, his handsome face annoyed. "Nay, but so help me, Chris, I will never go shopping for your wife again. Do you know how humiliating it was for Edward and I to purchase bolts of fine, feminine material and stockings?"

Christopher fought off a chuckle. "Humility is a fine quality in a knight," he said sternly. "I hope you selected pleasing colors and patterns?"

David rolled his eyes. "Aye, we did, we did. You want we should wear them for your approval?"

"Mayhap later." Christopher waved him off. "Get down off that horse. 'Tis time for the nooning meal and I had the cook hold it until your return. I am famished."

Edward and David dismounted, removing their gauntlets as their animals were led away.

"Lady Dustin's friend, Rebecca, will be up later to start on the other dresses you ordered," David told his brother as they walked to the steps of the castle. "She stayed up all last night to finish the three dresses we brought."

"I will pay her well," Christopher replied.

The great hall smelled wonderfully of roast venison and baked spiced apples. Huge loaves of bread and bowls of butter and honey were already on the tables and the knights sat, along with several senior soldiers and officers, pouring themselves wine and talking loudly.

A serving wench approached Christopher timidly, giving him a quick bob before whispering something to him. He nodded faintly and set his goblet down.

"Where are you going?" David demanded.

Christopher glanced up to the second floor landing of the stairs. "To retrieve my wife," he stood up. "I shall be back. Commence with the meal."

Dustin's door was open and he found her standing by the window, holding Caesar and gazing across the bailey.

"Why aren't you going to eat?" he asked her.

She didn't look at him. "I am not hungry, my lord."

He sighed, knowing she was still smarting from the licking he had given her earlier and knowing full well she was angry with him. To get angry with her would only inflame the situation, so he tried another approach.

"Please, Dustin," he said softly. "Will you please come and eat with me?"

She looked at him, then. "I cannot sit down."

He repressed the urge to grin. "That is your own fault. Mayhap if we bring a pillow for you to sit on?"

She shook her head. "I will not embarrass myself in such a fashion."

He thought a moment. "Then I will eat up here with you."

Before Dustin could protest, he was giving orders to two serving wenches and within minutes, the nooning meal was indeed brought up to her rooms and nicely displayed on her small cherrywood table. Christopher indicated a chair for her.

"My lady?" he said respectfully.

She eyed him a moment before setting down Caesar and moving for the chair. Yet she avoided the chair and reached down to her trencher, picking up a chunk of brown bread.

He watched her as she stood, eating. "Are you really that sore that you cannot sit and enjoy your meal?"

She glared at him. "Aye, I am. Your hand is big and you are strong and you hurt me."

He sat down, busying himself with his food. "Had you not been so disobedient, I would not have had to teach you a lesson."

"And what lesson is that? That you are stronger and bigger, and you can hurt me anytime you so choose?" she shot back.

He took a slow, deep breath and looked pointedly at her. "Nay, my lady. The lesson learned is that you will obey me at all times, and be respectful."

She pouted angrily and turned away, chewing on her bread. She didn't know quite how to respond to him, because in faith, she knew she had pushed him over the edge and what he had done was quite within his legal right. He could have done far worse. As it was, she only had a bruised bottom and nothing else.

Dustin was not daft, she knew that her mother had indeed let her have the run of the house the entire time her father was gone and she had gotten used to having her way in everything. No one would dare respond to her temper. But it was painfully evident that her new husband would not tolerate her willful nature or stubbornness. She sighed, thinking how they had come to this point this day. It had all started with Christopher slugging Jeffrey cock-eyed and she had gotten angry. Then the whole situation had blown itself way out of proportion because he wouldn't do what she wanted him to do, and that was tell her why he had struck Jeffrey.

She could not bend and twist this man the way she did everyone else and she was irked by it.

"Try the apples, they are delicious," he remarked, his mouth full.

She kept her stiff back to him. "I do not want any, thank you."

"So you intend to only eat bread and nothing else?" he asked. When she shrugged, he continued. "Dustin, you did not eat anything all day yesterday, and I know you did not break your fast this morning. You shall make yourself ill if you do not eat more than a simple piece of bread."

She shrugged again and he put his spoon down, getting out of his chair. "Come on," he grasped her shoulders and pushed her back to the table. "Eat something."

"Nay," she protested. "I…I can't sit on that chair, it will pain me."

He looked at her with annoyance, finally sitting heavily in his own chair and pulling his rigid wife onto his lap. She twisted and fussed, and tried to pull away from him.

"*Cease,*" he snapped softly, and she was instantly still, though she was glaring at him. "Now, my legs are a bit softer than the chair, so you may sit with me and eat your meal." As she shook her head, he raised an impatient eyebrow. "I shall feed you if I have to."

Her anger glazed with uncertainty, and she took the remaining piece of bread in her hand and shoved it into her mouth, still glaring at him as she chewed. He repressed a smile, reaching across the small table and pulling her trencher next to his.

"Try the apples, they are delicious." He picked up his spoon and resumed eating.

It was certainly the strangest meal Dustin had ever eaten. Torn between her anger for him and the comfort of his warmth and closeness, she somehow managed to eat everything in front of her. Christopher was pleased she was complying, realizing toward the end of the meal that his left hand had never left her waist. He was also hopeful that her anger was spent, for he had no desire to butt heads with her the rest of the day.

He finished his meal, watching her as she finished hers. As she was finishing the apple cider left in her cup, his right hand fingered the skirt of the indigo-blue surcoat she wore.

"David brought your new dresses," he said. "Why do you not wear one?"

She set the cup down, looking at his huge fingers grasp her dress. She could refuse, but she could not take another spanking this day.

"Very well," she said quietly, hating herself for sounding so damn submissive. "Which one would you like to see?"

"You choose," he replied.

She stood up, rubbing her bum as she moved over to the bundles piled next to her bed. The one on the top was the lavender. She picked it up and broke the strings that tied it.

Christopher rose, moving for the door. "I shall be downstairs," he told her. "Come and show me when you have finished."

"Aye, my lord," she responded quietly.

He gave her blond head a second glance as he exited the room, wondering if she were going to do as he asked or if she would find some other way to disobey him.

CB

CHRISTOPHER WAS OUTSIDE in the mid-afternoon, watching the de Velt twins' swordplay in the small arena to the west of the fortress. David, Edward and Leeton stood with him, all yelling encouragement or insults at the two burly men. Several other officers and soldiers were also watching, including Jeffrey. David nudged his brother.

"Why did you let him stay?" he asked.

Christopher glanced at Jeffrey before returning his gaze to Max and Anthony. "We can use all of the knights available," he replied. "I should like to see him fight the winner of this match."

His brother did not truly answer his question, and David was more curious than ever. Interrogation of Jeffrey earlier had given him no clues, either.

"Chris, I thought you were intent on seeing this man leave," he said again. "Why is he still here?"

"Do you want him gone?" Christopher asked.

"I care not," David answered, watching Max land a particularly heavy blow on his brother. "But you do not like him; that is apparent. Especially in lieu of the blow you landed him this morning."

Christopher sighed, clearing his throat. "I struck him because he touched my wife, and he knew it," he replied. "And it is not a matter of whether or not I like the man, but I understand him better now. We had a most productive talk this morning, which is why I let him stay."

David frowned wryly. "He didn't touch your wife, he was merely helping her with her dress."

Christopher's head snapped to his brother. "No one touches Dustin but me," he said sharply. "I will not have my wife being handled by my knights, for any reason."

David cocked an eyebrow. "What about me? Would you have slugged me, too?"

"You are different, David." Christopher turned away irritably.

"How so? I am your knight," his brother persisted.

"But you are my brother, and her brother-in-law," Christopher replied, as if David were daft. " 'Tis different for you to touch her. Why are you arguing this point with me?"

"I am not," David gave him a long look. "It's just, well, for a man who did not want a wife, you are being damn protective of this woman whom you married."

"What am I supposed to do, David?" Christopher replied, fully irritated now. "I married her, and I am obligated to protect her. Would you have me ignore her, allow her to do anything she wants with anyone she pleases? Would you have me care so little for the de Lohr name that I would pretend my legal wife did not exist?"

"I am not questioning your honor, calm down." David crossed his arms, watching Anthony trip over his own feet and nearly get clobbered by his brother. "It's just that I am starting to see more to this relationship than you are admitting."

Christopher looked at him with contempt. "You are mad, David, and I will hear no more. Lady Dustin is my wife, in name only. That's it."

David snorted a reply, causing his brother to grind his jaw. They watched the de Velt twins wind down their match in silence and Christopher motioned to Jeffrey across the arena. Without any words, Jeffrey knew what was expected of him and eagerly complied. It had been a long time since he had tested his skills on knights as fine as these.

Christopher watched the massively wide man take on Max, noticing immediately that Jeffrey wasn't particularly graceful, but he was as strong as an ox and any blow he landed to Max sent the man reeling. He became engrossed in the fight, forgetting his irritation with his brother and studying the ex-captain's skills. It didn't take long for him to discern that Jeffrey was very, very good.

He called a halt and the two men immediately stopped, facing him as he crossed over to them.

"Take a rest, Max," he instructed his knight. "I will finish your bout."

David tossed him his helmet and he latched it on, lowering the visor and drawing his sword from his scabbard. Jeffrey, seeing Christopher was moving into a defensive stance, immediately did the same.

"Let's see how good you truly are," Christopher said in a low voice.

Beneath his lowered faceplate, Jeffrey grinned. "A pleasure, my lord."

From her second story window, Dustin could see the battle taking place below. She had been watching for some time, having heard the first blows and her interest was piqued. She did not feel like leaving her room, being fatigued or the fact she was still wallowing in self-pity, she didn't know. But she and Caesar had been holed up playing with a little wooden ball and working on a half-finished piece of needlepoint.

There were so many other things she could be doing, like trying to retrieve the baby birds she had tried to save two days ago, but she knew in her heart that they were probably dead and she was saddened. She could also be out tending her rabbits, or seeing to the small flower garden her mother had loved so well. Aye, so many things she could be doing, but she simply didn't have the energy. Rather, she would watch the knights take practice on each other from a nice, safe distance.

She saw Christopher taking on Jeffrey, wondering if the match were only for practice or if indeed her husband intended to kill the man. With rising concern, she wondered if he was setting out to finish what he had started that morn. Forgetting the fact that she planned to be a hermit this day, she set the needlepoint down and intended to see for herself.

Although she wore the lavender dress, Christopher had yet to see it, as he had requested. Dustin was very pleased with the surcoat for Rebecca had done an outstanding job. It was very snug in the bodice with a plunging neckline, long trailing sleeves, and a full, voluminous skirt.

Dustin had pulled the front of her hair back and secured it to the crown of her head with her ivory clip, revealing her heart-shaped face. She usually kept her hair down because she thought her ears stuck out, but she had pulled it back when she had donned the dress to keep it out of her face and had simply forgotten to remove the clip. It was the one piece of jewelry or adornment she owned, and it had been a gift from her father. She only kept it because it had been a useful gift, but true to her nature, she hated fancy, feminine things of any kind.

All lavender silk and thigh-length blond hair, part of which was piled on top of her head, she dashed out of the castle and headed for the arena.

The field was surrounded by soldiers as she came up, slowing her pace and craning her neck to catch a better glimpse. She could hear metal slamming on metal and grunts of effort, but she could see nothing. Frustrated, she looked for higher ground. A few feet away was a log. Close to five feet tall and probably three feet in diameter, it was used for various practice drills and she knew she could have a birds-eye view if she could stand atop it. As good at climbing as she was, she managed to hoist herself up without so much as dirtying her dress, and stood her full height a bit unsteadily, her eyes riveted to the arena.

Christopher and Jeffrey were delivering blows so hard it made her body hurt just watching them. She assumed that if Christopher was going to kill Jeffrey, he would have done so by now, so the men must simply be testing each other. She knew that knights liked to prove themselves constantly.

She'd seen Jeffrey fight before and knew he had great strength, but she'd never seen her husband fight before and felt that familiar giddy warmth settle over her. His prowess was unmatched as he dealt Jeffrey blow after heavy blow, and the grace with which he lifted his massive sword unparalleled. It seemed to her that to every five or six offensive blows, Jeffrey could only return one or two and spent the rest of his time defending himself. She was amazed at Christopher's pure skill and precision, it was like Caesar toying with a mouse. It was obvious, even to her, that Christopher was far superior in strength and talent.

Jeffrey, however, was holding his own until he took a step backwards and tripped, landing heavily in his armor. Christopher was on him in an instant, the tip of his sword against the big German's neck.

Jeffrey let his sword fall from his grip and raised his hands in a gesture of defeat. "I concede, my lord."

After a moment, Christopher removed his sword and stood back, extending a hand to help the man to his feet. "You fight well, Jeffrey."

Jeffrey raised his visor and grinned. "Not as well as you, my lord. I had heard rumor that the savages called you the Lion's Claw and now I know why."

Christopher sheathed his sword and went to unlatch his helmet, but not before catching sight of Dustin standing atop the pole. She wasn't hard to miss in the bright color, perched like some exotic, beautiful bird quite comfortably atop the log, watching him.

He pulled off his helmet and tossed it in the direction of his men. "What are you doing up there?" he called to her.

"I came to watch," she answered.

The crowd surrounding the field parted as he walked through them towards her, his hands on his hips. "Did you climb up there all by yourself?"

"Of course," she answered the obvious.

He shook his head and glanced at his brother, who was grinning up at her with delight. He turned back to his wife.

"Come down from there," he motioned sternly.

She squatted and was preparing to slip down when he waved her off. "Nay, do not climb down and risk that dress." He stood next to the pole and held out his arms. "Jump and I shall catch you."

Without hesitation, she did, and landed easily in his arms. His hands instinctively tightened about her, and her arms grabbed hold of his neck for support, bringing their two faces very, very close. She kept waiting for him to set her down, but he didn't.

"So you like to watch swordfights?" he asked, feeling rather giddy at her closeness.

She shrugged, feeling the same giddiness he was. "Sometimes," she replied. "Truthfully, I thought you were still mad at Jeffrey and were planning to kill him."

He cracked a faint smile. "And you thought to stop me?"

She looked away. "I would have tried."

He chuckled then. "You are brave, my lady."

She didn't answer him as David and Edward and the other knights approached, all appraising her quite openly.

"I see that all of the humiliation and trouble we went through was well worth it, Lady de Lohr," David remarked.

"The dress is beautiful but not as beautiful as you, my lady," Leeton put in, bowing slightly and with a grin on his face.

Dustin hated sweet words but she controlled herself. "Thank you, my lords," she replied, letting go of Christopher's neck and pushing herself from his arms.

"We failed to see you at the nooning meal, my lady," Edward said. "An injustice I should hope would be corrected this evening?"

Dustin remembered her sore bottom, not daring to glance back at Christopher. "Mayhap," she replied vaguely. She was embarrassed by all of the attention, something she was unused to in large numbers. She could handle one man's attention, but several men flustered her. "I must go," she said quickly.

She started to move but suddenly there was a shout high atop the wall and all attention immediately turned to the source.

"Riders!" came the cry again.

"Are they flying a banner?" Christopher called back.

After a pause, there was a wave. "Prince John's colors."

Dustin looked up at Christopher in time to see his expression darken and she was startled, wondering why.

"Open the gates!" Her husband yelled back after a moment, then turned to his men. "Keep your swords ready, lads."

Dustin wondered what on earth he meant by that when suddenly he looked down as if he had forgotten she was there.

"Max," he gestured to the dark-haired knight. "Take my wife into the keep, if you please."

She ignored the soldier's outstretched hand. "Why would Prince John be here?" she asked.

"To see me," Christopher replied evasively. "Go with Max, Dustin."

"Wait," she said, putting her hand on his arm. "I want to see the Prince. I have never seen him before."

Christopher had so many other things on his mind that he did not want to deal with her at this moment. He turned to her swiftly.

"Mayhap another time," he said quickly. "Now, go. Please."

Puzzled and perhaps a bit rebuffed, she allowed Max to take her away and into the castle. Yet as soon as he had closed the entry door behind her, she waited until she heard the knight's footfalls fade back down the steps before opening the door again and slipping out onto the landing. She wasn't being deliberately disobedient more than she was simply curious. She'd never seen a prince before.

ᴓ3

CHRISTOPHER KNEW THAT Prince John himself would not have come to the far reaches of the realm, preferring to stay in London surrounded by his silly, pampered, evil courtiers. Yet he was tense and on guard, knowing exactly who would be riding though his gates, and he could taste the dislike on his tongue. There was only one man John felt capable of carrying his messages, a man widely hated for his conniving and diabolical mind. Christopher had been away for three years, yet even so, he could barely speak the name Ralph Fitz Walter without choking on it.

He stood in the middle of the bailey surrounded by his knights, waiting in silence. The riding party had been spotted from the east as it rounded the crest of the gentle hill leading into the small village, and would take time before they entered the gates. Time enough for him to reflect on his personal mission from Richard, on the answers he would give Fitz Walter.

When the party finally entered the gates, there were several gaily dressed men on colorful horses, surrounding a particularly dressed-down man in mail and black. The rest of the rather large group were soldiers of the prince, and Christopher ordered them kept outside the gates.

There was tension in the air as the man in mail and black dismounted his destrier and approached Christopher slowly, removing his gauntlets as he walked. His face was dark, his hair dirty and long. He was ugly and sinister-looking as he smiled thinly at Christopher.

"This is your gift from Richard?" he said, glancing about the keep. "Impressive. A most fitting gift for our king's Defender of the Realm."

Christopher's face was unreadable. "What do you want, Fitz Walter?"

"Not much for greetings, are you?" the man responded. "The heat of the Holy Land must have evaporated your manners." When Christopher didn't answer, he continued on. "I come from our glorious prince, de Lohr. He is requesting your presence in London. You came and left so quickly we scarce had a chance to enjoy your illustrious person."

"Surely John has enough fools to keep him entertained," he said coolly. "What does he want of me?"

"Your beautiful face and your commanding presence, who can say?" Fitz Walter gestured with his hands. "I have been sent to retrieve you personally."

Christopher crossed his arms over his broad chest. "I am busy. Tell John I will join him when time allows."

The tolerant look faded from Fitz Walter's face. "Your company is not a request, de Lohr, it is a command by order of our magnificent prince. He would not be happy to learn that you disobeyed his wishes."

Christopher gazed back at Ralph Fitz Walter, confidante and right-hand to Prince John. The man's soul ran as black as his hair.

"I take my orders directly from King Richard, not the prince," he said evenly. "As Defender of the Realm, I am answerable to Richard alone. John has no power over me, of which I am sure he is immensely displeased. I am the one man in this country who does not have to obey him, and the crown's troops in England are mine to command. You see, Ralph, I was there when Richard drafted the missive to his brother that I delivered to him from the Holy Land. I know exactly what it says and exactly what my sworn duties are." He took a step toward Fitz Walter and lowered his voice. "I am the strong-arm of Richard now that I am returned and I am sure that Prince John is furious at that fact. But it is of no concern to me. He cannot order me about as he does the rest of you idiots."

Ralph's face was dark and angry. "My orders come from the prince himself, de Lohr," he growled, then glanced at the troops waiting outside the gate. "I shall drag you back if necessary."

Beside Christopher, David flinched and his brother put out a calming hand. Fitz Walter looked at David, his lips peeling back in a sneer.

"Ah, the little Lion Cub," he said mockingly. "You would be brave and defend your big brother, wouldn't you?"

Christopher took another step toward Ralph, at least a head taller than the dark man. "I was, in fact, planning on returning to London," he said in a low voice. "But I will not be seen with you. I want you out of my keep, and out of my sight, or I will gut you."

Ralph gave him a weak smile. "For what?" His eyes suddenly moved beyond Christopher as if something had caught his attention, and a gleam came to his eye. "Oh, my," he breathed seductively. "Is that Arthur Barringdon's daughter?"

Christopher didn't know she was standing at the keep entry and he swung around rapidly to see that his wife was indeed standing at the top of the steps. David, Leeton and Edward saw his nostrils flare and his jaw tick as he turned back to Fitz Walter.

"Get out of here, Ralph," he growled. "I will not tell you again."

Ralph's eyes lit up with amusement, however dangerous. "Oh, de Lohr, you must bring her with you. John will be most pleased to see such a prize." He stepped sideways, as to better leer at Dustin. "Fine, indeed. A tasty piece of flesh. Had I known about her, I would have taken her for myself while you were still in Jerusalem."

Christopher's jaw was ticking so furiously that he was about to break teeth. Angry would not have been an apt word to describe his emotions at the moment.

"That is my wife, Lady Dustin de Lohr, and you will never again use those terms to describe her," he said in a controlled tone. "Now, remount your steed and get the hell out of my keep."

"But I only just arrived," Ralph pressed. "Surely you will invite me in to your new keep to meet your wife?"

Christopher stared at him but he wasn't going to tell the man to leave again. His next move would be to enforce his command at knife point. David, however, stepped forward.

"You have been told to leave," he rumbled. "Get out before I embarrass you in front of your men."

Undaunted, yet smart enough to realize that Christopher was sensitive where his wife was concerned, Ralph gave them all a slight bow and meandered back to his horse. Yet he would keep that bit of information tucked into his mind, for he was sure John would be interested in it. There was more than one way to control a seemingly uncontrollable man. Christopher watched Ralph mount his big warhorse and rein the animal about roughly.

"I give you one week, baron," he said loudly, more for the benefit of his men so they would not know that the baron had gotten the better of him. "One week to see you in London or I come back for you."

Christopher turned away, ordering the gates closed. Dustin, seeing that he was heading straight for her, bolted back inside the castle and raced madly for her rooms, desperately afraid he was going to spank her again. It was foolish to run from him, she knew, for he would only catch up to her, but she ran anyway. She was terrified.

She waited in her rooms for him to come. And waited. She sat tensely on her bed for nearly an hour before she heard a soft knock on her door. Jumpy as a cat, she shot up off the bed and bade whoever it was to enter.

Christopher's blond head appeared and he actually smiled at her. Dustin's eyes widened, off-balance and bewildered that he was smiling. He had a devastating smile when he wanted to, enough to make her knees go weak.

"I have a few moments to spare, my lady, and thought you might enjoy a trip into town," he said.

"For what?" she blurted, still waiting for him to come charging across the room and put her over his knees again.

"To take the material to Mistress Rebecca, of course," he stepped into the room. "My wife must be well-clothed at court."

She looked at him for a few long moments as his words sunk in. Then, her gray eyes widened. "I am going to court?"

"Aye," he nodded. "Actually, *we* are going to court. It seems that Prince John would have me there."

"And you are taking me with you?" she could scarcely believe what she was hearing.

"Of course," he said. "I would not leave you here."

She was speechless. Never in her wildest dreams did she ever imagine that she would go to London. Her life was simple and uncomplicated, and she never entertained dreams of rich courtly life. But now, with the impending prospect as the result of her marriage to a powerful baron, she found she was verily excited.

"Truly?" she grinned, her big eyes on him to see if he were teasing her.

He nodded, returning her smile. It was beautiful, bright and infectious. She clapped her hands together gleefully. "I have never been to London," she exclaimed. "What is it like?"

He feigned a thoughtful expression. "Full of greed, deceit, lust, and gluttony. It is a delightful place."

She laughed at him, her fear from moments earlier forgotten. Now, she was thrilled with the turn her future had taken.

"London," she said, turning away from him happily. Suddenly, her eyes fell on Caesar, sleeping lazily in the window bench, and she sobered. "But what of Caesar? Can he come, too?"

Christopher stepped up behind her, eyeing the cat. "That may not be wise, Dustin," he said honestly. "It will be a difficult journey for him, and he may run off. Cats like to stay where they are familiar."

She went over and petted the cat. "But I cannot leave him," she said mournfully, her mood increasingly sad. "Who will take care of him? And what of my rabbits?"

"Rabbits? What rabbits?" he asked.

"I have several pet rabbits I keep by the kitchens," she insisted. "What will happen to them?"

Christopher looked thoughtful, catching himself before he suggested that they could eat them. Even in jest, the recommendation would not sit well with her.

"The cat can take care of himself, I am sure." Christopher, not wanting to spoil the mood, took her hand away from the animal and enclosed it in his big, warm palm. "As for the rabbits, surely there is a child or servant who can tend them. Come along, now. Let us take the fabrics to your friend."

She let him hold her hand. She didn't know why she was letting him. Any other man who had ever tried to hold her hand had come away with a black eye. But she allowed him to lead her over to the other side of her bed where bundles of material were stacked. He let go of her hand and picked all the packages up himself.

As she watched him, she was struck again with how handsome he truly was. When she had been standing out on the landing, listening to him talk with the prince's man, he had been so controlled and powerful that her heart had swelled strangely. That strange, warm giddy feeling she was coming to associate with him. Knowing that he was her husband filled her with a sense of pride she had never known before. Even if he had spanked her, she found she wasn't angry with him anymore. If she were to admit it, she deserved it.

"Who was that man in the bailey?" she asked as she went to the door.

Christopher followed, the bundles in his arms. "His name is Sir Ralph Fitz Walter. He is Prince John's marshal.

He said it with some disgust, enough to cause her to look at him. "You do not like him," she observed.

"No one likes him," he replied, balancing the load as she opened the door. "The man is a snake."

Dustin watched him as he passed through the archway. "He called you by a title," she said thoughtfully. "What was it?"

"Baron?" he said.

"Nay, something else," she replied. "All I could hear was the word 'Defender.' What did he call you?"

They made their way to the narrow spiral stairs and he descended them with some effort, squeezing his bulk down the shaft. He waited until they had exited the front door of the castle before answering her.

"Defender of the Realm," he said.

"What is that?" she asked.

"It means that while Richard is away, I am his strength at home," he said. "I answer only to him."

She looked surprised. "You do not even take orders from Prince John?"

He shook his head. "Nay, only Richard," he replied. "His troops are mine to command. Prince John may only use their strength if he gains my permission."

Dustin was stunned. Christopher de Lohr, her husband, was the king's champion, Defender of the Realm. King Richard, of all England. Why hadn't she known this? Her mind was reeling with the enormity and surprise of it all and she almost tripped on the front steps. He cautioned her and she found she could not take her eyes from him. She had heard the dark man call him by the title, yet because she was so fearful for her own hide, it had made no impact on her. She felt the impact fully now.

"You have so much power?" she managed to ask, totally in awe.

He glanced down at her. "Why are you looking at me like that?"

Her mouth opened. "Because you are the Defender of the Realm and I did not even know it."

He shrugged, whistling to a soldier for his destrier to be brought around. Her mouth still hanging open, she walked around so she could look him in the face.

"Is there any other titles I should know about?" she asked, half irritated. "Mayhap, did God himself grant you a title you have failed to tell me of?"

He raised an eyebrow. "Not that I am aware of," he told her. "And I have no other titles. Except for one, which really isn't a title, simply a nickname."

"And what is that?" she demanded, thinking it was mayhap something even more auspicious than the titles she already knew of.

"Lion's Claw," he said, turning to watch his destrier being brought forth. "Saladin's men called me the Lion's Claw."

She gazed at him, her irritation fading. "Why?"

His attention went back to her, and he found himself drawn to the pretty style in which her hair was arranged. A bit careless, but pretty nonetheless.

"Everyone knows how powerful a lion is, but even a lion is limited without his claws," he said. "The Saracen's believed Richard to be the force, the power if you will. Yet I was his most deadly weapon, his claws."

This knowledge brought new respect to the man, in her eyes. She stared back at him as she absorbed the information, her mind completely overwhelmed with the knowledge. This man, whom she had struck, yelled at, baited, and struggled with at every opportunity was nearly the most powerful man in the kingdom.

Along with the new awareness came a new set of worries. No wonder he didn't want to marry her; a mere baron's daughter, she was not worthy of him in the least. The Defender of the Realm should have a refined, worldly wife, not a naive little waif with a bad temper and a stubborn streak. She struggled with insecurities she never knew she had, confused and overcome as she was, wondering why the man had even lowered himself to speak with her much less marry her. She felt self-conscious and unworthy to even be near him.

"Did you want Lioncross so badly?" she murmured as he loaded the items onto his charger.

He glanced at her. "What did you say?"

She just stared back at him, not sure if she wanted to repeat herself, unsure as to why she said it in the first place. But she suddenly knew one thing, she could not go to London and embarrass him. When the prince and his fine court people saw the champion's new bride, it would surely make him the laughing stock of London. She could not do that to him.

"Nothing," she was backing away. "I….I mean, I forgot something. You go on head; you do not need me."

She turned and bolted for the castle, hearing him shout her name but not stopping for one moment to respond. Once inside, she raced through the great hall, into the kitchens, and out through the back door and into the small kitchen yard that contained the buttery and the cold house.

There was a small, fortified gate in the wall. She yanked it open, slamming it behind her as she continued to tear out into the soft green countryside. Her legs pumped and her heart pounded, and tears of bitterness streamed down her face. She didn't know why she was so upset, but she was. For her and for him. The marriage was a disaster from the very beginning and it would only get worse.

She raced down a small incline and into a bank of trees, coming through on the other side and on into another dense bank of trees. She ran and ran until she could run no more, until her muscles burned and she had to stop or she would collapse.

There was a small pond to her right. She veered for it drunkenly, sobs rising in her throat until she finally flopped down into the soft, cool grass, crying her heart out for so many reasons. She could not stop to grasp just one.

CHAPTER SEVEN

CHRISTOPHER HAD FOLLOWED her into the castle, being informed by a serving wench that she had passed through the kitchens and had run out the back. Racing back out to his destrier, he mounted the animal and tore from the gates, reining around the side of his fortress until he came to the small tunnel that led from the fortified gate. A glance in the distance showed his wife running like the wind, disappearing into a heavy grove of trees.

She was not difficult to follow, but he made sure she did not know he was behind her. When she finally collapsed in a heap at the edge of a small lake, he kept his horse shrouded in the dense brush until he was sure she wasn't going to take off running again. Slowly and quietly, he dismounted and made his way over to her.

She was sobbing as if her heart was broken and he stood there for a long while, watching her and wondering what had upset her so. He knew she was surprised with the information that he was the king's champion, but he could not imagine that it would drive her to tears.

He should have simply let her go, but for some reason he could not. He had to know what was upsetting her.

"Dustin," he whispered.

Her head came up like a shot, her gray eyes wet with tears. "What…?" she gasped. "What are you doing here?"

"I followed you," he said softly, obviously. "Why are you crying?"

She pushed herself up into a sitting position, facing the lake, deeply ashamed. "You wouldn't understand, my lord," she said hoarsely.

She heard his armor creaking as he came and stood next to her, finally sitting slowly. She kept her eyes riveted to the water, now shades of orange and yellow from the setting sun. It was peaceful and serene, and the bugs were beginning to buzz about as night drew near.

"Would you tell me even if I would not understand?" he asked finally, his voice soft.

His tone disarmed her and she fought to maintain her control. When he was gentle like that, she could feel all of her self-protection dissolve. She was terrified to give in to the feelings he provoked.

"I am a silly girl, my lord," she said after a moment. "It matters not why I cry. I cry all the time, mostly for foolish reasons. I am sorry you felt you had to follow me."

He was gazing across the water as well, listening to the deep gulp of the bullfrogs. "I followed you because you are my wife and because I wanted to make sure you came to no harm," he said, then slowly turning his head to look at her. "And you are not a girl. You are a woman, and a beautiful one at that."

Shivers shot up her spine at his seductive tone and her chest throbbed with a curious dull ache. Why did he say such things when they simply weren't true? He had Lioncross, why did he still feel the need to speak sweet words to her? She stood up, wiping her eyes.

"Do not say those things to me," she snapped. "I do not want to hear them."

He watched her stiff back as she paced away from him. "Say what? That you are beautiful? 'Tis the truth, and I speak it."

She turned swiftly, her eyes flashing. "You do not have to say them anymore," she said. "Lioncross is yours and there is nothing to gain by flattery. I hate it when you say such things because I want to believe them."

Her voice suddenly trailed off to a strangled whisper and she whirled back around, appalled at what she had said. Her cheeks were flushing brightly, she knew it, and she wished the ground would open up and swallow her.

But it was an eye-opening statement. Christopher understood a great deal in that outburst. As beautiful as Dustin was, she didn't know it. That was why she chased off suitors and men with honeyed words. She didn't believe herself to be the least bit attractive, and she thought the men were liars because she knew Lioncross to be the real prize. Fact was, Christopher wasn't so sure Lioncross was the real prize anymore.

He stood up. "Dustin, listen to me," he said softly. "I never say anything that I do not mean. You are beautiful, and I have seen a great many women enough to know that. And I do not flatter, for I am not a charming man and I do not enjoy trivial romantic games. Look at me now."

It took a few moments, but she reluctantly complied and he could see that her cheeks were a pretty shade of pink. She looked completely miserable and it touched him.

"Lioncross is indeed mine, but so are you," he went on, softly. " 'Tis true, I married you to gain the fortress, but over the past few days I have come to acquaint myself with a remarkable woman whom I should like to know better, I think."

The setting sun behind him gave him an ethereal-like quality. Dustin sighed and lowered her gaze, inexplicably feeling the need to tell him her thoughts. She tried to control her mouth, to think of a smooth and believable explanation as to her actions, but she could not. She finally gave up.

"Do you want to know why I was crying?" she asked quietly. " 'Twas because I feel myself unworthy to be the Defender of the Realm's wife. I am unworldly, unmannered, unsophisticated and unrefined. Now you would take me to

London with you and I will do naught but embarrass you. I know nothing of court."

His face turned hard. "Unless you are planning a temper tantrum in the middle of the audience chamber, think not that you could ever embarrass me," he said pointedly. "In fact, I will be the envy of every man there because I have the most beautiful wife in the country. As for those other qualities you mentioned, you are nothing of the kind, and if I thought you unworthy of me I would have annulled the marriage by now. No fortress would be worth the grief you mentioned."

She gazed up at him as he approached. "I want to believe you, my lord, I do. But I cannot, not when I know how silly I am."

His hand caught her under the chin, forcing her to meet his eyes. "Naive, yes, but you are not silly," he said firmly. "I would never lie to you, Dustin. You will believe me."

She wanted to but she could not, at least not at this moment. She was still far too unsure of herself and still unsteady with the entire situation. "I shall try," she whispered.

The hand that was on her face began to caress her skin, timidly moving up her jaw until it reached her cheek. She could feel the warmth radiating down her neck, jolting through her spine, turning her limbs to mush.

"Your hand is as big as my head," she giggled, her warm feelings bringing foolish words to her lips.

As if to see her point, he brought up his other hand and effectively captured her whole head in his grasp. They grinned at each other.

"You are right," he said. "You fit most nicely in my hands." Christ, he wanted to kiss her, but he remembered his vow and it was the hardest thing he had ever had to do. If she wanted affection in the marriage, then she would have to establish it. He dropped his hands from her head, but his vow did not prevent him from holding her hand in his.

"Come, it grows late," he said, leading her back to his horse. "We shall seek out your friend tomorrow."

"Then you still want me to go?" she asked.

"Of course, Dustin," he said, reaching the animal. "I want you with me. You are my wife."

He lifted her up and sat her on the saddle and she winced, shifting on her sore bottom. He grinned. "Still hurting?"

"Aye," she said, eyeing him. "And do not look so pleased with yourself."

He mounted behind her. "You caused your own grief, my lady."

She made a wry face as he reined his horse around. "I shall be smarter next time. Or faster."

Grinning, he held her close to him the entire, leisurely ride back to the keep.

ƆƷ

LATER THAN NIGHT, it was well after midnight when Christopher heard the door to his room open quietly. Immediately alert yet remaining still, his right hand felt for the hilt of his sword and gripped it tightly, listening to careful footfalls crossing the floor, coming closer.

The footsteps stopped a moment, he guessed a few feet from his bed and then commenced once more, again very carefully, walking around the side of the bed. His eyes were mostly closed but he could see the figure in the dark as it rounded the bed and drew close to him. It was difficult to make out anything at all in the darkness of the room, and the muscles in his arm contracted as he prepared to strike.

Suddenly there were hands reaching down at him and he was forced into action, bringing up his sword with lightning speed to ward of his attacker.

Christopher was skilled, so skilled in fact that he purposely turned the blade flat side out to simply knock his accoster away as opposed to flat out killing him. Had he turned the sword a quarter inch more and lashed out with the sharp edge, he would have cut the intruder's head off.

There was a cry as the shadow went slamming back onto the floor, knocking over a small table in the process. Christopher was up in an instant, but it was not to protect himself; he recognized the yelp. Dropping his sword, he reached down for the small figure.

"Christ in Heaven, Dustin," he breathed, pulling her up against his chest and trying to soothe her. She was crying from fear and shock. "What are you doing here?"

Her tears were wetting his naked chest, her soft hands against his skin and it was a thoroughly wonderful experience, yet he was aware that his heart was pounding as he realized what he could have done to her. He held her back, trying to see her face in the darkness.

"Answer me, sweetheart. What are you doing here?" he demanded again.

He could see her quiver. "I....I came looking for Caesar," she gasped. "I did not want to wake you."

He let out a heavy sigh and pulled her to his chest again, feeling her tremble in his arms. Much to his surprise, she was actually holding on to him as well. He sat back on the bed, pulling her onto his lap and holding her close, scaring himself when he realized again that she could be lying dead at his feet this very minute. He didn't like being scared.

Dustin had suffered the fright of her life and she was quite shaken by it. Christopher had been so fast with the sword that she had scarcely seen the dim flash of steel before she was sitting on her bottom on the cold stone. Frightened, her arms were wound around his neck, and her cheek lay against his warm shoulder as he comforted her. It was almost worth the fright. He was so big and warm and gentle. She'd never needed the comfort of a man before and had fought those who had tried, but at this time she found his strength to be most reassuring and pleasant. Someday, she might even like it.

Christopher held her for the longest time, neither one of them saying a word. It was as if they both realized what could have happened and it brought the opinions of what they held for each other to new heights. Christopher could not even think about it anymore, every time he imagined the worst, he felt sick. Dustin, for her part, was feeling terribly lucky to be alive, and she was very content sitting on Christopher's lap.

A loud purring invaded their clinch and something warm and fuzzy bumped up against Dustin's back and Christopher's arm. They both turned to look at Caesar, purring wildly and meowing at the same time.

"Damnable beast," Christopher muttered.

Dustin turned in his lap, enough to reach out and pet the cat. In the process, she had ended up facing Christopher completely, face to face, chest to chest. It was a provocative position. Christopher noticed but Dustin didn't; she was more focused on the cat.

"You are a traitor and a troublemaker," Dustin whispered to the cat, scratching his ears. "What did I ever do to make you turn your back on me? Well?"

Caesar licked her fingers and then went over to Christopher's pillow, kneading it with his claws.

"Back away, rodent," Christopher said as he reached out a big hand and batted the cat away. Undeterred, Caesar jumped back on the bed and resumed his kneading in the exact same spot.

Christopher growled impatiently and Dustin giggled. "Caesar, the baron does not want you there."

"I tried to put him out tonight, three times," he said. "I closed the door each time, but somehow he got in. Where does he come from?"

Dustin shook her head. "I do not know. There must be a gap or a hole somewhere he can slip through," she gazed at the cat again. "He is a clever beast."

Christopher was looking at her as she watched the cat, her face so close to his that if he had stuck out his tongue, he would have licked her. He could smell roses, assaulting his senses until his limbs tingled painfully. How could a woman who shunned the more feminine things in life smell so damn sweet and womanly? Yet that was exactly what she was, extremely feminine and completely unaware of it.

The flames of desire licked at him and he knew he was going to have a hell of a time dousing the fire if she didn't leave right away. Damnation, he wanted her, but she would have to want him first. She would have to want him *first*.

"You have found your pet," he said, his voice husky and soft. "I would appreciate you removing him so that I might get back to sleep."

She turned her face and looked at him, jolted with his close proximity and riveted to the intense sky-blue eyes. She could feel his warm breath on her mouth and his masculine musk filling her nostrils. Her breathing began to come faster and with her reaction, she startled herself right off of his lap.

"I apologize again for surprising you this night," she said, her eyes inexplicably glued to him as she retrieved Caesar. "Goodnight, my lord."

She tore her eyes away and moved for the door, clutching the cat. By the time she reached the archway, she was almost running.

Ten minutes later, the cat was back.

Christopher appeared in Dustin's room, holding the cat away from him as if it carried a disease. Dustin, almost asleep, was startled to see him looming over her, his face grim.

"I have a theory, my lady, I would like to test," he said frankly.

She rubbed her eyes and sat up. "What?"

He threw the cat on the bed. "Move over."

"What?" her eyes opened wide.

He pushed his way into the bed, shoving her over. "I am curious to know if Caesar is attached to me personally, or simply the bed I am sleeping in."

Dustin tried to protest but the fact of the matter was that she was curious, too. Somewhere in the process of allowing him into her bed, she was caught next to him and his arm ended up around her. Pulled up against his muscular chest, she suddenly didn't feel much like protesting anymore. She rather liked the feeling.

"Now be still," he admonished, his arm squeezing her close.

"Pretend to sleep and let's see what he does."

Her cheek against the soft, smooth skin of the crook of his shoulder, Dustin obeyed and closed her eyes. Christopher feigned sleep as well, feeling the cat as it fidgeted and turned circles before finally plopping down, half on his legs. He heard the cat sigh contentedly, purring up a storm.

He lay there a long, long while, every so often taking a peek at the cat where it lay. Caesar was sleeping soundly. This fact worried him, for it proved that Dustin's cat was indeed attached to him and not to the bed upon which he had been sleeping. He winced inwardly, wondering how Dustin was going to react to this discovery. Hell, he didn't want the damn cat.

He glanced over at the top of her blond head. "Dustin," he whispered. When he received no answer, he gave her a little shake and tried again. "Dustin."

She responded by sighing raggedly and flinging an arm across his chest, burying her face half into his shoulder and giving another slow, languid sigh. He then realized she had fallen asleep and cracked a smile into the darkness.

With the cat draped across his legs and his wife burrowed against him, Christopher should have felt trapped but, instead, had the strangest feeling of satisfaction. He chuckled ironically and found himself stroking the top of Dustin's blond head.

"If you two aren't a maddening pair," he whispered, feeling the silkiness of the strands. "What in the hell am I going to do with you?" He didn't know if he meant the cat, or his wife, or both.

Unconsciously, Dustin's fingers drifted across his skin and he put his hand over them, pressing her soft hand against his flesh.

He lay staring at the ceiling for an indeterminate amount of time, his mind a jumble of curious emotions. He didn't even realize when he finally drifted off, for the next thing he knew the dawn was breaking, the cat was lying on his stomach, and both arms were wound protectively around his wife.

It was the best feeling in the world.

☙

DUSTIN WASN'T QUITE sure how to feel anymore.

She'd never needed anyone, much less a man, and as fiercely independent as she was, she was desperately confused. Puzzled because waking in Christopher's arms had been a most wonderful experience and she hated herself for thinking such betraying emotions. She absolutely refused to become attached to anyone, even her husband.

Dressed in the new golden surcoat that made her look like a goddess, she allowed Christopher, David and Edward to escort her into town to Rebecca's small hut. The peasants, who were well acquainted with the rough-and-tumble mistress of Lioncross Abbey, pointed and waved and smiled at her as she passed them by and Dustin was deeply embarrassed at the attention. She felt as if she were making a spectacle of herself, pretending to be a fine lady when the serfs knew very well that she was not.

She was riding in front of her husband, who had been inordinately quiet this morn. But, then again, so had she. She didn't know what to say to him, and when she donned the golden surcoat for their trip to town, she tried to tell herself it wasn't because she wanted to please her husband. Her thoughts were completely foreign to her.

David was the first to dismount when they reached Rebecca's cottage, lifting Dustin from Christopher's saddle. She thanked him when her feet hit the ground and tugged at her dress in a most unladylike manner to straighten it. David and Edward grinned while Christopher raised a reproving eyebrow. Dustin, still pulling at the neckline of her dress and scratching her right breast, caught the smiles of the two knights and realized what she was doing.

"Well, it itches," she declared and, thrusting up her chin, approached the door and rapped loudly. She ignored the knights laughing behind her.

Rebecca opened the door after a moment, her eyes widening at the sight of her friend. "Dustin. My God. You look gorgeous."

Dustin smiled broadly at her friend. "Thanks to you. It fits perfectly."

The two women squealed in greeting, babbling so quickly that the men could understand very little.

"How's your head? You had us so worried," Rebecca gushed.

"It's fine." Dustin pulled her hair back to prove her point. "Christopher put a stitch in it and it is healing quickly."

Rebecca glanced over her friend's shoulder at the three big men, suddenly a bit subdued with their presence. But Dustin wouldn't let the mood settle.

"We brought more material," she said, grabbing her friend's arm and dragging her inside. "The baron is taking me to London."

After that, the knights were completely forgotten. Even though they followed the women into the hut, bearing the material, they might as well have not even been there. Dustin and Rebecca chattered like magpies, about anything and everything, and ignoring all else.

The men stood back against the wall like huge silent sentries, listening with some amusement at all of the yakking going on. Rebecca unrolled the material and exclaimed gleefully over the colors and textures, holding them up to Dustin and telling her friend exactly how the dress was going to be. Dustin, uneducated in fashions and styles, simply nodded and went along with everything her friend said.

Christopher's eyes never left his wife, the way her face would light up with a laugh or a smile, the silly little giggle she had that could grow out of control so quickly. He noticed she had a thoroughly charming habit of wrinkling her nose when she was delighted. He'd never seen this side of her and he found he was utterly captivated.

"Oh, Dustin, I envy you going to London," Rebecca sighed as she rewrapped the material. "I have always wanted to go there."

"I know," Dustin said, helping her friend with the fabric. "I wish you could go with us."

"What are you going to do there?" Rebecca asked.

Dustin looked puzzled. "I do not know, exactly," she admitted. "I suppose we'll spend time with the prince." She turned to her husband for the first time since entering the hut. "Isn't that right? We will be spending our time with Prince John?"

He gazed steadily at her. Christ, if she only knew how much more there was to it than that. "Some."

Dustin gave him a small smile, a brief expression that unexpectedly warmed his heart, before turning back to her friend. "And guess what else? Sir Christopher is a very important man in England. King Richard himself gave him the title of 'Defender of the Realm.' Not even Prince John can give him orders."

She sounded suspiciously like she was bragging and Christopher cleared his throat, shifting his weight on his massive legs. "Dustin," he admonished softly.

Rebecca and Dustin both turned to him, and the expression on Rebecca's face was as if she were looking at God himself.

"My lord, what an honor," she said earnestly. "Why, to simply have you in my home is something I can tell my grandchildren about." Before he could reply in any way, the redhead turned back to Dustin. "You married a baron *and* the king's Defender? Dustin, how did you get to be so lucky? I can scarce believe it."

Dustin looked somewhat humbled, piling the material into a stack. " 'Twas my father's doing, not mine," she said, turning to Christopher with a twinkle in her eye. "The baron wanted Lioncross so badly he would have married Medusa to get it."

She saw him crack a smile and she was pleased at her accomplishment. To share a humorous moment with him brought one more facet to their deepening relationship. With Rebecca finishing storing the bundles of fabrics, it seemed that their visit was drawing to a close and Dustin was reluctant to leave. She and her friend were used to spending the entire day together, and with the prospect of her leaving shortly for an unknown amount of time, she missed Rebecca already.

She turned hesitantly to Christopher. "My lord, might I speak with you? Privately?"

He uncrossed his arms and immediately opened the door. Taking the silent cue, Dustin quickly passed through, and he followed. Outside, he faced her expectantly.

"I will not be seeing Rebecca for a while, my lord, and I was wondering if you would allow me to visit with her for the day?" She had never had to ask for permission to call on her friend and found it strange to form the words.

"Visit for the day?" he looked doubtful. "She needs to finish those clothes for you, Dustin. Your presence would only distract her.

"Nay, it would not," she insisted. "I could help her. I have done it before."

He eyed her, seeing how eager she was. He shrugged. "I will allow you to stay for the rest of the morning, then," he said. "I shall leave Edward here to escort you home."

She did not protest the guard, remembering well what happened two days ago. She smiled, a real smile. "Thank you, Christopher."

He cocked an eyebrow at her, a faint smile on his lips. "Christopher, is it? 'Tis 'my lord' when you want something, and 'Christopher' when you get it."

She giggled and before he could stop himself, he touched her cheek lightly with a gloved hand. It was a sweet gesture, not lost on Dustin. Her eyes gazed warmly back at him.

But Christopher was embarrassed with the display of tenderness and cleared his throat sternly. "I have work to do, my lady. I shall expect you home by the nooning meal, if you can stop chattering long enough."

"Aye, husband," she said saucily as he opened the door for her, causing him to do a double-take.

She'd called him 'husband.' He almost smiled, startled to hear the title from her lips. Hell, he almost looked around to see if she were addressing someone else, but he knew she was speaking to him. He *was* her husband and, much to his astonishment, he was growing to like it.

Dustin and Rebecca spent a pleasant hour as Rebecca began work on a surcoat. Dustin sat and watched as her friend carefully laid a pattern and cut it out. She had seen Rebecca do this many times before, but had never had the desire to learn to sew herself. She'd rather climb a tree or ride a horse.

Christopher and David had retreated to Lioncross while Edward stood vigilant watch outside the hut door. Dustin tried to coax him inside twice, but he smiled and refused politely. He was sworn to protect her, and if he were to sit comfortably inside the cottage, he could be caught off guard by danger.

"In all the years that we have known each other, and with as many times as I have been to your hut, I have never had to have an escort," she commented as Rebecca matched thread to the sapphire-colored fabric.

"But you are a baron's wife now," Rebecca replied. "You are too valuable to be allowed to run free and alone."

Dustin shrugged, leaning forward on her elbows. "I do not feel any different," she said, which was a lie. She felt very different. "What I mean is, I am still the same person I was four days ago, with the only difference being I am married now."

"And married to the Defender of the Realm." Rebecca was still having trouble coming to grips with the awesome nature of her friend's husband. "My God, when I think of that, my mind fairly explodes with disbelief."

Dustin smiled faintly. "How do you think I felt upon learning it? I am not a worldly, fine woman Rebecca. I am simply not worthy of the man."

Rebecca's head came up. "Ridiculous, Dustin. You are the most beautiful, kind woman I have ever known. Of course you are worthy of him. Did he tell you otherwise?"

"Of course not," Dustin replied. "He's never been anything but kind, at least for the most part. Except when he spanked me."

"*Spanked* you?" Rebecca repeated. "What on earth for?"

Dustin turned away, ashamed. "For throwing things at him and yelling."

Rebecca laughed heartily. "I have seen you do worse. He will be spanking you every other day if he considers that a grievous offense."

"Oh, be quiet," Dustin pouted. "You spank your children, not your wife."

"You do when your wife is as stubborn and spoiled as you are," Rebecca replied with a grin, noting her friend's expression. "Oh, Dustin, do not carry on about it. If I married a man as handsome as Sir Christopher, he could spank me thrice a day and I wouldn't mind."

Dustin looked at her friend. "You think he's handsome?"

"Aye, verily," Rebecca said, focusing on the material. "The most handsome man I have seen."

Dustin turned away thoughtfully. So Rebecca thought he was handsome, did she? To hear her comment only reinforced the very same thoughts Dustin was trying to ignore.

"This thread does not quite match," Rebecca commented, holding up the spool for Dustin to see. "Let's go see Mr. Codwalader. If he doesn't have it in his stock, then he can probably dye the correct shade for us.

Dustin nodded, following Rebecca into the small kitchen room where she had almost met her end. They went out the back door, heading for the heart of the village where the merchant's shops were, and completely forgetting about the knight who was standing watch at their front door.

Certain events happened purely by accident. Dustin and Rebecca stayed to watch Mr. Codwalader dye the thread a matching sapphire blue, an event that took a bit of time, which the two of them lost track of.

Edward, promptly at noon, stuck his head into the hut to announce their imminent departure and was baffled to find the cottage deserted. Concerned for his mistress and terrified that Christopher would blame him if anything happened to her, he set out in search of Lady de Lohr.

He had no idea where to look, of course, and after a half hour of searching, he made his way back to Lioncross. David was waiting for him in the bailey, his eyes widening when he saw Edward was alone.

"Where is she?" he demanded.

Edward was grim. "Gone," he said reluctantly. "David, I need help looking for her."

"Gone? What in the hell do you mean?" David asked urgently.

"Exactly what I said," Edward said, running a hand across his face. "Christopher is going to kill me. I was standing watch outside the front door the whole time and the two of them must have slipped out the back door. I have no idea where they went."

David's mouth went agape but he shut it rapidly. "Chris has got to know of this," he turned and dashed into the castle.

Edward dismounted and, not so eagerly, followed. Five minutes later, Christopher and the entire company of knights were mounted and tearing through the open gates toward the village.

Dustin and Rebecca, completely unaware of the uproar they had caused, sat quite happily in Mr. Codwalader's store and watched the man mix the dye to achieve the exact color of the material. They chatted with the wrinkled old man about different subjects, for Mr. Codwalader was very knowledgeable and they enjoyed his company. His wife had died years ago and he was alone, so he always enjoyed very lengthy conversations. Blissfully ignorant of the knights that were even now roaring into the village, they continued their discussion without reservation.

Christopher split up his men, sending half to one end of the village for a hut-to-hut search while he and David and Edward took the main street. His gestures were sharp, his commands brusque, and no one wasted any time carrying out his orders.

It was difficult for Christopher to express the emotions that were filling him. Anger, of course, but also a certain amount of apprehension after the attack the other day. He knew he had found his wife by pure chance and he had no desire to test his luck again. He had no idea where she might have gone but when he found her he hoped for her sake that her bottom had recovered somewhat from the other day because he was surely going to give her more of the same for filling him with a fear he had never experienced before.

To imagine something horrible befalling Dustin brought terror to his veins and he was greatly disturbed by it. Angry with her for causing it and angry with himself for being weak enough to feel it.

ଓ

MR. CODWALADER DYED the thread to perfection and, still wet, handed it back to Rebecca. She accepted the spool on a wire, still chatting leisurely with the little man and Dustin promised to pay him for it the next day.

After lengthy goodbyes and thank-yous, the two women left the shop and cut through the small village, back to Rebecca's hut. They had no way of knowing they had missed the search party by mere yards, as they had exited the rear of the shop while Dustin's husband and his knights had entered another shop a few doors down, nearly ripping the panel of the candlemaker's shop off its hinges in their haste.

Still neglecting to remember her watchdog, Dustin and Rebecca spent a good deal of time going over the dresses again as the baron and his men nearly ripped the little town apart by the seams looking for them. Finally, Dustin's stomach rumbled and she suddenly remembered about Edward and her promise to Christopher to return by the nooning meal.

"What time is it?" she exclaimed, throwing the front door open. She was verily surprised to find that Edward was gone.

"Well after midday," Rebecca squinted up to the sky. "Where is your knight?"

"I don't know," Dustin replied, puzzled. "Mayhap he got bored and went back to the keep."

She and Rebecca shrugged at each other, unconcerned with Edward, but Dustin was very concerned about being late for the nooning meal.

"I hope Christopher isn't too angry with me," she said, kissing her friend's cheek goodbye. "Thank you, Rebecca. I shall see you tomorrow."

As she had done hundreds of times before, Dustin gathered her skirts and walked casually back to the keep, enjoying the day and the birds and the sky, still totally unaware of the chaos that was erupting on her behalf.

That ignorance was not to last for long.

☙

THREE HOURS LATER, the knights rode back into the bailey, greeted by a host of soldiers and young squires to take their animals and their gear.

Christopher dismounted, tearing his gauntlets off and tucking them under his arm, his eyes riveted to the castle doors with his face set like stone. David walked up beside him.

"Try not to be too hard on her, Chris," he said. "Her friend said she did not deliberately disobey you."

Christopher didn't reply, which concerned David. He knew his brother better than anyone, and when Christopher was silent it was usually a sign of extreme anger. But there was nothing more he could say, so he slowed his pace and let his brother continue on into the castle, to deal with his wife alone. He wondered if he shouldn't follow at a safe distance, just to protect Dustin should Christopher go out of control. He had never seen that happen; still, he was concerned all the same.

A serving wench directed Christopher outside and he found his wife in the small kitchen yard, dressed in her usual peasant garb with her hair pulled back to the nape of her neck, feeding her rabbits.

Christopher marched up on her and stopped a few feet back, preparing to explode. He wanted to yell his head off but as soon as he saw her standing so innocently feeding her pets, he choked on his anger. But not quite; he was furious with her and had to clench his hands behind his back to keep from shaking her.

"Dustin?" he said in a remarkably controlled voice.

She turned around and he was caught off guard to see that her face lit up with a smile. "My lord, you have returned," she said pleasantly, shoving the rabbit she was holding back into his hutch. "I asked where you had gone and no one was able to tell me very much. Is Edward with you? He left Rebecca's hut before I did and I have not seen him."

This was not the manner or words of a disobedient, spiteful woman. He put his hands on his hips, trying not to glare at her as he realized she truly had no idea of what had transpired because of her thoughtlessness.

"Aye, Edward is with me," he said as evenly as he could manage. "You do not know where I have been?"

She shook her head, wiping her hands on her dress. "Nay. Where?"

Good Lord, he thought, turning away from her a brief moment, trying to maintain his composure. She truly didn't know. He had been out terrorizing the peasants because he thought she was in danger, and she was completely unaware of what she had caused.

"Inside, lady, if you will," he stepped aside and motioned to her.

Not sensing his conflict in the least, Dustin preceded him into the castle and then allowed him to lead her up to her rooms. Once inside, he closed the door softly and she turned to him.

She watched him as he slowly removed his helmet. It seemed to her that he was being rather thoughtful, and she wondered why.

"Is something wrong, my lord?" she asked.

He looked at her then, a bit calmer. "Where did you go today?"

She looked confused. "To....to Rebecca's cottage. You took me there."

He shook his head as he removed his mail hood. "Nay, I mean while Edward was supposed to be watching you. Where did you go?"

She blinked, pulling her long ponytail over one shoulder absently. "We went to Mr. Codwalader's store for thread. Rebecca needed an exact shade for the dress she is making, and he has the dyes. He always helps her with her sewing."

So that was it. Simple, straightforward. He still could not believe she didn't grasp the seriousness of the situation.

"That is where you went?" he raised his eyebrow. "Alone?"

She nodded. "Aye, we cut across...." Her eyes suddenly widened at him. "We forgot about Edward. Was he supposed to go with us?"

Christopher stared at her a moment before letting out an ironic sigh, sitting heavily in an oak chair. He put his hands to his head a moment, baffled at her innocence and suddenly lacking the desire or energy to get angry with her. He just couldn't manage it.

"Aye, he was," he mumbled. "He was your escort, Dustin, remember? That means he goes wherever you go. Do you have any idea how badly you frightened him when he went to bring you back and you were missing?"

She sat down on her bed, looking at her hands. "I forgot he was there, my lord. I am unused to escorts. When I returned, he was gone and I assumed he had come back to the keep. So I walked home alone, as I always have."

He eyed her. "There are certain things we need to establish at this moment, Lady de Lohr. I have a great many enemies, and when you married me they became your enemies as well. You are not free to come and go as you please, alone, for my enemies would take advantage of such a situation. As my wife, you are a valuable commodity and must be protected. You must remember this, Dustin. Your life will depend on it."

She swallowed. "You speak of the prince?"

"He's one," he replied softly. "Everyone has enemies, sweetheart. As Richard's envoy, I have more than my share."

She was still staring at her hands, thinking on his words. "Would they kill me?"

" 'Tis possible," he said. "But more likely, they would use you to get to me."

She looked at him then. "I do not understand all of this, my lord," she whispered. "Court intrigue is new to me. I know nothing."

He nodded. "You have indeed lived a sheltered, carefree life here at Lioncross. But no more, Dustin. You must grow up. It is not merely my enemies, but dangers in general. This world is not a safe place."

She hung her head and he felt himself relenting fully. He could see that she had not meant to cause any chaos, contrary to her nature. It was probably the first time in her life she had not meant to cause trouble, but had done so anyway.

"I apologize for my actions, my lord," she said regretfully.

"No need," he stood up. "Just remember yourself, my lady, especially while we are in London. There's no room for mistakes there.

"Then mayhap you should leave me here, just to be safe," she said.

He gave her a half smile. "Nay, wife, you will come with me," he said. "You will enjoy your stay, I am sure."

"With your enemies prowling the halls, looking for the first opportunity to kill me? I think not," she said with more irony than fear.

He laughed, causing her to smile. "I promise I will give you your own dagger to defend yourself. I have a feeling you would give any accoster quite a fight."

"I have my own dagger," she insisted. "Do you really think that I will need it?"

"I was jesting, sweetheart," he told her, gathering his mail, hood, and helmet. "You will never again need to defend yourself. I will do it for you."

"Why? Because you are my husband?" she teased lightly. "I do not recall that our wedding vows instructed you to defend me, only honor, obey, and trust."

He raised an eyebrow. "And you have already broken two of those vows, and I know not about the third."

She knew which ones he was referring to. "Aye, honor and obey have not always been my strong points, but I do trust you. Truly, I do."

He was standing by the door. "You had better," he said. "And before the month is out, I intend to have the other two."

She smiled a sort of noncommittal smile and rose, turning away from him. He found his eyes drawn to her full breasts, her shapely hips, and her whole figure. Christ, she was lovely and full and supple. Thoughts he had had before, yet thoughts that stayed with him the rest of the day.

CHRISTOPHER TOSSED AND turned that night. Every time he closed his eyes he saw Dustin, her sweet face, her luscious young body. Christ, it had been so long since he'd had a woman that his natural urges were getting the better of him and he'd been fighting off an erection most of the evening.

Yet he would not go to his wife. His vows were firm and strong, she would have to come to him first. But his body screamed to touch her, to hold her, to caress her and taste her like he had no other. He had every legal and moral right to go storming into her room and drive into her until he found his release and his seed beget an heir, but he just could not seem to do it. He knew she didn't want him, and that strengthened his resolve not to seek her out.

But he was terribly distended, thinking of her, and he knew he would have to do something about it or face great unrest. There were always serving wenches willing to relieve a man, no more than objects for a man to relieve himself with. Throwing the covers off and hearing Caesar squeal in protest as he was disturbed, he donned his breeches and left his room, searching with an overpowering urge for a woman to release him.

It wasn't difficult. The castle was full of willing wenches, even sleepy ones, and he returned to his room in no time with a big-busted brunette ready to obey his every command.

Christopher wasn't nice about it. He ordered the woman to strip as he removed his breeches and roughly squeezed her breasts, suckling hard on her as she moaned and writhed loudly beneath him. His huge hands bruised her soft breasts and her moans were partially of pain, partially of pleasure. He ran his hands all over her, his eyes closed, not even realizing that he was thinking her to be his wife. Wishing her to be.

That was the extent of his foreplay. He settled himself in between her legs and drove his massive organ into her so hard that she did scream from pain, and he slapped his hand over her mouth to quiet her. But her face soon awash with pleasure as he thrust into her, hard enough to bump her head against the wall. When he felt himself building quickly toward his release, he withdrew and turned the wench over on her stomach, propping her up on her knees. A trick he had learned of, so as not to deposit his seed and possibly beget a bastard, he eased himself into her anus.

The wench moaned and cried softly, rubbing her woman's center as he pushed his way into her. Within two hard thrusts, he was released, animalistic satisfaction washing over him, but nothing more.

When he finally opened his eyes and looked down at her dark head, he was suddenly struck by the fact he had been picturing Dustin in his mind all along and was horrified at what he had done. He had done nothing but mate in a purely bestial sense and he was disgusted with himself.

God help him, he wanted his wife in every sense of the word. He was ashamed that he was not strong enough to wait for her. Kicking the woman from his bed, he barely gave her time to dress before opening the door and practically throwing her from his room. He was hurried and urgent, wanting to get her out and forget about the whole affair. He was a man unused to regret, but regret he did.

ଔ

DUSTIN HAD NO more woken up the next morning than she began to hear the rumors that the baron had bedded one of the kitchen servants. Deeply shocked, she pressed the silly maid who was helping her with her bath until she was sure she had all of the horrible, humiliating details. Even when she had stopped asking questions, the wench continued to prattle on as if she were talking to another silly female and not the baron's wife. She went on and on and Dustin sat in stunned silence until hot tears began to sting her eyes and she chased the foolish woman from her room.

It seemed that all she did was cry anymore. She cried now because she was terribly hurt if the rumors were true, and she had no reason to suspect that they were not. Except for fatherly kindness, Christopher had never indicated the least bit of attraction for her and she knew it was because she was unworthy of him. Yet he had seen fit to take a kitchen wench to bed with him, and that information cut her to the bone. He did not believe her worthy enough to bed. The more she brooded, the more angry and hurt she became until her pain was a raging fire in her chest.

Why should she obey and honor him when he had seen it fit to dishonor her? True, it was not uncommon or even discouraged for the lord of the house to bed a servant. It was simply part of his privileges, yet her father had never done it because he actually loved her mother. She was blind and stupid to believe that Christopher would honor her in the same manner.

She was crushed. She simply could not deal with the thoughts anymore and decided from that point on she would never again allow herself to like him. Truth was, she was coming to like him a great deal and for her emotions, she had received a slap in the face. That would happen no more. Men, as she had always believed, were pigs and liars and cheats, and she hated all of them. Christopher had almost changed her mind, but fortunately his actions had brought her back to her senses.

She dressed in a standard dress, brown cloth skirt and a white blouse with a tight black girdle around her small waist. She was in the process of putting on her black leather slippers when she caught sight of her three new dresses hanging in her wardrobe.

Dustin didn't even think, the next thing she knew, she was yanking the dresses out and slashing them, tearing them, until there were shreds of lavender and gold and burgundy all over her room. The remaining material that refused to tear was shoved into the hearth where it burned brightly. Sweating and panting, yet somehow pacified with her venting for the moment, she secured her long hair back to the nape of her neck and quit the room.

It was mid-morning before Christopher went to seek her. He hadn't seen her when he and the other knights had broken their fast at dawn and had yet to catch a glimpse of her. Mayhap it was a guilty conscience that made him more eager to see her than usual.

He rapped softly at her door, calling her name. Twice more he tried and received no answer. Quietly, he lifted the latch and stuck his head inside.

What he saw shocked him and he knew instantly that someone had told her about his indiscretion. He should have known the stupid bitch would have run and told everyone who would listen. He felt sick to the pit of his stomach as he surveyed the torn dresses. Dresses he had asked her to wear. Christ, he knew the symbolic meaning of the ripped and destroyed clothing without even asking her and he was deeply distressed.

It was his own fault; all of it. Had he not been so proud, had he only been strong enough to wait, had he only...? It had taken hurdles and leaps and bounds to bring their relationship to the point it had reached, and looking at the chaotic room he could only pray that it had not been completely destroyed. He realized with growing concern that he didn't want Dustin hating him for the rest of his life. He wanted, nay, *needed* her companionship. He'd never needed anyone before the way he was beginning to need her.

He picked up a swatch of the gold, remembering how beautiful she had looked in it. He also remembered the way she laughed with Rebecca, her unrestrained comical sense and the beautiful shape of her mouth when she smiled. She had smiled at him like that on a few rare occasions. He wondered darkly if he would ever see that smile again.

There was a way out of this, of course. He could lie to her. Christ, he hated that thought. He was a man of impeccable honor and standards, and he knew he could not, in good conscience, lie to his wife. But he was feeling a peculiar sense of desperation, as if he would do anything to gain peace between them.

David came up behind him, surveying the room with surprise. "What in the hell happened here?"

Christopher was still clutching the piece of gold material. "I do not know for sure, but I have an idea."

"What idea? Where is your wife?" David asked with rising concern.

Christopher sighed. "Off somewhere, hating me," he said softly, looking at his brother. "I took a serving wench to my bed last night, David. I can only imagine that Dustin has heard the rumors."

David looked puzzled. "Why would you take a whore when you have a wife?"

"I haven't bedded her yet!" he suddenly snapped, disgusted with the whole situation, fighting for a grip on himself. He raked his fingers through his blond hair. "Leave it at that, David. I have to go find Dustin."

"You haven't bedded her? Damn, why not?" David grabbed his brother's arm, trying to understand. "She's the most beautiful woman I have ever seen, Chris. Why in the hell would you leave her untouched?"

Christopher was frustrated and agitated for too many reasons. "Because…oh hell, 'tis too complicated. Just leave me alone and say nothing of this to anyone."

But David wouldn't be put off. "Because you are too stubborn to admit you want her, isn't that right?" David's voice was low and controlled. "And she's too naïve and innocent to know what she wants. You have never had to fight a woman to get into her bed, Chris, and you think that Dustin will refuse you. Tell me I am right."

Christopher's eyes were dark as he glared at his brother. "If you know so much, then answer your own damn question."

David smiled wryly. "I already have. And I know something else, too. You care for your wife, and you don't want to."

"To hell with you," Christopher growled, throwing down the piece of golden silk and storming from the room.

David shook his head at his brother's foolishness, foolishness that just might cost him what he did so want, yet wouldn't admit it; his wife.

☙

CHRISTOPHER FOUND DUSTIN out by the rabbit hutches, feeding a big, fat white rabbit a bunch of greens. She looked like a serving wench, dusty and dirty with her hair askew under the bright sun. But she looked terribly beautiful and his heart did a strange little twist, a feeling he was coming to associate with her. He was coming to soften every time he looked at her. He stood there a moment, struggling to summon the courage to speak to her.

"Greetings, wife," he said softly.

She didn't look up at him or acknowledge him in any way. He waited a nominal amount of time for her to speak before clearing his throat. "I am speaking to you, Dustin."

She put the rabbit back in his cage. "I know," she replied.

"Why don't you answer me?" he asked.

"I have nothing to say to you, my lord," she said respectfully, busying herself with another rabbit in another cage.

"Why?" he asked.

She held up another bunch of greens to the little brown bunny, not answering him. He watched her as her jaw ticked and she blinked rapidly as if chasing off tears. He had never felt so guilty.

"Tell me what you heard," he said softly.

Dustin could not hold the tears back anymore and she sobbed quietly into the rabbit's silky fur. He waited patiently, wondering why she was feeling so hurt if indeed she were as indifferent to him as she pretended. But she was a prideful woman and he knew her honor was damaged.

"I cannot repeat it," she whispered.

He stepped closer to her, nearly touching her. "I would hear it. Tell me."

She cried into the rabbit's coat. "That… that you bedded a serving wench and she bears your bastard."

He sighed sadly, feeling as badly as he possibly could. "Put the rabbit down and come with me," he said gently.

"Nay," she suddenly hissed, moving away from him. "I hate you, Christopher de Lohr. I hate you with all that I am and I will never forgive you for shaming me, *never*. Go to London and leave me alone for I do not ever want to see you again."

She had every right to be mad and he had to force down an instinctive response. "Easy, my lady, easy," he said calmly. "Will you please put the rabbit down and allow me to explain?"

"Nay," her voice was louder, her crying gaining speed. "There is nothing you can say that I will want to hear. Go *away*."

He didn't care if they were creating a scene. He was going to speak to her and she was going to listen. He snatched the rabbit by the ears and tossed it into the cage. Dustin, startled and angered, started to scream at him but he caught her around the waist and threw her over his shoulder. He then carried her, kicking and hollering, all the way back through the kitchens and up to his room, where he proceeded to set her down and lock the door for good measure.

Dustin was like a wet cat, all fury and fight. She immediately started throwing things at him, anything she could get her hands on, screaming like a banshee. He removed his mail, his sword, until he was dressed only in a tunic, boots and a pair of breeches. The entire time she raged, he had yet to say a word, and spent most of his time dodging flying objects. But he let her go on; she had every right to be mad.

He stood and watched her as she stripped all of the covers off the bed, bashing the pillows against the wooden frame until feathers flew everywhere, all the while screaming of her hatred for him and for men in general.

As he watched her vent, it struck him that he could not lie to her if he wanted to build a good relationship with the woman. The relationship was probably already destroyed, but he still could not make up falsehoods simply to ease tensions. He must be honest with her, and as much as he found himself choking on the mere thought, to ask for her forgiveness.

He went over to the edge of the bed, standing in the flurry of feathers that stuck to his hair and clothing.

"Would you listen to me now?" he asked.

She glared at him with a look to kill, the tears and fury having expended most of her energy. Lacking the will or desire to go on anymore, she fell forward onto the mattress and rolled onto her back, an arm up over her head as she looked away from him.

Seeing she was calm and quiet for the moment, he sat on the edge of the bed. Forming the correct words were not easy.

"I am sorry for your hurt," he said softly. "Please know that I would never do anything to hurt you intentionally. I do mean that."

"Then it's true," she whispered. "You did bed her."

"I did, but it is not that simple," he answered, struggling with himself. "I didn't want to marry you; you know that. Yet, as the days passed and I came to know you, I came to like you. You are a priceless character, and a dazzling beauty, and the more I came to like you, the angrier I became at myself. Call it independence, pride, arrogance, whatever you wish. I felt threatened by you, I think."

"Why?" she hiccupped, still not looking at him.

"Because I knew once I lay myself open to you I would be vulnerable for your rejection," he replied. "You told me yourself that you did not want a husband. And the more I felt want for you, the harder it became for me. Last night, I wanted you, I will admit it now. But I would not go to you, knowing your feelings and knowing mine. The wench was a nonthreatening outlet for pent-up emotions. She was an object, Dustin, and nothing more. But I found that all the while I was with her, I was imagining she was you. 'Tis not an excuse I give you but an explanation. Whether or not it eases your humiliation, I will tell you all the same."

She lay back on his bed, staring off into the space of the room. Even in her state she realized that it must have taken considerable courage for him to admit his feelings. If he had the courage, mayhap she did, too.

Dustin sat up, drying her eyes before standing on her feet. Slowly she released her hair from its clip, shaking it until it fell all about her like a glorious coat of gold.

"Do you care for me, Christopher?" she asked softly.

He blinked slowly before answering. "Aye."

She turned to him with a raised brow. "You do?"

He nodded and stood up, turning away from her. "Aye, I do, and do not ask me why, either. You are the most bull-headed, obstinate, unyielding woman I have ever had the misfortune to marry, and after the disrespect you have shown me, I have no idea why I...."

"Christopher," she cut him off and he turned around. "I care for you, too."

He just stared at her, unsure of what to do next. He simply shook his head faintly, his blue eyes melding with her gray ones.

"I do not know what to say, Dustin," he murmured. "This is madness; all of it. Other husbands take servants to bed and not an eyebrow is raised, but I regretted what I had done the moment I did it because I felt as if I had betrayed you. And I have."

She lowered her gaze and leaned against the canopy post, deep in thought. "I know nothing of coupling, Chris. I have seen animals mate and know the physical aspects of it, but I am an innocent when it comes to the mating of people." Her hand absently caressed the post. "I know that it is the most intimate act a husband and wife can perform, yet a necessary one to perpetuate the family. I do not know why I feel so betrayed that you would choose to mate with another. It's not as if I am a desirable woman, not like some, so in a sense I do not blame you for seeking out a more experienced woman."

He came to her then, his hand closing over hers as it held on to the bedpost. "You are by far the most desirable woman I have ever met," he said quietly, reaching out his free hand to cup her face. "Think not for one moment that I do not find you attractive. You affect me, lady, and that frightens me."

Dustin's heart began to pound wildly against her ribs as his blue eyes bore into her. She didn't know why and she suddenly stopped caring why. He was so big and powerful and masculine and, yes, even though he was a man, she had to force herself to admit he was attractive and wonderful.

Even if he had bedded the wench, he wasn't entirely to blame for that. She knew she had not exactly been yielding and she was suddenly seized with the urge to know the feeling of his lips on hers. To her, a kiss was very intimate and it was difficult to comprehend much more.

"Chris," she whispered.

"Aye?" his voice was husky.

"I do not like honeyed words," she stammered back. "And I slug men who try to kiss me."

"Shall I go no further?" His eyes twinkled under half lowered lids.

She gazed back into them, her fear returning slightly. "Tell me you care for me, as a husband should."

"I care for you as a husband should," he repeated, very nearly upon her.

"Tell me you shall protect and defend me always, and that you shall never bed another woman," she whispered, feeling his hot breath on her face.

"All that and more, sweetheart," he whispered hoarsely.

"Dustin?"

"Aye?" she could nearly taste him, as close as he was and her arms and legs were tingling painfully, her heart pounding in her ears.

"May I have permission to kiss you?" he asked, barely audible.

"Aye," she replied.

"Chris?"

"Yes, Dustin?" He could nearly taste her, too, and it was driving him mad.

She hesitated a brief second, her eyes tearing away from his mouth long enough to look him in the eye. "Speak honeyed words to me," she gushed breathlessly.

He was on her before she could draw another breath, his mouth warm and soft and suckling her so fiercely she was overwhelmed. She'd never been kissed before. Dear Lord, is this what she had been afraid of? She knew instantly that she had been foolish for fearing something as sweet and wonderful as this.

Dustin was pliable and willing as Christopher's mouth did thrilling, erotic things to her own. His tongue gently pried her lips apart and she opened her mouth wide, crying softly as his tongue plunged into her sweet depths. Her arms wound around his neck, her hands pulling at his thick blond hair in movements that were purely instinctive and needful.

As Christopher increased his onslaught, he knew one thing, he'd never tasted anything so sweet in his life and he was afraid he would choke her trying to gain his fill. But he could not stop himself and when her fingers entwined in his hair, he whisked her up into his arms and laid her gently upon the bed, covering her up with his big body.

Christopher's hands moved to her full breasts, gentle yet insistent as he massaged her through her blouse and she arched into him, never having experienced such a thing but loving it instantly. They were losing themselves in each other, faster than either one of them imagined possible, until all that mattered was the feel and touch and taste of one another. *My wife*, Christopher thought with disbelief and glee. *This woman is my wife.*

"Chris?" a very loud male voice boomed from outside his door.

Christopher took his lips from Dustin's, albeit reluctantly, and pushed himself off of her and moved for the door. Dustin, suddenly embarrassed to realize the position she was in, jumped off the bed and tried to look nonchalant although her face was mightily flushed.

Christopher opened the door and David pushed his way in, his eyes wide. He looked right at Dustin.

"Is everything well?" he asked.

Christopher leaned against the open door, glancing at Dustin. "Everything is fine, David. As you can see, Lady Dustin and I are whole and sound. No blood or bruises."

David looked around, noticing the disarray of the room. The servants had told him of the way the baron had manhandled his wife out by the rabbit hutch and he was genuinely concerned for her safety.

"This room is a mess," he commented, looking back at Dustin.

She cleared her throat and straightened her skirt, feeling very self-conscious and ashamed of her wanton behavior. She walked very quickly to the door, pushing past David and Christopher.

"If you will excuse me, my lords," she said, her head down.

"Where are you going?" Christopher asked.

She didn't dare look up, knowing her face to be red. "I....I have a few duties to attend to. I must go."

"Dustin," Christopher tried to stop her, but she escaped him and David grabbed his arm when he tried to follow. He looked reprovingly at his brother. "What do you do?" he indicated the grip on his wrist.

"What were you doing to her up here?" David demanded. "This room is a sight."

Christopher was getting a bit tired of his brother's meddling. He sighed heavily. "David, she did this in her anger," he said impatiently. "I did not lay a hand on her. And, furthermore, you interfere like an old woman. Dustin is *my* wife, not *our* wife, and you will kindly remember that in the future. I do not like your constant hovering about."

David raised an eyebrow. "Someone needs to hover, Chris, since you obviously do not know the first thing about dealing with her. She's your chattel and that's exactly how you treat her, and I am ashamed for you."

Christopher stiffened. "I treat her better than that, and you know it. How dare you accuse me of neglect and ignorance."

David shrugged and stepped away from his brother, angry. "She's better than that, Chris."

Christopher saw a good deal in that softly uttered statement and his cheeks went red with rage as he faced off against his brother.

"Goddamn you, David," he hissed. "You have feelings for her. Can you deny it?"

David tried to turn away. "You are mad."

Christopher blocked him. "Nay, little brother, I am not," he said. "Now this all makes sense; that is why you have appointed yourself her personal defender. You care for my wife."

David's face turned red and his mouth tightened. "You do not know what you are saying."

Christopher glared at his brother, becoming aware that his actions certainly implicated him in a much larger problem. But David would deny it until he died and there was no use pressing the issue.

Christopher relaxed a bit and stood back, feeling strangely jealous that David should care for Dustin in something other than a brotherly sense. His brother, a man he had fought with and killed for, a man who was closer to him than anyone. It had always only been Christopher and David against the world. And now… there was Dustin.

"She is *my* wife, David," he said after a few moments, his voice hoarse and quiet. "Always remember that."

Their eyes met, steadily, and for a moment they simply stared at each other. David was the first one to break.

"It is something I will never forget," he said evenly.

Christopher waved his brother off, retreating back down the hall to find his wife, leaving David standing alone, struggling with himself.

☙

DUSTIN HAD ALL but disappeared, but Christopher didn't worry. He was coming to know her well enough to assume she was somewhere on the grounds. The nooning meal came and went and she did not appear, but still he did not concern himself. They had said a great deal to each other that morn and he was feeling confident with the progression of their relationship. In fact, he felt very hopeful. Instead of weakening it, his mistake seemed to have strengthened the bond they were forming.

He noticed that Jeffrey was also missing from the nooning meal, but thought nothing of it. He was far more concerned with David, who ate silently and did not as much as pass him a glance. Christopher was sure he had struck close to the truth when he accused David of caring for Dustin, and he knew his brother was angry at him, true or not.

Leeton and Edward were supervising the remaining repairs on the fortress as Christopher began arrangements for his departure to London. He even went in to the village himself to retrieve the dresses Rebecca had finished, and to pay her a lump sum for everything. He paid her far more than she was expecting to receive, and she was extremely pleased.

"My lord is generous," she said, thanking him graciously; almost embarrassed to be accepting such a sum.

He fought off a grin. " 'Tis worth it to see Lady Dustin in something other than rags," he told her.

Without a hind glance, his arms laden with three surcoats for his wife, Christopher moved for the door and opened it. Yet, something inexplicably made him pause, and he found himself turning back to his wife's friend.

Rebecca could read the uncertainty in his eyes and she was puzzled. "Is something wrong, my lord?"

"Nay, nothing is wrong." He cleared his throat hesitantly, eyeing Rebecca's mother. "May I have a word privately, Mistress Rebecca?"

Rushing to do such a great man's bidding, Rebecca hurried outside and closed the door behind her. She clasped her hands together, waiting patiently for him to speak. He loaded the dresses onto his destrier before he uttered another word, and then when he spoke, it was timidly.

"You have known Lady Dustin for some time," he said.

"Aye, my lord, since we were small girls," she answered politely.

He nodded, scratching his head underneath his raised visor. "I have never been very good at pretense. My wife is a mystery to me and I wish to know more about her. Will you help me?"

"If I can," Rebecca replied, wondering what he meant, exactly.

He could see her confusion and he hastened to clarify. "Tell me why she hates men so much," he asked.

Rebecca shrugged. "I do not believe she hates men but I think she resents them for the God-given power they have over women. She is very independent and she does not like to be given orders."

"I know," he said wryly. "I have been on the receiving end of such displays of rebellion."

As Rebecca giggled, he allowed himself to let his guard down a bit. He was now on the subject of Dustin and was genuinely curious about her. He wanted to know what Rebecca knew of his wife, a mystery more than any other mystery he had experienced.

"Will you tell me of the Lady Dustin you know?" he asked, almost pleadingly. "I would be grateful."

Rebecca could see that through all of the metal and muscle and titles and hardness that he was simply a man with human emotions. It struck her that he was sincere in his wish to want to know more about the woman he married so she felt comfortable divulging what she could. She hoped Dustin wouldn't mind.

"She is intelligent, yet simple," she said quietly. "She loves her flowers, her animals, and her keep. She was most distressed when her father turned it, and her, over to you. She thought she and her mother were getting along quite nicely by themselves."

"The keep was in disrepair," he remarked faintly.

"Because Lady Mary refused to do anything until Sir Arthur returned from the quest," Rebecca told him. "She believed it was his keep and she had no right to touch it."

"Ah," he nodded in understanding. "A wise woman. Continue."

Rebecca complied. "Dustin has never been ambitious. She would rather tend her animals and garden than go to court. She simply doesn't care for material things, which is why I am surprised she is wearing these fine dresses. She has shunned such things up until now."

He looked at her thoughtfully. "Yet she is not a fine and delicate woman, as flowers and animals would suggest."

Rebecca grinned. "She can fight like a man and climb a tree like a cat, and she is not afraid to dirty her hands with hard work," she said. "Yet she is the most beautiful woman I have ever seen and she reeks with feminine sensuality, which I suspect you already know. Does she puzzle you overmuch, my lord?"

He cocked an eyebrow at her. "Overmuch indeed," he said, shaking his head and mounting his destrier. He paused to gaze at the woman, his expression grateful. "Thank you, mistress, for everything. And I trust you will keep our conversation confidential."

"Of course, my lord," Rebecca agreed, stepping back as he reined his huge animal around. "And… my lord?"

He paused a moment. "What is it?"

Rebecca smiled impishly. "I approve of you spanking her. She needs it."

He cracked a smile and slapped his visor down. "More than she gets."

Rebecca laughed as she watched the man ride off, thinking that her friend Dustin was a very lucky woman, indeed. Gaze lingering on the big knight as he headed off towards the castle, she went back into her hut.

☙

TWO PAIRS OF eyes watched Christopher de Lohr ride off toward Lioncross, leaving the home of the pretty little red-headed wench. A lover, of course. She would be the first step in the quest to destroy de Lohr, as Sir Ralph had ordered. When he had returned to London, he had left a few men behind to spy, to linger, and to begin the no doubt long and arduous process of destroying the Defender of the Realm. It had taken nearly two days for the spies to decide where to begin, and the redhead was as good a start as any. Finally, they had their opportunity.

"His whore," one man mumbled.

His comrade, dirty and covered with oozing scabs that itched, nodded his scruffy head.

"Ralph told us to look for a link, and there she is," he replied. "We will start with her."

"Do we kill her?" the other man asked.

The oily man's gaze lingered on the neat little hut in the distance. "Ralph wanted insight and answers to the baron," he said. "We will get our answers, then we will kill her so she cannot tell what we have done."

The short, fat man nodded, making sure his dagger was concealed beneath his tunic. Together, they made their way to the hut in the near distance with nothing other than murder and blood on their mind. They had their orders and they had a plan. It would start here.

In the name of the prince and with the goal of destroying the king, the annihilation of Christopher de Lohr commenced.

☙

THE EVENING MEAL at Lioncross consisted of roast beef, Christopher's favorite meal. He had missed it dreadfully in the Holy Land and found goat to be a very poor substitute. His mouth fairly watered as he dug into a huge knuckle of succulent, stringy beef.

He didn't expect Dustin to join him. He had found her later in the afternoon tending an overgrown flower patch, at least that was what he had called it, but Dustin had stiffly informed him that it was a garden her mother had planted. He had been extremely annoyed to find Jeffrey with her, standing silently as she cut and pruned and pulled. He was not surprised to see that Jeffrey's hostility had returned full-bore, undoubtedly due to the wench-bedding rumors. Much to his disgust, he found he couldn't be too angry at the man's attitude. In fact, he didn't really blame him.

His wife did not seem particularly interested in his presence even though he tried to strike up a conversation. Several times, in fact. After the fourth or fifth attempt, he lost count, stopped trying, and excused himself. He should have ordered Jeffrey to leave as well, but the situation was tense enough as it was and he didn't want to make things worse. As he went about his business, he set Anthony to watch the two of them at a discreet distance.

He had nearly devoured his meal and was waving the serving wench to bring him more when his eyes suddenly caught a vision at the top of the stairs. His gaze trailed upward and he stopped in mid-chew, surprised and pleased to see his wife descending the stairs, dressed in one of the new surcoats he had retrieved that day. He had left the surcoats in her room, half expecting to never see them again, and pleased that he had been wrong.

He and the other knights rose as she approached. "I am pleased that you have decided to join us, Lady de Lohr," he said graciously, kicking David out of the chair immediately to his left and pulling it out for her. "Please, sit."

Without a word, Dustin accepted the chair and sat. Two serving women attended her with food and drink, and the knights sat.

Christopher could not take his eyes off her. She was wearing a striking sapphire blue that complemented her eyes and complexion beautifully. Her hair, long and straight and silky, was free down her back, and he spent so much time looking at her that it took him a moment to realize she had yet to look at him.

He was puzzled with her behavior. He had been sure that everything had been said between them that morning and that they were stronger for it, but he was forced to admit that mayhap he was wrong. She was brooding and quiet and he hated to admit that it concerned him.

"The beef is delicious," he remarked as she chewed.

Dustin swallowed, nodding. He watched her drink from her cup and take another bite, still not speaking. He respected her silence and returned to his food.

"I have never been this close to Wales," Edward piped up from across the table. "Tell me, my lady, when does winter set in?"

Dustin's haunting gray eyes turned to him. "Soon, my lord," she said. "By late October we will have snow, and will most likely last through February or March. Being so close to the mountains, our weather is always more severe."

"Snow," David sighed. "It has been three long years since I have seen it. There were days in the scorching heat I would dream of it."

Dustin looked at her brother-in-law. "The cook gathers great bowlfuls and pours fruit juice or honey on it for a treat."

David smiled at her. "I am looking forward to it."

Dustin grinned back. "As do I, but father said I would freeze to death eating flavored snow when it was all we could do to keep the great room a little above freezing itself."

Christopher watched his brother and wife smile at each other and felt a peculiar twinge deep in his chest. But he said nothing, knowing wisely that he would spoil the mood.

"I hear you have a cat, my lady," Leeton said, sitting opposite her.

"Aye, my lord, a big fat stripped cat," she nodded. "His name is Caesar because he rules this house and hold."

Leeton nodded. "I have seen him, skulking about. Not a particularly friendly animal."

"He is," she looked directly at Christopher, he thought, accusingly. "He is quite fond of the baron.

Christopher snorted into his goblet. "Ask me not why, for I do not know. He has taken a liking to me and I am at a loss to explain it."

"They say predators think alike, Chris," Edward said dryly.

Christopher nodded, the joke at his expense. "Which is why you and I get along so well."

The banter from that point on was light and amusing, although Dustin and Christopher never directly addressed one another. She spent most of her time listening and feeling her mood lighten, and it wasn't long before she seemed to pull out of her mood.

Dustin had indeed been brooding, although she truly didn't know why. She only knew that ever since Christopher had kissed her, she had been confused and disoriented. She had liked it and she had been willing to submit to him without a fight, and that had frightened her. Why had she relented so easily? What was the power the man had over her with just a simple touch? She didn't understand what her body was telling her.

The safest thing, she decided, until she could figure out her mind, was to stay a safe distance away from him. It wasn't that she was angry with him, but the feelings he awakened within her scared her and her fear kept her aloof.

The idea that scared her the most was the fact that she wanted him to care for her. She wanted him to like her, to protect her, to need her. He had told her that he did care for her, and even when she heard it, it was as if she didn't want to hear it. It was as if the stubborn, independent female inside her was fighting with the soft, willing woman that was begging to be let out.

The meal passed and even when the food was cleared and the senior officers left, and the knights were enjoying their wine and stories, she found that she was enjoying the company too much to leave. She was increasingly aware of Christopher's gaze on her but she tried desperately to ignore him. She didn't know what to say to him.

Two of the kitchen servants who also doubled as minstrels began to play their wooden flutes and Dustin listened dreamily to their soft ballad. David tried to get her to dance, twice, but she refused. She honestly didn't know how to dance very well and she would not embarrass herself. She'd never liked to dance.

The more they drank, the louder and wilder the stories became and the more amused Dustin became. She listened to the de Velt twins recall a particularly comical adventure they had shared and she laughed until tears came to her eyes. Max and Anthony were not the brightest men in the room, but they were gifted storytellers and she enjoyed their antics.

As Dustin loosened up, Christopher nursed his third watered wine. He sat back in his chair, smiling as he listened to his knights and watching his wife's reaction. She giggled and joked, endearing herself to men who had only seen her belligerent and surly side. This was the Dustin he wanted to know, to be a part of. He hoped to talk to her again before she retired for the night and was preparing his strategy when several of his soldiers entered the smoky hall. Christopher and the other knights were immediately on guard as a senior soldier saluted his liege.

"Trouble in the village, my lord," the man said.

"What sort of trouble?" Christopher demanded.

The soldier's gaze flicked in Dustin's direction. "It seems that a young woman and her mother have been killed, and the entire village is in an uproar," he said. " 'Tis said that the young woman was a friend of your wife's."

Dustin shot up from her chair in a panic. "Who is it? Who was killed?"

The soldier was hesitant, looking to Christopher for direction. "I...," he stammered. "I am not certain. They could be wrong, of course."

Christopher could see the man's reluctance but he needed answers. "Who have they said was killed?"

The soldier sighed faintly, knowing he had no choice but to relay what he had heard. "Comlynn," he said after a moment. "I was told her name was Comlynn."

Dustin's hands flew to her mouth. "Rebecca?" she gasped.

Christopher looked at her with great concern, instinctively reaching out to steady her. "Steady, lady," he murmured firmly before looking to his knights. "Mount your steeds. We ride."

The great hall turned into a shifting company of men, all moving purposefully to do their liege's bidding, but Christopher wasn't paying much attention to them. He was more concerned with his wife, who had quickly dissolved into tears of fright. Not wanting to leave her, alone and terrified, standing in the great hall, he swept her into his arms and carried her up to her bower.

Once in her chamber, he set her down on the floor but still kept a strong grip on her arms. She was gasping and crying, her face as white as snow. She didn't try to pull away from him or fight him, rather, she seemed afraid to let him go.

"Christopher," she gasped. "It cannot be true."

He felt terrible for her; losing her father, her mother, and now her close friend all within a few days. His huge hands cupped her face.

"I shall go see, sweetheart, I promise," he soothed her. "I shall see to your friend."

Her hands were gripping his wrists, her big gray eyes gazing up at him. "I would come."

He shook his head. "Nay, you will stay here and wait for me," he said calmly. "I shan't be long."

"Please," she begged. "I want to come. I must see for myself."

"Dustin, you will not, you will stay here," he said, pulling her to him fiercely, holding her to stop her struggles and comfort her. "I promise I will return quickly. I want you to stay here and calm yourself. The soldier could be wrong, you know."

Those seven words calmed her considerably. Her crying lessened but she still clung to him, her face buried in his tunic. He stroked her hair, her back and arms, unwilling to leave her until he was sure she was calming. When he felt her breathing slow, he pulled back and looked at her.

"I will go now," he said softly. "But I shall return. Promise me you will not leave your room."

She nodded unsteadily, her face wet and her lashes spiky with tears. She looked so pitiful that his heart went out to her and he leaned down, gently kissing on the cheek.

Dustin's hand went instinctively to the spot he had touched. She could still feel his lips there, soft and sweet. It had been a tender act, one of unspoken warmth, and as she continued to gaze up at him, somewhat awed by the gesture, he winked at her.

"I shall return," he said simply and quit the room.

She sat on her bed and waited.

CHAPTER EIGHT

REBECCA WASN'T SIMPLY killed, she was massacred. When Christopher entered the small hut, he was assaulted by blood everywhere; all over the walls, all over the floor. His stomach turned at the sight, but only on behalf of his wife. Her worst fears had just been confirmed.

Rebecca's mother was in the smaller room, tied to one of the posts and all but gutted. Her blood coated the floor and Christopher was sure she was completely drained of it. Whoever had done the horrifying deed seemed to have done it with particular malice, for the woman was so chopped up that she was barely in one piece. That sort of anger indicated madness.

But the sight of Rebecca, in the alcove where the beds were, disturbed him greatly. Whoever had killed her had done it with such viciousness that even a hardened warrior like Christopher was taken aback. David and Edward, having arrived several minutes earlier, had already had a chance to examine the body.

"What devil did this?" David muttered, gazing down at the corpse.

Christopher motioned at her. "Her throat is cut," he commented. "And it looks as if she had been gutted.

"Look at this," Edward lifted her wrist. "She is missing a few fingers. This woman was tortured, Chris."

Christopher let out a sigh of disgust. "Why in the hell would anyone torture this woman?" he wondered aloud. "What could they possibly gain by it?"

David flipped up her skirts, revealing bloodied thighs. "She was raped, too."

"Christ," Christopher muttered, looking hard before turning away, crossing himself. "Whatever you do, do not tell Dustin that. God be merciful."

The knights stood silently over the young woman, saddened at such a waste and feeling for the baron's wife. Christopher took a moment to compose himself before turning around once more and reaching down to gently pull Rebecca's skirts back over her legs. With a sigh of regret, he reached down and picked up the stiffening body.

"Take the blanket off the bed," he ordered softly. "Spread it out."

Christopher personally wrapped Rebecca up in a tight little bundle for burial while the de Velt twins took care of the mother. No one had seen the father and assumed he was dead as well, but just to be sure, Christopher sent a few soldiers out to search for the farmer. He wondered vaguely if Rebecca's father killed his family, but didn't dwell on it. What was done was done, and now he would have to deal with his wife's grief.

It seemed that death had followed him to Lioncross Abbey. He came bearing news of death, and three deaths had followed his arrival. He knew he wasn't directly responsible but he wondered if Dustin would blame him anyway. He hoped not.

As he was leaving the hut, his eyes were drawn to the hearth and he suddenly stopped, staring at what he saw. Two surcoats, nearly finished except for the hem, hung untouched by the gore and carnage surrounding them. He paused a moment before reaching up and collecting both of them, folding them over his arm as he left the cottage of death without a hind glance.

ଓ

REBECCA'S DEATH WAS too much for Dustin to take. She went hysterical and it took Christopher and David both to force down a poppy potion that knocked her out in minutes. They watched her twitch and fidget even in her sleep, looking so tiny in the middle of Christopher's huge bed. Both men were deeply exhausted from the day's events.

"Go get some sleep," Christopher told his brother. "I can handle her from here."

David nodded, moving for the door. "Damn, Christopher, what's going on around here?" he muttered. "Ever since we arrived there has been nothing but death."

Christopher looked down at his sleeping wife, deep in thought. "Everyone close to her has died," he said softly. "I wonder if this is some curse I have brought back with me, manifesting itself on her for the sins I have committed against the infidels."

David shook his head. "Any curse that strong would have attacked you first… why waste it on those around you?"

Christopher sighed heavily, removing his hauberk and moving for his plate armor. "I will see you on the morrow," he said, then stopped his brother before he could close the door. "Post extra guards, David. If we have a murderer on the loose, then I do not want him infiltrating my keep."

David nodded, quitting the room. Christopher proceeded to remove the rest of his armor and stripped off his tunic. He sat heavily on the oak chair and pulled his boots off, pausing a moment as he felt his fatigue. He rolled his shoulders and rubbed at his neck. Then he glanced over at Dustin, sleeping fitfully, and wondered if she would be better on the morrow. He hoped that Rebecca's death didn't throw her off the edge of madness.

Caesar appeared at his feet, rubbing up against him and he found he was actually glad to see the cat. He reached down and scratched the orange ears before moving to the bed, slipping in carefully beneath the covers and making sure his sword was at the ready.

Dustin twitched and let out a ragged sigh, turning over and pressing herself right into Christopher's chest. Contentment warmed over him and he wrapped his arms around her, pulling her close. Caesar, not to be left out, curled up against the nape of his neck and his head vibrated with the force of the animal's purring, yet it did not bother him.

He was coming to like it… all of it.

ଓ

DUSTIN AWOKE TO something tickling her cheek. She brushed at it, thinking it to be Caesar, but it tickled her again and again and finally opened her eyes when she heard a throaty laugh. Christopher, propped up on one elbow, was smiling down at her. She smiled back.

"Good morn, my lady," he said softly.

She stretched a bit. "Good morning, husband," she said, then memories from the previous evening flooded her and tears filled her eyes. "Rebecca!" she gasped.

His smile vanished and he enclosed her in his arms to comfort her. "I am sorry, sweetheart," he said quietly. "There was nothing I could do.

"She's dead," she cried softly.

"I know," he replied simply, not knowing what else to say.

Her crying was soft and mournful, deeply painful. Yet she spared him the hysterics from the previous night. She had cried so much the past week that it was becoming easier to gain control. The whole time, Christopher didn't say a word; he simply held her, trying to give her some consolation.

"We must bury her," she said finally, her face pressed against his naked skin.

"We will," he answered. "Whenever you are ready."

She shifted, pulling her hair free that was trapped between them as she looked at him. Gazes locked, devoured.

"Today?" she asked.

He nodded vaguely. "Do not rush. Whenever you are strong enough."

She gazed back at him, her tears and fears fading away as his sky blue eyes swallowed her up. They were so close, and with his nakedness, she began to feel that giddy warmth again. The longer she gazed at him, the stronger the feeling became.

"I should get dressed," she stammered.

"As should I," he replied, his voice raspy.

"I cannot get up unless you release me," she said.

"Do you want me to release you?" he asked.

"Do you want to release me?" she countered, embarrassed at the bold question.

"Nay," he answered, his voice silky. "I do not. Does that shock you?"

The giddy warmth was overwhelming her, causing her breathing to become ragged and her hands to sweat.

"What....what will you do to me if you do not release me?" she asked.

"What would you have me do?" he said in turn.

She shook her head slowly, her eyes never leaving his. "I don't know. Will you kiss me again?" It was a question, not a request, but he took it for his own interpretation.

He answered her by clamping his lips on hers, his lips soft and probing and his stubble scratching her silky skin. She knew instantly that it was as wonderful as she had remembered, and her arms went about his neck tightly. When he felt her acceptance, he let his inhibitions go. He would have her, and he would have her now.

He laid her back on the bed, his hands trailing down her body as he had dreamed of for so long. Her breasts beneath her shift were firm and round and felt wonderful against his big hands. And the way she pushed into him as he touched her drove him further over the edge of ecstasy. The moment he touched her, it was as if she had always been his, as if he had touched her this way a thousand times, each was sweeter than the previous. He found his hands were shaking with excitement when he reached up and tore her shift right down the front, all but destroying it.

Dustin let out a shriek but didn't stop him, instead, watched him as he kissed her shoulders, her chest, and his great hands were so gentle on her breasts. He kissed a circle around each breast, slowly and lingeringly, until her breathing was so rapid she thought she might faint. The sensations were beyond anything she had ever imagined. When he lifted his head and suckled on a peaked nipple, he took her to a whole new level of passion.

Dustin nearly came up from the mattress but his heavy body and firm hands prevented it. His mouth on her breasts was so wickedly lustful that she could not help herself from panting, spiraling out of control with his touch. Her hands found his thick hair, pressing his head against her nipples to encourage him. She never wanted him to stop, for the feelings were too wonderful to comprehend.

But he did leave her breasts, eventually, and his mouth kissed every inch of her supple torso, her sides, even the underside of her arms. How in the world he could turn something like a kiss into the most sensual experience she had ever encountered was a mystery, yet she had no desire to think on it. All she knew was that she loved what he did to her.

So far, every bit of loving he had done had been above her waist. But that soon changed and his huge hands began to touch her groin and inner thighs. Dustin jumped as his fingers drifted over her mound of dark-blond curls, the sensations strange and thrilling. It was such a private and intimate touch, and she was uncertain as to whether or not to stop him. Still, he had been completely gentle and wonderful thus far. She was struggling with herself and he seemed to sense it.

"Trust me, Dustin," he whispered, kissing her fingers.

"I do, my lord, but…."

He shook his head and kissed her hand again. "You will call me Christopher in private, always. I am your husband, your lover. I will come to know you better than anyone."

She looked down at him, reaching out to run her hand through his hair. He had trusted her with his very private feelings, once. There was so much she wanted to tell him, but it was difficult for her to lower her defenses long enough to do it. Yet in this environment, just the two of them, it became easier.

"The only person who knew me well was Rebecca," she whispered. "I would tell her everything; my hopes and dreams and dislikes. She was the only person I ever felt comfortable enough to confide in because she never laughed at me, nor made fun of my thoughts. She was the only person I ever trusted."

"Not even your mother?" he asked.

She shrugged. "Mother's ideals were different from mine, and she would only admonish me for being a nonconformist," she whispered in reply, stroking his hair. "She was my mother, yet she did not know everything about me."

His hand ran up the full length of her thigh and made her shiver. "I would know everything about you, wife."

She gazed back at him for a long moment. "Then know I am afraid of what we are doing, yet I think I like it all the same. Is that strange?"

He cracked a smile. "Not at all. 'Tis right to be uncertain of something you have never experienced before, but I can promise you that it will be wonderful. You must trust me."

She stared into his sky-blue eyes, as pure as air. Her reluctance was gone. "I do," she whispered.

He blessed her with his wide, curvy smile that sent her insides jiggling wildly, a smile rarely viewed but the most sexy, magnificent gesture she had ever seen. She could not help but smile back as he lowered his head and returned to running his mouth over her thighs.

She was once again losing herself in his touch when there was a loud rap at the door, accompanied by someone calling Christopher's name loudly.

Dustin jumped but Christopher merely paused, he face glazed with passion. "What is it?" he roared.

"Open the damn door, Chris!" It was David, irritated that the door was locked.

Christopher's mouth returned to Dustin's lower abdomen. "Go away."

"Stop arguing and get out of bed," his brother said, pounding on the door. "Ever since you arrived here, you have been the laziest bastard I have ever seen. Now open this goddamn door before I break it down."

Christopher sighed. Obviously, David didn't know Dustin was still in the room. He glanced up at his wife apologetically. "I shall see what he wants and send him away."

As he pushed himself up, Dustin scrambled out of the bed and pulled her torn shift about her.

"It's all right, sweetheart, get back in bed," he told her gently, not wanting to lose the entire mood. "Let me see what he wants."

Dustin snatched at the heavy coverlet and wrapped it around her like a mummy. Christopher sighed again; he knew the mood was already gone and she was very self-conscious. He was very annoyed with his brother.

He unlocked the door and David shoved it open from the outside, plowing it into Christopher's nose. Even as Christopher let out a grunt and put his hand to his face, David's look of irritation went to one of regret as he realized he hit his brother in the nose.

"Forgive me," he insisted. "But why in the hell did you lock the door?"

Christopher eyed him, his hand still on his nose. He lifted an arm in Dustin's direction. "To better protect my wife's privacy from idiots like you."

David's blue eyes riveted to Dustin, standing wrapped in a blanket, and he was immediately contrite. "Oh, Jesus, I am sorry," he said. "I did not know she was still in here."

"She is," Christopher gingerly wrinkled his tender nose. "What in the hell is so important?"

David looked at his brother, clearing his throat. "Uh… Mistress Rebecca's father came to the gates before dawn. He is insisting that the bodies be buried immediately to prevent demon possession."

"What?" Christopher demanded, incredulous. "What kind of nonsense is that?"

"I think I can explain," Dustin said timidly, rounding the corner of the bed. "Rebecca's father is Welsh, and still clings to the old religions of his forefathers. They believe that if a person is killed violently, then the angered soul will possess the body and wreak havoc on the living. He is very superstitious."

Christopher ran his fingers through his hair. "Very well, then. If that is what the man believes," he said. "David, go back to the man and tell him Lady Dustin will be there shortly."

David nodded, passing a final glance at Dustin. "I really am sorry, my lady. You must think me quite lacking in manners."

He seemed so remorseful that Dustin smiled and started to reply, but Christopher spoke before she could.

"Aye, she does, so get out of here," he said, all but throwing his brother from the room. When David was gone, he turned to his wife. "I am sorry, too. I was quite enjoying our time alone."

Dustin blushed. "I have a feeling that it will not be the last opportunity, my lord," she said, moving past him like a giant wrapped bundle, keeping her gaze averted. He smiled at her, pleased that she had all but given him permission to touch her anytime he so desired. And he was coming to quite desire her.

ꟹ

CHRISTOPHER NEVER LEFT Dustin's side.

From the moment he escorted her to the peasant cemetery next to the small church and throughout the ceremony read in the harsh Welsh tongue, he stayed close by her, his eyes constantly scanning the area for anything hostile.

Dustin was greatly comforted by his presence. She was so distraught at the death of her best friend that she had wept nonstop since they had left the keep. As she stood with Christopher underneath the trees, listening to the Welsh priest speak, she felt his arm around her arm but didn't give it much thought until he removed it, then she turned to look at him. Suddenly, she missed it terribly and he read her thoughts, replacing his arm and drawing her even closer to him.

Christopher's knights stood to the rear, their attention also drawn to the surroundings. With the murders yesterday, they were wary standing in foliage that would serve as perfect cover for an ambush.

Rebecca's father was absolutely stricken with grief. He had been out in the fields all day, returning to find soldiers in his house and his wife and daughter's remains spread all over the interior. He simply could not comprehend the loss and even now lay prostrate on the two fresh graves.

Dustin cried softly for the man's pain and for her own personal loss. She still could not believe her friend had befallen such a horrible fate and her agony was deep, deeper still for all of the losses she had suffered over the past week.

She wondered vaguely if she would ever be the same.

ꟹ

THE SAME TWO men that had killed Rebecca and her mother now hid among the trees, watching the mass take place for their victims beneath cloudy skies over the wind-swept cemetery.

"Look at 'im, standin' there with his grievin' wife as if he were an innocent," said the dark-haired, dirty man. "He as much as killed her, having her whore for 'im. 'Twas his own fault we had to kill 'er."

The fat man nodded grimly. "And she was loyal to until the end. Never did tell us anything much."

The oily man scanned their surroundings. "Virgil, do you think we could take the baron out? There's lots of trees for cover, you know. One good arrow and we could remove him forever."

Virgil shook his head. "Sir Ralph said to just spy on him, not kill him."

"But think on it," the other insisted. "We'd be doing John a favor. If we take out de Lohr now, he won't have to worry about him anymore. We'll be heroes," the other said enthusiastically.

Virgil looked doubtful, but he knew his friend to be smarter. "I don't know, Roy," he said. "What if we make John angry?"

"How can we make him angry for doing him a favor?" Roy demanded, then turned and crawled back through the underbrush to the belongings they had brought. "See here. A crossbow. I am a good aim with it."

Virgil scratched his head. "You will take out the baron?"

"With the first arrow," Roy bragged, motioning to his neck. "The mail is weakest there."

Virgil thought and thought. Mayhap Roy was right. He imagined the wealth and titles that would be bestowed on him for helping rid John of an archenemy. The more he thought, the better he felt about it.

"All right," he said. "But from a distance. And we run like hell after the baron is down, for I do not want to go up against any of those knights of his."

Roy nodded firmly. "The horses are tied up in the glen. A perfect getaway. Then we can return to London and tell Sir Ralph what we have done."

Virgil nodded, scratching his verminous head while Roy loaded the crossbow and took an extra arrow. Then, together, they snuck into the trees for a prime vantage point, confident in their loyalty to their prince.

They would be heroes.

CB

THE CEREMONY WAS over. Rebecca's father still lay in the dirt, weeping like a child. Dustin, sniffing and sobbing, watched as the priest tried to give the man a few words of comfort, but he was unsuccessful in convincing him to rise. Christopher's arm tightened around her as they stood there silently.

After several long minutes, Dustin could stand it no longer. She lowered the handkerchief she was holding, unaware when it fell to the ground.

"I must comfort him," she whispered to her husband, moving away from him and to the crumpled figure in the dark dirt.

Christopher and the knights stood silently as Dustin knelt beside the man. They could hear her soft voice, soothing and even, as she spoke to him, trying to persuade him to rise. And they could also hear the man refusing, lamenting loudly to whatever gods would listen as to why his wife and daughter had been taken from him. The more the farmer cried, the calmer Dustin became, until eventually she was able to convince him to get up and return with her.

Christopher watched his wife's gentleness, amazed that such a firebrand of a woman was capable of it. As she helped the stricken man to his feet, Christopher bent over to pick up the kerchief that she dropped.

As he straightened up, he heard a faint high-pitched whistle and knew exactly what it was before he even saw it. He had no time to react at all before the whine grew deafening and behind him, David let out a loud grunt and slammed to the ground in a crash of metal and bone.

The knights were in action before David had even hit the ground. The farmer be damned, Christopher pulled his wife to him and shielded her with his big body, moving her out of the trees and towards his destrier. Leeton and Edward had David each by an arm, dragging him free of the wooded area and back to the horses in the open field. The de Velt twins and Jeffrey were already mounted with swords in hand, spurring their destriers in the direction the arrow had come from.

The peasants who had attended the funeral were screaming and running for their lives. David, hit in the shoulder, was still able to control his own destrier as Leeton helped him mount. Christopher, having no idea who their attackers were, was desperate to get Dustin back to the keep. He thrust her at Leeton.

"Get her and David back to the keep and stay there," he ordered. "Edward, to me!"

Before Dustin realized what was happening, she was mounted in front of Leeton and, along with David, racing back to Lioncross.

The last glimpse she caught of her husband was of him astride his massive white destrier, huge sword in his equally huge hand, tearing off in the direction of the trees.

They reached Lioncross in short measure, helping David into the keep with a nasty-looking spine protruding from his shoulder. David's wound was not deep. The arrow had hit him in a weak spot in the armor, doing no more than embedding itself a couple of inches into the man's soft flesh. Leeton had removed it easily while Dustin had cleaned and patched it up.

Stripped to the waist, David was propped up with pillows as Dustin lay in a few stitches, cringing every time she stuck him with the needle. He did no more than smile at her and she was at a loss.

"Does this not hurt you?" she demanded.

"A tickle," he told her, studying her features at close range. She had been quite elusive as of late and he was not surprised to discover she was even lovelier up close.

She cocked an eyebrow, securing a stitch. "Somehow I doubt that," she said.

He turned a little, pointing to a large scar just below his rib cage. "Now, *that* one hurt. The scar is much smaller than the actual wound."

"What happened?" she glanced at it, a scar on an otherwise perfectly formed torso. Christopher had a slight matting of blond hair on his chest, but David's was as smooth as a baby's bottom and very beautiful. His arms were like thick oak branches.

"A Saracen," he said. "He caught me off guard, without my armor. But it was a good fight."

"How did he catch you without your armor?" she wanted to know.

David cleared his throat. "I was well….I didn't have any clothes on at all. I was… you see….there was this…."

"You were bathing," Dustin put in quickly, not wanting to know the rest. She had an idea of what he was about to say.

"Aye, I was bathing," he agreed rapidly, relieved. "What a bath."

She shot him a reproachful glance, returning to the next stitch. He smiled broadly, remaining silent as she finished mending the wound.

"Christopher will be pleased to see that you were not badly injured." She finally stood up, glancing at Leeton as he stood beside the bed. "Where do you think they could be? They have been gone a long time."

"They will be back," Leeton said. He had sent one hundred men-at-arms to assist the knights when they had first returned to the keep and was confident that any trouble had been swiftly quelled.

Dustin sat with David while Leeton went down to the bailey to check on the progress of the action. David insisted he was fine and able to resume a normal schedule, but Dustin had fits and demanded he stay abed. David complied reluctantly, knowing that Christopher would order him up as soon as he returned. Until that time, he was perfectly content to sit and gaze at his lovely new sister-in-law.

"I still find it hard to believe your father did not marry you off before he left with Richard," he said softly.

She glanced up at him as she cleaned up the items used to tend his wound. "Why do you say that?"

"Because you are so lovely," he replied. "Surely there were men beating down the door to marry you."

Dustin dropped her head again. "Idiots, all of them."

David grinned. "Including my brother?"

Dustin sighed irritably. "He did not beat my door down," she said. "My father simply handed everything over to him, including me."

"And that displeases you?" he pressed, although gentler.

She slowed as she gathered the last of the cat gut and needles. "Why do you want to know this? It is of no concern to you."

"My brother is my concern," he replied. "But if you do not want to talk about it, I understand."

"Thank you," she said, turning for the big wardrobe in the chamber to put everything away.

He eyed her. "Christopher didn't want to marry anyone, either. But he has reconsidered."

She busied herself at the wardrobe. "Is that so? Well, I care not. We are married whether either one of us wants to be or not."

He scrutinized her as she tried to ignore him. "Do you not like Chris?"

She looked at him. "He is my husband."

"That isn't an answer. Why do not you like him?" David persisted.

She cocked her head, not as irritated as she had been earlier. "You are the prying sort, aren't you? And I never said I didn't like him. I do."

He grinned. "Good. He likes you."

She shrugged, pretending indifference when she was secretly gladdened with his words. Not knowing what to say, she finished putting everything away and then went about straightening up the chamber just so she wouldn't have to sit and answer David's questions. He was nosy and, being unsure of her feelings and certainly not wanting to share them, she pretended to be busy.

David watched her work, surprisingly pretty and feminine for a woman who seemed rather rough. He could see the wall around her, the front she put up, yet the woman he had seen at the gravesite today had been completely open and vulnerable. She tried to be tough in front of everyone and David wondered if that still held true when she was alone with his brother. No wonder Christopher was afraid to lay himself open for her, even if he did like her. David had a feeling the woman could sting if she wanted to.

As he watched her wipe at a table, they both heard a loud shout from the bailey outside, and Dustin rushed to the lancet window that faced the northeast side of the bailey. She could partially see the big gatehouse, now with its gates opening wide.

"What is it?" David asked.

Dustin turned around. "They are returning," she replied, setting the needlepoint down. "I shall go see."

David almost stopped her, but refrained. It seemed to him that she wanted to go down to meet Christopher. As soon as she left, he got out of bed and went to the windows, gazing out over the bailey as the huge gates spilled forth men into the ward. He spied the knights, and saw that they carried a prisoner.

Hastily, he went in search of his clothes.

☙

DUSTIN STOOD IN the open door of the castle, shielding her eyes from the sun that had suddenly decided to make an appearance from behind the clouds. She'd never seen so many soldiers in her bailey, all mobilized and ready to fight when in fact they were returning. She knew these men to be a mixture of Christopher's loyal men-at-arms and men that her father had taken with him to the Holy Land, but under her husband's direction, they seemed to be much more disciplined than her father's troops had ever been.

The knights, including her husband, were congregating over near the eastern wall of the keep. Leeton was there, and she could see him wrestling with a man that had been trussed up on the back of Max's destrier. Curious, she stepped out onto the large stone step to get a better look.

Christopher dismounted his destrier and moved around to the prisoner, now held between Anthony and Leeton. Without a word, he motioned for the man to be tied spread-eagle between the two six foot poles near the wall. The man yelled and screamed and begged, but he was no match for the knights.

When the prisoner was secured, Christopher stood before him, his visor up and his eyes like blue ice. He stared at the man for several moments, enough to intimidate the hell out of him, and the man was visibly shaken.

"Now," Christopher's voice was low and controlled, "I will give you another chance. Tell me who sent you."

The man was weak and afraid. "I…I told you that no one has sent us. We were simply robbers, my lord."

"Robber's with a fine crossbow? Robbers bearing Prince John's colors?" Christopher pointed out. "I think not. Why did John send you?" He knew the answer already, but he wanted to hear the reply all the same.

"He didn't," the fat man insisted, spittle dropping from his pale lips. "We were, we are robbers."

Christopher's face was impassive as he stared at the fat little liar. Brusquely he motioned to Anthony. "Strip him."

The prisoner wailed loudly, his pleas for mercy going ignored. Anthony and Jeffrey proceeded to strip the man nude, leaving his shredded clothing at his feet. Christopher crossed his arms over his chest.

"Do not whip me, my lord," the man begged, crying. "Please have mercy."

"I am not going to whip you," Christopher informed him rather callously, glancing up to the gray puffy clouds that scattered in the sky. "Beg for mercy from the elements for they are your nemesis now."

With that, he turned on his heel and headed toward the castle. He was confronted by Dustin's puzzled face as she stood on the top step to the structure.

"Who's that?" she wanted to know. "What are you going to do to him?"

Christopher's gaze was kindly on her. "That, my lady, is a would-be assassin, and I intend to do exactly as you see," he replied. "A night in the cold ought to loosen his tongue."

Dustin gazed back at the prisoner, already shivering in the cool temperatures of the day. "You intend to freeze him to death?"

Christopher removed his gauntlets. "Perhaps, but I doubt it will come to that. I expect him to be spilling his life story before the sun sets." He returned his focus to his wife. "I hear my brother fares well. Where is he?"

"Here," David said, coming out of the castle, dressed once again in his armor. He rotated his shoulder gingerly. "A scratch."

Christopher raised an eyebrow. "That arrow hit you hard, little brother. Are you sure?"

"It was not a scratch, it was a deep puncture." Dustin frowned, angered that David had disobeyed her and gotten out of bed.

David smiled. "Mayhap to you, but to me it is a scratch," he said. "I am fine."

Dustin put her hands on her hips. "If you exert that arm, you are going to tear the stitches," she pointed out. "Would it kill you to spend the remainder of the day resting?"

"Probably not, but I do not feel like it," David replied, turning to his brother and motioning toward the captive. "Who's that bastard?"

"One of John's inept spies," Christopher replied. "We killed the other one."

"There were only two?" David asked. "Not an army to ambush us?"

"Nary a trace of an army," Christopher replied. "Just the two fools. I suspect we will have more answers by dusk."

Dustin, annoyed that David was ignoring her and Christopher seemed to have forgotten she was there, stormed back inside the castle. David and Christopher, still looking at each other yet completely aware of her display of temper, smiled at one another.

"She practically tied me to the bed," David said.

"Is it really a scratch? Should I take a look?" Christopher asked.

"It is," David insisted. "Look if you will, but you will agree with me. As it is, I have a training session I am late for over in the arena."

Christopher shrugged with resignation. "Very well, go to it. But if you tear those stitches, do not ask me to defend you from Dustin's wrath. She shall have your hide."

David grinned. "She can have it." When Christopher's smile vanished, he put up his hands in supplication. "A jest! Jesus, Chris, where's your sense of humor?"

David shook his head and took the steps to the bailey, followed by the de Velt twins. Jeffrey had left to attend to his duties, leaving Christopher with Edward and Leeton.

"He likes your wife," Edward commented.

"As my brother, I should hope that he would," Christopher replied evasively, wanting off the subject. "Don't you two have anything to do?"

Leeton and Edward looked at each other, then shook their heads simultaneously. "Nay."

Christopher glared at them. "Then find something or I shall find it for you," he said, his gaze trailing to the open castle door. "I will be inside."

He made his way to his rooms, passing by Dustin's chambers to see if she were there. When she wasn't, he went directly to his bedchamber and stripped off his armor and clothing, taking the time to wash himself from head to toe in the basin. As he washed, he was lost in thought. He knew for a fact that the man in the bailey was John's plant, and he knew the arrow had been meant for him, or worse, meant for Dustin.

Already John was starting his covert assaults and Christopher decided that the sooner he could get back to London and keep track of the prince, the better. He briefly debated as to whether or not to leave Dustin at Lioncross, yet he could not do that in good conscience. He would not be comfortable unless he was protecting her, and he would worry if she were left behind.

He splashed water on his face, chuckling bitterly at himself. When he had arrived on English soil, the greatest worry on his mind was Richard's throne and his own hide. Now with the added element of a wife he unexpectedly cared for, his problems were multiplied tenfold. Not only did he have to keep himself safe, but he had to worry over her as well.

It wasn't fair. He was entrusted with the most important mission of Richard's reign and although it was inadvertent, the king had given him the added burden of Dustin Barringdon. He briefly wondered if Arthur hadn't been a John loyalist and had planned the distraction all along, knowing Christopher's fondness for beautiful women.

He knew John to be clever and conniving. Christopher would have to be completely neutral in front of the prince when it came to his wife; otherwise, he knew she would be used against him. If John so much as suspected that he cared for Dustin in any way, then Christopher would be at a disadvantage.

He grabbed a towel, wiping his face and neck, his eyes distant in thought. He had to be honest with himself, how on earth could he remain neutral in regards to his wife? He could not, and he knew that. He was damn possessive of her and for good reason, he liked her. And, more importantly, he hadn't yet consummated their marriage. If someone else got to her before he was able to mark her….

He remembered his promise not to force her into his bed, yet as it stood, he was growing increasingly certain that he would have to break that vow. Dustin was his, and he would be the only one to brand her. He would kill any man who even as much as looked at her.

He had two nights in which to do the deed. He almost did it this morn, had it not been for David's interruption. The thought of sweet, soft Dustin in his hands was enough to make him groan with pleasure. Tonight would have to be the night, whether or not she liked it; otherwise, he would have to do it tomorrow night while they were on the road. After that, they would be in London and he didn't know when the opportunity would present itself once they arrived.

He changed into fresh clothing and donned portions of his mail and armor. He had duties to attend to, yet he had an overwhelming urge to seek out his wife.

He went with the urge.

CB

DUSTIN WASN'T INDOORS.

She was outside in the overgrown garden that her mother had kept, cutting the last of the summer blooms from the dying stalks. Still dressed in the flowing black dress she had attended the funeral in, she seemed intent on ripping flowers free of their confines as her long blond hair did wild dances when the wind caught it. Christopher stood at the gate leading into the walled garden, watching her movements. He could tell from her body language that she was still perturbed.

He came up behind her, watching her struggle with a huge stalk. " 'Twould be easier to cut it than to rip it."

She jumped in surprise, turning to look at him. "You scared me." She released the foxglove and tossed the other flowers she was holding into a big basket beside her. "What is it that you want, my lord?"

"Want? Oh, nothing." He crossed his arms casually. "I came to tell you that we will be leaving for London tomorrow. You had better pack all that you intend to bring this eve so we may load it up on the wagon."

"We leave tomorrow?" She suddenly looked forlorn.

His brows drew together. "What's wrong?"

She shook her head, regaining her composure. "Nothing, my lord. It's just that London reminded me of Rebecca again. Suddenly, I do not want to go so badly."

"Why?" he asked gently.

She shrugged, gazing about her. Then, she smiled ruefully. "Foolishness, my lord. I guess I was already homesick for Lioncross. How long will we be in London?"

He was standing a foot or so from her. Before he realized it, he was reaching out and pushing stray strands of hair from her face, tucking them over her shoulder. "A while," he replied, studying her face. "I am not sure exactly how long, but a while."

She sighed, excitement filling her as he played gently with her hair. "I shall be ready, then. How many trunks may I take?"

He cocked a blond eyebrow. "How many will you need? No pets, Dustin."

"I know that," she eyed him. "It's just that when mother traveled to Nottingham last summer, she took six trunks with her. Jeffrey said it was too many."

"Jeffrey is correct," he replied. "Pack everything you need and we shall decide from there if you need to cut back." He could not imagine she would manage to fill any more than two; three at the most.

Dustin gazed up at him as the wind whipped about her in the private walled garden. She did so want to take Caesar but Christopher had already told her that she could not. Well, he had said no pets, but Caesar was more like family, wasn't he? She knew she would miss the cat terribly and decided to try to persuade him one more time.

"Christopher," she began softly. "Can't I please take Caesar? I promise he will be no trouble."

"Dustin, I told you, he will not travel well," he repeated patiently. "He will not be happy."

"But I will miss him," she insisted miserably. "He will be happy if he is with me. He will be heartbroken and lost here when I am gone. He may run away."

"He won't run away from here, I promise you that," he said. "The cat is not stupid. He knows where he's fed and warm and pampered."

She made a wry face, signaling defeat, and lowered her gaze. He was sorry that he had to deny her, but he believed what he said, Caesar would still be ruling Lioncross upon their return.

She turned around and returned to picking the flowers. He continued to stand there and watch her, glancing up at the sky that was growing dark and menacing.

"It will rain soon," he said. "Let's go inside."

She glanced up, wiping at her cheek with the back of her hand. "I am almost finished."

He shifted on his massive legs, waiting patiently for her to finish, when suddenly there was a commotion over by the wall. They both looked over, watching the overgrowth shake violently.

Christopher stepped forward, wondering what sort of hellish wild animal was caught in the garden and wanting to protect his wife from any attack, when suddenly a great howl went up and Caesar came shooting out of the bushes, his ears back and his eyes wide. He tore after something neither human could make out.

Caesar tore a crazy path into the garden, screeching and running as fast as his fat body could take him. Dustin, watching her cat with her hands on his hips, wondered how long it would take him to catch the mouse so she could return to her task, when suddenly a tiny white rabbit burst forth out of the low-lying weeds, racing like the wind with Caesar hot on its heels.

"Caesar! Stop it this instant," Dustin shrieked, attempting to track down the cat.

But the cat and the rabbit were much faster than the mistress, and after running up a wild path through the garden, they were through the gate and into the area by the kitchens where Dustin kept her rabbit hutch.

Dustin was beside herself as she ran after the two animals, leaving Christopher following her far behind, fighting off his amusement as she yelled at the cat like an unruly child. Dustin dodged and dashed, trying to cut them off, then being double-crossed for her efforts. After racing a mad course through the small bailey, the little rabbit took Caesar out through the postern gate carved into the outer wall, and Dustin was forced to follow.

Christopher wasn't far behind, muttering a curse as he ducked into the tunnel and came through the other side. He could see Dustin running after the animals down the small grassy incline, still screaming at her disobedient cat. He was actually still quite amused, allowing himself to crack a smile now that he knew he wasn't being watched.

Then, it was as if the heavens opened up and suddenly there were sheets of water drenching him in his clean clothes and armor. Huge flashes of lightning lit up the sky and his immediate concern was for his wife, racing around like a madwoman in the field below him. He could see that she had stopped and had turned to look upward, and he wondered as he went toward her if she had indeed caught her cat.

But her hands were empty and she was absolutely soaking. Christopher went to her, picking her up and carrying her back up the hill. Once she was in the shelter of the cave-like passage of the postern gate, she pushed herself from his arms.

"What are you doing?" he demanded.

"I have to wait here for Caesar," she insisted, pushing her wet hair from her eyes. "He hates the rain."

It wasn't simply raining, it was pounding. Thunder and lightning broke every few seconds and the intensity was growing. Christopher shook his head.

"Nay, lady, we go inside," he said firmly. "The cat will take care of himself."

In spite of her protests, he swung her into his arms again and carried her into the keep. By the time they passed through the kitchens and into the great hall, Dustin was shivering and her lips were blue. Christopher bellowed for warmed wine and hot water even as he carried her up to her rooms.

"Off with the dress," he ordered, soaked to the skin himself but more concerned with Dustin.

Without a word, she tried to comply but her hands were shaking so that she could not manage the stays. He assisted her, releasing the fastenings and the surcoat slipped to the floor. She wore a shift underneath, plastered to her damp skin. Silently, Christopher had her lift her arms and he peeled it off of her.

As much as he would have liked to have stood there and gazed at her luscious nude body, she was as cold as ice and he ripped the coverlet off the bed and wrapped her in it tightly, using a portion of it to dry her hair. But she was still quivering, cold, so he steered her over to the fire that was snapping in the hearth.

"Stay there," he ordered. "I shall return."

"Where are you going?" she said through chattering teeth.

"To get something to warm you," he replied.

She was too cold to ask any more. Christopher returned a few moments later with warmed, mulled wine and a serving wench in tow, loaded down with linen towels. He set the servant to drying his wife's hair while he stood over her and watched her drink nearly half a goblet of the warmed wine. Outside, the storm was growing violent and Dustin kept turning her head to the window every time there was a crash of thunder or a bolt of lightning.

"Caesar hates the rain," she repeated softly, her gray eyes concerned.

"I am sure he is safe," Christopher replied. "How do you feel? Better?"

"Aye," she nodded, taking another sip of wine as she gazed at him. He was still in damp clothing. "Aren't you going to change out of your wet clothing?"

He glanced down at himself, knowing he should have dried the armor off immediately for it rusted easily.

"In a moment," he replied. "When I am sure you are not going to go charging off into the storm again looking for your cat."

She smiled in spite of herself. "I will not, I promise."

He smiled in return. "In that case, I shall take off these wet things before this armor rusts and traps me within it."

The wine was making her sleepy and silly. "Terrible," she said with mock seriousness.

"Indeed," he agreed, noticing that the wine was affecting her. "I would be quite useless, not to mention uncomfortable."

"Not to mention you could not relieve yourself." She suddenly looked up at him when she realized what she had said, her shock turning into bubbling giggles.

He grinned and patted her head. "You are feeling better, I see." He looked sternly at the maid. "Do not let her leave. And no more wine."

Christopher returned a half-hour later to find her curled up in a sturdy oak chair, still wrapped in the coverlet and munching on a hunk of bread with butter and fruit compote on it. In fact, there was a tray on the table next to her with more food on it. He was pleased when she smiled comfortably at him again.

"I had the maid bring this up," she said. "We missed the nooning meal."

"I know." He reached down and retrieved a large piece of bread, also pleased she had thought of him when she ordered the meal. Outside, the storm raged violently but her chamber was warm and cozy and he sat in the chair opposite her as he ate.

"Your hair is almost dry," he noted.

She ran her fingers through it. "Only on the top," she said. "It takes forever to dry."

He nodded faintly, finishing off the bread. "Your hair is beautiful."

She touched it again absently. "There is too much of it. It is forever in my way."

He raised an eyebrow. "You do not know how to accept a compliment, do you? I told you once you were beautiful and you told me you were too short."

Her cheeks went a soft pink but she didn't reply. He sat forward in his chair.

"The proper response to a compliment is 'thank you'," he said softly. "I know you know the words for I have heard you say them. Now, let us try this again; your hair is beautiful."

She looked at him from underneath her thick lashes, yet he could see a smile playing on her lips. "Thank you," she whispered.

He gave her a half smile. "And you are very beautiful."

"Thank you," she repeated, looking away from him.

"And I am glad I married you," he said, his voice gentle.

She looked at him, astonished. "You are?"

He held up a finger admonishingly and she corrected herself quickly. "I mean, thank you," she replied, then looked at him curiously. "Are you truly?"

He grinned and sat back. "Aye."

"But why?" she demanded, puzzled.

He looked amused. "Why not? You are beautiful and you have intelligence. You are a perfect match for me."

She continued to stare back at him just as he was gazing at her. She was quite amazed at his confession. Question was – was *she* glad she married him? She wasn't all sure yet, but she suspect that she was. What wasn't to like?

However, she was feeling quite playful and happy with the warm wine coursing through her veins and she felt a strange sense of power with his admission.

"In my view, this marriage could have been much, much worse," she said, feigning seriousness.

"Is that so?" he responded.

"Aye," she nodded firmly. "For instance, you could have been a horrible, ugly, mean ogre and I would have been forced into submission. I would say that I was rather lucky for that you are not, and I suppose my father did choose well."

"I thank you, my lady." He raised an eyebrow. "Then I must agree that I, too, have fared rather well. You could have been an abomination to the eye and I would have still had to marry you. What if you had been as fat as a cow? Or as homely as a pig? If I wanted this fortress, then I would still have had to marry you. Aye, I was fortunate on that account."

"You say that now," she shot back good-naturedly. "I do not think that was your reaction the day we met."

"Hmm," he said, lifting an eyebrow. "But we must do something about your disagreeable disposition."

She turned her nose up at him. "I have never had anyone complain before."

He laughed. "They wouldn't dare. You hit too hard."

She turned a coy gaze to him. "But you are not afraid of me, are you?"

He looked at her, falsely stern. "Your father was wiser than you know. He knew he must select a man who could hold his own against you in a fight. After seeing how I held off legions of Saracens, he was impressed enough to offer me the position. I was foolish enough to accept."

She sat up, the coverlet partially falling away. "With the good comes the bad," she teased. "You wanted Lioncross but I came with it."

He folded his hands under his chin, his eyes like blue flame as they smoldered at her. "How fortunate for me."

She grinned back, feeling his gaze licking at her. "Then tell me," she said thoughtfully, "were you his first choice? Or was there an entire company of men my father weeded through to make his choice?"

Christopher actually looked thoughtful. Hell, he didn't know, come to think on it. Was he indeed the first choice? Or had some other fool turned the baron down? Richard was close with Marcus Burton, now in the north determining the political tides of who was loyal to John. Could he have approached Marcus with the same proposal? Marcus was such an eloquent speaker that he could weasel his way out of anything, even a marriage contract.

He glanced at Dustin, suddenly jealous at the thought of her ending up in Marcus' arms. Foolish, of course. He was the Lion's Claw. Marcus was merely a general. He knew without a doubt that he had been the first choice.

"Nay, lady, I was his first and only choice," he said confidently. "I am the only one worthy of the treasure of Lioncross Abbey."

"Treasure? What treasure? We do have some wealth, but…."

He cut her off, taking her soft white hand, now warm, into his huge palm. "I meant you."

"Oh," she felt her cheeks go warm at the compliment. When he raised his eyebrows expectantly at her, she got his hint. "Thank you," she added quickly.

As the fire crackled and Dustin finished her bread, Christopher held her hand, lost in his own thoughts. Marcus Burton kept popping up into his mind, as much as he tried to ignore him. Marcus was his closest friend, outside of David, but the competition between the two of them had always been fierce. He wondered if Marcus would view Dustin as another contest, knowing the man's taste for women. His gaze turned dark as he stared into the flames of the hearth; friend or no, this was one treasure he would not share.

"What are you thinking?" came a soft, sweet voice.

Jolted from his train of thought, he smiled at her. "Nothing, my lady," he replied, letting go of her hand and rising to stretch his legs. "As much as I am reluctant to leave, I must go to make sure the final preparations are made for our trip to London."

She nodded, standing up as well, but the heavy cover made it difficult. "And I will get dressed. I must be ready to search for Caesar when the storm passes."

"You will not go without me, or another knight," he pointed at her. "Is that clear?"

"Yes, Christopher," she replied patiently.

He eyed her, wary of her too-obedient answer. "I am serious."

She looked at him, surprised. "So am I. I promise I shall take a guard dog with me." Then she smiled with mock sweetness.

He let out an exasperated sigh, trying not to grin at her. "Goad me not, lady.

I will take you over my knee."

She jumped back, pulling the blanket tightly about her. "Don't you dare!"

He did grin, then, and moved for the door. "I shall see you later, Lady de Lohr."

Dustin was still smiling as he closed the door. Even as she dropped the blanket and dressed in a green woolen surcoat with a tight green silk girdle, she grinned. Every time she thought of her husband, she grinned. She could not help it.

☙

IT RAINED VERY heavily for the rest of the afternoon and Dustin was growing increasingly concerned about Caesar. Yet she could do nothing until the rain ceased, so she busied herself by packing for their trip to London. The hours passed relatively quickly as she and a maid kept themselves occupied with storing her entire wardrobe and personal items into two medium-sized trunks.

Her husband, however, had spent a good deal of time out in the rain looking for the cat, among other things. His captive, standing naked and shivering in the bailey, still refused to talk and he was growing irritated with the man. He would alternately search the field where the cat and the rabbit were last seen and then return to interrogate the prisoner again. David and Edward joined him as he went from one duty to the next, as Jeffrey patrolled the wall, and Leeton and the de Velt twins prepared wagons and other effects for the trip to London.

Even though he was very busy, Christopher found that if he was not immediately occupied, his thoughts would drift to his wife and he found himself wondering what the night would bring. Would she be willing and responsive to him, as he had seen she was capable of being? It had been more than a day since she last had a tantrum or had showed her stubborn streak, and he was pleased with the woman he was coming to know. He wondered if she found him agreeable, too.

As dusk drew near and the rain showed no signs of letting up, Christopher abandoned the search for the cat and returned to the keep, making sure the gate was secured for the night and seeing personally that posts were set. Leeton and Max had the night watch in the miserable weather, although David and Edward would relieve them close to dawn. Christopher instructed all of his knights and senior soldiers to keep a close eye on the captive in hopes that once the rain turned freezing, the man would talk.

Inside the castle, the great hall was warm and a huge fire was blazing in the equally huge hearth. Cooking smells floated in the air from the kitchens on the ground floor level, reminding him of just how hungry he was. Soaked and itching with the damp wool, he dropped his armor in the foyer and had two soldiers carry it away to be cleaned. Dripping water, he took the stairs two at a time and made his way to his chamber.

Just as he was entering his door, he could hear Dustin's voice far down the hall. Glancing back, he could see her moving between her mother's room and her own, her arms laden with surcoats and other bulky materials. Curious, he went to see what she was doing.

Two maids were following her around and he could see with his initial observation that all of Dustin's mother's clothing was laid out all over the dead woman's room. Cloaks, dresses, fine surcoats, shoes… every inch of the room seemed to be covered with garments and accessories. He put his hands on his hips as he examined the mess, wondering what in the hell she was doing.

Dustin was in the process of shaking out a heavy fur-lined cloak, studying it for rodent holes or damage. She caught sight of her husband in the doorway and smiled sweetly at him. In that small gesture, he felt his heart soften and noticed he was verily pleased with her reaction. She was happy to see him.

"Greetings, husband," she said gaily. "You are all wet."

"Astute as always, Lady de Lohr," he said with a raised brow. "What is it that you are doing?"

She lay the cloak down. "Seeing if there are any of mother's things that will do me service in London," she said. "I have only two cloaks, and not very nice ones at that. Mother has armfuls."

"I can see that," he said. "But there are surcoats strewn about as well. You are not planning to take any of those, are you?" He ended with a warning tone, reminding her that he did not approve of her wearing her mother's too-tight garments.

She looked at him. "Only those of which you approve," she said patiently. "Since I have so few nice surcoats, I will try on every one of mother's and you can tell me which ones I can and cannot wear."

Sly, he thought. Rather than choose them herself and being obstinate about it, she would let him do the picking. That way there was no way he could disapprove of what she wore. "Very well," he said after a moment. "But only a few, mind you. We can have more made in London made to fit you."

She smiled. "Truly? More clothes for me?"

He shook his head at her, at her surprise at such a simple thing as having a surcoat made. "In case you haven't realized it, you are a baron's wife and you must be properly dressed," he said. "I believe we have been through this before. I shall order dozens of dresses made for you in London, and all the accessories to go with them."

She looked pleased with the extravagance, surprised he felt she was worth it. She'd never thought much about her clothing, but found that she was suspiciously interested in looking her best as of late.

"As you say, husband." She gave a happy little shrug, leaving the maids to finish shaking out the clothing. "Would you let me help you from those wet clothes?"

Now it was his turn to be surprised. "Aye, I would," he agreed.

They returned to his chamber and he sat on a chair, holding out his massive leg while she removed his boots one at a time. He watched her lovely face as she concentrated on removing his wet things, careful not to get herself wet. She was dressed in a soft knit woolen dress with a snug girdle that made the material drape over her breasts most invitingly. In fact, he'd never seen her look lovelier.

"Is your prisoner still out in the rain?" she asked as she hung his tunic up to dry.

"Aye," he replied, unfastening his breeches and they fell to the ground, rendering him nude.

Dustin had her back turned to him as she hung the tunic up. When she turned around to face him, she let out a gasp and quickly turned around again in shock. He grinned, picking up his breeches and walking over to her.

"You can hang these up," he said softly, hanging them over her shoulder and in front of her face.

She snatched them away and stiffly hung them up next to the tunic. "Where are your clothes so that I might get them for you," she asked primly, still not turning to look at him.

He was genuinely amused by her prudish stance. For a woman who melted under his hands like none other, he found it somewhat surprising.

"Do I make you uncomfortable like this?" he asked. "I am told I am quite exquisite."

She fidgeted. " 'Tis not that…well…indeed…'tis just…" She stamped her foot in frustration. "Would you *please* put some clothes on?"

He continued to grin. "I have seen you nude."

She closed her eyes for a brief second at the memory, remembering how embarrassed she had been the first time, and how she had not even noticed the second. She was ashamed that the second time had been so easy for her.

"Aye, you have," she conceded.

He studied her stiff backside, the way her hair fell so softly down her back like an impossible cascade. "There is no shame in seeing your husband naked."

She didn't know what to say. He was right, of course, but she was still embarrassed. She'd never seen a naked man in her life and the mere thought brought heat to her cheeks. Christopher, seeing how miserable she was, retrieved his breeches from the wardrobe and put them on.

"You can turn around now," he told her, feigning insult. "I have no desire to parade around nude for a woman who is appalled by it."

She turned around, slowly, her eyes falling to the leather breeches he now wore. She almost looked sad and he wondered why.

"What's wrong with you now? Do not you approve of these, either?" he demanded, half in jest.

She opened her mouth to say something, then reconsidered. Instead she bit her lip. "They are fine. 'Tis time for supper, I am sure."

He drew out his spare pair of leather boots, well-worn, and put them on. "What were you going to say?"

"Nothing," she insisted, moving to his wardrobe. "What tunic would you wear?"

"The woolen tunic with the snug neck, the color of eggshell," he said.

She pulled it free and helped him put it on. He straightened the tunic, smoothing it over his glorious chest as she watched. She fought off a disturbing urge to push his hands away and do it herself. When she moved away from the chair, he suddenly reached out and snatched her arm, pulling her to him.

Their eyes met, clear gray to pure blue. "Be honest with me, Dustin," he said in a low voice. "All I will ever ask of you in this marriage is that you be honest. Now tell me, what were you going to say?"

She met his gaze evenly. "You have asked a great deal more than that already."

He could have taken that statement as a challenge, but instead, the hand that gripped her trailed down her arm until he found her hand. He pulled her palm to his lips and kissed it.

"Tell me."

Her gaze continued to hold even, although he could nearly read the emotions in the pure depths. He thought he might have to ask her again, firmer this time, but after a moment he saw her relax as if she had considered her options and had decided to give in to him.

"I was going to say that I know I should not be embarrassed to see you without clothing, yet I am just the same," she said quietly. "I have never seen a naked man before."

"Not even a soldier? Or your father?" he asked.

She shook her head. "Nay, mother was quite strict about that. She believed flesh was a gateway to sin, and the less seen, the better," her gaze left him. "My mother's father was a deviant man, Chris. He used my mother for his own pleasure before my father married her. Mother was terrified of physical contact, even with my father. 'Tis why she insisted on separate bedchambers. You occupy his former rooms."

He was coming to feel remorseful that he had baited her. He let out a disgusted hiss. "There is no greater atrocity than incest," he muttered. "Arthur knew of this and still he married your mother?"

"Aye," she replied, meeting his eyes once again. "His father and my mother's father were friends, and my parents were betrothed as babes. Everyone knew what my grandsire did to my mother, yet they all feigned ignorance. Even on the wedding night, when guests demanded the stained sheets, my father cut his own hand and smeared blood on the linens."

Christopher was sickened on Dustin's behalf, yet he knew that sort of occurrence was all too common. He felt a good deal of sorrow for his young wife as she had come to hear of the worst life had to offer.

"Did your mother tell you this?" he asked softly.

"Aye, she did," she nodded. "One night right after father left with Richard. She was feeling sorry for herself, I suppose, and had too much wine. Father never knew she told me."

"Is your grandsire still alive?" he asked.

"Aye, he is," she answered.

His eyes suddenly narrowed. "Does he reside in Nottingham?"

She could see where this was leading and she timidly sat on his knee, putting her arms around his neck shyly. "I am not going there anymore, remember?" she reminded him. " 'Twould seem you would rather have me in London."

His arms went about her, their faces close. "Would you have truly exposed yourself to that potential hell simply to escape me?"

She shrugged. "I did not know you then, my lord," she said. "I reasoned that what awaited me in Nottingham could be no worse than what awaited me at Lioncross."

"Then you reasoned incorrectly, lady," he said softly, yet sternly. "You will never go near Nottingham, and if your mother were still alive, I would beg her for the privilege of championing her."

He was so close and she found him very strong and virile and powerful as he spoke of championing her mother. Her cheeks felt warm again. In fact, her whole body was on fire. She was gradually aware that she had been watching his mouth as he spoke, noticing his dark blond mustache and beard. It was very attractive. Before she realized it, she reached up and ran her fingers along his stubble.

He froze, watching her face as she played with his beard. The scratchy hair tickled her fingers and she smiled.

"I like your beard," she said.

He pulled her closer, rubbing it against her cheek skin and she giggled, trying to push him away. "Do you like it still?" he was still rubbing at her cheek.

She squealed, her hands shoving against his chest. "It scratches like briars."

He stopped and grinned at her as she rubbed her cheek. "A pity you will have to suffer through the winter with it," he said. "I will scratch you at every opportunity."

She rubbed the sides of his face roughly with both hands and then hopped from his knee playfully. "Not if I am in my bed and you are in yours."

He raised an eyebrow. "Think not, lady, that I am going through the entire winter sleeping alone, or through this marriage for that matter."

"So you intend to sleep with me always and forever?" she asked, still smiling.

"Aye, I do, and no argument," he stood up, facing her with his hands on his hips. "We will sleep in the same bed from this night on. When we return from London, I will see that all of your personal effects are brought to my chamber."

She was surprised that she didn't care in the least. She liked sleeping in the same bed with him, for he was soft and warm and comforting. "As you say, husband."

He expected an argument and was surprised when he didn't get one. Dustin continued to smile at him, her hands clasped behind her back. He braced his legs apart, clasping his own hands behind his back.

"I am pleased that you are learning well to obey my wishes," he said. "As much as I enjoy a good battle, I do not enjoy them with my wife."

"Why not?" she asked innocently. "I think we fight well together, do not you?"

"You are indeed a test for my formidable skills, but I would rather we act toward each other as we are now," he said. "I would rather talk to you than yell at you."

She was warmed by his words, feeling a sense of connection with him as she had never felt in her life. But smells from the grand hall were wafting into the room, reminding them both of how hungry they were, and they were both distracted.

"Lady de Lohr, I believe dinner awaits," he said after a moment, offering her his arm. Together, they proceeded to the meal.

All of the knights save Jeffrey and Leeton were at the table, already stuffing their faces with food. Christopher seated his wife next to his brother and took his own chair at the head of the table. Their trenchers were filled to overflowing and their cups topped.

The storm outside continued to vent its fury as the occupants inside Lioncross ate and drank and carried on a fine meal. Dustin's attention was riveted to Max and Anthony, again telling hysterical stories that had her in stitches. Christopher, silent as usual, was perfectly content to finish his meal listening to his wife's loud laughter.

They ate and drank, laughed and talked, until there was nothing left. It had been a fine evening. As the remains were being cleared from the table, three soldiers entered the front door of the castle, dripping wet from the terrible elements outside. They sought out their liege.

The soldier in the lead bowed quickly. "My lord, the captive wishes to speak with you."

Christopher glanced at David. "Well and good for him that he does," he muttered, then looked to his soldiers. "I shall come shortly."

The knights, all of them, quit the hall as the soldiers exited back out into the vicious weather. Dustin, alone at the table, looked after them and felt a bit lost all of a sudden. The abrupt silence was disorienting. She watched as David ordered Christopher's armor brought forth once more, and personally helped his brother don the metal plating. As they had been doing it all their lives, they worked as a team to adeptly dress in their protection. When Christopher finished strapping on a piece of plate armor over his forearm, he turned, almost as an afterthought, to his wife still at the table.

"I will not be long," he said confidently.

She nodded in response, watching as he and his men quit the castle. Beyond the door, the lightning flashed and the rain came down in buckets, yet it was eerily quiet in the grand hall.

Dustin sighed. When it had just been her and her mother, the grand hall was always this quiet and she was very aware of the difference before and after Christopher had come. She had come to enjoy the company of him and his men very much, and alone in the hall, she found the loneliness oppressive. As much as she had loved her mother, she felt it almost a sacrilege to admit that she liked life at Lioncross better now since the baron had arrived.

Even with everything that had happened, the deaths and fights and incidents, Christopher had somehow breathed life into the dying keep. Dustin was glad she hadn't gone to Nottingham, and glad circumstances had prevented her from leaving. Had she gone, she would have never come to know her husband and would have probably spent a good deal of time resenting him for marrying her and taking her keep.

Another clap of thunder sounded loud overhead and Dustin glanced up as if she could see it. With another sigh, she left the hall and went to her mother's small solar. There was a small fire in the hearth and Dustin moved for the windows, paneled with rare and expensive glass, for they provided protection and an excellent view of the bailey where she could watch what was going on between her husband and his prisoner. She was curious, for her father never kept prisoners, and she wanted to see what they were going to do with the fool who almost killed David.

☙

THE BAILEY HAD turned into a mucky, slippery lake as Christopher and his knights crossed it, heading for the wet, naked man near the eastern wall. Leeton and Jeffrey were already standing on either side of the man and Christopher could hear his wails as he approached.

He planted himself in front of the prisoner, spitting out the rainwater that had run into his mouth.

"I am here," he said coldly. "What is it that you wish to tell me?"

The captive was truly miserable, his entire body was blue and his teeth were chattering violently. "Ev-v-v-erything, my lord. I only ask shelter and clothing."

Christopher didn't react for a moment. Then, he leaned close to the man's face. "You had better be truthful, fool, or I will gut you on the spot."

"I am, I a-a-a-am," he insisted loudly. "I s-swear it on the bible."

Christopher motioned for him to be released, stepping back as Leeton and Jeffrey untied the man and handed him over to David and Max. He preceded his knights and the prisoner back into a side entrance of the castle that led into a row of small cubicles that were once used for confessionals as part of the original abbey structure. It was a seldom used place, full of ghosts, with a dim and musty smell. Although it wasn't warm, it was dry and the man was given a rough woolen blanket to dry off with.

Christopher waited impatiently for the man to speak until he could stand it no longer. "Well?" he demanded.

The prisoner wiped his face dry, letting out a heavy sigh. " 'Tis true what you have said, my lord, all of it," he said quietly. "Sir Ralph sent us here to spy on you."

"What were his orders?" Christopher asked calmly.

"To find out what we could and report back to him," he answered.

Christopher studied the man a moment. "But you tried to kill me."

"Aye, we did, but it was Roy's idea," the prisoner replied. "Sir Ralph never ordered us to kill you."

As Christopher interrogated the prisoner, a small access door at the far end of the room quietly opened, avoiding detection. A small silhouette stood still as stone, listening to the voices echo in the bowels of the old abbey. But Christopher didn't notice; he was too focused on gaining information.

He remained emotionless, standing with his legs braced firmly apart and his arms crossed. "Then what did you find out about me?"

The prisoner faltered a bit, eyeing Christopher. "Nothing much at all, my lord," he replied. "It seems no one around here knows you very well. Not even your whore would tell us anything."

Christopher showed a flash of puzzlement. "Whore? What whore?"

"The redhead," came the quiet reply.

Christopher was horrified. He snapped, grabbing the man by the hair and pulling him up off the seat, slamming him heavily against the wall. "You *killed* her?"

The captive screamed and twisted. "I didn't, Roy did!" he gasped. "He said she was your whore and we should kill her to keep her quiet."

Christopher's face reddened and he released the man, stepping back a moment to regain his composure. He was mad enough to kill but in a flash of reason, he knew if he killed the man, he might not know all of it. Gratification would have to wait.

"Bastards," he hissed as he turned away. "You goddamn bastards."

David, his handsome face tensed, stepped in because his brother seemed close to snapping.

"Who raped her?" he demanded. "And who killed her mother?"

The prisoner was scared, rubbing at his scalp where Christopher had yanked the hair right out of his head. "I killed her mother because I had to. Roy took care of the whore."

"What do you mean you *had* to?" David demanded.

Christopher turned around and the man met his eyes, fear glazing his face. "Because she interrupted us as we were trying to get information from the whore," he muttered. "She was going to run and tell, so I had to kill her."

Christopher glared at the man. "If you call her a whore one more time, I will cut your throat," he growled. "Now, answer his question. Who in the hell raped her?"

The captive wrapped the blanket about him tightly, cringing from the big knight. "Roy did," he said fearfully. "She said she was untouched, but he took her anyway. Even when she screamed... I think he violated her in many ways. He took his dirk and did... things to her."

Christopher's nostrils flared a spilt-second, disgusted and sickened by the admission. He would take the information with him to his grave. Dustin would never, ever know the details. Almost beyond rage, he shook his head slowly.

"You stupid bastard," he muttered. "She wasn't a whore, she was a friend of my wife's. Whatever possessed you to commit such a heinous crime against her?"

"We saw you leaving her house, my lord, alone," he answered. "We thought she was your mistress."

Christopher could see right through the fool's simple train of thought. "And you thought to gain knowledge of me." He shook his head at the irony, the stupidity, of it. "Tell me, then; have you sent any messages back to Sir Ralph?"

The fat man shook his head. "Nay, my lord. We have been here only a day or so."

Christopher nodded at the answer, mulling over what he was going to do with the man now. He felt a good deal of both relief and sorrow at having caught Rebecca's killer and he knew that, somehow and some way, there had to be justice served. Rebecca deserved that much and for her, for Dustin, he would make sure of it.

"What is your name?" he asked after a moment.

"Virgil," the prisoner replied without hesitation.

AS CHRISTOPHER DRILLED the man for any more useful information he could come up with, the collection of knights had yet to notice the shadow far down the narrow hall. The shadow had disappeared after the confession of Rebecca's murder and was now back, moving like a wraith, silently and swiftly, and suddenly it was in their midst. Yelling at the top of her lungs and wielding a heavy pick axe she had retrieved inside the keep, Dustin nearly clipped David as she swung the battle-axe with all her might straight at Virgil's head.

No one had a chance to react as the steel sang through the air and caught the prisoner half in the neck and half in the head, burying the blade deep. In a splash of blood and gore, the cubicle walls surrounding the man were colored crimson as his head slammed dully against the stone.

"You bloody bastard!" Dustin shrieked. "Consider that revenge for Rebecca!"

Christopher grabbed her tightly about the body but she struggled madly against him. The prisoner, dead, was a gory sight with a pick axe buried in his face. Dustin continued to rant and fight even as Christopher hauled her up in his arms, taking her back the way she had come. It was a chaotic and heartbreaking scene.

David and the other knights, stunned at the ferocity of Lady de Lohr, watched Christopher walk away with his screaming burden. They exchanged apprehensive and shocked glances before returning their focus to the dead prisoner.

"He got what he deserved," Max muttered.

Edward put a foot on the prisoner's fat chest and pulled the battle axe free, spurting more blood as the man fell to the floor in a spreading pool of the stuff.

"Gentle knights," Edward said softly as he tossed the axe to the ground. "I do believe we have seen a classic case of justice served.

David scratched his neck underneath his itching mail. "Damn, remind me never to rile her," he muttered. "Did you see the way she wielded that axe?"

"Did you see the power in her swing?" Anthony countered. "Put some armor on her and let her go into battle with us. She would do as well as any man."

David sighed, feeling his fatigue and wanting to be free of his wet and uncomfortable clothing. There was nothing more they could do for the prisoner. It was over.

"Let us move him out of here," he motioned to the de Velt twins. "We will burn the body when the weather clears."

ꕤ

BY THE TIME they hit the grand hall, Dustin was reduced to sobbing heavily in Christopher's arms. He held her tightly, whispering soothingly to her as he carried her up the last flight of stairs and into his chamber.

Once inside, he closed the door and tried to put her down, but she wouldn't let go of him. Awkwardly, he sat down on the edge of the bed in his bulky armor and held her, stroking her hair gently.

"Dustin, Dustin," he sighed, sing-song. "What do you do, lady?"

"I heard what he said," she sputtered. "I heard him say he killed Rebecca."

"I gathered," his voice was soft and comforting. "Why were you eavesdropping on us?"

Her head lay on his shoulder. "I wasn't, at first," she wept. "I watched you in the bailey and then when I saw you take him to the abbey, I followed because I was curious. Father never kept prisoners and I was just watching when I heard him. He said… oh, God, he said terrible things."

She wept heavily. Christopher took one arm from her and tried to peel back his hauberk, but it was difficult until she sat up and allowed him to remove it with both hands. By that time, her crying had lessened and she stood up, looking completely forlorn and exhausted. Now that he had the opportunity, he rose and removed the rest of his mail and wet things. Dustin stood silently, watching him with an occasional hiccup.

"Your breeches are wet," she hiccupped.

Silently, he undid the stays and removed his breeches. Dustin, meanwhile, had turned away from him and went over to the basin to wash her hands.

"His blood is on me" he heard her whisper but he didn't like the tone. By the time he reached her, she was rubbing harshly at the blood stains that were slow to come off and he grabbed both of her hands, stilling them.

"Come with me," he whispered into her hair, pulling her stiff body across the room and practically falling onto the bed with her.

She mumbled something, weakly struggling with him, but he ignored her and pulled the thick coverlet snuggly around them both. In his massive arms, she began to calm and he felt her shaking lessen and lessen. Outside his windows, the storm raged and pounded, but inside, in his bed, they were safe and warm.

Christopher lost track of time as they lay together, neither one speaking, yet neither one sleeping. Dustin didn't move a muscle as he stroked her back gently.

"I have never killed anyone before," she finally murmured.

He nodded faintly. "You used the axe with great skill."

" 'Twas my father's," she replied. "He didn't like it. He thought it was a messy tool."

"Not if used correctly." Christopher wasn't sure they should be speaking of this, but better to do it than to allow her to stew. "I am sorry you had to hear those things. I was going to spare you the details."

"I wish I hadn't heard," she mumbled, pressing her face into his shoulder. "But I did. I killed him, and I am not sorry."

"It is right for you to seek justice for your friend," he replied after a pause. "I do not fault you."

She suddenly raised her head, looking at him with her red-rimmed eyes. "Are you angry at me for interfering? I told you, I hadn't meant to, but when I heard him…."

He shook his head. "Nay, sweetheart, I am not angry," he said. "If there would be any justice to the man's execution, then it is right that you should dispense it for what he did to your friend." His eyes suddenly twinkled at her, crinkling at the corners. "You are ferocious, aren't you? I have never seen a woman with such bravery."

She lay her head back down, snuggling comfortably against his skin. The whole evening, day, and week was overwhelming her, and Christopher made her feel safe and warm as no one else ever had. Somehow she knew he would always be there for her, to protect and tease her. It was maddening and confusing and wonderful to feel the way she did about him. For someone who never wanted to be married, she was growing to like it a great deal. With warm and comforting thoughts, she drifted off.

Christopher felt her go limp and knew she was asleep. As exhausted as she was, he was glad but at the same time he was sorry. He had so wanted to play with her this eve, touch her, and warm her to him. She seemed to forget about everything when he touched her, and he wanted her to forget what she had done for the moment. He wanted to make her his in every sense of the word, and holding her up against his nude body was quickly escalating into torture.

Eventually, he fell into a light sleep. Dreams of Dustin filled his fatigued mind, images he could not quite grasp yet at the same time he could feel strong emotions of fear and anger. Eventually these images calmed and he began to dream of Dustin in a better light, her golden hair spread over him, her mouth on his stomach in his dream his hands grasped her buttocks, yet he could not quite feel her. It was almost as if she were made of liquid, he knew he was touching it, yet he could not grab hold.

Yet she was doing maddening things to him and he was in heaven, frustrated that he could not touch her. His hands left her buttocks slowly, moving up her arms and entangling themselves in cobwebs of golden hair until they reached her breasts. Suddenly, she felt firm in his palms and he began to caress her eagerly.

Christopher awoke suddenly when Dustin whimpered, and he was aware of his right hand on her breast, fondling her gently while his left arm held her fast to him. As one does when awakened from a vivid dream, he took no time to consider his actions and began to remove her laced girdle with great urgency. Dustin, still half-asleep, whimpered again and he tore at the top of her dress, baring her to the waist.

He was so eager that he found he was shaking as his hand reverently grasped her bare breast, observing the deep rosy nipple and delighting in the softness of her. His caresses, gentle at first, increased in intensity until Dustin gasped, entwining her fingers in his thick, blond hair.

His hot mouth descended on her sweet nipple, sucking her mightily and she cried out softly in response, now fully awake. He heard her call his name faintly, her hands in his hair and he was losing his control with all of it.

He tore himself away from her sweet flesh long enough to pull her dress completely off, rendering her quite nude underneath him.

They both froze for a moment, staring at each other in the dim light of the distant hearth. He gazed down at her, her perfect body posed delightfully, his knees between her calves. He was pleased that she was seemingly unashamed to look upon him this time.

"Your body is sculpted like a Greek statue I saw once when I visited Bath with my father," she murmured, her lids half closed. "How is it that you are as perfect as marble?"

He smiled, running his hands up both of her thighs, lowering himself gently on her. "And how is it that your body is the most perfect God has seen fit to form?"

He kissed her tenderly after that, every inch of her skin. He covered her arms, her legs, her stomach with kisses, driving her mad with a desire she had never known before. She needed him, somehow, though too naive to know exactly how. When he once again moved his great hands to her core, covered with dark-gold curls, she tensed beneath him and he looked up at her.

"Do not be afraid, Dustin," he whispered. "I shall be gentle, I promise."

He had told her that once before and they never went any further, due to David's interruption. She was so caught up in his touch now that if David had walked through the door at the moment, she would have taken his head off. She found she wanted Christopher desperately, all of her preconceived notions be damned.

She relaxed and lay her head back down on the pillow and he continued, stroking the exterior of her center before parting the thick lips and running his tongue gently within the pink folds of tissue.

Dustin could feel her apprehension rise but forced herself to calm, her mind whirling at the sensations he was creating. But his mouth did not torture her overlong for he knew she was very new to this. He came up on her slowly, kissing her stomach, the dip in her abdomen below her sternum, and under her breasts as his huge hands began to caress and stroke her.

He found a nipple once more, knowing how she responded to him, and fondled her more firmly as he suckled. It took virtually no time before she was slick and wet, her moisture running down onto the linens and he knew she was ready for him.

He parted her legs wide, his heart pounding in his chest with the desire and excitement he was feeling. Dustin opened her eyes and he lay atop her, supporting his weight with an arm and holding her tightly with the other. Below, she could feel his big organ throbbing at her threshold, pushing against her.

His eyes met hers, their gaze locking as he pushed into her very slowly, acutely aware of her tightness and small body. He was not more than an inch into her when he shuddered with utter ecstasy. Dustin, feeling as if she were being stuffed full, tightened with apprehension and he stopped.

"Relax, sweetheart," he kissed her cheek, her temple. "It will make it easier."

She didn't reply but he felt her arms tighten about him trustingly and that pleased him immensely.

He played a bit of a game with her, yet one that would help ease her. He would pull out completely, then push back into her slowly, going deeper and deeper each time, loosening her muscles. Her maiden's barrier was apparent and the next time he withdrew, he plunged back into her harder than he ever had, breaking the tissue and driving himself to the very hilt.

Because he had taken the time to relax her, the sting of losing her innocence was just that – a sting. Although it did not completely subside, it was not as frightening or unpleasant as Dustin had imagined it would be. Instead, she felt an overwhelming sense of comfort and pleasure with his closeness and not a hint of embarrassment. Of all of the things she knew she would feel, she had been completely wrong.

Christopher stopped, buried within her, and pushed himself up to look at her face. Her expression was soft and he smiled in surprise.

"Did I hurt you?" he rasped.

"A little," she admitted, her legs wrapping around his thighs of their own accord. "Is this all there is to it?"

He raised an eyebrow slowly, completely astonished at her reaction. He had expected screams, fighting, at the very least.

"Nay, lady," he whispered, dipping to kiss her nose. "We have only just begun."

He began to move in her then, slowly to allow her to adjust, but escalating quickly to ram-hard thrusts that rattled her teeth. Yet her nubile, innocent body responded to him with such intensity that she had no other choice but to go with it. Initially she had been puzzled with her wanton reaction to something she had never experienced before, but she rapidly gave in with the rest of her until she was riding with him, faster and faster, her nails biting into his broad back, feeling heat building in her loins but having no idea how to satisfy it.

Then, it happened; her body stiffened and her loins contracted with a sweetness that brought stars before her eyes and then she was falling, falling back down to earth and landing gently in a feather bed. Tremors rolled through her body, signaling rapture. The tremors faded but the rapture, the glow, remained.

But he was still moving within her, his breathing coming in hard grunts when finally she heard him give a low groan and his movement lessened and lessened and then eventually stopped. Dazed, Dustin lay clutched in his arms, her legs still wrapped around him, wondering why she had been so terrified of coupling. Her mother had clouded her mind with her own ideals, and Dustin thought for the first time in her life how wrong her mother had been.

Chapter Nine

CHRISTOPHER AWOKE BEFORE dawn, burrowed down into the thick mattress with his wife cradled against him. He smiled into the darkness of the room as the events from the night filled his sleep-warmed mind, and he kissed his wife's head softly, fondly remembering.

Outside it was still pouring rain, yet he had dozens of things to attend to. Dustin's trunks still needed to be loaded onto the wagons, something he had neglected to do last night due to the circumstances, and he intended to be on the road to London before noon. Thunder clapped and he was reluctant for Dustin to travel in such weather, but they had no choice. The prince and his bastards were waiting for him at Windsor, like jackals waiting for fresh meat.

He rose, carefully disengaging himself from her, and proceeded to order a bath for his wife. He sternly admonished the maids and serving men who brought the tub to be quiet, standing over them like a great sentinel, watching every move they made and glaring at them for any small sound.

When everything was prepared and waiting for her to awaken, he went over the wardrobe and drew forth the traveling clothes he would wear beneath his armor.

"Aren't you going to take a bath, too?" Dustin sat up in bed, her hair tousled wildly and a huge smile on her face.

He felt his heart go soft at the sight of her. "Nay, lady, I shall be wet enough this day, I assure you."

She scooted forward in the bed, her smile fading but her eyes alive. "I shall bathe you."

Christ, how could he resist her? Of course he could not, and within a minute or so he was submerged in the water and she was up, lathering a great horsehair brush with a cake of plain soap. He smiled as she came over to him and began to scrub him silently.

It was amusing and highly erotic. With the new heights their relationship had reached, they were both eager to explore it again. Dustin could not believe she was bathing a man, she being naked as well, no less. When did she become such an exhibitionist? She knew her mother, from her perch in paradise, must be having fits at her behavior.

As she soaped his chest she purposely grazed him with her full breasts, the second time drawing a growl from deep in his throat. She giggled with delight with his torment, feeling very powerful to affect him as she did. She even washed his hair, making sure her nipples teased his bronzed back mercilessly.

When she came around front to wash the rest of him, he would have no part of it. He snaked a massive arm out and pulled her right into the tub. Dustin squealed and giggled, her protests very weak because she was delighted with the newness of his intimate attentions.

"Now, you little nymph, I will wash you," he said in a husky voice that sent shivers up her spine.

He did just that as she sat between his legs in the great copper tub. Starting at the top of her blond head, he lathered her completely with rose-scented soap and didn't stop until he had soaped every one of her toes. Even after he rinsed her feet, he kept his eyes glued to her face while he brought a dainty foot up to his mouth and suckled passionately on her big toe.

Dustin went stiff with the sensation, her whole body running hot and cold and her loins turning warm and wicked. He grinned and returned the foot to the water.

She was sitting opposite him, her wet hair slicked back and her gray eyes wide and alive. All Christopher could think about was making love to her again and again, knowing he had many tasks to accomplish in a short time, yet not wanting to leave the warmth of the room and the company of his wife. It would seem that after last night, it was as if seeing her nude was like teasing a man who was dying from thirst with a drink of water. He had to have her.

"Come here," he growled.

She grinned, biting her lower lip, and complied, laying atop him in the tub of cooling water. He lay back, stroking her wet hair, touching her face.

"Why is it that you affect me so?" he whispered, more to himself than to her.

She gazed back at him, thinking the very same thing, yet afraid to admit it to him. She was feeling vastly comfortable with him now, yet she was not quite ready to reveal her most intimate self.

His hands ran down her back, to her buttocks, and out to her knees. He parted her legs and forced her to straddle him.

"Do you feel my want for you, lady?" he asked hoarsely. She nodded, indeed feeling his organ rub up the cleft of her bottom. "Aye, my lord."

"What do you intend to do about it?" he asked of her.

She shook her head. "What would you have me do?"

He cracked a lopsided smile and lifted her up in the water, bringing her core to bear on top of his pulsing shaft. Her eyes widened, but she quickly began to melt as her slippery passage gave way to his thick maleness. She was a bit tender from losing her innocence, but it was bearable. In a rush of heat and pleasure, she was impaled on him and she wound her arms around his neck for she was sure she would slide right under the water.

"Do you know how to ride a horse when it canters, so that you will not bounce up and down?" he asked in a husky whisper, almost mad with his need.

"Of course," she answered haltingly. "Move your hips with the animal's gait."

He caught her lips with his own, biting her lower lip gently, his rapidly filling-in beard scratching her. "Ride me."

Dustin threw her head back and was lost, riding him, feeling him full within her, creating her own heat. His hands were running all over her and she thought it terribly wonderful to be touched so gently, so caringly. She went with the motion, oblivious to everything else except the exciting new feelings and Christopher's big body underneath her.

Christopher was so far gone with excitement that it was no time at all before he was climaxing deep within her. When he felt his own release approach, he reached down and rapidly manipulated Dustin, bringing her to her own peak at nearly the same time. She cried out as her body stiffened with wonderful spasms before collapsing on his broad, beautiful chest.

He held her against him in the cooling water, never wanting to move ever again. She felt too wonderful exactly where she was.

"Did I hurt you?" he asked. "You must be somewhat sore."

"Not much," she replied. "Not enough to matter."

She sat up and he cupped her face with his big hands, completely swallowing her head up. "You are a remarkable woman, Dustin. I believe God had a plan in mind when he chose you for me."

"What sort of plan?" she asked.

He shook his head. "I do not know, at the moment. Mayhap it was to show me that I wasn't the only perfect soul on this earth. Mayhap it was to teach me humility. I simply do not know."

She shrugged vaguely and shivered. He suddenly realized that the water was cold and he did not want her to catch a chill.

"Out, sweetheart," he said briskly. "We have a busy day ahead of us.

☙

LIONCROSS WAS A chaotic mass of servants and soldiers, all preparing for the baron's trip to London. The rain had yet to let up, although the lightning and thunder had somewhat dissipated. The two wagons were led into the bailey and close to the front steps of the castle so that Dustin's trunks could be loaded and covered with straw to protect them.

After Christopher had dressed and left her, Dustin took more time than she could ever remember taking to prepare herself for the day. Usually, she tossed on the first dress she came across, but this morning she found herself actually debating about what she was going to wear. She finally chose a burgundy silk surcoat that had belonged to her mother with a wide, embroidered collar and long sleeves. It was heavy and very warm, and had a thick cloak to match. If she was going to be riding in rain, then she wanted to be well-protected.

The surcoat went on, albeit a bit tight, and she pulled on thick stockings and doeskin boots that she wore in winter. She also wore a heavy shift and a heavy off-white underskirt for extra warmth. When she was finally finished, she felt as if she were wearing an entire set of bedding. Her nearly dry hair was pulled back to the nape of her neck with her ivory clip.

Dustin made a trip a-purpose to look at herself in her mother's polished bronze mirror, and was not displeased with the woman she saw before her. The closer she looked, the more she realized that she had somehow changed over the past several days. It was difficult to put the change into words, but she could see it in herself and knew that her mother would have been pleased that her rough-and-ready daughter was finally starting to show signs of growing up.

She had had to grow up with everything she had suffered through and endured, yet mayhap even the negative had a positive side. Christopher had told her that he believed God had chosen her for his mate with a plan in mind. She wondered if the same theory applied to her, mayhap God had sent Christopher to her for a purpose. She wondered.

By the time she went back to her rooms, the knights were taking her two trunks out. She actually smiled at David as he passed by her, drawing a curious-but-amused stare from the man.

"My lady is jovial this day," he commented.

She shrugged. "Not jovial, but content. We are going to London!"

He laughed softly at her excitement. "I know," he let one of the soldiers take the heavy burden from him, wiping his hands. "It seems that I am going with you, as are Edward and Leeton."

"You are? How wonderful," she exclaimed. "Tell me, David, have you ever been to court?"

"I have been there," he said casually.

Dustin expected more of an answer, encouraging him to go on when he stopped. "And?"

He made a face. "*And* it is nothing but a gaggle of deviant, gossiping geese in fine clothing, trying to pretend they are better than the rest of the peasants."

She laughed happily. "I cannot wait."

He chuckled again at her enthusiasm, wondering how she would feel after a day or two of exposure. But he wasn't worried about her; with her temper and aggressiveness, she could hold her own easily against the catty court bitches… and with Christopher's reputation, she would have to.

Looking at her this morning, it was hard to believe she was the same wild woman who had killed a man the night before. She looked radiant and beautiful and he had a suspicion as to why. Christopher had the same look.

"Then I should hope for your sake, my lady, that the weather clears a bit," he said. "It will be miserable to travel in this weather."

She shrugged lightly. "We cannot control the weather." She looked at him seriously. "And another thing, call me Dustin. You are my brother now and I would have you address me as your sister."

He nodded, pleased. "It would be my pleasure, if Christopher approves."

She put her hands on her hips. "Approve or not, 'tis my name, and I say call me by it."

He put up a hand in agreement, not wanting to agitate her. With a smile, he extended his arm and they left her chamber, heading for the great hall.

Christopher was below in the foyer, his eyes riveting to his wife as his brother escorted her down the stairs. Christ, she was so beautiful he could scarcely believe she belonged to him. He left Max to meet her at the bottom of the steps.

"What do you do?" he sized David up and down. "Who gave you permission to touch my wife?"

"I did," Dustin said firmly. "As I have also given him permission to call me by my Christian name. Do you disagree?"

Christopher raised an eyebrow at her. "Nay, I do not, so long as he is respectful at all times. Get your hands off her, David. I shall take her from here."

David handed Dustin off to Christopher. "You always spoil my fun," he complained.

Christopher jerked his head at his brother, silently ordering him to make himself useful elsewhere. Good natured was the exchange, leaving all three of them grinning. When his brother sauntered off, Christopher turned back to his wife.

"You look lovely on this hellish morn," he said softly.

She felt her cheeks flush. "I dressed in the warmest dress I could find. David tells me that he and Edward and Leeton are coming with us to London."

" 'Tis true, although Max and Anthony are verily upset with it, but I feel strongly that their place is here, guarding my fortress," he replied. "Jeffrey seems to be content to stay. I was planning on leaving all of my knights here, but have since changed my mind."

"Since you captured the spy?" she asked quietly.

"Mayhap," he shrugged. "In any case, I feel better having adequate protection if I am indisposed."

"So you bring knights to protect me?" she asked, thinking it a bit excessive. "I can take care of myself, Christopher."

He gave her a reproving eye. "Nonetheless, Lady de Lohr, my knights will be your shadow."

She was standing on the third step up from the floor, almost eye-to-eye with him. Her eyes lingered on the golden beard and on the soft lips that had driven her mad with awakening passion. He saw her expression go soft and distant.

"What are you thinking?" he stepped closer to her.

She shook her head, flushing again. "I…about last night, I suppose," she said shyly. "Do you remember when you asked my permission to address me as Lady de Lohr, and you further told me that David said I hated the name?"

He nodded faintly. "I remember."

Her gray eyes found his blue. "I do not hate it anymore."

A slow smile spread across his mouth, broadening into the wide grin that near made her swoon. How she loved that smile!

"I am glad. I like using it," he murmured.

He lifted her hand to his lips, kissing it sweetly before escorting her off the steps and leading her into the grand hall. Because everyone was so busy, a scheduled meal had not been served. Instead, there were great plates of fruits and bread, honey and butter set out on the long table.

Dustin took a great slab of bread with butter and honey, chewing contentedly as Christopher conversed with Leeton for a moment, quietly. Since she could not hear their words, her mind wandered to Caesar and she wondered where the cat was. As soon as she remembered again that the feline was caught in the storm, her concern rose and she wandered out of the hall and disappeared into the kitchens.

The cook, a small woman, hadn't seen the cat, and neither had any of the other kitchen servants. The back door leading into the kitchen yard was wide open and Dustin finished her bread standing in the archway, watching the rain fall onto the already saturated ground. There was an icy wind with the storm, frozen fingers reaching out to touch her until she was shivering. Even after she had finished eating, she stood leaning against the doorjamb, wondering if the rain would let up enough to allow Caesar to return home.

"There you are," Christopher said, coming up behind her. "I was not even aware that you had left until I turned and found you missing. What are you doing?"

She glanced up at him and he noticed that her eyes were almost the exact color of the sky. "Watching for Caesar," she said, somewhat wistfully. "Where do you think he is?"

He gazed out over the muddy yard. "He's probably found a cozy spot somewhere in a thicket and is as dry as we are. You worry overmuch for him."

"He's old, Christopher," she admonished softly. "Of course I worry over him."

He caught her mood and put a hand on her shoulder. "Do you want me to go and look for him? I did yesterday, you know, and didn't catch a glimpse."

She was touched that he would go through that much trouble for her. "Nay, 'tis not necessary, I am sure. If he's hiding, you shall never find him." She let out a sigh, looking up at the dark clouds. "I suppose he will just have to wait until the rain clears."

Reluctantly, she turned from the rain and allowed her husband to lead her back into the warm hall. Jeffrey was there, as were the de Velt twins, eating everything that had been laid out. Dustin went to Jeffrey.

"Jeffrey, Caesar is caught out in the storm and I fear he will not return before I leave for London. Would you please take care of him while I am away?" she asked.

He nodded, "Yah, my lady. I shall find him when the rain stops. And he can even sleep in my bed if he wishes."

"Thank you," she smiled easily. "And my rabbits, too? Will you feed them?"

The cat was one thing, but the rabbits were another. Jeffrey cleared his throat, glancing at Christopher's stern face. "Yah, my lady, I shall feed the rabbits."

"Feed them to the cat," Max muttered and Anthony chortled loudly.

Christopher shot them both a threatening glare as Dustin turned to them, her pretty face menacing. "If you do, I shall have *you* for supper when I return."

The twins were immediately remorseful. "My apologies, my lady. We promise nothing will happen to the rabbits," Max said earnestly, though Anthony was still twittering.

"I shall take care of the bunnies," Jeffrey reiterated, glancing reprovingly at the two knights. "I am in charge while the baron is gone."

"Chris?" David bellowed at his brother from the front door. "The wagons are loaded and most of the men are assembled in the bailey."

"Very well," Christopher called back, putting his arm around Dustin's waist and pulling her with him toward the front door. "Gather your cloak, sweetheart, and anything else you would carry with you. I shall return in a few minutes."

"And then we leave?" she asked, her stomach fluttering with excitement.

"Aye, if everything is in order, we do," he gave her a wink and exited out into the pouring rain.

Exhilarated, Dustin dashed up the stairs to her room where her cloak and small traveling bag waited. The bag was her mother's, a small thing that hung on a golden rope that secured around her wrist. Inside, she had placed several of her mother's personal beauty items she wasn't sure she would need, but wanted to bring them just the same: a comb, a brush, a small hand-mirror of polished silver, a small glass vial of beeswax for chapped lips, another vial with a cake of ocher that her mother used to color her cheeks when she was particularly pale, a vial of rose-scented perfume, and a tortoise-shell hair clip.

She felt rather foolish for bringing so many vain, feminine items, especially in lieu of the fact that she didn't even know how to use the ocher, but she had them anyway. Just in case.

The cloak was terribly heavy as she slung it over her arm. Grabbing the small bag, she made her way to the door, her eyes lingering over her room, wondering when she would see it again.

There were so many memories that crept into her mind as she stood in the doorway; her father, her mother, Caesar, and Rebecca. So very many things, most of them happy, a few sad. And then came Christopher. It was almost as if there were two Dustins; one before the baron and one after.

With a faint smile, she closed the door, mentally trying to prepare herself for what lay ahead.

☙

EDWARD WAITED FOR her in the foyer, helping her secure her cloak as well as any mother, making sure it was securely fastened around her neck to prevent any rain from seeping in. Smart man that he was, he retrieved a shawl from a serving wench and tied it around her shoulders and neck before securing the cloak, adding another layer of protection. Dustin simply stood still and let him fuss over her, glancing at his face now and again and thinking him to be a very handsome man. His eyes were the most amazing gold color, and his manner confident and business-like. She knew Christopher put a great deal of trust in Edward, as much as he did in David.

She was also to discover that Christopher had seen to every little detail of the journey. Things she could have quite easily arranged, he had done. Two maids were to accompany her, older women who had served her mother and had always made sure Dustin's clothes were clean. She never had a maid of her own because she didn't want or need one, yet in London, she suspected she would need the help. Young boys, pages or squires that Christopher had brought with him, were dashing about and helping the knights finish with details.

Edward left her standing in the open front door as he went to inform Christopher that Lady de Lohr was ready, and she had a chance to see for herself what a madhouse the bailey had become. Soldiers, she suspected easily over one hundred, were in loose ranks in the bailey being hounded by the pounding rain. The big destriers were being brought out by grooms, snorting and dancing and snapping at anything that moved. Behind them, she could see a groom leading out her lanky warmblood. She'd never even told her husband that she had a personal horse, he must have suspected. She wondered with a grin if he had spent his time looking for a little palfrey and not a big-boned gelding.

Her horse, a beautiful rich brown with four white stockings, was named Hercules by her father because the animal was uncannily strong. But the animal was attached to Dustin and she could handle him better than any other, including the stable master. Yet he looked as calm and docile as a kitten as the groomsman led him out behind the harried destriers. Fact was, he could probably hold his own in a fight with a destrier and most likely win.

Someone began shouting orders and she jumped, for the voice was as loud as the thunder overhead. Her eyes found the source of the shouting and she was not surprised to see Christopher commanding his soldiers to straighten their ranks. He was walking toward her as he bellowed, moving quite easily in his bulky armor, with David and Leeton making sure his orders were carried out.

She watched him with his men for the first time, pride filling her when she saw how easily he controlled them, and how they obviously respected him. The presence and power the man radiated was unlike anything she had ever seen. Her father had been a good soldier, but he was more of a politician than a warrior. She realized that watching Christopher with his men charged her with a peculiar sort of excitement.

He mounted the steps and she stepped back, rain pouring off of him as he stepped just inside the threshold.

"Edward says you are ready," he said, his face and body soaked.

"I am, my lord," she replied. Lord, the man was big and imposing when he was still in his command mode. She'd seen him in full armor many times, but never when he had been directly commanding his men. It was as if there were two different personalities in the same man.

He shook his head, water spatting on the floor. "I think you will ride in the wagon under a tarp for a while, at least until this godforsaken rain lets up."

"I am not afraid of a little rain, my lord," she said. "I have ridden through worse."

"That was not a request, my lady." He seemed preoccupied and harsh. "You will do as I say," he turned and shouted to the nearest soldier. "Is the tarpaulin rigged on the large wagon?"

The affirmative reply came and he turned back to his wife. "Very well, then. Let us depart."

She nodded, putting her hood up to protect herself from the downpour and making sure the heavy cloak was secured.

"Dustin," he said softly.

Her eyes snapped up to him, aware of his tender tone. She was surprised to see him smiling down at her. He looked as if he wanted to say something, but instead he bent down and kissed her cheek, his wet helmet dripping water on her woolen hood.

"Come on," he said hoarsely.

He gathered her up in his arms, groaning aloud with all of the weight she was carrying. "Christ, woman," he pretended to huff. "You must weigh as much as I do."

She giggled at his feigned misery, wrapping her thickly-bundled arms around his neck. He winked at her, grunting again as he carried her out into the driving weather.

The back of the wagon was actually arranged nicely. Soldiers had secured a large oiled tarp over the entire bed and then had spread out a coverlet on the floor of the wagon. There were even a few pillows, and Christopher deposited her on one of them. Dustin glanced about, noticing that the two maids were at the far end, surrounded by their belongings.

Dustin turned back to her husband. "This is most comfortable, my lord," she said. "Did you really go through all this trouble for me? I could have just as easily rode Hercules."

He raised an eyebrow. "You mean that monstrous horse? We shall discuss him at a later time, wife. I am not at all comfortable with you astride that leggy beast, although the stable master assures me that the animal is as gentle as one of your rabbits when you ride him."

"He is gentle," she insisted. "And if you had doubts, why did you bring him along?"

"Because if I did not, you would be arguing with me just as you are now," he scowled at her, then flipped down his visor. "Make yourself comfortable, lady. 'Twill be a long ride until we stop for the night."

She fought off a smile. "Christopher," she beckoned him closer with her cocked finger.

He leaned down again. "What is it?"

Smiling now, she reached up and flipped up his visor, kissing him on the nose and then slamming his visor back down again.

"Nothing."

Underneath his closed visor, he was smiling broadly. He straightened again and shook his head at her. "Nymph," he muttered.

Dustin settled against the side of the wagon, feeling warm and dry as the rain poured all around her. Although she could not see him, she could hear Christopher giving orders and she sighed with satisfaction, looking forward to the days ahead.

☙

THE WEATHER WAS absolutely hellish. The closer they drew to London, the more thunder and lightning set in. Dustin alternately dozed and read in the wagon, very dry when the rest of the party was soaked and chilled to their very bones. A few times, she peered out from underneath the tarp to see if she could catch a glimpse of her husband, but the wagons were positioned midway in the column of soldiers and it was impossible to see the knights at the very front. Not particularly disturbed, she simply settled in for the ride and tried to keep herself occupied.

It was nearly the middle of the afternoon when the wagons halted and Dustin sat up expectantly, hearing orders echoing in the distance of a voice she knew to be Christopher's. She barely realized how excited she was to see him when suddenly he appeared beside her, his visor down on his massive helmet.

"How does my lady fare?" he demanded lightly.

Dustin's heart warmed. "Well, thank you, but I would like to stretch my legs a bit, if only for a moment."

"That can be arranged."

He held out a gloved hand to her and she placed her small hand in his, swinging her legs over the end of the wagon and standing on the mushy road. The other knights, all helmeted and looking quite alike, were suddenly standing around her and Christopher.

"The men are seeking shelter, as ordered," David said. "Thank God for all of these trees."

Christopher nodded. "At least it will provide them with some reprieve from the rain as they eat. As it is now, my wife and I will forge ahead and find our own bit of shelter."

Christopher took a bag from one of the soldiers and moved to pick up Dustin, but she balked. "Can I please walk? I have boots to protect my feet from the water."

He nodded, taking her hand instead and leading her into a big clump of trees. It was still damp, but they were clear from the driving rain under the heavy canopy.

Dustin stood eagerly while he opened the bag, she was famished. He handed her a wedge of cheese and chunk of bread and she accepted them happily. He watched her as she ate with gusto.

"How do you find the wagon?" he asked.

"Tiresome," she replied, glancing at him. "Can I please ride with you?"

He pulled off his helmet with a grunt of satisfaction, his blond hair wavy with moisture. "Nay, 'tis too wet still. I would have you ride dry in the wagon."

Dustin didn't even know what feminine wiles were, but she had a fierce load of them. She had seen her mother use soft words and actions to persuade her father, and it almost always worked. Mayhap if she used the same cunning on her own husband, he would allow her to ride up front with him and his knights. She was bored silly in the wagon.

She moved over and casually brushed up against him. When he looked away from the bread in his hand, she smiled sweetly. "Please, Christopher, allow me to ride with you and your men? I… I miss you."

He stopped chewing, gazing back into her gray eyes with some surprise.

"You do?" he managed to ask.

"Aye." She thought about it now, realizing it was true. "Aye, I do. Can I please ride with you?"

He swallowed his bite. He would like nothing better than to have her ride with him, better still, literally ride in front of him. But he was soaked through and he knew she would become, too, if she rode in the open.

"Dustin, 'tis far too wet," he said gently. "I must insist that you ride in the wagon."

Miffed, she turned away from him and he was remorseful that he had denied her request. Yet, for her own health, he knew he must.

"Do not move away from me," he ordered softly. "Come back."

"Nay," she snapped. "I will not."

He reached out a long arm and grabbed her, pulling her back against him. She gasped at the swiftness of his action, her eyes wide and irritated at him. Yet the eyes that gazed back at her were soft and warm. "Tell me you miss me again."

"Nay," she said firmly.

A smile played on his lips. "Tell me."

She tried to pull free but only succeeded in being held even tighter. "I won't. One time is all you will hear."

He leaned in, brushing her cheek with his rapidly filling-in beard. "Tell me, or I will scratch you to death."

She felt the giggles rising, the beginnings of a game afoot. "Torture me with fire and stone, my lord, but I will never utter those words to you again."

"You will," his voice was soft and seductive. "Tell me you miss me, wife."

His beard was scratching her neck, sending chills up her back and she struggled to pull away from him. "Never," she vowed with a smile on her lips.

"You stubborn creature, tell me," he insisted, his breath hot on her ear.

She pushed hard against his breastplate, managing to put a miniscule amount of distance between them. "I would hear the words from you, then, my lord."

He suddenly pulled back, looking quite serious. "Nay, for it would be untrue."

Her mirth drained and her mouth went agape. "What? You mean to tell me that you do not miss me?"

"Nay," he said callously, looking over at his food as if he suddenly remembered it were still there. "Men do not miss their wives. Their wives miss them because it is right that they should."

"Oh!" she gasped in outrage, slapping his hands from her. She managed to pull free from one hand and was staunchly fighting the other when he suddenly yanked her back to him again, so close that his face was a mere inch from her own. Dustin swallowed hard, suddenly forgetting her anger as his eyes bore into her.

"Where is your sense of humor, Lady de Lohr?" he whispered raggedly. "Of course I miss you. I ache for you. Why do you think I halted the column? My men need no rest. I did it so that I would be able to see you."

A twinkle crept into her eye and her arms found their way around his neck of mail and armor. "You are an arrogant man, husband," she said. "The most arrogant I have ever met. And cruel, too."

He raised an eyebrow, holding her bundled body against his own. "Arrogant, absolutely. Cruel, mayhap. Christ, you weigh as much as a horse in all of this material."

"Good," she said with a smirk, knowing the dresses were indeed heavy, but with this man's strength, they were practically nothing. "I hope I break your arms. Now, will you reconsider letting me ride with you?"

"Nay," he said flatly.

Dustin didn't want to hear that word, she didn't like it. She pulled herself up, closer to him, and began to pepper his face with quick, hot kisses. "Please?" she kissed. "Please, and again, p*lease?*"

He started to return her kisses when his better sense grabbed him and he put his hands up to stop her. "Dustin," he snapped, exasperated. "I said no. Do not harass me."

She latched onto his earlobe, sucking it as he had suckled her nipples, simply because the action seemed erotic. "Please?"

Christ, sucking his earlobe nearly undid him. Had he possessed any less control, he would have thrown her to the ground and bedded her right there. Her hot little mouth would be his undoing, he knew it, for all he could think of was that same pink orifice on his manhood and he shuddered, trying desperately to bring himself back to the world at hand.

"Dustin," he murmured, yet his arms were holding her fiercely. "Cease immediately."

"Only if you allow me to ride with you," she whispered, hot, into his ear.

He shuddered again, the exquisite torture too much and he knew she had won her battle. "Very well," he relented. "Now cease at once."

She released his earlobe and smiled broadly at him, her lips red from the activity. He rolled his eyes and kissed her hard.

"Do not ever do that again," he said against her mouth. " 'Tis a whore's trick to use sex to gain your own end."

She looked blankly at him and he knew she had no idea what he was talking about. "But you said I could ride with you," she said.

There was no use arguing the point, at least not now. But he would have to educate her soon, for the power she held over him even now was overwhelming. Should she learn to use that power intelligently, he would be as much as mud in her hands. It was a frightening thought.

He lowered her to the ground, helping her secure the hood of her cloak before putting his helmet back on. Then he looked sternly at her. "Well, come, wife. But if you soak to the skin, I do not want to hear a word of complaint."

"I promise, not a word," she said, biting her lip to keep from grinning. "Thank you for your graciousness, my lord."

He snorted in reply, gathering the empty bag and leading her carefully out of the trees and back into the harsh rain.

Dustin stood with David and Leeton as Christopher ordered Hercules brought forth. The warmblood was as tall as the destriers, his big brown eyes soft and liquid. Dustin went to the animal, hugging his great head and the horse pressed into her. Christopher shook his head faintly; she treated the horse just like she treated that damnable cat.

She moved around to mount and Christopher held out his hands to act as her boost. Putting her left knee into the sling of his interlaced fingers, she propelled herself up onto the animal and immediately swung her right leg over the pommel of the saddle. Even with all of the skirts and undergarment, Christopher saw that she was riding astride, as a man does.

He scowled in disbelief. "What are you doing?"

She looked completely innocent. "What do you mean?"

"Dustin," he lowered his voice. "I realize that you are used to riding astride, but you will not ride that way today. Both legs on the left, please."

She stared back at him, but she was already complying. "But 'tis easier for me to ride him astride. Hercules is used to me riding him that way."

"That may well be, but you will ride as a proper lady in the company of my men," his voice was low and patient. "You are my wife and I will not allow you to be seen in such an indecent position."

She honestly could not fathom his outrage, yet she knew that true ladies did not ride astride. Nodding compliantly, she tried to position herself comfortably and gathered her reins. With a lingering look, Christopher lowered his visor and moved to his own mount.

When the column moved forward, Hercules turned from a docile creature into a snorting, dancing beast that tried to throw his mistress off every few steps. Dustin struggled with the animal, shortening his reins tightly to give him less of a chance to throw his head around and to give her better control. Even as the big animal fought and grunted, she remained very much in control and rode him quite ably. Christopher and the others watched her closely, quite concerned for her safety, but were nonetheless very impressed by her skill.

"What's wrong with him?" her husband demanded.

"He does not like the way I am riding," she told him between grunts of exertion. "He prefers me astride.

Christopher didn't answer, continuing to watch his wife closely and making sure he stayed clear of the flying hooves. After several minutes of fighting, Dustin finally pulled the animal to a halt.

"Do you have a strip of leather I can use?" she asked, bailing from the animal and stroking his frothing nose. "Three feet or so should be enough."

David dismounted his steed and fumbled around in his saddlebags. He drew forth a length of rolled leather and handed it to her. Holding the horse's head still as she tied the leather onto the chinstrap of the bridle, Dustin ran it between his front legs and secured it to the cinch of the saddle. The knights watched her work quickly and expertly, tying a knot as well as any man. When she was done, she stood back and tested the strength and length of the leather.

"That should do well enough," she said, motioning to David to help her mount.

Christopher moved the company forward again. As before, Hercules danced and snorted and did fancy little sidesteps, but the strap she had secured under his chin kept him from throwing his head wild, saving Dustin's strength and her hands and actually calming the horse a bit. When she was sure the steed was somewhat under control, she glanced up at her husband and saw that he was looking at her, although she could not see his face. She smiled anyway.

Christopher was quite amazed with his little wife's skill with the horse. She was such a paradox to him; sweet and feminine and more sensual than any woman he had ever known, and yet she could ride better than most men and she could fight like a ruffian. And the most wonderful thing was, he realized, that she belonged to him. He told her once that he would know everything about her but he wondered if he ever truly would.

The rain was steady and they rode until after nightfall, when they came upon a small inn that looked as if it was leaning somewhat to the left. Everything sloped sideways. But it was presumably warm and dry. Christopher dismounted, ordering his men to set up a camp in the meadow adjacent to the inn, and made his way to his wife.

Dustin sat atop Hercules as David and the other knights saw to the men and to the horses. She smiled wanly at her husband as he approached and held up his hands to her. Wearily, she slid into them.

He lowered her to the ground, too busy making sure all was riding smoothly with his troops to notice much about her. He continued to give orders even as he opened the inn door for Dustin, finally quieting long enough to enter himself. He flipped up his visor, his blue eyes scanning the common room of the inn, which did not seem to lean as the outside structure would indicate. Smelling like unwashed bodies, the room was nonetheless dry. The innkeeper, a small man with a red face, dashed to greet his new guests.

"My lord, my lady," he said respectfully. "A room for ye on this miserable night?"

"Indeed," Christopher replied. "And for my knights as well. Three rooms should be adequate."

"Of course, my lord," the man glanced at Dustin. "And a bath for your wife?"

"She would be grateful," Christopher said as the maids were hustled in by Leeton. The door slammed once more and Christopher turned back to the innkeeper. "But now, we would eat."

The innkeeper looked at Dustin again and Christopher wondered what the man found so interesting about her other than her obvious beauty. He finally looked at his wife and was appalled to see how pale she was. And she was soaked to the skin.

"Christ," he murmured. "Bath now, man, food later. *Move.*"

The innkeeper jumped, yelling for his wife and for a bath to be prepared. Christopher put his arm around Dustin's shoulders, following the man up the stairs and to the right. He led them down two doors and into a small but comfortable room.

"The bath will be here shortly, my lord," the man said.

Christopher ripped off his gauntlets and set to removing Dustin's hood and cloak. "Feed my men when they come in," he ordered quietly. "My wife and I will take our meal in our room."

"As you wish, my lord," the innkeeper backed out and closed the door.

When he was gone, Christopher let out a hiss. "Dustin, why didn't you tell me you were wet through?"

Her teeth were chattering. "You….you told me no complaints."

He swore softly, pulling her wet cloak free and throwing it to the floor. "Take off your gloves, sweetheart," he said.

She held out her hands stiffly, looking somewhat embarrassed. "I can't. My hands are too cold."

He loosened the fingers of her right glove and pulled, startled when she let out a stifled cry. "What's wrong?" he asked.

She looked sheepish, embarrassed that she was causing so much concern. When she didn't reply, he gingerly pulled the glove free and saw her source of pain. Wrestling with the horse all afternoon had rendered her palms blistered, bloodied and raw. He clucked softly, examining her hands.

"Oh, Dustin," he murmured regretfully. "Why didn't you tell me?"

"Because you told me not to complain," she repeated. "Besides, I wanted to ride with you and the others. I do not like riding in the wagon."

He removed her other glove carefully, tossing it aside. There was a knock at the door and he went to open it, moving aside as a plump woman and three men brought in a large copper tub and began filling it with hot water. Dustin sank wearily on the nearest chair, waiting patiently while her bath was filled and wanting nothing more than to bathe and go to sleep. She was so exhausted that food had even lost its appeal.

An inn maid came in, bearing linen towels and a large bar of soap. Christopher could see that she expected to stay, but he sternly chased everyone out, bolting the door behind them.

"Stand up, sweet, let me get you out of that dress," he said, approaching her once more.

The dress, all the way down to the woolen shift, was wet. Her skin was pale and icy to the touch and he helped her into the tub, up to her neck in the hot water. The chill began to flee as she lay back, feeling her blood began to flow again. Reclining against the side of the tub, Dustin watched her husband remove his armor and the rest of his wet clothing, save his breeches. Then, he poured himself a cup of wine and faced her.

"Feeling better?" he asked.

She nodded. "Much. My blood is warming."

He nodded, taking a sip of wine before holding the cup to her lips. She took a healthy drink, thanking him with an appreciative look. He smiled and crouched next to the tub, his eyes grazing her.

"You will not be able to ride tomorrow with those hands," he said. "I shall bind them up tonight and tomorrow you can wear your gloves over the wounds to protect them."

Her face fell. "But I want to ride with you. I have ridden with my hands worse than this, and…"

"You can ride with me, sweetheart, in front of me," he put in, cutting her off. "Any woman who would withstand such vicious hardships on my behalf I would not dare deny."

Relieved, she took another sip of wine and he noticed that her cheeks were regaining their color. There was a knock at the door then, and he rose on his long legs.

"Who comes?" he demanded harshly.

" 'Tis us, milord," came an older female voice. "Your wife's maids."

He glanced at Dustin. "Are you content that I may go out and see to my men?"

She nodded. "Verily, husband. I feel much better now."

He smiled faintly. "Good. I shall return later."

"Can we sup downstairs, in the common room?" She sat up in the tub, looking eager.

His brows drew together. "What about your hands? And you must be exhausted, Dustin."

"Please?" she begged. "I have never supped at an inn before."

He put his hands on his hips. "There will be another time for that," he said. "Tonight we will sup in our room and go to bed early. I plan to be on the road to London before dawn."

Her expression went downcast but she didn't argue the point. He was sorry that he had to refuse her, but he believed it would be best if they kept to themselves. He had seen the way she became when she was around his knights. She demanded to be entertained and loved the company. He could only imagine that she would find a way to stay up all night if they supped in the common room with the various travelers. She wouldn't rest until she had talked to every one of them.

He opened the door for the maids and the two plump women bustled in, their arms laden with items for Dustin. He had one of the women help him on with his hauberk and he shook the water off his helmet before shoving it on. He paused, turning to his wife where she sat in the great tub, one woman drying her hair with a towel and the other scrubbing her right calf and foot with soap and a horsehair brush. Their eyes met and she smiled.

"I shall return shortly," he said, opening the door and closing it quickly behind him.

Dustin closed her eyes as the maid rubbed her head a bit too hard, yet her mind followed her husband back down the hall, down the stairs, and out into the elements. It was as if with every passing minute, she became more and more attached to him. If he were to suddenly leave her, she knew she would be utterly lost. She wondered if she clung to him because he was the only familiar person she had left and a recent acquaintance at that. But she also wondered if she clung to him because she felt more than simple fondness and comfort. Something told her it was much, much more.

Christopher returned to the inn almost two hours later, sputtering water and saturated through and through. David, Leeton and Edward followed close behind him, slamming the heavy inn door to block out the harsh climate. They stood for a moment shaking water off them as the innkeeper approached eagerly.

"Ready for your meal, good knights?" he asked anxiously.

Christopher nodded. "My knights will take their meal down here, but I will eat with my wife in our room."

"We're eating down here," Dustin said from the top of the stairs.

They all looked up at her as she descended the stairs, her damp blond hair flowing about her like a golden cape and dressed in a soft woolen surcoat of muted red. As simple as it was, it clung to her voluptuous form and Christopher was alternately admiring the picture she presented and highly irritated that she was disobeying his wishes. She approached him, the full skirt swirling about her and soaking up the water on the floor.

"Dustin, I told you we would eat in our room," he said evenly. Then he looked at his knights. "Take your meal."

"But I want to eat down here," she said, helping David remove the mail gloves he was struggling with. "Please, Chris? It is much nicer than our cramped little room, and besides, I have been having the most wonderful conversation with the serving girl," she pointed over her shoulder, "over there. Her name is Rachel."

Christopher flipped up his visor. "You have been in the common room conversing?"

"Aye, I have," she said, not registering his tone of voice. As she spoke, Christopher glanced around to the other occupants of the room. Three other knights sat at the far corner, partially obscured by the shadows. Three other tables were occupied by one or two men, most likely traveling merchants, but he was dismayed that his wife had been in the common room, unescorted, making a spectacle of herself. Her chatter roused him from his thoughts. "I ordered roast beef, and a beef and barley soup, and ale, and baked apples with honey and cinnamon. And do you know what else? The cook has a cat."

He looked at her, honestly stunned that she saw nothing wrong with her behavior. David, seeing his brother's reaction, put his hand protectively on Dustin's shoulder.

"Well and good, my lady," he said, eyeing his brother. "It sounds as if you have demanded a feast for us. Where would you have us sit?"

Dustin indicated a long table already set with trenchers and pitchers of ale. As she and the knights moved towards it, Christopher's shock moved to anger. He fought it down by telling himself that Dustin did not know of her transgression; he did not literally tell her that she could not go down into the common room. All he had told her was that they would eat in their rooms. She had disobeyed his wishes and for that, he would correct her. She was too headstrong for him to let it slide.

Dustin had just sat down as Christopher came up behind her and pulled her chair back out. Grasping her arm, he pulled her up to stand.

"We will take our meal in our room," he repeated the order she had already heard, glancing to his knights. "You gentlemen continue your meal and we shall see you on the morrow."

Dustin looked stricken. "But…but I…."

Firmly, he pulled her with him a step or two before the room was filled with a loud voice, directed at him.

"De Lohr, I have never known you to force a woman to do your bidding." The voice was deep and masculine. "What's wrong, Lion's Claw? Losing your touch with the fairer sex?"

Christopher's expression never wavered, but David, Leeton, and Edward stood immediately, hands on the hilts of their swords. Dustin's eyes were wide, for she could sense the tension in the men. Christopher's grip on her tightened.

"Show yourself," Christopher demanded steadily.

"In good time," the man said casually. "I cannot believe you do not recognize my voice, old man. You should. You heard it every day for three years."

Christopher didn't look overly worried, but Dustin was growing terrified. He let go of his wife and moved closer to the man and his two companions. His manner was steady but his body was coiled, his hand close to the hilt of his sword.

"I could scarce believe when you called that exquisite creature your wife," the man continued. "How in the hell did you get to be so fortunate? I have been watching her for the better part of an hour and I can tell you, she is beyond believing. Where did you find her and, more importantly, does she have any sisters?"

Christopher's eyes glittered, his jaw was twitching underneath his beard. "Show yourself, bastard, or I shall cut your heart out."

After an eternal pause, the man rose on long, muscular legs. He straightened his armor, taking his time about it, before stepping forward into the light.

Christopher was prepared to run the man through when the light fell on his face. Christopher's eyes widened.

"Burton!" he gasped in surprise. A smile crossed his face, with relief, and he took the extended hand in greeting. "Marcus Burton. What in the hell are you doing here?"

Sir Marcus Burton shook his liege's hand happily, his handsome face split in two with a wide smile.

"Coming to see you," he replied. "I was told your new seat is Lioncross Abbey."

"Indeed it is," Christopher said, his eyes twinkling warmly. "Christ, are you a sight. Come and greet my brother and my wife."

Marcus followed Christopher to the table, greeting David with a slap to the head and punching Edward in the chest. He knew Leeton vaguely and greeted him civilly, yet when his eyes fell on Dustin, his manner seemed to grow warm and serious. Piercing blue eyes gazed upon her, the color of cobalt, and he had chiseled features with a crown of cropped black hair. Big and muscular, he was extremely handsome. The cobalt blue eyes were intense as Christopher introduced them.

"Marcus, the woman you have been lusting after is my wife, Lady Dustin de Lohr," Christopher said as he drew her forward. "Dustin, this is my closest friend, Sir Marcus Burton."

Marcus ripped off a mailed glove and took Dustin's hand, bringing it to his lips. "My lady is too lovely for words," he said smoothly. "Forgive my boldness, but you were indeed a pleasure to watch. Since I saw the baron leave to attend to his men, I found myself your personal protector should any of these merchants be foolish enough to force their attentions."

Dustin blushed deeply as he kissed her hand, smiling when Christopher snatched it away. Marcus laughed. "Since when are you so damn possessive over a woman?" he snorted. "Jesus, Chris, with all of the woman that fawn over you...."

Christopher cleared his throat loudly. "They aren't my wife," he said, giving Marcus a quelling look. "Lady Dustin is, and I appreciated you watching over her while I was indisposed."

"My pleasure," Marcus said, his eyes once again on Dustin. "She needs watching over. Is she as disobedient as I gather she is?"

Dustin flushed pink, wishing he would stop looking at her as if she was a prize mare. Christopher looked at her, too, but with a reproving gaze.

"She is learning," he said. "She is better than she was."

The other knights were sitting down and Marcus drew up a chair. Christopher, reluctantly, sat as well, drawing Dustin down beside him.

"Tell me, Chris," Marcus said as David and the other two began to chow down the food. "Where did you meet her? You have only been in England a week. Was she waiting for you? You never mentioned that you were betrothed."

Christopher removed his helmet, running a hand through his blond hair. "Dustin is Sir Arthur Barringdon's daughter," he said. "She, and Lioncross, were a gift from Richard."

Marcus nodded in understanding. "Ah, yes, Arthur was dying when I left," he said softly. "The old man thought a good deal of you, Chris. So you married his daughter and gained the keep? An excellent arrangement. However, if I had known Arthur's daughter was such a beauty, I would have vied for her myself."

He was talking about Dustin as if she weren't even there and it irritated her. Since Christopher wasn't eating, she didn't either. She kept glancing at David as he gnawed away on a large beefy knuckle. He would glance at her every so often and smile.

Christopher didn't like Marcus' callous attitude, either. But Marcus was deeply acquainted with the Christopher before Dustin, the Christopher who would use woman for his own pleasure and who considered them no more than a necessary nuisance. But this Christopher was disturbed by the references to his wife, and he was unnerved that Marcus' words should upset him so. He felt unbalanced.

"I take it, then, you were coming to Lioncross to be in my service?" Christopher said, changing the subject.

Marcus smiled. "Absolutely, my lord. I would serve no other, except our glorious Richard, of course."

Christopher smiled faintly. "I am pleased. Who are your vassals?"

Marcus glanced over his shoulder to the two knights sitting in the corner. "The younger one is my cousin, Sir Trent Burton, and the other is Sir Thomas Dudley."

"Is that Dud?" Christopher studied the dark form in the corner. "Christ, I did not recognize him. He looks years older from when I last saw him on the sands of the Holy Land."

"He is," Marcus chortled. "But he, and my cousin, wish to serve you also if you will indeed have us."

Christopher looked as if he was thinking it over. "Very well," he said finally. "I shall take you and Dud on, but I will have to see Sir Trent in action before I can accept his oath."

"He has a good deal of skill and strength," Marcus assured him. "Now tell me, Chris; where are you traveling to?"

"To London," Christopher said, and his mirth faded. Marcus knew nothing of Richard's directive and here was certainly not the place to inform him. "You are coming with me."

"As ordered, my lord." Marcus did not look pleased, but held his tongue. He was far too wise to run off at the mouth in public.

Since they could not delve into the subject at the moment, Christopher relented and ordered his and his wife's trenchers filled, and they ate while conversation bounced about the table. Sir Thomas and Sir Trent joined them eventually, and Dustin was once again fascinated by the tales of the Holy Land. Sir Marcus was the consummate storyteller, but he always focused on her when he talked and she was uncomfortable with his attention. He reminded her of the honeyed-word fools that used to call on her.

She lost track of time listening to the men. When the food was finished and the plates had been cleared, she was still caught up in the stories. Marcus was in the middle of a particularly harrowing tale when the front door to the inn blew open in a crash of rain and weather and noise. Everyone turned to see several men in armor and mail storm in, filling up the room with their presence.

Dustin caught her husband's body language as he stiffened, as did the rest of the knights at their table. She was apprehensive, wondering why the men had suddenly gone on guard.

The knights that had entered the small inn were loud and rough, shoving and cursing each other as they made their way wearily to one of the worn eating tables. They demanded ale and food loudly, sending the innkeeper and the serving wench running.

Plates of food were brought to them and pitchers of drink. They dripped water all over the floor and in little time bones and bits of slop were falling to the ground as they began to eat. They were extremely loud and rambunctious, and Dustin eyed them distastefully.

"Pigs," she muttered.

Christopher did not want his wife in the same room as these hardened men. There was something unpredictable about them. The sooner he returned her to their room and bolted the door, the better.

"David, you and Leeton will escort my wife to our room," he said in a low, even voice. "One of you stay with her and bolt the door. I shall be up shortly."

David rose, pulling Dustin's chair out as Leeton came around and took her arm. Dustin glanced at her husband with concern, not understanding why he seemed so on edge, but he patted her arm.

"Go on up, sweet," he said quietly. "I shall be along."

A knight at the other table pinched the serving girl as she poured one man a cupful of ale, forcing her to cry out with pain. The men laughed and one of them did it again as the woman struggled to pull away from them. But they wouldn't let her go, like a cat in a snare, and they began to grab parts of her body that were sensitive and personal.

The serving wench was in a panic and Dustin looked to Christopher and his men to see if one of them would move to aid the wench. No one did. Frustrated, Dustin was about to say something to David but a cry from the serving woman interrupted her. The knights were starting to stick their hands up her skirt. Dustin, unable to control her mouth, burst out angrily.

"Leave her alone, you pigs," she snapped. "Keep your fat, filthy hands off of her!"

The entire table of knights turned to her, their anger quickly turning into open appraisal of the serving woman's defender.

"Come over here, wench, and I shall put my fat and filthy hands all over you," one man said and the entire table roared with approval. "God, you are a lovely little chit. Good knights, pray be kind to her. I should like to have your leftovers when you are finished."

Christopher got up, as did the rest of his knights. Huge and powerful and imposing, he rushed to the other table of men in less than a second, his sword drawn. He knocked one man who leapt up clear across another table, grabbing the offending knight by his armor and slamming him to the ground.

Everyone was shouting and bellowing, the sounds of swords being unsheathed filling the warm, stale air. Dustin lunged for the serving girl, pulling her out of the way as Leeton grabbed them both. David left them to plunge feet-first into the blossoming melee, sword in hand.

Leeton jerked her halfway up the flight of stairs when she realized that the skirmish had turned into an out-and-out brawl. She clung to the bannister as Leeton yanked at her, watching her husband beat the senses out of some hapless fool. She should have been mortified, but instead, she was mesmerized and strangely energized by the sight. She knew Leeton was trying to remove her, but she just didn't want to go. She wanted to see the fight, and help if she could.

"Give it to him, Chris!" she yelled, ignoring Leeton's tugs. "Beat him!"

Suddenly, a knight charged at her and Leeton thrust himself forward, kicking the man in the face and sending him tumbling back down the stairs. Dustin crowed triumphantly.

"That will teach you, you bastard," she said, clapping her hands.

Leeton looked at her with amusement and horror, a strange expression indeed. "My lady, you will come with me now or I will carry you."

She opened her mouth to reply when another knight was bearing down upon them. Dustin, gripping the railing, kicked the man squarely in the chest plate and sent him rolling, pleased with her handiwork. Shocked, Leeton didn't know whether to laugh or spank her. He could not believe what he was seeing, and he could not believe he was allowing it to go on.

The brawl transformed from a fistfight to a swordfight, and the air was full of the sounds of metal on metal. Dustin knew that the fight had gone beyond her, and she reluctantly followed Leeton up the stairs, watching what was going on over her shoulder. She could see Christopher engaged with a rather large man, their swords hitting so hard that sparks flew. David, Edward, and Marcus were involved in their own vicious battles, but Dustin's eyes were on her husband.

Christopher swung the sword with incredible confidence and power. He easily dispatched two of the men before kicking over a large table and marching over it to assist his brother. With David's opponent gored, it was no time before the hostile knights collected and turned tail, dragging their wounded comrades with them. As quickly as it started, the battle ended, and Christopher slammed the inn door behind the retreaters so hard that the entire building shook.

He was winded, but not because he was tired. He was so damn angry that he shoved his sword back in its scabbard hard enough to drive the tip through the reinforced end. His gaze went to his wife, standing at the top of the stairs with Leeton a step or two below her, and pointed a massive finger.

"To the room!" he roared.

Dustin jumped, truly puzzled at his reaction. Her shock turned to anger. "Well, you don't have to *yell* about it."

Christopher didn't reply, but his jaw was ticking. Clenching and unclenching his fists, he made his way through the debris and took the stairs two at a time. Leeton gave him a wide berth as he came up on his wife, huffing and puffing, his cheeks flushed with fury.

"To the room, now, or I will spank you right here in front of everyone," he seethed.

Dustin's eyes widened and she obeyed, gathering her skirts and hustling down the hall. Christopher, pausing a moment to utter a prayer to God to give him patience, followed.

The knights heard the chamber door slam close upstairs, and silently they began to right fallen chairs and see to the broken tables. They were moving silently and efficiently when Leeton began to laugh. Edward glanced at the man as if he were crazy, but caught onto his mirth before he knew it, and he too began to choke with laughter. David chimed in with his high-pitched giggle, followed by Marcus and the others until the entire room was screaming with laughter.

"Why are you laughing?" the innkeeper implored, devastated by the sight of his common room.

David wiped his eyes. "Because my brother has married a troublemaker and he is too besotted to notice."

"He notices," Edward corrected him. "But he chooses not to care."

☙

UPSTAIRS, CHRISTOPHER SLAMMED the door and bolted it as Dustin ran to the other side of the room, her eyes wide. He ripped off his helmet and tossed it aside, unbuckling his sword and scabbard and letting them clatter to the floor. Dustin watched his angry, jerky movements apprehensively.

"Are you going to spank me?" she asked fearfully.

He didn't look at her as his breast plate fell heavily to the floor and he ripped off his hauberk. "God knows I should," he muttered angrily. "I should spank you so hard that you blister, but then you wouldn't be able to travel to London. Hell, it would serve you right if I left you here."

Her big gray eyes filled with hot tears. "You wouldn't, would you?"

His head came up and he tried not to be swayed by the tears. "I should."

Her lower lip quivered. "I am sorry. I did not mean to start the fight."

He took a cleansing breath, calming his boiling blood. Her tears were cooling his fury. "You didn't start the fight," he struggled to stay calm. "But you know you should have left with Leeton. He was trying to be gentle in removing you. Next time I will give him permission to manhandle you like a sack of oats."

She blinked her tears away. "But I was in no danger on the stairs. I wanted to watch you fight."

"Why?" he implored. "In God's name, why, Dustin? Leeton was trying to get you to safety."

She could not answer him. Instead, she sat on the edge of the bed and pouted. He marched over to her, his massive hands resting on his hips.

"Listen to me well, lady, for I will not repeat this," he said lowly. "You will always do what is asked of you, without question or hesitation. You could have been in great danger in there. What if Leeton had been felled somehow and you had been at the mercy of one of those cretins? Would you have my attention divided in a swordfight so that instead of focusing on my opponent, I am worrying about you, giving my enemy an opportunity to gut me? I do not give you orders to hear my own voice, my lady. I do it because I know what is best for you. You will never again disobey nor question me, or so help me I will lock you in a room at Lioncross and throw away the key."

Dustin hung her head, completely remorseful. "I am sorry, Christopher. I…I did not think."

"I know you did not," he said harshly. "That is your problem, which is why I think for you."

Her head snapped up to him and he caught a flash of resentment. "Not in every matter, husband. I can think well for myself."

"Dustin!" he snapped, smacking a balled fist into his hand. But he forced himself to calm, turning away from her in agitation. "I am not arguing your ability to think for yourself, but you are a naive woman. You must trust me with your safety, and with other important matters. I am smarter than you are."

Her mouth opened in outrage, but wisely, said nothing. She stood up and unfastened her surcoat, allowing the garment to fall to her feet. Angrily, she tore off the woolen boots and woolen hose and kicked everything into a big pile. Then she moved to the huge bed and yanked back the coverlet, settling herself with loud, furious movements before jerking the covers back over her.

Christopher watched her, knowing how hard it was for her to bite her tongue. But he was right and she knew it.

"So that is it?" he said. "Not even a thank you for saving your virtue?"

Her blond head came up, her hair tousled wildly and her face red with fury. "Oh… go to… go sleep with your knights."

Her anger amused him, but he kept his humor banked. "Very well, then, you ungrateful creature, next time I shall let any man who pleases ravage you."

She brushed the hair from her face in outrage. "Just let them try. I shall drive their nose clear through their brain." She sat up, her anger gaining speed. "And I didn't need you to protect me, anyway. I do just fine by myself, or do I have to wield a pick axe to remind you?"

"You do not," he said, calmer now. "And you do need me, lady, whether or not you care to admit it."

She let out a grunt of frustration and fell back onto the bed, beating her pillow to make it comfortable. She was far too angry to respond, another word from him would have her throwing things, and she remembered what happened the last time she did that. So she chose to ignore him.

Christopher was nearly sedate again. He proceeded to remove his boots, breeches, and tunic, laying them on a frame by the fire to dry them out, and snuffed out the candle. Nude, he climbed in bed next to his wife's stiff body. They lay there in the darkness, listening to the rain, for a long while.

"How are your hands?" he asked.

"Fine," she snapped.

He sighed. "I should wrap them."

"Nay," she said harshly. "I do not want your help. I do not need it. I want to go home."

"Fine," he said shortly. "I shall send you home tomorrow. You cause too much trouble."

She rolled over, looking at his profile in the dim light. He was staring straight up at the ceiling.

"Fine," she agreed angrily. "I do not want to be where I am not wanted. Mayhap I shall petition the church for an annulment, and since you think I am too much trouble, I am sure you will not contest it. You can keep Lioncross and I shall marry somebody else, somebody who will treat me as an equal."

"And who would that be?"

She didn't know, but she thought quickly and blurted the first name that came to mind. "Jeffrey."

He turned to her in the darkness. "Kessler? Hell, he wouldn't know what to do with you."

Her anger was turning into hurt, and she rolled back over on her side away from him. "He loves me and would treat me well."

He flipped her onto her back, his angry face looming over her. "Did he tell you that?"

His big body was halfway covering her, and his huge hands were gripping her forearms. She was forced to admit that she was intimidated.

"Of course not," she said softly. "But I have heard the talk; I know what the men say."

He studied her in the light of the distant fire and his grip eased, turning soft and caressing. "Yet you do not return these feelings."

She shook her head. "Nay, husband, I only care for you," she murmured, then scowled. "Even if you are cruel and demanding and harsh."

He raised an eyebrow, but already she could see his gaze softening. "I am what you dictate, lady," he said. "Were you not so stubborn and willful and mischievous, I would not have to be severe with you."

The tenderness in his eyes filled her with warmth and awakening passion. She pulled her arm free of his grasp and ran her fingers through his hair. "Why did you attack that knight?"

"Why do you think? He insulted you and I could not allow that to go unpunished," he said firmly.

"But I yelled at him first," she reminded him, tracing her finger along his jawline.

He let out a long sigh. "You did, but no matter. You were defending the serving wench, which is admirable."

The mood between them quickly moved from irritation to desire. He reached up and pulled her hand away from his head, studying her blistered palm. "I really should bandage your hands, Dustin."

"Did you hurt your hands punching that man?" She turned the tables on him, looking at his knuckles. "You hit him very hard."

He shrugged. "My hands are fine," he said, looking at her again. "I saw you kick that soldier in the chest. Damnation, you are a ruffian."

She flashed a quick, embarrassed smile, moving both hands to his head, touching him tenderly. She didn't want to talk about it anymore, for she knew she had been wrong in nearly every way and he had done what had been necessary to protect her.

"Chris?" she asked softly.

"Hmm?" he closed his eyes to her touch.

"Are you really going to send me home?" she asked.

He opened his eyes. "Are you really going to divorce me?"

She grinned and giggled, "No."

"Then I won't send you back," he said, leaning down to nuzzle her neck.

His beard was scratchy and his breath warm and she began to melt against him. "Am I really a troublemaker?"

"The worst." His voice was husky as he gently kissed her neck, her shoulders.

She didn't say any more, giving herself over to him completely as his mouth caressed her gently at first, then more insistently. He had her lift her arms at one point so that he could remove her woolen shift, which then landed on the floor next to her surcoat and boots. He stopped a moment to gaze at her sweet body in the flicker of the firelight. She watched his face, shuddering as he ran his finger lightly down her torso.

"You are so beautiful," he murmured.

His voice was rich and seductive. She hated sweet words; she'd always hated them. But hearing them from his mouth meant something to her. As he bent down to kiss her again, she put her fingers up to his lips.

"Tell me more," she whispered.

His eyes glowed and he gave her a cocky sort of grin. "You are the most beautiful, sweet, luscious woman I have ever seen. Your eyes capture my heart and soul, Dustin," he said, gathering her closer to him, kissing her again. "You are as perfect as I am."

"More so," she whispered into his hair as he dragged his mouth over her chest.

"Aye, more so," he agreed, not wanting to talk anymore. He simply wanted to make love to her.

His manner was more urgent this night as the storm raged outside. He suckled her harder and his hands were more insistent than they had been, but she responded to him openly, matching his passion. His large hand stroked her tender folds, playing with her, arousing her juices. He put two fingers in her and she moaned, pulling at his hair.

"Christ, you are wet," he breathed.

"What does that mean?" she gasped.

He grinned, removing his fingers and placing his organ against her. "It means that your body wants me, sweetheart. It means that you want me to make love to you."

She nodded wildly. "Aye, I do."

He pushed himself up on his arms so he could look down at her and watch her body respond to him. When she brought her legs up, he pushed hard and drove into her in one thrust.

Dustin cried out softly, clutching at his hard buttocks. She felt his muscles contract as he thrust into her and it excited her terribly.

Christopher was riding on a haze of desire, driving into his wife as he had never made love before, watching her nipples harden in response to him. Aye, he desired her, lusted for her, but his actions this night were not limited to those emotions. He wanted to show his affection for her, to show her without words how deeply he was coming to care for her. He wanted her to care for him as much as he was coming to adore her. And he was rapidly coming to adore her, in spite of everything.

They achieved their pleasure together in a surge of contractions and emotions, with Dustin clinging to him and gasping so hard he thought she might be crying. But she wasn't crying, merely overcome with the newness of the sensations he was creating within her. He liked awakening her desire.

They lay together in the dark room, only the sound of the rain as it beat against the building. Christopher's lips rested on her forehead, his eyes staring into the darkness as he wondered how this little fireball of a woman managed to embed herself under his skin.

Dustin fell asleep in his arms, curled up against him like a kitten. As much as he wanted to join her in slumber, he had to go find Marcus and find out what the man knew. He was disturbed by the fact that Marcus had returned from the north quickly, which could only mean one thing, the lines were drawn quite decisively in either Richard's or John's favor. He must know what he was up against.

Leaving his wife tucked in with mounds of coverlets, he quietly donned his clothing and strapped on his sword and went to find Marcus.

Leeton was still downstairs, staring moodily into his cup of ale. Christopher strolled up beside him, wondering why he had not retired yet.

"You are still up?" he asked Leeton.

The big knight turned ale-sotted eyes to his liege. "Aye, still."

Christopher could see the man's moody expression and he knew why. Leeton drank too much and he was forever emotional about Rachel. "Go to bed, Leeton," he said quietly. "We leave before dawn and I need you alert."

Leeton sighed, belched, and set down the cup. "You know, Chris, it's on nights like these that I miss her the most," he said softly. "Rachel always loved the rain; in fact, she liked to run around in it and was forever catching a chill. And when I saw your wife tonight, the way she acted with spirit and with determination, it reminded me of Rachel again. Sometimes I think my grief will consume me."

Christopher patted his friend's shoulder gently, not knowing how to reply. Leeton stood up, weaving unsteadily.

"Will it ever go away, Chris?" he whispered beseechingly. "Or will I go to my grave with this agony in my heart?"

"It will fade, with time," Christopher replied quietly. "All memories fade with time."

"But if something were to happen to Dustin, would you be able to go on with your life as if she never existed?" Leeton pressed.

Christopher gazed back at him with uncertainty. "Of course not, but things are different with Dustin. You married Rachel because you loved her. I married Dustin because I had to."

"But you care for her, I know you do," Leeton said. "I have seen the way you are with her, and I'd venture to say that you are growing to love your wife. If she were to die, could you live with it?"

Christopher was growing increasingly off balance. "Go to bed, Leeton."

Leeton reached out and grabbed Christopher by his tunic, his drunk eyes awash with sorrow. "Sometimes I can't stand it anymore. I want to die."

Christopher snatched his friend's armor, giving him a firm shake. "You will not think that way, do you hear? You have a son to live for, Leeton. Do you think Rachel would approve of the way you are wallowing in self-pity, leaving your son to be raised by his grandparents?" He shook Leeton again, forcing the man to look at him. "Come to grips with yourself, man, or you are of no use to anyone."

Leeton stared back at his liege, his tears fading and his body going limp. "If it were Dustin, could you come to grips with it? What if she bore you a son that was the image of her and every time you looked at him, you felt your grief run fresh? Can you honestly tell me that you would ever be the same man again?"

Their blue eyes met with ferocious intensity, reading into each other's minds. Christopher was fully prepared to deny everything that had just been asked of him, but found in his heart that he could not. He released his hold on Leeton.

"Nay," he replied simply. "I would not be. Damnation, Leeton, since I married her, there are times when I do not even recognize myself. Now, go to bed. I will help you."

Christopher half-carried Leeton up the stairs to the chamber he shared with David. David, sound asleep and snoring loudly, was sprawled out over one small bed so Christopher sat Leeton down on the other. He undressed the man down to his breeches and pushed him back on the pillow.

He stood there a moment, gazing down at his once-mighty friend. So many thoughts were rolling through his head… is that what loving a woman did to a man? Sapping his will to live and destroying his soul? If that was the case, then Christopher wanted no part of it. He could not allow himself to love Dustin. Confused and frustrated, he quit the chamber.

Marcus was asleep in the next room. Christopher burst in, startling the man into brandishing his sword until he saw who his intruder was. Christopher smiled wryly and threw a tunic at him.

"Get up," he commanded softly. "We have much to discuss."

Marcus blinked, clearing his eyes as he sat up and pulled the woolen tunic over his head. He yawned. "So did you give your wife the lashing she deserved?"

"Tongue-lashing, yes," Christopher said, pouring himself a cup of wine. "I did spank her, once, but that was only because she gave me no choice."

Marcus chuckled. "Is she always that outspoken?" He was referring to her confrontation with the hostile knights.

Christopher drained his cup. "Always, Marcus," he said with weary irritation. "Arthur let her do anything she damn well pleased and never disciplined her in the least. Unfortunately, that left me with a job on my hands."

"Who cares?" Marcus stood up, easily as tall as Christopher. "If my wife were that beautiful, I would put up with a spoiled nature, too. It was a true pleasure to watch her earlier this evening as she spoke with the serving wench and the innkeeper. She is a lively one."

"Aye, she is." Christopher wanted to stop talking about his wife and get to the business at hand. "There is a stable outside. We will speak out there."

CHAPTER TEN

DUSTIN WOKE UP coughing. She sputtered and choked for a long time before finally sitting up in bed, rubbing her eyes. The fire in the hearth was a faint glow and she had no idea what time it was.

"Christopher?" she called softly.

She was answered with silence. Even the rain outside had lessened but she could still hear it. Coughing harder, she realized she was freezing and pulled the covers about her tighter, wondering where her husband was. She lay back down, trying to get comfortable, but then she was sweating and threw the covers off. A moment later, she was cold again. And then she was very thirsty.

She sat up in bed again and tossed the covers off, freezing, and ran to the pile of clothing that lay on the floor. With icy hands, she donned her woolen shift, red woolen dress, stockings and boots. She was so thirsty that she wanted to find a well or watered wine to slake it.

The corridor outside was quiet and she could hear faint snoring coming from somewhere. She walked silently down the hall to the staircase, shaking with chill as she went. Oddly, her palms were sweaty and her forehead was coated with perspiration, and she wondered if her strange condition had something to do with her wounded hands. Mayhap they had infected her somehow. Coughing again, she took the steps stiffly and wandered back into the kitchen.

There was a big wooden bucket on the counter with a ladle in it. Relieved, she took several large ladles of water, slurping the water. It felt cool to her parched throat and she wiped some on her hot face.

Then, she was so blasted hot again she could hardly stand it. The woolen dress was like a furnace, hot and cloying and restricting, and she was desperate to take it off or cool down any way she could. She was suffocating. Outside, the rain pelted the ground gently. *Cool rain.* Dustin threw open the door and stood out in the downpour, feeling the water cool her overheated body. She continued to stand there a few moments, coughing her lungs up and letting the cold water ease her.

"Dustin!" came a sharp voice behind her. "What in the hell are you doing?"

She turned to see David standing behind her, clad only in his boots and breeches. Astonished, he yanked her back inside.

"I am hot, David," she protested weakly. "And I was coughing, so I came downstairs to get a drink. Why are you up?"

"Because I heard you coughing," he informed her flatly. He put his hand up to her forehead, feeling her scorching cheeks. "Jesus Christ, you are burning up. You have a hell of a fever going."

She batted his hands away. "Stop that. I am not sick, 'tis this damn woolen dress. It is making me hot."

He cocked an eyebrow at her. "You are hot because you are ill," he said. "Where is Chris?"

"I don't know," she said softly, feeling weak and tired. "I woke up and he was gone. I don't know where he went."

David saw her sway and her lips went pale. He reached out and scooped her up, heavy wet dress and all. David wasn't near as tall as Chris, but he was wonderfully broad and muscular and smooth. Dustin, not feeling like fighting him, wrapped her arms around his neck and lay her head on his shoulder.

"I guess I do not feel very well," she admitted in a whisper.

"I can imagine," David said, trying to ignore just how sweet and soft she felt in his arms, carrying her through the common room and up the stairs. Her long hair licked at his skin and he found he deeply envied his brother his wife.

He kicked the door of her room open and carried her in. He set her on unsteady feet, but she was sopping wet and he knew he had to get her out of her clothes.

"Stay here, Dustin," he said softly, crossing the hall and throwing open a door. "Edward! Get out of bed and go find Chris."

Edward, dazed, rolled around in his bed. "What is wrong?"

"Dustin's taken ill," David said. "Find Chris. Mayhap he is in the camp somewhere."

Edward was up, donning his nearly-dry clothing. David retreated back into Dustin's room. He didn't want to undress her, but she was standing in the middle of the room, shaking like a leaf, and he knew he had to do something. He could not wait for Christopher to come and take care of her.

"Come on," he said softly. "Let's get you out of that dress."

Dustin didn't protest. David deftly undid the stays of her dress and peeled the wet garment from her. He then sat her down on the bed and removed her boots, biting his lip when he peeled off her stockings. Her legs were like silk. He was struggling with himself more than he ever had, because he knew without a doubt that Dustin was the most desirable woman he had ever come across, a woman that was unknowingly endearing herself to him. A woman who was his brother's wife.

Dustin remained clad in her damp shift, but David would go no further. He wasn't strong enough to remove the shift and he suspected his brother wouldn't take kindly to it, anyway. Dustin, still sitting on the bed with her wet hair, shivered violently and spurred David into another sort of action. He stoked the hearth until it was a roaring blaze then moved her over by the fire.

"Come and sit over here and dry out," he said.

He sat her in a chair right next to the fire, covering her legs with a thick blanket. Dustin, her eyes closed, sat and shivered. He stood back, wondering where in the hell his brother was and wondering why he could not have been offered Arthur Barringdon's daughter.

Several minutes later, Christopher charged into the room with Marcus on his heels. He was winded, having run from the stable yards at top speed when Edward found him and relayed David's message. His handsome face a mask of concern as his eyes fell on Dustin.

"What in the hell is wrong?" he demanded, falling to one knee beside her.

"She awoke coughing and went downstairs to find something to drink," David explained as Christopher felt her hot face. "I heard her coughing and followed her into the kitchens. By the time I got there, she was standing out in the rain being soaked."

"Out in the rain?" He cupped Dustin's warm face, forcing her to look at him. "Why were you in the rain, sweet?"

"She was hot," David answered for her. "I brought her back to your chamber and removed her dress, but her shift is still damp and she should probably take it off as well."

Christopher nodded, pulling the blanket off of her. "Thank you, David. I appreciate your assistance," he said. "One last thing, if you will; find the innkeeper and have his wife prepare a hot willow brew for her fever."

David was gone without a word. Christopher glanced at Marcus. "I fear our conversation is ended, for the moment," he said quietly.

Marcus nodded, his serious gaze on Dustin. "She cannot travel, Chris," he murmured. "She is too ill."

Christopher did not like the idea of leaving his wife behind, even if it be for only a day or two. He glanced down at her blond head.

"We shall see how she fares on the morrow," he replied.

Marcus shook his head. "Look at her, Chris. She will not be well enough to travel by dawn."

Christopher's head snapped to his friend, banking the surge of emotion he felt. "What would you suggest, then?" he demanded quietly. "I must be in London by the end of the week and I will not leave her here."

Marcus could see how agitated he was becoming. "I do not have to be in London by the end of the week," he said. "I can stay behind and tend her until she is well enough to travel. I do not think you have much of a choice."

Christopher looked at him for a long moment before gazing back at his wife. Dustin's bright eyes were turned to him.

"You would leave me here?" she whispered.

He sighed, stroking her damp head. "You are sick, sweetheart. I can't let you travel in this foul weather until you are well enough."

Her eyes welled up. "I do not want you to leave me."

Marcus discreetly vacated the room. Christopher stood his weeping wife on her feet and pulled off her shift before bundling her back up in the blanket and carrying her to bed. He removed his tunic and crawled in next to her, cradling her shaking body next to his.

"I do not want to leave you, but I have no choice," he whispered against her hair. "I have to leave for London tomorrow."

She pulled her arms free from the blanket and wound them tightly around his neck. "Please do not leave me, Chris."

He kissed her. "I do not want to, Dustin, you know I do not. Now go to sleep, my love. I shall watch over you 'til morning."

She calmed down a bit, snuggling against him and coughing. He held her tightly, yet his mind was reeling.

He had called her "*my love.*" Christ, what had he vowed just this evening? That love was a weakness and that he could not allow himself to love his wife, no matter what. He could care for her, like her, be fond of her, but he could not, *would* not, love her. It would kill him if he did.

Dustin sighed raggedly, shivering and coughing. His heart ached to see her ill. It was his fault; he should not have allowed her to get so wet and he felt terribly guilty. But he could not allow his concerns for her to override the more pressing concerns that were facing him in London. And after his conversation with Marcus, there were problems aplenty.

He never did manage to sleep that night.

☙

CHRISTOPHER WAS UP before dawn, dressed in full armor. The innkeeper's wife brought Dustin a brew of wine and herbs, and Christopher patiently coaxed an entire cupful down. Her fever was minimal, but she was coughing and sneezing and generally miserable, and he was deeply sorry that she would not be able to go with him that day. Dustin felt so rotten that in spite of her crying the night before, she didn't care one way or the other.

Christopher called a meeting with his knights in the common room; seven huge imposing men sitting around a rough oak table. The entire purpose of the meeting was to see who would stay behind with his wife until she was able to travel.

"I plan to leave twenty-five men-at-arms behind to serve as escort when my wife is well enough to travel," Christopher told his men. "Marcus has graciously volunteered to stay with her and I will accept his offer. However, I would like at least two more men to stay in addition."

"Did you have any one in mind?" David asked.

"Not you, little brother," he replied. "I want you with me. I would like to leave Dud and Edward, if that is acceptable."

Sir Thomas Dudley and Edward glanced at each other, nodding. "It is," said Edward.

Young Trent Burton, newly knighted last year, was honored and thrilled at the prospect of accompanying the Lion's Claw to London. According to Marcus, Christopher was the greatest knight who had ever held a sword. He looked forward to the opportunity to prove himself, suspecting that he had not been asked to guard the baron's wife because he was not yet trusted. That was fine with him, for he would rather serve the baron personally.

Christopher stood up. "It is decided," he said. "Edward, I do not want Dustin on the road unless the fever is completely gone and her symptoms have subsided, and do not let her convince you otherwise. Her powers of persuasion are great."

Edward had already seen much evidence of that. "Understood, my lord."

Christopher moved away from the group, confident that his wife's safety would be well-tended in his absence. "See to your duties," he told his men as he headed for the stairs. "I will say farewell to my wife and join you shortly."

The knights disbursed as Christopher took the stairs. He entered the bedchamber quietly, noting the innkeeper's wife as she sat beside the bed, watching Dustin sleep fitfully. Her two maids sat in the far corner with the soiled red woolen surcoat between them. All he did was motion to them and the room was cleared and the door closed. He went over to his wife, gazing down at her pale face and watching her labored breathing. He was so very sorry to be leaving her, but he trusted Marcus and Edward to take care of her.

He bent over and kissed her forehead, twice, and smoothed errant bits of hair away. Dustin sighed deeply and her eyes fluttered open.

"Greetings, husband," she stretched and coughed. "Are we leaving?"

He kissed her forehead again. "I am leaving, sweetheart, you are staying. Remember?" he said quietly. "But I shall see you in London in a few days."

She nodded sleepily and he wondered if she even understood what he was telling her. She seemed very groggy with the potion the innkeeper's wife had given her. "I am leaving Edward and Marcus here with you, and you will obey them implicitly. Do you understand me?"

"Obey, aye," she murmured, her eyes closing as sleep tried to reclaim her. "Chris?"

"What is it?" he whispered.

"I think I shall miss you," she muttered. "Will you miss me?"

She was speaking like a drunkard and he smiled faintly; it was rather humorous. "I will."

She smiled, eyes closed. "Do you know what else?"

"Nay," he whispered. "What else?"

"I think that I shall tell you I love you," she whispered, so softly he hardly heard it. "I love Caesar, I love my rabbits, I love my mother and father, and I love you, too. Did you know that?"

He was stunned. He didn't even know what to say so he simply shook his head. "Nay," he breathed. "I did not know that."

"Now you know."

He stared back at her, overwhelmed. Christ, did she even realize what she had said? She was sick and tired and filled with a good amount of wine, but did she even understand what those three little words meant?

He took a step back and stumbled, trying to get a grip on himself. Did she love him or was she simply running off at the mouth? He didn't know, but by God, he had to get the hell out of there and clear his mind. If she did indeed love him then it would be too easy for him to....he bolted from the room like his arse was on fire.

By the time he had reached the common room, he was in control again, at least outwardly. David was waiting for him.

"Are we ready?" Christopher demanded, slamming on his helmet.

"Aye, we are," his brother replied, then lowered his voice. "Chris, do you think it is such a good idea to leave Marcus in charge of Dustin? You saw how the man looked at her."

Christopher cocked an eyebrow. "I see how you look at her, and how every man in my command looks at her," he replied steadily. "I trust Marcus, David, as much as I trust you. He would never do anything so stupid as to forfeit his life."

David didn't reply. He was not keen on the idea of Marcus Burton protecting the lovely Lady Dustin, but any more words on the subject would make him appear *too* concerned. Christopher had already accused him of having feelings for her once and he would not do anything to further justify those suspicions.

Slamming down his visor, he followed his brother out into the rain.

ꝏ

THREE DAYS LATER Dustin was fit to be tied.

Her fever had dissipated the first day, and the cough and runny nose were practically gone. Her guard dogs, Edward and Marcus and Dud, never let her from their sight. She was not even allowed to go outside into the new sunshine.

She wondered how Christopher was faring. She was angry at him for not even saying goodbye to her and she would tell him that when given half a chance. But to do that, she had to get to London, and she decided on the morning of the fourth day that they would leave that morn. She was the baroness, wasn't she? And they were her vassals. Well, her husband's vassals, but nevertheless, they would do her bidding.

She dressed carefully in a burnished gold surcoat, one Rebecca had made, with a plunging neckline and long sleeves. She pulled the front of her long hair back and secured it at the back of her head with her ivory clip, and made sure the two maids packed everything into her trunks except the pretty brown cloak with the rabbit lining. She would wear it because even though the sun was shining and the birds were singing, it was still quite nippy outside. Winter was in full swing.

She found Marcus and Edward downstairs in the common room, playing some sort of card game. Squaring her shoulders, she marched down the stairs and made her way purposely to their table.

The two knights rose when she approached, their eyes grazing her appreciatively. "Lady de Lohr, a pleasure," Marcus said fondly.

She raised a dark brown eyebrow at him. "Marcus, I wish to go to London today. I am well and can travel, and I am sick of this little hovel. Can we go? Please?" She added the "please" purely for courtesy's sake so she didn't sound like a tyrant.

Marcus glanced at Edward, who was glad she had not focused her willfulness on him for once.

"Mayhap, my lady," he replied. "Are you sure you are feeling well? No more cough?"

She shook her head hard. "No more cough. I am as healthy as a fat baby."

Marcus sighed dubiously, glancing again at Edward for moral support, but was being ignored. He cleared his throat. "Very well, my lady. If you say you are well, then I shall take a lady's word. We will leave whenever you are ready."

She was fully prepared to argue with him, but his gracious acquiescence had her smiling. "I am ready now. Can we leave now?"

Marcus and Edward chuckled. "I suppose so," Marcus said. "Can Edward and I gather our things at least?"

She nodded happily. The knights put away their cards and Edward threw open the door of the inn.

"Dud," he called to the knight standing watch outside. "We leave within the hour. Move the men."

The innkeeper, hearing that his most loyal customers were preparing to leave, rushed to the kitchen. When he returned, he brought a plateful of delightful apricot and apple pastries, some glazed with honey. Dustin's eyes widened with delight and she downed the first gooey confection with glee. When she started on her second, Edward admonished her gently.

"Not too much, my lady," he said. "A full stomach and travel do not go well together ofttimes."

She made a face at him and shoved another bite in her mouth. "What you mean to say is that if I eat too many, I shall become as fat as a pig."

Both Marcus and Edward glanced at her voluptuous figure. She was neither thin nor plump, but in the perfect state in between. Her waist was pleasingly narrow, her hips generous and her breasts large and firm and round. Aye, she was a flawless handful for any man. Much better than those reed-thin, highbred noble wenches. Dustin reeked of health and life and sensuality.

"I would doubt you could ever become fat," Marcus said diplomatically.

Dustin shrugged, eating the last of the apricot pastry. "I suppose Chris would divorce me if I did become fat, or lock me away somewhere."

Marcus laughed. "Nay, he would not. I'd take you even then. I rather like round women."

She shoved him playfully and he missed the bite he was trying to put in his mouth, smearing it on his cheek instead. She laughed loudly at his misfortune until he turned to her and smeared the rest of the goo on her chin. She jumped back with a yelp, but her laughter overtook her and she was once again screaming with her delightful, happy laugh. Edward stepped back. If this deteriorated, he did not want to get caught in the crossfire.

It was as he feared. Dustin, seeking revenge, picked up an apple confection full of nuts and dates and charged Marcus, smashing the whole thing right into his face, even shoving nuts up his nose. He sputtered, alternately licking and wiping his face as Dustin laughed herself weak.

"If you were not my liege's wife, I would make you lick it off," he growled, although he was not angry in the least.

Edward shook his head. "I shall go find something to clean you two up with," he muttered, disappearing back into the kitchen.

Dustin was still giggling as Marcus sat down, wiping his face. There was one more pastry left and, unable to resist the temptation, she picked it up and pretended to eat it. Instead, she came around behind him and smashed the whole thing into his face.

Marcus' hands flew up and snatched her arms, yanking her so hard that she and the remainder of the pastry flew into his lap. They were both laughing and struggling with each other, not realizing that Dustin had landed in a very compromising position until it was too late.

Dustin was clutched to Marcus' chest, her face not an inch from his own goo-smeared one. His cobalt-blue eyes bore into her, as much from shock as from the excitement. Dustin's face grew very warm as she stared back into his eyes. She didn't know why she didn't pull away; it was as if he had somehow hypnotized her. She could not quite seem to tear her eyes away from him and the whole time her mind screamed of the impropriety of it. Christopher was her husband, this man was his vassal – she cared for Chris, not this man she had only known a matter of days.

But it was more than that. Dustin thought she was going insane, for she had known dozens of suitors and not one of them ever appealed to her. Then she married a man and grew to find him extremely attractive, and then on his heels comes another man she finds attractive, too. But it was of no matter; she knew right from wrong. Sitting on Marcus' lap was wrong and, awkwardly, she tried to climb off.

Unfortunately, Marcus had her tightly. She was too close, too beautiful, too tempting. Against his better judgment and all that he stood for, his lips descended on Dustin's, hard and forceful and firm. There was pastry everywhere on his face, now on hers, and Dustin yanked away from him, twisting free of his grip and stumbling several feet away. Somehow, she ended up on her feet, glaring at him.

Marcus could only look at her, his eyes as wide as her own. He could still scarcely believe what he had done.

Dustin stopped glaring and her eyes welled up with confused, frightened tears. "Marcus…," she breathed, tears spilling over. "How could you do that?"

Before he could find his tongue and apologize, she dashed up the stairs and he heard the door to her chamber slam. Edward reappeared out of the kitchen, holding a wet cloth.

"Where is Dustin?" he asked innocently, handing the linen to Marcus.

Marcus was still in shock. He accepted the cloth and wiped his face clean of the sticky mess. He was struggling to cover up his blunder.

"Up in her room, I suppose, gathering her things," he said, unable to look Edward in the eye.

But Edward was unaware of Marcus' manner. "Good," he said. "The sooner we get to London, the better. Chris must feel fairly exposed without his full complement of men."

Marcus didn't reply. He was anxious to get out of there. He set down the cloth and took the stairs to his own room to collect his belongings, leaving Edward to follow him in blissful ignorance.

☙

LATER ON THE road, Dustin was determined to ignore Marcus. She blamed him for what happened, yet in the same breath she blamed herself and her guilt was terrible. As they rode side by side along the road, she was pleased that he seemed to ignore her, too, and that allowed her to collect her thoughts.

Dustin was naive, but she wasn't scatterbrained. She accepted the fact that she found Marcus attractive, and she accepted the fact that she had grown to consider him a friend over the past few days. He had been kind and gentle and attentive to her needs, and she had inadvertently fallen victim to his charms.

But she missed Christopher terribly. She thought of him constantly and looked forward to the moment when they would be alone together again. When she thought of his hands on her, his hot mouth and scratchy beard, she went warm and liquid inside. The more she thought of Marcus and their kiss, the more she missed her husband. She knew everything would right itself once they were together again. She wondered if he had missed her, too.

She had been so caught up in her train of thought that she hadn't seen Marcus steer his destrier over to her until it was too late. She caught a glimpse of the dark-brown animal from the corner of her eye.

"My lady is quiet," Marcus said softly.

"I have nothing to say, my lord," she replied evenly. "I am trying to conserve my strength for the remainder of our journey."

He didn't say anything for a moment. "Dustin, I am sorry. I never meant...."

She jerked her head around, looking to see who might be around them. Edward and Dud were several yards back, talking between themselves, and the men-at-arms were behind them still. She and Marcus were quite alone where they rode.

"I do not wish to discuss this, Marcus," she hissed. "It happened. Leave it at that and we shall get along fine."

He sighed. "Aye, it happened, but I wanted you to know I was sorry. I never meant to do it. It just happened somehow."

She nodded curtly, her only reply. He watched her as the horses plodded along, her stiff back and taut features.

"Are you going to treat me like dirt for the rest of my life?" he asked, half in jest.

She turned to him in irritation, her gray eyes dark. "What is it you want from me, Marcus? Why can't you simply leave well enough alone?"

He flipped up his visor, his dark blue eyes riveted to her. "I am going to be serving your husband for a long time, my lady, and it would make both our lives considerably easier if we could move past this incident. I do not want your hostility every time I come near you, for sooner or later Christopher is going to deduce that something is going on and he will demand truths. I, for one, do not wish to divulge this particular moment of weakness. He would be most unforgiving."

Dustin's anger faded and she swallowed hard, looking away. Then she sighed. "I am sorry it happened, too. 'Twas no one's fault alone."

Marcus was greatly relieved. They rode together for a few moments in silence, each feeling the tension draining away between them. But Dustin found the need to clarify something.

"I...I care for my husband, Marcus," she said softly, looking at him. "Had I met you first, things might be different, but I did not meet you first and I am married to Christopher. You must understand that."

He nodded. "I understand completely," he said. "Since you are being truthful, I shall be with you. I am intrigued by you, Lady de Lohr, yet it will go no further than that. You have my oath as a knight of the realm.

She still wouldn't look at him. She wished he would simply drop the subject. "I believe you."

That was the end of their conversation. There were two more days of minor conversation and Dustin avoided Marcus as much as she possibly could. Essentially, they rode together in silence the rest of the way to London with Dustin struggling to forget what had happened.

Marcus, however, was not. He did not want to forget.

ɞ

Windsor Castle

BUILT OF BLOND stone with the biggest walls she had ever seen, the sight was enough to fill Dustin with awe and dread. She almost fell off Hercules gazing up at the massive, turreted structure as the party rode in from the northwest and she heard Marcus laugh at her.

"It's so big," she gasped.

"Aye, it is," Edward said, riding behind them. "The seat of the great Christian Empire."

Dustin shook her head, overwhelmed with the all of it. As they rode under the portcullis of the western gatehouse, soldiers yelled of their arrival and Dustin swore she had never seen so much activity in all her life. There were hundreds, even thousands, of men everywhere and it suddenly dawned on her that her husband was in charge of all of them. It was nearly too much to comprehend. She very much wanted to see her husband at that moment.

"Do you see Chris, Marcus?" she asked excitedly.

"He will not be out here on the walls, my lady," Marcus replied. "More than likely, he is over in the practice arena or in the knight's quarters. We'll find him."

Even more than her excitement of arriving at Windsor, she found she was shaking with excitement to see her husband. She had felt so lost without him, and the whole incident with Marcus had frightened her. The past three days of travel had been hellish and she was anxious to find comfort in his arms.

As they approached the massive round keep of the castle, several stewards in silk tunics and hose came rushing out to greet them. Dud and Edward took charge of the men-at-arms as Marcus helped Dustin dismount. There were servants dashing about everywhere, stripping her belongings off her horse and unloading the wagon.

A thin man as tall as she was approached her and bowed deeply. "We were told that you would be arriving, Lady de Lohr. Your husband has requested that you take to your rooms and he will seek you later," the man said.

Dustin eyed him. "How did you know it was me? We sent no word ahead announcing our arrival."

The man bowed quickly again. "If it pleases my lady, your husband instructed us to watch for the most beautiful woman in the realm with hair like spun gold. When we saw you passing through the portcullis, we assumed he meant you. Were we wrong?"

Dustin grinned bashfully and Marcus answered. "Nay, you were not. 'Tis indeed Lady de Lohr," he said formally. "Show her to her rooms for she is weary from her ride."

The man bowed again, motioning to a few men behind him. They began rushing forward to assist in carrying Lady de Lohr's belongings.

"Where is Baron de Lohr?" Marcus asked.

"He is over on the tournament field, my lord," the steward replied. "Our illustrious Prince John has scheduled a tourney the day after tomorrow, and he and his knights have been practicing. He asks you and your knights to join him immediately after seeing to his wife's comfort and safety."

"Very well," Marcus nodded curtly, motioning to Edward and Dud.

After a brief conference to divide up the duties, Marcus went with Dustin and the herd of servants while Edward and Dud went to see to the men. Marcus and Edward would join up later, on the practice field, leaving Dud to guard Dustin.

Windsor had more than just a massive cylindrical keep and a few outbuildings. It also had a block of apartments that stretched all along the west side of the castle. Inside the cavernous block, Marcus took Dustin's cloak personally as she followed the stewards and porters with her baggage. She could not take her eyes off the women and their beautiful dresses, having never cared about her appearance before, but now she felt extremely self-conscious. Her gold surcoat was simple and tasteful, but these women had surcoats with studded jewels and gold leaf embroidery. She did not mean to stare, but she was.

She fell back in step beside Marcus, clutching his elbow. "Marcus, have you ever seen so many richly dressed women?"

He had and was not in the least impressed. "Rich surcoats are all they have in their favor, my lady. I would wager to say that their intelligence equals a stalk of celery."

She giggled, noticing the women were starting to stare back at her. One woman's gaze was particularly hostile and Dustin stiffened.

"Why is she looking at me like that?" she demanded. "I am going to teach her some manners."

She meant what she said, but Marcus clamped a huge hand over her arm and stayed her. "Now is not the place, my lady," he said evenly. "She is simply envious of your beauty, surely you cannot fault her that. In fact, I'd say that rumors of your loveliness are even now spreading through court like wildfire. If I were you, I would learn to accept the openly hateful looks from jealous women or you are going to be fighting a great many of them."

She turned to look at him, seeing that he was sincere. "Do you know that you are only the second person to tell me that I am beautiful? Chris was the first, but I though he said it because....because he wanted something."

Marcus had a good idea what she meant. "He said it because it is God's truth, and I say it for the same reason. You had better become accustom to hearing it."

They followed the steward into a cathedral-like foyer and ascended a massive staircase to a second floor. There were great open-beamed ceilings and plaster walls. After that, Dustin was completely lost. She knew they traveled down a corridor until they came to a large oak door, one of several in the length of the hall. The head steward threw the big iron lock and opened the door.

Dustin was speechless. The huge antechamber she had entered into was resplendent with silk curtains and big hides covering the floor. Finely carved furniture decorated the room and there were two doors, opposite each other on parallel walls. A fire burned softly in the huge carved hearth. The chamber smelled like freshly cut wood and she could see fresh rushes skirting the perimeter of the room.

While she was gaping at the room, the army of servants that had been following her slipped into the room and disappeared through the door on the far right. They worked efficiently, like ants, and shortly had her trunks and other small effects brought in. Her maids were ushered in, as well, and they too disappeared through the door to unpack for their mistress. Dustin had yet to notice the activity; she was still appraising the room.

Marcus lay her cloak on a chair, grinning at her reaction to the room. "A far cry from Lioncross?"

She nodded faintly. "Have you ever seen such luxury, Marcus? We are staying in rooms meant for royalty."

"Nay, my lady, you are staying in rooms meant for the Defender of the King's Realm," he said. "Christopher is worthy of such attentions."

She shook her head again, moving to the windows and delighted to notice a garden-like courtyard below. Her awe was turning into giddy happiness, and she spun away from the window in delight, relishing the newfound luxury and space of her chambers.

"This is wonderful," she exclaimed. "Are you going to see Chris now? Can I come?"

"Aye, I am going to see him now, but you cannot come," he replied. "He wants you here, but I am sure as soon as he sees you have arrived, he will join you. You will not be alone for long."

She dutifully nodded, not particularly disappointed because now she could explore her new home. Marcus left her with a formal bow, telling her to bolt the door behind him and open it to no one save someone she knew. When he was gone, she did as she was told and immediately began to investigate every corner of the pretty antechamber.

RISE OF THE DEFENDER

BIRTH OF THE LEGEND

PART 2

CHAPTER ELEVEN

London, England
The Tower of London

PRINCE JOHN SAT in his silk and oaken chair, a chair he likened to be the throne of England. His dirty black hair was stuck to his oily face as he watched Ralph Fitz Walter from across the polished and well-used table that was one of the centerpieces of his lavish solar at Windsor Castle. His father had used this table. To John, it reeked of power. He could still see his father, Henry the Second, standing over it, yelling about something or another. It seemed to him that his father had always been yelling.

"She has arrived," Ralph said with a leering smile.

John was distracted from the ghost of his father. "She? Who?"

"Lady Dustin Barringdon de Lohr," Ralph enunciated every syllable with relish. "She's in the baron's chambers with only one knight as a guard."

John, hit with the news, sat forward in his chair. "De Lohr's wife? How damned fortunate for us."

"Hmpf, fortunate indeed, sire," Ralph agreed. "I still believe we would have been successful in a kidnap attempt had you so allowed. She had only twenty-five men-at-arms and three knights as escort."

"Mayhap," John waved him off. "But de Lohr was very vague with where she had been, and why she was delayed. I will not risk men with such scant information. But she is here now and I am pleased."

Ralph nodded, scratching the louse that had just bit him on the back. "Shall I bring her here, sire?"

John sat back in his chair thoughtfully. "One knight, did you say? We can get around one knight." His gaze lingered on Ralph a moment longer. "Have we heard anything from your spies at Lioncross Abbey?"

"Not a word, sire," Ralph said, a bit embarrassed. "I have sent out a few good men to follow up with them. It shan't be long."

John nodded slowly, still in thought. Finally, he took a deep breath. "It is probably of no importance now, considering de Lohr and his wife are here," he said "Aye, bring her to me. I would meet this woman."

"And de Lohr?" Ralph wanted to know.

John shrugged. "What of him? I will tell him I simply could not wait to meet his wife," he said. "I won't touch her, at least not today. So tell me, Ralph, how goes preparations for the tourney in two days?"

The subject changed and Ralph went with it. "Nearly complete, my lord," he said. "The lists have been built and the banners are being raised as we speak. It should be a grand spectacle. Oh, and sire, another thing, Marcus Burton was one of the knights who escorted Lady de Lohr to London. 'Tis said he serves de Lohr now."

"Burton?" John looked surprised. "Damnation, I didn't even know he had returned. Serving de Lohr, did you say?"

Ralph watched John's face twist with frustration, but the man turned to his wine and said no more. Ralph, feeling the conversation over, moved for the door but John stopped him.

"Ralph, why did I not know Burton had returned?" he asked evenly.

Ralph swallowed, John was bloody well angry when he used that sweet tone. "Because I was not told, sire," he replied steadily. "I would have informed you immediately, as you know."

John was contemplating his gold cup. "I would have Burton champion me. You will relay the order, Ralph. I want Burton bearing my colors at the tourney. If he and de Lohr fight side by side, they will tear through the other participants like a knife through butter and there will be no chance to fell de Lohr."

"Burton will not fell de Lohr, sire," Ralph said frankly. "You know that as well as I."

John's head came up. "As my champion he will do as he is ordered."

Ralph sighed. "Sire, I am forced to remind you that de Lohr commands the fighting men, as per Richard's command."

John suddenly slammed his fists on the table. "But knights are of a different breed. They are not commanded as the common troops."

"But they fall under the same provision," Ralph argued back. "Knights are sworn above all to the king, which means de Lohr has command of their loyalty."

John threw his cup, standing up so fast that his chair fell over. His ugly face was red with fury.

"How is it that a lowly baron commands all of the fighting men in England?" he seethed. "I am a prince! I command England and England cowers at my feet, as it should. Now get out of here and do my bidding. Bring me de Lohr's slut, and then find Burton and inform him of his new duties."

Ralph bowed slowly, eyeing his liege as he quit the room. John, his nostrils flaring with humiliation and anger, forced himself to calm. He picked up his chair and sat slowly, forcibly.

All would be right, eventually, he told himself. To be rid of de Lohr at this point was his primary goal, and rule of England second. And, hopefully, the Lion's Claw's wife would provide an easy end to her husband's claim.

ꕥ

SIR THOMAS DUDLEY was in a panic.

It was all he could do to keep from running full-bore to the tournament arena where he knew Christopher would be. As it was, he was jogging at a rapid pace in spite of nearly one hundred pounds worth of armor. Sweat dotted his dark brow.

The arena to the east of the castle was crowded with knights on horseback, men on foot, practicing for the approaching games. It was a vast area with newly built lists that men were still hammering on. Dud immediately spied David's blond head on the opposite side of the arena near the horse corrals, and ran straight to him.

David was with Edward, Leeton and young Trent. It was obvious they had been practicing heavily, coated with perspiration, and now stood at rest before the next bout. When Dud came racing up, crashing into the fence in his haste, all of the men looked at him with alarm.

"Dud!" David exclaimed sharply. "Why aren't you with Dustin?"

Dud was beside himself. "Where's the baron?"

David grabbed him. "He is by the barracks. Answer me, dammit, is something wrong?"

Dud's faded green eyes focused on David. "Sir Ralph came for Lady Dustin not fifteen minutes ago with an entire company of soldiers. He was polite, but there was no mistaking the message he gave me; turn the lady over to him or the soldiers would seriously disable me. I had no choice, David."

"Jesus Christ," David hissed even as Leeton took off for the barracks on a dead run. "Why didn't you go with her?"

"Think about it," Dud said, as he removed his helmet and threw it to the ground in anger. "If I did, then there would be no one to inform Christopher of what had happened. And if I had refused to let the lady go with him, then I would probably now be drowning in my own blood, which brings us back to my first point. Someone had to tell Chris."

David understood and paced about like a caged animal. There was naught else to do but wait for his brother. He knew better than anyone that Ralph was a dead man.

Christopher and Marcus crossed the compound and headed toward the castle faster than anyone had ever seen men run in armor. David and the others, seeing them running in the distance with Leeton trying to keep pace, ran after them. The group came together just as they were entering a side gate.

"Chris," David called as his brother charged into the inner courtyard. "What are you going to do?"

Christopher was so angry he was white. He stopped running long enough to collect himself and catch his breath, facing his six faithful knights.

"I am going to find her first, and then I am going to kill Ralph," he said evenly.

"I was under the impression that he took her to the prince, my lord," Dud said. "I am truly sorry to have failed you in this."

"You didn't fail me, Dud," Christopher said shortly. "To have gotten yourself killed would have been to fail me. I have no doubt my wife can hold her own against the prince until I get there."

He turned and charged headlong into the castle with the knights behind him, creating a chaotic scene as they raced down the halls, nearly running people down in their haste. Soldiers on guard saw the Lion's Claw running and began joining their liege. By the time Christopher mounted the massive staircase leading to the second floor, there were no less than fifty soldiers following him. Had he not been so concerned for his wife, he would have been pleased with the show of loyalty.

John's apartments were in the royal wing. Christopher and his men blew past the honor guard, who made a feeble attempt to stop them but went ignored. They tore up the fragile woolen carpets that led to John's chambers. Marcus and David barked orders to the soldiers to cover the exits and to position themselves. Christopher, without a word, kicked in the prince's door.

He burst into the room, having no idea what he would find. He was therefore completely shocked to see his wife sitting opposite John, a goblet of wine in her hand and a plate of sugared confections between them.

Dustin's half-full goblet clattered to the floor, splashing out its contents. He could see by her face that he had scared the hell out of her, but no matter. He knew John and knew what the man was capable of, and he was vastly relieved to see that she was untouched in any way.

"Chris!" she exclaimed. "What did you do?"

He ignored her and faced off against John. "Why is my wife here, unescorted?"

John sat back easily in his chair, a thin smile on his lips. "We are enjoying one another's company, baron. Certainly there is no harm in that. And in answer to your question, my apartments are full of soldiers willing to protect a young woman's virtue."

Christopher was having a difficult time controlling himself. He walked over to his wife, his gaze never leaving the prince. Dustin, confused and a little frightened, watched his movements anxiously. When he stood next to her, he finally tore his eyes away from John long enough to look her over.

"Are you all right?" he asked.

"I am fine," she said, a timid smile on her lips. "The prince and I were talking of my father, and…."

"Get up, Dustin. We're leaving," Christopher said abruptly, grasping her by the arm and pulling her to her feet.

Stunned, Dustin obeyed silently, allowing her husband to pull her toward the door.

John stood up. "But I am not finished with her yet. Could you come back in an hour?"

From out of the walls there suddenly appeared several soldiers of the prince's special guard. They were elite troops, mostly mercenaries, and Christopher had no command over them. They followed the prince and the prince's money.

"Tell your cockroaches to fade back into their hovels, John," Christopher said lowly. "I have six knights and nearly one hundred soldiers out in the hall that say your conversation with my wife is concluded."

Dustin heard what was going on, yet did not fully understand the gravity of the situation. As Christopher took her to the door, she felt hands reach out and take her from him protectively. She glanced up to see Marcus' grim face, and then her husband was partially blocked from view by David's muscular body.

John was up and walking as if to show them to the door. Christopher never made a move to put his hand on the hilt of his sword, but the rest of his knights did. Honestly, Dustin was as confused as hell because the prince had been cordial and polite toward her. Why was everyone so deadly serious that she leave the room with a massive escort?

"I enjoyed our talk, my lady, even if it was cut short," John said, craning his neck to get a look at her. "And I would ask a favor of you, if you would be so gracious to grant me. We are holding a tournament in two days, as I am sure you have been made aware, and I would be honored if you would dispense with the trophies for the winners."

Dustin was flattered but before she could reply, Christopher spoke.

"She will not," Christopher said flatly. "She is my wife, not some whore issuing favors to the fortunate. Find another slut to do your work."

"Chris," she said, tugging at him. "I would like to do it."

He didn't react, but John's face lit up. "There? You see? She will do it. Oh, de Lohr, do not be so selfish. Allow the less fortunate to gaze upon this rare and precious beauty. 'Twill make the men fight harder if they know they are to receive a kiss from such an angel for their efforts."

"Nay," Christopher repeated firmly.

"Yes," Dustin countered, pulling away from Marcus' iron grip. She shoved David aside and moved away from the knights before anyone could grab her. Angrily, she faced off against her husband. "I do not understand your rudeness. What he has asked of me is a great honor, and I should like to do it."

John grinned broadly. "Ah, a woman who stands up for herself. I like it."

Christopher's jaw ticked angrily. In fact, he was angrier than he had ever been in his entire life.

"Dustin," he said as evenly as he could. "You will not do this, and you will come with me now without another word."

Something in his tone scared her. Puzzled and angered, she did as she was told and once again found herself in Marcus' grasp. He led her from the room, with David and Christopher backing out of the room still facing the prince until the door slammed shut.

Christopher took his wife from Marcus while David and Edward dispersed the soldiers. With her firmly by the arm, he dragged her the entire way back to their rooms. Dustin, sensing she had done something very, very wrong, didn't utter a word of protest.

When they finally reached their luxurious apartments, Christopher flung her into the antechamber and slammed the door furiously behind him. Dustin, having had time to build substantial fear of his wrath, scooted to the other end of the room. A safe distance, she assumed.

Christopher was shaking with fury and, aye, fright. He took a few moments to breathe and calm himself before dealing with his fully disobedient and highly willful wife.

"Dustin," he began in a controlled tone.

"What?" she jumped at the sound of his voice. Then she began to speak rapidly. "Christopher, I am sorry. I didn't mean to contradict you but the prince had been very kind to me and he seemed to know a bit about my father, and I have never been to London before and awarding prizes in the tournament is such a wonderful honor, and I have never...."

His brow furrowed and he cut her off. "Why are you jabbering like a fool?"

She looked frightened and he saw her swallow hard. "Because I am trying to explain myself before you spank me. Mayhap you won't spank me quite so hard if you understand my excitement."

He calmed considerably to see that she was truly remorseful. It furthermore occurred to him that she knew nothing of what was going on here in London, except for a few tidbits he had fed her.

Of course she saw a charming prince; John could be that if he wanted to. As inculpable as she was, she fell under his spell, and when he asked her to present prizes at the tourney, she was understandably flattered. John was very right in his description of his wife, and for that he could not fault the man, but Dustin did not understand the greater implications of doing John a "favor."

He visibly relaxed. "I am not going to spank you," he said. "But you have made me angry."

"I am sorry," she repeated, not knowing what else to say.

He took a good look at her in her burnished gold surcoat; she looked absolutely ravishing. To think of John and Ralph drooling all over her drove him white with anger all over again, but he banked it. He hadn't seen his wife in three days and he didn't want to spoil their first meeting even more than circumstances already had.

He unlatched his armor and removed his mail gloves and hauberk, leaving them in a pile by the door. Then he removed his heavy leather vest and tossed it across a cherry wood table, leaving him clad in only a damp linen shirt, breeches and boots. He proceeded to wander over to a silk and oak chair, sitting heavily in it.

Dustin watched him closely. He seemed preoccupied and she wondered if it was because he could not decide how to properly punish her.

"Come here," his voice was soft again.

She obeyed and he drew her down onto his lap, his eyes drinking in her beauty for a long moment before speaking.

"Dustin, I know you do not understand politics or intrigue, but unfortunately, sweetheart, you are right in the middle of it," he said. "I told you that I had enemies, with one of them being John because of the title Richard bestowed upon me. Understand me when I tell you that he will do anything, anything at all, to destroy me. And he will use you if he can."

She looked shocked and angered. "I would not help him destroy you."

"Knowingly, no. But John is a clever man, and he would use someone of your innocence to his advantage," he said, caressing her arm gently as he spoke. "He knows I will do anything to keep you safe and protected, and he's right. I'd give my own life to keep you from harm, Dustin."

She gazed back at him, at his sky blue eyes, and her hand came up to caress his bearded cheek.

"He was very kind to me," she said simply.

"He would be, for he has everything to gain by obtaining your trust," he replied. "Listen to me well, you must never again go near the prince. Do not speak or even look at him, or Ralph either. They are on this earth for one reason and one reason only, to destroy all that is Richard's and to obtain England for themselves. As Richard's champion, they must kill me if they are to accomplish this."

The thought of Christopher dead scared the hell out of her. He saw her eyes go wide and she threw her arms around his neck and squeezed him tightly.

"You cannot die," she whispered tightly. "They cannot kill you, Christopher, they simply cannot."

He held her close. "They won't, sweet. They are not smart enough."

She pulled back and looked at him, and he was surprised to see tears in her gray eyes. "If you die, I shall be all alone. My father and mother are dead, and Rebecca is gone. But you…I would not want to live if you were dead."

He was touched by the passion in her statement, her apparent devotion to him. He remembered what she had said to him the morning he left her at the inn, and he believed her now. It scared him to death.

"I will not leave you," was all he could say, and pulled her to him once again as he tried to compose himself. He could not think straight with her looking at him as she was. "I shall never leave you, Dustin. I vow it."

She held on to him for a few long moments before wiping at her eyes. He brushed her hair back with his trencher-sized hands, smiling at her until she smiled back.

"No more cough?" he asked lightly.

She shook her head. "Nay, I am healed," she replied. "Marcus was worse than any nursemaid. Twice he sat on my legs to keep me from getting out of bed."

Christopher laughed softly. "Good man. I knew you could not get around him."

Her smile faded as she remembered her encounter with Marcus. But she pushed the thought away, ignoring it, focusing on her husband.

"You did not say goodbye to me," she commented, moving the subject away from Marcus. "Why not?"

Confusion crossed his features. "I did, Dustin. Don't you remember?"

She shook her head. "You did not. I would have remembered, but you left me without a thought. I am angry with you for that."

It occurred to him that if she didn't remember him bidding her farewell then she didn't remember what she had said to him before he left. He realized he was deeply disappointed.

"I did, I assure you, so your anger has no basis," he said.

She eyed him dubiously but relented, obviously not too terribly angry with him. Arms still around his neck, she cuddled up against him happily. "What will we see first in London? I want to go see the Tower, and Westminster Abbey, and the Thames, and...."

"One thing at a time," he cut in, though he was smiling. "There will be very little time for seeing the sights, but I have decided that there is one trip we will most definitely make."

"And what is that?" she asked.

"To the Street of the Jewelers," he said, noticing her puzzled look. "When I married you, I neglected to give you a bridal gift. I would make amends now."

"But...but you gave me a ring," she glanced down at her pretty little band. "I remember you told me it was a bargain."

He let out an embarrassed sigh. "Well, yes, I did," he said. He had told her it was a bargain so she wouldn't think he had gone to any trouble for her. He was sorry for his statement now. "Nevertheless, I want to select something pretty for you."

She shrugged carelessly. "My mother had coffers of jewels. I do not care much for flashy jewelry."

"I know that," he replied, "although you are the one woman in this world who would justify such an extravagance. I want to select a gift that you will wear, always. Something you will be proud to wear. Something that will remind you of me."

She cocked her head. "We could have a jeweler smelt a gold mask of your face and I could wear it on a chain so everyone would know who I was married to."

He laughed. "Everyone already knows who you are married to. That was established following the first few moments of your arrival."

She watched him for a moment, his handsome face creased with mirth. "Chris?"

"What, sweet?"

She looked at him hesitantly for a moment. "If I…if I were to purchase a wedding ring for you, would you wear it?"

His smile faded and his expression turned amazingly tender. "Aye, Dustin, if you were to buy me a ring, I should be proud to wear it."

"You would?" she was astonished.

"I said I would," he answered.

She grinned. "Then when we go to the Street of the Jewelers, I shall buy you a ring just like mine, only much bigger."

"Not too big. I want to be able to lift my hand without assistance," he quipped.

She giggled, very pleased that he would wear a token of their union. They continued to sit together a few moments in silence, happy to be together again. Christopher had a great many things to attend to but was reluctant to leave Dustin, considering the boldness of the prince. He quickly decided the best way to protect her was to keep her with him, even in improper situations like drilling the troops or practicing on the field. He knew she wouldn't mind, and he would feel much better knowing she was only an arm's length away. 'Twould be much harder for Ralph or John to contact her if he were only a stone's throw distance.

"How would you like to go with me about my duties?" he asked.

Dustin's face lit up, as he knew it would. "Can I? Oh, yes, I would like that."

"Good," he smiled and stood, letting her fall gently to her feet. "Gather your cloak, my love, for it promises to be brisk."

She smiled happily and moved quickly to the mirror to straighten her hair as he cursed himself silently. There he went calling her "my love" again. He would have to stop himself from calling her that before it became a nasty habit.

He moved swiftly to his armor in the corner, donning most of it before Dustin helped him with the mail hood and gloves. But before he could put his helmet on, she jumped up and latched onto his neck, kissing him hard on the lips.

"Thank you, husband," she whispered happily.

He grinned back at her. "For what?"

She shrugged and let go of him, securing her cloak. "For taking me with you, for protecting me. For everything."

"You may thank me as you did anytime," he winked at her, putting his helmet on.

Taking her hand in his huge mailed fist, he led her from the room.

ග

EVEN THOUGH IT was late in the afternoon, Windsor was alive with people. Christopher took her to the tournament arena where his men were and she was awed at the sight of the stands and the colorful banners that were going up all around. There were hundreds of servants and craftsmen seeing to every detail of the arena and surrounding vendor booths.

"Where is your banner?" she asked her husband.

Christopher pointed to a massive banner in the shape of a three-point shield, a rich blue with a golden lion set into it. The lion was rearing on its hind legs, a sword clutched in its claw and a laurel wreath on its head. It was a truly magnificent banner and easily outshone the others.

"It's beautiful," she said sincerely.

Christopher pointed to a banner a couple of flags down. "That is the de Lohr banner, for Lohrham Forest." It was a green and yellow banner with a hunting bird on it.

Dustin studied it. "Why are there two different banners for you?"

"Nay, sweetheart, *my* banner is the blue and gold," he told her. "It stands for my title and Lioncross Abbey. The other one is for my uncle and our family name."

"Are there going to be knights from Lohrham Forest competing?" she asked.

"There are only three knights at Lohrham, and yes, they are going to be here," he said. "They will compete for my uncle's honor. I will compete for mine."

He took her around the arena where several men were practicing jousting with straw-stuffed dummies. Dustin was so involved with watching them that she nearly tripped twice.

Christopher held her hand tightly, amused at her fascination. He had been around knights and tournaments for so long that it was refreshing to see it through the eyes of one who had never seen the spectacle before.

In a clearing next to the arena, Christopher's knights were practicing hand-to-hand fighting with several other knights. The two of them stood on the perimeter for several minutes, watching Marcus plow through several knights and not even raise a sweat. He stopped when he caught sight of Christopher and Dustin and smiled brightly.

"An audience," he said loudly, removing his helmet as he approached them. "Just what I like to have."

"Marcus, you are a wonderful fighter," Dustin gushed. "Those men didn't have a chance."

Marcus glanced at Christopher. "Obviously you have not seen your husband in the ring, my lady. The gods are envious of his talent."

Dustin grinned, catching sight of David and Leeton. She called out to them and David motioned her over, and she went to him as eager as a child.

"What is she doing here?" Marcus murmured casually to Christopher.

Christopher's eyes were on his wife as he replied. "I felt it safer to keep her with me at all times," he replied quietly. "After what happened, I will not let her out of my sight. Besides, this is all new to her and she loves it. She will be no trouble."

Marcus nodded in agreement. "I must confess I had no idea what we would find in John's apartments," he muttered, fussing with his gauntlet. "With the prince hung like a bull, he has torn many a young woman asunder and I half expected Dustin to fall prey."

Christopher shook his head. "You do not know my wife very well," he said. "She may be innocent, but she packs a punch. She would fight him with her dying breath."

Dustin turned around and called out to them, motioning them to join her. Christopher started to comply but Marcus backed off.

"I have got more rounds, Chris," he said, replacing his helmet.

"Then we shall see you in my apartment before supper," Christopher replied. "I should like us all to attend the meal together in a show of unity."

"Agreed," Marcus nodded. "That will throw the fear of God into John. With the Lion's Claw and Richard's premier general in the room, he ought to be throwing fits on the rushes before the night is out."

Christopher grinned as the two went their separate ways.

Dustin spent the rest of the fading daylight watching her husband and his men work over the other knights on the combat field. Someone had brought her a chair and she sat on the edge of it, her eyes riveted to the fighting before her.

It was clear early on that Marcus had been right.

Christopher was easily the best soldier there. She has seen him fight before, but briefly. Here in this setting, he was constant and omnipotent, dropping men easily. Her heart swelled with excitement and pride when she thought of him winning the tournament tomorrow.

He joined her after an hour or so of knocking over weaker men. When he removed his helmet, she promptly stood up and kissed him loudly on the cheek.

"What was that for?" he asked.

"For being brilliant and strong," she said giddily. "And Marcus. I must congratulate him, too, for being almost as good."

"Do not kiss him," Christopher said in a low voice, shaking out his helmet. "A simple handshake will do."

She gazed at him for a moment, her joviality fading. It was becoming increasingly apparent that Christopher must never know what happened between her and Marcus. As protective and possessive as he was, there was no telling how he would react, and Marcus' life might be in serious jeopardy. Mayhap her life, too.

Trying to gage him, mayhap trying to anticipate his reaction, she pressed forward in her usual manner.

"No handshake," she teased. "I will give Marcus a big, wet kiss right on the lips."

He simply shook his head, removing his gauntlets and shaking the perspiration out of them. Not receiving an immediate answer, she turned her attention back to the field.

"Your kiss to Marcus would be the kiss of death." He said it so casually that she almost didn't catch his words. "I would run him through and take delight in it…Marcus!"

She jumped when he yelled to his knight, feeling sick inside. Even as Marcus jogged over and the two of them engaged in a tactical conversation, she still felt dulled and nauseated. She decided to never again bring up the subject and to pretend that it never, ever happened. Mayhap if she pretended long enough she would come to believe it.

Dustin looked up at the two men as they spoke, each distinctly handsome. But she found it was Christopher who drew her gaze, who warmed her heart. She thought of the tournament, and of him winning. If he were to win and she were not awarding prizes, then it would mean that another woman would have the honor of publicly touching her husband. With that thought, she flared.

"Christopher?" she called to him.

He and Marcus turned to look at her. She fixed her husband with a miffed gaze.

"You are going to win the tournament, are you not?" she demanded.

He cocked his head, unsure of her tone or her question. "I would hope to."

"But you are the best soldier in the realm. You fight all of these men as if they are children, so I would venture to say that you are going to win the tournament," she said firmly.

He cleared his throat modestly. "There are two categories, my lady, the joust and field combat. To win both would be a task."

She stood up, rigid with the jealousy she was feeling. "But you are the very best; therefore, you will win." He cocked his eyebrow at her and she continued almost angrily. "If you win and I am not allowed to bestow the prize to the winner, then that will mean that another woman will have the pleasure of kissing you and rewarding you publicly. You will not allow me kiss Marcus to congratulate him for a fine fight, yet you would allow another woman to kiss you in front of the entire court."

Both men were taken aback by the ferocity of her statement, yet Christopher had to agree she had a certain amount of logic. Silly, but logical. Before he could answer her, she jumped at him again.

"Think on it this way, husband," she raised her chin. "If I am to bestow prizes, then what better incentive for you to win? You would not want me favoring another, would you?"

Marcus snorted. "She has a point," he mumbled, then suddenly looked struck. "What does she mean congratulate me for a fine fight?"

Christopher gave Marcus an irritated glare before focusing on his wife again. "What brought this up again?"

She stuck out her lip. "Nothing. I....I just want to be the one to congratulate you, 'tis all."

"And you shall, in the privacy of our bedchamber," he replied evenly. "Not in front of the whole of Windsor and London."

She scowled. "And why not in front of them? Are you ashamed of me?"

Marcus started to laugh and Christopher was highly annoyed at both of them. "Of course not, Dustin, but what we do between ourselves is a private matter, not to be displayed for public scrutiny."

"We are married, Chris. They know that we do far more than merely kiss," she shot back, putting her hands on her hips. "If you won't let me award trophies, then I will not come at all."

Christopher moved toward her and away from the hysterical Marcus, gripping her arm tightly and leading her several feet away. She frowned fiercely at him.

"Do not look at me like that," he snapped. "And do not speak to me in that tone, either. I have warned you about that."

"Then why cannot I award the prizes?" she persisted. "Oh, please? Do not deny me."

As much as he hated to admit it, her reasoning was sound. He knew he would be the victor, and he would like nothing better than to be kissed by his wife. But she would be kissing him in front of John and Ralph, and he knew he would not be able to control his emotions when he held her in his arms. They would see right through the rigid facade he was trying to maintain.

"Very well, I will think on it," he said finally, watching her face light up with a huge smile. He held up a warning finger. "But I promise nothing other than that."

"That is enough, husband."

She threw her arms around his neck and kissed him two or three times before he peeled her from him.

"Dustin, not out here, sweet," he admonished her softly. "Not in front of the men."

She pouted. "You are ashamed of me, then. You do not even want your own men to see me touch you."

He gave her a stern glare. "That, lady, is a lie and you well know it. But there is a time and place for everything, and kissing me in front of my knights is not the correct place for that action."

She was still put off, turning away from him and crossing her arms. He watched her as he adjusted his armor and put his gauntlets back on.

"I will say this, Lady de Lohr," he said, softly and richly. "I am more proud of you and your beauty than you can imagine. Mayhap that is why I wish to keep what is between us private. To see you display affection inflames every man who sees it; to see nothing more than courtesy and warmth between us only fuels their imagination and nothing more. What I do with you is my private heaven and no one else's."

She gazed up at him, deeply touched by his words. "Cannot I at least kiss you once in a while, should it be appropriate?"

He gave her a half grin and leaned down, kissing her on the lips so sweetly that she lost her balance. "Aye, you may. And I give myself permission to kiss you wherever and whenever I damn well please. Satisfied?"

She nodded, her cheeks flushed. "Aye."

Marcus watched them from afar, trying to busy himself with his armor and sword, trying to pretend he didn't notice the exchange. But he did, and it cut through him. He tried to ignore the twisting in his chest, venting his frustration with his jerky movements. He'd never been jealous in his life but knew that he was feeling his first at that moment, and he was disgusted with himself for it. His infatuations usually lasted a mere day or so, but this one had not only failed to dissipate, it had increased in strength.

But it could go no further, he told himself. Lady Dustin was married to his liege, and he was not about to jeopardize everything he had ever worked for simply for a woman. Mayhap if he told himself that enough he would believe it, although a fleeting thought told him that she would be worth every heartache should it come to that.

☙

DUSTIN DRESSED CAREFULLY for her first formal supper. She knew that there would be scads of elegantly dressed women, and she would simply have to make do with what she had. She had never in her life cared for fine clothes or jewelry, but she wished she had some now. She wondered if Christopher would be ashamed of her because she was not swathed in expensive finery. He had disappeared to parts unknown but Leeton and Dud were out in the antechamber acting as her protectors.

She had her maids hem up a surcoat Rebecca had not quite finished, a surcoat of exquisite ruby-red brocade, almost a garnet it was so rich. The neckline was wide-open, hugging her arms just below the shoulders and clinging to her figure with long sleeves and a snug bodice. Her white breasts were displayed most provocatively, and she smiled when she knew that Rebecca had made it this way with her trip to London in mind. The skirt of the surcoat was huge and flowing, creating a train in back when she walked.

She sat in front of a lovely carved vanity, absently brushing her hair and wondering what she should do with the unruly mass. It was so long and she had so much of it that it would completely cover up the surcoat if she let it, so again for the first time in her life, she was sorry she knew nothing of the latest hairstyles.

One of her maids, a short plump woman with a fat face, watched her young mistress for some time before approaching timidly.

"Do ye want yer hair properly done, my lady?" she asked with a smile, gazing at Dustin in the reflection of the mirror.

Dustin sighed. "I do not know. I don't know what to do with it. I want to look fashionable, but I do not know how."

The maid put the shift she was holding down on a chair. "If ye would allow me, my lady, I will help ye."

"Would you, Marta? I would appreciate it greatly," Dustin said sincerely.

The woman nodded, beaming, and scooted from the room. Dustin waited several minutes before the woman came hustling back with a strange-looking device in her hand. She immediately went to the hearth and lay it upon the coals.

"What's that?" Dustin asked distrustfully.

"A French frizzing iron," the woman announced. "We shall do wonderful things with that mane of yers. Another maid is coming to help me, with your approval."

Dustin nodded, trusting that the women knew what they were doing. She certainly didn't.

An hour later, curled and brushed and primped, Dustin was allowed to look at herself for the first time. Initial shock was immediately replaced by a wide, happy grin.

The frizzing iron had done just that, it crimped her long hair until it was a mass of wavy brocade. The castle maid had pulled the hair around her face back, braiding it, and then wrapping that braid around her head to keep the hair off her face. Yards of wavy, silky hair cascaded down her back in glorious fashion. Tiny tendrils of crimped hair caressed her lovely face.

Dustin hardly recognized herself, and she was absolutely delighted with her hair. She knew that only unmarried women wore their hair free at court, sometimes adorning it with pretty barrettes or thin nets, but she had far too much hair for those trappings. She had no choice but to leave it free and lovely. She admired herself in the mirror, turning around and around until she was dizzy and laughing, hoping her husband liked it, too.

With her hair dressed and finished, she pulled on delicate cream-colored hose and slippers to match, which too tight because they had been her mother's. But she didn't care, she was actually pleased with her appearance this night and nothing could spoil her mood.

The castle maid had one more trick up her sleeve before leaving. She took the beeswax and ocher that Dustin had brought with her and mixed it together until she had a shade that was barely colored red. Then, she added a bit of oil, just enough to make it workable, and then deftly painted Dustin's lips with it.

Dustin studied herself in the mirror, vastly pleased with her slightly red, slightly glossy lips. She kept rubbing her lips together nervously, unused to the cosmetic. Yet with her hair up and her lips painted, she didn't feel like quite such an outsider. She could not wait to be seen, positive the results were pleasing.

She wasn't disappointed. Leeton and Dud could only stare at her in awe. Leeton was the first to remember his manners, taking her hand and kissing it softly. Dustin simply beamed.

"Do you really like it?" she grilled them.

They nodded firmly. "Aye, my lady, there is no one who can match your beauty," Leeton said truthfully.

" 'Tis not too much? Too red? Too much hair?" she pushed, wanting to know if they were being honest with her. She could probably wear an old sack and they would tell her she was the fairest maiden in all the land.

"Nay, my lady, you are.....ravishing," Leeton assured her.

Dustin blushed appreciatively. "Thank you. Do you think Christopher will think so?"

Leeton's smile faded a bit. "Oh, yes, my lady, he will. I promise you that."

Pleased with herself, she wandered over to the window to wait for her husband to return for her.

There was a knock on the door several minutes later. Leeton unsheathed his sword as Dud rose to answer.

Edward and Sir Trent stood in the doorway, dressed in their armored best. They pushed their way into the room, stunned into reverent silence when they beheld Lady de Lohr. Edward, after a moment of gaping at her, swallowed hard and turned to Leeton.

"Go and change into appropriate attire," he said. "Trent and I will keep the lady company. Return here when you are finished and we will escort Lady de Lohr to the feast."

"Why would you escort me?" Dustin wanted to know. "Where is my husband?"

"He is indisposed, Lady de Lohr, nothing to be concerned with," Edward replied evenly. "He will join us shortly."

Dustin, disappointed, wandered back over to the window and sat in a chair, staring at her hands. Edward followed Leeton and Dud out into the hall, making sure the door was closed tightly before turning to them.

"What is wrong?" Leeton wanted to know. He could hear something in Edward's tone.

"I am not sure," Edward replied in a whisper. "Marcus was cornered by Ralph an hour ago and was ordered to champion the prince in the tournament. Marcus, of course, refused and nearly killed the man. Now they are all in the prince's apartments, and Christopher and David have gone with him for support. Unfortunately, the prince demanded a private meeting and Christopher and David are waiting in the hall like caged beasts. 'Tis not a pleasant situation, to say the least. That is why we are to escort Dustin to the feast and wait for them there."

"Damn," Leeton muttered. "Champion John? Who in the hell would want to do that?"

Edward cocked a wry eyebrow. "No one, which is why they are trying to order Marcus into the position," he replied. "Even though Christopher commands the troops, knights are not truly considered a part of that vocation. John is trying to insist that knights fall under the command of the ruling body."

"If Marcus were to champion John, then he would be competing against Christopher," Dud thought aloud. "As awesome a prospect as that is, it is also frightening. They would surely kill one another."

The men stood a moment in silence, each contemplating their own horrific thoughts until Edward stirred for the door.

"Off with you both," he commanded softly, "and a quick return."

Without another word, Leeton and Dud disappeared down the corridor.

CHAPTER TWELVE

MARCUS STOOD STIFFLY in Prince John's antechamber, his jaw ticking with frustration. Ralph and the prince sat several feet away, side by side, as if they were an ugly pair of statues. The conversation had reached a lull with Marcus refusing to budge and Ralph nursing a sore jaw. If it were up to Marcus, he would be nursing a broken neck as well.

John sat back in his silk chair, angry at the refusal of this mere knight to champion him but holding his temper for the moment. He would gain nothing if he erupted and he knew it.

"Tell me again why this proposal is so distasteful to you, Burton," he asked nicely, hoping to cool the enraged man. An angry Marcus Burton was not healthy for anyone.

Marcus gazed at him impassively. "I serve Baron Christopher de Lohr, and King Richard is my liege. I will serve no other."

"But I am Richard's brother," John pleaded. "As crown prince, 'tis right that you should serve me as well, is it not?"

"Nay," Marcus said flatly. "I serve my king."

Ralph muttered something but John cut him off, switching tactics. It was obvious Marcus Burton could not be ordered, pushed or tricked into anything; they had been trying that for the better part of the hour. Therefore, he would try another route.

"Burton, you are the best knight in the realm, everyone knows that," John said. "You should have titles, glory, everything you deserve, but instead you choose to serve a mere baron when you, in fact should be a baron yourself."

Marcus merely cocked an eyebrow. John continued. "I could grant you a baronetcy, Burton. You could have lands, a magnificent keep, and the most beautiful wife in the land. Everything you deserve and desire can be yours for doing me a simple favor."

Marcus looked away, outwardly disinterested when, in fact, he knew John had the power to grant exactly what he promised. If accepting a baronetcy from John would compromise his standing with Richard, then he would absolutely refuse. Still, much to his regret, he found himself remotely interested. As a powerful baron, he could control much in England and maintain the country for Richard's return. And there was truth to the feeling that he was somewhat jealous of Christopher for his new lands, wishing Richard had seen it fit to bestow the same glory on his head.

And why hadn't he? Christopher was not a better man than he. He had two years of service on Marcus, that was all, and although he was a better tactician, he was not a better soldier. The resentment he pretended didn't exist suddenly seeped through his veins, and for another reason as well; Lady Dustin.

John watched Marcus' impassive face, knowing the man must at least be thinking on his offer. He would be a fool not to.

"Think on it, Burton," John repeated, quieter. "I shall grant you your heart's desire if you do one small, simple thing for me as being my champion."

Marcus looked at him. "I must refuse again, sire. I want no part of you."

Ralph and John glanced at each other and Ralph stood up, though keeping a safe distance from the huge man. Something unspoken was passed in that glance, something that hinted of a darker purpose. Marcus didn't catch it, but Ralph knew what he had to do. Information had come to them earlier that day, by way of a soldier's comment and rumors that were too valuable to pass up. Like any good tactician, Ralph would use it to gain their wants. He went for the throat.

" 'Twould be a shame if Sir Christopher happened to find out that you kissed his wife," he said casually. "I wonder what he would say?"

Marcus could not stop himself from reacting. His head snapped to Ralph and the cobalt blue eyes flamed. His first instinct was to kill them both outright, but he controlled himself so forcefully that his body began to shake.

"Who told you such outrageous lies?" he demanded in a low, hostile growl.

"Not lies, but fact, I am told," Ralph said smugly. "Did you really think you were all alone with her in the common room at the inn? With twenty-five soldiers milling about, preparing to leave, wouldn't it make sense that at least one of them would see you?"

Marcus knew he went pale. His stomach churned wildly and he fought off the overwhelming urge to react outwardly, when in fact he knew he could not. His life, mayhap Dustin's life, depended on his control.

"I am also told you spent a good deal of time alone with her in her room," Ralph went on. "Mayhap there was more than kissing going on? Should Lady Dustin bear a child some months from now, 'twill be interesting to see if the child has black hair or blond hair."

Marcus could not breathe with his fury. "Such vicious lies should not be allowed to go unpunished," he seethed. "To make it easy, I will kill every one of the soldiers that accompanied the lady and I to London. That should eliminate your spy."

Ralph smiled. "They are Sir Christopher's men and you will have to answer to him if you commit such a crime. What would you tell him was your reasoning?"

"To kill a liar and nothing more," Marcus replied evenly, trying to regain control of his wits. "For that is the only true reason. You should execute your spy yourself for relaying such falsehoods. I have had enough of this conversation."

He moved for the door and they let him. John called after him.

"Think on my offer, Burton," he said. "Titles and lands shall be yours. And, if you happen to mortally wound de Lohr in the tournament, I will also grant you Lady Dustin."

Marcus was out the door, slamming it behind him in his rage. John and Ralph looked at each other and chuckled wickedly.

"He will be yours, sire," Ralph said confidently. "Did you see how he rigidly denied it? Of course it is true. He will not allow de Lohr to become privy to such damaging knowledge."

John was quite pleased. "Are you sure the soldier is trustworthy?" he asked.

Ralph nodded. "Not just one, but two men saw him through the small window as they were guarding the door," he replied. "It was worth five gold crowns apiece to learn that he practically raped her right in the front room."

John grew thoughtful, thinking of Burton and his strong character. "He will not admit it, though. We may have to divulge the information to select people to start a wildfire of rumors. Mayhap it would cause a great enough rift between de Lohr and Burton, enough to force the man to our side. Mayhap we do not have to blackmail him at all; let the rumors do the damage."

Ralph agreed. "If you wish it, I am sure we could accomplish that very task tonight at supper."

John liked the idea. "Make it so."

"As you wish, sire," Ralph replied, an evil gleam to his eye.

☙

MARCUS WAS OUT of control with anger. He plowed into David in the hall, nearly taking the man down as Christopher reached out a huge hand to ease him.

"Steady, man, steady," he admonished, gripping Marcus' arms. "What in the hell did they say to you?"

Marcus was so undone he could hardly think. He looked up into Christopher's blue eyes, the eyes of a man he loved dearly, and could not speak for a moment. But he had to say something, anything, for he knew that one way or the other, Christopher was going to hear of his indiscretions with his wife. He would rather explain now, albeit most likely a lie, than defend himself later. He wanted to be upfront with Christopher even if he was not planning to be entirely honest. He could not seem to tell him the truth, for even though he didn't bed Dustin, in his heart he already had a hundred times.

"He is attempting to force me to champion him," he rasped after a moment, "any way he can do it."

"What does that mean?" Christopher demanded, studying him closely.

Marcus prayed that God would forgive him for what he was about to say. "Apparently there were some spies traveling with us," he said softly. "Soldiers who are willing to tell them anything for a price."

Christopher's expression never wavered. "What stories?"

Marcus took a deep, fortifying breath. "Somehow, Ralph uncovered a story about Lady Dustin and I in a compromising position. Ralph intends to use the story to blackmail me into championing John." He gazed into Christopher's eyes as he spoke. "They were told that I ravaged your wife. They were also told that Lady Dustin and I spent a good deal of time alone together, in her room, which was true. But nothing ever happened, my lord, I swear it on all that is holy. I never touched your wife when we were alone in her room."

Christopher let go of him, his eyes unreadable but his body tense. He stared back at Marcus a long, long time and Marcus was sure he was reading right through him. He fought off the urge to fall to his knees and beg for forgiveness.

"That," Christopher said after a long and pregnant silence, "is a lie."

Marcus' eyes widened at Christopher. He saw the man smile faintly and knew it would be the last thing he saw on this earth before gazing upon God's holy face.

"My lord?" he choked.

Christopher lifted an eyebrow. "Dustin told me you sat on her legs to keep her in bed," Christopher explained softly. "So you did touch her. You could have spanked her, too, if she needed it."

Marcus closed his eyes, his fury and anxiety draining out of him and he slumped against the wall. He was positive every bone in his body had deserted hm. Christopher stood over him, knowing what a mind-wracking interrogation it must have been with John and Ralph, yet he had never seen Marcus so weakened. He was the strongest man he knew.

Marcus grappled with his emotions, turning his pale face up to his liege. "I thought you were going to run me through," he murmured, which was the truth.

Christopher took his arm, pulling him up from the wall. "You have no control over rumors and lies, Marcus. People will believe what they will," he said. "Yet you had the courage to tell me what was transpiring, and for that I am grateful. Now we can deal with what comes."

Marcus shrugged weakly. "I suppose they mean to break us down, to split Richard's loyalists from the top."

Christopher began to pull the man down the hall with David trailing after them. "Nay, we must stay together, no matter what," he replied. Then, he grunted disgust. "Who would have believed that John and Ralph could have tried to use a woman to drive us apart? Of all the stupid and ludicrous ideas...."

He trailed off, shaking his head. But David, who had managed to walk up beside them, was focused on Marcus.

"Aye, he told us of the rumors," he said evenly, "but he did not deny them."

Christopher came to a stop, as did Marcus. They looked down at David, and Christopher actually glared, but David stood his ground.

"Well, he didn't," he insisted to his brother. "Mayhap he was trying to save his own ass by telling you first, lying about it, so that you would not believe the truth when you heard it."

Marcus' jaw ticked as he faced off against David. He was bigger and broader, but by no means the better warrior. David was one of the elite.

"Do not let your jealously be so apparent, Lion Cub," he growled.

David twitched in Marcus' direction but Christopher threw out a massive arm between them.

"What is going on with us?" he demanded angrily. "Three years in the sands and never a harsh word, but we return to England, I take a wife, and suddenly everyone is at each other's throats? David, you will apologize to Marcus for your blatant insult."

"Not until he denies it," David muttered.

Christopher looked to Marcus. The man continued to stare David down, his jaw working furiously. The cobalt blue eyes were hot enough to burn.

"I did not ravage Lady Dustin," he said simply. *No, I kissed her softly.* There was definitely a difference between kissing and ravishing, minor though it might be.

Christopher had heard enough. Leaving David and Marcus glaring at each other, he had larger problems to worry over than two of his men quarreling.

There were several soldiers guarding the door to his apartments and he brushed past them, opening the door and slamming it in his wake. Edward and Sir Trent were in his antechamber, but Dustin was nowhere to be seen.

"Where's my wife?" he demanded, then eyed Trent. "In the hall, boy."

Trent obeyed quickly, leaving Edward with a furrowed brow at Christopher's manner.

"What happened?" Edward asked.

Christopher glanced at him on his way to the wine decanter. He poured himself a healthy amount before answering.

"Christ, what isn't happening?" he snapped. "Ralph and John tried to blackmail Marcus into championing the prince by telling him that their spies saw him ravish my wife back at the inn. Marcus did the correct thing by telling me about it, but that does not mean the rumors will not run rampant. I can only imagine how Dustin is going to react."

Edward sat on a chair, his expression cool. "What did Marcus say?"

"The truth; that nothing happened," Christopher said staunchly.

Edward nodded, his eyes growing distant. Christopher downed his goblet and poured himself another, eyeing his silent friend.

"What is with you?" he demanded.

Edward glanced up at him, then looked away, shrugging. "Not a thing. Are you going to dress for supper?"

Christopher set the goblet down, eyeing Edward. "What were you thinking, Edward? What have you heard?"

"Heard? Nothing," he said truthfully, then looked at his liege a long moment. "But I would be lying if I did not tell you that I think there may be some truth to the rumor."

Christopher ran cold. "What do you think? Damn, Edward, you were there. What do you think?"

Edward drew in a long, deep breath. "What do I think? I think that your wife has fallen in love with you, and that Marcus has fallen in love with your wife."

Christopher's gaze didn't waver for several long moments. Then he broke away and wandered slowly across the cold wooden floor. After a pause, shook his head.

"Damn," he muttered, then turned to Edward again. "Are you sure?"

"As sure as I can be without asking either one of them."

Christopher looked at the man, his expression torn with shock, before finally emitting a hissing sigh. "Why is this happening, Edward?" he demanded without force. "Never in my wildest dreams did I imagine when I married Dustin Barringdon that she might prove to be the downfall of the mightiest knights since Arthur's Roundtable. Had I only known, I would have told Richard to forget everything. No keep is worth his kingdom, which might be exactly what this boils down to."

"What are you babbling about?" Edward demanded.

Christopher's passion was in his gestures, his voice. "Christ, Edward. David thinks himself in love with her, Jeffrey has told me he is in love with her, now you tell me that Marcus has fallen under her spell. And every time Leeton looks at her, he thinks of Rachel and becomes absolutely useless. That leaves me with you, Dud and that young Burton boy who seem to be unaffected by my wife's charms. How is it possible that this is happening?"

Edward shook his head slowly, seeing Christopher's point. But his liege had failed to mention one very important point. "What about you, Chris? Have you fallen for the woman you didn't want to marry?"

Christopher stopped pacing and looked at him. "Oh…hell, I do not know," he whispered, his agitation evident. "All I know is that I cannot go for a minute without thinking about her. How could I not? She is beautiful and sweet and full of spirit. I am very fond of her, true, but I do not love her."

Edward gazed back at him, not about to contradict him. But Edward knew better; Christopher did indeed love his wife, but he was too damn proud to admit he actually depended on someone other than himself.

As they pondered the revelations, the questions, something came whistling through the air and missed Christopher's head by a mere inch. Both knights instinctively ducked as the pewter cup banged against the wall behind them, and they turned with astonished expressions to see Dustin's tear-stained face glaring at them from the bedchamber door.

Christopher's heart sank when he saw her. She had heard it, all of it, and he could only curse himself for being stupid enough not to control his mouth. But as soon as he saw her, he also realized one thing; she was by far the most beautiful woman he had ever seen. Her hair was incredible, and the surcoat flattered her in every way. He wanted to take her in his arms but she threw another cup at him and he dodged it.

"Get out of here, Christopher de Lohr," she cried. "I hate you. I told you I hated you before, but I mean it now. Go away. I do not ever want to see you again!"

"Dustin," he began feebly, moving toward her.

She screamed at him "You bastard! All the time you were being kind, you were thinking hateful things about me all along!" She bolted into the bedchamber and slammed the door, crying hysterically.

Christopher sighed and looked helplessly at Edward, who didn't feel the least bit sorry for him. He sought to offer the man advice before he quit the room.

"Chris," he said pointedly, making sure the man was looking at him. "If you ever thought to tell your wife that you love her, now would be a good time."

He left, leaving Christopher listening to Dustin's miserable wailing and feeling enough guilt to flood a moat.

☙

HE COULD NOT fold to her. He *would not* fold to her. Christopher dressed for supper, his armor having been polished by his squire until it gleamed like crystal. He listened to Dustin's cries fade until there was complete silence, but even then he didn't go to her. His heart was screaming for her forgiveness, his body ached to hold her, but his damnable pride prevented everything from being as it should. He would not show weakness.

His knights joined him an hour later, having been informed by Edward that Lady Dustin would most likely not be attending supper with them. Hesitant to ask why, they congregated in the antechamber and eyed each other with uncertainty as Christopher finished dressing. Their liege had yet to look at them and tension was evident.

Finished fussing with his armor, he went to the bedchamber door and rapped softly. "Dustin? Are you ready?"

"Go to hell!" Dustin spat from behind the door.

The knights had to look away, but not before broad smiles crossed their lips. They could not even look at each other for fear of bursting into laughter. Only

Marcus and Edward didn't smile.

Christopher sighed slowly. "Open the door, sweetheart. 'Tis time to go."

The door seemed to explode with pounding and kicking on the other side of it. "I said go to hell!" she screamed, louder.

He wouldn't acknowledge her profanity. "Open the door, Dustin, or I shall open it from this side."

"You do and I shall…I shall jump out the window!" she hollered, kicking the door one last time for good measure. "Go away. Go eat your supper and I hope you choke to death!"

They began to hear things breaking and a huge crash that shook the entire room. Christopher's brow furrowed.

"Dustin?" he called, standing next to the door. "Are you all right?"

"What do you care?" she yelled, dissolving into sobs. "You do not like me, anyway. What do you care if I die? Then your knights will not be divided and you can continue your mission for your all precious and powerful Richard. You can sleep with him from now on, because you won't be in my bed!"

He sighed heavily, looking at his knights for the first time.

"Go ahead without me. I shall be down….in a minute."

They turned to go, except Edward. Christopher nodded to him, silently telling him that all would be well. Edward closed the door softly behind him.

When the men were gone and the room empty, Christopher ran his hands through his hair, a weary, defeated gesture. As much as he vowed he would not bend to her, he could not leave her like this.

"Open the door, Dustin," he sounded curiously as if he were begging. "I just want to talk to you, I promise."

"Nay!" she wept.

"Please?" Now he was begging. "I swear, I only want to speak with you. Please open the door."

He thought he was going to have to break the door down and was amazed when it swung open quietly. He waited a moment before pushing it all the way open just to make sure she wasn't lying in wait for him with a club or broken chair leg. He spied her sitting quite calmly on the bed, her tears dried and her hair in place. In fact, she looked stunning and he was completely off guard.

He stood by the door, eyeing the destruction of the room. He was hard pressed to admit that her anger mattered to him, that he didn't want her to be angry with him.

"I am sorry you heard that," he offered finally. "I did not mean to upset you so."

"You blame me," she said in a scratchy voice. "You blame me for everything, don't you? For Marcus, for David, for everything."

"Nay, Dustin, I do not blame you," he said softly. "You have no control over your beauty or your charms, and being men, they naturally succumb."

"But you do not," she whispered.

"That is not true," he said firmly. "I am very, very fond of you. You are my wife."

Her head came up, her eyes dark with hurt. Oh, why did she have to be so tormented by his words? She was stupid, foolish and completely out of control….and she didn't care. Her pride was already damaged. She could not suffer much greater shame.

"My father and mother loved each other," she whispered. "If I ever had a husband, I hoped that someday we would grow to love each other, too. You love David, and Edward, and the others. You even love Richard. But you cannot love me, and it pains me. I should not care, but I do."

Her words reached into his chest and grabbed hold of his heart, twisting and squeezing until it was bled dry.

"Do you love me?" he whispered.

Her fierce pride was badly wounded. "I do not know… I think so. Otherwise, why would I hurt so?"

He could not stop himself from reaching out and pulling her soft hand to his lips, kissing her fingers until she started to cry again, softly. It was a painful and tender moment for them both.

"All things take time, Dustin," he murmured. "Especially love. 'Tis the most difficult of emotions to achieve and the most difficult to be rid of. The kind of love I feel for my brother and for my knights is nothing compared to the love I would feel for my wife. For you. But I never expected to marry, much less love the woman I married."

"You are speaking in riddles," she sobbed.

He was. Damnation, he was. Christ, he knew he loved her. He could not remember when he hadn't and the revelation of it nearly blew his mind to cinder. But he simply could not bring himself to spit it out. No one, not even Dustin, must ever know his weakness.

He was suddenly on her, his mouth sucking her lips with blinding ferocity. She cried harder, responding to him, aching with her need and her confusion. Why did he kiss her so when he didn't even love her? Mayhap he sought to comfort her, or to comfort himself, but all he was succeeding in doing was confusing her even more and she suddenly tore away from him, flailing off the bed until she stood unsteadily several feet away.

"Don't," she said, her whole body shaking violently. "Don't kiss me like that."

He sat on the bed, gazing at her with a look she had seen before, always before he made love to her. It was an expression that usually weakened her, but not now.

"Why?" he pleaded. "Dustin, what do you want me to say that will make things well between us again? Is it that you want to hear me tell you that I love you? Would that make things right again?"

She shook her head. "Even if you were to tell me that, I'd know you were lying." She put her shaking hand to her lips. "I have been so stupid; stupid enough to believe that I could be happy in this marriage. But it appears that our marriage will go the way of so many others, whereon we will simply tolerate each other. Even so, I seem to have driven a wedge between you and your men, and mayhap for that you will grow to hate me."

"Dustin, Dustin," he sighed softly. "I told you I care for you deeply, and I do. I thought you were happy. I know I have never been happier, yet in the same thought I have never been more confused. If you are not happy, what is it you want from me?"

"Nothing," she said shortly, moving to the dressing table and smoothing at her hair. "They are expecting us downstairs."

Her back was stiff, her manner reminiscent of the first day he had met her. Cold. Hard. Distant. His stomach twisted with regret and sorrow.

"Do not do this," he said softly. "Please… don't."

"Do what?" She turned to him, her look innocent. "I am Lady de Lohr in name and body, and I will act the part. That is all you want from me, anyway, isn't it? What did you call me once 'additional baggage?'"

He let out a hissing curse. "And I also told you that I was sorry I said that," he snapped. "You are not additional baggage, Dustin. Damnation, woman, I'd take you over that bloody keep any day of the week."

Her eyes widened but she controlled her reaction. She knew how much Lioncross meant to him and for him to make that declaration astonished her. She should have been deeply flattered, but she wasn't. She was still stinging from his words to Edward and they were the only thing that filled her mind.

She lowered her gaze. "I am hungry. Let us go downstairs."

He stared at her a moment, knowing that would be the only reaction he would get from her. She was deeply hurt and he had only himself to thank for that. He could right it if he were strong enough, but he wasn't. He simply wasn't strong enough to open his heart fully to her and risk the destruction of his soul.

&

CHRISTOPHER AND DUSTIN entered the cathedral-sized great hall of Windsor Castle with great flourish. As Christopher knew it would be, every man in the room turned to stare at his wife as they passed by on their way to the head table. Everyone knew Christopher and had heard he had married, but this was the very first anyone had seen of lovely Lady Dustin de Lohr.

Dustin was awed by the spectacle before her but tried not to show it. She tried to be as expressionless and aloof as possible, but it was difficult not to let her eyes wander over the magnificent trappings of the hall. And the people,

Lord, the people were dressed finer than any she had ever seen and she thought that surely even Heaven could not be this resplendent.

Christopher didn't say a word to her as he led her to the table and seated her between David and himself. The knights had all risen respectfully as she entered the hall, their gazes never wandering from her or their liege. They were, in fact, surprised to see her at all.

Dustin actually smiled at them as Christopher pulled out her chair, noticing that several seats down were Prince John and Sir Ralph, and they both smiled seedily at her. She quickly averted her gaze and took her seat.

The room was abuzz with conversation as the servants brought out the first of several courses. Various boiled vegetables were set in front of Dustin and, her stomach being twisted in knots, made no move to eat them. Christopher and the other men dove into their food with gusto, but Dustin found her attention still drawn to the entire room and its occupants.

"Aren't you going to eat?" Christopher asked softly.

"Later," she said, not looking at him.

He continued with his food and Dustin continued to ignore him, noticing how the women were variously dressed and thinking that she did fit in, at least somewhat. She was so caught up in her observations of women with sleeve cuffs that trailed so long that they went all the way to the floor that it took her several minutes to notice a particularly solicitous serving wench on the other side of her husband.

The woman, a bit older than herself, had been hovering over Christopher since the meal began, refilling his goblet and offering him her apron to wipe his beard with. He was ignoring her for the most part, but Dustin flared with jealousy. Hurt or no, angry or no, no serving wench was going to lust after her husband.

She shot out of her chair, her face flushed with fury, and grabbed the unfortunate woman by the hair. Christopher was hit in the back of the head by the struggling women, astonished to hear his wife's calm, low voice as she called the wench every insulting name she could ever think of as she led her away from the table and towards one of the exit doors. There was no mistaking her meaning.

Christopher and his men watched as Dustin practically threw the girl from the room and then returned to the table as if she had done nothing more than have a pleasant conversation with the wench. Calmly, she reclaimed her seat and picked up her spoon. Everyone exchanged stunned glances as she, quite calmly, resumed eating.

"Would you mind telling me what that was all about?" Christopher asked her.

She took a mouthful of vegetables. "I did not like the way she was serving you."

He raised an eyebrow. "So you bodily removed her from the room?"

She fixed him with a hard gaze. "I did, and I shall do the same thing to any other wench who tries to 'serve' you."

He did grin, then. "Dustin, I am…flattered."

"Don't be," she snapped. "I am your wife and am simply protecting my honor."

His smile vanished. With a heavy heart, he resumed his meal.

They were being served a course of venison in a sweet sauce when Ralph suddenly appeared in front of them, his oily face focused on Dustin. Dustin nearly choked when she looked up and saw him leering down at her.

"What do you want, Ralph?" Christopher demanded coldly.

"Me? Nothing," he said. "But our glorious prince has sent me to offer his hearty approval to Lady Dustin's bold action. A protective wife is a wonderful thing, de Lohr. Yet if she is that aggressive with a woman who had not even touched you, I wonder how you, baron, would deal with a man who had indeed done more than lay a hand on your wife?"

Christopher returned to his food. "I would kill him, of course."

"Even Marcus Burton?" Ralph's gaze flicked two chairs to Dustin's left.

Dustin's head came up, her eyes wide. But Christopher didn't flinch. "And what lies do you have to tell me about Marcus?" he asked disinterestedly.

Ralph smiled directly at Dustin. "Ask your wife, de Lohr. She will tell you."

Dustin was close to exploding. With all of the raging emotions she was feeling, they were begging for a release. She could not believe what she was hearing and, before she realized what she was doing, she stood up and slapped Ralph Fitz Walter across the face as hard as she could.

"You evil little bastard," she hissed.

The entire table shot to their feet, Christopher with his hand to the hilt of his sword but making no move to stop his wife. The front portion of the room that witnessed the action went silent and the silence spread as the explanation went from person to person.

She had hit him hard. Ralph's head snapped sharply to his left with momentum and slowly, he brought it around to face Dustin again. Her face was angry and flushed, but her gaze didn't waver. Ralph knew he could not seek revenge now, in front of her husband, but he was deeply humiliated. He forced himself to smile at her.

"Too close to home, my lady?" he said thinly. "Mayhap you should have used the same tactic on Marcus in the common room at the inn."

Dustin was livid and unthinking. She bound onto the table, skirts and all, and would have throttled Ralph had it not been for Christopher grabbing her. He hauled his hissing, kicking wife against him and had to yell at David and Marcus to keep them from charging Ralph in her stead. Edward grabbed hold of Marcus to control the big man.

"Dustin," Christopher said harshly. "Stop it. You are making a scene."

She stilled, aware that he was right and trying desperately to control her fear and anger. But she was reeling with shock and disbelief; how in God's name did Ralph find out about Marcus and her? More importantly, what would Christopher think now? If Christopher wasn't sure he loved her before, then surely this would kill any affection he had for her.

Ralph, having accomplished what he had set out to do, abandoned the table, leaving everyone in an uproar.

Dustin simply wanted to die. She fell back into her chair, her hands covering her face miserably, as Christopher and Edward tried to calm the table and each other. She could not even look at Marcus; she wondered if he were even still at the table. Surely he would turn and run for his life. Mayhap she should go with him.

There was a cup thrust at her, big hands forcing hers around it. "Drink this, sweetheart," Christopher murmured. "Be a good lass and drink up."

Shaking, she took several large swallows. Christopher had one hand on her wrists, helping her drink, while a big arm was draped over her shoulders. Dustin thought that mayhap he would get her drunk to lessen the pain when he killed her, but his expression looked deeply concerned, and that puzzled her.

"That's my good girl, take another drink," his voice was soft and rich, caring even. She gazed up at him, wondering when he was going to take her head off, but he simply smiled at her. "Are you all right?"

She could not even answer him. She was looking at him, but not really comprehending anything. His smile faded. "Dustin, are you all right?" he asked again.

She opened her mouth feebly but words refused to come forth. She was suddenly quite warm.

Christopher snatched the cup from her, reaching down to pick her up. David was standing up on her other side, aiding his brother as he collected the huge skirt.

"I am taking her out," Christopher told his brother. "Stay here and enjoy the evening. Come and see me when the festivities have ceased."

"What about Ralph?" David demanded.

Christopher fixed him with a deadly glare. "I shall deal with Ralph." He swept Dustin from the room amidst the chaos.

Marcus saw them go from the corner of his eye, feeling sick and angered. He wished it could be he who comforted Dustin, for God only knew how mad and ashamed she was. He should have sought her out earlier, to explain what had happened and to tell her what he had told Christopher. He hadn't exactly lied, but he hadn't exactly told the full truth. He wondered if he would indeed be a dead man come the morn.

Leaving the great hall in chaos, Christopher carried Dustin to their apartments. It was quiet and dark except for the banked fire in the hearth.

Christopher was as gentle as a mother as he carried Dustin into their bed chamber and laid her upon their bed.

Dustin lay there, curling up into a big red and blond ball as if she could fold in on herself and hide. Christopher removed his armor in silence, stripped off his shirt and pulled off his boots. He then proceeded to bank the fire in the hearth before finally turning to his catatonic wife.

"Did Ralph's words upset you so?" he said quietly.

She closed her eyes and hot tears ran across her face and onto the pillow. "Are you going to kill me?"

He looked shocked. "Kill you? Why on earth would I kill you? Do you actually think that for one moment I would believe that snake's lies?"

Her eyes opened after a moment. Then, slowly, she turned to look at him. He looked like a great ethereal being with the firelight silhouetting his massive frame. It took her several long moments to grasp what he had just said.

"You do not...you do not believe him?" she whispered before she could stop herself.

"Of course not, Dustin," he said curtly. "I know Marcus better than that, and I would hope that I would know you better, too. Ralph and John will spare nothing to gain their ends and destroy me. Using you and Marcus was nothing short of vile, even for them."

She sat up, her hair spilling over her. Her relief was immense but she was afraid to say anything lest he suspect that her relief was a bit *too* great. Yet there was one point in all of this that bothered her tremendously; he obviously trusted her, and she had done naught to earn it. She felt guilty all over again.

"Thank you, my lord," she said softly, for she could think of naught else to say.

"For what? For rejecting their lies?" he said, sitting on the edge of the bed.

Something occurred to her at that moment; when she had heard the rumors about her husband having bed a serving wench, she had confronted him and he had confessed. With that knowledge, she was able to deal with it and move on. Yet here the same opportunity presented itself and she took the coward's way out by omitting the truth. Mayhap if she placed the blame on herself, where it truly lay, then he would not be so harsh with Marcus. The thought of her living with this lie hanging over her head was unbearable.

Out of respect, out of guilt, mayhap to hurt him as he had hurt her, she realized she was about to confess. Perhaps there were many reasons for it. All she knew was that she had to. Her great gray eyes turned to him and she could see that his expression was soft. She met his gaze steadily.

"Chris, Ralph spoke the truth," she said softly. "Marcus did indeed kiss me in the common room at the Inn. It was short and went no further, but it happened. His guilt is as great as mine."

Christopher stared at her a long time. In faith, he didn't trust himself to speak. He could see simply by her expression that she was being open and honest with him, and that drove a knife into his belly. So it was true. Though he kept his gaze on her, something in his expression changed. The warmth fled, replaced by shock and ice.

Dustin could see the change come over him. She hadn't expected anything different. "You were truthful with me, once, when I asked you about the serving wench you bedded," she said softly. "I cannot lie to you about this and I can only pray that you forgive me as I forgave you."

He bolted off the bed, pacing toward the windows aimlessly. His hands began to work, great plate-sized hands, clenching and unclenching, finally dragging through his hair. His body was tensing more and more with each step he took.

"Is that all that happened?" he asked, his voice tight. "What about all of the time he spent with you in your room?"

"He never touched me, I swear it," she said evenly. "He was never anything but perfectly courteous. He kissed me, once, that was all."

"Did you like it?" he snapped, then regained hold of himself. "I did not mean that. Christ, Dustin...."

She was incredibly calm, much more than she thought possible. "Nay, I didn't," she said quietly. "I was shocked and angered. I can only tell you that it wasn't planned, that I do not hold feelings for Marcus, and that it will never happen again."

His hands were still moving, tensing. "Then he lied to me."

"If he did, it was only to protect me," she said. "He fears you, and he respects you, and he realized the gravity of the mistake. We both do."

He looked at her then, and she saw anguish in his eyes. Dustin was suddenly inflamed by the pain, for he had caused it in her heart many a time and she was outraged that he should act as though he had been hurt. He wasn't hurt; the only thing injured was his honor.

"At least I didn't bed the man," she exclaimed, hurt and anger filling her. "You did not extend me any consideration before you were pumping your seed into another woman. And do not act as if you are wounded by this action, my lord, for the only thing that is damaged is your pride."

She expected him to fly at her, but he didn't. He looked as if she had taken a dirk and stabbed him in the heart with it. "How can you say that?"

"Because it's true," she fired back. "I am your chattel, your wife whom you profess to be fond of, a pretty little chit whom you subject to your commands and moods and politics. That is all there is to Lady de Lohr in your eyes."

He clenched his teeth, trying so very hard to maintain himself but not doing a very good job. She had hurt him, perhaps more than anyone ever had, and his primal need for satisfaction lashed out at her.

"What else are you good for?" he growled.

He might as well have hit her. Her jaw clamped shut and her eyes softened with agony, but she did not look away from him. She maintained her gaze, her dignity, for all she was worth.

"If nothing more," she whispered, "of giving you a fortress."

He stared at her, deeply remorseful for what he had said. She was so easily crushed, but the truth was he was hurting, too. As much as he tried to convince himself that it was merely his honor at stake, he knew that his heart was gravely wounded. He was bleeding.

With nothing more to say, Dustin turned away from him and climbed off the bed. Her movements were lethargic and slow, as if it was taking everything out of her simply to move.

"I would sleep in the other bedchamber," she said quietly.

When she moved past him, he called out to her softly. "You will not," he said. " 'Tis not safe for you to sleep alone. You will sleep in here, with me."

She looked up at him. "Under the circumstances, I am sure you can...."

He shook his head, cutting her off. "Nay, lady, you will stay here. You may have the bed and I shall...sleep on the chair."

Pain such as she had never known welled in her as she began removing her tight surcoat, anything to busy herself. She wanted to go to sleep, to forget about this for a short while. Mayhap when she awoke, fresh, she would be better able to cope. As it was, she was as brittle as kindling and Christopher's presence only made her feel worse.

"You are not going to kill Marcus, are you?" she asked softly, fumbling weakly with her stays.

Christopher was as close to emotionally numb as he had ever been. He was gazing off across the room, not looking at his wife.

"He lied to me," he said simply.

Dustin's head came up, fear filling her veins. Even if she carried no feelings for the man, she could not let her husband kill him.

"You will *not* kill him, Christopher. I would as soon throw myself on your sword."

"This matter is between my knight and me," he said.

"Nay, it is not." Her rage was surging again. "I am as involved as either one of you. If you kill him, then you must kill me as well. For that matter, mayhap I should return to Lioncross and kill the serving wench you bedded. The one who carries your bastard."

She ended bitterly and his eyes snapped to her. "She does not carry my child," he said.

Dustin simply turned away from him, still undoing her stays. She was too exhausted, too emotional, to say anymore. She blocked him out, unable to cope.

Christopher sat there as she undressed, digesting everything that had happened that evening, trying to regain his shattered composure. As shocking as her confession was, and as stunned as he was that Marcus had lied to him, it was nothing compared to the ache in his heart that Dustin had betrayed him. He could deal with Marcus, but handling his feelings for his wife was a matter he had never had to confront before.

Love was pain and weakness, and this example was living proof. He moved past his wife, heading through the antechamber and to the front door. Opening it, he barked orders to one of the dozens of soldiers guarding the hall and the man took off running. With his knights still in the dining room, he wanted extra soldiers guarding his wife.

He left to seek out Marcus. It would seem that there was much to discuss.

CHAPTER THIRTEEN

CHRISTOPHER FOUND HIMSELF out in one of Windsor's elegantly manicured gardens by the massive motte, sitting in the cool air staring out into nothingness. He was so consumed with emotion that he was absolutely useless.

He had intended to find Marcus, but somehow he had gotten sidetracked on his way to the great hall and had ended up outside, his mind filled with Dustin and the myriad of feelings he had for her.

She had confessed, she had apologized. She had forgiven him for his indiscretion, and compared to what he had done, hers was barely mentionable. After all, she had not lain with the man and he was sure of that. With all of the admissions, he was sure she had told him everything because she was not very good with concealing her emotions. He was furthermore sure that what had happened between her and Marcus was not planned and not premeditated, for he knew her enough to know she was incapable of planning such indiscretions; she was far too innocent.

Which was most likely her problem; she became giddy with Marcus' overbearing attention and allowed it to happen without thinking. Yet how could he blame Marcus? The man knew a beautiful woman when he saw one and probably kissed her before thinking, even if she was his liege's wife. That thought frightened him, for if Marcus committed such a sin with full knowledge, then it must mean he was more than infatuated with Dustin. Mayhap Edward was right after all and Marcus was truly in love with Dustin.

Christopher kicked at the dirt, frustrated and tired and miserable. Miserable because he loved her and could not tell her, miserable because she wouldn't believe him, anyway. He was frustrated with this tremendous distraction while he was supposed to be on a mission from the king, and he was tired because his mind was working too hard trying to sort itself out.

Across the garden came a tall, dark figure. Christopher heard the footsteps and saw the shadow, knowing his sword was a mere inch or so from his hand. Edward's face came into focus under the soft moon glow.

"Why in the hell are you out here?" he asked, sitting on the stone bench beside Christopher. "I should think you would be in bed with your wife."

Christopher didn't say anything for a moment. "She told me that she and Marcus shared a kiss."

Edward wasn't surprised, but he was concerned. "And? God, Chris, you didn't hurt her or…."

Christopher rolled his eyes wearily. "In Christ's name, of course not. She is sound and whole, probably asleep with thirty-five soldiers guarding the door and the halls. She is perfectly safe."

Edward let out a sigh of relief. "I knew you would not touch her, but sometimes we do strange things in anger." He looked long at his liege. "What about Marcus? Are you going to call him out?"

Christopher's jaw ticked. "I do not give a damn about Marcus," he hissed. "It is Dustin I am concerned about. I do not know what I am going to do with her."

"What do you mean 'do with her'?" Edward asked, his brow furrowed.

Christopher hissed a long, exasperated sigh and stood up, stretching his legs. It was going to take courage to say what he was trying to spit out and he struggled with it.

"You were right, Edward, about everything," he finally said. "You knew….how I felt about my wife, but God help me, I cannot bring myself to admit it or say it, even to myself. As I sit here wallowing in misery, I realize that it has taken something of this magnitude to bring me to grips with my feelings for Dustin." He shook his head in defeat. "The woman will be the death of me, Edward. John already knows she means a great deal to me, but if he finds out that she is becoming my reason for living, then he will use that against me and if anything ever happened to her, I would lose what is left of my mind."

Edward smiled faintly. "I never thought I'd ever hear you say you love her."

"I have not," Christopher almost shouted.

Edward grinned broadly. "Yes, you have, in your own way. Tell her and draw strength from her, Chris. She loves you, too."

He shook his head hard. "She wouldn't believe me. She would think I am telling her simply because I know that is what she wishes to hear."

Edward watched him pace. "Why does she frighten you?" he asked.

Christopher stopped. "Because she holds my life in her hands and she does not know it. Love frightens me, for it is a weak man's disease and I do not wish to catch it."

"Too late," Edward said frankly. "And you are so wrong. Love is the most powerful strength of all. Remember your Bible, Chris; there is no greater strength. You fought in the Holy Land for the love of God and it made you invincible."

Christopher shrugged. "I fought for my love of Richard, and he made me what I am. But what I feel for my wife is so unexpected and overwhelming. It overshadows even my devotion to Richard. How is that considered strength?"

"It will be what you make of it," Edward stood up. "You may use it as your life's blood, or you may spend the rest of your life cowering from it. You are married to that young lady for better or worse, for the rest of your life. The fact that you have fallen in love with her is more than anyone could ask for. Do not you realize how fortunate you are?"

Christopher eyed Edward a moment before turning away, his pacing slowing but his body rigid and agitated.

"Do you truly believe Marcus is in love with her?" he asked.

Edward shrugged. "Who can say? But I believe so. Mayhap the only way you can find out is by asking him."

Christopher shook his head vehemently. "If he were to say yes, then I would most certainly kill him. And I need Marcus, Edward. He is the best knight in the realm and I need him."

"Nay, *you* are the best knight in the realm," Edward corrected him. "You and Marcus are so much alike that it is frightening. Talk to the man, Chris, I implore you. If you do not, this madness of yours will eat at your soul and destroy you from within."

Christopher kept his head bowed, watching his feet. "I cannot have this conflict, Edward. Not when Richard's throne is at stake."

"Is it?" Edward asked quietly.

Christopher finally sat down, heavily. "Marcus said that the barons in the north are very opposed to John, yet some of the upper nobility support him because they are as deviant as he is. With Richard gone, the entire country feels as if their king has deserted them and dissatisfaction grows. It is difficult at this point to say who has the edge in loyalty, but both Marcus and I feel that one thing is certain, if John makes a move for the throne, then it will throw the entire country into civil war."

"What of Richard's betrothed?" Edward asked. "Mayhap if she were to assume her rightful place...."

Christopher waved him off. "She is a child, Edward. And she is not yet the queen. Nay, unfortunately, John is gaining power and Ralph along with him. Do you know that he bestowed upon Ralph the title of Sheriff of Nottingham?"

"I heard rumor," Edward said distastefully. "Richard has a marshal, now John must have a sheriff."

Christopher sat forward, his elbows resting on his knees and his great blue eyes staring off into the darkness.

"How do I allow myself to become involved in these things?" he muttered. "Such a simple matter as taking a wife has grown into my greatest concern when, in fact, my greatest concern should be for my king. Sometimes I think I should board a merchant vessel and sail off into the world, and leave all of this mess behind."

"And leave Dustin here?" Edward asked softly.

Christopher paused a moment before shaking his head. "Nay," he whispered. "I would take her with me and pray that someday she overcomes this hatred she bears. Mayhap someday she would consider me a fine husband."

"She doesn't hate you, and she is deeply proud of you," Edward told him, rising to his feet. "Go to her, Chris, and surmount your pride. 'Tis the only way."

Christopher nodded faintly. "Mayhap."

Edward stretched the weariness out of his lanky body. "If you are finished with your emotional crisis, let us return to the dining hall and show John that Richard's presence is indeed heavy at Windsor."

Leave it to Edward to put things into perspective. Without an argument, Christopher rose, silently, his mind on his wife as he followed Edward to the great hall of Windsor. He was, in truth, glad for Edward's presence. The man always had the ability to calm him, to help him to see reason. Christopher was frankly concerned how he was going to react when he saw Marcus and was glad for Edward's presence. At least the man would provide a buffer between him and Marcus should the situation grow ugly.

Unfortunately, Marcus was the first man he saw upon entering the hall. Oblivious to Christopher's thoughts, he went right to him.

"Is Lady Dustin all right?" Marcus asked with concern.

Edward glanced at Christopher, but his liege was expressionless. "She is in bed," he replied.

"Good," Marcus issued a sigh of relief. "When I forewarned you about Ralph and John's plans, I neglected to tell your wife. I hope the shock was not too great."

The man is digging his own grave, Edward thought. Discreetly, he left the two men standing near the door, alone, but didn't go far. He wanted to be close in case the conversation deteriorated.

Seeing Edward move away from the corner of his eye, Christopher was much calmer than he thought possible. He crossed his arms, his gaze lingering over the crowd that was now up and dancing to minstrels.

"Considering Ralph spoke the truth, her shock wasn't so great more than she is simply distraught," he said, his eyes then falling on his knight. "She told me what happened at the inn, Marcus. More than anything, she is deeply concerned for you. It would seem that she does not want me to kill you."

Marcus met his gaze for an eternal moment, frozen in time, no feelings nor reaction forthcoming. He wasn't really surprised that Dustin had confessed. In fact, he felt rather relieved by it. Oddly relieved.

"Is that what you plan to do?" he asked quietly.

"Nay," Christopher replied, as steadily as he could manage. "But I would like to know why you lied to me."

Marcus sighed faintly and averted his gaze. "I do not recall lying to you, Chris," he said softly. "Specifically, I told you I did not ravage your wife, and I didn't. We shared a small, stolen kiss for which I am completely guilty, and nothing more. It was over almost before it began."

Christopher's big body tensed as he studied Marcus' profile, but it occurred to him that he was right. He never actually denied kissing Dustin; he only denied ravaging her. His anger was fed because of the small technicality upon which Marcus was basing his answer.

"Why, Marcus?" he finally managed to whisper, his pain breaking through and hating the fact that he sounded so hurt. "Why did you do this?"

Marcus met his liege's eyes, his composure slipping because of what he heard in Christopher's tone.

"I do not know," he murmured. "Mayhap the three days I spent with your wife proved to be too much for me. I told you I thought she was absolutely beautiful, and I believe my infatuation with her got the better of me. I cannot tell you how sorry I am, Chris, for everything. You know me well enough to know I am an honorable man."

"I thought I did," Christopher said. "I trusted you and you betrayed me."

Marcus' jaw ticked with the severity of his words. " 'Twas never my intention. I can only beg your forgiveness."

Christopher held his gaze a moment longer before looking away. Marcus, too, looked away, his eyes distant and painful.

"Do you have feelings for my wife?" Christopher asked quietly.

Of course I do. Marcus had been grappling with them ever since he kissed her. But he had a suspicion that this honesty would not be well received.

" 'Twould be futile, my lord, for she cares only for you," he said quietly, "and I am a man unaccustomed to futility."

"Pretty words, Marcus, even for you," Christopher said. "But you did not answer me."

Marcus sighed softly, forming his answer carefully. "I told you that I am infatuated with her, but that is all. It will pass."

"What if it does not?" Christopher asked. "Will I find myself being challenged by you in the future, the prize being my wife?"

"Nay, my lord, I would never do that," Marcus insisted softly. "She is your wife, in the eyes of God and England. I would not, nor could I, take her from you."

Christopher was more hurt now than when he had entered the room. His anger was banking, manifesting itself into sorrow. He had trusted this man, his dearest friend, and he had been betrayed.

"Do you love her, Chris?" Marcus asked after a moment.

Christopher didn't look at hm. "I do not see how that is any of your affair."

"It isn't," Marcus said. "But I think had this incident been more a matter of pure honor, I would be lying on the floor right now in a pool of blood. Yet I see a look in your eye now that I have never seen before, a great pain. If you did not love her, you wouldn't be so agonized nor indecisive."

Christopher clenched his teeth. "She is my wife, Marcus. Of course I am hurt by this, but at least she confessed. I had to drag it out of you."

Marcus knew that was the closest thing to an admission as he would get. "Shall I seek another liege?"

"Nay," Christopher said shortly, regaining some of his composure. "I need you, Marcus, and we must hold together if for nothing else than for Richard's sake. No woman will drive us apart."

Marcus bowed shortly. "As you say, my lord."

The air between them grew stiff and formal, as if there was an understanding between them yet the camaraderie had vanished. Christopher was distrustful of Marcus' intentions, and Marcus resented his liege for the one thing he truly desired; his wife. It was a horrible circumstance, one they both struggled with.

From the best of friends to distrustful comrades, the fall from grace was a painful thing, indeed.

☙

LATER ON THAT evening, Marcus walked alone through the corridor heading toward his chamber, feeling distinctly saddened and ashamed. He was so caught up in his thoughts, wandering, that he was genuinely shocked to see Dustin emerge from the darkened corridor.

Dustin came upon Marcus, her beautiful face pale and furrowed. She was dressed in some sort of simple surcoat, wrapped in a heavy shawl. She looked ill and lost.

"Dustin?" he asked softly, deeply puzzled. "What in the hell are you doing out here? Where's Chris?"

"I do not know," she said wearily. "He has not returned and I was concerned. Are you all right?"

She was looking him over for injury and he knew what she meant. "I am fine," Marcus reached out and took her arm, turning her around in the direction she had come. "Let me take you back."

Dustin allowed him to lead her back down the hall. Truth was, she was feeling terrible and sickened, and was grateful for the assistance. But she was desperate to find Christopher for he had left so abruptly that she was terribly worried.

"I told him," she said softly, leaning into his arm. "I am sorry, but I had to. 'Twasn't fair to lie to him."

"I know," Marcus replied quietly. "We have spoken of it."

"Does he hate you?" Dustin looked up at him. "He hates me, you know. He left me alone in our room. He just… left. He never wanted a wife and I am sure now that he is doubly sorry."

Marcus shook his head. "That is nonsense," he said, helping her up the stairs. "He does not hate you, and he does not hate me. He is grieved, 'tis all."

"He took a serving wench to his bed right after we were married, you know," she mumbled, tired and defeated. "When I found out I was hysterical. He hadn't even bedded me yet, but I forgave him. Why can he not forgive me?"

"He will, Dustin," Marcus murmured. "He will forgive us in time."

She stumbled and he paused, lifting her into his big arms and carrying her the rest of the way down the hall. There were several soldiers in the hall and Marcus lay into them.

"Who's in charge?" he bellowed.

The soldiers snapped to attention, the voice of Sir Marcus Burton sending bolts of fear through them.

"Crag Armitage," one soldier replied firmly. "He is inside with the baron now, my lord."

Without another word, Marcus pushed past the soldiers and kicked open the door to the antechamber.

Christopher was reaming the unfortunate sergeant as Marcus breezed in with Dustin cradled in his arms. One look at Marcus holding his wife and Christopher practically kicked the soldier out, his face contorted with rage.

"What do you do?" he demanded ferociously.

"I found her wandering the halls downstairs," Marcus replied steadily. "She's exhausted."

Christopher snatched Dustin from Marcus' arms, setting her down roughly and she stumbled, falling back even as he reached out to steady her. But his attention, his anger, was solely focused on Marcus. Veins were bulging and his outrage had reached its limit. It began to overflow, spilling out all over the place, and Christopher spoke before he could think about what he was truly saying.

"You are dismissed, Burton," he growled.

Marcus' eyebrows rose, off-guard. "I… what did you say?"

"You heard me," Christopher snapped. "You are dismissed from my corp. I want you away from Windsor, and away from my wife. If I ever see you again, I will kill you."

Marcus' dander rose, fury to match Christopher's. "For what? For God's sake, Chris, I was just…."

Christopher cut him off. "You will address me as 'my lord' from now on," he roared. "Get out of my sight, Burton, or so help me, I shall drop you where you stand.

Marcus' expression turned deadly. "You may try, my lord," he said in a low voice, "but I will defend myself wholly, for I have done nothing wrong."

"You have done nothing but covet my wife and break God's holy commandment," Christopher seethed. "If the only way I can keep you away from her is to banish you from my sight and service, then so be it."

Marcus was stunned. He stared back at the baron in complete disbelief, not wanting to believe his words. He finally shook his head slowly.

"You are mad," he hissed. "Would you have preferred that I left her wandering the halls for John or Ralph to find?"

"Get out." Christopher turned his back on his former friend and knight. He could not stomach the sight of him anymore. "I have nothing more to say to you."

Dustin, having sat in shocked silence throughout the exchange, suddenly found her voice. "You are not being fair, Chris," she said. "Marcus did nothing."

"Nothing but lie to me, nothing but covet you," he whirled around to Marcus again. "Is there anything else you have failed to mention? I never asked you if you bedded my wife back at the inn. Did you?"

"I told you he didn't," Dustin insisted.

"And I swore to you on the Holy Bible that I never touched your wife in that manner," Marcus said. "I can do no more than that."

"What you have done is driven an irreversible wedge in Richard's loyalists," Christopher said. "You always were a womanizer but I never believed that you would stoop so low as to pursue my own wife. 'Tis your own actions you must blame for this."

"And what of you," Marcus shot back, his massive body rigid. "How dare you speak of betrayal when you saw it fit to bed a serving wench after you had taken your vows with your wife. Mayhap you are ignoring your own guilt by focusing on me."

Christopher's eyes widened, cut down by the information, now used against him. It had been a weak moment that was coming back to haunt him. But he stood his ground. "I have no guilt," he insisted, jaw ticking. "Dustin has forgiven me, which is of no concern to you."

Marcus was still posturing furiously. "It is not my concern, but you stand here accusing me of a heinous crime when, in fact, 'twas a kiss I stole. I did not bed the woman." He jabbed a finger at Christopher. "How dare you act the hypocrite!"

"You are jealous," Christopher said as if the entire concept had just dawned on him. "You are jealous of me, of my titles and land, and of my wife. Aren't you? So you intend to destroy what you cannot have."

"Stop it!" Dustin shrieked. "Listen to what you are saying!"

They were ignoring her, their eyes spitting venom at each other. Finally, Marcus turned for the door. He was afraid of what would happen if he didn't. Dustin, her hands on her mouth, took a few timid steps after him.

"Please, Marcus," she pleaded softly. "He did not mean it."

"Leave him alone, Dustin," Christopher snapped, turning his back on Marcus. "He must go."

She backed off, her eyes extending a thousand apologies to Marcus. He gazed at her, his body riddled with pain and jealousy, wishing he could take her with him, but more concerned with the ending of his relationship with Christopher. He simply could not believe what was happening. Shocked and furious, he quit the room.

When he was gone, Dustin turned her tear-streaked face to her husband. “How could you do that?” she demanded. “You had no reason!”

He didn’t answer her, leaning against the wall and staring out of the window into the night. His jaw was still ticking, beads of sweat on his forehead. He was angered and sickened, devastated and grieved. He was so much at the moment that he couldn’t single out one particular hurt. It was all hurt.

“Go to bed, Dustin,” he said finally.

Devastated, Dustin let her wrap fall to the floor and she wandered woodenly toward the bedchamber door. She paused a moment, trying to think of something to say, but no words would come. All she knew is that something horrible had happened this night, and she was responsible for it.

If there was any doubt that he hated her before, there was none now.

CHAPTER FOURTEEN

MARCUS, FURIOUS AND irrational, found himself wandering aimlessly through Windsor's great corridors. All of his senses were reeling, his mind focused on Christopher's rage and words, and wondering if he should return to protect Dustin from his wrath. Yet he knew the anger was focused on him and him alone, and that hurt him to the core. A moment of weakness would apparently cost him what he had worked for all his life.

He found himself wandering the royal wing, padding along the fine woolen rugs. He stopped and turned himself around, not wanting to be anywhere near John, but there was a body behind him, blocking his path.

Ralph's lip curled in a sneer. "Took a wrong turn, Burton?"

Marcus wasn't in the mood for the man. "Move aside, Fitz Walter."

Ralph, amazingly, did as he was asked and Marcus brushed past him.

" 'Twould be a shame if anything happened to Lady Dustin, don't you think?" Ralph said leadingly.

Marcus froze, turning around with slow restraint. "What are you babbling about?"

Ralph shrugged and it just occurred to Marcus that there were no other soldiers in the hall. Ralph had confronted him alone, a rare happening, but it put him all the more on guard.

"Just that," the sheriff said lightly, leaning against the wall. "Lady Dustin is a beautiful woman, obviously loved by a great many men. 'Twould be a pity if an accident were to befall her."

He had Marcus' full attention. "Ralph, let me make this as plain as I may. If Lady Dustin so much as stubs her toe, I will come looking for you and I will kill you. Is that understood?"

"Perfectly," Ralph said. "But I am sure you will have to stand in line for that honor behind her husband. Unless…unless, of course, you *were* her husband."

Marcus' steely facade was invaded by a hint of annoyance. "That again? I told you once that I would not consider being John's champion."

Ralph stared Marcus down for a brief moment, then examined his nails. "Baron Marcus Burton has a certain ring to it," he said. "And I understand there is a lovely baronetcy in Somerhill simply waiting for a deserving man. You are from York, are you not? Surely Somerhill is of your acquaintance. A perfect place to raise a family with a beautiful woman, far from London and Lioncross."

Marcus was actually listening to him. He was alternately appalled and interested. Ralph looked up, catching the gleam in Marcus' eye for a split second. He knew when to strike.

"All you have to do is champion John at the tournament," he insisted. "Burton, you can joust in your sleep. Surely I am not asking too much."

Marcus fought off the urge to agree with him, closing his eyes and turning away. Yet, for the sake of argument only, he pictured what Ralph was suggesting; with Christopher gone, he could marry Dustin and take her away to the north. Alone, he could champion Richard's cause and rally the northern barons for their support. And Christopher's knights could pledge their loyalty to him, with Lioncross falling into the ward of the crown.

But Christopher had to be out of the picture. He tried hard to imagine his friend gone and he simply could not. Tens of thousands of Saracens had tried to kill the Lion's Claw, what made him think that he could do it, legally, at a tournament?

Marcus shook himself from those thoughts, shocked and disgusted for plotting Christopher's demise. He could no more kill Christopher than kill himself. How in hell could a simple woman cause him to rethink his morals, his devotions, and his entire life? He wasn't even sure what he felt for her, but whatever it was, he had never experienced it before and it was making him crazy.

Nay, he could not and *would* not kill Christopher, no matter how angry he was with him. But he could compete against him.

There was nothing wrong with that, except it was too late to seek a sponsor… except for John. If Marcus won, mayhap regardless if he won, he would have his title and his lands. And, mayhap as well, he would have a bit of revenge.

Slowly, he turned to Ralph, surprised the man was still there looking questioningly at him.

"I will hear more of this," he mumbled, hating himself even as he said it.

☙

DUSTIN HAD BEEN asleep for hours. Lying on the huge bed, alone, she looked like a small child. She lay on her back, one arm over her head and the other resting on her stomach, with the firelight reflecting softly on her pale face.

Christopher hadn't slept at all. He didn't even enter the bedchamber until he was positive she had fallen asleep, and even then he did nothing more than stare at her.

His mind was still cold with shock and anger, but he was beginning to come around. His anger with Marcus had not abated and standing at the foot of the bed watching his wife sleep somehow intensified his feelings.

Yet it was more than anger, because the bitter twinge of jealousy filled his mouth – jealousy because he knew Marcus to be a fine man and Dustin, being so naïve in ways of the heart, could have just as easily fallen for Marcus.

Mayhap that is why he sent Marcus away. With the man out of his hair, he could better deal with his own feelings toward his wife. With Marcus around, he went out of control so easily and it scared him.

Gazing down at Dustin's beautiful face, he knew in his heart that he loved her dearly. He always would, no matter what happened. Damn, she could have slept with Marcus and he would have forgiven her simply because he could not stand the thought of being without her.

He meandered around the side of the bed and reached down, stroking a wayward strand of hair from her forehead. She sighed raggedly, turning in the direction of his hand and he felt the heat of desire lick at him. His hand lingered on her forehead, touching her face for a moment before he sat beside her. His fingers combed through her incredible mane, feeling its silkiness against his rough skin and lifting it to his nostrils to inhale the faint rose scent.

The same hand left her hair and traced ever so delicately down her neck, tracing her breasts through her shift. He was aware of his engorged shaft straining against his breeches but he was content to touch her for the time-being, knowing she would spurn any sort of advance once she awoke. He would steal this time, then, to worship her.

He didn't know how long she had been awake, watching him, for when he happened to glance up from delicately tracing her nipples, her wide gray eyes were on him. Startled, he stopped his exploration and stared back at her, wondering if he should say something. He opened his mouth to tell her he was sorry for waking her when he could not seem to remember the words and before he could stop himself, his mouth and body descended on her.

Dustin should have fought him, but she could not seem to find the strength or the desire. Once his great hands scalded her and his expert tongue licked her lips into a frenzy, she turned herself over completely, forgetting about the anger and fear and hurt that had constituted her day. All that mattered was Christopher, on her, in her, touching her. Even if he didn't love her, his touch said otherwise and it was easier to pretend.

Her shift was torn down the middle in one swift move and his clothes came off hurriedly as they bit and sucked at each other hungrily. His hands found her breasts, his lips found her nipples, and Dustin's cries of ecstasy filled the room. He was moving furiously, almost roughly, but she loved all of it and encouraged him onward.

He was absolutely consumed with her. His fingers stoked her most delicate center, coaxing forth her juices that told him without words how badly she wanted him. She was soaking before he could insert a finger into her, and he forewent the finger in lieu of his throbbing manhood.

They came together in a cataclysmic clash of pure desire. He thrust into her in one long, powerful movement and she moaned loudly, biting her lip to keep from screaming. He drove into her, again and again, watching her nipples harden in response to his force, watching her breasts shake with the power of his thrusts. She was so tight and slick that in no time at all he was convulsively spilling himself into her. Dustin, feeling him throbbing and pulsing within her, could not help but answer in volcanic triumph.

When the tempest passed and they were basking in the warm musk of their lovemaking, Christopher felt her stiffen in his arms and he knew that her guard had gone back up.

"Dustin," he said softly. "I am…I am sorry that you had to witness my exchange with Marcus. But you must understand that I had to do what I felt best for you. For us."

"As you say, my lord," she said, aloof.

He sighed into her hair. "Do not be angry with me, sweetheart."

"What does it matter? You have made it obvious that I am good for naught much else but bedding and appearance," she said. "As you have just proven, you can easily take what you want from me no matter how I feel."

He pushed himself up, away from her. "Do not place the blame on me, lady. You responded quite easily."

She didn't look at him. "That is because sex is all we have between us, my lord. You respond to my body, I respond to you, and soon we will beget an heir. Do you think it possible that you could love your child even if you do not love the child's mother?"

He rolled off the bed, angrily pulling on his breeches and boots. "Go back to sleep, Dustin."

She closed her eyes obediently. Angry and bitter, he pulled his tunic on and moved for the door, but not before gazing back at her face, preparing for one final retort. But the words died in his throat when he noticed two wet trails leading from her eyes to the pillow.

CHAPTER FIFTEEN

"I STILL DO not believe it," David growled.

It was a bright and lovely morning. The knights, all of them, and Christopher were marching purposefully for Prince John's audience chamber. They had been summoned by a triumphant steward, requesting their presence by order of the prince. The purpose of the meeting was to announce that John had finally selected a champion.

They were met in the halls by several other competitors, all summoned for the same purpose. There was talk of who had been foolish enough to accept John's offer, but no one was positive as to who it might be. David and Leeton kept pestering Christopher as to where Marcus was, but Christopher would only shake his head and change the subject. Edward already guessed what might have happened, and furthermore suspected just who the new champion was. Christopher suspected it too.

As the doors to the audience chamber opened and the knights and men began to file in, Edward made sure he walked in beside his liege.

"It's Marcus, you know," he murmured.

Christopher's face hardened. "If it is, then I pity him. He is a bigger fool than I thought."

"You two had words last night," Edward remarked, a statement and not a question.

Christopher didn't answer, making sure he found a place as close to the door as possible. He didn't want to be in the very front for John's scrutiny.

"Marcus no longer serves me, and if he is John's champion, then he no longer serves Richard, and is considered the enemy," Christopher finally said, quietly.

Edward shook his head regretfully. "Marcus isn't the enemy any more than I am," he said. "If he is John's champion, then he must have a damn good reason."

"He does," Christopher snapped. "We are sworn enemies and he wishes to defeat me."

"Sworn ene…?" Edward's brow furrowed. "What in the hell are you talking about?"

Christopher shook his head harshly, not wanting to answer, noticing that the prince and Ralph were entering the room. Edward continued to eye him even as the crier announced the prince, as the man graciously acknowledged his subjects.

"Thank you for coming, loyal vassals," John said with a sappy overture. "I know that your day is busy, yet I found this announcement too important to wait until tomorrow, so I will make it short and to the point. A new baron has joined your ranks, a man entirely worthy of the title I have bestowed upon him. A man who served our king and my brother in the Holy Land, and whose reputation for fairness and righteousness is unparalleled."

David and the other knights eyed each other and Christopher. He refused to look at any of them.

"This new baron will be my champion tomorrow in the games, and I expect to win," John said, laughing at his jest, though it was not a jest. "I know that you are extremely curious to know just who this man is, so with no further delay, I will introduce you to the realm's mightiest warrior, Marcus Burton, Baron Somerhill."

Christopher's knights were beyond shocked. Their eyes bugged out as Marcus took his place beside John, in full armor and draped in John's colors. Christopher gave no reaction, but inside, he was sickened. Was Marcus so angry with him that he would cast Richard aside and carry on with John? Marcus was like a brother to him and regardless of their falling out, he was disgusted by the treason the man had committed. But he did not react outwardly in any way. He knew he was being watched.

John looked directly at Christopher as he spoke. "I have granted Marcus the baronetcy of Somerhill," he said, listening as murmurs of disbelief spread throughout the room. "Be pleased and be warned; the competition tomorrow will be as tight as history has ever recorded."

He had finished his pretty little speech, his eyes still on Christopher. Disgusted and depressed, Christopher grew more and more disheartened as his eyes met with Marcus' cobalt-blue orbs, a silent challenge coming forth from them. Without a word or another glance, he spun on his heel and quit the room.

His knights caught up to him several doors down the corridor.

"Chris," David hissed. "What in the hell is going on? Why is Marcus championing John?"

"Ask Marcus," Christopher replied.

"But…he is sworn to Richard," Leeton said. "What happened?"

Christopher waved them off, too angry and repulsed to answer them at the moment. Anything he said would come out as too personal, too selfish, so he ignored their questions. Later, when he was calmer, he would speak with them.

David knew they would not receive any answers. Motioning the others away, he continued to walk in silence beside his brother as they continued down the hall.

When they reached the door to Christopher's apartments, David put a hand on his brother's arm.

"Truth between us, brother," he said quietly. "It is her, isn't it? Did Marcus make advances to her?"

Christopher looked at his brother and he could feel his walls coming down. Visibly, he relaxed. "Aye, he did," he whispered. "He neglected to tell me the whole truth. Dustin spilled out her soul, which is typical for her, but Marcus danced around it even when I confronted him. I can no longer trust the man, David, and I will not have him under my command."

"Over Dustin?" David asked incredulously. "I cannot believe that, Chris. That is not the Marcus Burton we fought with for three years."

Christopher shook his head. "I do not mean it as it sounds. As a knight, he is still the only man, aside from you, that I would have as my right hand. Yet sometimes, where jealousy and emotion are involved, men have been known to do strange things." He let out an irritated sigh. "Damn, David, I just do not know anymore. Since I have returned home, nothing is as I had planned. I feel as if the natural order of things are unbalanced; I do not know who to trust or believe anymore."

"Because of Dustin?" David asked softly. "Jesus, Chris, if you'd only open yourself to her and quit fighting everything you feel, maybe things would be right again. If you would only trust her, you would be at peace. Your insecurity is making you mad."

Christopher smiled faintly. "You sound entirely wise. But are you right?"

"He is."

The voice came from down the hall. Both men turned sharply to see Marcus coming toward them, in full regalia, his handsome face calm. The tension in the air soared; they could all feel it. David eyed his brother, wondering if he was going to have to somehow hold the man back when he unleashed on Marcus. But Christopher made no provocative moves as Marcus drew closer.

"Before this goes any further, before irreversible damage is done, I want you to know my reasoning for what I have done," Marcus said quietly.

"No need, Burton," Christopher said stiffly.

"Oh, but there is." Marcus' eyes glittered. "You see, I understood your words to me last night, Chris. I see now that you love Dustin desperately else you would not have blown up at me as you did. You perceive me as a threat because you are uncertain of your wife's feelings towards you. Mayhap I am a threat; but be that as it may I have no intention of trying to steal your wife from you. As for my decision to champion John, I did it for several important reasons, namely, because John had granted me a title and lands for which I am deserving, powers that can be used for Richard's advantage. It matters not who bestows the authority, for once it is mine it is mine to keep." He approached slowly. "Chris, John told me that if I mortally wound you in the tournament that he would award me your wife. Naturally, I refused. Last night, Ralph outright threatened Dustin's life if I did not reconsider. So I did, and I accepted, but not before every one of my demands and stipulations were put into writing and signed by the prince and by Ralph, with an additional copy sent to the Archbishop of Canterbury."

Christopher and David were stunned. "And what requirements did you make?" Christopher asked softly.

"That in the tournament, no matter how I fared, that my titles and lands could not be revoked," Marcus replied. "So you see, I have gained a great deal, but at a great price. My reputation has been severely compromised, yet I believe redeemable in time. I saw immediate advantages to becoming John's champion."

Christopher swallowed, feeling his guilt growing by the moment. "And my anger toward you pushed you into this?"

"In a sense," Marcus agreed honestly. "You have so much and I have very little. Your distrust and fury cut me, Chris, because it was irrational. 'Tis true I have given you reason to distrust me where Dustin is concerned, but we have been fighting side by side for so long that I would hope that fact alone would weigh heavily in your mind."

Christopher looked away, unable to meet Marcus' eyes anymore. Marcus watched his former liege, slowly removing the gauntlet on his right hand. "With everything that happened yesterday, I do not expect an instant apology, nor would I accept one, but mayhap over time we can be friends again," he said. "But I will give you one last display of loyalty, baron. I will not fight against you, in battle or in tournament. No one short of God can order me to do that."

Without warning, he slammed his right fist into the wall as hard as he could, crunching bone and cartilage against stone and mortar. Something had to give; it was his hand. Bone spurs and shattered metacarpals thrust up through the flesh and blood was streaming everywhere. Christopher and David flinched, but through it all, Marcus never uttered a sound.

Bitterly shocked, Christopher could only stand there as David rushed to Marcus, passing a critical eye over the destroyed hand.

"Jesus, Marcus," David swore softly. "Why in the hell did you do that? You shall be lucky if that hand will ever be useful again, much less hold a sword."

Marcus, his face pale the only indication of the level of pain he was experiencing, continued to meet Christopher's eyes steadily.

"I will not fight against the baron," he repeated weakly.

David passed a glance at Christopher as he wrapped Marcus' hand in a scarf to stop the gushing blood. Without another word, David led Marcus back down the hall and disappeared with him, leaving Christopher standing in stunned silence, alone in the corridor, with tears in his eyes.

CS

CHRISTOPHER FOUND DUSTIN sitting in their great antechamber with a piece of needlework in her hand. She did not acknowledge him in any way when he stormed in, tossing his cape aside and marching to the closet that held his armor. He was still reeling with shock, and was far more determined than he had ever been to win the tournament tomorrow and laugh in John's face. He felt as if he were fighting for both Marcus and himself, as well as Richard and the entire crown. Sometimes it was as if the weight of the world were riding on his massive shoulders and it would merely take a feather's burden to break him into a thousand pieces.

The feather's burden could very well come in the form of his wife. He didn't glance at her as he put on his armor, even as her maids came out to help him with his mail hood and gauntlets. Dustin ignored him, as well, her beautiful face buried in her needlepoint. If the maids questioned her behavior, they did not show it.

Christopher chased the serving women away and strapped on his sword, moving to pick up his helmet. He did glance at Dustin then, his eyes raking over her in a pretty purple surcoat and her hair pulled back softly. She looked beautiful.

"You are coming with me," he said shortly.

Her head came up. "Where, my lord?"

He adjusted his helmet before slamming it onto his head. "To the practice field, lady, as you did yesterday. Gather your cloak."

Still clutching the needlework, she retrieved the other cloak she brought, an off-white heavy cape with ermine lining, and swung it over her shoulders. He watched her secure the neck and pull it comfortably about her, wanting to help her, to touch her, but restraining himself from even trying.

As his wife, he had every right to touch her any way he pleased, but she was quite distant and cold and he found his guard was up as well.

"Come, Lady de Lohr," he held out his arm formally and she accepted stiffly.

He took her down to the practice area with him where several dozen knights were already going about their practice rounds. He sat Dustin down by the new lists where he could keep an eye on her and went to join his men over by the eastern wall of the arena.

David saw him coming. He was working out a scratch in his sword as his brother approached. "How is your wife this morn?" he asked.

"I do not know," Christopher replied disinterestedly, then turned to the rest of his men. "We will practice between ourselves this morn. Baron Sedgewick's men wish to challenge us to light rounds later, as do Lord Darby's men. We will take them on after the nooning meal."

Everyone moved to the arena but Edward. He moved close to Christopher. "David told me what happened with Marcus."

Christopher nodded, slamming down his face plate. "How does he fare?"

"Marcus? His hand is crushed and he will be fortunate if he can ever hold anything in it again, but he's resting comfortably in his quarters," Edward replied, eyeing Christopher. "You really should go see him, Chris. The man ruined his life because of you."

Christopher's head snapped to him. "Don't you think I know that? Don't you think that I'm completely guilt-ridden that my insides are eating themselves out? Leave me alone, Edward. I would deal with this myself."

"Does Dustin know?" Edward asked softly.

"Hell no, she doesn't," Christopher snapped. "She already resents me and I will not add fuel to the fire."

"She's going to hear about it, you know," Edward pointed out. " 'Twould be better if she heard the truth from you first. If she hears it secondhand, 'twill only worsen her feelings."

Christopher sighed, unsheathing his sword and examining it. Then he lowered it, jamming it into the cold earth.

"Marcus found her wandering the halls last night and brought her back to me," he said quietly. "He held her in his arms as if she were the damn Virgin Mary or something. When I saw the look on his face, and the way she was pressed against him, something....I snapped, Edward. I ordered him out of my service, and away from my wife. It was if I were listening to someone else shout at Marcus and I had no control over it. Dustin was there, of course, and heard everything. She told me I was not fair and she was right, but I honestly felt I was doing what was necessary to preserve our marriage. I just did not go about it properly."

Edward nodded in understanding. "And Marcus, distraught, ran right to John and accepted a reward for representing him in the tournament."

"Something like that, I am sure," Christopher murmured. "He insisted that Ralph had threatened Dustin's life and that fact contributed to his decision. But he, like me, has had time to think about the rashness of our actions. The only escape for him was to injure himself so he could no longer fight, thereby saving his pride and reputation. But I do not know what escape there is for me; I have made a mess out of everything because of this goddamn pride I carry."

Edward gazed off across the arena, seeing Dustin sitting in the stands with her nose buried in her needlepoint. "Do you want my opinion?

Christopher snorted. "Absolutely."

"Then apologize to Dustin and beg her forgiveness for being so harsh and cold and cruel," Edward said. "I have a feeling she would be most understanding if you were to only be honest with her. And as for Marcus, apologize as well and hope for the best. He worships the ground you walk on, you know."

Christopher nodded vaguely, drawing his sword forth from the ground deliberately. "You are most likely right, my friend," he said. "Come now; let us see who is sharper this morning in the arena."

Glancing up from her needlepoint, Dustin stole glances at her husband as he fought Edward effortlessly. To watch him fight again caused her heart to swell with enormous pride and she again remembered the passion and fire between them last night. But since yesterday he had returned to the cold, unfeeling baron that had come to Lioncross over a week ago, a man who married her in dirty armor and whose steely demeanor filled her with loathing. It made her eyes fill with tears to think that he would be that way the rest of their lives, unable to forgive her for an innocent mistake.

She had let her guard down for this man and had welcomed him, albeit reluctantly, into her heart. She had grown to love the man whose strong hands and warm smile made her feel warm and safe. But stung by his words and by his actions, she would be damned to make the same mistake twice.

Lost to her thoughts, she became aware that there was a body next to her and she glanced over, seeing that it was Ralph Fitz Walter. She scooted several inches away from him, still with her needlepoint lifted as if to create a barrier between them.

"Lady de Lohr," he greeted formally. "How lovely you look today."

"Thank you, my lord," she mumbled.

"Ah, I see your husband out there," Ralph remarked. "A fine warrior. The best. I trust that he and Marcus have come to an agreement over you?"

Dustin lay the needlepoint down in her lap, her gray eyes guarded and dark. "I know not what you mean, my lord. There is no agreement to reach."

"Of course not, my lady, my mistake," Ralph said quickly. "But did, in fact, your husband tell you that Marcus will be competing against him in the tournament? It will prove to be a priceless match."

"Against him?" Dustin stared at Ralph. "Nay, my lord, he said nothing."

Ralph smiled narrowly. "Then let me be the first. Mayhap the prize will be more than a simple reward, eh? Mayhap there will be a trophy involved."

Dustin shot to her feet, her anger and hatred of this man filling her. "I am no trophy, sire, and I resent being labeled as such. I am Christopher's wife and will always be, Marcus or no Marcus. The man is inconsequential to me."

Ralph's eyebrows rose. "Pray forgive, madam, 'twas not my intent to offend," he said soothingly. "I simply meant… well, 'tis well known that there is a struggle of the heart where Marcus and your husband are concerned."

"You are so wrong, Sir Ralph, that I resist the urge to laugh in your face," Dustin snapped. "There is no struggle, other than the continuing struggle of honor and morality. I married Christopher for duty and honor, nothing more. I am his legal wife and would do nothing to jeopardize that station. Now, if you will kindly leave me alone, I would appreciate it."

Ralph rose to his feet. He was aware of several mailed forms approaching him from all sides. Christopher came up to stand by his wife with his sword held tightly in his hand. Ralph smiled and bowed deeply to Dustin.

"Thank you for your company, my lady," he said graciously. "And I look forward to seeing your beautiful face at the tournament tomorrow."

Dustin didn't reply, averting her gaze. Ralph, amused, looked at Christopher. "Greetings, my lord," he said. "I see you are in fine form today."

"Be gone with you, vermin," Christopher rumbled.

Ralph laughed. "Not much for compliments, are you? Well, tomorrow will tell just how fine your form is. I look forward to your bouts with Burton."

Christopher took Dustin's arm and gently began to lead her away. Ralph, ignoring the knights breathing down his neck, watched her go. He did so enjoy goading her and the baron.

"My lady, will you reconsider awarding prizes tomorrow?" he called. "John is most anxious that you do it."

Dustin waited for Christopher to answer for her, looking up at him when he didn't. She could only see his eyes and the bridge of his nose through his raised visor. He was looking at her.

"Do you want to?" he asked.

She was shocked but after a moment, managed to nod once. Christopher turned to Ralph.

"Tell John that my wife will grant his wish," he said. "She will be most gracious and award trophies and, considering I will win all, she will be awarding them to me."

They left Ralph standing alone in the stands with a shocked look on his face for a change.

Christopher took her around the other side of the arena where their squires and a few soldier were camped. The knights were trailing after them, like a protective group, and Dustin was having a difficult time looking at her husband. She was incredibly confused as they came to a stop near a horse corral.

"Why?" she finally asked.

Christopher glanced at her. "Why did I allow you to award prizes?" he removed his helmet. "You heard my reasons, I gave them to Ralph."

She looked up at him a moment, trying to determine his true motive, but could read nothing on his stoic face. She found a stump and sat on it.

"Why are you fighting Marcus?" she asked, quieter.

Christopher looked at her. He had a feeling Ralph had come to gloat. "Marcus is a baron now, a title granted by the prince last night. In return, he is championing the prince in the tournament tomorrow."

She lowered her head, not uttering a sound and he knew she was deeply upset. As he gazed at her, he knew he had to tell her the truth of the circumstances. To keep it from her would further destroy what was already badly damaged between them, and he very much wanted to repair it. He crouched down next to her.

"Dustin, I will not be fighting him," he said softly. "Marcus had an…accident this morning and he is unable to compete."

"Accident? What sort of accident?" she looked at him suspiciously.

"He broke his sword hand," he replied softly.

Dustin was concerned. "Is he all right? How did he do it?"

"He will be fine," Christopher replied, avoiding her second question. "Tell me, my lady, would you like to go to the Street of the Jewelers later today? I promised you a trip."

She shook her head. "Nay, I do not feel like shopping."

He raised an eyebrow. He repressed an urge to leave her alone to her self-pity, instead resorting to a seldom-used tactic; he begged.

"I would like you to come with me," he said softly, gently. "Please?"

She shook her head again. "Nay, I do not want to go," she repeated.

That was as much begging as Christopher was going to do. Abruptly, he rose and began fumbling with his armor. There was frustration and disappointment to his movements. Dustin watched him from the corner of her eye first, then more openly, watching his sharp and rather reckless movements.

"Do you really hate Marcus?" she asked.

"Nay," he replied. "I do not. I never did."

"Do you hate me?" she questioned.

He came to a halt and looked at her. "Of course not, Dustin. I could never hate you."

She stood up, her body rigid and her beautiful face intense. "Then tell me you forgive me or tell me you will never trust me again before you take another breath," she pleaded. "I cannot go on with this any longer, Christopher."

He stared back at her. "Is it so important that I forgive you? Are you not satisfied to let things pass over?"

"Nay, I am not," she said passionately. "I will not have this between us, not for the rest of our lives. I will not have a seed of bitterness or a gram of mistrust that you can throw back in my face."

"Why would I do that?" he asked, puzzled. "But if it is so important to you, then I do forgive you."

"And Marcus?" she pushed.

He lowered his gaze, pretending to busy himself with his helmet, but she reached out and stopped his hands, her fingers curling around his great mailed gloves. He tried not to look at her but he knew he was fighting a losing battle. Their gazes locked and she lifted her eyebrows.

"Do you forgive him?" she whispered, enunciating each word.

"Would you have me forgive him?"

She nodded firmly so there would be no mistake. Christ, as he looked into the depths of her haunting gray eyes he knew at that moment that there was nothing on earth he wouldn't do for her.

"Then I do," he whispered.

"Will you tell him or shall I?" she asked.

"I will when I see him," he replied, trying to shake off the effect her gaze was having on him.

She shook his hand, trying and succeeding to regain his attention. "Nay, Christopher, you will tell him *now*."

"Dustin, I am not yet finished with my bouts and….."

She cut him off. "The man is crippled, Christopher. 'Twould greatly improve his outlook to know that you do not carry a grudge," she said softly, her tone honey to his ears. "And know this, husband; a clandestine relationship takes two people. Even if Marcus were willing, which he was not, I certainly would not jeopardize my marriage to you by taking part. 'Tis you I love, husband, not Marcus Burton."

He stared back at her, her words sinking in. *'Tis you I love, husband.* Her words filled him more than he ever thought possible, hearing it again from her and knowing that this time, she meant it. She wasn't ill or sleepy. She was clear-headed and rational. When she smiled as if to emphasize her words, he came apart, kissing her happily more times than he could count, listening to her giggles and sighs and, finally, her soft pleas to stop. Her arms were wound around his mailed neck, her face against his beard.

"I am so glad you do not hate me," she whispered against his cheek.

He kissed her chin. "Dustin, there is nothing you could possibly do to make me hate you," he replied. "I am so sorry for the things I said. I didn't mean them."

"I know," she rasped, cuddling against him.

His kisses slowed and he grew thoughtful. "You said something to me last night, something that has irked me ever since." He relaxed his hold and she slipped down to stand on her feet. "You said that sex is all we have between us. It isn't, is it?"

She shook her head and put her fingers on his lips to quiet him. "I just told you I love you, Chris. Obviously, there is more than a physical relationship on my part." Her smile faded. "But what about you? When I asked you, you gave me a pretty speech that I still find difficult to understand. You said love was difficult to achieve and that it took time. It took me less than a week to know that I loved you. Is that enough time?"

He grinned and kissed her fingers. "It is."

She caught his knowing grin, eyeing him. "And?"

"And what?" he said with good-natured evasiveness. "Do you wish me to tell you that I would die for you a thousand times over? That I worship the ground you walk on? That I find myself living simply to see your smile, to hear your laughter, to feel your fist on my jaw?"

She giggled, closing her eyes briefly and drinking in his words happily. "Aye, tell me all that and more," she breathed. "Tell me you love me."

His smiled faded and his grip tightened, his blue eyes boring into her. "I do.

More than anything."

Her breath caught in her throat. She hadn't truly expected to hear him admit it and she was surprised, but at the same time an overwhelming sense of elation swept her and she smiled broadly. She grabbed his beard and shook his head gently.

"Then say it, Chris," she demanded softly. "I would hear those words from your lips."

He pulled her to him, nipping at her ear. "In time, sweetheart. But know that I do."

She would be satisfied with that for now. She did not understand why it was so hard for him to utter the words, but it mattered naught. He admitted his love and she was delirious with joy.

"Now we must go and find Marcus," she said, pulling away from his probing lips.

"Now?" he repeated, his thoughts lingering more on seeking their bedchamber.

"*Now*, Chris," she said firmly. "He feels terrible, I know it."

Christopher gave her a long look before sighing with reluctance. "Very well."

He took his wife's hand and escorted her to the low, squat outbuildings that housed visiting knights. The knight's quarters were cool and dark as the two of them entered, the smell of the corridor dank. As they progressed, she became apprehensive, wondering if Marcus would throw them both out on their ear. But she had to try; she was sure if she hadn't hounded her husband then he would not have come. The man's pride was legendary.

Christopher stopped before an iron-clad door and gave a sharp rap. They heard Marcus' voice demand identification of the caller.

" 'Tis me, Marcus," she said softly before Christopher could respond. "Dustin."

After several moments they heard the latch to the door lift and slowly, the door swung open.

Marcus' pale face loomed in the door, his right hand bandaged almost to his shoulder. His eyes were riveted to Dustin, and then with surprise they focused on Christopher. But there was no emotion whatsoever and the silence was uncomfortable.

"We came to see how you are faring," Dustin offered, feeling the tension rise. "I am so sorry you had an accident. Is it bad?"

Marcus looked at her a moment before opening the door wide and allowing them entrance.

"It's bad enough, my lady. I will not be fighting in the tournament tomorrow," he replied politely.

"What did the physician say?" Christopher asked.

Marcus didn't look at him as he pulled up a chair for Dustin. "That it is broken."

"How bad?" Dustin asked, concerned, her lovely face upturned to him.

Marcus sat on his bed. "Bad," he said with a nod of his head. "Very bad."

Dustin glanced at Christopher, who was looking at his friend. As Christopher gazed at the man, the waste and the selflessness of Marcus' actions gripped him like a vise and he felt his pride, his rigidness abate.

"*How* bad, Marcus?" he pressed quietly.

Marcus looked at the bandage, touched it. "Most of the bones in my hand are broken, as well as my elbow," he said. "The physician seems to think that my arm, when it heals, will be virtually useless."

Dustin gasped, a hand flying to her mouth. "Oh, Marcus, that's terrible," she exclaimed softly. "But surely the physician is wrong. Why, once your hand is healed, 'twill only be a matter of building your strength again."

"Or learning to fight with my left hand," Marcus smiled at her, his eyes dulled.

Dustin returned his smile sympathetically. "Marcus, I am truly sorry for you. You are the greatest fighter I have ever seen, next to Christopher, of course. You will be again, someday, I know it." She reached out and gingerly touched the stiff bandage. "How did it happen?"

Marcus didn't even look at Christopher, keeping his eyes focused on Dustin's blond head. "It's not even worth mentioning, my lady, truly. What's done is done, and I've moved on."

Dustin didn't press anymore. Christopher wouldn't tell her how it happened, and neither would Marcus, and she suspected that one had to do with the other.

"I hear that you are now a great and powerful baron," she said, trying to shift the subject to something less morose. "Congratulations, Marcus. Richard will be most pleased."

He nodded. "I hope so, as I am eager to see my holding," he said. "The winters are hell that far north, though."

She grinned, her eyes alive. "They cannot be worse than winters on the Welsh border. We freeze sometimes for six straight months."

"Do you hear that, Chris?" Marcus actually looked at him. "You have six months of the deep freeze to look forward to."

Christopher cracked a half smile. "Then I am pleased to have you to commiserate with."

Marcus snorted. "I am not entirely sure I am equipped to handle a cold winter any longer," he said. "Winters in the Holy Land were beautiful and mild. I fear I have been spoiled."

Christopher nodded. "As have I," he said. "I am ashamed to admit it."

Dustin, happy that they were at least talking civilly, took the opportunity to slip from the room. She rose from her chair and put her hand on Marcus' shoulder.

"My husband wishes to speak with you, Marcus, so I will leave you two alone." She patted his shoulder before moving for the door. Christopher, standing in front of her like a huge movable wall, crossed his arms.

"And where do you plan to go?" he asked pointedly. "I will not have you wandering the halls of the knight's quarters alone."

"That is true, my lady," Marcus rose. "I am sure your husband doesn't mind if you hear what he has to say."

Christopher looked over her head to Marcus. "Nay," he said after a moment. "I simply....Marcus, I know that whatever I say is grossly inadequate considering what has happened, but all the same I wanted you to know that....well, that I am so very sorry for the way I acted, and for what I said. I cannot explain myself except to say that I was foolish. Whether or not you forgive me is your privilege, but I wanted you to know my feelings just the same."

Marcus gazed back at him, his cobalt blue eyes unreadable. Christopher, positive the man was going to throw him bodily from the room then and there, cleared his throat and continued.

"Dustin will be awarding prizes at the tournament tomorrow," he said. "I would consider it an honor and a personal favor if you would act as her protector."

Marcus knew how hard that request must have been for Christopher. Truth was, he would like nothing better. He was almost as good with a sword in his left hand, as he was with his right hand, although most people didn't know it. But Christopher knew it, else he would not have asked.

Marcus didn't blame Christopher for anything, for all of the events stemmed from his blunder. If the situation had been reversed, he doubted he would have acted with as much control as Christopher had, in spite of everything that had happened.

" 'Twould be my pleasure, my lord," he said after a moment, his heart melted by Dustin's huge smile.

Christopher nodded shortly. "My thanks," he said. "What did John say of your injury?"

That seemed to bring some humor to Marcus' lips. "He was only just here moments before your arrival," he replied. "His personal physician tended me, you know. To say the prince is furious is an understatement, especially in light of the fact that I had all of my conditions put in writing and he cannot do a damn thing about it. I am a baron by his hand whether or not he likes it, and he has no champion at the tournament tomorrow."

Dustin, feeling the tension of the room drain away, was happier than she had been in a few days. She leaned into Christopher, feeling his arm go about her waist.

"We are going to the Street of the Jewelers, Marcus," she said. "Please accompany us."

Marcus waved her off. "Nay, my lady, as much as I would like to, I have been ordered to rest and I must say that my arm throbs."

"Of course," Dustin nodded. "Then mayhap we will see you at supper?"

"I would not miss it," he replied. "That is, if the baron is gracious enough to allow me the company of his knights and wife."

"You are my vassal, it is expected that you are with me at all times," Christopher said firmly, rescinding his order of dismissal he had issued the night before and hoping to make it sound firm enough that Marcus would not dare back down. But the man was a baron now, too, and was no longer subject to Christopher's orders. "If that is agreeable," he added.

Marcus grinned at the addition of the last sentence. "It is," he replied. "Did you know that John granted me five hundred troops to take with me to Somerhill? As big as your force, I might add. The task at hand is selecting my knights. If you have no objection, I will be taking Dud and Trent with me."

"None at all, as they are your men," Christopher replied. "There are many fine knights at Windsor because of the tournament and tomorrow should provide you with a great opportunity to view their skills."

Marcus nodded. "I already have at least two men in mind."

"Who?" Christopher was suddenly all talk, all business.

Dustin listened to her husband and his vassal, almost weak with relief. Once again they were talking as they had when she had first met Marcus, before all of the ugly scenes and words. Therefore, she was perfectly content to stand there patiently whereas before, she would have whined to leave.

They left Marcus to rest almost an hour later. Dustin by then was truly bored, twitching restlessly until Christopher finally excused himself. They left the knight's housing and proceeded back across the grounds, their pace unhurried and their talk light. She could scarce believe that this morn she had been desperately angry at him, unsure of any feelings she had. Strange how everything became abundantly clear in a matter of minutes.

"To the Street of the Jewelers, then?" Christopher asked as they left the knight's quarters, taking her hand and all but forgetting about the practice rounds going on in the arena down the slope.

She nodded. "I would buy you that massive ring now."

He was grinning, scratching at his beard underneath his mail hood. "This beard itches something fierce when I perspire. What say you were I to shave it off?"

She was amazed that he had asked her opinion and took the question seriously. "You are most handsome with it off or on," she said. "If it irritates you, then shave it off."

"But I will no longer be able to scratch you when I kiss you," he teased, grabbing her and rubbing her cheek with his beard until she screamed.

"Shave the bloody thing off!" she yelled, smiling, as he released her. "You like to use it to torture me."

"True," he agreed. "Then mayhap I shall keep it."

They laughed together and continued to the stables.

CHAPTER SIXTEEN

FROM WHERE RALPH stood, he had a perfect view of Baron de Lohr and his wife as they wandered leisurely down to the stables. He watched them hug and laugh until they disappeared from view before turning to John, seated several feet away and sitting in front of a chess set.

"Well?" John asked, considering his next move.

"De Lohr and his wife," Ralph told him. "Looks as if he will be taking her out for a ride."

"I'd like to take her for a ride," John mumbled suggestively, moving a piece. Ralph pushed himself away from the window and sat back down.

"What do we do now with Burton nonfunctional?" he asked, moving his knight.

John chewed his lip as he thought. "The bastard probably broke his hand himself," he said. "He gave me some lame excuse about a horse stepping on it. Why does this always happen to me? Just as I seem to gain the upper hand, disaster strikes. Waste of a perfectly good baronetcy for nothing. Well, now, de Lohr continues to be a problem."

Ralph watched the prince make another move and began contemplating his own. "I am a firm believer in destroying the man at the source," he said. " 'Tis obvious that we can trust no one else for this task. He is quite fond of his wife, my lord. I suggest we start there."

"What? Kill her? You used that threat on Burton but I did not believe you to be serious," John replied. "She's far too lovely to kill, Ralph, and I have not yet had a chance with her."

"Nay, not kill her," Ralph said. "But it would not be impossible to abduct her and spirit her far away. How could de Lohr focus on your destruction if he was consumed with worry for his wife?"

"De Lohr is out to destroy me, isn't he?" John murmured, moving another piece. "Why else would he be here as Richard's eyes and ears." Suddenly, he stopped in mid-movement and looked at Ralph. "Do you believe it possible that Richard sent him here to kill me?"

"An assassin? 'Tis possible, I suppose, but knights as righteous as de Lohr are not keen on premeditated murder." Ralph countered the prince's move. "Nay, de Lohr is here to spy on you and report back to your brother. With him distracted in the search for his wife, 'twill be much harder for him to spy on you."

"Sweet Jesus, what would we do without lovely little Lady de Lohr?" John murmured, moving his queen. "My brother unknowingly undermined his own mission by ordering de Lohr to marry the woman. Who would have known that he would have fallen in love with her?"

"How could he not?" Ralph moved his knight. "Check." "She's a thoroughly delectable piece of meat, not unnoticed by Burton or any other man who sees her."

John sat forward, studying the board. "Which one of our loyalists holds the most fortified castle?"

Ralph thought a moment. "There are several, my lord," he said. "The trouble is de Lohr commands all of the crown's troops, which total thousands of men. Were he to use the force and attack the hold where his wife is being held, he could easily destroy the fortress and our vassal with it. Nay, sire, if we abduct her, we must hide her until the time is right to use our leverage."

"Hide her where?" John, irritated he was losing, demanded.

Ralph sat back in his chair, drumming his fingertips against each other as his elbows rested on the arms of the chair. "Wales, Ireland, Scotland, France. Anywhere but England."

John looked thoughtful for several moments. He may have lost the game, but he had not lost the fight. "I have a holding in South Glamorgan, in Wales. I saw it once; a Godforsaken, miserable piece of dung. St. Donat's Castle sits on the coast among sharp cliffs and sheer mountains, a gloomy depressing place that is said to be haunted. The caretaker is a member of the family that built the place and I obtained the castle. 'Twould be a perfect place to keep Lady de Lohr while her husband frantically scours England in search of her. He'd never think to look in Wales, do not you agree?"

"Absolutely, sire," Ralph agreed. "Especially with winter coming, who would want to brave south Wales? We could keep her there comfortably for months."

John was suddenly not so angry that he lost the game. His hard brown eyes found Ralph. "Make it so, Ralph. And no mistakes this time."

Ralph nodded. "Trust me, sire. Lady de Lohr is as good as ours."

☙

DUSTIN WAITED PATIENTLY while her husband conversed with the stable master, looking about the stables with interest. Christopher had his back turned to her and she wandered a few feet away, watching the people and the children, hearing the dog's bark and the horse's bray.

Absently, she began to wander slowly, noticing everything and smiling shyly when a groom would give her a bow or a nod. She stopped for a moment to admire a particularly beautiful black gelding, trading a few words with the groom before continuing on, completely forgetting about her husband. She was filled with the stables and the smell of horses and hay.

She rounded a corner and paused to study the reddest chestnut she had ever seen when suddenly she heard tiny little squeaks, like pathetic whimpers. The sounds grew louder and she followed them, mounting a ladder to the hay loft curiously. It was there she found the source of the sounds, three tiny pups flailing about in the hay.

She cried out softly and crawled across the dried grass, taking the first friendly puppy she came upon and cuddling him sweetly. His brothers, seeing movement, stumbled toward her.

She studied the pups, noting from their teeth and eyes that they were five or six weeks old. She cradled a short-legged blond puppy, while his siblings were black with white and all brown, respectively. It was no time before they were crawling all over her, snagging her surcoat with their sharp baby claws and she was thoroughly delighted. She wondered where the Mama dog was. The straw was dented and a little dirty, and the pups were thin. She decided that the mother must have abandoned them and the pups were obviously too small to find their way down from the loft. As she cuddled and cooed, she heard her name being shouted loudly.

"I am here," she called out.

Christopher didn't answer for a minute, marching into the stables with the rage of the devil. "Where?" he boomed.

"Up here," she answered, looking down. He was directly below her.

He heard her voice and looked up, seeing her through the slats and the hay. "What in the hell are you doing?" he demanded. "Dustin, you know better than to wander off."

"Come to the ladder," she said softly. "And hold up your hands."

"What?" he scowled, putting his hands on his hips.

"Please, Chris, just come to the ladder," she said, picking up all three pups. "Hold up your hands."

With a snort of annoyance, he came around and mounted the first step of the ladder, holding up a hand as requested. Dustin scooted to the edge of the opening and handed the first puppy, the black and white one, down into his mailed glove.

"Christ," he hissed, clutching the puppy quickly to him so he would not drop it. "What is this?"

She put her feet on the top rung of the ladder, holding two puppies in one hand. "I found them up here. Their mother must have abandoned them. Aren't they cute?"

"Delightful," he said dryly, noticing that she was trying to descend the ladder with one of her hands occupied. "Hold, lady. Give me those mongrels before you fall and break your neck."

Carefully, she handed the other two down to him and quickly descended the ladder; gently taking back the pups she had given him. He continued to hold the black and white one, eyeing it critically.

"And what, I am afraid to ask, are you planning to do with these rats?" he asked sternly.

She turned her wide, innocent eyes to him. "Keep them, of course. I miss Caesar so much, and holding them helps ease the pain a little."

He bit his tongue. Every negative word he was about to say simply slipped away and he could not deny her. Exasperated at her, and at his own weakness, he put his huge hand on her back and guided her from the stable.

"Where will they sleep? Surely not in our bed," he said.

"Nay, I will make them beds of their own," she said, rubbing noses with little blond puppy. "I think I will call this one Alex, in honor of Alexander the Great. And this one," she nuzzled the brown puppy with the long legs, "I will call Cabal."

He cocked an eyebrow at her. "King Arthur's dog? A sound name, though he does not look deserving enough."

She pursed her lips at him in irritation and gazed fondly on the little black and white mutt cradled in her husband's massive hand. "And that one, I will name Harold."

"After King Harold, no doubt," he muttered, then looked at the wriggling little pups. "Al, Hal and Cab. What a trio."

He snickered as she protested strongly, though not without cracking a smile. "You will not call them that," she demanded. "You will call them by their proper names."

He ignored her, lifting the pup he held against his chest so he could look at the little black-and-white face. "How goes it with you, Hal? Do not think to overrun my house like that vicious beast disguised as a cat does. You will know your place or I will have roast dog for sup."

"Do not say that," Dustin admonished, laughing loudly when Harold licked Christopher's nose. Christopher, goaded by her laughter, kissed her soundly on the lips and smeared puppy saliva on her cheek. Dustin giggled, licked her lips, and returned the kiss. Christopher almost forgot about the dog and pulled her to him with his free hand, his lips sweetly invading hers. They were about to become even more involved when someone shouted his name.

They looked up to see Edward approaching, smiling but puzzled as he came up on them.

"What is this?" he pointed at the pups.

"Dogs, Edward, or are you truly that ignorant?" Christopher said sarcastically. "My wife has acquired three new pets, God help us."

"Charming," Edward sniffed. "So you have been here playing with puppies while Baron Sedgewick and Lord Darby demand you fight them both? They refuse to take us on of lesser rank."

Christopher made a face. "Damn, I was hoping they would occupy themselves elsewhere this morn," he said. "I wish to take my wife into London."

"So take her." Edward was thrilled to see that Christopher and his wife were getting along again. He had been concerned for them. "I shall simply tell the baron and the earl that you cannot be found."

Christopher glanced at Dustin's eager face. "And so I shall," he said, handing the pup he was holding over to Edward. "Take this canine and his brothers to Marcus. Tell him to feed them or something, at least until we return."

"What about his hand?" Edward demanded, taking on Dustin's puppies.

"His other hand is fine, as is the rest of him," Christopher said. "He is wasting the day by lying around like a weakling, so he can busy himself with these little maggots. This one is Al, this one is Hal, and this one is Cab."

Dustin rolled her eyes and pushed forward, shoving her husband aside. "This one is Alex, this one is Harold, and this," she eyed her husband impatiently, "is Cabal. Make sure you tell Marcus and tell him I shall come for the pups in a few hours."

Edward was vastly relieved. If Dustin was speaking of Marcus, and Christopher was beaming like a fool, then things must be right in the world. He wondered if Christopher took his advice and apologized for his rashness; obviously, something had happened and he was thankful, for everyone's sake.

"As you wish, my lady," he said, grasping the puppies awkwardly as he strode away.

Once the dogs were gone, Christopher took her hand. "And now, we go to London."

THE STREET OF the Jewelers was where every fine gold and silversmith in London kept shop. Christopher brought six trusted soldiers with them because he wanted his wife protected while he selected her gift alone, for he wanted it to be a surprise.

Dustin, not one for jewelry, was not particularly interested in the wares displayed, but in more of the people and buildings. She watched fine women walk by, taking note of their surcoat or hair, then her head would whip around to study another individual. Christopher watched her with a great deal of amusement.

"One more snap of your neck like that and your head will come free from your shoulders," he remarked after she intently studied a man dressed in flowing black with an odd sort of cap on his head.

"Who was that?" she asked, pointing to the man walking away from them.

"A Jew," he replied.

Dustin turned once more to watch the man disappear into the crowd. "Oh," she acknowledged with wonder. "I have never seen a Jew before."

He reined his destrier in front of a busy shop and Dustin rode alongside. He dismounted, moving towards her. She was too busy observing the people around her to notice that he held his arms up to her. She ignored him, though not intentionally.

"Are you going to sit up there all day?" he asked with feigned annoyance.

She grinned at him sheepishly and slid into his waiting arms. He held her just a bit longer than necessary, smiling at her. "This is the shop where I bought your wedding ring," he told her. "Mayhap they have another ring to match."

She nodded as he took her arm and led her into the dark shop. The goldsmith, although busy with another customer, recognized him and waved enthusiastically.

"Baron," he said happily. "So good to see you again. How was it in Wales?"

Christopher removed a gauntlet. "I was not in Wales, I was on the border, and it was acceptable. I have brought my wife; she wishes to purchase a ring for me like the one I gave her."

Dustin held up her hand and showed him the pretty gold band with five tiny diamonds. The man nodded firmly.

"Ah, yes, I have something that will match quite nicely for you, baron, a very princely ring," he said, rummaging through his wares.

Dustin and Christopher watched him as he dug around and mumbled to himself. Suddenly, he drew forth a ring gleefully and thrust it toward Christopher.

"Now there is a fine ring for a baroness, don't you think?" he said.

Christopher took the ring and scrutinized it closely. It was an exquisitely cut diamond, as big as a fair-sized pebble, set in a thin gold band so that the diamond nestled atop the band and caught the light brilliantly. He moved it around, noting the quality and color of the gemstone.

"Give me your hand," he told his wife.

She held up her left hand and he slipped the band on her finger, placing it flush against her wedding band. It was a perfect fit.

He examined the ring closely, turning Dustin's finger from side to side. "I shall take it," he said as easily as if he had just purchased a loaf of bread.

Dustin stared back at the ring in awe. It was a magnificent diamond and the rainbows of colors that radiated forth from it were unimaginable. But it was also quite large and, she thought, gaudy. Although it matched the wedding band beautifully, she believed it looked sorely out of place on her hand with the chewed nails.

"Christopher," she said softly. " 'Tis a lovely ring, but I am very happy with the band you gave me. Surely I do not need another wedding ring."

"You do, and now you have one," he replied in a tone that she dared not argue with.

Resigned to the rock that now hugged her finger, she gazed at it again, holding it in front of her and watching the colors as it caught the light and growing to like it better by the second. Suddenly, the jeweler let out a small cry and brought forth what he had been searching for. With great flourish, he handed it to Dustin.

It was a horribly gaudy ring with a diamond on it as big as a bird's egg. She turned her nose up at it and handed it back.

"I want a man's ring, not a woman's," she sniffed.

"But this is a man's ring, a baron's ring," the goldsmith insisted. "See the workmanship? The craftsmanship?"

Dustin shook her head firmly. "I want a strong ring, solid and beautiful and simple. That thing is for the court dandy."

Christopher hid a smile as the jeweler began to sort through his wares again. Dustin stood on her toes, trying to see over the man's shoulder as he shuffled about. He would hold up a ring to her and she would shake her head. The gaudier the ring, the harder the head would shake. Finally, desperate and down to his very last ring, he held up what he considered to be a grossly inadequate ring for a man of the baron's status.

She was pleased. It was a large, wide band of gold, strong and solid and perfect. It was exactly what she wanted, exactly like her husband. Christopher watched her face as she looked the ring over.

"Are you pleased? Is this what you had in mind?" he asked.

Dustin took the ring from the jeweler. "Take off your gauntlet," she asked her husband.

Obediently, he removed the glove and she slid the big ring onto his finger easily. She smiled and looked up at him. "It's perfect. What do you think?"

He looked at the ring. "I think my wife has very good taste."

She smiled broadly and he tapped her lightly under the chin before turning to the goldsmith. "It would seem that we are satisfied," he said. "What is the price?"

Dustin watched her husband's hand. He held the gauntlet in his right hand, leaving his left hand bare as he bartered for the price of the rings and when he was satisfied, he paid the man with several gold coins. Dustin swallowed hard when she saw the exchange of money; her ring had cost him a great deal and she wasn't even that fond of it. Yet, since it was a gift from him, she would treasure it.

Purchase complete, Christopher took Dustin out of the shop and into the faded late morning sun.

"Would you like to look about?" he asked.

She looked down the street, busy with hundreds of people. "Aye," she replied. "Are there any bakers down there? I am hungry."

Perfect, he thought. She could occupy herself with food while he selected her gift. He feigned irritation at her. "You keep eating like you do and you are going to be fat as a pig," he said sternly, although it was far from the truth. He liked to see her healthy appetite.

She stuck out her lower lip in a pout. "And then you will not want me anymore?"

He could not help but break into a smile, giving her a few coins. "Eat yourself sick. I have business to attend to."

He turned to his soldiers and gave them a few sharp orders, putting one of the men in charge. Dustin grinned at her husband as she walked down the street with her escort, noticing he hadn't put his glove on yet. Even from where she was, she could see the wide gold band gleaming in the weak sunlight and she was immensely pleased. Selecting it had been much easier than she thought.

She walked down the street with her guards, glancing here and there when vendors would call out to her, but shaking her head and passing on. She asked the soldier who was in charge where the baker's shop was and he pointed to the junction where two roads crossed. Dustin truly was famished, for she had had no morning meal and the nooning meal was rapidly approaching. The streets were alive with people and things, and she was thrilled with the new sights and smells.

On the corner was a man with a little monkey on a leash. Dustin had never seen a monkey before and was entranced at the little thing as it danced about and held out its little hat for coin. She laughed with delight when the monkey would take a bow after receiving a coin. The vendor, a thin man with bad teeth, politely answered her questions about the animal and gave her permission to pet the beast.

The monkey was affectionate and soon curled up on Dustin's lap as she stroked it tenderly. It was a tiny little thing with a beard that moved comically when the vendor gave it something to eat. Dustin forgot all about the baker.

She lost all track of time petting the monkey and playing with it, laughing when it would smile a big monkey-smile. Her guards never said a word and neither did the vendor, although she was costing him money the longer she played with his source of income. But after a while she realized that she was taking the man's valuable time, although she was depressed at the thought of leaving the monkey.

Thanking the man for his kindness, she gave him all of the coins that Christopher had given her for the baker. She turned around to the soldier in charge and shrugged carelessly.

"I guess we are not going to the baker, after all," she said. "We should go back and find my husband."

The soldier nodded and they started back the way they had come. They hadn't moved five feet when there was great screaming and a commotion behind them. Dustin whirled around to see the vendor viciously fighting with the little monkey. The monkey was flipping over and over on the end of the leash, biting the man when he tried to grab him. She continued to watch in horror as the man swatted the monkey heavily on the side of the head, as the little animal fell, dazed, to the ground.

She rushed forward as the vendor picked the monkey up by the scruff of the neck, mumbling curses at the creature.

"How dare you strike that monkey!" she accused loudly. "Put him down, I say!"

The nice vendor was suddenly not so nice. " 'Tis my beast, missy, and I shall thank ye to stay out of my affair."

Enraged, Dustin grabbed his arm. "I shall not stay out of it, not when you go about beating tiny defenseless animals. You should be ashamed of yourself."

The monkey was beginning to come around, squirming and crying just like a human baby, and the vendor struck it again to keep it still.

Dustin shrieked. "Don't do that!"

The man bit off a retort and turned his back on her, moving to gather his things. Dustin was furious.

"Don't you dare ignore me," she snarled, yanking his arm so hard that he nearly lost his balance. "I will not allow you to mistreat that monkey no matter what it has done. Give it to me."

The man shoved her back roughly, still holding the monkey cruelly. "Go away, ye fancy bit of chit. This is none of yer affair as I warned ye before."

Before her guards could even make a move, Dustin balled up a fist and slugged the man squarely in the jaw as well as any soldier. The vendor sailed back, tripping over his own feet and the monkey fell from his grasp. The men-at-arms were moving in to kill the man but Dustin beat them to it, pouncing on the fool and pounding him twice with her hard fists until he struck back and caught her in the face, sending her off him and onto the cobblestones. By that time the soldiers were there and Dustin was pushed aside.

Dustin hopped to her feet, furious and ready for another go around, when there was suddenly a huge hand on her shoulder. Startled, she looked up to see her husband walking past her, pushing his way through the soldiers and grabbing the vendor by his hair. He then removed his dagger as swift as a desert wind and slit the man's throat. The vendor's life slipped away in a gurgle of blood and mucus.

As fast as it had started, it was over. The people on the street who witnessed the event quickly moved away and went about their business, pretending to be busy. Anything to keep from making eye contact with the massive knight lest they be the next victim. But they all knew why he had done it, even Dustin. The vendor's mortal mistake had been to touch the knight's woman.

Christopher wiped his dagger on his mail and sheathed it, turning to his wife as calmly as anything.

"Are you all right?" he asked. "He hit you fairly hard."

"I am fine." She let him turn her face to get a look at her cheekbone. Her anger was fleeing and she was beginning to feel tremendously guilty for what she had caused. "I hit him first, Christopher. He was beating the monkey and...."

"I know," he replied, eyeing her cheek. "You are going to have a slight bruise. It's already swollen."

That was the extent of his comment, no lecture, no anger, and no questions. Dustin wondered if she should explain what happened anyway. He had killed for her so easily and the thought frightened her. Did she have so much power?

He let go of her chin and took her by the arm, but she suddenly balked. "The monkey!" she cried. "Where did it go?"

"Monkey?" Christopher repeated, watching his wife bound away, cooing into crevices and under tables and carts.

Dustin was determined to find the monkey. Christopher turned to his men, demanding to know what she was talking about and they eagerly told him. They also told him what events had started the fight, for in faith, he had only seen his wife strike the man and the return blow. Now, with an explanation from his soldiers, he understood completely. It was a good thing he had finished his business when he had and had gone in search of her, for there was no telling what would have happened to the man had his wife been let loose on him. Her passion for animals were deep. She would have done anything to protect the weaker creature and the man could have very well been beaten to death by an enraged female. As it was, his death was relatively quick and painless, a hard lesson learned for touching the Lion Claw's wife.

Christopher continued to watch her search for the little creature until she stopped by a storm drain and he could see her talking to something inside of it. He moved forward slowly, listening to the soft tone of her voice as she extended her hand gently. It was virtually no time at all before a tiny little monkey with a white beard gingerly came out of the pipe and held onto one of her fingers. She smiled and spoke to it as if it were a child, capable of understanding every word she said.

He paused a moment, his heart warming at the sight of his beautiful wife, resplendent in silk and brocade, crouching in the filthy gutters of London coaxing, of all things, a monkey from a hole. Had he not seen it he would not have believed it, and the confirmation of what he had been feeling for nearly a week hit him full-bore. He was hopelessly in love with her.

The monkey climbed onto her hand and Dustin rose, cradling the frightened little thing against her warm cloak as she went back over to her husband.

"Look at him," she crooned. "Isn't he sweet?"

He raised an eyebrow. "A monkey? You recently acquired three dogs and now you need a monkey?"

She looked up at him. "I do not need him, he needs *me*. Just look at him, the pathetic little thing." She kissed the monkey's head.

He snorted. "Lips that touch monkey fur will not touch mine."

She gave him a saucy little grin. "Is that so? And how long can you be faithful to that vow? An hour? Two?"

He shook his head reproachfully, wondering what he was going to do with the menagerie she was collecting. He chose to ignore her taunt, knowing she was correct.

"That vendor, mayhap, had a family," he said. "If that is the case, this monkey belongs to them."

She looked stricken but surprisingly she didn't protest. "I am sure you are right," she said softly, hugging the monkey closer. "Mayhap it is only right to turn the monkey back over to them." Considering that because of her, her husband had just killed the family's source of income.

Christopher could see her downfallen expression. As she hugged and kissed the monkey, he felt sorry for her. Turning around, he caught the attention of the nearest vendor.

"You, man," he said sharply, then pointed to the dead peddler. "Do you know if the man had family?"

The vendor was a silversmith. His eyes widened and he scraped the ground a couple of times before answering. "Nay, sire, he was all alone," he said. "His wife died a couple of years ago and they had no children."

Christopher turned back to his wife, noticing that her expression had brightened considerably. He felt himself relenting.

"Very well, you may keep it," he said reluctantly. "But it had better behave or I will spank you for any transgressions it commits."

She laid her cheek on the top of the monkey's head and smiled at him. "Sir George will be a perfect gentleman," she promised.

He rolled his eyes. "Sir George? You named it after the greatest knight who ever lived? The Dragonslayer?"

Her eyes took on a warm glow. "You are the greatest knight who ever lived," she whispered.

He gazed back at her, a smile spreading across his lips, pleased and flattered yet knowing just the same that she probably said it simply because he granted her desire.

"Well for you that you have finally come to realize it," he said, winking at her.

She lowered her lashes coyly and he smiled broader, taking her arm and leading her back up the street from the direction they had come.

CHAPTER SEVENTEEN

SIR GEORGE HAD entwined himself in Dustin's hair and refused to come out. He sat on the collar of her cloak, completely covered by her thick mane and screamed every time she tried to remove him.

Even now, back in their apartments, she could not coax him forward and told her irritated husband that George would come out when he was ready.

Resigning his wife to her fate, which would probably include a case of monkey warts, Christopher moved beyond the situation and ordered the nooning meal, albeit an hour late. He sent a soldier to find his knights, including Marcus, and request their presence at the meal. He then proceeded to remove his armor, eyeing his wife as she tried to talk to the monkey in the polished bronze mirror.

"Sweetheart, I need your help," he told her, holding out his arms so she could help him remove his hauberk.

Dustin pulled off the heavy mail and let it fall to the floor. His quilted shirt underneath was wet with perspiration and his hair was slicked with moisture.

"Why don't you change into clean clothing?" she suggested helpfully.

"Why?" he asked, moving to pour himself a goblet of wine. "The clothes would simply become soiled just as these are since I am going to fight all afternoon."

"But you smell," she pointed out bluntly. "And I, for one, find it unappetizing."

He raised a blond eyebrow. "You who speaks with a louse-ridden monkey in your hair? If we have to cut all your hair off because of that miniature creature, Dustin, I swear I will kill it."

She shushed him loudly. "He will never come out if you say things like that."

There was a knock at the door and he moved past her. "It had better be out by tonight or I shall rip it free myself."

"Why?" she teased boldly. "Can't you make love to me with a monkey screaming in your ear? I scream in your ear."

He shot her a reproving look and jerked the door open for David, Edward and Leeton. They scarcely had time to enter the room when Dustin was excitedly showing them her latest pet, while Christopher shook his head with resignation. She was more excited about the monkey than she was about the huge diamond ring he had bought her, but he didn't particularly care. It was a tribute to his wife's lack of materialistic value and he was pleased all the same.

"Show them what I bought you, Dustin, if you can spare the time," he remarked dryly.

She smiled at him and held up her left hand, shoving the ring right in David's face. All three knights grunted with approval.

"A fine ring," David said. "Jesus, had she been any closer that thing would have knocked my eye out."

"Where on earth did you find a monkey, Chris?" Leeton asked, trying to urge the animal out of its hovel.

"My wife found it," he replied disinterestedly. "David, did you have the destriers reshod as I asked?"

"This morning," his brother replied, picking through Dustin's hair to get a better look at the monkey.

Christopher eyed the men as they gingerly lifted his wife's hair in search of the great hairy beast within.

"I do not appreciate you manhandling my wife," he said with disapproval.

"Chris, if you call this manhandling, then I pity the poor fool who actually ever lays a hand on her," Edward quipped.

"He is dead, in fact," Christopher said, pouring himself more wine. "Where do you think she got the monkey?"

The knights looked to Dustin in mild surprise and she met their gaze, although her expression was downcast.

"He was a street peddler and the monkey was on a leash, doing tricks," she said. "He started to beat the monkey and I could not simply stand by and let him, so I… well, I tried to stop him and he was very rude. In fact, he was so rude that I hit him and we fought."

Edward nodded in understanding. "And your husband stepped in and killed him."

"Aye," Dustin said, lowering her gaze, but came back passionately. "I am truly sorry the man is dead, but he was cruel and evil and I had to stop him."

Christopher could see that she was becoming agitated. "We know, sweetheart, you were protecting God's creature," he pacified her. Then he glanced at the waterclock on the mantle. "Where in the hell is our meal?"

David was trying to stick his hand underneath Dustin's hair to remove the monkey when there was another rap on the door. Edward opened it and Marcus came into the room, holding the three puppies against his chest with his good arm.

"How long have you been back?" he demanded of Dustin. "Do you know that these mongrels have been eating constantly? And pissing all over my floor. I am not a….Jesus, what in the hell is that on your neck?"

"A monkey," David said, moving closer to the animal as Leeton pulled her hair back.

"I can see that." Marcus put the dogs down. "What is it doing there?"

"Nesting," Christopher said. "How's your hand?"

"It throbs, but the physician gave me a colwart and boiled willow concoction to ease the pain," Marcus replied.

The puppies began to whimper and yelp, running about the room and the monkey suddenly came alive. It bit David and scratched Dustin's neck as it literally flew onto a chair and then scrambled to the top of a large wardrobe. The puppies continued to yelp and wriggle all over the floor. Every time a puppy would yap, the monkey would scream, as if it were being stabbed. Dustin stood atop a chair as she tried to coax it down.

Christopher, composed and regal as always, shook his head with disbelief at the chaotic scene in his elegant antechamber. Marcus could not hide his smile and broke into choked giggles every time Edward looked at him. David, meanwhile, was nursing a substantial monkey bite on his finger and wondering aloud if he was going to die from it.

As havoc ensued in the room, the two maids bustled into the chamber with several kitchen servants in tow, setting out the nooning meal on the large oak table by the hearth. Dustin yelled at the servants to close the door so the dogs wouldn't escape while Christopher and his knights moved for the table, preparing to feast. Dud and Trent, the last two knights to join the disorder, almost had the door slammed in their faces by a servant eager to do Lady de Lohr's bidding.

Dustin could see that the monkey was frightened and decided to leave it be. Snatching the puppies, she handed them over to the maids and asked that the women feed them and take them outside so they wouldn't pee all over the polished floor. She would retain a couple of the kitchen servants to serve the meal and, with an exhausted sigh she sat heavily at her husband's left hand.

Christopher was already well into his meal of roast mutton, baked apples and stewed vegetables. The others, too, had dug in with gusto and Dustin followed suit. She ate and listened to the men, relieved to the core that Marcus and her husband were acting as if nothing was amiss, as if the heavy bandages on Marcus' arm were nonexistent. She wondered if it were all an act, keeping up a front for the sake of Richard and his vassals, but she didn't think so. Mayhap they would forgive and forget sooner than she hoped. It was almost too good to ask for.

She was so busy eating and listening to her husband that she neglected to see the monkey scoot off the cabinet. The very next thing she realized, George was sitting on the end of the table by Leeton and Dud. He nearly had heart failure when he looked up and saw the little creature pick an apple off his trencher. Dustin shushed the knights sternly when they started to laugh and throw food at the monkey. Like small boys, they obeyed the female command. The money ended up sitting on the edge of Dud's trencher and ate everything but the meat.

When the meal was over, Christopher got his men moving for they all had bouts to fight, getting in the last bit of practice before the tournament tomorrow. Dustin left the monkey in the apartments but clutched the puppies as she followed the men down to the arena and seated herself comfortably in the lists, much more excited to watch than she had been earlier. As the dogs fumbled about and explored, she was riveted on the field before her.

She was surprised to see Marcus swing a sword against Trent, obviously instructing the young man. He clutched the blade in his left hand, maneuvering it as expertly as he did with his right. She knew Marcus to be skilled, and she should have realized that his talents were well-rounded. He had joked about learning to fight with his left hand. What she didn't understand was that he already knew how to fight with it.

But as she watched him, a new set of fears clutched at her; if he were still able to fight, would he then be fighting her husband on the morrow? If not, did the prince know Marcus was still functional and would he, in fact, force Marcus to fight, broken hand and all?

She chewed her lip with worry, noticing that the field was quickly filling with people. Knights on horseback with huge jousting poles, squires, various servants and grooms were all about the field like busy insects. Christopher and his men were over to her far left under a group of trees and she could see that the squires were helping them with their armor and weapons.

Christopher's squire was a tall, well-built blond-haired boy that she had seen but three or four times. He had never spoken a word to her and she had been too busy with her own problems to notice him, but she watched him now and how he deftly handled her husband's possessions, and she made a mental note to at least discover the boy's name.

Her husband's squire and the other squires; for each knight had one, were experts at making themselves scarce, and were only around when they were needed. A few of them looked to be about her age. She also recognized some of the grooms that were handling the destriers and knew at least two of them to be from Lioncross. Strange, she thought, how she never noticed the people beyond the knights; these were people who obviously knew their jobs because her husband's small camp ran much better than most of the others, and she decided that she would get to know who these competent vassals were.

The stands were virtually empty except for a few observers here and there. Christopher had posted three soldiers behind her as guard, men who were chasing the puppies as much as they were watching over her. Glancing about at all of the color and activity, she noticed a young woman sitting several yards away from her, almost to the opposite end of the stands. Dustin studied the girl quickly; she was very pretty with long, straight medium-brown hair. She was probably about her own age, sitting with a much older woman as a companion. She made eye contact with her and turned away quickly, but not before catching a slight smile on the girl's lips.

David and Leeton were the first of Christopher's knights to go against Baron Sedgewick's men. Dustin felt her spirits lift as the two men skillfully handled their opponents, not intending to defeat them at first since this was practice. The intent was to gain strength and ease with repetition, then move in for the "kill." Dustin yelled encouragement to her husband's men, applauding as loudly as a saloon wench when first David and then Leeton sent their adversary to the ground. Caught up in the excitement, she stood up and stomped her feet and hollered until she realized she was making a fool of herself and, sheepishly, sat back down.

Edward and Dud were preparing to take the field when one of the soldiers assigned to her, respectfully and somewhat fearfully, told her that one of the puppies had slipped away, underneath the grandstand. In a panic, afraid the dog would hurt itself, she jumped up and ran down the wooden stairs, hunting frantically for the little dog. Usually the puppies yapped constantly, but she didn't hear a sound as she nosed in and around the structure. The soldier who had informed her followed, concerned.

"Are you looking for this?" asked a pleasant, female voice.

Dustin looked up and saw the girl from the stands approaching her, a smile on her pretty face and clutching Alex in one hand. Dustin nodded and smiled timidly.

"Aye, I was," she said. "Where did you find him?"

"He came over to me to where I was sitting," she said, pointing up to the lists. "When I saw you leave in a hurry and bob around as if you were looking for something, I knew immediately what had happened."

"Thank you for finding him," Dustin said. "His name is Alexander."

The girl rubbed noses with the pup just as Dustin did. "Hello, Alexander," she said, then looked back up at Dustin. "My name is Gabrielle."

Dustin nodded, feeling a bit nervous and shy; she didn't make new friends very easily. "Dustin. Do you live here?"

"What a pretty name," Gabrielle said. "And no, I do not live here. My husband is in the tournament tomorrow and we are leaving shortly after. What about you? Do you live here?"

"Not really," Dustin said. "My husband is in the tournament tomorrow, too, but I believe we are staying on for a while."

Gabrielle grinned. "I saw you cheering for your husband, am I to assume?"

Dustin nodded, smiling bashfully. "His men. This is the first tournament I have ever been to."

"Truly?" Gabrielle put Alex down, for the puppy was wriggling endlessly. "This is only my second, but they are most exciting. Who is your husband?"

"Christopher de Lohr," Dustin replied.

Gabrielle's eyes widened a bit. "The Lion's Claw? You are his wife?"

Dustin nodded, self-conscious with the star struck acknowledgement, but

Gabrielle smiled broadly.

"My husband speaks very highly of him," she said. "My husband is Lord de Havilland, Earl of Fenwark. He is jousting tomorrow, although the mere thought of it scares the wits from me. I begged him not to, but he insisted."

"Why would you not want him to compete? 'Tis an honor," Dustin said, scooping Alex up as he ran past.

Gabrielle shrugged, averting her open gaze for the first time. "Charles is....well, he is not as young as the other competitors. I am afraid he is going to be seriously injured."

"If he is older than the others, then that should mean that he is more skillful because of his years of experience," Dustin said. "Do not worry about him overly."

Gabrielle smiled. "Mayhap," she said. "Would you like to sit with me and my sister-in-law? We would enjoy your company."

Dustin glanced back at her guard, preparing to decline, but not wanting to because she instantly liked Gabrielle. Why shouldn't she have someone to talk to?

"Aye, I'd like that," she replied, turning back to her guard. "Go and get the other puppies. I am going to sit with Lady de Havilland."

The guard didn't leave her until she was back up in the stands and seated beside Gabrielle and her sister-in-law, the earl's sister, Isobelle. The older woman was homely and fat, but nice enough, and Dustin relaxed with Gabrielle's easy manner. She was talking so much that she missed Edward, Dud, and Trent's match. The next time she looked up, Christopher was taking the field opposite a man in beautifully sculptured armor. Her expression went soft.

"That's Christopher," she pointed him out to her friend.

Gabrielle nodded. "I know, I have seen him," she said. "He is exquisitely handsome, don't you think?" They all giggled and Gabrielle flushed pink. "Of course you think he is handsome because he is your husband. You are so lucky, Dustin. He is gorgeous."

Dustin was alternately peacock-proud and jealous-green, but she smiled anyway. "I think so," she said as she glanced over the field. "Point Charles out to me so that I might see what a handsome husband you have also."

Gabrielle found her husband's camp, flying green and white banners, and pointed. "He's there, in the bright armor, the shorter one. See? He is inspecting a pole."

Dustin squinted and nodded. "Aye, I see him, but I cannot see his face. You will have to introduce me to him later."

"As you will have to introduce me to the great Lion Claw," Gabrielle said.

In faith, Dustin never thought of Christopher in that context, but she nodded in agreement, turning her attention back to the field as the marshal started the match.

"Who is he fighting?" Dustin asked.

Gabrielle leaned toward her, studying the other knight. "That's Lord Darby, I believe. This ought to be an interesting fight; the earl believes himself to be the best fighter in the realm."

Dustin snorted. "Mayhap behind my husband and Marcus Burton he is, but that will remain to be seen."

"I understand Marcus Burton is going to champion the prince tomorrow," Gabrielle said.

Dustin shrugged. "He had an accident and will not be fighting. See him beyond the fence, with the bandage around his arm?"

Gabrielle did indeed. "Oh, the poor man. What happened?"

"I do not know," Dustin replied truthfully.

The bout below was beginning. Lord Darby, a small man, believed himself to be quite clever and skilled and darted about the field in a frenzy. Christopher, a temperate man on the battlefield, paced himself and easily fought off the onslaught of blows. But it was like watching a large cat toy with a mouse; eventually the patient cat was going to win. The earl may have been faster, but Christopher was by far superior and Dustin watched with awe.

Gabrielle watched the expression on the face of her new friend and in spite of her sweet nature, she was deeply envious. She wished that she cared for her husband they way Lady Dustin obviously cared for hers. The light in the gray eyes spoke volumes of untold words and emotions. Although she had yet to see the baron with his wife, rumor had it that the feeling was mutual. Gazing at Lady Dustin's obvious beauty, she could see why the man among men had broken down and married her.

The earl believed himself to be doing quite well when, in fact, he was barely holding his own. He would not acknowledge that he was getting tired and when he reached his threshold, he resorted to tricks to bring the baron down. He threw a heavy strike and feigned movement to the right instead, rolling quickly to the left, and then landed a heavy blow on Christopher's shoulder and neck.

Dustin gasped and shot to her feet just as Christopher brought his broadsword around as fast as lightening and caught the earl on the side of the torso. The diminutive man went hurtling to the damp, dark earth.

"Let him have it, Chris," Dustin hollered like a rowdy. "Take his bloody head off."

As soon as she said it she remembered just who she was keeping company with and, chagrinned, she turned around to see their reaction. One look at Dustin's sheepish face and Gabrielle and Isobelle broke into gales of laughter.

"Oh, Lady Dustin, you are a prize," Gabrielle wiped her eyes. "I should like to yell like that, too, but I haven't the nerve. I admire your spirit."

Dustin didn't know what to say. She grinned, embarrassed, and averted her gaze, seeking out her puppies who were roughhousing a few feet away.

Christopher had knocked the wind from the earl and the bout was declared over. Instead of returning to his camp, he turned for the lists and Dustin stood up, followed by Gabrielle and Lady Isobelle. When Christopher reached the platform, he beckoned his wife with a crooked finger.

"Who was it that was yelling at me like a serving wench at a cockfight?" he asked, unlatching his helmet and pulling it free of his sticky head.

"Who do you think?" Dustin grinned down at him. From where she was standing, his head was level with her thighs.

Broadsword and helmet in one hand, Christopher pulled his wife off the dais, hugging her around the knees as he carried her one-armed across the arena. Dustin squealed with delight, bracing her arms on his broad shoulders and waving goodbye to her new friends. He set her down when they had reached the safety of his camp.

"My puppies," she insisted. "They are still over there."

"They will be well watched," he told her, glancing at the soldiers that were still under the awning. "Who were you talking to?"

He held out his arms to her and she removed his hauberk, glancing at the squire when he whisked it away.

"Lady Gabrielle de Havilland," she said. "Her husband is the Earl of Fenwark. The other woman is the earl's sister, the Lady Isobelle."

"You will not speak with her anymore," he said, holding up his arms while his squire unstrapped his sword.

"But why?" Dustin demanded earnestly. "I like her."

Christopher didn't reply until the sword and gauntlets were off. Then, he pulled his wife aside, under a young oak where they were allowed some privacy.

"Because her husband is very loyal to the prince," he said quietly. "Did she ask you anything? What did you speak of?"

"Nay, she didn't ask me anything in particular," Dustin replied. "And we spoke of little things, really. The only thing she said in regard to the prince was that she heard Marcus would be championing him in the tournament tomorrow."

"What did you say?" he pressed.

"That he was injured," she answered, eyeing him. "We were having such a nice talk and she never pressed me for any information. Why can't I be her friend? I do not have any friends in London."

"There are plenty of other women you could become acquainted with," he said. "But not her. You will stay away from Lady Gabrielle."

Dustin crossed her arms stiffly and pouted. "I do not want to become acquainted with any other women. I like Lady Gabrielle and I do not care if her husband is bloody Lucifer himself. Why must you think that everyone is so subversive?"

"Because they are," he said flatly. "Do not argue the point with me, Dustin."

She frowned and leaned against the tree, ignoring him. He watched her for a moment before resting a big arm on an overhead branch and bending down to kiss his wife on the nose.

"Do not scowl like that," he said softly, with a smile.

She stuck her tongue out at him for an answer and he laughed deep in his throat. "Careful, lady," he cautioned. "One might consider that to be a proposition."

She smiled faintly in spite of herself, but she was still frustrated. "I promised Lady Gabrielle that I would introduce her to you."

"Out of the question," he said without missing a beat, his gaze still soft on her.

Dustin felt herself melting with his look and decided to use it to her advantage, she knew she could not keep up the stiff front for much longer. Her arms wound around his neck and he hugged her close, although she pulled back when he tried to kiss her.

"Oh, why cannot we be friends? Why do not you at least meet her before you pass judgment," she said, making sure she was very close but dodging his lips every time he moved for her. "She said you were handsome and gorgeous."

"And she is correct," he said, finally capturing her lower lip between his own. "But I will not meet her."

"You are not fair, Chris," she whispered as his lips suckled hers.

"Fair?" he whispered back, kissing her chin. "Fair is not having to watch over my wife every moment for fear that someone will harm her. Fair is trying my damnedest to keep you safe when others would see you come to tragedy. Not much in this life is fair, lady."

"Lady Gabrielle would not harm me." She was having a difficult time keeping her train of thought as his lips moved to her neck.

"Not another word, Dustin." He said it so seductively she didn't know if he meant Lady Gabrielle or just in general. To be safe, she shut up and let his mouth devour her throat and shoulders.

Behind them, someone cleared his throat loudly and Christopher's head came up from the swell of her bosom, his expression less than tolerant. David's expression was unwavering.

"John is in the stands," he said.

"What's he doing?" Christopher asked.

"Sitting with that woman Dustin was sitting with and fondling the puppies," his brother replied.

"My puppies!" Dustin cried softly.

Christopher shushed her. "We shall go and get them," he said evenly before returning his attention to his brother. "Where's Marcus?"

"Talking to John," David answered.

"Damn," Christopher hissed.

Dustin followed her husband around the group of trees and back across the arena where the prince and Sir Ralph were indeed sitting with Lady Gabrielle and Lady Isobelle. Ralph had one of the puppies by the scruff of the neck, inspecting it carelessly, and Dustin had to bite her tongue to keep from yelling at the man. Even as they approached, she could see Marcus grabbing onto the remaining wandering pup and holding onto it for safekeeping.

"I shall thank you to hand over my wife's pets," Christopher said coolly, taking Harold from Marcus and handing him to Dustin.

The prince gazed disinterestedly at Christopher, still clutching Alex as he continued his conversation with the two ladies. Ralph, however, extended Cabal as if the animal were contaminated somehow.

"Common gutter beasts the pets of a noblewoman?" he said haughtily. "How distasteful."

"Coming from another gutter beast, I am sure the pups are not offended," Dustin snapped, her gray eyes glittering. "Give me my dog."

Ralph smiled narrowly, still holding the crying pup away from him. "You know, baron, I am considering competing in the games tomorrow," he said casually. "I have not yet practiced. Do you think I have lost my competitive edge lounging around the castle for the past several months? I sincerely hope not, but I wonder just the same. Mayhap I should find out."

With that, he suddenly tossed the little pup into the air and withdrew his sword in the blink of an eye. Before anyone could stop him, the sword arced upward in a flash of blinding metal and sliced the puppy in two clean halves, blood splattering on the floor and onto the sheriff. The two puppy parts thudded like wet balls onto the wooden floor of the lists.

Dustin screamed and turned away sharply, burying her face in the first available body which happened to be Marcus'. Christopher bound up onto the platform and had Ralph by the throat, his huge fist driving into the man's face like a hammer into soft metal. The prince yelped at being jostled and dropped Alexander, and the two women next to him screamed horrifically and covered their eyes.

All of Christopher's knights, save Marcus, jumped onto the stands but no one attempted to stop Christopher from beating Ralph's brains in. In fact, there were several dozen soldiers witnessing the entire brawl and no one made a move to intervene. John, seeing that his cohort was receiving a heavy thrashing, began spouting off to any soldier he made eye contact with to restrain the baron, but he was blatantly disobeyed. Frustrated, he took to jumping Christopher himself and found himself bridled by David and Leeton.

Christopher had reached his limit with Ralph. He didn't kill him when he took his wife the day she arrived, although he should have, and he didn't kill him when he pressured and threatened Marcus, but he should have done something. Every blow had Dustin's or Marcus' or name on it and after pounding the man senseless, he threw him over the side of the lists to the cold earth below.

Ralph wallowed around aimlessly, trying to stand but not knowing which way was up. Christopher descended the short flight of wooden stairs, stalking the sheriff like a lion for a kill. Ralph saw him coming and struggled to his feet, throwing an off-balance punch that Christopher easily subdued before driving his fist into the Ralphs' gut and the man collapsed on the dirt.

"And that," Christopher said in a strange raspy voice, "was for the puppy."

Ralph vomited the contents of his stomach into the dust, breathing loudly. "You bastard," he heaved. "I should have killed your wife when I had the chance."

Christopher's features stiffened and he moved for him once more, but David stopped him.

"No more," he said quietly. "You shall kill him if you do."

Christopher looked at David, who nodded his head slightly in Dustin's direction. He looked to her, crying against Marcus, and knew it would not be a good thing to commit murder in front of his wife. As it was, she had to witness a sound beating on top of seeing her puppy dismembered. He forgot all about Ralph.

"De Lohr!" John came rushing down the stairs. "Leave him alone, I say. How dare you lay a hand on someone of higher rank!"

Christopher swung on the prince. "I wouldn't have had to lay a hand on him if you disciplined him once in a while. Unfortunately, your lack of control has forced Ralph to learn a very hard lesson, one I will repeat gladly, if needed."

John began to shake and twist, and all present could see a fit coming on. His face grew quite red and he began to froth at the mouth. From that point on the man was incoherent, and Christopher turned his back on him as he fell to the ground in great convulsions of rage.

"Come on, sweetheart," he said gently, taking her from Marcus. "Let's go back to the apartments."

She was sobbing pitifully, like a child, clutching Harold to her chest. "Alex," she managed to choke out.

"Where's the other one?" Christopher looked around, as did Marcus and David.

"He's here, sire." Lady Gabrielle stood on the edge of the platform and handed Alexander down to David.

Christopher looked up at the woman, her pretty face pale and tear-streaked. "Thank you," he mumbled, eyeing her for a moment. "Where is your husband, my lady? Do you have an escort back to your rooms?"

"Aye, sire," she nodded, pointing to the older man several feet away from her.

Christopher recognized the earl and, nodding shortly, handed the other puppy to his wife and led her gently away. His knights followed in a group, with

Marcus bringing up the rear. He had been watching John throw a fit next to Ralph's limp body, disgusted to the bone that his greed and envy had caused him an alliance with the man. Again, he could only pray that Richard was in a forgiving mood when he informed him of his treasonous act.

Practice was over for the day.

CHAPTER EIGHTEEN

DUSTIN WAS EXHAUSTED and ill by the time they reached their apartment. She gently set the puppies down on the floor and wandered into their bedchamber, too distraught to do anything more than throw herself on the bed and curl up into a ball.

Christopher threw a few table scraps on the floor to keep the pups occupied and followed his wife into the bedchamber, unlatching what remained of his armor and letting it clatter to the floor by the door. All the while, his eyes were riveted to his wife as she lay in a shaking heap upon the bed, and he silently cursed Ralph again for his dastardly act.

He tore off his tunic and went over to the bed, lying carefully on the bed next to Dustin. Although her hysterical crying had ceased, she continued to hiccup and sob and chewed her nails absently. His heart ached for her and he found himself stroking her head gently, pulling her hair back away from her face and tucking it behind her ear, watching the colors in the dim light. He didn't say anything because he knew what she needed at the moment was simply to be comforted, and he hoped his soft touch and warm body pressed against her back at least offered some.

He watched her pale face, her eyes becoming heavy-lidded as she lay there. She was such a strong and independent woman that it were moments like these where her true vulnerability came through; she was as fragile as a flower. This was the Dustin that needed him the very most.

The monkey suddenly appeared on the pillow above her head. Christopher continued to stroke her hair as he watched the monkey, blinking rapidly and moving its little beard crazily. The little monkey inched forward, resting on its haunches, then inched forward again. He continued to watch it, wondering what it was going to do, until it was practically sitting on top of Dustin's head. He found himself tensing, waiting for the beast to go crazy again, when a tiny little hand shot out and began rubbing Dustin's hair rapidly, mimicking Christopher's much longer strokes.

He smiled broadly at the monkey. "That's right, George. Be sweet to my lady, she has had a difficult day."

"What's he doing?" Dustin whispered, a finger between her teeth.

"Comforting you," Christopher replied, leaning over and kissing her cheek softly.

Dustin sighed raggedly, closing her eyes. Christopher began to rub her shoulders and arms therapeutically as George progressed beyond stroking her hair to picking it apart, inspecting her scalp for vermin. Christopher laughed softly at the monkey, undoing the stays on his wife's surcoat and loosening it to allow his caressing hands better access. Her muscles were tight and her whole body tensed, but she was gradually relaxing under his expert hands. After several long minutes, she fell into a fatigued sleep.

He continued to touch her even though he knew she could not feel him simply for the pleasure and comfort it brought him. George, finding nothing of interest on Dustin's scalp, took to playing with her hair.

Christopher pulled the coverlet up over his wife and quietly admonishing the monkey to be silent, gathered his armor and moved into the antechamber. The puppies had curled up on one of the rugs and had fallen asleep, exhausted after their busy day. He walked past the sleeping dogs and opened the front door, ordering one of the soldiers in the hall to summon his squire.

Dustin slept through the afternoon. Christopher checked on her every few minutes, keeping himself busy in the antechamber with various things in preparation for the tournament on the morrow. David came up to sit with him, lounging about like a gentleman of leisure when they both knew he could be out in the arena practicing. Edward and Leeton, Dud and Trent all came by at various times with various excuses for their visit, but Christopher knew they had come to see how Dustin was, and he told them frankly that she was exhaustedly sleeping. Since it seemed his knights could not practice without him hanging over their shoulders, Christopher sent each man about on a particular errand for the morrow.

Late in the afternoon, Marcus called. His handsome face was grim as he pulled Christopher into a private corner.

"John is out for blood, Chris," he said quietly. "He is spreading the word that any man who mortally wounds you in the tourney tomorrow will be awarded ten pieces of gold."

Christopher shrugged. "So?"

Marcus looked hard at him. "And I have heard from reliable sources that if you are killed, John intends to auction Dustin off to the highest bidder."

Christopher met his gaze for a moment before raising his eyebrows in an unconcerned gesture. "Then make sure you or David are the highest bidder."

"You are not upset?" Marcus asked, surprised. "Hell, I was livid."

Christopher crossed his arms confidently. "Marcus, legions of Saladin's men could not kill me. There is no possible way in the world that an English knight, no matter how good, is going to kill me. However, were you competing against me tomorrow the odds would have been considerably higher. Quit worrying."

"I am not, I am simply informing you of the latest from the den of jackals," Marcus said. Then he shifted the subject. "How is Dustin?"

"Sleeping," Christopher replied, moving back into the room.

Marcus sat in a chair, trying to move his right arm to a comfortable position. "I saw Edward working with the jousting poles down by the arena," he said. "He's mounting the new crow's foot tips on them instead of the spears."

"I know, I told him to," Christopher replied. " 'Tis too easy to kill someone with those spear tips; I simply want to unseat them. Most everyone is mounting their poles with crow's foot."

"So I have seen," Marcus replied. "But 'twill be easy to pick out the men who have in mind to kill you tomorrow; I suspect they will be the ones that still bear the spear tips."

Christopher smiled flatly. "I shall bear that in mind."

The sun was low in the sky and it was just the two of them, sitting comfortably before a glowing hearth. The events of yesterday, of the morning, seemed years away. The silence was comfortable, thoughtful.

"There will be civil war," Marcus said softly, staring at the dying embers.

Christopher rubbed his beard. " 'Tis hard to say," he replied. "I have been back in England for over a month and have yet to feel the true pulse of favor. You seem to think England divided from your trip to the north. I simply do not know yet."

"Do you intend to send word to Richard soon?" Marcus inquired.

"And tell him what?" Christopher gestured with his hand. "Nay, Marcus, I will not waste Richard's time with gossip and rumors. I must have more solid evidence before I send him a missive."

Marcus leaned on his good arm, letting out a heavy sigh. "John will start a civil war, you know. He's already amassing a mercenary army, which he thinks is a secret."

"And he has already bled the coffers dry so I cannot imagine what he expects to pay the army with," Christopher replied.

"But they are amassing nonetheless and when he strikes, 'twill be your duty to quell him in the name of Richard," Marcus reminded hm. "That, my friend, constitutes civil war."

Christopher sat, deep in thought. Marcus was right, although Christopher refused to be an alarmist. Civil war was a long way off, in his opinion. But he, too, felt it was inevitable and the thought depressed him.

"Tell me," he said, changing subjects. "When do you intend to inspect this great fortress of Somerhill?"

"Whenever circumstances allow me to leave," Marcus replied. Then, he grinned. "John is really furious about that, isn't he? He wasted a perfectly good baronetcy on a crippled knight."

Christopher snorted humorously. "Score another victory for Richard's cause."

They snickered and insulted John, sharing a carafe of wine between them as the sun sank lower in the fall sky. Days were growing shorter and colder, signaling the onset of winter's approach.

As the conversation faded, Christopher noticed a swaying figure in the doorway to the bedchamber. Dustin was standing there, her loosened surcoat all but falling off as she rubbed her eyes sleepily. Christopher set down his goblet and rose.

"So you decided to wake?" he teased gently. "Did you sleep well?"

She nodded, yawning. "George is still asleep on your pillow," she said. "Hello, Marcus."

Marcus waved with his good hand. "Good morn."

Christopher pulled up the sagging dress at her shoulders. "Are you hungry? We were just contemplating going down to supper."

"Aye, I could eat," she said. "I shall change my surcoat."

She stumbled back into the bedchamber with Christopher in tow. Marcus turned back to the fire, to his wine, darkly wishing that it could be him in the bedchamber helping Dustin change her surcoat and disgusted with himself in the same breath. Christopher had been right of one thing during his earlier tirade; Marcus was guilty of breaking the tenth commandment.

Christopher came back out after a few minutes, acknowledging Marcus' questioning glance. "She will be out in a minute," he said.

Marcus noticed his liege wore a fresh tunic and his hair was combed. Muscled legs bulged through dark breeches and disappeared into black leather boots. Marcus felt quite ill-dressed in his dirtied tunic and worn boots. But there was no time to change, for Dustin emerged from the bedchamber a few moments later dressed in a wine-colored surcoat of brocade with gold leafing that hung off her exquisite shoulders and molded to her torso. It was exquisite and rather indecent.

Christopher did a double-take at his wife. "Is that one of your mother's surcoats?"

She looked defiantly back at him, fussing with a slipper. "Aye, it is, and you approved of it. And you just fastened the stays not a minute ago and said nothing about it."

He raised an eyebrow. "I must have been drunk. 'Tis too tight."

"It fits me well, thank you," Dustin insisted. "I am not going to change again. What do you think, Marcus?"

Marcus glanced at Christopher before forming a carefully-worded answer. " 'Tis a lovely surcoat, my lady."

"You are no help," Christopher muttered, then looked at his wife again. "Well, then, I suppose it is a good thing you have both Marcus and myself for escorts, considering we will be beating the entire male population of Windsor away from you."

She giggled and he held out his arm to her. When Marcus stood beside her she instinctively reached out to take his arm, as well, but clutched bandages instead. "Oh, Marcus, I am sorry." She snatched her arm away. "Did I hurt you?"

"Nay, dear lady," he said as he opened the door. "You could not if you tried."

There were still over a dozen soldiers in the hall and Christopher took half with them down to the great dining hall where supper was already being served in high fashion. Leeton and Edward were there, but David and the rest of the knights were attending to the final details for the tournament as Christopher seated Dustin and then took the chair next to her. He didn't bother to glance at the head table to see if Ralph was there; he hoped the man had died of a hemorrhage.

Dustin seemed to be in good spirits. Mummers were moving about the room, making fun of the guests and doing acrobatics. Dustin had seen mummers, once, when she had traveled with her father to Bath as a young girl and was fascinated by their tricks and brightly colored costumes. One fool wore lively bells on the end of his three-cornered hat that jingled wildly.

She devoured her meal of capon and venison with a plum sauce, watching with bright eyes as the mummers danced, oblivious to the conversation her husband was having with Marcus over the top of her head. She was thoroughly enjoying herself until she glanced away from the fools and caught sight of Lady Gabrielle sitting a few tables away with her husband and sister-in-law.

The smile of greeting that was forming on her lips turned to horror when she saw that Lady Gabrielle's face was bruised and her lip was swollen. The woman averted her eyes when she saw Dustin, turning back to her trencher and Dustin went stiff with distress. She turned to her husband.

"Chris, look at Lady Gabrielle over there," she pointed as discreetly as she could manage. "Look at her face. She looks to have been in an accident."

Christopher glanced nonchalantly at the lady. It took him all of two seconds to see that the woman met with no accident, unless she mistakenly threw herself on her husband's fists. He turned back to his own food, disgusted at a man who could beat his wife.

But Dustin wanted his opinion. "What do you think happened? Can I at least speak with her for a moment?"

"That would not be wise," he said quietly, suspecting that Lady de Haviland's husband disciplined his wife for consorting with an enemy's wife. "Leave well enough alone, Dustin."

She looked at him curiously. "Leave what alone?"

"Lady Gabrielle," he said quietly. "I wouldn't even look at her if I were you."

She was thoroughly puzzled by now. "For God's sake, why not? What's the matter?"

Christopher put down his spoon, wondering how he could delicately phrase his answer so his wife wouldn't fly into a frenzy.

"I told you that her husband was sympathetic to John," he replied. "After what happened this afternoon with Ralph, I can only deduce that the earl punished his wife for befriending you. Anymore contact between you and it could result in more than a beating for her."

Dustin's eyes widened and her mouth opened slightly, but she didn't look back at the woman. Instead, she looked quickly down at her trencher. "He hurt her?" she whispered. "But…she did nothing. Why did he have to hurt her?"

Christopher picked up his wife's hand and kissed it, returning to his own food. "I do not know, sweetheart. Some men do not think twice about beating a female."

Dustin was sick. She sat back in her chair, trying desperately not to look at Lady Gabrielle but wanting to comfort the woman somehow. She was such a nice lady and Dustin was quickly becoming distraught on her behalf.

Suddenly the mummers were in front of her, two effeminate men in tight little costumes, dancing and cavorting in front of her. They leap-frogged over each other a few times, singing some sort of crazy song. Minutes earlier, Dustin would have been thrilled but at this moment she wanted nothing to do with them.

The first mummer, a little man with graying hair, hopped up to the table and gave Dustin a wild-eyed look.

" 'Tis said the Lion's Claw married the most beautiful woman in the realm," he began. "The man who single-handedly tamed Saladin finds himself tamed by a mere slip of a girl with enough hair to weave a rug."

The two of them bounced around crazily as the tables closest to them laughed at Christopher and Dustin's expense. Dustin frowned impatiently as the second mummer bobbed forward.

"Eyes like silver, hair like gold, will she tarnish when she grows old?" he blurted in a silly fashion, rolling his eyes. "The face of an angel and fists of steel, will she be the Claw's Achilles heel?"

Christopher sat quite calmly, his gaze never wavering and his expression never changing. Dustin, however, wasn't so adept at hiding her emotions.

"Go away," she snorted as the first mummer rolled forward for his turn.

His face fell exaggeratedly. "Oh, my lady doesn't appreciate our humor. Should we use smaller words?"

It was a blatant insult, unusual for mummers. Christopher suspected the prince had paid these fools well for a daring chance. Before he could stop his wife from reacting, she stood up and smashed a half-eaten custard tart into the mummer's face.

"Obviously you do not understand words at all, otherwise you would have respected my wishes," she snapped. "Get out of my sight before I do more than rub custard in your face."

Surprisingly, the mummer didn't react except to stand there with his mouth agape. Then, in a silly move, he licked his lips and face, smacking loudly. "Mmmm. Tasty, tasty. As tasty as you, lion tamer?"

Marcus was half out of his chair before the mummers frolicked away, their mood unspoiled.

"Sit down," Christopher tugged on her arm.

"Are you going to let them get away with that?" she demanded.

"*Sit!*" He pulled hard and she plopped into her chair. Then, to Dustin's amazement, he put his big arm around her shoulders and pulled her close to him, lips against her ear. "John sent them over here to get a rise out of me. I shall not oblige him."

She looked up at him, her face so close she could feel his heat. "And I did. I apologize."

He smiled softly. "I expect no less from you, Lady de Lohr. Those mummers had better run for their lives."

She grinned, embarrassed. Knowing how he felt about public displays of affection, she was feeling warm and giddy with his nearness in front of a roomful of strangers.

"You are very close," she murmured.

"Aye, I am."

"Are you going to kiss me in front of the prince?"

He did, tenderly and sweetly. To hell with his restraint; John and Ralph already knew that he was smitten with her and there was no use in pretending otherwise. He remembered the mummer's words, thinking the term Achilles' heel to be quite apt. She was his one and only weakness, and the sooner he acknowledged that, the better to deal with it. He realized he was finished resisting her. There was no point. He was a much happier man embracing the joy of emotion than denying it. It made him feel strong and empowered.

He was going in for another kiss when a figure stood in front of the table, interrupting. Christopher looked up to see William Marshal, Earl of Pembroke. The tall, older man was Richard's marshal, of greater rank than Christopher and was more an administrator than warrior. Christopher had had a long, arduous meeting with William the very day he arrived in England, even before he had delivered Richard's message to John. William was a man of good moral character who understood John's ambitions better than anyone, and despised him greatly.

"I have a need to speak with you, baron," he said quietly, barely acknowledging Dustin.

Christopher took his arm off his wife and rose steadily, concerned with the look in the marshal's eye. "Of course, my lord." He turned quickly to Marcus. "Entertain my wife until I return."

Marcus agreed, his eyes riveted to Christopher and the marshal as they left the hall, knowing that something was amiss from the stiff stance of the earl. He wondered darkly what fresh new hell they were about to enter. William Marshal and a stiff stance could only convey something very bad.

Dustin's eyes followed her husband, hoping he would return shortly and having no idea who the older man was. She also had no idea that the eyes of John were on her, raking over her beauty and trying to formulate a plan for getting the baron's wife alone again. Every time he saw her, his lust for her grew. He hoped the tournament tomorrow would provide such an opportunity. If truth be known, the only man in the realm he did fear other than his brother was Christopher, yet he knew that the baron could not punish him in any way should he lay hands on his nubile young wife. John had bedded the wives of earls and dukes, and all were powerless to revenge him. But de Lohr was different; the pure presence of the man intimidated and angered him at the same time.

He knew how to seek revenge for Ralph. True, they had planned to abduct the woman anyway, but to seek true revenge rather than use her for a pawn was never the original objective. The purpose was now altered.

As John plotted and schemed, William Marshal took Christopher into a small antechamber, one of a hundred in Windsor. Music from the great dining hall could still be heard even when William closed the door and faced the expectant Defender. The mood was already grim.

"Chris, we have just received word from Palestine," he said softly. "There is no easy way to tell you this, lad, so I shall come out with it. Richard is missing."

Christopher's brow furrowed. "Missing? What do you mean?"

"He sailed from Acre to the coast of Corsica and simply disappeared," the earl replied. "His general believes him to be traveling across the continent incognito, trying to reach his Duchy of Normandy before crossing to England, but no one is certain."

"Damn," Christopher hissed, relaxing against a massive oaken table. "Why would he do that when he knows Duke Leopold of Austria is out for his blood? Not to mention Emperor Henry, or Philip Augustus. Christ, they are all out for his hide. Why would he chance such a stupid action?"

"Richard is a wise man, Chris," William replied, as perplexed as the baron was but trying to remain confident in Richard's ability. "He must have had damn good reasons whatever they might be. The fact remains that John is going to run rampant with this knowledge."

Christopher's handsome face was grave, his eyes dark. "What do you suspect?"

The earl shrugged, examining a particularly fine chair. "He's already amassed quite a mercenary army, you know."

"I know, but how large? My sources tell me conflicting stories," Christopher said. "And how in the hell is he paying these cutthroats?"

"His loyalists," William said frankly. "He has some very wealthy backers, Chris, and they are feeding their wealth directly into his coffers. Believe me, he has the means to pay an army. A massive army, nearly ten thousand men as near as we can gather."

Christopher nodded. "I'd been told that," he said. "But I have not been in England long enough to verify the information myself."

"You have had other things to attend to," William acknowledged, then fixed him with a reluctant gaze. "But that's not the only problem. 'Tis rumored that John is trying to establish an alliance with Philip Augustus which, if successful, will supply him with almost limitless power and men."

Christopher sighed heavily, studying his boots for a moment. "I fought with the French king in Palestine," he said. "He and Richard were like two roosters, each vying for the dominant position. There is no love lost between them and he will surely find allies in Richard's enemies. Leopold is out for Richard's blood for what he did to him at Acre," he shook his head slowly. "Richard is in danger of losing his throne, isn't he? With his disappearance, 'twill be easier for John to claim the kingdom."

William nodded. "I am afraid that is what it will come down to," he said quietly, sitting in the chair he had been examining. "Richard has very powerful allies, his largest being the church. But if he is missing and presumed dead, then there is no use defending a kingdom for a dead king. John will rule."

Christopher stared thoughtfully at the floor for several long, pregnant minutes. Neither man spoke, the severity of the situation sinking in and a great cloud of doom settling.

"Does John know yet?" he asked.

"When I sought you, he had yet to be informed," William replied. "But that may have changed since then."

Christopher sat still a moment longer before pushing himself off the table and crossing his arms. "It would seem to me that if Richard is missing, then someone should go looking for him. As his champion, it must be me."

"Nay, lad, not you," William said firmly. "As his champion, it is important you stay here and control the crown's troops so that John cannot use them. If you leave, there will be no one to stop him. You cannot appoint your own replacement; only Richard can do that."

"We cannot simply sit here while Richard may be in grave danger," Christopher said passionately in the first real display of emotion. "He very well may require assistance."

"There is nothing you can do," William said. "Even if you were to find him, 'twould be you and he against the whole of the continent. You said yourself that Leopold and Henry and Philip were out to get hm. You alone could not defend him against every troop on the continent, formidable as you are. And most certainly if he is traveling in disguise, don't you think that Richard's champion riding into France and Germany would attract attention?"

Christopher looked at him a moment, hard, before turning away in frustration. He kicked at the floor, scuffing his boots. "So what do we do, my lord?"

"At the moment, nothing," William replied. "The justices will be meeting on the morrow regarding this crisis, I am sure. I go now to deliver the message personally to all of them."

Christopher turned to him. " 'Twill take you all night. Allow me to assist you in this so that we may both be in bed before the sun breaks the horizon."

"I would be grateful," William admitted, rising. "I am not as young as I used to be; not as young as you."

Christopher snorted. "At thirty-five years, I am hardly young. Richard is a mere three years older than myself."

"You are young," the earl insisted with a weary smile. "When you reach my age, you will know what old is. By the way, Chris, I have not had the chance to congratulate you on your marriage to Lord Barringdon's daughter. A fine match."

"Thank you, my lord," Christopher mumbled.

William moved for the door, eyeing Christopher. "You know, if I were you, I would return her to Lioncross. 'Tis not safe for such a beautiful woman here in John's court. The prince will set his sights on her, if he hasn't already."

Christopher's jaw ticked. "I am well aware of the prince's lust," he replied. "As for returning her to Lioncross, I feel better able to protect her here. My knights are with me and she is never alone, whereas at Lioncross there is less protection."

William's hand rested on the door latch and Christopher stopped, facing him in the dim room. "Chris, before John makes his move to seize Richard's holdings, you must leave Windsor and return to your keep if you expect to preserve your life. He shall go after everyone loyal to his brother, especially ranking officials such as you and myself."

"I can handle John's mercenaries," Christopher said confidently. "Yet in faith, the only thing that concerns me is if John does indeed ascend the throne. My only hope is that he will allow me to live out my life in England in peace, although I have grave doubts that that will be the case. I fear I may find myself fleeing to Ireland or Scotland."

"All of us, lad," William smiled wryly and opened the door. " 'Twould make a fine commune living amongst Richard's ousted loyalists. Now, I shall deliver the messages to the clergy justices. That leaves you with the nobles."

Christopher nodded curtly. "Most of which are at Windsor, except for a very few. I should be done by midnight at the latest."

"Waste no time," William said. "I will see you on the morrow."

Christopher left the marshal and made his way back to the fragrant and stuffy dining hall. His great sense of foreboding was overshadowed by the urgency he felt. The feast had finished and the orchestra was filling the hall with a lively tune. As he moved toward his wife, he made sure to take note that John had already left the hall and his sense of urgency multiplied.

Dustin smiled happily as he approached the table and was pleasantly surprised when he bent down and kissed her on the cheek.

"I have business to attend to, sweet," he said in a low voice, though there was no mistaking the serious tone. "Marcus, will you see my wife safely to our apartments?"

"Of course, my lord," Marcus replied, deeply curious as to the marshal's message but knowing better than to ask.

Dustin, however, looked crestfallen. "Where are you going?"

He glanced at Marcus a moment before forcing a smile at his wife. "Do not concern yourself," he said, kissing her cheek again. "I shall return as quickly as I can. Enjoy the rest of the evening."

He left quickly so she could not ask him any more questions. However, outside the hall beneath the blanket of brilliant stars, Marcus caught up to him.

"What's happened?" he demanded.

"Who's with Dustin?" Christopher countered sharply.

"Edward and Leeton," Marcus replied. "She is fine. Now tell me what's happened."

Christopher glanced about to make sure there were no prying ears. "Richard's missing," he said grimly. "He disappeared from his ship off the coast of Corsica and William thinks he may be traveling inland to Normandy. I go now to deliver the message to the noble justices."

Marcus closed his eyes briefly and crossed himself with his good hand. "Dear God, with half the continent after him it will be a miracle if he survives."

Christopher nodded. "Keep close watch on Dustin and yourselves," he warned quietly. "John will undoubtedly try testing his reins of power now that Richard has vanished and I fear his first move will be against his enemies, Richard's allies. Find David and Dud immediately and warn them of the events, but let the information go no further this night."

"Rest easy, Chris, your wife is in good hands," Marcus assured him. "We won't leave her until you return."

"Thank you." Christopher slapped him on the shoulder and left him standing in the hall, wondering grimly what the state of the country would be in come the dawn.

Marcus sent two soldiers in search of David and returned to Dustin, who was seated between Leeton and Edward, watching the dancing before her. She smiled politely as Marcus took his seat.

"Are you a dancer, my lady? Surely you must be." Marcus didn't want her pestering him about Christopher and immediately delved into another subject. "Edward is a fine dancer, aren't you, de Wolfe?"

Edward waved him off. "Of course I am, but if I were to dance at this moment, my entire dinner would come up."

Dustin shook her head. "I learned to dance as a child, like every well-bred young lady, but I haven't danced since then. I do not remember how."

"A travesty," Marcus said gravely. "The most beautiful woman in the kingdom has forgotten how to dance."

Dustin grinned and shrugged, watching the women's surcoats twirling before her. In faith, she would love to dance but she knew all eyes would be upon her and she would only end up embarrassing herself. So she watched, content for the moment, and enjoyed the company. Yet her mind was with her husband, wherever he had gone and hoping he wasn't in any danger. Danger seemed to follow him.

Time passed and songs were played, people enjoyed themselves. Dustin had imbibed a bit too much wine and was enjoying herself immensely, laughing and joking with the three knights at her side. David, Dud and Trent joined the group eventually and Marcus took David aside to explain the latest developments. David, as always, overreacted but controlled himself for the sake of appearance. Feeling particularly protective over Dustin with his brother about, he seated himself directly behind her and kept detached from the conversation as his eyes roved the hall for John's henchmen.

Almost as soon as David took his seat, a young woman approached the table and curtsied deeply in front of them. They all eyed her suspiciously, except for Dustin and Edward. Edward thought her to be quite lovely and Dustin simply wasn't naturally distrustful. The woman was tall and her luxurious blond hair was pulled back primly. When she looked up, Dustin thought there something familiar about her eyes but could not place her.

"Do not you even recognize your own family, David?" the girl said. "I realize that it has been over five years, but surely I have not changed that much."

David's eyes widened and he shot to his feet. "Deborah!" he croaked, vaulting over the table and taking the woman into his arms. "Jesus Christ, it *is* you. But...we still believed you to be in Bath. What are you doing here?"

The Lady Deborah Valeria du Reims de Lohr smiled, her smile exactly like her eldest brother's. With her lovely blue eyes and pert nose, she was a beauty.

"The tourney, of course," she answered her brother. "I came with the earl and his wife. I only heard upon our arrival this day that you and Christopher were here. Where is our illustrious big brother?"

David was still flabbergasted. He hadn't seen his sister since she had been twelve years old, and the gawky girl he remembered did not resemble this exquisite creature in the least. "He's about," he answered. "Jesus, Deborah, I still cannot believe it is really you. Christopher will be thrilled."

"Not as thrilled as I was to hear that our Lord kept you safe in the Holy Land," Deborah said, studying her brother's face. "Christopher's reputation has been a great source of pride for me. How magnificent he must be."

David nodded, recovering his shock and remembering Dustin. "Ask his wife," he said, indicating Lady de Lohr on the other side of the table. "This is Chris' wife, Deborah, the Lady Dustin Barringdon de Lohr."

Deborah's eyes fairly sparkled as her gaze settled on Dustin. Dustin rose, feeling the love and acceptance flowing from the woman even though they had just met. It was an unusual, wonderful experience and she felt as if she should throw her arms around her newly-found sister-in-law.

"Lady Dustin, 'tis indeed an honor to meet you," she said sincerely. "I had no idea my brother had married and I apologize that I have no wedding favor for you, a situation I will immediately remedy. But please accept my congratulations."

"Thank you," Dustin replied. "I am so happy to meet you, Lady Deborah. Will you be staying in London long?"

"A week or so, mayhap," Deborah said. "Long enough for us to get to know one another. I finally have a sister!"

She clapped her hands together gleefully and the entire group laughed at her delight. David pulled up a chair for his sister and she joined their conversation, sitting next to Dustin as if she had known her all her life.

Dustin liked her immediately. She was cultured and vivacious and her blue eyes twinkled the same way her older brother's blue ones did when she smiled. She was very lovely in a subdued sort of way, a creamy, glowing beauty. Dustin realized quickly that she did not want Lady Deborah to return to Bath and would speak to her husband about it forthright. She wanted Lady Deborah to return with them to Lioncross Abbey.

The evening moved on rapidly and before they realized it, it was past midnight. Dustin was having a wonderful time with Deborah and didn't want the evening to end, protesting loudly when Marcus called a halt to the fun and demanded to return her to her apartments.

"Marcus, you spoil my joy," she accused with a pout, "I am not tired in the least."

He was on his feet, giving her a fatherly-sort of reproving glance. "I am sure that is true, but your company of knights have a tourney tomorrow and would like to get their rest. The only way they might accomplish that task is if *you* retire for the night."

She gave him an exaggerated frown and turned to Deborah. "I am afraid our time is ended," she said. "Will you sit with me at the tourney tomorrow?"

Marcus cleared his throat before Deborah could answer. "You will be awarding prizes, my lady, if you will recall, and will be isolated from the crowd."

Dustin's face fell a bit. "Oh," she said. "Then… I will see you tomorrow, Lady Deborah, I promise."

The women giggled as if they were planning some sort of covert action. Marcus grasped Dustin's arm and helped her to her feet, not an easy task considering she had had far too much wine and was as tipsy as a loon. David had his sister, escorting her back to the Earl of Bath's group.

They were on their feet in preparation of leaving when Marcus and Edward were confronted by two young women in gaudy court surcoats, layers upon layers of fabric and embroider and their cheeks over-rouged. They were giggling as one woman put her arm upon Marcus' good hand.

"Baron Marcus Burton," she exclaimed loudly. "Do you know that I have waited all night for you to dance with me?"

Marcus cocked a tolerant eyebrow at the brown-haired woman. "I apologize, Lady Lucinda, truly. But I have been else occupied."

The woman and her companion eyed Dustin openly and Dustin. Even with her alcohol-induced high-spirits she immediately bristled.

"I can see that," Lady Lucinda said cattily. "Lovely, isn't she? I see that she has you and Sir Christopher occupied."

"This is Christopher's wife, the Lady Dustin," Marcus said, eyeing Dustin and the women, wondering if they were in for a round of punches. "My lady, this is Lady Lucinda Bartley and Lady Maryann de Bohun."

The two women looked at Dustin with new eyes but not necessarily friendlier eyes.

"I had heard he had married," Lady Lucinda said, "but I had no idea this lovely little thing was his wife. She's so small."

Dustin's eyes narrowed. "Aye, you knew I was his wife," she growled. "Everyone in the whole bloody castle knows it. And as far as my size is concerned, I have yet to hear my husband complain."

Lady Lucinda curled a thin lip. "I meant no offense, Lady de Lohr. It's just that....well, your husband is known for his appetites and you do not seem to fit the bill."

Marcus pursed his lips and stood back; he did not want to be caught in the crossfire but he wanted to be close enough to prevent Dustin from committing murder.

Dustin put her hands on her hips, swaying. "Have you been bedded by my husband?"

Lady Lucinda looked away coyly. "Surely, my lady, I have not for I am not yet married and….."

"Save it for your husband, if you ever get one," she snapped overbearingly. "If you are a maiden, then I am the Queen of France. If I were to take a headcount of all the men in the room you two sluts have bedded between you, it would most likely constitute half the room. That is, if they were brave enough to admit they touched women as ugly as you."

Lady Lucinda and Lady Maryann were appalled and angered, emotions increased by the snickering of the knights. Dustin grinned, a humorless gesture.

"That's what I thought," she said smugly. "Whores disguised as fine ladies. And let me guess, you pursued my husband relentlessly but were unsuccessful.

He has much better taste." She suddenly pushed forward and waved her hands sternly at them as if to sweep them away. "Be gone with you, piglets. And leave Lord Marcus alone or you shall have to deal with me."

"How dare you!" Lady Lucinda cringed but did not do as she was ordered and leave. "You are an ill-bred little wench who was lucky enough to marry a baron, and he married you purely for the inheritance. Everyone knows that you are a simple country waif with no claim to court other than your husband."

Dustin's jaw ticked but she did not lose her smile. Her gray eyes bore holes into the woman.

"If you intend to spread rumors about me, then you had better get the facts straight," she said, her delivery quiet and rapid. "My father, Lord Arthur Barringdon is a cousin to Richard and John; my great-grandmother and their great-grandmother were sisters and my mother is directly descended from King Harold. Now, do you have any more questions about my lineage?"

Lady Lucinda looked as if she were about to retort but thought better of it. In a swish of blue silk and finery, the ladies swept away with their noses in the air and disappeared back into the crowd. Dustin made a face and turned her back on them.

"Bitches," she snapped, reaching for more wine.

Leeton and Edward put their great mailed gloves together and clapped slowly, appreciating the lady's bravado. She grinned at them and they laughed softly. Even Marcus was smiling.

"You did well with your first test," he said, taking the goblet from her.

"Test? Was that a test?" she asked, frowning as he set her drink down.

"Of course," he replied, holding out his elbow to her. "Now they will go back and tell their friends and all will think twice before confronting you again."

"Hmpf," Dustin snorted, taking his arm. "It wasn't much of a test. I need someone better to sharpen my claws on."

Marcus chortled, leading her from the room. "Let me get you out of here before you turn the whole room into one giant ruckus."

The halls of Windsor were dim and silent as they made their way back to the apartments. Dustin clutched Marcus and Edward, feeling the floor beneath her rolling about and wondering why she could not keep her footing.

Edward had to practically carry her up the stairs and she giggled the whole way up, banging on his plate armor and singing a crazy tune. When he set her down at the top of the stairs, she laughed loudly and whirled away from him, right into Marcus' chest.

Marcus caught her with his good arm, grinning as he straightened her out and they resumed their trek. Tipsy as she was, she began to dance and bounce her way down the hall, crowing about her first victory with the court wenches and insisting that the knights, all five of them, sing her praises. They did and she threw up her arms in triumph.

"Where is my husband?" she said, falling against Marcus and grabbing his armor, causing him to lose his balance.

"I do not know," he answered truthfully, regaining his feet and trying to keep her from falling. "I am sure he shall return shortly."

"Marcus!" She grabbed his neck, trying to force him to look her in the eye. "Where is he?"

Edward could see that Marcus was at a disadvantage and grabbed Dustin around the waist, pulling her off of him. "He is seeing to business, Dustin," Edward said steadily. "Do not worry about it."

"I am not," she insisted, stumbling when he set her down. "I just want to know where he is." Her knees gave way a little and she fell against Edward, who wrapped his arms about her instinctively to keep her from going down. She looked up at him, a silly-sweet smile on her lips. "Thank you, Eddie. Eddie, Eddie, *Eddie!*"

Edward chuckled in spite of himself and picked her up, knowing they would never make it to the apartments if she kept on like this. He hoped Christopher wouldn't be angry that they allowed her to get drunk; truthfully, they hadn't even noticed the amount of wine she imbibed. Hopefully, she would sleep most of it off before her husband returned.

They were approaching the apartments and the hall seemed particularly dim. Several of the torches were out and Marcus found it peculiar that there were no soldiers on guard out in the hall. He put up his hand, halting the group, and shushed Dustin loudly when she tried to question him.

"Dud, Trent," he motioned to the knights. "Clear the way."

Unsheathing swords, the two knights cautiously made their way up the hall and toward the door. They nearly disappeared in the darkness, the reflection of the torchlight catching their armor here and there. Edward put Dustin down, moving for his own sword as he watched the knights up ahead.

"What do you think?" he asked Marcus.

Marcus shook his head, his cobalt-blue eyes intense. "I am not sure, but the absence of soldiers cannot be good. There should be at least a half-dozen men guarding the door."

Dustin pushed herself forward, her head hurting and the floor moving. "I want to go to bed. What are you doing?"

Marcus grabbed her before she could move forward. "Making sure all is safe for you, my lady," he said evenly.

There was a richly clothed chair against the wall. Edward gently sat her in it, making sure he was standing directly next to her should anything happen because he, like Marcus, was leery of the darkened hall.

In the darkness up ahead came a crash of metal on metal and a groan of pain followed. Marcus, Edward and Leeton had their swords in hand, ready to do battle when they saw that their enemy was none other than John's cockroaches, his elite force. Urgently, Marcus turned to Edward.

"Get her out of here," he ordered.

"Nay, Marcus," Edward countered. "If we can get her into the rooms and bolt the door, she will be safe. Besides, I cannot leave you. You are compromised."

Dustin, jolted from her drunken stupor, shot off the chair with a yelp of surprise. Soldiers in black and green charged forward, immediately clashing with the three knights and Dustin found herself cringing behind Marcus as he fended of several soldiers with his left hand. With every blow she gave a little gasp of fear, feeling the concussion through Marcus' body.

Even with his good arm useless, Marcus was remarkable. He found himself fending off an onslaught of soldiers, too many to count, but he knew they were in grave danger. He could hear Dud yelling something but could not make out the words and beside him, Leeton and Edward were fighting for their lives. He knew very early on that they had to get Dustin out of there; there were simply too many soldiers for them to hold off.

Behind him, he heard yelling of a familiar sort. David raced up the hall with his sword in hand and plunged into the turmoil, his sword flashing like bolts from heaven. The man was as fast and as furious as a madman, his well-aimed strokes striking down men where they stood. Yet even with the considerable addition of David, they were still badly outnumbered. Marcus retreated slowly with Dustin tucked behind him, trying to fight his way free of the rolling mass of fury as he hustled Dustin to safety. He could feel her hands gripping him tightly about the waist.

There were at least two dozen men against the six of them, impossible odds even for the best of knights. Dustin was terrified; all she could think of was running for help or finding a weapon to help in the defense.

Then it occurred to her; down the hall and high on the wall were a display of weaponry, arranged quite artfully. Her mind's eye focused on the mace she knew was there and she was seized with hope that if she could retrieve the mace, she could help her knights. She had used a mace before; Jeffrey had taught her when he had showed her how to use the pick axe and the sword.

Trouble was that it was damn heavy and she wasn't even sure if she could be effective, but no matter; she had to try. Releasing Marcus, she charged back down the hall in a fit of panic.

The mace was there as she remembered. Breathing heavily, she pulled a chair across the corridor and stood on it, ripping the spiky ball-on-a-chain off the wall and nearly falling off the chair with her effort. As she knew, it was terribly heavy, but she heaved it over her shoulder and jumped off the chair, tearing the maroon surcoat with one of the spikes and causing her shoulder to bleed as she tore back down the hall, anxiety filling her. She was close to tears of horror and did not realize that by the time she returned to the fight, hot tears were already streaming down her pale cheeks.

Dustin took no time to pick and choose her targets. With a yell that a Scot would have been proud of, she swung the mace over her head a few times to gain momentum and plowed it into the first enemy soldier she came to. The helmet caved in and smashed his skull into fragments.

Dustin didn't even stop to see what her handiwork had caused; she continued to swing the mace, killing two more unsuspecting soldiers before one man actually turned on her, brandishing his sword high. Dustin didn't back down in the least; she swung the mace again and aimed well, but she ended up entangling the chain in the soldier's sword. In a panic, she tugged as hard as she could to release it, but the man's strength was greater and he nearly tore her arms from her sockets yanking the mace from her grip.

He snapped his sword sideways, disentangling the mace and bringing the sword to bear once again on Dustin. She was momentarily stunned; all she could do was stare back at the soldier who held her life in his hands.

She could hear shouting going on and suddenly there was a man standing beside the soldier in front of her. The visor to the faceplate went up and she found herself face to face with Ralph Fitz Walter. His bruised, circled eyes glittered evilly at her and Dustin knew she was trapped.

"My lady looks ravishing as always," he said as easily as if they were at a social gathering. "Accompany me and I shall spare your husband's knights."

Dustin knew that if she went with Ralph, she might never see the sun rise again. After what had happened this afternoon, she knew he would seek revenge on Christopher. Panic surged in her chest and she stumbled backwards, her mind completely blank except for the lone thought of escaping the sheriff.

"Nay!" Ralph screamed as she moved, unable to grab hold of her. As Ralph pushed forward, the soldier, thinking Ralph had just given him the order to kill the lady, brought the sword down and buried five or six inches of the blade lengthwise in the top of Dustin's left thigh.

Dustin screamed loudly with pain and shock, twisting away with blood streaming all down her surcoat and spattering on the floor. Marcus and Edward, the closest to her, saw what transpired and were overcome with desperation to reach her. All Marcus could see was the blood and his heart crashed to his heels in agony.

Suddenly the hall was filled with a legion of soldiers, crown soldiers, fighting off John's guard simply by sheer number. Frightened residents of the wing had summoned the company when sounds of a battle filled the corridor, it was a matter of honor to kill John's mercenary bastard troops. The hate for the elite guard was great among the crown's men-at-arms.

The black and green soldiers retreated down the hall, yet not without resistance, as Ralph hurled himself at Dustin and snatched her by the arms.

"You are coming with me," he snarled into her ear.

Dustin tried to kick and fight him, but the shock of her wound was rendering her weak and faint. She did manage to slug him in his bruised face, and he dropped her with a loud curse. But when she stumbled away from him, he hit her brutally across the back of her head and she faltered, allowing him to get a grip on her waist. Gasping with triumph, he hauled the dazed Dustin against him and attempted to find a way free of the melee.

"Ralph!" came an unmistakable roar and the sheriff looked over to see Marcus jostling toward him, his face deadly.

Ralph ripped his dagger free of its sheath and pointed it at the baron. "You are the prince's champion. You should be assisting me, you traitor."

"I shall kill you, you bastard!" Marcus bellowed furiously, shoving soldiers aside with his bad arm, oblivious to the pain. "Let her go."

The dirk pointing at Marcus was suddenly at Dustin's gut. "I shall kill her if you come any closer, Burton. Call back your men or she dies."

Dustin heard the words through her stupor and suddenly came around, twisting violently against Ralph and throwing her hands up in the general direction of his face. As she hoped, her palm found its mark and Ralph yelled in pain as his nose was again struck. His hands on his face, Dustin fell to the floor and scrambled on her hands and knees, persevering with every ounce of strength she had as she tried to get away from him. There was a heavy silk curtain several feet away; she pushed toward it, thinking if mayhap she could hide in the folds, Ralph would leave her alone to die. And with the amounts of blood she was losing, she was sure that heaven was her next destination.

Ralph was in his own world of pain. His broken nose was moving loosely about his face and he forgot all else but retreating before further damage could be dealt. Hollering in frustration and anguish, he staggered back down the hall, yelling retreat to the elite guard. Hearing the command, swords dropped and the stampede was on.

Marcus raced to Dustin, propped up against the far wall half-hidden behind the huge silk portiere. She was trying to wrap her surcoat around her bleeding leg without much success and he pushed her hands away, wiping at the blood as he tried to assess the wound.

"Jesus Christ," he breathed. "Oh, God, Dustin, I am so sorry."

Through her weakness and pain, Dustin could see how agonized he was as he ripped her surcoat away to get a better look at her leg. She reached out and touched his thick black hair.

" 'Tis nothing compared to your hand," she said shakily. "Are you all right? Is everyone all right?"

David was there, letting out a small cry of panic when he saw all of the blood on his brother's wife. He dropped to his knees, shoving Marcus aside as they both tried to get a better look at the wound.

Edward and Leeton rushed up, nicked and breathing heavily as they gazed down on their liege's wife. Yet before they could do or say anything, Dud stumbled up, blood all over him.

"Marcus," he croaked, "Trent is in a bad way."

Edward pulled Marcus to his feet and the two of them followed Dud back up the hall to where young Trent Burton lay in a puddle of his own blood, having been lanced in the side of the neck. He was bleeding volumes by the second. Edward and Leeton picked him up between them as Marcus opened the door to Christopher's apartments.

David was left alone with Dustin, having seen the wound and was now wrapping her leg tightly in strips of her destroyed surcoat. His handsome face was so very serious and Dustin watched him work; the pain in her leg unbearable but she maintained her composure. 'Twould only upset David more to see her tears, and he was doing the very best that he could.

"There," he said in a breathy voice when he had finished tightening the cloth. "Let's get you back to your room."

He reached down and picked her up, holding her against him as he rushed back down the hall and into the antechamber of Christopher's apartments. Behind him, Leeton slammed the door and bolted it.

Trent lay on the floor and Dustin caught sight of him, twisting in David's arms. "What happened to Trent?"

No one answered her, for they were more concerned with stopping the flow of blood from the man's neck. David carried Dustin into the bedchamber and laid her gently upon the bed.

"David, where is Christopher?" she asked as he pushed her down on the pillows.

"I do not know, but I intend to find him," David said grimly, then turned to the open door. "Leeton! Get in here!"

The tall, blond knight was immediately by David's side, his fair face glazed with distress.

"Stay with her," David instructed breathlessly. "I am going for Chris and for a physician."

Leeton nodded shortly, removing his helmet even as David raced for the door. Dustin pushed herself up on her elbows, her face pale and her eyes unnaturally bright.

"I am fine, really I am," she insisted.

David nodded once, glancing at Leeton before quitting the room. As he moved past Marcus and Edward in the antechamber, trying desperately to save young Trent's life, one look at the mess told David that the efforts would be in vain. A major vessel had been breached and the poor young man's life was slipping away. David paused a moment, watching their attempts, and he was gripped with utter contempt for Ralph and John.

"How's Dustin?" Edward managed to ask, up to his elbows in blood.

"It's long and fairly deep, but not too serious," he replied. "I am going for the physician and for Christopher now. Bolt this damn door after I leave."

He didn't wait for an answer before he was gone, tearing down the hall with the rage of the devil filling him.

CHAPTER NINETEEN

CHRISTOPHER RETURNED CLOSE to dawn, having no idea that anything was amiss until he approached his apartments and saw the bloodstains on the floor. Terror seized him, even as he raced the last several yards and saw a dozen soldiers guarding his door. Without a word or a glance, he shoved into his apartments, his eyes wide with fear.

David was near the door, his sword drawn in reaction to his brother's violent entry. When he saw who it was, the sword clattered to the floor.

"Chris!" he exclaimed. "Where in the hell have you been? I have been looking...."

"What happened?" Christopher only wanted his questions answered. "Why is there blood in the hall?"

"We were ambushed," David said gravely. "Ralph lay in wait with John's troops out in the hall and jumped us when we returned from supper. They killed the six guards that were protecting your apartments and stored the bodies in the maid's alcove at the other end of the wing."

Christopher's face washed with a menacing expression. "Bastards," he hissed. "Where is Dustin? Is she well?"

"She took a blow to the leg," David said, hoping his brother wouldn't tear him apart in his grief. "A decent cut that bled a great deal, but the physician stitched her up and gave her something for the pain. She is sleeping."

Christopher's face went from sheer anger to chalky pale very rapidly. He stared at David a moment.

"But she's all right?" he rasped. " 'Twas not a severe wound?"

"Nay, not overly," David replied. "The doctor says there was no great damage, though she will have a scar."

Christopher could hardly catch his breath, so great his shock and grief. His gaze wandered from his brother and traveled to the closed bedchamber door, so incredibly furious at John and Ralph but immensely grateful for Dustin's life. He took a moment to glance about the room, noting the blood on the floor.

"What is that?" he demanded, pointing. "Is that my wife's blood?"

"It is Trent's," Marcus said from his chair in the corner, his head resting on his hand wearily.

"Trent? What happened? Where is he?" Christopher asked insistently.

"He is dead." Marcus' hand fell to his lap, his face lined with fatigue. "He took a blow to the neck and bled to death, right there on your floor. We tried to help him but there was nothing we could do."

Christopher's eyes washed with sorrow for the knight's death. Even though he had not truly fought with the boy, Marcus thought a great deal of his cousin and, therefore, so did Christopher. He had seen him in practice for the tourney and knew the lad to be an aggressive and eager fighter.

"I am sorry, Marcus," he said softly. "I did not know the boy very well, but he was your blood and I am truly sorry for his death."

"As am I," Marcus said hoarsely, averting his gaze.

Christopher looked about again, at his bloodied and weary knights and at the blood on the floor, and was suddenly seized with a ferocious rage. Damn John and Ralph; would the bastards stop at nothing to destroy him? An attack against him was understandable, even welcomed, but to ambush his knights and wife in the very halls of Windsor was inexcusable. Christopher knew damn well that Ralph had convinced John the undertaking would be a success, revenge for the pounding Christopher had dealt Ralph that afternoon.

Instead of going to the bedchamber as expected, Christopher whirled and stormed to the front door. David, Edward and Leeton leapt out to stop him.

"Where are you going?" David demanded.

"Where do you think, little brother?" Christopher snapped. "This time they have gone too far. They have wounded my wife and killed one of my knights, and I will avenge myself on them. They have played with fire and now they shall be burned."

"Nay, Chris." David grabbed him by the arms as Edward wedged himself between his liege and the door. "Do not you see? That is what they want. John is looking for an excuse to dispose of you and an attack on the prince would sentence you to a life in the dungeons. Not even Richard could release you."

"John is not looking to dispose of me; he is looking to destroy everything that I am," Christopher raged. "I cannot allow this crime to go unpunished."

"You can and you must." Marcus was up, standing next to David. "John is above the law, unanswerable to all except God and Richard. You cannot touch the man, Chris. You *know* that."

Christopher was shaking with fury, his jaw clenching and unclenching. "I can still kill Ralph."

"John would have you executed for murder," Marcus said evenly. "You are not thinking clearly, Chris. Go in and see your wife and calm yourself."

Christopher's eyes met Marcus' and David's. He gnashed his teeth with the helplessness he was feeling.

"Christ," he muttered. "I command the crown's troops and I can do nothing against an attack on my family."

"Go in and see Dustin," David repeated Marcus' suggestion.

Reluctantly, he moved from the door, his great body tensed. The knights dispersed themselves, weary from the day's events.

"Who shielded my wife?" he asked, as he moved for the bedchamber door.

"I did," Marcus said. "And then she shielded herself. Do you know the woman can use a mace, and use it well? She felled three soldiers herself, if you can believe it. I was amazed."

Christopher looked at him without surprise. "I can believe it," he said.

"What about Richard, Chris?" David asked. "Have you heard anything else?"

"Nay," Christopher replied, his hand on the latch. "He is missing and the justices meet today after the tournament to discuss the future of Richard's government. John, I am sure, is claiming two victories this night."

"Two?" David asked.

"Aye," Christopher nodded absently. "The attack on my knights and my wife, and the vanishing of his brother."

Edward and Leeton had not heard of Richard's disappearance, and they turned astonished faces to their liege. He acknowledged them with a wave of the hand.

"Marcus will tell all," he told them quietly. "I will see to my wife now."

Christopher quietly opened the chamber door and entered, shutting the panel softly behind him. It was dark inside and his gaze found his wife upon the great bed. Dustin was asleep, snoring softly and buried under a mound of covers. Dustin's maid sat by the glowing hearth, rising to her feet when she saw Christopher.

"How is she?" he whispered, his eyes on his wife's sleeping face.

"She fell asleep not an hour ago, my lord," the woman replied. "The physician gave her a medicine for the pain but she fought sleep, waiting for you to return."

He nodded briefly and dismissed the woman. With grunts of relief and fatigue, he stripped off his armor, peeling off his clothes until he was nude. As he moved around the bed, he noticed the puppies sleeping soundly on a pile of rags and he skirted around them quietly.

Dustin was on her back, both arms over the top of her head. He was flooded with relief as he sat on the bed beside her, knowing her fate could have been that of young Trent. He so tremendously thankful that a slice to her leg was all she had suffered.

He reached out and stroked her hair and touched her silk cheek. It began to occur to him that bringing her here to London had not been a wise choice. He had convinced himself that he would be able to protect her better were she with him, but that had been far from the truth. Now, with Richard's fate unknown and John's imminent plans to usurp the throne, he knew that she would be safer at Lioncross Abbey. They would all be safer, the knights included. But if John planned to conquer Richard's holdings and his loyalists, he would have to do it keep by keep, and Lioncross would surely be at the top of the list. Christopher, as commander of the crown's troops, would find himself fighting John at every turn.

He sighed, caressing her head tenderly. Mayhap she would not be safe at Lioncross; if not, then where could he send her? Certainly not Nottingham, nor Lohrham Forest. Then a thought occurred to him; Marcus' new keep was in the north, near York. That was nearly as far north as one could get, terribly far away from London.

Marcus could not fight, not with that arm. But he could protect Dustin and defend his keep from any attack. And if Christopher reinforced Marcus' troops with two hundred more crown troops it would provide ample protection for his wife. But, *Christ*, he didn't want to be away from her, not even for a minute. He knew now that keeping her here at Windsor was entirely selfish on his part; he could not protect her any better here, and tonight's incident was a prime example.

But to send her with Marcus… his thoughts lingered on the obvious. The two of them, alone in the north, with Christopher far away… Marcus was greatly attracted to Dustin, still. Christopher knew that. He had to admit that he didn't trust Marcus not to make another move on his wife and if he were honest with himself, perhaps he didn't trust Dustin not to resist. They were the foolish thoughts of a weary man and, for the moment, he pushed it all aside. He didn't want to think about it anymore this night.

George jumped onto the bed, his beady little monkey eyes blinking rapidly at Christopher as he crawled around Dustin's head and settled himself on the top of the pillow. Christopher sighed and moved over his wife, snuggling into the bed beside her and being mindful not to jostle her leg. He knew from experience how painful such wounds could be.

With two hours until dawn, he slept.

CHAPTER TWENTY

THE MORNING DAWNED bright and clear, unusual for the time of year but very pleasing to the occupants of Windsor. There was a cool breeze lifting the banners about the tournament field as the grounds came alive with knights and servants, groomsmen and squires, all preparing for the exciting day ahead.

Christopher had risen and bathed in the antechamber so as to not wake his wife. His squire and two other young boys sat in the corner polishing the rust from his armor. George, ever curious, had followed Christopher into the room and sat perched on a chair as the baron bathed, screaming a monkey scream when Christopher flicked water at him and drawing laughter from the boys.

Christopher donned his breeches and heavy linen shirt, pulling on his boots, as one of Dustin's maids brought the morning meal into the room, followed closely by David. His brother had brought his own squire and soon four boys sat in the corner polishing two sets of armor.

"How is Dustin?" David yawned, breaking apart a hunk of cheese.

"Still asleep," Christopher replied, drinking a warmed mulled wine brew. "What about you? Did you get any sleep?"

"About an hour," David replied. "Marcus probably didn't sleep at all. He is devastated with his cousin's passing."

Christopher grunted in sympathy, sipping at his cup. "David, I made some decisions last night," he said. "With the uncertainty of Richard's future, I have decided to leave Windsor. I am afraid that last night was only a foretaste of what is to come."

David nodded. "That is wise," he said. "Dustin shouldn't be here with John and Ralph on the prowl. They came for her last night, you know. She belongs back at Lioncross."

"She's not going back to Lioncross," Christopher said, noting the expression of surprise on his brother's face. "David, when John goes through with his plans to seize the throne, and have no doubt that he will, Richard's loyalists will be his first targets. Lioncross is too close to London to be safe for my wife."

"So… what?" David wanted to know. "Where will you send her?"

Christopher took a healthy drink of his brew. "With Marcus to Somerhill."

David eyed him warily. "Chris, what are you talking about?"

Christopher sat forward, his expression grim. "David, John is raising a mercenary army and the justices believe he intends to forcibly seize Richard's holdings, especially now that Richard is missing," he said in a lowered tone. "Obviously, if that happens, you and I, and all of Richard's troops will move to halt him and civil war will ensue. I intend that Dustin should be as far away as possible, with Marcus, at Somerhill."

"Marcus will not be fighting with us?" David demanded, his emotions running high as usual.

"With his arm useless? I would not allow it," Christopher said.

"But you will allow him to protect your wife, to be with her day in and day out, while you defend Richard's throne?" David hissed. "You may save your king's throne, but you may also lose your wife in the process. Think on it, Chris. Marcus loves Dustin and in your absence, you know what could happen."

"It will not," Christopher snapped quietly, eyeing the squires in the corner. "Dustin is my wife and she loves me. I will have to trust them both, David. What else can I do?"

"Send her to Lohrham. Or to Bath," David insisted. "Jesus, Chris, do not send her into the wilds with Marcus. You shall never get her back."

Christopher sat back in his chair, his expression icy. "I have made my decision, David. I must do what's best for my wife."

David acted as if it was *his* wife being sent away. "You are wrong."

Before they could argue the subject further, the door to the bedchamber opened. The men turned to see Dustin standing in the doorway.

"You are back," she said, her focus on Christopher. "I thought I heard your voice."

"Dustin," Christopher said as he got out of his chair. "You shouldn't be up, sweetheart."

She met him halfway, throwing herself into his arms. He hugged her deeply and then tried to swing her into his arms, but she protested with a grunt of pain.

"I am sorry," he said gravely, lowering her back to the ground. "I did not mean to hurt you, sweet."

"I am fine, really," she said, but she was pale. Then she glanced over at David. "Good morn, David."

Before David could answer her, Christopher lifted her gingerly. "Back to bed with you, lady. That leg requires rest to heal."

Her brow furrowed. "The physician said it is not too deep and I do not feel like staying in bed. The tournament is today."

"No tournament for you," he said firmly, swinging her back into the bedchamber.

"But, Chris," she protested, gripping his neck tightly to prevent him from laying her down on the bed. "My leg will heal. The physician stitched it and wrapped it tightly, and I can walk on it. I must get ready for the tournament."

David listened to them argue, hearing Dustin challenge and complain and cajole in response to Christopher's firm denials. When Dustin got mad and called him a less-than-ladylike name, David shot a reproachful glare to the gigglers in the corner. The sun rose steadily and the fight ensued, much to David's amusement.

As he sat there listening to his brother's wife rant, it occurred to him how much this woman had become a part of their lives. Not just Christopher's, but his as well. It was as if she had always been a part of their lives and he almost could not remember what it was like before she graced them with her light.

His infatuation with her had banked to respectful appreciation, but he had to admit he was fiercely protective of her when it came to Marcus. Mayhap it was jealousy, but whatever the case, he didn't trust Marcus where Dustin was concerned and he thought his brother's intention to send Dustin north with the new baron to be foolish.

The door to the bedchamber suddenly slammed shut with a resounding noise, rattling the utensils on the table before him. Even with the door closed, he could hear Dustin shouting and Christopher's even responses. David took a last swig of wine and rose, going across the room to see how his armor was coming along. The squires, proud of their work, displayed the shiny pieces for him.

Something banged heavily in the other room and he heard Dustin yelling loudly. He couldn't really make out her words, but whatever they were, they were angry. Casually, he held his arms out while his squire pulled his hauberk on, acting as if there was nothing unusual occurring at all. But the young squires had big eyes as the banging and shouting continued. David thought it all rather comical.

He finished dressing, including the tunic bearing Christopher's colors. This was a newer tunic, made a few days ago when he had tunics made for Marcus, Dud and Trent. David wondered if Marcus would even be wearing colors today, even though he would be acting as Dustin's escort. And he had no doubt Lady de Lohr was coming, although he pondered the question of whether or not she would award trophies.

Time was passing and they had to get to the tournament field to begin preparations. He knew that the other knights were most likely already there, but he hesitated to leave without Christopher. The fight coming from the bedchamber had grown suspiciously quiet and he suspected it was either because Dustin was crying or because Christopher was making mad love to her.

David waited about as long as he dared, finally donning his helmet and headed for the door, just as the bedchamber door opened and Christopher exited, not looking the least bit sheepish.

"Well? Is she coming?" David demanded, fumbling with his gloves.

Christopher shot him an impatient glance as he went to his squire. "She is," he said, forcing the words out. "Go and make sure the preparations are complete. I shall escort my wife down to the field."

David snorted and Christopher glared at him menacingly, conveying silent threats of pain and death to his brother should he laugh at him. David bit his lip and feigned a serious look.

"Edward and Leeton are at the field, I am sure," he said, fighting off a bad attack of the giggles. "I shall wait for you and your lovely wife."

Christopher ignored him as his squire helped him with his armor. Dustin's two fat maids bustled in and out of the bedchamber, carrying in hot water and linens and other things. The young squires sitting against the wall watched with great interest as the women scurried in and out, back and forth. They dug into the massive wardrobe in the antechamber at one point and retreated with a pile of cloaks.

"How is her leg?" David asked, watching the competent young squire handle Christopher's leg armor.

"'A mere scratch', she says, to quote a more experienced warrior," he replied, shaking his leg to adjust the greave. The armor settled down over his boot. "If she bleeds to death up in the lists, then it is her own fault."

"Are you going to let her award trophies?" his brother inquired.

Christopher tugged at the tunic as his squire straightened his breastplate. "I already told her that she could," he said, looking at David. "As much as I loathe the idea of her anywhere near John and Ralph, there is naught they can do to her with Marcus by her side or with thousands of people as witnesses."

David stood with his legs braced apart, arms crossed, watching the squire finish his brother's dress. David had seen his brother in armor for as long as he could remember, and words that came to mind this day were imposing…indestructible…powerful…fearless. Defender of the Realm and Richard's Champion. His brother was all of that and more.

"Chris, with all of the excitement, I forgot to tell you that Deborah is here," David said after a few moments. "I saw her in the dining hall last eve. She's a damn woman grown; I never would have recognized her if she hadn't come to me first."

"Deborah?" Christopher looked surprised, then nodded with sudden understanding. "Of course; how could I have not realized? The Earl of Bath is here. Christ, I shall have to seek her out and see if your words are true. How old is she now, seventeen? By the way, have you seen anyone from Lohrham?"

"Nay," David answered. "They probably arrived late yesterday, as did the rest of the competitors who weren't already here." He grinned suddenly. "It shall be a route, Chris. Lohrham's knights are all old warriors who fought with father and Uncle Philip. There are only a few worthy knights in the contest worthy of your skills, most of them having recently returned from the quest."

"And not even they can defeat me," Christopher said with customary arrogance, as casually as if he were discussing the weather. "You are correct in your observation, little brother. This tourney will be a route for Richard's forces."

His squire was securing his sword when Dustin entered the antechamber.

All male eyes in the room, young and old alike, were glued to her like flies to honey. She wore a surcoat of rich royal blue silk, the same color as Christopher's tunic. The flattering lines along her bosom and shoulders brought out the beauty of her neck and torso, and she had pulled her hair back softly to reveal her heart-shaped face.

She smiled as she approached her husband, noticeably limping. "Do you like it? It matches your colors."

Christopher was deeply pleased. He smiled faintly, touching her gently under the chin. "The color makes your eyes as dark as storm clouds," he said softly. "Aye, I like it a great deal. Never have my colors looked so good."

She grinned triumphantly and Christopher had to chuckle; she was always as happy as a child when she got her way.

"Thank you, my lord," she curtsied coyly, lowering her lashes. She was becoming quite practiced with her feminine gestures, for they came naturally to her.

Christopher grinned openly at her, holding out his hands for his squire to pull on his gauntlets. Dustin stepped back as the tall lad silently and deftly pulled on the gloves. She eyed the young man curiously, now at close range. She had never been this close to him before and she was interested.

"I have never met your squire, Chris," she said. "Would you introduce us?"

Christopher looked as if the idea had never occurred to him. The squire stopped what he was doing, his cheeks flushing bright red as he looked up at his liege.

"Darren, this is my wife, the Lady Dustin de Lohr." He looked at his wife and turned the boy to face her. "Dustin, this is Darren Ainsley, son of Lord Robert Ainsley. Darren served with me three years on the quest. His father served Richard."

Dustin nodded to the embarrassed young man. "Is your father still in the Holy Land?"

The poor squire looked as if he were going to die from sheer fright. "Nay, my lady, he perished over a year ago," he answered, his voice cracking.

"How terrible," Dustin said sincerely. "Then it would seem that you and I have something in common."

"Aye, my lady," the boy nodded rapidly, his eyes too shy to meet hers.

"How old are you, Darren?" she asked.

"Seventeen, my lady," he replied, then added, "I was sent to foster at Lohrham Forest when I was seven years old. Lord Christopher took me as his squire when I was twelve."

Dustin smiled at him and Christopher felt the boy sway under his grip. As amusing as it was to witness Darren's abject terror, time was pressing.

"If you are ready, then, we shall proceed to the field," Christopher said.

As Dustin nodded, he let go of Darren, positive the lad would collapse without the support. He didn't, but bolted for the corner as if he had been burned, gathering Christopher's weapons and shield hastily. Christopher had to smile to himself; he barely remembered the same fear when he had been a lad barely over the threshold of manhood, speaking to a beautiful woman for the first time. But no woman he had ever seen nor spoken to had ever compared with his wife, so he felt doubly sorry for Darren on that account.

"Do you think I will need my cloak? I do not think I will need it." Dustin was rambling on. David simply shrugged.

"Bring it," Christopher ordered. "The day may grow chilly."

"But the sun is shining," Dustin pointed out, "and this silk is heavy. I will not need my cloak."

Christopher picked up the deep blue cloak and threw it at her. "Take it."

She dropped it on the floor purely from spite, smoothing her surcoat primly. "I do not want to," she said disagreeably. "The silk is warm enough. Besides, it will cover up this lovely dress and I want to show it off."

He glared threateningly at her, about to suggest that her surcoat gave an ample view of her lovely breasts and that the cloak would cover her from lustful eyes, but he didn't want to upset her. Instead, he sighed heavily and picked the cloak up.

"Take it or you do not go," he said in a low, even tone. She scowled but took it, for she was wary of the level of his voice.

The squires preceded them from the room, with the boys laden with Christopher and David's shields as well other implements. Dustin fastened the cloak around her shoulders and took David's and Christopher's arms. Outside in the hall were a full company of soldiers lining the walls. They snapped to attention when they exited from the antechamber and Dustin startled at the loud salute as they greeted the baron. They were all Christopher's troops, their sharp blue and gold tunics indicating such, their mail polished to a sheen.

It was extremely impressive, even to her. Twenty-four soldiers escorted her, Christopher and David down from the apartments and through the bulk of the castle. There were very few people in the castle, most of them either getting ready for the tournament or already down at the field, and the cadence of synchronized bootfalls echoed loudly in the cavernous halls as they made their way outside.

Dustin gripped the elbows of the two knights, almost running to keep up with the pace that had been set and her chest swelling with the enormous pride she was feeling. She could not keep the cocky smile from her lips.

She glanced up at her husband, so tall and strong and powerful that he was nearly surreal. His helmet was on and his visor lifted and it was impossible to see most of his face, but she stared at him anyway. She could not describe the pride filling her veins, proud that he was hers, that all of this loyalty was theirs, that her husband and his knights were the envy of the whole of Windsor.

"How's your leg?" he asked, as his helmeted head looked down at her.

Truth was, it ached a great deal but she forced a smile. "Not too bad."

"Are we walking too fast for you?" he asked.

She didn't want to be a bother, especially when she had put up such a fuss earlier. But her expression gave her away and before she could answer he was barking orders at the sergeant to slow the pace. Slower, and much better for her, they continued on to the arena.

The lists were already filling up with women in gaily decorated dressed and men with brightly colored tunics and shoes. The royal box was decorated with flowers and ribbons and silks, but John and Ralph were nowhere to be seen. David excused himself and Christopher positioned the color guard personally.

"What are you doing?" Dustin asked, watching him place the men in strategic places about the stands.

"Making sure each man has an unobstructed view of you," he replied, distracted. "Marcus will act as your personal protector and these men will assist him. Their duty is to you and you alone."

Dustin watched the strong, silent soldiers take their places, a little overwhelmed that all of the men were assigned to her. The early morning sun was remarkably warm and she was heating up rapidly underneath the cloak, so she removed it as her husband placed the last of the guards. Finally, he turned to her.

"That should be sufficient," he said, his eyes raking her bare shoulders and chest. He almost forgot himself, but cleared his throat and continued. "You will sit up there."

She turned and looked to see where he was pointing, noting that there were several chairs in the royal box.

He continued, "Marcus should be here momentarily, and I do not want you straying from him." He grasped her chin, forcing her to look at him. "Do you understand me?"

"Aye," she nodded. "Will I see you at all?"

"Of course, sweet. I shall be fighting for the honor of Richard and England, out there on the field," he said, smiling. "And then, of course, you will award the trophies to me."

She smiled in return, her eyes suddenly growing concerned. "You shall be careful, won't you? Promise me that you will not get hurt."

"I promise," he replied sincerely. "Do not worry about me."

"I *do* worry," she said insistently. "I cannot help it. I have heard that tournaments can be very dangerous."

"Not to me," he snorted, bending down to kiss her when she eyed him dubiously. "And there is one thing more." He fumbled under his tunic and was digging beneath his mail while Dustin watched him curiously. Finally, he drew forth a black silk pouch and proceeded to open it with his thick fingers.

"Do you remember I told you that I wanted to buy you a proper wedding gift, something you would wear and remember me by?" he asked softly.

"Aye," she said. "But you bought me the diamond ring and I think of you every time I look at it."

He smiled warmly at her. "Close your eyes."

She did as she was asked, feeling something heavy and cold lay against the white skin of her bosom like a great block of ice.

"Open your eyes, sweetheart," he ordered quietly.

She did and immediately looked down to see what he had placed upon her. Her breath caught in her throat when she observed a large golden cross, inlaid with glittering sapphires and strung upon a beautiful gold chain. It was simple and elegant, entirely gorgeous, and she turned it over and over in her hands as she admired it.

"Oh, Christopher," she gasped. "It's lovely."

"Do you like it?" he watched her expression and could only read joy.

"Oh, I do," she exclaimed, her face lighting up with a huge smile. "I shall never take it off, I swear it. But why do you give it to me now, in front of everyone, where I cannot thank you properly?"

His great gloved hand caressed her cheek and her heart fluttered at his warm, loving gaze. "You thank me properly by being my wife, by bearing my colors, by your beauty and your spirit. 'Tis the greatest thanks I could receive."

"I will thank you later in private, nonetheless," she promised quietly.

"I will live on that vow the rest of the day," he said, turning as a knight roared by on a gaily colored destrier and the crowd applauded loudly.

"Who is that?" Dustin asked.

"Sir Stephen Marion," he replied. "A pompous fool if there ever was one."

Dustin watched the knight remove his helmet and acknowledge the cheers of the crowd, eyeing her husband as he pretended to ignore the cries. "Lord, he's a handsome devil," she teased.

Christopher tightened his gauntlets. "Not after I get finished with him," he said. "Take your seat; Marcus should be here shortly."

"Where are you going?" Dustin grabbed his arm, suddenly afraid to let him go.

He put a hand over hers. "I must prepare, sweetheart." He could read the anxiety on her face and patted her hand reassuringly. "Do not worry. Enjoy yourself. This will be exciting, I promise."

He tried to steer her toward her chair, but she balked. "Wait; I haven't given you a favor."

"Aye, you have," he said, holding up his left hand. "I wear it on my finger."

"But…it's just a wedding ring," she grappled for her surcoat. "Let me give you a real favor you can carry in your gauntlet."

"This ring means more to me than any slip of material, Dustin," he said softly, stilling her hands. "I really have to go now."

Again he moved her toward her seat but she stopped dead in her tracks like a stubborn old horse. "Kiss me."

His brow furrowed. "I cannot, sweet. I have got my helmet on and…."

"Kiss me, *please*." She was insistent.

He sighed, wondering what was bringing on this case of nerves. True, she had never been to a tournament before, but she was acting as if he were going to his death. With thick fingers, he unlatched his helmet and removed it. Before he could take another breath, she grabbed his mailed head and planted an urgent, hard kiss on his bearded lips.

"Dustin, what's the matter with you?" he demanded quietly.

"Nothing," she insisted, still holding his head. "It's just that I have never been to a tourney before and I know there is always a chance that you could…"

"Do not say it or you shall curse me," he warned lightly. "My sweet love, I have been competing in tournaments since I was twenty years old and I have yet to be injured in one. You worry overly."

She started to pout but he thankfully caught sight of Marcus rounding the stands. "Look, there's Marcus," he said quickly before she could stall further. He waved at the man. "Marcus!"

Marcus caught sight of them as he entered the lists, his eyes warming at Dustin. She looked absolutely beautiful in the dark blue surcoat. Christopher took her hands from his head and kissed them before placing them on Marcus' arm.

"Take her before she convinces me not to compete," he said. "I have yet to see to my horse or to my men."

Marcus' hand closed over her two small ones. "Why? What's the matter?"

"She's afraid," Christopher said, putting his helmet back on. "She has never been to a tournament before and she's concerned that I will end up impaled on a pole or some other sort of nonsense."

"It's *not* nonsense," Dustin insisted hotly.

Christopher and Marcus passed glances and Marcus began to lead her toward their seats. "Aye, it is," Marcus said. "You are in for a great treat, my lady. Tournaments are a test of skill and tactics, not a fight to the death."

She allowed him to settle her, but her eyes were glued to her husband as he strode away across the busy arena. They were barely seated when Marcus found himself the object of several young women's attentions, all in a rush of giggles and perfume.

Dustin lost sight of Christopher and turned her attention to the flock of young ladies fawning over Marcus, cooing like silly sappy fools about his arm, lamenting the fact that he would not be competing. Dustin sighed irritably, if there was anything worse than a cow-eyed man, it was a cow-eyed woman. She turned her back as Marcus politely fended off his admirers.

The arena was alive with knights and horses and servants. Banners of nearly every great house in England whipped about in the brisk wind that was picking up, blowing the dead leaves across the field. Dustin's fear for her husband was gradually replaced by the building excitement as the competitors prepared for the great meet ahead. She quickly lost her anxiety as she eagerly watched a knight's last practice with his new joust pole, or mayhap a few final light blows against another knight. Everyone was busy, making ready for the events in one form or another.

Marcus found it very strange to be watching the games from the stands. He had never in his life watched a tournament from this vantage point and realized he was very restless. He tried to concentrate on various opponents, evaluating them as if he were actually going up against them, but the constant stream of female admirers were distracting and he was losing his good nature. The more the stands filled with various houses and nobility, the more women seemed to occupy themselves with the great Marcus Burton.

Dustin was peppering him with questions, but she was a welcome diversion. Her view of life, of the world, in general was refreshing and he was happy to answer her inquiries. But no sooner would he respond to her than another lady was tugging on his arm, vying for his attention. He began to wonder if sitting in the stands was such a wise idea, if he continued to be as distracted as he was, he would not be able to keep an eye on Dustin.

Dustin, over all of her excitement, could see Marcus' irritation. The women about him were fluffy little chits with shallow brains and even shallower hearts, and she suspected that there was only one way to get rid of them.

"Do you want me to fight them off?" she asked.

He turned greatly amused eyes to her. "Hopefully that will not be necessary," he responded, then eyed a particularly busty woman as she approached him with a smile. "Yet, on second thought, I may have to accept your gracious offer."

Dustin eyed the woman, too, a few feet away. "I think I know a way to be rid of them," she said. "Do most of these people know who I am?"

"A few, not all," Marcus replied. "I doubt the women have made the association that you are Chris' wife; those gossipy little whores. They come up to me in groups and then retreat to tell their friends, and then their friends move in. Why do you ask?"

Dustin grinned a mischievous grin. "Go along with me, Marcus, whatever I do."

Before he could respond, she bounded onto his lap and threw her arms around his neck. "Of course I shall marry you, Lord Marcus. We shall be ever so happy at Somerhill and…!" She suddenly looked up at the busty woman innocently. "Greetings, ladies. Congratulate me!" She fixed Marcus with as sweet and loving expression as she could muster. "The baron and I are to be married immediately. Tell everyone we will have a big, expensive wedding. Won't we, darling?"

Marcus was watching her with astonishment but didn't miss his cue. "Of course, my love, whatever you say." For good measure he kissed her loudly on the cheek.

The big-chested woman was appalled and outraged. She took a step back, glaring at Dustin's smirking face, and put her handkerchief to her lips as if to stop the scream of shock rising in her throat.

Dustin just beamed up at her, pulling Marcus' face into the soft curve of her neck. "Remember, tell everyone. Marcus Burton is no longer a free man, and I am the jealous sort with a belt full of daggers that I am quite good with."

The woman shrieked, nearly stumbling over her own feet in her haste to leave. Dustin's fake smile turned into a real one and Marcus tore his face away from her silky neck, not because he wanted to but because he knew if he kept it there any longer, Dustin might become suspicious.

"There," she said smugly. "That should take care of that."

She climbed off his lap and took her seat, gloating at her cleverness. Marcus, however, was still a bit stunned. Having her so close, so sweet, so warm against him only served to reinforce his desire for her. For a brief, clandestine moment he actually held her, actually put his face against her incredible skin and the faint scent of roses permeated his nostrils.

Marcus was a strong man, but he was not perfect. His want for his liege's wife was multiplying and he was having a devil of a time controlling it. He knew her actions were innocent, but they had provoked the banked flames in him nonetheless.

"Thank you," he managed to say. "Mayhap that will keep the foolish birds away from me."

"The rumors will spread like wildfire," Dustin agreed. "At least for today, they will believe it. Only when they see me with Christopher will they become confused and then, eventually, discover our game."

"Are you really good with a dagger?" Marcus teased. "You are damn good with a mace."

"Oh? You noticed, did you?" Dustin shrugged, somewhat embarrassed. "I can handle a dagger, too, I suppose. Why? Do you want me to follow through on my threat?"

He laughed. "No, truly, you have done quite enough."

Something over Dustin's shoulder caught Marcus' attention and he stiffened. Dustin saw his expression and whirled around to see the prince and Ralph mounting the stairs to the lists, surrounded by a dozen elite guards.

Marcus rose, his face like stone as he watched John and Ralph make their way to their seats, a few feet from where he and Dustin sat. As Ralph and Marcus glared daggers at each other, John extended his hand graciously to Dustin.

"Lady de Lohr, how lovely you look." he loudly exclaimed.

"I'm so pleased your husband allowed you to grace me with your company."

Dustin realized she was shaking as she rose and placed her hand in the prince's, watching him with veiled disgust as he kissed her palm. But the prince didn't bother her nearly as much as Ralph did; standing a mere few feet away, she felt his presence like a harsh December wind. Every time she looked at him her leg began to throb unbearably, reminding her of what happened last night.

Ralph's face was one massive bruise. He stopped glaring at Marcus long enough to focus his beady eyes on Dustin.

"My lady," he greeted skeptically, his eyes roving her body. "You look entirely healthy and whole."

Dustin, twitching, could not hide her contempt. "No thanks to you, sheriff, but at least I am alive."

Marcus, seeing an invitation for an explosion, gently grasped Dustin by the arms and pulled her down to sit once again.

John eyed Marcus. "You know, for my champion, you do not seem to be inclined to wear my colors."

"I wear no colors today, sire, for I am not competing," Marcus replied steadily.

"Yet you sit with Lord Christopher's wife," the prince pointed out.

"As do you, my lord," Marcus returned.

John pulled back a bit, rethinking his strategy. He scrutinized Marcus once more before leaning back in his chair in a relaxed motion.

"I must say I was quite disappointed to learn of your injury," he said without sincerity. "In fact, I found myself searching for another champion right away and although I found no one of your caliber of skills, I was able to find a suitable replacement."

Marcus gazed back impassively, wondering who had been foolish enough, besides himself, to champion the prince. "Anyone I know, sire?"

"Possibly." John let his gaze wander out over the arena until it came to rest on a group of men underneath a massive oak tree just outside the perimeter of the field. Marcus and Dustin followed his eyes, immediately spying the black and green colors of the prince. Beside her, Marcus visibly stiffened.

"Good Christ," he muttered.

Before Dustin could ask him what he meant, John glanced over at the two of them, looking rather pleased with himself. "His name is Sir Dennis le Londe."

"Dennis the Destroyer," Marcus hissed. "The man is no champion, sire, he's a butcher."

"And he's worth every penny," John shot back. "Although I paid him far less than what I paid you, Burton. He and two of his men, along with three of my elite knights, will be competing for my glory."

Mercenaries. Marcus felt his chest swell with disgust and anxiety. Dustin, her eyes wary, tugged at his arm.

"Who is that man?" she asked.

Marcus controlled himself, for Dustin had only recently quelled her fears and anything he said could send her off on another fit of terror. "A mercenary, Dustin," he said quietly. "He fought with the French in Palestine a year or so back and was known for his....aggressive fighting."

What he didn't tell her is that the man single-handedly destroyed two Muslim settlements, mostly women and children, under the guise of peace. He was a completely brutal, unscrupulous man and Marcus wished to God he were fighting in these games for the simple pleasure of humiliating the bastard.

He didn't know if Christopher was aware of Dennis' presence, but one thing was certain; Christopher was going to have his hands full. If the baron believed these games to be an easy victory, the stakes had suddenly changed.

"Is he good?" Dustin's voice broke into his train of thought. "He cannot beat Christopher, can he?"

Marcus' jaw ticked. "No."

Ralph came alongside of John, taking a seat to the left of the prince and placed himself nearly next to Dustin. "What did you expect, Burton? The prince must have a champion, and a fine one can be bought for the right price," he said. "And after Lord Christopher rendered me quite unable to compete yesterday, I was forced to make other arrangements."

Marcus bit back several harsh retorts, cursing himself for ever becoming involved with these two jackals. "So you hire three bloodthirsty mercenaries to compete in a field of honorable knights."

"Exactly," Ralph said with a fake smile. "I would wager to say that de Lohr will have to fight for his trophy, don't you think? 'Twill not be the easy ride he would have believed it to be."

Marcus' big body tensed and he fought down the urge to rant and yell and destroy everything within his reach. Dustin, however, had not caught on to his concern as she continued to watch the prince's champion prepare.

"Look at his helmet, Marcus," she said, leaning into him. "It has horns on it. And his horse's armor has spikes all the way around."

Marcus' cobalt blue eyes were as dark as midnight. "I know."

He glanced at Dustin after a minute, her beautiful face openly surveying the field. He was so thankful that his fears had not rubbed off on her, but he found himself more and more apprehensive by the moment. Jesus, what if Christopher were indeed killed in front of her? As ruthless and conniving as le Londe was, anything was possible. Christopher had told him, in jest, to be the highest bidder should he in fact perish and Dustin was put on the block. He knew now that if anything did happen, Somerhill be damned. He would take Dustin and flee the country.

The marshals were taking the field and the stands were filled to overflowing. The air fairly bristled with excitement now as the knights were beginning to form two lines in anticipation of the pageant of colors that would begin the tournament. Dustin could see her husband's knights but she did not see him.

"Where's Chris?" she asked Marcus, pointing to the knights.

Marcus, still under a cloud of doom and gloom, managed an ironic chuckle. "He doesn't like the pageantry or the pomp, so he lets David and the others soak up the adoration," he said, then turned to Dustin. "But just you wait; it has been over three years since the population has seen Chris in a tournament and they will welcome him back with open arms; they love him."

Dustin, with a look of surprise, looked back over the stands at the hundreds of people waving their hands and kerchiefs and yelling for their favorite champion.

"Truly?" she faced front again. "I didn't realize he was so popular."

"Oh, Dustin, there is none more so," Marcus said fervently. "Chris has been the reigning champion of the joust and hand-to-hand since he was twenty-two. Only in his absence have there been others, but the king has returned to regain his crown and the crowd will go mad for him."

Dustin smiled faintly, a prideful smile. "What about you? How well did you do?"

He shrugged and looked over the field again. "I have fought Chris seven times on the field," he said. "I have beat him twice in the joust and thrice with my sword. I am the only one who's ever come close."

"And you are very good," she said agreeably, eyeing his bandaged arm underneath the mail. "I am sorry you will not have a chance to improve your record."

"If I improved my record, it would be at your husband's expense," Marcus reminded her with a smile.

She brushed a stray bit of hair off her face, openly studying his arm again. "Will you ever be able to use it again?"

"Only God can say for sure," he replied. "The feeling is there and the bones will heal. 'Twill be up to me to work it back to strength."

She shook her head, her hand lingering on his arm for a moment longer before she folded it in her lap and turned her attention back to the field. Marcus stared at her until the trumpets heralded the start of the games and the crowd roared with enthusiasm.

CHAPTER TWENTY-ONE

THE JOUST WAS first and the knights drew lots to see who would compete against each other in the first round. After the opening bout, Dustin had already had enough. One young knight nearly lost an arm, and her fear for Christopher returned full measure. He was not scheduled to go on until almost the end of the round, and her anxiety was making her mouth dry and her hands tingle painfully.

Marcus, cool and calm, sat impassively as he watched, commenting on every right or every wrong move. By the third bout, she was ready to throttle him if he spewed forth one more gem of criticism.

David's turn was up and he neatly disposed of his opponent on the first run. Dustin cheered wildly for him, yelling like a roughhouse wench until Marcus yanked her back into her seat. She shut up, but she continued to grin and wave at David until he waved back.

Edward was up two bouts later, taking on one of John's mercenary knights. Two passes and two hard hits later, Edward ended up on his arse and was automatically disqualified. Shaken, he made his way from the field under his own power and the crowd acknowledged him politely. Leeton came immediately after him, taking down the Earl of Warkworth's captain with one powerful blow. He was quite triumphant until he learned he had caved the man's chest in and, an hour later, the man died.

Dud won his bout as well, up against the formidable Earl of Norwich. It took four passes to take the earl down, and even Marcus roared his approval when the earl clattered to the ground in a thump of armor.

As long as Christopher's men were winning and unharmed, Dustin was ecstatic. She screamed and hollered, much to the disapproval of John and Ralph. Ralph even went so far as to admonish her to be neutral since she was awarding trophies, but a deadly look from Marcus shut him up.

John's champion, Sir Dennis, broke the neck of the man he was jousting against by bringing his pole up at an angle in the very last seconds before they clashed and caught the man in the neck.

Everyone in the stands heard the snap and the knight was dead before he hit the ground. The entire crowd shot to their feet in horror and Dustin gasped aloud, her hand to her mouth in disbelief.

Sir Dennis pranced around the ring, gloating in complete disrespect of the dead knight even as his comrades hurried out to the field to take the body away. Dustin was sickened, for all she could see was Christopher laying there, dead. Marcus gently sat her down once again and she found herself turning to him for comfort. She was terrified.

"Well, well, accidents will happen," John said carelessly.

Dustin looked at him with scorn, preparing a sharp reply, but Marcus whispered in her ear and she bit her tongue.

Christopher's bout was next. Dustin's attention was riveted to his imposing form as he rode out onto the field on his great white destrier. At the very moment the animal's hooves hit the brown dirt of the arena, the crowd knew their champion had arrived and went absolutely mad.

Even though Marcus had forewarned her, Dustin was still startled when the roar went up. Beyond excitement or any other rational feeling, she could do naught but stare at him as he accepted his pole from his squire and moved it to a comfortable position.

"Oh, lord," she moaned. "Marcus, I cannot watch this."

He grinned at her; she was as white as a sheet. "Be brave, Dustin. There is none better at this than your husband."

She stared at Christopher for a moment longer before turning away and shutting her eyes tightly. "I cannot look. Who is his opponent?"

"Sir Stephen Marion," Marcus answered.

"Him?" She jerked her head around to look again and then just as quickly looked away. "Christopher said he was a pompous fool."

"He is," Marcus agreed. "But he is an excellent knight. This should be an exciting bout."

"Cease," she snapped, covering her eyes with her right hand.

Marcus laughed softly, enjoying her terror. "Here comes the marshal," he commented.

"Do not tell me anymore," she ordered, pressing her hand tighter against her eyes.

He leaned closer to her. "He's holding up his flag and the knights are preparing their poles."

"Marcus!" she yelled softly. "Shut up or I will kill you myself. I cannot watch this."

"You are not," he reminded her. "So I will be your eyes."

"Nay, do not!" she shook her head, terror and excitement and apprehension filling her full to overflowing.

"There goes the flag," Marcus announced.

Dustin was seized with dread. She could hear the destriers charging, their hooves thundering loudly as the two knights approached one another with their poles aloft. She began to whimper softly with mounting fear as the rumble grew louder and louder and she could hear Marcus laughing quietly.

There was a deafening crash and the crowd cheered uproariously. Dustin's hand flew from her eyes and she whipped her head around to see her husband, still mounted, reining his horse to a halt at the opposite end of the arena. Sir Stephen, also still mounted, was fumbling with his pole as a young squire ran out onto the field to retrieve his shield.

Dustin sagged into her chair, her hand to her forehead. She was absolutely drained.

"You see? He's fine," Marcus said. "Watch the next pass."

She eyed him, too weak with emotion to respond. The marshal was again on the field with his little yellow flag. Dustin watched the flag fall and in spite of her great apprehension, found herself unable to cover her eyes the second time.

Christopher spurred his steed forward, the horse digging deep holes with the power of his leap. Man and beast became one as they charged forward, aiming for the opposition's shield, waiting for the correct moment to lower the joust pole. The seconds that passed were both elongated and shortened; it seemed to take forever to reach one another, yet suddenly, they were clashing with cataclysmic force.

Dustin jumped with shock when Sir Stephen went sailing to the ground in a crash of metal. The crowd roared their approval and ladies' favors filled the air like rain, falling softly to the dirt of the arena for Christopher as he swung his destrier around and made a pass in front of the stands in a rare display of acknowledgment. Mayhap it was because he was sentimental for his first bout since returning home, yet for whatever the reason, he drew strength from the roar of the crowd.

Dustin's heart surged with pride as he thundered past her, not realizing she had the most amazing smile on her lips. As he had promised, he was uninjured and her doubts were quelled for the moment.

He brought the horse around again and came to an unsteady halt directly in front of her. Dustin, oblivious to the cheering crowd, jumped to her feet and rushed forward.

Christopher didn't say a word. Raising his visor, he reached out and took her hand, bringing it sweetly to his lips. Dustin blushed mightily as he gave her a wicked grin and, slamming his visor shut, tore off across the arena. Dustin simply stood there, watching him ride off as if he were God himself.

"Charming," John said dryly.

The spell was broken. Dustin stiffened and turned back to her seat, choosing not to dignify John's comment with a response. Marcus eyed her as she lowered herself to the chair.

"You see? There is nothing to worry over," he said.

She tossed her hair over one smooth shoulder. "There are more bouts to come though, aren't there? This was merely the first."

Marcus shook his head. There was apparently no convincing Lady de Lohr that a tournament could be fun and exciting. He briefly wondered if she would show such concern for him if he were fighting.

The field was raked smooth in preparation for the second round and the combatants were paired against one another by the high marshal. Everyone in the stands were milling about or buying food from one of the numerous vendors, waiting for the next round to start.

"Marcus, I am hungry," Dustin said. "Can we go and get something to eat?"

Marcus glanced at the field. "It looks as if it will be a few minutes yet before the games begin," he said, and stood up and held out his arm. "What would you like?"

Dustin wanted everything. Marcus ended up buying her a fat tart with raspberries, chicken grilled on a stick, and a pie-like concoction filled with beef, onions and cheese. She downed the chicken in no time, chowed down the pie, and then started in on the tart. Marcus watched her eat with enjoyment.

"Has Chris been starving you?" he demanded suspiciously.

"Why do you ask?" she asked, her mouth full of custard.

"Because I have never seen a lady eat so much," he said. "Yet there's not a bit of fat on you."

She shrugged, taking another bite. "I like to eat."

He grinned, glancing out over the field to where the different competitor's camps were set up. He could barely make out Christopher's quarters, isolated away from the others. He nudged Dustin.

"Would you like to go see Chris?" he asked.

Her face lit up. "Can we?"

He took her arm in response, leading her around the field and between various encampments. He had an ulterior motive for bringing Dustin to see her husband, he wanted to confer with the baron regarding Sir Dennis. In fact, if Chris would allow him, he would gladly fight in the melee. He was highly uncomfortable with the Destroyer in the competition, especially when John had put a price on Christopher's head.

They passed by a tent bearing the colors of the knight Sir Dennis had killed. Inside they could hear a pathetic female sobbing and Dustin instinctively stopped, her eyes welling with sympathetic tears. Lord, it could so easily be her crying over her husband's body. She still may be. She turned her wide gray eyes up to Marcus sadly and he did nothing more but urge her onward, away from the grief.

Her sadness faded when she caught sight of Christopher's tent. David and Edward were outside, adjusting the tip on David's joust pole. Dustin called out their names and gathered her skirts, hopping over a puddle and skipping the rest of the way.

She threw her arms around David happily with a congratulatory hug, then gazing apologetically at Edward.

"Oh, Edward, I am sorry," she said. "But it was a good fight. Did he hurt you?"

Edward shook his head, though he had a ripe bruise on his forehead. "Nay, my lady, he did not. I hit my head when I fell to the ground. 'Twas my own clumsiness, really."

Christopher burst out of his tent, his eyes riveted to his wife. "I thought I heard your voice," he said. "What are you doing here?"

Marcus moved forward. "I brought her," he said, making note of Christopher's disapproving look. "Well, I could not leave her alone in the lists. Not with John and Ralph a few feet away. Besides, all they want to do is brag about le Londe. Did you know he was here?"

"Not until he killed one of Derby's men," he replied, as Dustin ran up to him and wrapped her arms around his waist. Marcus watched with cloaked envy as Christopher kissed the top of her head before continuing. "I had no idea he was even in London, and I have been here over a week. I wonder where John has been hiding him."

"Mayhap he wasn't," Marcus said. "It is entirely possible that le Londe was in France with Philip Augustus and just yesterday sailed the channel. We know that John is in contact with the French king and more than likely relayed his troubles about you, whereupon Philip sent le Londe to champion the prince's cause."

Christopher nodded. "As logical an explanation as any," he agreed. "What remains now is what to do with him. 'Tis without a doubt I will be facing him at some point."

Marcus eyed Dustin, silently relaying to Christopher to be careful what he said. But Christopher was well aware of his wife's fears, and he was also fully aware that she did not know of the price John had put on him.

"Your wife has been on an eating binge and I have no money left," Marcus said, changing the subject.

Dustin grinned. "And I still did not get to sample the cream pastries."

"Take Edward with you, then, and get your pastry," Christopher said. "I am sure Marcus would appreciate being free of you for the moment."

Dustin gazed up at him, her face positively glowing. "Do not joust until I return to my seat."

His gaze on her was equally warm. "I seem to remember seeing my wife with her hand over her eyes as I took the field," he said with a raised brow. "Do you intend to actually watch me this time?"

"I watched your second pass," she insisted weakly. "I saw you unseat the pompous fool."

He nodded reluctantly as if he didn't believe her, then kissed her head once again. The show of affection from him had been remarkable, considering he tried to be very private with his feelings for her. But Dustin savored the affection, public or private.

"Go with Edward, sweetheart," he patted her gently and yelled to his knight. "Edward, feed my wife and return her to the stands."

Since Edward was not competing until the melee in the afternoon, he readily agreed to escort Dustin. All blue silk and silken blond hair, Dustin laughingly took Edward's arm and they disappeared from view.

The moment they were out of sight, Christopher turned to Marcus. "Dennis will try his hardest to mortally wound me," he said in a low voice. "Ten marks of gold will inspire him to conquer me any way he can."

"I know," Marcus replied. "Let me fight with you in the melee, Chris. I can watch your back."

Chris looked at him, disbelievingly. "With that arm? Forget about it, Marcus. You'd end up getting yourself killed."

"Chris, we've seen Dennis fight." Marcus would not be denied so easily. "We both know how ruthless he is. He shall stop at nothing."

Christopher's sky-blue eyes grazed the tents until he came to rest on John's encampment nearly a quarter mile away. "He cannot best me, Marcus, but he can make my life miserable," he replied. "I am not worried about the melee so much as I am the joust. If he pulls a trick, then there is virtually no time to react. And I worry for my brother and my men, as well. Dennis does not play for fun, he plays to kill."

Marcus stared at the ground thoughtfully for a few moments. "Do you want me to take Dustin back to the apartments?" he asked softly. "She's terrified as it is, and seeing you or one of the others injured will ruin her."

Christopher shook his head. "Nay, she would worry more penned up in a room where there were nothing to do but imagine the worst," he said, then looked at Marcus with unguarded eyes. "Just….if something does happen, even though it won't, take care of her as best you can."

"Then you are worried," Marcus declared softly.

"Nay, not worried, but cautious," Christopher corrected him. "Dennis the Destroyer requires me to act in that manner."

Somewhere back toward the lists, trumpets sounded, informing the wandering crowd that the games were about to commence again.

"That's my call," Christopher said, adjusting his sword. "Take care of my wife, Marcus."

"She doesn't need me to take care of her," Marcus retorted lightly. "As long as I keep her supplied with food, she's happy as a fool."

"No, Marcus," Christopher's voice shocked him with its intensity and he found himself staring into the sky blue orbs. "I mean take *care* of her. If anything happens to me, I will depend on you."

Marcus had never known Christopher to be wary, ever. The man was a perfect model of confidence and perfection, and he found himself licked by apprehension. He wanted to dismiss Christopher's caution, to insist that none could touch the Lion's Claw, but he bit his tongue.

"As you say, sire," he replied softly, turning for the stands.

By the time he reached his seat, Dustin and Edward were already there and filling their bellies with two great cream pastries. He eyed the pastries with distaste, wondering aloud how they could eat such sickly sweet confections. Dustin simply smiled.

John and Ralph had been up walking the grounds, acting God to the inhabitants of Windsor. They returned to their seats shortly after Marcus' arrival, both men gazing haughtily at Edward.

"So, de Wolfe, you are out of the competition," John said flatly. "A pity. Your father was a fine jouster, you know."

"Aye, your grace, I am well aware of my father's skills," Edward replied in his rich, steady voice. "But he, like me, found cheating beneath him. Obviously, not everyone has our scruples."

John laughed aloud. "Oh, de Wolfe, as righteous as your father in every way. Thank God not every knight is as moral as you two are or this country would be quite colorless."

Edward didn't reply, finishing his pastry when in fact he had lost his appetite. Dustin licked her fingers with gusto, frowning like a child when Marcus snatched her hands and wiped them off with a kerchief.

The joust competitions continued on for the rest of the morning, with the field of knights narrowing down little by little. There were two more substantial injuries, but for the most part, the majority of the combatants walked away unharmed. By midday, the list had been narrowed down to only two men and, as expected, Christopher was to face off against Dennis the Destroyer.

Dustin had actually enjoyed the rest of the bouts and was even able to watch her husband dispose of his final three challengers with nary a twinge of apprehension, but when it became apparent that his final round would be against John's champion, her anxiety returned worse than before.

Sitting between Edward and Marcus, her stomach was twisting into painful knots. Christopher was at the opposite end of the field and she could see his spiral-decorated shaft pointing up to the sky as he adjusted his shield over his left side. Sir Dennis was closer to her, his horned helmet quite imposing as he sat stock still, watching Christopher settle himself.

Dustin found herself staring at the man, her eyes shooting daggers at him, and every inch of her body conveyed pain and hatred. She didn't even know him yet, she hated him all the same. From what she had heard, he was a disgrace to the brotherhood of knights, and for the simple fact he was competing against her husband, she hated him all the more.

Sir Dennis reined his steed over to the lists where John and Ralph were sitting. He raised his visor and Dustin was able to catch a glimpse of the despised face.

"Ten marks, did you say?" the knight said in a heavy French accent. "Seems like a small amount for a man's life. He is married, *n'est-ce pas*? Where is his wife?"

Ralph jerked his head leisurely in Dustin's direction. "The Lady Dustin de Lohr."

Dennis' bright, pale eyes immediately focused on Dustin and she went rigid under his naked scrutiny. He was probably as old as her husband, plain-faced, almost boyish-looking. She found it hard to believe that this man had the nickname of "Destroyer". He smiled and she quickly averted her gaze.

"I want her, as well," Dennis said to John. "Ten marks and the *mademoiselle*."

As he reined his horse away, Dustin's lovely face washed with shocked anger.

"What is he talking about?" she demanded hotly of John and Ralph, ignoring their titles completely.

The prince glanced casually over his shoulder at the sheriff, who shrugged lazily. "I wouldn't know," he replied. "Ralph? Do you know what he's talking about?"

"I have no knowledge, sire," Ralph lied. "We will have to ask him to clarify his statement when the joust is finished."

Dustin was shaking with fury and confusion and Marcus reached out to pat her arm. He and Edward exchanged disgusted glances, each man knowing exactly what the knight had meant. Had Christopher heard it, there would be French guts spilled out all over the ground.

The tournament marshal took the field, looking at both competitors to make sure they were ready. A hush settled over the crowd and Dustin's palms began to sweat terribly. She wanted to cover her eyes but she could not seem to lift her hands. The stands grew quieter and quieter until it seemed that all she could hear were the screams of the hawk riding the drafts high above the arena. She wondered vaguely if it were a bad omen.

Dustin closed her eyes a brief second, fighting off her lurching stomach. She swore at that moment that if Christopher survived, she would make him promise never to compete in a tourney again. She simply could not take the terror it provoked, excitement be damned.

The marshal dropped the flag and Dustin's heart surged into her throat as she watched her husband and Dennis charge at one another like rolling thunder, poles leveling out as they closed the gap. Dustin's fingers flew to her mouth and she bit hard to keep from screaming, seeing the two mailed and colored knights come together in a scream of wood and metal, horse and man. Yet a split second before their poles collided with one another, she saw her husband jerk sideways in the saddle and then came a thunderous, shattering crash.

Christopher's whole body snapped like a rag-doll from the force of the blow, but he remained seated as his destrier came to a halt at the end of the run. The crowd let up a collective groan and rose to their feet, concerned for their newly-returned hero. Dustin shrieked as Marcus and Edward shot angrily to stand.

"Damnation!" Marcus shouted. "He brought that pole to bear on Chris' head."

Edward furiously agreed. "Had he not ducked when he did, he would have had his head torn off."

"Jesus, his shoulder must be broken from that blow," Marcus raged. "How does he look, Edward?"

Edward was standing at the end of the platform, scrutinizing Christopher closely. His liege seemed to have righted himself adequately, but he could see that his left shoulder was bleeding through the mail.

"He shall live," Edward said reluctantly, turning back to his seat. "But that shoulder is going to need attention."

Dustin was still seated, her hands folded at her mouth and her huge gray eyes full of tears. Marcus gazed down at her, realizing they must have terrified her further with their shouting.

"He's fine, Dustin," he said softly, sitting beside her. "Another pass and he shall have the bastard on his arse."

She shook her head and closed her eyes, wiping at the tears as quickly as they fell and trying hard to be brave. "I know," she said with courage she did not feel.

The field marshal and a few other officials were conversing with Christopher and they could see his head nodding faintly. John turned to gaze at Dustin, his eyes grazing over her.

"I do hope your husband is well enough to continue," he said. " 'Twould be a shame to lose de Lohr. The competition wouldn't be the same without him."

Dustin looked hard at the prince, sick and tired of his deceptions and games. "Why do you offer me such bold-faced lies? You hate my husband and would like nothing better than to see him dead."

Only Dustin and her forthright manner could get away with such blatant disrespect. John's eyes widened with feigned surprise.

"How untrue, Lady de Lohr," he insisted. "I greatly respect your husband and his skills. To lose him would be to lose the Defender of the Realm and leave us all vulnerable."

Dustin's face twitched with fury. "You are a liar, my lord, and a disgrace to the crown," she snapped. "I should have listened to my husband when he told me to stay away from you."

Ralph turned on her savagely. "Anymore from your mouth, madam, and I throw you in the dungeons for blasphemy."

Marcus and Edward were up, preparing to rip Ralph joint from joint but

John put up a quelling hand. "Sit down, everyone, or I shall have you all removed." His hand fell limply to the arm of the chair. "Emotions are high, especially with an injured comrade, which is why I forgive Lady de Lohr her words. Look, now; the marshal is moving to centerfield."

Dustin, her beautiful face dark, sunk back into her chair as Marcus and Edward regained their seats. The whole day had been draining on her and it wasn't even noon yet, she could not even fathom what the afternoon might hold.

Dustin wasn't mentally prepared when the marshal dropped his flag. Christopher and Sir Dennis stormed toward each other with a deafening roar, shafts leveling out, and Dustin tried to close her eyes but she could not manage the action. She could only stare, frozen in her seat, waiting for what would happen next.

Two glancing blows and naught else occurred. With the next pass, Christopher broke his shaft and took his brother's one as a replacement. As he handled the heavy pole, Marcus and Edward glanced at each other over Dustin's head, silent words acknowledging that their liege was definitely favoring his left shoulder.

The crowd's feelings were rising and falling like waves upon the shore, and Dustin's emotions with them. Every time Christopher made it through a pass unharmed, she whispered a prayer to God that his next one would be as successful. It was completely maddening and frustrating and she was so sick to her stomach that she thought she might vomit, but she didn't want to leave the lists. As much as she was terrified to watch, she knew there was no other place she would rather be.

At the other end of the field, Sir Dennis switched from his crow's foot shaft to a spear-tipped one. Marcus saw the exchange and his body went stiff with fury.

"Damnation," he spit, then turned to see if Edward had caught the switch. Indeed, Edward had and his golden eyes were wide with apprehension. In the midst of their anxiety, Dustin suddenly shot to her feet.

"He has got a dagger on the end of that shaft," she gasped with realization. "He is going to kill Christopher with it."

Marcus grabbed her arms and set her down as the combatants took up position. But Dustin would not be so easily sated.

"You must stop this!" she said frantically.

"I cannot," Marcus said quietly. " 'Tis perfectly legal for Sir Dennis to joust with the spear-tipped shaft."

"Like *hell*!" Dustin shot out of her seat again, thrusting herself forward towards John and Ralph. "Sire, surely you will not allow your champion to compete with a blade on the end of his pole?"

John looked amused with her terror. "My lady, 'tis painfully obvious that you have never been to a tournament before. Until a year or two ago, spear-tipped shafts were the only type used in a joust. The crow's foot tip is very new."

Dustin looked back at the prince in disbelief, her eyes trailing to the field helplessly as the competitors prepared for their run. The field marshal raised his flag and with the drop, the destriers sprang into a rumbling gallop.

Dustin could not move. It took all of her concentration to stand there and watch, her breath caught in her throat and her heart quivering in her chest as her husband and the prince's champion raced toward each other at breakneck speed. Behind her, the crowd slowly rose to their feet in anticipation of what was to surely come.

When it happened, it happened too fast for the human eye to comprehend. The shafts came down and suddenly there was a deafening noise; Sir Dennis went flying from his destrier as if unseen hands had thrown him. Dustin's heart soared until she saw a split second later that Christopher, his destrier gored by the 12-foot shaft, went down hard enough to shake the ground. Dust and chunks of earth spewed into the air and before she could react, Marcus and Edward flew from the lists and were racing across the arena.

Dustin was in shock. In fact, almost the entire lists were rushing onto the field. Even Ralph had jumped from the platform and were running toward the mass of people, all swarming around the two competitors. The arena turned into a boiling pot of knights and officials and she completely lost sight of her husband and his horse.

The crowd in the lists were loud with their concerns, but Dustin could not hear them. It was as if she were locked in her own little world, her entire life hanging on what was happening out on the dirt in front of her. She tried to pick out her husband's knights, any familiar head, but there were so many men in armor that it was impossible to single out any one person. She could hear shouting and see all sorts of movement surrounding her husband and his animal.

"My, my." Prince John was standing beside her, shielding his eyes from the glare of the weak sun as he gazed out on the field. "Quite a finish to an exciting bout. I do hope everyone is all right."

Dustin could not even manage a retort. Her mind was like mud. Before she realized it, she was descending the stairs and making her way across the field like a woman hypnotized. She saw nothing, heard nothing; her focus entirely on where she last saw her husband. The honor guard that Christopher had left in charge of her broke rank and began to follow, wondering if they should prevent her from going any further. Yet they did not, instead, acting as an escort and shoving people out of her way as she went. Dustin didn't even notice their assistance.

Sir Dennis' men managed to get him back on his feet. He was several feet to her right, quite shaken as he leaned on his comrades for support. Dustin snapped out of her trance long enough to stare him down with a look of complete loathing. He didn't see her as he was helped from the field.

She pushed into a crowd of knights and suddenly the legs of Christopher's horse became visible through the crowd. Seized with anguish, she tried to shove her way further but was grabbed with large, firm hands.

"Lady de Lohr." It was an older knight, his visor raised and his face coated with perspiration. "I am Lord Lyle Hampton, Earl of Canterbury. Certainly there are better places for you to be than out here on a dirty field. Please allow me to escort…."

Dustin jerked away from him roughly. "I would see my husband."

The earl eyed the sergeant of the escort as he grasped Dustin again, more firmly this time. "I understand completely, my lady," he said gently, "but it would be much better if you wait in the lists to see your husband."

"Nay!" she screamed. "Let me go or I shall scratch your eyes out."

Lord Hampton, fortunately, was a man of even temper, having three daughters of his own. He was a friend of Christopher's and also a friend of Christopher's uncle, Sir Philip. Christopher had proudly pointed out Dustin to the earl before the competition, which was how the earl knew who the lovely lady was on sight. And he also knew without a doubt that she should not be here.

"As you wish, my lady," he said, holding her with an iron grip. "But it will have to wait. We must get you out of this dirt. Sergeant, your help would be appreciated."

The sergeant-at-arms gripped Dustin's other arm and between he and the earl, were able to direct her back toward the stands. But Dustin would have no part of it and turned into a wild animal. She slugged the earl in the nose, drawing blood, before she turned like a banshee on the sergeant and kicked him in a weak point in the armor by his groin. Free for the moment, she grabbed her skirts and tore through the crowds of knights and men, knowing her greatest advantage was the fact that men in armor lack decent balance and are not quick on their feet. With enough shoving, she knew she could throw them off enough to reach Christopher.

As she rounded a particularly tall bank of knights, she caught sight of Edward's head and she screamed his name loudly. At the sound of his name, Edward whirled around and rushed to her as she moved toward him. He snatched her firmly around the torso and she twisted and punched him.

"Let me go!" She fought Edward with every ounce of strength she possessed. "Where is Christopher?"

Edward was having a devil of a time holding onto her. "Come on, Dustin," he said, grunting when she elbowed him in the gut. "Let's get you back to the lists."

"I will not," she shrieked. "What happened to my husband? Is he dead?"

"Nay, he's not dead," he said, getting a better grip on her when she relaxed a bit. Mayhap if he were honest with her she would stop fighting so much. As it was, she had no idea what was transpiring with her husband and was understandably terrified. "He's trapped under his horse, Dustin. They are trying to free him now."

As he hoped, she stopped struggling and instead strained around Edward to get a better look at what was happening.

"Oh, Lord," she whispered, seeing only seas of mailed legs. "Is the horse dead?"

"Aye," he replied quietly. "The spear went right into his chest."

"Is Christopher alright?" She turned her brimming gray eyes up to him. "Please tell me, Edward."

Edward could see her anguish. He loosened his grip and put his arm around her waist. "Come with me," he said softly.

He led her around the crowd and soon Christopher and his horse came into view. Dustin's hands flew to her mouth to stop the sobs as she viewed the scene closely; the destrier, mortally wounded, fell sidelong into the dirt and trapped her husband's right leg underneath thousands of pounds of horseflesh and armor. Christopher, helmetless, was supported by David and Leeton as dozens of knights and soldiers and grooms tried to truss the horse up with rope, enough so they could lift him off Christopher.

Dud was near the animal's head, and Marcus, his brow sweaty from exertion, was controlling the entire operation as he shouted orders loud enough for the king of Scotland to hear. Seeing her husband so helpless nearly drove Dustin over the edge.

She was standing yards away from Christopher, watching the urgent actions of the men working furiously to free her husband. Had Edward not been holding her firmly, she was sure she would have slipped to the ground from sheer grief. She found herself leaning against him, her head against his armored chest. As long as she could see Christopher and see that he was alive, she could keep herself calm.

"So this is where you went." The Earl of Canterbury strolled up casually, a handkerchief to his nose. "I thought as much."

Edward glanced over at the earl. "What happened to your nose, sire?"

The earl snickered. "Lady de Lohr and I were introduced," he said, studying her lovely profile as she watched the rescue effort on her husband.

Edward raised his eyebrows in horror but the earl waved him off, still chuckling. Together, the three of them watched the last of the rigging go around the destrier's body. The task had been difficult and time-consuming due to the angle the horse had landed and also for the fact that the men had to dig trenches underneath the animal to run the rope through.

Marcus tested the ropes himself and when he was satisfied, ordered the men to be ready. Dustin tensed as the ropes were pulled taut, moving the beast inch by inch as David and Leeton grasped Christopher's arms and tugged. In synchronization the men would pull at the horse as Christopher's men attempted to slide him out from underneath the animal.

It took several tries until finally, after a lifetime of torturous waiting, Christopher slipped free. Dustin let out a cry of relief and Christopher heard her, twisting around to see his wife.

"Dustin!" he called urgently.

She tore free of Edward and raced to him, collapsing in the dirt beside him and covering her good silk surcoat with filth. Even as David and Leeton and Dud were steadying him into a sitting position, Dustin was throwing her arms around his neck and weeping hysterically.

Christopher's armored arms went about her stiffly, distracted with the pain and disorientation he was feeling. Marcus was kneeling beside him, demanding to know where he hurt. He waved Marcus off, focusing instead on his crying wife.

"Sweetheart, I am all right," he whispered softly into her ear. "Stop your weeping."

Naturally, she disobeyed. He so wanted to comfort her more, but his ribs were absolutely killing him and he was in agony. He turned his head to David slightly.

"Help me with her," he said, voice raspy.

David reached down to pull her free but she responded by tightening her grip on Christopher. Pained and exhausted, he patted her gently.

"Go with David, sweet," he said softly. "Be a good girl."

Dustin pulled her tear-stained face back, looking him deeply in the eyes, so incredibly grateful he was whole. He kissed her, his beard scratching her face, and smiled faintly. "Stand up," he whispered.

She kissed him anxiously three or four times, kisses soft and quick and sweet, before doing as she was asked. Her legs were shaking so that David found himself literally supporting her as Marcus knelt beside Christopher.

"Where are you injured, Chris?" he asked.

Christopher took a deep breath. "I am well enough, except for my ribs and shoulder."

"What about the leg?" Marcus asked.

"It does not hurt," Christopher replied, bending it at the knee slowly. "Amazing. I thought he damn near tore it off when he went down."

"Can you stand?" Marcus inquired insistently.

Christopher nodded and his men reached down, carefully lifting him to his feet. Immediately his head began to swim and his knees went weak, but he fought it. After a fall as brutal as the one he took, 'twas a natural reaction and he was grateful for Leeton and Dud's strong arms to lean on.

The crowd of knights applauded loudly when they saw the champion on his feet. Christopher nodded vaguely to acknowledge the cheers, reserving a worn smile for his ashen-faced wife.

"Can you walk?" Marcus asked him, wondering who was paler; the baron or his wife.

"Aye," Christopher replied, shifting a bit as if something inside his armor was itching him. "Christ, I can hear my ribs grinding."

The castle surgeon who tended the knights was a big, burly man with wild red hair. He appeared beside Christopher as the men tried to steady him, eyeing the man critically.

"I came as soon as I could," he said. "I was off tending the Earl of Norwich. What's this? I hear a horse fell on you? Why are you walking, man? You should be on a gurney."

In faith, Christopher was feeling fairly weak but knew he had to keep up the strong front if only for Dustin's sake. She looked as if she were about to faint. He flicked a hand at the surgeon.

" 'Tis nothing, really," he grunted. "A bit of rest and I shall be fine."

"He broke some ribs," Marcus told the doctor flatly. "And his shoulder is injured."

The surgeon nodded curtly. "To your apartments then, baron. We waste no time with broken ribs. One could steer loose and puncture your liver and you will bleed to death in minutes."

Dustin gasped in horror and Christopher eyed her with concern. "I assure you, it's not that severe," he told the doctor, wishing the uncouth man would keep his mouth shut.

But the surgeon wasn't finished, he glared at Marcus. "And what are you doing running about here with that crushed arm? I told you to keep it immobile and to rest a great deal. If it turns gangrenous, we have to cut it off and no one wants a one-armed knight."

Dustin let out another strangled cry and looked at Marcus with fear. Marcus echoed Christopher's thoughts, he wished the fool would shut up before he had Dustin swooning.

"My arm is healing nicely, Burwell," he said evenly "Let's focus on the baron, shall we?"

The group of knights and men were dispersing and the field marshals were conferring in the center of the arena as Christopher and his group passed slowly by. The crowd, seeing their champion up and walking, albeit with help, began to stomp and cheer wildly. In no time the lists were literally quaking with the excitement and appreciation of the crowd as Christopher crossed the field.

Two of the marshals approached Christopher. "My lord," the head marshal bowed quickly. "The officials have conferred and we all agree that you are the winner of the event."

Christopher's guts were hurting him the longer he stood. He leaned heavily on Leeton. "And just how did you come to that decision?"

"Sir Dennis hit the ground first, my lord," the man replied. "You unseated him without question. Had he not gored your destrier, you would not have met with the dirt."

Christopher glanced over his shoulder as a couple dozen grooms and stable servants were towing his horse from the field. He was deeply saddened; Boron was nearly seventeen years old and the two of them had seen through every campaign and tournament since he had been a squire. With Boron beneath him, there was never a worry, for the animal could read his mind and he knew he would miss him greatly.

"Very well," he replied wearily.

The marshal turned to Dustin, who was behind her husband and clinging to David. "My lady, will you award your husband his just reward?"

Dustin was so drained she could barely walk, but she nodded unsteadily. Christopher looked over his shoulder at her.

"You do not have to, sweetheart," he said softly.

"We need to wrap those ribs, my lord." Burwell boomed.

Christopher shot the man a withering look. "I have won the joust and will accept what is mine." His eye caught the horse as it cleared the arena and headed for the outlying area. "Considering the cost of victory, I would say the prince better award me the whole bloody treasury."

"I shall do it," Dustin said hoarsely, letting go of David and brushing a wayward strand of hair from her face.

The marshals went to the lists and, after a brief discussion with John and Ralph, waved Dustin and Christopher over. David and Marcus escorted Dustin up the stairs to the dais as Christopher made his way slowly toward the foot of the platform. John and Ralph were on their feet, scowling contemptuously at Christopher as he approached.

Dustin watched her husband as he made his way toward the royal box and disengaged himself from Leeton and Dud. The crowd went mad as he walked the last few feet under his own power and halted, as tall and proud as he could manage, in front of John. Dustin found herself drawing comfort and strength from the cheers of the people as they showed their respect for the man they called the Lion's Claw.

Even with his battered body, his spirit soared to conquer the pain. The agony was not readable on face. He was, in every sense of the word, the champion and Defender of the Realm.

Dustin moved beyond her shock and weakness. Before she realized it, tears were filling her eyes and spilling in hot streams down her cheeks. She wiped them away, but they kept reappearing and the more she wiped, the faster they seemed to fall. Marcus saw her quaking and leaned next to her ear to whisper words of encouragement. She sniffled and nodded quickly in response, stepping forward as a steward ushered her to John's side.

John was not in the least bit happy. Sir Dennis was fine after his vicious fall, but he had lost the bout nonetheless. The prince eyed Christopher, lifting his hands irritably to silence the screaming crowd.

"It seems that the champion has returned from the quest as skilled as if he had never left," the prince said with mock sincerity. "He has bested the finest England had to offer and for that, he will be duly rewarded."

The steward handed Dustin a ribbon made from red brocade, embroidered with gold thread into fantastic patterns. It was a beautiful ribbon, though hardly worthy of the pain and effort expended for such a tourney. She accepted it graciously and moved forward when John motioned to her. The tears were falling faster than ever, dripping off her chin and onto the top of her breasts, and the sobs began to rise as the prince lamely indicated that she pin her husband with the ribbon.

Christopher's heart was breaking. Dustin was trying so hard to be brave, to award him the prize, but she was quickly crumbling. He took a few stiff steps forward, standing at the very edge of the platform as she stood above him, shaking so badly that she could hardly place the ribbon on him.

"It's all right, Dustin, my love," he whispered for her ears only. "Give me the ribbon and be done with it."

She heard him call her "my love" and she dissolved, the sobs coming forth like great choking sounds. He wanted desperately to reach up and cradle her against him, but his ribs were screaming with pain and he knew the action was impossible. He raised his hand and took the ribbon from her, for she was unable to go any further. With a quick nod to David, the man swept Dustin against him and Marcus moved close on her other side. They were moving for the stairs when Ralph moved before them, his oily face glazed with humiliation.

He boldly glared at Marcus and David before his black eyes came to rest on Dustin. "Next time, my lady….," was all he said. It was a challenge and a promise that could have encompassed any number of references.

Dustin's tears disappeared as she stared back at the sheriff. Anger and hatred filled her, racing up her spine until she was fairly hot with the stuff. No longer was she the weakened wife, she yanked herself from David and Marcus and moved to within an inch or so of Ralph's disgusting face, her lips parting seductively as she looked him up and down, scrutinizing every inch of the hated face.

Ralph found himself quivering at her closeness, wondering if she were going to strike him again, but her face was calm, even passionate. The gray eyes belied nothing as she looked him over and then came to rest on his.

"To hell with you," she spat so deliberately that there was absolutely no mistaking the meaning.

Ralph actually swayed back as if her words had a physical effect on his person. Without another glance, Dustin stood straight and proud, and preceded David and Marcus from the lists.

CHAPTER TWENTY-TWO

BURWELL WAS NOT gentle when he wrapped Christopher's ribs. In fact, Christopher insisted his wife leave the room before the surgeon even started so that she wouldn't hear his grunts or see his agony. Reluctantly, but without tears, she did as she was told and returned to the antechamber with Marcus and Dud. The surgeon required David and Leeton's strength, as they remained behind with their liege.

Someone closed the door to the bedchamber and Dustin wandered absently to the windows that overlooked the fading garden below. She didn't know how long she stood there, picking at the lattice work that covered the windows and staring out at the sky, the trees, and the birds. George jumped onto the sill at one point and kept vigil with her, and Dustin passed the time playing with him and feeding him grapes.

Alex and Harold, who had been sleeping underneath the wardrobe, wriggled out from underneath and happily jumped all over Dustin's legs, vying for her affection. She would pet them and croon to the pups, but George was still deathly afraid of them so she didn't pick them up. Instead, she tried to convince George that the little dogs weren't trying to make a meal out of him.

Marcus sat by the hearth, watching every move she made and hearing every word she said. He was trying so hard to fight down his feelings for her, but when he saw her like this, it was impossible. Every time she laughed at George, he was smitten anew and he began to realize with mounting horror that his infatuation had deepened to the point where it had grown into love. God help him, he was in love with her. With all of the women he had been with and had been courted by, the one woman he did fall for was a married one and he found it bitterly ironic.

Somewhere in his train of thought he glanced up and caught her looking at him. She smiled when their eyes met.

"What are you thinking, Marcus? You are a thousand miles away," she said.

He forced a smile. "Not really," he said. "I was thinking on le Londe and wondering how he fared."

Dustin's smile vanished. "Dead, I hope. What did he mean when he said he would take me and ten marks?"

"I don t know," Marcus lied. "Mayhap he was stating his price for beating your husband."

She turned back to George as he climbed onto her arm and toyed with her hair. "John could not give me to him, could he? I mean, if Christopher were killed?"

"Nay," Marcus said through clenched teeth. "Sir Dennis would never have you, I swear it."

She mulled over his statement seriously until George crawled onto her neck and she began giggling uncontrollably. She jumped up and began dancing about strangely, much to Marcus and Dud's amusement.

"What is the matter with you?" Marcus demanded.

"He tickles," she giggled, scrunching up her neck in an attempt to dislodge the monkey. "He likes my neck."

"Come here and let me remove him," Marcus motioned to her, still seated.

She twisted her way over to him and leaned over. Marcus unwound the uncooperative monkey from her hair and gently pulled him free. Dustin straightened and took the screaming monkey from his hands.

"Thank you," she said, petting George and setting him down on the table. He immediately scampered over to a bowl full of apples and began gorging himself.

There was a knock at the door and Dud rose to answer it. Lady Deborah, her lovely pale face even paler, was in the archway with terror in her eyes. Dustin rushed to her.

"Come in, Deborah," she bade eagerly.

Deborah hugged Dustin tightly. "Oh, Dustin, I saw everything. Is Christopher all right? Are you well?"

"The surgeon is wrapping his ribs," Dustin told her as Dud closed the door behind them.

Deborah closed her eyes tightly for a brief moment and crossed herself. "God be praised he was not killed," she said. "I have never been more terrified in my entire life."

Dustin nodded; she knew exactly how she felt. "Come and sit down."

Deborah smiled and bobbed a curtsy for Marcus, who acknowledged her with a vague nod. She and Dustin sat next to one another, yet neither woman said a word for a moment. Dustin felt a great deal of comfort from Deborah's presence.

"I did so want to go to you when Christopher was felled," Deborah said. "But the countess would not allow it. She said it was better that I wait until the situation calmed."

"And she was correct," Marcus said, eyeing Dustin. "We had our hands full with the injured baron and his unruly wife."

Dustin's eyes narrowed at him. "Quiet, baron, or I shall break your other arm." She turned back to Deborah. "Deborah, I do not want you to return to Bath. I want you to return to Lioncross with me. Would you consider it?"

Deborah's face regained some color. "Truly, Dustin?" she asked, thrilled. "I would like nothing better. To be with my brothers and my new sister-in-law would be wonderful."

"Honestly?" Dustin was surprised she gave in so easily. "I know you grew up in Bath, but I want you to come home with me. You do not object?"

"Nay," Deborah insisted. " 'Twould be a wonderful dream."

Dustin smiled broadly, a bright spot in an otherwise hellish day. "Then I will speak to Christopher on it. How can he say no?"

They hugged and smiled at one another, the conversation turning to other subjects and time passed by. Marcus sat and listened to them talk like geese in a gaggle, wondering how two women who had just met could find so much to talk about. It was amazing how well Deborah and Dustin got along, almost too good, he thought, but didn't dwell on it. Deborah was a de Lohr and, in his mind, beyond any ulterior motive.

Almost an hour later, the surgeon came from the room, eyeing Dustin critically as he rolled his sleeves down. She, as well as the two knights and Deborah, were on their feet anxiously.

"Your husband has at least five broken ribs, my lady, as well as a shoulder that was gored and popped out of socket," he said sternly. "I treated the wound on the shoulder and replaced it, but the ribs will take time to heal. I understand you are the only one who can control this man, am I correct?"

Dustin looked as if she didn't understand the question. "I… I can only try."

"Then try hard," Burwell said. "The man must stay abed for a few days to allow those bones to soft-heal. After that, only light movement and plenty of food and rest. Will you do this?"

Dustin nodded firmly. "Aye, my lord, I will."

"Good." The surgeon stood away from the door. "Well, get in there to see him before he comes out here to find you."

She scurried past the doctor and nearly collided with David and Leeton as they were exiting the room. They moved out of her way and she proceeded into the room. Behind her, the door closed softly.

Christopher was laying back on the pillows, his arm and ribs bound tightly together. His face was pale, but he smiled weakly at her as she approached the bed. She returned his smile with pure relief.

"So you have five broken ribs?" she repeated softly.

"Aye," he replied, his voice weary. "But at least the shoulder wasn't broken. I heard the surgeon. Just how are you planning to keep me abed for days on end?"

Without intention, warm, passion thoughts filled her mind and erotic heat seared her veins. Even when she realized what she was feeling, she could not stop herself. Her eyebrow rose slowly and a seductive smile molded to her lips.

"Any way I can, baron," she said provocatively.

He caught her tone with a good deal of surprise and pleasure. He laughed low in his throat. "I have but one good arm, my lady. You would take advantage of me in my state?"

She crept onto the bed, her face glazed with desire and hunger; a direct result of the relief she was feeling that he was alive and on the road to recovery. Like a cat, she stalked toward him until both arms were braced on either side of his head and her soft body was hovering over him. Their gazes locked, a thousand soundless words of pleasure and thankfulness filling the silence as their eyes devoured one another.

"I would take advantage of you, baron," she whispered. "I would do anything I had to do to make sure you recover fully from this injury, and if that means making love to you all day and night, then so be it."

She could feel his hand moving up her back. "I look forward to my infirmary, then," he said.

Her lips came down on his with infinite softness, licking at his lips the same way he licked at hers. Their tongues met and engaged, tasting the sweetness that they had to offer and taking pure pleasure in life itself. Dustin felt his hand in her hair, holding her head down to him as he sampled his fill of her. When she did pull back, his huge hand was on her face, savoring her.

"My sweet little love," he whispered, kissing her again. "I am sorry for what happened. This is the first time I have ever been injured in a tourney."

She looked at his bandages, her hand running lightly over them. " 'Tis not your fault, but that of that diabolical Sir Dennis. Do you know that he wanted ten marks and me to dispose of you? I was sitting there when he told Prince John."

Christopher's eyes went from softly passionate to deep blue with fury. "He said that?"

She nodded, putting her face in the crook of his neck. Christopher grabbed her head and pulled her back up to look at him.

"He said that?" he pressed. "Exactly?"

His expression frightened her. She hadn't meant to anger him, only tell him what the man had said. "Aye, he said that exactly," she said. "When he rode up to the prince before your bout, Dennis asked John if you were married. John pointed to me and then Sir Dennis said that he wanted me and ten marks."

Christopher's hand went from gripping her head firmly to caressing her, as if he were forcibly trying to calm himself. His gaze lingered on her and she could see the fire in his eyes banking. She took to stroking his face tenderly, hoping he would calm down. In his present condition, there was nothing he could do about what was said. At least, not at the moment.

Finally, he cracked a smile. "Would you do me a favor?"

"Anything, husband," she replied.

His grin widened. "Would you shave this bloody beard? It itched something terrible today and nearly drove me mad."

She nodded. "If you wish it, of course."

He kissed her once, twice. "Go get my razor and soap."

She bounded off the bed, being careful not to jostle him too much. He noticed as she went to the cabinet that she was still limping a bit. "How's your leg?"

She shrugged, drawing out the necessary utensils. "Sore, but not overly. The wound wasn't all that deep, but I fear I shall have an ugly scar on the top of my thigh."

"Your thigh could never be ugly, Dustin," he said. "You could not be ugly if you tried."

She poured some water in a bowl and began to lather up the soap. "Do you know that I like you better with your beard?"

"You do?" he asked, frowning. "But you said I looked handsome either way."

"You do." She turned to him with the items in her hand. "I love you either way. But I like your beard best."

He smirked and shook his head as she sat down and proceeded to shave off his dark blond beard. She was careful and thorough and he wanted to know where, and on whom, she had practiced. She laughed at him, ignoring his questions playfully, until his entire face and neck was as smooth as new skin. When she was done, she wiped him off and handed him the polished hand mirror.

He eyed himself critically. "Hmmm," he said critically. "I look like a fresh-faced squire."

"You look wonderful," she said. "How old are you, anyway?"

His eyes crinkled as he handed her back the mirror. "You do not know? No one has told you?"

"No," she set the mirror down. "I never thought to ask, and you never told me. How old are you?"

"Thirty-five years," he said.

Her eyebrows rose. "You are? You are old."

He laughed. "You say that because you are only nineteen. Thirty-five isn't so old."

"I shall be twenty on the first of December," she told him. "That seems old to me."

"Your birthday is coming soon," he said thoughtfully. "I am glad you told me. We will have a fine party for you."

She shook her head, grinning shyly. "Nay, no party. I do not want a party."

"And why not? Every young lady wants a party," he insisted.

She shook her head firmly. "No party, Chris. I would simply like us to spend it together, at Lioncross."

His smile faded. How could he promise her that when he wasn't even sure where they would be tomorrow, much less a month from now? But that was what she desired and he would not deny her.

"Anything you want, sweetheart," he said softly.

She put all of the items into the bowl and carried them back across the room. "When is the day of your birth, Chris?"

"April," he said. "The seventh."

"Good," she said, setting the paraphernalia down. "I will always remember that."

He shook his head. "Birthdays are of no consequence. They simply remind us of how old we are growing."

She came back over to the bed and prepared to sit on it when she looked down and saw how dirty her surcoat was. She hadn't noticed or cared until this moment.

"This is ruined," she said softly.

He glanced at the surcoat, feeling his fatigue and pain catching up with him. "No matter," he said softly. "We shall have more surcoats made, as I promised. But I do like the color on you."

She reached around and undid the stays, and the surcoat fell to her feet in a billowy swish of silk. She kicked the surcoat into the corner and removed her slippers and stockings, gazing at the pile with disturbing memories. She wondered if she would ever be able to wear deep blue silk again.

Distressed once more, she turned away from the mound of clothing and opened her mouth to speak, but promptly clamped it shut again when she saw that Christopher had fallen into a deep, exhausted sleep. Silently, she tip-toed over to the bed.

He did indeed look like a young lad with his clean face. She smiled as she delicately touched his blond hair, running her hand down his smooth cheek. She had fairly forgotten just how full and sensual his lips were, lips that made her feel more wonderful than anything on earth. Her fingers traced the granite-squareness of his jaw, glad that the beard was off because it had covered the gorgeous deep dimples in his cheeks.

A shudder ran through her when she realized just how close he came to death. Tears threatened her again, but she fought them off, telling herself firmly there was no need to cry anymore. He was going to be fine.

Tenderly, she kissed his cheek and went to her wardrobe to retrieve another surcoat. She donned a pretty pink surcoat with a braided brocade rope that hung around her hips and pulled her hair back to the nape of her neck and plaited it into one thick braid. She had seen a woman in the grand dining hall with her hair plaited in such a way and decided it looked very pretty. Sans hose, she put on her slippers and exited quietly into the antechamber.

Marcus was there, standing by the window as if in a daydream. He turned around when Dustin entered the room.

"How is he?" he asked.

"Sleeping." Dustin glanced around the room. "Where is everyone?"

"The melee is about to start," he said. "Everyone is down at the arena."

"They are competing after what happened to Christopher?" she said angrily. "What of Sir Dennis? Is he able to compete?"

"Aye, he is." Marcus wasn't the least bit happy about it. "It would seem that David and the others have a score to settle with the man and they would not be deterred."

Dustin looked long at him a moment. "Why didn't you go, too?"

"Because someone needed to stay here with you," he replied.

She sank wearily into a chair and curled her feet underneath her. "It is unfortunate that Christopher cannot kill the man himself," she said. "If I were Chris' size, I'd don his armor and pretend to be him."

Marcus looked thoughtfully at her a moment and she picked up on his line of thinking, shaking her head. "You will not do it, Marcus. You cannot fight with your arm."

"I was able to defend you yesterday," he said. "I can handle a sword with my left hand fairly well."

"But Christopher hurt his left shoulder," Dustin pointed out. "Don't you think that someone would notice, particularly Sir Dennis?"

"I doubt anyone was paying that much attention," Marcus replied, glancing over at Christopher's discarded armor and tunic. "Besides, Chris and I are about the same size."

"He's taller than you," she said flatly.

"Not by much," Marcus insisted. "He is six inches over six feet, and I am nearly five inches over six feet. What is an inch or so?"

"You weigh more than he does," Dustin told him.

"Ten pounds or so," Marcus said. "With a helmet on and all that armor, who will know the difference?"

"I will," Dustin said softly. "I won't allow you to, Marcus. If something were to happen to you, I would die of guilt. Now sit here and keep me company and let us hear no more talk of the melee."

Reluctantly, he complied, yet thinking it was wonderful to have her all to himself for the afternoon. It was almost as if they were a normal, married couple sharing a quiet day together, and for a brief few moments he allowed himself the fantasy.

Later on that night after the sun had set, Dustin went into the bedchamber and lit the tallow candle by the bed. Christopher was still soundly asleep, snoring softly. She smiled and gently touched his hair, turning to remove her surcoat. The surcoat, shift and slippers ended up on the chair and she dashed to the hearth to stoke the fire before sliding into bed, nude, beside her husband. He was warm and she was freezing as she snuggled up against him. Even in his sleep, his arm went about her and she pressed close against him and wallowed in his heat.

She wasn't particularly tired and found herself running delicate fingers over his magnificent chest, feeling his soft skin and smelling his musk. She forgot he was asleep as she played with his nipple, making it peak just as he hardened hers. Curious, she stuck her tongue out timidly to taste it.

Christopher let out a groan and his eyes opened drowsily. "Any more of that and you will kill me," he said huskily.

"I am sorry," she reached up to stroke his forehead.

"So am I," he replied. "Were I not so weak, I'd throw you on your back and make love to you until the dawn."

A slow smile crept onto her lips. "Why must you always make love to me? Why cannot I make love to you?"

His eyes blinked slowly and then he smiled. "You can, if you wish," he replied. "But I can do naught to help you."

She was feeling brave and sat up on her knees, her beautiful body bathed golden in the candlelight. "Then do not. Just tell me what to do."

He sighed, his eyes closing briefly. "Do what feels right, sweet love," he said. "Do what tastes good, what makes you feel good. Do what I do to you."

She smiled, running her hand up his bandages to his unwrapped chest. "As you say, sire," she whispered.

She started at his neck, kissing him softly, running her tongue over his flesh, suckling his earlobe until he moaned with frustration. She delighted in his massive chest, kissing and licking him, working around the bandages and loving every moment of it. The terror of the day was still with her and her movements and actions were her way of telling him how glad she was that he was still alive, and still hers. And he understood every word.

She straddled him and her mouth, her hair, caressed his lower abdomen, below the bandages. Her tongue invaded his navel and he shuddered, the fingers of his good hand entwining in her luxurious hair. Her mouth went lower and lower and he felt her hot little hands timidly grasp his huge organ.

"Does it hurt if I hold you like this?" she asked.

He lifted his head weakly and looked at her, her hair was wild, covering her entire body and her lips were red and swollen. If he could have managed any one feat at that moment, he would have taken her in his arms and bed her until she fainted.

"Nay," he rasped. "It feels wonderful."

She looked down at his throbbing manhood, running her hands up and down the length of it. "Can I kiss you there?"

"Please." He lay his head back down on the pillow, anticipation filling him.

The very moment her hot lips touched him, he thought he was going to spill. But he restrained himself with every ounce of strength, feeling her become bolder by the moment.

"Dustin, do you know how I put my tongue in your mouth?" he whispered.

"Pretend that my organ is my tongue."

"Put it in my mouth?" she asked with surprise.

"If you wish to, then do it," he responded quietly.

She put her mouth around him, uncertainly at first, but with growing confidence as she moved her tongue around him, running it under the ridge of the head. He stifled a moan as she plunged her whole mouth down on him and drew up slowly, sucking him hard.

"Christ," he shuddered. "I shall explode if you do that again, sweetheart, I swear it."

She grinned, arrogant with the power she held over him. "Do you like it? Truly?"

"Truly," he whispered in response, never more sincere in his life.

So she did it again and again until he yanked her hair roughly, pulling her up. They were breathing heavily with want, sweat already coating their bodies as Dustin crawled over him, bringing her lips to bear on his again, kissing him wildly. His hand was still entangled in her hair as if to never let her go.

With eager, shaking hands, Dustin grasped his massive shaft and straddled him, slowly lowering herself onto him as she had done once before. As slick as she was, it still took her two tries to completely embed him within her tight little body and they both released moans of pure ecstasy.

As weak as he was, Christopher had never felt more pleasure and his explosive release came within seconds. Dustin, however, was still in full passion and continued to move up and down on him, relishing the fullness of him within her. She could feel herself building to her peak when he reached down and manipulated her taut bud of womanhood expertly, bringing her to climax in a burst of stars.

When her cries of pleasure ceased and her body went warm and weak, she fell beside him and cuddled up to his musky body. He cradled her tightly, wishing he could do more than simply hold her against him.

"Did I hurt you?" she asked softly.

He was so weary and relaxed he was very nearly asleep. "Nay, sweet love, you did not. 'Twas a thoroughly miraculous experience, one I hope to repeat nightly. Go to sleep now."

She squirmed against him a moment longer as she got comfortable, finally sighing with contentment. It was a beautiful end to the most harrowing day of her life, but she was willing to put it behind her as long as Christopher was safe and in her arms. Within minutes, she was in a deep, dreamless sleep.

Christopher felt her go entirely limp against him, so desperately tired yet not quite able to fall back asleep yet. What Dustin had done to him, with him, was still in his mind and he relived it for a moment. Her hands, her mouth, her incredible body lingered in his brain and he considered himself so unbelievably fortunate to have her. 'Twas but one more reason to be loyal and grateful to

Richard, had it not been for the man's insistence, he would have never married Arthur Barringdon's daughter.

Dustin snored softly in her sleep and he smiled, caressing her with his right hand. "Dustin?"

She was asleep, unable to answer him and he knew it. Yet his feelings for her would not be stopped and were brimming to be expressed. She could not hear him to know precisely how weak he was and, somehow, he felt safe with the knowledge. And terribly cowardly.

"I love you," he whispered, stoking her soft arm. "More than life, sweetheart, I love you."

Dustin snored on into the night.

CHAPTER TWENTY-THREE

SIR DENNIS WON the melee after nearly killing David. John, pleased with his new champion, granted the man a title and lands to accompany in Dorset, prime lands to be sure. With yet another new baron at Windsor, Christopher was dealt another worry.

The justices met after the tournament and decided that until they had a body or confirmation of Richard's death, the man was still England's king and they would continue administering the country in his absence. Christopher, in full agreement with their conclusion, decided to delay his return to Lioncross until there were any changes regarding Richard's well-being. It did not, however, sway his mind to send Dustin northward. He had yet to speak with Marcus about it, but knew the man would do as was asked of him.

The trouble was, he could not seem to bear to part with her. He was in bed an entire week with his ribs and shoulder injury. She did everything for him, and he was becoming quite dependent on her. She was the first thing he saw in the morning and the very last thing he saw at night. His attachment to his wife was growing by the minute, as was hers to him. Before the week was out, they were absolutely inseparable.

Deborah did indeed stay on with Dustin as expected. Christopher and David were pleased to have their little sister under their wing, and Dustin was grateful for the company. Deborah and David occupied smaller apartments next to Christopher and Dustin, and the two women got along as if they had known each other all their lives. Dustin felt the loss of Rebecca less and less each day and was better able to cope with life at Windsor with Deborah's courtly manner. Christopher also had another motive for keeping his sister with him; John and Ralph knew exactly who she was and he felt better able to protect her if she were under his roof.

Weeks passed and Christopher healed rapidly, as did Marcus. Toward the end of November when the wind was freezing and ice covered the ground, Christopher was completely healed and Marcus was able to flex his fingers. The arm had atrophied a bit, but he set to sword practice to strengthen it, as much as he was able to hold anything in his stiff hand.

John and Ralph had kept a remarkably low profile. Even with Sir Dennis and his henchmen as the prince's constant companions, there were no confrontations, threats, or attempts on Christopher's life. In fact, it was almost too good to hope for and Christopher was increasingly concerned that John was merely attempting to lure him into a false sense of security. There was, however, one point of great distress in the midst of the calm. John's mercenary army were growing in strength and size and Christopher, as well as the justices, suspected that Philip Augustus was channeling funds into England somehow to pay for them. There was also the unmistakable fact that a great majority of the mercenaries were Frenchmen.

Dustin matured a great deal in those few weeks. The simple young woman with simple tastes was growing into the flower of Windsor. Everyone knew who she was and she was the target of most of the social events at the castle. If someone were having a gay party, then it was a must that Lady Dustin de Lohr attend. If she didn't, the party was an immediate failure. At first the attention was due to the fact that she was the Defender's wife, but as people gradually got to know her, she began to build her own formidable reputation.

The fact remained, however, that Dustin was not a frivolous, party-minded individual and she found most parties extremely boring. Her clothing had gotten more trendy, thanks to Deborah, but she still wore no jewelry other than the cross Christopher gave her and her wedding rings. And she never, ever went anywhere without her husband. It became a standing joke around Windsor that there was an invisible umbilical cord that linked the two together. Not only that, but for as much as Marcus and David and the others were with her, more lewd jokes suggested that each man took his turn with her on different nights. Baron de Lohr's group was a tightknit, impenetrable clique.

'Twas the very end of November when Dustin awoke one morning after Christopher had left and proceeded to take a long, hot bath. She bathed almost every morning in the winter to get her blood warmed and flowing. As her maids fussed and fretted, she hopped from the tub and into a thick linen towel, drying off in the chill of the room.

"Nay, not that surcoat," she told the maids. " 'Tis too tight. I would wear the blue woolen surcoat this morn."

Obediently, the blue surcoat was brought and one of the maids had a bit of a time trying to fasten the stays on the back. Dustin would suck her breath in and then exhale loudly, stay by stay, until they were all secure. Even then, the surcoat was far too tight. She gazed back at herself in the mirror.

"Look how tight this surcoat is," she demanded with disgust. "I am getting as fat as a pig."

The maids passed glances at each other as Dustin tugged and pulled at the surcoat.

"And look at my breasts. They're growing as large as melons," she said, pushing at her breasts and then flinching when they hurt. "I have got to stop eating so much."

"My lady, if I may be so forward," the plumper of the two older woman spoke. "Did your mother not speak to you of the ways of men and women?"

Dustin looked at the woman as if she were daft. "Of course, Lottie. Even so, I am a woman married and surely would have figured it out by now."

"Nay, my lady, 'tis not what I meant," the older woman said patiently. "Did your mother ever speak to you of breeding?"

"Well, of course," Dustin said impatiently. "She told me that a man and a woman consummate their marriage and eventually…." The huge gray eyes widened to the point of bulging from her skull and she was actually shocked speechless. "A child? I am to bear a child?"

The maids giggled. "From the looks of it, one the size of the baron," Lottie said. "When did you last have your menses?"

Dustin was shaking with excitement and surprise, and it was difficult for her to hold a thought, any thought, but try she did.

"Let me see," she struggled to think. "Lord, it's been so long and I didn't even realize it. I suppose the end of September."

The maids nodded at each other, satisfied. "Then you are nearly two months along with this child, and it should be due in early summer." "June," the other maid said helpfully.

Dustin put a hand to her mouth, half covering the silly grin on her face. She could scarcely believe it and was absolutely thrilled. "Truly?" she breathed timidly. "A son for Christopher?"

The maids giggled again and Dustin twirled about with delight, wanting to laugh and cry and jump for joy all at the same time. She grabbed George and did a happy little dance, and then scooped up Alexander and bounced him around while Harold barked loudly at her feet.

"I must go find my husband immediately." She put George down on the bed and tugged at her surcoat, and then laughed at herself for trying to make it fit. "I suppose I shall have to get all of my dresses altered."

She dashed out into the antechamber, warmed by a huge fire roaring in the hearth. Outside, the sky was nearly black with storm clouds even though it was almost mid-morning.

The maids scurried after her, demanding that she wear her warmest cloak. She was so scatterbrained that she put the cloak on backwards before realizing her error and turning it around correctly. Laughing at herself again as Lottie pulled it tight, she opened the front door to the apartments and met with the usual half-dozen guards.

"Where is my husband?" she demanded swiftly.

The sergeant on duty saluted her smartly. "At the training grounds, my lady, drilling the troops."

"Will you take me there?" she asked.

"My pleasure, my lady," the sergeant said, commandeering two other men to act as additional escort.

Dustin was so excited she practically ran. The sergeant led her down to the first level of the castle and out into the freezing weather. It was misting already, promising the massive storm that was to come, but Dustin didn't care. All that mattered was that she tell Christopher about his son.

By the time they reached the training grounds, icy rain was pelting them. The cloak Dustin wore was very heavy and lined with fox, rendering it extremely warm, and she wasn't feeling the elements in the least. The sergeant found a large tree for her to stand under while he sent word to the baron.

The training ground was a huge, flat field on which the troops were practiced and drilled. At this moment, there were no less than eight hundred men milling about the grounds in various maneuvers. She could see several knights on horseback working with the men, but she had yet to see her husband. Then, before her, an entire column of men marched by and she immediately saw that the knights in command were none other than her husband and Marcus.

Both men were riding in armor, but helmetless. The rain was beating down on them, soaking their heads, and Dustin's eyes riveted to her husband as he passed by her on his new destrier. He was riding the dancing animal effortlessly and bellowing orders to the men-at-arms. His cropped blond hair was soaked and he kept shaking his head like a dog to keep the rain out of his eyes. She watched him move on down the field until the sergeant who had escorted her dashed out to his side. After a couple of exchanged words, she saw the sergeant point directly at her.

Christopher spurred his horse in her direction and the unruly animal came to an unsteady halt several feet away from her, snorting and pawing the earth, and Christopher cuffed the animal across the neck. The horse calmed enough for him to be able to dismount without being thrown. Once down, he rushed to his wife's side underneath the tree.

"Dustin," he said harshly. "What in the hell are you doing out here?"

She opened her mouth but in that instant her excitement turned to hurt at his tone.

"I...I....," she sputtered.

He gave her an impatient glare. "Go back with the sergeant, sweet."

"Nay," she said firmly. "Christopher, I....can we talk somewhere?"

He looked at her with disbelief. "Dustin, I cannot. I have got two hundred new recruits to drill this morn. Now go back to the apartments and we shall talk this afternoon."

She wasn't returning without telling him the news, but he was being difficult to convince. However, she had learned something about Christopher in the months she'd been married to him; he hated to see her cry. Big, fat tears immediately welled in her eyes and his expression instantly changed.

"Do not do that," he ordered quietly. "I shall be back for the nooning meal and we can talk then."

She blinked and the tears spilled down her cheeks, turning her back to him. Behind her, she heard him sigh.

"What is so important, Dustin?"

She shook her head, letting out a sob for effect. He reached out with his huge hands and turned her around to face him.

"What is so important that you are out here in this hellish weather?" he asked, more gently.

She shook her head again and sniffed. "Not here," she said. "I do not want to talk about it out in the rain."

His jaw ticked impatiently and he glanced over his shoulder to see that Marcus had the recruits well in hand for the moment.

"Very well," he said in a low voice. "Come with me."

He pulled her to him and led her to a fairly deserted bank of stables. He took her into the very last stall, smelling strongly of fresh straw and rain. He shook his head to rid the water from his hair as Dustin lowered the hood of her cape. He put his hands on his hips expectantly.

"Well?" he demanded softly.

The moment was upon her and she found she was actually frightened to tell him. She had been so eager that she hadn't even thought of how she was going to deliver the news. She wiped her eyes and cleared her throat a couple of times, a thousand words spinning about in her flighty brain.

Christopher sighed impatiently. "Come now, Dustin, I have no time for games. What is so important?"

She opened her mouth to speak but again lost her nerve. "Kiss me."

He looked at her, disbelieving. "What?"

"Please?" she moved forward, her sweet face upturned.

He scowled but did as he was asked, a quick kiss turning into a long, lingering kiss of delicious promises. When she had finished with him, his loins were heating up and his whole body was languid.

Dustin licked her lips, running her finger over his lips and then kissed him again.

"Talk to me, wife," his voice was a seductive growl. "What is so important?"

Her courage returning, Dustin disengaged herself from his arms and stood back, unfastening her cloak and removing it.

"Do I look any different to you?" she asked.

He was thoroughly puzzled. "You are as beautiful as you ever were. Why?"

"Do I look fat?" she persisted.

He looked at her ripe, supple body and shook his head. "No Dustin, why the questions? What are you driving at?"

"Do you know that none of my surcoats fit me anymore? They are all as snug as skins on a grape," she said insistently.

He raised an eyebrow, his eyes raking her body once more. "I see no difference. If you are worried about it, then we shall have more surcoats made. Is that what you wanted to talk about?"

"Nay," she said quickly. "Yes. Oh, Christopher, it's just that... *oh*!"

She stomped her foot with frustration and lowered her gaze, again searching for the correct words. He reached out after a moment and pulled her against him.

"If you are worried that you are putting on weight, do not," he said softly. "You are a delightful, delicious morsel for my tongue, sweetheart."

"I *am* putting on weight," she agreed.

"I care not," he replied, thinking what she wanted was reassurance that he still found her desirable. "You look better than you ever have. Your breasts are more than a handful for me and your beautiful legs are supple and..."

"Chris," she put her hand to his lips to quiet him. "We are going to have a baby."

His eyes widened and beneath her fingers, his mouth went agape. Her eyes met with his for an eternity of long seconds before he even trusted himself to speak.

"A *baby*?" he whispered. "Dustin, are you pregnant?"

She nodded, trying to gage his reaction. "Are you happy?"

He tried to laugh at the idiocy of the question but all that came out was a choked gasp. Complete, unexpected joy surged through his veins as his disbelieving mind tried to comprehend her words. "Happy? Christ in Heaven, Dustin. Happy isn't a word I would choose to describe my feelings."

She looked at him with uncertainty. "Tell me, then. Are you not happy?"

He responded by kissing her feverishly, every inch of her face and neck until she was laughing and gasping with delight. She tried to speak, but every time she uttered a word his mouth was on her again and sucking at her with furious joy. He stopped long enough to allow her to catch her breath, cradling her against him with the utmost reverence.

"Christ, sweetheart, I cannot describe in words how thrilled I am," he whispered against her, then held her back to look her over urgently. "How do you feel? Are you all right?"

She smiled. "I am fine, just fat," she said, winding her arms around his neck. "I love you, Chris. I hope to give you a fine, healthy son."

He kissed her tenderly. "That would be the ultimate gift, sweet love. As long as you come through unscathed, tis all I will ask of God."

Their lips met again, so sweetly and worshipful of each other, growing increasingly passionate by the moment. The storm outside was a full-blown climate upheaval, but inside the deserted stable, their love was filling the air like a warm breeze.

He lay her back on her cloak, throwing off pieces of armor and hearing them hit the straw in reckless disorder. Not a word was spoken, but there was no need, his gentle touch and eager lips spoke volumes to her. Between tender, urgent kisses and reverent caresses, she helped him off with his hauberk and underclothing.

He ran his hands over her nude body for the longest time, kissing her slightly rounded belly over and over, worshiping the miracle they created inside her. He still could not believe the good news.

She moaned softly at his touch, closing her eyes to savor every sensation he was bestowing upon her. From her breasts to her toes, he was unstoppable, his huge body prowling over her like a graceful beast. When he finally did mount her, it was with more tenderness than she dreamed possible, his strokes even and measured and erotic.

He made love to her as he never had, his throat tight with emotion. The child she carried, *his* child, meant more to him than anything on earth and he was so, so grateful that Dustin loved him enough to bear him the gift.

When they did climax together, tears of joy found their way down her cheeks, clinging to Christopher for dear life. She never wanted to let him go, just simply remain as they were forever, listening to the storm outside yet warm and happy with their contentment.

He dressed her carefully, managing to touch her stomach a dozen times in the process. He wouldn't allow her to help him with his armor, only his hauberk because it was bulky and awkward. When he was fully dressed, he pulled her to him once again and kissed the life from her.

"Now I want you to go back to the apartments and rest," he said softly.

"But there's to be a grand luncheon in the great dining hall and Deborah and I promised to attend," she protested. "There will be entertainers and…."

"Nay," he said firmly. "You will return to our apartments and relax. I do not want you exerting yourself in the least."

She frowned at him. "Chris, I have been pregnant for almost two months and have yet to injure or exert myself in that time. Be reasonable about this, I won't break."

He raised an eyebrow at her. "Do not argue with me."

"I am not," she insisted. "But I have seven more months to go and refuse to be treated like an invalid until June. Can I please go to the luncheon if I promise to leave the moment it is finished?"

He eyed her and she was hopeful with his indecisive pause. "If you promise to leave the very moment you have finished eating, then I will allow it." He pointed a massive gauntleted finger at her when she smiled triumphantly. "But if you so much as vary in your plans but a moment, I shall chain you to the bed myself until my son is born."

She stood on tip-toe and kissed him on the tip of his nose. "I promise, I promise."

He smiled and swatted her on the bottom. "Delay me no further, wife."

He took her out of the stable, shielding her with his huge body from the driving rain and to the waiting escort of his men. He suddenly found it difficult to let her go with them, wanting more than ever to protect her himself and reluctant to leave the duty to anyone else. But he forced himself to let her go, waving a hand at her in response to her huge smile as they led her away.

Behind him, Marcus rode up and kicked mud all over his legs. "Where in the hell did you go?"

He looked up at his vassal, rain pelting his face, and smiled the broadest smile Marcus could ever remember seeing.

CHAPTER TWENTY-FOUR

WORD SPREAD THROUGHOUT Windsor that the Defender's wife was expecting. Dustin was the recipient of thousands of items for the baby, all of them designed for a boy, and she prayed to God every night that the child would be male. She knew Christopher would be tremendously disappointed if she bore a daughter.

Deborah was mayhap even more ecstatic over the baby than she was, if such a thing were possible. She sewed endlessly, making mounds of blankets and little suits and booties until Dustin's wardrobe was fair to overflowing with the stuff.

Dustin's twentieth birthday came and went with very little fanfare, as she requested. Christopher held a small dinner party in her honor with only a very few select guests, mostly other knights. She was embarrassed with all of the attention and gifts, but it was a lively party and she was sorry to see it end. The greatest gift came later in their bedchamber, however, when Christopher presented her with a beautiful bejeweled hair clip and matching ear-bobs. He stripped her of her surcoat, piled her considerable hair on top of her head and secured it with the clip, and put her ear-adornments on her and proceeded to make love to her deep into the night.

It was around this time that Dustin noticed how distant Marcus had become. No longer was he the humorous, personable man, but rather detached from everything. Deborah had a mad crush on the man and Dustin suspected that mayhap he was uncomfortable with the attention, and was concerned for him. When she tried to talk to him, he would always excuse himself before they could delve into any manner of conversation.

Around Dustin, he was even worse. Whenever she would come around, he would leave before she could say a word to him. Dustin was concerned, of course, but the impending baby seemed to wipe all else from her mind. Whatever was troubling Marcus, she couldn't be bothered by it.

It was a few days before Christmas when John decided to have a mask. It was a season of celebration and prayer, but the prince took it to the next level. He wanted a mad party. The mood struck John to have a mask, and a mask all of Windsor would have.

Dustin had been planning on the dance since she had learned of it days before. Even though she didn't dance, she still thought it would be great fun to attend, and she and Deborah had spent the entire afternoon selecting a surcoat.

A clear red brocade was her choice, complementing her skin beautifully. Deborah's finest surcoat was an elaborately embroidered black and white brocade which Dustin thought to be gaudy, but with her simple tastes, everything seemed gaudy.

She still could not believe a tiny life grew inside her. Days after the discovery, she kept running her hands over her stomach in disbelief, grinning when Deborah would touch her belly also. In fact, Deborah seemed to touch her belly more than Dustin did, so excited was she.

Christopher returned from the practice field in the late afternoon, grimy and sweaty and smelling like a horse. Deborah retreated, leaving Dustin alone with her filthy husband.

He tried to kiss his wife but she ducked away from him, wrinkling her nose. "Not until you bathe."

He gave her a half grin, removing his gauntlets. "I must bathe simply to kiss you?"

"You must bathe if you plan to sleep beside me tonight," she told him. "Moreover, I will not be seen with you tonight at the mask if you do not clean yourself up."

"Mask?" he repeated. "You mean John's deviant party?"

She eyed him. "Aye, that's what I mean. Did you forget? You promised we could go."

"But that was before you told me of your condition," he said sternly. "You will not cavort about the dance floor and exert yourself."

"I do not dance, you know that." she said sharply. "But you promised that we could go, and I want to very much."

"Go and do what? Sit?" he shot back. "Nay, Dustin, you will stay here and rest tonight. You should not be out and about."

She frowned, putting her hands on her hips. "Do not start that again. I am fine, I told you. And I want to go to the party simply, well, to see the fine surcoats and talk with people. Our friends will be expecting us."

"Our friends will understand when I explain to them why you were unable to attend," he said as he removed his breastplate. "Your health is more important than a party."

Her pretty mouth set in a stubborn line. "Are you breaking your promise to me? Is your word no better than water through my fingers?"

He raised an eyebrow reprovingly. "You know better than that. I promised you before I knew you were carrying my son and the circumstances have changed. I do not wish to discuss this anymore."

"And we shan't." Dustin stomped an impudent foot. "I am going, and so is Deborah. The only way you can stop me is to tie me down, but know that I will fight you every step of the way if you try."

She dashed into the bedchamber and he tossed his breastplate and hauberk to the ground with frustration. "I will tie you down if I have to," he yelled to her. "Do not think that I won't."

"And risk injuring your precious son?" she exclaimed angrily, suddenly standing in the doorway. "You already care more for this child than you do for me. Will you forget about me completely when he is born?"

He turned to scowl at her, but she was already gone. He could hear her rummaging about in the bedchamber. With a sigh of annoyance, he shirked off the rest of his armor and tossed his boots over by the hearth.

Dustin was digging through a chest in the bedchamber.

"What are you doing?' he asked, yanking his shirt off.

"Looking for my stockings," she snapped.

He watched her for a moment, his jaw ticking. He could feel himself relenting to her, as he knew he would. He was coming to realize that her happiness meant everything to him, even in the smallest matters. He knew she had been looking forward to the ball, but he had hoped to discourage the strenuous activity.

"Are you that determined to go that you would fight me tooth-and-nail for the privilege?" he asked.

"Aye, I am." She stood up quickly, her hair a giant wild mass. "You *promised.*"

He had, and he was cornered. He scratched his itchy scalp and sighed in resignation. "Very well, then. If you are hell-bent on attending this orgy, I shall not stop you. But you will not overextend yourself in the least, do you understand?"

She pushed the hair from her face, her willful stance instantly softening. "I won't, I promise. Will you bathe now so you do not go into the grand hall smelling like a stable?"

He nodded wearily, although it wasn't a physical fatigue. This woman taxed his emotions like a syphon.

Yet he would not be alone. He ordered every one of his knights to attend, and they were not reluctant. A mask meant a myriad of beautiful young women and they were most eager to see the goods. Bathed, shaved and combed, they were dressed in their finest tunics and boots, sans armor. It was the first time Dustin had seen them all without their armor, although they were well fortified with an assortment of small daggers.

Dustin looked absolutely radiant in the red brocade. She had pulled the front of her hair back to reveal her face and the heavy golden cross hung most prominently against her breasts. Christopher was as proud as a peacock, his formidable arrogance fed with his beautiful wife and her pregnancy. The knights knew, and they all smiled knowingly as Dustin appeared on her husband's arm. Flushing a pretty shade of pink, she averted her gaze shyly.

David escorted Deborah to the grand hall. The group arrived as the ball was in full swing, gay music and tables of food and thousands of candles filling the massive room. Christopher immediately took his party over to a vacant table and sat his wife down promptly, but Deborah begged to dance and David obliged.

Dustin watched happily as Deborah took David through three dances, granting him a rest while she continued with Leeton. Dustin found herself wishing she remembered how to dance, if only to be close to her husband. As it was, he was sitting at the table, his eyes roving the room suspiciously and she snorted ironically to herself. She could dress him up and make him appear as a gentleman, but she certainly could not conceal the soldier in him. He actually appeared ill at ease, and she would learn later that it was because he felt positively naked without his armor.

John and Ralph and their group of shady characters arrived late, as usual, and the prince made a grand occasion out of his first dance. He acted as a child in a sweet shop, pretending to be very selective with the women he would dance with. His gaze fell on Dustin and he smiled, but one glimpse of Christopher's face sent him on his way. Christopher watched him like a hawk as he made a move for a lovely brunette on the opposite side of the room.

There was something remotely familiar about the woman as the music commenced and the dancing began, but he did not recognize her until John swung her by his table. Then, realization dawned.

"Isn't that Amanda?" David leaned next to him, casually nursing a large goblet of wine.

"Aye," Christopher said faintly, watching John swing the woman about.

"Jesus, I'd nearly forgotten about her," David replied. "I didn't even know she was here."

Christopher didn't answer, averting his gaze to another part of the room. David wandered back over to Marcus, who happened to have heard the exchange.

"Who's that woman?" he asked David.

David took a healthy swig of wine. "The one dancing with John? Her name is Lady Amanda de Fortlage. Her father is the Earl of Chaumont."

Marcus nodded, "I know who she is. I meant what is she to Christopher? He seems disturbed to see her."

David glanced over his shoulder to make sure Dustin wasn't listening. "She and my brother were… well, involved once. But her father heartily disapproved of Chris. I think she was the only woman he ever felt anything for, other than Dustin."

Marcus raised a black eyebrow, looking more closely at the dark-haired woman. "Was he in love with her?"

"Hell no," David snorted. "He said she was good company, and good in bed, but that was about all."

Marcus nodded slowly, mildly surprised at the information. He usually heard all of the rumors, and he hadn't heard that one.

"Did he want to marry her?" he asked.

David did chuckle, then. "Not a chance. He only married Dustin because Richard forced him to. Chris did not want to marry anyone."

Marcus let the subject go, but he kept glancing with interest to the pretty woman as she danced with the prince. When the dance was over, she returned to her friends along the opposite wall, but not before she had caught sight of Christopher.

He knew she had seen him and he was actually nervous. He didn't want Dustin knowing of his past relationship with Amanda, but he knew she would approach him eventually. He tried to brace himself for the encounter.

Dustin was blissfully oblivious to the conflict in her husband's mind. She and Deborah were talking up a storm, joined eventually by Baron Sedgewick's wife, the Lady Anne. She was a vivacious, petite woman and Dustin enjoyed her tremendously. The group was rounded out by Lord Hampton's two daughters, Emilie and Nathalie, who had become fast friends with Dustin after learning she had punched their father at the tournament. The party complete and chattering away, it sounded to the men like a conference of magpies.

Actually, David thought Emilie Hampton to be quite fetching. She was a very pretty girl with blond hair and brown eyes, the same age as his sister. He kept eyeing her, smiling coyly and turning away when she would fix her gaze on him. Dustin caught on to the game early on and goaded Emilie endlessly.

Christopher knew of the game, too, but he was more preoccupied with keeping Amanda at a safe distance. He was afraid the woman might say something, however inadvertent, and send Dustin into a frenzy.

He could see Amanda across the room, talking with her friends. She was more lovely than he had remembered, although she could not compare to Dustin. No woman could. Indeed, he had been very fond of Amanda, of her wit and intelligence, and she had been a veritable wild woman in the bedchamber, but his interest had been limited. He knew she had fallen in love with him and had pleaded with her father to accept Christopher, but much to his relief, her father wanted nothing to do with the lowly knight. It had saved Christopher from having to tell Amanda he did not want to marry her, and they had parted amiably.

Undoubtedly she had heard that Christopher was married and he was curious as to what her reaction would be. Would she be bitter? Happy for him? He wondered, for Amanda was the only woman other than his wife that he had truly liked as a person. She had a good heart, although she could be catty, and would make some man an excellent wife someday.

A pretty ballad started and the women all bound to their feet, all except Dustin. She looked confused as the ladies around her insisted she rise and dance with them.

"Dance?" Dustin sputtered. "But....but I haven't danced in ages. I do not remember how."

"This is a woman's dance, Dustin," Anne said, taking her arm. "Just follow what we do and I promise you shall love it."

Christopher stood up, the first time all evening, and eyed the women sternly as they attempted to persuade his wife to retreat with them to the dance floor.

"I have forbidden her to dance, ladies," he said firmly.

Deborah looked up at him. "But why, Chris? There is no harm in dancing."

He sighed, looking his wife in the eye. Not all of the women knew of Dustin's condition. They would all know eventually, anyway, and he saw no harm in revealing their joyous news. "Because she is with child and I do not want her to exhaust herself."

That bit of information sent the women into cries of congratulation and happy kisses, but it did not deter their determination that Dustin should dance. They tugged her free of the table only to run headlong into Christopher's huge body as he blocked their way.

"Surely, sire, your wife must dance this dance," Nathalie Hampton said. " 'Tis an ancient fertility dance."

The women giggled and Christopher crossed his arms sternly, yet there was a faint smirk on his face. "I know what the dance is, my lady, I have seen it many a time. I simply do not want my wife to tire."

"This dance will not tire her, my lord," Anne Sedgewick said. " 'Tis slow and beautiful. Surely you do not intend to forbid Dustin from any sort of activity until the child is born. She will not break."

Where had he heard that before? He raised a disapproving eyebrow and looked at Dustin's smiling face. He could see that she wanted to go with them. "Very well, then. But no jumping or cavorting about."

"Cavorting about?" Dustin repeated. "Why do you always say that as if I jump from table to table? I have never cavorted about."

He grunted at her and moved out of the way, allowing the women to pass. His knights stood about, watching the ladies and grinning. Especially David. He smiled broadly at Emilie as she brushed past him.

"Can't I dance, too?" he asked her.

She turned her pert nose up in the air. "Nay, sire, 'tis a woman's dance."

"But I want to dance with a woman," he persisted.

She shot him a blatantly flirtatious look. "Then you should have asked sooner."

The knights laughed at David's expense as the women took to the huge parquet floor. Even Christopher laughed until he saw that Dustin took up a position two spaces away from none other than Lady Amanda.

His smile faded as the possibilities rolled through his head, so lost in thought that he failed to notice Baron Sedgewick approach.

"Greetings, Defender," Sedgewick said. "I hardly expected to see you and your men here after the grueling day you put in."

Christopher looked down at the baron, he was nearly fifteen years older than himself, compact and well built, a very companionable and distinguished man. Christopher respected him a great deal, not only because he had fought with his father, Myles de Lohr, but because he continued to fight even at his advanced age.

" 'Twas a mere training session, Miles," he said. "Besides, my wife would not take 'no' for an answer. And speaking of wives, do you know your wife is most pushy?"

"Aye, I do," Sedgewick nodded confidently. "She is that and more, Chris, although I will respect the privacy of marriage and not delve into details. Suffice it to say that I am well aware of her aggressive nature."

Christopher grinned, watching the ladles as they tried to teach Dustin the moves to the dance. "Then it would seem we have something in common, stubborn wives."

Miles snickered. "You should see our daughters. Both of them, just like her. God help me."

Christopher nodded. "I find myself with the very same prospect. Only recently have I been told I am to be a father."

Miles congratulated him heartily. "Pray for a son, boy. The women folk already threaten to outnumber us."

They stood and small-talked through the entire dance, watching the women laugh and trip over each other as they tried to teach Dustin the dance. She wasn't particularly graceful and was glad when the music finished, although she had enjoyed herself tremendously.

"I told you I could not dance," Dustin said as she attached herself to her husband.

Anne fell against Miles, kissing his cheek. "You did fine, Dustin. Now tell me, my lord, does your wife look tired?"

Christopher gazed down at Dustin's smiling face. "Nay, but I know she is. Sit down and I shall get you something to drink, sweetheart."

Miles put his arm around his wife. "Well, then, I will excuse myself and my pushy wife. We have our own guests to attend."

Dustin waved at Anne and took a seat. Deborah and Nathalie were in the process of giggling as David paid attention to Emilie, but Dustin's eyes followed her husband as he crossed the room. He was so tall and broad and powerful and she realized then and there that she had never been happier in her life.

Marcus watched Dustin as her eyes followed Christopher, and his jealousy was getting the better of him. What he wouldn't give if she would only look at him the same way. But now, with the baby, it would seem that Christopher and she were fused together permanently, and he felt a sad sense of hopelessness.

Up until this point Marcus had always held out some sort of belief that, given the correct circumstances, he could convince Dustin to go away with him. But with the child on the way, the chance was gone and he felt betrayed somehow. It was strange to put his feelings into words, for he knew of none strong enough, but betrayed was an apt term. Miserable, he returned to his drink.

Meanwhile, Christopher had retrieved a goblet of mulled wine for Dustin and was looking over the table of confections when he felt a gentle tug on his arm. Off-guard, he turned to find himself staring into soft brown eyes he knew very well.

"Hello, Chris," Amanda said softly. "I had heard you were here."

"Amanda," he knew he appeared startled. "I...how have you been? It's been a long time."

"Almost four years," she supplied. "I heard that you got married. Congratulations."

"Thank you," he replied, fumbling for words. "And you? Surely by now some man has stolen you for his own."

"Two years ago," she said. "I married the Earl of Reivne. A likable man, Chris. He reminds me a lot of you in some ways."

"I am pleased," he replied, feeling a bit more comfortable knowing she was handling the news of his marriage well. "Is he here?"

"Nay," she shook her head and her earbobs jingled. "He is too old to travel, truly. He prefers our chateau near Brittany and allows me all of the freedom I wish. Unlike you."

He cocked an eyebrow. "I was only thinking of your safety, Amanda, and you know it."

She smiled. "I do, and I miss your protectiveness. Surely you are as protective with your wife?"

"Absolutely," he said firmly. "Sometimes I wonder how Dustin ever got along before I married her."

"Dustin?" Amanda repeated. "What a lovely name. Which one is she?"

Christopher turned to look at his party and was not surprised to see Dustin gazing back at him questioningly. "In the red surcoat," he said.

Amanda squinted to get a better look. "Oh, Chris, she is exquisite. I saw her during the dance earlier and she has a lot of spirit. No wonder you married her."

He let the statement go, not wanting to delve any further into the subject. In fact, his nervousness was returning. "Honestly, Amanda, it has been damn good to see you," he held up the goblet. "My wife is waiting for this."

Amanda nodded understandingly. "Of course," she said, but then she suddenly put her hand on his arm. "Chris, I must speak with you later. 'Tis most important that I see you alone. Would you oblige me?"

He certainly didn't want to, but he nodded faintly. "If it is that important, I will. Where would you have me meet you?"

Amanda's eyes flicked to Dustin and back again. "Before you leave the hall tonight? Mayhap outside in the corridor? There is a small alcove at the base of the stairs."

"I know the place," he said, wary of her true intentions. The woman was a firebrand of passion. The room she was suggesting was very secluded. "Why don't you go there now and I shall try to get away for a few minutes."

"Good," Amanda said, turning away with a final glance at Dustin.

Christopher took a deep breath, wondering what sort of fresh hell he was getting himself into. He hoped she would not try and rekindle the old flame of passion. He returned to Dustin and handed her the refreshments. She drank down the wine as he sat.

"Who was that woman you were talking to?" she asked.

"A woman I knew once," he said.

"What's her name?" she set the goblet down and looked at him.

"Lady Amanda de Fortlage," he replied, hoping she wouldn't press anymore. "Do you feel all right? Mayhap we should retire."

"I am fine," she said, starting in on the pastry. "Did you know Lady Amanda well?"

"Fairly well," he replied. "But that was a long time ago. Where did Lady Emilie go?"

"She's dancing with David." Thankfully, her attention turned to the dance floor and she was smiling. "They make a handsome couple, don't you think? I would certainly love to have her as a sister-in-law."

He snorted. "David? Marry? I think not."

"Why not?" she demanded "You did."

"But I was forced…I mean, I had no choice, but I do not regret it," he said, grinning smugly at her. "In fact, I cannot imagine my life without you."

She raised a reproving eyebrow. "You say that now, husband," she said, watching him snort. "Tell me; if you saw me here tonight and you did not know me, would you want to meet me?"

He rubbed his jaw. "Mayhap. I would certainly think you were the most beautiful woman in the room."

"Mayhap?" she repeated his word deliberately. "You are unsure if you would want to know me?"

"I did not say that," he said, his lip twitching with a smile. "You asked if I would want to meet you, and I said mayhap. I do not demand introductions to women, Dustin. Usually, they introduce themselves to me."

Her eyebrows shot up in outrage. "I certainly would not have introduced myself, so I guess we would never have known one another."

"Why wouldn't you have introduced yourself to the Lion's Claw?" he asked earnestly, baiting her.

She raised her chin, looking away from him. "Because I wouldn't give a lick about you or your lofty title."

He was trying not to laugh. "I can hardly believe that I would fall in that category," he said. Then he leaned forward, his chin on her shoulder. "You would not have introduced yourself? Truly?"

"Nay," she said, crossing her arms.

He gave a soft chuckle. "Oh, sweetheart, of course I would have asked to meet you. In fact, I would have wooed you endlessly."

She eyed him, still miffed. "Would you have married me?"

"Probably not. But we would have had a grand time of it," he said, laughing.

"Oh!" She jerked away from him, facing him indignantly. "What do you mean by that?"

He giggled uncontrollably. "Nothing, sweet, nothing. Suffice it to say that we are married and I am glad of it."

"You do not get off that easily," she said, grabbing his tunic. "What do you mean we would have had a grand time? Do you mean to say you would have taken advantage of me, used me like a whore, and then moved on? I would not have been worth marrying?"

He tried to kiss her but she dodged him. "You are the only woman in the realm worth marrying," he said softly, catching her face in his hands. "But whether or not I would have been wise enough to realize it is another matter."

She softened considerably at his words, trying to remain wounded but not succeeding. When he kissed her sweetly, she relented fully.

"Now," he said, "I have some business to attend to for a moment."

He called to Marcus and the man looked over at him from where he was talking to two young ladies. When Christopher beckoned, he excused himself politely and approached.

"I have something to do that shan't take me but a few minutes." Christopher stood up and offered Marcus his chair. "Entertain Lady de Lohr while I am away, please."

Marcus sat down and Christopher winked at his wife before he quit the hall. Dustin watched his massive frame leave through the ornate doorway, focusing reluctantly on Marcus. The man merely smiled at her, pleasantly, before finding interest elsewhere. He never left her side but he didn't pay much attention to her, either. Such was the situation between him and Dustin these days; she accepted it, but she was sorry. Whatever was troubling him, she hoped he would soon be over it.

She missed the old Marcus.

ଓ

AMANDA WAS WAITING in the alcove. Christopher slipped into the small room, pulling the heavy silk portiere closed behind him. Impatiently, he faced his old flame and crossed his arms.

"What is so important, Amanda?" he demanded in a low voice.

Her smile vanished. She had expected more than this surly attitude from a man she had devoted her life to for a year and a half. Rebuffed by the demeanor, the old familiar hurt began to creep into her veins.

"Not only to me, but to you, Chris," she said softly. "I haven't seen you since we last parted ways. You were preparing to leave with Richard, I believe, when I last saw you. I am glad to see you returned home whole and safe, and a legend, no less. I was very proud to hear…"

He cut her off irritably. "My wife is waiting for me. What is it that you wanted to say?"

Amanda was not an aggressive, overbearing noblewoman, as so many of them were. She had a genuinely sweet character and Christopher's brusque manner was upsetting her greatly.

"Why are you acting like this?" she whispered. "I have done nothing to warrant this treatment."

His stiff stance softened, nay, she had not. But he was terrified to be alone with her, not because she was a weakness for him, but he was afraid someone would see them.

"I am sorry," he said. "It's just that I have had a busy day and I am fatigued. Please tell me what was so important that I must meet with you privately."

She gazed back at him a moment, the man she had loved so dearly. He was even more handsome and powerful than she had ever remembered; her life that could have been. But in the same thought she knew in her heart that he had never truly wanted her.

"Your wife is very lucky, Chris," she said softly. "And very young. Where did you find her?"

He sighed. "Richard betrothed us and we have been married less than four months."

"She's a beautiful girl," Amanda observed. "Is she kind, too?"

He almost smiled. "When she wants to be. But more often than not, she's a stubborn, spirited wench who always gets her way."

Amanda smiled. "Most women do. Pray be good to her; I know how you hate disobedience in a woman."

He nodded, avoiding her knowing gaze. "May we come to the point, Amanda? Or did you simply wish to get me alone and talk about my wife."

Amanda shook her head. "Nay, I can find out all I want about her from the gossips. Your wife is a favorite subject right now. And what's this I hear about Marcus Burton?"

Christopher blinked slowly, rolling his eyes up to her. "Lies, all of it. Marcus is a good and loyal vassal, as you well know."

She could sense his impatience with her and knew she had better come to the point of their clandestine meeting or there would be hard feelings between them. She was hurt to realize he did not want to be around her in the least, whether it was because of her personally or because he was truthful when he said he wanted to return to his wife, she wasn't sure. But to avoid a most uncomfortable situation, she decided to come to the point.

"I asked to meet you here for a valid reason, Chris," she began softly. "There is something you should know. When we last met, before you left for the crusades, I had come to tell you of something. Do you remember? I sent you a missive saying that I was coming specifically to see you?"

He nodded slowly. "I do. You told me you were returning to France."

"True, but I didn't tell you everything I had intended to," she said softly, lowering her gaze for the first time. She suddenly seemed ill at ease and he saw her take a deep breath. "I had gone to London to tell you…to tell you that I was pregnant with your child."

His eyes widened. "What?"

She nodded shortly and stood up from the chair. " 'Tis true. I had gone to London to tell you I was pregnant, but when I saw how consumed you were with Richard and the quest, I knew that it would be futile to divulge the information," she said, looking at him. Her brown eyes were filled with sorrow. "You would have gone, anyway. I know you too well, Christopher. And if you hadn't and stayed simply to marry me so that our child would not have been a bastard, you would not have achieved your auspicious reputation. So, you see, 'tis a good thing you went after all."

He looked stunned. His hand went to his head and he sagged against the wall, mulling over the revelation. "So you didn't tell me? Amanda, I find this difficult to grasp."

"I know," she said softly. "But I did what I thought was best. Father was returning to France and I with him. Should anyone ask about my pregnancy, I simply told them that my husband had been killed in the crusades. An excellent lie, if I do say so."

He stared at her, slowly shaking his head. "Good Christ, Amanda…where is the child?"

"In France," she replied softly. "His name is Peter Myles de Vries, my husband's last name."

He could only look at her, astonished and seized with a tremendous sense of shock. She watched the emotions play on the face of a man she had seldom seen emotion from, and it brought her pain anew, as well, even though it had been nearly four years. God, she had loved this man more than life itself and she had known very well that the feelings were not returned. Aye, she bore his bastard because she knew it was all she would ever have of him. The elderly man she eventually married never questioned her about her son's paternity, and he had loved them both unconditionally. Although she did not return his love, it was a stable environment for Peter, and her son was her utmost concern.

Yet she didn't blame Christopher for simply being himself. He was far too independent for a wife, so she thought. Four years had done a lot to ease her bitterness. She went over to him and put her small hands in his massive arms.

"I named him Peter Myles, after my father and yours. He's the exact image of you, Chris, truly," she said softly, seeing his shock. "I am sorry, I do not mean to throw this overwhelming news on you, but I felt you should know. 'Tis your right."

He gazed back at her, his hand enclosing one of hers. "Oh, Amanda, I do not know what to say."

"Say nothing," she forced a brave smile. " 'Tis all past now and you have a bright future with a beautiful young wife to look forward to. She will bear you many strong children, I know it."

"She is pregnant now," he whispered as if the thought suddenly occurred to him. "She insists this child is a boy."

"It probably is," Amanda agreed. " 'Tis only right that a de Lohr bear male heirs."

He was staring off into space, digesting this bit of news that left him shaken to the core. His eyes met Amanda's brown ones. "I have a son?" he echoed with disbelief.

She nodded, a smile still playing on her lips. "A big, healthy boy with your blond hair. He knows about you, Chris. I felt he had a right to know who his true father was, although my husband has raised him as his own. Peter is a happy, well-mannered boy and you would be verily proud of him."

He was shocked. He remembered telling Leeton once that if he had a son, he would never let him out of his sight. Now he discovered he had a son, and he found that demanding access to the child to be the farthest thing from his mind. His son was a boy, happy, living with his mother and the only father he had ever known. What right did he have to demand the child be returned to him? He had no right at all and he would never be so very cruel. Furthermore, he would never do that to Amanda. She didn't have to tell him, but she had out of courtesy and respect. He would not turn on her like a madman and demand to take her child away. But his heart ached for his little boy. His son.

Amanda sensed his confusion and knew it was time for her to leave. She patted his hand and kissed him on the cheek. "Good fortune to you, baron, and your new family. I must go now."

He looked up at her, the sky-blue eyes dark with misery. "Thank you for telling me, Amanda. I am only sorry… sorry we had to go our separate ways. I am sorry you felt that you could not tell me you were pregnant when last we saw each other."

"It was for the best," she insisted bravely. "Had you stayed and married me, you would have been miserable. You didn't love me; you loved Richard. 'Tis better this way, Chris. I would prefer it as such than being married to a man who didn't want me."

She gave him one last smile and blew him a kiss as she yanked the curtains open. He heard her give an audible gasp and he stiffened, turning his attention to the hall before her. Marcus Burton was standing in the middle of the corridor, staring at both of them quite emotionlessly. His eyes glittered in the torchlight and Christopher could feel the disgust emanating from the man.

"Your wife is feeling ill, baron," he said coldly. "She is returning to your apartments."

Christopher pushed past Amanda and on into the hall. "Marcus," he glanced at Amanda's apprehensive face. "Lady Amanda and I were simply having a private conference, nothing more."

Marcus spun on his heel. "Why should I care about anything you do, baron?"

Christopher reached out and grabbed Marcus, causing the big man to tense as if preparing for a fistfight. His cobalt-blue eyes were blazing with fury.

"It is not what it looks like, Marcus," Christopher insisted in a low voice.

Amanda found her feet and slipped past the men without a word. Marcus eyed her with contempt, as if she were the castle prostitute. Then, he stopped trying to bank his anger and faced Christopher.

"You have got a hell of a lot of nerve lecturing me on the fidelity of marriage when you go out and find the nearest bitch to bed," he seethed.

Christopher kept himself calm. "I wasn't going to bed her, Marcus. She's an old friend."

"I know," Marcus snapped. "I know exactly who she is. You had a relationship with her. Jesus Christ, it isn't enough that you married the most beautiful woman in the realm? You do not even have the decency to remain faithful to your wife, while accusing me of lusting after her. You hypocritical son-of-a-bitch."

"Watch your tongue," Christopher growled. "You know not of what you speak."

"Then, pray tell me." Marcus was agitated, trying to keep himself from physically attacking Christopher. "I came out here looking for you because the wine has made Dustin sick. She vomited all over her surcoat and even now David and Deborah are taking her back to your apartments. And I find you alone with that French whore in a secluded alcove? What in the hell am I supposed to think?"

Christopher's jaw ticked ominously. "I realize how it looks, Burton, but trust me when I tell you nothing went on. I swear on my oath to Richard that nothing happened between Lady Amanda and I." His tone lowered to a husky growl. "But since you seem to think the very worst, I will tell you my reasons for being alone with her. Lady Amanda and I did indeed have a relationship before I went on the quest. We parted ways shortly before I left, and she came to tell me that she found herself pregnant around the time I sailed with Richard. My son is four years old now, living with the Earl of Reivne in France," he said, and found that repeating the news filled him with sadness and longing all over again. "That, baron, is why I was alone with her. This is the first time I have seen her since I left with Richard and she felt I had a right to know, as the boy's father."

Marcus looked back at him doubtfully, but sedate nonetheless. "You didn't know she was pregnant when you left?"

"Of course not," Christopher said. "If I had, I would now be married to Lady Amanda instead of Dustin. I would not have allowed her to bear my bastard in shame."

Marcus' hot stance cooled in mere seconds as the full impact of the explanation weighed down on him. "I do not know what to say," he lowered his gaze. "I heard your voice and was about to pull the curtain back myself when Lady Amanda opened it. I saw you, and I saw her, and I drew the only natural conclusion I could think of."

"I realize that," Christopher said. "God only knows, I know exactly how it must have looked. But I assure you, the lady simply wanted to tell me of my son. That was all Marcus. Surely you know I care for Dustin a great deal. I'd never do anything to jeopardize my relationship with her."

Marcus shrugged, off-balance, and ran his hand through his hair. "I know."

Christopher began to walk, taking Marcus with him. "Is Dustin all right?"

"Sick to her stomach," he replied. "She's more upset about ruining the surcoat than anything."

Christopher nodded, quickening his pace as they headed for the stairs.

"Chris, about everything I said," Marcus offered feebly. "I didn't mean it. I was angry."

"I know you were, and you had every reason to be," Christopher replied.

They took the stairs two at a time, reaching the dimly lit corridor on the second floor.

"I am sorry you never knew about your son," Marcus said quietly, sounds echoing off the wall. "I can only imagine your surprise."

Christopher nodded. "Shocked is more apt a term. And sorrow. Sorrow that I will most likely never know him," he said, looking at Marcus. "This knowledge goes no further, Marcus. Not even David, and especially not Dustin. Agreed?"

"Absolutely," Marcus nodded.

"Thank you," Christopher said sincerely as they rounded the corner into the wing where he was housed. He knew that Marcus would take his secret to the grave, but he was still reeling from the news. But it filled him with an even greater love for the child Dustin carried.

He was denied one child, mayhap he could make it up to the next.

CHAPTER TWENTY-FIVE

THE WEEKS FOLLOWING Christopher's announcement of Dustin's pregnancy brought happy mentions from friends and allies alike. David in particular seemed thrilled with the news. But the one person in Christopher's inner circle, however, who seemed to be increasingly distant from the mother-to-be was Marcus.

Dustin noticed, of course, every hour of every day. She had hoped he would come around, or at least tell her what was bothering him, but he had made no such attempt. As the days passed, so did her sense of concern. Finally, she'd had enough. His aloofness was beginning to wear on her and she was determined to know what his issue was.

One day when he had come to discuss a few matters with Christopher, she slipped out and followed him from her apartments, cornering him in a deserted hall as he was heading for the narrow servant's staircase at the end of the corridor.

"I would know what is troubling you, Marcus," she demanded softly.

He studied her coolly, his cobalt-blue eyes glittering in the torchlight. She was dressed in a heavy woolen surcoat, a bit too long due to her expanding waistline, and her gray eyes stared back at him with concern.

"I do not know what you mean," he replied.

"Do not insult my intelligence," she snapped. "You have been sulking around here for weeks now and I want to know why. Have I said something to offend you? Has Chris?"

His hard stance softened a bit. "No, Dustin, no one has offended me. There is nothing the matter, truly."

She sighed with frustration. "Marcus, I thought you were my friend. You have always been excessively kind and sweet and attentive, but lately it's as if I do not know you at all. You are not the same man I have come to know and love."

He blinked at her. "Love?"

She flipped her hand in a careless gesture. "Yes, of course, as my friend. Won't you please tell me what is bothering you? I do not like seeing you like this."

He could see she was genuinely concerned and felt his guard go down. For her, and only her, would it go down.

"Truly, Dustin, there's nothing wrong, at least nothing that can be solved," he said softly.

"What is it?" she begged softly. "Will you please tell me?"

She moved towards him as he shook his head. God, he had been fighting his feelings for her ever since he met her and when he found out she was with child, it was as if a white-hot blade had been thrust through his heart. It had only gotten worse with time. The happier Dustin and Christopher were, the more distressed he became. He knew his attitude had reflected his feelings, but he simply could not help himself. He loved her and probably always would, and would have given twenty years of his life if the child in her womb could have been his.

He put his big hands on her arms in a reassuring gesture. "There is nothing to tell, Lady de Lohr. But I appreciate your concern."

Dustin touched his hand, the hand that was slowly coming back to strength. "I am not as naive as you think, Marcus. I know a great deal, or at least I sense it." She pulled his hand off her arm and held it between them. "This is a good example, I know you injured your own hand, although I do not know why, but I suspect I had something to do with it. You lied to me."

His black brows drew together. "When? I would never lie to you."

She smiled faintly. "You are right now," she murmured. "You told me that your infatuation would pass. It hasn't, has it? And now you are angry with me because of it."

He gripped her hand in his healing one. "I am not angry with you, Dustin." He felt his composure slipping. It was a dark, quiet, lonely hall, who would hear his words except her? It was suddenly as if he had to confess and get all of the bleak feelings out of his soul. Mayhap if she knew the truth, if he could put his emotions into words, then he could gain much needed relief. As he struggled to say something, she spoke softly.

"Then tell me what is bothering you, Marcus," she said quietly. "Let me help."

The statement struck him as sad and ironic. He gave her a wry smile and released her hand.

"You cannot, unless you are planning to leave Chris and marry me," he said. "I apologize for my actions for I never meant to upset you or infer that I was angry. It's…it is sometimes difficult for me to realize that I have fallen in love with my liege's wife, as horrific as it is."

Her face went slack. "You have fallen in *love* with me?" she gasped. "Marcus, how could you? You know I can never… Marcus, I love Christopher."

His face hardened. "I know you do and I know he would probably kill me if he knew I was telling you this, but tell you I must for my own sanity." He was growing agitated. "Call me mad if you will, but I cannot help what I feel. I kissed you once, Dustin, and I haven't kissed another woman since. I do not know if I ever will."

Dustin felt as if the entire weight of the world had just been laid on her shoulders. She stepped back from him, denial all over her face. "And you blame me? I have done nothing to encourage you."

"Nothing except what comes naturally, and I cannot blame you for it," he shot back passionately. He stopped to compose himself, running his hand over his cropped black hair. "I am sorry, Dustin. For everything, I am sorry. I have tried to put you away in my mind, but I have been unsuccessful as of yet. I suppose I need time to suppress my feelings and I apologize if I am distant or cold in the process. But what I feel for you, Dustin…it scares me."

She gazed back at him, feeling so badly that she was the cause of his distress. "Christopher said the same thing to me, once," she whispered. "He said I frightened him. Why do I scare the two of you so? I am a simply woman, for God's sake, not Lucifer in a disguise."

Marcus let out a strangled chuckle. "You are simply the most remarkable woman either of us has ever met. Unfortunately for me, Christopher was the lucky one. Yet I know that you would have loved me had I met you first, and that is my foremost regret in life," he sighed and slapped his thigh in defeat. "Ah, well, there is no use in dwelling over what could have been."

She looked back at him a moment, studying him, before sighing softly. "I think I could have easily loved you, but I married Christopher and I love him dearly," she said. "I am sorry to cause your pain, Marcus, I would never hurt you knowingly."

"I know," he said with a weak smile. "And I am sorry to have been such a bear. I shall try harder to return to my sweet, charming self."

She grinned. "Do not fret over it," she said. "If you are gruff, 'twill give me an excuse to slug you and it will be the most exercise I have had in weeks. Christopher practically talks for me so that I will not strain myself."

Marcus laughed softly. "He is driving you insane, isn't he? The child is all he can talk about."

"I know," she nodded. "He talks to it every night, puts his mouth right against my belly and tells the babe what he expects of him."

Marcus could just see Christopher talking to Dustin's naked belly and he chuckled. She giggled in return, pleased to see that the "old" Marcus was on the mend. Without warning, she went over to him and put her arms around him, squeezing him affectionately. She probably shouldn't have, but she hated to see him upset. He responded stiffly, and she stepped back with a bashful grin on her face.

"I am glad you are not angry with me," she said.

"Never," he insisted, glancing over his shoulder to the steep stairwell behind him, partially shadowed in the darkness. "Well, I am expected on the field. Go back to your rooms before Christopher sends out a search party."

He turned for the stairs and was most of the way down the flight when he heard Dustin calling him from above. He turned to see her standing in the doorway, the light from the corridor behind her silhouetting her figure. She was saying something he could not quite hear and he asked her to repeat herself. Confused, she did not hear his response and started to descend the steep, narrow stairs.

Marcus was two or three steps from the bottom, looking up at her and thinking it was not such a good idea for her to be descending the flight. It was too steep and angled. He took another step toward her and called out to her to return to the top. Dustin took her eyes off the stairs for a moment because she hadn't caught his words, and when she did, she inevitably stepped on the long hem of her surcoat.

Marcus saw it coming and there was absolutely nothing he could do to prevent the fall. He saw her pitch forward, heard his own hoarse shout, and then she was tumbling down, down, down in a mass of wool and hair. He tried to run to catch her but he was simply too far away and by the time she crashed into him, she had fallen nearly the whole flight of stairs.

Marcus caught Dustin in his arms as she tumbled into him, her body limp with unconsciousness. Her head was cut and blood was coming from her nose, and Marcus was filled with complete and utter horror. He tried to force his legs to move, to run up the stairs with her cradled in his arms, but he could not seem to function. His whole body was shaking, running hot and cold with disbelief and panic.

But move he had to; Dustin's life depended on it. With a shout of agony, he propelled himself back up the steps and ran as fast as his legs could carry him.

☙

BY THE TIME Christopher barreled back to his apartments, the entire corridor was lined with soldiers and various knights, all parting out of his way like the Red Sea to Moses. David was with him, for it was he who went to find Christopher after Marcus had stumbled into the apartments with Dustin squeezed against him, her arms flopping about loosely and her neck hung over his arm.

Christopher could not even think. His mind was a black bog of terror and anguish, only knowing that his wife had been injured in some way but not much else. Marcus had been nearly incoherent in his explanation to David and the others. All they knew was that she was badly injured and a surgeon had been summoned.

All of his knights were in the antechamber, their eyes wide with concern as Christopher and his brother bolted into the room. Christopher's eyes immediately found Marcus, standing near the bedchamber door. Marcus knew what had happened and Christopher would tear the man apart if the explanation was not clear and forthcoming.

"What in the hell happened?" he roared at Marcus.

Marcus was coming apart, desperately trying to control himself. "She fell down a flight of stairs, Chris. I tried to save her, but I was too far away."

Christopher let out a strangled cry and put two huge hands over his mouth to prevent any more sounds from escaping. He was breathing so hard and so fast he was nearly hyperventilating.

"What stairs?" he asked through his hands.

"The flight at the end of the hall; the servant's well," Marcus whispered in reply, closing his eyes and turning away in agony.

Christopher could only stand there and stare at his friend's dark head. He was incapable of moving or speaking while his frenzied mind sorted out the information.

"Who's with her?" he choked.

"Burwell and his assistant," Leeton supplied. Marcus was too devastated to speak. "They have been in with her for a while now."

As if on cue, Burwell came bursting out of the room and dashed to the front door, completely ignoring the occupants of the antechamber. He yelled to a few of his men out in the hall to retrieve a midwife and slammed the door shut again, only then noticing Christopher and the others.

His ruddy face was intense to the point of anger, but it softened when his eyes fell on the baron.

"How is she?" Christopher demanded.

"She is injured, my lord, injured," he said. Burwell was not the great communicator, but he was an extremely competent surgeon.

"*How* injured?" Christopher could hardly bring himself to ask.

Burwell approached him, his gruff manner easing as he reluctantly met Christopher's eye. "No broken bones, I think, but she is bruised and battered." Then, much to everyone's concern, put a beefy hand on Christopher's shoulder. "There will be other babes, my lord, for she is young and strong. But my biggest concern at this moment is stopping her hemorrhaging, for she is losing too much blood for my taste."

His assistant said something to him and Burwell turned into the gruff and crusty physician again. He dropped his hand from Christopher and began ranting about something or another, storming back into the bedchamber and slamming the door, leaving Christopher standing in the middle of the room in shock.

After an eternal minute, he sank slowly into a chair. Gripped with grief, he hung his head.

No one knew quite what to say to him. David moved over to the chair but his tongue caught in his mouth and he could think of nothing that would be remotely comforting.

"I am sorry, Chris," he said quietly. "But there will be more children and...."

Christopher shot out of his chair, his face red and his body as tight as a spring.

"Goddammit, I do not care about the baby. My wife is in there bleeding to death and that is all I am concerned with." He staggered about aimlessly, dragging his hands over his face. "Christ, why did this happen? Why did this have to happen to the only good thing that has ever come into my life? What have I ever done to deserve this grief?"

His speech was as passionate and moving as any of them had ever seen him. The silence that met with his plea was deafening, for he wanted answers to questions no one was able to give.

"God is wise and merciful, Chris," Marcus said in a strange, hoarse voice. "You must trust that He will pull Dustin through."

"To hell with God!" Christopher snapped with fury and force, whirling on Marcus. "And to hell with you, too. This is all *your* fault, Burton. What was she doing on the stairs? And why were *you* there? Why are you always around my wife?"

"Because you ask it of me." Marcus pushed himself off the wall and glared at Christopher. "You ask me to protect her, remember? And I didn't push her down those stairs; she tripped. It was a goddamn accident!"

Edward was up, pushing Marcus away from Christopher as the two men came dangerously close to one another.

"Sit down, Marcus," he said with quiet firmness. "David, pour your brother a cup of wine and set him down."

David gripped Christopher's arm to steer him toward a chair but he pulled away roughly. "I do not need wine," he barked. "I need to see my wife."

The door to the apartments opened and a small, old woman came through, escorted in by one of Christopher's soldiers. She curtsied to the roomful of agitated men.

"My lords, I am Griselda Warwick, the midwife," she said. "Burwell sent for me."

Christopher moved forward and grasped the woman by the arm. "In here," he told her.

He pulled her toward the bedchamber and opened the door. It became apparent that he intended to follow the woman in, and Edward reached out to grab him.

"Where are you going?" he asked with concern. "Leave them to work on your wife alone. You shall do no good in there."

Christopher glared at Edward and yanked his arm away. To Edward, it almost looked as if the baron was about to cry for his eyes took on a most unfamiliar haze. Without a word, he lowered his gaze and pushed forward into the bedchamber, closing the door behind him.

The room was dim. The midwife rushed over to the bed where Burwell and his assistant were administering to Dustin, swathed in a disarray of linen sheets and other bedclothes. Her legs were up and her thighs parted, just as they parted for him when she drew him down into her. His eyes immediately went to her face; she was as white as the sheets and there was a bandage on her forehead, misshapen and crude.

Christopher's breath caught in his throat at the sight. Never in his life had he felt more helpless or anguished over anything. His chest twisted painfully, making it difficult to breathe as he took halting steps toward her.

"Get out," Burwell spat at him, moving aside to give the midwife better access.

Christopher ignored him, moving to the head of the bed and falling to his knees beside his wife's head. The bed had been lowered at the head and the foot of it raised high with chairs. He noted the angle of the bed as he raised a shaking hand and touched Dustin's forehead tenderly.

Burwell stood there and alternately glared at Christopher and paid close attention to what the midwife was doing. "I gave her something for the pain, baron. She is asleep and I do not want you upsetting her.

"I won't upset her," he whispered, gently stroking her head, his gaze compassionate on her sleeping face.

Dustin suddenly twitched and her eyes fluttered open. Immediately, she let out a groan of pain and everyone put their hands on her body to still her twisting.

Christopher threw his huge arm across her chest. "Be still, my love, be still," he whispered urgently. "I am here."

Her drugged eyes tried to focus on him and the tears began to fall uncontrollably. She cried feebly, like a child, and he buried his face against her head, murmuring words of comfort to her and stroking her head sweetly.

"The bleeding is growing darker," the midwife announced softly, throwing a saturated towel on the floor. "It will lessen now."

Burwell let out a sigh, the evidence of his relief. He had been positive the baron's wife was going to bleed to death in front of him and he had no desire to confront the man with the news, for he would most likely have been the recipient of a blade to the belly.

Christopher heard the woman, too, and was flooded with relief so great he went weak. His grip tightened on his sobbing wife, so very, very grateful for her life.

"You will be fine, sweetheart," he kissed her cheek, brushing his lips on her hair.

"My baby," she squeaked miserably.

"I know," he whispered. "I am so sorry."

She coughed and twisted with discomfort as the midwife did something Christopher could not quite see.

"Your son is gone," she sobbed. "Oh, Christopher, can you forgive me?"

He didn't even realize there were tears in his eyes. "There is nothing to forgive, Dustin, 'twas an accident."

The midwife closed Dustin's thighs and pulled the coverlet over her. "Let her rest a bit, baron. I shall check her in a few minutes."

Christopher nodded, his attention still on his wife. Burwell leaned over him and lifted the bandage on her forehead, checking on the huge bruise underneath.

"Well, at least you did not crack your skull open," he commented. "Great Gods, it's amazing you survived at all."

Christopher turned to shoot the man an angry look but the surgeon was already moving across the room, helping his assistant with the dirtied instruments.

Dustin's sobbing had lessened, sounding more like weak whimpers and Christopher tried to hold her as close as he could with the strange angle of the bed.

"Do you hate me now?" she murmured.

"Of course not, Dustin, I love you," he responded before he thought about what he was saying.

He froze, and her crying stopped. Then, her head moved a bit and her swollen gray eyes focused on him questioningly.

"Tell me again," she begged.

He blinked at her, almost refusing, but he didn't know why he should. He loved her, she knew he loved her, but the matter of saying those three simple words had been the most difficult of tasks. To say them was opening him up, laying himself vulnerable, and giving her power over him.

But she already had power over him. She was his wife and he loved her like nothing else on earth. The time had come for him to stop being such a coward and tell her over and over how much he loved her until she grew tired of hearing it. He hated himself in that it took something of this magnitude to bring him to his senses.

"I love you," he whispered, gazing into the depths of the stormy gray eyes. "You are my reason for living, lady, and I love you with all my heart."

Her clammy hand came up to weakly caress his cheek and her pale lips formed a wonderful smile. "Tell me again."

He grinned. "I just did, but I will say it again if you wish it. I love you madly."

Her eyes closed but the smile was still there, and her hand dropped limply to the bed. "I love you, husband," she sighed.

He clutched her hand tightly, holding it reverently to his lips. They stayed in that loving position the longest time. The midwife continued to check Dustin periodically to make sure the hemorrhaging had stopped, offering an encouraging smile to Christopher now and again. Burwell and his assistant remained, seated quietly in the corner of the bedchamber in case they were needed again. The afternoon passed into early evening.

Finally, the midwife was satisfied that the bleeding was minimal and would stop in a few days. She instructed Christopher to keep the head of the bed down for the night and in the morning she would return to see how Dustin was faring. Burwell, too, was full of instructions as to the care of Lady de Lohr and Christopher listened intently.

When the man turned to leave, Christopher stopped him.

"Burwell," he said in a scratchy voice. "Is.....is there enough of the babe to bury?"

Burwell looked thoughtful. "The babe was about as big as my thumb. Intact, I might add."

Christopher swallowed at the distaste he felt at even asking the question, then hearing the answer. It bordered on disgust, but for some reason, he had to know. The fetus was his flesh and blood and a part of him, a part of Dustin.

"Was....what was it?" He hated himself for asking, for sounding so petty.

"A son," Burwell's voice was hushed.

Christopher's eyes stung and he lowered his head. "I would appreciate a Christian burial for my son," he said, his voice choked with emotion as he gazed on Dustin's sleeping face.

Burwell merely nodded, closing the door softly behind him.

In the darkness of the room, with his wife sleeping and the world around him silent but for the crackling of the logs in the hearth, Christopher allowed himself the luxury of tears.

CHAPTER TWENTY-SIX

DUSTIN'S RECOVERY WAS terribly slow. With the loss of the babe, she seemed to have lost her spirit. She sat in the antechamber day after day, eating little and working on pieces of needlepoint. There were several of them; as she would become bored with one and move on to another. It was her only form of entertainment because she absolutely refused any visitors, including the knights and Deborah.

Christopher was miserable watching his wife waste away. Her beautiful hair had lost its luster and her lovely face was a constant pale shade, lacking any color whatsoever. The wide gray eyes were circled and lifeless. Even after the midwife said she was nearly physically recovered, Dustin refused to leave the apartments.

Christopher was in a very difficult position. John and Ralph were beginning to create a stir again, most notably with the party they held on the eve following Dustin's accident for their closest friends. Rumor had it that it was a celebration for Christopher's loss, and the knowledge drove him beyond rage. If Dustin were to hear of it, he knew she would lose her sanity for sure.

Missives had been coming from the continent regarding Richard's whereabouts, and the justices were positive the man was alive, but they had no way of knowing where their king was. That portion of Christopher's responsibilities began heating up, only adding to the tremendous burden of Dustin's infirmary. He found his attention focused solely on her, and his concerns with Richard, although grand, paled in comparison. His one desire was to return his wife to her former wonderful self, and for the first time in his life, he was completely dedicated to something other than Richard.

A week or so after Dustin's accident, Christopher cornered the midwife in the hallway outside his apartments. He was greatly concerned for his wife's mental health and wanted the old woman's opinion.

"My wife has not been the same since her mishap," he said in a lowered voice. "Is this a normal occurrence with women when they lose children?"

"Aye, sire, 'tis perfectly natural," the woman replied. "She feels unworthy and a failure, even though it was an accident. Give her time, my lord. She shall come around."

He looked at the woman doubtfully, he so desperately needed reassurance. "But she mopes about and refuses to eat or leave the apartments. Her body is sound, is it not?"

The woman nodded. "She is a very healthy lass and her recovery has been remarkable."

He crossed his arms with frustration, finally nodding. "Very well. Thank you for your advice, madam."

The old woman's eyes twinkled at him. "Do you want more advice, sire? Give her a few months or so, and then beget her with child as quickly as possible. Sometimes that helps ease the ache."

"But will that be safe?" he wanted to know. "Christ, the woman nearly bled to death from the womb."

"She will have healed completely by then, I assure you," the midwife said. "Your wife is young and strong, my lord. She will bear you many children to come."

Christopher nodded shortly, satisfied with the woman's knowledge. "Thank you again, madam."

The midwife curtsied and scurried several feet down the hall before pausing a moment and turning back to Christopher, who was just about to enter his apartments.

"My lord?" she called out to him. When he turned, she retraced her steps quickly. "There is but one more thing you can do to help your wife recover physically, though this task may prove to be unbearable to you."

"What is it?" he asked.

"Rubbing her breasts will help her womb contract and heal faster," she said, motioning over her own breast with a circular pattern. "I recommend it to all of my patients."

He cocked an eyebrow at her. "Rubbing her breasts? Now why would I find that unbearable?"

The woman grinned. "Because you cannot bed her for another six or seven weeks, and some men find the duty, shall I say, painful."

He nodded, a faint smirk on his face as she left him again. When he turned back to the door, he noticed a half dozen guards with smirks on their faces. Eyeing them all dangerously, he entered his apartments.

Dustin was sitting in her usual chair by the windows, playing with George. The monkey was dancing and doing flips in her lap and she watched the little beast without much enthusiasm. Christopher meandered up to her, watching the monkey's tricks.

"The sun is out this day," he said casually. "Would you accompany me on a walk?"

She shook her head. "I do not feel like walking."

He knelt beside the chair, his eyes going to her pale face. "I miss you walking beside me," he said. "You used to go everywhere with me."

She didn't look at him but continued to play with the monkey. "I do not want to go anywhere."

He studied her features, so incredibly beautiful. The bruise on her forehead was fading. His heart was wrenching to see her so. "Please, sweetheart, come walk with me. How would you like to go into town?"

Abruptly, she stood up and the monkey fell from her lap. "Nay," she snapped. "I told you I do not want to go anywhere and I would appreciate it if you would stop asking."

He rose on his massive legs, trying to maintain a calm manner with her. "I am only thinking of you, Dustin. You have been holed up in these rooms for over a week and it would do you good to get out and move around."

She swung her great mane of hair angrily and bolted past him into the bedchamber. "I do not want to move around," she said angrily. "I do not want to walk."

He followed her, his irritation growing. "Why are you being like this?"

She flopped on the bed. "Go away."

"I will not," he said with annoyance. "What is the matter with you?"

"What is the *matter* with me?" she repeated, incredulous. "In case you have not realized it, I killed your son. How can you ask me that question?"

He sighed heavily, trying to bank his anger once again. "You did not kill the babe, Dustin," he said softly. "We have been over this a thousand times. You tripped, and you fell, and I am extremely grateful for your very life. We can always have another child, but there will never be another you."

"No more children," she frowned, frustrated. "No more. I do not want anymore."

"Why?" he asked.

She simply shook her head hard, wallowing in self-loathing and self-pity. He approached the bed.

"Why not?"

"Because….no more dying." Her voice was reduced to a whisper. "They die; everything I love dies. My mother, my father, Rebecca, my child… I cannot love anything else and watch it die."

"You love me and I am not dead," he said softly, sitting carefully on the bed beside her. "I shall never leave you, Dustin. I swear it."

"You almost did," she said, meeting his gaze painfully. "I watched you go down in the joust and I thought you were dead too."

He took a deep breath, reaching out deliberately to clasp her hand. He rolled it over, inspecting it, before bringing it back to his lips.

"I will not compete in any more tournaments," he said softly. "I do not want to worry you needlessly. I have a wife to think of now; 'tis no longer simply me."

Dustin's eyes widened. As magnificent as he was, as powerful and as skilled, for him to make that statement spoke incredible volumes as a testimony to his devotion to her.

"But…but you are the champion," she insisted, turning the tables in the conversation and focusing on him. "You are the best, Chris. For you not to compete is a waste of your talent."

He cocked an eyebrow at her. "I thought you would applaud my decision."

She lowered her gaze and shrugged. "I cannot ask you to stop doing what you do, Chris. You are a soldier, and the very best in the realm. You must maintain that reputation in spite of my worries. You said yourself that I worry overly, and I do." She put her hands up to his face, rubbing his stubble affectionately. "I am very proud of you, husband. And I love you dearly."

He put his hand over hers, dwarfing it. "I am getting too old to compete, anyway. I would leave it to the younger men who have not yet established a reputation."

She shook her head. "You are not too old."

He chuckled at her, remembering what she had said when she found out how old he was. She grinned, too, remembering her words as well.

"Walk with me," he said in a low tone.

Her smile faded and she pulled her hands away. "Nay, Chris. I do not want to."

He reached out and pulled her to him before she could crawl off the bed. "Why, Dustin? You cannot keep yourself locked up in here the rest of your life. David and Marcus and the others are very distressed that you will not allow visitors; they miss you. And Deborah is reduced to tears every time I see her. Why do not you want to see them?"

"Because I do not." She struggled against him, trying to loosen his grip. "I do not want them looking at me, thinking about what happened, because I will see it in their eyes and I do not wish to be reminded of it endlessly."

" 'Tis only their sympathy you will see in their eyes," he said quietly.

"I do not want it," she said snappishly. "I do not want their pity."

He looked at her but she would not meet his gaze. She was still clutched against him, stiff and uncooperative, but he leaned close and kissed her cheek anyway.

"They do not pity you as a weakling or as a failure, Dustin," he murmured. "They simply wish to tell you how very sorry they are for our loss. They are our friends, our family, and they love us. They love *you*."

Her eyes filled with tears that spilled over in little rivers down her cheeks. Her angry, defiant stance dissolved and she relaxed, falling against him. He held her tightly, comforting her, kissing her, loving her.

"I cannot," she sobbed quietly.

"It's all right, my love, you do not have to do anything you do not want to," he assured her. "If you want to stay in these apartments and rot, then so be it."

Her tears turned to choked giggles. "Do not tease me."

He grinned. "I am not. If you want to stay here and become part of the fixtures, I shall not stop you. But can I bury you if the dogs start gnawing on your rotting corpse?"

She let out a cry of disgust and slapped playfully at him. "That's a terrible thing to say."

"So sorry," he said with mock sincerity.

She eyed him, wiping her eyes. "You are not."

He stroked her dull hair, watching her compose herself. "Will you at least bathe this morn and don a clean surcoat? It might make you feel better."

She glanced down at herself, her dirty shift and robe. She suddenly wondered how Christopher could have stood her appearance for an entire week.

"Aye, I shall do that," she nodded.

He had the delightful duty of bathing his wife. She was still rather weak and needed his help to wash her thick hair, but she insisted she was quite capable of soaping her own body. He ignored her statements and ran soapy hands all over her skin until he was fully engorged and bordering on miserable. She had lost a substantial amount of weight during her infirmary, her stomach completely flat and her breasts somewhat smaller, but her body was as incredibly luscious and desirable as it had ever been.

The bath did indeed seem to perk up her spirits and they deteriorated to throwing suds on each other. After receiving two hefty bombardments of white froth, Christopher grabbed her to him, wet and all, and kissed her hard. He was miserable when she responded intensely, pressing her naked breasts against his shirt until he had to let her go or go mad.

She smirked at him from her perch in the tub. "You started it."

He raised an eyebrow at her, wiping his hands on a towel. "Started what? Oh."

She was pointing at his swollen crotch and he turned around so she would not see him. "Get out."

She laughed. "No. Turn around."

"No," he said flatly. "Get out of the tub before you catch chill."

She leaned on the edge of the tub, her gray eyes glittering up at him. "No. Turn around and lower your chausses."

His head snapped around and he looked at her wanly. "No, Dustin."

"Then I shall get out and lower them for you," she said seductively.

He gazed at her with disbelief. "Dustin….no. We cannot you are still weak and…."

She reached out and managed to grab hold of his breeches, tugging him toward her. "Come here."

He could have easily pulled free of her grip, but instead found himself responding to her. He didn't want to, but it was as if some invisible force was pushing him forward, moving for him and he was powerless to respond. He watched his wife unfasten the stays on his chausses and release his great organ, helpless to stop her but anticipating her actions with more excitement that he could imagine.

Her warm, wet hands fondled his great size eagerly and when, with an evil grin, her hot mouth plunged down on him, he was completely lost.

He never knew he could climax so quickly. It could not have been more than a couple of minutes and he was erupting convulsively, his hands entangled in her wet hair and he heard himself murmuring her name over and over again.

When it was over, he swept her from the tub and wrapped her in a giant linen towel. Cradled against him, he carried her over near the fire and began to dry her off vigorously. She was still grinning at him.

"Why are you looking at me like that?" he asked.

She shrugged, not answering. He slowed his rubbing. "Why are you grinning?" he asked.

Again, she shrugged saucily and he fought off a grin, returning to toweling her hair. "You will tell me why you are smirking so or I will wrap you up in this towel and throw you in the hearth."

She gave him a look that let him know she didn't believe him. "I was simply thinking how wonderful you are, that's all," she replied. "And how much I like making you submit to me."

He gave her his own disbelieving look. "Is that so? Do you intend to abuse your power, lady?"

"Never," she replied, closing her eyes as he combed out her hair. "Chris?"

"What, sweetheart?"

"I would take that walk with you now," she said softly. "Can we go into town to the baker's? I have a craving for a sticky bun."

He smiled with relief. "Of course we shall go. But we will ride if you want to go into town."

"Can David and Deborah and the others go, too?" she asked.

Mildly surprised at her turn of heart, he spun her around to face him. "If you wish it, of course. Are you sure?"

She nodded. "Aye."

He smiled and kissed her head. "David and Edward and Leeton should be at the training grounds," he said thoughtfully, setting the comb down. "But I do not know where Marcus is. I shall send someone...."

"No," she said firmly.

"What do you mean?"

"I mean that I do not want Marcus to come with us," she said, her joviality slipping as she turned away from him and toward the wardrobe.

He observed her stiff back. "Why not?"

Her eyes met his insistently. "Because I do not...I do not want to see Marcus Burton ever again. I hate him, so leave it at that."

He put his hands on his hips. "I will *not* leave it at that." His eyes narrowed. "Does this have something to do with your accident?"

She didn't answer him as she went to the wardrobe and began fumbling with a surcoat. He approached the wardrobe. "Answer me, Dustin. Does this have something to do with your fall?"

Her head snapped up to him, her face dark. "He was there."

"Aye, he was there, at the base of the stairs," Christopher agreed. "He is not responsible for what happened."

She turned around and ripped a pair of slippers from the wardrobe. "I do not want to see him ever again, Chris. Tell him, or I will."

"I do not think you are being fair, sweetheart," he said quietly. "Marcus is devastated over what happened. He feels terrible."

"He should," she snapped, but clamped her mouth shut and pulled her shift over her head.

Christopher watched her angry, jerky movements a moment. For some reason, she blamed Marcus for her loss but he could not understand why other than the fact that the man simply happened to be there when it occurred. He wondered if she blamed him because he did not, or more correctly, could not help her.

Whatever the reason, he knew Dustin to be somewhat reasonable and knew that with time, she would forgive and forget.

At least, he hoped so.

☙

THEY MADE QUITE a caravan. Christopher, in full armor along with David, Edward, Leeton and Dud, escorted Dustin and Deborah into London simply because Dustin was dying for a sticky bun. To be out in the fresh air, although quite freezing, was refreshing nonetheless and Dustin's pale face received color simply from the icy chill that turned her nose and cheeks red.

Michaelmas was upon them and the streets were lined with decorations and happy people. Old snow congregated in the gutters and stank with the sewage, but Dustin was feeling much better with her outing. In fact, she actually felt like shopping, much to Deborah's delight. Christopher would have bought the bloody White Tower for her if she wished it, anything to raise her spirits.

David led them all to a delightful bakery on the outskirts of town. All seven of them entered the small, warm establishment and Dustin proceeded to eat two sticky buns, two chunks of hot bread with apple butter, plus a slice of dark bread with butter, nutmeg and honey. The more she would eat, the more the fat baker would feed her.

Since she was so full, Dustin and Deborah wholeheartedly agreed to visit the popular dressmaker on the other side of the Thames. Christopher wasn't thrilled about taking a ferry across the frozen river, but agreed to keep her happy. They proceeded to the river's edge and he wrapped her in his arms to keep her warm as they waited for the river boat.

"Now that you are drunk on bread and sweets, you intend to spend all of my money?" he teased her.

She nodded firmly. "All of yours, and all of David's, and all of Edward's, and…"

Edward shook his head. "I will have my own wife for that soon enough. Leave me out of this."

"But your wife is only three years old, Edward," Dustin said. "I must prepare you for what is to come."

He snorted. "By the time I marry her, I will probably die of heart failure the first time she spends an extravagant amount."

They laughed and joked as they waited, but Deborah seemed distracted. Finally, she turned to her eldest brother.

"Where is Marcus?" she asked.

"At Windsor," he replied, careful of what he said. "The last I saw, he was working with a group of squires in the jousting field."

"Why didn't he come?" Deborah asked.

Dustin's mood sank again, but she said nothing. Christopher felt her press closer against him. "Because I did not tell him we were going into town," he told his sister. "He's very busy, Deborah."

Deborah sighed a regretful, pretty sigh and looked over her shoulder again as if expecting Marcus to ride up any moment.

The trip to the dressmaker's had been an expensive one for Christopher. Dustin had purchased one surcoat that the woman had ready-made, a surcoat a noblewoman had ordered and neglected to pay for, and ordered two more for herself and for Deborah. Christopher not only found himself paying for his wife, but for his sister.

"When are you going to find yourself a husband?" he asked Deborah with feigned irritation. "You are an expensive habit."

She grinned coyly. "No one has asked for my hand yet, my lord."

"Hmm," he eyed her critically. "I believe I will have to sell you off to the highest bidder to recoup my losses."

"I doubt there would be anyone who would pay such a price for me," she said.

"Aye, there is," Dustin said, knowing Deborah meant Marcus but not wishing to go into it any further. "We simply have to find him."

Deborah blushed prettily. "I have a suggestion."

Christopher wasn't oblivious to what his sister was inferring; he'd known she had her eye on Marcus for months but Deborah was too much of a lady to broach the subject. Her latest words had him eyeing her warily, fearful of Dustin's reaction if Deborah's suggestion was going to be Marcus. He decided it was best all around to simply skirt the subject.

"You will forgive me if I do not ask for your suggestion," he said. "It is my duty to find you a husband and I plan to select the wealthiest old man I can find so you can spend your days tending his gout, wiping his dribble, and turning all of his coffers over to me. How does that sound?"

As he'd hoped, the women were properly distracted. Dustin burst out into laughter while Deborah, grinning, was mortified.

"You would not dare do that, would you?" she asked fearfully.

He cocked a stern eyebrow. "If you keep costing me so much money, I will have no choice."

Deborah looked worried, eyeing the bundled dress she held. "Then you can return the dress and get your money back. I do not want to be a burden."

He wasn't about to return the dress. He pinched her chin lightly. "You are not a burden," he told her, "but it is more than likely that you fear I really will select a fat old husband for you who lies in bed and farts all night long."

Dustin giggled loudly and even Deborah was smiling. "Like David does?" she asked innocently.

David, having stayed out of the conversation to this point, heard her insult. "What is this?" he said, outraged. "Who told you such lies?"

"They are not lies," Edward said from his other side. "I have seen it for myself. A fearsome and pungent talent you have, David."

David slugged Edward, who nearly toppled off his charger. It set the stage for laughing ladies and insults being slung all around the entire ride back to the castle.

CHAPTER TWENTY-SEVEN

BACK AT WINDSOR, the hour was rapidly approaching for supper and Dustin decided that she would attend her first formal meal in over a week. Christopher was doubtful as to whether or not she was strong enough, mentally and physically, but he did not want to deny her. She seemed happy as she and Deborah admired her new surcoat and fussed over each other as they experimented with different hairstyles, and he was deeply relieved that she was returning to her happy self.

There was a knock on the antechamber door and Christopher left his wife and sister to go and open it. Marcus barged into the room, dressed finely in his new tunic bearing his coat-of-arms.

"Well? What do you think?" he demanded, turning around so Christopher could see the whole thing.

Christopher was wary of the man's presence because of his wife's attitude, but he admired the crest just the same.

"Magnificent," he said, stepping back to study it better. The colors were a crimson field with black and gold, the silhouette of a massive bear with a crown around his right arm and a sword in his left hand. "Very impressive."

"Dud is wearing his tonight," Marcus said. "And Sir Stephen Marion has pledged to me this day, of which I am extremely pleased."

Christopher nodded. "The man is a fine knight, very strong," he agreed, wondering if Dustin could hear Marcus' voice.

"And do you know who else has pledged to me? Sir Dalton le Crughnan," Marcus said proudly.

"Le Crughnan? Christ, Marcus, he's the biggest man in England. How in the hell did you earn his loyalty?" Christopher demanded.

"I bested him this afternoon in a fight," Marcus said, a huge smile on his lips. "He said he would only serve a man who could beat him in a fair battle, and I did. He's mine."

Christopher shook his head. "Good Christ, I will never again say a bad thing about you lest le Crughnan come after me to avenge you. Hell, I do not even know if *I* could have bested him."

"He is not such a fearsome animal now that I have spent some time with him, but Dud is scared to death of the man," Marcus said.

Christopher snorted. "Me, too. He's a giant."

Marcus grinned, glancing past him to the open bedchamber door. "I hear your wife is up and about. Glad to hear it."

Christopher looked quickly at the door and moved to close it. "She and Deborah are preparing for supper," he said. "We shall see you in the grand dining hall this evening."

Marcus nodded. "I am relieved she is feeling better, Chris. How is her mood?"

Christopher cleared his throat, wondering how to answer him. "Rotten, at times," he admitted. "She is still quite affected by the whole thing, Marcus, so do not take offense too quickly if she….well, if she isn't acting herself."

Marcus agreed, wishing he could at least speak to Dustin. He had really rushed to their apartments to show her his new crest and hear her praise, but that would have to wait until supper.

"Well, I suppose I had better gather my men," he said, retreating to the front door. "I shall need them to beat the women off me now that I have established my own house. I suppose I am considered quite a catch."

Christopher gave him a lopsided smile. "Christ, why? Get out of here, you arrogant whelp."

"You will help me select my wife, Chris," Marcus said. "Considering you landed the most beautiful, desirable woman in the realm, I will trust your opinion."

"Choose your own wife, Burton," Christopher opened the door for him. "I shall not be blamed for the poor woman's misery."

He closed the door on Marcus and turned to see Deborah and Dustin exiting the bedchamber. Deborah's face was tight with emotion.

"So he wants a wife, does he?" she said. "Why didn't you mention me? You are so eager to get rid of me."

"Deborah, I am not a matchmaker," Christopher said firmly. "You and Marcus will have to form your own relationship without my help."

Deborah looked decidedly displeased, but Dustin's face was cold. Christopher noticed her expression and sought to get rid of his sister for the moment.

"Go dress for dinner," he told his sister. "Dustin and I will come and retrieve you in an hour or so."

Deborah quit the apartments with an injured ego while Dustin merely turned back for the bedchamber. Christopher followed.

She was dressed in a long shift, fumbling with her new surcoat in preparation for wearing it.

"Are you still angry with Marcus?" he asked. "He shall be sitting with us at supper tonight."

"For Deborah's sake, I will tolerate him," she said. "Help me with this surcoat, please."

He held the surcoat up for her and she slipped the luscious gold brocade on, smoothing it over her trim torso as he did the stays. Christopher stood back a moment, watching her as she observed herself in the mirror and he let out an appreciative sigh.

"Christ, you look marvelous," he said with approval. "The surcoat was well worth the price."

Dustin gazed back at herself; the surcoat clung to her like a second skin, the wide, scoop neckline barely off her shoulders and the sleeves long and bell-shaped at the wrist. The skirt was long and narrow, emphasizing her figure to a fault. She looked like a golden goddess and Christopher was growing lustier by the minute.

When she moved to put her hair back, he stopped her. "No," he said, putting her hands back to her side. Still looking at her reflection in the mirror, he ran his fingers through her hair, playing with it and combing it, until it was a glittering erotic mass. He pushed a healthy portion of it over her right shoulder, allowing it to cascade over her breast and hang past her waist, while the rest of her hair hung down her back to her buttocks.

She closed her eyes as he touched her, her heart pounding with excitement and her breathing growing rapid. She loved it when he played with her hair, relishing his touch. He stroked and touched and played to the point when he was finished, she was panting for him painfully and he buried his face in her neck. His arms went about her and she relaxed into him, feeling his hot mouth kiss and lick at her neck.

"Chris," she moaned.

"What?" he mumbled into her neck.

"We cannot… well, we cannot *do* anything and you are driving me insane," she murmured. "Stop this torture, husband."

He stopped only to spin her around to face him, his hands gripping her arms and his face dark with passion. "Kiss me," he demanded.

She grinned, hearing her own plea in his words. She kissed him long and hot and feverishly, a kiss of pure desire.

"Now who is torturing whom?" he asked in a raspy voice. "I cannot touch you for at least six weeks, the midwife told me so."

"I know," Dustin replied. "She told me as well."

They looked regretfully at each other for a moment before he hugged her briefly and pulled away, preparing to dress for supper.

"Do not wear that surcoat again until I can do something about it," he instructed her firmly, then mumbled more to himself. "Christ, this will be the longest six weeks of my life."

ଓଃ

WILLIAM MARSHAL, EARL of Pembroke, and William Longchamp, Bishop of Ely, were their supper companions that evening. Dustin sat between Christopher and David, her husband entirely occupied by the chancellor and the marshal. David did his best to keep her entertained, but she was restless and out of sorts. Deborah sat on David's other side and Marcus next to her.

Dustin was determined to ignore Marcus. She could not bring herself to look at him, knowing how he felt, knowing he was the reason she fell down the stairs. If he had only come up when she had called to him, she wouldn't have descended the stairs. Aye, she blamed him, although she knew deep in her heart that it wasn't his fault. Yet she had to find a focus for her grief, and Marcus made a convenient whipping post.

All of their friends had made a grand fuss over Dustin's appearance and she tried hard to be gracious. But her patience wore thin quickly and she was grateful when the meal commenced. After a fine supper of meats and winter vegetables, the king's minstrels began the entertainment with a slow folk ballad and soon the floor was filled with dancing couples. Dustin watched, remembering her mother had taught her the dance when she was young, and suddenly wishing her husband would dance with her.

Marcus made a number of attempts to start a conversation with her, but she would respond with one-word answers or not at all. Frustrated, he resorted to conversing with Leeton and Edward, and kept his back to Deborah, which upset her immensely.

Ralph was on the dance floor with a very young, pretty redhead, dancing lightly. Dustin didn't even realize he was there until he stopped in the middle of the song right in front of her. Christopher, aware of Ralph's attentions on Dustin, turned menacingly to the sheriff. If the man so much as mentioned their loss, he would kill him where he stood.

"I am surprised to see you out and about, Lady de Lohr," he said thinly. "From what we had heard, you were near on your deathbed."

Dustin met Ralph's gaze steadily. "Nay, sire. As you can see, I am well."

Ralph had imbibed a bit too much wine. He pushed his dancing partner away and leaned forward on the table. "Call me not sire, my lady. Relatives should not be so formal."

Dustin looked confused as well as irritated. "What?"

Ralph laughed low in his throat. "Are you feigning ignorance or are you truly unaware of our ties?"

Christopher stood up. "Stop harassing my wife, Fitz Walter."

Ralph smiled openly. "I am not harassing her, truly, de Lohr. Your wife and I are related by blood."

"My wife would never be related to the likes of you," Christopher growled. "If you value your life, you will leave this table posthaste."

Ralph stood back from the table but he didn't leave. "I can see you are puzzled, so allow me to explain. Lady Dustin, your mother was from Nottingham, was she not?"

Dustin was seized with horror. *How did he know that*? By not answering, she answered him completely.

Ralph's smile was back. "You see, my lady, your grandsire and my father are brothers. I did not know until I visited Nottingham last month. Your grandsire is most anxious to see his only granddaughter."

Christopher slammed his big fists down on the table. "You are a liar, Fitz Walter."

"Not at all," Ralph insisted. "Lady Dustin's mother, Lady Mary Fitz Walter Barringdon, is Lord Bruce Fitz Walter's daughter. Lord Bruce's younger brother is my father, Charles."

Dustin went white and she thought she might literally become sick. Ralph could only beam at the two shocked people.

"We're related, de Lohr," he crowed happily. "Isn't that amazing?"

Christopher was furious. He pointed a thick finger at Ralph, his manner slow and deliberate. "You will stay away from my wife, and you will stay away from me. I want nothing to do with you, you bastard. Get out of my sight."

"Anything you say, cousin," Ralph said flippantly, then gazed at Dustin. "Lord Bruce sends his love and regards, my lady. He hopes you will visit him soon."

Christopher moved menacingly but William Marshal grabbed him to halt any advance. "No, Chris, not here," he said quietly. "He is baiting you. Let him go."

Ralph flitted away, leaving everyone at the table shocked and bewildered. Christopher, still inflamed, looked at Dustin.

"You didn't tell me your mother was a Fitz Walter," he said sharply.

Dustin looked horrified. " 'Tis a common name," she choked. "I didn't know…Oh, Lord…."

Then it is true. Christopher regained his seat and quickly took his wife's hand in a reassuring gesture. He fought to calm himself.

"I am sorry, sweetheart, I did not mean to snap at you," he squeezed her hand. "Calm down. Eat your sweets."

Much to his sorrow, she started to cry. He immediately stood up and drew her with him, conveying his apologies to the chancellor and the marshal, promising to return shortly. He would comfort his wife first.

He never received much of a chance to do so. By the time they reached their chamber, a messenger from John was waiting for them. As much as he wanted to ignore the summons, Christopher's curiosity had the better of him.

଼

"DID YOU TELL them?" John asked from his vantage point.

"I did," Ralph said, he was so damned pleased with himself. "Quite a bit of luck, wouldn't you say, sire?"

"Indeed," John gazed off across the room to the big table where Richard's loyalists were gathered. "I see her reaction was as expected."

"Of course it was," Ralph replied. " 'Twas only by chance I discovered the information myself. I know she had no idea that I was her second cousin."

John glanced at him. "You look nothing like lovely Lady de Lohr," he said. "She must take after her father's family. Now tell me, sheriff, now that the entire de Lohr camp is unnerved, what shall we do about it?"

"Do, sire? What do you mean?" Ralph sat down.

"What I mean is, we planned several months ago to kidnap Lady de Lohr and spirit her off to St. Donat's Castle," John said shortly. "With the most recent developments, it is more imperative than ever that de Lohr is put out of the way. My mercenary army is even now in Nottingham with your uncle preparing to strike Gloucester and it will only be a matter of time before de Lohr mobilizes the crown troops. I want Lady de Lohr taken away and hidden for safekeeping."

"You are planning to go to Nottingham, are you not?" Ralph said. " 'Twould be suspicious if you were both to vanish at the same time. She either goes before or after you."

"Ralph, in light of the information we received this day, I leave for Nottingham tomorrow," John said irritably. "With Richard a captive of Leopold and Emperor Henry, he is completely helpless and I can rule England before the summer is out if I launch my army now to gain control of his holdings. De Lohr will do everything in his power to stop me, and I want his wife to be my secret weapon. I care not when she goes, just make sure you follow through with it."

"I promised you I would, sire," Ralph said softly. "But 'tis the heart of winter now, and Wales will be hellish to travel through."

John let out an annoyed hiss. "Then take her somewhere else, Ralph, or do I have to do your thinking for you? Damnation, I shall take her to Nottingham with me and she will be in good company with her grandfather."

Ralph shrugged. "Verily, 'twould make better sense," he said.

John liked the idea. "De Lohr would be busy fighting your armies at Gloucester or wherever they go, never dreaming his wife was with you, holed up in Nottingham. For her to be with you would be so logical, he shall think it illogical."

John's gaze lingered on Ralph. "For months now we have kept a low profile, building my army with Philip's wealth, the stupid bastard. He thinks he controls me by it, when in fact, I may turn on him like an ungrateful son." He sat opposite Ralph, drawing forth his gaudy, gleaming dirk and inspecting it absently. Suddenly, he tossed it sharply and it sailed, blade first, into the banister of the balcony.

Ralph eyed the blade, 'twas only inches from his shoulder. "I look forward to leading your armies, my lord. Sir Dennis and I will be an unbeatable team."

John watched his blade quiver, his thin face thoughtful. "Victory is all that I ask. And de Lohr's defeat."

Ralph nodded slowly. "Success will be ours, my lord."

"Send word to de Lohr," John commanded quietly. "In fact, send word to all of my brother's loyal men. It is time to put the last nail in my brother's coffin, so to speak. I have need to speak with his loyalists, and especially de Lohr."

Ralph carried out the prince's directive without another word.

CHAPTER TWENTY-EIGHT

MARCUS AND DUD were in charge of Dustin while Christopher answered the prince's summons. Reluctantly, Marcus had come simply because Christopher had no one else to turn to because most of his knights were too drunk or missing to attend his wife. Marcus was still smarting from her rebuff earlier and he wanted to return to his bed. He hadn't even fully dressed, only taking the time for breeches, a shirt and heavy boots.

Dustin had been asleep several hours and, a little after midnight, Dud complained of a sour stomach and left the antechamber to seek relief. Marcus played with the monkey for a while before ending up pacing listlessly in front of the windows.

She was angry with him, he knew it. He felt that if he could talk to her, reason with her, then mayhap she would see things clearly. He had spent the week of her infirmary convincing himself that loving Dustin de Lohr was a waste of energy, and vowed to move forward and put her from his mind. It was growing easier bit by bit, day by day, and he knew he would eventually be successful in chasing the woman from his mind. Already he could look at her without feeling the strange, fluttering sensation in his chest.

But he needed to speak with her to settle the air between them. With Christopher gone, he was alone with her and he wasn't sure when he would have another opportunity to talk to her, just the two of them. His courage rose and fell until finally, he bolstered the nerve to open the bedchamber door. He hoped she wouldn't be angry at him for waking her, but he felt strongly that he needed to do this.

She was curled up at the edge of the bed, and he could see that she was sleeping nude. Familiar feelings raced through his veins, but he stopped them angrily and moved forward toward the bed.

Bedclothes were bunched all around her, covering her most intimate parts but leaving little to the imagination. Marcus took a deep breath, trying to keep his mind on what he had come for. The room around them was pitch dark, the only faint light coming from the dying fire that hardly radiated beyond the hearth. Everything else was blackness as he knelt beside the bed.

He tried to speak her name but he choked. Trying again, he leaned close to her. "Dustin?"

She twitched a bit and he tried once more. "Dustin, wake up," he whispered.

She sighed deeply and stretched, and his mouth went agape as the bedclothes fell away from her magnificent breasts. Marcus almost staggered back. *Jesus, I shouldn't be here!* But he forced himself to stay. He had to talk to her, he admitted to himself, to ease his own conscience.

"Dustin?" he whispered smiling. " 'Tis me, Mar....."

Her arm suddenly snaked up and grabbed him around the neck, unbalancing him in his crouch so that he toppled over on her.

"You are back," she murmured sleepily, latching onto his earlobe. "I missed you."

Marcus' mind went into failure. Before he realized it, his arms were going about her, responding to her. He knew he should yank away from her, at least tell her who it was she was kissing, but he could not force the words from his mouth. Guilt exploded within him but at the same time, desire and lust such as he had never known flooded him like a wildfire and he ceased to think, like a rational, moral being. All he could think of was her, in his arms, as he had always wanted.

In his blind lust, he was rough with her. The fact that it was so dark in the room worked in his favor because she could not see who it was and he had yet to utter a word. His mouth was all over her, tasting, licking, sucking and she panted heavily in response to his less than gentle ministrations.

His clothes were coming off, she was helping him. When his broad, bare chest met with her peaked nipples, he groaned so low in his throat that he rattled his own teeth. Dustin laughed softly, pulling him against her.

He could not seem to touch her fast enough, every inch of her skin covered with his hands or his mouth. His lips suckled her nipples until they were raw, but she loved every moment of the sweet torture and Marcus' mind was a black void, neither feeling nor hearing anything but Dustin beneath his hands.

He forged a trail down her flat belly to her most intimate center, trying to be gentle with her but not being able to control his want or his shaking. When his mouth came to bear on the pink folds hidden behind the soft blond curls, Dustin nearly came off the bed with pure passion. Her fingers delved into his hair, pulling at it insistently as she encouraged him onward. His tongue was wild and wicked, driving her mad with sweet torture as he savagely orchestrated her taut little bud. His hands, his huge hands, never left her breasts.

His tongue probed her passage, tasting her with all of the hunger he had felt for her. He was beyond rationality, he knew exactly what he was doing and who he was doing it to, but he suddenly didn't care anymore. Had Christopher walked through the door at that moment, Marcus would have fought him to the death. Some things in this life were worth dying for, and she was one of them.

When he could stand it no longer, he shoved himself between her legs and drew her knees up, positioning his great shaft against her orifice. Dustin had him by the hair.

"Chris," she whispered. "We shouldn't do this. The midwife said...."

He cut her off by thrusting headlong into her, driving himself in the full long length and Dustin let escape a moan of utter rapture. Marcus was unstoppable; he drove in to her again and again, feeling her tightness like nothing else he had ever known, knowing indeed this would be the greatest mistake of his life but knowing in the same breath that he would die a contented man. He would live on this moment the rest of his life.

When he erupted, it was through clenched teeth in the greatest explosion of pleasure. He pulled Dustin to him fiercely, holding her with the most reverent of touches. He held her for the longest time, caressing her, kissing her beautiful hair, until he felt her relax and he knew she had fallen asleep.

He was already beyond the limits of safety, for Dustin's sake. She thought he was Christopher and would be entirely innocent of her husband's wrath, but wrath she would receive. The hardest thing Marcus ever had to do in his young life was let her go.

He dressed quietly, watching Dustin sleep peacefully, wondering if she would ever realize what had happened this night. He hoped that one day she would, and he furthermore hoped she wouldn't hate him for his weakness. But he had done more than taste her, he had feasted and for that, he would go to his grave satisfied.

He would never be rid of her now and it would slowly kill him to see her living her life with Christopher. There was only one way to be clear of her beautiful, face forever, as much, as the thought pained him. Yet for his sanity, he knew he must. But his moment in time with her would linger on him forever.

With a long glance, Marcus Burton quit the room.

CHAPTER TWENTY-NINE

CHRISTOPHER PACED THE floor of John's audience chamber calmly enough, but inside he was as cagey as a cat. He was almost frantic to know why John had called an audience of Richard's loyalists, he and the justices, and a few close advisors of the absent king. Yet even as he wondered, he knew the reason and his stomach tightened in response, word must have come about Richard. He didn't know why his instincts told him that, but he knew it just the same. All of the justices sat or stood in relative silence, waiting in the chill of the ornate audience hall, their minds riveted to the same thought, they knew why they were here, too.

William Marshal watched Christopher pace, his aged face creased with fatigue and worry this night. Whatever the reason they had been summoned, it could not be a good one and he would not let his concern show.

"Would you sit down, Chris? You are going to wear a hole in the damn floor," he said quietly.

Christopher eyed William, slowing his movement but not sitting. William raised an eyebrow at him.

"I realize that you believe sitting in John's presence is a sign of submission, but force yourself," he said with suppressed sarcasm, trying to lighten the mood a bit. "You are making me nervous."

Christopher continued to eye him doubtfully but did as the elder man asked and took a seat next to him. William relaxed back into his chair, eyeing Christopher's stiff body with faint amusement. He shook his head and smiled; Christopher hated John more than any of them, and for good reason, and was preparing to shoot to his feet the moment the prince entered the room. He might as well still be standing for all of the relaxing he was doing on his arse.

"Tell me, how is your wife?" William asked.

"Well, sire," Christopher replied. "Her appetite and vigor have returned, thankfully."

William nodded. "Well and good," he eyed Christopher. "Any thoughts on returning her to Lioncross?"

Christopher shrugged vaguely. "Thoughts, of course, but no action."

William nudged the big man with an elbow. "You'd miss her too much, wouldn't you?"

Christopher lifted his shoulders again, not meeting William's knowing gaze. "I'd rather have her here with me."

William laughed softly; Christopher was not a man to admit attachment to anything or anyone other than Richard, even though it was painfully obvious his wife had usurped their king in the Defender's heart. Yet before William could goad him further, a small door behind the throne swung open and Ralph marched through. He hadn't taken two steps when Christopher was on his feet, his huge body coiled with anticipation.

Everyone rose out of pure protocol when John entered the room, waving benevolently at the group of men and followed by his closest advisors. Christopher eyed the small group of seedy, shady characters, even if they were some of England's most noble blood. Bringing up the rear was none other than Sir Dennis le Londe.

He spied Christopher and gave him a wolfish sort of smile. Christopher met the expression with an unreadable face, wishing he could get the man alone just long enough to snap his neck like kindling. They never had gotten along, merely tolerated one another because they were fighting for a common cause. Dennis was a devotee of Philip Augustus, as passionate about his king as Christopher was for Richard. Since Richard and Philip Augustus despised each other, it was only natural for Christopher and Dennis to feel the same way. What had happened in the tournament had not increased Christopher's loathing, but simply reinforced it.

John took his seat, adjusting his robes as a woman would fuss over her surcoat. The justices sat and waited patiently while John deliberately stalled, conferring with various men around him before finally clearing his throat and facing the expectant throng.

"Loyal vassals of Richard," he began. "I am afraid 'tis bad news I must give you. I received word from the continent today regarding Richard's whereabouts and well-being and, I am sorry to say, the information is most disturbing."

Christopher braced himself mentally, not daring to glance at William Marshal but so wanting to. John continued.

"On December 12, Richard was captured by forces of Duke Leopold. He and Emperor Henry are holding our king hostage and the inclination seems to be that they will demand a ransom for him, a ransom I am sure we as a country cannot meet." He was relishing the open reaction of some of the justices. "As Richard's heir, 'twould seem that England would be mine in that case."

William rose beside Christopher, eyeing John with disbelief. "Is Richard well?"

"He is healthy and whole, as far as we are told," John replied without a hint of distress.

"Then ransom or not, sire, Richard is King of England until his demise," William said evenly.

"But England needs a king who is not being held prisoner," John said, trying to control the temper that threatened to flare.

"Richard cannot rule from a cell."

"Richard is king," William repeated. "The throne of England is his. And it is quite possible that we may deliver the requested ransom; has any amount been discussed yet?"

John's jaw ticked. "Nay, not yet," he replied quietly. "But surely it will be overwhelming and the royal coffers are already near to bone dry. There will be no way to pay it."

"Begging you pardon, sire, but how do you know?" William said. "Richard has many loyal, wealthy vassals and it is quite possible that the booty will be raised. Mayhap we should wait and see what Leopold and Henry demand before we draw any conclusions."

John was thoroughly agitated. Already the meeting was not favorable in his behalf, as he had hoped. William Longchamp, Richard's chancellor, suddenly bolted from his seat, wringing his hands behind his back.

"How dare they take Richard prisoner as if he were a common thief," he raged. "By what right do they possess the power to take our sovereign hostage?"

"They consider Richard a criminal, my lord, as you well know," William said steadily, hoping Longchamp would calm down and realize now was not the place for dissension amongst Richard's ranks. "We have known that for a long while now, yet it changes nothing. Leopold and Henry the Lion hold Richard and we must deal with them."

Christopher was surprisingly collected. He crossed his massive arms over his chest, listening to Marshal's voice of reason.

"Would an armed incursion be possible, my lord, were we to find out where they are holding him?" he asked William quietly.

"I will not allow it." John shot out of his chair, shaking his fist at Christopher. "You will not take an army into the empire to free my brother. Such acts could be deemed provocative and before we would realize it, we would be at war with the entire empire."

Christopher's gaze was cool on John. "We are already at war with Henry, so to speak," he said. "He has captured our king. Would you not consider that act the least bit provocative?"

John's mouth worked furiously. "No armed excursion, de Lohr. I forbid it."

"You cannot," Christopher responded flatly. "You have not the power. Only the justices can deny me."

The veins on John's neck bulged. "But I am the bloody prince and heir to the throne. 'Tis well within my royal right to approve or deny the use of crown monies and power."

"The troops are mine, as pursuant to Richard's decree," Christopher reminded him, wondering how long it was going to be before John was having seizures on the floor. "Your use of them is limited."

"They are crown property and I am the crown," John shot back. "But you are not king." How Christopher loved to say that.

"They are Richard's troops and he has given the responsibility to me in his absence. Why must we go over this, sire? You read the missive and know full well the royal appointment. 'Tis not up for discussion, and certainly not with me. I am simply following Richard's orders."

John was bordering on another fit and Ralph leaned closed to his liege, whispering in his ear until John visibly relaxed. All in the room watched as he regained his seat with mounting control over himself. He seemed to calm with amazing speed and Christopher wondered what in the hell Ralph said to him, but not really wanting to know.

"My brother will never leave captivity alive, you know," he said finally. "Philip is akin to this kidnapping and he and Henry want him dead, almost as badly as they want money. Mayhap they will decide that his death is more important to the good of the free world after all. 'Twill be interesting to see if there is a ransom demand at all."

A rapid change of attitude, no doubt to throw the justices off guard. Christopher raised an eyebrow at the prince, but William remained impassive.

"Mayhap, sire," he replied. "I suppose we will find out in due time. Was that all you wished to speak with us about?"

John stared back at William, mulling over the question, before letting out an ironic snort. "I should think it would be enough, yet you do not seem overly concerned. It is possible you care not what happens to your king or that you have become accustomed to running the country in his absence?"

William smiled wryly. "I both care what happens to our king and look forward to his return, sire. As do you."

They all knew the final three words to be a flat-out lie. John merely turned away, this meeting had not gone favorably in the least and he was eager to be done with it. He had expected outrage, pleading and cursing at the very least, but the seams of Richard's governing body were strong and showed no signs of deficiency. Informed of their lord's fate, they were now sure of his whereabouts and grimly determined to resolve it. John was not at all pleased with the show of strength, yet it did not mar his plans. He had an army waiting for him in Nottingham. He had hoped Richard's captivity would allow him a fairly bloodless route to the throne, but he could see that it was not going to happen.

So be it, then. He would take what was rightfully his by force. There would be no better opportunity.

He rose, signaling dismissal to the vassals. Christopher stood back and allowed the justices to file from the room, almost as if protecting their retreat from John's horde. Marshal was the last man from the room, and Christopher fell in behind him as a broad human shield. He wanted no surprises from the rear, and as unpredictable as John was, that was always a possibility.

"De Lohr!" came a heavily-accented call.

Christopher instantly knew who hailed him, turning with a stone stare to Sir Dennis. The man smiled amiably, but there was no mistaking the deadly glitter to his eyes.

"Your wife…is she well?" he asked, laced with venom.

Christopher felt his control slipping. "She is none of your concern, le Londe."

"Of course not, but my concern is genuine after her most unfortunate accident," the Frenchman said.

Christopher could not help the look of contempt that crossed his face. Without answering, he turned for the door once again and attempted to leave, but Sir Dennis was on his heels.

"What will happen to her, I wonder, if you take an army to rescue Richard?" he pondered thoughtfully. "If you were not to survive, I mean. She is most beautiful and…."

Christopher whirled around and grabbed Sir Dennis by the neck, slamming him with all of his power into the nearest wall. A framed tapestry crashed to the floor as William and a few other justices raced back into the room to control the Defender.

But Christopher was out of control; le Londe was a big man, but he was no match for the provoked husband. Christopher's face was red and his veins bulged as he held Sir Dennis like a cornered mouse.

"Wipe my wife from your mind, le Londe," he seethed, hearing William begging him to back off. "You will not look at her, nor speak of her, nor even think of her or so help me, by all that is holy, I will gut you like a pig to the spit."

Sir Dennis actually had the stupidity to smile. "Mon frère, your passion for your wife is touching, but misplaced in this case. I was simply voicing my concerns for her safety, nothing more."

Christopher went for his sword, halfway unsheathing it until William and the others grabbed hold of his arm and wouldn't allow him to remove it any further. His eyes were boring death into le Londe, and he was forced to release the hilt as Marshal and Longchamp pleaded urgently beside him; beseeching him to control himself. In a flash of sanity, Christopher reluctantly obeyed and let le Londe slip from his grip, although he knew not why he should release the man.

Sir Dennis adjusted his armor, not the least bit disturbed by Christopher's display and now quite confident that the way to destroy de Lohr had just been confirmed. With a sharp salute and an equally taunting smile, he disappeared through the door behind John's throne.

Richard's faithful watched him go, realizing they had a problem on their hands in the form of Lady Dustin de Lohr. If the woman could incite such behavior in her husband to the point of irrationality, then John could use that against them. De Lohr out of control was a terrifying sight to behold, and it had taken five of them to restrain him. And even that would not have been enough if he hadn't cooperated.

"Come on, Chris," William said, grabbing him around the neck and pulling him toward the door.

Christopher was shaken, tensed and angry that he flew at Sir Dennis so easily. He tried to tell himself that it would not happen again, but it was lie. The words of the mummer came floating back to him, their inane songs and dance making sense to his furious mind. Dustin was indeed his Achilles heel, and now everyone knew it. He should have been embarrassed, but he found he was not. She was his wife and he would let all know he would kill without hesitation where she was concerned.

The faithful of Richard marched down the darkened corridor with not a word spoken between them. At the end of the hall where it branched off, all of the men took their leave with the exception of Longchamp, Marshal, and Christopher. Marshal dismissed the others with a promised meeting to further discuss the subject come dawn, giving everyone time to mull over the situation in their own mind and come to grips with it. At the moment, he wished to discuss the predicament with Richard's two most trusted men.

Longchamp's apartments were the closest. The three men settled themselves in, with heavy doses of fine burgundy going around. By this time Christopher was in control again and waited patiently for William to speak.

"My gentle men," he began softly. " 'Twould seem that we have problem."

Christopher thought he meant him until the chancellor piped up. "Richard was a fool to leave the safety of his ship and take to the continent," Longchamp grumbled. "What on earth possessed the man?"

"Pirates, bad weather, who can say?" William replied. "Richard never was fond of the sea. But what is done is done, and we must think of a way to return our king to England."

"Queen Eleanor would know of this, sire," Christopher said, focusing on William. "Being French, she must carry some weight with Philip."

William shook his head. "They despise her, too, Chris, you know that. She is nearly as powerful as the king with all of her holdings. Nay, we will notify Eleanor, but I am afraid she will be of no use in gaining her son's release."

The silence that filled the room was heavy and still. Christopher finished off his wine and poured him and Longchamp another goblet.

"Do you think John knows where they are holding him?" Christopher asked.

"I would tend to doubt it, considering the man never could keep a secret," William replied. "If he knew, he would have told us."

"The little bastard," Longchamp growled. "He sees this as his golden opportunity to seize the throne. There's no telling what he shall do now."

"My informants tell me that he has moved his mercenary army north," Christopher said. "Away from London and away from me."

"North where?" Longchamp demanded. "York? Durham?"

Christopher shook his head. "Nay, not that far north. Besides, his brother, Geoffrey, is in York and they loathe the mere sight of each other. My guess is Nottingham, mayhap even planning to shield the troops in Sherwood Forrest."

"Sherwood is haunted, everyone knows that," Longchamp spat out, as if Christopher were a moron. "The men will not go near it no matter how much John pays them."

"Nottingham Castle is large enough to conceal a mighty army," Marshal murmured thoughtfully. "Besides, Fitz Walter's uncle is lord of the keep."

Christopher's face went hard and both men immediately remembered the exchange earlier in the evening.

"Your wife is indeed Ralph's cousin?" William asked softly.

"Aye," Christopher nodded his head, running his fingers though his hair with irritation. " 'Tis all my fault, really. She told me her grandsire lived in Nottingham when we were first married but I never pursued the thought. I was too caught up with my own problems. Now I find out the hard way that my wife's grandsire is Ralph's uncle."

"Has Lady Dustin ever met her grandfather?" Longchamp asked.

"Nay, never, and she never will," Christopher said firmly. "Dustin told me of things that the man did to her mother… vile things. She's never going near the place."

William shook his head with regret after a moment. "How is it that all of the Fitz Walter men are so foul? Ralph's father, 'tis said, had a taste for human flesh. Is there nothing more despicable than that? 'Tis no wonder why Ralph is as evil as he is."

Christopher sat down, beginning to feel his fatigue. "And yet Lady Mary, Dustin's mother, was the very epitome of feminine grace and manners, a true lady," he said softly. " 'Tis still hard to believe such a woman was bred of Lucifer's loins."

"All of the Fitz Walter men are Lucifer in the flesh," Longchamp said with a sneer. "Yet your wife must take after her mother – a lovely and refined lady she is."

Christopher smiled for the first time. "Lovely, yes, but she is certainly not the gentle soul her mother was," he said. "She takes after Arthur and his family, I think, though at times I have wondered if she is not the devil's spawn."

"Arthur descended from King Harold, didn't he?" William rubbed his chin thoughtfully. "A punchy man, but hardly the devil. Now William the Bastard; now, *there* was a devil."

"My ancestor came over the channel with Duke William, his top general, I might add," Christopher said softly. "But my family's roots are German and French, from the continent, although my mother was from the house of du Reims. My uncle, her brother, was the Earl of East Anglia."

William's eyes suddenly grew soft, catching Christopher's attention. He thought he caught a flash of emotion in the faded depths, but it was quickly gone. "What?" he demanded softly of the marshal.

William glanced at Christopher, a bit embarrassed at his display of feeling. " 'Tis nothing, really," he said, shrugging. "You did know that I knew your mother, didn't you?"

"Aye," Christopher said evenly. "Uncle Philip told me you were in love with my mother, once."

William grinned. "Once, many years ago," he said. "I was newly knighted at the time and your mother, God rest her soul, was part of a fighting force I was attached to. Never did I see a lovelier woman, Christopher. Skin as pure as cream, hair like a golden fire. Aye, Val du Reims was indeed a beauty." He finally drew up a chair. "But she did not even know I existed, especially after dashing Myles de Lohr came on the scene. Lord, your father was an imposing sight."

Christopher gazed at William steadily, impassively listening to the man reflect. "I lost both of my parents when I was fourteen years old, and David was ten," he said softly. "I was squiring at Derby, as was my brother. I had been a page there since I was six, so I remember very little of my mother. But I remember her giddy laugh and her endless affection towards David and me. We were the only survivors of five births, you know, with Deborah being the last."

William reflected on Val de Lohr, the woman who had been allowed to fight like a knight, and was a very good one, until she married Myles de Lohr. De Lohr had put an end to his fighting wife rather quickly.

"Your mother passed away when Deborah was very young, as I recall," William said quietly.

Christopher nodded. "My parents were quite old when I was born, and older still when David and Deborah were born," he said, thinking back. "My mother passed away when Deborah was less than a year old and my father passed away shortly after her. A fatal disease, the physic told us. 'Twas a malady of the lungs that took them both. Fortunately, the physic spirited Deborah away before she could catch it. She was raised in Bath."

"I remember hearing of the tragic circumstances," William replied quietly, his eyes warm with remembrance. "Aye, Val de Lohr will always remain the most beautiful woman I ever had the fortune to gaze upon. You remind me a great deal of her, actually. Sometimes when you smile, I see her. David is a duplicate of your father, I think."

Christopher shrugged, sitting back in his chair. "I would hope so. My father was a great knight."

"He was indeed, Chris, he was indeed," William agreed passionately. "You must forgive me for wandering. We are far from the subject at hand."

"Indeed we are," Longchamp interjected with a bit of sarcasm. "Let's return to Richard, shall we?"

Christopher glanced at the taciturn man. Longchamp was bitter, stubborn and aggressive and Christopher held little like for the man other than he was able to deal with John on the prince's own level.

"My apologies, my lord," he said, not meaning it. "As for Richard, mayhap it would be best to wait until we receive word from Leopold as to his demands. Truthfully, there is nothing more we can do until we have more information."

"Chris is right," William agreed, yawning. "We must play the waiting game and send word to Eleanor in the interim."

Longchamp drained his glass and set it down heavily. "I must say, you are all being rather calm about the whole thing," he said.

"Richard is being held captive and neither of you barely raise your voice. Are you truly unconcerned or is it a grand act for John's sake? Well?"

"What would you have us do, William?" Marshal asked. "Scream? Rage? Shout to the rooftops that Leopold and the Lion will suffer greatly for their acts? We knew Richard was in danger and have already had time to accept it; now we finally know the result of the danger. 'Tis not a matter of remaining calm, but of keeping a clear head to better deal with events. But you are correct in your assessment that we remain collected for John's sake; unfortunately, the man is gaining advantage as we speak and I will allow him no opportunity to exploit our weaknesses. Whatever happens, we must remain strong and united or Richard's throne is lost."

Longchamp's agitated gaze visibly relaxed. "You are right, of course," he said with resignation, rising. "Then it would seem we should retreat for the remainder of the night and see what the morrow brings. I will call the justices together after the morning meal and we will continue this conversation to include them."

Christopher was up, moving for the door, his mind rapidly moving from Richard to Dustin. "Then good sleep to you, my lords."

"Sleep well, Chris," Marshal said after him.

With the Defender gone, Longchamp faced Marshal.

"Will he survive this?" he asked softly.

William shrugged. "He's the best knight who has ever lived, William, and we are mightily fortunate that he fights for Richard. But John will try to seize the throne by force, and Christopher will be compelled to defend his king's holdings." He sighed wearily, feeling older than his years. "I hope he survives whatever John is planning, for with Christopher gone we will be hard-pressed to defend ourselves."

"Civil war is imminent, William, we both know that," Longchamp said flatly.

"I know." Marshal turned a distant gaze out of the grand windows in Longchamp's antechamber, smelling the freshness that was his beloved England. He had served two kings, knowing his service had aged him beyond his years. Yet his duties had been administrative for the most part, not field oriented as

Christopher's were. As hard as the justices worked to maintain Richard's throne, it was nothing compared to the physical toll the Defender was in for. The governing body would make the decisions from a comfortable chair, and Christopher would enforce them with a thirty pound blade in his massive hand.

William had lived a full life. He wondered if Christopher de Lohr would do the same.

CHAPTER THIRTY

WHEN CHRISTOPHER RETURNED to his apartments, he was satisfied to see that the soldiers he had positioned in the hall were making a good show of strength. When they heard Christopher's bootfalls approach, without seeing his face first in the darkness, they made a calculating and intimidating show of force. But once they realized the intruder was their liege, they resumed their posts in the dimness of the corridor. Feeling confident in the protection he had lodged in the corridor, Christopher entered his apartments.

The antechamber was dark when he entered, smelling of smoke and rushes. Dud was sitting near the fire, half asleep, as Christopher shut the door and bolted it. Startled, Dud bolted to his feet with his hand on the hilt of his weapon.

"Easy," Christopher admonished, holding up a quieting hand. " 'Tis only me. But it could have been a swarm of cutthroats. You know better than to sleep on duty."

Dud was embarrassed. "Too much wine this evening," he offered weakly. "Truly, I was not asleep but I wish I were."

Christopher fought off a grin, motioning to the door. "Go, then, you old woman," he said. "I will… wait a moment; where is Marcus? I left him here with you."

Dud was already heading to the door. "Aye, you did," he said, "but he disappeared about an hour ago. I went to use the privy and when I returned, he was gone."

Christopher's brow furrowed. "Gone?" he repeated. "He left?"

"Aye, my lord."

Christopher went from puzzled to annoyed. "He left Dustin alone?"

Dud didn't want to incriminate Marcus and he shrugged weakly. "He must have had a very good reason, my lord," he said. "He would not have simply left without one."

Christopher was angry. He went to the bedchamber door, opening it quietly and peering in. It was so dark that he had to step into the chamber and lean over the bed in order to see his wife sleeping soundly. Satisfied she was whole, he went back out into the antechamber and quietly shut the door.

"Go and find Marcus," he snapped softly. "Tell him that I want to see him."

"Now, my lord?"

Christopher was gruff. "Tomorrow at sunrise he had better be on my doorstep," he said. "And tell him if I have to go hunting for him, he will be in a greater mess than he already is."

Dud knew that Marcus was in for a row from the look on Christopher's face. He also knew better than to argue. Nodding smartly, he quit the antechamber and shut the door behind him.

Christopher bolted the door behind the man, wondering what in the hell Marcus was thinking to have left Dustin unprotected. Retreating to the bedchamber, he went inside and softly shut the door.

It was so dark that he stumbled into the bedframe and stubbed his toe, biting off a curse as he quietly removed his clothing. Or, at least, he thought he was doing it quietly; he ended up hitting his elbow on the wardrobe and muffling a groan. He took his boots off and was removing his breeches when he heard Dustin stir.

"You are loud enough to wake the dead," she said sleepily. "Hurry and get into bed before you end up breaking something."

He grinned in the darkness although she couldn't see it. "I think I broke my arm against the wardrobe."

"That is not an illustrious injury for a man of your stature," she giggled. "Tell people you broke it fighting off one hundred angry men."

He snorted and felt his way to the bed. "I will make up a good story, have no doubt," he said as he fell onto the mattress and pulled the covers up. "I am sincerely sorry to have awoken you."

Dustin snuggled against him as he settled in. "Twice in one night," she murmured. "At least it was worth it the first time. I wonder if it will be worth it again."

He pulled her up against his chest, settling down for sleep. "Twice?" he repeated. "What do you mean?"

Dustin's eyes were closed, already half-asleep. "Do not tell me you have forgotten already," she muttered. "How could you?"

"Forget what?"

His chest was next to her face and she kissed him softly. "Now do you remember?"

"Remember what?"

She put her hand on his thigh, moving across it seductively until she came to his flaccid manhood. She gripped it, gently but firmly, and began to stroke him.

"This," she whispered, kissing him again. "Shall we go a second time tonight?"

Her hand to his manhood instantly inflamed him but he put his hand on hers, stopping her from working him into a frenzy.

"I have no idea what you are talking about," he whispered, kissing the top of her head, "but you know as well as I do that we cannot do anything for six more weeks. The midwife said so."

She laughed softly. "That is not what you said earlier."

"I was not *here* earlier," he said, shaking his head. "Sweetheart, whatever you think we may or may not have done, you must have been dreaming. Pity; I would have liked to have joined you."

Dustin's eyes opened, staring out into the darkness. Her head came up. "You do not have to deny it," she said. "I will not tell the midwife, I promise."

He could barely see her silhouette against the backdrop of the dying fire. "Sweetheart, I swear that you were dreaming."

"I was not!"

"Aye, you were," he said, reaching up to pull her down against him. "There is no shame in a vividly erotic dream. It happens all of the time."

"It does *not* happen to me," she insisted, although she let him pull her down to him again. "Chris, you were here. We made love. Do you truly not remember any of it?"

Christopher was growing amused. His wife was having hot and sexual dreams and refused to admit it. He hugged her tightly.

"If I said I remembered, will you go back to sleep?" he asked.

Dustin could sense that he was laughing at her and she was not humored in the least. "Why are you laughing?" she demanded. " 'Tis not funny at all."

He started chuckling, then. "I am flattered," he purred, his hands moving down to caress her naked buttocks but just as quickly pulling away. "I thought men were the only ones who dreamed of sex."

"I did *not* dream of sex."

"Admit it. You did."

She was pouting now, torn between knowing what happened but now perhaps thinking it did not happen at all. More than that, she was confused. Was it really possible to have such dreams? Shifting against her husband, she could smell his familiar musky scent mingled with the faint smell of sandalwood. Christopher had soap that smelled of sandalwood that he had brought back from the Holy Land, and the scent reminded her strongly of him. It was soothing and comforting, and she began to calm down.

Perhaps he was right, after all. Perhaps she had only dreamt it. As she settled against him and sighed with contentment, her nose itched and she brought up a hand to scratch it. As she did so, she caught a whiff of pine. It was strong and distinctive, unexpected in this safe haven of their bed chamber for one very good reason; Marcus smelled of pine.

Dustin's eyes flew open and her heart began to thump against her ribs. She sniffed her hand again, discreetly, and was again assaulted by the smell of pine. Growing increasingly confused, perhaps frightened, she carefully rolled over, away from Christopher, so that they were spooning. It also gave her a chance to smell her arms, which also seemed to have the faint scent of pine on them. A distinct sense of foreboding swept her.

"Chris?" she whispered.

He was nearly asleep. "Aye?"

"Where...," she began, stammered, and then started again. "Where were you tonight?"

He yawned. "Attending business," he said vaguely. "Why do you ask?"

She didn't want to tell him. Not in a million years did she want to tell him, but she had to know something first. She struggled to be clever about it.

"Was David here as my protection?" she wanted to know.

He sighed faintly, sleepily. "He was not," he replied. "Dud and Marcus were left to protect you."

So Marcus *had* been here. Dustin felt sick all over, thinking about what Christopher had referred to as her dream, remembering it in such detail that she knew it had not, in fact, been a dream. She remembered every touch, every sensation, and every move and, in hindsight, she should have realized something was different about it. The more she remembered, the sicker she became.

It had been so very dark in the room when he had appeared. He had whispered and she had naturally assumed it to be Christopher. Who else would have come into their bedchamber? She had been half asleep and happy to see him, and had pulled him into bed with her. Christopher, or more correctly, Marcus had never said a word. He had simply ripped his clothes off and made wild and passionate love to her.

His touch had been electric, almost brutal, but she had loved every minute of it. It had been exciting beyond words. It was as if...as if there had been no love involved whatsoever and they were acting on animal instincts. When he had mounted her, it had been with power and brutality and when he had climaxed, it had been with the instincts of a rutting bull. No real emotion, but simply blind and crazed attraction.

Oh, Lord, she thought with horror. She could smell the pine on her body, reminding her every second of the horror of her unknowing infidelity. Her stomach lurched and the tears came, and she threw herself out of bed and slammed around in the darkness, searching for the water basin. She could hear Christopher behind her, wanting to know what the matter was, as she found the basin purely by touch and vomited into it.

Dustin continued to vomit even as Christopher climbed out of bed and put his hands on her soothingly, pulling her hair out of the way so it would not get soiled. His soft words and gentle hands threw her into hysterics that she could not explain away. All Christopher knew was that she was ill and he wanted to send for a physic but she would not let him. She allowed him to help her back into bed and cover her up, where she quickly fell into a fitful sleep.

It wasn't a dream, was her last coherent thought. *Oh, God, it wasn't a dream!*

Dustin remained in bed, sick and distraught, for nearly a week.

CHAPTER THIRTY-ONE

THE NEW YEAR came and went. The justices had sent two envoys to see to Richard's well-being and to see to negotiations with Henry and Philip Augustus. While they were waiting for news on that front, Christopher's spies informed him that, indeed, John and his mercenary army were holed up at Nottingham Castle and that it appeared the troops were preparing to mobilize. Toward the end of January, Christopher began to mobilize his own troops in anticipation of John's first move.

Marcus had disappeared the night of Dustin's vomiting fit and no one had been able to find him. A month of worry and fear went by as to his whereabouts. As a last resort, Christopher sent a messenger to Somerhill on the chance that Marcus had retreated to his new holdings and the messenger was fortunate enough to lay eyes upon Burton himself. But the new baron was taciturn and inhospitable, and would not allow the messenger into his fortress. So the messenger returned to London with the news, and Christopher began bombarding Somerhill with missives and messengers.

But Marcus had yet to respond to Christopher's missives and ignored all of Christopher's pleas to return to London. Christopher was at a loss to understand the man's behavior and would have liked to go north himself and beat the stubborn man to a pulp, but he could not risk leaving London with John preparing to strike. Moreover, he would have to pass fairly close to Nottingham to gain his way north to Marcus' keep and he would not hazard the possibility of getting captured or cornered by John's buffoons. But he simply could not understand Marcus' attitude, nor did he have the time to decipher it. Either Marcus was with him, or he wasn't, and he was deeply saddened and puzzled that it was most likely the latter.

Marcus' absence cast a dark shadow over Christopher and his knights, for they all felt as if a piece of the puzzle was missing. Although no one knew for sure why Marcus had deserted them without a word, they suspected it had something to do with Dustin. No one voiced their opinions, not even to themselves, but they were all of the same belief. There was no animosity towards her, for there was nothing to be bitter about since Marcus' decision was his own, but each man wished that Marcus would come to his senses and forget about the woman.

Dustin, of course, had put him completely out of her mind. He didn't exist to her as far as she was concerned and she was happy he was gone. Her focus, love, and attention was solely on her husband, fearful if she didn't keep him completely in her thoughts and mind, her guilt would consume her. Although she hadn't knowingly responded to Marcus, still, that night of passion those weeks ago had wracked her with turmoil. She loved her husband with all that she was, and Marcus had been persistent in threatening to destroy that. She hoped she never saw the man again.

'Twas the beginning of February, bleak and cold. Dustin had seen very little of her husband for the past several days. She and Deborah would busy themselves as much as possible and they were even allowed a good deal of freedom to roam the castle now that John was vacated, but still, Dustin missed Christopher terribly. Yet she had grown a little in her time at Windsor, and she knew something was in the air without her husband even telling her. She'd never seen a battle, nor even been near one, but she knew that Christopher was preparing the crown troops for a big clash with the prince.

True, she'd heard all of the rumors there were to hear. It would seem that every gossip at Windsor always ran to her with the latest to discover if she could confirm or deny anything, which she never could because Christopher rarely told her anything. In spite of the fact that her husband was closed-lipped about his affairs, she had learned a great deal about what was transpiring. It never seemed to be the right time to question him about anything when he returned to her at the end of the day because they saw each other so infrequently that she did not want to waste her time with him on rumors and gossip.

This particularly icy night he returned to their apartments unusually fatigued. His face was chapped and red from the weather and his brow seemed to be permanently furrowed. Dustin, dressed in a luscious robe of pale yellow silk, tried to make sure his meal was perfect, but even that didn't seem to snap him out of his mood. He ate silently, only speaking to insist she sit on his lap the entire meal.

His moods were growing darker and darker these days, just like the weather. Dustin played with his hair as he ate, her eyes raking over him appreciatively. She found herself living her day around him, his face always on her mind, and the taste of him on her lips. She fully realized that the fiercely independent Lady Dustin Barringdon had become the highly dependent Lady de Lohr, but she didn't care. She lived for him, and only for him.

"I want to show you something," she suddenly bound off his lap, hoping to cheer him up. "Watch Hal."

Obediently, the medium-sized dog came trotting out of the bedchamber. Harold had become quite attached to Christopher and he, strangely enough, found himself attached to the stocky mutt with the big jaw. The animal was also inordinately strong and protective, and he was verily pleased to have him protecting his wife. No one could get within a few feet of Dustin without Hal barring his huge teeth.

"Now, watch," Dustin said, snatching George from where he was enjoying a piece of fruit on top of a small table, and set the monkey on Harold's back. With a nudge, Harold trotted off with George clutching the dog's neck, looking like a miniature horse and rider. Dustin giggled gleefully as Harold rounded the room with George perched stiffly on his back.

Christopher wiped his hands on a cloth and smiled wearily at the trick. "I shall have a saddle made for him at once," he said. "George looks positively terrified on his bare back."

Harold stopped in front of Christopher and wagged his tail, accepting with relish the tidbit Christopher tossed to him. Then, with George still clinging to his back, he trotted off into the bedchamber once more.

"Is that what you have been doing with your time? Saddle-breaking my dog?" he asked.

Dustin always thought it funny when he referred to Harold as "my" dog. For a man who wanted nothing to do with the pups, he had changed his mind fast enough when he discovered the animals could be beneficial.

"What else am I to do? I have been bored out of my mind with you gone all of the time," she said, sauntering back over to him and curling up on his massive lap. "I have missed you terribly, husband."

He wound his arms around her torso. "I know, and I have missed you, too. But I have been very busy."

"And very secretive," she said, instantly sorry she had. She hadn't meant to sound as if she were prying. "I am sorry, I didn't mean that."

"I have not been secretive on purpose," he said. " 'Tis just that I have been extremely busy and when I see you, I do not want to talk about the trivia of the day. I want to talk about you, about us. What did you do today?"

Dustin shrugged. "Nothing much. Deborah and I went for a walk about the grounds, but that was all," she said, suddenly perking up. "I nearly forgot. I saw the Earl of Fenwark today across the courtyard. Do you suppose Lady Gabrielle is with him?"

He gave her a reproving look. "I thought we agreed about Lady Gabrielle, Dustin."

She pursed her lips. "I know, I know, but with the prince gone from Windsor, I thought well, I'd hoped…."

He shook his head. "Sorry, sweet, 'tis no good. Remember what happened to Lady Gabrielle the last time you two met."

She swallowed, indeed remembering the woman's bruises. Then, she shrugged again. "I did like her, Chris. She was a nice lady."

He kissed her cheek soundly and stood up, depositing her on the floor gently. "I know, but you have Deborah now to keep you company. You'd better forget about Lady Gabrielle altogether."

He removed the last of his leg armor and stretched with exhaustion. His heavy linen shirt landed on the floor for the maids to wash and Dustin found her want for him rising as she watched him strip off his clothes. It had been over six weeks since her accident and, true to his word, he had not touched her. But she could stand it no longer; tonight, all of that would change.

She followed him into the bedchamber, closing the door softly behind them. Harold and Alex were curled up in front of the hearth, sleeping, as he passed by them and to the large basin. As he washed himself, his glorious back to her, Dustin let the robe fall to the floor and, nude, slipped under the coverlets. She had been planning this evening all day, having taken a leisurely bath and washed her hair earlier. Clean and smelling like a bed of roses, she hoped it was enough to entice him out of his fatigue. The longer she waited, the more she began to tremble with anticipation.

He came over to the bed, drying his face with a linen towel. "Why are you in bed already? I thought we might play a game of Fox and Hounds."

She raised a slow, provocative eyebrow at him and suddenly threw back the covers, revealing her luscious body to him in the soft light. "I thought we might play a different game."

He froze, staring at her beautiful shape. "It has been seven weeks, hasn't it? Christ, I'd lost count after the first two for it seemed like an endless eternity." The towel went sailing and his breeches were already half-off; it was miraculous how his fatigue suddenly disappeared. "Are you sure, sweetheart? Are you up to this?"

She reached up and pulled him down even as he struggled to free his feet from his breeches. "More than up to it, husband. I want you to make love to me all night."

The breeches were off and his lips were on hers, his exhaustion vanished at the warm softness of her flesh. She moaned in response as his huge hands latched onto her breasts, giggling against his fervent lips and he smiled as he kissed her eagerly.

Truth was, with everything on his mind, he had nearly forgotten about the sweetest thing a man could taste; his very own wife. He thought he had banked his urges quite well until he saw her nude form in front of him; then, it was as if he had no control whatsoever.

He was trying to be gentle, to pace himself but, Christ, he wanted her so badly he found himself being rough. Yet Dustin didn't complain; in fact, she encouraged him and even yanked his hair cruelly as he suckled a nipple, causing him to raise his head up and she descended urgently on his lips with her own strong drive. The rougher he became, the more she liked it.

Suddenly she rolled him over on his back, her hot little lips blazing a scorching trail all over his broad chest, peaking his nipples with her tongue and grunting with pleasure the whole while. He groaned with his own satisfaction as she moved down his abdomen before closing on his engorged organ with relish. Yet he could stand no more than a second or two of her ministrations; winding his fingers in her wild hair, he pulled on her hard enough to bring a scream to her lips.

He was fearful that he had been too rough, but his fear turned to overwhelming lust and desire when he saw her gazing up at him with a grin to seduce God himself. He'd never known his wife to enjoy brutality in their lovemaking but, Christ, he was loving it, too.

Dustin was on her back before she realized it, whispering words of encouragement as he fell atop her and positioned his great shaft at her threshold. He was trying to be gentle, but she simply would not allow lt. He knew it was likely to pain her a great deal when he entered her, but her legs were wrapping themselves around his thighs and he could feel how slippery she was, throwing him over the edge into oblivion. As Dustin told him in no uncertain terms what she wanted him to do to her, Christopher coiled his rock-hard buttocks and drove into his wife like a great battering ram.

Dustin cried out with the thrill of pleasure-pain, her nails digging crescent-shaped wounds into the flesh of his arse. He was unstoppable, thrusting into her hard enough to rattle her teeth, feeling her tightness enclosed over him, so pleasurable it was painful.

She rose to meet his every thrust, crying out his name and begging him to move harder, swifter, and hotter. He was absolutely mad with his wife, filling every corner of his mind until nothing else in the world existed but her. His plunges became more forceful, his hands squeezing her breasts, the sweat of his body mingling with hers until he finally climaxed in a great searing blast of convulsions. He heard her soft screaming pants and he knew she had achieved her own pleasure, their pulsing muscles interacting with each other, responding one to the other. The warm glow that was descending on them was almost visible.

He held her tightly, not withdrawing, overwhelmed with the passion between them. Never had he made love to a woman with such blind desire and force, and he found he was actually astonished with the drive they shared. The seven weeks had been well worth the wait to have it peak in such a glorious fashion.

"Dustin de Lohr," he growled into her ear. "You are a reckless, wanton wench."

She pulled her head up, smiling through her tousled hair. "You make me that way, husband. I have been dreaming of your magnificent body for seven long weeks."

"I know, you told me six weeks ago," he teased her. "Was this more wonderful than your dream?"

Dustin was suddenly struck with the remembrance of Marcus. Lord, she'd almost forgotten and inadvertently Christopher caused all of the pain and guilt and confusion to flood over her again. But she was strong and fought it for all she was worth. She threw her arms around his neck tightly, hoping if she held on firmly enough, that Marcus' memory could not disturb her.

"More wonderful than anything in this world," she whispered fervently. "Promise me it will always be like this, Chris."

"If I have anything to say about it, it will," he kissed her cheek. "You are choking me, sweet."

She loosened her grip but didn't let him go, laying her head back to look him in the eye. His gaze was loving and warm, drinking in her face just as she was devouring his.

"You are going away, aren't you?" she whispered after a moment.

He blinked at the rapid change of subject. "Where did you hear that?"

"Do not be evasive with me. I have heard the rumors, I know John has a large army and is preparing to strike King Richard's holdings, holdings which you will have to defend." She ran her fingers through his hair. "When are you leaving?"

She could see his expression become unguarded. "Dustin…."

"Please tell me," she begged. "I am not a silly, simpering female who will fall into swoons like a weakling. Just be honest with me, Chris, *please*. I want to know when I will be losing you so I can prepare myself."

After a moment he reached out and stroked the stray hairs away from her face, tracing a finger over her lower lip. "I do not know exactly when," his voice was hoarse. "But soon. Mayhap within the next week or so."

Dustin suddenly felt like crying, but she had promised to be strong. Her sweet Christopher fighting against the evil bastard John, possibly dying for a king who had never actually ruled England from English soil, angered her to the point of madness. But she had promised to be strong, and she intended to keep that promise. Even if it killed her.

"Are you going north to Nottingham?" she asked. "My grandsire is housing John's troops, is he not?"

He nodded slowly, kissing her hand. "He is, and north we will ride when John moves."

"Are you taking David and Edward and Leeton?" she asked.

"I must," he replied. "And Marcus, too, if I can ever get through to the man."

Dustin was glad Marcus was gone. It was much easier for her to recover without having to deal with his face every day, and without having to face an additional level of guilt. If he were gone it was easier to pretend nothing ever happened.

"Marcus' keep is far north of Nottingham," Christopher was saying. " 'Twould be a good thing to launch an attack against John from two fronts, me from the south and Marcus from the north. But Nottingham is so damned fortified, we must wait until we know John is moving his army from the protective walls. 'Tis the only way to destroy him – out in the open."

Moving off the subject of Marcus, Dustin's guilt shifted to her grandfather, a man she had never even met, and his loyalty to John's cause. She wondered if Christopher blamed her somehow for causing so much grief.

"I am sorry," she whispered.

"For what?"

"For my grandsire's evil nature, for helping John," she said softly. "Lord, Chris, Ralph is my cousin. Doesn't that make you angry or repulsed?"

He shrugged. "Why should it? You cannot choose your relatives, sweetheart, and you certainly are not responsible for bloodlines."

"I consider you a noble Barringdon, Dustin, not a Fitz Walter."

"I am a de Lohr," she whispered.

He grinned. "Aye, you are, aren't you?"

They kissed sweetly, lingeringly. Kisses of love grew into kisses of desire and they made love until the dawn.

CHAPTER THIRTY-TWO

CHRISTOPHER LEFT SHORTLY after the sun rose for the troop field. Dustin slept until mid-morning, rising happy and full of spirit. She took a quick bath with rosewater and dressed in a heavy surcoat of pale blue silk with the cross Christopher gave her being the only piece of jewelry she wore. Her mood was light and gay and the maids kept passing her giddy glances as they went about their daily routines.

Deborah joined her later, excitedly telling her that she had heard rumor that a merchant from Venice was in the forecourt and suggesting they go down to see his wares. Having nothing else to do, Dustin agreed.

With the weather being so miserable outside, several merchants were moved into the lower foyer of Windsor. There was no mistaking the merchant from Venice, dozens of women were ogling over his wares and bolts and bolts of exquisite material were stacked in neat rows.

Deborah immediately delved into the material while Dustin sniffed at the vials of perfume. Deborah eagerly asked Dustin's opinion of several fabrics and colors, but Dustin would merely shrug, Deborah knew much more of fashion and taste than she. While Deborah began to barter with the merchant, Dustin lost interest in the perfumes and turned her attention to the people who were filling the foyer and grand hall. From the corner of her eye, she spied the Earl of Fenwark several feet away inspecting feminine goods.

Dustin watched the average-sized man pass an eye over the wares, wondering hopefully if Lady Gabrielle was with him. But he seemed to be quite alone and Dustin found her courage to go and ask him of his wife; after all, Christopher never actually saw the earl beat his wife, so therefore he could only speculate about her bruises and the reason behind them. Mayhap he as wrong. And since Dustin hadn't talked to Lady Gabrielle since their first meeting, she could simply pretend she hadn't seen the bruises on the countess. Christopher would be angry she had disobeyed him, but she wanted to try and speak with the earl for the sake of Lady Gabrielle.

She walked right up to the earl and curtsied deeply. When she rose, she noticed his scrutinizing gaze on her.

"My lord earl," she said. "I am Lady Dustin de Lohr; I believe you know my husband. I saw you had come to Windsor yesterday and wondered if your wife had accompanied you. She and I met at the tournament in October and I enjoyed her and the Lady Isobelle very much."

The earl was impassive and rather cold. "She did not accompany me, Lady de Lohr, for good reason. My wife passed away after Christmas."

Dustin was shocked. She took a step back from the earl, her hand going to her throat in an unconscious gesture. "Oh....my lord, please accept my condolences," she stammered helplessly. "I am...I am speechless, sire, truly. Was she taken suddenly ill?"

His lip twitched in a most frightening manner, disturbing Dustin all the more. "Nay, my lady," he said. "She fell down a flight of stairs and broke her neck. Now, if you will excuse me."

He pushed past her as if she were a leper, leaving Dustin coming to grips with her dismay and sadness. She watched him move toward the merchant from Venice, saying something to his aide and then laughing merrily with the man. His callous attitude and stone-cold manner turned her heartache in to growing anger.

Deborah saw her sister-in-law's face and quickly moved to intercept her before Dustin said or did anything rashly.

"Let's go, Dustin," she said steadily. "I have what I want."

"Did you hear him?" Dustin seethed. "His wife is dead and he cares not a lick."

"I heard him." Deborah was growing nervous, she was not nearly strong enough to control Dustin if she went into a rage. "I am tired. Let's go back to the apartments. Please?"

Dustin started to nod her head when she caught sight of Lady Isobelle several feet behind the earl. Without a word to Deborah, she pushed through the shoppers toward the fat woman.

"Lady Isobelle," she curtsied quickly. "I am Lady Dustin de Lohr, I met you and Lady Gabrielle at...."

Lady Isobelle's eyes fell on Dustin with alarm, then quickly banked. "Of course I know you, Lady Dustin," she said quietly. "Please; you mustn't...."

Dustin ignored the woman, bent on finding out more about her friend's death. "What happened to Lady Gabrielle?" she asked. "Her husband said she fell down the stairs?"

Lady Isobelle's cheeks flushed and she kept glancing nervously at her brother, who happened to be facing away with his back to her. She took out her handkerchief and fanned her face. "Aye, she fell," she stammered. "There was... she was dead before she hit the floor."

Dustin's face went gentle with sympathy. "I am so sorry, Lady Isobelle. She was a very nice lady and I am sorry she is dead."

Lady Isobelle nodded shortly and whirled away from Dustin, thrusting herself through the crowd blindly. It seemed to Dustin that she was desperate to get away from her. Puzzled and saddened, she turned with Deborah and retreated from the foyer.

The halls were busy with the inhabitants of Windsor, walking the halls because they were unable to go outside in the freezing rain. There were soldiers lining the corridors, all of them acknowledging her in some way as she passed. It was a very common occurrence since her husband commanded the troops and she was used to it now, but when it first started happening, she had been embarrassed at the attention.

There was a spread of bread, wine and cheese in the grand dining hall since it was close to the nooning meal. Dustin and Deborah gathered as much as they could carry and found a cozy window seat in a deserted corridor to share their meal.

"Do you think Marcus will return?" Deborah asked before Dustin had even taken a bite.

Dustin kept her gaze averted. " 'Tis difficult to say. Chris says he cannot get through to him, whether he means literally, I do not know. Mayhap Marcus doesn't want to come back."

"But why?" Deborah lamented. "Did I say something to send him away? Was I too forward with my feelings?"

Dustin glanced up at her sister-in-law, sweet, faintly pretty, feminine. Marcus would have a good wife in Deborah. "I do not think you were at all. Mayhap….mayhap he wasn't happy here, or mayhap he was overly desperate to see his new keep. I simply do not know, Deb….Chris doesn't know, either."

Deborah gazed out of the window, miserably chewing on a piece of cheese. "He doesn't like me," she said sadly, then looked at Dustin. "He likes you, though."

Dustin knew her eyes were wide with surprise. "Why do you say that?"

Deborah shrugged, picking at her cheese. "I have heard the gossip, Dustin. 'Tis hard not to. I didn't believe any of it until I began to see the way he looked at you." When Dustin shook her head vigorously, Deborah put up a placating hand. "I know you do not return his feelings. Christopher has made himself blind to Marcus' desire for you, probably because he respects the man so much. I suppose as long as Marcus didn't act on his feelings, Chris would feign ignorance. David hates Marcus for the dissension he has caused within Christopher's ranks."

Dustin's eyes were guarded; she didn't know what to say. Deborah smiled softly. "How can I blame him for loving you? You are so beautiful and you do not even know it. I wish I were more like you, Dustin."

Dustin did speak, then. "You are mad. 'Tis I who am envious of you, Deborah. You are refined and lady-like and elegant, everything I am not. I could never be like you in a million years. My daughters will have to learn to be a lady from you, because I certainly cannot teach them anything but how to ride a horse and how to tend a sick animal." She touched her sister-in-law's hand gently. " 'Tis you who are beautiful and do not know it."

"Then I will trade you some of my beauty for some of yours," Deborah quipped, and Dustin giggled in agreement.

They were finishing the last of the bread when they heard footsteps coming down the hall, rapid steps. They glanced up to see Lady Isobelle bearing down on them, her fat face worried. Dustin stood up.

"Lady Isobelle!" she greeted in surprise.

Lady Isobelle put up a hand. "I have no time, my lady. I have come to tell you a few things, items you must pass on to your husband."

Dustin nodded quickly, stunned at the urgency of the woman. "Of course. What is it?"

Lady Isobelle glanced around anxiously as if to make sure they were alone, and Dustin and Deborah found themselves doing the same. Anxiety settled over them.

"Lady Gabrielle didn't fall down the stairs; the prince fancied her so my brother gave her to him as a gift," she whispered quickly. "Sweet Gabrielle is at the mercy of a madman. It is simply easier to tell everyone that she is dead so he will not have to tell the truth of what he has done."

Dustin's eyes widened and she gasped in horror, but Isobelle wasn't finished. She grasped Dustin by the wrist.

"Know this; my brother has threatened to kill me if I so much as look at you," she said quietly, urgently. "He holds a great deal of hate for Richard and for your husband, my lady. But the most important news you must carry to your husband is this: I heard my brother speaking with other men, men loyal to John, and I heard him say that John is planning to lay siege to Tickhill before the week is out."

Dustin was rather overwhelmed at all of the news. She swallowed hard, feeling herself being unwantedly sucked into covert political dealings. "I will tell him, Lady Isobelle, I swear it," she said. "But why...why are you telling me this and betraying your brother?"

"Because my brother is vile and corrupt, and sweet Gabrielle must be helped," she said passionately, pulling her cloak about her tighter. "My brother and his army are riding to John's aid this night; your husband must be made aware."

Dustin could see what a great risk this woman was taking and she forced herself to swallow her apprehension and put on a brave front. "I shall go and tell him now. Thank you, Lady Isobelle. Truly you are very brave."

Lady Isobelle nodded shortly and glanced about her again. Satisfied she hadn't been followed, she swept away from Dustin and went back down the corridor. Dustin took a few steps further into the hall, watching the rotund woman as she slipped down the way. An intangible darkness swirled about them, as if they had been made privy to the plans of Lucifer himself and Dustin felt an unconscious chill run over her.

"What was that all about?" Deborah gasped, suddenly standing behind her.

Dustin shook her head faintly, still watching the cloaked figure. "We must find Chris. He should be at the barracks."

"Do you believe her, then?" Deborah demanded softly. "Who is she?"

"The Earl of Fenwark's sister," Dustin replied. "Damn the man. He whored his own wife to the prince. Christopher said he was evil and I should have listened. My Lord, what if…."

She started to turn toward her sister-in-law when a bloodcurdling scream filled the still air of the corridor. Both women whirled around to see Lady Isobelle being stabbed repeatedly by a shrouded figure in black. Astonished and horrified, they continued to watch in frozen terror as the assailant cut Lady Isobelle brutally, not even stopping when the woman fell to the ground. The pounding was merciless and driven, speaking of unmentionable hatred and anger.

Dustin was shocked to the core, too stunned to even turn and run. She could hear Deborah's shrieks and felt her pulling on her arm. Even as the attacker turned to the both of them, several more mysterious figures appeared, and she could not seem to make her feet move. But her shock quickly wore off when she realized the figures were now coming for her. And she knew they would kill her in the same grisly fashion. Panic surged through her.

"Run!" she roared to Deborah.

Dustin had always been able to run like a deer, but Deborah was having difficulty keeping up and the pursuers were gaining. Unfortunately, they were in a deserted wing of the castle and there was no one to hear their cries for help. Yet, they were also fairly close to the rear courtyard and the paths that led to the barracks. Terror filled every inch of her body like flowing fire and her chest burned with exertion as she tore through the hall with Deborah on her heels. Lord, if they could only make it to the outside door, they would have a chance.

The door at the end of the hall that led to the outside was locked. They pulled and tore at it, but the bolt was locked and they obviously had no key. Despair swept over Dustin and Deborah began a panicked chant, but neither would give up. Being intelligent woman who were fighting for their very lives, they saw a chance to escape through the latticed windows.

Dustin smashed the wood with her hands, scraping and cutting them, but that was nothing compared to what would happen to her if the molesters caught up to them. She boosted Deborah up through the window first, shoving the woman roughly through the small opening. Then, with Deborah's help, she managed to thrust herself through the orifice, tearing her surcoat to shreds with the jagged wood as she squirmed through, all the while hearing the footsteps growing deafeningly loud as the men caught up to them. With every footstep, her heart pounded harder and when she finally slipped through the window and fell to the ground, it was with a shout of triumphant relief.

Deborah yanked her to her feet and they were off and running again, pounding over the frozen earth but sweating rivers with the exertion. A glance over her shoulder told Dustin that at least two pursuers had made it through the window and were even now racing after them.

"Deborah," she gasped. "Can you make it to the barracks?"

Deborah was losing ground, jeopardizing them both. "I....I can try."

Dustin's heart was sinking even lower; she could not leave Deborah behind but she obviously could not carry her. Dustin knew she could make it to the barracks easily, slowing now to keep pace with her sister-in-law. But any slower and they would be caught.

"Go for the castle," Dustin heaved. "Find the soldiers!"

An entrance to a main portion of the castle was off to the right; Deborah could make it and then find help. The crown soldiers would protect her to the death. There was simply no way Deborah was going to make it all the way to the troop grounds, and Dustin knew she had to make it to her husband or she would never see him again. She knew instinctively the pursuers were after her. If she and Deborah split up, she hoped they would concentrate more on her and give Deborah a chance to escape.

"But... Dustin!" she cried. "I cannot leave you."

"Leave me or we're both lost!" Dustin shrieked. "Into the castle. Now!"

She heard Deborah's panting cries as she darted off for the castle. Dustin didn't even look to see how many were pursuing her sister-in-law; she was confident Deborah could find help before they were able to catch her.

Dustin bound down one of the paths that led through the wall and out into the open. As she was entering the short tunnel, something hit the wall beside her and she shrieked; she caught a flash of metal and knew it to be a well-aimed dagger. Driven by new terror, she tore through the tunnel with amazing speed and emerged into the clearing that preceded the troop grounds.

The dead shrubs provided no coverage as she raced through them, snagging her legs on the dry branches. Her chest was close to exploding with the pain of her run, but she forced the discomfort away. She knew she must be completely focused on her destination or all would be lost.

Dustin could hear the footsteps behind her, faint but unmistakable. It was no time before she emerged onto an open field, sloping toward the vast arena and training grounds of the troops. It had begun to mist, freezing water coating her, but she tore down the slope hearing her heart pounding in her ears and praying to God to let her make it to Christopher. She could not even think of Deborah anymore; she was only concerned with her own precious hide.

She rounded the side of the arena and was met with the sounds of a horse thundering toward her. Knowing it was a pursuer coming to catch her, she dipped under the wooden rail of the arena to separate herself from the horseman, catching a glimpse of him from the corner of her eye and hearing shouts as he re-routed his men. Dustin tore a wild trail across the arena, the very same arena where Christopher had been injured, and scampered out the other side into a bank of dormant oak trees.

Dustin could see people up ahead of her at the stables and she screamed at the top of her lungs to them to find Baron Christopher. Her whole body was aching desperately and she knew she could not go much farther; she could only pray that the stunned groomsmen would help her.

She could hear that damnable horse again, behind her and gaining rapidly. Fortunately, she was closer to the stables now and she ran an obstacle course through a couple of wagons, pulling the front of one askew to slow her pursuers. She raced inside to one of the enclosed stable wings and ran down the wide open corridor, hoping the man on horseback wouldn't pursue her inside the stable. Her ears peaked, for she no longer heard the hooves and a fleeting bit of hope touched her. Mayhap she would make it, after all.

But the hope was premature, for as soon as she exited the stable, the man on horseback was waiting for her. Dustin skidded to a halt and crashed into the horse, slamming heavily into it and landing on her arse. Panic surging through her, she scrambled underneath the dancing animal and fought off an assailant who tried to grab her skirts. Screaming bloody murder at them, she stumbled and ran off as fast as her shaky legs would carry her.

There was shouting going on all around her, but she was too consumed with her own fear to see that the stable hands were fighting off her attackers, stabbing them with pitchforks and trying to slow their progress. She continued to run, her breathing coming in ragged gasps, straining to keep the pace as she madly dashed along the L-shaped back of stalls and rounded the corner. Relief began to fill her when she saw the barracks and several hundred troops not far ahead.

But her head was beginning to swim and her arms and legs were beginning to feel strange, as if she were losing control over them. But she pushed, pushed, pushed; pressing onward because her very life hung in the balance. She had to make it to the soldiers or die.

Through her swirling vision, she saw men in armor running toward her and she knew with flooding relief she had reached safety. But she could not seem to stop running until one of the men reached out and grabbed her.

"Jesus. Dustin!" It was David. "What is the mat…?"

He was cut off and she heard a huge crash of metal on metal. Dustin screamed and fell away from David, trying to scramble away from him as she heard the unmistakable sounds of a sword fight over her head. There was a great deal of shouting and yelling, and suddenly she was surrounded by soldiers. Someone grabbed at her, but she slapped at them and whirled away, taking two or three swaggering steps before collapsing in an exhausted heap on the frozen earth.

Dustin was still conscious but so miserable and wiped out that she almost didn't care what happened to her anymore. She lay on her back, harsh gasps for air filling her ears and her head was rocking wildly. Tears of pure agony filled her eyes as the sounds of swordplay grew fainter and then there was someone beside her. She jumped, making a feeble attempt to rise, but a huge hand stilled her.

"Christ, Dustin, are you all right? What happened?" Christopher gathered his wife up against him.

Dustin could not breathe because sobs were constricting her throat, and she could not talk because she could not breathe. The sobs won over the talking, but she was gasping so she sounded as if she were dying. She felt like it, too.

"Calm down, sweetheart, calm down," Christopher said soothingly, ripping off his helmet. "You are safe now. Just breathe, sweet, *breathe*."

She was trying to, truly, but she could not seem to catch her breath. "Deborah," she rasped.

Christopher was already filled with panic as his wife struggled to breathe in his arms, but when she spat his sister's name, his panic doubled. He whirled to the nearest knight. "Go find my sister," he barked. "Take a company of men with you."

"In....in the castle," Dustin gasped. "The west w-wing."

The knight heard and was gone, roaring to the men-at-arms as he went. Dustin could only lay there, in agony with every breath she took, trying to calm herself down.

Edward bent over her, his handsome face creased with concern. Christopher held out his gloved hand to him and Edward silently ripped the gauntlet off. Christopher's left hand, the wedding band gleaming dully in the dim daylight, caressed Dustin's flushed face. He didn't speak, knowing she needed a moment to collect herself, and then he would know all.

Dustin's hands flew to her face, covering it for a moment as her breathing calmed. Then, the fingers splayed and the great gray eyes opened and focused on her husband.

"Earl....the Earl of Fenwark tried to kill me," she finally whispered. "You must find Deborah."

"What?" Christopher said, outraged. "What are you saying?"

She struggled to sit up, Edward gently pulling her arm and Christopher supporting her back. Between coughs and sniffles, she managed to spit out the entire story. When she was finished, Christopher's face was the picture of fury and it scared the wits from her.

"Then those men chasing you were assassins." It was more a statement than a question, and he looked at Edward. "All of my knights to me. *Now*."

Edward nodded grimly and rushed off, his armor jingling. Dustin, infinitely more composed, brushed stray bits of hair from her face and watched her husband closely. His gaze seemed to be following Edward, even after the man had disappeared from view, before returning to her once again. When he saw how intently she was looking at him, he smiled bravely. *Too* bravely.

"My courageous little wife," he said as he leaned forward and kissed her head. "Do you feel well enough to stand from this damp earth?"

Dustin, suspicious of his ready smile, nodded and rose unsteadily to her feet. Christopher kept a good grip on her, watching as his soldiers hauled away one of the men who had been chasing after his wife. He saw, with pleasure, that his men had literally disemboweled the bastard. Dustin watched, too, with morbid curiosity but turned away as they passed by.

"What are you going to do now?" she asked. "Lady Isobelle said the earl was moving his army north tonight and that he plans to attack Tickhill Castle. She wanted you to know. But her story about Lady Gabrielle… can you imagine that her husband gave her to the prince as a gift? I have never heard of such a vile thing."

Christopher digested the information, his cunning mind beginning to calculate the course of the immediate future. He wasn't surprised to hear the information; in fact, he was grateful, at least for the intelligence on Tickhill. There had been rumors but nothing concrete. Now, he had a starting place.

"I am not shocked," he admitted. "What else did she say?"

Dustin shook her head. "That was all before… before…," she trailed off, unable to voice such horror. Her gaze moved to Christopher's face, seeing that he seemed inordinately calm. "What are you going to do? Are you going, too?"

He stroked the top of her blond head. "I do not know, sweet. I am only concerned with you right now."

"And Deborah," she insisted. "She cannot run as fast as I can and…."

He glanced down at her lowered head and saw she was trying hard to fight off the tears. God help the earl if his sister had come to any harm; as it was now, he was going to kill the man mercifully. If the worst had happened to Deborah, then Christopher would make sure the earl's death was a slow, painful one.

David jogged up, his eyes riveted to Dustin. "Are you all right, Dustin? Did they hurt you?"

She sniffled, wiping quickly at her eyes. "Nay, David, I am unharmed."

He looked her over, her disheveled surcoat and bleeding hands and shook his head. Then he looked to his brother. "Edward is rallying Nicholas de Burg, Sean de Lara and Guy de le Rosa to reinforce our ranks. With Marcus and Dud missing, we could use the strength." He felt the familiar taste of a fight in the air and was tense with anticipation, knowing not who they would be fighting to avenge the attack on Dustin, yet knowing soon they would be facing a battle.

Christopher nodded curtly, obviously preoccupied as his wife clung to his waist. "I have been working with them since I have arrived here and I feel they have proved themselves worthy of my inner circle. Edward and I talked on this subject yesterday," he said, then his gaze fell on his brother. "David, go with Dustin and help her pack."

"Pack?" Both Dustin and David repeated loudly.

David eyed his brother with displeasure, knowing that Christopher planned to get to the bottom of who had attacked his wife, and furthermore wanted to accompany him. He didn't want his brother fighting without him. "Send a company of men with her to help her pack. My place is with you."

"You heard me," Christopher said in a low voice. "She returns to Lioncross today. Deborah, too, and I want you with them while I tend to the earl. Send word ahead to Max and Anthony that they are coming; I want them to meet my wife and sister on the road."

David shook his head. "My place is with you," he repeated steadily, advancing on his brother. "You have got an entire squadron of men assigned to your wife. They will protect her while we take care of whoever has attacked your wife."

Christopher raised an eyebrow at his shorter, younger brother. "Do not argue with me, David."

"I am not," David replied evenly, clenching his fists. "But I am going with you."

Dustin watched the two of them, not at all happy with their body language for they looked as if to brawl any moment. It was a terrible cap to a terrible morning and she began to cry.

"Stop fighting," she sobbed.

They both looked at her and were instantly remorseful. "We are not fighting," Christopher said, pulling her close. "We never fight. We disagree, but we never fight. David?"

David made a wry face at his brother. "Never."

Christopher ignored the implication and kissed Dustin on the top of the head. "I need to talk to David alone a moment."

He let her go, concerned when she wobbled, but she waved him off. He pulled David aside.

"John is preparing to launch a strike against Tickhill Castle before the end of the week," he told him quietly. "The Earl of Fenwark's sister informed Dustin of his plans and asked her to tell me, having overheard her brother speak of them. I want Dustin out of Windsor and back to Lioncross immediately; you saw what nearly happened to her. She is being pulled deeper and deeper into something that does not concern her."

David was confused. "Is that what this is all about? Jesus, why should the earl's sister tell Dustin of his plans?"

"Because Dustin befriended Lady Gabrielle, the earl's wife." Christopher had no time to explain all of this. "The earl killed his own sister because she relayed the information to my wife, for Christ's sake. Had he been successful in his attack on Dustin, we would most likely be picking up pieces of her, and God only knows what's become of Deborah. I want both of them away from this place."

David looked as if he had completely forgotten about his sister. "Jesus. Where is Deborah?"

"I sent Sean de Lara and a company of men out to find her. She and Dustin were together at the beginning of the chase but split up, so I hold hope that our sister has found safety," Christopher replied. "But I want you to find out what has become of Deborah when you have settled my wife. And keep Sean with you; I am demanding his loyalty to me, as well."

"I thought you wanted me to help Dustin pack?" David pointed out.

Christopher gave him an intolerable look. "I changed my mind. My wife has an entire company of soldiers assigned to her, no one will get past them."

David nodded without the grin he was feeling. "Then we leave tonight?"

Christopher glanced at Dustin, longing already filling his heart. "Aye," he replied. "After I take care of the earl, we leave."

David's adrenalin flowed quicker and harder than just about anyone. He could feel his energy surge, eager to get a lick at the earl for what he had done to the ladies, and eager more to be on the battlefield once again. The man was a born warrior.

As requested, Christopher's knights were soon congregated around him. Edward, Leeton, and David were joined by three new faces. Dustin had seen the men before, serving her husband, but he had not allowed them around her. She knew from Marcus that Christopher was extremely selective about the knights who personally served him and assumed that these men must have met her husband's standards.

Sir Nicholas de Burg was a nice looking man in his mid-twenties, his dark hair longer than the others. Sir Sean de Lara was a very young, very handsome knight with a massively muscular build, and Sir Guy de le Rosa spoke with a heavy Spanish accent and had a broad smile that showed every tooth in his head. Dustin watched her husband explain the situation to the men and saw their pleased faces when Christopher asked for their pledge to him. Actually, he demanded their pledge, but the men were more than willing to give it. These men were knights, independent of a liege other than Richard, and were pleased to be committing service to the Lion's Claw. Satisfied that his knight ranks were growing stronger by the day, Christopher gave each man individual orders and dismissed them.

David came to Dustin, taking her shaking arm. "Time to pack, Lady de Lohr."

Christopher broke away from his private conference with Edward to see his wife and brother off. "I shall meet up with you later," he told his brother, then affectionately stroked his wife's cheek. "Are you going to have enough trunks?

God only knows how much we have acquired since we have come to London."

"I shall manage," she replied wearily, exhausted to the bone and still frightened for Deborah. Yet her husband, remarkably, had remained fairly calm throughout the entire occurrence and she wondered about it. "Are you going to help Deborah now?"

Christopher wasn't looking at her as he put his gauntlet back on again. "I have men going to Deborah's rescue, Dustin. She will be amply protected. You will make sure she packs her things, as well. And try to limit the baggage to four trunks for each of you, if you please."

He was talking casually, yet there was no mistaking his tense manner. Dustin eyed him warily. "Where are you going?" she asked.

He put his helmet back on, adjusting his mail hood beneath it. "To pay a call on the earl."

Dustin's eyes widened. She wanted to protest, to beg that he simply go with her and that they leave this place, but she could not and she wouldn't. Christopher was a soldier, the best in the realm, and fighting was his vocation. She hated the thought of him fighting for any reason, wishing he were a simple scholar so she wouldn't have to worry about him so, but in faith, she loved his strength and his power. He was the Defender, and she loved him more than life. As afraid as she was for him, she would never ask him to be less than he was.

"Are you going to kill him?" she asked, already knowing the answer.

He didn't answer her, instead bringing her hand to his lips and kissing it sweetly. "I shall see you later."

He turned abruptly and she cried after him, rushing to him when he paused. Tired and scratched and damp, she put her arms around his neck and kissed him through his helmet.

"I love you, husband. Be safe," she whispered.

He stroked her cheek with a mailed hand and was gone.

David took her arm gently. "How are we going to pack George?" he wondered aloud as he led her away.

CHAPTER THIRTY-THREE

WINDSOR WAS IN an uproar. Between Deborah's screams for help and Christopher's men tearing up the place trying to find the Earl of Fenwark and his men, the entire castle was running for cover.

Sir Sean de Lara found Deborah quite safe but thoroughly shaken in a small room, well protected by several crown soldiers. He returned her to Dustin's apartments, whereupon he and David took a group of about thirty men-at-arms and went to meet up with Christopher, leaving the other thirty men guarding the women. Alone and terrified, Dustin and Deborah busied themselves with packing.

Christopher was hell-bent. He had forced himself to be calm in the presence of his wife, but in faith, he was beyond fury. It mattered not to him that the earl was loyal to John and was preparing to join him in the north; what mattered to him was that the earl had tried to kill his wife. He was terribly angry for Deborah's sake, too, but the outrage he felt on Dustin's behalf was consuming. The man dared harm his wife and he would pay for the action with his life.

He had seen the Lady Isobelle's mutilated body and had been sickened by the fact that the same bastards had been chasing his wife. He and three companies of troops, all of them his personal men that he had brought from Lioncross, went through Windsor like a violent storm in search of the earl. Servants and residents alike scattered out of his way, terrified that the Lion's Claw was obviously bent on blood and wondering who the unlucky man was. Inevitably, it began to spread that he was looking for the Earl of Fenwark to kill him.

The earl knew Christopher was coming and was ready for him. By the time Christopher and his men reached the wing where the earl was housed, there were at least a hundred of the earl's troops waiting and the clash that ensued could be heard all over the castle.

ଓ

BACK IN CHRISTOPHER'S apartments, Dustin and Deborah were busy packing away the last of Dustin's things when Dustin's two maids came scurrying in, their faces lit with apprehension.

"The baron has taken on the earl," the fatter of the two managed to gasp.

"The battle threatens to destroy the entire north wing."

Cold fear clutched at Dustin, but she faltered only a split second before continuing her packing. "Then we must hurry and finish, for when the fight is over, we will be returning to Lioncross. Help Lady Deborah with the linens."

In a nervous huff, the maids did as they were told.

Dustin eyed the ladies in her bedchamber, watching them as they quickly packed and cleaned, feeling their anxiety. She was trying hard to remain cool, but the knowledge that her husband was engaged in a massive fight shook her to the core. She knew it was coming, mayhap wondering if it had already occurred when the women had come barging in with the information that set her mind to swirling again.

She didn't care about revenge, or of the bloody honor Christopher spoke of when discussing Richard. True, he was fighting on her behalf now, but somehow Richard was ultimately responsible for everything that happened to her and her husband, and she hated the man for it. Everything except for ordering Christopher to marry Arthur Barringdon's daughter.

Dustin was thinking crazy, irrational thoughts in her attempt to remain calm, but she could slowly feel her composure slipping.

ௐ

IN THE HEAT of battle, Christopher's composure wasn't damaged in the least. He was at home in a battle, more comfortable than most men were in their favorite chair. Reinforcements had arrived to bolster his number and he found himself in a full-blown war. With as many men as there were crowding the broad corridor, each fighting the other in such close quarters that men of the same army were cutting each other down, Christopher had yet to see the earl and suspected, correctly, that the man was behind barred doors.

Yet it was of no matter, he would tear the door from its hinges in his quest for revenge. He shoved onward through the melee, cutting down enemy troops, using his armored arms to knock men down before slitting their throats, all in a raging attempt to reach the earl's apartments. The blood, the noise, the smell of battle and death were everywhere. Pretty woolen rugs beneath their struggling feet were shredded.

He glanced over his shoulder to see David standing atop a chair, slicing one man's head clean from his shoulder and kicking another man to the ground. He always marveled at the energy his little brother exhibited in a crisis; David lived for a good fight. He may have lacked the size of other knights, but by damn, if he wasn't the quickest fury on two feet. Opponents often underestimated David's strength because of his stature, and that was often their last mistake before seeing the fields of paradise.

Edward and Leeton were fighting around him, engaging as many as three soldiers at one time. Leeton fought so easily that it looked as if he were bored by the conflict, as if it were no test for his skills. Edward, however, fought each man as if he were fighting the greatest warrior in England. He grunted and groaned with his efforts, always victorious but acting as if it had taken all his strength to emerge successful. Christopher had decided a long time ago that Edward would make a fine earl when his father passed on, for he would rather tend to more gentlemanly pursuits than brandish a weapon.

Christopher pushed on with Sir Nicholas and Sir Guy close on his flanks where he could watch them in an out-an-out battle. Practices and tournaments were one way of surmising a knight's talents, but there was no substitution for a good fight. Christopher was pleased to see that these men were exceedingly efficient and capable. Just as they worked their way through a group of particularly zealous soldiers, they came upon Sir Sean as he gored his opponent with a hearty yell. He grinned enthusiastically at Christopher as he withdrew his sword before starting in on the next unfortunate man.

Christopher smirked, shaking his head at the knight's zeal. But his smile was cut short by a heavy sword against his back, smashing against his helmet. He turned and defeated his opponent within three stokes of his sword, but his ears were ringing and he could feel the unmistakable warmth of blood from his split scalp. Cursing himself for being stupid enough to allow himself to be caught from behind, he moved toward the door at the end of the hall.

The earl's door was bolted from the inside, but Christopher and Sir Nicholas made short work of the locked panel. The door swung open with a crash and Christopher was the first man through, his eyes settled on the earl at the far end of the room. The earl had surrounded himself with a few dozen men, all fighting with ardor as the baron and his troops poured in through the shattered doorway, but even that number of men would not be enough to save the earl from the wrath of the Lion's Claw.

In spite of his advanced years, Charles de Havilland was an accomplished fighter and met Christopher's sword without hesitation. Furniture went up on end and furnishings were destroyed as the baron and the earl went head on. Christopher knew he would beat the man without a doubt, wondering how such a distinguished-looking man could be such a brutal, cold-blooded beast. To send his wife to whore with such a devil of a man was an inconceivable horror to Christopher. With the anger of that thought, he brought down his sword so hard that the earl lost his grip on his own blade and the steel went clattering to the floor.

The earl froze, his face one of haughty contempt. He waited patiently for the final blow, but instead, Christopher lowered his sword and raised the faceplate of his visor. Icy sky-blue eyes met brown ones, each man feeling nothing but hatred for the other.

"You tried to kill my wife," Christopher said in a low, slow voice. "I know why. But I have trouble dealing with the idea that you actually believed you could get away with it. Do you know your assassins followed her all the way to the training ground? Now, tell me; how intelligent was that?"

"Apparently not intelligent enough," the earl said evenly. "Had my men been armed with a crossbow, your precious Dustin would now be as cold as the winter ground. 'Tis my only regret, baron. My only one."

Christ, but the man was cool in the face of death. Christopher's anger threatened to flare, but he contained himself.

"I hear that Lady Gabrielle is now John's whore," Christopher said with disgust. "I am curious as to how a man of your status could damn your lovely young wife to a life of misery."

The earl raised an eyebrow. "You have come here to talk of women? What of Richard and John? Surely you must realize that John is the rightful king of England. His father, our illustrious Henry, wished for John to ascend him and not his brother."

"What Henry wished and what birthright declared are clear, my lord," Christopher retorted. "Richard is the rightful heir."

"I beg to differ, baron, but you are fighting on the wrong side," the earl said. "As our king, Henry had every right to choose who would succeed him, and he did not wish it to be Richard."

"Ridiculous," Christopher responded. "The king cannot choose his successor, only birthright can establish rule. I will discuss this with you no further; Richard is our rightful king."

"There are many who feel otherwise," the earl replied tightly. "Richard is driving England to civil war by not turning rule over to Henry's chosen. Why do you insist upon serving a man who had never actually ruled a day from English soil? Richard is monarch in absentia, de Lohr. John may not be the best choice for king, but at least he loves England enough not to leave it."

Christopher stiffened. "John drives England to civil war with his greed and petty jealousies. Were he to rule from the throne, he would destroy this country and every man with it."

"You are a fool," de Havilland hissed in the first real show of emotion. "Cannot you see that? Your loyalties are misplaced."

"My loyalties lie with the true king of England," Christopher snapped quietly. "Now, earl, returning to the reason I am here. You made an attempt on my wife's life, and for that, you shall pay dearly."

The earl wasn't impressed. "Is that the only reason you are here? It could not possibly be because you know I am loyal to John, and because of the information my sister relayed to your wife?" The earl shook his head, trying to provoke Christopher, to unbalance him. "Are you going to kill me because of one small, insignificant woman? She is nothing in the scheme of the world, de Lohr, as you would do well to remember. The only thing of importance is

England and her rule."

Christopher cracked a dangerous smile. "Nay, my lord, 'tis you who would do well to remember that the only thing of importance is my wife. England and her rule come second." He stood back from the man and motioned with his sword. "Retrieve your blade. I do not strike down an unarmed man."

The earl eyed him for a moment before mechanically picking up his sword. Before raising the weapon in a defensive posture, he shook his head with genuine confusion.

"You are a bigger fool than I ever thought you to be," he said. "How can you place any value on a woman? From what I had heard and seen of you, you were Richard's most devoted servant. When you tore Windsor apart to get to me, I was confident it was because I was riding to John's aid. And now you tell me it is because I had my men chase your wife? 'Tis madness, de Lohr. How can you tell me your wife comes before your king?"

Christopher lowered his visor and raised his sword. "Because she does, as I am about to demonstrate. Defend yourself, my lord."

The earl promptly raised his sword. "You are a pathetic excuse for a Defender, de Lohr, if you would use your strength to protect a woman, a woman who was unfaithful to you, no less."

"And now you add slander to the charge of attempted murder," Christopher said. " 'Twill be a pleasure to dispense justice."

"Then I thank God Marcus Burton isn't here, lest I'd be fighting off the two of you on Lady de Lohr's behalf," de Havilland snorted cruelly. " 'Tis beyond me how the two of you could be bewitched by the bitch."

Christopher brought the sword down, every ounce of power in his body surging to his arms as he slammed into the earl with unearthly strength. The earl brought his sword up, the force of the blow so powerful that it drove his own sword backward and buried it into the soft flesh of his neck.

The earl stumbled back, his windpipe cut and the horrible rasps of a man dying filling the room. He knew we was going to die and his eyes were wide as Christopher loomed over him again, raising his sword and delivering the merciful deathblow that severed his head from his body.

Christopher's fury was beyond rational. He stood over the earl's body, shaking with all of the raging emotions he was feeling, his breathing coming hard and fast. Behind him, there were still pockets of fighting in the room and he suddenly reached down and grabbed the earl's head by the hair, raising it high above his head.

"It is over!" he roared, reverberation through the walls loud enough to be heard by every soldier involved.

He pushed through the room with his grisly trophy held above him, scattering the earl's men like rabbits. Out in the corridor, he shouted his words again and the fighting immediately stopped. All eyes turned to the Lion's Claw and his prize.

The battle was indeed over.

ᏂᏰ

THE SOLDIERS GUARDING the door would not allow Dustin from her rooms to see what was transpiring with the skirmish. Wise, seasoned men that they were, they listened empathetically as she pleaded and begged, but there was no possible way she was going anywhere, especially out to find her husband, and the men in charge tried to reason with her. Dustin had stopped trying hours ago to control her fear for Christopher, and she even tried tears to sway the soldiers. It didn't work.

When she eventually tried to bully her way out, the Irish sergeant picked her up and bodily placed her back in the antechamber, closing the door politely behind him as he went back out into the corridor. Dustin was too concerned about her husband to fight anymore, knowing it would be futile, and took to pacing the floor of the room nervously while Deborah and her maids pretended to be busy with other things.

Dustin was close to hysterics. He'd been gone the entire afternoon and she was sick with worry for him. Surely if he had been victorious, he would have returned to her immediately. Yet if the earl was triumphant, then… Dustin squeezed her eyes shut at the thought; she wasn't able to pursue it. She would have to trust Christopher and know he would return to her. Lord, with him taking his army north tonight, she would have endless days of this worrying to look forward to. The sooner she learned to control her anxiety, the better.

Eventually she grew tired of pacing and sat while Deborah read aloud from a bible that she had brought with her. Dustin was disinterested, her mind was drifting across the compound to the north wing, reaching out as if she could see Christopher if she tried hard enough. Deborah droned on and the maids finished packing quietly, retreating to Deborah and David's apartments to pack their items. Dustin sat and waited, her anxiety being replaced by a sort of numbness she was becoming accustomed to. There was naught else to do but sit and wait.

The sun had set and she knew supper would be served shortly in the grand dining hall. Her stomach rumbled but she wasn't hungry. One of her maids returned long enough to stoke the hearth in both the antechamber and the bedchamber before hustling back to her duties. Dustin had lost track of time as it grew dark outside and she waited for her husband to return.

A peculiar droning sound permeated the room and Dustin turned to look curiously at Deborah, who lifted her head from her reading and gazed back at her sister-in-law questioningly. Then, at the same time and without a word, they both looked to the front door of the apartments.

Dustin was a second faster than her sister-in-law. She rushed to the door and threw it open. She was met by a host of surprised male faces.

"What's going on?" Dustin demanded of the soldiers congregating in the hall. The Irish sergeant looked down at her; he was a great stocky man with a bushy red mustache. "News of your husband, my lady."

"What news?" Dustin snapped at him.

He looked at her a moment as if debating whether or not to tell her. "He fared well in the skirmish, 'tis all," he said steadily. "He lost only four soldiers, a fine statistic."

She raised a well-arched brow at him. "Who cares about a bloody statistic? Where is he?"

"I don't know, my lady," he said truthfully. "But I am sure he will return soon."

"But it is dark outside. Where could he be?" she demanded.

"Honestly, my lady, I know not," the sergeant insisted. "You must be hungry. I shall send someone to fetch dinner for you."

"I am not hungry!" she yelled at him. "I want to know where my husband is. What were you all talking about out here? We could hear you all the way inside the chamber."

The sergeant shook his head patiently. "Soldier talk, 'tis all, I swear it," he replied. "Why don't you return to your room and I shall have someone bring your meal."

Dustin's face was red with fury. "If you say that one more time, I shall punch you right in the nose. I do not want food, I want someone to tell me where my husband is. If you do not know, then find out, for if you do not, I swear I shall jump from the window and go find him myself."

"We are on the second floor, my lady," the sergeant reminded her. "You would break your neck at the very least if you jumped from the window." He glanced over at the group of new soldiers that had only moments before arrived with the victorious news. "Do any of you lads know where de Lohr is?"

"His knights are with the troops," one man replied. "I haven't seen the baron."

The other soldiers looked at each other, nodding in agreement, no one had seen Christopher.

"With the troops? Why?" Dustin asked the man firmly.

"The army is mobilizing, my lady," the soldier answered. "An awesome sight to behold, indeed; over one thousand men and knights."

Mobilizing. Dustin swallowed hard, feeling the pit of her stomach twist. Dear Lord, he really *was* leaving tonight. And she hadn't seen him all day, and there was no telling when she would see him again. It was all happening so fast that she could scarce believe it. Her apprehension and agitation was suddenly overtaken by a fierce desire to be held by her husband.

The sergeant put a gentle hand on her. "Go and rest, my lady. The baron will be here shortly."

She didn't even answer him as she turned and went back into the antechamber. Deborah, her pale blue eyes wide, gazed back at her with concern.

"What's wrong, Dustin?" she asked softly. "You look as if about to cry."

Dustin glanced at her. "Oh.....no, I am fine. But would you mind terribly if I retired? It might be a good idea if we both get some rest. After all, Chris said we would be leaving tonight and I never could sleep on a horse."

Deborah nodded quickly. "An excellent suggestion, Dustin. You shall let me know when Chris returns, won't you?"

"Of course," Dustin nodded, accepting a quick kiss on the cheek from her sister-in-law before she quit the antechamber.

The room suddenly felt empty and Dustin felt as if she were in a fog. A day that had started out normally had become the absolute worst and she was reeling with the rapid events. She sank into the nearest chair, her mind working itself into muddled confusion. So he was leaving, and she was returning to Lioncross. When would she see him again? Dear Lord, would she see him again? He would be fighting against John and his army of cutthroats, and she was utterly terrified that he would meet his end.

Dustin covered her face with a hand. Lord, if they could only retreat to Lioncross and forget about John and Richard and the whole bloody country. She simply wanted to grow old with her husband and to hell with the rest of the world. Living the rest of her life without him was her very worst nightmare, and with the wars that were rapidly approaching, she had to face the very real possibility.

One moment she was staring at the fire and the next, someone was shaking her awake. She startled, nearly falling out of the chair except for strong hands that held her steady.

"Careful, sweetheart," Christopher bent down and scooped her into his arms. "I shouldn't have awoken you, but the time to leave is coming upon us and...."

Instantly alert, Dustin threw her arms around her husband and peppered his face with kisses. "You are back," she managed to say in between kisses. "I was so worried for you. Where have you been? What's happened?"

He returned her kisses, capturing her lips with his own and slowing her urgency considerably. Only when he had suckled and kissed and licked her quiet did he speak.

"Are you all packed?" he asked against her neck. "My men are ready to take your things."

She forced his head up. "Where have you been all this time? What happened to the earl?"

His soft expression hardened imperceptibly. "The earl is dead. And I have been with the justices for the past six hours listening to them debate."

"And?" she bade him to continue.

"And the army does indeed ride tonight to destroy John," he said. "You leave tonight as well and return to Lioncross."

She forced him to look at her. "Are you taking me back to Lioncross yourself or are you riding north with the army?"

His eyes drank her in, memorizing every feature of her beautiful face and he felt despair of separation filling him. Never in his life had he faced this situation and he found it overwhelmingly distressing.

"I ride with my army, sweet love," he said softly. "You and Deborah, along with Leeton and Sir Nicholas and 250 men-at-arms will be returning to Lioncross this night."

In spite of the fact that Dustin had promised herself she would be brave, hot tears instantly filled her eyes. Before she could say anything, Christopher was kissing them away, lapping at her cheeks with his tongue and tasting her salt.

"No tears, Dustin," his voice was raspy. "I want to remember you smiling, not crying with sorrow. Please be brave, for me."

She tried terribly to stop her tears, responding to his kisses with kisses of her own. "How much time do we have?"

"An hour, mayhap less," he said. "I'd like to be moving as quickly as possible."

She squirmed from his arms, taking his hands and pulling him in the direction of the bedchamber. He had been thinking the exact same thought and without a word, followed her into the darkened room.

They were completely silent as they fervently removed each other's garments, such great pain filling them that it was difficult to put into words. All they could think of was each other, touching, holding, caressing, tasting. Even as the clothes fell to the floor and Christopher lifted her onto the bed, the anguish of their impending separation filled Dustin so that the moment he lay his body atop her, she began to cry softly.

He heard her faint sobs and felt his eyes sting with tears of his own. His mouth tasted of her fully, gorging himself on the sweetness of her flesh, trying to ignore the salt he tasted from her tears. There was not an inch of skin that did not go unexplored by his worshipful mouth and not a limb nor a joint that did not go carefully caressed by his massive hands. When he did enter her hot, slick body, it was with a gentle and passionate thrust.

Dustin wrapped herself around him, memorizing every stroke, every sensation, every marvelous feeling he created within her. She was so very, very terrified this would be the last time she ever felt him.

Passion overcame her tears for the moment and she turned into the wanton woman he loved so well. Not content merely to make love with him atop her, she pushed him over onto his back so that he could watch her while she slid up and down on his great shaft. Sobbing intermittently, she flipped her incredibly mane over so that it covered him from his neck to his stomach and she watched, upside down, as she made love to him.

She heard him groan and he grabbed her by the hair, pulling her onto her back once again and driving his wet organ into her throbbing body. It was too much for Dustin, she was so aroused that it was no time before she was pulsing with pleasure, her panting cries answered by his own grunt of satisfaction, and she heard her name in his throaty cry.

The musk of the love making mingled in the cool air as he gathered his wife against him, kissing her hair over and over again. The warmth of her passion quickly faded and Dustin once again felt herself being overcome with despair, dissolving into tears as he held her.

"Oh, Dustin," she heard him murmur against her head. "Do not cry, my love. I won't be able to leave you if you cry."

"Good," she sobbed. "I do not want you to go."

He sighed, snuggling down into the feathered mattress and holding her tightly. "I have to. I do not want to, but I have to."

Sniffling and choking, she looked up at him and he kissed the end of her tear-streaked nose. "You *do* want to. You must go and protect your beloved Richard's properties. He matters most to you, Chris, he always has."

He laid his head back on the pillow, studying her lovely, tear-stained and angry face. " 'Tis true, our king has always been my priority," he said softly. "But I truly cannot remember when, indeed, he began running a distant second to you."

She sniffled loudly, wiping at the tears on her neck and eyeing him with a mixture of anger and doubt. "What do you mean 'second to me'?"

His face was soft and thoughtful as he pushed a stray bit of hair from her face. "Just what I said," he murmured. "You are the greatest priority in my life, Dustin. What I do now, I do because it is my duty and because I am sworn to it. But my heart, my love, is with you. Were that I had a choice in all of this, I would retire to Lioncross with you and raise a huge family. No more war, no more king, no more bastard prince."

She looked at him, astonishment filling her. "But…but you are the Defender. You are Richard's chosen and you have always made it clear that Richard was the most important thing in your life."

"I know, and I am sorry," he said softly. "At one time, that was true. But no longer. You, Lady de Lohr, are the most important thing in my life and I love you with every last fiber of my being. I have known that for some time now, but I have never been fully able to admit it. It is still difficult to believe."

Miraculously, her tears vanished and were replaced by the most radiant of smiles. "But you already told me you loved me. I was satisfied with that."

He grinned lazily, "I thought I was, too. But I was wrong. You consume me, lady, and I can think of nothing but you. This separation that we face is paining me more than you can possibly know."

"I know your pain too well," she said softly. "It eats at me like a cancer. With every step you take, with every mile of distance between us, I feel as if my life is slipping further and further away. I am so scared, Chris, I cannot think straight sometimes. 'Tis all happening so fast."

He continued to stroke her hair, devour her face. Then, he smiled. "Do you know that for two people who didn't want to be married, we are acting like a couple of sotted fools. Do you suppose marriage agrees with us?"

She smiled broadly. "It does. My mother would be most pleased, I think. She did so want us to like each other."

"Lady Mary would be in her heaven to see that we have fallen in love with one another," he agreed, pulling her down to the soft curve of his shoulder. "And your father, too. On his deathbed, he asked that I wed you and give you children; that was all. He said I didn't even have to like you."

She felt him chuckle and she made a wry face. "Marry me and give me children, eh? I am sure my father was in fits because I was nineteen and not yet wed; not even betrothed." She ran her hand over his faintly hairy chest. "But why you, Chris? Of all the men my father could have chosen, why you?"

He had wondered that, too, of course. "I do not know, sweet," he said with a sigh. "But we really must show our thanks to your father and his brilliance. Mayhap we will name our firstborn son after him."

"Arthur? Pah!" Dustin's head came up and she made a face at him. "I do not like that name. Our son will have a strong name, as I have told you before. His name will be Curtis."

"Curtis?" he pretended to greatly disapprove of the name when, in truth, he had agreed on it once before, months back. "I do not know. Why cannot we name him after me? Actually, I have always liked the name Percival."

"Percival?" she said in outrage. "No child of mine will bear the name Percy. Our son will be named Curtis, or I swear I shall bear you only daughters."

He laughed. "Good Christ, you would, wouldn't you? I'd have a household full of stubborn, willful little wenches just like their mother and I would surely go mad."

She grinned at him. "Ten of them, just like me. Are you properly frightened now? Will you agree to the name Curtis?"

He put his hand over his face in defeat. "Anything, anything if you will spare me that living hell."

She continued to grin at him as he looked at her from underneath his hand. Then he dragged it the length of his face and pulled her down to him once again.

"I love you, Dustin," he said softly. Against him, he felt her snicker. "Why do you laugh?"

"Because that is the first time you have ever told me without me telling you first," she said. "Lord, Chris, you are turning into a sappy fool with enough honeyed words to fill a cesspool."

"And you hate honeyed words, I know," he agreed with an exaggerated roll of the eyes. "Please do not slug me."

"I won't, I promise," she said, snuggling against him. "Only from you will I hear those words."

He held her for the longest time, staring up at the dark ceiling, wondering what the future would hold for them both. He knew they needed to get up and moving, but he simply could not bring himself to break the spell. When Dustin fell asleep she began snoring softly, he listened to her every breath as if it would sustain him. The depression he was experiencing was overwhelming.

Eventually he forced himself to rise, donning his clothes. Darren had his armor and would soon be pounding on the door of the antechamber, demanding to dress his liege. He glanced at Dustin, reluctant to wake her, but knowing it was necessary. With a final loving gaze, he roused his sleeping wife.

CHAPTER THIRTY-FOUR

AROUND MIDNIGHT, DUSTIN and Deborah were loaded onto their horses to begin the journey back to Lioncross. Temperatures were well below freezing and a light snow was falling as Christopher and his knights made sure the two armies were well prepared and organized.

There would be two armies leaving Windsor this night, over a thousand going with Christopher north to Nottingham and two hundred going with Dustin to Lioncross. The massive outer courtyard was full of soldiers and torches lit the area brightly. Dustin sat atop Hercules, watching what was going on solemnly. Her eyes on Christopher as he moved like an efficient war machine, completely competent in what he was doing as he put hundreds and hundreds of people in order. He constantly amazed her with his perfection and intelligence.

Hercules stirred uneasily underneath her and she comforted the big horse, knowing the cold was hard on his limbs as he stood unmoving. Deborah was beside her on a pretty gray palfrey, while Harold, Alexander and George rode in one of the wagons. Harold, however, broke free of the confines of the cart and dashed across the compound to where Christopher was giving orders. Dustin almost called to the dog but she saw Christopher lean down and give the mutt a pat on the head, and she smiled. The Christopher that had brought her to London months ago would have rather cut off his own hand than pet a dog.

Leeton came around loaded down with traveling blankets, thick things that weighed a ton. He proceeded to wrap Dustin in one of them, covering her completely from the waist down and covering the majority of Hercules, as well. Even though Dustin was swathed in layers of warm clothing, she was still glad for the protection. Deborah looked like a swaddled baby when he got finished with her and Dustin giggled.

The snow was falling harder now and hot breath hung like fog in the still night air. The armies were now properly in order and ready to move as the knights, their duties complete, began to mount their destriers. Christopher was taking nearly 300 of Richard's loyal knights with him and the sight of all those men in armor was truly a scene to behold. Never had Dustin seen so many men dressed to the hilt for a battle and it was an awesome experience. The power her husband held within the kingdom began to take on new dimension in her eyes, for she could not truly grasp the concept until she saw the reality before her. And with the new respect came a new hope; surely with all of these men protecting him, it was inevitable that Christopher come home to her unscathed.

Christopher moved back across the courtyard toward his wife and her party with Harold scampering at his feet. His armor acted like one giant block of ice with all of the snow coating it, yet he wasn't cold. As was usual with him before a battle march, his energy flowed and he felt nothing but the power within him focusing on the fight ahead. There was no one more singularly-visioned in a battle than he, breathing and eating war. But he found that the most unusual thing was happening to him; he could not get his wife from his mind and he was constantly distracted by her presence. He wanted to be with her so that he had to stop himself from rushing through the necessary preparations and give them the full attention they required. Distraction could be deadly in his profession.

He approached his wife, his gaze good-naturedly reproving. "You are as big as that horse with all of the material you are wearing."

"You made me wear all of this clothing," she shot back. "I can barely move with all of the weight."

He snorted. "You shall be grateful for the weight and the warmth when the weather worsens, Lady de Lohr, and you shall thank me." He glanced at his sister, eye-level with him on her small palfrey. "Are you sure you do not want to ride with Leeton? That little animal doesn't look entirely hearty."

"She is quite hearty, I assure you," Deborah answered. "She has taken me many places without incident."

He frowned doubtfully but didn't argue. Instead, he moved closer to Dustin. "Leeton has instructions to stop and allow you two to rest come morning, but sleep no longer than a few hours. I want you back within the safety of Lioncross as soon as possible."

She nodded, curling her gloved hand around his great mailed one. "Why the urgency, Chris? We cannot even sleep the night and leave when dawn breaks?" She nodded her head toward Deborah. "I worry for her health; she is not as strong as you or I."

He raised an eyebrow, but she could feel his hand gently squeezing her own. "You ask me that now? You have known for a while now that you would be leaving come nightfall."

"I know, but the urgency to leave Windsor seems to be gaining. It didn't seem quite so pressing this morning, even after the earl attacked me." She lowered her voice. "What is so wrong that we must leave in the dead of night?"

"I must leave tonight if I am to rendezvous with John's forces before he can reach Tickhill," he said. "I will not leave you here alone, even for a night. When I leave, you leave. Simple enough?"

"Aye," she nodded, feeling foolish to question his wisdom. "When…when do you think you will be returning?"

The pressure from his hand grew stronger. "I know not, sweet love. Within a month, hopefully, but I cannot know."

She gave him a sad, resigned smile. "Spring is coming. Lioncross is beautiful in spring."

"I look forward to it," he said softly. "And you."

"I can only pray that this ugly business is over with quickly and you can return to me permanently," she said. "Mayhap you will dispose of John quickly enough that…"

A shout cut her off. "Chris. We await you," David yelled.

Christopher waved at his brother and turned back to his wife. Dustin braced herself; the time had finally arrived and she was trying hard to keep her promise and not cry, but gazing into his sky-blue eyes forced sobs into her throat. When he smiled sweetly at her, she blinked and fat tears rolled down her cheeks.

"No, Dustin, do not." He reached up and brushed the tears away. "No tears. I want to see you smile."

"I cannot." she squeaked.

He laughed softly and kissed her gloved hand. "I shall return as soon as I can, I promise. Know that you mean the world to me, wife. I shall always return to you."

She could only nod, afraid if she opened her mouth she would start bawling like a baby. He tried to release her hand but she held onto it tightly, her head bowed as she tried to compose herself.

"It is time to leave, sweetheart," he said gently. "I have to go."

She nodded again, swallowing down all of the tears and sadness she was feeling. "I know I just wanted to tell you…tell you that I love you."

He winked at her and kissed her hand again, pulling his fingers away more firmly this time and she had no choice but to let him go.

He took a couple of steps away and Harold danced around him eagerly. He frowned at the dog.

"Dustin, I cannot take this mongrel with me," he said sternly. "Control him, would you?"

She sniffed, forcing herself to be brave as she focused on the wriggling dog. "He wants to go with you. Why cannot you take him?"

He eyed her reproachfully. "Dogs do not go into battle. Call him to you so that I might leave."

"Harold won't get in the way, Chris," she said. "You have been taking him to the practice field with you; he likes the excitement of battle."

"Dustin, I will not be responsible for Hal being gored on the battlefield," he said, picking the chunky dog up and put him in front of his wife. "Take him."

Dustin gripped the fat mutt in front of her, struggling to hold him as he twisted and fought. He eventually plunged from the horse and raced back across the courtyard to where Christopher was preparing to mount up. She saw her husband say something to the dog, point at her, and then eventually give up when Harold refused to cooperate. He mounted his steed and motioned to

David, reining his horse in Dustin's direction as David shouted orders.

He thundered over to his wife as Harold raced beside the animal, very careful of the hooves that were as big as he was. Christopher swung past Leeton and relayed his orders, and immediately the column of men were set in motion. Hercules lurched forward as Christopher reined his destrier beside her.

Dustin didn't say anything, content to gaze at his powerful face. His eyes roved over the two moving armies, scrutinizing every man and bellowing to his officers when he detected an anomaly. Although they had just begun to move, she could tell by his manner that for all purposes, he was already at war.

It made an awesome sight, over a thousand soldiers moving out in the falling snow, countless torches lighting their way. The courtyard was alive with dancing shadows and shouting men as the rhythm of the march picked up, with the armor and swords jingling in synchronization.

Dustin was very warm in spite of the freezing temperatures, and was actually feeling some of the excitement that was in the air. And it was excitement, not fear or apprehension as she would have expected on a battle march. These men were seasoned, trained soldiers, preparing to do Richard's work by defending him against his raging brother. The confidence she sensed around her served to boost her failing spirit and she knew these men gained their assurance from her husband. She gazed at him, pride filling her.

He sensed her eyes on him and turned to her. "Why are you looking at me like that?"

She shook her head, a faint smile on her lips. "No reason, husband. Am I not allowed to look at you whenever I please?"

"You are, provided that you tell me why you are smiling," he answered.

Her smile twisted with mock irritation. "Did you tell me not five minutes ago that you wanted to see me smile? Now I am smiling and you demand to know why."

He snickered and shook his head, glancing off in the direction of a particularly loud shout before returning to his wife. Even then, he would only smile slyly at her.

Dustin liked his smile, it was flirtatious and she responded with a coy look of her own. Their separation was a mere minutes away, but she wasn't thinking on it. She was enjoying his mood.

"How's your horse handling these days?" she asked.

He cuffed the horse affectionately on the neck. "He is doing much better. I think he will do very well on this campaign."

"What did you finally decide to name him?" she inquired.

He shrugged. "I have been calling him 'horse'. His trainer called him Brutus, a name I detest. You are good with names, think of one."

She looked closely at the animal, a magnificent silver dapple with a salt-and-pepper mane. "You were so intent on naming a son of ours Arthur. Why not name your horse Arthur?"

"Your father would rise from the grave if I named a horse after him," Christopher snorted. "Ah, well, think of a name while I am gone."

Dustin's party passed under the portcullis first, and Christopher with them. When the entire column of troops had passed onto the road and turned northwest, Christopher took hold of Hercules' reins and pulled his wife from the procession, waiting until it passed by them completely before speaking. Behind them, his massive army was passing through the gate and turning due north.

He flipped up his visor, delicate flakes of snow touching his face as he gazed into the face of the woman he loved with all of his heart. He ached with loneliness already.

"Leeton and Sir Nicholas will be joining me as soon once you are settled," he said, his throat tight with emotion. "Max, Anthony and Jeffrey will be remaining with you at Lioncross. Obey them, Dustin, for I do not want to have to worry about you while I am away."

Much to her surprise, she found her tears were gone and replaced by a warm feeling of trust and love. Christopher seemed more distressed than she did.

"I promise, I will obey them," she said with a saucy bat of her eyelashes. "Even if it kills me, I shall be agreeable."

Her courage soothed his own aching heart and he managed a smile. "If you are agreeable, 'twill be a small miracle. Now ride on and join Deborah, sweetheart. Take care of yourself."

She smiled beautifully, gathering Hercules' reins. He wanted to see her smile, and she would oblige him. "Be safe, husband. Take care of Harold."

He glanced down and saw that the dog was indeed sitting politely by his destrier. He groaned. "Christ, Hal. What am I going to do with you?"

"Feed him, let him warm your bed," Dustin teased softly.

Christopher reined his horse close to her. "You are the only one to warm my bed, wife. But I will feed him," he reached out a massive gloved hand and swallowed up half of her head. "Give me a kiss."

Dustin almost unseated herself as she responded to him, the most loving kiss either one of them could remember.

"Go," he said. His throat was tight again. "Leeton is waiting for you."

Dustin turned Hercules around, throwing one last glance at Christopher. He waved at her, watching as she spurred her horse like a man and raced back along the column toward Leeton, waiting patiently by the road on his roan destrier. Christ, he felt as if his heart was being ripped from his chest, but he forced himself to tear his eyes from her.

Slamming down his visor, he drove his destrier in the direction of his northward-bound army.

RISE OF THE DEFENDER

LONG LIVE THE KING

PART 3

CHAPTER THIRTY-FIVE

CHRISTOPHER AND HIS mighty army were not in time to save Tickhill Castle from being consumed by John and his forces. Led by Sir Dennis and his band of mercenary generals, they were a surprisingly strong and disciplined army. The crown troops laid siege to Tickhill for nearly two weeks before retreating. John was anchored in deeply at Tickhill and Christopher reluctantly decided to pull back to a safe distance to anticipate John's next move. Tickhill was lost for the moment and it was difficult for him to admit it.

As Christopher knew, the army was not to stay at Tickhill. After establishing jail-like security in and around the fortress, the army banded together once again and moved northwest toward York. Christopher found himself chasing after the army as a mother after an unruly child. The mercenary army would attack every fortress in their path and the crown troops would be there to defend and repel, losing a few castles but saving more than they lost.

It was frustrating and exhausting work. John was grimly determined to seize England castle by castle, hoping to shut off the north from the rest of the country; to conquer it keep by keep.

Christopher knew the tactical planning to be Sir Dennis'. The man was a cunning soldier, if not a bit reckless. He had a huge army with voracious fighters that he used handily, moving from one castle to the next with incredible speed. Christopher had a devil of a time keeping up with them.

February moved into March, and March into April. His thirty-sixth birthday came and went on the battlefield, the same day that Edward suffered a nearly mortal wound to the groin. The knight hovered one step above death for nearly a week before showing any improvement, so Christopher sent him back to Lioncross as soon as he was able to travel. Edward carried with him a special written message for Lady de Lohr from her husband. Christopher had slept the night before with the message clutched to him, knowing it would soon be touching Dustin's own hands. He missed her more than words could express.

Spring came and went, moving into summer and Christopher found himself in East Anglia outside of Norwich. He had relatives here but did not stop to visit. The justices had been sending him regular communication regarding Richard's situation; a circumstance still unimproved. Richard was well and was still being held captive, and the justices were in the process of raising the ransom demand. All they asked of Christopher was to control John as best he could. More and more of Richard's troops were coming home from the Holy Land every day and soon Christopher would have another army larger than the one presently under his command waiting at Windsor. With over four thousand men, he would surely destroy John and regain the seven keeps he had been unsuccessful in defending.

With the heated summer months, the battles seemed to wane and eventually there was a strained standoff. John still held seven castles, but he had made no more advances, and the majority of his field army, including Sir Dennis, had retreated to Nottingham. The situation was at a stalemate, a state Christopher guessed would remain for a length of time while John rethought his strategy. At the beginning of August, he saw his opportunity to return to Lioncross for the first time in almost a year.

With his troops taking a well-deserved break in London, Christopher set off for home. He and his five knights rode all day and all night, not pausing to rest, for they knew how eager their liege was to see his beautiful wife. And, in faith, they were eager for the coming rest they so very much needed.

The humidity of August was bearable as he crossed onto his land, his stomach twisting with excitement to be closer to Dustin than he had been in six months. He wondered how she would react upon seeing him, for he had sent no word ahead. He wondered if she still loved him, or if she had forgotten about him altogether. The humidity of the day meant nothing to him as the late morning sun beat down on his oven-like armor. He felt nothing but relief as he rounded a crest and the mighty fortress of Lioncross loomed in the distance.

David reined his horse alongside, smiling at his brother's face. "Jesus, Chris, you look like you are seeing a ghost."

"I feel as if I am living a dream," Christopher said quietly. "Christ, David, has it been so long? I cannot believe we have actually arrived."

"We have," David said with a nod, gazing off at Lioncross. "I only hope your wife does not kill you for giving her the surprise of her life."

Christopher nodded in agreement, not replying as they drew closer to the village. Harold, racing alongside Christopher in his customary place, suddenly took off after a rabbit and Christopher whistled loudly to the mutt. The dog had been his constant companion throughout the campaign and the two were inseparable. He and David had taken to treating the dog like one of the family, feeding it from the table and letting it sleep in its own bed. Harold had become a kind of mascot, a tough little scrapper of a dog with a heart as big as England herself.

Passing through the town, he saw that it had not changed a lick and was mildly surprised when the villagers recognized him and turned out to give him welcome. Pleased as he was, he did not acknowledge them. His mind, his attention, was on his fortress. Anticipation and excitement shook his belly until his hands quivered. He simply could not wait to take his wife in his arms and tell her how much he had missed her.

Lioncross Abbey loomed before them, the squat and powerful walls embracing the oddly-shaped keep. Shouts went up on the wall of the fortress and the huge gates began to yawn before him. His men had seen him coming and had turned out en masse to greet their liege. He could not fight off the grin as his troops cheered him wildly as he passed through the gate, his eyes raking over his structure to make sure everything was as he had left it. Much to his pleasure, the fortress was as strong and solid as ever and he reined his horse to a halt in the middle of the dusty bailey.

Max and Anthony rushed to him like eager children, welcoming him home with handshakes and claps. Christopher slapped Max on the side of the head, demanding his wife before any words of greeting were exchanged.

"I should have known," Anthony said. "He returns not to his fortress or his men, but to his wife who has been ruling us like Nero."

"Nero, did you say?" Christopher shrugged. "That sounds about right. Where is my little Caesar?"

"In back with her garden," Max replied. "She has spent nearly every day there and it thrives. Keeps that damn monkey with her, too, and that little blond dog."

Christopher whistled to Harold, who was immediately beside him. "Go find your mistress," he told the animal, and it darted off as if it knew exactly what he was saying. He looked at Max again. "Did the cat ever return home?"

"Aye, it did, and it sleeps with your wife, along with the other pets," Max said. "You are going to have quite a fight on your hands trying to claim your rightful place in bed. But, in truth, the monkey has become rather fond of Edward and sleeps with him at times."

Christopher grinned and removed his gauntlets. "Where is de Wolfe?"

"With your wife, I imagine," Max answered. "He has hardly let her out of his sight."

"Good man," Christopher said firmly, pushing past the group of them. "Make yourselves useful, men. I would see to my wife now."

Jeffrey exited the castle just as Christopher entered, exchanging words of pleasant surprise with him before pointing him in the direction of his wife. As Christopher ducked inside, Jeffrey descended the stairs and greeted the group of returning knights.

"I see battle agrees with you," he remarked, sizing up the familiar men, as well as unfamiliar men. "The baron looks healthy enough."

"The man is immortal," Leeton sighed, leaning against his destrier. "But I am not. I want food and sleep, in that order."

The other knights agreed heartily, yelling for their destriers to be tended. With the horses taken care of, they were free to proceed into the castle and to the first decent meal in months. Max and Anthony were chattering like magpies, filling the returning warriors in on all of the happenings during their absence. The group of knights mounted the stairs, all running off at the mouth like children.

"Was the baron surprised when you told him of his wife?" Jeffrey asked.

Max shrugged. "We did not tell him. He will see for himself."

"See what?" David demanded. "Is Dustin all right?"

Max grinned at his brother. "She's fine. Better than fine," he smirked at David. "She's with child."

David's mouth opened in astonishment. "She's pregnant?"

Anthony put his arms out in front of him, mimicking a rounded stomach. "Verily."

Jeffrey shot them all reproving looks. " 'Tis disrespectful to speak of Lady Dustin in such a manner. You should show more consideration and tact."

Max punched Jeffrey in the arm. "Do not be so serious, Kessler. You know we hold the utmost esteem for Lady Dustin."

Jeffrey scowled as he entered the castle. "Uncouth heathens, the lot of you."

Christopher was quivering with excitement. He passed through the grand hall, making note of the interior of his keep as he moved through and into the kitchens. The servants bowed and scraped as he passed by, surprised their lord had returned home and scurrying to prepare a hasty welcome.

They were all in awe of the man, having heard of his exploits from Lady Dustin. The cook caught sight of him and promised him a meal fit for a king, and was rewarded in turn by a smile. Truth was, he would have been even more pleased at the respect of the servants, had he not been so preoccupied with finding his wife.

He exited the castle and went into the small kitchen bailey where Dustin kept her rabbits. It looked the same as when he had left it. The hutch was still against the wall and was well kept, loaded with bunnies. He veered to his left and toward the great walled garden where Dustin's mother had kept flowers, the same garden that his wife was tending now. His palms began to sweat with anticipation as he passed through the arched gateway.

Inside, the garden was absolutely lovely. He paused, his eyes falling on the blond head several feet away, sitting on the ground with her back to him. Edward was immediately to his right, seated in a chair made from willow branches.

Edward's eyes were huge with surprise and he bolted to his feet, his mouth opening but Christopher held up a silencing hand. Edward caught himself before he spoke, answering Christopher with a broad smile and a quiet handshake. Christopher tore his eyes from his wife long enough to look his knight over, seeing the man had not regained the weight he had lost from his infirmary, but appearing healthy enough. He motioned Edward away with a nod of his head.

Dustin was busy doing something he could not see. The monkey sat atop the garden wall, screaming at Christopher as he approached Dustin, and he thought for sure the little beast had ruined his surprise. But Dustin ignored the monkey.

"Shut up, George," she snapped. "You are so damn loud."

Christopher grinned, sneaking up behind his wife and drinking in the sight of her. A few feet in front of her, Alexander rose from his crouch and wagged his tail at Christopher. Yet Dustin was still focused on the bush in front of her.

"Edward, is it time for the nooning meal yet? I think the animals are hungry," she said. Receiving no answer, she turned her head. "Edward?"

The first thing she saw was a pair of legs. Massive, tall, armored legs. Startled, she jerked her head up to see who it was.

Christopher smiled back at her. "Greetings, wife."

Dustin's mouth fell open; stunned was an understatement. She thought she was daydreaming, but when he laughed softly at her astonishment, she seemed to snap out of her trance.

"Chris?" she gasped. "My God… is it really you?"

"Aye, Lady de Lohr, in the flesh." He put his hands on his hips. "What? No feverish kisses? No screaming or jumping? 'Tis most unlike you to be so calm."

Tears filled her eyes and she threw the basket off her lap onto the ground, dumping the flowers it held. As she struggled to her feet, it was Christopher's turn to be immensely surprised. The first thing his eyes fell on was her rounded belly.

"Dustin!" he gasped in shock. "You are pregnant!"

She was on her feet, her arms going about him tightly. He responded to her fiercely, pulling her to him but in the same breath remembering her delicate condition. He had thought to surprise her by his unannounced arrival but it would seem that the joke was on him.

He held her so reverently, listening to her soft sobs, unbelievable happiness filling him. His hands stroked her magnificent hair, her back, his lips kissing her with utter sweetness. It was a long while before either one could speak as their mutual surprise settled.

"Are you all right, sweetheart?" He held her face in his huge hands. "Christ, I cannot believe… I am astonished. Thrilled and astonished."

She smiled at him, kissing him a few times before answering. "I hoped you would be," she said softly. "I could only hope that you would return home before your son was born."

His eyebrows flew up. "You thought not to tell me before that time?"

She grinned, wiping at her eyes. "I would have told you."

His hands moved over her rounded belly, amazed. Her first pregnancy had ended before her stomach had enlarged and he was seriously delighted to feel the firm curve of her stomach.

Dustin watched his face, his expression so completely astounded, and laughed softly at his reaction.

"Aye, there is a baby in there," she told him. "The village has a new midwife since Rebecca's mother was killed. She comes every day to visit me."

He shook his head faintly, still caressing her belly. "My God, I still cannot believe it," he breathed. "A baby."

"A son," Dustin said firmly, touching his face and he kissed her hand. "Oh, Chris, I cannot believe you're actually here. Why did not you send word to me?"

He shrugged. "Because I did not want to take the time to send the missive. I simply wanted to come." He pulled her to him again, so completely worshipful of her. "I missed you terribly, Dustin. There was not a day or an hour that passed that I did not think of you, and wondered how you were."

"I thought about you all day and all night," she rubbed her stomach. "It was hard not to."

He grinned, kissing her happily. "Do you feel well?"

She made a face. "Better than I did. But I still cannot eat mutton. It makes me gag. And I cannot even look at raw meat."

He laughed. "Then I will order that no raw meat be anywhere within your proximity." He suddenly lifted her high above him as if she were no more than a feather's weight.

"I am to have a child!" he bellowed.

Dustin laughed, bracing her hands on his huge shoulders as he brought her down to kiss her and then lowered her completely to the ground, afraid he had jostled her too much with his excitement. He helped her straighten her dress.

"Did I hurt you?" he asked rather anxiously. "I am sorry; I should not have done that."

She sighed with mock irritation, eyeing him. "Are we to go through this again? Lord, Chris, I shall not break. Edward wants to do everything but walk for me, and he is driving me mad. If I have two of you to deal with, I shall scream."

He had no sympathy for her. "Not only two, but nine. I brought all of my knights with me and I can promise you, Lady de Lohr, that you will want for nothing." He hugged her happily. "You shall be lucky if your feet touch the ground at all."

She batted at him playfully. "Untrue, my lord. I will do my own walking, thank you. And I want no nervous men following me about."

"I am afraid it goes without saying," he said, kissing her cheek. "When is the child due?"

"The midwife believes a month before my birthday, the first of November," she said.

He looked thoughtful. "That would stand to reason considering the last we made love was the beginning of February."

She shook her head. "You keep track of these things as well as I do," she said. "I have never heard of a husband who remembered details so very well."

"I remember everything." His voice suddenly went seductive and Dustin felt chills of desire run through her. "I look forward to this eve, wife, when I can inspect every inch of your luscious body in private."

"As do I." She wound her arms around his neck as he buried his face in her shoulder. "Lord, Chris, I have dreamed about you for so long."

"I know of your dreams," he teased. "Erotic and highly real. Yet they cannot compare to real life."

He meant her episode with Marcus so many months back and her smile faded. She had completely forgotten about Marcus Burton until that very moment and now, she felt sick again. The guilt, the horror, washed over her again as if it had never left, but she struggled to put it aside. She didn't want anything dampening his homecoming. Not even memories of Marcus.

"Take me inside," she said softly, her mood spoiling. "I would greet your warriors home."

His arm about her waist protectively, they went inside with George and Alex in tow. Inside the grand hall, the knights had gathered and were talking loudly over ale and cheese. When they saw Dustin, those who had not seen her since her pregnancy, crowed with delight and congratulated Christopher on his virility. He grinned at them, waving them off as he and Dustin sat at the table.

Dustin's somber mood quickly fled as life was once again breathed back into Lioncross' great hall. To hear the familiar voices again and to listen to the camaraderie was pure pleasure, and Dustin realized how much she had missed it. Even Christopher had a few stories to tell and she listened with great interest. And as soon as he started to speak in his deep, rich voice, the little life inside of her began kicking fiercely.

"Give me your hand," she demanded, quieting all of them. She placed Christopher's huge hand over her stomach and smiled broadly as he felt his child move for the first time.

Christopher's face lit up like a bank of Christmas candles. His mouth opened with surprise as he indeed felt his child kick violently in Dustin's stomach. The babe was extremely active and Dustin grabbed David's hand and put it next to his brother's.

"Jesus," David exclaimed, feeling the thumping. "What power! Does it hurt?"

She shook her head. "Of course not. But it is very bothersome when he does it in the middle of the night."

"Does he do this often?" Christopher asked, still in awe.

"All of the time," she said wearily.

"Get your hand off my wife," Christopher growled at his brother, then his tone went immediately sweet again. "Are you sure it doesn't hurt? He is amazingly strong."

"He is like his father," Dustin's eyes twinkled.

Christopher removed his hand from her belly and took her hand, kissing it. His eyes never left her face.

The conversation resumed around them, but they were lost to the world. They could only see and feel each other. The conversation between them was quiet and private until Christopher finally rose and excused them both. He would wait no longer to get her alone.

Dustin was as giddy as a new bride as he took her up to the chamber he had occupied before leaving for London. He was not surprised to see that she had moved all of her personal belongings into them, as he had told her he would do when he returned.

He smiled and sat her down in a hide-covered chair. "Now, I would get a good look at you without all of those infatuated schoolboys hanging about," he said softly, moving to remove his armor.

Dustin saw what he was doing and stood up again. "Let me help you."

"Nay, sweetheart, I will do this alone," he waved her off. "I left Darren in London to visit with his mother and I forbid you to take his place."

"But I have helped you with your armor on numerous occasions," she insisted.

"But you were not carrying my babe on those occasions," he said with a twinkle in his eye. His breastplate clattered to the floor and he pulled off his tunic, moving to his hauberk. "How have things been around here?"

"Well," she said, watching him with his leg armor. "Jeffrey has been keeping the collections from the border revenues in some secret place; he wouldn't even tell me. He said that only you would know their location and worth. And the village has been peaceful."

"No raids?" he asked.

"Not since I have been home," she replied. "Strange; the Welsh seemed to have stopped their aggressions altogether. The merchants and travelers that come over the border have been very friendly and honest."

"How would you know?" he looked at her in the process of removing his tunic. "You haven't been out carousing the village in your condition, have you?"

Her chin jutted up. "I have gone into the village a few times, husband. I have always taken Jeffrey or Max or Anthony with me, as you requested."

He frowned. "They know better than to allow you to roam about and tire yourself. I will have to have a talk with them."

"You shall do nothing of the sort," she said firmly. "They had no choice in the matter; I was going with or without them."

His look was most reproachful as the tunic hit the floor. "You are most obstinate, Lady de Lohr. Now that I am home, things will be as they should."

She suddenly smiled up at him. "Say it again."

"What? That things shall be as they should? Or that you are obstinate?"

"Nay," she said softly. "Lady de Lohr."

He met her smile, sinking to his knees in front of her and enveloping her and the chair with his massive arms. "Lady de Lohr," he whispered. "The Lady Dustin Mary Catherine Barringdon de Lohr."

She giggled and ran her hands through his blond hair, tracing his features and reacquainting herself with his thick face.

"I am so glad you are back," she whispered. "Do you have any new scars to report to me before I find them and become upset?"

He looked as thoughtful as he could under her silky touch, paying more attention to her hands than to her question. "Scars?" he repeated. "A few, mostly on my arms and one on my leg. Nothing terrible."

"Then you were not wounded severely in any way?" she pressed, ceasing to stroke his head and pulling his left arm in front of her where she could inspect it.

He flipped his wrist over so she could inspect a two-inch scar on the underside of his thick forearm. "I got that when my horse disobeyed a command, damnable beast. But in answer to your question, no, I was not severely wounded in any way. Edward was the only knight in my command to be severely wounded."

She ran a finger over his new scar. "He still has trouble walking, Chris. And I have heard the knights say that he is afraid to pick up a sword. Do you suppose he does not want to fight anymore?"

Christopher's heart sank a little; he had had the same suspicions about Edward. The man just had not seemed himself since he had been wounded. Mayhap now that he was returned, he could convince Edward otherwise. The man was a fine knight, one of the very best, else he would not have been in the Defender's service.

"Edward was nearly killed, sweetheart," he replied. " 'Tis natural that he may be afraid to go into battle again, but I shall deal with him. Now tell me; how is my sister and why have I not seen her?"

Dustin smiled most marvelously. "Oh, Chris, you will be so happy to hear that Deborah is in love."

"In love?" he repeated sharply. "With whom?"

"A man from the village," she replied. When Christopher's mouth opened in outrage, she put a hand over his lips to allow her to finish. "He is a scholar, Chris. He teaches the children in the village to read and he is deeply admired and respected. He and Deborah have fallen in love."

"My sister is in love with a scholar?" he said through her hand and she removed it. "Where is she, Dustin?"

"With him," she replied, still smiling. "He holds class three days a week and Deborah helps him. Even now, he is teaching a whole room full of children to read. The class is over at the monastery."

He was truly flabbergasted. How could he possibly be angry that his sister was missing? Deborah was in love, properly escorted in a monastery filled with priests, helping her lover teach a class of children. Nothing suited her more, but that was not the point.

"This man is not even a knight?" he asked.

"Nay," she replied. "His father was a scholar, and his grandfather a bishop. He is very smart, almost as smart as you. I think you will like him."

Christopher stood up, rubbing his chin absently. "He is not of our station, Dustin. I do not know if I can allow this to continue."

Dustin stood up. "Why not?" she asked. "No one else has asked for Deborah's hand, and she truly loves this man. You cannot possibly condemn them."

He sighed; it was so much more complicated than that. "Dustin, it is not a matter of condemning them or not. Deborah is my sister, a de Lohr, and when I choose her husband I must be sure that the man is capable of protecting her. Deborah is nearly as vulnerable as you because of her relationship to me."

Dustin saw his point but she was greatly distressed on Deborah's behalf. "Chris, Deborah has known so little happiness in her life. She was raised from infancy by strangers because you and David were off on your own, and for the first time in her life she has a sense of belonging and of family. She loves Gowen. She wants to be his wife and have her own family."

"Gowen. The man's name is *Gowen,*" Christopher snorted ironically. "Christ, even his name sounds scholarly."

Dustin put her hands on her hips irritably. "Well, if you are so worried about your sister's safety, then send a troop of soldiers to protect her. Why does the husband always have to do the protecting, as if that were part of the husbandly oath?"

"Because it is," he said. "A husband is required to protect his wife, and to bear arms to be able to defend what is his. What is *Gowen* going to do when confronted with those who would harm my sister? Read them to death?"

He said the name "Gowen" as if the man was a feminine little frill, and Dustin was greatly annoyed.

"Where does it say that in order to be a good husband, you must know how to bear arms?" she demanded. "The knowledge of warfare and weapons does not guarantee a satisfactory husband. Take the Earl of Fenwark, for example; the man fought admirably, yet he was a terrible husband. If you had to pick between Gowen and the earl for Deborah, which choice would you make? A man who would love her and be kind to her, or a man who would simply protect her should the need arise, and to hell with everything else."

He gazed back at her, impressed with her argument, but firm nonetheless. "I must do what I feel is right for my sister," he said. " 'Tis not her choice to make, nor yours, nor Gowen's. 'Tis mine."

Dustin crossed her arms angrily over her rounded stomach. "And what if Deborah were your daughter, Chris? Would you marry her off to a man simply because he could protect her and forget about her happiness?"

His stance softened imperceptibly. "Dustin, you are asking me to make a decision of the heart when I must make it of the head."

"And you are avoiding answering me because you know I am I right," she said, feeling herself gaining the advantage. "If you are so concerned with Deborah's protection, then why can't she and Gowen live here, with us? That way, you will be able to protect her always. Would you deny her the happiness we have found?"

He stared back at her for a few moments. When he spoke, his voice was soft and warm. "When did you become so wise?" he asked. "Did this miraculously happen while I was away?"

She grinned. "I have had to do several things on my own since you were away, including sleeping alone in your great bed."

"No longer," he said, returning her smile. After a moment, he sighed with resignation. "Very well, wife. I will meet this Gowen and decide for myself whether or not he is worthy of my sister."

"Stop saying his name so disdainfully," she insisted. "I have known Gowen since we were children. He is a fine man."

He reached out and grabbed her hand, pulling her over to the bed. "He was not, perchance, one of the many suitors you had while your father was away?"

She shook her head. "Nay, he wasn't interested in me or the keep. But he is very interested in Deborah."

Christopher grumbled. "Well for him that he did not set his sights on you, else I would not allow him near my fortress."

She only smiled, thinking how firmly he spoke of other men's feelings for her when he had allowed Marcus, mayhap the biggest threat of all, to be so close to her. She remembered Deborah's own words, how Christopher had feigned ignorance where Marcus was concerned because of his respect for Marcus, and she saw the words to be true. He had killed on her behalf before and was not hesitant to do so again, yet he completely overlooked Marcus Burton. She wondered if he knew of the full extent of her relationship with Marcus, if he would still continue to overlook the obvious.

She doubted it.

ꝏ

DEBORAH RETURNED TO the keep by mid-afternoon after being informed her brothers had returned. She would have left sooner but she did not want to leave Gowen in the middle of a class, so she waited eagerly for the session to end. She gazed out of the lancet window up to the massive fortress on the rise, excited to see Christopher and David, and excited to tell them about Gowen.

Gowen accompanied her to the fortress, much more nervous than he would admit now that he was about to meet mayhap the most powerful warrior in the realm. He could scarce believe Deborah returned his feelings, and he furthermore knew he wasn't the least bit good enough for her.

But he kept his ideas to himself, hoping beyond hope that the baron would somehow bring forth a miracle and accept him. If he did not, then Gowen knew he would surely never marry because he loved Deborah far too much to consider another woman. But if he did, then he would be truly astonished. He prayed harder than he ever had that the baron would receive him, considering he was the father of Deborah's unborn child.

Max opened the gates for Deborah and Gowen, smiling amiably at the tall young man, not missing the chance to throw in a few good jibes at the scholar's expense. Gowen laughed but Deborah angrily shushed Max as they made their way to the front door.

The interior of the castle was dark but faintly warm, with smells of meat roasting for supper hovering in the air. A stocky black-and-white mutt appeared out of the darkness and growled menacingly at them, but reconsidered after smelling at Deborah's dress. Then, as if he gave approval for their presence, trotted off.

"*What* was that?" Gowen whispered, watching the frightening dog disappear.

"Hal," Deborah told him. "He's my brother's dog."

Dustin appeared from the hall, her face lit up with a beautiful smile. Gowen smiled back immediately, for Dustin always had that effect on him. He'd always thought her to be the most beautiful woman in the world, a dream so far beyond his grasp he had never thought to pursue it. Instead, he had been happy to be her friend.

Deborah and Dustin hugged each other tightly. "He's back," Deborah sighed. "Oh, Dustin, I am so happy. And David, too. Are they well?"

"In fighting form," Dustin said gleefully, then watched as Gowen's face paled. "So sorry, Gowen. I did not mean fight you."

They giggled as Gowen pretended to wipe his brow. "Did you tell him?" Deborah asked softly.

Dustin nodded. "Aye, I did," she replied, her voice quiet. They could all hear voices coming from the great hall directly ahead and knew the baron to be in there. "I told him everything I dare."

Deborah nodded. " 'Tis up to me to tell him the rest." She gazed back at Gowen and held out her hand. "But I appreciate you preparing him."

Dustin looked serious. "You have got to tell him everything, Deborah. Even if he rages and tears the place up, he must be told. 'Twill only be a few more weeks and he will guess everything."

"I know." Deborah and Gowen held hands tightly. "Oh, Dustin, you do not think he will hurt Gowen, do you?"

"Absolutely not," Dustin said emphatically. "I will not allow it. I shall throw myself in front of Gowen if I have to, if that is what it takes to stop him."

Gowen tried to get a better look at the occupants inside the room. "Which one is he?"

"At the head of the table, with the beard," Dustin said, her eyes finding her husband immediately.

"Which one? Oh....*that* one?" Gowen swallowed. "Good Lord, Dustin, you never told me that he was as big as a mountain. Oh, my dear God...."

He trailed off, looking sick, and Dustin shook her head. "Stop that," she admonished gently. "He is as gentle as a kitten."

Deborah gave Dustin a disbelieving look but said nothing, and Dustin took Gowen's other hand.

"Come now and meet him," she said, then fixed him with a pointed look. "And relax."

Dustin was the first one into the dining hall, smiling brightly at her husband. He returned the gesture and kissed her hand. He was about to say something to her when he caught sight of his sister leading a very tall, lanky young man behind her. Instantly, the smile vanished.

"Lady Deborah," he said formally. "How good of you to break away from your busy schedule to welcome me home."

Deborah let go of Gowen and went to Christopher, kissing him dutifully on the cheek before moving around to David. Gowen, meanwhile, felt the weighty stares of Richard's most powerful knights and he had never in his life been so scared. But Deborah smiled at him, putting her hand on Christopher's shoulder.

"Chris, I would like for you to meet someone very dear to me," she said softly. "This is Gowen Olmquist. Gowen, I'd like you to meet my brother, Baron Christopher de Lohr."

Gowen bowed gallantly, even though he was shaking like a leaf. "My lord, 'tis an honor and a pleasure," he said kindly.

Christopher did not say a word. He scrutinized Gowen, his silence sending the terror of the devil through the young man. He was extremely tall and thin, but was a nice-looking boy with dark blond hair and a thin mustache. His blue eyes were wide and honest, giving him a rather innocent look.

Dustin was feeling very uncomfortable for Gowen. She glanced at Deborah, seeing that her sister-in-law was also very uncomfortable. When she squeezed Christopher's hand insistently, he ignored her.

"How old are you, boy?" Leeton asked, not sounding at all like the friendly man they all knew.

"Twenty-five years, sire," Gowen replied. He had a wonderful speaking voice.

David, having studied his fill of Gowen, cleared his throat loudly and reached for his goblet. Dustin was about ready to kill all of them for their inexcusable rudeness, wondering why Christopher was being so bloody cold.

"Gowen and I met when we were five years old," she said, as she let go of her husband and went to her friend, entwining her arm in his. "He had a beehive and I used to pester him endlessly for honey. But being a true gentleman, he always granted my requests."

She made sure she was looking at Christopher when she said "true gentleman." Christopher did not so much as raise an eyebrow at her and David sat his goblet down and looked at Gowen curiously.

"Do you still raise *bees*?" he asked distastefully.

Dustin was infuriated with their arrogant attitude and condescending tone, and was preparing to tell them so when Gowen replied to David's question.

"Nay, sire, I do not," Gowen answered politely. " 'Twas a childhood hobby, nothing more. I spend my time teaching these days, and translating."

"Translating what?" David asked.

"The Bible," Gowen replied evenly. "I am in the process of translating the Bible from Latin to Welsh for a few of the Welsh border lords."

David cast Christopher a long look before turning away. Christopher, however, continued to stare at Gowen, analyzing every move the man made. The other knights ignored the young man as if he were no more than a spider in the corner, and Dustin was incensed. Christopher stared at the young man for several more tense moments before looking back to his ale.

"He may stay and sup with us," he said.

Dustin was mad enough to spit. "Oh, thank you, Your Holiness," she said with great exaggeration. "Your gracious benevolence is appreciated."

Anthony snorted into his goblet, the only reaction to her sarcastic remark. Christopher drank what was left in his cup, eyeing his sister.

"You look well enough," he commented. "How is Lioncross agreeing with you?"

Deborah was close to angry, embarrassed tears. "Well, my lord," she said. "Gowen has been most helpful acclimating me to the surroundings."

Christopher acted as if he didn't hear her. "I fought with someone you knew at Norwich, Deborah," he said casually. "Sir Liam Donavan. Do remember him? He certainly remembered you."

Dustin's mouth went agape. She squeezed Gowen's arm encouragingly before moving back to her husband.

"What does she care about Sir Liam Donavan?" she snapped softly. "We were speaking of Gowen."

Christopher gave his wife a lazy glance. "Mayhap *you* were. I was simply curious if she remembered a man who she seemed to have left an indelible impression on. David, do you remember Sir Liam?"

"Aye," David said with a firm nod. "A hell of a fighter. Swings a broadsword as well as anyone."

Deborah turned away, fighting off tears. She went over to Gowen and took his arm, urging him with her. Dustin watched them leave the room, enraged like the devil. When she heard the front door slam softly, she turned to her husband as if to kill him.

"How *dare* you treat him as if he were as common as dirt!" she exclaimed. "I have always known you to be arrogant and pompous, but I have never known you to be so utterly rude. I cannot believe you did not even respond to his greeting. Of all the conceited, nasty, haughty….."

She was raging and he put his hand up to still her, but she yanked away from him, telling them all what horrible, insensitive creatures they were. They were terrible, mean and cruel. Even Edward received an earful, for he had befriended Gowen over the past few months and she berated him for not defending him. No one was safe or spared from her tirade. Christopher sat and listened to her, knowing every word was true. But he had intended for it to be exactly as it was.

"Dustin," he said calmly.

"Do not talk to me," she snapped. "I am not finished with you yet."

"Aye, you are," he said. "I have heard enough."

"No, you have not," she threw back at him. "Christopher de Lohr, if you do not go and apologize to Gowen and Deborah right now, you can sleep with your soldiers tonight."

The knights, their heads lowered liked scolded dogs, glanced around at each other in anticipation of Christopher's reply. Their liege rose slowly to his feet, his gaze fixed on his wife.

"Do not threaten me," he said quietly. "Come here and sit down before you upset yourself."

"I will not," she snapped, turning her back on him and marching from the room.

Christopher went after her, his boots clapping loudly on the stones as he pursued his wife to their bedchamber. She slammed the door a few seconds in front of him, only to have it swing open violently and slam again, hard enough to rattle the furniture. The knights looked at each other and shook then heads; another bout was about to begin between the baron and his enraged wife.

Dustin stormed to the other side of the room, completely ignoring Christopher as she began to dig through the wardrobe and throw his clothes all over the room. He watched her with building irritation, but also with a certain amount of amusement; she could be very physical when riled, but her movements were so jerky and magnified that they were comical. He had heard that pregnant women were often moody and volatile, but he honestly imagined Dustin more animated than she already was. He was wrong.

"What are you doing?" he asked calmly enough.

"Do not talk to me, you…you *ogre*," she growled, yanking a tunic off her head that had inadvertently landed there. "You are the meanest, nastiest man alive. I cannot believe how cold you were to my friend, and Deborah's lover. Gowen is a very nice man, but you wouldn't know anything about being nice, would you?"

He bit off a smile as her arms flailed about, determinedly tossing his clothes into a pile. "What are you doing with my clothes?" he asked.

"I told you not to talk to me!" She tugged roughly at a pair of lodged hose and nearly fell over when they suddenly pulled free. Christopher took several rapid steps to steady her, but she regained her feet and dashed away from him. "Don't touch me!"

He put his hands on his hips. "Dustin, I have not seen you in six months," he said. "Are we to spend our first night together quarreling?"

Her face was dark and pouting, but he saw a flicker of doubt in the gray eyes. "Well you…you should not have been so mean. Why were you so mean to him?"

"I was not mean; I never said a word to him," he said, putting up a hand to silence her as he proceeded to explain. "Sometimes, my lady, one can deduce a great deal by simply being still and watching. I simply sat and watched him as he reacted to you, to Deborah, to David and Leeton. There is nothing 'mean' about that. There is a great deal to learned about one's character and behavior when facing a new situation."

"You made him terribly uncomfortable," she insisted. "And Deborah, too. She was crying when she left."

"I know, and for that, I am sorry," he said sincerely, taking a step toward her. "But I want to observe her Gowen before I speak with him."

"Why? To determine if he is worthy of your attention?" she said cynically. "Even I am not that prideful, husband. I do not think everyone is beneath me."

"Nor do I," he said, standing directly in front of her, gazing down into her face. "But it is undeniable that certain people have certain stations in this life. If I deem Gowen unworthy of our family, I will deny him."

"You cannot," she insisted but quickly caught herself, horrified that she almost slipped with the most private of secrets.

"I can, and I will if it is necessary," he said evenly. "Now, I do not want to fight about this anymore. I want to walk about my keep, with you, and see what has happened to it in my absence."

"Will you go and apologize to Gowen and Deborah?" she asked.

"To my sister, yes. But tonight will tell whether I apologize to Gowen or throw him out of my keep," he said, tapping her chin with his forefinger.

Up on their bed, Caesar awoke and stretched a long, cat stretch. He yawned contentedly and licked his chops, his eyes focusing on his master and mistress and emitting a loud meow.

"So you awaken after the storm has passed, you wicked beast?" Christopher said. "Have you become acquainted with Harold yet? I forbid you to make a meal of him."

Dustin smiled, rubbing her belly as the baby kicked. Christopher put his hand on her stomach, too.

"He's so strong," he said, the joy of the baby's movements alight in his eyes. "He is not even born yet. Aye, this lad will be the most powerful knight that England has yet to see."

"And fight with you?" she turned her sweet face up to him, her eyes soft and caressing. "I do not think I want my son to fight."

"Why not?" he insisted. " 'Tis well enough for your husband to fight. Why not your son?"

"Because," she shrugged. " 'Tis different, that's all."

He smiled, pulling her into an embrace. "Your motherly instincts are showing, Lady de Lohr. You cannot protect your child always."

"I know," she lay her head against his chest, sighing with contentment. Lord, she had missed him. "Chris, when are you returning?"

"I don't know," he said, his hands caressing her. "John is quiet now, holed up at Nottingham. I suppose whenever he moves again, I shall leave. But I fully intend to be here for the birth of my son."

"But that is almost three months away," she said.

He kissed the top of her head, not knowing what to say. Quite a lot could happen in three months.

CꞫ

THE SUPPER HOUR rolled around and the servants set out a splendid meal for their master returned. The knights, having enjoyed a leisurely afternoon, appeared at supper bathed and dressed and fully intended to stuff themselves ill on the well-prepared food. Dustin and Christopher were also finely dressed in celebration of Christopher and David's return, and they sat down to a table loaded with delights.

The beef was a bit too rare for Dustin and Christopher laughed as he ordered it back to the kitchens, cooked until it was black so as to not upset his wife. Conversation was light and pleasant, the room fragrant and warm, as they waited for Deborah and Gowen to return.

And they waited. Christopher bade the men to go ahead and eat, irritated at his tardy sister. Everyone ate until they could hold no more, but Deborah and Gowen had yet to arrive and Christopher's mood was darkening.

"She is probably heartbroken," Dustin said, scolding her husband softly. "You'll be lucky if she ever speaks to you again."

He raised an eyebrow at her but remained silent, listening to Leeton relay an amusing story as he toyed with his goblet of wine.

It became ridiculously late and it was obvious that Deborah and Gowen were not going to show. By this time, Christopher had had enough and slammed his emptied goblet loudly on the table as he rose.

"Dustin, where does Gowen live?" he asked.

Her eyes widened at his authoritative tone. She'd only heard him use it in crisis situations.

"Why?" she wanted to know. "What are you going to do?"

"Answer me," he returned firmly.

She stood up as well, eyeing him. "Christopher….."

"Dustin, I am not going to kill the lad," he assured her. "I simply want to know where he lives so I can retrieve my sister."

She looked at him as if she did not believe him. "Then I shall go with you."

Christopher motioned his knights up. "Nay, you will not," he said. "You will go to bed and wait for me."

"Nay, Chris," she insisted. "If you fly into a rage, someone has to stop you. I forbid you to lay a hand on either of them."

He gave her a reproachful gaze as his armor was brought to him by two young pages. Other young boys had brought in the armor of the other knights and began to help them dress. It always amazed Dustin how well Christopher's men could read his mind; he'd not uttered a word to call for his armor, yet here the young boys were, ready to assist him. The depth of fear and respect for the baron ran even to the lowliest of pages and she knew they hovered about, anticipating his every wish.

" 'Tis not my intention to lay a hand on them, merely to bring Deborah home," he said, bending down as his hauberk was slipped on. "Now tell me where he lives."

She watched the pages work like busy, eager bees over her husband, removing his fine silk tunic and replacing it with the standard tunic and armor. She might as well tell him, for someone else easily would.

"On the southern tip of the village, near the monastery," she said quietly. "The cottage is small and rundown, and there is always a light in the window."

"Why is that?" he asked.

"Because his father works through the night," she replied. "He does work for the monks."

His eyes met hers for a moment as the little squire pulled Christopher's gloves on. "Where do you think they are?"

She was surprised he would ask, for he always knew everything. She could not remember him ever asking her a question like that.

"I truly do not know," she said. "But I do not think they will be at his cottage. Mayhap they are at the monastery."

The page handed him his helmet and he plopped it on his head, adjusting the hauberk beneath it. His knights were dressed and awaiting orders.

"Go on to bed, sweetheart," he said, accepting the sword that the squire was struggling to hold and moving around the table. "I shall return soon."

Dustin nodded, watching Christopher and his men exit the front door of the castle and hearing the shouts as the destriers were brought around.

Indecision clutched at her, wanting to tell him of Deborah's condition so he would not be too harsh with her, yet afraid to tell him for fear he would become enraged. She stood in the archway, watching them mount their mighty warhorses and seeing the bailey come alive with soldiers and torches. The massive gates began to unfold like a huge mouth, waiting to be fed.

The more Dustin watched the commotion, the more apprehensive she became. She was sure that Deborah and Gowen had done something desperate and she was terrified that Christopher's wrath would be unmerciful. He was issuing orders in a loud voice and frightening her with his intense manner, as if he were riding into a battle and not simply forming a search party. Her indecision peaked and she knew, for Deborah's sake, that she had to tell him about his sister. It was not her right and she was aware of that, hoping that he would be merciful if he knew the reason why his sister and her lover were so determined to be together.

"Chris!" She suddenly bolted from the doorway and scampered down the steps. "*Chris!*"

Above all of the shouting, he heard her and reined his horse around. "Dustin, go back inside."

"I must speak with you!" she yelled.

He shook his head as his horse danced beneath him. "Not now. Go back in the keep."

The gates were open wide and the destriers dug into the earth and launched themselves into a full gallop. Christopher's horse swung around with a great snort, tearing after the others.

Dustin stood there in the bailey, watching them race off with several men-at-arms. She kicked at the ground in frustration, wondering where indeed Deborah was and praying her husband would keep a level head. He had said he was simply riding out to retrieve Deborah, and she believed him. What concerned her is what he was going to do to Gowen.

She returned to the castle but her heart was heavy and she found herself pacing the long corridors, lost in thought. She was genuinely terrified for Deborah and Gowen, for there was no telling how Christopher was going to react without Dustin to stop him. He was as unpredictable as she was, yet he was blessed with far more common sense. She only hoped he would utilize that gift and not do something rash.

In her wandering, she passed by her mother's room. The door was slightly ajar and she entered, her gaze sweeping the bedchamber. Everything was the same as it had been when she passed away nearly a year ago and Dustin sat on the bed, trying to draw strength from her mother's memory. She went to her mother's grave often and told her of events; in fact, her mother had been the first to know about the child she was expecting. But it seemed as if the Dustin Barringdon from a year ago was a distant dream, so completely removed from the life she now led that she wondered if the girl had ever even truly existed. Dustin certainly was not the same girl she had been a mere year ago.

She was a baroness, married to the Defender of the Realm, and with all of the prestige and honor that went with that station. That alone would have been enough for most women, but not for Dustin. She had the additional pleasure of actually loving her husband, and receiving his love in return.

Aye, she had grown up in this keep. She knew everything about it, as it was her home. She knew the village and the surrounding area for miles. She was so happy to be here, to have her husband home, and to await the birth of their son. But just as her spirits were lifting, they came crashing down again with one thought; Gowen knew the area, too, if he and Deborah were truly hiding, then Christopher would never find them.

଼

DUSTIN HAD BEEN asleep for a short while. She was startled awake by shouting coming from the bailey, and she rose stiffly to see what was happening. She knew before she even looked that her husband must be returning and she was not surprised to see nine destriers pouring through the open gates. But she was shocked to see a female figure seated in front of David, and another figure trussed up and thrown haphazardly over the back of another.

Deborah and Gowen had been found.

DUSTIN SNATCHED A robe and wound it tightly about her, not even bothering to find her shoes before she was dashing downstairs. She should have been furious that Gowen was being treated like a common criminal but she found she was more frightened than anything. The stones were like ice beneath her feet as she charged to the front door and yanked it open.

A chill wind greeted her, sending shivers up her spine. Yet the shivers were for another reason as she watched the horses come to a halt, their breath hanging heavy in the damp air. Torches and soldiers were everywhere and for a moment, she lost sight of Gowen as they removed him from Leeton's destrier.

Christopher dismounted his dancing steed and slugged the horse as it tried to bite at him, his action indicative of his mood. He raised his visor and snapped orders to his knights even as David lifted Deborah from his destrier and half pulled her toward the castle. Dustin could see, even from a distance, that Deborah was devastated.

"Get your hands off her!" she yelled, racing down the steps, jerking Deborah from David's grip. "You will not manhandle your sister like a common wench."

Deborah was sobbing softly and Dustin threw her arm around her protectively, glaring daggers at David. He met her gaze steadily, almost as hostilely, and turned back to the other knights. Christopher, several feet away, saw the exchange but had greater concerns on his mind at the moment. He yelled his brother to him.

Dustin took Deborah into the castle and slammed the great door closed. She did not speak nor ask questions as she led Deborah up to her smaller bedchamber. Once inside, however, she sat her sister-in-law down and demanded answers.

"What happened? Where were you?" Dustin asked sternly.

Deborah was positively white. "Oh, Dustin," she sobbed. "You must stop him from killing Gowen. He won't even listen to me."

Dustin grabbed her wrists, forcing her to be still and calm down. "Answer me, Deborah. What happened?"

Deborah faced her sister-in-law, knowing she was the only friend she had in the whole world. "We....we were married this afternoon. The priests at the monastery performed the ceremony and granted us sanctuary. Christopher violated that sanctuary."

Dustin's heart sank and she dropped her head in sheer disbelief. "Dear Lord, no," she whispered. "Tell me everything."

" 'Twas horrible," Deborah cried. "After the meeting this afternoon, Gowen and I were positive Christopher would refuse our marriage and we felt we had no other choice, so we asked the priests at the monastery if they would marry us. Gowen's father paid for the ceremony. When Christopher came looking for me, the priests denied him entrance and told him why. Oh, Dustin, he went mad; Leeton and Edward tried to stop him but he tore the door down with his bare hands and searched every room in the church. One of the monks helped us escape through the kitchens, but David saw us and caught up to us. Then they tied Gowen up and brought us back." She broke into heavy sobs. "Christopher has not said a word to me and I know he is going to kill Gowen."

Dustin was pale. She let go of her sister-in-law's hands and stood up, her beautiful face set.

"Nay, he will not," she assured her. "I will go speak to him right now and find out what on earth possessed him to violate a church and handle you and Gowen as if you were outlaws. Did you tell him you were pregnant?"

Deborah shook her head, wiping at her eyes, and Dustin touched her damp head. She softened.

"Take off your shoes and relax," she said quietly. "I shall send a servant up with warmed wine."

"I cannot relax," Deborah insisted. "I must find out what is happening to my Gowen."

"I will find out," Dustin said firmly. "I promise you that I will find out."

She left Deborah a sobbing heap by the fire and returned to her bedchamber. Dressing in a heavy woolen dress, an equally heavy woolen scarf around her head, and thick hose, she proceeded back out into the bailey.

The soldiers were clearing the courtyard and the knights were going about their business. The first one she came across was Jeffrey.

"Jeffrey," she called. "Where is my husband?"

He turned to her, his sharply angled face pinched from the cold. "In the abbey, my lady. But you should be inside where it is warm."

She ignored him, steering for the doors that led to the abbey. Jeffrey caught up to her and cut her off.

"Let me take you inside, Lady Dustin," he said in his thick accent. "The abbey is no place for you."

"Why did you let him do this?" she demanded harshly. "You have known Gowen almost as long as you have known me. How could you let Christopher treat him like this?"

"I had no choice, you know that," he said softly. "Gowen is a good boy, but he was very wrong in this case. Your husband will deal with him appropriately."

"How can you call killing him appropriate?" Dustin argued loudly. "He and Deborah are in love; what is so wrong about them wanting to be together?"

"Who said he was going to kill him?" Jeffrey countered. "Punishment does not necessarily mean death, my lady. Now return to the castle; you should not be out here in the cold."

"Do not tell me what to do," she snapped, pulling away from him. "I am going to find Christopher."

Jeffrey snatched her arm firmly. "That," he said, "would not be wise. 'Tis best that you listen to me."

Dustin shoved at him to dislodge his grip, beating him on the shoulder when that didn't work. Furious, she shoved at his face and ended up smacking him in the nose. Blood trickled but he didn't let go. He began to drag her towards the castle.

"Kessler!" came a voice so loud it echoed off the buildings. They stopped their struggles and turned to see Christopher standing in the doorway that led into the abbey. "Let her go. Dustin, come here."

She dashed over to him, angry and frustrated. "Where is Gowen?"

"Go to bed," he told her firmly, his face set and hard.

She shook her head, "I will not. I must speak to you first."

"I have no time, Dustin," he said sternly. "For once, do as you are told."

Dustin clenched her jaw. "I am *not* leaving until you let me speak with you."

His jaw ticked and his blue eyes were dark and angry on her. "Dustin, do as you are told or God help me, I will spank you, child or no child."

Tears, Dustin thought. *Tears always soften the rock of a man.* Her eyes glistened with tears and she walked away from him, sobbing loudly but purely for effect. She continued to walk, waiting for him to stop her, and was enraged when he did not. Frustrated that her ploy hadn't worked, she ran into the castle and wound her way back to the rear entrance to the abbey. There was more than one way to gain her end.

Quiet as a mouse, she slipped in through the rear door, her eyes adjusting to the dark and cool interior. She heard voices in the distance and she took the stairs, her eyes wide and alert to her surroundings. The abbey had two levels, the lower level used for prisoners, and she assumed they had taken Gowen there. There was only one way in and out, which concerned her, but she would have to try. She had to see him, to protect him.

Suddenly there was a massive body in front of her. "No, you don't, you little vixen," Christopher said sharply. "Back up the stairs. Now."

He yelled and she jumped, but she did not turn tail as ordered. Instead, she pressed herself flush against the wall as he mounted the stairs and stood over her in a great, huffing mass of armor and flesh.

"Wife, I have no time for this foolishness," he said severely. "If I have to take you back to our chamber, I shall tie you to the bed until I return, I swear it."

The tears were real this time. "But I have to talk to you." Her lips were trembling. "Please, Chris. Just for a moment."

His features did not soften, but he did not reply right away. He continued to gaze at her for a moment. "What, then?"

She sniffed and cleared her throat. "Deborah told me what happened. What are you planning on doing with her husband?"

His brow rippled at the mention of his sister's husband. "First and foremost, I have sent for a priest to annul the marriage," he told her. "After that, I have yet to decide what to do with Master Olmquist."

Dustin forced her fear down. She reached out and grasped her husband, wanting to touch him so he would know her sincerity.

"Please do not annul the marriage," she begged softly. "They love each other so. They only did this because you were so cold this afternoon and they feared you would deny them."

He cocked an eyebrow. "What they did was disobedient and wrong, Dustin," his voice was so low he was growling. "Whether or not they love each other is not the issue but the fact is that I cannot allow such blatant insubordination. 'Twas my decision to make; not theirs."

Dustin shook her head. "The decision has already been made," she sighed, suddenly very tired. He read her fatigue and helped her to sit on the stairs. She gazed up at him. "Why did you violate the monastery?"

He raised an eyebrow as he sat on the stair below her. "Because they had no legal or moral grounds to grant them sanctuary."

"What?" she asked, confused and outraged. "They had every moral and legal right, Chris."

He shook his head. "Deborah and Gowen were not fleeing death, nor great harm, nor famine, nor were they in any imminent danger of being separated or imprisoned. They requested sanctuary on purely groundless reasons."

"Since when is love a groundless reason?" Dustin said quietly. "They did what they did because they were afraid of you. And because Deborah is pregnant."

His gaze lifted, meeting her wide gray eyes. She held her breath, knowing the next few moments would determine his reaction, waiting and wondering what her husband was going to do.

"She *is*?" he asked. He pulled off his helmet and it went sailing, angrily, to the bottom of the stairs. A mailed hand raked through his damp hair. "Christ in Heaven, I cannot believe my ears. Dustin, she's *pregnant*?"

"Aye," Dustin reached out and touched his face, hoping to soothe him. "As am I. She and Gowen are madly, deeply, hopelessly in love with each other. Now tell me, husband, if the situation were reversed and if it were you and I acting out the roles, would you have stopped at nothing to make me your own? She carries his child, Chris. Surely you can appreciate that."

He was fuming. "Appreciate it? Damnation, I should spill his innards this very minute!"

"But you won't," Dustin said steadily. "He is the father of your future nephew, Chris. And Deborah's husband."

"Damnation," he spat, his big body tensed as if he were contemplating some horrible action. Then he looked at her. "You knew about this all along, didn't you? You even…even *approve* of this disgrace."

" 'Tis no disgrace to love someone and to want to have children," she replied calmly. "What's done is done, Chris. They are married now and the child will not be a bastard."

He did not look at her, his expression hard as he stared off into the dimness of the abbey. She watched his face, continuing to stroke his hair lovingly and hoped beyond hope he was reconsidering his stance.

The truth was that Christopher knew he should be furious, but he could not seem to bring himself to a rolling boil. Had he not loved Dustin as he did, then his fury would be out of control and Gowen would surely suffer a painful death. Yet because of the feelings he held for his wife, he understood and could not bring himself to be overly angry.

Still, he was enraged because they had taken matters into their own hands, but he knew now why they had done it. And he furthermore knew there was no way he could annul the marriage. Everything now suddenly made sense; all of the pleading, begging, the clues his wife had given him that he had been too narrow to see. As always, he saw what he wanted to see.

After several long minutes, he simply shook his head and she slipped up behind him throwing her arms around his neck and pressing her face against the side of his head.

"Be merciful to them, my lord," she whispered in his ear, sending chills up his spine. "Imagine if it were we who were separated, subject to our fate by the decision of another, afraid yet so desperately in love that we did not regret our hasty actions. If there was a chance I were to be taken from you, would you not do everything in your power to keep us together? That is what Gowen did. Do not fault him for loving Deborah."

After a moment she felt his huge gloved hand grasp her arms gently, and she felt him sigh. "I am given little choice in the matter," he muttered.

She kissed his ear softly. "Please, Chris. Let them be happy."

He closed his eyes at her touch, his mind torn between the issue at hand and her closeness. "Lady, your reasoning and wisdom improve by the day. Soon you will be as wise as your husband."

"Who do you think I learned everything from?" she smiled, kissing his ear again. "I love you, Chris."

He squeezed her arms around his neck. "Where is Deborah?"

"In her room," she replied. "I told her to wait there for me."

Christopher sat broodingly another moment, trying to remember when his life went so out of control. He was unused to anything other than perfect obedience and order, but within the past year, he felt as if his command over something as simple as his family was slipping away. Not with David, but with the women, Dustin and Deborah were giving him fits.

"I would go see my sister's husband now," he said in a low voice, gently unwinding her arms and helping her to stand.

"Can I come? Please?" she asked.

He kissed her cheek. "Nay, sweetheart. Go see to my sister, as I am sure she is in desperate need of reassurance."

Dustin dared a little smile. "Then you will not annul the marriage? You will let them be?"

He tried to glare at her, but his heart wasn't in it. "Aye, I shall leave them be. But they live here, under my roof, where I can protect my sister. And to hell with Gowen if he does not approve."

Dustin smiled broadly and kissed him. He relented his hard stance with a throaty chuckle and kissed her again.

"You have a heart as big as a lion, husband," she said softly. "Surely there is not a more understanding, generous man on this earth."

"You have cast a new understanding on the term Lionheart," he said, his eyes warm. " 'Tis usually a phrase to describe fierceness and bravery. But you have always seen through me, haven't you? You are the only person in this world who can read me like a book."

"Not always," she admitted. "You can be mightily unpredictable. And frightening."

"Speaking of frightening," he raised an eyebrow, "why did you fight with Jeffrey like that? You know the man was only doing his duty."

"I have done worse to him," she shrugged. "And he has hit me back on occasion."

"He's done *what*?" her husband responded sharply.

She laughed softly. "Mother gave him permission to discipline me if needed and, on occasion, he has. Did you think you were the first person to spank me?"

He frowned severely. "Of course not, but I never imagined Kessler was the enforcer."

Dustin shrugged. "Father did not have the heart, so mother put Jeffrey in charge of dispensing punishment."

Christopher shook his head. "Amazing," he mumbled. "Go upstairs, now. I shall join you later."

She kissed him again before retreating up the stairs. He watched her, waiting until the door closed softly before retreating to the sub-level of the abbey.

Dustin was nearly weak with relief as she made her way back to Deborah's room. She knew Deborah would be ecstatic with the turn of events, and Dustin was thrilled that the newlyweds would be living at Lioncross. She and Deborah would go through their pregnancies together, and their children would be constant companions. She was full of dreaming of the future as she mounted the stairs and passed into the second floor corridor, her heart and mood soaring with joy.

Deborah's door was closed and she knocked, softly calling her name. Receiving no answer, she lifted the latch.

Four stories below her, Christopher heard the scream.

CHAPTER THIRTY-SIX

"JESUS CHRIST, SHE has slit her wrists," David hissed as he struggled to stop the bleeding from Deborah's arm.

Christopher was bent over his sister's other arm, tying a tight tourniquet in an attempt to stop the blood flow. He did not answer his brother as he concentrated on his task, making sure Gowen was applying tight pressure to the wound he was tending. In the corner, Dustin was sobbing loudly.

"Is she going to die?" she asked anyone who could answer.

No one could, in fact, answer her. Deborah had been bleeding for quite some time and Christopher was unsure if his sister was going to survive. His heart twisted with remorse for the actions that had driven his sister to the brink of despair, yet he regretted nothing. If he had to do it over again, he would have changed nothing but for the fact that he would have explained things to Deborah and not assumed that she understood his reasons. He felt guilty, although he tried not to.

"Where did she get the goddamn dagger?" Edward wound another piece of linen around the wrist David was securing, but it was bleeding rapidly.

"It is hers," Christopher replied, checking his sister's condition by lifting up an eyelid.

"Lower the head of the bed, Chris," Leeton said. "And keep her arms up. The blood needs to stay in the vital areas."

Christopher nodded and between him and Leeton, they lowered the head of the bed while the others kept Deborah's arms aloft as they tried to control the bleeding. In the corner, he could hear Dustin crying.

"Jeffrey, get my wife out of here," he said softly, not looking at her.

"No, please," Dustin said, pushing against Jeffrey as he came to her. "I would stay here. Deborah needs me."

"We are doing all we can for Deborah," Christopher told her, trying to be gentle. "Please go and rest, sweetheart. Let us take care of my sister."

Next to Christopher, Gowen was weeping quietly. He was holding Deborah's arm as Christopher and Edward bandaged it. Dustin's eyes fell on him and she forced aside her grief to focus on the anguished young man.

"Gowen," she pleaded softly, "please come with me. Let them work in peace."

He shook his head, dirty and disheveled from the night's events. "I shall not leave her to die alone," he whispered. "She needs me now."

Dustin looked at Christopher and saw that his expression was grim. She curbed her hysteria, presenting a calmer picture.

"I do not want to go, Chris," she begged quietly. "Please let me stay."

He did not reply, seeing that she was easing somewhat after her initial shock. He knew that she certainly wouldn't rest if he sent her away; indeed, she would be much worse off with worry.

"Sit down, then," he replied hoarsely. "Sit down and be still."

Dustin obeyed and Jeffrey took position beside her like a huge watchdog. Sir Nicholas and Sir Guy stood in the doorway, watching with great concern as their comrades struggled to save the life of their liege's sister.

"If Burwell were here, he'd have her under control," David muttered, distraught. "Jesus, why did she do this?"

"Fear," Gowen answered quietly, staring at Deborah's white face. "The baron drove her to it."

Tension of another kind filled the room. Dustin's eyes went to Christopher, who was focused on his sister. Even though her husband had been harsh with his sister, even she did not believe he was responsible for this disaster. Anger filled her, her emotions surging from one volcanic peak to the next.

"That is not fair, Gowen," she said fiercely. "Christopher did nothing of the kind."

Gowen looked up at Dustin and she could read the irrational grief. "He might as well have put the dagger in her hand himself," he said. "You know how unbalanced she has been lately. Of course he drove her to this with his cruelty and his arrogance."

Dustin shot out of the chair. "How dare you speak of my husband like that," she said, shaking an angry finger at him. "No one is to blame but Deborah for her own foolishness."

Gowen stood up and Deborah's arm went slapping to the bed in spite of Leeton's attempts to grab it.

"Everything that has happened this day has been his fault," he snapped at her. "Had he not been so haughty, we would not have felt it necessary to be married immediately. He broke the sanctuary of the church to bring us back and then threw me in the dungeon. Deborah had no way of knowing my fate and, assuming the worst, has tried to take her own life. How can you be so blind?"

A huge hand reached out and grabbed Gowen around the neck, fairly lifting him off his feet as he was shoved away from the bed, away from the others. Dustin gasped, her hand flying to her mouth.

Christopher's eyes glittered like deadly sapphires against Gowen's pale, frightened blue.

"You may say what you will about me, sirrah, for your words do not offend, me nor provoke this action," he rumbled. "But you will never raise your voice to my wife. Ever."

"It is all right, Chris." Dustin went over to them, her eyes wide and her anger banked. "He did not mean it; he is upset. Please do not be harsh."

Christopher did not look at her. "Do you understand me?" he said to Gowen. "If we are to live under the same roof, then you will come to understand a great many things."

Gowen was nearly blue. "I....I did not mean to shout at her," he rasped. " 'Twas not my intention to offend, sire, but Dustin and I have known each other a great many years and I treat her as I have always treated her."

"With such disrespect?" Christopher shot back, his eyebrows raised.

"Nay, sire," Gowen was struggling for breath. "As a sister. Who does not yell at their sister?"

Christopher stared back at him, reading truth in his eyes. Moreover, he was right; were Deborah conscious at this moment, he'd yell his head off at her. After a moment he dropped his hand and stepped back, still eyeing Gowen unsteadily. Before Dustin could touch him, he took long, quick steps back over to his sister.

Dustin watched her husband sadly for a moment before turning her attention to her friend and new brother-in-law. Her panic was slowly subsiding and she was resigning herself to the fact that her husband and his knights were doing everything possible to help Deborah. She doubted Burwell or God himself could do much more. As hard as it was, she would have to place her faith in them, for there was nothing she could do and her sense of helplessness was overwhelming. Quietly, she moved over and took Gowen's arm.

" 'Twill be all right," she said softly. "They will help her."

Gowen was gray with horror and apprehension, too overcome to speak as he watched the men work on his wife. Dustin watched, too, forgetting about her endless fatigue and swelling ankles. The only thing that mattered at the moment was preventing Deborah's life from slipping away.

They struggled with Deborah into the night. The only reason she hadn't died immediately was because she had slit her wrists cross-wise and not vertically. Christopher was able to stitch the wounds up tightly, lessening the bleeding and promoting coagulation. Dustin sat, wrapped in a coverlet, watching as they strapped her arms up to the bedposts to keep them elevated and to further prevent her from doing any more damage to herself. From that point on, it was a waiting game. If she had lost too much blood, she would die. But there was all the possibility in the world that she would survive, yet no one seemed particularly optimistic, and Dustin was greatly disturbed.

It was close to dawn and Dustin had eventually fallen into an exhausted sleep in Deborah's overstuffed chair, wrapped like a cocoon in the feathered blanket. The knights had retreated, save David and Leeton, as Christopher stood vigilant watch at the foot of Deborah's bed, his eyes never leaving her pasty face. He was damn angry at her for attempting to take her own life and the guilt he had been struggling with most of the night hung heavy about his shoulders. He could feel the weight. Perhaps Dustin had been right; perhaps he had been arrogant and cold. For a man of his ego, it was a bitter pill to swallow.

The sun was barely peaking over the horizon when he turned from his post and looked at Gowen, still awake but looking an ugly shade of gray as he stared at his wife.

"Go and sleep," he said quietly. "I shall stay with her."

Gowen shook his head. "This is my place, sire. I shall not leave her."

Christopher did not argue, for he knew his reaction would have been the same. He turned to his brother.

"See about the morning meal, if you would," he said. "I am famished."

David nodded, glancing at Dustin as he passed her on his way to the door. Her face was half shoved into the blanket and he could hear her snoring softly.

"She snores?" He looked at his brother, his face lit up with a tired smile. "You never told me that."

Christopher glanced at his wife. "Leave her alone. Go get my food."

David snickered as he quit the room.

Christopher continued to stare at Dustin long after his brother was gone. She was curled up like Caesar, sleeping so peacefully that he was tempted just to leave her be. As tired as she was and in her condition, she should be in the comfort of her own bed, but he knew the moment he touched her that she would awaken. He left his post and wandered over to her, daring to touch the blond head tenderly before moving to the fire and stoking the embers.

"I never thought I'd see Dustin married," Gowen said dully.

Christopher looked up from the hearth and saw his brother-in-law looking at him.

"She was more boy than most boys, you know," Gowen went on. "She could fight, run, and swim… anything. All of the boys in the village loved to be around her, and she thought it was because they accepted her as one of their own, when in fact it was because she was so beautiful that they simply wanted to gaze upon her."

"Yet no one was truthful with her," Christopher said. "Even when she became of age?"

Gowen smiled weakly. "And risk getting our nose broken? I think not. She could be your very best friend in the entire world, yet at the same time, your biggest fear."

"Fear? Why?" Christopher stood up.

"Because she is nearly perfect," Gowen replied. "Isn't that reason enough for fear? Dustin Barringdon was something above the rest of us mortals, my lord, somewhere in that mystic realm of fairy princesses and legends. She was not meant for any of us mere peasants to have."

Christopher gazed down at his wife's head. "Yet, I have her."

" 'Tis right you should have her," Gowen insisted. "You are Richard's warlord and deserving of such a woman. But, in faith, when I heard she had married, I laughed with pity for the fool who had been brave enough to marry her. Surely he had no idea what she-devil he had been saddled with."

Christopher's cool demeanor cracked in the slightest and he grinned faintly. "And you thought not to warn me?"

Gowen smirked smugly. "Some lessons in this life must be learned the hard way," he said. "When I heard rumor that you were a favorite of Richard, I assumed your life had been an easy one and found fiendish delight with the thought of the unmanageable Dustin as your wife. But I see that I was wrong, for she obviously cares for you a great deal. You are all she could speak of while you were away."

Christopher stood behind the chair, looking down on Dustin as she slept. "We missed each other," he said simply.

"I know," Gowen said softly, his eyes trailing to Deborah once again. His smile faded. "She looks like a prisoner tied to the bed like that."

Christopher looked to his sister. " 'Tis necessary that we keep the blood away from the wounds to allow them to scab over."

"I realize that, but it looks so barbaric." Gowen rose from his seat and went over to Deborah, his eyes trailing the length of her long, slim body. "I worry for the child."

"Dustin tells me the village has a midwife; I will send for her this day," Christopher told him.

Gowen raised an eyebrow. "That woman? She is more witch than midwife. She has fairly convinced Dustin that she bears the next emperor."

"Is that so?" Christopher glanced at his wife, not as confident about her health and the baby as he was just a moment prior. "A witch, you say?"

"A charlatan," Gowen said firmly. "I cannot stand her near Deborah, but the old crone is very convincing and tells the women what they want to hear."

Christopher was growing increasingly concerned. "Then I will refuse the woman admittance to my keep," he said. "There are no other midwives in the village?"

"A few with lesser reputations," Gowen replied. "None that I would trust with Deborah's life or the life of our child, yet the choice is nil."

"Like hell," Christopher grumbled. "There was a woman who took care of my wife when she had her accident last year, an excellent midwife. I will send one of my knights to Windsor to retrieve her. I will trust the life of my wife and child to no sorceress."

"A wise decision, baron," Gowen said, relieved. "How fortunate I am that my brother-in-law can command even mighty Windsor to do his bidding."

Christopher lifted an eyebrow in agreement; angry Dustin could be so naive as to believe the tales of a witch. He was greatly concerned for the child now, knowing the midwife to be an imposter, but resisted the urge to awaken and scold his wife. With Deborah's injuries, it would not be wise to upset her further. But he would bide his time until the moment was right.

Christopher and Gowen spent a great deal of time alone together, watching their respective sleeping wives, speaking of things small and large. They grew to know each other bit by bit, and even after David joined them with the morning meal, continued their deeply philosophical conversation about the morality of Hadrian's invasion. David, way out of his league, dozed off in a chair.

Christopher discovered rapidly that his new brother-in-law was indeed a sharp man. Well-read and opinionated, Christopher found himself greatly enjoying the intellectual conversation. Of his knights, Edward and mayhap Leeton were the only two he could hold a truly intelligent conversation with, for the rest, including his brother, were not as bright. David was an outstanding soldier and lived for the battlefield, but he was lacking in deep intelligence. Christopher thought at one point, with humor, that if he could combine David and Gowen into one man, he would have the greatest warrior in the world.

Toward noon, Dustin awoke and began moving, groaning as she did so. Christopher looked at her with concern.

"What is wrong?" he demanded.

"Ohhh," she groaned again, twisting her body gingerly. "My entire body is sore. I can hardly move."

Grinning with relief, Christopher held out his hand. "Let me help you, then."

He pulled her out of the chair, steadying her as she gazed over at Deborah. "Has she awoken?" she asked.

"Nay," Christopher replied. "Are you hungry?"

"A little," she said. "But I would rather have a bath."

"Go take one, then," he said gently. "I shall join you in a few minutes."

Dustin nodded wearily, straightening her surcoat and moving for the door. She passed by David, unconscious in a chair and snoring like thunder. With an irritated purse of the lips, she smacked him on the side of the head.

David jumped, disoriented, until he saw his sister-in-law's scowling face. "What was that for?" he demanded.

"For waking me up, you lout," she snapped. "Good lord, you snore louder than anyone I have ever had the misfortune to hear."

"Ha!" David sneered. "Look who is accusing me of snoring? You would wake the dead with your snoring."

Outraged, Dustin slugged him in the arm hard enough to make him wince. "I do not snore," she cried. "What a terrible thing to say."

David rubbed his arm, looking to his brother for support. "Am I wrong? Am *I* wrong?"

Christopher turned away, a smirk on his face. " 'Twas a most unsavory thing to say, David, right or wrong."

Dustin punched him again for good measure and quit the room.

David rubbed his arm where Dustin had smacked him, eyeing his brother. "As always, your support is appreciated, brother," he said sarcastically.

Christopher snorted. "She only slugged you. If I were to have agreed with you, 'tis more than likely she would do a great deal more to me."

"And you fear retribution?" David asked. "Since when?"

"Since I married her," he said, glancing at Gowen who smirked knowingly.

David shook his head, standing up to stretch the stiffness out of his sculpted body. "And I say I have had enough of both of you. I am going down to the practice field."

Christopher waved him off, feeling pretty damn tired and stiff himself with an entire night of standing. Deborah's breathing was even and her pulse steady, but she had yet to wake. He pondered whether or not she ever would.

"I shall leave you here with my sis.....your wife, then," he said, crossing for the door. "I will not go far and expect to be notified immediately if she awakens."

"As you wish, sire," Gowen replied, sinking wearily into the nearest chair.

Christopher paused at the door. "You may address me as Christopher in private. To call me sire seems stiffly formal, and I would hope that tonight we have gone beyond such prescribed standards."

Gowen nodded. "It has been an eventful night, I will concur. And I appreciate the gesture."

Christopher nodded weakly and left to join his wife.

☙

GRISELDA WARWICK AND Burwell rode in with Sir Nicholas and Anthony exactly eleven days later. Darren, the young squire, had also ridden escort. His mother had been thrilled to see her only son, but his visit was concluded and he, too, was anxious to return to Christopher. He was positive his liege could not get along without him.

Dustin was in the bailey with the dogs when the party rode in. She smiled at Anthony and Darren, flirting with the young man as he dismounted until his face was as red as a beet. She laughed at him, glad to have him in their midst again. Griselda, seeing Dustin's advanced state, hopped off her wagon faster than she should have and scolded her for being out and about.

Dustin laughed at the old woman. "I have got two more months to go, Griselda. I feel fine."

Griselda passed a well-practiced eye over Dustin's body. "If I did not know better, I would say you had two or three weeks to go at the very most. You are far too large for only six and a half months."

Dustin's smile faded, turning into simmering horror. It simply wasn't poss….*No.* She stepped back from the woman, suddenly seized with apprehension such as she had never known. She had to be only six and a half months pregnant, for that is when she and Christopher had made love for the first time after her accident. But her encounter with Marcus had been a full five weeks before that. Try as she might to suppress the knowledge, in the recesses of her mind, Marcus Burton fought to make himself known. *It could not be Marcus' child!*

"Nay!" Dustin burst, drawing looks from everyone around her. "This child is due around the first of November and you shall not say otherwise."

Griselda, undaunted, took Dustin's arm and noticed she was shaking. "Come inside now, my lady. I shall make you a soothing brew of chamomile and rosehips. Come on, now."

Burwell eyed Lady de Lohr as well, stretching the stiffness out of his fat body. Behind him, his assistant dismounted and deftly gathered their baggage.

"My lady is looking far better than when I last saw you," Burwell said. "Two months, did you say? If that is true, then the baron's child will come out as big as he is."

Dustin was growing overwhelmed with their comments, but the more she tried to ignore them, the more they slammed into her. If she were forced to admit it, then she would have realized that the thought had been with her all along, but she had convinced herself early on that such probability was impossible. But the midwife's innocent comment had her entire world crashing in around her.

Christopher met them at the front door of the castle. "Ah, Burwell, Mistress Griselda, I see that…..what's wrong with my wife?"

"Fatigue, sire, of course," Griselda replied. "She should rest as much as possible now."

Christopher looked at Dustin, his face furrowing with concern. "Do you feel all right, Dustin?"

She snapped out of her train of horrid thoughts when she realized he was talking to her. One look at his face and she burst into tears.

"Here, here, sweetheart." He took her from the old woman, cuddling her tenderly. "What is the matter now?"

"*Now*?" Dustin sobbed. "What do you mean 'now'?"

He silently cursed himself for the slip; he hadn't meant it to sound as it did, although it wasn't far from the truth. Everything upset her these days.

"I did not mean it that way," he assured her quickly. "Let us go upstairs. Mistress Griselda says that you must rest."

"I do not want to rest," she wept.

"Yes, you do," Christopher insisted firmly as he took her up the stairs. "And I want Mistress Griselda to examine you."

"No!" Dustin snapped, trying to jerk away from him. "I do not want anyone looking at me."

"That is foolish, Dustin," he said calmly. "Let's go lie down."

Burwell snorted as they wrestled with Dustin. "At least my patient isn't fighting back," he said. "If you would kindly direct me to your sister, baron, I shall be about my business."

Christopher jerked his head skyward. "Up the stairs, fourth door on the right. Her husband is in the room with her."

Burwell pushed past the three of them with his wispy little helper in tow. Dustin grumbled and muttered and sobbed the entire way back to their rooms, irritably slapping her husband away as he tried to help her off with her cloak. He stood back with his hands on his hips, greatly approving of the firm, matronly way Griselda handled his wife. It was obvious this woman was used to cranky, irritable, witchy pregnant woman. He, for one, wasn't.

Griselda managed to partially disrobe Dustin to get a good look at her belly. Her warm, expert hands probed and prodded gently, her old face glazed with concentration. Dustin snapped at the old woman, grunting when she probed near her tender groin.

Christopher stood back and watched with anticipation, vastly relieved he had brought Griselda to Lioncross to care for his wife. He would sleep easier knowing the old woman was under his roof. After an impatient eternity, Griselda pulled Dustin's skirt down to cover her belly.

"The child is already head-down," the old woman commented. "Even as I was feeling his position, he was active and moving. I'd say you are going to have a very large baby on your hands, my lady."

Dustin, now interested in what the woman had to say, looked concerned. "How big? Am I going to be able to birth the child without trouble?"

Griselda prodded her pelvis, helping her lift her knees as she internally probed her passage. Dustin was uncomfortable with that part of the examination; only Christopher had truly touched her there, although after her accident she had been examined, but she jumped anyway when Griselda first tried to probe her. At her side, her husband murmured reassuringly and she calmed. After a few silent minutes of poking and grunting, Griselda moved to the basin to wash her hands.

"Your hips are wide enough," she commented. "Baron, might I have a word, please?"

Relieved, Dustin let out a blustery sigh and pushed her skirts down. Christopher straightened her surcoat the rest of the way and helped her sit up. Patting the top of her head, he followed the old crone out into the corridor.

"What is the matter?" he asked, dread filling him.

"I do not want to alarm you, sire, but the child is already large enough to be born, and your wife says she has two months yet," Griselda said quietly. "If she gets too much larger, and I have no reason to believe that she will not, then I may have to take… steps."

Christopher went cold with fear. "Christ, woman, what steps? Make yourself clear."

"I may have to take the child from her," the old woman said as evenly as she could; an enraged, nervous father was not always the most rational of creatures. " 'Tis not as horrible as it sounds, truly; I simply give her a potion to induce her pains and hope that it will take care of the problem. If not, then I may have to open her belly and remove the child that way."

"*Open* her belly?" Christopher raised his voice before he could stop himself, instantly mindful that his equally nervous wife was on the other side of the closed door, and he did not want her to hear him. "Explain yourself," he said again, much more quietly.

Griselda cocked an eyebrow. "Bank yourself, sire, for if it is the only way to save the life of your wife and child, then so be it," she said. "I make an incision thusly in her belly and the child is quickly removed. Stitches will close your wife up and she will heal in a few months' time. I have done it before, several times, when there is no other alternative."

Christopher was horrified at what the woman was suggesting, but fascinated as well. "And it is always successful?"

Griselda shrugged modestly. "I have had more successes than failures, sire. But I will need your help in the matter should it come to that, as new mothers do not wish to be put under the blade for obvious reasons."

He raised an eyebrow dryly. "Obvious indeed. What help can I give?"

"Comfort her, convince her it is necessary and, if required, hold her down while I complete the task," she answered.

"I shall knock her out myself before I allow her to feel the pain of a blade to her belly," he snorted firmly. "But I will support whatever you feel is best, mistress."

"Thank you, sire," Griselda replied. "Now, why do not you comfort your wife and make sure she rests. I will make her a soothing brew."

They went back into the bedchamber to find Dustin out cold on the bed, snoring softly in slumber. The midwife smiled and picked up her bag, quickly bobbing a curtsy for Christopher's benefit before quitting the room.

Christopher sat beside the bed and watched Dustin sleep for a long time, his mind mulling over many things. As much as he loved Dustin and as much as he desired this child, he would have the midwife save Dustin's life over that of the babe. He had made that decision firmly before God, that over all else, Dustin should survive the births of their children. He'd rather be childless than lose his wife.

His head ended up resting in his hand and he could hear noise from the bailey faintly wafting up through the windows. He ironically wondered who was having a more difficult time with this pregnancy, him or Dustin.

Then he did something he hadn't done since he had left the Holy Land; he prayed.

BURWELL TRIED A number of remedies to bring Deborah out of her state. He said she was no longer unconscious, merely in a very deep sleep as her body tried to regain some of its strength. But she needed to wake up and begin taking nourishment if she and the child were going to survive, so he opened a small vial and waved it in front of her nose a few times. After a moment, he tried once more and, miraculously, Deborah stirred. A third and a fourth time and Deborah's blue eyes fluttered open, rolling back in her head as she tried to come around. Gowen called her name loudly a few times and eventually, she focused on him.

Christopher stood and watched as his sister regained her senses, terribly relieved when she recognized all of them and began to cry weakly in Gowen's arms. But Burwell broke up the tender moment by insisting she take some nourishment, and he stood over Gowen and watched him fed her several spoonfuls of beef broth. Deborah sputtered, coughed, but did as she was ordered in spite of the fact that she was weaker than a baby.

"Chris," she whispered. "I am so sorry to be such a bother."

He raised his eyebrow with mock sternness. "As well you should be, lady."

The tears started as Gowen tried to feed her. "I was so wrong and I humbly beg your forgiveness." Her eyes gazed lovingly up at her husband. "When you took Gowen away, I was positive you were going to kill him and I did not want to live without him. I know my actions seemed rash, but to me, they were necessary. Yet I see that your mercy is infinite, brother, and I shall always be grateful."

"I cannot forgive you for your attempt on your life, Deborah. Only God can pardon your sin," he said. "As for marrying without my permission, we shall discuss that later. Right now I want you to become healthy and whole once again and bear me a strong nephew."

Her eyes widened a bit and she looked to Gowen in confusion, but he only smiled tenderly and spooned another bit of broth into her mouth. She was deeply ashamed that Christopher should know of her weaknesses, as she had so many. But, as she had always known, her brother had a heart as big as the heavens.

In spite of the fact that she was unworthy to be a de Lohr, he acted as if it mattered not. A man who was feared by the entire realm for his fierceness and unforgiving manner was gentle and compassionate with his loved ones, and she was entirely undeserving in her opinion.

"Thank you," she whispered again, wishing she could demonstrate her thanks somehow.

He waved her off with a slight smile, simply relieved she was back with them once again. Convinced his sister was in good hands, Christopher left her to those more knowledgeable and ordered a huge meal in celebration of his sister's recovery.

The day outside had grown black as coal and as he went to his bedchamber, he noticed that it had begun to rain.

☙

AND RAIN IT did, for days on end. Deborah grew stronger, Dustin grew fatter, and between the two of them Christopher was quite possibly going insane. Neither one of them were in the best of moods, even in the best of times. Deborah's strength returned and so did her pregnancy sickness. If she wasn't vomiting, she was laying down. Gowen was miserable with her sickness and sought solace with the knights whenever he could.

In spite of the fact that the man wasn't a warrior, he fit in quite well with the knights and enjoyed their camaraderie. Christopher even began to trust him with the records of the estate as well as the records of the border revenues, and the keep ran more efficiently than it ever had.

Gowen was brilliant and had a mind for numbers, and Christopher was grateful to have him. True, he had accepted Gowen much faster than was usual with him, for he was a man whose loyalties and friendships were long cultivated. He honestly did not know why he had let Gowen come to know him as rapidly as he had. Mayhap it was because he felt guilty for the actions that led to the marriage of Deborah and Gowen, and then the subsequent attempted suicide of Deborah. In a sense he felt as if he were making up for what he had inadvertently caused, but he would rather cut off his head than admit it to anyone, especially to himself.

By mid-September, the weather had turned bitterly cold and the rain was almost constant. The midwife had confined Dustin to bed because she had grown so enormous and had begun to indicate to Christopher that she was considering inducing her pains in the near future. Terrified for his wife, Christopher avoided the midwife, as if not seeing her would somehow erase the problem. Foolish, he knew, but he did it just the same.

'Twas the twentieth day of September when he entered the castle from the bailey, a bluster of icy wind following close behind him. He let out a grunt as the chill swept over him, shaking himself like a dog. Cold did not usually bother him, but the day was particularly bitter as he shirked his helmet and portions of armor into Darren's waiting hands. Instructing the boy to clean his armor and then report to Leeton for sword practice, he was intending to seek his bedchamber to see his wife when Gowen stopped him.

"Chris, this missive came in not an hour ago. We tried to find you." Gowen handed over a scrolled piece of vellum.

Christopher eyed the parchment, reading the seal. "It is from Longchamp," he murmured as he broke it. "I was out behind the keep, in the clearing where David and I plan to build a troop house and practice arena."

Gowen watched Christopher's face as he read the missive, but could see no particular emotion. After a few minutes, Christopher rolled the parchment back up.

"How much money do we have in the coffers?" he asked.

Gowen blinked. "A substantial amount," he replied. "Are you interested in coinage or overall wealth?"

Christopher chewed his lip thoughtfully, looking at the rolled vellum. "Longchamp demands money for Richard's ransom. Henry and Leopold have demanded one hundred thousand marks of gold for his release."

Gowen's eyes widened. "My God, Chris, even we do not have that much. Surely the justices aren't demanding...?"

Christopher cut him off. "Nay, they are not looking for me to pay all of it." He shook his head, leading them both into Gowen's small office which used to be Lady Mary's solar. "Damnation, with everything I have done for them, they should be paying *me*. Nay, they simply want to know how much I can donate."

Gowen pondered the question a moment, moving around his cluttered desk. "Dustin's dowry is fairly hefty, Chris. You could donate that to Richard's cause and leave the rest untouched, including your own individual wealth acquired from the quest."

Christopher looked at him. "She came with two thousand marks of gold plus an assortment of heirlooms and jewels. What is the total worth?"

Gowen shrugged. "Offhand, I would say ten thousand marks if the jewels were sold on the market. An extremely hefty donation."

Christopher nodded, tossing the vellum onto Gowen's desk. "Sizable enough for their needs," he said. "I shall ask that you prepare the donation, then, and I shall send my men to London with it."

Gowen looked at him, then chuckled. "How can you so easily part with that amount of money? I realize, of course, that it is for Richard's release, but ten thousand marks is more money than most people see in a lifetime."

Christopher nodded. "I realize that, and I also realize that I am depleting my wealth by one-third, but the king must be ransomed for the sake of England," he said, scratching under his coarse mail. "I must make sure there is a future for my family, and for yours."

Gowen raised his eyebrows in agreement as his liege quit the room.

As Christopher mounted the stairs, he found himself remembering a time when all he cared about was money and material wealth. Within a year his priorities had changed so drastically that it was almost as if he did not know the Christopher before Dustin; the almost-mercenary warrior committed to only himself and Richard.

He was still the same man, but he had acquired many new characteristics that he had considered himself incapable of at one time, and the person responsible for that change was a petite blond woman with the unlikely name of Dustin. Fact was that he did not care if he had grown the least bit soft and sentimental, as long as she and his close friends were the only ones who knew it.

He opened the bedchamber door fully expecting to be greeted by her smiling face and was concerned to find the bed empty. He called her name, searching a small adjoining solar but finding no trace of his wife. His concern turning to irritation and his bellows for Dustin lifted the roof off the castle.

The entire place was in an uproar searching for the errant wife when the kitchen servants told their master that his wife had passed by them on her way to the small bailey outside of the kitchen. Enraged, he stormed outside, knowing exactly where she had gone.

Wrapped in a heavy cloak and swathed in yards of heavy material, Dustin stood next to the rabbit hutch, clutching two of the fuzzy creatures as her husband marched up beside her. He was fully prepared to ream her for her disobedience and foolishness, but when he saw her sweetly holding the rabbits and changing their bedding, he felt himself go soft. He knew she had been concerned about her bunnies, and even though she had a peasant boy caring for them, she still fretted. Beside her, Hal and Alex sat wagging their tails, looking for handouts.

"What are you doing?" He sounded almost calm, certainly not like the man who had nearly torn the castle apart just moments before.

Startling her, he could read the guilt in her eyes. "I came to make sure they were warm enough," she said quickly. "With the weather so bad, I was concerned."

He gazed at her sternly, his hands on his hips. "Dustin, the boy is doing a fine job with these rabbits. I see him out here daily."

Her lips molded into a pout. "If he's doing such a fine job, then how come I am missing three of them?" she demanded. "Three of my biggest."

He peered inside the hutches. "Are you sure? How can you tell? There must be thirty or forty rabbits in there."

"Only thirty-eight," she said with a pout. "I had forty-one."

"Forty-one," he repeated, shaking his head with some exasperation. "Mayhap they escaped, sweetheart. 'Tis not unusual for rabbits to slip out of tiny holes."

She frowned sadly, replacing the rabbits she were holding and securing the cage. "I think the boy is stealing my rabbits. I want you to find someone else to tend them."

He eyed her, crossing his arms. "If you are positive he is stealing them, then I will cut his hand off. And *then* I will find someone else to tend them."

Dustin gasped, her wide gray eyes the exact color of the storm clouds above. “I do not want you to cut his hand off. I simply want you to find someone else to tend them.”

“Stealing in my baronetcy will not go unpunished, Dustin,” he said sternly. “If the boy has stolen your rabbits, then he shall pay the price.”

She eyed him, glancing back at the hutch again. “Mayhap I miscounted,” she said after a moment. “They do look to be all here, don’t they?”

“You shall not count them again,” he said. “You must return to bed immediately.”

“But my legs ache from lying about all day,” she whined, taking a step back from him. “I need to walk about, Chris. I simply cannot lie still all of the time.”

He scowled. “You can and you will until this child is born,” he said firmly, his fists on his hips. “I shall sit on you if I have to, Dustin. Your health and the health of my son mean everything to me.”

“But I am bored out of my mind,” she insisted. “I can only sew so much, and Caesar and George offer minimal entertainment. I hate it. I want to be out and about.”

He was not unsympathetic and his manner softened.

“I know, sweet, but it will only be for a little longer,” he assured her. “After the babe is born, you can run your head off if it pleases you. Now, come upstairs and I shall read to you from Beowulf.”

“Nay,” she said petulantly, seeing his gaze turn hard and suddenly receiving a mental picture of herself slung over his shoulder as he carried her to bed. “I….I want to see my garden first. Please?”

He pursed his lips in frustration. “Blatant disobedience one moment and sweet pleading the next,” he grunted. “Dustin, surely you are going to drive me right out of my mind. I shall be glad when this child is born if nothing else than to rid you of these mood swings. Well? If it is your garden you wish to see, then see it you will or else I shall never get you out of this hellish cold.”

She smiled sweetly at him and took his arm as he rolled his eyes at her with exasperation. “You are making me daft,” he murmured sternly.

“I love you, husband,” she said, laying her head on his arm affectionately.

Her garden was dead, as she knew it would be, but she took great delight in planning the flowers she was going to plant for spring. Christopher listened, gave her his opinions when she asked, and spent the majority of his time watching her pace from plot to plot, explaining to him in great detail what she had in mind.

Now and again, he would glance to the sky above, for he could smell the rain and he knew they were in for a hell of a storm. He was eager to get his wife inside, but she was happier than he had seen her in weeks fluttering about in the dead garden, and so he allowed her a bit of freedom.

The cold had turned her beautiful face a healthy rosy shade and the pregnancy had filled her cheeks out, making her appear like a round little cherub. Christopher was entranced by her glow, her beauty, and her spirit as she made her way back over to him, all smiles. He held his arms out to her and she fell into him, still chatting happily about her flowers.

He hustled her up to their bedchamber, helping her with her cloak and heavy overdress she had put on. The closer he came to view the true figure of his wife, the more he suddenly realized that Griselda was right; she was absolutely enormous and he felt a bolt of fear shoot through him. She certainly could not go another six weeks. He silently vowed to seek the old woman out when he left his wife, to begrudgingly comply with whatever she wanted to do with Dustin.

"Sit down," he told her and she lowered herself onto the bed, holding up her feet so he could remove her boots.

It had been weeks since she had been able to put her own shoes on. This morning before she went outside, she had had to lie on her back on the bed and hold her legs up in the air so that she might struggle to pull her boots on.

"Now lie down, sweetheart," he said, pulling the coverlet up around her. "I shall return in a moment with some mead and the book."

"I have already read Beowulf," she told him, unhappy.

"I see," he blinked thoughtfully. "Have you read Song of Roland?"

She nodded. "The Iliad, too."

He pretended to give her a stern, pondering look. "Hmm," he rubbed his chin. "I see that I shall have to make up my own stories to keep you abed."

Her eyes lit up. "Tell me of your adventures in the Holy Land."

That will keep her busy for days, he thought as he sat on the bed next to her and drew her into the curve of his torso.

"So you want to hear of the Holy Land, do you?" he said thoughtfully. "Well, now, where shall I begin?"

"At the very beginning," she insisted, cuddling up against him and waiting expectantly. "Tell me of when Richard first recruited you. Where were you serving?"

He obliged her. He'd barely gotten to the part where he was placed in command of a division before they sailed for Turkey when he felt Dustin go limp beside him. When she began to snore, he smiled and wrapped his free arm around her, his mind relaxing from its remembrance, and his eyes drifting to the window where freezing rain was spattering the sill.

He eventually left Dustin sleeping in the early afternoon and went downstairs to partake of the nooning meal. Even before he entered the great dining hall he could hear his sister's bad temper as she turned her nose up at everything Gowen was offering her. Deborah had such an even temper that it was surprising to hear her get upset at anything at all. He and Gowen passed glances as he took his seat.

"Deborah, with all of that complaining, you are surely going to wake the dead," Christopher told her as he reached for a well-done knuckle of beef.

Deborah turned a pouting face to him. "I am not complaining," she insisted unhappily. "I simply do not like beef and Gowen is trying to force it down my throat."

"You had better eat something, else that child will be born grossly underfed," Christopher said sternly. "Griselda has warned you."

"I know she has warned me," Deborah snapped, immediately contrite. She forced herself to calm. "I am sorry, Chris, I try to eat, truly I do. But nothing appeals to me."

"Then find something that does and eat only that," Christopher said with a mouthful of beef. "Surely there is something that takes your fancy?"

"There is," Gowen announced loudly. "She'd eat honeyed fruits all day long, the kind the cook makes with cinnamon and nutmeg."

"Fine," Christopher said decisively. "Then I shall order the cook to make platefuls of the stuff and Deborah can eat until she explodes."

Deborah made a face, letting them know exactly what she thought of the both of them. Christopher snorted into his cup, wondering if all women turned into such banshees when they were with child. He never thought it possible of his mild-mannered sister.

David, Edward, Leeton, and most of the other knights save Jeffrey and Sir Nicholas entered the dining hall loudly, dropping weapons and armor and bellowing loudly for food and ale.

"Christ, shut up, would you?" Christopher waved at them irritably. "You make more noise than a heard of stampeding cattle."

"Look who's calling us loud," Edward said, sniffing as he sat. "The man that bellows orders so loudly that Philip Augustus can hear him over in France. Ah, what is on the menu this day?"

The knights dug into their meal with the usual enthusiasm, licking fingers and throwing the bones to the floor. Harold and Alexander had a feast cleaning up their droppings. Outside, the weather worsened and they could hear the thunder deep into the dining hall.

"Jesus, this climate is terrible," David exclaimed. "I would take the searing sands of Jerusalem over this mess."

"This 'mess,' as you call it is nothing you have not dealt with before," Christopher said dryly. "I think you are growing soft in your old age, little brother."

David eyed his brother menacingly at the insult but said nothing because his mouth was too full. "Where's Dustin?" he asked after he swallowed.

"Sleeping," Christopher answered. "That's all she does anymore. She's almost stopped eating, too."

"You see?" Deborah chimed in. "I am not the only one."

Christopher was patient with her. "Aye, sweet, but you are not as far along as my wife," he said. "Our child is already huge and grown and if she eats anymore, she will probably explode. Your babe needs nourishment yet."

Properly put in her place, Deborah lowered her head and picked at her boiled vegetables.

The meal finished and the knights took the opportunity to enjoy some fine wine that Gowen had purchased in Gloucester. David and Max announced it was too sweet and promptly deemed it a woman's drink, but Edward thought it delightful. Christopher raised his eyebrows at the lot of his boisterous knights, thinking to take some of the drink up to his wife when she awoke.

Jeffrey and Sir Nicholas burst in through the front doors with a violent slam, the elements howling and whistling around them. They looked like huge, mythical beasts in their soaked armor and tunics and the knights inside immediately yelled at them to close the doors.

"My lord!" Jeffrey ignored the demands of the others. "Raiders!"

The knights were up, bellowing for their armor, as Christopher rounded the table even as Darren was rushing at him.

"How many?" Christopher asked.

"A large party, as large as I have ever seen." Jeffrey actually sounded concerned and that, in turn, concerned Christopher.

"Raiding for winter supplies, no less," Christopher said as Darren competently pulled on his hauberk. "I was wondering how long it would be before we had trouble."

"This winter promises to be fierce," Jeffrey agreed. "The Welsh are panicking early."

"Where will they go first?" Christopher asked as his breastplate was latched.

"Most likely the harvest stores at the edge of the village," Jeffrey replied as David, fully armored, dashed past him outside and began shouting for the warhorses. "And the sheep. They love to target the sheep."

"Waste no time, then." Christopher motioned to his men, strapping on his sword. "They will not raid my village."

As the knights blew out of the hall, Gowen and Deborah were left sitting at the massive table, flabbergasted with the speed in which the men had mobilized and moved out. They looked at each other, a bit dazed, before Gowen picked up a honey-crystalized raisin and placed it in his wife's mouth, smiling weakly.

The rain was fierce as the knights rode out of Lioncross with about fifty men-at-arms, armed to the teeth with crossbows and swords. Christopher, too, carried a crossbow on the back of his saddle. The raiders were not much for confrontations and he doubted he would have the chance to use his sword, so most of the defending would be done from a distance.

Jeffrey led the way to the southwestern portion of the village, where the church stood. Even as they arrived, the Welsh raiders were intently attacking the place of worship. Christopher grabbed his crossbow, taking aim at the five or six bandits who were charging the front door. A well-aimed arrow from him and from Leeton took down two of the villains while the rest fled in terror.

But there were plenty of them to go around. They hooped and hollered like animals as they ran and sometimes fought the soldiers and knights who were surrounding them. They were a dirty, verminous lot of scruff, peasants and rabble who populated border towns. Christopher felt as if he were herding a band of unruly children as he chased the swarthy men down and killed them mercifully.

Surprisingly, their chaotic appearance seemed to be some sort of ploy to confuse and unbalance the English, hoping that the complete irrationality of their attack would throw them off guard, for they continued to stay and fight instead of escaping back across the border.

Christopher fought off the dirty men who tried to charge him, using his huge feet to kick them away or a giant mailed fist to cave their faces in. He set up a perimeter around the church and, for the moment, the parish and her winter stores appeared to be holding. He was focused on driving the Welsh bastards back where they came from.

Off to the side of the melee, standing near a line of trees, was Edward. He appeared to be observing the entire clash, occasionally fighting off anyone who ventured close to him, but for the most part he was not involved in the scuffle.

Christopher was enraged; he had spoken with Edward, even practiced with the man and his knight showed every sign of returning to the competent warrior he had been before his injury. Confident in Edward's recovery, Christopher had not pushed him in any way, but now to see Edward standing clear of the fight had infuriated him and he would not stand for it.

He spurred his destrier toward Edward, running over several Welsh as he charged. Controlling the destrier with pressure alone from his thighs and knees, Christopher drew his sword and raised his shield. Edward saw him coming, merely watching Christopher approach. Yet, in hindsight, he should have known better when he saw the broadsword go up and the shield move into a defensive stance. He and Christopher had known each other since they had been pages and he never truly believed his friend would attack him, not even when he hit the ground in a painful crunch of bone and steel did he believe it still.

Christopher loomed over Edward as he lay on the ground, grunting loudly with the shock of the fall.

"You will raise your sword and plunge into that battle this moment, de Wolfe, or you can gather your things and be gone before the sun sets," Christopher said icily. "I will coddle no bastard coward in my ranks."

With that, he was gone, leaving Edward who struggled to rise and struggled to come to grips with his phobia. He had never heard Christopher use that tone with him and he was as ashamed of himself as his liege was. Finally on his feet, he staggered to his destrier and mounted, swallowing hard before spurring his steed forward into the heat of the brawl. He knew he had no choice.

Christopher forgot all about Edward as Max was taken down by several raiders who had ganged up on him. The destrier screamed as it went over on its side, trapping Max even as Christopher and Leeton fought their way to him. The man received a good pounding but was spared any real injury thanks to his armor. Back on his horse, he was distressed to see that the animal suffered a terrible gash above his fetlock and blood was gushing onto the hoof.

"What did you say to Edward?" David reined his dancing charger alongside his brother.

"Where is he?" Evasively, he answered his brother with a question of his own.

"Fighting off a group of raiders, fighting as I haven't seen him fight in a long time." David's helmet turned in the direction of Edward.

Christopher felt a small amount of satisfaction, although he was still disappointed in his knight. He did not bother to turn and look. "Damnable bastards are heading for the church again," he said, spurring his animal forward.

The skirmish that should have been handled in mere minutes turned into a scuffle that lasted all afternoon. The Welsh were like crazed dogs, moving about in waves and vandalizing cottages and businesses more than actually destroying anything.

It was frustrating to chase the wily bastards about and Christopher finally had enough; he sent to Lioncross for one hundred reinforcements and before the hour was up, they had the raiders turning tail for the border. He sent the majority of his knights chasing after them, not only to make sure they retreated across the border, but also to check the border garrison he kept manned. Max and Sir Guy accompanied him back to Lioncross.

The very moment he entered the gates, Gowen was there to meet him.

"It is Dustin, Chris," he said as the man dismounted.

Christopher ripped off his helm and nearly tore his head off with it. "What?" he asked, panicked. "What's happened?"

"Her pains started nearly three hours ago," Gowen replied. "Griselda and Burwell are with her."

All of the color drained from Christopher's face as he charged past Gowen, oblivious to everything in the world except the plight of his wife and child.

CHAPTER THIRTY-SEVEN

PAIN ON THIS magnitude was something entirely new for Dustin. Her pains had started slowly enough and she thought that mayhap giving birth was not such a terrible thing after all, but they quickly escalated and she rapidly decided she wanted no part of it.

As vocal as she was, it was no time before she was panting loudly with each contraction and cursing everyone she made eye contact with. Burwell was simply in the room to view the birth; in his line of work he did not get much practice and Griselda was the very best to learn from. Dustin did not want him in the room and nearly got out of bed to bodily remove him.

She cursed Christopher for not being at her side, for bringing the pain upon her, and for thinking that ridding the village of raiders was more important than the birth of his child. She was fully prepared to slug him in the jaw for his priorities, but the moment his pale face entered the room, she broke down into sobs.

Griselda wouldn't let him in the room with all of his armor on, and still wouldn't let him near his wife without washing the grime off his hands. Then, and only then, was he allowed to comfort Dustin.

Christopher had never been around a laboring woman before and he was the first to admit it scared the hell out of him. He was doubly terrified that the babe was almost five weeks early, but Griselda did not seem overly concerned. She assured him that everything was progressing nicely and by the morning, he would be holding his son.

Dustin did not want to wait that long. She wanted the babe out that very minute and was rolling with the contractions as best she could. She then plead with them to tie a rope around the babe and pull him out. They had all laughed at her, but she did not think it was the least bit funny.

He rubbed his wife's back and massaged her shaking legs, stopping every time she had a contraction and closing his eyes as if by sheer force of will he could absorb her pain. He could not stand to see Dustin in so much pain, even though he had known full well what he had been in for. Finally, toward midnight, Griselda gave Dustin a drink of poppy that seemed to take the edge off her contractions and make her very sleepy. With her tensions relaxed, he was able to relax a bit, too.

Her contractions worked all night and into the morning, dissolving Griselda's prediction that the babe would come by sunup. Instead, the poppy potion was making Dustin sick and she would vomit it up every time she tried to take it, rendering her pains merciless and causing her to scream with agony every time a wave would roll over her. Seventeen hours into her labor, Christopher was ready to climb the walls.

"What is taking so long?" he demanded in a harsh whisper, making sure his wife could not hear him.

"Patience, sire, patience," Griselda assured him. "Some women take longer than others, that's all. She is progressing slowly but everything appears fine. Why, I have seen women in labor for three days, and their children were perfectly healthy."

Haggard and unshaven, Christopher glanced at his wife. "The child is early, mistress."

The child wasn't early and Griselda knew it, but obviously the baron did not. 'Twas not her place to involve herself in the puzzling situation.

"The child is large and I am sure will be fine, sire," she said. "Now do not fret so. Why do not you go and eat something? We will still be here when you return."

He started to refuse but Burwell clapped a meaty hand on him. "Come, baron, let the women do their work, and let you and I do ours on a plate of venison."

Dustin had another contraction and moaned loudly, too weak to do the screaming she had been doing earlier. Christopher closed his eyes briefly, sickened with her necessary pain.

"All right," his voice was a whisper, but then he said rapidly "but I shall be right back."

Griselda nodded, waiting before the door was closed before moving back to Dustin and swabbing her clammy brow.

Christopher was met downstairs by every one of his knights and Gowen, all clamoring to pester him with questions. Christopher ignored them for the most part, weary to the bone as a serving wench placed a trencher of food before him. He did not even realize he was hungry until the smells filled his nostril, and then he ate everything on the plate.

His men and vassals were waiting quite impatiently as he finished the last of his bread and downed the remainder of his fruited water.

"How is she?" David could stand it no longer.

Christopher wiped his mouth and looked at his brother. "She is in labor, David. Not exactly a party atmosphere."

"No babe?" Leeton asked, his face pale and Christopher suddenly remembered what had happened to the man's wife in childbirth.

"Not yet," he said, a little less snappish. "But Griselda assures me all is well. At any rate, Dustin is miserable but coping."

"We could hear her screaming down here," Leeton said. "It sounds as if she is being beaten."

Christopher made a wry face. "Mayhap that would be preferable."

The other knights began assaulting him with questions but Leeton simply looked away. He was reliving a nightmare and not at all pleased. He knew the screams of childbirth all too well, and he had seen what bearing a new life had done to his beloved Rachel. Abruptly, he quit the hall.

Christopher watched him leave, a twinge of sorrow for the man. Now that he was experiencing the same action that had taken Leeton's wife from him, he could relate to the man's pain completely. Leaving his men for a moment, he found Leeton in Gowen's office.

The knight was sitting in a hide-covered chair, staring out across the dismal compound. A low fire crackled in the hearth, making the room rather cozy.

"Leeton," he said quietly.

The knight turned to look at him, quickly dashing away the tears on his cheeks. Christopher was miserable for him. "What is it?"

"You asked me once, a long time ago, that if anything ever happened to Dustin, would I ever be the same. Do you remember?" he asked.

Leeton nodded, trying to compose himself. "I remember."

Christopher fixed him with a gentle, unguarded look. He seemed hesitant to go on, but he did. "The answer is no. If my wife dies as a result of this, I will not be the same. For the fact that you have maintained your life and character in the face of the death of the woman you loved, I admire you greatly. I do not believe I am that strong."

"Aye, you are," Leeton said, his voice faint. "You are stronger than you know, Chris. You have no weaknesses."

"Yes, I do," Christopher looked up to the ceiling as if he could see his wife through the mortar and stone. "She's a slip of a woman whom I love with all of my heart and soul."

He turned and left, leaving Leeton coming to grips with his terrible memories yet, somehow, stronger with them. Mayhap it was the fact that time was passing and easing his pain, or mayhap it was Christopher's understanding. Whatever the case, he did not feel quite as desolate as he had when he had entered the room.

Christopher fully intended to return to his wife when he came head-to-head with Burwell at the base of the stairs. The physician smiled at him, instantly throwing Christopher on his guard.

"Leave the women to their work, my lord," he said firmly. "You shall be of no help up there now. Come, let's enjoy a game of Fox and Hounds to pass the time."

Christopher's face was set. "I promised Dustin I would return, and I shall. Get out of my way."

Burwell shook his head. "Son, at this point you will simply distract her, and she needs all of her concentration to birth that enormous child of yours." He put his thick hands on Christopher and attempted to turn him around. "You will do now as men have done for centuries; you will wait and drink and see your child after it is born. If you tend her now, you shall do more harm than good. You must allow Griselda to work."

A shadow of a doubt crossed Christopher's mind as he thought that Burwell's words made sense. He wanted to be with his wife; well, not really, but he was scared to leave her alone to face the impending birth, terrified that something would happen and he would not be there if she needed him. But, in faith, he had had just about all of the pain and moaning he could take from her. He hated feeling so helpless.

Feeling like a dumb animal, he allowed Burwell to turn him around and steer him toward the grand hall. The healer began bellowing for wine and the game pieces to be brought forward, and in spite of the misgivings tormenting his heart, Christopher allowed himself to be swallowed up by his company of knights as they sat around the massive table.

Christopher was very good at keeping track of time. Although he played a couple of games with Burwell, he was acutely aware that the hours were passing and nothing was happening. His anxiety was running rampant and he took to pacing the cold floor of the hall absently, listening to his men as they played their games to pass the time but not really hearing. His heart, his mind, his soul, everything but his body, was up in the bedchamber with his wife.

Several times during the afternoon he tried to push his way upstairs, but he was thwarted every time by Burwell and a host of knights. He tried threats, intimidation, reasoning, and finally pleading, but they would not let him pass the stairs. Frustrated and frayed, he sank into a heavily padded chair by the hearth and put his head in his hands. He knew without a doubt he was going insane with worry.

Dustin's two maids had joined in the waiting, helping Griselda with her every need so that the midwife could focus her complete attention on Dustin. Thirty-two hours into her labor, the baby's head was finally beginning to crown. After two hours of hard pushing, even Griselda was growing concerned, but when she saw the dark little head forcing its way into the world, she felt a certain amount of relief.

"The child's head is appearing, my lady," she encouraged Dustin. "Push as hard as you can with your next pain."

Dustin was spent. She had been spent for hours and hours but there was no mercy for her weary body. She, the bedclothes, and the mattress were absolutely soaked with perspiration and fluids. When the next unbelievable pain hit, she grunted loudly and tried to push, but she honestly did not think she could. She'd been pushing for hours, or was it days, and nothing had happened. She was so very, very tired that she did not care at this point if she died or not.

But this contraction did not subside like the others had, it continued until Dustin was shrieking with agony. She could hear Griselda's matronly voice, light and reassuring, encouraging her onward, but she has ceased to hear her words long ago. She was wrapped up in her own world of agony until the pain suddenly subsided a bit and she felt a great, slippery rush and the pressure diminished substantially.

"Is…is it born yet?" she breathed heavily, feeling one of the maids swab her clammy brow.

"Almost," Griselda said. "Another push and 'twill be free."

Dustin seemed to snap out of her lethargy then; *one more push*. She began to live for that one more push and when the contraction came, she bore down with her remaining strength and was rewarded with a tremendous sense of relief. Almost instantaneously, she heard a thin wail.

More alert than she had been in over a day, she struggled to sit up to see the babe as Griselda and the maids fussed over the infant.

"Well? Is he all right? Is he healthy?" she demanded.

Griselda smiled and suddenly there was a fat, squalling, red infant displayed for Dustin to see. "Your daughter is fine," she said. "Look how big and strong she is."

Dustin was immediately entranced. She realized that she did not care that it wasn't a boy; it was a beautiful, healthy daughter and she reached out and touched the tiny, sticky fingers. Tears of relief and joy coursed down her cheeks.

"She is big, isn't she?" she whispered. "Oh, give her to me, please."

Griselda cleaned the infant a bit and wrapped her in warm, clean swaddling. Dustin had never experienced anything so sweet as holding her daughter in her arms for the first time. She cooed to the baby, examining her tiny hands and touching her little face, all the while completely unaware that she was crying. All of the pain and exhaustion from the past day and a half was suddenly worth the effort.

Griselda and the maids stood back a moment, watching the new mother with her new daughter, smiling happily between them. But Dustin was very pale and very weak and needed her rest; the babe would still be there when she awoke. Sending one of the maids for the wet nurse enlisted from the village, she gently took the babe from Dustin and handed it off to the other maid for more serious cleaning.

Dustin protested weakly at her child being taken away, but Griselda shushed her firmly. "You will be holding that child for years to come, my lady. Now we must take care of you."

With that, she bade Dustin to drink a nourishing concoction that tasted terrible, but settled her stomach. Now that the newness of the moment had passed, Dustin began to quiver as if terribly cold and Griselda bundled her up in layers of coverlets and furs.

Warm, bone-tired but elated, Dustin was asleep before she even realized it.

☙

CHRISTOPHER MUST HAVE fallen asleep with his head resting on his palm, because the next thing he knew, he heard David's astonished voice and he shot out of his chair, instantly alert. It took him absolutely no time at all to spy Griselda descending the stairs with a swaddled bundle in her aged arms.

Christopher felt his knees go weak, be it because he rose too fast or because he was overcome with rampant emotion, he wasn't sure. All he knew was that the old woman approaching him with a smile on her face was cradling his child and he could not take his eyes off of the white blankets.

"Dustin?" he managed to croak.

"Fine, my lord, fine as I told you she would be," Griselda replied. "And your daughter is a fine, healthy baby."

Daughter. He had a daughter. Disappointment was nonexistent as he timidly took the babe and gazed for the first time on the chubby red face. At that very moment there were no possible words to describe his emotions, for all that he seemed to be feeling was a peculiar euphoria that filled his body like warm honey. He could only stand there and stare at the miracle he and his wife had created, his gratitude for both lives spared were immense. When the baby stirred and made little sucking noises, he was instantly, deeply, in love.

The infant mewed like a kitten and the entire roomful of men and vassals let out a collective sigh of approval, moving forward to get a better look at the baby, but Christopher backed away from them and shielded the baby's face with his free hand.

"I shall not have you breathing on my daughter like a pack of jackals," he snapped, although it was done gently. He then turned to the midwife. "She is fine? I mean, my daughter?"

"Fine, fat and saucy," Griselda nodded confidently. "Look at her for yourself, baron, and see how large she is."

"I see," he said softly, pushing a massive finger into a tiny palm and being rewarded with a strong grip. He could not stop himself from smiling broadly. David pushed forward, trying to peer into the creases of the cloth and Christopher took mercy on the man. "See your niece? Isn't she the most beautiful female you have ever seen?"

"Aye, verily," David agreed sincerely. "She looks just like her mother."

Being reminded of Dustin again, Christopher looked at Griselda. "I must see my wife now."

"She's sleeping, baron, and in good hands," the old woman assured him. "She will not know the difference if you spend a few extra minutes admiring your daughter."

And admire he did. He crooned softly to the infant, announcing with satisfaction that she opened one tiny eye when she heard his voice. His knights had ignored his warning and were crowding around anyway, so he threw back the folds of the blanket and displayed her quite plainly for all to see and cherish. She was so very beautiful and perfect and in all his life he had never known such pride.

David was admiring her, too. But as he admired his new little niece with pride, another sinister, darker emotion entangled itself within the others and he uncomfortably shirked off the jealousy he was feeling. Yet, as persistent as the rising sun, it bloomed again, stronger than before and David took a step back, hoping the evidence of his envy wasn't visible on his face.

He took a good look at his brother, as happy as he had ever seen him, yet there was more to it. There was a contentment he had never seen before and suddenly, he was wildly jealous. His brother had a beautiful wife, a daughter, a keep and loyal vassals. Once, David fit into those plans but he suddenly felt like an outsider. For so long it was only he and Christopher, against all others, but now he suddenly realized it was he alone against all others. Christopher had changed before his eyes and he had been left behind.

There were no flaws to Christopher's and Dustin's marriage. They loved each other desperately, that was obvious. The only negative intrusion had been that of Marcus Burton, and even that influence had simply faded away. Aye, his brother and Dustin were stronger than ever, and with the introduction of the baby, David's place in Christopher's life was dissolved. He had been shoved aside and he knew it. The longer he looked at the babe, the more consumed he became.

"What are you planning to name her?" Leeton asked, touching the silky skin.

Christopher raised his eyebrows slowly. " 'Tis likely to create a bit of a problem for, you see, my wife selected only one name, a male name. I have no idea if she had even considered a female name."

Christopher caught sight of a figure descending the stairs and looked up to see his sister. Her face was a mask of thrilled astonishment as she saw what her brother held.

"The baby!" she shrieked. "Dustin had her baby. Oh, why didn't anyone awaken me?"

She rushed to Christopher, begging to hold the infant and he reluctantly complied. She cooed and ogled and gushed, declaring the babe to be the most beautiful one she had ever seen. Then, she began calling the baby Curtis and Christopher stopped her.

"It is a girl, Deborah," he informed her.

Deborah looked at him blankly for a second before her face spread into the most marvelous smile. "A girl? Thank God. There are too many men around here for my taste as it is."

They all snickered as Deborah kissed the baby and told her over and over how very perfect she was. Christopher crossed his arms across his weary body, simply content for the moment to watch his daughter as she was admired by all. He felt as puffed-up as an arrogant peacock, but as the seconds passed, his heart was being pulled to the second floor bedchamber where his wife lay sleeping.

The baby began to fuss and wail lustily and Christopher was alarmed. "What's wrong? Why is she doing that?"

"I am sure she is hungry, my lord," Griselda said. "I have seen to securing a wet nurse from the village so that your wife may recover uninterrupted."

"That was wise," Christopher agreed, looking with concern on the red-faced babe. "Take her and make sure she is fed. I would see to my wife now."

The midwife moved to take the baby but Deborah begged to hold her just a bit longer but Christopher intervened. "Deborah, soon you will have a squawking infant of your very own. Now, unhand my daughter so that she might eat."

With a smile, his sister reluctantly handed the child over.

Dustin's room was dark except for the light from the fire, casting dancing shadows on the walls. Christopher entered quietly, waving away the maid who was sitting vigilantly by his sleeping wife. The woman left the room quickly, leaving him alone with Dustin for the first time in days.

He moved around the bed and sat in the great hide chair, removing his boots as quietly as possible. But his eyes, the entire time, never left her face. She looked so entirely peaceful and beautiful and it occurred to him that she wasn't snoring. Boots off, he removed his tunic and leaned forward in the chair to tenderly stroke her head, knowing he should not because it might disturb her, but wanting so desperately to touch her. His love for his wife was so great it was more a part of him than his heart or his brain, he knew he literally could not live without her.

"So, coward, you come in when all of the screaming and blood has vanished," Dustin mumbled, her face half into her pillow.

He smiled, his hand caressing her head. "You are supposed to be sleeping."

Her face was pale and there were dark smudges under her eyes, but her beautiful smile lit up the room. "I could not. Not until I saw you."

He took her hand and kissed it so reverently that it brought tears to her eyes. "Did you see her?" she asked.

His eyes were misty as well. "I did and she is absolutely beautiful, as is befitting your daughter," he whispered. "Thank you, Dustin. From the bottom of my heart, thank you."

He kissed her hand again and she sobbed softly, not bothering to wipe the tears away that were streaming down her temples. "Lord God, I am tired. She was not easily born, Chris."

"I know." He laid his cheek on her hand, his eyes drinking in her face. "I suppose I am to blame for that. 'Tis my tremendous size."

She shrugged. "As large as you are, I am equally as small. I believe we are both to blame."

He smiled broadly and leaned forward to deposit the sweetest of kisses on her lips. His forehead touched hers, his huge hand still caressing her head and feeling her softness. He was content just to feel her, to touch her, and to know she had survived something as deadly as all of the battles he had ever faced. His hands touched her face and he could still feel her warm tears, and he kissed her entire face until all of the tears were but a damp memory. Beneath his touch, Dustin sighed raggedly.

"I love you, sweetheart," he murmured, his lips against her temple.

Dustin burst into soft sobs again and he shushed her gently, knowing how tired and emotionally drained she was. They both were.

"I think we have a problem," he said after a moment, trying to lighten the heady mood. "You selected only one name, a male name. We certainly cannot name my beautiful daughter Curtis."

She blinked at him, sniffling. " 'Tis true that we cannot," she answered hoarsely. "But I had selected a girl's name, as well, only I wasn't going to tell you because I wanted so badly the babe to be a boy."

His smile faded. "Are you disappointed, then?"

"Nay." she insisted and he instantly believed her. "How could I be? The moment I looked at her, I wanted her more than any scruffy male child. She's so pink and perfect and...are you disappointed?"

"Perish the thought, Dustin," he said with soft sternness. "She is my daughter, my flesh and blood, and I love her more than anything on this earth, other than you. I wouldn't take a son for her if God himself marched into this room and proposed a trade."

She smiled faintly. "I am so glad. I know that all men want sons and ...."

"Not me," he insisted. "I am perfectly happy with a gorgeous daughter in the image of my gorgeous wife."

She put her arms around his neck and he could feel for himself just how weak she was. She needed to sleep, and so did he.

"What is this name you have selected for her?" he asked, unwinding her arms gently.

She looked thoughtful. "I was hard pressed to think of the most wonderful name I could. Anne, Eleanor, and Catherine are too common and I do not like them. And since I have an uncommon name, I wanted our daughter to have a beautiful and uncommon name, too."

"And?" he pressed.

She smiled. "I wanted to name her after you, and after me, so I put our names together. Her name will be Christin. Christin Valeria de Lohr."

"Christin," he repeated softly. "I like it very much. 'Tis as fragile and feminine and perfect as she it. And Valeria after my mother. Christ, I am lucky to have such a clever wife." He leaned down and kissed her loudly on the forehead.

She smiled, her fatigue catching up with her and her lids suddenly very heavy. He stroked her forehead. "Sleep now, sweetheart. I shall not leave you."

She nodded feebly, trying to adjust her sore body into a comfortable position. He thought about sleeping next to her this night, but he knew she was terribly stiff and he did not want his presence impeding her. If she wanted to sleep crosswise on the bed because it was more comfortable for her, then so be it.

He settled back in the hide chair, his hand resting on her arm, and lay his head back with a sigh of contentment. He stared at the ceiling a moment, silently thanking God for his infinite mercy and the blessings he had seen fit to bestow on him. Still touching his wife, he drifted off into a dreamless sleep.

☙

GRISELDA STOOD LIKE a silent guard as the wet nurse fed the baron's new child, making sure all was well. When the infant had eaten her fill and slept contentedly, she retrieved her and carried her into the new nursery that had been decorated for her and her soon-to-arrive cousin.

She lay the babe down and re-swaddled the wrappings, tightening them as she went. At one point a tiny hand found its way out of the bindings and Griselda started to put it back when she noticed just how small the hand was. The rest of the baby was large and she was healthy, but her hands were tiny and wrinkled. Curious, Griselda undid the rest of the blankets and examined the feet. They, too, were small in proportion to the size of the body and wrinkled.

Griselda looked thoughtful as she wrapped the baby up again. The small hands and feet were indicative of a premature infant, although the child was as big as any she had seen. Properly swaddled and laid on her side, the old woman watched the dark-haired infant for a moment, pondering her discovery.

After a moment, she shrugged to herself and turned away; mayhap the infant was premature, after all mayhap Lady de Lohr had been right all along.

CHAPTER THIRTY-EIGHT

IT WAS EVIDENT from the beginning that no child was ever loved more than Christin de Lohr.

Dustin dismissed the wet nurse after a week of service and insisted on caring for her daughter exclusively. After all, she had birthed the babe and 'twas only right that she tend her. Christopher tried to reason with her, but Dustin would not listen. As usual, he let her have her way but kept a careful watch on her diet and sleep habits, not wanting her to tire herself.

But the spoiling and doting was equal from both parents. Christopher would sit with the baby and rock her for hours, singing to her in his delightful deep baritone and Dustin would stand in the doorway and listen with tears in her eyes. Deborah could not listen at all, the sweet tenderness of a father and daughter sent her sliding into sobs. The shortening days of autumn were spent with his daughter when they should have been spent outside with his men, but he wasn't overly concerned. David and Edward were driving them like slaves and he knew they were being kept at the ready.

Christin would awaken every two hours during the night like clockwork and Christopher had made it his duty to collect the hungry babe and bring her to his wife for nourishment. The pleasure and contentment he derived from watching his new baby tug at his wife's breast was well beyond words. He had oft wondered what true peace of soul and spirit was, and if he would ever achieve such a thing. Watching little Christin suckle Dustin's swollen nipple made him realize that he had achieved true contentment in life and had not even known it.

September passed into October and into November. The snows came and they were all in the deep freeze, but inside Lioncross, there was always a warm fire blazing and food enough for all. It was truly a place of happiness and love and Christopher was sure there was no better castle in all of England. All of his life he had been searching for himself, and here he had found it.

Christmas came and Christin had turned into a fat, red-cheeked cherub with an infectious toothless grin. Christopher adored the baby; she was rarely, if ever, out of his sight and he took to carrying her everywhere he went, much to Dustin's irritation. Christin was her daughter, too, and she was hardly ever allowed to hold her. Fortunately for the irate mother, Christopher would not dream of taking the babe with him outside and during those times, Dustin bonded with Christin eagerly. She almost felt the outsider the way Christopher demanded he be allowed to hold his daughter at all times.

But she wasn't jealous, nor did she feel neglected, for the nights were theirs and theirs alone. Christin finally started sleeping from dusk until dawn, and Christopher always made sure he reserved that space of time for his wife. Most often, they would take a bath together, soaping each other sensually until the heat of passion would overtake them and they would make slippery-wet love to one another. The first time Christopher had made love to her after Christin's birth had been so sweet, she had cried with the pure joy of it.

And she felt in top form, too. Her luscious figure had returned better than before, she thought, and Christopher could not get enough of her. She was so truly happy for the first time in her life that she had completely pushed John and Ralph and Richard out of her mind, for fear of hexing her good fortune. She never wanted Christopher to leave her again and the thought of him returning to battle made her sick to her stomach.

But as time passed and Christin grew, quite another thing was turning her stomach into knots. Christin was absolutely beautiful with dark, wavy hair and her mother's huge gray eyes, and Dustin was verily pleased to see that she looked like her. The eyes and the shape of her little mouth were definitely Dustin's, but it was the color of the hair that upset her so. With her and Christopher so blond, the dark-hair of the babe stood out obviously. With every passing day, Dustin began to imagine she saw something of Marcus in the sweet baby face.

Foolish, she scolded herself, for her mother had possessed black hair and it was entirely possible that little Christin had inherited her grandmother's dark hair. But the fear, the apprehension, and the overwhelming guilt plagued her.

Two days after Christmas, Dustin went out to the rabbit hutches to make sure the peasant boy had given the animals enough warm bedding and food. Christopher had the babe, as usual, in the great hall. Alexander had followed her out into the hellish cold, dancing around her feet to keep warm. As she was poking into one of the cages, a figure came up beside her.

"It is awfully cold to be out here," David said, his nose red with the ice. "What are you doing?"

"Making sure they do not freeze to death," she said, slamming a little door closed and securing it. "I thought you were tending to the new men-at-arms?"

"I was," David said. "But Edward and Leeton are drilling them in battle rules and I want no part of it. Where's Chris?"

"Inside with Christin, where else?" she snorted. "Sometimes I think he loves her more than me."

There was something in David's eyes that met hers strangely. "I doubt it," he replied evenly, then paused a moment. His gaze was intense on her as he spoke. "I know, Dustin."

She blinked at him, tilting her head. "Know? Know what?"

He let out a hissing sigh, all of the friendliness gone from his face. "Jesus, do not lie to me," he snapped. "You can lie to Chris because he loves you and he will believe anything you tell him, but for God's sake, do not lie to me. I *know*."

She honestly had no idea what he was talking about and her irritation grew. "Know what, David? What are you talking about?"

He suddenly grabbed her arm, his fingers biting into her flesh and she gasped. "You slept with Marcus, didn't you?" he hissed. "Christin isn't Chris' child at all, she is Marcus'."

Dustin's mouth went agape. His words had hit her in the face like a slap and left her reeling, but she had the presence of mind to calm herself before she tore into him like a hurricane. Roughly, she tore her arm from his grasp and glared daggers at him.

"How dare you accuse me of infidelity," she seethed. "Christin is Chris' daughter, David, in spite of your wild imaginings. I cannot believe you would think so lowly of me."

He grabbed her again, this time with both hands, and she struggled angrily with him.

"You are a liar and a whore," David snarled. "Christin looks just like Marcus; admit it! She bears his dark hair. Explain how two blond people such as you and my brother can bear a dark-haired child!"

Dustin yanked free and slapped him hard across the face. David responded by slapping her just as hard and sending her reeling. She slammed into the rabbit hutch, grasping the first thing that came into her hand and swung it back at David with all her might. The short piece of wood caught David in the neck and he grunted, a mighty gash in his flesh. He put his hand to his skin, drawing it away sticky with blood.

"You *bitch*!" he hissed.

"I was defending myself!" she fired back at him, wielding the wood like a club. "How dare you accuse me of such terrible atrocities! I cannot believe you would think such despicable things about me when I have never done anything to deserve such distrust. And who are you to confront me with such things? You are not my husband!"

He reached out and disarmed her, but not without a struggle. The log went sailing and Dustin backed away from him, preparing for the next barrage.

"Somebody has to confront you," he growled. "Admit it. Christin is Marcus' child. I knew it from the very moment I laid eyes on her that she was not of Chris' loins."

"You did not, because it is not true!" Dustin shrieked. "I swear to God I shall kill you for such lies, David."

He charged at her, grabbing her by the shoulders and slamming her against the rabbit hutch. Dustin grunted and gasped, struggling in David's grip, but it was like fighting iron.

"They are not lies," he rumbled, his face close to hers. "So help me, Dustin, I shall kill you before I allow you to hurt Chris. He is the mightiest knight since Galahad and you have already turned him into a soft, simpering fool who cares only for the comforts of his home and family. He used to be the toughest, mightiest warrior in all the world and I have watched him turn into a tender family man right before my eyes. Jesus, he was right all along. You will destroy him."

Dustin's fear-filled eyes gazed back at her brother-in-law, his words overwhelming her. The hatred, the hostility, frightened her and after a moment, she could only shake her head slowly.

"I will not, David," she said, pain in her eyes. "I would never do such a thing."

"You already have," he spat with contempt, releasing her and stepping back, his big hands clenching nervously.

Dustin's fear was overshadowed by her anger. "Christin is his daughter, and I am his wife," she said, trying to figure out what the motivation was behind his fury. It was very unlike David. "If a family makes a man weak, then I suppose he is weak. Weak of his own choosing, David. I did not force it on him. If you want to be angry with someone, then be angry with him. I did nothing but love him and he chose to respond. I did not shove my affections down his throat like a stuffed goose."

He turned away from her but she refused to let him go that easily. She was starting to make headway with him.

"What do you want from me, David?" she wanted to know. "To swear to you that Christin is his daughter? Then I will. On the Holy Bible, I swear to you that she is his own daughter, and I furthermore swear to you that I never touched Marcus Burton!"

The latter was only a half-truth, yet, it could be the full truth. After all, she had once thought her encounter in her dark bedchamber to be a dream. Mayhap it was after all. Mayhap if she told herself enough it really would only be a dream again and not the reality of Marcus in the flesh.

David's jaw was ticking and he refused to answer. Dustin could see that there was so much more to his outburst but she still wasn't sure what it was. "This isn't just about Christin, is it?" she said, her tone considerably softer. "There is more to this than you are telling me. Why have you decided you suddenly hate me so, David?"

He wouldn't look at her, nor answer. He pulled free of her grasp and paced a few feet away, trying to collect himself. Dustin stood there, watching him, wondering if he were ever going to answer her when Christopher came out into the small courtyard, his face grim.

Dustin's eyes widened and she covered her cheek where David had struck her. David, however, had a bloody gash on his neck that was impossible to cover up as Christopher's eyes bore into him.

"I heard a nasty rumor that you struck my wife," he said calmly to his brother. "Is this true?"

David knew what he had done and fully realized the consequences. "I did."

Christopher's jaw flexed dangerously. "Might I ask why?"

David looked away. "Ask her."

Dustin watched the two of them apprehensively, knowing a servant must have heard the struggle and had run straight to Christopher. She feared for David's life.

"I am asking you," Christopher said. "Answer me and I may be merciful."

David turned to face him, then, and his face was glazed with scorn. "Do you truly wish to know, brother? I struck her because she's been playing you for a fool. Look at Christin; does she *look* like you? She does not and do you know why? Because she isn't your daughter, she's Marcus'!" He gestured wildly toward Dustin. "She has been Burton's whore all along and God only knows why you haven't done something about it. Why do you think Marcus left? Because he was in love with her and he could not stand to see her with you. Goddammit, you are both in love with her and she has been playing both of you for idiots. I stuck her because I will not allow her to damage you any further. She's already brought the mightiest knight in the realm to his knees and now she threatens to drive a dagger into your heart!"

Christopher was astonished at his brother's tirade. He always thought David had adored Dustin and he was honestly at a loss to understand his breakdown. But the fact remained that he had deeply insulted Dustin as well as injured her, and he would pay the price.

"David," his voice was calm, controlled. "Christin is my daughter, my flesh and blood. She has her mother's gray eyes, her grandmother's dark hair, and my nose. Never think for one moment that Marcus had anything to do with that child. My wife was not his whore, merely his friend, and it is his misfortune to fall in love with a woman he could not have. You, little brother, have no right to accuse her of such a heinous crime and you furthermore have no right whatsoever to strike her. And as far as weakening me, she has done the opposite and has made me the strongest man in all the world. Mayhap if you ever fall in love, you will understand. But I am afraid you will not have the chance; get yourself armed and stand ready to pay for your actions."

Dustin gasped, knowing that Christopher intended to kill his brother. "Nay, Chris," she begged. "Do not!"

He ignored her as David brushed past both of them and he waited until his brother was out of sight. Then, he took a few slow steps to his wife.

"Let me see what he did." He took her hand from her cheek and examined the bleeding welt. "He cuffed you good. Does it hurt?"

"Not much," she grasped his hand pleadingly. "Oh, Chris, you are not really going to kill him, are you? He was only trying to protect you."

"I do not need protecting," Christopher replied, caressing her fingers. "And I cannot allow him to be a threat to you or to Christin."

Dustin could not believe her ears. "You cannot kill your only brother. Chris, what are you thinking?"

"I am thinking that my brother has crossed the line," he answered. "He has injured you and insulted you grievously, and I will treat him as I would treat anyone who would damage you. I will defend your honor."

She was appalled and scared. "I do not want you to kill him."

"And I do not want to, but I must do what is necessary," he said more calmly than he felt. "Dustin, what would have happened had I not come out here to stop my brother from further harming you? As difficult as it is for me to believe, the proof of his brutality is standing out on your face and I cannot allow that. Brother or no, he will pay."

Dustin's eyes welled with tears. "But I am only your wife," she whispered. "He is your brother."

He grasped her face between his hands, swallowing up her head. His gaze was hard and soft at the same time.

"You are my life, Dustin," he whispered. "Everything else in this life, including my own brother, pales in comparison. He knows what he did was wrong, but he did it anyway."

She blinked and fat tears fell onto her cheeks. "Please do not kill him."

He kissed her and took her hand, leading her back toward the kitchen door. "Christin is sleeping. Go and relieve Griselda the sitting duties."

"Chris, I...." she started to protest, but he stopped abruptly at the entrance to the kitchens.

"Not a word, Dustin," he said hoarsely and she suddenly saw the pain in his eyes. "Please, sweetheart, not another word. Just do as you are told."

"But Chris," she tried one last time to defend David. "I struck him first in anger."

Christopher sighed. "Be that as it may, he should not have struck you in return. And I will never forgive him for calling you a whore. Now, go tend to Christin, sweet."

She put her face in her hands and dashed away from him. He followed not far behind and he could hear her sobbing all the way up the stairs. He paused a moment in the great hall, listening to the door to their bedchamber slam and feeling enough grief and sorrow to flood England.

He was deeply shocked at his brother and his behavior was inexcusable. Yet in his heart, he would rather kill himself than take his brother's life. Torn, increasingly despondent, he made his way outside.

David was waiting for him in full armor.

ↂ

CHRISTOPHER WAS UNARMED and without his protective gear, and he eyed his brother from a distance. Edward and Leeton had dismissed the men and stood with Jeffrey, Max, Anthony, Nicholas and Guy on the edge of the practice field, hardly believing what they were seeing. Edward was the first to approach Christopher.

"What in the hell is going on?" he demanded. "David said you called him out. Why?"

Christopher continued to eye his brother. "Because he called my wife a whore and accused her of bearing Burton's bastard."

"Christin?" Edward repeated with disbelief. "That is insane. Why would David say that?"

Christopher shrugged. "I do not know, and I furthermore do not care. He did it and he shall pay."

Edward grasped his arm. "You cannot kill your brother, Chris," he said firmly. "Banish him from your presence forever, disown him, but do not kill him. You shall never be able to live with yourself."

Christopher looked at Edward for the first time, mulling over his advice. True, he certainly did not want to kill David, and banishing him was indeed a viable alternative. "I must punish him, Edward. What he did was unforgiveable."

"Indeed, but discover his reasons and make your judgment," Edward replied. "Good God, he's your brother, *Chris*. Your very best friend, your flesh and blood. Can you, *will* you, truly kill him over one incident?"

"One incident?" Christopher repeated sharply. "Suppose I allow this to go unpunished and one incident becomes two, and Dustin suffers more than a bruise on the cheek? Suppose she suffers serious injury? Nay, Edward, I must punish my brother for his actions."

"He hit her?" Edward echoed, eyeing David. "My God, Chris, what is going on in his head?"

"I do not know." Pain inflected itself into his voice. "But mayhap you are correct in suggesting I should find out."

He left Edward and walked deliberately toward his brother, who raised his sword defensively. Christopher stopped a few feet away, glaring at his brother with a mixture of anger and sorrow.

"Before I pass judgment, David, I would hear why you committed such terrible sins against Dustin," he said quietly. "I would like to understand what provoked this event."

David did not lower the sword. "She has blinded you," he said. "Christin is Marcus' child as surely as I am Myles'. Can't you see how much she looks like him?"

"If that were true, then it is my problem to deal with, not yours to handle in my stead," his brother replied. "I told you once before that Dustin is my wife, not *ours*. If there is any revenge to be sought or any punishment to be dealt to her, it will come from me and not you. You have no right to interfere in my life."

"Interfere?" David spat, suddenly dropping the sword and tearing his helmet off. "Someone has to. She has turned you into a soft, gutless fool. The Christopher who used to be my brother would have killed Marcus the first time he laid hands on her. He would not have spared his life and allowed this liaison to continue. What has happened to you?"

Christopher understood a lot in that tirade. David simply didn't understand what it was to love more strongly than anything else on earth, a love that was forgiving and divine and complete. Marcus wasn't the issue here; it was David. David was jealous, perhaps feeling alone and left out, and he could not accept it.

"What's happened is that I have fallen in love with my wife and child and for the first time in my life, I am truly happy," Christopher replied softly. "David, I am sorry if you cannot understand that. Mayhap if you take a wife, someday you will understand. But my loving Dustin and Christin in no way diminishes my love for you. Perhaps you are trying to drive a wedge between Dustin and me simply because you feel left out of my life. Marcus, although you have always been jealous of him, is just an excuse."

David tried to glare at him, to hold his edge, but it was rapidly slipping. It always amazed him just how insightful his brother was. "Are you going to kill me or not? Get on with it."

"Do you hate my wife?" Christopher asked.

David looked confused. "I…she's made you weak, and…."

Christopher shook his head. "Answer me. Do you hate her?"

David's chin went up. "Aye."

Christopher studied his brother's face. "And when did you discover this? There seemed to be no problem until Christin was born." He took a few steps closer and slammed the sword away from David's hand. "You are jealous. You are jealous because I have a beautiful family and you do not. And you are trying to destroy it. Christ, David, why would you do this?"

David faltered, stammered. "It was only after Christin was born that I began to see what was truly going on. We had all been blind to it until she presented you with a dark-haired daughter. We did not want to think the worst until we saw the proof with our own eyes."

"There is no proof because nothing ever happened," Christopher said sharply. "As I told you, Dustin's mother had black hair. There is no mystery to it. You are the one who is being blind, David. I never expected this of you, little brother, and it pains me greatly. I always thought you were my greatest supporter."

David's hurt became evident in his face and he lowered his gaze, moving slowly to pick up his sword. "Kill me if you are going to."

Christopher was devastated that his brother was being so stubborn. He was having a difficult time accepting all of it.

"You will not apologize?" he asked.

"Nay," David said firmly. "I am not the one who is wrong."

Christopher ground his jaw, irritation and fury sweeping him. His obstinate brother was leaving him with no choice whatsoever.

"So be it," he growled. "I will not kill you, although God knows I should. You are my only brother and the bind of blood saves you from certain death. But I will exile you from Lioncross forever. You will never again be allowed near me, or my family, and you are banished from my service as Richard's Defender. I care not where you go or what you do because you no longer exist to me. Get out of my sight, David. I want nothing more to do with you."

He turned on his heel and left David standing in the courtyard, his young face a mask of rage and grief. Death would have been preferable than his brother's rejection. Within a half hour he had packed his things and was gone.

Christopher watched his little brother from the solar that used to be Lady Mary's. His twisted heart grieved him deeply and his torment was unimaginable, alternately raging and cursing his brother for his violent, sudden actions and then wondering why he did not have the foresight to see the storm coming.

He and David had always been so very close, as if they could read one another's thoughts, but this time Christopher had had no idea what David had been thinking and he was overridden with shock. When David's white charger exited the gates, Christopher allowed himself the privilege of hot, bitter tears.

"He is going." Dustin stood in the doorway, having seen David load his destrier and turn for the gates. She went in search of her husband and found him in the private little room that her mother had favored.

Christopher's back was to her and she stood there a moment, wondering if she should leave him alone when she suddenly saw his shoulders heave. Shocked, she moved into the room and her ears met with a muffled sob.

Dustin rushed to him, throwing her arms around him and pressing herself against his back. She felt a warm hand gently grasp her arms and beneath her embrace, he began to shake with sobs.

"Oh, Chris," she murmured soothingly. "My love, my sweet husband, I am so very sorry. Please do not cry."

His sobs were unbridled, like a child's, and Dustin's face was soon wet with her own tears. She felt so guilty, so helpless, and so pained with his grief. She blamed herself for David's departure one moment, yet knew the next moment she had done nothing. She continued to hold her husband tightly and croon to him soothingly, hoping she would be able to comfort him somehow. His deep tears cut her to the bone.

He continued to stand by the window and weep and she allowed him time to grieve before pulling him away from the sill and sitting him in a chair. She then sat on his lap and cradled his great head against her breast, caressing him tenderly until his crying ceased. Even after he stopped, they continued to sit together for an endless eternity, lost in their own thoughts and both devastated from the loss of a brother.

CHAPTER THIRTY-NINE

"CHRIS!" GOWEN CAME barreling into the great hall, a huge scroll of vellum in his hand. "Missives from London!"

Christopher was up, moving to take them already. It was nearly a month after David's departure and the snow on the January ground was enough to freeze the devil from hell. On the fresh rushes, Dustin was helping Christin sit up, and her eyes flew to her husband apprehensively as he took the parchment.

Christopher glanced reassuringly at her as he broke Longchamp's seal and read the message clear through. Unemotionally, he looked directly at his wife.

"Richard is released and on his way home," he said. "But John is drumming up more mischief in the north and I am ordered returned."

Dustin's mouth opened in horror but she clamped it shut and rapidly lowered her gaze. Even as Christopher returned the missive to Gowen and ordered Leeton to prepare the men, his eyes were fixed on his wife.

He moved around the table to the hearth where his wife and babe were playing, his heart already aching for the departure at hand. When he returned, there was no telling how old Christin would be or how much of her growing he would have missed. But that was nothing compared to the pain of separation he was already feeling for Dustin. She kept her blond head down, pretending to busy herself with the infant even as her husband loomed over her.

"Dustin," he said softly.

It took a few long moments before she lifted her head and he could already see tears in the huge gray eyes. Without a word he scooped Christin into his arms and pulled Dustin to her feet, pulling her against him as he took the babe back to her nursery.

Griselda was there, folding freshly washed linens. The old woman had elected to stay until Deborah's babe was born in the spring. Meanwhile, she made an excellent nanny and had become an important part of the family.

Christopher handed the old woman his daughter. "I believe she could use a nap."

Griselda took Christin, cooing and giggling to the babe as Christopher closed the door quietly behind them. Alone in the corridor with Dustin, he fixed her with a gentle smile.

"Ride with me," he commanded softly.

He took her by the hand and down to the stables, where he saddled only his destrier and lifted her up onto the beast. Sans armor or any weapon, he galloped from the bailey and out into the cold, bleak countryside.

The temperature was freezing, but Dustin was warm wrapped in Christopher's arms. He let the dappled charger have his head for a couple of miles until finally reining him to a halt by the banks of a frozen stream. Dustin slid off and wandered to the water, studying the ice crystals absently.

"I must leave by tonight," he said. "I am sorry, sweetheart."

She shrugged. "I knew you would leave me again, someday. Only I hoped that someday would never come."

"As did I." He swung his leg over the saddle and dismounted, giving the horse an affectionate slug. His eyes moved over the beast, which had matured considerably over the months. "You never did name my horse."

Dustin glanced back at the animal and he noticed with fascination that her eyes were the color of the landscape that surrounded them. "I have thought on it somewhat, and I believe a suitable name is Zephyr."

"Zephyr? A fitting name," Christopher said with satisfaction. "He is indeed as wild and unpredictable as the wind. You have a knack for names, wife. And other things."

Wrapped in dark gray, Dustin only nodded faintly and turned her attention back to the stream. He came up behind her, enveloping her in his massive arms.

"I am eager for Richard to meet you," he said softly. "And likewise thank him for ordering me to marry you."

Dustin knew he was jesting but she did not feel like humor. "You would have him meet the woman that drove his mightiest warriors apart," she said softly.

His smile vanished. "You have done nothing," he said. "Whatever happened with David and Marcus happened in their own hearts; you did nothing."

She turned in his arms, embracing him and laying her head against his chest. "I miss you already," she said sadly. "Where are you going?"

He held her close. "To London, and then north. I do not know exactly where," he said softly. "It will be strange not having David by my side in battle. It was strange enough not having Marcus at the beginning of the campaign, but I got used to it. I suppose I will have to get used to David's absence."

"Do you know where David is?" she asked softly.

He sighed, caressing her back. "I heard tale that he had gone to Canterbury, but I am not sure. I expected him to go straight to Lohrham Forest, but he did not."

"Does he know anyone in Canterbury?" Dustin inquired.

He smiled. "Aye, and so do you. Emilie Hampton."

Dustin looked up at him. "Emilie!" she gasped in realization. "Of course. Chris, do you think…?"

He shrugged, cutting her off. "I do not know. David is not who I thought he was, so mayhap marriage is in the realm of possibility after all."

Dustin was delighted, hoping secretly David would marry Emilie and he and Chris would make up so they could all live happily at Lioncross. But she did not voice her thoughts, although her husband knew exactly what she was thinking.

The sky above them opened up and a heavy snow began to fall. The wind kicked up and within a minute or so, white ice was swirling about them and growing stronger. Christopher hustled Dustin onto the destrier and mounted himself, although he knew they might possibly freeze to death before they reached Lioncross.

"Is there a small farm or shelter where we can wait this out?" he asked her above the noise of the wind.

Dustin thought a moment. "If I remember correctly, there's a hunter's shack back in the woods to the south," she pointed in that direction. "As children, we would often play there and pretend it was our fortress to defend."

He reined the animal in the direction of the dead trees. "It will defend us now from the elements."

The shack was indeed there as she remembered, and Christopher carried her inside. It was neglected and run down, but at least they were out of the snow. Dustin felt a sense of giddy adventure with it all, alone with her husband in an isolated hut. Christopher flashed a grin at her as he gathered the old wood that was lying about and after several tries, started a fire in the dirty hearth. It was no time before he had stoked it into a roaring blaze.

"Now, let's hope we don't choke on the smoke should the chimney malfunction." He sat down next to his wife and pulled her into his arms.

Dustin laughed softly. She cuddled against him, all alone in their private little haven. Outside the wind was vicious, but inside the old shack, they were warm and dry.

"I would stay here forever with you," she sighed contentedly.

"Without Christin?" he asked.

"Her, too," she said quickly. "You can ride back for her."

He smiled, feeling the warmth of the blaze. "On second thought, I agree with you," he said. "I would stay here with you, alone."

He kissed the top of her head, her temples, and she closed her eyes at his touch. Her stomach lurched with excitement for she knew what would follow, and she could not stop herself from responding to him aggressively. He had wanted their lovemaking to be slow and tender, but Dustin turned on him like a cat in heat and he could not help but follow her fervor.

She spread her cloak on the dirty ground and pulled him down on top of her, pulling his woolen tunic over his head and going to work on his under tunic. His fingers deftly undid the stays on her surcoat and it was no time before they were both naked, frolicking on the fur of the cloak.

The passion between them was indescribable. With every touch, Dustin nearly wept with delight, and every kiss spoke thousands of unsaid words too deep to express. His hands kneaded her full breasts, wet with milk, and he lapped up the sweetness and then suckled her for more. She was ultra-sensitive because she was nursing, but it enhanced their lovemaking all the more. His mouth devoured every inch of the flesh on her torso and arms, moving to the secret place between her legs and making her writhe with desire. His tongue peaked her little bud, probed her slick depths eagerly before he took mercy on her and placed his organ at her threshold.

He paused a moment, wanting to tell her everything that was in his heart, but she wouldn't let him. She wanted him to show her what was in his heart, and he did. Driving into her hard enough to bring a scream to her lips, he rode her as hard as he ever rode his horse, bringing them both to a climax in mere minutes. Descending from heaven on a cloud of pure contentment, Dustin held him close and refused to let him withdraw. Within a half-hour, she turned him onto his back and rode him erotically until he exploded again in a scalding blast of seed. Four times in that afternoon, they climaxed one with the other.

The snow let off enough toward late afternoon and he took Dustin back to Lioncross. Jeffrey and Leeton, greatly relieved to see them, recalled the three search parties they had sent out and were better able to focus on mobilizing the troops bound for London.

As soon as Dustin was settled and he had a chance to check on Christin, Christopher joined them in the bailey in full armor, mentally turning himself from the loving husband and father to the battle-bound warrior.

The Defender had returned.

DUSTIN THOUGHT SHE was handling Christopher's return to London quite well. But when it became apparent departure was imminent, she grew hysterical and took to her bed. When Christopher entered the bedchamber in full armor preparing to bid her goodbye he was verily distressed to find his wife huddled in bed, weeping into the pillows. He coaxed her out of bed and half carried her into the nursery where he could say his goodbyes to Christin.

Dustin sobbed miserably as he kissed the baby and spoke softly to her, and she grinned her sweet little smile at him. His heart was breaking that he had to leave her, but he promised he would buy her some pretty baubles and toys in London. He also asked the babe to take good care of her mother, a silly statement that nearly brought Dustin to the brink of collapse.

Leaving his daughter and fighting off the tears, he gently took Dustin into the vacant corridor and pushed her against the wall, wiping her eyes for her with a handkerchief.

"Get hold of yourself, sweetheart," he lectured gently. "I shall not leave you a weeping, quivering mass. Be brave for me, love. *Please*."

She was trying but every time she looked into his eyes, the tears started fresh. Finally, he gave up trying to calm her and took to holding her instead.

"I really must go," he whispered into her hair. "Will you watch me from the window?"

She nodded unsteadily and he kissed her forehead. "That's my girl," he whispered. "Now, is there anything you want me to bring you from London? How about some new dresses? It has been a long time since you have had any new clothes."

She sniffed, looking thoughtful. "Why don't you get Christin and I clothes to match?"

He smiled brightly. "What a delightful idea. I shall do that."

She was pleased that he liked her idea. She smiled as much as she could at him and he kissed her gently. "I have got to go, sweetheart. I promise I shall return as soon as I can, and I am leaving Jeffrey and Edward here with you."

"Edward?" Dustin repeated. "But… I thought you wanted him in the battle."

Christopher shook his head. "I have Leeton as my right hand, plus Max and Anthony and the others. I shall not be lacking for knightly power," he said. "Besides, even though Edward says otherwise, he is still afraid to brandish a sword. 'Twill be easier on him this way, although I have no doubt that he will protect you should the need arise."

Dustin nodded, running her hands over his face one final time, touching his features and memorizing them. "Be safe, my love," she whispered. "Return to me."

He kissed her sweetly, leaving her standing in the corridor as he descended the stairs and disappeared into the foyer. When she heard the front door slam, she went into their bedchamber and stood watch by the window as his army moved out.

Christopher was the last man through the gates. He turned and caught sight of her watching him and waved a massive, gloved hand.

She waved weakly in return and he swung his charger about, disappearing though the gates and out into the snowy, dark night.

CHAPTER FORTY

THE STOP IN London had been for the sole purpose of picking up the crown troops, now numbering nearly three thousand strong. Christopher viewed his huge army with satisfaction, knowing they would surely quell John easily and he could return home soon. Richard was crossing the channel as he met with the jubilant justices, but Christopher could not wait for the king. John had to be controlled as he laid siege to the mighty stronghold of Gowergrove Castle.

Richard's return had indeed pleased Christopher, but with the focus his life had taken, he hadn't felt the excitement he once would have. He no longer lived solely for his king, but for his family, and he wondered how well Richard would receive that knowledge. Christopher intended to step down from his title as Defender and become a mere baron once again, leaving the duties of the realm to a successor he would surely handpick. Marcus was the first man that came to mind.

The troops were retrieved and the three thousand man army headed northwest to the great castle of Gowergrove, a favorite holding of Richard's at the southern tip of Sherwood Forest. John had always had his eye on the fortress, and if Gowergrove were under his command, 'twould be near impossible to pass from southern to northern England without passing through his territory. Christopher had to secure the castle at all costs, and early on the eleventh day after leaving Lioncross, he lay siege to John's troops at Gowergrove Castle.

John's mercenary army was dug in like a tick on a dog. The walls of Gowergrove were nearly thirty feet tall and the moat surrounding it was filled with nasty, rotting filth, very undesirable for the men-at-arms to go plunging into, to say nothing of the knights in their armor. Leeton set two hundred men to building ladders to mount the walls, but until that time, there was naught else to do but besiege Gowergrove with archers; fine Welsh archers whose accuracy was legendary.

Three days into the siege, the ladders were complete and after a day and a night of attempts, they were finally able to cap the walls and the battle truly began. When the bridge went down, Christopher was the first man inside.

The fighting went on for days. Long, exhaustive days. Christopher saw barely five hours' worth of sleep and spent his entire time in the saddle dueling mercenaries. Ralph was nowhere to be seen, but he saw Sir Dennis on several occasions and made it his focal point to seek the man out and destroy him.

The battle had spilled out into the surrounding areas and the moat was filled to overflowing with the bodies of the dead. Christopher had suffered tremendous losses, as had John, but he refused to withdraw because John's army was considerably weaker. He knew it would not be much longer and he would have Gowergrove secured.

As is usual in February, the winter weather turned extremely foul and the worst storm Christopher could remember doused them day and night. At night, the rain would turn to ice and pelt the armor like a thousand stones being thrown, but in the day, it was miserable freezing rain. The land outside the castle soon turned into a deep, mucky bog and the destriers were up to their knees in the stuff, making fighting extremely difficult.

Christopher was exhausted, as they all were. One morning, he found himself fighting outside of the great wall, trying to help Leeton subdue a particularly hearty band of criminals. They were trying to steer them toward the moat, corner them in, but the unruly horde were proving to be most disobedient and Christopher was fed up with all of it. His frustration had reached a frenzied level when something huge and powerful tore into his body, plowing through his mall and shoving his breastplate aside as it invaded his midsection brutally.

Stunned, Christopher's hand flew to his left side and he was anguished to feel the shaft of a great spear protruding from his torso. The rain had begun to fall again, in great blinding sheets, washing his life's blood down his saddle and onto the ground before it could collect on his armor.

He still retained enough of his wits and reined Zephyr around, heading with speed for the trees. He wanted to be away from the battle zone so there would be something left of his body to return to Dustin. And he knew, with great remorse, anger, and agony that he was going to die. He had seen wounds like this before and they were always fatal.

Christopher barely made it to the edge of the forest before weakness overcame him and he fell from his horse in a great, dying heap. He struggled through the haze of darkness that threatened to crawl further into the underbrush, his breathing coming in harsh gasps and feeling pain radiate throughout his body like nothing he had ever known.

His eyes burned with tears, but not for himself. He would never again know the sweetness of his wife's flesh, nor would he have the joy of watching his daughter grow into a beautiful young lady. The torment of cruel fate surged through him and he cursed himself the first day he ever picked up a sword. If he could have changed it, he gladly would have. He missed Dustin already. *Goddammit, it just wasn't fair!*

There was someone beside him and he recognized Leeton, rushing at him in panic.

"Jesus, Chris," Leeton's voice cracked. "The bloody bastards got you. Oh, Jesus, let me see!"

Christopher tried to wave him off, knowing any attempt to save him was futile, but Leeton roughly yanked off his breastplate and shoved his mail aside.

"A spear," Leeton spit with contempt. "Goddamn cowards could not get you with a sword, so they took to hurling spears. I have got to get this out."

Christopher started to shake his head, but he was far too weak to do anything but utter a strangled yelp when Leeton yanked the spear from his guts. Bright red blood gushed freely as Leeton slapped a few rags of linen on the spot, knowing they would be nearly useless against such a flow. He already felt the loss of his liege deeply and his handsome face was pale with sorrow.

"Leeton," Christopher groaned, grabbing at him.

"Aye, Chris, I am here," he said, grasping Christopher's hand and holding it tightly.

Christopher could barely speak. "Take....take my wedding ring," he whispered. "Take it back to my wife. Tell her....tell her what happened and tell her my last thoughts were of her. And tell her I love her, Leeton. I love her with all my heart."

Leeton, a seasoned veteran, found himself choking back tears. "Chris, I...."

"Take it!" Christopher tried to yell, but he had not the strength to press his point. His life was fading away and his strength with it.

He held up his left hand. Leeton hesitated for a tormented moment before ripping off the gauntlet and pulling off the ring. He did not know who was the more miserable; him or Christopher. He wanted to scream, to yell, to demand that God show pity and take him instead, but he could only focus on his liege with tears in his eyes. Christopher, satisfied that his last wish would be carried out, let his hand fall to the ground. His blue eyes closed and there was a faint smile on his lips.

"Thank you," he whispered.

Leeton heard a horn and turned his head in the direction of the battle. "Chris, they have got the mercenaries boxed in. I have got to go, but I swear I shall be back. Do you hear me? I shall be back. I shall find Burwell and return. He will save you."

Christopher weakly grasped his wrist. "No one can save me, Leeton," Christopher murmured. "You and I both know this is the end of me. One more thing....find David and tell him that I am sorry for everything. Tell my brother than I love him and ask him to take care of Dustin and Christin for me."

Leeton could not stop the strangled sob, but he nodded his head furiously. "Aye, anything you say," he said tearfully, grasping Christopher's shoulders with his big hands. "Just... please hold on. Burwell ought to have something to patch up that hole."

Christopher did not reply; he had already slipped into unconsciousness and his breathing was slowing. Swallowing hard, Leeton took one last look at his liege, his grief overflowing, wishing he was not the one charged with the horrible duty of informing Lady de Lohr of her husband's passing. Already, he felt the agony to his bones.

But he would do what had been asked of him in one last show of obedience. He would have much rather stayed with Christopher as he breathed his last, but more pressing duties were calling and he answered reluctantly. Leaving Christopher lying beneath the trees to protect him from the rain, he put the wedding ring on his left hand for safekeeping and mounted Zephyr. His own destrier, suffering a huge gash to the chest, was left grazing on the edge of the forest.

Leeton reined Zephyr in the direction of the battle, taking one last glance at Christopher's still form under the trees. Dear God, it wasn't fair. Christopher was The Defender, entitled to immortality, deserving of divine grace. To die fighting the bastard prince was unworthy of such a great man, and Leeton felt a great surge of anger wash over him.

Leeton swore to himself that he would find Ralph and Dennis and John and run each one of them through on Christopher's behalf. If it took him the rest of his life, he would do it. Every one of those bastards would pay for what they had done to his beloved liege and friend. And with each stroke of the sword into their flesh, he would be sure to mention Dustin's name.

He made it several hundred yards from the wall, fighting alongside other knights in the blinding rain. Aboard Zephyr, the men thought he was Christopher and the fighting was furious. They were inspired by him. Yet they were not the only ones who thought he was Christopher; a barrage of crossbows unleashed arrows as plentiful as rain, and Zephyr went down in a scream of agony. Leeton tried to bolt free, but the horse fell quickly and with all of his armor, he was weighted severely. There was no chance for him to escape.

Twenty-five hundred pounds of horseflesh buried him face-first in the mud, and in Leeton's last wild thoughts, he never imagined he would actually drown on the field of battle.

☙

THE BATTLE FOR Gowergrove was over.

Crown troops victoriously let Richard's pennant fly from the walls and took to killing any remaining mercenary soldiers. Word of The Defender's death hit everyone hard, as hard as if their own beloved father had been taken from them, and they were committed to doing everything they could to make John's army pay. As the men moved slowly and lethargically about their duties, as exhausted men usually do, disbelief filled every face.

Anguish and grief were hand in hand among the men, and especially the knights. But none were harder hit than Christopher's personal stable. They set about their tasks mechanically, although each and every one of them had taken the time to view the body in the mud, half-buried underneath his destrier. Seeing had to be believing, yet none wanted to believe.

"We lost Leeton, too," Max mumbled, gazing down on the body of their great liege. "Has anyone even seen him?"

"Nay," Sean de Lara replied, turning away from the rotting corpse underneath the horse. Sean had remained in London when Christopher had gone to Lioncross last year, but then rejoined Christopher when the man had come to London to collect the crown troops. He had been by the baron's side for weeks. "He is probably buried underneath this muck, somewhere. I saw his horse three days ago, over by the line of trees."

Anthony de Velt had shown an amazing amount of responsibility in the past three days. A rotting hand, a wedding ring around the left finger, was jutting up out of the rancid mud and he reached down and plucked the gold band free. "For Lady de Lohr," he said softly. "She will want to keep it. Now, we must bury the body."

"We are not returning him to Lioncross?" Max stood up from his crouch and faced his brother. "To be buried on his soil?"

"Max, if we bring this sickening corpse back to Lioncross, you know Lady Dustin is going to want to view her husband," Anthony said pointedly. "We will try to prevent her, but you know she will gain her way. Do you truly want her to see Chris in this state? It will drive her insane."

Max glanced down at the corpse, so bloated and unrecognizable that the skin was splitting on the head where the helmet was restraining it. The only thing of any recognition was the blond hair, and the ring.

"Nay," he said after a moment, crossing himself and uttering a prayer. "God, no."

Anthony nodded curtly. "Then set up a detail to dig Chris a grave. Leeton one, too, if we can find his body. Pick a nice place, perhaps on that little rise up there."

Max tore his gaze away from the body and motioned to Guy de la Rosa. "Come on," he muttered. "Let's get to it."

Sean and Anthony were left gazing down at the grisly scene. "What in the world happened?" Sean asked. "I mean, look at the way the horse has fallen. Impaled through the heart, he is. Is it possible it fell on Chris and he drowned in the mud?"

Anthony shrugged. "Mayhap we shall know after we free the body. Meanwhile, we have a whole keep to clean up." He glanced over at the men-at-arms who were beginning a funeral pyre and he stomped off in their direction. "Hey! You men over there! Do not burn bodies so close to the keep unless you want to render everyone in the castle ill!"

He was off shouting, leaving Sean standing a depressing watch over the remains of his liege. The thought that The Defender was gone was so overwhelmingly bleak that the man hesitated to believe another day would dawn over England.

He glanced at the sky above, bleak and gray. That was the world to him at the moment without his liege, bleak and gray and colorless. He could not stand to look at the body anymore; with a sting to his eyes, he went to help the others dig graves.

CHAPTER FORTY-ONE

WORD OF THE Defender's passing spread through England like wildfire. Ralph and John, having been at Nottingham when Sir Dennis had brought them the news, partied for three days. Lady Gabrielle, on John's arm, wept through the night. Surely nothing could save England now.

Richard disembarked at the Tower to be met by the justices, welcoming him home to English soil with one breath and notifying him of the current situation with the next. John held fourteen castles and Christopher de Lohr was dead, killed in battle at Gowergrove Castle. Deeply distressed and seriously exhausted, Richard had shed public tears at his brave friend's passing. Sir Philip de Lohr, disembarking with Richard, crossed himself and went immediately to Winchester Abbey where he prayed for two straight days.

David, now betrothed to Emilie Hampton and serving Lyle Hampton, heard from the earl of his brother's passing. His pain was so great that Lyle ordered David locked in his room with a constant guard on his person, terrified his future son-in-law would take his own life. He knew of Christopher and David's falling out, and he furthermore feared David would never be the same.

A violent argument between two brothers would now never be resolved, and David was inconsolable. Even Emilie could not bring him out of his depression. But David was made of strong blood, and after his initial shock and pain dulled, he kissed Emilie goodbye and set out for London to see Richard. He knew the king would want to see him, but his stay in London would be short. After that, he vowed to continue to Lioncross and beg Dustin's forgiveness, hoping she would allow him to comfort her. And mayhap, she could comfort him as well. He could not deal with the fact that Christopher had gone to his grave hating him.

Marcus Burton even heard of Christopher's death and Richard's return by way of a traveling Scot lord. Holed up at Somerhill, Marcus had had virtually no contact with the outside world, shunning missives and denying entrance to any outsiders. The less he knew of London and the ways of the world, the easier it was to forget about Dustin. He had been fairly happy for the past year at his new keep, ruling the baronetcy fairly and justly; he was greatly loved by his vassals. He had even selected a woman he thought would make an excellent mother for his sons, but the moment he heard of Christopher's death, everything was dashed.

The pain and loss he felt was overwhelming and he spent two days in his solar, drinking away his guilt and pain. But when the liquor dried up, so did he, and he immediately decided to set forth to Lioncross. With Christopher gone, he planned to do what he had always wanted to do. He would claim Dustin, and woe to any man who would try to stop him.

Richard, John and Ralph… he cared not for their problems anymore. With each passing moment, the only thing of importance to him was Lady Dustin de Lohr. Somehow he knew Christopher would approve of him taking care of his wife and, by God, he would not only take care of her. He would worship the ground she walked on. How could Christopher want for anything more than that?

THE ONLY PERSON who had not immediately heard of Christopher's death was his wife. Dustin went about her business every day, taking care of her growing daughter and running Lioncross with Gowen. In the morning she would see to the day's needs, and in the afternoon, she would till the frozen ground in the garden in preparation for the spring plant. She was happy as she tried to keep busy, easing the pain of separation from her husband, but she consoled herself with the knowledge that he would return home to her. She had grown confident in his ability to stay alive and counted the days until his return. She could hardly wait to hold him.

Late one afternoon in February, the returning army was sighted. Dustin was in her bedchamber with the maids when she heard the cry go up from the wall, and all three of the women raced to the window to catch sight of the approaching troops. They could see the blue and gold of Christopher's banners in the distance.

Glee surged through Dustin. Chasing the maids out, she donned her very best surcoat, one of burnished gold that Christopher loved so much, and carefully brushed her long hair. She wanted to look good for him and make him glad that he had returned to her. In her excitement, she called into the nursery and had Griselda dress Christin in a clean frock so the baby could greet her father properly.

All of Lioncross was in an uproar. Edward was in the foyer, moving to the front doors when Dustin hung over the balcony overhead and yelled at him not to detain her husband with a bunch of silly war tales. There would be time for that later. He grinned and waved her off, joining Jeffrey in the bailey. He noticed that Jeffrey's' face was grave.

"What's wrong?" Edward demanded, still smiling from Dustin's comments. "How can you possibly have a sour face on this day of days?"

"I count only five knights," Jeffrey said. "And I do not see the baron's horse."

Edward shrugged. "Mayhap he remained in London. Richard is, after all, returned and I am sure there is much to discuss."

Jeffrey shrugged in agreement, but his sense of uneasiness did not dissipate. In fact, as the huge gates yawned open and the knights spilled in through the opening, his apprehension increased. He did not know why; mayhap it was simply an overactive feeling on his part.

Edward wasn't concerned in the least as the knights rode in. He did, however, notice Leeton was missing and that concerned him a bit, but not overly. The knights rode directly to him, reining their weary mounts to a halt in the dusk.

"Max and Anthony," Edward greeted pleasantly. "Good Lord, don't tell me Chris was detained in London with Richard. My lady is going to have fits."

Anthony dismounted, followed slowly by the others. By their sheer movements, Edward was alerted and his heart leapt into his throat. Without a word, they had conveyed much. Edward's smile vanished.

Anthony removed his helm. When his brown eyes met Edward's, there was nothing more to say. His expression said everything. Edward's face went as white as plaster and he felt bile rise in his throat.

"Oh....no, Anthony," he breathed. "Please... Chris is not coming home, is he?"

Anthony dug into his tunic and with the most reverent of gestures, held Christopher's wedding ring out to Edward. The man simply stared at it, unable to make a conscious decision to move and do anything with it. It was almost as if he were not truly grasping what he was seeing.

Jeffrey finally took the ring. "How did it happen?" he asked quietly.

Anthony did not look anything like the man who had left Lioncross a mere month earlier. He looked older, more haggard.

"The last day of the battle for Gowergrove," he said quietly. "We are not sure how it happened, but we found him in two feet of mud buried beneath his horse. You understand there wasn't much left to bury, Edward. We buried him on a rise overlooking Gowergrove. We did not want to bring him back here for....her....to see."

Edward blinked and two fat tears rolled down his cheeks, dashed away by his shaking hand. "You did right, of course," he said softly. "And Leeton? He perished also?"

"Aye," Anthony nodded wearily. "We never did find his body. With the rain and mud, 'twas nearly impossible. Then when the mud dried up before we could completely clear the field of battle, there was no chance to find him."

Edward wiped his hand across his face. "God be merciful," he breathed, trying desperately to compose himself. "Does Richard know?"

"All of England knows," Anthony replied. "We had to stop in London to leave off the crown troops, and Richard had declared a day of mourning. Sir Philip is inconsolable. I do not even know if David knows."

"No doubt he does by now, if he is in Canterbury," Edward replied, struggling for his composure. "I wonder if he will return to Lioncross now that…."

Anthony's eyes widened and Edward stiffened, knowing Dustin had been sighted. He knew he should rush to her and take her inside to deliver the news, but he could not seem to move his legs. It took all of his energy to turn around and face her as she descended the stairs, a quizzical smile on her lips. When he saw the smile, he nearly snapped.

"Where is Chris?" she asked curiously, glancing about. Then, she looked annoyed. "Do not tell me he stayed behind in London with Richard. Why could not he have come home first?"

No one could answer her; all of their tongues were glued to the roof of their mouth. Edward tried to force himself to move forward, to return her to the keep, but he could not make his body obey. Dustin's mouth pressed into an irritated line as she waited for an answer and he knew he had to say something, but he simply couldn't find the correct words, praying to God to give him the strength to tell her that her husband was never coming home.

"So is it a surprise and he's sworn everyone to secrecy?" She put her hands on her hips. "Well, somebody had better tell me or no one is going anywhere. Where is he? Did he go to Canterbury, by chance? I shall kill him if he attends David's wedding without me."

Jeffrey was the first to move, and even he did not say a word. He thrust his hand at Dustin, an object between his fingers. She glanced at it and smiled, thinking it to be a gift from her husband. But the moment she snatched it away to examine it, she knew what it was. Her smile fled and her knees went weak. God help her, she knew what it was.

She stared at it for a long, long time. "Why do you have his ring?" she finally asked.

Edward snapped out of his trance. Around them, the bailey was completely silent and even with the hundreds of men, there was absolutely no movement. Filled with people, it was as quiet as if it were deserted.

"I am so sorry, Dustin," he whispered, his eyes filled with pain.

The gray eyes came up, swallowing him whole. She stared at him until he felt uncomfortable. "What are you sorry for?"

"He is gone," Edward's voice was tight with tears. "He is a soldier and he has died in battle, as so many others. But his knights have recovered his wedding ring, a keepsake that meant more to him than anything material he possessed."

Dustin stared back at him, the color draining from her face. No one moved or said a word, waiting for her to fly into a hysterical rage. After several moments, no rage was forthcoming. In fact, she had yet to move a muscle. She simply stood there, holding the ring before her face, staring at Edward as if he had just spoken to her in a foreign language. Some wondered if she had understood what he had said.

"He has not," she said simply.

"He has," Edward insisted gently.

Dustin shook her head, her nostrils flaring and Anthony stepped forward. "He has, my lady," he said quietly. "I saw the body myself. I retrieved the ring for you to keep."

Dustin blinked slowly, absorbing the words. It was almost as if she had become a statue, for she moved nothing but her eyes. It was clear that she was having a difficult time comprehending their words, her stunned mind struggling to process the truth.

"It is not true," she said again, but her voice was quivering now.

Edward sighed faintly, putting his hands out to her. "Let me take you inside," he murmured.

She yanked away from him. "Do not touch me," she hissed. Then, she looked at the men surrounding her, more than anger in her eyes. There was pure, unadulterated hatred there, a thousand accusations of blame firing out at them. "You are lying. You are all lying!"

Max and Anthony passed concerned glances. "My lady, I swear that we are not." Anthony tried not to sound as if he was pleading with her. "I saw him myself. I swear we would not lie about this."

The quivering in her voice had taken over her body. They could all see it in her face, in her movements. Somewhere in the distance, thunder rolled across the sky as another storm moved in and Dustin, with her husband's wedding ring clasped between her fingers, lowered her arm slowly. With a lethargic, baleful blink at Edward, she stumbled back and turned, weaving unsteadily as she made her way back to the castle. The moment she hit the stairs, she collapsed in a heap.

The knights came running. Edward picked her up and carried her, weeping, the entire way up to her bedchamber.

☙

DUSTIN'S DAYS WERE filled with pain. Too shocked to cry, her pain went beyond tears. In fact, her pain rendered her unable to do anything but sit and stare out of the window as if expecting Christopher to ride through the gates any minute. Her whole world was numb, mindless, and in total denial.

The wet nurse from the village had to be re-employed because Dustin had stopped eating and Griselda knew she should not nurse. In fact, Dustin had ceased to do anything even remotely human and began to take on the cold, unfeeling characteristics of a stone wall.

Everyone worried desperately for her, but she wouldn't talk. Edward spent whole days with her trying to get her to open up, but she wouldn't even acknowledge him. He seriously feared for her mental stability. Her feelings remained locked up inside her, building to the point where there was nothing else to do but explode.

When the tears did come, they came in torrents. Days upon days upon days of hysterics, fainting deteriorated into breaking things and destroying her surroundings. She destroyed every one of her fine dresses and at one point cut her arms terribly when she broke a precious porcelain vase her mother had given her and ground the razor-sharp chips into her forearms.

After that, Edward ordered someone to be with her at all times and Dustin turned into a surly, snapping bitch who hated the sight of anyone. The only person she would warm up to was Christin, and even then, all she did was hold the baby and cry.

It was a miserable time for all of the occupants of Lioncross. Dustin was quite mad with grief, taking to wearing her peasant clothes again and ignoring anyone who said a word to her. Her sorrow and agony had turned her into a shell of a human being, neither feeling nor caring what went on around her. Her days were spent with her daughter or her garden; she had even let her rabbits go free because they reminded her of Christopher. Nothing mattered to her at all anymore. Her world was pain.

One night after dinner, Anthony was sitting with her in the solar as she sat motionless by the hearth. Her gorgeous blond hair was a rat's nest of filth and she had dropped quite a bit a weight to the point where she was almost skeletal. She did not look at all like the same robust woman they had come to know and love. It was a horrific sight.

"How did he die, Anthony?" she asked.

It was the first rational statement she had made in weeks. Startled, Anthony looked up sharply from the sword he was sharpening. Should he tell her? God, even he did not really know. He was extremely careful in how he answered her.

"Truthfully, I am not sure, my lady," he said. "We found him several days after his death and it was difficult to tell."

She absorbed this, still staring off into the flames. "John killed him."

"My lady?" Anthony inquired politely.

She turned to him, her eyes clear. "John killed him," she repeated. "It doesn't matter how he died, because John killed him."

Anthony was careful in his reaction. "In a sense, he did."

Dustin turned back to the flames.

Later after Dustin had gone to bed, Edward and Anthony were alone in the solar sipping fine French wine and Anthony expressed his concern for Dustin.

"What are we going to do with her?" he asked Edward wearily. "I have never seen anyone grieve so hard or so long. She knew Chris was a soldier when she married him; she should have prepared herself for the eventuality of this moment."

"I doubt one can be truly prepared for the death of a loved one," Edward replied. "However, I am worried for her also. Her mental health is unstable and she verges on total madness at times. Dustin was so strong I never thought to see this happen. She even keeps a distance from Deborah because she says the woman possesses 'his' eyes. I can only imagine she sees Chris every time she looks at his sister, but Deborah is understandably bewildered."

Anthony raised an eyebrow. "We all are. Edward, I am worried about her."

Edward sat opposite his friend. "There is nothing we can do" He shook his head sadly. "I wish David were here. He would be able to get through to her."

"David?" Anthony repeated, dubious. "After what happened, do you truly believe that?"

Edward nodded firmly. "Aye, I do. David was jealous of Christopher and Dustin. With Chris gone, there is nothing to be jealous of anymore. They say that sometimes grief is the most binding of emotions, and I am sure David would be able to snap her out of this madness."

"Should we send word to him?" Anthony asked.

Edward gazed off into the darkness of the room a moment, listening to the popping of the wood in the hearth. "If I know David, and I do, he is probably already on his way here. We will give him a week or so and if he still had not arrived, I shall send word to Canterbury."

Anthony nodded, downing the last of his wine and wondering why life for all of them had ceased to exist the moment Christopher's life slipped away. There seemed to be the past, and only the past; there was no future at all.

☙

RICHARD WAS COMING to visit to express his sympathy to Lady de Lohr. And, not surprising, David was coming with him. Edward and the other knights rejoiced with this news, hoping it would be enough to bring Dustin out of her stupor. With each day that passed, she seemed to grow worse and they worried for her very life now. She was so thin and pale, nothing like the healthy, vigorous woman they knew her to be.

The early March morning dawned amazingly bright and cheery. It was not long after sunrise that the sentries sighted an approaching army and the horn was sounded. Edward, knowing it to be Richard and David, hustled to find Dustin. He had purposely kept the information from her, afraid that if he told her she would fly into a fit. Now it was too late for her to do anything, so he sought her out in the garden.

She was hoeing like a farmer, dressed in the peasant garb that she favored these days. Gone were the fine dresses, the hose, and the jewelry. She was back into her blouses and rough cloth skirts, with the black leather girdle trussed up as tight as it could go and even then, it was too loose. Her long hair was dirty, hanging almost to her knees as she chopped the ground furiously.

"Dustin?" Edward had long since stopped addressing her as "My lady" or "Lady Dustin."

She did not look up nor did she answer him, as was usual these days. She continued to hoe. Edward continued.

"Riders are coming, someone I think you might like to see," he said. Then, he paused. "David is coming."

She stopped hoeing. Her head came up and she fixed him with her dull gray eyes. "David? Here?"

He nodded and smiled timidly. "Are you pleased?"

She blinked at him, mulling over the question. Was she pleased? Of course not. Nothing pleased her anymore. There was no pleasure in life. She hated everyone and everything, hated them for taking away her beloved. Her head went down and she started chopping at the ground again.

"Nay," she muttered. "Tell him to go away. He is not welcome here."

Edward's smile faded. "He brings the king with him, Dustin. Richard is here as well."

She stopped again and her head shot up. "Richard is here?" She raised the hoe and her eyes flashed like lightning in a storm. "He is most certainly not welcome here. Tell him to go away or I shall take this hoe to him."

"This is Christopher's home and Richard is most welcome," Edward replied steadily. "You, as dutiful Lady de Lohr, will welcome the returned monarch. Go upstairs and change."

"Nay!" Dustin shouted. "I do not want him here; I do not want either one of them here. I hate them both. Tell them to go away, Edward, or I shall strike them down where they stand."

"Why?" Edward asked softly.

"Why?" Dustin shrieked. "Because Chr…., my husband, is dead because of Richard, and David is not welcome in our home. That is why."

She could not even bring herself to say Christopher's name and Edward could feel her pain. She hadn't really spoken of her feelings in all this time and now he was coming to understand something; she blamed Richard, she blamed John; she blamed everyone. His heart was very sad for her with so much agony and no way to ease it.

"Nonetheless, they are here, and I will not turn them out before they are fed and rested," Edward said quietly. "If you cannot behave yourself, I will lock you in the abbey until they have left."

She threw the hoe to the ground and glared at him. "This is *my* home, Edward. Not yours."

He tried not to become angry with her. "Like it or not, you have a great station in this life. You have certain duties you may not shirk for any reason, Dustin. Christopher would take you over his knee if he heard you right now and well you know it." He took a step toward her sternly. "Now go upstairs and bathe and put on a clean dress. I shall not have you meeting our king looking like a madwoman."

Dustin's jaw worked as she slowly reached down to pick up the hoe, he could see that her palms were blistered and bloodied. "Go to hell, Edward."

She resumed her hoeing without another word and he turned with frustration for the house.

By the time he reached the bailey, the gates were open and the army was filing in. However, he noticed immediately that it was not the king or David. The colors were and black and gold, and he realized with shock who had come.

Marcus Burton rode into the bailey on a pure white steed, looking taller and prouder and stronger than Edward had ever seen him. The other knights turned out, eyeing him and his knights warily as they came to a halt in the center of the bailey. Jeffrey, sensing the tension, ordered the baron's army to remain outside the wall. Marcus and six knights remained on horseback as the gate closed again.

Edward was truly surprised. As he approached Marcus, the man tore off his helmet and his cobalt-blue eyes locked onto Edward's gold ones.

"Edward," he said in his smooth voice. " 'Tis good to see you again."

"And you, baron," Edward replied steadily. "To what do we owe the honor?"

He knew why Marcus was here; they all knew. It was a foolish question.

"I heard of Chris' passing and I came to express my sorrow to Lady de Lohr," Marcus replied, somewhat subdued. "How is she faring?"

"Terribly," Edward said honestly. "She borders on madness, Marcus. You have never seen anything like it."

Marcus let his gaze wander over Lioncross. "May I see her, please?"

"That may not be wise," Edward said. "She does not want to see anyone."

Marcus leveled his gaze on Edward. "I would see her, Edward. I have ridden over a week to see her, and I will not leave before I have had a chance to speak with her."

Edward knew where this had been leading all along. From the look of determination on Marcus' face, he knew exactly what his presence meant. Pleasantries were gone and now they were at the meat of the situation.

"You have come here to take her," he stated softly. "Haven't you?"

Marcus' jaw flexed and he lowered his gaze, fumbling with his reins. "I have simply come to see Dustin."

Edward took two long strides and was upon him, gazing up at Marcus' guarded expression.

"Do not lie to me," he hissed. "You heard Chris was dead and you could not wait to claim his widow."

Marcus' eyes were like ice. "You make it sound heartless, de Wolfe," he said. "I would offer her stability, protection, anything she desires."

"She has a child, you know," Edward said. "She bore Chris a daughter in September. It would be an instant family, Burton. There is no longer simply

Dustin to think of anymore."

"And I would love the child as my own," Marcus replied without missing a beat. "It makes no difference to me."

"Stop thinking of yourself, Marcus," Edward said heatedly. "Consider her feelings for a moment. She just lost her husband; do you truly think she wants another so soon? Give her time to heal, for God's sake."

Marcus' jaw began to tick again and he swung his leg over the destrier, dismounting in a jingle of armor; it was the latest and most expensive armor Edward had seen. He approached Edward until he was an inch from his face and lowered his voice so that only Edward would hear him.

"I love her, Edward. I have always loved her, more than anything," he muttered. "I have crossed the whole of England to see her and I am not leaving until I do. You can announce me or I can find her myself; the choice is yours."

Edward met his gaze with eyes as hard as stone. " 'Tis no choice, Burton," he growled. "You have given me an ultimatum and I do not take kindly to them."

"Then raise your sword and make your attempt to stop me," Marcus said, glancing sidelong at the other knights. "I can take on all of you, even the de Velt twins. 'Tis only David that concerns me."

"David is not here," Edward replied. "He left Lioncross around Christmastime."

Marcus' face rippled with surprise but he caught himself. "All the better for me, then. Will you show me to Dustin or must I find her myself?"

Edward eyed him harshly for a moment. "She is not as you remember her, Burton. Chris' death has changed her a great deal."

"She is still Dustin," Marcus replied evenly. "I shall always love her as such."

Edward glared at him a moment longer before turning on his heel. "Kessler, offer the baron's men refreshment," he told him. "We shall return shortly."

Edward took Marcus through the great hall of Lioncross and Marcus appraised the place, comparing it to his own keep, but his mind was focused on Dustin. He was so damned excited to see her that his stomach was taut with nerves. As they passed into the kitchens, a tall young man with a thin mustache met them and smiled inquisitively at Marcus. Edward stopped abruptly.

"Marcus Burton, this is Gowen Olmquist, Deborah's husband and Lioncross' steward," he said shortly.

Marcus and Gowen barely had time to exchange pleasantries before Edward was forging onward, taking Marcus out into the small kitchen bailey and pointing to the iron-worked gate that led into the garden.

"She's in her garden," he said with restrained anger. "I shall leave you to talk to her alone, but be aware that I will be within earshot. Bank yourself, Marcus; her mind is very brittle, as is her manner. Be shocked with nothing she says or does."

He turned sharply and marched away, leaving Marcus a moment to compose himself before seeing Dustin for the first time in a year. The anticipation was nearly too much to bear as he opened the garden gate.

Even though Edward had warned him, he was still shocked at the sight of her. She looked like a prisoner, dressed in rags and hoeing the ground furiously. Her luscious hair hung in dirty clumps and she was far thinner than he had remembered. Disheartened, Marcus swallowed hard as he stepped forward.

"Dustin?" he said softly.

She hoed a split second longer before stopping. Slowly, her head came up and Marcus was distressed to see her gaunt, pale face. Still incredibly beautiful, but so terribly haunting. He smiled and her eyes widened.

"Hello, honey," he said. "It has been a long time."

The hoe fell out of her hand and she straightened, brushing her ratty hair from her face. "Marcus?"

He nodded, taking a few timid steps forward. Dustin took a step backward and he stopped.

"What are you doing here?" she asked in awe.

"To see you, to see how you are," he replied. "I came to tell you how sorry I am about Chris."

She shook her head faintly. "You ran away," she said softly. "He was so worried about you. He went off to fight John and he was angry because you did not fight with him."

Marcus' smile faded. "I had to leave, Dustin. I....something happened unexpectedly and I had to leave."

"You mean you made love to me and fled in guilt," Dustin said, remarkably clear-minded. "Aye, Marcus, I know what happened that night. I thought I had dreamed it, but I knew soon enough that I hadn't. 'Twas good that you left."

He lowered his gaze. " 'Twas never my intention to take you, Dustin," he said, reliving that night so long ago. He had lived on the memory for over a year. "I went into your bedchamber that night to talk to you and in your sleep, you thought I was Christopher. I could have stopped it from happening, but I did not want to. I have always loved you, Dustin. You know that."

"Is that why you are here? To tell me you love me?" Dustin asked, then smiled ironically. "I do not want to hear this, Marcus. The only man I will ever love is dead, and I do not want anyone else. I am sorry you have come all this way for nothing."

"Think on it, Dustin," Marcus said softly. "I can offer you protection, companionship, and my undying devotion. And your daughter; I would be her father-figure."

Dustin stiffened, flooded with memories of how much Christopher had loved his daughter.

"You shall never be her father, Marcus," she said, rather angrily. "Her father is dead."

"Mayhap so," Marcus said hoarsely. "But I would love her as if she were my own."

Her eyes snapped to him but she bit her tongue. She didn't want to argue with him and she surely didn't want to hear of his proposal. In fact, she felt nothing for the man as she gazed at him. Not even friendship. There was no feeling at all. As she stood there, trying to figure out how to get rid of him, Griselda brought Christin out into the bright sunlight and Marcus' jaw dropped.

At six months old, the babe had his black hair and Dustin's gray eyes. The old woman passed the child over to her mother and left the three of them standing in uncomfortable silence.

Marcus' eyes were wide at the black-haired infant. "Dustin…?" he began timidly.

"I do not know!" Dustin snapped harshly, bouncing Christin when the baby whimpered at the sharpness of her mother's voice. She softened her tone. "I do not know, Marcus."

Marcus' mouth was hanging open. "But… the hair. And the shape of her face," he stammered.

"My mother had black hair," Dustin shot back. "And her eyes and her face are as mine. She…she is Chris' child, Marcus."

He forced himself over the shock and approached the two of them, holding out a timid finger to which Christin gleefully latched on to.

"She has my hair," he said softly.

Dustin did not answer. Marcus smiled at the baby and was rewarded with a wide grin, displaying two new teeth. "Can I hold her?" he asked.

Dustin bounced the baby a moment longer before reluctantly handing her over. Christopher had been very timid with his daughter at first; Marcus held her with great confidence that made her heart jump strangely. Christin grabbed his nose and stuck her hand in his mouth. He was delighted.

"What's her name?" he asked.

"Christin," Dustin replied sullenly, torn between Marcus' joy in the babe and the guilt that was sweeping her.

"Christin," Marcus repeated. "What a pretty name. Jesus, she's beautiful. She looks just like you."

Dustin looked away from him, emotions within her numb heart stirring again. Christin cooed and gurgled and Marcus was instantly attached to her. He continued to play with her even as Dustin meandered over to her hoe and picked it up. He watched her pick it up and begin scratching at the dirty again.

"Come home with me, Dustin," Marcus said softly. "You shall love Somerhill. There are lots of children in the village and Christin would have playmates, and it would be a fresh start for you. Away from Lioncross and its memories."

Dustin hoed haltingly at the thawing ground, her misery becoming evident. "I do not know, Marcus," she whispered. "This is my home and I belong here. It is Chris' home."

"And look what it is doing to you," he said with more firmness. "You are wasting away with grief. You must get away from this place."

Her head snapped up and she prepared a sharp reply, but the sight of him holding her happy, gurgling daughter brought tears to her eyes and the hoe fell to the ground. As her hands went over her face, Marcus went to her and wrapped her in his free arm.

Dustin went to pieces. To feel a massive, strong, warm arm around her once again threw her back into Christopher's arms and she allowed herself to imagine, for a second, that it was he who was holding her.

The more she wept, the tighter Marcus' grip became and her arms found their way around his waist. She could hear him comforting her softly and felt him kiss the top of her head at least twice. She also felt a different pressure on the top of her head and heard Marcus scolding Christin softly for eating her mother's hair. It was comical and she actually laughed, lifting her head to see that Marcus was smiling as well as he unwound her hair from Christin's death grip.

Edward was standing by the kitchen door with a birds-eye view of what was going on in the garden. He could see Marcus holding Dustin and Christin, and he was seized with a great anger. Anthony and Jeffrey joined him.

"I want him gone," Edward growled. "I do not care how, but I want him out."

"Why?" Anthony asked. "He's the only one who's gotten Dustin to respond in any way. Look; she's actually smiling."

Edward gritted his teeth. "The bastard comes swaggering in here to collect Dustin as if she was a prize," he seethed. "I shall not stand for it. And neither would Chris."

"Chris would want her to be happy," Jeffrey said quietly. "I have known Lady Dustin longer than anyone. If she wants to go with this Marcus, and in your judgment he is a just, fair man, then I know her mother would have no objection. She only wished for Dustin's happiness also."

"Marcus Burton has a reputation second only to Chris," Anthony told him. "Richard loves the man. He is as fair and just as they come. But you never told me he was in love with her, Edward."

Edward did not answer for a moment. "Verily," he replied faintly. "As much as Christopher, at least. But she only had eyes for her husband, and now Marcus sees this as his opportunity."

Anthony watched them for a moment before turning away. "If she will be happy with him, then I am sure Chris would approve."

Edward shook his head, eyeing Marcus and Dustin menacingly. "She is Chris' wife," he said.

"And Chris is dead," Jeffrey said, slapping him on the shoulder as he followed Anthony back into the kitchens.

CHAPTER FORTY-TWO

MARCUS STAYED ON for several days, trying desperately to convince Dustin to return north with him. He would much rather have her agreement in the matter, but whether or not she consented, he intended to take her with him. He was resolute that he would not leave without her.

Even with Marcus' presence, her habits changed little. She bathed at least now and brushed her hair, but her clothes were still of the peasant style and her appetite was nil. Marcus went into town and ordered three new dresses for her as a surprise and ordered pretty accessories to go with them, hoping to brighten her spirits. She was so sullen and depressed all of the time that it broke his heart to see her moping about. At first, taking her with him had been completely selfish, but the more he stayed on to observe her situation, the more he was convinced that it would truly be in Dustin's best interest. He only hoped that he could convince her that it would be best, also.

But Dustin wanted little to do with him other than conversation. She kept a cool distance, keeping her protective wall up with him at all times because she knew how easy it would be to succumb to him. He would give her what she was so desperately seeking, comfort, love, protection, but the problem was that she wasn't seeking those things from him; she wanted her husband. Any touch from Marcus would be compared to Christopher, and with any kiss she would close her eyes and pretend it was her husband. Marcus was a man who could stand on his own merits, no doubt. He was so much like her husband it was frightening – strong, incredibly handsome, powerful, and brave. Had she never met Christopher, Marcus Burton would have been the love of her life.

But the fact remained that he wasn't. Marcus surprised her with the dresses one night after supper and Dustin showed little interest, although she did thank him sincerely. Beautiful clothes reminded her of her husband because he had taken such delight in seeing her dressed to the hilt. She tried to explain her reasons to Marcus but she doubted he could understand. She could see that he was hurt by her reaction and she was sorry, but it did not change her feelings.

Nearly a week after his arrival, Dustin appeared one morning in his bedchamber. It was well before dawn and he was startled to see her standing next to his bed, dressed in a soft white nightshift. There were circles under her eyes and he wondered if she had slept at all.

"What is wrong, honey?" he asked with concern.

Dustin opened her mouth but nothing came out. Hot tears began to spill from her eyes and she angrily wiped them away.

"I….I had a nightmare again," she whispered, embarrassed and exhausted.

He pulled the coverlets back. "Come here, with me."

She shook her head hard and jumped back. He swung his huge legs over the side of the bed. "Then tell me," he said gently. "What was the dream about?"

She was shaking. "Chris," she whispered. "Ever since he died, I have had the same dream every night. I dream that I am just awakening in the morning, and it is bright and lovely and the sun is streaming in through the windows. He's lying next to me with his arms around me, and I can hear him talking about something, I never know what." She cracked, sobbing pitifully. "I can smell him, Marcus. I can smell his skin and feel its texture, and I feel so warm and content. And then I wake up to a cold, empty bed and I feel as if my grief is new. Every time I feel as if my heart is being yanked out and smashed. I cannot take it anymore."

His eyes were soft with sympathy. "Of course you cannot." He opened his arms to her. "Come here, Dustin. Let me comfort you as I have so wanted to do."

She stopped fighting him for the moment and allowed herself the luxury of his comfort. He was warm and soft and wonderful, and in no time she was asleep in his arms.

Marcus held her well into the morning hours. She slept limply, dreamlessly, and he knew it was because she felt safe with him. He would chase all of her bad dreams away. She curled up against him, her face pressed into his chest and he knew right then that he was taking Dustin back with him on the morrow. No one had taken charge of her since Christopher's death, they had all let her run her life her way and she was going to kill herself if she continued. Someone had to take charge of her, and that someone would be him.

Late in the morning he tucked Dustin into his bed, kissing her temple sweetly and allowing himself to feel some happiness. He had what he had come for. Washing his face, he donned his clothing and set out with determination.

Marcus took over Lioncross that day. Not since Christopher had left had it run with such purpose or fortitude. All of Christin's belongings were packed as well as everything Dustin owned. Bedding, linens, carpets, everything was loaded into two wagons that were secured in the bailey. The army camping outside the wall were given orders to prepare for departure.

Edward was furious that Marcus was taking over Lioncross as he was. But Marcus was a baron and technically Edward was of a lesser station, so there was very little he could do. He certainly did not want Dustin to leave, but as he saw it, he only had two options; either talk some sense into her or hope that Richard arrived before they left. Even with the latter, he could not be certain that Dustin would stay. Richard loved Marcus and was most likely to grant him anything; even the dead Defender's wife.

Edward cornered Dustin in the afternoon when she went out to her garden. As she had done day after day, she began to hoe and he stood by silently and watched.

"Are you really going to go with him?" he asked her.

Dustin hoed absently. "I guess so. I am so confused, Edward, I do not know what to do anymore," she looked at him. "This is my home. It is Chris' home and I do not want to leave, but I almost feel like I have to. Staying here day after day, seeing the things we loved together, cuts me to the core. Mayhap if I go with Marcus, I shall clear my mind and see things more rationally."

"He wants to marry you, Dustin," Edward said, his voice low. "Who's to say that once he gets you to Somerhill that he will ever let you return to Lioncross? Will you indeed marry him?"

Dustin shrugged. "I do not know, Edward I do not know anything anymore."

Edward sighed, feeling the situation slipping away from him. "Do you love him?"

"Nay," Dustin shook her head. "I shall never love anyone but Chris. I have told Marcus that, but he doesn't seem to care."

"Is it fair to give the man false hope by returning home with him, then?" Edward pressed quietly.

"I have never given him any hope whatsoever," Dustin insisted. "I have made it very clear that I will only love Christopher. But Christin needs a father, and I will eventually need companionship. I like Marcus, Edward. He is a decent man and he was my husband's best friend."

Edward leaned against the wall, running a weary hand over his brow. "There is nothing I can say to stop you?" he asked. "I think you are acting rashly. I think Marcus is making your decisions for you."

The hoe dropped. "No one makes my decisions for me," she said sternly. "But I must decide what is best for myself and for Christin. I am sorry if you cannot accept that, Edward. But Lioncross is mine now and I would hope that you would run it ably in my absence. Gowen will still keep the books, but you are in charge of the castle. And have no doubt that I will return."

He gazed at her, a hundred thoughts tumbling through his mind. He knew she wasn't thinking properly and that Marcus was very persuasive. The man had caught her in a weak moment and somehow had convinced her that returning to Somerhill was best for her.

But Christopher was gone, never to return. Mayhap it was for the best that Dustin go with Marcus and start a new life for herself and for Christin, away from the grief and memories that were slowly killing her.

"Then I will say nothing more than to wish you complete happiness, Dustin," he said after a moment. "Chris would want you to be happy."

Her eyes filled with tears and she bit her lip. "I know," she whispered. "Lord,

Edward, sometimes I do not think I can go on anymore. His absence is like a huge gaping hole in my soul, never to heal and I swear to you that sometimes it is all I can do to keep from killing myself. But I promised Chris that I wouldn't if anything ever happened to him, and I should not like to be spanked in Paradise in front of the heavenly hosts for disobeying him. 'Twould be most embarrassing."

He grinned. "No doubt. And knowing Chris, he would stop at nothing to take his hand to your behind."

She brushed a tear away. "Did they tell you how he died? They won't tell me. And where is this Gowergrove Castle that I might visit his grave someday?"

Edward's smile faded. "Archers, I believe, felled him. Zephyr, too; they found them together. Gowergrove is at the southern tip of Sherwood and should you decide to go there, I would wish to go with you and pay my respects, also."

She nodded, absorbing the information with a blustery sigh. Now that she had some idea as to how he died, she felt a strange sense of peace. But it did nothing for the ache in her heart.

"I miss him so, Edward," she murmured. "Will the pain ever go away?"

He put his arm around her shoulders comfortingly; this Lady Dustin sounded more like the lady he had grown to know, not like the crazy, irrational creature that had been raging about the keep for weeks.

"In time it will fade, that I promise," he assured her. "But it may never truly go away."

Dustin sighed, letting him comfort her for a moment. Marcus entered the garden, then, and they could both see the possessiveness in his expression.

"What goes on here?" he asked mildly.

"Nothing," Dustin said, letting go of Edward. "We were speaking of Lioncross and other things."

Marcus eyed Edward with a great deal of suspicion, much to Edward's annoyance. "Good God, Marcus, we weren't plotting," he snapped. "We were saying our goodbyes, considering you are planning on leaving tomorrow."

Marcus' gaze was cool at the sharp tone but he let it slide. "Come along, Dustin," he said. "I want you to make sure everything you will need or want is packed."

Dustin preceded him from the garden, but Marcus paused at the gate to throw Edward another hard glance.

"She is mine now, de Wolfe," he hissed. "You would do well to remember that."

He moved away, leaving Edward fuming.

Before sunset that evening, an approaching army was sighted and Edward knew that it had to be Richard and David. There was no other alternative. With renewed vigor, he ordered the dinner portions doubled and the remaining unoccupied bedchambers prepared. He waited until everything was moving smoothly before seeking Marcus out.

As he suspected, he and Dustin were holed up in Lady Mary's solar playing a game of Fox and Hounds. Marcus kept her very much to himself and very isolated from the others. Edward could not help the satisfaction that crept into his voice.

"Richard and David are approaching, my lord," he said evenly. "Mayhap you would like to greet them in the bailey?"

Marcus lifted an eyebrow as Dustin shot to her feet. "Richard and David?" she repeated, agitated. "I do not want to see them."

"Mayhap so, but they are here nonetheless." Marcus put up a hand to calm her. "Why don't you go upstairs and change into one of your new surcoats? That would please me."

"Nay!" she yanked away from him, toppling the game board. "I do not want them here, either of them. They are to blame for my misery and I hate them."

Marcus stood up. "Calm down, honey," he said softly. "You shall only have to see them a moment and then never again. I promise I shall keep them away from you."

Edward did not like the wild look to her eye. All of the healing that had occurred with Marcus over the past week was rapidly slipping away.

"Richard killed Christopher," she said pointedly. "He is responsible for everything that has happened."

"Be reasonable, Dustin," Marcus said steadily. "Christopher served Richard of his own accord; no one forced hm. He is not the first man to die in the service of his king, and he certainly won't be the last. Richard is not responsible in the least and I am sure his grief is great. Chris was his dear friend."

She eyed Marcus with doubt and agitation, knowing his words made sense but not wanting to admit it. She had to blame someone for her husband's death, and Richard was the most obvious target.

"I hate him," she seethed. "And I am going to beat David to a pulp if he sets foot in my keep."

Marcus never did ask what had happened between Christopher and David, but at this moment he decided to find out. Dustin was obviously very angry with her brother-in-law.

"What happened between Chris and David that you should hate him so?" he asked her.

She jutted her chin out, turning away from him. "He accused me of horrible things and we fought. Christopher banished him from Lioncross."

"You fought?" Marcus repeated with mounting disbelief. "Do you mean that you actually exchanged blows?"

"I slapped him and he slapped me back," Dustin replied. "Christopher was going to kill him, but he exiled him instead."

Marcus shook his head. "What did he say to you that was so horrible? I know for a fact that David adored you, Dustin. What happened?"

She looked him in the eye. "He accused me of being your whore and of bearing your child. So I hit him."

Marcus was almost physically impacted by the statement. Edward watched him as he tried to keep his steady demeanor, but it was apparent he was shocked. After a moment, the veins on his throat throbbed.

"Then David does not set foot in this castle," he said in a low voice. "I shall run him through if he tries."

"You will have no choice," Edward informed him. "He comes with Richard, and Richard will gain him entrance. You cannot go against our king."

Marcus glared at Edward; he did not like the way this was going already. He could not take Dustin with him tomorrow as planned if Richard were here, and he did not want David near her, yet Edward was correct in that he had no power to deny him entrance to Lioncross.

Muttering a curse, he turned away. Horns sounded on the wall outside and they knew that the army's arrival was imminent. The huge outer gates were already swinging open.

Marcus turned to Dustin. "Honey, go upstairs. Wait for me there."

Dustin turned immediately and quit the room. Edward and Marcus exchanged glances before proceeding out into the foyer and onward to the bailey.

As they expected, David and Richard entered the courtyard side by side. Slightly behind them rode Sir Philip de Lohr, and a host of other distinguished knights that had come to pay their respect to Lady de Lohr. Edward and Marcus were stunned; they thought that only Richard and David and a few vassals were coming, when in fact, the army that had come with them was made up entirely of knights that had served with Christopher in the Holy Land. Marcus recognized every man he lay eyes upon, as did Edward, and they swapped awestruck gazes.

The courtyard was full of men in full armor and regalia, and even then the party still spilled out of the gates and down the road. The men-at-arms were astonished at the show of support for their liege; they, of course, had always known the baron to be a great man. But they could not imagine that the whole of Richard and his court respected him as much as they did. It was an awesome sight to behold.

Dustin saw the men from her bedchamber window, her hate and agitation fleeing when she saw all of the knights that had accompanied the king. Without even being told, she knew that they had come to pay their respects to her for the loss of her husband, and all of her fortitude and mental stability returned in one fell swoop. Out of their love and respect for her husband, they had come to pay him homage and she would not disappoint. They wanted to see the Lion's Claw's wife, and see her they would. She could feel the reverence radiating from the army, the very deep admiration they held for Christopher evident and she was deeply touched. They would not see the crazy, dirty woman who had run mad with grief for weeks on end, nay; they would see regal, composed Lady de Lohr as befitting the baron's wife.

Dashing from the window, she bellowed for rosewater and a towel.

☙

RICHARD, HIS TUNIC of scarlet with three fierce lions as clean as anyone had ever seen it, held up a hand in greeting to Edward and to Marcus.

"Marcus, I thought you might be here," he said. "Ever the faithful vassal to Chris, aren't you?"

Marcus nodded slowly. "Sire, our prayers were answered with your safe return."

Richard raised a heavy eyebrow and dismounted stiffly. "Indeed. Yet I come home to discord and chaos, even amongst my own ranks." He removed his gauntlets and passed an eye over Edward. "De Wolfe, you are looking well. I understand you have been taking care of Lady de Lohr."

"In a sense, sire," Edward bowed. "I am making sure Lioncross is running smoothly."

Richard nodded shortly then glanced over his shoulder at David. "Are you going to sit there forever?"

David dismounted, his eyes guarded against Edward and outright hostile on Marcus. Richard was no fool; he could plainly read the distrust and animosity between his men. All of his joviality and good feelings fled.

"Enough of this," he snarled. "When we were together in the Holy Land, you men were inseparable. There were no stronger bonds anywhere in my ranks, and I return home to find everyone at odds. I shall not stand for it any longer. I heard rumor that Dustin Barringdon is the root of this problem, but I refused to believe it. Since when does a mere woman come between my knights of the realm?"

The three men looked decidedly uncomfortable and Edward cleared his throat. " 'Tis not that simple, sire, truly," he said softly.

Richard was impatient. "Then we shall discuss it later, but for now, I wish to see this woman on whom my kingdom hinges. Where is she?"

"Inside, sire," Marcus replied. "I shall retrieve her for you."

"No need," Philip walked up on the small group, his faded blue eyes gazing over their heads at the front door to the keep. "She has come."

All eyes turned to see Dustin emerging from the door, and not a man who laid eyes upon her beauty dared to breathe. She was dressed in royal blue silk, Christopher's color, the color that enhanced her gray eyes like nothing else. Her hair had been brushed within an inch of its life and pulled softly back from her face, revealing her true loveliness. Around her neck hung the huge cross

Christopher had given her and those closest to her noticed color to her lips. She looked as beautiful as ever, her head held high as she paused at the top of the steps.

Without introduction, the host of knights knew who she was. It was as if she possessed an aura about her that distinguished her from another mere lady. When she paused at the top of the stone stairs, waiting to be summoned forward to meet Richard, every man in armor dismounted and dropped to their knees, driving their swords into the dirt before them. It was a unified show of support and respect, a sea of mighty knights in armor displaying their undying devotion to the wife of their fallen Defender.

Dustin was stunned at the swift, decisive movement of the collective group. There were so many of them that it was a truly awesome sight to behold, and her eyes widened in astonishment. Every man was on his knees before her, some with their faces turned toward her, some with their heads bowed reverently in prayer. Dustin's chest swelled with pride, wishing Christopher could be here to see the show of force.

A smile crept onto her lips, a smile of pleasure and genuine hope. She could feel the respect coming forth and touching her, silently enveloping her weary body and helping to heal the gaping hole in her heart left by her husband's passing. Strange that it took no words, no magic, and no medicine to start the healing process. A simple gesture, mighty as it was, became the catalyst.

It was completely silent, the only sounds being the nighthawk that was riding a draft somewhere high above. The sun sunk lower in the sky and a faint breeze had picked up, but Dustin stood frozen to the spot as the knights of Richard's realm paid mute homage to her fallen husband. Behind her, she heard sniffles and she recognized the source.

"Gowen," she said softly without turning around. "Get Christin. *Hurry*."

Frozen for a moment in time, she was entranced by the overwhelming support and continued to gaze back at the men until Gowen finally appeared at her side, holding Christin. Dustin took her daughter into her arms, murmuring softly and pointing to the bailey below, filled with hundreds of silent, powerful knights.

The baby chewed her fingers, wide-eyed. Dustin took the steps, coming upon Edward and Marcus, who had kneeled with the rest of them. In fact, they had all kneeled, even Richard, and when she came upon him, he took her hand and kissed it genteelly.

"Lady de Lohr," he said hoarsely. "Am I to assume this is Chris' daughter?"

"Her name is Christin, sire," Dustin answered.

Richard rose unsteadily to his feet, alternately eyeing her and the baby. Finally, he held out his hands. "May I?"

She handed the baby to him and the first thing Christin did was stick her finger in his eye. Richard laughed loudly and kissed the tiny fingers.

"She is beautiful," he responded, handing her back to Dustin. "I can see Chris in her face most definitely. Arthur would be proud, my lady."

Dustin nodded graciously, deeply pleased and in awe of the king's presence. Richard's gaze was open on her. "I came to meet you, Lady Dustin, and to extend my condolences on the passing of your husband."

"Thank you, sire," Dustin answered softly.

Behind him, Sir Philip rose from his crouch and smiled faintly at her, and Dustin instantly saw the family resemblance.

"You must be Sir Philip," she said. "Chris told me so much of you, I feel as if I have known you a lifetime."

"An honor to meet you, my lady," Philip replied.

Dustin glanced down at Philip's side and saw David's bowed head. Forgiveness filled her and she knew now that whatever had happened in the past, it had been foolish and ridiculous. She and David had always liked each other a great deal and the tiff had been a freakish event. She realized that now, for suddenly she realized everything with a clear, solid mind. Christopher was dead and she was forever altered, but life would continue and she was somehow stronger for it. Her strength was in the love they had once shared and for the character he had built in her through his devotion. She understood that now.

She moved past Richard and Philip and touched the top of David's head.

"David," she said softly. "Get up and greet your niece. It has been a long time since she saw you last."

He raised his head. His entire face was wet with tears. Dustin shushed him softly, encouraging him to his feet and then falling into his embrace. Against her, David let loose with his sobs as she whispered comfortingly to him. Forgiveness was more, and better, than he had ever hoped for.

Not releasing David, she turned back to Richard. "Sire, we have refreshments for you and your party. Would you please come in?"

Richard smiled at her and cupped her chin gently between his fingers. She gazed up at him, watching his face ripple with emotion. At thirty-eight years old, he looked much older and haggard from his tumultuous life.

"I understand Chris found love with you, my lady," he said softly. "I can see why."

She flushed, the first color to her cheeks in weeks. Passing Christin to Marcus, she took Richard's arm and escorted him inside.

As Richard and Dustin headed for the keep, David didn't move. His gaze was on Marcus, as hostile and confrontational as ever. Marcus met his gaze, steadily, feeling the tension between them explode.

"How long have you been here?" David finally asked.

"Over a week," Marcus replied steadily.

David's jaw ticked. "You couldn't even wait until my brother was cold in his grave, could you?"

Marcus didn't want a fight on his hands, not with Christin in his arms, so he kept his manner calm. "It is not like that, David. Give me more credit than that."

David wouldn't back down. "Then you can leave; now."

Marcus' jaw ticked. "Not without Dustin. She is returning with me to Somerhill.

David's nostrils flared but he kept his cool because of Christin. "No," he said flatly. "She is staying here."

Marcus did not reply, knowing that if anymore were said it could result in raised voices and frighten the baby. He simply turned away from David and started back toward the house when a knight nearby called out to him.

"Lord Marcus?" The man stood up, taking a step forward. "I am Sir John de Monfort. I served with you and Lord Christopher during the siege of Acre."

Marcus nodded coolly. "I remember you. A fine knight."

The man nodded. "Thank you, my lord. I was wondering…the babe. She is Lord Christopher's, is she not?"

Marcus looked at the baby in his arms, who was still chewing furiously on her fingers. "The Lady Christin de Lohr."

The knight nodded faintly. Without another word, he approached Christin and fell to one knee, touching her little foot and bowing his head in a silent prayer. Abruptly, he rose and wandered off, but immediately behind him was another man to take his place. Marcus soon realized that the entire group of knights were falling into line to pay their respects to Lady Christin.

David stood behind him as the knights filed past, some touching her foot, some gently touching her head, and simply others making the sign of the cross before her and murmuring a prayer. And still others placed small medallions in her little hands, bright objects for her to play with, which were undoubtedly expensive. Marcus was silent, protective, and deeply touched on Christopher's behalf.

Christin, being the good-natured baby that she was, thought all of it was great fun and cooed and babbled the entire time. She would grab the hair of the men who bowed before her or reach out and snag a piece of tunic. More than once Marcus had to pry her hands free of someone, to which she would scream baby talk and wave her wet hands angrily at him. More than once, she batted him in the face with her wet fingers, leaving damp streaks. But Marcus didn't flinch.

David, watching his niece with her developing personality, could not help thinking just how much like her mother she was. The more he watched her, the more he realized how very wrong he had been; except for the hair color, she looked nothing like Marcus and he, too, was beginning to see Christopher in her features. He only wished his brother were alive so he could tell him so.

The knights camped in and around Lioncross that night, their bonfires sending eerie blobs of fire glowing into the blackness of the March night. Each man felt closer to the Defender, walking the very earth that Baron de Lohr had come to love so well.

CHAPTER FORTY-THREE

THE FIRST THING Christopher was aware of was dull, aching pain. And, Christ, he was so damn hot he could barely stand it. His mind was groggy and muddy but he gradually became aware of voices around him and he was immediately concerned he had fallen into enemy hands. He thrashed a bit but he was far too weak to do anything more. Gentle, strong hands were holding him steady.

"Easy, my lord, easy," came a male voice. "Stop moving about like that or you shall re-open your wound."

Christopher struggled to speak. "Who...where...?"

"Shush, do not talk now," the man said. "You have got to use all of your strength to get well. Could you take some broth?"

Christopher opened his eyes a peep, his lids felt as if they weighed a hundred pounds apiece. His focus was all out of sync and he blinked several times to clear his vision. Two men and one woman slowly came into view.

"Who are you?" he rasped.

One man smiled slightly, a nice-looking man perhaps his own age. "My name is Rob," he replied. "This lovely woman who saved your life is my wife, Marianne. Can you tell us your name?"

Christopher cleared his parched throat and thought a moment; his mind was so muddled he could not seem to remember. "Christopher de Lohr," he finally said. "How did I get here?"

"My man brought you here," Rob indicated a big, burly red-headed man standing next to him. "He found you in the trees after the battle for Gowergrove. You were as good as dead, but he brought you back anyway. Seems he took pity on you because you fought against John."

Christopher's eyes opened wider, though they were red and crusty. His vision was a little clearer, but he was still so bloody hot. "How long... long have I been here?"

"You have been unconscious for over two weeks, my lord," Marianne replied, placing a cool compress on his head. "We thought you were dead until just last night when your fever broke. It has not gone completely, but it is certainly not what it was. How do you feel?"

"Like I am dying," Christopher croaked. "Two weeks?"

"Aye," Rob replied. "Are you one of Richard's knights?"

Christopher nodded once, weakly. "Aye."

He drifted off to sleep and Marianne shushed her husband when he tried to ask him another question.

"Leave him be, Rob," she admonished. "The man still has one foot in the grave, so let him sleep. He will answer your questions in time."

Rob stood up, a head shorter than the burly man next to him. "I wonder if he's close to Richard," he glanced over at the mail, sword and tunic in the corner that belonged to his guest. "What did he say his name was? Christian?"

"Christopher," the big man reminded him. "Christopher de Lohr. The name sounds familiar, Rob."

"Does it?" Rob gazed down at the massive man again. "I cannot place it. Well, we can do no more for him at the moment. We shall return shortly."

"Where are you going?" She stood up, brushing her thick auburn curls out of her face.

Rob kissed her. "Business, love. Not to worry."

She pursed her lips in irritation. "Business. You mean robbery. Rob, no wonder John has labeled you an outlaw. All you do is steal and rob and burn."

Rob's handsome face lost some of its humor and he put his vest on. "What do you expect? The man stole my castle and tried to kill me. He is to blame for the life I lead, not I." He jerked his head in the direction of the man sleeping on the floor. "Mayhap that one can help us seek justice if he is one of Richard's knights. Mayhap it was a good thing that Jonathan here found him when he did."

Marianne watched her husband strap on his arrow pack and sling his bow over one shoulder. Her face was still furrowed and Rob planted a kiss on her nose. "We shall return shortly, love. Take good care of Sir Christopher."

Marianne shook her head as Rob and Jonathan ducked out of the hut, wrestling with the hide flap. It was always the same with him – *revenge, revenge, revenge*. Would it end? Not until John was dead, most likely, or Rob had had a chance to seek audience with Richard and regain his keep. Aye, Marianne would certainly love to live at Tickhill again and not in these rotting little huts in the middle of Sherwood.

"Take care of yourself, Rob of the Hood," she muttered, turning back to her patient. "Somehow, you always manage to."

☙

CHRISTOPHER DID NOT come around again for another three days. But when he did, the fever was completely gone and he awoke remarkably clear-headed. He gazed at his surroundings, listening to the snoring inside the hut. He could pick out at least three, possibly more.

He shifted a bit and was met with stiffness and soreness such as he had never known and decided to simply rest easy. His slight groan roused Marianne, who was immediately up and moving to his side.

"Sir Christopher," she exclaimed softly. "You are awake."

"Indeed, my lady," he replied, his voice returning to the rich, soothing tone Dustin had loved so well. "But it would seem I chose the dead of night to awaken to."

Marianne smiled; she was a pretty woman, if not a bit plain. " 'Tis an hour or so before dawn," she replied. "My husband and his men will rise soon. How do you feel?"

He raised an arm ever so slowly and lay his left hand on his forehead. "Not too terribly, actually," he said. "Horrible compared to what I usually feel like, but better than I felt when I awoke earlier. But I am rather thirsty."

Marianne nodded quickly and rapidly drew a wooden ladle of water. She coaxed him to drink slowly, but he was so thirsty most of the water ended up running down his face and into his hair. Slaked for the moment, he thanked her.

By this time, her husband had heard the voices as he was rising, pulling on his rough linen tunic.

"Sir Christopher, you are awake," he said as he rolled to his knees. "God be praised. How do you feel?"

Christopher's weak left hand found his unkempt beard. "As if I have just gone several bouts with Lucifer himself. Christ, I need a shave."

Rob and Marianne laughed, and big Jonathan bolted upright on his pallet at the noise. "What goes on?" he demanded. Then he noticed Rob and Marianne hovering over Christopher, who was quite awake. "Oh, my lord, you are come to life."

Chris let his hand fall to his chest. "That, sirrah, is a mere opinion. What is your name?"

"Jonathan Blackwelder, sire," he replied. "I was the young earl's troop master."

"Young earl?" Christopher looked puzzled and he saw Rob wave Jonathan off. "You are an earl? What…where am I, then? Are we at your keep?"

"Nay." Rob's usually pleasant face was suddenly morose. "For I no longer have a keep, my lord, at least in the personal sense. John has it."

"John?" Christopher repeated. "What is the name of your keep?"

"Tickhill," Rob replied quietly.

Christopher stared at him a moment, slow understanding coming over him. He remembered the battle for Tickhill all too well, even with his haze-clouded mind. "You are the Earl of Longdon?"

Rob's head came up to Christopher. "You are familiar with my keep? Were you at the siege of Tickhill?"

Christopher closed his eyes. "Aye, my lord. 'Twas I who led the crown troops against John's mercenary army." His voice was weak again, weak with defeat. He hated admitting his failure to the man who had saved his life. "We arrived too late to save your fortress, sire, and I am sincerely sorry for it. By the time we arrived, there was little to do."

"You led the crown troops?" Rob glanced at Jonathan. "Are you the knight they call the Defender?"

Christopher nodded weakly. "Hard to believe, is it not?"

"Richard's Defender?" Jonathan said with wide eyes. "The man they call the Lion's Claw?"

Christopher nodded again, opening his eyes to stare at the ceiling. Marianne and Rob and Jonathan exchanged astonished glances; the man lying in their modest little hut was the all-powerful Defender of the Realm.

"We are honored by your presence, sire," Marianne stammered.

Christopher gazed kindly at her. " 'Tis I who am honored, my lady, and forever in your debt. Will I heal completely?"

She nodded, lifting the bandages on his left side. "Your wound was terrible, sire, to say the least. Never have I seen a man with such a gaping hole live. But I'd venture to say that since you have survived thus far, you should heal completely. You have an amazing will to live, sire. 'Tis the only explanation other than God's divine grace."

"I have everything to live for," Christopher replied quietly. "A wife and daughter await me at home. 'Twould it be possible to get word to them?"

Rob and Jonathan exchanged glances. "That may not be possible at all, sire. John has placed a price on my head and on the heads of my associates. To send a message would be to possibly reveal our whereabouts." He looked genuinely sorry. "The only way your wife will receive a message is if you take it to her yourself. We could not risk one of our men being followed."

Christopher sighed heavily. "I see," he said sadly. "And what was this heinous crime you committed to warrant a bounty? Stick your tongue at the prince? Mayhap, given him a less than polite expression?"

Rob smiled again. "I see you understand John too well. Nay, sire, my only crime was trying to defend my keep and killing four of his elite guards in the process. But he has deemed me an outlaw, and my people and I eke out an existence in Sherwood waiting for the opportunity to present itself so that I might return home."

"You mean that as a result of John, you truly are an outlaw now," Christopher said. "Forced to steal to live."

"We could become farmers, but why?" Rob shrugged. "John has declared us outlaws, and outlaws we will be. But only against his loyalists; we only rob and steal from those we know are loyal to the prince. We may be small in number, but we are as pesky as a horde of fleas. Annoying to the point of distraction."

Christopher smiled. "My lord, I think I like you already."

"That is good," Rob replied. "For someday I may need your help to explain my actions to Richard. I do intend to regain my keep, but I shan't be able to do it as an outlaw."

Christopher's smile faded. "I can promise you I will do everything in my power to persuade Richard to return your holdings. He's returned to England now and I can only assume he will be taking back England fortress by fortress."

"He has returned from the quest?" Rob repeated; he had been out of touch a long time. "God be praised; now mayhap England can return to some normalcy."

"One can only pray," Christopher replied softly.

Rob scratched his scalp and buttoned his tunic. "Well, I must be running along. Our spies tell us that the Earl of Dorset is on the road this day with a load of cash and other valuables destined for John at Nottingham. I think I shall relieve him of his burden."

His manner was so carefree and light that Christopher thought he sounded much like a naughty boy, not at all like an earl. As Rob and Jonathan left the tent, a pretty maid entered bearing a steaming bowl. Her soft brown eyes immediately fell on Christopher and she flushed, handing the bowl to Marianne. Marianne was not daft; she saw the look on the maid's face.

"Lizabetha, be pleased to meet Sir Christopher de Lohr," she said. "We must make him well so that he might return to his wife and child. My lord, this is my niece, Lady Lizabetha du Bois."

Christopher glanced at the woman, she was very young, younger than his wife, and pretty. She blushed virginally and lowered her gaze. *Very practiced*, Christopher thought. Seeing the girl made him long for Dustin all the more.

Marianne chased Lizabetha out and fed Christopher herself, a rich beef broth. He was hungry and ate the whole bowl, feeling the fuel in his veins already. He watched Marianne put the bowl away and prepare another compress for his healing wound.

"My wife must think I am dead," he said softly.

Marianne raised her face to him. "No doubt that she does, sire, I am sorry we cannot risk sending a message."

Christopher shook his head. "Nay, madam, I did not mean to imply that I was insistent upon sending her word. I understand your husband's situation, and I understand John. It is just that…well, it pains me deeply to know that my wife believes I am dead."

Marianne began to change his bandages. "I can only imagine her torment, my lord, and yours. But you will not be able to leave until your strength has returned, and that could take weeks. To travel any sooner will surely do further damage."

He glanced down at the wound in his side, purple and puckered and scabbed. It was just below his ribcage. "I ought to have a lovely scar."

Marianne smiled. "Hopefully, these herbs will lessen the scarring."

"Nay, madam, I am worried over no scar. I am simply grateful for my life," he replied, greatly fatigued again.

Marianne watched his strong, handsome face as he drifted off to sleep once again. She could hardly believe his identity and she said a quick prayer to Fate. Fate had brought Jonathan to the wood's edge that day in search of battle souvenirs, instead finding a dying man. *Why had he brought him back?* Even Jonathan hadn't truly known the answer to that, but she knew Fate had brought him here so that she could heal him. The Defender, in thanks for his life saved, surely would help her Rob get his fortress back. Hope soared within her bosom; aye, Fate was to thank for this.

Christopher slept until noon. He was roused by a gentle voice, knowing it wasn't Marianne's and not surprised to see Lizabetha hovering over him, a smile on her pretty face.

"My lord, I have brought food and a razor," she said softly. "Marianne said you lamented about needing a shave. If you will allow me, sire, I shall both feed and shave you."

He nodded, blinking the sleep out of his eyes. He allowed Lizabetha to prop him up with a few blankets so that he was sitting up a bit. After the world stopped spinning, she fed him the broth of a stew that had been made from the remainder of their beef. It was thick and delicious and he ate the entire bowl, gratefully accepting a cup of watered ale to wash it down.

The entire time, Lizabetha said not a word but smiled endlessly. He was polite but cool, for he did not want to encourage the girl and her obvious infatuation.

She lay him back once again and carefully shaved his face. He made sure she left the beard, but she cleaned it up a great deal. She even washed his hair with a bit of soap and dried him gently with a towel. He knew he looked much more presentable when she blushed. He could not help but grin.

"Your assistance is appreciated," he said, rubbing his hand over his smooth neck. "Amazing that something as simple as a shave can improve one's spirits."

Her blush deepened as she collected the bowl and razor. "You are welcome, my lord," she said. Then, her gaze lingered on him, daring to look him in the eye. "Is there anything else you require?"

It was a leading question, one that made him slightly nervous. "Nay," he replied evenly. "You have been a great help and I appreciate it."

Lizabetha's gaze lingered on him, suggestively, but she said nothing more as she quit the hut. Christopher kept his gaze averted until she left, only then daring to look at the door to make sure she had truly gone. Even then, he could only roll his eyes and pray the infatuation was a passing thing.

CHAPTER FORTY-FOUR

DUSTIN AND CHRISTIN had sat with Richard and the knights for most of the evening, listening to the fighting men tell tales of battle upon the sands of the Holy Land and stories of valor involving Christopher. Even though Christin couldn't understand the stories. Still, Dustin wanted the baby there, basking in the aura of her father's memory. It was as if he were holding her once again, so strong and vivid the tales. He was there, in spirit if not in body.

It had been evident since the meal commenced, however, that David and Marcus were deeply at odds. Edward sided with David and Marcus seemed to be on his own island of righteousness, defensive when it came to Edward and David, yet warm and accommodating when it came to Dustin.

He told his own stories of Christopher. Some involved Christopher, David, himself, and Christopher's cousin on his mother's side, a knight by the name of Kieran Hage. Another great knight on the quest, he had been killed by assassins before the quest had been complete. Christopher and David had grieved long for the man who had been like a brother to them. When Marcus brought up his name, even Richard grew saddened.

"War is the widowmaker and kings the executioner," he muttered philosophically. "I have seen many good men fall, all in the name of religion or conquest. I do not believe that Christopher had gotten over the death of Kieran."

David reflected on his massive and intelligent cousin. "Nor I," he said softly. "To lose him as we did, to assassins no less, was tragic."

"We never recovered his body, did we?" Richard said before he could think. "The last I was told, he was tracked to Nahariya, but after that, he all but vanished."

David and Marcus, rather anxious, passed glances at Dustin, who was sitting next to Richard, with the baby sitting on the table in front of her. Richard realized they were on to a very bad subject and quickly shifted focus.

"My lady, I understand your mother is a Fitz Walter," he said the first thing that popped to mind, watching David wince. Another bad subject. "I… I never met your mother. Arthur spoke very fondly of her."

Dustin looked up from the baby, whom she was playing patty-cake with. The subject of Christopher's cousin's missing body did not escape her; much like her own husband, they had nothing to bury. That was all she could seem to focus on. She was struggling not to linger on those morose thoughts as Richard attempted to engage her in other conversation.

She smiled weakly at the king. "My mother and father were married for over twenty years," she said. "They were quite fond of each other."

"No brothers or sisters?"

She shook her head. "Only me," she said. "If my father wanted a son, he never said so. He was very attentive to my mother and me."

Richard was growing worried; there didn't seem to be many safe subjects with Lady de Lohr except for the baby. That one seemed safe enough. When Christin squealed happily as her mother played with her, Richard was glad for the diversion.

"The child is good natured," he said. "You are very blessed."

Dustin smiled at her daughter as the little girl slapped at her hands. "She is a happy lass."

The baby was animated, finding a used spoon from her mother's trencher and putting it in her mouth. Marcus, across the table, made little clucking noises and Christin turned to look at him. He smiled at the baby and she grinned back, broadly. Marcus set down his cup and reached across the table, pulling her into his arms.

He tickled the baby and made loud kissing noises on her fat little hands. Christin was delighted, but seated next to Marcus, David was clearly unhappy. He continued to watch as Marcus played with Christin until the baby grew fussy and Dustin called for Griselda. The old woman whisked the baby from the hall and they could hear her crying upstairs, unwilling to settle down for sleep. As the sounds of her sleepy and unhappy daughter faded away, Dustin sat next to the king and sipped on her wine, thinking back to the stories of her husband's valor and trying not to miss him too much. It was a difficult struggle.

And it was not a struggle missed by David or Marcus. They were watching her as Richard was watching them. Now that the baby was gone, the tension at the table was increasing. They had behaved for the sake of the baby but now that she was gone, there was no longer any reason for good behavior. They ended up glaring at each other over the rim of their cups. Finally, Richard reached his limit.

"Enough of this," he snapped quietly. "This behavior will end. Am I clear?"

Marcus averted his gaze but David continued to stare the man down. Richard slammed his cup on the tabletop to get David's attention.

"David," he hissed. "Do you hear me?"

"I hear you, sire."

"What is your issue with Marcus? Tell me now and let us get this out in the open."

David took his eyes off Marcus, then. He looked at the king, seeing the man's extreme displeasure.

"It is not a simple thing, sire," he said, realizing it was difficult to explain. "I do not think that...."

Richard cut him off. "Marcus," he addressed him. "You will tell me why you and David are at each other's throats."

Marcus was considerably less hostile when facing his king. "He is angry with me."

"Why?"

"Because... because I have come to Lioncross to take Lady Dustin away from here and marry her."

Richard wasn't surprised. It all but confirmed the rumors of Burton's attraction to lady de Lohr. "Is this so?" he said. "Do you intend to take her and the baby back to Somerhill?"

"I do."

Richard pondered that as he looked back to David. "And you disagree?"

David nodded his head, his eyes on Marcus. "Aye, sire, I do. Lady de Lohr belongs here at Lioncross."

"Alone? Or with you?" Richard demanded. "David, you are betrothed yourself, are you not? Do you intend to break your betrothal to Emilie Hampton and marry your dead brother's wife?"

David faltered. "Nay, my lord, I still intend to marry Emilie," he said. "But Lady Dustin's home is here, within these walls. And Chris would want his child to be raised in his own keep."

"So you would have her stay here, alone, simply to raise a child who will not even remember her true father?" Richard shook his head. "If that is truly Chris' desire, then it seems most selfish to me. Or is it that you object to Marcus personally, David? I am curious."

David looked at Richard. "Marcus is the best knight in the realm now that my brother is gone, but...."

Richard interrupted him. "That was not my question. *Why* do you object to Marcus marrying your brother's wife?"

David lowered his gaze, toying with his goblet. "Because she is Chris' wife, sire," he said softly. "She is his legacy. If she marries Marcus, she will cease to become Chris' wife. She will be Lady Burton, and it will almost be as if Chris was never married or never had children. Lioncross will be empty of his family and his legacy will die."

Dustin fought off the tears and lowered her head so no one could see her pain. But Richard saw her pain and he placed his palm over her soft, white hand.

"Christopher *is* a legend, David," he said quietly. "So long as there are a thousand knights to remember him and pass on his story, his legacy continues endlessly. And that beautiful babe in the nursery is the fruit of his loins, his legacy in the flesh. Marcus Burton would never change that."

David's head shot up sharply to Marcus and then focused on Richard once more and the king could see the doubt and grief.

"David, Christopher will live forever in our hearts," he said. "What Marcus is doing is offering to wed Lady Dustin and provide her with a stable, safe life. He is offering his companionship to her and I, for one, think he is being quite selfless. I should think you would appreciate knowing Chris' wife would be well taken care of."

David lowered his gaze.

Down the table was the tall figure of Philip de Lohr. He had been listening closely to everything. He drew his nephew's sullen glance and the attention of everyone else at the table when he cleared his throat quietly.

"Every time I look at you, David, I see my brother," Philip said softly. "I know what it is like to lose a brother, someone I admired above anyone else. When Myles passed away, I felt toward Val much as you do toward Dustin. She was Myles' wife and I felt that she was my personal responsibility." He sat forward on the table, his handsome face weary. "But Val followed Myles shortly after in death. I honestly believe she could not live without him and allowed whatever ailment that claimed him to claim her. But if that had not been the case, I would have wished for someone to offer her a new life, someone I knew and respected, and someone who would treat her as my brother had treated her. I think Lady Dustin is very lucky to have Marcus as her savior."

"Savior is a strong word, Philip," Marcus replied softly.

David's hard facade was faltering and Philip faced him. "I suppose what I am saying, David, is I know how you feel. I lost my older brother, too. Had Val lived, I know he would have wanted her to be happy. Allow Dustin her happiness, lad. If it is with Marcus, then be happy for them both."

David's handsome face was tired and uncertain. Dustin's head was bowed, trying so hard to fight the tears that were nonetheless spilling onto her lap. Time ticked by as David mulled over his uncle's words.

Finally, David shook his head. "Uncle Philip, Chris loved her more than anything on this earth. I just cannot believe that he would want her to leave Lioncross and take Christin away." His eyes flicked up to Marcus. "I cannot in good conscience, let her go with Marcus. I just cannot."

Oddly enough, the tension had drained out of the room. Now there were only men trying to understand the position of each other. But Marcus wasn't leaving without Dustin, David or no David.

"She is going with me," he told David firmly. "If I have to cut through you and every other man here, she is going with me back to Somerhill and I am going to marry her. I do not care if you approve or not, David. It is not up to you."

David had been very calm until Marcus' reply, which sounded suspiciously like a challenge. He stiffened in his chair.

"I am not surprised," he snarled. "Hell, you tried everything in your power to take her away from my brother. Why shouldn't I think you would kill me to get to her?"

He bolted to his feet and Marcus bolted to his feet. Marcus' knights followed suit, as did Christopher's until Richard was shouting above the clanging of armor and the unsheathing of swords to restore order.

"Sit down, all of you," he roared. "Damnation, sit down or I shall have you all thrown in irons. David, sheath that damn sword or I shall shove it down your throat."

The king was furious. Marcus stepped back from the table angrily, his chair toppling over as he paced aimlessly toward the hearth. The other knights obeyed their king, taking their seats again, except for David and Philip. Philip was trying to calm his nephew down, coaxing him back to his seat.

Dustin couldn't take it anymore. She was already emotionally brittle and spiritually spent and her breaking point was low. She stood up, marching over to her brother-in-law.

"You do not own me, David," she snapped. "I must decide what is best for me, not you. I hate it that you are constantly fighting with Marcus. You used to be the best of friends before I came along, I know. Edward told me that you and Chris and Marcus were inseparable. And now you are ready to kill him. I cannot take your hostilities any longer."

"I am thinking of your best interests, Dustin," David said. "You are still grieving, for God's sake. I do not want you making a quick decision you will regret."

"But it is *my* decision," she fired back. "Let me make my own mistakes, David. Let me live my own life, which happens to be a life without your brother." She spun around, gesturing to the heavens of the great hall. "This place is my home, my wonderful home until a year ago. Ever since then, I have seen the pinnacles of joy and the very depths of grief here. My family has lived here for five generations, but do you know that when I look at the dining table, I only see Christopher sitting at the head? And 'tis only him I see mounting the stairs to our bedchamber, or stoking the hearth because I am cold. David, the man lived here slightly over a year, yet he left his mark as indelibly as if he had lived here one hundred years. With every turn, with every flash of light, I see only him and I am haunted."

She suddenly realized she was giving this speech for every man present, opening up her soul as she hadn't opened it up for anyone. The fire crackled in the hearth as she took a cleansing breath and faced off against David and Marcus.

"I do not want to leave Lioncross," she said softly. "This is my home; it is Chris' home. But sometimes I feel as if I will go mad if I stay here a moment longer. Marcus is well aware of my feelings on the matter, and I accept his offer to go with him to his keep because I believe I need the change. I shall return to Lioncross, someday, mayhap as Lady de Lohr, mayhap as Lady Burton. But it is my decision to make and my life to live. I have to do what is best for Christin and best for me."

David was clearly torn after her speech. "But why with him, Dustin?"

"Why not?" she asked him deliberately. "Why on earth not, David? Surely you do not want me; you have Emilie. And I will not go with your uncle to Lohrham Forest for the man doesn't need me banging about there. Why is it so hard for you to let me leave this place? You are making a difficult decision even harder."

David was slipping. "Because…oh, hell, Dustin, I do not know. I cannot think on it anymore; I suppose I cannot fight you anymore. If you truly want to go, the truth is that I cannot stop you."

"Good," Dustin breathed, satisfied. Still, she could see the pain in his expression and it saddened her. "I appreciate your concern as my husband's brother, but you must let me do what I think is best."

David gave up in that moment. There was nothing more to fight and nothing more to say. He stared at Dustin for several long moments before walking to her, pulling her head against his lips and kissing her hair.

"Be happy, then," he whispered. "He would want you to be."

He left the hall, ascending the stairs wearily to his bedchamber. Dustin visibly relaxed, her gaze moving to Marcus where he stood, handsome and strong, by the hearth. He smiled weakly at her but she did not respond, instead, facing against Richard.

"If you will excuse me, sire, I shall be retiring," she said quietly.

Richard nodded faintly and Dustin curtsied, quitting the hall and going the same path of David to the second story. Only when she was in her bedchamber, the chamber she had shared with Christopher, did she let her guard down. She lay heavily on his side of the bed, on the linens she hadn't changed since he had left because she could still smell his musk in the sheets. Inhaling deeply, she again smelled the faint scent and it brought tears to her eyes.

With a ragged sigh, she lay her cheek on his pillow and let her mind wander to happier days.

ᘛ

MARCUS COULD NOT sleep that night. He found himself wandering the halls of Lioncross, feeling Christopher's presence like a ghost, following him everywhere. He paced the second floor completely, made his rounds on the third floor, and then found himself down on the ground floor, not even aware of his wandering because he was so deeply lost in thought.

Was he pushing Dustin to do something she did not want to do? Had he taken advantage of her weakened state for his own selfish reasons? Clearly, he was, but he was afraid if he did not take her now, then she would never go with him. She was an heiress and valuable to Richard as a commodity, and Marcus was deathly afraid if he did not marry her now, then Richard would find a husband for her to somehow strengthen his empire. He had to press his advantage now, while there was time. If he allowed her time to grieve and recover, then his chance might be past. And he could not stand the thought of Dustin in someone else's arms.

He found himself in the abbey. Curious for the first time of his surroundings, he glanced about the dark, forbidden place and wondered how in the hell he got there. As he turned to remount the stairs, there was an unmistakable ring of a sword as it was being unsheathed from its scabbard.

Marcus stiffened, not particularly surprised to see David looming several steps above him, a sword in his hand.

"I am unarmed, David," Marcus said quietly.

A sword suddenly landed at his feet with a clatter. "Not anymore," David replied. "Here and now, Marcus. We will end this here and now."

Marcus did not move for his sword just yet. "Why do you hate me so much, David? We used to be best friends. Is it truly Dustin, or is it something else I have done?"

"You changed, Marcus," David said in a low voice. "You coveted my brother's wife. You shamelessly pursued her and embarrassed yourself and the de Lohr name. You showed no restraint or control whatsoever. It was as if you would stop at nothing to have her, and even though Christopher overlooked it, I was deeply offended. And now, I am going to do what my brother should have done all along."

"Kill me?" Marcus said with raised brows. "Your devotion to your brother is touching, David, but do you truly think my 'pursuit', as you call it, is worth taking my life?"

David lowered his sword a bit, taking a step. "Then let's see it from a different angle, Marcus," he said. "Let's assume that it were you who married Dustin, and Christopher who was so madly consumed with her that he was not shy about his feelings in the least. Let's say that he kissed Dustin, your wife, and tried to hide the fact. Let's say that he was with her always, never actually voicing his feelings, but not having to because they were written all over his face. Let's say that he was so relentless that everyone began spreading rumors, but he did not care. He looked like a fool, you looked like a fool, and Dustin looked to be nothing short of a whore. Now, how would you react to such a thing?"

Marcus' face was dark. "I was never like that, David. I admitted my infatuation to Chris and banked it well. I was never shameless in my pursuit of Dustin until now."

David smiled thinly. "It hurts, doesn't it? If the situation were reversed, then you most certainly would not have been as forgiving as Christopher was. He overlooked everything you did because of his love and respect for you, and it made him look like an idiot. Now ask me again why do I want to see justice served?"

Marcus inhaled deeply and looked to the ground where his sword was. Slowly, he reached down and picked it up.

"You won't kill me, you know," he said quietly. "I shall disembowel you first."

David shrugged faintly. "Tell me one thing, Marcus," he muttered. "Did you bed her?"

Marcus lifted his sword, examining the blade in the faint torchlight. "Does it matter?"

"Not really. Whether or not you did it physically, you have already done it in your mind a thousand times," David replied. "I was simply curious to know if you indeed followed through with your desires and if she responded."

Marcus was focused on the ridge of his blade. "It is none of your business."

A bolt of fury shot though David at the evasive answer. "Then you just answered my question."

Marcus glanced up at him, cocking a black eyebrow. "I did. I told you it was none of your affair, which it isn't. What goes on between Dustin and me isn't anyone's concern."

David's nostrils flared angrily. "Then I was right all along; she was your whore. And Christin? She's your daughter."

Marcus kept his calm. "Dustin was never, ever my whore, David. And Christin is Chris' daughter."

"Did you bed her?" David roared, enunciating each word and they reverberated off the thick abbey walls.

Marcus raised his sword slowly, moving it into a defensive position. "I did."

David was actually stumped at the short, precise answer. He had expected more denials, more maneuvering. But his shock was gone in a second, his fury returning tenfold.

"You bloody bastard," he growled. "You filthy son of a bitch. How could you do that to Chris? He trusted you, goddammit. *He trusted you!*"

Marcus could see David's pain more than his anger, and his own pain surfaced as well. "It wasn't that simple, David. When it happened… Dustin did not even know it was me. She thought I was Chris and she took me into her bed," his voice was a whisper. "I am a weak man, David, not at all as perfect as our Defender was. I could have stopped it, but I did not. I wanted to. Aye, I freely admit it to you. I took advantage of the situation. Never blame Dustin, David, for she thought I was her husband. Are you satisfied now that you have a confession? I have simply given you more reason to kill me."

David raised his sword, fighting back his considerable anger. If he lashed out and tired himself at the beginning, then Marcus would show no mercy and finish him off in his fatigue.

"I do not blame her," he said. "I have never blamed her. She's young and impressionable. But I fully blame you."

"As you should." Marcus gripped his sword with two hands on the hilt, preparing for the first strike. "You may try to kill me if you think you must, David. I am ready."

David did not reply. Instead, he came hurtling down from the stairs and met Marcus with the force of his fury. Metal met on metal, screaming at the pressure and sparks flew into the damp air of the abbey.

Marcus was fully prepared for the onslaught, and for David's fury. A whole year of anger and resentment and jealousy was releasing itself. David was faster than any man alive with a sword, but he could be reckless. Marcus, however, was far more controlled and more powerful than his opponent. It was dark in the abbey, working to neither man's advantage as they plowed their way through pieces of old furniture and bounced off the walls.

David tripped at one point and staggered against the stone wall, narrowly averting being decapitated by Marcus as the big man descended on him with all of his might. The clang of broadsword against broadsword echoed loudly and roused a few servants, who instantly panicked at the fight in the abbey and Richard was awakened from a deep sleep.

Angry as hell, the King of England grabbed his serrated broadsword and marched for the bowels of the abbey. He had no doubt as to who was doing the fighting.

CB

MARCUS AND DAVID stood before Richard in the grand hall, a few of the king's officials surrounding the tired monarch as he glared back at his disobedient vassals. He was so damn tired all he wanted to do was sleep, but instead, found himself breaking up a serious fight. Had he not intervened when he did, David de Lohr would now be preparing for his burial.

"I know why you were fighting," Richard said in a low voice. "I need no explanation. And from what I am told, it was a long time in coming. But I will tell you this now; I will hear of no more fighting between you two. There is no one in this world I am at peace with, including my brother, and I shall not stand for any goddamn fighting within my own ranks. I should like there to be just one minute measure of stability in my life right now, gentle knights. I should like it to start with my loyal warriors, or I swear I shall take Lady Dustin with me and keep her at Windsor if you two cannot make peace with each other. Is that understood?"

Marcus and David nodded simultaneously. "Aye, sire."

"Good," Richard exclaimed, eyeing them both critically. "I will ask one thing, however; who started it?"

David piped up before Marcus could speak. "I did, sire. I sought Marcus out."

"David, you know better than to cause trouble." Richard jabbed his finger at him. "Good Lord, you are just like your father. Hotheaded and aggressive. But I will tell you now, no more of it. Christopher, thank God, controlled himself better than most men and you should have learned from him. And Marcus; you are David's superior officer. You should not have responded to his challenge."

"I was given little choice, sire," Marcus responded. "It was either defend myself or die."

Richard shot David a withering look. "Get a hold of yourself, Sir Knight. Come to grips with your grief and the future will work itself out. It does not need your interference."

David lowered his gaze, his jaw ticking. Marcus didn't dare look at him, both of them feeling like naughty children being caught with their hand in the candy jar. Marcus didn't hate David, but he hated the animosity he was creating. If David would only surmount his guilt and anger, he was sure his feelings would calm.

"Back to Canterbury with you on the morrow, de Lohr," Richard said finally. "Go back and marry your Emilie and I will hear no more about you and Marcus Burton."

"Aye, sire," David said softly, bowing as he quit the hall.

Marcus passed a glance at Richard when David was gone, waiting to be dismissed also but surprised to find Richard staring at him.

"Do you love her, Marcus?" he asked softly. "Is she worth dying for?"

"Without a doubt, sire," Marcus replied. "I love her with all my heart."

Richard held his gaze a moment longer before shaking his head in resignation. "What is it about this woman? The two greatest knights who have ever lived love her, and I am frankly astonished. Why, Marcus? What makes her different?"

Marcus shrugged. "I can only tell you why I love her, sire, not why Christopher did. She is beautiful, innocent, compassionate, and spirited. She is everything a woman should be."

Richard absorbed the answer, lowering his gaze to the tabletop. The seconds ticked away with deafening silence, but Marcus knew the conversation wasn't over yet.

"Marcus, with Christopher gone, I am in need of a champion. Will you do this for your king?"

Marcus stared back at Richard a moment, unsure of what he had just heard. But the realization of it hit him and his eyes widened a bit. "You want me as your champion?" he repeated.

"You are the best knight in the realm; even David has acknowledged that," Richard said. "I need you, I need your strength. Will you do this?"

Marcus did not know what to say. Being Richard's champion was his lifelong ambition. God, how long had he yearned to hear that question asked of him? A lifetime, a bloody lifetime, but he found now he could not positively respond to it. Being Richard's champion would mean living in London, away from his keep. Aye, Dustin would be with him, but he wouldn't want her to bear the scandal that would surely fall upon her shoulders. All who would see her would think that she certainly did not wait long to fall into Marcus' arms after the death of her husband. Nay, he could not allow Dustin to go through that.

Being Richard's champion would mean fighting his battles at his side, as Christopher had done. And Christopher was now dead. Marcus knew Dustin could not bear to be a widow twice in one lifetime, and he decided at that moment that living his life with her within the safety of his compound was greater glory than living by the sword as Richard's right hand. He could hardly believe he was about to turn his king down.

"Were you told that I agreed to champion John once?" Marcus asked quietly.

Richard nodded. "For which you received Somerhill. A clever ploy to gain lands, Marcus. I will admit it and it's understandable. Yet I also know that you met with an unfortunate accident and were unable to champion my brother, but still you managed to retain your baronetcy."

Marcus lifted his eyebrows. "I oft wondered how you would react to such knowledge, sire," Marcus replied. "Even as I agreed to it, I deemed it a most treasonous act. I am grateful that you do not see it as such."

"We all do what we must in this life to gain our own ends," Richard said. "I am certainly guilty enough of that. But tell me now; will you be my champion?"

"Sire, as honored as I am that you have asked this of me, I am saddened that I must refuse," he replied steadily. "My single greatest desire in life is to return home with Lady Dustin and her child, and live my life fully."

Richard gazed at him a moment before giving an ironic chuckle. "This woman intrigues me that she would cause you to give up everything you have worked for in life. You are a soldier, Marcus, the very best. You would give this all up for her?"

"Aye, I would." Marcus met his eyes clearly.

Richard sighed heavily, scratching at his unkempt hair. "Amazing. Well, then, I suppose there is nothing more to say. Are you sure of this, Marcus?"

"Verily, sire," Marcus replied.

The king scratched his head again and stood up, moving stiffly around the table and toward Marcus. Marcus met his monarch tall and straight and proud.

"Mayhap if Lady Dustin is so great, I should make her my queen," Richard joked. "Or, better yet, send her to Philip Augustus and bring down the entire French Empire."

Marcus smiled. "You'd have to fight me for her, sire."

Richard guffawed loudly and slapped Marcus on the shoulder. "Will you at least answer the call to battle if I send for you, Marcus? Can I expect your assistance?"

"Of course, sire," Marcus replied. "I shall always bear a sword for you when asked."

"But you will not champion me," Richard prodded gently.

"Nay, my lord," Marcus replied regretfully.

Richard shrugged and slapped Marcus again. "I could but try once more. Well, it would seem I am forced to choose a champion again. Who would be worthy of me, I wonder?"

Marcus gave his opinion as the two of them wandered from the hall.

CHAPTER FORTY-FIVE

CHRISTOPHER'S STRENGTH WAS slow in returning. It was a full week before he was able to sit up unassisted, greatly setting back his timetable for returning home. Marianne and Lizabetha tended him every day, making sure he was fed and comfortable, and he was deeply indebted to the both of them. He knew the way to reward Marianne would be to regain Rob's keep, but he was at a loss how to thank Lizabetha. The girl was far gone in love with him and he would do nothing to encourage her.

During the fourth week after his injury, he got it in his mind to stand. He knew he must stand if he was ever going to completely recover, and he pestered Marianne until she covered her ears. Finally, to keep him quiet, she promised to ask Rob and Jonathan to help him when they returned from the hunt. Satisfied, Christopher let the matter rest.

But it did not last long. Rob and Jonathan were gone nearly the entire day and by late afternoon Christopher was antsy. Lizabetha sat with him, quietly doing her needlework in the corner when Christopher decided he was going to stand that very minute. Panicked, Lizabetha pleaded with him not to try it, but he ignored her. Finally, in desperation, she agreed to help him. He would do it with or without her help, and she knew he could not do it alone. And besides, she did so want to be near him.

But it was a long, slow process. First, he sat up. When he felt strong enough, he braced himself against a stool and pushed himself onto his knees. Kneeling, he was as tall as Lizabetha and her eyes widened when she realized for the first time what a giant he was. After several long minutes of panting and resting before the next move, he flashed Lizabetha a triumphant smile and put one foot in front of him, so he was kneeling on one knee as if in a bow. Lizabetha wrung her hands nervously. She was excited and terrified at the same time.

Laboriously, Christopher tried to push himself up and Lizabetha instinctively grabbed hold of him. As soon as he tried to put his weight on his legs, he realized that his idea was not a good one and toppled back onto his pallet, taking Lizabetha with him. She fell on top of him, her light brown hair splaying and emitting a yelp of surprise. Christopher was concerned that he had hurt her somehow with the fall and started to voice his concerns when suddenly, she began kissing his face.

Light, quick, hot kisses peppered his left cheek and part of his chin before he grabbed hold of her and pulled her back. He opened his mouth to order her to cease, but her fingers went over his mouth and sweet, virginal Lizabetha turned into a squirming body of lust.

"I know it is wrong, my love, I know," she whispered breathlessly. "But I have loved you from the very moment I lay eyes on you and I simply cannot help myself any longer. Please do not deny me, my sweet, powerful knight."

"Lizabetha!" Christopher snapped as non-forcefully as he could, holding her at arm's length. "My lady, you are correct when you say that your actions are wrong. As flattered as I am, I am afraid that I have a wife and babe, whom I adore. I cannot and will not carry on a liaison with you, child."

"I am not a child!" Lizabetha insisted hotly. "I am a woman of flesh and blood, and I have never loved anything more in my life as I love you. I want to give myself to you fully, my love, my sweet, and I ask nothing in return. No one will know."

He was at a distinct disadvantage. He was not tempted in the least, but she was pressing herself mightily and he knew from experience that a scorned female was a bitter, spiteful creature. He owed these people his very life and he was sorely pressed to reject her.

"Lizabetha, listen to me," he said calmly, gently pushing her off of him. "I am flattered, sweetheart, really, but I will not take advantage of you. Moreover, I love my wife and would do nothing to jeopardize our marriage. Someday when you have a husband of your own, you will understand. Be a good girl, now, and get me a drink of water. Please?"

Lizabetha pouted darkly. "Forget the bloody water," she said dramatically. "I want you to take me, my lord, do away with this troublesome virginity. Take me or I shall surely kill myself."

"Not before I kill you first!" Marianne ducked into the hut and Lizabetha screeched, pleading for her hide to be spared. "Leave us now, niece. I shall deal with you later."

Lizabetha fled in terror and Marianne turned back to Christopher, her face flushed with dismay.

"My lord, I humbly beg your forgiveness for Lizabetha's rashness," she said, deeply ashamed. "She is young, sire, and…."

Christopher waved her off. "Say no more, my lady. I understand completely, although I must say I was a bit worried there for a moment," he admitted. "You came in the nick of time; otherwise it might have been her word against mine."

Marianne shook her head. "We all know Lizabetha has been smitten with you. We wouldn't have believed anything she said if she had accused you of being less than chivalrous. I apologize for her again, my lord."

He smiled at the woman's embarrassment. "No need, my lady. No harm done, except to her feelings, mayhap."

"The pain she is feeling in her heart now will be nothing compared to the pain of her blistered backside," Marianne remarked. "A willful one, she is."

Christopher thought of his wife and his smile went soft. "I have one of those on my hands, also. Stubborn, too."

Marianne saw his expression and was touched by the love she saw in it. "Your wife? Surely not. A man of your station would have the most obedient, perfect wife in the realm."

He laughed loudly. "My wife is the most willful, disobedient, frustrating woman God ever saw fit to create. I cannot count the times when we have fought over the simplest of things or the number of times I have wanted to blister her backside. Actually, I did on one occasion."

Marianne looked dismayed, but he could see she was fighting off the giggles. "Say not so, my lord. Did you not know of her nature before you married her?"

"Nay." Christopher relaxed on his pillow, thinking back. "I did not know her at all, although I knew her father well. Richard betrothed us and I had no choice but to marry her."

Marianne could hear the adoration in his voice and she smiled. "How fortunate you married someone you could care for, my lord. These days, 'tis truly a miracle to be fond of your mate."

Christopher eyed her. "Fond of her? Christ, I love the woman. Why do you think I am so desperate to return to her?"

Marianne touched his arm gently. "You shall, my lord. I promise you shall. Tell me of this woman, your wife. I am sure she is most beautiful."

He closed his eyes, picturing Dustin. "She has blond hair that falls to her knees, silken, like spun gold. Her face is the most beautiful on this earth, and her eyes are the color of storm clouds. It's an amazing shade of gray, which our daughter has inherited."

"What's her name?" Marianne asked.

"Dustin," he said reverently. "Lady Dustin Mary Catherine de Lohr."

"Dustin? An unusual name," Marianne remarked "And your daughter? What is her name?"

"Christin," he replied. "What a devil she is. Smart, too."

Marianne was truly touched by this massive knight's devotion to his family; he obviously adored them. Strange, she usually pictured knights as God-fearing warriors, bound only to themselves and to the king. But this man, Richard's champion no less, had a definite love for something other than himself. The romantic, womanly part of her was fulfilled somehow and she envied Lady Dustin his devotion. Not that Rob was any less devoted to her and to their son, but he did not speak of them as Sir Christopher spoke of his family.

Later on that night, Lizabetha returned with his supper and he suppressed a grin; she refused to sit down or even look him in the eye as she tended him. *Poor thing,* he thought. Rejected and spanked all in one day. When he was finished with the rabbit stew, he thanked her politely and she nodded, backing out of the hut with as much dignity as she could muster. He waited until he was sure she was out of earshot before falling into a fit of giggles.

Rob and Jonathan descended on him after supper. They seemed very energetic and rousing, and he wondered why.

"I hear you wish to stand, my lord," Jonathan said loudly. "God be praised. The sooner you are out of here, the sooner I get my bed back."

Christopher raised his brows in agreement. "True enough, sirrah. But I will need both of your help to stand, I am afraid."

Rob held out his hand to Christopher and he looked at it hesitantly. "Now?"

"Now," said Rob. "No better time to start anything than now."

With a shrug, Christopher allowed both men to take him by the arms and slowly, gently, pull him to stand. But Christopher was hunched over like a troll, breathing heavily and his knees wobbled like a newborn foal.

"This is not such a good thing," he rasped. "I think I am going to be ill."

"Nay, you are not," Jonathan said firmly. "Just rest a moment; the sickness will pass."

Christopher took several deep breaths and his stomach eventually calmed, but his torso was as sore as if he had been working it day and night for months on end. Shaking and gray, he gripped Rob and Jonathan tightly.

"All right, then," he whispered. "Let's see how tall I can stand."

By sheer force of willpower, he stood as straight and tall as if he had never been injured. Both men were astonished to see just how tall he truly was.

"A damnable giant, you are," Jonathan boomed. "And I thought I was tall."

Christopher laughed a soft, weak snort. "I feel as if I am on top of a tree, looking down. I'd gotten used to the view from the ground up."

"Can you take a step?" Jonathan persisted.

"One thing at a time, Jon," Rob admonished him. "The man is standing up for the first time in a month; give him time to adjust."

Christopher cuffed Jonathan gently on the side of the head. "I promise I shall be out of your bed as soon as I can," he said. "But right now, I think I would like to sit down again."

CHAPTER FORTY-SIX

MARCUS AND DUSTIN left just after dawn. Bundled up against the cold, she rode Hercules out of the massive gates, tears stinging her eyes. David had left without a word before she had even awoken and her heart was saddened. She suspected that Marcus knew the reason, but she would ask him later. Now, as she left her home, was not the time.

Alexander, George, Caesar and Christin were huddled in a large, protected wagon, watched over by the wet nurse who would be doubling as Christin's nursemaid. The woman was big and shy, and wet-nursing was her vocation since her youngest child was twelve. Dustin had found it hard to believe that the woman would like breastfeeding so much that she would continue it for years on end. But she loved Christin and Marcus felt comfortable with the woman, so he allowed her to accompany them to Somerhill.

Marcus had remarked that the wagon looked more like a zoo than a nursery, for the animals outnumbered the people, but Dustin insisted on taking all of her animals. Especially Caesar; he was old but she would not leave him behind as she had when she had left for London. She wanted her oldest friend with her, and she needed him now more than ever.

Richard saw them off, begging the privilege of staying on at Lioncross a few more days to rest before returning to Windsor and the troubles that awaited him there. Dustin was happy to comply, and Edward was the perfect host. They had spoken privately earlier about her future plans and Edward assured her that Lioncross would still be standing should she ever choose to return. It was a bittersweet goodbye between them, for Edward seemed to be the last of Christopher's knights who hadn't been affected by everything that had happened.

As she left the gates, Harold came racing up beside her, barking furiously. Dustin almost went to pieces. Harold had not accompanied Christopher on his fateful mission because the dog had been ill after killing and eating a whole chicken. Christopher had been sorry not to have his mascot and as Dustin looked down at the dog, all she could think about was her husband falling and dying in battle without his dog there to comfort him. Hot tears fell on the breast of her cloak as she tried to reason with Harold to stay behind. He belonged at Lioncross, if for no other reason than to protect Christopher's phantom. She truly believed the dog belonged there.

Harold, remarkably, stopped at the gate and sat down, still barking and wagging his tail as Dustin continued on. She watched the little mongrel for a few moments, still waiting for him to follow and pleased when he did not. Mayhap all of his barking was not asking to accompany her; it was asking her to stay. Dashing away the remainder of her tears, she turned forward and found Marcus smiling at her. She gave him a small smile and lowered her gaze.

Her last glimpse of Lioncross as they crested the hill and turned north was amazingly clear and bright. The sun was out and the snow had melted, cleaning everything and making the world fresh and new. Her heart lurched with longing and grief, but Marcus reached out and touched her arm, murmuring encouraging words. With a resigned sigh, Dustin turned her back on Christopher's home. She never looked back.

THEY STOPPED FOR the night and made camp. Marcus and Sir Thomas Dudley, or "Dud" from their London days, rigged up an excellent tent using the bed of the wagon for a bed. Christin was asleep next to the wet nurse as soon as Dustin lay her down. Marcus and Dustin then shared a quiet supper later that evening as his men rigged several tarpaulins to keep the moisture away through the night. Dustin wondered if Marcus expected her to sleep with him.

She was not surprised to learn that he did expect them to sleep together, giving her a myriad of sound reasons as to why she should not sleep alone. Dustin begged off politely, saying she would rather sleep in the wagon with her daughter. She could see that Marcus was disappointed, but he graciously backed off and made sure she was given the very best and thickest blankets. The knights retired for the night, as did the men-at-arms, and the camp quieted rapidly, leaving Dustin and Marcus alone by the camp fire.

"Well, I am rather tired," she said softly. "I would retire now. Goodnight, Marcus."

"Dustin," he said quickly, pausing almost uncomfortably when she turned around and looked at him. "Are you quite sure… I mean, the tent would be less crowded and…."

Dustin smiled faintly, shaking her head. "Thank you, but no," she replied, seeing that he truly was disappointed. She understood his feelings, but he had to understand hers. "Marcus, I am simply not ready for you. Your presence is comforting and I am grateful for your generosity toward Christin and myself, but I am simply not ready for your affections."

He kicked at the ground a moment, embarrassed at his eagerness. "Is it that obvious? I am sorry, Dustin. I am not trying to push you."

She walked over to him, putting her hand on his arm. "I know you are not, but you are nonetheless. Give me time, Marcus. I need time to heal."

He took her hand and put her palm to his scratchy cheek, his cobalt-blue eyes soft. "I know you do. And I want to help you, if I can. Dustin, I do so want to be close to you. I have always wanted to be close to you."

She raised an eyebrow and smiled. "You are pushing again."

He pretended to slap himself in the head. "Old habits die hard. Well, let's get you to bed."

He took her arm and started to lead her toward the wagon when she suddenly stopped. She reconsidered sleeping with him for a split second and the thought of massive, strong arms around her and a warm body to snuggle against was very inviting. Lord, it had been so long since Christopher had held her and there was a huge void inside her wishing to be held and comforted. Marcus understood she was not giving him permission to ravage her, and she was confident he would not. But lying in his arms, she might even be strong enough to pretend it was Christopher; just for a moment.

"I think you are right," she turned her face up to him.

"About what?"

"Sleeping under your protection. Plus, the wagon is crowded. I will probably not sleep at all with the baby snoring and the dogs in my face."

He looked surprised. "Are you sure?"

She nodded slowly. "Aye, I am."

Snuggled against Marcus was a thoroughly cleansing experience, cleansing in that it helped dash some of her doubts and fears about her future. She could close her eyes and feel his strength and it helped her a great deal. But as she lay in his arms, she was equally sure of one thing; she could never love Marcus Burton. She could be fond of him, bear his children even, but she could never love him. Her love would always and forever be Christopher's.

☙

THE REST OF the trip was uneventful, even if the weather was miserable. After the first night they slept in each other's arms, Dustin found that her wall was up with him. Sleeping in his arms was well enough, but he wanted more and she wasn't willing to give more. So Dustin kept her wall up between her and Marcus, and the more her mind cleared, the more she wondered just what in the hell she was doing with him.

The plan to go to Somerhill had seemed so positive from the beginning and she was sure that a change of scenery would be the best thing for her, but as her wits returned, she missed Lioncross terribly. With each mile passed, she regretted her decision more and more and was forced to admit that David and Edward may have been right. She had acted in haste, wanting some sort of relief from her grief but not knowing what, and she took the first opportunity that arose.

But she would not return home, at least not immediately. *Give Marcus a chance*, she told herself. *Mayhap he can at least bring a ray of joy back into your life if you will only let him.* With the shock of Christopher's death wearing off, and the return of normalcy to her character in sight, Dustin realized that the rest of her life was to be a very gray, bitter thing. The only person who could possibly give her any happiness was Marcus Burton.

The very last day before they reached Somerhill dawned gray and foggy and heavy with mist. Christin had been up all night long cutting a new tooth and Dustin was exhausted, even though Marcus had spoiled her for a few hours. Her fatigue, coupled with the constant travel, had upset her stomach terribly.

She coaxed a few bites of breakfast down, hoping to calm her jitters, but everything she ate came right back up again and she felt worse than before. Marcus was gravely concerned for her and insisted they rest for the day, but she insisted more firmly that they continue. Two hundred men-at-arms and six knights were eager to return to their keep, not to mention Dustin and Marcus and the rest of them. She would not halt progress due to her nervous stomach.

Pale and sick, Marcus loaded her up onto Hercules with great hesitation. He wanted her to ride with him, but she waved him off. She would ride to Somerhill alone.

She was truly miserable. Hercules had a smooth gate, but the very rocking motion worsened her condition. The constant taste of bile coated her mouth and all she wanted to do was lay down and sleep for a week. In fact, her breasts ached terribly with each jostle of the horse and her stomach wasn't only upset, it was sore as well. She could only remember feeling this badly once in her life, when she was first pregnant with Christin, and....

Dustin forgot all about her churning stomach and her shaking hands. In that instant, all of the clues came into focus and she realized with an explosion of jubilation that she was pregnant again.

Her hand flew to her abdomen, trying to remember when she had her last menses and she could not. In fact, she hadn't had her cycle since she conceived Christin and she was nearly wild with excitement. *Thank you, God!* She cried silently, over and over again, singing it in her heart and soul until tears of joy filled her eyes and rolled down her cheeks. She dashed them away, wanting her moment of happiness to be a private one for now. If Marcus saw her tears, he would demand to know why she was crying and she did not feel like sharing her secret with him yet. This was her personal moment to share with her deceased husband, wherever he might be. As much as Christopher had loved Christin, she knew he would be absolutely ecstatic with another child. Another legacy.

Dustin blinked back more happy tears as she touched her stomach gently. She knew without a doubt 'twas a son she carried beneath her heart.

SOMERHILL WAS A lovely place. As lovely as Lioncross was. Somerhill was magnificent and well kept, and Dustin knew Marcus was responsible for the condition of the keep. It sat on a rise overlooking the river and protected a fairly large village. Even as they rode into town, peasants turned out to greet Marcus, and Dustin was impressed with the respect the man had earned from his people. Christopher hadn't had the time to mingle much with his vassals since the majority of his time had been spent away from Lioncross, but Marcus had had ample time to get to know his people considering he had been holed up in the structure for nearly a year.

Women handed Dustin several bouquets of new spring flowers and she buried her nose in them, inhaling their heady fragrance. The world around them was thawing in the early spring and Dustin's mood was lightened. A new baby, a new world, and a new keep that loomed before her against the late afternoon sky.

"Marcus, it is beautiful," she remarked.

He reined his white steed close to her. "Do you like it? I am rather proud of it. It's not as massive as Lioncross, but I like it."

"Oh, no, it is much taller than Lioncross," Dustin said, indicating the two massive towers that stretched heavenward. "We do not have any towers."

The gates were already open and Marcus' men were greeting him home with shouts and waves. The party entered into the outer bailey, for there were two, and Marcus' knights began disbanding the army and ordered the wagons unloaded. The bailey quickly turned into a rushing mass of people, all moving about their assigned tasks. Dustin simply sat high atop Hercules, absorbing it all.

Marcus was then beside her, holding up his arms to help her. With a smile that she truly felt this time, she slid into his arms and he lowered her gently to the ground.

"I hope you shall be happy here, honey," he said softly. "I have come to love it a great deal."

She patted his arm reassuringly. "I can see why. It is a beautiful place." She only remarked on the latter of his statement.

Marcus did not let her go for a moment and Dustin felt a distinct pull between them; those cobalt-blue eyes were captivating. She remembered the very first time she ever looked into them, she had felt the exact same pull. She knew it would be very easy to love Marcus, but she could not let herself. She only loved Christopher, and the thought of even considering loving Marcus brought floods of guilt.

Clearing her throat, she stepped back as Sir Stephen Marion brought Christin over to them. Her daughter was wrapped in enough wool and fur to keep several peasant children cozy and looked as round as a fat, ripe melon. Her sweet cherub face was the only thing visible, but the wrappings waved wildly when she saw her mother.

"Hello, sweet pea." Marcus touched the babe's cheek as she was placed in her mother's arms. "Jesus, Dustin, unwrap that babe or she will suffocate."

Dustin grinned, indeed taking off the outer layer of clothing. "The wet nurse is fearful she will catch cold this far north."

Marcus raised an eyebrow. "Bundled like that, she is going to sweat to death first." He turned to Sir Stephen. "Tell Dud we have gone inside and help him with Lady Dustin's belongings. They will go in the chamber next to mine. And ask Iris which room the baby and the wet nurse are to be housed."

Stephen, a very handsome blond man that reminded Dustin a good deal of David, saluted smartly and was gone.

"Who's Iris?" Dustin asked.

"My chatelaine," he replied. "But I am sure with you here, I will not be needing her services any longer."

"Marcus, keep the woman," Dustin insisted. "I am a terrible chatelaine."

He took her arm and turned her toward the inner bailey. "You are not. Lioncross is the best run keep I have ever seen."

"Thanks to Gowen and Edward," she told him. "Surely you saw that they were in charge, and not me."

He shrugged. "I assumed that was because you had been grief-stricken for so long that they had voluntarily taken over your duties."

Dustin shook her head. "Obviously, you know nothing about me," she said lightly. "In hindsight, I suppose I should blame my parents for not insisting that I learn things all young ladies should learn, but they let me do whatever I pleased. I hated dancing, sewing, managing a household, all the things that well-bred young women needed to learn. I did learn to do needlepoint and paint because my mother absolutely insisted. But most of the time, I ran with the peasant boys and learned to ride and hunt and fish. Do you know that I can build a boat, and raise a hut in a mere few hours? Certainly not things required by a chatelaine."

He grinned, noticing the looks from his men as he brought her into the inner bailey. They were looking at Dustin as if she were the goddess Aphrodite on his arm.

"So you can build?" he said. "Impressive. What else can you do?"

She warmed to the pleasant mood. "I can fight, but, of course, you already know that."

He raised a black eyebrow reprovingly. "I have no firsthand knowledge of it, but I have seen you. Were you any taller, I would take you into battle with me."

She laughed and his heart skipped a beat. It was so good to see her laugh.

"I would be your very best knight, too, and you know it." When he shrugged in agreement, she continued. "My father taught me to read and write, and I can do mathematics and debate philosophy. Father was proud of my accomplishments, even though they were not the usual accomplishments of noble ladies."

Marcus wriggled his eyebrows. "True enough, but you are not a usual noble lady," he replied as they mounted the low step that led into his keep. He stopped her there, focusing on her beautiful face. "Truly, Dustin, I want you to be happy here. I am well aware of your feelings and your fears, and I promise I shall do naught to antagonize you. But you know my feelings, too, and I am not usually a patient man. But I shall be with you, I promise."

He kissed her free hand sweetly and she felt her wall going down just a bit. His manner was gentle and she liked that.

"Thank you, Marcus," she said softly. "I appreciate everything you have done for Christin and myself, and in spite of what David and Edward think, I believe Christopher would approve."

Marcus nodded his head chivalrously in thanks just as a big, bosomy woman with a tall white bun on her head appeared at the door.

"Great Walls of Jericho!" she roared. "Is this your Lady Dustin, Marcus? Get her in here before she and that babe catch their death of chill."

Dustin looked at the woman with surprise as a fat hand shot out and hustled her inside. Marcus, with a quirky grin on his face, followed close on her heels.

In the warm, dim entryway, the woman put up a tremendous fuss over Christin, and Dustin wasn't sure if she should protect her child or hand her over. Obviously, this was Iris.

"You never said we were going to have a babe in the house," Iris scolded Marcus, then turned sweetly to Christin. "Oh, Marcus, she is beautiful. I cannot remember when there was a babe in the keep last. What is her name?"

"Christin," Dustin replied. "And she's cutting teeth, so beware."

"Teeth!" Iris said it as if it were the most wonderful thing on earth. "I shall give her a bone to chew on. That will take care of her teeth."

Dustin could not help grinning as she glanced at Marcus, and he returned her expression. Iris was holding out her hands expectantly.

"Give me the sweet little peapod and I shall take care of her," the old woman begged firmly. "You, my lady, look as if you could use a bath and some rest. Sara is upstairs filling a tub for you already."

Dustin looked uncertain; but Marcus smiled. "Thank you, Iris. My lady could indeed use the rest."

Reluctantly, Dustin handed Christin over to the woman and the housekeeper immediately began crooning and singing to the babe, her manner gentle as one has to be around infants. Marcus watched Dustin's face as Iris took Christin away.

"Do not look like that," he said softly. "She has six children of her own and is quite competent. She will see that Christin is bathed and fed."

"But I wanted to do it," Dustin lamented.

"And you shall, starting tomorrow," he told her firmly. "You need to relax and collect yourself. Christin is in good hands, I promise."

She gave him a doubtful raise of the eyebrows and he took her arm, leading her up a flight of stone stairs that clung to a massive wall and opened up onto the second floor. At the very end of the corridor, he took her into a spacious bedchamber with the biggest bed she had ever seen in the middle of it. Over near a great carved fireplace was a large copper tub, and the girl that was busying herself next to it stopped abruptly and curtsied.

"My lady, I am Sara," she said rather boldly. "Your bath is ready."

Dustin eyed the room before her gaze fell on the servant. She was about her own age with bright red hair and a long face. Marcus was focused on Dustin's beautiful face as she absorbed the room, the new sights and atmosphere. He fully realized he had both hands on her protectively, although Dustin wasn't even aware of it.

"I should get my men settled," he told her. "Will you be all right for a while?"

Dustin moved to undo her cloak. "Of course," she said. "Where did Iris take Christin?"

"Probably to show her off to the servants and then, I would imagine, she will settle her very close to your room." He could see she was lost without her daughter and he smiled, kissing her on the cheek. "She is fine. Do not worry so much."

"I am not," Dustin insisted with a shrug.

He laughed softly at her and quit the room, leaving her feeling strange and alone.

Sara quickly bustled over to Dustin and deftly helped her remove her things. But Dustin refused the girl's offer to help bathe her, preferring to do it alone. The only person she ever allowed to bathe her was Christopher, and baths in general were a sore memory. He had so loved to bathe her.

Alone in her new surroundings, Dustin slid into the great tub and washed her hair twice, soaping her skin until she was sure she had scrubbed herself raw. The tub was so big it would have been perfect for two people, and before she realized it, tears welled and fell, mingling with the warm water.

"Why, Christopher, why?" she whispered painfully. "Why did you leave me? You promised you would return."

Soft sobs filled the room, not unheard by young Sara in the alcove. She had slipped in through a servant's door to hang Dustin's surcoats to rid them of wrinkles and had heard the heartfelt plea like a stab to her romantic heart. Distressed, she silently exited the room and ran immediately to find her mother. Iris sought out Marcus in mere minutes.

There wasn't a person at Somerhill that did not know of Dustin's plight by dinner. Dustin showed up on Marcus' arm for dinner, dressed in an apricot-colored silk he had purchased for her. She looked pale and tired, but was polite as she was introduced to the various occupants of the keep and hearing the stories of those who had been at Somerhill some length.

Iris had been at Somerhill since she had been a young girl. The baron that had occupied it before Marcus had been the last of a long, distinguished line and when he passed away, he left no heirs and the property reverted to the throne. But Iris and two of the old man's knights had stayed on to run the keep before Marcus took it over, and he had kept them.

The knights that had come with the castle were older, seasoned men who had served King Richard's father, King Henry, and spoke favorably of the man. Sir Alan Armstrong and Sir Nels McCullogh each had younger wives, Lady Margaret and Lady Emma, respectively, and five young children between them. As for the other knights Marcus had brought with him, Sir Stephen, Dud, and Sir Dalton le Crughnan, they were a respectful bunch and she had appreciated their professional attitude toward her on the journey.

Dud had fought with Christopher on the quest and she found herself engaged in a pleasant conversation with him, listening to the exploits of her late husband with delight. At first, he had been very reluctant to speak of Christopher, but she had persisted and he obliged. Dud soon found himself telling Christopher's tales for the entire table and they hung on every word. Dustin likened it to the days at Lioncross with Christopher and his men seated around the meal table, listening to Anthony or Max tell tall and wonderful tales. Those times would always have a special place in her heart and she missed them terribly. The de Velt twins were gifted story actors and had the ability to entertain greatly, even though Dud did well on his own as he told of their exploits in Jerusalem, and had his audience enthralled.

All except Marcus. He had been there, and done it all, too. He found himself staring at Dustin's turned back as she listened to Dud and the slow fire of jealousy crept surely into his veins. How in the hell could he compete with a dead man? The way Dud was talking, Christopher was an immortal god of war, not the mere mortal man Marcus knew him personally to be. He knew winning Dustin over was going to be difficult, but if tales of Christopher bombarded her ears every night, he'd never have her attention. Aye, Marcus was jealous of a dead man.

Dustin enjoyed hearing Christopher's legend from Dud's point of view. She did not know why she wanted to hear talk of her husband when all she did was feel a stab of pain at the mere mention of his name, but suddenly she decided she wanted to hear Dud's tales. When he had finished one particularly long story, he immediately begged off from any more, and she had no idea it was because Marcus was giving him the evil eye over her head. Still, she was satisfied, and she finished the remainder of her bread with Christin sleeping in her arms. She hoped Dud would tell her daughter and unborn son of their father's great adventures.

Marcus slept in the chamber next to hers. There was an adjoining door which had made Dustin wary in the beginning, but she purposely left it unlocked to prove to Marcus that she trusted him. She did not think she'd be able to sleep in the great, strange bed, but the moment her head hit the pillow, she was asleep. Marcus, on the other hand, spent most of the night sitting in a chair staring at the adjoining door. Lord God, he wanted her so badly he could hardly stand it. To have her so close, yet untouchable, was cruel torture at the very least.

He slept in the final hour before dawn and then was up again as the sun cleared the eastern horizon.

The days were getting longer as spring bore down on the north, and Dustin grew more and more comfortable with her new surroundings. As lovely as the countryside was around Lioncross, she grew to love the gently rolling hills of the north and truly loved the view of the river from the turrets of the castle. Marcus would take her up there every evening at sunset and they would speak of trivial things as they watched the sky turn colors together, and it became an integral part of the process of healing and contributed toward becoming intricately acquainted with one another.

True to his word, he did not pressure her in the least. He let Dustin make her own timetable, as hard as it was for him, but was rewarded at the end of the second week when she took his hand for the first time without him touching her first. A small step, but one he lived on. To have Dustin's affection was all he strove for.

The people of his keep came to like Dustin a great deal, and Christin was the most popular person there. She was a crawling, sitting, gurgling bundle of joy and Marcus adored her as if she were his own flesh. Even as much as he loved the baby, he could not help wishing for a child of his own from Dustin. He wondered how long it would be before she agreed to marry him and admit him to her bed.

But he found the more time he spent with her alone, the more he wanted everything from her. At one time he would have been satisfied with her companionship and fondness, but he was greedy now and wanted more; he wanted her love. He wanted to see Dustin look at him the way she had looked at Christopher. He wanted her devotion, her adoration, everything.

But he would have to be patient, and that did not come easily to him. He hoped that time would prove to work in his favor.

CHAPTER FORTY-SEVEN

BY THE SIXTH week, Christopher was able to stand without assistance. But stand was all he could do; walking was painful and still and it took both Rob and Jonathan to help him. But he was driven to stand and walk alone, and almost exactly two months from the day of his injury, he was able to stand and walk from the hut unassisted.

He had gotten to know Rob's people bit by bit over the past weeks, and was pleased when he was able to meet them standing on his own feet. They, of course, knew exactly who he was and he found himself the object of worship. The people knew that the Defender would help them regain their stolen lands and possessions and they were as determined as he was to help him regain his strength again. Christopher had no shortage of assistance.

Rob and some of the other men had built Christopher his own little hut and he was grateful. Also, he knew that Marianne would be glad to have him out from underfoot, and he and Jonathan had laughed about that. His hut was complete and he was able to at least hold his own weight on his legs. His attention then turned to regaining his fighting form and he knew without a doubt that he was in for the biggest challenge of his life.

Christopher had lost a great deal of weight during his infirmary. At six feet and six inches, he usually carried about two hundred and seventy pounds on his big frame, but he was well below his fighting weight. His muscles had atrophied a bit from sheer disuse and he set forth the very day he could walk without shaking to get himself back in shape. He knew that he would have to build up to swinging a sword again, so his first order of business was to chop wood. It would help loosen the damaged muscles in his torso and begin to strengthen him.

Every day, he would chop enough wood for the entire encampment. From dawn to dusk, he chopped and chopped. Rob and his men would go out on "errands", as they called them, and Christopher would watch them go with envy, wishing he were strong enough to ride a horse all the way home.

His heart, his mind, his body ached for his sweet wife and he had many sleepless nights wondering what had become of her. Had David returned to marry her in his absence? What of Richard; had he married her off to someone else? Or, his worst nightmare would come to light and he would wonder with agony if she had taken her own life. God only knew what Dustin had gone through over the past months and he shuddered to think of her reaction when she saw that he was indeed alive. Would she hate him for being such a cruel prankster?

Christopher's injury had been so severe that he wasn't surprised when his stamina did not return quickly. But it did, eventually, show itself and within three weeks of starting his new regime, he could already see a marked difference. His muscles were beginning to resume their natural shape and grow, and he began taking long walks in the forest to strengthen his big legs.

The walks turned into runs, and every child in the camp wanted to join him. He thought he looked rather like the Pied Piper with dozens of children running after him on leaps and bounds through the forest. He began to enjoy his runs a great deal, delighting in the innocence of the children who accompanied him. He could not even remember his childhood, yet these children somehow brought him closer in touch with it.

Yet with every step, he drew closer to Dustin and prayed to God that she hadn't forgotten him. He truly had no idea what to expect. He hoped, of course, that nothing had happened and everything remained as it was. But somehow he knew in his heart that the great Lion's Claw's wife would not be left alone. There was no one to blame, of course, so he tried to prepare himself for any situation, yet he knew with deadly certainly one particular fact. Dustin was his wife and his alone, and no man, nor king, would keep them apart.

He liked the nights in the camp best. Christopher had mingled with kings and nobles, yet with the salt of the earth, he found a likable peace. Their life was hard, no doubt, but they were a happy bunch without the political turmoil he was so accustomed to. They had an easiness about them, a simplicity that he found comforting. True enough, Rob was the Earl of Longdon, but he did not act like it. He was much more in his element with these outlaws than in the trappings of his title. Christopher envied the man that he had the ability to relax and accept his situation, waiting for the time to present itself to reclaim what was his, in the interim, making life as miserable as possible for John and Ralph.

Christopher would have liked nothing better than to help Rob and his hoods antagonize the prince and the sheriff, but he lacked the strength yet and was bent on focusing his entire attentions to his recovery. And he furthermore had suspicions that if John and Ralph knew he were alive, they would stop at nothing to get to him. He could be Rob's greatest strength, or his deadliest weakness. He suspected Rob knew that, also.

One morning, early, Christopher was distracted by his wood chopping by Rob's young son, Simon. The boy was ten years of age, impish and quick, and was a great admirer of the Defender. He'd been fishing with the boy a couple of times and liked him.

Simon was fairly shaking with excitement as he watched Christopher rip apart a large stump, and even when Christopher stopped chopping the boy continued to twitch. Finally, Christopher leaned against his axe and eyed Simon.

"What is it with you?" he asked, not unkindly. "You are dancing around here like you have termites in your breeches. What is it?"

Simon flushed and kicked at the ground. "Sire, I was….well, I mean, we were all….I was wondering when you were going to practice with your sword?"

Christopher fought off a grin, trying to look stern. "Is that why you are as jumpy as a rabbit? Because you want to be the first in line to fight me?"

"Nay!" The boy looked terrified, but recovered with a hard swallow. "I was wondering…if… well, if…."

"Speak out, Simon, for Christ's sake," Christopher said. "I cannot understand you when you mumble. Knights of the realm do not mumble."

Simon stiffened and he fixed Christopher in the eye. "I want to see you practice with your sword, sire."

Christopher did smile then, and he put his huge hand on Simon's shoulder and nearly swallowed up half the boy in his grip.

"You do, do you?" he said. "Well, I was thinking about working with my sword today, as a matter of fact. Do you suppose that you read my mind?"

Simon smiled eagerly. "Shall I go fetch it?"

"Wait," Christopher admonished him as he tried to dash away. "We need to prepare the field if I am going to practice. It will take time between the two of us to accomplish this, for I need a thick log, and preferably a quilt or some batting, and…."

"We all will help," Simon announced and, on cue, there were suddenly a dozen boys coming out of the trees toward them, all smiling like fools.

Christopher grinned at the boys. "Why am I not surprised?" He tousled Simon's hair. "Very well, Simon. Retrieve my sword and send your knaves to find me suitable dummies to practice against."

"How about my Dada?" one boy called, and they all screamed with laughter.

Christopher shook his head. "Nay, not *that* kind of dummy," he snorted. "Two or three logs, about my height, if you can find them. Waste no time, lads. *Go*."

By the time Simon returned with Christopher's sword, the entire camp was made aware that the Defender was preparing to bear arms again. When Simon returned to the clearing, he did not return alone.

Christopher was a little embarrassed at all of the people who had turned out to see him practice for the first time. He wasn't sure just how good he would be and he wished Simon had kept his excitement to himself, but he could understand the thrill.

Lugging thirty odd pounds of broadsword, Simon could barely lift it to Christopher's outstretched hand. But the moment Christopher took hold of the hilt, he felt the familiar magic and raised it as if it were made of feathers.

Rob and Jonathan turned out to see Christopher, smiling broadly and commending themselves on doing a fine job of healing. The day was surprisingly warm and Christopher stripped off the rough linen tunic he had been wearing, revealing his magnificent body. His skin was faintly tan and smooth, his muscles well-formed even if they weren't quite as bulky as they once had been. He was sweating lightly and the newly-warm sun glistened on his skin. The only flaw in an otherwise perfect form was the puckered, purplish scar just underneath his ribcage on the left side of his torso. It was the size of an apple, and even then it had shrunk considerably.

"Sir Christopher, do you intend to show us ignorant wretches what true swordplay should be?" Jonathan quipped.

Christopher rubbed the blade with a rag. "Can you swing a sword, man? If so, you will be my sparring partner."

Jonathan guffawed loudly. "Me? Go against the Defender of the Realm, the Lion's Claw? Never!"

Christopher snickered, rubbing out a few faint marks on his blade. He needed a rougher polishing cloth for the others, but this would do for now. Christ, he hadn't realized how much he has missed having his sword in his hand until now. Standing underneath the warm sun preparing for a practice bout made him realize just how lucky he was to be alive.

"And you, my lord?" he addressed Rob. "Surely you are skilled with such an instrument?"

Rob shrugged. "Of course. But I won't fight you, either."

Christopher raised his eyebrow at the two of them. "Well, somebody should or else you will have a camp full of disappointed people. They are expecting a battle."

Jonathan turned away as if he had better things to do. "They will not get it from me. No, sir; not me."

Rob chuckled, watching as Christopher became reacquainted with the grip on the sword. "Jonathan said that when he found you, you had that sword clutched to your chest as if you were fearful someone would take it. It is a beautiful piece, indeed."

"It was my father's," Christopher said, inspecting a nick closely. "And it survived three years on the quest with me. It means a great deal to me." He lowered the sword and focused on Rob with a twinkle in his eye. "Are you still going to play the coward, my lord? Even in front of your son?"

Rob glanced over at Simon, eagerly helping his friends steady one of the logs Christopher had asked for. "Are you trying to provoke me, sir knight?" he cocked an eyebrow.

Christopher snorted. "Not at all," he said. "By the way, I am a baron by title. Not as great as an earl, but I consider it an accomplishment beyond a mere knight."

Rob looked stricken. "God's Bones," he said. "We have been sorely insulting you all this time by calling you 'sir' instead of 'lord'. I must certainly practice with you to make up for our lack of manners."

Christopher smiled and lowered his blade. "A pleasure, my lord."

Rob shot him a fearful glance, knowing Christopher was going to take advantage of the situation. Leaving the clearing, Rob returned shortly bearing a blade. It was a magnificent piece of work with a gilded pommel and jewels set into the hilt. Even Christopher was impressed.

"Where did you get this?" he said, carefully examining the sword.

"Stole it from one of John's elite troops after I killed him," Rob replied, not particularly proud of the fact. "I lost my own sword in his chest, so I took his."

"A fair trade," Christopher handed it back to hm. "Sire, if you are ready, I believe your son is waiting most impatiently."

Rob blew out his cheeks as if to summon courage and followed Christopher into the clearing.

"Be easy on me, my lord," Rob pleaded with a smile. "I do most of my fighting these days with a crossbow."

"If you aggravate his wound, I shall take a switch to you," Marianne yelled from the edge of the trees.

"Do not listen to her, Rob," Jonathan hollered in response. "Cut a few inches off those tall legs."

Rob, who had just assumed a defensive posture, suddenly stood up straight and glared back into the crowd. "Will you kindly shut up? How do you expect me to survive this bout if you distract me like that?"

The group tittered and Rob returned to his defensive position. He grinned at Christopher. "Whenever you are ready."

"After you, sire," Christopher replied lightly.

They were both out of practice, but it was obvious in the first minute or so why Christopher had earned his considerable reputation. He was toying with Rob, but in truth he was glad he was not going against anyone more seasoned. To start slowly was the best thing he could do and he could feel seldom-used muscles coming back to life again.

Rob concluded the match before any more harm was done to his pride and Christopher thanked him graciously for demeaning himself. But already establishment had been made that, indeed, he was who he said he was.

The Defender was on the road to recovery.

CHAPTER FORTY-EIGHT

DUSTIN WAS BENT over the basin when there was a loud rapping at her door. She told whoever it was to go away, but Marcus announced himself and she had no choice but to respond. She did not want him to see the contents of her stomach on display in the basin, so she put it in the wardrobe to hide it from him. Quickly brushing her hair, she straightened her surcoat and went to open the door.

Marcus raised an eyebrow at her. "What? Are you hiding a lover in here?"

She stood back as he entered the room, trying not to look suspect. "Can I at least put a surcoat on before you come barging in here?" she snapped.

He looked at her, ignoring her tone. "What's wrong with you?"

"What do you mean?" she lowered her gaze and moved away from him.

"I mean, Iris says you have been sick ever since you got here," he said, concerned. "What's wrong, honey? Isn't the food settling on your stomach?"

Dustin pursed her lips with frustration. "And what else does Iris tell you about me? Damnation, that woman knows everything that happens to me two seconds after it happens. This castle is a damn rumor mill. I hate it."

"Calm, lady." He put up his hands soothingly. "They do not mean to be that way, but it is a close knit group. They are not trying to be malicious, just concerned."

"I do not need their concern," she shot back. "I do not need them nosing into my business, or going through my trunks, or worrying about me in any way."

"Going through your trunks?" he repeated. "What are you talking about?"

She waved irritably at him. "Just that. Someone went through the belongings I left in my trunks. Marcus, I swear I am ready to take my fist to these people."

"Did they steal anything?" he asked.

"No," she said. "But that is not the point. They seem determined to allow me no privacy, and with everything that happens, they go running to you."

He was calm as he watched her pace. "It is because they know I care about you and I want to know when something is wrong."

"I shall tell you myself if something is wrong," she said forcefully. "I do not need the tattlers to do it for me."

He sighed and went over to the bed, sitting heavily on the pretty coverlets. "Come here."

"Nay," she spat, pacing in front of him.

He reached out and grabbed her, pulling her onto his lap. She struggled for a moment, but relaxed when she realized how comforting it was to have him close. With these weeks she had spent with him, her wall had come further and further down and it was becoming easier to respond to his affections. And she so desperately craved affection at times it made her cry. She reasoned that if she could not have Christopher, then Marcus was the next best.

His dark blue eyes met her gray orbs tenderly. "Would you please tell me what's wrong?" he asked softly. "Are you ill?"

She shook her head. "Nay," she replied, not wanting to tell him of her secret, increasingly concerned as to how he was going to react to know she carried her dead husband's child. She knew Marcus loved her, but every man had his limit. What would the people of his keep think if they learned Marcus was in love with a woman pregnant with the child of a dead man? It would make him look like a fool. She did not want to do that to him. To save his honor, to do him this one favor when he had done so many for her, she knew what she had to do.

Dustin remembered the time long ago when they had made love. She remembered it had been powerful and lusty, but she felt as if she were betraying Christopher all over again by contemplating taking Marcus into her bed. Still, her pregnancy was early enough that she would be able to tell Marcus the child was his. But they would have to consummate their relationship soon.

Christopher was gone and she was being faithful to a memory. She loved him so much that she could not help it. Yet Marcus was here and he was real and she had grown to become very fond of him over the past several weeks. As hard as it was for her, she knew for her best interests, she needed to do what was necessary to perhaps save them both.

Marcus jolted her out of her train of thought. "Then what, Dustin?" he pressed gently. "What is it?"

She looked at him and felt the pull again. It wasn't love, but more a sheer animal magnetism. For once in her life, she gave into the pull.

"I....Oh, Marcus!" She threw her arms around his neck in resignation. After a moment, she kissed his ear hotly. "I am glad you brought me here." Half lie, half truth.

Marcus was pleasantly surprised. Dustin's hot breath sent chills up his spine and the fire of desire kindling in his loins, but he banked himself. He was becoming used to banking himself where she was concerned.

"As I am, honey," he replied. "Do you feel like going downstairs? Dud told me of a whole field of wildflowers in bloom. We can bring Christin and...."

She cut him off, pulling back to look at him with a seductive smile that made his heart leap into his throat.

"I do not want to go anywhere," she used a tone he had never heard before. "I want to stay here. With you."

His eyes widened and she caught the look of utter surprise. "And?" he wanted to know.

She focused on his lower lip, a masculine, sensuous thing. "I need you. I need you now."

His jaw hung. "What?"

She ran her finger along his lower lip, feeling the desire in her veins build. What had started out as a fine job of acting was quickly becoming the real thing. He was so astonished that he wasn't reacting to her, so she stopped her onslaught and suddenly stood up.

"Very well," she said, rather primly. "I can see that I hold no interest to you."

He snatched her back to him as quickly as she had risen, pulling her against him firmly. His face was an inch from her own, their eyes devouring each other.

"Are you sure?" he whispered, not even daring to hope.

She kissed his lower lip, only his lower lip, and caught it between her teeth erotically as she pulled away from him. "I am," she whispered. "Truly, I am."

Marcus could not believe it. His eyes raked her from her hair to her toes and he was completely at a loss for words. Forgoing the words, his mouth latched onto hers and in a great release of desire and passion, he pulled her back onto the bed with him.

What started out slow and completely sensual quickly grew in strength. He literally tore her surcoat from her and she let him, encouraging him with passionate words that sent his blood boiling. His own clothes came off faster than he thought possible and Dustin moaned with pure pleasure when their naked flesh came together for the first time. It was an explosion of erotic pleasure, comfort beyond imagining as his hands moved the length and breadth of her body.

For Dustin, it was purely therapeutic. She needed to be touched, needed to know that she was loved and that she was not alone. She tried to close her eyes and pretend it was Christopher, but she could not. His presence was so different from Marcus' and she knew him better than she knew herself, and it was nearly impossible to pretend that the man holding her now was her deceased husband. She was momentarily disappointed, for she had hoped to imagine for just a moment that 'twas Christopher back with her, one more time. But her disappointment was momentary in that Marcus Burton was a man among men, not inclined to take second to anyone, especially a dead man.

He was rough with her, as she had remembered, but it fired her desire tremendously. His teeth bit at her nipples, already engorged and tender from nursing, but he was skilled enough to know how far he could go without actually hurting her. A little pain was pleasurable.

He sucked her dry on both breasts, giving Dustin so much pleasure that tears filled her eyes. She tried to make love to him, to run her hands over his massive chest or move to cup his testicles, but he would gently push her back down again and continue his attentions. Lord, he had wanted her so badly and for so long that she was going to lay there and enjoy everything he did to her, whether or not she wanted to join in. This experience was so entirely unexpected that it left him giddy.

She tasted so sweet and he sucked and tongued her in every possible place, feeling her warmth against his face Dustin relaxed completely, panting softly with his most intimate touch and giggling when he suckled her toes. He smiled back, meeting her desire-hazed gaze before quickly flipping her over on her stomach and descending on her bottom with his mouth.

Dustin moaned and writhed underneath him, even blushing when he parted her buttocks and ran his tongue the length of the crack, toying with her anus. He bought her up to her knees while her face and shoulders were still lowered into the pillow and pressed his mouth into her private center, manipulating her little bud from an entirely new angle.

Dustin immediately started to thrash with passion and he could not wait any longer. Turning her over on her back, he lowered his massive frame onto her and gently kissed her mouth.

"I want to look at your face when I make love to you," he whispered hotly.

Breathless, she met his eyes and wrapped her pretty legs around his thighs. "Take me, my lord."

He did. He drove into her wetness with a shout of triumph, rocking the bed with the measured power in his thrusts. She met his thrusts firmly, clinging to him as he moved within her. *Christopher, Christopher, Christopher*! Her mind sang over and over but she had the presence of mind not to voice her thoughts. This was Marcus now, her future husband, and she would not degrade him by thinking him to be another. Yet it wasn't easy, her mind, her body, was geared to Christopher.

When it was over and they lay entwined in each other's arms, Dustin thought she might actually grow to enjoy this completely one day. True, her body was satisfied by his lovemaking, but it was her mind he had to win over.

☙

THE NEXT DAY was a difficult one for Dustin. She was embarrassed that she had responded so physically to Marcus when her heart and soul still belonged to Christopher. She was confused and angry at herself, second-guessing her reasoning for taking Marcus to her bed. Was it right to let him believe the child was his merely to save his honor? Was it then right to deny Christopher his own flesh and blood?

She just did not know anymore and was sickened over it. She knew she was a silly, weak woman and she could not truly fathom why the strongest men in the realm had loved her. She certainly did not deserve them.

She was out walking with Christin in the bailey, avoiding the curious gazes of the peasants and soldiers alike, ignoring them because she was afraid to open herself up in any way with a smile or a word. She wanted to stay to herself to try and sort out her surging emotions, hoping the sun and air would help her do just that.

Alexander jogged beside her, yapping and dancing about. Christin watched the dog intently, yelling and screeching at the animal as Dustin all but ignored the two of them, entirely lost in thought. Caesar and George had opted to stay inside and keep each other company, although Caesar was a bitter old thing these days. And he hated Marcus.

Dustin remembered when Christopher had first come to Lioncross, and how Caesar had taken to him immediately. If she hadn't known better, she would have sworn that the cat was instrumental in drawing her and Christopher together. His timing had been impeccable and his moves, planned. But here at Somerhill, he hissed and scratched at Marcus as if the man were the devil. She wondered if it was because the cat felt that only Christopher had a right to his mistress.

A shadow fell across her path and she stopped, looking up to see Dud smiling at her. He was a kind man with a beaten face, and she had remembered his loyalty to her husband. She smiled back.

"My lady looks well this day," he commented. "May I be so bold as to ask to accompany you?"

She did not want company, but she did not have the heart to refuse him. "Of course."

He fell in beside her and they walked in silence, pacing the dusty ground of the bailey.

"Your lady daughter is looking more like her father every day," he remarked.

Dustin looked at Christin. "Do you think so?"

"Aye," he agreed. "Verily, she has the shape of his face, and his mouth. I can see him when she smiles."

Dustin studied her daughter's face a moment. "She will know about her father, Dud. I want Christin to grow up hearing of him every day so that she feels that she knows him."

Dud's smile faded a bit when he remembered the look Marcus had given him as he had told stories of Christopher. The man was bitterly possessive about this woman and her child. "She will, my lady," he said. "I will tell her myself when she is old enough to understand."

"Would you?" Dustin turned to him earnestly. "I would like that very much. You have known him much longer than I have."

He was not surprised by the sincerity in her voice; he knew how much she and the baron had loved one another and it almost made him resent Marcus for interfering.

"I promise that Lady Christin will know all there is to know about her father. Well, *almost* everything," he chuckled.

Dustin smirked and shook her head. "I do not even want to know about *those* things," she said stiffly, then glanced at him sideways. "Was my husband….I mean, did he have other women when you knew him?"

Dud looked thoughtful, hell, he could think of a dozen offhand, but nothing more than passing fancies. Christopher loved to admire beautiful women, women who had thrown themselves at him, but he had never shown much interest in them beyond a roll in bed. Dud had known Christopher since they had been young knights, many years ago, and he had seen and heard of Christopher's escapades with Marcus and David. But did he have a serious woman? He recalled one, a Lady Amanda, but naught much else to the story.

Dustin was waiting for an answer as he recollected. He saw her expectant face and cleared his throat. "Outside of a wench here and there, no one that I am aware of. Christopher lived cleaner than most knights."

Relieved, Dustin smiled and nodded, shifting Christin to the other hip. "Tell me more of his adventures in the Holy Land."

Dud grinned, clasping his hands behind his back as he thought. "Let me see, now. Did I tell you the story of the inn in Damascus? Aye, I told you that last night." His brow furrowed. "How about the road to Antioch? Or the two nights we spent in Joppa when the Muslims were running rampant about the place looking for us?" When Dustin shook her head, he smiled broadly and continued with his story.

He was nearly finished with the exciting story about Joppa when one of the main players of the tale marched up in jingling mail. Marcus' face was grim; he knew Dud had been filling her head full of Christopher's tales and he was angered.

"Don't you have duties, Dudley?" he asked coldly.

Dud's eyes actually narrowed, a rare occurrence for the no questions asked obedient knight. He was doing nothing wrong and did not appreciate the tone taken, yet he knew it was Marcus' jealousy talking.

"They are completed for this morn, my lord," he replied respectfully. "I was simply talking to Lady de Lohr." He deliberately used her title if for nothing more than to remind Marcus as to who she was.

Marcus' stiffened with hostility. "Then find something else to do. I shall take the lady from here."

Dustin could sense the animosity and it confused her. Dud bowed quickly and was gone before she could thank him and Marcus instantly took his place.

"Where were you walking to?" he asked nicely.

She eyed him. "Why were you so rude to him?"

He raised his eyebrow. "I wasn't. Where are you going?"

"Aye, you were," she snapped, turning her back on him and beginning to walk away.

He caught up to her. "Do not turn your back on me. I asked you a question."

"And I asked you one. Answer mine and I shall answer yours," she said evenly.

His first reaction was to flare but he calmed himself. They walked several feet before he answered. "Let me make myself clear, Lady Dustin. I do not take orders from you. Requests I will honor, but anything other than a polite question will not receive an answer. Additionally, I expect you to respond to and obey me as a proper lady should. I am master here, not you."

Dustin did not answer a moment, feeling particularly stubborn. She was so used to having Marcus bow to her every whim that she did not like it when he pulled rank on her.

"Do you understand me?" he asked when she kept silent.

She shrugged, looking away from him. He reached out and snatched her arm, whipping her around to face him. Poor little Christin's head snapped with the suddenness of the movement and Dustin gasped.

"Answer me," he said in a low voice.

He only succeeded in making her mad. "I understood you perfectly. And I do not like being handled like a rough-house wench."

"Then do not act like one," he replied smoothly.

"I shall act as I please, Lord Marcus," she said. "If you do not like it, then send me home. I did not ask to come here."

He stared back at her a moment before releasing her arm. "Yet you are here nonetheless and will abide by my wishes," he said quietly. "I do not wish to fight, Dustin. Would you take the nooning meal with me, alone, in my chambers?"

She gazed at him a moment. "Do you mean to ask if I will bed you again? I do not feel like it."

He let out a hissing sigh and stepped back from her, his exasperation showing for the first time. "If I wanted to bed you, then I would do it. I do not need to ask your permission. I was simply looking to spend some time alone with you."

Her mouth opened in outrage. "You would not bed me without my approval," she said hotly. "You are not my husband, Marcus Burton, nor are you my lord and master, and I shall not be treated like your concubine."

He grabbed her again and pulled her close to him, his eyes blue flames. "I shall treat you like my wife if you will let me," he snapped with quiet ferocity. "Damnation, Dustin, what do I have to do you to make you believe that my love is sincere? All I want to do is love you."

Her hostility, fed by her own confusion, drained away. He was so vulnerable, so open, that she could see his soul in his eyes. How terrible to love someone so completely and not receive just a little in return. Now there was another item to add to her guilt.

"I am….I am scared," she whispered before she could control herself. "Everything I have ever loved has died. I cannot love anymore, Marcus."

His anger fled at her open confession. He could see she was being entirely honest and his heart ached for her.

"I won't ever leave you, and I won't die," he whispered earnestly. "I swear to you, Dustin, with God as my witness. Do not be afraid, honey. Please. I will not hurt you."

She stared at him a moment, wanting to believe him but still afraid. Christin reached out and grabbed at his face and he kissed her little hand, still staring at Dustin. That sweet, simple gesture brought tears to Dustin's eyes.

"I just don't know, Marcus," she whispered.

He sighed faintly. "If anyone should be afraid, it should be I," he said quietly. "Hell, Dustin, I have wrestled with a demon greater than myself for the love of you. I'd walk the fires of hell or swim from here to eternity for you, and that in itself is scary. I love you desperately and know even so that you do not love me, yet I lay myself open to you every day, hoping beyond hope that you shall come around. I risk great personal anguish for you. Now, tell me; who should be more afraid? Me or you?"

Christin batted at his cheek, entranced with the scratchy stubble. Dustin continued to stare into his eyes, battling a demon of another sort; she still loved her dead husband and she knew she could never love Marcus, but she could not bring herself to tell him that.

"I shall try," she said after a moment. "I can only promise to try."

"And marry me?" he pressed gently.

"And marry you," she agreed, feeling as if she had just lost some sort of battle.

He smiled and kissed Christin's hand again, then kissed her. Even if she did not love him, his kiss could still curl her toes.

"You won't regret it, I promise," he said.

She forced a smile at him as he took Christin from her and put his arm around her waist, resuming their walk.

"Won't you tell me why you were so rude to Dud?" she asked again, nicer this time.

Marcus cleared his throat softly, averting his gaze. He did not want to admit the truth to her.

"Because he was neglecting his duties," he said simply. "Didn't Chris ever tell you not to question any order he gave to his men?"

"In a sense," she said, knowing Marcus was right. "He told me never to question any order."

"And he was right," Marcus teased, although the underlying tone was serious. "Never question my orders, my lady. Each command serves a purpose or function, and is well thought out. Understand?"

"Aye," she nodded.

He sensed her melancholy mood but refused to give into it.

"Shall we ride into town? The man at the livery had a beautiful pony I thought would make a fine mount for Christin."

"A pony?" Dustin repeated. "Marcus, she's only seven months old. She cannot ride a pony."

"Not now, but give her a few months." He nibbled on the baby fingers. "She will ride like a knight."

Dustin shook her head. Even if he wasn't Christopher, sometimes he sounded a good deal like him.

CHAPTER FORTY-NINE

DAY BY DAY Christopher worked with his sword, repetition and drills constituting his regimen. The dummies the boys had rigged for him worked well for the first week or so, but after that he simply wore them out. Simon and his friends insisted on repairing the barriers, but Christopher gently turned them down. 'Twas easier to simply practice against a solid tree, and the clearing was surrounded by plenty of them.

Simon wanted to be a knight and Christopher knew the boy's desires all too well. But he was in no mood to teach the boy skills, for he was preoccupied with his own recovery. But he almost felt obligated to take Simon under his wing, for if it hadn't been for the boy's parents, Christopher wouldn't have survived at all.

So, with reluctance, he began training Simon. It slowed his own progress down considerably to work with the boy, but much to his surprise, he found he actually enjoyed training the lad. Not that his determination to return home had lessened in anyway, but he wasn't so disturbed at his slow pace anymore. Simon was an eager, dedicated student.

But along with Simon came his friends, and soon Christopher found himself fostering fourteen boys between the ages of nine and fifteen. Every morning, the boys would be waiting for him in the clearing to begin their daily drills and Christopher would instruct them fully before starting his own drills. Rob and Jonathan, when they weren't out on business, took to supervising.

Christopher should have been irritated that his focus was being diverted and his progress slowed, but he truly wasn't. He came to enjoy teaching the young boys, and they were so damned eager he had not the heart to deny them. He remembered when he was their age and all he lived for was the feel of a sword in his hand, dreaming of the day when he would be the realm's greatest knight.

He found it hard to believe how much he had changed since returning from the quest. The self-centered, arrogant man had grown a heart in the interim and he found himself doing and saying things that the Lion's Claw would have never done or said. His compassion, no longer suppressed, was allowed to express itself and his sense of humor had found an escape. He was still the dedicated, controlled person he had always been, but he had matured. He had become something quite wonderful, and he knew he owed everything to his wife. He would be nothing without her.

His heart yearned for her more every day and sometimes the impatience threatened to drive him insane, but he was wise in that he knew he could not make the trek before he was physically able to complete it.

His strength returned more and more each day and he had gained some of his weight he had lost, thanks to Marianne's cooking and his rigorous training. In fact, he thought his body looked and felt better than it had before, leaner and tighter. But he still had time to go before he was perfect and he focused every morning on that one goal to be perfect again, to return to Dustin.

April was a beautiful month, even in the middle of Sherwood. The cold weather began to warm a bit and the birds and animals were alive in the trees. Christopher's young knights were progressing very well and he was immensely proud of them, as if they were his own sons. Rob even took to sparring with Simon, receiving a good nick on his arm one afternoon and congratulating his son for his prowess.

Christopher was practicing on horseback now, strengthening his legs and torso as he sparred with straw dummies atop poles. The muscles where his wound was had been severed and badly damaged and he was stiff, but he worked hard to loosen his body and firm up the muscles that had been unused for months.

It was at this point in time that he decided he could indeed ride back to Lioncross. Hell, he could do what he was doing here at home, and make love to his wife in his off time. He felt strong and whole, mayhap not quite as strong as he had once felt, but he felt good just the same. With a rush of excitement and relief, he decided it was time for him to leave.

Rob was not surprised to hear of his decision. "I knew you'd leave us someday," he said. "The more I saw you work, the more I knew it would be soon. Do you truly feel up to it?"

"I do, my lord," Christopher answered. "The sooner I get back to my wife and family, the more completely I shall recover."

Rob nodded. "Simon will be crushed," he said. "Who will continue their training?"

Christopher smiled sympathetically. "Send him to foster with me at Lioncross; send them all. I have many fine knights who will train them."

Rob rubbed his chin slowly, "Do you know I have been thinking just that?" he looked around at his encampment. "Look at this place, baron. 'Tis no place to raise a son. I should like a better life for Simon, away from his father, the outlaw."

Christopher could feel the man's melancholy at the situation. "If I might ask, my lord, why was he not sent away when he was six or seven, as most boys are?

Rob shrugged. "His mother could not bear to be away from him," he said frankly. "He is our only child. Marianne wanted to keep him as long as she could, although I have chided her on the subject many a time."

Christopher nodded, noticing Lizabetha in conversation several yards away with a tall young man. She was animated and smiling, and Christopher found himself thanking God that her attentions to him had been brief.

"I shall consent to sponsor him if you wish, my lord," he focused on Rob. "I would consider it an honor."

"God's Blood, baron, the honor would be ours," Rob insisted. "Our son fostered by the great Lion's Claw? What prestige."

"Think on it, then," Christopher said. "I shall be leaving on the morrow, with your permission.

"I shall speak with my wife," Rob said, eyeing Christopher in the filtered sunlight. "I am sorry to see you go, baron. You have made our dingy world a little less gray."

Christopher smiled, standing back to salute him formally. "And I, my lord, owe you my very life. Consider me always your humble servant."

"All I ask is that you put in a good word for me to Richard," Rob insisted. "I am not an outlaw or a bandit, baron. I am simply a man trying to make a life."

"I know," Christopher replied. "And I swear I shall do my very best."

As Christopher went back to his tent to prepare for his departure, he could hardly believe the time had come. He could picture Dustin in his mind, smell her hair, and feel her skin, and it nearly drove him insane. But he was terrified for what he would find upon his return and with each passing second, his excitement and anxiety grew.

☙

MARCUS AND DUSTIN were married in the small chapel of Somerhill. It was a lovely little sanctuary and Dustin was married in a dress of ivory silk, with Christin all dressed up in rose and pink. Marcus held the baby throughout the entire ceremony, and after he had placed a chaste kiss on his new wife's lips, he kissed the baby on the head. Christin had contentedly sucked her fingers, unaware of what had transpired.

Dustin wore the cross Christopher had given her and the wedding rings from him as her only adornment. Marcus saw the jewelry but said nothing until they were seated at the wedding feast.

"Why are you wearing those rings?" he said casually. "I had to put my ring on your right hand."

Dustin glanced down at the gold band and diamond ring. "I…I do not know. I always wear them. I have never taken them off."

"I would appreciate it if you would, at least, wear my ring on your left hand," he said. "You can wear those rings on your right hand if it pleases you."

Dustin could not bear to remove the rings. She had bedded this man, and married him, yet she could not stand the thought of moving Christopher's rings to her other hand. To remove them would to be admitting that she was no longer Lady de Lohr, no longer Christopher's wife. She knew in her mind that she wasn't married to him anymore, but her heart had yet to accept it. The rings did not belong on her right hand and Marcus could not force her.

The minstrels began to sing a lovely ballad for the newlyweds as Dustin faced Marcus firmly.

"I do not want to move them, I want to wear them where they are," she said. "I….I am not ready to move them yet."

His face darkened. "That's ridiculous. You just married me, Dustin. I shall not allow you to wear your dead husband's wedding rings in lieu of mine."

"Do not say that!" she screamed, shooting out of her chair. The musicians kept playing, but all eyes had turned to the newly-married couple.

"Sit down, Dustin, you are making a scene," Marcus said in a low voice.

"I will not," she snapped, turning to take Christin from Lady Emma. "I will return to my room now."

He ground his jaw, pulling Christin out of Dustin's arms and handling her back to Lady Emma. "Come with me."

She took a swing at him but he ducked, throwing her over his shoulder and the small crowd in the hall went wild with approval. Dustin kicked and twisted, drawing even greater applause from the audience, as he carried her from the dining hall and up to his bedchamber.

Inside, he set her down roughly and she stumbled away from him, her pretty face flushed. Without a word, she tried to push past him and escape the room, but he grabbed her arm and flung her onto the bed. His huge body fell atop her, pinning her to the mattress.

"Get off me!" she yelled.

His voice was low. "You are my wife now and I may do anything I please. 'Tis time you accept that."

She glared at him, knowing his words to be true. "God forgive me for what I was thinking when I consented to marry you. I must have been mad!"

He was stung but he did not show it. *Patience*, he kept telling himself. Be patient and she will come around.

"I love you, Lady Burton," he said quietly. "I have always loved you, and nothing you can say or do will change that. Is it so hard to accept my love?"

She turned her face away, still struggling against him. "I married you, Marcus, what more do you want?"

"I want you, your heart, your mind, as well as your body," he said steadily. "Jesus, Dustin, why do you treat me as if I am a leper? You act as if I am a twisted, disfigured troll instead of the man I am. Do I truly repel you?"

She stopped her fighting, looking at him then. "Is that what you think? That you repel me?"

"What am I to think?" he returned softly.

She shook her head slowly. "Marcus, of course you do not repel me. You are the most handsome man I have ever seen."

"Besides Chris," he added.

She nodded. "Aye, besides my hus…Chris." Her face went soft, her struggles ceased for the moment and he relaxed atop her. "I remember the first time I saw you. You are so striking that I had very unladylike thoughts about you, and I was embarrassed because I had only been married a week. I was guilty for thinking someone gorgeous other than my husband."

"Is that right?" he smiled faintly. "I remember the first time I saw you, too. Once I got past all of this hair, I realized you were absolutely beautiful. And I wanted you. Even after I learned you were Chris' wife, I still wanted you."

"I know," she said. "You kissed me."

"I did," he agreed evenly. "Admit it to me now, Dustin. You liked it. Before the shock set in and you pulled away, you liked it."

She gazed back into the dark blue depths and offered a little grin. "Perhaps," she said ambiguously. "But you scared me because you made me feel vulnerable."

"Why?" he wanted to know.

"Because you were willing and I found you attractive," she said honestly. "But the more I grew to love Chris, the easier it was to ignore you. I remember thinking that if you had showed up at Lioncross first, you would have been the love of my life."

His smile faded. "Had I but known, honey, I would have been the first man to come for you, believe me."

Her hand came up, timidly, and she ran her fingers slowly through his wavy black hair. Lord, he was a handsome devil.

"Why am I so blessed that the two most important warriors in the kingdom both found love with me?" she whispered in awe. "What did I ever do right in the eyes of God to warrant such a reward?"

He shook his head, dipping his head to kiss her softly on the neck. "Do you know that I have never loved anyone, or anything, in my life? Especially not a woman."

"What about your family? Mother?" she asked, closing her eyes at his soft, warm lips.

He was working his way up her neck. "I left to foster when I was six years old, so I have little attachment to my mother," he said, his mouth against her skin. "Other than Richard, and my fellow knights, I have loved no one. Mayhap that is why I lose control around you so easily."

She melted into his touch, his caresses, and soon their clothes were off and their bodies were melding erotically. Dustin pushed him over on his back, dragging her mouth all over his broad chest, closing her eyes and trying hard not to imagine him to be Christopher. She straddled him, her buttocks nearly resting on his neck, and fondled his arousal endlessly before plunging her hot mouth onto him. She could feel him kneading her bum and nipping at her skin.

He had all he could take of her mouth and pulled her underneath him, turning his attentions to her plump breasts and slim torso. She writhed beneath him as his big hands moved about her, telling her wordlessly how glad he was that she was finally his wife.

Dustin had realized something about Marcus' lovemaking early on; he liked a bit of roughness, and he liked to put her in strange positions. Not that she minded, for it excited her as well. He put her knees up and plunged his face into her intimate place, his tongue caressing and lapping and stroking long and hard until she was nearly screaming with need. When she was dripping wet, he put her legs together and Dustin looked at him with great disappointment.

"What's wrong?" she panted.

He grinned wolfishly. "Nothing."

Legs pressed together, he pushed them up so her knees were in her face, exposing the most private part of her to the celling. She could not see his face because her legs were in the way as she was nearly folded in half, but when she opened her mouth to question him further, she felt his huge member pressing against her and he slid easily in his full, hard length. Gripping her knees to keep her legs aloft, he pumped into her with sensual force and Dustin quickly realized she liked this a great deal.

He thrust and thrust, his grunts of pleasure matching hers. She felt herself building quickly, wanting the explosion that came with the relief, but he suddenly stopped and parted her legs, pushing his body down onto her as she wound her thighs around him.

"Is this the only way Chris made love to you?" he asked breathlessly.

Her eyes were glazed with desire, nearly incoherent. "What do you mean? Did he make love to me atop, as you are? Nay, sometimes I made love to him, riding him like…."

"Nay, that's not what I meant," he whispered, running his hand along the crack of her buttocks and coming to rest on her anus. "Did he ever make love to you here?"

"No," Dustin shook her head, curious but apprehensive at the same time.

He smiled, kissing her chin, her neck. "Then you are a virgin."

"I am no virgin, Marcus," she snorted. "I have birthed a child. I have been married before, and…."

He snickered. "You are a virgin, here." His finger wiggled into her anus ever so slightly and she squirmed, feeling uncomfortable but liking it just the same.

"Do you… do you want to make love to me there?" she asked a bit fearfully.

"Nay, honey, not if it makes you uneasy," he pulled out the hard length of himself and drove into her again as if to emphasize his point. "I am perfectly happy where I am."

He thrust into her a couple of times, trying to regain his rhythm, but she stopped him. "If you want to….isn't it right that a bride should be virgin for her husband?"

He smiled. "What are you saying? That Christopher took your first virginity, so you are offering me your second?"

She giggled. "Will it hurt?"

"Did it hurt to lose it the first time?" he asked.

She shrugged. "Not really. Will I like it?"

"Oh, I think so," he whispered, thrusting into her again. Dustin turned herself over to him, trusting him with whatever he wished to do. He continued to make love to her as he was, drawing out his thrusts and making her so slick and wet she was sprawled beneath him like a wanton wench, begging him for more. When he was sure her anus was drenched with the moisture from her vagina, he withdrew and slowly inched into the puckered hole.

Dustin's eyes opened wide as he slowly drove into her, but she did not utter a sound. In fact, she was so aroused that she felt her climax start before he was even fully imbedded in her and he drove into her three times before spilling his seed. Gasping and calling his name softly, she wound her arms around his neck and he withdrew from her anus, driving once again into her vagina and feeling the last of their combined convulsions.

Seated to the hilt as his arousal diminished, he was sure nothing on this earth was greater. He had found his happiness, his contentment, in everything.

Dustin lay in his arms, her legs wrapped around him, feeling very naughty but liking it just the same. How was it that this man made her feel so wicked? She may not have loved him, but he made her feel daring and womanly. She fully intended to tell him her feelings, but somehow sleep claimed her before she could speak the words.

DAYS PASSED AND spring descended fully on Somerhill. Marcus spent nearly all of his time with Dustin and Christin, taking them into the small town, or down to the river, or off into the countryside for a ride. He was convinced that if he bombarded Dustin with his presence, that she would put Christopher behind her more quickly and begin to focus on him. He was positive that they could have a happy life together if she would only give him a chance.

Try as she might not to, Dustin seemed to linger on Christopher constantly, especially when she saw Marcus with Christin. He was so loving and good with the babe that it made her heart ache to think what Christopher was missing. Yet she also began to see that he truly loved the both of them, selflessly, and she was moved. It was growing increasingly more difficult to fight off her growing feelings for Marcus. He was a kind man, a good husband, a wise father, and an exciting lover and she knew she would be happy with him if she would only let herself. But she could not seem to let her wall down completely, not even for him.

News arrived from Lioncross in late April announcing the birth of Michael Christopher Myles Olmquist. Mother and son were doing very well and Dustin was thrilled that Deborah bore a son. She mentioned returning to Lioncross for the christening, but Marcus was vague and changed the subject. Dejected and somber, Dustin realized he would probably never let her return home. Edward had been right. Somerhill was now her world, and Lioncross was a memory. Marcus knew how she felt, but he could not risk taking her to Lioncross only to have her never want to leave.

One bright day, Marcus took his wife and daughter into the land ablaze with spring flowers and set out lunch while Christin scrambled through the sweet grass. Dustin sat on the ground and watched her daughter play, taking leaves out of her little mouth as Marcus approached and offered her a bit of cheese.

"Spring time is glorious this far north," he commented, sitting down beside her and lounging back. "There is far more color than in the south."

"Oh, I do not know," Dustin replied, taking a bite of cheese.

"Lioncross is fairly colorful this time of year."

"Aye, but you are closer to the Welsh border," he said. "London is so filthy and drab that the flowers refuse to grow."

She smiled. "How close are we to Scotland?"

"Two day's ride," he said. "We have actually had a few marauders since I have been here, but they have kept to the woods."

Christin scooted past and Dustin reached out to tickle her tummy. Marcus smiled at the baby, catching the reflection of Dustin's diamond ring in the sunlight and feeling his mood dampen. He reached out and took her hand, studying the ring.

"If I bought you a diamond ring, would you wear it?" he asked.

She pulled her hand away, guiltily trying to hide it. She wasn't sure how to answer him. "I do not like diamonds, really. I only wore the ring because Christopher made me."

"Then take it off," Marcus said shortly, immediately cursing himself for sounding so blunt. "I mean, he's no longer around to force you to wear it. And you are married to me now, and I should like to see you wear my ring."

Her light mood was ruined. Her wedding rings were a sore point and they both knew it. "I do wear your ring, Marcus."

"On your right hand." He sat up swiftly. "When are you going to stop holding onto Christopher? He is dead, Dustin. I have courted you for weeks and weeks now, praying that you would come to your senses, but you continue to live for a life gone by. You would do well to realize that."

So much for patience. Dustin hung her head, tears welling. "I do realize that. Why do you think I came north, with you?"

He stood up, agitated. “I do not know I truly do not know. You tell me, why *did* you come?”

She looked up at him, her eyes wide with outrage. “Because you all but got down on your knees and begged me to come,” she reminded him. “You nearly killed David when he tried to stop you and threatened Edward at every turn. What choice did I have?”

He looked at her for a moment; of course she was right. He had done everything but tie her to his horse. With a long sigh, he turned away.

“Dustin, I want you to let me love you,” he said softly. “I thought I had enough love for the both of us, but I cannot continue to give and not receive. You have got to give just a little, honey.”

She stood up. “I told you I would always love Christopher, Marcus. You knew that when you brought me here. I have never lied to you about that and I told you I needed time, but you continue to push me and eventually you are going to push me away from you.”

He just hung his head and she felt sorry for him. Lord only knew how hard he had tried to make a life for her, to love her and care for her, and she knew she had been difficult.

With a stab of pity, she went to him and wrapped her arms around his waist. She held her hands up, making sure he was looking down at them, and switched her wedding rings to the opposite hands.

Marcus’ bright gold and garnet wedding band gleamed on the third finger of her left hand. He smiled weakly and clenched her hands against his tight stomach.

“Don’t be angry, Marcus,” she said softly. “You have been more than patient and I hope you do not find out too late that I was not worth all of the grief I caused you.”

He turned around and took her into his arms. “Never in a million years.”

Christin, ignored, let out a whooping yell and they both turned to see her grinning happily back at them, chewing on a piece of harmless grass.

“Is she my daughter, Dustin?” he asked softly.

Dustin shook her head. “I see Chris in her, Marcus. The only thing that resembles you is the color of her hair.”

He drew in a long breath and kissed the top of Dustin’s head. “There will be more babies for me; for us. And they will all look exactly like me.”

“Never,” she scowled at him. “They will all be fair like me, not dark as the devil.”

He grinned at her, nipping at her ear playfully and she pulled away, moving back over to retrieve her daughter before she began grazing like a cow.

Marcus felt as if he had won a great battle that day. Little by little, Lady Dustin was slowly becoming his.

CHAPTER FIFTY

CHRISTOPHER'S LAST EVENING in camp was a special night. Lizabetha and her host of silly adolescent friends sang a song in his honor and he applauded graciously at the end of the warbled tune. Simon, a poet at heart, said a special prose he had made up about the Defender and Christopher hid a smile as the boy told of greatly exaggerated exploits. When the boy came to a part where Christopher single-handedly captured a thousand Muslim soldiers, it was all he could do to keep from bursting out in laughter.

But he was nonetheless touched by the show of respect from these people whom he had come to know over the past few months, and he shared a stew of venison and early carrots with Rob privately. The two of them sat in the doorway to his hut, watching the rest of the camp cavort around the fire and entertain themselves. The forest around them was dark and silent as they finished the last of the stew.

"What now, baron?" Rob wanted to know.

Christopher sat down his bowl. "I return home and pray I still have a home to return to."

Rob watched him for a moment. "You are worried about your wife?"

"More than anything," Christopher replied. "She's been a widow nearly three months now, a wealthy widow at that, and it is difficult to say what's happened in my absence."

"I am truly sorry we could not send word of your whereabouts," Rob said. "I hope you understand I simply could not risk the well-being of everyone in camp."

Christopher waved him off. "I understand only too well, my lord, and your apologies are unnecessary. We all must do what we think is best, and even though I am not nearly in prime health, I must go home."

Rob nodded, taking a drink of stolen wine. "I wish I could go home."

Christopher looked at him, the faint firelight reflecting off his young face. "Someday you will. I swear it. And I shall take great delight in ridding your keep of the prince."

Rob grinned. "He seems to be rather fond of it, and Nottingham, I am told."

Christopher nodded in agreement. "After my affairs at home are settled, I promise you that I will seek Richard out and plead your case."

"I am loyal to Richard," Rob said. "And to you, Defender, whether or not you regain my keep. But until I know that Richard won't put a noose around my neck if I show myself, I would just as soon stay to Sherwood. I am rather fond of the place."

Christopher looked about him. "I had heard this place was haunted as a boy."

"Haunted with thieves and rabble," Rob snickered. "And with an earl with no lands."

"John had no legal right to declare you an outlaw," Christopher said firmly. "You were defending what was yours."

Rob shrugged. "That may have well been true then, but he has every right now. I have been stealing from his vassals for quite some time now and that, my friend, makes me an outlaw in the eyes of everyone."

"That may be true, my lord, but I shall still plead your case to Richard, and our king always listens to me," Christopher said.

Rob tried not to sound too hopeful. "We can only pray," he said quietly, then picked up the bowls. "Well, I am feeling fatigued this night. I shall see you off on the morrow."

"My thanks, Lord Robin of the Hood," Christopher stood up, too. "Were it not for you, I would not be alive, and I owe you my life."

"No, you do not," Rob said with a faint grin. "What you have done and will continue to do more than makes up for what Marianne did for you. God must have been watching out for both of us that day when He brought you to us."

Christopher nodded, watching the young lord traipse back across the compound. He turned away, feeling his exhaustion but not sure if his excitement would allow him to sleep.

He stretched out across his pallet, his mind roaming to Dustin as it always did at night, remembering the smell of her skin, the feel of her hair, thinking that within six days he would be at her side. It was almost too much to bear, as if tempting a starving man with food not quite within his reach. His ache, his longing, was consuming him, but eventually he drifted off to sleep.

He was awakened that night by an unearthly howl and immediately he was up, feeling the surge of adrenalin in his veins. His breeches were barely fastened when Rob came barging into his hut.

"Raiders, Chris," he said breathlessly.

Christopher yanked on his last boot and clutched his sword. "Raiders?"

Rob simply nodded and rushed out with Christopher on his heels. At the far end of the camp, mailed men on horses were bearing down with torches in hand. The shouting, the noise that resulted from their appearance was frightening.

But Christopher saw them immediately for what they were, and anger swept him. "Those are no raiders, Rob, they are John's forces," he said quickly. "Get Simon and Marianne into the woods. Hurry."

Rob, customary arrow pack slung over his left shoulder, disappeared into the camp and Christopher quickly mapped out a strategy. The soldiers were already beginning to burn and kill, moving through the village like a plague. He raced back inside his hut and grabbed everything he had come with, his tunic, his armor, his weapon and his scabbard. He knew the hut would be burned and he did not want to lose his possessions, and with his arms full he ducked back outside and made a dash for the woods.

Nearly half the village was burned before he made another appearance. He emerged from the trees dressed to the hilt for battle; his armor secured and his stained tunic announcing just who in the devil he was. There was no mistaking Christopher's banner, for it was one of the most recognizable in England. Dark blue and gold told everyone that this warrior was loyal to Richard.

Even though he wasn't mounted, he was a hell of an imposing sight. He marched straight up to the first mounted soldier and deftly disarmed the man before yanking him clear of his steed. As the fool lay dazed on the ground, Christopher put the tip of his sword against the man's neck.

"Return to your commander," he said with deadly authority "Tell him to cease this raid by command of the Defender of the Realm, or he shall suffer at my hands personally."

The soldier snorted and blinked his eyes, frozen on the ground. "The Defender of the Realm is dead. Killed in battle three months ago. Everyone knows that."

"Have you ever seen the man?" Christopher asked.

"Aye, I have." the soldier said indignantly. "Tall bastard with blond hair and…."

Christopher ripped off his helmet, fixing the man in the eye. After a moment, the soldier's eyes widened and his mouth hung open.

"It *is* you," he gasped with fear and awe. "But they said…said you were dead. How is it you are here?"

Christopher jabbed him in the neck to stop him from talking anymore. "Aye, it is me, and know I mean what I say. Return to your commander and tell him the Defender of the Realm is back from the dead. You will leave this place."

"But you defend outlaws," the soldier snapped. "These scabs continue to commit crimes against the crown."

"Against John, you mean," Christopher replied icily. "These people are no outlaws in the eyes of our king, I assure you. Go now, before I change my mind and remove your head from your body."

He backed off and the soldier rolled to his knees, regaining his shaky feet. Christopher corralled the man's big-boned war horse and ripped off the green and black colors. He then swung himself astride the charger without the use of stirrups, although it had taken a bit of effort to do so, and pointed his sword at the soldier.

"I confiscate this horse in the name of King Richard," he boomed loudly.

"Go, man, and deliver my message."

He spurred the animal in the direction of the fighting even as the soldier wobbled off at a dead run, bearing unbelievable news.

The Defender was returned.

ℭ𝔅

AS QUICKLY AS Christopher's death had spread through the realm, the news of his resurrection spread even faster. John and Ralph were the first to hear of it, and they killed the messenger in their disbelief.

Safe and sound in Nottingham, away from the wrath of Richard for the moment, they were gravely concerned with the rumors that Christopher de Lohr was indeed alive. Having Richard on the attack was threat enough, but if the Defender were indeed alive, then there was good reason to be terrified. Between the king and his champion, surely there was no hope in retaining the keeps gained in warfare.

Christopher had single-handedly saved Rob's camp that night. Although substantial damage had been done, few lives were lost and John's troops turned tail when they realized just who they were fighting against. It had taken them months to find this den of bandits and they were fully prepared to destroy it and capture Lord Robin of the Hood. But when they saw Christopher de Lohr returned to battle like Lazarus arisen, superstition got the better of them and they retreated. Christopher purposely fought with his helmet off so John's men could witness his face and return with the news. He had hoped that his presence would make John think twice before attacking these people again.

Rob and Jonathan were quite amazed to see him in battle. They knew his reputation and assumed that he had not gained it by being a loaf, but to see him in action was a sight to behold. He moved with such ease and grace that Rob was nearly nailed twice by enemy soldiers as he watched him fight, hypnotized.

When the soldiers retreated and the camp grew quiet in the last couple of hours before dawn, Christopher slept a short time but arose quickly to depart. Rob, Jonathan and Simon saw him off aboard his confiscated destrier, and Christopher had to be stern with Simon, for the boy was on the verge of tears the entire time. *Knights do not cry*, he told him with gentle firmness, although it was a lie. He had cried his share since he had met his wife. His body tingling with excitement, he loped from the burned camp without a hind glance.

Christopher drove himself hard. His body was still weakened, but he forced it down as much as he could as he rode the endless green miles toward Lioncross. Evidence of spring was everywhere and he inhaled of it deeply, grateful to be alive.

IT WAS THE near the first of May. He had been injured around the beginning of

February and found it difficult to believe he had been gone that long. Had it truly been so long? Would he return to find all as he had left it, or would he discover his world had been turned awry? He was excited and apprehensive, so desperately eager to return to his wife and tell her how very sorry he was that his death had been a mistake, and in the next breath tell her how very much he loved her. He never told her often enough, in fact, hardly at all, but he would remedy that. He had vowed once before to tell her he loved her until she was sick of hearing it. He would keep that vow.

He passed through Gloucestershire, a lovely portion of the country that he was fond of. The mount beneath him had a pleasant gate that made it easier for him to stay in the saddle for lengthy amounts of time. But eventually, he had to rest and eat, but he made sure it was no longer than absolutely necessary and then he was in the saddle again, riding for home.

A trip that should have taken six days took just over four. The horse was hearty, fortunately, so he had been willing and able. Christopher rode the crest that overlooked Lioncross and the little village, pausing a moment to drink in the sight. It was strange how a year or two could change the way a man looks at life, he thought.

When he first came to Lioncross, he was only concerned with securing the mightiest keep in England. The wife, the village, the perks that came with it were secondary. How his priorities had changed was amazing; how his life had changed was beyond comprehension.

IT WAS DARK and the gates were closed. He rode up to the massive gatehouse and bellowed a greeting for the sentries. The moon was a sliver, offering the guards little light with which to view the caller, but they opened the gates anyway, as was customary.

Christopher smiled to himself as the gates opened and he was beckoned in, thinking they were in for one hell of a surprise. Jeffrey was the first man to see him, his angled face severe.

"Name yourself, man," he said sternly.

"Defender of the Realm, and your liege," Christopher replied. "Do not take that tone with me, Kessler."

Jeffrey cocked an eyebrow, going for his sword, but something made him stop. *The voice*, by all that was holy… did he recognize the voice? As if in a nightmare, he washed with cold fear and stepped back from the horse and rider.

"Show yourself." His voice was a whisper.

Christopher removed his helmet and fixed Jeffrey in the eye. The soldiers standing around him let out a collective gasp and instinctively jumped back, afraid that it was a phantom come to kill them. Christopher gazed around him with patience.

"I am not going to bite you," he assured them, understanding their shock. "It is me. Truly."

Jeffrey was as white as plaster. He was the only man brave enough to step forward and give Christopher close scrutiny.

"Can you see through me?" Christopher asked, holding up his hands. "Do I hover above the horse? Look at me, Jeffrey."

Jeffrey did, meeting his eyes with astonishment. "What…?" he stammered. "I do not understand this."

Christopher swung his leg over the charger and dismounted. All of the soldiers, save Jeffrey, jumped back a step when he hit the ground and Christopher scowled.

"Enough of this nonsense," he scolded. "I am alive, I am whole, and I want to see my wife. Where is she?"

Jeffrey shook his head, trying to regain his reeling senses. "What happened to you, my lord?" he asked, awe and shock in his voice. "Anthony and the others said you perished in battle. They even buried you on a hill overlooking Gowergrove."

"I was not killed, but I was severely wounded," Christopher replied. "I fully realize that it appears I have returned from the dead, but I assure you, I am quite alive. Where is Dustin?"

He caught movement over Jeffrey's shoulder and looked up to see Edward emerging from Lioncross, looking at Christopher as if he were looking at a ghost. His eyes were bugged and his face had the same strange pallor that Jeffrey's did, and he seemed to have forgotten how to take stairs. He tripped, recovered, and slowly continued his approach as if he were walking in a dream.

"Oh… my sweet God," Edward breathed. "Is it really you?"

"It is really me," Christopher said gently, smiling at his close and dear friend. "I am very much alive and in the flesh, and I have returned home."

Edward stopped, swaying as he put his hand to his mouth. Christopher held out his arm. "Would you like to touch me to see if my rotting flesh is peeling from my bones?" he asked. "Mayhap you would prefer to address me as Beelzebub or Mephistopheles? Yet, I assure you, I will answer to Chris.'"

"This cannot be," Edward gasped. "You are dead."

"I am not dead," Christopher said patiently, realizing he had collected quite an audience in the bailey. "As I told Jeffrey, I was severely injured and it has taken me all of this time to recover from the wound. It is only now that I am able to ride a horse and return home. Honestly, I am not the walking dead."

Edward took his hand from his mouth and approached him, still eyeing him with a great deal of disbelief.

"Where is Dustin?" Christopher asked softly.

Edward blinked and turned a darker shade of gray. "Oh, God, I think I am going to be ill."

Christopher cocked an eyebrow at him and reached out to grab his arm. With a tug, he pulled him toward the keep. "Christ, Edward," he swore softly. "When did you become such a weakling?"

They entered the dark and cool keep where Christopher went straight to Lady Mary's old solar. There was wine there, on the heavy oak table, and he shoved a cup at Edward and forced the man to drink it. Edward did, all of it in two big gulps.

"Have some more," Christopher poured Edward a second of wine. "Perhaps that will bring you to your senses."

But Edward needed more than wine; he needed a slap in the face and someone to tell him he wasn't dreaming. All he could do was stare at Christopher, absolutely astonished.

"I thought I was seeing a goddamn ghost when I saw you in the bailey," he whispered. "Jesus Christ, Chris. You are supposed to be *dead*."

"I very nearly was," he replied. "But I shall go into that later. Where is Dustin? Do I have to ask again?"

Edward closed his eyes and took a long, hard swallow of wine. "She is not here," he said, closing his eyes and wondering how Christopher was going to react to the events since his alleged death. When he opened his eyes again and saw Christopher staring back at him, as healthy and whole as when last he saw him, he rolled his eyes again and put his face in his hands. "My God, I am talking to a dead man."

Christopher grabbed him roughly, pulling him to stand and leaving no doubt in Edward's mind that he was, indeed, alive.

"Have no doubt that I am not dead, de Wolfe, but if you do not tell me where my wife is, you may find yourself in that very state," he growled. "Where in the hell is Dustin?"

Edward finally relaxed, gazing back into his liege's eyes. Perhaps that brutal action, small as it was, had convinced him that Christopher was indeed alive. There was so very much to say he did not know where to begin.

"She's with Marcus," he said. "He came to Lioncross when he heard of your death and took her back with him. They are probably married by now."

Christopher let him go, anger and grief flashing in his eyes. "Marcus took her? And she went?"

Edward scratched his head and sank back into his chair; he was feeling distinctly weak. "It is just not that simple, Chris. Dustin was… well, she was beyond devastated to hear of your death. Jesus, I have never seen anyone grieve the way she did. I think she quite literally went mad. She wasn't the same person after she received the news."

Christopher's eyes stung with tears and he found himself taking the seat opposite Edward. He looked down at his folded hands. "And I can never make it up to her for causing her so much pain. I'd sooner gut myself than hurt her like that, but it was out of my control."

"I know," Edward replied softly, still finding it hard to believe he was talking to Christopher. "She wouldn't eat, she took to wearing that peasant garb she was so fond of when you first married her, and she cried all of the time. At one point, she broke a fragile vase and cut herself terribly with the shards. It was just awful."

Christopher shut his eyes tightly and his eyelashes glistened with tears. "Christ, Edward…."

Edward was feeling a bit more in control as he talked. "Marcus arrived to express his condolences, but there was no mistaking his intent," he continued softly. "He came for Dustin and he would not be dissuaded. I tried and he threatened me. David and Richard arrived nearly a week after Marcus did and our king was pulling David and Marcus apart at every turn; it was a nightmare, totally chaotic." He poured Christopher some wine. "Richard was in a foul mood with your death and with John's rampages; David and Marcus were at each other's throats, and Dustin was crazy. I have never seen such madness."

Christopher's head came up, his eyes wet with tears. "Did Marcus force her to go with him?"

"Yes and no," Edward replied. "Her mind was brittle, and Marcus, as you know, can be persuasive. He convinced her that a change of scenery would be the best thing for her, and he furthermore wasted no time in declaring his intentions. I think he simply overwhelmed her."

"Bastard," Christopher growled. "Has he so little respect for me that he would not even allow Dustin to grieve? And what did Richard say to this?"

"Marcus respects you, Chris, but he loves Dustin more," Edward replied. "Richard gave him his blessing to take Dustin and marry her. David was livid."

Christopher's jaw ticked. "So David returned, did he? I knew he would."

"Your brother was in agony, Chris," Edward told him softly. "He was consumed with guilt for what had happened between you two and he was as protective of Dustin as a lioness. He only left Marcus alone when Richard ordered him back to Canterbury."

Christopher sighed, running his hand over his face. "This is all so overwhelming."

"I know how you feel," Edward said ironically, watching Christopher as he absorbed the events of the past few months. "Now, tell me, what in the hell happened to you?"

Christopher looked at Edward a long moment before fumbling with his armor and mail. He pulled everything aside and yanked his tunic up to allow Edward a glimpse of the large, purple scar on his torso. Edward visibly paled.

"That," Christopher said softly, "is the result of a mercenary spear. I was gored like a wild pig and left to die on the outskirts of the battle when a man found me and took me back to his village. There, I was tended by a woman and her husband and nursed back to health. Hell, Edward, I did not regain consciousness for two weeks. They thought I was dead, too."

Edward shook his head. "Could you get no message to us, to let us know you were alive?"

"Nay," Christopher replied regretfully. "The village was a den for outlaws. John is seeking these people and they could not risk letting their place be known. There was no way to send word. The only way to let you know I was alive was to tell you myself, so, here I am."

Edward was beyond overwhelmed; he was having difficulty grasping the entire event. He wiped his hand over his face. "This is incredible. I simply cannot believe any of it."

"Believe it," Christopher murmured. "Christ, Edward, now I have to go north and fight Marcus to get my wife back? Life gets more complicated all the time."

"Indeed," Edward agreed fervently. "But I warn you, Chris; Marcus will not let Dustin go easily. He was quite adamant when he came here for her, like a man possessed."

Christopher ground his jaw. "She's *my* wife, Edward. He has no choice but to return her to me. If he doesn't, then he will die."

Edward averted his gaze, the clash between Christopher and Marcus was bound to tear up the north. He had seen the look in Marcus' eye when he came for Dustin; the man would die for her. So would Christopher.

"Chris," Edward ventured after a moment. "Do you think it wise to go charging up to Somerhill to retrieve you wife? I mean, there is no doubt in my mind that Marcus will do everything in his power to keep her, which will only result in a full-scale war. Do you think that wise for Dustin to witness? After all, the shock of seeing that you are alive will be strong enough without witnessing the ensuing war. And then, suppose, you do not survive; how do you think she will react?"

Christopher's face was dark as he absently studied his goblet. "She's my wife, Edward, and Christin is my daughter. I appreciate Marcus taking care of them, but the fact remains that they are mine. And I will take back what is mine."

"At what cost? Dustin's sanity?" Edward fired back gently. "Think long and hard on this approach, Defender. Use your mighty wisdom now, more than ever."

Christopher started to reply when there was a rap at the solar door. Max, Anthony, Jeffrey, Nicholas, Sean, and Guy pushed the door open before being invited, and Christopher motioned them into the room. He knew how stunned and curious they were.

" 'Tis really you, my lord?" Anthony asked timidly.

"Truly, Anthony," Christopher smiled wearily.

The men shook their heads, astonished. "But you *died*. I saw your body."

Anthony insisted.

"I do not know whose body you saw, but it wasn't mine," Christopher replied.

Something shot in through the doorway, a wisp of an animal level with their shins. Harold threw himself into his master's arms, licking crazily and wagging his stubby tail so hard he threatened to shake it off. Christopher grinned as he fought off the affectionate attack.

"Hal, you fat little maggot," he exclaimed softly. "I was wondering where in the hell you were."

"Well, that is good enough for me," Max said softly. "He's no ghost or the dog wouldn't go near him."

Hal was in dog heaven as Christopher scratched him roughly. Edward shook his head at the two of them. "He wouldn't leave with Dustin, you know," he said. "She took every animal but him. It was as if he was rooted here."

" 'Tis because he knew I would return," Christopher said, throwing Hal off his lap only to have the dog spring up again. It was a game they played, the harder Christopher tossed him, the more eager he was to return for more. He ended up throwing the dog across the room and Hal raced back, wagging his tall and dancing with delight when Christopher put his hand down to let him know he was sincere about not wanting him in his lap.

Anthony was still shaken. He watched Christopher and the dog, letting out a blustery sigh. "You....I mean, the body, was wedged beneath Zephyr. I even retrieved your wedding ring for your wife."

Christopher looked at him a moment as if he suddenly realized something. "Leeton," he whispered. "I gave my wedding ring to Leeton to give to Dustin. He was wedged beneath Zephyr, did you say?"

Understanding spread between the men, as if the pieces of a puzzle were suddenly coming together.

"He must have taken your horse," Anthony said quietly. "His steed sustained a heavy battle wound and he must have taken Zephyr when you were injured."

Christopher closed his eyes for a moment, feeling the loss of his dear friend. "Did you send word to Derby?"

"Aye, we did. His son turned two years old on the very day of Leeton's death," Max replied. "The earl sent a long missive back, informing us of Richard's progress. A smart little lad, he says. I suppose it was not a tragedy from the boy's point of view, considering he never knew Leeton."

Christopher sighed, rising on his long legs. "I suppose. But I do not understand one thing, other than the wedding ring and the destrier, why did you think Leeton was me? We look nothing alike. Surely you could have seen...."

Anthony shook his head. "The body was rotted so badly that we could not tell any facial features, except for the blond hair. You both have blond hair."

Christopher nodded in instant understanding. “Naturally, you assumed it was me. I understand a great deal now.”

He wandered over to the window overlooking the bailey and his men watched him closely, still finding it very difficult to believe he was returned. Half of them expected to blink their eyes and he would be gone, but several minutes in his presence convinced them that he was no apparition. This was the baron, the powerful Defender, and then joy began to override their disbelief.

“Surely we must send missives to King Richard, and David,” Anthony said after several moments. “They must know you are alive. And we shall send a missive to Marc....”

He suddenly looked to Edward, who shook his head darkly. It occurred to all of the knights at the same time that Christopher's' wife had gone with Marcus.

Christopher turned around and eyed his men with the sudden silence. Then his eyes fell on Edward. “I ride for Somerhill come the morrow,” he said quietly. “I go to retrieve my wife.”

Edward hung his head. “ ’Tis wrong, I tell you. You shall only upset her further.”

Christopher bit off a harsh retort, instead, turning back to the bailey again. “I have returned from the dead, Edward. That fact alone will upset her; it doesn't matter how it is presented,” he said, and suddenly turned to Anthony and Jeffrey. “How many men do I carry now?”

“Eight hundred, sire,” Jeffrey replied.

“Mount all but one hundred of them,” Christopher ordered swiftly, the excitement of the march filling him. He was in command once again. “And, indeed, send word to Richard. Tell him I am riding for Windsor and that I will be taking two thousand crown troops with me to Somerhill. Then send word to my brother; tell him of my plans, but do not ask him to join me. I simply wish for David to know I am alive.”

Jeffrey and Anthony took Nicholas with them as they went about carrying out their orders. Christopher focused on Max and Sean.

“I want the men carrying crossbows,” he said, “and I want the border post reinforced with ten men. I want no Welsh surprises while Lioncross is running with a skeleton guard.”

Guy was the only knight left in the room without duties. He faced Christopher expectantly. “You will carry the missive to Richard. You will not wait for a reply and you will join my army as quickly as possible.”

Guy saluted sharply and spun on his heel, quitting the room in a jangle of armor. When all were gone, Christopher turned to Edward and, satisfied, drained his cup.

“Ah, I see the mighty Lion's Claw has indeed returned,” Edward said with a faint smirk. “But, in faith, you look a bit pale and underfed. How do you feel?”

"Pale and underfed," Christopher agreed. "But that will take care of itself. My concern right now is to return my wife home."

Edward nodded in resignation; he knew there was nothing more he could say. "I am riding with you," he said flatly. "Leave Kessler in charge of Lioncross."

Christopher eyed him with an amused smile. Edward was becoming quite adept at giving orders, even to him. "Aye, my lord."

☙

GOWEN HAD NEARLY passed out from the sight of Christopher, turning a sickly green until Christopher gave him a sharp slap on the cheek to bring him about. Thrilled and stunned, he went to inform his wife and prayed the shock wouldn't turn her milk sour. Little Michael was having a difficult enough time feeding and Griselda was worried for the infant.

Deborah shrieked and cried with disbelief, crying even harder when Christopher entered her bedchamber and took her in his arms. Deborah sobbed over and over how mad Dustin had become, how consumed with grief she had been, and strongly urged him to go and get his wife. Christopher swore that he would, but not before he held his new nephew a good, long time, remembering his sweet little Christin with great longing.

NEWS OF CHRISTOPHER'S return spread through Lioncross and the village like a raging fire and before the hour was out peasants were turning up at the gates, clamoring to catch a glimpse of their lord. Christopher was touched, but he was more concerned with preparing for his journey.

Trouble was, he was feeling distinctly weakened from his ride home and he still wasn't up to full strength. He knew the ride to Windsor and then north would be a rough one, and to take on Marcus immediately in battle frankly worried him. He had always been able to outfight Marcus, but in his weakened condition, he wasn't sure if he would be successful. He actually began to think that Marcus might have a chance to beat him but he quickly shoved that thought from his mind. He was the Defender. He was unbeatable.

"What's wrong, Chris?" Edward was standing at the door to his bedchamber, gazing at him with concern.

Christopher realized he was hunched over, leaning on a chair for support. Quickly, he stood up. "Nothing at all," he said. "Are the men preparing?"

"As you ordered, sire." Edward came into the room. "Look, Chris, we both know you have seen better days. You are still recovering from that wound, I'd say. Mayhap your age is finally catching up with you."

"I am only thirty-six," Christopher replied. "I am not that damn old."

"Aye, you are, and your body isn't healing as well as it has in the past," Edward said. "Just look at you; you are thinner than I have ever seen you and you lack the vigor of the Christopher I know. Mayhap you should wait before you try and tackle Marcus."

"Nay," Christopher snapped. "I am fine, Edward, so leave me alone. We ride tomorrow."

Edward shook his head. "You cannot fight Marcus like this. He will murder you."

Christopher flared, clenching his fists. "What would you suggest, then? Dustin is my wife, Edward, and the thought of her was the only thing that kept me alive. I must have her, I *will* have her, and if tearing down Somerhill is the only way to get her back, then so be it."

Edward saw this situation for much more than it was. Christopher wasn't at all well, yet he still intended to charge north to take back what was rightfully his. But it was more than that; he loved Dustin so fiercely that he was willing to risk his life to get her back. His heart ached for his friend.

"Why don't you simply send a missive to Marcus and ask him to bring her back?" Edward said. "With you alive, his marriage to her is void. He has no claim on her."

"Oh, Edward," Christopher waved him off in irritation. "You said yourself how determined he was to keep her. He will not bring her back."

"If Richard told him to, he might," Edward said hopefully. "Richard would deny you nothing."

Christopher shook his head and stripped off his tunic, giving Edward another view of the scar and his body. Not so much sheer mass anymore, but leaner and more defined. Aye, he was thinner, but he certainly did not lack for muscle. In fact, he looked better than Edward had ever remembered.

"If I cannot fight for what is mine, I certainly will not have anyone else do it for me," he replied, grunting as he stretched out his torso muscles. "I appreciate your advice, Edward, but my mind is set. I go for Dustin tomorrow."

Edward shrugged in defeat and quit the room, moving swiftly down the corridor and descending to the first floor. It would seem that he had a couple of missives of his own to send this night.

CHAPTER FIFTY-ONE

DAVID'S HANDSOME FACE was white as he stood by the ornate glass window, looking over the inner courtyard of Canterbury Castle. Beside him, Philip de Lohr sat motionless.

"He's alive," Philip whispered in disbelief.

David was overwhelmed with the contents of the missive, so much so that he did not trust himself to speak immediately after reading it. But now, having had the chance to mull it over in his frazzled mind, he would speak.

"Dustin is with Marcus," he murmured. "And I let her go. After he kills Marcus, he is going to come and kill me."

"Don't be ridiculous," Philip snapped softly. "You were obeying a direct order from Richard. He ordered you away, and you had to go. If Chris is going to kill anyone, let it be our king. He gave Marcus his blessing.

David turned away from the window, his face sunburned from an entire afternoon of practicing in the late spring sun. The past three days had been the most cataclysmic of his life, getting married and learning that his late brother was not at all dead. It was almost more than he could take.

"How is it that he was mistaken for dead?" David wondered aloud. "I don't understand how Anthony could have made such a mistake. Even Burwell declared him dead. I don't understand any of this."

Philip picked up the missive from Edward; it had come alongside the message from Christopher. " 'Twould do you well to ride for the north and prevent your brother from tearing Marcus apart. Edward seems to think it will be a full scale war."

"Edward likes to overreact," David said flatly. "But he is right in assuming I would want to know of my brother's plans. If anyone can stop him, I can."

"He rides with Richard by his side, and you cannot stop our king," Philip said. "According to Edward, Christopher is riding to Windsor to seek reinforcements and then to Somerhill to retrieve Lady Dustin, who by now is probably Lady Burton."

David eyed Philip for a moment before turning away. "This is all madness. Jesus, if Christopher had just killed Marcus the first time he made a move on Dustin, none of this would be happening. Now the whole goddamn country is going to fall apart because my brother and his former best friend cannot keep their hands off the same woman."

"What are you going to do?" Philip asked softly.

David thought a moment. "Take a couple of hundred men with me and ride for Somerhill, I suppose, but I do not know what good it will do. Lord Hampton may want to go, even though he considers himself retired after turning his troops over to me." He glanced at Philip. "What about you? You have a hundred men lodged here in Canterbury. Will you go with me?"

"You forget, I brought Edward here for the wedding, and I shall not allow my twelve-year-old son to ride into battle," Philip said. "Nay, when I leave, it will be to return to Lohrham Forest. I shall let you deal with Christopher; I never could. The only man who could remotely handle him was Richard."

"Christopher respects you, Uncle," David said. "He always listened when you spoke."

Philip snorted. "He listened to me and then did exactly as he pleased anyway. Nay, David, whatever happens is between Christopher and Marcus. Richard is likely to be torn in two if he intervenes."

There was a soft rap on the solar door and the Lady Emilie de Lohr stuck her head in, smiling tenderly at her new husband.

"Mother is serving refreshments in the smaller hall. I promised I'd tell you."

David smiled back at his new wife, truly fond of the woman to the point of falling in love with her. And why not? She was a soft, gentle beauty and a tremendous flirt. He liked that.

"You did, my sweet," David replied. "Tell Mother we shall be there in a moment."

Emilie nodded, then cocked her head quizzically at her husband. "Is something wrong? You do not look well."

David snickered ironically. "No, sweet, nothing is wrong. We shall be along."

Emilie took the hint like a good wife and closed the door behind her. David glanced at Philip. "Now, if that were Dustin, she'd be in here beating me to a pulp until I let her read the missive. I was terrified to take a wife because I was afraid they were all like her."

Philip laughed. "And this is the woman a country is tearing itself apart over? Most confusing."

David was jesting, of course, trying to alleviate some of the tension. As he turned to his uncle again, the door to the solar flew open and a tall, gangly blond youth appeared.

"Father!" he exclaimed. "The mare is foaling. Lord Hampton promised I could have the foal."

"So he did," Philip rose, eyeing his son critically. "Eddie, are you old enough to see an actual birth?"

Edward de Lohr scowled at his father. "I have seen worse. Come quickly. David, you come, too."

David waved him off, watching his uncle and cousin quit the room.

When they were gone, he sighed heavily and sank into the nearest chair. He could scarcely believe that Christopher was alive, but all the more thankful that the rumors of his death had been untrue. He could only imagine the turmoil his brother was going through, knowing his wife was with another man. There were so many unanswered questions that David was wildly confused.

He knew he had to go north, if nothing more than to show support for his brother. He would apologize to Christopher for the things he had said about Dustin and prayed his brother would forgive him. He could only hope that with all of his other troubles, Christopher would be willing to put theirs aside. Dustin had forgiven him and he hoped his brother was in the same spirit.

Emilie was waiting for him in the hall. He saw her sweet, rounded face and took her into his arms. She blushed as he kissed her, feeling flushed and warm.

"Ah, let me guess," David said seductively. "You cannot wait for me to bed you again."

"David," Emilie gasped in mock outrage. "Do not say such things. My sisters are liable to hear and…."

He frowned. "They hear everything, Emilie, no matter if it is whispered or shouted. Nathalie and Elise have ears all over this damn place. They are probably around the corner right now, giggling their heads off."

Emilie smiled at the mirth of it. "They are only children, for God's sake. Don't get so angry."

"Children? Ha! You mean the Devil's own offspring," he snorted. "At fourteen and sixteen years of age, I would hardly call them children."

Emilie kissed him softly, making him forget all about her annoying sisters. "No wonder your father was so glad when I came along," he purred against her cheek. "He has had his fill of women."

David rolled his eyes as he rubbed his cheek against hers. "The poor man is outnumbered."

"You have evened out the odds somewhat."

"Not enough."

Emilie giggled, letting him hold her and kiss her for a few moments. "What did the missives from Lioncross say?" she asked casually.

He pulled back and cocked an eyebrow. "You little minx, using affection to gain information."

"I am not," she replied indignantly. "I simply wanted to know if it said something about Dustin and Christin."

He looked at her a moment before releasing her from his embrace and taking her hand. "Let's go find your father, then. I think he would like to hear this, too."

RICHARD TOOK THE news of Christopher's reappearance with great shock and relief. Such things as a mistaken death were possible, he only knew too well, and he had a mass said immediately in thanks. Two missives had arrived from Lioncross Abbey, one from Christopher and one from Edward de Wolfe.

Christopher's missive gave a brief explanation and outlined his request and future plans, and Edward's was far more concerned with Christopher's march on Somerhill. The man was extremely concerned that Christopher and Marcus were going to stage an all-out battle for Lady Dustin, and Edward was furthermore concerned with the fact that Christopher had no intention of sending word to Marcus of his impending visit.

Richard sighed after he read the missives; the situation was to take a turn for the worse, he could see, and he rapidly made a few decisions. He would grant Christopher his request for troops, yet he himself would ride with the Defender to Somerhill in hopes of preventing a bloodbath. He could, of course, deny Christopher's request, but with everything the man had done for him, he could not refuse him in good conscience. Secondly, he personally would send word of their plans to Marcus Burton so the man would be somewhat prepared for their arrival. If Christopher was to be angry about the leak of information, then let him be angry with the king. Richard felt it was only right to let Marcus in on what was going on.

The king was torn between his two greatest warriors; who to support, who to defend, and most importantly, what to do about Lady Dustin. He could hardly believe these two seasoned soldiers were fighting over the same woman, like two dogs over a bone. It was ridiculous at best, but nonetheless very grave. Both of them loved her, and matters of the heart were always the most serious. But she was, after all, Christopher's wife first and he himself had ordered them wed. Marcus Burton had no legal claim over her now that Christopher was returned and any marriage was dissolved, but Richard knew the solution would not be as easy as that.

He dreaded the ride north, of what would take place. And he was very, very sorry for he knew that he would lose at least one of the two to death's vile clutches before all was said and done.

CHAPTER FIFTY-TWO

THE ARMY WAS sighted at dawn.

Nearly three thousand troops descended on Somerhill under the summer sunrise, looking like an army of ants in the distance. Like a black tide of men and horses, they approached the keep in a steady rhythm, scrutinized by the troops atop the massive wall of the castle.

Marcus Burton watched them closer than anyone, knowing exactly who they were, yet his heart still sank when he saw Richard's and Christopher's banner flying side by side. He could not fight the king; he had contemplated holding out, but he knew that would be disastrous. He had no choice but to open his gates to Richard or face the consequences, and he was greatly troubled.

The missive announcing Christopher's resurrection had been nothing short of a blinding shock. Marcus would not have believed it except that one of Richard's personal knights delivered it and vouched on behalf of the king that the Defender was, indeed, alive. Marcus had raged for an hour after reading it, accusing the king of subversion, and went so far as to throw the knight from his keep. But he recalled the knight an hour later, sat down with him in the great hall of Somerhill, and questioned him most of the night. Only then had he been satisfied that Christopher de Lohr somehow, someway, had returned from the dead. It was as sickening as it had been astonishing.

After his disbelief had settled into edgy acceptance, his focus inevitably turned to Dustin. Marcus purposely kept the missive contents from her, simply waiting for the right time to tell her, but it never seemed appropriate. Truth was, it had taken him a long time to advance their relationship to what it had become and he knew the moment he told her that her first husband was alive, it would dash it all out the window. He loved Dustin too terribly to risk that until it was absolutely necessary. Selfish, he knew, but he didn't care. But now, three weeks after he received the missive, the time was upon him.

The army came to a halt about a quarter of a mile from the fortress and set up siege lines; Marcus could see the careful battle lines from where he stood. It was classic de Lohr tactics. After the lines were drawn, two riders broke off from the main body and thundered towards the gatehouse. Marcus ordered the gates open, ushering in the riders. Marcus saw very shortly that is was Christopher and Richard. He met them in the outer bailey, his big body tense and unfriendly.

The silence between the three of them was uncomfortable and electric. No one seemed to want to speak first or even move; it was a standoff, each man waiting for the other to break. Christopher finally flipped up his visor and met Marcus' cobalt-blue eyes for the first time. For Marcus, it was a distinct shock looking into the eyes of a dead man.

"You cannot have her," he growled.

"Dammit, Marcus," Richard snapped. "What kind of greeting is that?"

Marcus cleared his throat, glancing at Richard and then back to Christopher. "I am pleased to see that you are not truly dead."

Christopher snorted rudely. "Somehow I doubt that. Where is my wife?"

"*My* wife is inside," Marcus corrected him coldly. "I did not tell her you were coming."

"What?" Richard gasped before Christopher could speak. "She does not know we have arrived?"

"Nay," Marcus was dangerously close to insubordination as he spoke to his king. "In fact, she does not know Christopher is alive. I did not tell her."

Christopher flew off his destrier, his boots thumping against the earth and his big body posturing angrily.

"You *bastard*," he hissed. "You filthy, lowlife bastard. I ought to…."

Richard bailed off his destrier in time to grab hold of Christopher. "Easy, baron, easy," he said, looking to Marcus again. "That was most unwise of you, Marcus. And selfish."

"Selfish?" Marcus repeated as if he hadn't heard correctly. "Sire, I beg to differ. 'Twas a choice I made for the sanity of my wife, who is with child and quite easily upset."

Christopher visibly swayed in Richard's grasp and Richard glanced uneasily at the man; the veins on his neck throbbed erratically and his pale lips were open in shock. Christopher didn't look at all well. With a long look at Marcus, he pulled himself from the king's grasp and struggled to compose himself.

Marcus was so torn it was unbelievable. Christopher had been his best friend, once, but now he was his sworn enemy. Yet he couldn't help feeling vastly relieved to see the man alive, in spite of everything. He had a difficult time believing things had deteriorated the way they had, but truthfully the only thing that mattered was Dustin. She made him blind to everything else.

Richard's gaze lingered on Christopher with some concern before returning his focus to Marcus. The meeting wasn't going at all well, and these men who had once been like brothers were seething with hatred. It was disheartening, on so many levels. Richard struggled to keep the meeting from deteriorating even more.

"May I see Lady Dustin?" Richard asked after a moment.

Marcus braced himself. "I would ask that you not, sire."

"That is of no matter to me," Richard said, more firmly. If Marcus was going to be difficult, then so was he. "This is not a request, baron."

Marcus ground his jaw, knowing he could not deny his king. "I shall retrieve her for you, then," he said with strained politeness. "Would you come inside?"

Richard tugged at Christopher but Marcus put out a hand. "Not him," he said pointedly. "Just you, sire."

Christopher turned to face Marcus. "I am coming and nothing short of God can stop me."

"I can stop you," Marcus said through clenched teeth.

Christopher flared and Richard found himself caught in the middle, ordering both men to stand down. But it was like trying to separate two raging bulls so he bellowed to one of the nearby soldiers and sent the man back to the army for reinforcements. Richard spent his time pushing Christopher one way and literally kicking Marcus the other until, thankfully, a pair of knights came charging into the dusty bailey and leapt from their destriers. Richard turned Christopher over to Edward and Anthony, to keep the man calm, before turning his attention to Marcus.

Richard was exhausted and edgy, frustrated that Marcus was being so stubborn. More than that, it made him physically ill to see how much hatred there was between the two former friends. His patience was gone.

"You are making this most difficult, Marcus," he said in a low voice. "Stop being so bloody obstinate and gain us entrance to your keep before we burn the damn thing down. Am I understood?"

Marcus eyed Richard, resigning himself to the inevitable. "As you say, sire."

Before he moved to do the king's bidding, there was a clatter of footsteps on the great stone stoop and Dustin appeared out of the keep. She gazed with excitement over the group, too caught up with the arrival of an army to even look at the banners or at the men. She had been out by the beehives with Iris in the kitchen yard, not even imaging the old woman was purposely detaining her. But an errant soldier had told her of the approaching army and she had run off before Iris could stop her.

They all looked at her, including Christopher. Had Edward not been holding onto him, he would have collapsed in a heap. Never had he seen her look so beautiful, so incredibly healthy and sound and whole. Dressed in a simple yellow surcoat that revealed her blossoming belly, he was weak with the sight of her. His mind went blank and all he wanted to do was run to her and take her in his arms, never to let her go. After months of waiting and dreaming, it was almost too much for him to take in his weakened state. Tears found their way onto his cheeks. He couldn't stop them and didn't care.

"Marcus?" Dustin gasped, her gray eyes alight as she looked at him. "Who has arrived? Why did not you tell me? Oh!" Her eyes suddenly fell on Richard and she curtsied, surprised. "Sire, I did not know… oh, my goodness… I apologize I was not here to greet you."

Richard smiled weakly at the woman who was tearing his kingdom apart.

"Lady de...," he caught himself, "Lady Dustin, you look lovely, as always."

"Thank you, sire," she said pleasantly, amazingly, still not bothering to look at any of the knights that had accompanied the king. "Truly, forgive me for not greeting you personally, as my husband did not tell me you were arriving. To what do we owe the honor of your visit?"

Richard was at a loss for words. Dustin was smiling expectantly at him and he honestly could not answer her. Marcus, too, seemed momentarily stumped. Dustin passed an irritated eye to Marcus, waiting for a reply. But no one spoke until a soft, deep voice suddenly filled the air.

"Greetings, Dustin." Christopher pushed past Edward and Anthony, only a few feet away from her, his sky-blue eyes drinking in her face. He wiped at his wet cheeks, smiling when she turned to him. Their eyes met, and it was magic. "You look wonderful, sweetheart. It is so good to see you."

She heard the voice, and then she turned and saw the face. After that, she remembered little. She remembered thinking she was dreaming, seeing Christopher walk toward her as magnificent as she had ever remembered him, and then thinking that she was losing her mind. Was it possible that his ghost was haunting her, come to punish her for marrying Marcus?

She could only stare at him as he loomed over her, seeing him yet not seeing him, and then her entire world went blissfully, peacefully, welcomingly black.

☙

DUSTIN AWOKE WITH a hysterical gasp, tears flooding from her eyes as she sat bolt up in the bed. Warm hands steadied her and she could hear Iris' soothing voice before she even focused her eyes.

"I saw him!" she wept hysterically. "I saw him, here. He was here and if I reached out, I would have touched him."

"I know, peapod," Iris said soothingly. "Lay down and calm yourself."

But Dustin was having fits. "Christopher was here, at Somerhill. Why did I see him, Iris? *Why?*"

"Because he *is* here," Iris replied steadily.

She and Sara were the only people in the room; the men were down in the grand hall screaming and yelling at each other. Never had Iris seen so much hatred and anger and emotion, and she was frightened. With King Richard in the middle of it, the situation was larger than she could even comprehend. But Marcus had left it up to her to break the news to Dustin because he was fully intending to rip Christopher's throat out.

"He is... *what*?" Dustin breathed in horror. "What are you saying?"

Iris fixed her with a patient look. "I am saying that Baron de Lohr is indeed here, in the grand hall. It seems that he was not killed in battle after all, merely wounded. He has returned to claim you and Marcus refuses to let you go."

Dustin was overwhelmed; stunned, shocked, beyond comprehension were all too light a term. She was shaken to her soul, her disbelief so great that she almost passed out again, but she controlled herself. She began to breathe unevenly, clutching at her throat as the news sunk in. He was alive and come for her? *Alive? Alive? Alive?*

Iris tried to stop her from leaving, but Dustin's mind was too far gone with shock and anticipation. She only knew she had to get to Christopher. With bare feet, she tore from the room with Iris and Sara shrieking after her and raced down the corridor to the stairs. She took the stairs much too quickly and nearly tripped on the bottom step, but she recovered and kept going. All that mattered was seeing Christopher. She had to see him or die trying.

Dustin could hear the shouting in the hall, the angry words, and things banging about. She blew into the room like a madwoman, with her surcoat gathered around her knees, and her hair wild as she desperately sought out Christopher. She was terrified that she had been lied to, that he really wasn't alive, and that she was simply going mad.

But that wasn't the case. Her knees went weak when her gaze fell on him several feet away, standing near the hearth. Their gazes locked and Dustin could feel the emotion pouring out of him, into her, and vise verse. Without a word spoken, she knew everything that was in his heart and it filled hers to the brim, exploding in a burst of gladness like she had never experienced. She gasped at the sensation of joy, of adoration, but she caught movement out of the corner of her eye and saw that Marcus was moving toward her. She bolted away from him, throwing out her hands to stop him, and he indeed came to a halt. She didn't want his intrusion. Dustin refocused on Christopher, making her way haltingly towards him.

"Is it truly you?" she breathed. "Or am I dreaming again?"

Christopher's goblet went clattering to the floor and his arms opened up for her, his heart bursting with agony and elation. She threw herself into his arms in a mass of hair and material and pregnant belly. Her hysteria returned tenfold and he fell to his knees with her in his arms, his face buried in her hair, with the smell of it making him faint. He simply could not believe he was holding her again, feeling her, and touching her. Good Christ, how long had he waited? *How long*?

Christopher's tears came and his deep sobs joined her high-pitched weeping. Cries from the soul filled the room. He held her so tightly that she could not breathe, but it was joyful suffocation. It was a moment that Dustin thought would never come and if she smothered for it, then she was glad to. His huge arms enveloped her, with one plate-sized hand at the back of her head swallowing up her skull.

Even though he was real and breathing in her arms, Dustin still could scarcely believe it. If this was true insanity, if she had indeed crossed the threshold, then she would be content to be a lunatic the rest of her life. There was such bliss in it.

There wasn't a dry eye in the room. Battle-hardened warriors dashed away tears, turning away from each other so no one would know of their weakness. Richard stood a few feet away, his own throat constricted with sobs as Christopher and Dustin wept together.

Edward was sobbing openly with his hand over his mouth. Anthony had tears running down his ruddy cheeks as he put his hand on his friend's shoulder. Above, on the loft overlooking the great hall, Iris and Sara were weeping in one another's arms and were joined by several serving wenches who had heard the yelling. One would have had to have been dead not to have felt the very depths of the emotion involved.

Time was stilled for just a moment, a warm sliver in the span of ages opening just for them, allowing them a second chance in life. Love had conquered, consumed, and persevered until Christopher and Dustin were where each rightfully belonged, in one another's arms.

Only Marcus wasn't weeping. He was so consumed with anguish and jealously that he turned his back on the scene, racing for his sword. Blackness clouded his vision, pure and simple, and he would have it out with Christopher here and now. By tonight, Dustin would be a widow either way.

Dustin clung to Christopher as if she were afraid he was going to disappear. They were both on their knees, clutching each other fiercely, afraid to move or speak. Dustin finally pulled back after a few minutes, running her hands all over his wet face, touching him to make sure he was real. His stubble scratched her hand and he kissed her palm as she dragged it over his mouth, closing his eyes to feel her again.

"Oh my God, Chris," she wept. "Are you real? Are you true?"

He kissed her fingers, her mouth. "As real as rain, sweetheart. Christ, Dustin, I am so sorry. Please, my love, forgive me for putting you through this."

She kissed him eagerly, feeling his scratchy beard with delight and even laughing with the glee of it. Her emotions were beyond description.

"Do you still love me?" she begged hoarsely.

He focused on the face, the eyes. "More than my own life, Dustin. I will love you in this life and beyond."

She put her hands on either side of his massive head and he kissed her with sweet urgency until she put her hand over his mouth. "Say the words, Christopher."

"I love you," he whispered against her cheek, closing his eyes with the bliss of it. "I love you, Dustin, with everything I am. Know that I will always love you, no matter what."

She giggled, quickly returning to sobs as he kissed her with all of the reverence they both felt. It was then he realized they were both kneeling on the floor and in her condition, he wanted her off the ground.

"Get up, sweetheart," he staggered to his feet and pulled her with him. "You should not be on the floor."

Dustin struggled up with him but immediately noticed the change in him. "You have lost weight," she cried softly. "Oh, Chris, what happened? Why did they tell me you were dead?"

He pulled her close, not ever wanting to let her go. "Because they thought I was," he murmured. "I was wounded in battle and they mistook Leeton's body for mine. But let's not get into that now. There will be all the time in the world later. Just let me hold you. Where's Christin?"

"In her nursery," she told him, running her hands over his face again. "She is looking like you more and more. She is even starting to walk."

He kissed her hands, his whole body shaking with emotion and glee. "I have missed her terribly," he murmured sincerely. "She probably won't even remember me."

"She will," Dustin whispered, kissing his mouth again. "She loves you."

She pressed against him, sniffling, laboring to gain control of her emotions. The shock of it still wasn't over, but she was starting to understand that he really had returned to her and her hysteria was being replaced by overwhelming joy.

Christopher glanced over her head at Richard, smiling at the man's red-rimmed eyes. The other knights had moved discreetly over to the other end of the room, allowing them some privacy, and he was grateful. He did not even notice Marcus was missing until the man charged back into the room, brandishing his broadsword and armor.

"Let my wife go," he ordered Christopher. "Prepare to meet your God, baron."

Christopher's smile faded and Dustin whirled around as if she could protect him with her swollen body. Instantly the mood of the room changed.

"No, Marcus!" she cried.

"Marcus, put down the sword," Richard put himself between the concerned parties. "Put it *down*."

Marcus flipped up his visor. "Sire, that man holds my wife and I will defend what is mine.

"She is his wife," Richard reminded him.

"She's *mine*," Marcus shot back. "The child she carries is mine."

"No, it is *not*," Dustin said deliberately, seeing the look of disbelief in Marcus' eyes. She felt a good deal of pity for him, and guilt for herself, but she was selfishly unconcerned for Marcus at the moment. "Marcus, I was pregnant when I came here, only I was afraid to tell you. I let you think the babe was yours, but it was not. It is Christopher's."

Marcus' expression fell. "That is not true."

Dustin nodded emphatically. "It is," she said. "Do you remember how ill I was when I first came to Somerhill?"

Marcus well remembered that time. "I do."

Dustin felt Christopher's massive hand move to her belly and she put her own hand over it. "I am sorry I deceived you, Marcus," she said sincerely, "but under the circumstances, I thought it best to let you believe what you would."

His cobalt-blue eyes stared back at her miserably. "I suppose I knew you were pregnant," he said softly. "Whether or not Christopher is the true father, I accepted the child as mine. It is my child, and you are my wife."

"I am Christopher's wife," she said earnestly. "You *know* that; you have always known that. He is my husband, dead or alive."

Marcus slammed the faceplate down and raised the sword and Dustin bolted forward, suddenly furious.

"So help me, Marcus Burton, if you harm Christopher, I shall hate you for the rest of my life," she snarled. "Do you hear me? I shall despise and loathe you, and I shall kill myself if you try to touch me. Do you understand me?"

The sword lowered slightly. "Do not say that."

"It is true!" she shrieked. "I shall hate you forever, Marcus. I want Christopher. He has returned to me, and I want him. Can you not understand? As badly as you want me, *I want him.*" Her last three words were deliberate and stressed.

"Dustin," Christopher came up behind her. "Leave him be, sweetheart. He must do this, as I must."

She whirled to Christopher, seeing that he was donning his helmet. "Nay!" she gasped. "I forbid you! Christopher, I just got you back. I am not going to lose you now."

"You will not," he said evenly.

From the shadows, Anthony suddenly came charging forward, sword in hand. Marcus didn't hesitate as he engaged Anthony head-on, landing a clean strike to the groin within the first four blows. Mortally wounded, Anthony fell to the floor in agony.

The room sat in stunned silence, realizing Marcus was deadly serious about fighting for Dustin. Dustin, too, realized Marcus meant what he said, but she was horribly shocked to see that he had gored Anthony. She watched Edward drag Anthony across the floor, leaving a thin trail of blood.

"Marcus," she said, scared and incredulous. "You killed him!"

Marcus did not reply and Richard moved forward, eyeing the two men severely. "How is it that we have come to this?" he wondered quietly. "My very best knights, dueling each other over the love of a woman. How in the hell have we come to this?" He looked down at Dustin. "My lady, sometimes I wish I had never heard the name Barringdon. You, dear woman, have come closer than anyone to toppling my throne."

Dustin felt guilty as sin, lowering her gaze. Richard hadn't meant to blame her, though, and put a fatherly hand on her arm. His gaze fell on Marcus and then Christopher.

"I do not relish what this has come to, but I had better let you two fight it out or there will never be peace within my ranks." He pulled Dustin along with him, out of the line of fire. "Get on with it then, and I shall await the victor with Lady Dustin in another room." So much for the glorious speech he had prepared to give at this moment; he knew any words would be wasted on them. The die was cast and nothing he said would make any difference.

But Dustin wasn't ready to go. She pulled away from Richard and rushed to Christopher. "Nay," she cried softly. "Do not do this. Christopher, I do not want to lose you again. I could not take the pain, not when I just got you back."

He flipped up his visor and kissed her with painful sweetness. "You won't, sweet love. Go with Richard."

Dustin could not believe this was happening. To have him in her arms for mere minutes and then suffering the threat of death again was too much to take. She started to cry again, but he kissed her tears away.

"Nay, Dustin," he murmured, his lips on her face. "No tears."

He gently turned her toward Richard, but instead, she veered toward Marcus. He observed her coolly as she approached.

"If you win, Marcus, you lose everything," she whispered viciously. "You will not have won a wife, but an enemy for life. Leave well enough alone and we can remain on good terms, but kill Christopher, and I will turn your life into a living hell."

He gazed at her a moment. "Would it be so terrible to remain with me?"

"Not if I loved you," she said honestly. "But the man I love is alive, Marcus, and I want to be with him. Why is that so difficult for you to understand? I certainly do not want to hurt you, for you have been more than generous, but would you truly want a wife who did not want you?"

She saw pain in his eyes and she reached out to touch him. "Marcus, the time we have shared has been wonderful and I shall always have fond memories of Somerhill. But my place is with Christopher, and you must find a wife who will worship the ground you walk on. But that wife isn't me."

She turned to gaze adoringly at Christopher as Richard moved forward and took her with him. The rest of the knights and officials cleared out after them. Alone in the room, Christopher and Marcus faced off.

"You did not have to kill Anthony," Christopher said, posturing defensively.

"I did. He wanted to kill me," Marcus replied.

Christopher suddenly stopped his advance. "Marcus, what would have become of us if Dustin did not exist?"

Marcus stopped, too. He thought a moment. "I suppose we would still be the best of friends, carousing Windsor and bedding wenches."

Christopher head bobbed in a nod. "Do you remember the Countess of Ixloe?"

Marcus nodded. "Absolutely. The biggest tits I have ever seen."

Christopher snorted. "She paid you as if you were a common whore."

Marcus snorted in return. "And you got a sable cloak out of her."

"Better than money," Christopher insisted. "Or what about the time we got into that fight in Constantinople? In the beer house?"

Marcus lowered his sword and raised his faceplate. "Those idiots deserved it. French bastards, insulting Richard as they did."

"Richard beat the hell out of them," Christopher said, lowering his own sword, grinning. "He always intimidated the hell out of me after that, although I never let on. And David; Christ, do you remember when David bedded that ambassador's daughter?"

Marcus laughed, warming to the conversation, all but forgetting his hurt and anger. "Hell yes, I do. We had to smuggle him out of the city because there was a damn price on his head."

"We were clever bastards, weren't we?" Christopher's eyes twinkled, his smile fading as he fixed on the man he had loved like a brother. "What in the hell happened? One minute you were my best friend, and the next minute we are preparing to kill one another."

Marcus' smile faded, too. With a grunt, he sat heavily on the nearest chair. "We fell in love with the same woman."

"Is that it?" Christopher sat across from him, wincing when his armor jabbed his scar. "I thought it would be something much more complicated than that to make us want to kill one another."

Marcus sighed heavily. "I do not want to kill you, Chris. But I love Dustin."

"As do I," Christopher said softly. "She was my wife first, Marcus. The children are mine, no matter how much you love them. I do not want to die; I do not want you to die. I am sorry for all of this, I truly am, and I appreciate the fact that you took my wife and child as your own. God only knows not many men would do what you have done, and I am deeply thankful. But I am back now, and I want my family. You would kill me for wanting what is my right?"

Marcus met his gaze a moment before looking away. After several long seconds, he slapped his leg in defeat. "I love her, Chris. I have always loved her."

"And she loves me," Christopher returned gently. "I shall not share her with you, my friend. You shall have to find your own wife."

Marcus gazed back at him, resignation and hurt written in his eyes. After a moment, he let out a hissing sigh and turned his head. "Sometimes I wish I had never heard the name Dustin Barringdon, either."

"Then that is where we part opinions," Christopher replied. "I cannot imagine my life if I had not married Arthur's daughter."

They sat together a long while in silence, each man to his own thoughts, Christopher wondering if Marcus was still going to fight him. He hoped not, for he would surely kill his friend. It might take some time, but he had no doubt he would be the victor. His heart ached for the friendship they used to have, for the way things used to be.

"I shall let you take Dustin on one condition, then," Marcus said finally. "That you leave Christin here with me."

Christopher was surprised. "Why would you say that?"

Marcus cleared his throat, dropping his gaze. "I think…I think she is my daughter, Chris, and I shall tell you why. You may want to kill me after you hear this." He stood up. "The night I left London, do you remember you asked me to watch over your wife while you met with the justices?"

"I do," Christopher nodded, seriously curious.

Marcus swallowed, finding this confession harder than he once thought. "Dud left me alone with Dustin, and if you recall, she had been very angry with me over her miscarriage. Hell, Chris, I had to talk some sense into her, so I went into her bedchamber hoping to have a few words with her." His voice was quiet. "It was almost black in the room; I could scarce see my hand in front of my face. When I knelt down to wake her, she thought that I was you and immediately pulled me onto the bed with her. I could have stopped her, but I am guilty in that I was far gone in love with her and I did not want to stop her. She thought it was you the entire time, Chris. She kept calling your name, but I didn't care. I took her and I did not regret it. But I left London because I could not bear to see her with you after that."

Christopher's face went hard with shock and anger but he kept his customary composure. "And you think Christin is your daughter?"

"She was born early, wasn't she?" Marcus said. "She has dark hair, like me. Dustin isn't even sure if she's your daughter."

He stared at Marcus a moment. "Then she did, in fact, know it was you who took her that night?"

"She said she thought she dreamed it, and I assured her that she did not," he replied. "I never meant to betray you, Chris. But I could not help myself."

Christopher looked away, those events suddenly rushing back to him with amazing clarity. He remembered well when Dustin accused him of making love to her, and he had insisted that she had only dreamed it. *Damnation*! Then it hadn't been a dream, after all. He remembered her moods, how bitterly she had hated Marcus. All of it suddenly became clear and he felt distinctly less benevolent toward his friend. To think that his sweet little daughter may, in fact, not be his after all spread anguish in his heart. And he felt doubly foolish for denying the very fact to his brother. Had David been wiser than he when it came to Dustin? Had he been right all along?

"I see," he rose stiffly, feeling his anger rise. "Damn, Marcus, was David right? Should I have killed you the very first time you kissed my wife? Would that have spared me all of this pain and anguish?" he focused on Marcus. "I trusted and respected you till the very last, Marcus. But from what you have just told me, any last shred that existed is gone. Hell, even as I rode here with Richard, I was hoping beyond hope we could remain friends, but I see that you have rendered that quite impossible. I always knew you to be cunning and sly, but never against me. You have betrayed me, Marcus, beyond repair."

Marcus looked deeply saddened and guilty. He knew Christopher was right and he was disgusted with his lack of control. But the fact remained his motives had been true, even if his tactics weren't.

"I can only apologize, Chris. 'Tis your right to accept or reject it," he said.

Christopher paused a moment. "I reject it. And Christin goes with her mother."

Marcus looked away a moment, feeling the grip of his sword in his hand. "Then I guess there is nothing left to say. I have enjoyed our friendship, Chris, in spite of everything."

Christopher had returned to the hard Defender, his face emotionless as he secured his helmet and lowered his faceplate.

"Now I must do what I should have done a year ago," he said. "May God have mercy on your soul, Marcus."

Marcus lowered his visor, not the least bit apprehensive. "And on yours, Christopher."

The Defender of the Realm faced off against Richard's mightiest general. Each man knew the other's skills and weaknesses, having fought with each other long enough to know his opponents responses. When the first blow came, from Christopher no less, the clash of blade upon blade shook all of Somerhill to the very rafters.

☙

INSTEAD OF FEELING weakened, Christopher had never felt so powerful. It was as if he had never been injured, and Marcus fought as if his right hand had never been crushed. Blow upon blow slammed against each other with unimaginable strength, their teeth rattling and their heads jarring at the force. But this was the fight of their lives, as if all of the preparing and practice that they had gone through their entire lives was now suddenly coming to bear. This was the pinnacle they never thought to achieve, yet were just the same.

They plowed their way through the great hall, grunting and snorting with effort, tearing the place apart until it looked as if a platoon of thieves had gone through it. The only thing remotely spared was the massive oak table, but it had suffered greatly in the clash.

Christopher's stamina was holding very well as he slashed away at Marcus, all of the anger and pain of betrayal finding an outlet through the serrated broadsword. He would have much rather beaten Marcus to a pulp with his fists, but David's words kept ringing true in his ears; *you should have killed him when he first lay hands on Dustin.* He would not make the same mistake twice, as much as it pained him.

Marcus deftly danced around a huge cabinet, pulling it down behind him and it crashed with a deafening roar to the ground. Christopher acted as if it wasn't even so much as an obstacle, he charged over it, smashing through the wood as he plowed his way to Marcus. Broadswords met with the stone wall, emitting a shower of sparks as Marcus dodged Christopher's fury.

All of Somerhill was in hiding, waiting until it was safe to come out. Everyone knew that Lord Christopher and Lord Marcus were going at it, and the knights purposely kept all of the soldiers outside in the outer bailey, as far away as they could from the fighting. Edward was nearly frantic to get inside, but Sean and Nicholas restrained him uneasily. Several feet away, Sir Stephen, Dud and Sir Dalton eyed Lioncross' knights with a mixture of suspicion and regret. The tension in the air was tangible.

Marcus took the offensive well into the bout, hoping that Christopher had tired himself out enough to the point that defeat might be in sight. He charged headlong at the Defender and they both went tumbling down a short flight of stairs, ending up in a dimly lit corridor that led to the small chapel where Marcus and Dustin were married. It was fairly dark and their blows met with each other a good deal more than they had out in the well-lit main hall. Christopher landed a particularly vicious strike to Marcus' torso, in the weak point where the breastplate met the lower body armor, and blood stained the mail.

It was a bloody nick, but not too severe, and Marcus strove onward, fighting Christopher for all he was worth. The power, the strength coming from a man who was declared dead not four months ago was amazing; in fact, he hadn't seen Christopher stronger in spite of his weight-loss. If anything, he was more agile than ever.

With renewed determination, Marcus met the onslaught and countered.

ᘓ

"I CANNOT STAND this anymore," Dustin whispered painfully. "I do not hear them. Where did they go?"

Richard cocked a well-trained ear. "I still hear them, but they have moved away from us. Aye, they are both still alive."

Dustin clutched her stomach. "Oh, lord, I think I am going to be ill. Why are they doing this? Why?"

Richard smiled ironically, his gaze averted. "For a reason I never thought I would see. For the love of you."

"But I only love Christopher," she insisted. "Why does Marcus insist on going through with this battle? If he wins, I shall hate him until I die."

"Men do strange things when they are in love," Richard said vaguely.

Dustin looked at the king, forgetting about her own anguish for a moment. "This distresses you greatly, sire. You love both Christopher and Marcus, don't you?"

"As if they were my brothers," Richard replied wearily. "Oh, my lady, the stories I could tell you of them, their bravery and devotion to me. To see it come to this is unbelievable."

Because of her. All of this, because of her. Richard was losing his throne and the two men who could help him regain it were fighting over her. She felt guilty and worthless. Mayhap if she had died in childbirth, the wrongs would have righted themselves. Christopher and Marcus had loved each other, once. And that love was gone because of her. All of this was her fault.

Mayhap if she left, things would go back the way they were. But where would she go? Her father had been a friend of the Earl of Wrexham. Mayhap he would take her. What of Lord Sedgewick? She could go and live with him and Anne, and serve as Anne's lady. Mayhap if she explained the situation, they would take her in. But she would swear them to secrecy; Christopher must never know where she went. For all he would know, she had run away and disappeared.

Hot tears stung her eyes; she loved Christopher so much that she could not stand to be away from him, yet she would have to put her feelings aside. Lord, she had only this day learned he was alive and now she was considering leaving him. But the value of his life and Marcus' life was more important than her feelings, and considering she had caused all of this havoc, she did not deserve anyone's love. Besides, Christopher could not truly be happy with her; all she had done was cause dissension and misery among him and his men.

She had been a weak, indecisive mass of humanity ever since Christopher had "died." She knew that he was alive and for that, she was somehow made whole again. But the division she had caused made her ashamed of herself, even though she had not knowingly done anything. She truly believed if she left, then all would right itself. There would no longer be any reason to fight if she were gone.

Dustin was intelligent, but she was naive. She believed more with each passing moment that if she were gone, Christopher and Marcus would stop trying to kill each other, and Richard would then stop resenting her. Then, mayhap, someday, she would seek her husband again. Mayhap he would have a chance to clear his mind and decide if she was truly worth the pain she had caused.

She rose unsteadily, eyeing Richard where he sat in the corner. Fighting off the tears, she approached him.

"Sire," she said softly. "I am....I am not feeling very well. I would retire to my rooms to rest, if I may."

He gazed at her. "You look tired. Go as you will, my lady. Would you like me to escort you?"

"Nay," she shook her head quickly. "I am quite able, sire."

He watched her go, only imagining the toll this turmoil must be causing her. But she was handling herself remarkable well, he thought. She was handling it better than he was, in fact. Yet, in truth, there was nothing else they could do but sit and wait.

☙

CHRISTOPHER AND MARCUS ripped the chapel apart beam by beam and had, amazingly enough, rendered little damage to each other. Neither man's strength was waning, feeding off their adrenalin as they fought each other as if either man was Lucifer himself. Strangely, neither man felt hatred, only a sense of duty. They ceased to see each other as Christopher and Marcus and began to view the armored opponent as just that, a faceless enemy. It was the only way to keep the deep, deep emotions from tearing them apart.

Dustin was shaking with nerves and purpose. She had dressed in a thick woolen surcoat and had packed an extra surcoat and items for Christin in a small satchel that could be easily concealed beneath her heavy cloak. She knew what she was planning was hastily thought of, and that it was dangerous for a woman and child to travel alone, but she ignored her common sense. She could fight well and protect both herself and her daughter, and with renewed determination, she went to find Christin.

Sara had the babe in the nursery, playing with her on the floor. Dustin breezed in and snatched her child, dismissing Sara rudely. When the maid left, she quickly dressed Christin in layers of warm clothing and took her back into her own chambers.

Gathering her things and wrapping herself and her daughter in her warm cloak, she left the room without a back glance. She was leaving and she was never coming back.

It had been remarkably easy to slip out of the castle unseen, for the halls were deserted. She could not hear the fighting anymore, but she did not think on it. She had to force her fear and terror from her mind and focus on her task ahead. Urgency filled her as she raced from the keep and into the inner bailey.

Marcus had shown her a tunnel that led through the inner wall to the outer bailey, and she slipped through, ducking when a sentry passed too close. The sun was setting as she dashed, unseen by the hundreds of soldiers to her back, as she raced to another gate and stealthy snuck into the stables.

Hercules snickered softly and she shushed him, setting Christin down while she bridled and saddled the horse. Christin was perfectly happy sitting in the clean straw, sticking pieces in her mouth and smiling sweetly at her mother.

Stable boys and grooms passed by the stall on a few occasions, but Dustin was able to prepare the horse undetected. The trick would be, however, taking him out of the stable.

There was a small, arched tunnel that led from the outer wall to the countryside beyond. If she could lead Hercules to it, she was sure he would fit and she could take him out unseen. Otherwise, she would have to go through the front gates, and that would mean meeting up with Edward and the rest of the knights. She had no doubt that whatever excuse she gave them, they would refuse to let her leave. But leave she would, and she finally decided as she cinched the saddle that she would ride to Baron Sedgewick's in Wiltshire. She could make the journey in three days. She prayed the weather and her courage would hold out.

With Hercules ready, she tied Christin to the front of her with a thick scarf, forming a little cocoon for the babe. Christin cooed and sucked her thumb and Dustin was so thankful she was blessed with a good-natured babe.

Keeping her eyes alert, Dustin led Hercules from his stall and immediately spied the gated tunnel. A few stable boys milled about several stalls down, but for the most part, the stables were deserted. Everyone had gone to see who would be victorious in the fight between Christopher and Marcus, and the diversion worked in her favor.

With a kiss to Christopher and a prayer to God, Dustin led Hercules through the old gate.

RICHARD LOST TRACK of all time sitting, waiting for the victor to come and collect the spoils he had worked so hard for. In fact, he even dozed off and was surprised to awaken to a dark room, knowing that he had slept much longer than he had intended.

A servant entered the room, bearing cheese and wine for the king, and Richard took a big bite of cheese before wondering if Lady Dustin would like some. Still resting, he presumed, he decided not to wake her up. Instead, he wandered out into the corridor to see how the battle was progressing.

A harried-looking servant told him that Lord Christopher and Lord Marcus were still going at it in the opposite end of the castle, and furthermore told him that they had destroyed everything in their path. But they were still remarkably whole, considering the battle had been raging for over four hours. With a sigh, Richard decided to see for himself.

He passed Iris as she descended the stairs and the woman nearly prostrated herself at his feet.

"Beg pardon, my lord king, but is Lady Dustin well? I have not seen her since this morning when she...."

"She is resting in her room," Richard said, distracted. As he moved past the woman, she stopped him.

"She is not in her room, your grace, and neither is Christin," Iris told him. "I presumed they were with you."

He paused and looked at her. "She went up to her room three hours ago, woman. I have not seen her since."

Iris' eyes bugged slightly. "Do you suppose… she could not have done something foolish to herself or the child? She was quite distraught with everything that has gone on."

A light went on in Richard's eye. A strange gleam, the beginning of an idea. He suddenly knew how to end the battle, at least for the moment. Mayhap it would be enough time to settle the differences less violently. He fleetingly wondered if Lady Dustin had planned something like this all along.

"Have you searched other rooms for her?" he demanded.

"Nay, sire, I have not," Iris said. "But I shall go this minute and…."

"Nay," he put out his hand to stop her, his eyes glittering thoughtfully. "Return to her room and see if anything is missing. I shall lead the search for Lady Dustin."

Iris scooted off and Richard marched away purposefully, heading to the other end of Somerhill where the combatants were fighting. He found them in an area that housed the chapel, with dank cellars and storage rooms that houses phantoms at this time of night. There was very little light and he was surprised that Christopher and Marcus hadn't hacked themselves to death because of it.

"Cease!" Richard roared from the top of the stairs.

At the bottom of the flight, Marcus was dealing Christopher a heavy blow, but both men came to a jerky halt. Weaving and panting, they faced the king.

"Lady Dustin is missing," Richard said gravely. "We must search for her now; we have no idea how long she has been gone."

He made it sound more severe that it was on purpose; he wanted the two stubborn men to think of something other than themselves. Properly distracted, he hoped they would forget about their mortal combat.

"Gone? What do you mean gone?" Christopher breathed heavily. "Where could she go?"

Marcus raised his faceplate, his face dripping with perspiration and lined with fatigue. "There are a thousand places to hide in this labyrinth."

Richard raised an eyebrow. "Or a thousand windows to throw oneself from," he said. "Honestly, you two are the most selfish bastards I have ever seen. Did either of you stop to think how this was affecting her?"

Christopher raised his faceplate, a trickle of blood coming from his mouth. "She wouldn't do anything so foolish. She must be hiding somewhere."

"Has anyone checked the north tower? She loved the view of Somerhill from there." Marcus' sword was lowered and he was moving for the stairs.

"That's not all, good lords," Richard saved the best for last, hoping that would jolt them into action. "Christin is gone, too."

Christopher froze a moment, as did Marcus. Then, they glanced at each other apprehensively and Richard's heart soared.

Bravo, Lady Dustin, wherever you are.

ᴄᴏ

A SEARCH OF the entire castle turned up nothing. It was close to midnight and Richard was gravely concerned. He had honestly believed that she would turn up, but it soon became obvious that she was not within the confines of the keep.

Christopher and Marcus were men possessed; searching every inch of the castle with complete disregard of their hatred of one another. It was as Richard had hoped, only the circumstances had grown quite concerning. He had been sure that Lady Dustin had gone to some outlying corner of the castle to weep, but when hours of searching failed to produce her or the babe, he felt guilty that he had even let her out of his sight.

Christopher was the one to discover that Hercules was gone and his heart sank. But that was quickly followed by explosive anger and immediately, he sought out Marcus.

"Her horse is gone," he boomed, marching up on Richard and Marcus. A massive mailed fist lashed out and caught Marcus right on the jaw, sending the man staggering. Richard put himself once again between the two of them.

"Chris!" the king snapped in warning.

Marcus spun around, his hand on his jaw and charging back toward Christopher, only to be halted by Dud and the king. His eyes were blazing with fury.

"You goddamn bastard, this is all your fault," Christopher raged. "If you had only kept your bloody hands to yourself, none of this would have happened. You went after Dustin like a dog goes after a bitch in heat."

"Christopher!" Richard shouted again; he was not in a pleasant position between two huge, huffing men. "Shut your mouth. You are not making this any easier."

Marcus' eyes narrowed, ignoring Richard's command. "To the devil with you," he seethed. "You never cared for her until I showed interest. I loved her from the start, which is something you failed to do."

Christopher put his hands out but Edward yanked him back roughly, assisted by Nicholas. They pulled and pushed the two men apart, tension and uneasiness flowing through all of them. It was frightening to think the whole situation was so desperately out of control.

"So she is gone and has taken the babe with her," Richard said loudly, trying to divert their attentions from each other. "Marcus, this is your land. Where could she have gone?"

Marcus sighed, attempting to control his fury. "I do not know, sire. She was not out of the castle very much. She does not know the terrain well."

"Is it possible that she is trying to return to Lioncross?" Richard wondered aloud.

Christopher shook off his knights, running his fingers through his hair as he, too, struggled for calm. "As possible as anything else," he said. "We must search for her immediately."

"Agreed," Richard replied quickly. "Assemble your men, baron, and set to the road south. Marcus, gather your troops and send them in search of your land; every nook and hovel. I shall join Christopher on his trek south."

Orders delivered, there was nothing more to do but carry them out. Making sure Christopher and Marcus kept a distance between them, the men of Richard's command went quickly to do the king's bidding.

Christopher was so tired he was nearly ill, but he ignored it. His wife and daughter were missing and he had to find them, no matter what physical toll it took on him. He cursed Dustin under his breath for being so foolish even as his heart twisted with agony. Richard had been right; he and Marcus had been selfish and had given little regard for Dustin's emotions. Edward had tried to warn him, too, but he had ignored him. The only person to blame for this was him, and he knew it.

His horse saddled, he mounted up with his knights and charged into the bailey just as Marcus and his men were preparing to depart the gates.

Christopher stared across the bailey at Marcus, his guilt overwhelming him. He was a rational man, but he had acted most irrationally and unreasonably, and he was ashamed. He had let his emotions rule him and the results had been less than pleasant. He wondered regretfully if he could ever right the wrongs he had committed, not against Marcus, but against his wife and his king.

The fact also remained that Marcus' marriage to Dustin was not covert, nor was it betrayal. With Christopher dead, Marcus moved to take his place. Had the situation been reversed, Christopher would have done the same. The only treasonous act, and a grave one at that, was that Marcus had bedded his wife at Windsor. Any other acts, he could forgive, but he doubted he could ever forgive Marcus that.

Slowly, he dismounted his charger and made his way over to Marcus.

Marcus eyed him warily, as he should have. Christopher shot an angry glare to Dud as the man tried to intervene between the two of them, then crooked his finger at Marcus to join him in a private conference.

Marcus did not move. Christopher sighed, unstrapped his sword, and let it fall to the ground. Moving away from the weapon, he raised his hands as if to show Marcus he was unarmed and tried again. With the second beckon, Marcus responded.

"See here, Marcus," Christopher said wearily. "This has gone too far. Dustin may be in grave danger and I will admit it is because of me. I do not care if you or I die, but I certainly do not want her placed in jeopardy. I will not fight you for her anymore; I just want her to be happy. If it is with you, or with me, I shall allow her to make her own choice. I have put her through too much already and driven her to this. I am finished with this."

Marcus was harsh, controlled. "That is not fair. You know she will want to go with you."

"Not necessarily," Christopher replied. "She may hate me tremendously for all of the pain and grief I have caused her and quite possibly does not want to have anything more to do with me. Her leaving is a good indication of that."

Marcus looked at him a moment. "All right, then," he said slowly. "I would agree to those terms."

"If it is me, no more protesting from you," Christopher pointed his finger at him. "And if it is you, I shall bow out quietly. You shall never hear from me again."

Marcus nodded stiffly. "Agreed."

They parted and went back to their steeds, and Christopher found he was a good deal more fatigued than he had been just moments earlier. It took him a moment to realize that, for the first time in his life, he was putting someone else's needs before his. He could not make Dustin miserable anymore; whatever would make her happy would make him happy as well. Just as long as she was healthy and safe, it did not matter who she was married to. He was willing to make the sacrifice simply to have her returned.

CHAPTER FIFTY-THREE

DUSTIN, REMARKABLY, WASN'T the least bit tired as Hercules loped along through the darkness of the night. Christin, long since fed and asleep, curled against her mother's chest.

Dustin knew basically where she was going; she had a good sense of direction and remembered this as the same road she and Marcus had traveled from Lioncross. Wiltshire was more westerly, but she guessed she had another day of traveling before she could make the directional turn. She would stop and ask someone as she drew closer.

Sherwood Forrest was a dark, scary place, loaded with ghosts and phantoms and bandits. Dustin tried not to think on it as she cantered along the road, not daring to glance into the trees for fear she would see something terrifying. Especially in the dark; it was frightening, but she focused ahead and ignored her superstitions. She was on the northern tip of the massive forest and had at least a day's travel before she could steer clear of it.

She wondered what had happened back at Somerhill. Her heart tightened with anguish when she thought of the needless deaths that had occurred because of her. Almost since the very first, she had heard of how Christopher had changed and how the once-mighty ring of knights had been driven to fight and quarrel.

Why hadn't she seen it before? She was a horrible influence, a wicked woman to have divided the mighty as she had. There had been too much pain and destruction going on around her, too much confusion. Mayhap leaving wasn't the wisest decision, but it was the only thing she could think to do. She had to get away, but her love for Christopher was making her question her decision with every passing mile. To be so close to him and then to be separated again was like a dagger in her gut, but she forced herself to believe it was a necessary choice.

Tears filled her eyes as she loped into the night; tears for her love lost, tears for her future, for herself.

☙

CHRISTOPHER AND RICHARD took the southern road, riding into the night. They knew they were on the right track when one of the scouts identified Hercules' hoof prints, and they immediately sent word back to Somerhill. Christopher knew that Marcus would catch up to them in a matter of hours and his jealously was fed, but he controlled himself. He wished Marcus would just stay the hell back at his keep, but he knew his former friend would do no such thing.

They estimated that Dustin had at least a three hour jump on them and Christopher honestly expected to find her sleeping by the side of the road. He could not imagine that she would ride into the night, especially in her condition, and was surprised to realize that she had done exactly that. A three hour head start was a substantial lead, and they tried to spur the horses faster to make up for lost time.

Richard said very little to him the entire time and he knew it was because his king was disappointed in his Defender's behavior. Christopher decided to save the man the trouble of relieving him of his post, since he had already decided months ago to resign as Defender of the Realm.

"Sire, there is something I must speak to you about," he said over the noise of the horses.

Richard looked at him. "What is it?"

"I will resign this night as Defender of the Realm," he said. "I feel that with my…."

Richard looked shocked. "You will not. I shall not hear of it."

Now Christopher was surprised. "But… sire, with everything that has happened, surely you are ashamed to have me as your champion."

Richard was appalled. "Ashamed? Good Christ, Chris, how can you in all honesty say that? That is the most ridiculous statement I have ever heard."

Christopher looked at his king, at a loss for words. Richard actually looked angry as he explained.

"Chris, you are worth your weight in gold one hundred times over," he said firmly. "I would give up an army of a million men if I could have a mere one hundred of you. I will not consider giving you up as my champion."

"But, Richard," Christopher lowered his voice as much as he could over the pounding hooves. "I have not acted the Defender very well since returning to England. The situation with Marcus and my wife is a good example."

Richard made a face. "Chris, this incident is a result of nothing but my own stupidity," he said. "I should have rewarded Marcus when I rewarded you, given him his own wife and keep, but I did not. Arthur suggested Marcus first, you know, but I thought you were more deserving. This little 'situation,' as you call it only proves to me that you are a man of flesh and blood, with human weaknesses. It pleases me to know that your heart is not made of stone."

Christopher stared back at his king, a confused look on his face. "Why was Marcus considered before me?" he asked.

Richard shrugged. "Because you were all too powerful and too consumed with your profession," he answered. "I knew you would never get married, and

Arthur thought Marcus might be easier to force into an arranged marriage. It was not because he preferred Marcus over you. He just did not think you would consider it."

Christopher looked away, his eyes roving across the darkness. He wasn't particularly offended, for he knew the king's words to be true. Arthur simply wanted Dustin married, to either the Lion's Claw or the general, and Richard saw it as an opportunity to reward his faithful. In Richard's view, Christopher had been the more faithful and received the prize.

"Not only have I reconsidered my stance, but I am most grateful to you for ordering me to wed," Christopher said finally.

Richard smiled faintly. "In spite of everything you regret nothing?"

Christopher shook his head deliberately, his only answer.

The endless road loomed ahead under the silver moon, beckoning them faster.

ᘓ

MORNING DAWNED AND Dustin was exhausted finally. She slowed Hercules to a halt beside a small stream off the beaten path and dismounted carefully. Grateful that Christin was still asleep, she moved to lay her down, but the moment she jostled the baby, big gray eyes opened and Christin was ready for the new day. With a weary smile, Dustin resigned herself to the fact that she would receive no sleep this morn.

She fed Christin and gave her a quick little bath in the icy stream, which the baby loved in spite of the chill, and bundled her back up again for the journey. Splashing her own face with water and tying her hair back, she feasted on a piece of bread and a hunk of cheese before re-securing her daughter and mounting Hercules.

Back on the road, she let the horse walk instead of lope, for she was afraid the rocking motion would put her to sleep. The forest was losing its density and as she crested a small hill, she saw a group of riders approaching from the east.

Fearful, Dustin urged Hercules onward at a run. The last thing she wanted was to meet up with riders, for a woman traveling alone was a foolish creature. Bandits and cutthroats lined the roads closer to London, but she hoped that this far north, she might escape them. Kicking Hercules until he grunted, she made rapid time south.

Much to her horror, the riders had seen her and moved quickly to cut her off. She was no match for men who knew the forest intimately, and within minutes, she was routed. She reined her horse around and tried to make an escape, but quickly discovered that she was boxed in from all sides.

Dustin's heart was pounding as she eyed the group of men who had surrounded her. She cursed her stupidity, but it was too late. Divine intervention was the only way she was going to make it out of this predicament.

One of the soldiers dismounted and made his way to her, studying her openly.

"Pray, my lady, what are you doing out here, alone?" he asked pleasantly.

Dustin was so terrified she could hardly speak. "Ride…riding, my lord. Riding to Wiltshire."

The soldier eyed her. "You are a pretty piece of fluff. What is your name?"

She paused, wondering if she should tell the man who she was married to. Mayhap if she told him who she was, he would let her go.

"Lady Dustin de Lohr," she said.

The man looked at her a moment, then cocked his head. "Are you related to the Defender de Lohr?"

"I am his wife," she said, suddenly brave. "Now, allow me to go on my way and I won't mention to my husband that you detained me."

The man looked stunned. Then, suddenly, his eyes widened and he smiled a terrible smile. "By God. I remember you. In London, I remember the fuss that was made over you. Oh, this is grand, indeed."

He went off into gales of whooping laughter and Dustin glared at him.

"What's so funny?" she demanded harshly. "Get out of my way."

He stopped laughing when she tried to steer Hercules around him. Reaching out, he grasped the horse's reins and pointed a finger at her.

"That will be enough from you, little miss," he said sternly.

"Let go of my horse," she snapped.

He did not, of course, and cuffed Hercules when the horse snapped at him. "I can see the animal is about as well tempered as the mistress," he remarked. "I know of a man who would be quite interested to see you, Lady Defender."

Dustin was torn between fear and anger. "Who?"

The soldier smiled, but it was entirely fake. "Your greatest admirer, of course. Prince John."

Dustin gasped. "Prince John?"

The soldier motioned to the men behind him. "Take her. Secure her horse."

Dustin shrieked as he reached up for her, startling Christin into a screaming bundle. Immediately the men halted.

"What's that?" the soldier demanded.

"My daughter, you fool," Dustin said nastily. "You have upset her. Now let me go and I will not tell my husband of your actions."

The soldier reached up and grabbed her, noticing before he even set her on the ground that she was pregnant.

"By God, woman," he hissed. "What fool let you travel alone?"

Dustin twisted away from him, holding Christin fiercely. "Do not touch me," she spat in return. "Give me back my horse."

The soldier put his hands on his hips; he was a nasty, fierce man, but he seemed to have something most of John's soldiers lacked; a bit of control.

"You shall ride with me," he said firmly. "Foul-tempered little chick."

Dustin scowled. "I shall not go with you to the prince. I shall kill myself first."

"With what?" he asked. "If you have a dagger, you had better give it to me now and save us both a lot of trouble."

"I have no dagger," Dustin said with contempt. "But if I did, I'd use it on you."

He nodded in agreement. "No doubt. Come, now."

He yanked her by the arm and pulled her, struggling and twisting, over to his mount. His men collected Hercules and grinned as he lifted the spitting, fighting female onto the back of his horse.

"Stop that or you shall hurt yourself," he ordered. "I shall not be responsible for the death of the babe you carry."

Dustin stopped, looking at him with fear and hatred. "You are already responsible for kidnap, and when John is finished with me, you shall be responsible for murder as well."

"Is that what you think? That he's going to kill you?" the soldier asked, mounting behind her. "Lady, he would never dispose of a pretty thing such as yourself. You shall be added to his collection."

The men laughed bawdily and Dustin glanced around, bewildered. "What are you talking about?"

"Surely your husband, the great Lion's Claw, has told you about harems?" the man said, gathering his reins. "I understand he had a magnificent one in Ascalon."

Dustin did not even know what a harem was, but she did not like the sound of lt. "I am no offering to be made to a deviant prince."

"Aye, you are," the soldier answered firmly. "You will be my great contribution to John's cause. The wife of the Defender delivered personally by me."

"But he's in Nottingham," she pointed out.

The soldier looked at her. "Do not you even know where you are?"

Not really, she did not, but she refused to answer him. The soldier laughed.

"To Nottingham, ladies," he said to his men. "This prize ought to get us a week of women and ale."

The men cheered and yelled, confusing and frightening Dustin all the more. Against her body, Christin started to cry. Dustin tried to comfort her daughter, not knowing what else to do or say.

Fighting them was not an option because of her condition and she resigned herself to the fact that she was now a captive of Prince John. She wondered what was a worse fate; outlaws or the bastard prince. She would almost rather take the outlaws.

She had taken a foolish gamble and she had lost, and now her fate and the fate of her children rested in the hands of a morally corrupt man. She could not help wondering that if Christopher ever did catch up to her, she was in for the spanking of her life.

ଓ

"I DO NOT like this," Richard growled. "I do not like this at all."

Christopher was on the ground, studying the myriad of hoof prints and boot prints on the soft earth. His sky-blue eyes turned easterly as he studied the horizon.

"Well?" Richard demanded harshly.

Marcus wandered the perimeter of the hoof prints, his eyes glazed with thought. He came to within a foot or so of Christopher and his eyes trailed off in the same direction as the Defender's.

"Nottingham," he murmured.

Christopher did not respond for a moment. He continued to stare to the horizon as if in a trance. "John is so bloody bent on protecting his holdings that he would indeed have a patrol this far north. Christ, I cannot believe they actually found her."

"Look, Chris," Edward pointed to the ground. "Smaller boot prints. Female boots."

Christopher did not turn around. "I know. I saw them." He turned around then, slowly. "The patrol found her, took her off Hercules and put her on with one of them, and then headed back for Nottingham."

"It is at least a day's ride to Nottingham," Marcus said. "We can catch them if we ride hard enough."

"We have already ridden hard enough," Christopher looked at the sweaty, tired horses. "We shall succeed in killing our mounts if we do not rest them before proceeding." He slapped at his leg armor, weary and defeated, and wandered back over to his horse. "We shall rest now for a few hours. The horses need it."

"But she's with a roving band of soldiers," Marcus said quietly. "We have got to get to her as soon as we can."

Christopher knew that; with every fiber of his being he felt it. But he could not, would not allow himself to get caught up in the panic.

"We shall never get to her if we kill our horses," he said calmly.

Marcus flushed and Richard jumped in. "You are right, of course. We must pray that my brother's soldiers show mercy on an expectant mother and her babe and do naught to harm either of them." He eyed the two men, so powerful and large, yet so helpless at the moment. "I furthermore suspect that John would kill any man who touched her before he has a chance to. I would not worry about her until she reaches Nottingham."

"Jesus Christ," Marcus muttered, turning away with disgust.

"Calm yourself," Richard snapped.

Christopher was far calmer than he should have been. He was trying so hard to keep everything inside that he came across looking callous. But, God help him, his insides were tearing themselves apart.

"Edward, send riders back to Somerhill. Tell the sergeant in charge to send the remaining troops to Nottingham," he said steadily, focusing at Marcus full on. "We're going into battle."

Marcus straightened, feeling the familiar smell of a fight in the air. But this time, he would be fighting for something that meant more to him than all of the battles in the Holy Land combined.

Richard bowed his head a moment, in silent prayer. "I shall send back to London, then. I have fifteen hundred men armed and waiting at Windsor. Not an excessive amount, considering how fortified Nottingham is."

"I'd say that the six hundred men from Somerhill plus the fifteen hundred men from Windsor is a bit much, sire," Christopher said softly. "We can take the castle with a thousand at the most."

Richard pulled his gauntlets back on. "John holds fourteen of my properties. I intend to regain all of them, and I might as well start with Nottingham. We not only ride to retrieve the Lady Dustin, but we ride to secure my holding." He eyed Marcus and Christopher sternly. "I ride with my Defender and my premier general, and I have no doubt that victory will be ours."

Strains of sand and heat began to flow about them, the air faint with the smells of myrrh and the sounds of Muslims as the faithful were called to prayer. They began to feel the familiar taste of the quest, even though they were in the heart of England.

Suddenly, the fighting, the dissension, the hatred, were foolish and misplaced. They were warriors, soldiers, the men that they were before they had ever heard of Lady Dustin Barringdon.

But heard of her they had and, unfortunately, both men loved her deeply. Yet when it was all over and she was safe, only one would be the victor. And neither man was used to defeat.

CHAPTER FIFTY-FOUR

CLUTCHING CHRISTIN, DUSTIN was hustled from the huge bailey of Nottingham and ushered into the cool interior of the keep. The castle was larger and darker than anything she had ever seen, short of Windsor, and the cold fear she felt consumed her and the open doors swallowed her up.

The same soldier who had found her continued to be her shadow, never letting her stray more than an arm's length. Rather than feeling protective, he was pleased with his capture and wanted John to know exactly how loyal he was to the prince. He hoped for a promotion at the very least.

Soldiers, people, were everywhere as Dustin was rushed down corridors and up a flight of stairs. She was extremely tired and nauseous and struggled to keep herself in check. She mustn't lose control, for she had no idea what would become of her daughter should she lose consciousness, and her fierce desire to protect Christin overrode her own illness.

John and Ralph had no idea what gift was to be deposited in their laps. They were together, as was usual, in John's great audience hall when the doors flew open and soldiers filled the doorway.

"What is the meaning of this?" Ralph screamed at his soldiers, cuffing the first man he came to. "Since when do you come barging in unannounced?"

"Forgive, my lord sheriff," a soldier said respectfully. "But we have brought you a prize."

"Prize? What goddamn prize…?" Ralph's eyes fell on Dustin in the center of the mailed men. His eyes nearly bugged from his skull and he pointed a helpless finger at her. "You? It is *you!*"

Dustin was on the verge of tears but she met his gaze without a word. Ralph stumbled and pushed through the soldiers until he reached her. He could scarce believe what his eyes were telling him, but believe he did. As if to make sure he was not dreaming, he reached out and fingered the material of her cloak.

"Where on God's earth did you find her?" John's eyes were dancing with surprise and glee.

"Riding to the north, through Sherwood," the soldier that had found her replied. "She was quite alone, my lord."

"Alone?" Both John and Ralph looked at her with shock. "Why were you alone, Lady Dustin?" John asked.

His voice was kind but she knew what he was capable of. "I…I was going home, to Lioncross."

"But where was your husband? Oh, excuse me, *husbands*," Ralph deliberately drew the word out.

Dustin flushed, tired and angry and scared. "Dead, I suppose. When I last saw them, they were dueling to the death." Her chin came up bravely. "It no longer matters, sire. But what matters is that I would like to continue my journey. Will you allow me to pass?"

John looked taken aback by her question. "Certainly not," he said. "A lovely lady such as yourself will ride nowhere unescorted, and especially not before you have had time to rest and enjoy the hospitality of Nottingham."

Dustin eyed him warily. "Then I am not a prisoner?"

John shook his head and took her arm. "Absolutely not, my lady. You are an honored guest."

Christin, underneath the cloak, let out a squeal and Dustin pulled the heavy cloth back. A little head covered with curly dark hair popped up, the gray eyes focusing on John. The prince was deeply shocked. The child was the image of her mother and he swore he could see Christopher's features, but the black hair was surprising. He had not heard that Lady Dustin had bore the Defender a child.

"Another de Lohr, I presume?" he asked.

"Aye," Dustin shifted Christin's weight and patted her rounded belly. "And another."

John was stunned. It was almost too good to ask for, too unbelievable to imagine. The Defender's expectant wife and child right in his very own lap. And with Richard preparing to take back the holdings John had confiscated, the luck was beyond believing.

He relaxed, a benevolent smile crossing his face. It would seem that God and fortune was to be on his side.

"Come, my lady," he pulled her along. "You must be exhausted."

ꟹ

LATER, AFTER DUSTIN and Christin were safely tucked away, Ralph met John on his usual walk around the compound. The gray-stoned castle cast long shadows in the early afternoon as the men converged in the inner bailey.

"Well?" Ralph asked his liege.

"Well *what*?" John answered.

Ralph sighed impatiently. "Lady de Lohr, sire. What are you planning for her?"

John picked at his teeth. "Nothing, for the moment. I have already prepared a missive to London informing my brother of our 'guest'. The rest will be up to him and up to de Lohr, whether or not I am allowed to keep my holdings and whether or not Lady Dustin and the children live."

"You would kill them?" Ralph asked.

John shrugged. "Mayhap not. Lady Dustin would make a fine concubine, don't you think? But I have no use for children, especially de Lohr's children. Mayhap I would sell them off."

Ralph raised an eyebrow. "Indeed. Sell them to Marcus Burton."

They both giggled. "Oh, what I wouldn't give to see de Lohr and Burton battling to the death. I'd place my money on de Lohr, of course, although Burton is nothing to trifle with," John said.

Ralph agreed. "Richard has one more problem on his hands with his two best knights fighting over a woman," he said. "Do you suppose he himself started the rumor of de Lohr's death to throw us off the track?"

"No," John snapped. "You forget, Ralph, that la Londe saw de Lohr go down. 'Twas no rumor, although I am most curious to know how he survived."

"The man has God on his side, most assuredly," Ralph commented. "Three years in Jerusalem could not kill him."

John stopped at a small vendor's shack, inspecting the copper bracelets. "This would look lovely on Gabrielle, do not you think? And Dustin, too."

"Do you plan on sharing Dustin with la Londe and my Uncle Bruce as you have Gabrielle?" Ralph asked, a bit snidely.

John took the bracelets that pleased him and did not bother to pay for them. "I will not," he said frankly. "La Londe was most insistent about Gabrielle, but he will not touch Dustin. At least, not until I have had my fill of her. And I doubt her grandfather will want that sort of relationship with his own granddaughter, although I would not be terribly surprised to be wrong."

Ralph gave a crooked smile. "My lord, you have the most beautiful harem in all of England."

John grinned lewdly. "I have never bedded a pregnant woman before. I wonder what it will be like?"

Ralph shrugged carelessly. "Start a new fad, my lord. Make it the rage of the palace."

John snickered, "Bedding pregnant woman? It could prove to be messy."

They smiled, snickered, and continued on their walk, feeling more light-hearted than they had in months.

ଓ

DUSTIN AWOKE FROM a deep sleep to a soft, female voice in her bedchamber. She opened her eyes slowly, looking around and suddenly remembering where she was. She lay in the middle of an opulent bed, surrounded by finery on the top floor of Nottingham Castle. The voice that she heard was coming from the opposite side of the room. Slowly, she sat up and focused on the source.

Lady Gabrielle de Havilland sat on the floor with Christin, playing with the babe. Christin was cooing and standing up with assistance, trying to take off walking, much to Gabrielle's delight. Dustin propped herself up on one elbow, watching the two of them and pleased to see her old acquaintance. She looked as lovely as she always had, in spite of the life she had been forced to lead.

"Greetings," she said softly.

Gabrielle's head snapped up. "I am sorry, my lady. I did not mean to wake you."

Dustin shook her head. "That's all right," she smiled. "Christin needs to be fed soon. 'Tis good to see you again; have you been well?"

Gabrielle lowered her gaze, focusing on the babe. "Well as can be expected, my lady. How have you fared since we last met?"

Dustin rolled out of the bed. "Well, I suppose, in spite of everything. And do not call me 'my lady.' Please call me 'Dustin.'"

"And you will call me Gabrielle," her friend responded with a smile. "Truly, Dustin, there is so much that has happened and so much that should be said. I do not know where to begin."

Dustin rubbed her belly. "You heard of your husband's death?"

"Aye," Gabrielle said without emotion. "I was told it was your husband who killed him."

Dustin eyed her apprehensively as she sank into a chair. "He did, but only after the earl killed Lady Isobelle and threatened my life as well. I am sorry, Gabrielle."

"Why?" Gabrielle asked seriously. "He was an evil, vile man and I am glad he is dead. I do not have to worry if he's going to beat me, or starve me, or lock me in a room to rot. Your husband did me a great favor, Dustin."

Dustin swallowed, looking at her hands. Gabrielle glanced at her friend as she rolled a little ball to Christin.

"How did you come here?" she finally asked.

Dustin's eyes came up, filling with tears. She struggled with herself for a moment. "Oh, Gabrielle, everything is so awful."

"Tell me," Gabrielle insisted gently.

Dustin sniffled, trying to find a starting point for her horrible story. "I suppose it started when I first met Chris," she said. "I drove his men apart until they hated each other. After I was told Chris was dead, I married Marcus Burton because it seemed the right thing to do, but then Chris returned and he and Marcus had a battle to the death."

Christin had crawled off. Gabrielle stood up, making sure Christin wasn't anywhere near the hearth, and went to her friend. "There, now, Dustin," she said soothing, patting her on the arm. "Who won?"

"I do not know," Dustin sobbed. "I left before it was over. Gabrielle, I have caused all of this strife and anger. I had to leave. If I am gone, there will no longer be a reason for them to hate each other."

Gabrielle felt for her friend. "Then they do not know you have gone?"

Dustin shook her head, wiping her eyes. "I did not tell anyone, but I am sure they know by now. And they are probably glad."

"I doubt that," Gabrielle still remembered how Christopher had looked at his wife, and how envious she had been. "I know your husband loved you, Dustin. He was very proud of you."

"Proud of what?" she wept. "Proud of the fact that I drove him and his best friend apart, proud that because of me, he exiled his brother? Gabrielle, he's better off without me. They all are. Mayhap things can be right again with all of them if I am not around."

Christin crawled past and Gabrielle picked her up. "Dustin, how can you be so silly? Your leaving will not change anything."

"Yes, it will," Dustin insisted. "Don't you see? I am the cause of everything. With me gone, they will stop hating each other and be friends again."

Gabrielle shook her head, Christin's fingers entwined in the rich brown tresses. "It is not that simple and you know it," she scolded softly. "Where were you planning on going? Surely not here to Nottingham."

"Home," Dustin said vaguely. She did not want to tell her everything, lest she mention it to John. She hated to think that she did not trust Gabrielle, but she did not yet.

"Alone, pregnant, and carrying a child?" Gabrielle pointed out. "You are not thinking clearly, Dustin."

"Of course I am not," Dustin snapped, shooting out of the chair, agitated. "My dead husband returns from the grave, my current husband challenges him to fight for the wifely prize, the king wishes he had never even heard of the name Dustin Barringdon, and half of the kingdom is being torn apart from within because of me. Tell me, Gabrielle… would you be thinking clearly?"

Gabrielle looked at her. "No," she said quietly. "But at least you have men who love you. I am nothing more than a royal whore."

Dustin stopped her raging and looked at Gabrielle. Lovely, gentle Gabrielle. Dustin's problems were severe, but she was not the only one with problems. Her self-pity vanished and she threw her arms around Gabrielle.

They cried together for several long minutes, Christin pulling hair from both their heads. They found comfort in one another and strength, and Dustin began to see just how foolish she had been.

She was suddenly desperately concerned for Christopher, and for Marcus. She began to wish she had never left.

"What now?" she asked with a sniff.

"We become strong together," Gabrielle said firmly. "With you here, I can face John and Ralph."

"But I have got to return to Somerhill," Dustin said. "I have got to see what has happened."

"You cannot escape, Dustin, trust me," Gabrielle said with resignation. "I have tried. There is no way out."

"There is always a way," Dustin said firmly. "You just have not found it yet. We shall find it together."

Gabrielle nodded weakly, running her hand over Christin's dark hair. "She has such dark hair. Marcus must be very proud."

Dustin looked at her daughter a moment. "She is Christopher's child, as is the babe I carry. Marcus and I did not have any children together."

"But you and Lord Christopher are so fair," Gabrielle insisted. "How did she come with this thatch of black?

"My mother had dark hair," Dustin said, suddenly remembering her mother's relations. This place, Nottingham, had been her home. She silently vowed not to mention the fact to Gabrielle.

Gabrielle smiled at Christin. "I envy you, Dustin. One babe and another on the way. I conceived my first month here with John, but he had a witch-woman give me bayberries to eat and I miscarried. It was the most awful…"

Her voice faded away and Dustin looked completely horrified. Of all the cruel and inhuman things to do… she was sickened for her gentle, lovely friend.

"With your husband gone, there will be ample opportunity for you to find another husband," she assured Gabrielle timidly. "I will plead King Richard to select a handsome, kind husband for you."

Gabrielle looked at Dustin with honesty. "Who would want me, Dustin? The prince's whore? No self-respecting man would accept me."

"You are not to blame to your situation," Dustin replied firmly. "You mustn't give up hope."

Gabrielle shrugged and turned away, her composure shattered. Dustin set Christin on the bed, not knowing what else to say. After a moment, Gabrielle turned around with renewed courage.

"You must be starved," she said briskly. "I shall have the servants bring you a meal. And a bath, too. Do you have any clothes to change into?"

"Nay," Dustin said. "I did not pack much, just necessary items for Christin and myself."

Gabrielle nodded sharply. "There is a fine seamstress here. I shall put her to work on a few surcoats for you. Mayhap she can finish one this afternoon."

Dustin never could get excited about clothes. She simply nodded as her friend prattled on, acting as if she had some control of the situation. Even Dustin could see that it was all a brave front, a facade for a woman with no true place in the world.

Dustin bathed later that day as Gabrielle took care of Christin, relieved to have a bit of time to herself. Gabrielle had brought her a flowing robe of pale blue and Dustin wrapped herself in it as her hair dried, watching her daughter and Gabrielle play as she listened to the sounds of the massive bailey floating in through the lancet window.

To hear the sounds reminded her of Lioncross and Somerhill, and the stab to her heart deepened. She shook her head faintly at her own stupidity and recklessness, yet there was naught to do about it now. She was in a dark situation and knew she must rely on her wits to help her escape.

For once in her life, she could depend on no one but herself for protection.

CHAPTER FIFTY-FIVE

NEVER WAS A mightier army to be assembled.

Christopher, Marcus and Richard intercepted the army riding from Somerhill and took command of the nine hundred man force. With the additional fifteen hundred men riding north from Windsor, they would not only lay siege to Nottingham; they would mow it to the ground.

Richard made the decision to wait for his army from Windsor. Christopher highly disapproved of the conclusion, but he was unsuccessful to convince his king otherwise. Marcus actually became quite irate and he and Richard had exchanged angry words. For a change, Christopher had had to separate the two of them.

Richard's logic was simple; he believed Dustin to be fairly safe and saw no need to go charging in and risk a great number of casualties. With the troops from Windsor, mayhap the casualties would be minimal simply because of the sheer number of men. Additionally, Dustin was not the primary concern; he intended to regain Nottingham for the crown and he knew he must show overwhelming force. When mercenary French soldiers returned to Philip Augustus after seeing battle with the returned King of England, he wanted the French king to know that Richard the Lionheart would not tolerate the French meddling in his country.

So they waited outside of the village of Grantham, a little over twenty miles to the east of Nottingham. Somerhill was over a half day's ride, and within a day after discovering where Dustin had been taken, they had their nine hundred troops. Camp was set up and the wait for the army from Windsor was met with impatience by all. Christopher was nearly insane with grief and worry, but he knew that within two days, they would be marching for Nottingham and for his family. Until then, he was helpless.

Marcus got a grip on himself and was handling the wait better than Christopher. He and Christopher would talk of items that related to the battle, but that was the extent of their contact. For two men who had shared a tent for three years, it was a little strange being without the camaraderie and support of one another. They would gaze at each other across the compound, eyes meeting sometimes, but with no emotion. Yet even with the hurt and jealousy and anger, each man sensed an unfillable void the other had left within him, although they would not admit it. The pain of losing one's best friend was too deep for words.

On the second day of camp, an army was sighted riding in from the south and immediately the battle cry went up. Marcus expertly set up skirmish lines under the eagle eyes of Richard and Christopher as they studied the incoming troops.

"Now who in the hell could this be?" Richard mumbled.

Christopher could see colors being flown, but they were too far away. He tightened his reins. "We shall soon find out."

The dark brown destrier charged forward, kicking up great clods of dirt as Christopher ran at breakneck speed down the slight incline before leveling out on the flat, grassy land. As Christopher drew closer, he could see that there were no more than three hundred men and he was truly curious. Who would be riding with a small army this far north?

The answer came to him when he spied the yellow, gray and black of Lord Lyle Hampton, Earl of Canterbury. *David.* His little brother had come.

David met Christopher well in front of his army, the familiar white destrier he rode catching Christopher's eye. Christopher was so damn glad to see his brother that he was off his destrier before the horse even came to a halt, pulling his brother into a great bear hug in spite of the bulky armor they both wore. His anger, his grief, his disgust with David was dissolved in an instant.

"David," he managed to choke after an emotional minute. "What in the hell are you doing here?"

David wiped at his eyes, not ashamed to let his brother see how caught up he was. "Here to support you, of course," he said, then gestured to the massive army on the rise. "What is all of this?"

Christopher was so emotional he was ready to crack. He cuffed his brother affectionately on the side of the head.

"Dustin was taken to Nottingham," he said hoarsely. "How did you know we were here?"

"Because I rode to Somerhill, knowing you would be heading there to collect Dustin, and they told me what had happened," he replied, his blue eyes drinking in his brother's face. "I came to help."

Christopher laughed softly. "And so you have," he murmured, his hand still on his brother's shoulder as if incapable of letting him go. "We are waiting for reinforcements from Windsor before we go charging in and raise the place. Christ, David, you do not know how good it is to see you."

David's face was lit up like a candle. "What about you? Jesus, you were *dead.* What in the hell happened to you?"

Christopher waved at him. "It is a long story. I was severely wounded and it took me three months to find my way back home again, but we shall delve more into that later," he said. "What matters now is retrieving my wife and daughter."

David shook his head, still reeling with emotion. "What about Marcus?"

Christopher shrugged. "A truce, for now. At least until we get Dustin back."

"That's why I came, you know," David said. "I thought you were going to have an all-out war with Marcus, and I wanted to fight with you; even if you did not want me."

"Did not want you…?" Christopher repeated, realizing how very foolish they had both been. "You are my brother, David. My only brother. What happened….well, we both said and did things in the heat of anger that we should not have."

David shook his head hard. "I am all to blame, Chris. You did nothing but protect your wife." His voice lowered regretfully. "You were right when you said I was jealous. I was jealous of everything you had. When you first married Dustin, it was a sort of game to try and get you to like her. But when you came to love her, I felt left out. I guess I had to find something wrong with her to make you not love her so that things would be as they had been. Can you ever forgive me?"

Christopher's eyes were warm. "I understand you returned to Lioncross to act as her protector. That proves to me how sorry you were for what happened."

David snorted ironically. "A lot of good I did. She married Marcus anyway."

"Richard said you tried to kill Marcus in a sword fight," Christopher said. "Very brave of you, little brother. I spent half the day yesterday trying to do the same thing."

David shrugged, not voicing what he was thinking. That their friendship had come to this still bothered him greatly. He glanced back at his troops after a moment.

"I have got three hundred men to reinforce your ranks," he said, "if you shall have me."

Christopher smiled broadly. "I would have no other." He slugged his brother again and moved toward his destrier. "What is this I hear that you have taken a wife?"

David snickered at his brother's disbelieving tone. "I did, and a lovely woman she is. But she came with two sisters and they are driving me crazy."

Christopher crowed with laughter as he mounted. "You deserve all that and more. You never could handle a woman."

David mounted his dancing animal. "They are *not* women. They are the spawn of Satan."

"Not Nathalie," Christopher said. "She is an obedient, thoughtful girl.

"That is what she wants you to believe," David sneered. "She puts on a prim and proper front, and then when your guard is down – boom. And Elise, the youngest, is even worse. Do you know that they put honey on my pillow? And charcoal in my helmet? I went for half a day with black hair and had no idea why my men were laughing at me."

Christopher laughed heartily at the mental picture of his high-strung brother dealing with two disobedient children. "David, I think I like these girls. You must tell me more sometime."

David made a face. "Later."

Christopher waved at him and they turned tail on one another, returning to their respective armies. For them both, the world suddenly seemed a little brighter, a little more hopeful.

David's men set up camp and it was truly like old times. Richard had his inner circle of knights about him and he could not have been more pleased. In spite of the tension in the air, David and Marcus had barely acknowledged one another and kept their distance, dampening Richard's mood a bit, but it could not be helped. He would have rather had them ignoring each other than trying to slit one another's throats.

The army from Windsor was expected on the morrow and Richard took leave of his men and went to bed early. Christopher and David were standing around the massive pyre, watching the sparks fly into the dark night and speaking of insignificant things. Christopher wanted to know more of his new sister-in-law, Emilie, and was eager to hear of David's exploits with her younger sisters. He laughed until he cried picturing his brother trying to handle two spirited young girls.

They were laughing about something or another when Marcus strolled past the fire, eyeing the two brothers impassively. Christopher gazed back, as did David, and immediately the tension rose. Harold, at Christopher's feet, rose and snarled menacingly.

"Marcus," he greeted formally.

Marcus merely nodded his head, crossbow strung over his shoulder, and continued on his way. David watched him disappear into the night before letting out a hissing sigh.

"Be mindful that he doesn't use that thing on your back," he referred to the crossbow. "Marcus is the best archer in the realm."

Christopher nodded. "I am well aware of his skill," he looked at his brother and slugged him playfully. "That is why I have you here, to cover my back."

David grinned, gazing at his brother a moment. "I told you once that you had changed. I cannot believe how much you have changed."

"How so?" Christopher raised his brows.

"Jesus, Chris, how *haven't* you changed?" David snorted. "The Lion's Claw I knew had little sense of humor and ate and drank and slept war on the field. The only time I ever saw you relax was with a woman in your arms. But right now...I mean, look at us. Since when did we like and slug each other like a couple of lads? And that ugly dog is constantly with you; you always hated animals. Furthermore, you smile all the time. You never used to smile at all. I wondered at times if you even knew how. You have taken on a dimension I never knew you had."

Christopher shrugged. "There is much in life to be happy over, I suppose. I love my wife, my daughter. Why should not I smile?"

David grinned at him and shook his head. "Then you were right. Love hasn't made you weak; it is made you invincible."

Christopher nodded deliberately, pleased his brother was seeing the truth of it. "And Emilie? Do you love her?"

David looked embarrassed, kicking at the ground "I don't know. I'm very fond of her, God knows. But love… well, it scares me."

"As it frightened me," Christopher looked thoughtful. "I seem to remember a close relative of mine, male of course, tell me once that if I would only allow my wife to love me that everything in this world would right itself. Quit fighting her, I was told. Now I wonder who told me that?"

David looked away sheepishly. "Some idiot, I am sure."

Christopher smiled. "A wise idiot. He should follow his own advice."

David crossed his thick arms and drew in a deep breath. "Mayhap. But I swear I am going to kill her sisters one of these days."

Christopher chuckled. "Don't you dare. I am pleased that they are proving to be a thorn in your arrogant side."

"Arrogant," David choked. "Now look who's calling me arrogant. Jesus, out of the mouth of the man who invented the term."

They grinned at each other, watching the fire burn in comfortable silence. Bootfalls caught their attention and they both looked through the flames to see Marcus appearing out of the darkness.

"Posts are secured, my lord," he told Christopher formally.

Christopher nodded slightly. "Very good."

Marcus gave a slight bow and turned on his heel, but Christopher stopped him. He did not know why he should, but somehow, it just wasn't right for them to hate each other. It was as if the earth was out of balance, or the stars out of alignment. It was unnatural and went against the grain. With everything that had happened, he still yearned for his friend.

"You did not eat," he said.

Marcus' face was unreadable. "I wasn't hungry."

Christopher sighed. "Will you join us?"

Marcus' eyes widened a bit and he eyed David. "Nay, my lord, I do not think so."

Christopher sat on the log behind him and rested his ankle on his knee. "Sit down, Marcus."

David took his own seat, not looking at Marcus. Marcus looked at the two brothers, once his very best friends, and he, too, yearned for the way things had once been. But there was so much hurt and anger in his heart that it was difficult to see past it. Yet he could see that Christopher was making some sort of effort to be civil, and he decided to reciprocate. But he wondered if David was hiding a dagger in his belt with his name on it.

Slowly, he lowered his big body onto an upturned log and sat stiffly, his hands clasped in front of him. Harold growled threateningly at him and Christopher admonished the dog sternly.

"Have you seen your father since you have returned?" Christopher asked.

Marcus shook his head. "Nay, even though Leicester is less than a day from Somerhill," he said. "The last I heard of my father, the earl, he and his new wife were busy on a family of their own. He has no time for his second son from his first wife."

"What of your brother? Surely you have seen him?" Christopher asked.

"My brother, the monk?" Marcus said with some contempt. "The man will inherit the earldom when my father dies and doesn't know a damn thing about running it. As far as I know, he's still at Westminster. I did not even see him when I was in London."

Christopher looked at him a moment before staring back into the flames. It began to occur to him that Marcus felt alone in the world, abandoned by his father and forgotten by his brother. He had no one at all, which was probably why he was so determined to hang on to Dustin. He needed the security of a family from her desperately, and Christopher wondered if he was even aware of it.

"Tell me something, Marcus," he said after a moment. "Are you so resolved to keep Dustin because you love her or because you have no family ties whatsoever? Is she and Christin your ready-made family or are they the love of your life?"

Marcus' features grew dark. "How in the hell can you ask me that? I told you once and I shall tell you again, I love her."

Christopher kept calm; he truly wasn't trying to rile Marcus, but simply help him think. "It could not be because your mother died when you were young and your father deposited you on the Earl of Derby when you were five? You have never had the closeness or strength of a woman or a family as I have. Is she somehow filling a role for you, a role you have forced upon her whether or not she is willing?"

Marcus stood up, his big fists clenched. "To hell with you," he snared. "How dare you judge me."

David sighed heavily and shook his head. Christopher glanced at his brother, pleased that he was keeping his calm but knowing it was difficult for him.

"I am not judging you," he said softly. "I did not mean to upset you, Marcus. I am just trying to understand. Please sit and we shall speak no more about it."

Marcus did not sit, but he did not leave, either. "How dare you probe me, Chris," he hissed. "How dare you try and analyze my actions. By what right?"

" 'Tis my right because it is my wife you married," Christopher reminded him.

Marcus' jaw ticked. "And my daughter she bore."

"You *bastard.*" David could hold still no longer. He snarled at Marcus. "You are the most…."

"Shut up, David." Christopher cut his brother off, returning his gaze to Marcus with less calm than before. "If she is your child, kindly explain how it is she looks like me?"

"We all see what we want to see," Marcus said quietly. "You see yourself, and I see me. But I know without a doubt that she is my flesh and blood."

"Wishful thinking," David snapped. "She's not your child, Marcus. She is as much your daughter as Dustin is your wife, which is not at all."

"Stay out of this, David," Marcus warned. "This does not concern you."

"The hell it doesn't!" David snarled. "Anything that concerns Chris concerns me. I should have spilled your guts when I had the chance."

"You never had the chance," Marcus said smoothly. "If you recall, I was winning our bout when Richard separated us. If anyone's guts were to be spilled, it would have been yours."

"Arrogant son of a bitch," David rumbled. "Jesus, Marcus, what has Chris ever done to you that you would try and destroy his life?"

Marcus stopped in his tracks. He was preparing for an all-out verbal fight with the two brothers when David's words suddenly struck him. Faltering, he turned away from the two of them because he honestly could not reply. He never thought of the situation in that context; what *had* Christopher ever done? My God, was he being vindictive for the fact that Christopher had earned a greater reputation, or had found more favor with the king and he did not even realize it? Confusion swept him.

"Is…is that what it looks like? That I am seeking some sort of revenge?" he murmured, turning back around to face Christopher. "That I am out to destroy you?"

Christopher just looked at him, not replying. Marcus had asked the question with such bewilderment that it was difficult not to feel his honesty. The white-hot tension that had surrounded them was draining away and even David began to relax.

"What do you think?" David said earnestly. "Of course it looks like you are trying to take everything away from my brother. His wife, his child, his life… why, Marcus? Did he wrong you somehow?"

Marcus shook his head vehemently, his puzzlement overwhelming. "Nay," he breathed. "I am not trying to punish him for a wrong against me. We just happen to love the same woman."

Christopher sighed, leaning forward with his arms resting on his knees. "Marcus, she is my wife and Christin is my daughter. Your marriage to her is void anyway because I was alive when you married her. She was never your wife, and she was always mine." He looked up at him. "I have tried to be patient. I have tried not to become angry. I have threatened you and I have fought you.

Dustin has even told you that she doesn't want you. What will it take, then, for you to leave us in peace?"

Marcus, a man of considerable pride, lowered his gaze uncertainly. Everything that was said, albeit unpleasant, made sense even to him. He did not want to admit it, any of it, but it was clear even to him that he was in the wrong. As if a fog had lifted and revealed a scene as clear as heaven itself, he suddenly realized how very terrible he had been.

But, God, he loved her. His motives had always been very sincere toward Dustin; he simply loved her. But David's words and Christopher's words seeped into his brain, and even as he tried to fight off their meaning, his common sense and moral character could not deny their correctness. They were right; they had always been right, and he had been selfish and absorbed. He had been right when he told Christopher that both of them saw what they wanted to see. He only saw his love for Dustin and completely disregarded her feelings, as well as Christopher's. Only his wants had mattered to him because he was used to having his desires fulfilled.

But Dustin did not want him; she had told him that, but he had chosen to believe that he could make her love him if he tried hard enough. Mayhap for the first time in his life Marcus realized he could not manipulate the situation to his advantage. With a stab of pain to his chest, he realized that he had indeed been self-indulgent and ignorant. God help him, he did not want to let her go, but as much as he loved her, he knew he had to.

His strength drained from his body and he collapsed on the upturned log. He stared into the flames of the pyre for an endless amount of time, weary and defeated.

"I love her," he murmured slowly. "I was blinded by her beauty, her innocence, her charm. She made me forget all that I am and all that I stand for, and I will tell you now that I am deeply ashamed to admit my guilt. I took it for a game, at first, but my obsession with her grew and I could not control it." He looked up at Christopher's sad eyes. "I will not fight you for her anymore, Chris. I can see now that I have already done enough damage."

David was shocked to see Marcus fold so quickly. He blinked at his brother, whose expression was one of sorrow.

"I trusted you once and you betrayed me," Christopher said hoarsely. "I am having difficulty believing you."

"No doubt," Marcus said with defeat. "I could swear to you on the Bible, but I think mayhap even that would not be strong enough. If I swear to you on my oath as a knight, will you believe me?"

Christopher looked at the fire, not wanting to doubt Marcus' oath, for the man was the best knight in the realm. But he was bitter and weary and tired of deceit.

"Mayhap in time," he whispered. "Mayhap your actions will speak louder than words."

Marcus was bewildered and frustrated, at himself, at everything. "I am not completely guilty in all of this," he said. "You proved to be spiteful and irrational, too. If there is any betrayal to be felt, I should be allowed a small portion."

Christopher's head came up. "What are you talking about?"

"In London, Chris. Do you remember how crazed jealous you were when I was around your wife? We had done absolutely nothing at that time, yet you were wild with envy," Marcus reminded him.

"You had kissed her," Christopher returned.

Marcus threw up his hands. "An innocent taste, I swear to you. I felt nothing for her at the time. It was, as I said, a game. My feelings for her followed shortly thereafter."

Christopher let out a laborious sigh. "I do not know, Marcus. I just do not know what to think or believe anymore."

Marcus watched his former friend as he stared at his hands. "Do you know that even after I married her, she refused to take your wedding rings off?" he said. "I am not daft, Chris. I knew she did not love me, but I hoped with time that things would change. And they would have, but with you returned, even I know that there is no hope."

With that, Marcus stood up and walked away, leaving Christopher drained and David astonished.

"Do you think he is sincere?" David asked.

Christopher ran a hand through his hair. "Oh, hell, David, I don't know," he sighed heavily. "I would like to hope so, but he has lied to me before where Dustin was concerned. I will not allow myself to be sucked in again. We shall just have to wait and see."

David puffed out his cheeks and sat down, shaking his head in wonder. He never thought he would live to see the day when Marcus Burton backed down from anything. Surprisingly, he wasn't leery as his brother was.

He believed him.

ଓ

IN THE SHADOWS, young Darren watched his liege and the other two men. He remembered well how close the three had been and was deeply distressed to see the bitterness and mistrust between them.

Their animosity was because of Lady Dustin, yet they were all united because of her. She had split them, but she had pulled them together. It was a strange paradox and one he never thought to understand. He could see how terribly upset they were over her capture and in his smart, quick mind, he was formulating a plan.

He had learned about life from his liege, and had experienced enough adventures with the man to hold him for the rest of his life. As exciting as they sometimes were, he was intelligent and had learned from them. He only hoped his liege would agree to what he planned to propose.

Christopher and David were subdued as Darren approached from the darkness and cleared his throat respectfully.

"Greetings this night, my lords," he said.

Christopher glanced up at the broad, blond youth who could pass for his son and smiled faintly. "Still up, Darren? I would think you to be asleep by now."

"Nay, my lord," Darren replied. "I think that if I fall asleep, I will awake to find that I have merely dreamed you were alive."

Christopher shook his head and patted Harold on the head affectionately. "Nay, lad. I am alive."

Darren cleared his throat again, mayhap a bit nervously, and moved stiffly to the log Marcus had occupied. "May I sit, my lords?"

David waved him down and he sat perched rigidly on the edge of the log. Not knowing exactly how he should broach the subject, he decided to simply jump in with both feet.

"Lord Christopher, I have a….a plan regarding your wife," he said.

Christopher looked up from the fire. "Plan? What do you mean?"

Darren felt his face flush as all attention was on him and prayed they did not think him a fool.

"I have been thinking," he said, rather quickly. "Lady Dustin has no protector in Nottingham. She is alone and I know how you must fear for her safety. When we attack come tomorrow, the gates will be closed and the castle sealed and her fate will be in the hands of Prince John and Sir Ralph. She will have no one."

"What are you getting at, Darren?" David demanded.

Darren cleared his throat for the tenth time and forced his courage. "I am thinking that Lady Dustin needs a protector at Nottingham. Of course, the prince and the sheriff know you, my lords, and all of your knights. They even know a good deal of your men-at-arms. They know everyone who is loyal to Richard and it would make it impossible for you or virtually anyone else to slip into Nottingham unnoticed to rescue Lady Dustin."

"We know this, Darren, which is why we made no attempt at a covert rescue mission," Christopher said patiently.

"But they do not know *me,*" Darren insisted. "I could slip in unnoticed and make myself available to your wife."

It was out there. Christopher and David stared at him a moment before turning to look at each other. Darren held his breath as no words were spoken between the two, yet a wordless discussion passed between them. He could tell; the brothers had that ability. Pins and needles of anticipation pricked at him as

Christopher turned away from his brother and gazed into the crackling fire again.

"They have seen you before," Christopher said finally.

"But they paid me no mind, my lord," Darren insisted. "I blend in with the other squires and they believe me to be no one of importance."

Christopher raised an eyebrow thoughtfully, mulling over the possibilities. "You would do this?"

Darren nodded eagerly. "Aye, my lord, I would," he insisted. "I am almost seventeen years now, and I can handle a sword well and…."

"Christ, Darren, you do not have to tell me your qualifications; you are my squire," Christopher said with more emotion than Darren had seen all night. "You can handle a sword almost as well as I can, of that I have no doubt. But you place yourself in grave danger should I allow you to go."

Darren relaxed for the first time. "As you did when you broke your brother out of jail in Antioch? As you did when you took on Saladin's general El-Hajidd on the dunes to rescue the fifteen Christian knights he held captive?" He smiled with admiration. "I was there, my lord. If there is no danger, there is no glory, and if there is no glory then there is no point in being a knight."

Christopher and David gazed back at his strong, young face for a moment, hearing the words and reasoning of a much older man.

"Jesus, Darren, when in the hell did you grow up?" David mumbled.

A slow smile spread across Christopher's lips. "Well said, Darren," he said, rather proud of the lad. "But I do not know if I can allow you to be placed in such jeopardy."

"I wish it, sire," Darren said firmly. "I would do this to help your wife, and to help you. Please do not deny me. There is so much you have done for me. Won't you allow me to repay the debt in the least?"

Christopher shook his head and turned to his brother. "Christ, he pleads as well as you do." He slapped at his leg and sat up straight on the log. "I will think on it, then. Go to bed now and I will let you know when I have made my decision."

Darren slid off the log and bowed respectfully. He began to leave when something stopped him and he paused. "My lord," he said hesitantly. "I would give my life for Lady Dustin. She has been kind to me. I am unconcerned with being placed in danger if it will save her."

Christopher's gaze lingered on the infatuated boy. His wife had power over men she did not even realize. "Thank you, Darren."

He left and Christopher turned to his brother. "What say you?" he asked.

David shrugged. "I am encouraged," he admitted. "Darren is a fine swordsman and will make an outstanding knight in a few years. If we cannot be there to protect her, then I am comfortable with him in our stead."

Christopher agreed. "He is an intelligent, quiet boy and not given to rash judgments," he observed. "He can think for himself."

David stood up and stretched the knots from his legs. "If you want my advice, let him go," he said, rubbing at his neck. "I think it would ease your mind to know that Dustin and Christin are not entirely alone."

Christopher nodded vaguely. "But if they discover him, they will kill him."

"That is a risk we all must take."

Christopher thought on it a moment longer before replying. "I must seek out Edward on this matter. If he gives approval, then I will agree to it."

"What of Richard?" David asked.

"Richard will concur with whatever I decide," Christopher said confidently.

They rose and went their separate ways. Christopher felt a good deal of comfort with Darren's suggestion and was more positive with every step he took. Christ, if it were only that easy. Surely Darren could enter Nottingham unnoticed, for it was a large keep, but to find Dustin and stay with her would be nearly impossible. Especially if John had tight control of her, as he suspected he did.

But he was desperate. He knew what John was capable of, and if anything happened to his wife and child, he would surely die himself. He would not want to live without them.

ೞ

DUSTIN WAS SURPRISED when dresses of every color and flattering style began arriving in her room. But she was shocked when expensive jewels and shoes began arriving, too, and clothes for Christin, as well. She could not believe that Gabrielle had ordered all of these fine clothes for her and wondered furthermore who was going to pay for them. Surely the prince was not so inclined to spend his money on her, his enemy's wife, and she was deeply curious. She would refuse to touch them until she knew all of the details.

Gabrielle arrived later on in the morning and immediately fawned over the new clothes. When she tried to dress Christin in one of the outfits, Dustin stopped her.

"Nay, Gabrielle, she stays as she is for now," she said firmly.

Gabrielle looked perplexed. "But why? Her clothes are soiled and she could use a bath."

Dustin was firm. "Because I do not know who has sent all of these things," she explained warily. "I will not touch them until I know where they came from, and why."

Gabrielle looked at the piles of surcoats. "I ordered you three coats and paid for them myself. They are the ones on the chair, I think. The pale silks," she stood up, holding Christin. "But truthfully, Dustin, I do not know where the rest came from."

Dustin eyed her treasures. "They came from someone who doesn't know me very well," she said, picking up a luscious sapphire and diamond necklace carelessly. "Now, what am I going to do with this? Caesar would love to play with it."

"Caesar? Who's Caesar?" Gabrielle asked.

"My cat," Dustin replied, letting the necklace fall to the table with a clank. "My old, fat, spoiled cat who keeps to himself these days. I took him with me to Somerhill, but he made himself scarce. He did not take to Marcus very well."

Dustin sat in a chair, her pregnant belly looking as if she were harboring a pumpkin underneath her surcoat. Her beautiful face was rested and rosy with her condition, not looking like a woman who had spent a night and day traveling alone.

"When is your baby due, Dustin?" Gabrielle asked, as Christin chewed on her fingers.

"October," Dustin replied. "I have still got a good deal of time to go."

"It is nearly July now," Gabrielle said. "You do not have that much longer."

Dustin sat back in the chair and stroked her belly. "Believe me, Gabrielle, come the heat of August, October will seem like an eternity."

Gabrielle smiled. "And you know it to be a son?"

Dustin nodded firmly. "A son for Christopher," her face suddenly went distant and mournful. "I wonder if he will ever know his son."

"What will you name him?" Gabrielle asked softly.

"Curtis," Dustin murmured. "Curtis Arthur."

"But what if it is another girl?" Gabrielle asked with a twinkle in her eye. "Then what?"

Dustin shrugged. "One girl is all I need," she smiled at her daughter. "But if it is, then I do not know. I cannot think of any female names."

"My mother's name was Arianna," Gabrielle said. "I have always liked that name."

"My mother's name was Mary," Dustin said. "Too plain and too common. Nay, I must think of a wonderful name such as Christin's is."

They took the nooning meal in Dustin's room. In fact, it was sent up without even being ordered and Dustin suspected that she was not such a guest after all. Either that, or John did not want to see her face at his table and spoil his appetite. Whatever the reason, she ate nearly all of the food on the table and then demanded hot water to bathe her daughter. Gabrielle was right; little Christin could use it.

She dressed Christin in one of the little garments she had brought for her and tied a strip of cloth around her head to keep the curly dark hair from getting in her eyes. Already, the babe had a considerable amount of hair. Bathed and fed and happy, Christin crawled about and stuck the rushes in her mouth as her mother tried to discourage her.

Gabrielle seemed determined to spend all of her time with Dustin and Christin. Not that Dustin minded, but the woman seemed desperate for companionship. She was a sweet, funny girl and even in the short time they had spent together, Dustin had come to know her well. She was extremely comfortable with her, but she was still wary about trusting her. Dustin had no idea what her relationship was with the prince and wasn't sure if anything she said wouldn't be immediately repeated.

But, lord, if she wasn't a beautiful, elegant creature. Everything about Gabrielle reeked of breeding and nobility, from the top of her light brown hair to the bottom of those long, long legs. She was several inches taller than Dustin, of which Dustin was highly envious, and she had a silly, squeaky laugh Dustin found hysterical. In some ways, she reminded her a lot of Rebecca. She was sad when she thought of those days with Rebecca that seemed so very long ago.

They were passing away the afternoon chatting about nonsensical things when there was a sharp rap at the door. Gabrielle set Christin down to open it, bowing immediately to the tall, graying man in the archway.

"Lord Bruce," she said formally, assuming he was looking for her. "I apologize that I have not been in my room, but …"

He waved her off. "Not you. I have come to see my granddaughter."

Gabrielle blinked in confusion as Dustin rose slowly from her chair, her eyes fixed on the man whose features were remotely familiar. Frightened and curious at the same time, she openly studied the tall, distinguished looking man.

He smiled at her. "Lady Dustin, of course," he said, stepping into the room, shoving Gabrielle aside. "Great Lucifer, you look like Arthur. I see nothing of my dear Mary in you."

Dustin was nervous. "My lord," she greeted.

"None of that," he snapped. "I am your grandfather and will be addressed as such. You were probably three or four the last time I saw you and surely you do not remember, but you called me Poppa."

"Poppa?" Dustin barely remembered the tall, dark man who had been her mother's father. "I am sorry, sire, I do not remember. But I shall…address you as 'Poppa' if it pleases you."

"It does," he said firmly. "And where is my great-granddaughter?"

They all turned to Christin, playing with a comb on the floor. She smiled innocently up at her great-grandfather and he went wild with delight.

"At last! A child who looks like a Fitz Walter," he crowed. "Look at that hair. Only my side of the family has such pleasingly dark hair. All of Arthur's people were colorless."

Dustin was uncomfortable with the loud, tall man and scooped Christin up into her arms protectively. Lord Bruce continued to smile and announce his pleasure with Christin's dark looks.

"She looks nothing like her bastard father, I am pleased to see," he went on.

"God help me, harboring a de Lohr. Well, I am pleased to see that at least my great-granddaughter is indeed a Fitz Walter."

Dustin was appalled by his words and lowered her gaze, lest he see her angry tears. Lord Bruce, having no idea he had upset his granddaughter, turned to the room laden with expensive items.

"I see you received my gifts," he said with approval, then looked at her. "Why do you not wear them? I demand to see you in one of the surcoats I selected for you."

Dustin, shaken and unnerved, nodded. "Aye, mi....Poppa. I shall put one on immediately."

He nodded curtly. "And jewels. Lots of jewels. My granddaughter will be the best dressed in the keep."

Dustin nodded, keeping her eyes averted. With a final approving glance, he turned for the door. Gabrielle, still standing with her hand on the door latch, curtsied.

"I would have you service me in my rooms before the hour is up," he tapped her on the chin. "Do not be late."

He left with a slam of the door, leaving both women in stunned, embarrassed silence.

Dustin had no idea what to say. She was afraid that Gabrielle would never speak to her again for not divulging the fact that she was Lord Bruce Fitz Walter's granddaughter, yet she was deeply humiliated for her friend with regard to her grandfather's last orders. Summoning her courage, she turned slowly to her friend.

Gabrielle was staring at the floor, her lovely face glazed with shame and shock. Sensing Dustin was looking at her, she met her gaze.

"You are his granddaughter?" she whispered.

Dustin nodded feebly. Gabrielle stared at her a moment longer before letting out a painful sigh. "And you did not tell me? Why not?"

"I was afraid of what you would think," Dustin said honestly.

"What *I* would think?" Gabrielle repeated. "My God, Dustin, you just heard the man order me to his bed like a common whore. What must *you* think?"

"I think that your situation is beyond your control and that you are not to blame," Dustin replied firmly. "I could never think badly of you, Gabrielle."

Gabrielle looked dazed as she sat on the edge of the bed. "I hate Lord Bruce," she murmured. "He likes to make love to me in my arse. 'Tis painful and degrading."

Dustin sat down beside her. "Marcus liked to do it that way, too, but I found it enjoyable. He never hurt me."

Gabrielle looked at her, surprised. " 'Tis a deviant way to make love, I say. What about Lord Christopher?"

Dustin shook her head. "Never like that. He never even suggested it."

Gabrielle looked back at her hands and sighed. "Well, I had better go, then. I shall see you later?"

Dustin could not help it, she impulsively threw her arms around Gabrielle and they hugged each other fiercely.

"Be strong," Dustin whispered.

Gabrielle rose and went to the door, turning to pause. "Oh, Dustin, do not ever let them treat you as they treat me."

"I won't," Dustin insisted firmly.

With a weak smile, Gabrielle was gone and Dustin dissolved into a flood of tears.

☙

JOHN HAD PLANS for Dustin. He intended to have her that eve, but he knew it would not be that simple. He knew she would fight him every step of the way and as much as that excited him, he did not want her to injure herself before he had a chance to feast on her amazing body. The most logical and convenient solution he could think of was Christin.

He had no intention of harming the babe, but he could hold her somewhere where her frantic mother would never find her. At least, not until she had pleased him. Cruel and simple was the ploy and he looked forward to it with glee.

As he sat in his solar watching the temperature rise in the bailey, he was as happy as a child with Christmas candy, but he wondered seriously what had become of de Lohr and Burton. Surely at least one man had survived their mortal bout, and surely he would lay search for his wife. Since John had sent word to Richard regarding Dustin's presence, he expected some sort of contact within the week. He waited with relish, fully intending to play his advantage for all it was worth. Meanwhile, he intended to play with Lady Dustin, pregnant or not.

LATER THAT AFTERNOON, Gabrielle took Dustin and Christin into the bailies that were Nottingham. They were huge and were a village unto themselves, and Dustin studied everything with interest. Soldiers followed the three of them a short distance behind and she knew it was for spying as well as protection, so she kept her manner neutral and tried to not let them see when she was searching the walls for any doors or gates. There had to be a way out of this damnable place.

More peasants than she had ever seen populated Nottingham. They were happy people who genuinely interested her. They would fawn from a distance over Christin and two of the ladies gave the babe a type of root to chew on to help her teething. Christin, happy as always, chewed contentedly on the dried root and drooled all over her new surcoat. Dustin thought the people to be remarkably open and friendly despite the dastardly men who ruled from the castle.

Dressed in a lovely blue linen surcoat, she broke away from Gabrielle and Christin to admire a particularly fine pair of doeskin boots hanging on the cobbler's shed. People were milling about and around everywhere, and business was going on, so she thought nothing of the figure who had brushed by her and leaned against the wall of the shed. Finished appraising the boots, she started to turn around when she heard her name.

"Lady Dustin!" came the urgent whisper. "Do not turn around, my lady, lest you give me away."

Startled, her first reaction was to indeed turn around to the source of the voice, but she caught herself instead. She forced herself to calm down and feigned interest in another pair of shoes, hoping her shaking did not show.

"Who is it?" she whispered as casually as she could manage.

" 'Tis Darren, my lady, your husband's squire," Darren whispered. "He has sent me with a message."

Dustin was overwhelmed in that moment with relief and joy. *He was alive!* Christopher had survived. But in the same instant she knew he was alive only because Marcus had met his death and grief flooded her. But her happiness overcame all other emotions and she suppressed an urge to scream her elation.

"He lives, Darren?" she hissed.

"Indeed, my lady," Darren replied. "He wants you to know that Richard and his army are riding to your aid. They will be here on the morrow."

"The king?" Dustin was stunned, her mind spinning. "What…what of Marcus? Is he dead?"

"Nay, my lady, he rides with the king," Darren whispered. "They have put off their duel in order to save you."

Dustin was shocked and fought to maintain her composure. *The king was riding to her aid?* It did not make sense, especially since the man hated her. And Christopher, was he coming because he was obliged to or because he wanted to? After everything that had happened, how could she be sure? And Marcus was alive, after all. She was relieved, of course, but she did not like Darren's words…*'to put off their duel.'* Did this mean the moment she was returned, they would try and kill each other again? She simply did not know; how could she be sure of anything anymore?

She could not, but she knew one thing for certain; she wanted Christin away from Nottingham. If there was to be a battle, she wanted her daughter safe. She believed she could handle John and Ralph, but if they were to threaten Christin….she would be lost. Anxiety clutched at her.

"Darren, you must take Christin out of here," she whispered, glancing from the corner of her eye to see where her guards were. "If there is to be a fight, she must be safe."

"But...my lady," Darren protested. "I am to protect you. I cannot leave."

"You must!" she snapped, drawing attention and recovering nicely by grabbing a shoe and yelling to the cobbler that he must make the shoe in her size. When the soldiers looked away, she took her first look at Darren. "Darren, she must be taken to safety. She is in great danger here."

"But what of you?" Darren asked urgently. "You are in danger, too."

She scowled at him. "I can take care of myself, but I cannot take care of myself and Christin. You must take her to her father."

Darren was speechless. This was not part of his plan, nor was it part of his orders. He dreaded telling her "no." "My lady, I cannot leave you," he whispered feebly. "Lord Christopher sent me here to protect you."

She glared at him, her pretty jaw ticking. "Protecting Christin is the most important thing in the world. Darren, so help me, if you argue with me, I shall tell Christopher you were most disobedient."

His young face washed with apprehension. "Please, my lady, do not...my orders were to protect you."

She ignored him, glancing behind her again to see that Gabrielle was looking at her curiously. Quickly, she pretended to straighten a pair of shoes. "Meet me out here in an hour. Right here, behind the cobbler's shed. Do you understand?"

Darren sighed with resignation. "Aye, lady, I do. Unfortunately."

Behind her, there was a bit of commotion and she turned around to see Sir Dennis la Londe approaching. Her heart sank; she hadn't seen him since her arrival and was hoping to avoid him. Darren faded away as Dennis smiled leeringly at her.

"My lady," he greeted in his heavy French accent. "I was told of your arrival. May I say, it is delightful to see you again."

She barely nodded, moving away from Darren and back toward Gabrielle. Sir Dennis followed her closely, like an eager dog.

"It was certainly a surprise to hear of your visit," he said, then glanced at Christin. "Oh, my, is this the *enfant* de Lohr? Strange, she looks like a Burton with that dark hair."

Dustin whirled to him, her teeth clenched. "My mother had dark hair, and if you will, ask Lord Bruce, who happens to be Christin's great-grandsire. Now, if you will excuse me."

She tried to push past him, but he stuck to her like grease on a spoon. "Your grandpapa is Lord Bruce? I did not know, *chèrie*. How fortunate."

She hated his sickly-sweet accent and rolled her eyes at him in disgust. He responded by grabbing her sharply by the arm, his big fingers digging into her soft flesh.

"If I were you, I would behave with a bit more respect." His voice was cold, not at all friendly as it had been just a moment before. "A warning this time."

Her nostrils flared angrily and she yanked her arm away. "Do not presume to give me a warning of any kind, Sir Dennis. My grandsire is your host, as is your prince. I do not answer to you."

She twisted away from him and walked away with her entourage in tow. Sir Dennis watched her go with beady eyes, imagining all sorts of deviant things in his warped mind.

"You will, *chèrie*," he murmured. "Soon, you will."

CHAPTER FIFTY-SIX

RICHARD'S ARMY WAS barely rested from their march from Windsor before they were mobilizing again in preparation of the siege of Nottingham. The summer morning dawned warm and clear as crystal, and Christopher was already sweating as he positioned the nearly two thousand troops.

It was good to be working with Marcus again, for the man was as capable as he when it came to tactics and intuition. He knew where Christopher wanted the men and he knew exactly where to position the archers for maximum effectiveness. It was no time before Christopher merely hung back and supervised while Marcus and David streamlined the massive army.

His heart swelled with pride as he watched his brother and his former friend, remembering what it had been like in the Holy Land. David and Marcus were extensions of himself and he need not utter a word for them to know exactly what he wanted. For the moment, the hostility and sorrow were forgotten as he watched his men work. Edward and his other knights were serving Marcus and David well, making sure their orders were carried out. The precise chain of command was perfect, as always, and Richard rode up astride his dark gray steed to watch the final preparations.

"Just like old times," he remarked, watching Marcus and David work like a fine-tuned team. "I'd almost forgotten."

"I never thought to see this again," Christopher said softly. "Marcus and David have been working together for over two hours and nary a harsh word between them."

Richard gave a wry smile. "Amazing."

They watched the last of the archers being positioned and then Edward and Sean began moving the wagons into place.

"Darren should have found Dustin by now," Christopher said. "He rode into Nottingham yesterday morning and I would think he has had ample time to locate her."

"Most likely," Richard agreed. "But I am concerned for the lad. He is not a spy, you know. He is taking a great risk."

"He is an intelligent boy," Christopher said. "I have faith that he will be cautious."

"Nevertheless, you know I was not very agreeable on the proposal," Richard said firmly. "I do not know what possible good he can do except to get himself caught. Then we shall have one more person to rescue."

"I trust Darren, Richard," Christopher said softly. "He has proven himself many a time, and I trust him."

"But do you trust him with your wife's life?" Richard asked, shaking his head. "I cannot believe you would send a seventeen-year-old squire into the pit of hell and expect him to perform as a knight."

"I shall knight him next year myself, and I will be proud to have him in my stable." Christopher looked at Richard. "Don't you trust my judgment when it comes to warriors?"

"Of course." Richard waved him off. "It is just that he's not a full-fledged knight yet and….oh, hell, I don't know. There are too many people to worry over. Darren certainly cannot protect your wife if John sets his sights on her. To do that would be to kill a prince of England, and I will not allow it."

Christopher put up a hand in supplication. "Darren's orders are to shadow Dustin and protect her from harm, not to kill John. Richard, I simply feel better having him with her if I cannot be. I thought you understood that yesterday?"

"I understand," he muttered. "I understand that I am growing soft and that you are going mad."

Christopher chuckled. Then, he sobered and changed the subject. "Marcus and I talked last night."

"And?" Richard looked at him.

Christopher sighed. "He says he will not fight me for Dustin anymore."

"Do you believe him?" Richard asked.

"I don't know," Christopher replied. "He's lied to me before where my wife is concerned, so I suppose time will tell."

Richard studied the face of his mighty Defender. "You look tired. Did you sleep?"

"Barely," Christopher said. "I shall sleep when Dustin is safe beside me."

Richard did not say anything, glancing at his army as David raced like hellfire the length of the column for some unknown reason. He could hear the knight yelling.

"That fool is going to kill himself one day doing that," he murmured, then looked at Christopher again. "That wound has taxed you greatly, hasn't it? You are still not completely well and this march is draining your strength."

Christopher drew in a deep, slow breath, looking to his king. "I shall admit that I do not feel as strong as I am used to, but I will eventually. I am well enough to raze Nottingham and retrieve my wife."

Richard shook his head. "You are either the bravest man alive or the biggest idiot. Who would have thought you would raze a castle for anything less than my glory?"

They shared a small chuckle. "Not I, Richard, and well you know it," Christopher said. "My devotion to you was legendary."

Richard's smile faded. "You say that as if it were a thing of the past. You are still my Defender and champion, Chris. I shall not release you from your duties."

Christopher shrugged and gazed back over the army. "You will have to while I heal completely. I would suggest David or Marcus in my stead."

"David is a wild man," Richard snorted. "And Marcus is too caught up in his own personal problems. Damnation, when did things become so complicated? I think I shall return to Jerusalem; the situation was a lot less complex."

Christopher laughed softly. "I shall send word to Philip and Henry and make sure they meet you when you set foot on the continent," he jested.

Richard snorted again, louder. "Hell yes," he agreed. "Why not have them add to my problems?"

Christopher smiled broadly at his king when a loud whistle pierced the air and he saw David give him the high sign, indicating the army was ready to move. Christopher lifted his mailed fist in response.

"We are ready, sire," he said to Richard. "At your command."

Richard gazed out over his army, drinking in the sight of the power under him. "I have spent most of my life fighting," he mumbled. "I know nothing else. My army is my family and the battlefield, my home." He latched his helmet. "I envy you, Chris, that you would find something more to this life than dying and fighting and blood. That you would find love is an amazing accomplishment indeed, and I will most likely never know the joy." He paused, looking to Christopher as he gathered his reins. "Let us get your wife back."

Christopher slammed his visor down in response. Richard watched a change come over the man, as visible as the rising sun. He morphed from the concerned husband to pure warrior.

Richard watched the transformation with satisfaction; this was the Christopher he knew and loved. The Christopher he had grown to know over the past few days confused him greatly, for it was almost as if it weren't the same man. The new Christopher felt emotion and showed depth of character, admirable traits indeed, but confusing when one considered that the man had never shown emotion before. Richard had felt disoriented until this moment, this was his Defender. This was Christopher de Lohr, the greatest warrior since Galahad or Lancelot. He was the legend.

"Why are you looking at me like that?" Christopher broke into his thoughts.

Richard suddenly realized he was smiling. Clearing his throat, he put his faceplate down. "No reason," he muttered.

Marcus and David thundered up, followed closely by Edward, Dud, and the rest of the knights. They all stood atop the slight rise, gazing down on the mightiest army England had ever seen assembled, and nodded with gratification.

"My loyal knights," said Richard. He loved to give pre-battle speeches, but he found this morning that none came to mind. He decided to speak what he felt. "I am deeply pleased that we are together, fighting as one body again. May victory be ours!"

All of the knights responded by the customary cry, "God and King Richard!" and spurred their destriers from the crest, riding to their positions along the column. Only Christopher and his king would ride in front, leading the troops to certain glory.

ଓ

DUSTIN WAS SHAKEN and encouraged by her encounter with Darren. Thrilled that Christopher was alive and wildly relieved that he was coming for her, she tried to maintain a calm attitude for the benefit of her captors. She was tremendously eager to remove Christin from harm's way and thanked God for sending Darren to her. She could take care of herself, but she was terrified for Christin's safety. Terrified that somehow John would take advantage of the infant.

The afternoon passed and the heat was bearable, but sticky. In her condition, she was always hot and felt miserable and damp as she dressed Christin in a durable linen outfit that would protect her and wear well. She doubled her nappy so she wouldn't leak all over Darren as he carried her to safety, and put a matching hat on her head to protect her little ears and scalp. Christin, hating anything on her head, kept pulling it off until Dustin gave her a piece of dry bread to chew on to distract her.

Dustin felt as if the Devil were nipping at her heels and her sense of urgency was paramount. She did not know why, but it was as if an unseen force was pushing her, making her race against herself to get her daughter out of Nottingham. She was almost panicked in her urgency, but she forced herself to calm for Christin's sake. How would she explain Christin's absence to John and her grandfather? Surely they would demand to know where the child was. She would simply have to think of a logical, believable explanation, at least until Christopher and the army arrived. After that, she did not care. Christin would be safe and that was all that mattered.

Time went quickly and before she realized it, the hour was upon her and it was time to take Christin to the bailey. She could only pray that Darren was obedient, that God and luck were with them, and that they would make it safely out of Nottingham. As she prepared a final tiny bag with food for her daughter, Gabrielle knocked softly and entered the room.

"I thought you might like to.....what are you doing?" she asked.

Dustin thought about trying to hide her plans, but there was no use to it. Gabrielle was her friend, and she would have to trust her.

"I am getting Christin out of here," she said. "Today. Now."

"What?" Gabrielle's eyes widened. "What are you talking about?"

Dustin took a quick breath to bolster her courage and pulled Gabrielle down on the bed beside her.

"My husband's squire is here," she said softly. "He came to watch over me, he says, by order of Christopher, but I in turn ordered him to take Christin out of here. Richard is riding to my aid, Gabrielle, and Nottingham will be a living hell. I do not want my daughter to perish or be used as a pawn in this evil game John plays. I want her safe."

Gabrielle looked deeply fearful, but there was also a glimmer of hope in her eyes. "Richard is coming for you? And your husband? Dustin, how marvelous!"

Dustin nodded swiftly. "I must get Christin to Darren. I told him to meet me by the cobbler's shed and he should be there now. I must go."

Gabrielle shook her head. " 'Tis dangerous, Dustin. John usually takes his walk about this time and if he were to see you...."

Dustin swallowed hard and squeezed Gabrielle's hand. "I shall just have to take that chance. Nothing is more important than Christin's life."

As she rose to gather Christin's things, Gabrielle grasped her arm gently. "Dustin, will you...will you take me with you? I have nowhere else to go and...."

Dustin did not even let her finish her sentence. "Of course you are coming with me. You do not think for one moment that I would leave you here?"

Gabrielle smiled weakly. "Nay, I suppose not. But I had to ask."

Dustin flashed her a quick smile and gathered Christin. "Now, I must make my little trip," she said, her gaze going to her innocent daughter's face. "Say goodbye to Lady Gabrielle, Christin. Tell her that you will see her later, at Lioncross."

Gabrielle kissed the baby several times. "I miss her already, Dustin. But you are correct; she is not safe here."

Suddenly the door swung open and Ralph was in the doorway, his beady black eyes focusing on Dustin immediately. Dustin's heart went into her throat; she was terrified that Ralph had heard everything as he wandered slowly toward them.

"My ladies," he greeted, eyeing Christin as if she were a lower life form. "The prelude to the evening meal is being served in the main hall. Lady Dustin, I have been asked to accompany you."

Dustin blanched; her plans and her daughter. She began to shake, praying Ralph could not see her despair and fought the urge to tell him to go to hell. She must remain polite and neutral if she were going to get through this.

"I see," she said hoarsely, clutching Christin. "May I at least change clothing?"

Ralph's eyes raked over her pregnant form in the soft linen surcoat. "No need, I'd say. You look ravishing."

With one attempt to stall foiled, Dustin cleared her throat and glanced at Gabrielle, a plan formulating quickly in her mind. "Is Lady Gabrielle to attend, also?"

Ralph looked at Gabrielle disinterestedly. "Not that I know of. The whores do not usually eat with the privileged."

Dustin was stung on behalf of Gabrielle, who met the statement unflinchingly. Suddenly, she saw the way clear and felt a gush of relief as she handed Christin into Gabrielle's arms.

"Very well, Ralph," she said briskly. "Gabrielle, be sure and take Christin for her walk in the bailey or she will never get to sleep. And be sure to stop by the cobbler's shed as I was planning to and see if he has made those shoes in my size."

Gabrielle's stunned face suddenly registered realization, and she nodded. "As you say, my lady. 'Twill be my pleasure."

Dustin smiled at her, her body quivering with anxiety and relief. Ralph didn't notice, however; he reached out, taking her elbow.

"Come then, Lady Dustin," he said. "Your admiring throng awaits."

She avoided his gaze, wondering who composed this "admiring throng" and allowed him to lead her from the room.

WHEN THE DOOR closed, Gabrielle let out a loud exhale and looked at Christin.

"Come now, little one," she kissed her shakily on the forehead. "Your escort awaits."

Darren was indeed waiting. Even though he did not know who the strange woman was who was holding Christin, she seemed to focus on him immediately and walked directly toward him. She was a beautiful, refined woman and he found himself speechless as she reached him.

"You must take Christin," she whispered, handing the babe to him. "There is no time to waste."

He took the child, open-mouthed, a hundred questions bubbling forth in his mind.

"Who are you? How do you know me?" he stammered, all the while glancing about to make sure none of John's soldiers were watching.

"I am a friend of Lady Dustin's," Gabrielle explained quickly. "Hurry. You must leave."

"Wait!" Darren insisted. "Where is Lady Dustin? And how do you know me?"

Gabrielle looked over her shoulder nervously. "Lady Dustin is with John and Ralph at the moment. I knew you were Lord Christopher's squire because you have that look about you. Now go."

"What look?" Darren demanded.

Gabrielle gave him a small smile. "The look of goodness and purity. You are soon to be a knight, are you not? Now, please hurry before you are discovered. They would not take kindly to you, young squire."

Darren tore his eyes off her lovely face and looked about, not wanting to be found out, especially with little Christin in his arms. Everything was happening so fast and nothing was as he and Lord Christopher had intended. He had barely been in Nottingham half a day and already, he was leaving. But he was leaving with a most precious cargo, and he knew that his liege would not fault him for straying from the objective.

He glanced down at Christin's wide gray eyes, looking up at him with interest. He felt his heart soften, the unmistakable swell of protectiveness filling him. She was so young, so trusting, and he would not fail her. He *could* not. This was his liege's child, his flesh and blood, and he would protect her with his life. He was still torn for the fact that he would not be remaining behind to shadow Lady Dustin, but he saw that this little life was more important, as her mother had insisted.

"Thank you, then, my lady," he whispered, covering Christin's head with his heavy black cloak. "I shall do as ordered."

Gabrielle turned her back on him, not so much as acknowledging his reply. She was shaking with fear, afraid that someone had seen her pass the baby off. John's men were everywhere and she was constantly watched, but she was as sure as she could be that this time, no one had followed her. They were beginning to trust her more and, therefore, hound her less.

With a straight back and the confidence of knowing that her plight would soon be ended with the approach of Richard, she made her way back into the castle.

☙

DUSTIN WAS IN a living nightmare. With John on one side of her and Ralph on the other, she fought off wave after wave of nausea. Sir Dennis and her grandfather, Lord Bruce, rounded out the lovely little group and she knew she had a permanently sour expression, but it did not matter. She did not care what they thought.

"You are not wearing the jewels I sent to you," Lord Bruce said firstly, forgoing any greeting.

Dustin was tired of being nice, tired of being respectful to the point of servitude. Her husband and the bloody king of England were coming for her and with that knowledge, she felt confident. With men so potent on her side, how could the likes of John and Ralph and her grandsire harm her? She fixed Lord Bruce right in the eye.

"Obviously, you do not know me well, sire," she said coldly. "I hate jewels and frivolous clothes. I will wear what I deem comfortable."

She had John and Ralph's attention with that statement. They looked to Lord Bruce to see how he would react. Lord Bruce did not disappoint; his eyes narrowed the same way his granddaughter's did when she was displeased.

"You will wear what I request, Lady Dustin," he countered. "And furthermore, you will not take such a tone with me lest you find your backside blistered."

"You wouldn't dare!" she shot back, tired and irritated and full of pregnant hormones.

His eyebrows shot up. "Do you test me, then? I shall put you over my knee as I did your mother when she was disrespectful."

Dustin raised a disbelieving eyebrow at him, glancing at John and feeling the need to play one man against the other. She had created dissension within Christopher's ranks unknowingly; she wondered what she could do to John's men should she set her mind to it. She could confuse and anger them so greatly that mayhap they would be glad to hand her over to Richard and Christopher without much of a protest. For whatever the reason, she would give them the respect they were giving her.

"My mother is dead, Lord Bruce, and unable to verify your story," she said, giving John her full attention. "What would you recommend to eat, sire? This dish looks interesting."

John was amused to see her ignoring Bruce plainly. The man had boasted endlessly about his family ties when he had discovered his granddaughter was a woman of importance, but she clearly wanted nothing to do with him. John himself actually spooned her a helping of the capon in fruit sauce and sat back while she delved into it.

But Bruce was furious with her behavior. He was embarrassed at the very least. "Sire, I would speak with my granddaughter alone, with your permission," Lord Bruce said, and got up from his chair.

John put up a hand. "You may speak with her if that is all you truly intend to do," he said. "I forbid you to lay a hand on her, Bruce. I mean it."

Bruce flushed red, eyeing Dustin angrily but seeing the situation for what it was. John wanted his granddaughter for himself and he would not be allowed to lay a hand on her, at least until he had grown tired of the game. John did not like damaged goods.

Slowly, he regained his seat and tried to focus on something other than his damaged pride. Dustin, fully aware of her grandfather's embarrassment, continued to eat what was in front of her and ignored Bruce completely. It was strange that she felt safer with John than with her own grandfather. Yet in truth she felt safe with none of them, and she was hard pressed to decide the lesser of the evils.

"Tell me, my lady, what was it like being married to the two greatest warriors this realm has ever seen?" Sir Dennis asked, his eyes glittering over the top of his bejeweled goblet.

Dustin's head snapped up; she had expected as much from the man and fought to control her emotions.

"That depends, Sir Dennis," she said. "They were both kind, noble men."

"That's not what he meant," Ralph quipped snidely. "He wanted to know who is better in bed."

Dustin cringed inwardly; how could they speak so callously of such a wonderful, loving act? Shocked, she swallowed her mouth of food and prepared to reply when Sir Dennis cut in.

"You always know what I am thinking, do you not?" Dennis laughed. "Let's make a bet, *mon frere*. I say the de Lohr is the better lay. What say you?"

Ralph grinned lewdly. "I have heard that Burton is a tiger, but then again, what would I know?" He looked at Dustin. "Here sits his former wife. Why not ask her?"

Dustin stared back, disgusted and sickened at the conversation. But she could play lewd games with the best of them rather than let them see how badly they had upset her. Mayhap if they saw she wasn't the least bit sensitive about her "marriages," then they might leave well enough alone. Primly, she folded her hands and collected her thoughts before fixing Sir Dennis in the eye. Let her beat them at their own game.

"They are both men among men, let me assure you," she said softly with a trace of seduction. "Marcus Burton can bring a scream to my lips within thirty seconds and Christopher de Lohr can play games until the sun rises. Any more questions?"

John paused with a spoon half way to his mouth. Sir Dennis and Ralph gazed back at Dustin with surprise, glancing at each other after a moment. They had thoroughly hoped to upset and unbalance Lady Dustin, but instead, she was meeting their challenge. This small slip of a woman who had managed to snare the love of the greatest knights of their time was holding her own against her formidable rivals and they felt the game slipping away, losing interest. There was no point in playing if she was not going to respond.

"But...who is better?" Sir Dennis tried one last time.

Dustin sat back in her chair, her eyes glittering like storm clouds. "Christopher, without a doubt. Although Marcus is no amateur." She offered a triumphant little smile to cap off her performance.

John was looking at her with a great deal of amusement. "My, my, you are frank, aren't you? True ladies do not boast of their conquests, you know."

"Since when have I been considered a true lady?" Dustin shot back with a smirk. It was becoming easier to play their game as she went along. "With the exception of a few, every woman at Windsor disliked me intensely and I was considered something of a passing fad."

"Not true," John returned. "I know you were very popular, for a fact."

"My *husband* was very popular, sire," Dustin corrected.

"Popular with the women. They only wanted me around because I was his wife. I must say, those bitches were a bore."

John laughed softly and Dustin joined in boisterously, eyeing Ralph and her smile vanished unnaturally fast. "What is it with you, Fitz Walter? Don't you have a sense of humor?"

Ralph raised a greasy black eyebrow at her. "My lady is…most different without her husband hanging about."

Dustin threw up her hands. "He is a bore, too. *Do not do this, Dustin. Do not sit this way. Do not ride astride.*" She mimicked Christopher's sternness. "The man kept me bridled like a brood mare. Acted like my damn father more than my husband."

"But you love him," Ralph stated.

A stab of pain went into Dustin's heart; Lord, she loved him more than life itself. Her loud demeanor faltered slightly. "Aye, I do. He is a kind man. But I did not say *what* kind."

John laughed loudly and slapped his hand against the table, calling for more wine in the process.

"I know what kind," he said, then eyed Dustin slowly. "You are putting on quite a show for our benefit, my lady."

Dustin twitched with surprise; mayhap her acting wasn't all that grand. But she had to pretend they did not frighten her, that she really did not care about Christopher or Marcus. They could not see just how terrified she was.

" 'Tis no act, I assure you, sire," she said, lowering her lashes. "Before you is the real Lady Dustin Barringdon de Lohr."

He raised a questioning eyebrow but said nothing. He wasn't sure what to think anymore, but he was not so gullible that he sincerely believed her. Mayhap there was part truth to her statement, but he doubted it. In his experience, women were scheming cows.

"Tell me my lady, will you compare me to de Lohr and Burton's expertise in the bedchamber?" he leaned close to her. "I wonder what you will tell others about me?"

Dustin went white; the fear she was trying desperately to control returned fully. "I will tell…..nothing, of course, sire."

"Lying wench," he hissed, moving away and drinking deeply of his goblet.

Dustin was quivering but controlled it well; she had known all along that John planned to couple with her, but she prayed he would take pity on her physical condition. She had heard through the palace rumor mills that the prince was hung like a prize stallion and she had no desire to see firsthand for herself. The thought of him touching her in such a manner almost made her retch right there at the table.

John laughed at her. He could see her discomfort and he knew immediately that her entire facade was an act.

"Do you know that Ralph and I were planning to abduct you from Windsor?" he said with a smile on his lips.

Dustin looked at him. "What?"

He nodded, amused at her shock. "We were planning on kidnapping you and taking you far away, to Wales in fact, simply to bring de Lohr to his knees." He leaned forward, toying with the cross around her neck. "The trouble was that he never left you unguarded and the one attempt we did make was costly. There was never the proper opportunity and I had too many other bloody things on my mind to make your capture a firm priority."

Dustin was shocked but the prince prattled on, having imbibed too much wine. "After you fell down the stairs and lost your child, he never left you alone and we knew it would be futile to make another attempt. But it was always in our mind, wasn't it, Ralph, to somehow abduct you and hold you over de Lohr's head. Our plans were grand, indeed, but somehow we never had the chance to carry them out. We wanted to bring you here to Nottingham and hide you from de Lohr, but the moment was never right. I had too many pressing problems. Yet when de Lohr was said to have been killed in battle, most of my problems seemed to have resolved and we forgot about abducting you."

Dustin was sitting as far away from him as she could get, her eyes wide with horror. She realized how much she had helped John's cause by walking right into his lap, and she furthermore prayed to God that Gabrielle had managed to get Christin to Darren. She knew John and Ralph were conspiring against her husband, but she never truly believed she would be their tool. Christopher had told her once that they would try to exploit his weaknesses and she saw now how right he had been. The thought processes of John and Ralph were exactly as her husband said they were.

"What do you intend to do with me?" she heard herself asking, hating herself for sounding scared.

John smiled lazily, drinking more wine. "Nothing, for the moment. I do not have to. Richard is aware we have you and no doubt, so is de Lohr. I want to thank you, Lady Dustin, for helping us accomplish a great deal with very little effort."

If Dustin had had a dagger, she would have killed herself for her own stupidity. What on God's earth had she been thinking when she had set out alone? She had been scared, confused and disoriented, but she had not been stripped of her common sense. What had Christopher said to her once, a long time ago? That John would find a way to use her to destroy her husband? Now, thanks to her lapse in judgment, Christopher was probably in more danger than he had ever been in his life because she knew he would walk through fire to rescue her. And so did John.

She could not speak anymore. She looked away from the prince, cursing herself silently with every breath.

"What? No more chatting? No more frankness?" John stuck out his lip. "I am disappointed, Lady Dustin. Surely you would entertain us more."

Dustin shook her head. "Nay, sire, I am quite weary," she whispered. "I would retire now."

John shrugged. "Very well, if you must. Ralph, you will escort Lady de Lohr."

Ralph stood up and pulled Dustin out of her chair. "With pleasure, my lord."

"Do not touch her," John spat, pointing a finger at his sheriff. "I will not have your leftovers."

"As you say, my lord," Ralph agreed, gripping Dustin's arm as he led her from the hall.

Ralph took Dustin to her chamber and opened the door, lingering a moment as she entered. Dustin refused to meet his eye, wishing he would go away.

"You know, you struck me once. Do you remember?" he asked.

Dustin looked at him, then. "Aye, I do."

He nodded faintly, studying her face and trying to read her emotions. She did well at hiding her feelings.

"Then know that I intend to seek revenge on you, one way or the other," he said. "I may slap you back, or I may take it out of your hide. I just wanted you to be aware of my plans, my lady."

He did not frighten her, merely made her angry. "And I shall be sure and inform the prince of your plans, also."

He smiled ever so slightly, the fire from the hearth playing on his greasy black hair. "That, my lady, would not be wise," he said softly. "God, how long have I dreamed of you within my grasp? I can scarce believe the good fortune we have befallen. I am still shocked with it all. I will bid a good eve to you, then."

He left and Dustin kicked off her shoes in frustration. She was so desperately tired and sick that she did not know how much more of this torment she could take. She could hardly wait to find Gabrielle to make sure Darren took Christin with him. She had to know her daughter was safe.

Christopher, wherever you are, hurry!

CHAPTER FIFTY-SEVEN

THE ROAD WAS flat and from the absence of activity along the path, they knew they had been sighted. Nottingham lay beyond the horizon and Christopher mentally lingered on the fortress; Dustin and Christin were holed up in that horrible place and his stomach twisted with agony. He could not think of what might be possibly happening to them now as he rode to the rescue, because to imagine the worst drove him insane. Over his right shoulder, several feet back, Marcus was having the exact same thoughts.

A rider suddenly appeared on the road ahead, riding toward them at breakneck speed. It was just one man and no alarm was sounded, but Christopher sent Marcus and David out to intercept. However, the closer the horse came, the more Christopher recognized the animal and he bolted forward with terror in his throat.

Darren was returning to the army.

David and Marcus reached Darren first, their horses dancing and snorting with excitement. They barely had time to speak when Christopher roared up, plowing his animal forward and pushing David and Marcus out of the way.

"Darren!" he bellowed. "What in the hell is going on? Why have you returned?"

Darren threw back the hood of his black cloak. "She would not let me stay, my lord," he said loudly, sensing his liege's apprehension. "She insisted I return with a gift for you."

Christopher's composure was rapidly slipping. "Gift?" he roared. "What kind of damn nonsense is this? You had your orders, boy."

Marcus and David were waiting for Christopher to behead the squire right then and there, and they both cringed inwardly when the young man had the audacity to smile.

"My orders came from a higher source, my lord," the squire said. "My lady was fearful with the approaching battle and wished to have her most valuable possession taken to safety. She wouldn't let me stay, my lord. She insisted I bring you this."

He moved the cloak from his chest and Christin de Lohr's bright gray eyes blinked in the sudden light. Christopher's eyes widened and he heard himself gasp as he laid eyes on the daughter he had not seen in months. Immediately, his heart softened and he forgot all of his anger and anxiety. Without thinking, he reached out and took her.

"Oh, my God," he whispered. "Look at her; she is beautiful."

Marcus could only stare at Christin, his heart breaking into a million pieces. The hardest thing he had ever had to do was not reach out instinctively for the babe, and he felt as if the weight of the world was pressing on his chest.

David, his face soft and smiling, flipped up his visor to get a better look at her. "By damn, if she isn't starting to look more and more like you," he told his brother. "Poor child."

Christopher smiled at his brother's comment, not taking his eyes off the baby. Warm, fluid emotion rippled through him and he was in love all over again.

"Hello, sweetheart," he murmured. "Do you remember me?"

Marcus flipped up his own visor, mayhap in challenge. He wanted to see if Christin would react to him instead of to Christopher. He had promised he wouldn't fight anymore, but his aching heart demanded one last bit of satisfaction. He loved Christin more than anything; almost more than Dustin.

Christin looked at Christopher, chewing her fingers. Then, she looked at David disinterested and finally to Marcus. He got a reaction; she smiled broadly and crowed, but then she abruptly turned back to Christopher and slapped at his face with wet fingers.

Christopher melted. He kissed her little fingers and her face, careful not to bump her with his visor. The more he kissed her, the more she giggled and slapped.

"Just like her mother," David remarked warmly. "She thinks it funny to punch you in the face."

Christopher's throat was tight, too tight to speak. He did not trust himself not to break. Marcus could not take anymore, his heart was ripping in two, so he reined his horse away, back to his position in the column. David was aware of the pain in the man's eyes but did little more than watch him trot back along the line before turning his attention back to his brother and niece. He was saddened, though, at Marcus' pain; even with all of the hatred and fighting that had gone on between them, David wasn't cruel. He did not wish sorrow on anyone.

"What are we going to do with her?" Richard asked, as he rode up and watched the touching reunion.

Christopher held the babe close to his chest, watching her as she banged on his armor and nibbled the little fingers she put in his mouth.

"Keep her back in the wagons," Christopher replied, his voice filled with incredible gentleness. "Christ, I cannot believe how beautiful she is."

"Your wife was wise to send her to safety," Richard said.

"Absolutely," Christopher agreed, taking his eyes off his daughter for the first time and focusing on Darren. "How is Dustin?"

"As well as can be expected, my lord," he replied, his expression hesitant. "I saw her only once, this morning, when she was out walking with John's hounds in tow. Her friend, a Lady Gabrielle, delivered me the baby for safekeeping. I was told Lady Dustin was with John and Ralph."

Christopher's face hardened like stone and he took a deep, calming breath. Richard was again amazed to watch him transform from doting father back to hardened warrior.

"We ride," Christopher growled. "David, get the column moving while I deliver my daughter to Burwell."

Richard scratched his cheek. "He should be thrilled with the prospect of child-watching," he said with a smirk.

The army was moving and Darren took up a place of honor beside Christopher as they rode. It was a reward for a job well done, and Christopher furthermore had more questions to ask of the young man. A young man who had so recently seen his precious wife.

"Was Dustin looking well?" he asked his squire.

"Aye, she was, my lord," Darren answered. "I have never seen her look better."

There was something in his voice that caused Christopher to turn and look at him. "What is it that you are not telling me?"

Darren looked uncomfortable, his eyes on the road ahead. "Nothing, truly, sire. 'Tis just that I saw your wife only once, and I had to keep in the shadows when that bastard le Londe approached her. He was less than gentle with your wife, sire, and it was extremely difficult for me not to intervene. But I had no choice if I were to bring your daughter out of Nottingham. I could not risk being caught."

Christopher's face was impassive, but his hands underneath his mailed gloves gripped the reins with white-knuckled intensity. "How was he rough with her? Did he strike her?"

Darren shook his head. "Nay, sire, he did not, but he grabbed her by her arms," he told him. "He was less than respectful and she gave him an earful. And she mentioned something I found strange; she said her grandfather was the Lord of Nottingham."

"Indeed he is," Christopher said evenly, thinking what a vile, disgusting man Lord Bruce was. He could only pray that he hadn't taken to Dustin the same way he had taken to Dustin's mother. Whether or not he had, he was a dead man. They were all dead men. Even John was, whether or not Richard knew it.

Richard knew it, but he had said nothing. John was his brother, hated or not, and he would not allow his Defender to kill him. If he had touched Lady Dustin, then the fight would be a grand one for Richard intended to defend his brother himself. Bloodlines dictated it. But if John had kept his hands off the Defender's wife, then mayhap reasoning would prevail over might. His conflict was tremendous; he did not want to lose his Defender, but he could not allow the man to kill his brother, no matter what he had done. It would seem their goals, for once, were not the same. Richard only wanted his property returned; Christopher only wanted his wife.

"Chris," Marcus rode up, tipping his head in the direction of the castle. "Nottingham on the horizon."

Christopher strained his eyes to see that, indeed, the tiny dots that represented peasants were scattering like flax in the wind and up on the massive wall, they could see a flurry of activity.

"Prepare the men, Marcus," Christopher said and he could hear orders being barked almost simultaneously. "Darren, fall back with the other squires."

Darren obeyed, a bit disappointed. He was hoping to ride into battle at the front of the column. He wasn't wearing any body armor but he could don his scant pieces when time allowed. Hell, he was almost a damn knight. In fact, he had seen more action than men who called themselves knights.

Doing as he was told, Darren reined his animal about and returned to the rear of the army. Like any good knight, his adrenalin began to flow and he was eager to fight the battle alongside his liege and King Richard. Already a battle veteran at his young age, Darren looked forward to seeing Lady Dustin again. And he had no doubt that he would. Surely God himself could not have raised a mightier army, with mightier leaders.

The army rode toward Nottingham, the first of fourteen keeps that Richard planned to retake from his brother. The summer sun sank in the sky and the heat of the day stagnated, and the hawks high above riding the warm drafts screamed to their mates. Below them, knights in armor slung their shields over their left knees and adjusted their swords, preparing for the coming battle; the clash between the brothers Plantagenet.

Christopher's determination was unmovable, unwavering. His shield slung and his broadsword at the ready, his eyes were focused on the looming gray shape coming into view, assessing the structure tactically.

His heart sank a little; Nottingham was mayhap one of the best fortified castles in England. The thirty foot walls were nearly impenetrable and he let out a small sigh. He wasn't disheartened in the least, but considered it a challenge to his considerable skills.

He would get his wife back, walls or no walls. Prince or no prince. King or no king.

ଓ

DUSTIN HAD NOT seen Gabrielle or Christin since she left them to attend John, and that had been nearly two hours ago. She sat by the hearth, listening to the noise of the bailey, so wild with worry that she could do naught but sit and stare. And movement or any words would be like removing the plug from the dam;

everything would go and she would lose her careful control. So she sat and waited for any word of what had transpired.

There was a knock on the door and she jumped, flying to open the panel. But her excitement quickly turned to apprehension when she saw that Sir Dennis stood in the hall, grinning suggestively at her.

"Ah, *chèrie!* You are so eager!" he said gleefully. "I am flattered."

Her blood ran cold. "What do you want?"

He gave her a look of mock hurt. "Tsk, tsk, *mon petite.* Why are you so unfriendly? I have simply come to keep you company."

"I do not want your company." Dustin tried to shove the door closed, but he blocked it firmly.

His eyes glittered dangerously as he pushed into her bedchamber, the smile on his lips becoming something more sinister. "Do not ever shut me out, *chèrie.* I do not like it."

Dustin backed away, although she wasn't particularly frightened. She had seen the way John had ordered his men not to touch her and was confident that Sir Dennis would obey the order. But she was perturbed and angry; she had been confronted by Lord Bruce, Ralph, John and now Sir Dennis and she was frankly sick of the games they seemed to like to play. She had tried to play their game, but it had backfired in her face and she was wary. But she had not lost her fighting spirit, bolstered in the knowledge that her plight would soon be over.

"I do not give a damn what you like," she growled. "Get out of here or I shall tell John you tried to force yourself upon me."

Dennis pushed in so hard that Dustin stumbled back, almost tripping in her attempt to get away from him. When she recovered, she could see that he was indeed moving for her and she dashed away, scampering for the hearth and the fire poker she could see within her reach. She reached the poker a second before Dennis closed in on her and she swung it around with all her might, catching Dennis across the chest. The sharp tip left a long, thin gash on his flesh and he stopped instinctively, his hand flying to the wound.

Dennis' eyes widened as he drew his hand back, covered with blood. "You little bitch," he hissed with surprise. "Why did you do that?"

Dustin held the poker between them, fully preparing to use it again. "Get out."

He looked at her, perplexed and angered. "But why? I have done nothing. You, *mademoiselle*, attacked me without provocation."

"Without provocation?" Dustin repeated incredulously. "You entered my bedchamber uninvited, sir. I'd call that a most provocative move. Now, get out before I drive this poker through your heart."

Dennis' face lost its confusion and he charged her, snatching at the poker. Dustin swung hard and hit him twice, once across the arm and once on the face before he dislodged the poker and sent it sailing. Panicked, Dustin tried to flee but in her lethargic state, Dennis was faster and grabbed hold of her arms.

He yanked her, twisting and fighting, to the bed and slammed her down hard. Stunned momentarily, she attempted to roll away, but he flopped his body atop her and effectively stopped her escape.

Dustin was near hysteria, fighting and struggling for all she was worth. Dennis had her arms trapped and threw his big leg across her thighs to pin her down, leaving his sword hand free to assault her. She could feel his hand moving up her leg, skimming her hips and moving across the roundness of her belly.

"What joy Burton must have had planting his seed in this exquisite body," he breathed heavily.

Dustin jumped and shrieked, twisting violently, anything to get away from his offensive hand. Tears were close to the surface, but she refused to give in. Once spilled, Dennis would have a great advantage and she could not allow that. She had to fight.

His hand caressed her stomach, moving upward and she realized with horror that he was moving for her breasts. His big hands cupped her fullness, fondling her roughly and she bit off a scream, trying with all of her might to dislodge him.

"Do not fight me, *chèrie*," he panted. "I can give you much pleasure or much pain. Yours is the choice."

Dustin was growing quite weary with her struggles. Her body was not in prime condition and she realized reluctantly that she would not be able to beat this man in a physical sense. The only thing to do would be to defeat him on a mental level. Dustin wasn't very good with mind games, but she would have to try in order to save herself. Forcing herself to calm, she desperately cleared her mind of its panic and set forth rapidly to formulate another plan.

Her struggles lessened, she moved to look Dennis in the eye. His plain face met her beautiful one, his eyes glazed with lust.

"I....I choose pleasure, my lord," she choked, her heart pounding in her ears.

He flickered a small smile. "Wise, *chèrie*. I am quite good, I am told."

Dustin forced a smile, she was shaking so badly that she could feel her lips shaking. "We shall see. Might I rise and prepare myself?"

He eyed her. "Not so easy as that, *mon petite*."

Dustin cleared her throat and drew in a breath to relax, to prove to him that she was sincere. If she was going to retrieve the fire poker again, then he had to let her up. And once she had the poker, she fully intended to gore him. It was either that or he would surely kill her.

"It is, I swear it," she said softly, trying to appear submissive. "I am tired of fighting. My body aches for a real man's touch. Mayhap that is you?"

"Mayhap," he replied, eyeing her now that she was suddenly cooperative. "You will certainly find out."

Dustin gulped, trying desperately to convey compliance. Surely he could feel her shaking. "I have not had but two lovers, my lord. You will be gentle with me, will you not? My husbands were often rough. It frightened me."

She was lying through her teeth, anything to appear vulnerable. Dennis lapped it up, knowing she was lying but feeling comfortable enough with her submissiveness. As long as she wasn't biting and kicking, he could handle her resistance. He felt himself growing warm, looking forward to their coupling. He had been planning this since he had seen her the day before, and to hell with the prince. He was confident he could explain his impetuousness.

He grinned. "Very well, then. Rise and prepare yourself," he said, releasing her. "But no tricks, mind you. I shall thrash you soundly, prince or no prince."

Dustin nodded solemnly, straightening her surcoat as she rose. With a shielded gaze, her eyes rapidly searched the floor for the fire poker. As she rounded the side of the bed, she was flooded with relief to see it lying close to her wardrobe, which just so happened to be her destination. Taking a deep breath to bolster her courage and ease her quaking knees, she blessed Dennis with a sweet smile and moved toward the wardrobe.

"Something pink, *chèrie*," Dennis said, stretching his legs out on the bed. "I like to see my women in pink."

Dustin did not answer; she was close to the poker and was trying to maintain her posture so he wouldn't see that she was moving for it until it was too late. Her feet moved rapidly across the scrubbed floor, every step bringing her closer to Dennis' death. Her palms began to sweat; she had to be swift and sure. There would be no room for mistakes.

With quaking hands, she was upon the poker and she dropped to her knees, snatching it confidently within a firm grip. Dennis, moved from the warm anticipation of sex to a stab of anger at the sight of his prey preparing to defend herself again, shot off the bed with the agility of an attacking tiger.

"*Non!*" he bellowed. "You scheming little whore. I shall take that iron to your backside."

Dustin heard him coming, hearing his angry footfalls hit the floor and rush toward her. Panic surged through her and she stumbled as she attempted to rise, ending up on her behind. In the great rush to protect herself, she swung the poker around just as Dennis descended on her like an avenging angel. The combination of her rapid movement and his swift action drove the head of the poker right through his sternum, burying it deep within the muscle of his beating heart. He was dead before he hit the floor.

Dustin sat on the floor, gasping with shock and terror. Sir Dennis was slumped over her feet, bleeding all over her legs and surcoat and she was so petrified with horror that she could do naught but sit and stare at him. It took her several long moments to realize that he was no longer a threat and only then did she try to calm herself.

She yanked her feet out from under him, panting with the effort and the disgust she felt. Her legs were shaking so that she could not stand, so she simply scooted a few feet away and leaned against the wardrobe, making desperate attempts to slow her breathing and regain her senses. Now that the initial danger was over, she had to clear her mind and decide what move to make next. After all, she had just managed to kill Prince John's champion, self-defense or not, and she was positive the prince would not take kindly to her offense.

Just as she was getting a grip on herself, the door to her bedchamber flew open and Gabrielle stood in the archway. Her pleasant expression instantly went to one of absolute horror when she saw Sir Dennis' crumpled body lying in a pool of blood.

"Dustin," she cried. "What….?"

"Shut the damn door," Dustin croaked.

Gabrielle, stunned, immediately slammed the door shut and bolted it for good measure, turning back around to face the gory scene with disbelief.

"What happened here?" she demanded shakily. "Is he…is he…?"

"He is dead," Dustin said, more calmly than she felt. "He tried to rape me, and I killed him, although it was truly an accident," her eyes sought out her friend in earnest. "I could not let him have me, Gabrielle. He might have hurt my child somehow, and….," she trailed off, swallowing the bile rising in her throat.

Gabrielle, her hand clutching her throat, walked hesitantly toward the body, viewing it in astonishment. He was in a heap on his side and the fire poker jutting from his chest was stark evidence of what had happened.

"You killed him with the poker?" she pointed. "My God, Dustin, what bravery! I simply cannot believe it."

Dustin was feeling distinctly limp now that she was calming. She gazed impassively at the bloodied body, wondering what in the hell she was going to do now.

"He charged at me just as I picked it up," she said quietly. "He impaled himself on it."

Gabrielle was overwhelmed. How many times had she imagined herself doing the same thing but had lacked the simple nerve? She hovered over Dennis' body, her legs like water, delight and terror hand in hand.

"What are we going to do with him?" she whispered.

Dustin felt the impact of the word "we." Gabrielle would not allow Dustin to be alone in this, and she was deeply grateful. But what remained now was, indeed, what to do with the body. With a deep breath for courage, she rose to unsteady feet.

"We have got to hide it somehow to get rid of it," she said. "But where?"

Gabrielle shook her head. "I don't know, Dustin. We cannot very well carry him anywhere and…." She suddenly looked up at Dustin. "I am scared. If John finds out what you have done, he will….."

Dustin wouldn't let her finish. "I know," she cut her off, though not unkindly. "We must hide him somewhere where he won't be found, at least for a while."

"At least until he starts to smell," Gabrielle added, almost dryly.

Dustin looked from the body to her friend and back again. Then, her gray eyes scanned the room in thought, desperately trying to think of a way out of this situation. What to do, what to…?

Her eyes fell on the massive wardrobe, filled with her new, hated clothing. A light went on in Dustin's mind; surely she could hide the man underneath the mound of clothing and he would be out of view from anyone who opened the wardrobe, at least until they went digging. Rapidly, she bent down and pushed Dennis over on his back.

"In the wardrobe, Gabrielle," she said with quiet urgency, yanking the poker free with disgust. "We shall put him in there and cover him with my surcoats."

Gabrielle sucked in her breath sharply and glanced at the open wardrobe. It was certainly large enough. Lacking a better suggestion, she grabbed hold of Dennis' legs. With Dustin dragging him by the arms, it took them several tries to get the dead man up into the wardrobe. Blood was everywhere as they lay several surcoats atop him as well as any other accessories they could find, covering him completely. They worked quickly and quietly, a tremendous sense of urgency filling them.

Only when Dennis was covered and the wardrobe doors closed did Gabrielle rush to clean up the trail of blood on the floor. Dustin, spent emotionally and physically, flopped into a chair as her friend did a fine job of covering the evidence.

"Where is Christin?" Dustin managed to ask, afraid, yet knowing if there had been trouble, Gabrielle would have told her first thing. "Did you give her to Darren?"

Gabrielle threw the last of the bloody rags into the hearth and covered them with ash and soot. "I did," she said, looking up at Dustin with a small smile. "She is safe, my lady. Have no fear."

Relieved beyond words, Dustin simply nodded and rested her head on her hand. Her daughter was safe and Christopher was coming for her; she should have been thrilled, but she was so spent that she could not manage it. There was naught to do now but wait for her husband and pray the corpse in the closet wasn't discovered before he arrived.

"What if John asks for Dennis?" Gabrielle asked, washing her hands in the basin.

Dustin shrugged wearily. "We have not seen him."

Gabrielle nodded silently, her stomach twisting in knots. She was so terrified she could hardly think, but she would have to trust God that everything would work out as it should. Wooden with shock, she sat next to her friend and the two of them passed the afternoon in stunned silence.

ঙ

RALPH WAS IN fits. He had run from the bailey, through the length of the castle and up a flight of stairs before he allowed himself to slow down and catch his breath. Without a knock, he plunged into John's chambers.

"There is an army approaching," he announced severely.

John nearly fell off his chair in haste to rise. "An *army?* Richard?"

Ralph nearly choked over his words. "They are flying your brother's banner, as well as de Lohr's and Burton's."

John's eyes bulged to the point where Ralph thought they might pop from his skull. "All three?" he gasped. "How on God's earth is it possible that the three of them are here? Why, Dustin has only been here a mere three days and it 'twould be impossible for my message to have been received in London, and then have the armies mobilized." He was starting to shake, an early sign of the fits he was famous for. "And it would have been impossible to rouse de Lohr and Burton so quickly. Ralph, I do not understand any of this."

"Nor do I, sire, but the fact remains that they are here," Ralph said grimly. "I have sent men in search of le Londe and have already set to mobilizing our troops."

John, twitching, nodded unsteadily. He had not expected them nearly so soon and was totally unprepared. He thought he had ample time, time to use Lady Dustin, time to control her, time, time, time....

"How far out is the army?" he asked.

"Mayhap four hours, according to our patrol," Ralph replied, smelling the battle that was to come. "They are moving quickly."

John's lip jerked unconsciously; he moved to the window as if he could see the approaching army for himself. His frazzled mind was working furiously, formulating a rapid plan of action.

"I am leaving this place, Ralph," he said. "I will take Dustin with me."

Ralph shook his head. "I must disagree with you, sire. She would serve us better here. If you take her, there is a chance that she could be wrested from you in the open. 'Twould be best to keep her at Nottingham."

John quivered a moment before whirling on Ralph. "Then I take the child."

Ralph shrugged. "To what avail? I would wager to say that as valuable as the child is to de Lohr, his wife is more valuable." He was, for once, calmer than his liege. "I would suggest keeping them both here. De Lohr will think twice before destroying Nottingham if we use his family correctly."

John's eyes narrowed. "Correctly? What do you mean?"

A smile tugged at Ralph's thin lips. "Simply tell the man you will kill both the child and his wife if he launches an attack. Put Lady Dustin up on the ramparts with a crossbow to her back so he can see for himself that we mean what we say. I would wager to say that he will reconsider any hostility on that basis."

"But what of Richard?" John wanted to know. "He wants his property back regardless of what we do with Lady de Lohr. So we kill her? So what? He will surely attack us then."

Ralph shook his head. "You will have to trust that de Lohr, and Burton for that matter, will convince Richard otherwise," he said. "How fortunate for us that Richard's two strongest knights love the same woman."

John looked dubious. He was more afraid of his brother than de Lohr or Burton, and prayed he was wise enough to use his advantages. He also prayed that Ralph was right and that Richard would not attack Nottingham if de Lohr and Burton convinced him otherwise. At any rate, an army was approaching and preparations must be made.

"Find le Londe," he growled, resuming his twitching and pacing. "The man is in charge of my army, is he not? He had better be on the ramparts or I shall castrate him myself."

Ralph nodded, feeling amazingly confident in the face of mayhap the greatest army ever assembled. The king, his Defender and the king's premiere general were bearing down on them, yet he found his apprehension somewhat easing. He knew that he and the prince held the advantage.

"I shall seek Lady de Lohr as well and make sure she is well taken care of," Ralph said.

"See that you do," John snapped, his mind moving beyond his prisoner and ahead to more pressing concerns. "But I want her displayed blatantly when the army closes in to avoid an instantaneous attack. When they see her, surely they will stop any advance and give us a chance to press our advantage."

"As you say, sire," Ralph replied steadily.

As he marched down the cool corridor toward Lady de Lohr's rooms, he felt distinctly omnipotent. It was obvious to him who held the true power in England, and it wasn't the king.

CHAPTER FIFTY-EIGHT

DUSTIN AND GABRIELLE had finally calmed enough to the point where they could sit and read without their book shaking so bad they could not see the words. Gabrielle, who was unusually educated for a woman, read passages from the Book of Job, a particularly depressing subject. Dustin changed out of her bloodied surcoat and into a fresh one.

It was one of the newer garments Gabrielle had ordered for her, an eggshell-colored linen with a voluminous skirt and long, billowy sleeves that made her feel especially fresh and feminine.

A thin gold and black rope ran underneath her breasts for decoration, emphasizing the beautiful swell of her chest and allowing her blossoming belly ample freedom in the heat, she had pulled her hair into a thick braid, letting the heavy thing fall over her right shoulder and trail to her groin. Tendrils of damp hair framed her face as she took a seat opposite Gabrielle and demanded she read something lighter; she did not want to hear about the trials of Job any longer, for she was having a few trials of her own.

Dustin dozed off as her friend read softly, not even realizing it until she was roughly awakened by Gabrielle's shaking hand. Startled, she twisted around to see Ralph entering the room.

"Ladies," he greeted tightly.

Dustin was filled with panic, wondering if Ralph would read her mind and go to the wardrobe in search of her victim. She rose as steadily as she could, fixing him with a stern gaze.

"What do you want, Ralph?" she asked.

He did not smile. Instead, he turned to the door and the two ladies noticed several of John's elite guards standing in the hall. Ralph glanced back at the women, pleased to see the expressions of doom on their faces.

"I would ask, Lady de Lohr, that you remain in your rooms for the time being," he said formally. This Ralph was not the sniveling, taunting man she had grown to know. He was firm and decisive and it scared the devil out of her. "You will not leave these rooms under any circumstances. Is that clear?"

Dustin looked from the guards to Ralph. "Why? I thought I was a guest here, not a prisoner."

Ralph raised an eyebrow. "True enough. I ask that you remain here for your own safety, considering that an army approaches and I would hate to see you injured in the crossfire."

An army! Dustin knew immediately that it was her husband and she could not help the smile that crossed her face. Her plight, Gabrielle's plight, was drawing to a close and she could not suppress the gloating feeling welling inside of her.

"It is my husband, isn't it?" she asked.

Ralph's expression was hard. He wouldn't lie to her for she would know the truth soon enough. "Perhaps," he answered.

The fear and panic Dustin had so recently felt was vanished. "My husband has come for me as I knew he would," she said arrogantly. "How do you feel, Ralph, knowing that you will be dead in a matter of hours?"

His eyes narrowed. "Do not be so confident that it will be me meeting my death."

"He will not let you live," she said confidently. "He has come for me and you, my lord, shall pay the ultimate price for confining the Lion's Claw's wife."

Ralph's jaw ticked. "Do not be so certain, bitch."

Dustin took the challenge, for she truly felt she had nothing to lose. Her husband was within sight and that, to her, made her untouchable. Even if he wasn't physical with her, Christopher's reputation alone would keep Ralph at bay, knowing the wrath he would face.

Her first instincts had been to play dumb to Ralph's revelation, but she found she could not. She was so thrilled that the army was arrived, that he had come for her, that she could not contain herself.

Dustin had never in her life been arrogant about anything. She'd never had any reason to be. But she was suddenly extremely arrogant about her husband, his reputation, and the fact that she was his wife. She tried to ignore the fact that she was his trouble-making wife and that she had left him for the very same reason. She briefly wondered if he was going to take a strap to her behind when he caught up to her for being such a bother, and she furthermore would not blame him.

But Dustin did not regret leaving as she did. She had turned men against each other and she was not rueful in her decision. Her one and only regret was that she had been caught by none other than her husband's most declared enemy. God or the Devil was working against her, she wasn't sure which. It would be a miracle if Christopher did not hate her for everything she had caused.

"You show your apprehension by resorting to name-calling, sheriff," she said, not the least bit offended. "And you should be afraid."

"Nay, woman, 'tis you who should be afraid," Ralph returned sharply. "For it is you who have lured your husband to his demise. And he will not be resurrected the second time around, I assure you."

Dustin stiffened ever so slightly. "Christopher will not die, sheriff. He cannot."

Ralph gave her a thin smile. " 'Tis not just de Lohr, but Burton as well. You have lured two men to their deaths. Can you live with yourself?"

Dustin cleared her throat softly, her arrogant stance draining. She wanted to lower her gaze from Ralph's piercing black eyes but she could not, for she meant what she said.

"They will not die, Ralph," she assured him. "They are too powerful for you to kill and you know it. They will have the keep by morn."

"But they will not have you or your child," Ralph said deliberately. "Our mighty prince will see to that."

Dustin blinked, a bolt of fear shooting through her. She wasn't afraid to die, truly, but she feared for the life of the child she carried. Suddenly, her arrogant front was not such a wise move and she felt herself backing down, but only for the sake of her child. Selfish as she was, she had only been thinking of herself and not of the babe within her.

Ralph saw the wind go out of her sails and felt infinitely more in control of the situation. He slapped his heavy leather gloves against his thigh.

☙

THEY WERE RIDING for battle. Christopher could smell the excitement in the air, permeating the warriors like a drug. They fed off it, breathed it, touched it until the only thing they were capable of focusing on was the approaching storm.

Christopher's face was set like stone. His sky-blue eyes drank in the massive shape that was Nottingham, set like a great stone phantom against the colors of the setting sky. The peasants had long since taken cover and the only movements visible were the soldiers moving about on the walls.

"Skirmish lines," he grumbled to Marcus, who set the men to moving.

It was an awesome sight to behold when Marcus, David and Christopher set up the skirmish lines. A devotee of Roman legions, Christopher set up his troops into blocks of 40 men, moving them out in sharp military style across the rolling green fields around Nottingham. Ten blocks formed a row, each block with a crude ladder for breaching the walls, and there were three rows. The closer they drew to the actual fortress, the more the blocks would spread out and move to surround the castle. There were, in effect, three waves of soldiers instead of one giant front, and it was a very effective method of laying siege.

Richard sat back and watched with the pride of a father as his Defender positioned the troops. Christopher was a master of tactics, especially when it came to laying siege to a fortified structure or city. Not usually content to be a passive observer, he was wise enough to know that Christopher was better at this than he was. Out of the way, Richard mentally prepared himself to take on his brother and regain his holding, the first of many such battles.

Christopher returned to him after checking the position of the troops himself with Marcus and David hot on his heels. Sean, Guy, Dud and the rest of Christopher and Marcus' knights were not far behind. Visors went down and shields were secured over the left knee, grips checked and the leather straps adjusted until they were comfortable. After securing himself, Christopher passed a practiced eye over his knights to make sure all were in order, even going so far as to readjust a piece of armor on Marcus' destrier that had slipped.

Marcus held the animal steady as Christopher worked through thick gloves to secure the errant piece of metal. He thanked Christopher smoothly, like the Marcus of old whose very best friend had been the man they called the Lion's Claw.

Christopher, knowing Marcus as well as he did, gave an appreciative smile at his tone and found himself looking at the man through his lowered visor as if he could indeed see the smile. He was jolted from his battle-hard attitude for just a split second, wondering if Marcus was trying to unbalance him for some reason. They had been so cold and formal with each other that the friendly tone caught him off guard.

Marcus saw Christopher looking at him and flipped up his visor, his smile fading. "What's wrong?"

Christopher shook his head but Marcus reined his animal around so he could better speak to him. "You still do not trust me, do you?" he asked quietly.

"In battle there is no one I would rather have by my side, save my brother," Christopher said without hesitation. "I trust you with my life, Marcus."

Marcus looked hard at him. "But you do not trust me where Dustin is concerned."

Christopher's shielded face turned away. "I…I am trying, Marcus, I want to."

Marcus's gaze lingered on him a moment before he lowered his visor once again. "Then do."

Marcus whistled to his destrier and the horse thundered forward, leaving Christopher struggling to regain his composure.

Another destrier rode up beside him and he looked up to see Edward looking at him. The man had kept an extremely low profile since they had left Somerhill and Christopher was almost surprised to see him.

"He is sincere, you know," Edward said.

Christopher looked at him. "I want to believe that, Edward, I really do."

Edward sighed and adjusted his helmet. "Listen to me for once, Chris. I am usually right."

"You are *always* right," Christopher returned. "Why would you say that?"

Edward shrugged, moving to turn away but Christopher put out a hand and grabbed him before he could get away.

"Why do you say that, Edward?" he asked. "Why have you been avoiding me so?"

"I haven't been," Edward replied. "It was plainly obvious that you refused to listen to me so I stopped talking."

Christopher flipped up his visor, frowning. "You mean about Dustin?"

Edward nodded, speaking reluctantly. "I told you not to go charging up to Somerhill, but you ignored me. I told you not to fight Marcus, but you ignored me again. I finally gave up."

Christopher gazed at him a moment. "And you were right both times, Edward. God help me, I should have indeed listened to you and I shall forever regret my rashness. I am sorry I hurt your feelings, old man. I never meant to."

Edward lifted his visor, a faint smile on his lips. "I can die happy now. I do not think I have ever heard you apologize for anything you have done, Chris. It makes all of my humiliation worth it."

"Humiliation? I have never humiliated you," Christopher said, fighting off a grin. "Bullied you, scorned you mayhap, but never humiliated. You are by far my wisest friend, de Wolfe. You are invaluable to me."

Edward snorted. "Is this what death has done to you? Made you humble and sentimental beyond belief?"

Christopher scowled. "David said the same thing. I have not changed that much."

Edward's eyes twinkled and he lowered his visor. When he spoke, there was amazement in his voice. "Oh, yes, you have."

☙

LINES WERE SET and there was naught else to do but position the senior knights and move out. Christopher reined his destrier between Richard and Marcus, waiting for the final command from his liege.

But Richard was a thousand miles away, staring at the dark hulk of Nottingham as if he were hypnotized by the sight. His men waited patiently, silently, listening to the murmurs among their own men and the distant shouts from the soldiers in the fortress, all waiting for the final command that would move them forward and toward their destiny. Some would die, some would live, and the excitement for the battle made their blood pump loudly in their ears. The wait for the command merely served to feed their drive.

"Sire?" Christopher finally inquired after several minutes.

Richard drew in a long, slow breath as a man usually does when he awakens from a deep sleep. "I have not seen my brother in four years," he said softly. "A pity we have to meet like this." He turned to Christopher and lowered his voice. "John is not to be touched by anyone. Is that clear?"

Christopher stiffened; he knew Richard was referring to him. In hindsight, he had known that Richard was going to demand this of him and he had tried to prepare himself, but the answer still came hard and forced. John, by virtue of birth, was untouchable, and it cut Christopher to the bone, especially if the prince had touched Dustin in any way. To cut John down would surely be his own death, and he had promised Dustin that he would not die. The paradox was overwhelming.

Slowly, he nodded once and Richard was satisfied. The king's gaze then sought out Marcus and demanded the same of him, also met by an equally reluctant affirmation. Relieved that mayhap the most important point was clear to all of them, he turned his attention back to the fortress and prepared to give the supreme order.

Before the command could leave his lips, the man-sized door within the massive outer gate opened and a figure spilled forward. Although they were several hundred feet away, everyone recognized the Sheriff of Nottingham, dressed in black leather and armor. Ralph stood just outside the door, his arrogant gaze moving over Richard's army.

"Archers," Marcus rumbled a command next to him, but Christopher held up a hand quickly.

"Nay, not yet," he said. "He has something to say. Let him say it and then we kill him. Aim for the neck."

Marcus relayed the order to the sergeant, his eyes trained on the sheriff and his massive body tensed like stone.

"I wonder what in the hell he wants?" Richard ventured.

Ralph did not keep them waiting. "Greetings, King Richard… de Lohr….Burton. How nice of you to come."

No one replied and Ralph smiled humorously. "I would admit you to the keep but we have, well, little room with all of John's troops and the peasants huddled inside. It seems your army scared them soundly."

"We scared your troops?" David yelled back before anyone could stop him. "I would believe that."

Richard's men in earshot laughed uproariously but Ralph did not miss a beat.

"Ah, Lion Cub, I see you are still as biting as always," he said. "Strange to see you bearing arms with your brother and Marcus Burton again. I had heard you had been exiled to France for bedding their wife."

David's horse jerked when the rider tensed. Marcus and Christopher sat like stone, but inside, they were white with anger and hatred. Ralph was deliberately provoking them and they knew it.

"What is it that you have come to say, Fitz Walter?" Richard inquired in his booming tone.

Ralph half-bowed to the returned monarch, acknowledging the sound of his voice. "Sire, 'tis good to see you riding the green fields of England again. I am sure it is something entirely foreign to you, to ride in your own country," he jabbed. "Can I assume, then, that you received our message?"

"Message? What message?" Richard repeated.

"Regarding Lady de Lohr, sire," Ralph reminded him as if he were a child. "She is our guest here at Nottingham."

Christopher twitched but Richard quietly, sharply, stilled him. "I am fully aware of Lady de Lohr's whereabouts," Richard replied. "As much as we appreciate your hospitality, her husband has come to take her home."

"Is that the reason for this sea of escorts?" Ralph asked dryly. "Or, mayhap, is there another reason for this show of force?"

Richard sighed, tightening his grip on the reins. "I have come to replace my brother's men with legions of my own, as is befitting *my* holding. A changing of the guard, as it were."

Ralph crossed has arms. "We rather like it here, sire, and furthermore have no intention of leaving."

Richard was finished with the pleasantries, the foolishness. "Let us cut through the charade, Fitz Walter. Baron de Lohr wants his wife and I want my holding. Will you turn them both over peaceably?"

Ralph did not answer for a moment. "I am afraid that we cannot, sire. We have become quite attached to them."

Richard shifted aboard his great destrier. "We would like Lady de Lohr returned without a fight, please. Surely we can work toward a pleasant conclusion."

Ralph grinned ironically. "Sire, I am sure our opinions would not match in that case."

"Then what is it that you want?" Richard said impatiently. "You try my tolerance, man."

Ralph took on the look of the hound who had cornered the fox. Now they would determine just where this confrontation was going.

"John wants the holding he has collected, sire," he said. "It is a simple enough request considering how many you have. Surely you can indulge him."

"Where is my brother?" Richard said irritably, tired of dealing with the middle-man.

"Inside, of course," Ralph replied.

"Coward," Richard muttered, then spoke loudly to Ralph. "I have no time for you, Fitz Walter. Either give me back my holding and return Lady de Lohr to her husband, or we will take them both from you. And I promise that the latter will not be pleasant."

Ralph's face took on such a devious smile that the knights were on their guard. The sheriff turned and motioned to the open door and bodies began passing through the opening. It took Christopher all of a split second to see his wife being escorted forward between two burly mercenaries, one of them pointing a massive crossbow at her rounded belly.

Marcus heard Christopher whimper low in his throat but he was too slow to stop the man from bailing off his destrier. The chargers danced about as they felt their rider's tense, as they sensed the change in mood and smelled the fear in the air. Richard did not call Christopher back for he knew it would be of no use; the man was already halfway to his wife, his armor clanging in sharp, rhythmic tones as his boots met with the earth.

"Stop where you are, de Lohr, or I skewer your wife," Ralph said sharply, seeing visions of himself being crushed to death by the Defender's bare hands.

Christopher froze, a good twenty feet or so from Dustin. His heart was breaking into a million little pieces as he gazed upon his wife. She was quivering with fear, her head lowered and her eyes closed. He could see how terrified she was and had he any less control, he would have ripped apart Ralph and the two soldiers holding his wife with his bare hands. But he steadied himself, not wanting Ralph to have any more of an advantage than he already had. Jumping from his horse had not been the wisest move, but he had acted blindly. He only knew he had to get to Dustin, no matter what. Now that he had a moment to think, he got a grip on himself and stopped any advancement.

His eyes were drinking in the sight of his wife, dressed in flowing white robes with her considerable hair pulled into a thick braid. She looked so lovely and angelic, so completely fragile, that it nearly brought tears to his eyes.

Yet one thing struck him – since she had appeared, she had yet to look at him. Or any of them, for that matter. His heart constricted painfully, for he knew that she refused to look at him because of the hatred she harbored. His selfish actions, his complete ignorance of her feelings, had been why she had left. Aye, he knew that now, and he could think of only one way to make restitution to her.

"Dustin, sweetheart," he said hoarsely. "I love you."

Her eyes flew open and her head jerked up, the huge gray eyes he knew so well boring into him like bolts of steel. Her eyes were swimming with unshed tears, held back by her astonishment.

"You *do*?" she gasped.

"Silence!" Ralph snapped.

Christopher ignored him. "Of course I do," he said, longing in his tone. "Dustin, you know that. I love you more than my life, sweetheart. I always will."

"But…," she sputtered, relief beyond description filling her. "How can you say that afte…?"

"I told you to be silent!" Ralph boomed. "One more word and I take your wife back inside."

Christopher wisely held his tongue; he was so desperate to see his wife that he did as he was told. Tearing his eyes away from her, he glared icily at Ralph.

"Let her go or I shall rip out your testicles with my bare hands," he rumbled.

Ralph believed him, but he also knew that he wouldn't do anything so long as he held Dustin captive. Christopher wouldn't make a move with a crossbow aimed at his wife. The sheriff raised a cocky eyebrow.

"The mighty Defender," he said sarcastically. "All of your skill and strength will not help you now, will it? It would seem that I hold all of the power now. And I will use it, have no doubt."

"She's of no use to you," Christopher said evenly. "Richard is going to take this holding whether or not you hold my wife."

"I think not," Ralph snorted. "You won't let him. If so much as an errant dagger flies in my direction, your wife will be instantly impaled, as will the child she carries. I would be doing the world a service by killing de Lohr's son."

Christopher kept his calm outwardly, but inside he was raging like a wildfire. He looked from Ralph to Dustin again. "Are you alright, sweet?"

She nodded unsteadily. "I am fine."

He smiled at her, much to Ralph's displeasure. "I am sorry, sweetheart. For everything. Please forgive me."

"De Lohr?" Ralph yelled, moving himself so that he was in the line of sight between Christopher and his wife. "Mayhap you do not understand my words? I told you to be silent."

Christopher was focused on Ralph. "You will not take that tone with me, Fitz Walter."

"I can do anything I damn well please," Ralph retorted. " 'Tis I who hold the power… *and* your wife."

He did. Christopher forced himself to acknowledge the fact that Dustin was in serious danger and further forced himself to realize that he was going to have to deal with Ralph on his own terms.

"What is it that you want, then?" he asked coldly.

Ralph looked him over as if contemplating something vile. A sickening smile came to his mouth. "I want to see you kneel, de Lohr," he said. "I want to see you kneel before me and beg for your wife's life. I may be merciful."

Dustin heard the words, watching Christopher's reaction. When Ralph had come for her an hour ago in her rooms, awakening her from a dead sleep, he snatched her to him rapidly, only to keep her standing in the inner bailey. She had no idea what he intended to do. The thought of humiliating Christopher publicly never occurred to her, and she was stricken with the cruelty. She could handle anything he dealt her, but she was consumed with protectiveness for her husband.

Christopher loved her. He had said it and begged for her forgiveness. She was confused and thrilled and anguished all at the same time. She wanted nothing more than to collapse in his embrace but the soldier holding her arms and the one setting his sights on her belly would have something to say about it. She wondered if fainting would do any good. Would they leave her in a heap? Would it distract Ralph enough so that Christopher could gain the upper hand? She just did not know and she was too fearful to attempt anything. So she watched and waited, like everyone else.

Christopher eyed Ralph a moment, knowing he had no choice. The thought of kneeling to the man sickened him, but he would do anything to gain Dustin's release. Yet he was well aware that Ralph could just as easily kill her anyway. Still, he could only do as he was asked.

With a movement as fluid and graceful as a cat, he went down on one knee and faced Ralph.

"I would then beg you to release my wife, Fitz Walter," he said with nary a quiver of disgust in his voice.

Ralph chuckled softly and took a few steps towards him, his hands on his hips. "You can do better than that."

"No, Chris!" Dustin yelled, twisting in the grip that held her. "Do not beg him, the evil bastard!"

Christopher did not look at his wife, he was focused on the sheriff. "I will again beg for mercy, my lord. Release my wife and I will be ever grateful."

"Better, better," Ralph inclined his head. "Mighty Defender. You do not look very mighty now."

Tears came to Dustin then. She could not stand to see Christopher so humiliated, humbled in front of Richard and all of his knights. Big sobs came bubbling forth and she stopped struggling, hanging her head in sorrow.

"Do not beg him," she moaned. "Please, Chris, do not."

He could hear her sobs and they broke his heart. His careful control was slipping. "Give her to me, Ralph. Have you no compassion?"

"No," Ralph said flatly. "Not for you, and not for your wife."

Dustin would have done anything to get Christopher out of his predicament. Anything at all. Then the first crazy idea that popped into her mind was the one she went with. With a scream that would have made many a woman proud, she suddenly clutched her stomach and buckled her legs.

"My God!" she cried out. "The baby.....something is wrong."

All men were afraid of pregnant women, and the battle-hardened soldiers of Nottingham and Richard's forces were no exception. All eyes snapped to her, even the soldiers on the wall who had heard her, and for a brief moment, confusion reigned in all of them. Christopher, seized with panic, shot to his feet and started to run for his wife, but Ralph was closer.

The sheriff saw the Defender on a dead run toward his wife and panic of his own set in. Using a pre-arranged signal, he raised his arm with the yell of a barbarian, signaling the archers on the wall to let loose their arrows. Dustin, still clutching her stomach, really did scream as a rain of arrows cascaded down in Christopher's direction. Ralph was suddenly on her, bull-dogging her and the two soldiers back inside the small door. The last glimpse Dustin had of her husband was of him being slammed with a hundred arrows.

The battle started in that split second. Richard sounded the battle cry and his troops moved, their yells filling the humid summer air and the sounds of unsheathing swords deafening.

Dustin, shrieking and crying, was dragged into the bailey and hastily thrust into the arms of several waiting guards.

"Take her to my room," Ralph yelled above the noise of the infant battle. "Keep her there until I come for her."

Dustin could not fight, she was far too stunned with witnessing what she was sure had been Christopher's death. How could he have survived the hail of arrows? Her mind went to mud and her knees collapsed, and she felt herself being lifted and carried into the dark coolness that was Nottingham.

She welcomed the blackness of unconsciousness as it swallowed her up.

☙

CHRISTOPHER WAS VERY much alive. His reinforced armor had protected him from the arrows and even now he was mounting his destrier and swung the animal in the direction of the massive gates. His troops were taking the walls and he and his knights were able to focus on breeching the door.

Edward was beside him with two hotly burning torches in his hand. "We can set fire to the gates, my lord. With this heat, they will burn in no time."

Christopher nodded, motioning for him to hand off a torch to David, and together the two of them set to burning the rope trappings of the gates. Marcus gouged out great holes in the wood for David to ignite, speeding up the process. With the ladders going up on the walls and the gates igniting like kindling, Christopher stood back and waited for his opportunity to tear Nottingham apart.

He could not even think about Dustin or he would surely go mad. He had to keep his wits about him or he would be no good at all, and there were too many people depending on him. Nay, he would have to keep a clear head and wait for the gates to burn down and only then would he allow himself the luxury of thinking of his wife. Only when he was able to do some good would he let thoughts of her fill his brain.

"What happened to Dustin?" Marcus rushed up to him, his charger dancing and snorting.

Christopher rolled his eyes in defeat; just as he was gaining control of himself….. "I do not know, Marcus. It could have just been the excitement of everything."

Thankfully, Marcus did not pursue it and Christopher was able to return his focus to the gate. As was usual with old wood, it began to go up quite nicely in spite of the rain of arrows around the perimeter of Nottingham that prevented them from moving much closer. Already, the men-at-arms were racking up casualties due to the arrows and Christopher ordered his men to fall back from the backside of the fortress. With the gates burning, he would form ranks to charge in once the gates were down.

ଓ

INSIDE NOTTINGHAM, CHAOS ruled. Ralph and Lord Bruce were positioning the troops to protect the bailey and the castle from the breach, but they were having a hell of a time with all of the peasants running about. Moreover, and most importantly, Dennis le Londe was nowhere to be found.

"Where in the hell is le Londe?" Ralph sputtered to anyone who could answer him. Several of le Londe's men were assisting at the moment and were unable to answer, feeding Ralph's anger.

"I am going to gut him when I find him," he said between clenched teeth, cuffing a soldier who was foolish enough to bump into the sheriff. "That lazy bastard has seen his last day of comfort within John's protective company, I vow it."

Lord Bruce, too old to do much fighting, followed Ralph around breathlessly. "Mayhap he is in hiding. At any rate, we shall have to handle this onslaught between us."

Ralph looked at Bruce scornfully. "You are no good to me, old man. I need le Londe. When this is over with, I am going to kill him myself."

A young soldier ran up to Ralph, scraping the ground. "The prince demands your presence, Lord Sheriff."

Ralph hit that soldier, too. "Tell the prince I am trying to protect his bloody hide," he snapped, then thought better of it. "Tell the prince I am indisposed at the moment. Inform him that Richard's troops are burning the gates and that I expect them to be breached soon."

The young soldier, his jaw bruised, bowed again and was gone. Ralph paused a moment in disgust, watching the boy run away and shaking his head with the damn foolishness of everything. He was missing the commander of the troops, the prince was demanding his presence like a spoiled child, and on top of everything Lady Dustin had apparently taken ill.

Damnation, why did everything bad always happen to him?

ଓ

THE BRIDGE TOOK a long time to burn. It was well after sunset before Christopher, Marcus and David were able to dislodge enough of the cinder to allow a man to pass through. But the hole was only big enough for one man, and Christopher demanded by rank to be the first one through. Yet Richard outranked even him, and Christopher found himself following his king through the smoldering opening.

As they expected, they ran headlong into a skirmish line of mercenary troops. Richard took the full brunt of the line, yet Christopher and Marcus, followed by David and Edward and the rest of the knights, were quickly there to defend their monarch. Limbs were hacked off, heads were severed by sheer force of sword power, and the mercenary troops began backing off quickly.

With every step they took back, another man from Richard's force pushed in through the breech. It wasn't long before there were several hundred crown troops inside the outer bailey, fighting in such close quarters that there was barely room to move.

Christopher was smashed up against Marcus and Edward, fighting a seasoned group. But his mind was already moving to the castle where his wife was and he was increasingly desperate to get to her. She was trapped in the hulking structure, extremely ill, and he could not stand it anymore. He had to get to her.

"I am going for the castle!" he yelled to Marcus over the noise. "Take command here."

"You cannot go it alone!" Marcus yelled back. "I shall cover your back."

"Nay!" Christopher boomed. "Richard needs you here. I must do this alone."

Marcus speared a mercenary soldier in the throat before answering. "You cannot take on the whole goddamn castle, Chris. Let me come."

"I am coming!" David ran over two soldiers as he reined his horse next to his brother; he had heard the entire conversation. "If anybody is assisting Chris, it is me."

A fresh wave of enemy troops rushed them and Christopher found himself fighting off several men at one time. He would parry and thrust with amazing speed and skill, goring one man and cutting off his comrade's head with the same stroke of the blade. The fighting was furious and wild, but Christopher's cool demeanor never wavered. Never was there a finer warrior in the heat of battle.

With the wave of soldiers subdued, Christopher turned his biting, kicking charger for the castle. Richard was several feet away, under control with Edward and Sean at his side, and Christopher was confident that the king was well-protected. With that peace of mind, he knew he had to get to his wife.

Marcus saw Christopher break free and head for the inner bailey. He muttered a curse as he impaled another mercenary soldier with his broadsword, fully intending to follow Christopher into the castle.

The further Christopher rode from the heat of the battle, the less the resistance became. The gates to the inner bailey were completely gone, he noticed, allowing him to pass through unhindered. A few soldiers engaged him, but nothing of importance, and he thanked God that luck was on his side. It would seem that the majority of the mercenary soldiers were at the frontline, trying to prevent the mass of crown troops that were pouring in through the gutted front gate.

The battle was raging behind him and he was consumed with reaching his wife as he bailed from his destrier, taking down two soldiers who tried to prevent him from entering the castle. More soldiers dashed into the doorway just as Christopher was preparing to enter, and he raised his sword to brace himself for another go around. But, as quickly as they appeared, the soldiers were gone and Christopher did not ask why. He simply raced into the cool interior of the castle, intent on keeping to the shadows and moving fairly undetected.

He had barely rounded his first corner when somebody grabbed him from behind. His sword came up, crashing down against another blade of equal strength. He heard Marcus grunt.

"Goddammit, I *knew* you were going to do that," Marcus said frankly.

Christopher felt relief flood him, but also irritation. "I told you to stay with Richard."

"Aye, you did, but I did not listen," Marcus said. "Besides, Richard is well-protected with David and Edward. You need me more."

Christopher scowled. "All right, then. But keep quiet."

Marcus did as he was told and they made their way up a flight of stairs to the second floor of Nottingham Castle. "Do we know where we are going?" Marcus asked dryly.

"She has got to be up here, somewhere," Christopher's eyes trailed the length of the corridor. "We shall simply have to check every room until we find her."

Marcus wiggled his eyebrows but said nothing, following Christopher closely as they made their way down the hall. It was silent and dim, wall sconces offering the only light. At a junction where one corridor met with another there were four or five bodies in front of them, mercenary soldiers, all bearing Prince John's colors.

Marcus stepped away from Christopher slowly, sword raised, with his eyes never leaving the menacing group. "I shall take the ugly one."

"Which ugly one? Be specific," Christopher snapped, although there was no mistaking the mirth in his voice.

It was as it had been for three years in the Holy Land, two men, the best of friends, fighting side by side and knowing each other as well as they knew themselves. It was the familiar feelings of camaraderie that they never thought to feel again.

"The ugly one on the right," Marcus snapped back lightly. "In fact, I shall take both of the bastards on the right."

"You bloody coward, leaving me with the rest," Christopher grumbled.

Marcus grinned. "You are the one with the reputation, earn it."

They looked at each other for a split second, silent words passing between them, knowing exactly what was to come next. They had done it together a thousand times before.

At the same time, they raised their swords and let out a spine-chilling yell, charging at their opponents like crazed men. It rarely failed; the enemy soldiers were startled just enough to give Christopher and Marcus the advantage, and they cut down two men before ever engaging in a sword fight. Yet even the broadsword battles were short-lived; Marcus disposed of his man a split second later than Christopher.

"You are getting slow in your old age," Christopher commented.

Marcus opened his mouth in feigned outrage. "You only had one. I had two."

"Cease your complaining," Christopher said, looking around to make sure there were no more soldiers waiting to ambush them. "You always did like to complain."

Marcus shrugged and motioned to the corridor. "After you, sire."

Christopher eyed him arrogantly. "As it should be."

Marcus chuckled, following Christopher's lead down the hall. It was so strange, yet so completely natural for them to be fighting together, jesting their way through it as they had done for three years in Richard's service. The fighting between them, the anger and hatred, seemed like a god-awful far away dream. It was now as it should be, as it has always been. It was as if the Christopher and Marcus that had fought over Dustin were two completely alien people.

Now, things were normal again. And they were two men on a mission.

CHAPTER FIFTY-NINE

RALPH HAD A plan. He would destroy de Lohr once and for all. When it was apparent that the gate was going down, he had vacated his post and raced into the castle, moving immediately for the prince's rooms.

John was dressed in travelling clothes and surrounded by his elite guard. He knew that Richard was coming to kill him and he was terrified. De Lohr, Burton, and Lady Dustin were completely forgotten as he struggled to keep himself from falling into fits over the swing in luck. Everything had happened so bloody fast that his head was still spinning, yet he knew that he must leave this place if he were going to survive.

He had hoped to use Lady Dustin as a bargaining tool to keep Nottingham, but those plans were long forgotten. John was fabulous at making big plans but was terrible at following through. At this very moment all he was concerned with was his own hide. Nothing had worked out to his advantage, not one damn thing.

Ralph found his liege chomping at the bit and he personally escorted the prince down the winding staircases to the cavernous underground of Nottingham. There was an escape route through one of the dug-out tunnels that led to a shielded exit in the wall. John was adamant that Ralph go with him, but Ralph was firm. He had unfinished business to attend to. Promising to meet up with Ralph at Tickhill, Prince John was ushered out of the fortress covertly by his elite mercenary guard.

With John being skirted to safety, Ralph could better concentrate on the de Lohrs. His plan was to confiscate Dustin and her babe, taking them the same route as the prince and leaving Nottingham. He still felt firmly that they had the advantage of keeping Lady de Lohr as hostage, although the siege on the castle was in direct conflict with that reasoning. Mayhap it wasn't a wise idea after all, and mayhap Lady de Lohr served no purpose other than a nuisance. But Ralph knew one thing for certain; Christopher de Lohr loved his wife desperately, and Ralph was determined to wreak misery on that man.

Dustin sat in Ralph's bower wringing her hands nervously. She could hear the sounds of battle far below and tears of fear were still in her eyes for her husband. She refused to believe she had seen him killed. Surely he was on his way to rescue her even now. She was shaking with terror and fatigue, and her mind invented terrible scenarios of what was transpiring outside, around her.

Thank God Christin went to safety. If her daughter were still in Nottingham, surely she would be mad with grief right now. As worried as she was for herself and for Christopher, she was also terribly worried for Gabrielle. She hadn't seen her friend since Ralph had so cruelly separated them and she worried for the woman's safety.

The door to the bedchamber jolted and Dustin was seized with panic; she knew it to be either John or Ralph come for her. But in the same breath she remembered that she had feigned illness for Ralph's benefit. Hoping they would have some pity on her, she threw herself back on the bed and grabbed her stomach, moaning softly.

After a jerk and a pop, the old door flew open and in came Ralph, his thin face flushed. Dustin eyed him through slit eyelids, moaning loudly this time. Ralph marched up on her and snatched her wrist barbarically.

"Get up," he wheezed.

Dustin yelped in surprise as he yanked her off the bed and pulled her toward the open door. Forgetting about her ploy, she began to twist and fight, beating his arm with her free fist.

"Let go of me!" she demanded.

Ralph was in no mood to fool with her. Hauling off, he hit her across the face with a mailed glove, leaving a huge scrape already oozing blood. Dustin's hand flew to her face, stunned.

"Do not resist me," he seethed, spittle forming on his lips. "I have had enough of you and enough of your bastard husband. Where is your daughter?"

Tears stung her eyes, but her anger superseded her pain. "Go to hell," she spat. "I will not tell you anything!"

With a grunt of frustration, he exited the room and yanked her so hard after him that he nearly dislocated her shoulder. Dustin grunted and almost tripped, but she caught herself and started to fight Ralph with everything she had.

Dustin's shrieks and grunts filled the deserted hall as Ralph literally dragged her after him. For his wiry build, he was amazingly strong and Dustin was having a hell of a time against him. She tried grabbing onto chairs, portieres, anything that would anchor her against the force of the sheriff. But Ralph would simply pull with all of his might and dislodge her, and she would trail after him cursing and fighting.

He pulled her down a small spiral staircase to the second floor of the castle and she tripped on purpose, crashing into the man and nearly sending both of them to the bottom in a heap. Angered, he cursed and took another swing at her, but she ducked and kicked him in the thigh. Nothing happened against his armor, but the gesture satisfied her just the same. Undeterred, Ralph persevered onward with his fighting prisoner, determined to reach her rooms and collect the babe de Lohr.

He reached her chamber, tossing her inside viciously. Dustin flew with the momentum and crashed against the bed, fortunately, not hard enough to hurt her. Her eyes were spitting venom as Ralph raced to the small crib where Christin had slept.

"Where is she?" he demanded, his jaw ticking and his face sweaty. "Where is the damn baby?"

Dustin's chin went up defiantly. "Not here, you loathsome bastard."

"I can see that," he yelled, rushing to her. "Where's the goddamn baby?"

Dustin opened her mouth when suddenly there was a figure in the doorway. Gabrielle entered the room, quite calmly for all of the yelling that was going on. She fixed Ralph in the eye.

"The babe is gone," she said frankly. "Le Londe came here before you and took her. I know not where they went."

"Le Londe?" Ralph's eyes widened with surprise. "He was here? Where did he go?"

"I do not know, my lord," Gabrielle said, as cool as rain. "He snatched the babe and fled mere minutes ago."

Dustin, shaking with shock, still retained sense enough to see what Gabrielle was doing. Weak with emotion and grateful for her friend's assistance, she decided to play along. "And you let him? You bitch! Why did not you stop him?"

Gabrielle's head jerked to Dustin, an amazing look of devilment filling the soft hazel eyes. "She is not my child. Besides, had I tried to stop him, he probably would have killed me."

Dustin shrieked and moaned, throwing Ralph into fits of indecision and confusion.

"Shut up!" he screamed at her. "Shut up before I slit your throat."

Dustin quieted, but not entirely. She pretended to cry weakly, overacting a bit, but Ralph did not notice. His mind was soaring with le Londe's sighting.

"I must find him," he said absently, looking to Gabrielle again. "Which way did he go?"

Gabrielle was a brilliant actress. She lowered her gaze demurely and stepped away from the door, pointing out into the hall. "I saw him take the stairs toward the grand hall."

Ralph was seized with a sense of purpose again. He grabbed Dustin once again, jerking her past Gabrielle. Gabrielle looked at Dustin with such indifference that Dustin almost believed she truly did not care what was happening. Ralph, however, knew better than to leave her behind. He did not know why he should take her, only that he should.

With his free hand, he seized Gabrielle by the hair. "You are coming too."

With his quarry, Ralph awkwardly raced down the hall. Dustin was still shrieking and struggling and Gabrielle had begun to fight back, adding to Ralph's woes. He seriously considered throwing Gabrielle down the stairs just to be rid of her, but thought differently of it. He was so confused and so anxious he simply couldn't think straight any longer.

They reached the top of the stairs where Dustin could see soldiers dashing about below at the beginning of full-scale chaos. She grabbed at the banister to throw Ralph off balance while Gabrielle, seeing what Dustin was doing, moved to do the same. Ralph began to bellow and yank at them unmercifully. From below, it was actually quite comical to see the Sheriff of Nottingham struggling with two women, listening to him ranting and cursing. But to the participants, it was anything but comical.

Dustin had a death grip on the railing, anything to prevent Ralph from dragging her down below. She glanced at Gabrielle, fearful for her safety because she was closer to the stairs. As she looked at her friend, something caught in her peripheral vision and she looked back down the second floor corridor, positive soldiers were coming to Ralph's aid and terrified that she and Gabrielle would be hurt in the struggle.

She was therefore astonished to see Christopher and Marcus at the very end of the hall. They were hundreds of feet away, but even at that distance she could read the surprise on their faces. It took her less than a second to react instinctively.

"*Christopher!*" she screamed.

He heard her; Christ, he heard her and was moving even as she cried his name. But Ralph saw him, too, and was screaming to the soldiers down below to aid him.

The distance closing between Christopher and his wife was never ending. The more he ran, the farther away she was until he felt as if he were gaining no headway at all. Panic filled his veins and anguish filled his throat, threatening to choke him to death. He could see Ralph dislodging her grip and yanking her away from the stairs, retreating down the opposite direction of the hall, even as a dozen soldiers mounted the second story landing and separated the sheriff and the approaching Defender. Cut off from Dustin, Christopher tore into the soldiers like a man possessed.

Marcus and Christopher fought valiantly, yet it was two against twelve and they were not gaining much ground. But they fought with renewed vigor, now knowing where Dustin was and were desperately intending to reach her. The grunts of effort sounded every time broadswords came in contact with each other with bone-jarring force. Within a minute or so, they had cut down four men and were moving furiously on the rest. Yet with every passing second, Christopher's anxiety was growing.

Suddenly, from the second story landing, they heard a rebel yell that made their hair stand on end. Christopher could not help but grin; without even looking, he knew it to be David. Only his brother howled like a wild man in the heat of battle.

Yet it was not only David, but there was Edward, Dud, Sir Stephen Marion and Sir Dalton le Crughnan as well. They had fought their way through the hysteria of both wards in search of their lieges, knowing instinctively that they could use the help. Even if they did not, every man in the service of the Defender and the general knew the prime objective; to rescue Lady Dustin. If one failed, there would be another to take his place until the last man had died trying. They were not about to leave the place without her.

Christopher watched with satisfaction when the swords of his loyal vassals met with the mercenary soldiers. The troops, fighting now from two fronts, were a sight less confident. Especially when Sir Dalton, as big as a bear, began grunting and yelling like a caveman and intimidated the hell out of them. The fight was not long for the running.

Christopher fell back, moving around the squirming mass of men and picking up speed as he raced in the direction his wife had been taken. Even as he rounded the corner at the far end of the hall, he could hear her screaming and knew he was on the right track. Her screams were distinctive, and he remembered when they had once, long ago, saved her life.

And they would save her life again. He thanked God for her healthy lungs and pursued the sound with a vengeance.

He met with a dead end at the extreme end of the hall. He could hear her yelling and cursing from the other side of a locked door, a massive oaken panel that was movable. Marcus raced up beside him.

"She's in here," Christopher breathed heavily.

Marcus thrust himself against the door in a futile attempt to break it down. He turned to Christopher, his cobalt-blue eyes wide with anxiety. "How are we going to get in there?"

Christopher glanced around, searching for anything that might help him bust the massive door into splinters. Other than the swords they held, there was nothing of substance in the hall and Christopher felt his panic rise. On the other side of the door, he heard Dustin shrieking again and he threw himself against the door, his fingers digging into the wood.

"I am here, Dustin!" he bellowed, yet pain was evident in his voice. "I am coming!"

He could hear her screaming his name and he was close to buckling, again searching the hall for anything that might assist him in his venture. Immediately, his eyes fell on two things that rapidly calmed him; an open, arch-shaped window and a torch. He ran to the torch, snatching it off the wall and thrusting it at Marcus.

"Burn the door down," he barked, turning for the window. "I shall try another way in."

"Jesus, Chris, we are fifty feet up," Marcus said earnestly. "You shall be killed if you fall."

Christopher jumped onto the windowsill with the agility of a child, for all of his immense size. “I will not fall,” he said, inspecting the six-inch ledge that ran along the outside of the wall. “Get started on that damn door.”

Marcus watched him sheath his sword and snatch several silken cords from the massive curtains that lined the hall. He tied the ends together and then secured the very end of the patchwork rope around his waist. Marcus moved forward and secured the opposite end of the rope to a heavy iron wall sconce directly beside the window.

Christopher flashed him a grin, already halfway out the window. “A bit of insurance never hurt,” he remarked.

Marcus raised a quirky eyebrow. “So you *are* afraid of falling,” he said. “Even you cannot fly.”

Christopher was out on the ledge. “Not last time I checked. Get to work on the door.”

He was gone, inching along the ledge like a crab. His destination, he could see, was about twenty feet away and he estimated he would have to untie the rope and go the last five feet on his own. Dustin’s yelling wafted through the open portal, just large enough for him to slip through, and he had to keep himself in check. The urge to move quickly was overwhelming, but he knew that he would not even be allowed one mistake. Even if the rope held, he would have to start all over again and time was of the essence. He had to get to his wife.

Marcus set the door ablaze as ordered, waiting impatiently for it to burn, and rushed to the window every few seconds to make sure Christopher was still there. He, too, could hear Dustin yelling and his heart was twisting with anguish. Even if he rescued her first, it was not him she wanted. Marcus thought he was being selfish by insisting he help Christopher rescue his wife, simply to be near her. It never occurred to him that he was doing a completely selfless thing by risking his own life.

Inside, Dustin wasn’t shrieking because she was scared, at least not truly scared. She had seen Christopher and her courage surged, knowing that he was indeed alive and coming for her. Ralph had brought the women into a massive room, almost devoid of any furnishing, and was spending most of his time trying to corral them. Gabrielle and Dustin scampered about, throwing things at the sheriff as they tried to keep him away from them. It was hysterical and chaotic as Ralph tried to chase them down.

He had brought them to the room for a reason. Sir Bruce had told him that this room, having once served as a chapel, had a secret exit by which the priests used to come and go. He saw no outward signs of the exit, concentrating more on capturing Lady de Lohr and Lady de Havilland. After the women were trussed up he could then continue his search. He was not apprehensive that de Lohr and Burton were going to be able to break the door down, the door was like iron.

Smoke suddenly started to billow underneath the door and Ralph stopped chasing the women, looking at the smoke curiously. It occurred to him that they were going to try and burn the door down, as they had burned the gates of the keep down, and he felt his first twinge of apprehension. His confidence waned and he set out with determination to capture the women.

Gabrielle was the first one cornered by the sheriff, and Dustin yelled and threw things in their direction. She was true with her aim and hit Ralph on the back of the head with a candle sconce, drawing a curse and a promise that he would blister her hide. She continued to yell and cause an uproar as Ralph tied Gabrielle to a chair. The only reason she did not physically attack Ralph was because she was afraid he would capture her, too, and decided to keep a safe distance from him for as long as possible.

Smoke began to assault her nose and she briefly considered rushing to the door to try to unbolt it, but the heat from the fire had rendered the bolt scalding. Unable to do anything, Dustin continued her verbal assault on Ralph and dashed across the room to one of the large arch-shaped windows, squeezing back on the sill as if to hide from the sheriff. He was almost finished with Gabrielle and she knew that she was next. Her fear began to creep back.

Ralph had tied Gabrielle particularly tight with a strip of cord. Wearily, he turned about in search of Lady de Lohr and immediately spied her huddled on the window sill. Dustin blanched, telling Ralph to stay the hell away from her, but he was not listening. Slowly, he made his way toward her, knowing there was naught she could do and nowhere she could go.

Dustin watched his advance, her back to the open window, wondering if she should threaten to jump. Scared to death of heights, she decided against it and was preparing to run amuck in the room again when a massive arm suddenly went around her from behind.

The Defender had arrived.

☙

MARCUS STOOD WITH his sword in his hand, watching the door go up in flames. Christopher had disappeared into the room and he was desperate to assist his lord. He kept glancing behind him to make sure no one was advancing on him, the heat of the door so intense he had to step back.

Piece by piece, the door began to buckle and he knew that soon he would be able to kick it in. Yet, for now, Christopher was on his own against Ralph. It was not a difficult task, but the Defender had two women to protect, making the job more complex.

Marcus was standing several feet away watching the door burn when he was hit from behind and a sharp, stabbing pain radiated through his back. He knew immediately he had been gored and he let out a grunt of surprise, spinning around to face his accoster. He fully expected to see a horde of soldiers or the sneering face of John, but instead, was confronted by an older, distinguished man he did not know.

His face was a mask of pain and surprise as he raised his sword against his attacker. The man's face was expressionless.

"Richard's bastard within my walls," he mumbled. "You shall die here, then."

Marcus could feel his wound throbbing, bleeding. Warm, sticky blood ran down his right leg. "Who in the hell are you?"

"Lord of the keep," the man informed him with a boom. "This is my castle, you whoreskin. You have no right to be here."

"I have a right by decree of Richard," Marcus answered. "We shall take this fortress back in the name of the king and you, sir, shall be executed for treason."

The man let out a growl and charged at Marcus. Swords met and sparks sprayed, although Marcus knew immediately that the man was no match for him. Even in his weakened state, he would have no trouble dispatching the man who called himself lord of the keep. Within five strokes of the broadsword, John's sympathizer lay in a pool of his own blood, his head half-severed from his neck.

Marcus stood back a moment, breathing heavily and feeling the sharp pain of his wound. He put his hand to it, trying to assess it as best he could. The man caught him between the joints of his armor, in the flesh and muscle of his torso. It was a deep puncture, but it could have been far worse and Marcus sighed with relief when he realized it was not a life-threatening wound. Even so, he was bleeding moderately and his hands were shaking, but he ignored it. Smoke was thick in the corridor and he turned his attention back to the smoldering door.

☙

DUSTIN WAS SO surprised when she was grabbed from behind that she instinctively tried to pull away, swinging her balled fists at her unseen molester. Christopher caught a punch on the jaw, unbalancing him slightly as he tried to come in through the window and he muttered a curse as his foot slipped out over nothingness.

"Dustin!" he snapped gently. "It is me. It is me, sweetheart."

She let out a cry, ceasing her struggles and turning with the utmost shock to see Christopher's face not a foot from her own.

"Christopher!" she gasped, throwing her arms around his neck with a great rush of relief and joy.

He grabbed her with one arm, steadying himself against the sill with the other; he still wasn't completely through the window. As great as his relief was that he finally held Dustin in his arms, his eyes immediately found Ralph on the opposite end of the smoke-hazed room and he hastened to climb out of the window sill with his wife clinging to his neck.

He kissed her face feverishly, as much as he dared to allow his attention to be diverted for one sweet, heavenly moment. But there was no time for anything else, and he released her with great reluctance and gentleness, pushing her against the wall.

"Are you all right?" he demanded with tender harshness. His hand moved to her belly and she realized he was speaking of her "attack" outside of the outer gates. "I am fine, truly," she gushed.

He nodded stiffly, touching her face. "Then stay here, sweetheart," he told her, his eyes riveting to the sheriff.

Ralph could not believe his eyes, yet in same token, he wasn't really surprised at all. He immediately unsheathed his broadsword in a slow, deliberate move and took a few stalking steps forward.

"So you have taken to climbing walls now, have you?" Ralph remarked snidely. "Mayhap you truly are a phantom, de Lohr, in league with the devil for restoring you your life."

Christopher raised an eyebrow. "Nay, Fitz Walter, the devil has enough henchmen with you and John to do his bidding. In fact, you shall be able to greet Great Satan personally in but a few moments."

Ralph raised his sword in front of his face. "I do not think so. I have defeated you before, de Lohr. Do you not remember?"

"Aye, I remember," Christopher's sword was in his hand, though not raised, as he approached the sheriff. "As I recall, you had one of your young friends trip me before you tried to kill me in practice. I still bear the scar."

"No one tripped you, you simply stumbled over your own feet," Ralph said. "Not difficult for a boy of twelve."

Christopher shook his head. "You shall never change, Ralph. You were a liar when I first met you and you are still a liar," he said, his voice turning cold. "I have known you since you were nine years old, Fitz Walter. You have never changed."

Ralph's face continued to hold a slightly cocky, amused expression. "I do not like to admit that we squired together, either."

Christopher shrugged. "The fact is inconsequential. What remains now is that I intend to avenge myself upon you for the grief you have caused me. Have you any last words before I spill your innards?"

Ralph was beginning to feel trapped. His sure manner, his advantage, was quickly slipping away and he knew he would be forced to defend himself against de Lohr. Strange, he felt no fear until this very moment when he realized he no longer held the edge. But now, terror flooded his veins.

Dustin watched, pressed against the cold stone wall, as her husband and the sheriff moved toward each other. Her gasps of surprise had died down, and now that her fears were alleviated at the arrival of her husband, she found she was remarkably calm in spite of her shock.

With loving adoration, she watched Christopher move on Ralph like a cat stalking a mouse and she knew her plight had ended. A very small detail was to be taken care of; the elimination of Ralph Fitz Walter, and she could go home. She almost wanted to tell Christopher to simply leave well enough alone so that they could depart immediately, but she wanted to see Ralph punished, too.

Her calm vanished the moment the clash of broadswords echoed though the room, and she gave a little shriek of surprise as Christopher plowed into Ralph. Gabrielle, too, tied to the chair on the opposite side of the room, cried out in alarm. Momentum picked up and the noise of the meeting swords grew more painful as Christopher and Ralph worked their way across the cavernous room.

Dustin's hand was at her throat as she watched the fight; terrified. She was always terrified when she watched her husband fight, be it in a tourney or in an actual battle. She wanted to cover her eyes but she was afraid to, afraid that something would happen to Christopher while she was cowering like an idiot. So she watched, afraid to breathe as her husband and the sheriff tried to kill one another.

Christopher was like a man possessed as he ripped into Ralph. The sheriff, however, was fresh, and met his blows steadily. Christopher chopped and parried, knocking Ralph over and goring him in the thigh before the sheriff could recover. Bleeding profusely and swearing, Ralph dodged another, possible mortal blow and scrambled a few feet away to regroup and respond.

But Christopher was unmerciful. There was nowhere for Ralph to hide, nowhere for him to seek refuge as the Defender pursued him, literally tearing the room apart in his wake. Several old candle stands met with their death at the hands of Christopher, toppled and dashed as his sword swiped them. Ralph dashed behind a silk portiere and was promptly swaddled in it as Christopher slashed the supports. Rolling away in panic; he twisted his way free of the confining material a split second before Christopher came down heavily with his sword. Had Ralph been any slower, he would have been cut in half.

The fight progressed, each man sweating and grunting with sheer physical exertion. Ralph was rapidly tiring and growing despondent because Christopher showed no signs of the same. He had no way of knowing that Christopher had been fighting and moving for more than a week, greatly taxing the man's already weakened state. What Christopher was doing was accomplished on pure willpower alone. His strength and his energy were gone, and his body was feeding off of the love for his wife. After months and months of separation, he could taste her again and that thought alone gave him the strength of ten men.

The door was burning hotly, crumbling, and falling away. The room was filled with acrid smoke, causing Dustin and Gabrielle to cough and choke. Dustin was by the window, which afforded her a small amount of relief, but Gabrielle was virtually trapped on the other side of the room and was unable to escape the smoke. Dustin was panicked to help her friend, but Ralph and Christopher were fighting directly between the two women, separating them, and Dustin could not make her way safely to Gabrielle. With the ferocity of the fight and the swift movement, she could easily become caught in it should she try to move.

Dustin's eyes were riveted to Christopher as he gracefully hacked away at Ralph. His face was expressionless, no hate and no anger as she would have suspected. He almost looked calm compared to Ralph's expression of total anxiety. He was so focused and so at ease tearing Ralph down that it made her feel calmer, too, although she was shaking and would yelp every time Ralph landed a blow against him. But she knew he would be the victor; he always was and she had the utmost faith in his abilities. She only wished he would hurry the hell up so she could hold him and tell him how very much she loved him.

But they were taking their time with it, cutting and striking against each other. Ralph had several decent nicks whereas Christopher showed signs of none and Dustin felt her heart lighten, for she knew the fight would be over soon and Christopher would emerge whole. She had no doubt of it until she noticed ugly red blood soaking the bottom of his hauberk on his left side and staining the top of his leg armor.

Horror gripped her, *where had this come from?* Perhaps he had been wounded in the battle outside somehow, yet she had not noticed it when he had first come into the room. The more she watched, the more he bled, and she was more terrified that he would bleed to death than be speared by Ralph.

Suddenly, the massive burning door gave way and splinters and burning cinders of wood exploded into the room. Dustin cringed, turning her face away as she was pelted by bits of wood and debris. Before she could even turn back around, someone was grabbing her and she cried out in fear.

"Dustin." Marcus had her by both arms. "Come on; let's get you out of here."

"Nay!" she was terribly glad to see him but she wasn't about to leave Christopher. "I am staying with Chris. Marcus, go help Gabrielle. *Hurry.*"

He looked puzzled for a split second until he caught sight of Lady de Haviland tied to a chair on the opposite side of the room. He glanced once more at Dustin.

"Are you all right?" he asked, his eyes raking over her.

Again, she found herself explaining her seizure outside of the gates and she nodded firmly. "Fine, Marcus, I am fine. Are you all right?"

He nodded, although he was paler and pastier than Dustin had ever seen him. She eyed him even as he lied to her, her own eyes moving over his body. "Why are you so pale?" she demanded. "Are you ill?"

"Nay, Dustin, I am not ill," he replied hoarsely, letting go of her and passed a wary look at Christopher and Ralph as they destroyed the remains of an altar.

He turned his back on her, preparing to cross the room to her friend, when Dustin cried out and grabbed him.

"You are hurt!" she exclaimed. "You lied to me. Let me see."

He pulled away from her firmly but gently. " 'Tis only a scratch, I assure you."

She opened her mouth to argue with him, but he was gone, skirting the room as he made his way to Gabrielle. Dustin watched him go, seeing the blood on his lower back and down his right leg and thinking that it did not look like a mere scratch to her. A huge crash from the direction of Christopher and Ralph diverted her attention from Marcus and she was instantly refocused.

Marcus heard the smash signaling the total destruction of the carved altar, but he was intent on rescuing Lady de Havilland and paid little heed. Gabrielle was trussed up tightly in the oaken chair, the ropes so tight they were cutting off her circulation to her arms. She smiled wanly as Marcus reached her, slicing through her bindings with his dagger.

"Thank you, my lord," she said softly. "I was losing feeling in my hands."

He gently pulled her to stand but her legs were so shaky that she fell against him. Instinctively, he put his arms around her to shield her from the fight at hand as he led her to safety.

Dustin and Gabrielle fell into each other arms, tremendously grateful that their lives were spared and that all would soon be well. Marcus provided a shield against the fighting that was going on in the room, but Dustin shooed him away; she knew instinctively that the fight was waning and she wanted to see for herself. Reluctantly, he moved aside, watching with the two women as Christopher beat Ralph down.

Ralph was spent, he was certainly not as fine a warrior as Christopher and it sorely showed. He found himself bouncing off walls in his fatigue, no longer swinging his sword because he was simply too tired. His entire motivation was to keep away from Christopher's broadsword any way he could, and eventually he simply took to running around like a crazed idiot. Christopher gave little chase; he would wait for Ralph to collapse before delivering the final blow.

A hush settled in the smoky, cluttered room; the death watch had begun.

Christopher stood in the center of the room, breathing heavily and sweating, filthy and exhausted to the bone but his posture was as straight as a tree, his stance unshaken. He looked completely in control as Ralph staggered about in a futile attempt to delay death. Dustin's eyes were wide as she alternately watched her husband and passed pathetic glances at the sheriff.

"Christopher…," she ventured softly.

He put up a gentle hand to silence her, not taking his eyes off Ralph. He was still caught up in the fight and could not allow his attention to be diverted lest Ralph suddenly come to life and run him through.

Ralph knew he was done for. He tripped over his own feet and slammed heavily into the wall, scraping his face and shoulders against the stone as he turned to eye Christopher with contempt.

"This isn't over, Defender, not by a far sight," Ralph rasped. "John shall persevere, mark my words."

Christopher took a slow step toward him. "Richard is king, Ralph. Why is that so hard for you to come to terms with? He is the rightful heir, as his birthright dictates. John is nothing more than a petty, jealous boy."

"Henry wished for John to ascend him," Ralph wheezed back. "He was going to kill Richard himself so that John could take the throne before he himself was claimed by death."

Christopher shook his head slowly. "Speculation, pure and simple," he said. "Even so, Richard is king and shall remain so as long as I have breath in my body."

Ralph's eyes spit hatred and fear before he lolled his head away, his gaze falling about the room as he knew it would be the very last he saw of his beloved England. He did not want to die, for he knew he would be doing penance in hell for years to come for his sins. Ah, well, he was too tired to fight anymore and he knew full well there was no chance to escape. Yet he regretted nothing he had done, nothing at all, and he would not denounce his actions before God.

He pushed himself up, a little straighter, although he was still leaning against the wall. Inadvertently, he bumped a heavy iron wall sconce and it gave way. A panel in the wall opened up immediately to his left and Ralph realized that it was the secret exit he had been searching for.

His heart soared with delight and he bolted off the wall. With a triumphant shout, he threw himself into the hidden doorway. Christopher, breaking from his still stance the moment the panel had opened up, knew there was no time to stop the man. He was exhausted and frustrated, disbelieving that Ralph was going to somehow escape him. In desperation, he pulled out a long, thin razor-sharp dagger from a hidden sheath on his upper left arm. He threw it, well-aimed at Ralph, as the man entered the doorway. It had been an unsteady throw but his aim had been true; and before Ralph could disappear the dirk caught the man squarely in the throat.

Ralph toppled over, hands to his throat. He yanked the dirk free but that was his undoing; blood flowed freely from the severed artery. Christopher reached the secret doorway, with Ralph half in and half out of it, in time to see the man bleed to death on the cold stone floor.

It was finished.

He just stood there a moment in disbelief. Dustin, having witnessed the entire climax, released Gabrielle and walked toward her husband, her entire body aching, her dress torn and dirty, and feeling as if she could sleep forever. But the newness that was hope and joy was seeping into her soul, telling her that, indeed, her trial was over. She wanted all of it to be over, and she wanted her husband.

"Chris," she breathed.

He looked at her, standing in the open doorway for a small eternity before pushing himself away. He continued to stare at her as if he was having difficulty believing the rapid occurrence of Ralph's death. It had happened so quickly that he was rather numbed by it all.

"Is it over?" Dustin asked timidly.

Christopher nodded, glancing once again to Ralph's supine body. "It is."

"Swear it?"

"I do."

"Then take me home," Dustin whispered fervently, tears suddenly welling in the huge gray eyes.

Christopher broke, rushing to her and capturing her in his embrace with the passion and want and tenderness of the ages. Her tears turned into full blown sobs of joy as she felt him against her. His face was in her hair and his armor was jabbing her with familiarity. He was here, in her arms, and she would never leave him again. She was so choked with emotion that her mind turned into a warm haze, where the only thing that mattered was that he loved her. Her hair felt wet and it took her a moment to realize it was due to her husband's tears.

Time had no meaning as they held each other, too consumed by emotion to speak. Christopher embraced his wife to him, his eyes closed, smelling and feeling her to the very core of his soul. It was a magical moment, the sweetest of times, and he did not even realize he was rocking her slowly.

"Why did you leave?" he managed a rasp whisper.

She sighed raggedly, pulling back from him. Her hair, half of it out of the braid, was ensnared in the shoulder joints of his armor. "Because you and Marcus were fighting," she sniffled. "You were fighting because of me. You hated each other because of me. I thought…thought if mayhap I left, you would stop fighting. You would have no more reason to."

His hands gripped her face, swallowing her head. "How could you think that?"

She shook her head, lowering her gaze. "I do not know. I was going to leave and never come back."

His sky-blue eyes bore into her. "Do you hate me so much that you would be so desperate to escape me?"

She choked on his words and her eyes widened. "I do not hate you at all. I love you, Chris, but you should hate me for causing you so much trouble."

It all became painfully clear to him why she had left and he shook his head slowly. "Christ, Dustin. I could never hate you, sweetheart, and in spite of your crazy ideas you have done absolutely nothing to cause trouble," he said, his voice infinitely tender. "I thought you ran away for all of the pain and grief I had caused you. It was not easy on you to think me dead, and it certainly unbalanced you when I returned. I thought you hated me, sweetheart."

Her mouth opened in surprise. "Of course not. Chris, I *love* you."

He let out a heavy sigh and pulled her to him once again with all of the reverence and satisfaction he felt. He was so terribly relieved that his body threatened to collapse on him. In fact, he discovered that his hands were indeed shaking and it puzzled him. But he continued to hold his wife and said a silent prayer to God for her safety. So what if there was a battle raging around them; they could do without their Defender for a moment longer.

Suddenly, the burned-out doorway were filled with knights and Christopher looked up to see his brother standing in the doorway, his eyes wide.

"What took you so long?" Christopher demanded softly.

David almost collapsed with relief. "Jesus Chri....are you all right?" he asked, entering the destroyed room. "Where in the hell are Ralph and John?"

"Ralph is dead but I do not know where John is," Christopher said, releasing his wife. "How goes the siege?"

"Nottingham is ours," David replied confidently. "The mercenary troops are already disbanding. Say, who's this bastard in the hall?"

"Some fool who was stupid enough to challenge me," Marcus replied, touching the puncture wound in his back.

Gabrielle, on the opposite side of Marcus, craned her neck around and let out a gasp of surprise. "Lord Bruce."

Dustin's eyes widened and she broke away from Christopher, only to be met with the gory sight of her dead grandsire. Christopher moved quickly behind her, afraid she was going to fall into fits, but instead, she shook her head.

"He got what he deserved," she murmured, turning to Marcus. "Thank you, Marcus. You did my mother and me a great service."

"That is your grandfather?" Marcus repeated incredulously, not sure whether to beg her forgiveness or acknowledge her thanks. He looked to Christopher, who shook his head faintly. *Let it go.*

Most of Christopher's and Marcus' knights were crowding the corridor, waiting for a command of action and were wholly glad to see Lady Dustin. It was Christopher who moved first.

"Let's get the hell out of here, then," he said, his voice strangely dull.

Marcus moved to escort Gabrielle, who made a valiant attempt to walk but found her knees buckling. In an instant, she was in Marcus' arms and he found himself gazing back at an extraordinarily lovely woman. He truly hadn't noticed before. Gabrielle flushed and started to apologize, but he shushed her.

"You have had a time of it, my lady," he said, noticing the clear hazel of her eyes before tearing himself away. "I consider it an honor to assist you."

He swept her out of the room, followed closely by Dustin, Christopher and David. Yet suddenly, when they filtered into the hall, Christopher came to an unsteady halt and weaved dangerously. Dustin turned around to ask him what the matter was when he suddenly plummeted to his knees.

Dustin screamed and grabbed hold of one of his massive arms. "What's wrong?"

David and Edward were there, grave concern written all over their faces. Christopher, breathing hard, ripped off his helmet and sent it crashing before putting a hand over the left side of his torso.

"Goddamn wound is acting up again," he mumbled.

"Wound? What wound?" Dustin demanded severely. "Let me see it."

He tried to stop her, but she pushed his shaking arms away and shoved his mail and armor aside. An oozing, puckered scar the size of an apple confronted her and she gasped loudly.

"What's this? How did this happen?" she cried.

"Shush, sweetheart, you are going to get yourself all worked up," Christopher said, his voice soft and a tired smile on his face. "This, my love, is why I was away for three months. This is what nearly killed me, and I see it is trying to accomplish its unfinished task."

Dustin's pallor turned ashen and her hand flew to her mouth. "Oh my dear God," she whispered. "Oh, Chris, you have reopened it. Are you going to die?"

"Nay," he said flatly. "All I need is some rest and my wife by my side and I shall recover fully. David, take Dustin. Edward, help me to stand or we shall never make it out of this Godforsaken place."

CHAPTER SIXTY

DUSTIN HAD NEVER experienced such complete, utter satisfaction as the army crested a small hill and Lioncross came into view. Her home, Christopher's home, loomed in the distance and tears of relief sprang to her eyes. Surely heaven was not as gracious and welcoming.

Christopher viewed Lioncross with a great deal of relief and joy as well. A smile creased his lips as his gaze devoured his lands, his keep. He had returned once more and he swore silently that, barring any great catastrophe on Richard's part, he would never leave Lioncross again. He was home to stay.

Dustin rode in front of Christopher, clutched against him as she had been the entire journey. He was exceptionally weak, but he refused to let her ride alone. It had been far too long since he had held her and he was determined to make up for lost time. Dustin reveled in his touch, ignoring the jab of the armor and her own aching back. Wherever Christopher was, she was content and comfortable.

Everyone had accompanied them back to Lioncross, save Richard. With his brother on the run, he was obliged to follow. Pleased beyond words that the situation had righted itself and all was well with his knights, he allowed Marcus and David only a few days' time to accompany the Defender home and then return to the troops. Christopher had earned the right to recover fully at home and was therefore spared any further service to subdue John. Considering the price the man had paid against the prince, Richard was more than willing to be generous to his Defender.

Christopher had learned that Richard's first destination was Tickhill. With sincere earnest, the Defender fulfilled a promise to the man who had saved his life and had pleaded the case of Lord Robin of the Hood to the King of England. On pure faith from his Defender's words and as a result of the gratitude he felt, Richard promised to fully look into the charges and restore the earldom. Christopher could ask for no more than that.

Riding in front of her Uncle David, Christin crowed happily and chewed her hands as the army skirted the village en route to the keep. Christopher and Dustin smiled over at the fat, happy cherub.

"She looks more and more like you daily," Dustin commented.

"Yet it would seem that she harbors your characteristics," Christopher replied, splaying his great hand on her belly. "Mayhap this child will be like me."

"Ha!" David scoffed. "That will remain to be seen. You shall probably have a house full of women before this is through, every one of them like your wife."

Christopher raised an eyebrow as Dustin chuckled. "Now where have I heard that threat before?"

" 'Tis no threat, sire, but a promise," Dustin snickered. "This child will be a girl."

"Christ," Christopher muttered. "And just what are you planning to name this spawn? Curtis?"

"Nay." Dustin insisted with a grin, passing a glance at Gabrielle, seated in front of Marcus. "I was thinking on naming her after a friend."

"Friend? What friend?" he asked.

Dustin sighed with content and snuggled back against him. "Lady Brielle de Lohr has a nice ring to it, doesn't it?"

"Brielle?" he looked over his shoulder to Gabrielle and Marcus, as well. "Ah, of course.

"Tis a fine name."

The gates of Lioncross yawned open wide to welcome home their lord and lady. Men were shouting and several peasants had turned out to shout their welcome as the large company passed through the gates. Christopher acknowledged the horde, he was so very glad to be home.

Jeffrey and Max were there to greet them and Christopher was immediately reminded of Anthony's death at the sight of his brother. Edward rode close to Christopher, reading his thoughts.

"I shall tell him," he murmured to Christopher.

"He died in battle, Edward," Christopher said softly. "He died with a sword in his hand."

Edward nodded. To tell Max that Marcus had killed his brother would surely create another battle, and it was best to omit certain facts to the man in this case. Christopher was tired of battles.

"What took so long?" Jeffrey greeted, a rare smile on his face. "We thought you went on the bloody quest again."

Christopher reined his charger to a halt and carefully lowered Dustin into Jeffrey's waiting arms. She surprised her father's former captain by hugging him warmly.

"Nay, no quest," Christopher said, dismounting stiffly. His wound was still tender and raw. "No more quest. No more war. No more fighting of any kind anymore."

Jeffrey raised an eyebrow as Dustin walked away from him, making a beeline for Deborah on the front steps of the keep. Christopher watched his wife and sister embrace happily and he could hear their chattering from where he was standing. Weary but happy, he turned to supervise the dismantling of his troops when Jeffrey suddenly took hold of his arm.

"I must speak with you immediately, my lord," the German said quietly.

"What is it?" Christopher removed his gauntlets.

Jeffrey glanced at Dustin briefly. "You have a visitor, my lord," he said. "He arrived nearly three weeks ago."

Christopher looked puzzled. "Who?"

Jeffrey cleared his throat. "Your son."

Christopher stared back at him. "My son?" he repeated slowly. "What are you talking about?"

"Peter Myles de Vries arrived with his nurse and a male servant from France," Jeffrey informed him. A missive accompanied him from the Earl of Calais. It would seem that young Peter's mother, a Lady Amanda, and her husband, had been killed in an accident and the boy was orphaned. The earl felt himself too old to raise the lad and decided the boy would be better off with his father."

Christopher was thunderstruck. *His son? Here?* He closed his agape mouth. "Where is he?"

"Out back, where your wife kept her rabbits," Jeffrey replied. "It would seem that the boy has a fondness for rabbits, as well, and has already amassed a collection."

Christopher's eyes trailed across the compound as if he could see his son though stone walls.

Marcus walked up, removing his helmet. "Where do you want the wagons, Chris?" he asked, oblivious to the look on Christopher's face. When his friend did not answer, he looked closely at him. "Chris?"

Christopher jerked his head to Marcus. "My son is here."

Marcus had no idea what he was talking about. "Son?"

Christopher nodded. "My son," he repeated, murmuring. "Lady Amanda's son."

Marcus looked puzzled a moment longer before realization dawned. "The lad you told me of? He is here?"

Christopher could only nod his head. Dustin suddenly reemerged from the castle and he seemed to snap out of his shocked state. "Christ, I must tell Dustin."

"Too late," Jeffrey murmured, and they all turned their head to see a young boy crossing the courtyard toward them. It was obvious to anyone who looked at him that he was Christopher's son; he was an exact miniature copy. Christopher's breathing stopped as his eyes beheld his son for the first time.

There was nothing they could do to stop the inevitable. Dustin was closer to the boy than they were and she immediately smiled curiously at the lad. The boy stopped and returned her smile.

Christ, Christopher thought, *he even smiles like me.* He should have been apprehensive as hell, but he found he was not. He knew his wife well enough to know she would be rational about this unexpected turn. At least, he hoped so.

"Hello," she said. "Who are you?"

"Peter Myles de Vries, my lady," he replied with a practiced bow.

"What are you doing at Lioncross, Peter?" she asked pleasantly. "Are you visiting someone?"

"Nay, my lady, I am here to meet my father," he replied. At six years old, he was very mature for his age. "My father is Baron Christopher. Do you know where he is?"

Dustin's smile vanished. She stared at the boy a long moment before tearing her gaze away and seeking out her husband. Christopher stood with Jeffrey and Marcus, all three men were staring back at her with different degrees of apprehension, yet none more pronounced than Christopher's.

Christopher's son. She looked back at the lad and saw that he was a smaller version of her husband, perfect and handsome and mannerly. She fully realized she should become furious, incensed, shocked at the very least, but she knew in the same breath that she could not muster the emotions. She knew Christopher as well as she knew herself, and she knew he would not be deliberately deceitful or try to hurt her. It just did not matter anymore. They had been through too much together and she simply could not be angry with him.

The boy was looking up at her with a sweet, innocent expression and she warmed to him; he was indeed her beloved's son and she would treat him as if he were her very own. She had enough love for a houseful of children; not limited to her own flesh and blood.

Dustin held her hand out to the boy and her smile reappeared. "Come with me, Peter. I shall introduce you."

Christopher watched in stunned silence as his wife led his son directly to him.

"Christopher, this is Peter Myles de Vries," she said. "Greet your son."

Christopher tore his eyes from his wife and faced his son. "Welcome to Lioncross, Peter."

Peter bowed like a gallant little gentleman. "Thank you, my lord. I like it here already."

"I am pleased, then," Christopher answered, recovering his shock. "I am sorry to hear of your mother's passing."

Peter's handsome little face rippled. "Me, too. But mother always told me that if anything were to happen to her, then I would come and live with you in England. Is it true you are the greatest warrior in Richard's army?"

"Without a doubt, lad," Marcus said over Christopher's shoulder. "Your father is the greatest knight who has ever lived."

Peter's young face lit up with pride. "My mother said that. I want to be a great knight, too."

"You will be," Dustin said softly, putting her hand on his shoulder. "You are most definitely your father's son. I can see it already."

Peter was nearly bursting with pride. He grinned unabashedly at his father and Christopher smiled faintly, tousling the boy's hair. "Return to the keep, then, and I shall speak with you after my men are settled."

His face as radiant as the sun, Peter turned tail and raced back into the castle. Christopher looked at his wife when the boy had disappeared through the door.

"Dustin," he began softly.

She put her fingers to his lips as Marcus and Jeffrey made themselves scarce. "He's a beautiful boy, Chris. Have you known about him all along?"

He shook his head. "His mother informed me only last year," he replied softly. "I am sorry I never told you. I never thought to see the lad and simply saw no point in it."

"Who's his mother?" Dustin asked.

"Lady Amanda de Fortlage," he replied. "Although you were never introduced to her, you did see her last year at one of the parties John gave. She was at the grand ball we attended right after you discovered your pregnancy."

"I remember," Dustin nodded. "When David first met Emilie, Lady Amanda was the dark-haired woman you spoke with."

"Aye," he nodded. "Are you angry?"

She smiled. "Should I be? I am not, truly. He seems like a very nice young man."

He let out a sigh of pure relief, pure disbelief in the realization that his son was here, at Lioncross. "Lady de Lohr, you are a wise, remarkable woman. I cannot tell you how glad I am that I married you."

She wound her arms around his waist. "Or were forced to marry me, as it were."

He grinned and brushed his lips against hers. "Aye, forced to indeed."

They gazed at each other, love and adoration filling the air engulfing them. Never had Christopher been so happy. Never had Dustin been so entirely content.

"HERE, TAKE YOUR daughter." David walked up to them, holding Christin out to her parents. "She smells fully ripe."

Dustin took Christin with a chuckle. "Do not be such a coward, David."

"I am not," he insisted, propping his helmet up on his head. "By the way, who was that young boy? He looked familiar."

Christopher looked at his daughter, his wife. "He's your nephew, David. The result of a liaison between Lady Amanda de Fortlage and myself. Lady Amanda and her husband passed away recently, so the boy has come to live with me."

David's eyes widened. "Jesus Chr… your son? No wonder he looks familiar."

Dustin patted Christopher's cheek in an affectionate gesture. "He is beautiful, just like his father. Now, I really must go and change Christin out of these smelly clothes."

Christopher watched his wife walk away, still astonished with the ease in which she had accepted his bastard. No questions, no anger, no tears of humiliation. He was stunned and so very relieved at the same time, but he saw a definite wisdom that had come to his wife since he had been married to her. She was calmer, more accepting, far more in control of herself. He knew he had the extreme situations to thank for her maturity, although he would not have put her through any of them had he had the choice.

"I am shocked, Chris," David murmured. "You never told me that Amanda was pregnant."

"I did not know until I saw her at Windsor last year," Christopher said. "I honestly never thought to see the boy, so I told no one, save Marcus."

"Marcus knew?" David asked, incensed that his brother had seen fit to tell a friend, but not him.

Christopher put up a placating hand. "I had no choice but to tell him; however, we shall get into that later. Right now I would see to my wife and daughter, and then become better acquainted with my son."

David watched his brother cross the compound, watching as the Defender's eyes roved his keep, making sure there was nothing out of the ordinary or changed. He shook his head and turned away, life was certainly full of surprises. Now if he could only hope Emilie would be as understanding as Dustin when he explained to her that he had pledged his services to Richard to help his king reclaim his holdings. Wives, like brothers, were confusing creatures.

Marcus passed David and was good-naturedly surprised to be the recipient of a slug to the arm. He eyed David with a grin, just like old times. David pretended to ignore him as he joined Edward in disassembling the men-at-arms. Picking up a rock, he sailed it at David and struck the man in the back of the helm. David flinched, turned and shook his fist at Marcus menacingly.

Gabrielle was waiting patiently by Marcus' destrier, expecting to be shown into the keep by the general. Marcus grabbed her few items from his saddlebags and rounded his horse, his smile pleasant upon her.

"I would thank you again for the kindness you have shown me, sire," she said. "I will be forever in your debt."

He held out his elbow to her. "Nonsense. You owe me nothing."

She flushed a pretty shade of pink as he led her toward the keep. Her eye deliberately avoided him, instead, skimming the castle. "This is a large place. Well kept, too."

"Thanks to the baron," Marcus replied. "You shall like it here."

"I know I will," she replied. "Lady Dustin has been very kind to me."

He nodded, his smile fading. "She is a kind person."

Gabrielle looked at him, her heart going out to the man who had loved and lost. He was so very handsome, so very strong, and she could feel her own heart breaking. She could never hope to have a man as grand as Marcus Burton, not after what had happened. But even so, she wished him much happiness someday when he had gotten over Lady Dustin.

"The weather is much more severe here than in the south where you are from," Marcus said. "Even the summers seem warmer."

Gabrielle snorted lady-like. "I doubt it. Summers were most miserable in Penzance."

Marcus grinned, leading her up the steps. "Summers at Somerhill are very pleasant. You shall have to visit sometime."

Gabrielle's heart leapt into her throat, fighting back the wishing and hoping that was flooding her soul. "I would like that, sire," she replied evenly, although she felt as if she could gush like a fool.

He paused at the top of the steps and faced her, studying the fine-boned lines of her face. "Call me Marcus, if you will. Might I call you Gabrielle?"

Gabrielle thought she was going to faint with sheer happiness. "I would consider it an honor, si….Marcus."

He grinned at her and she smiled back. Together, they entered the great keep that was Lioncross.

GRISELDA HAD MET Christopher at the top of the stairs. The old woman had stayed on after the birth of Deborah's son because of the difficulties the child had and had never left. Even now, Deborah was expecting again and Griselda had no shortage of patients. Christopher could see that the old woman was greatly concerned.

"Welcome home, my lord," she bowed quickly.

He eyed her. "What's wrong?"

Griselda came straight to the point. "Your wife, sire. After her long trip, she must rest and she is refusing to listen to me."

Christopher shrugged, his fatigue catching up with him. "She seems healthy enough to me, but I will see that she rests well for the rest of the day."

Griselda held up a finger. "Not just this day, sire, but until the child is born. We do not want a repeat of what happened with your daughter."

Christopher's brows came together. "What do you mean?"

"I mean that the child was early," Griselda said. "We must make sure that this child she carries is not early."

Christopher froze. "Christin was early?"

"Aye, she was," Griselda repeated patiently. "You yourself mentioned that fact, even though I did not believe it, but you were nonetheless right. We must make sure this child comes full term."

It took him a moment to realize he had stopped breathing. Slowly, he resumed his intake of air but there was no mistaking the shock of emotions that were filling him. The old woman had just made his life complete and she did not even know it.

"You are sure Christin was early?" he asked, his voice strangely raspy.

"I'd stake my reputation on it, sire," Griselda said confidently.

He stared at the old woman a moment. Then, he grasped her gently by her bony shoulders and planted a loud kiss on her wrinkled old forehead.

"Thank you," he whispered.

Griselda watched the baron lumber down the hall, his gait slow and tired, wondering what in the world was wrong with the man. But her puzzlement did not prevent a faint blush from creeping into the aged cheeks.

DUSTIN WAS LYING down when he entered the bedchamber. She had only meant to rest a moment, but the minute her head hit the pillow, she was asleep. Christin was snoring baby-soft in the little cradle next to the bed and he smiled at his daughter. *His* daughter.

Dustin stirred the moment he touched the bed. "You are here," she murmured. "I am sorry, I did not mean to fall asleep."

He put his hands on her as she tried to rise. "Nay, sweetheart, lay down. You are tired."

"But I have a house full of guests," she protested softly.

"Gowen and Deborah can handle the masses," he said gently, moving to pull her shoes off. "You need to rest."

Dustin watched him, his movements slow and unenergetic. "You are exhausted, too. We both need to rest."

He smiled wanly. "I am all right."

She reached out and tugged on his mail. "Lie with me."

He eyed her, instantly half-aroused with her tone. Christ, it had been months since he had touched her, but now was not the time.

"Nay, my love, I shall not," he said with gentle firmness. "We would most definitely not get any rest if I did."

She sat up, her beautiful face rosy and glazed with love. "It has been months, Chris. Will you truly deny me? After everything we have been through?"

He felt his composure evaporating. "Of course not, Dustin, but look at us. I am still recovering from a near-fatal injury, and you are exhausted and pregnant."

"Then neither one of us will tax the other," she said softly. "Lie with me, husband. I need to feel you."

He lost it. His armor and mail came off and he was next to her within seconds, pulling her most fiercely to him and burying his face in his hair. The scent of roses filled him.

Dustin sighed with utter contentment, her eyes closed at the pureness of his touch, the absolute reverence she felt in it. Tears of such joy stung her eyes that she did not bother to dash them away. The tears were well-earned.

The Defender of the Realm made love to his wife that afternoon, every touch and every kiss a song of love unto itself. He loved her with the endless devotion of time, always and forever would he love her. And she responded to him with the blind worship she had always felt for him; she could not remember when she hadn't loved him.

God had given them a second chance and they would not be so foolish as to waste it.

The Defender had come home.

EPILOGUE

"THEY ARE HERE!" Dustin was running as fast as her shapely legs could carry her. She dashed out of her bedchamber and hit the stairs like a runaway horse, almost crashing into her daughters at the base of the stairs.

"Mama, they are here!" Christin announced with excitement.

Dustin grabbed Christin's hand. "Come along," she said as she snatched her other daughter's hand. "Come, Brielle."

The three ladies raced outside, excitement filling their veins. Dustin was near to bursting with anticipation; it had been so long since she had seen her sons. Fostering was a cruel thing, she thought bitterly as the great gates of Lioncross swung open. To separate a family for the sake of training was inexcusable to her, although her husband thought differently.

Christopher was crossing the bailey with his youngest son in tow. Five-year-old Myles was the spitting image of his Uncle David, whom he would soon be greeting. He stopped a moment and shielded his blue eyes from the sun as he watched the gates lurch to a halt, eager to catch a glimpse of the incoming party but being foiled as his father hoisted him onto his shoulder.

"But I want to see!" Myles protested with a grin, gripping his father's neck.

"You can see better from up here," Christopher told him. "Down on the ground, someone might run over you."

Myles strained to look over his shoulder as his father made his way to the front steps of the keep, watching with excitement as the large party entered the gates with great noise and fanfare.

"Do you see them?" Dustin demanded of her husband before he even reached her.

Christopher fought off a grin, stopping at the base of the steps turning around to face the party. "Nay; not yet. They are probably riding with Emilie and the girls."

Dustin was so excited she could hardly contain herself and her daughters were catching on. "Do you think they have changed much, Mama?" Christin asked.

"Christin, they have only been gone six months," Christopher said. "I doubt they have changed to the point where you wouldn't recognize them."

"But six months is a long time, Dada," Brielle chimed in. "Curtis and Richard are bound to have grown some."

"They have not grown beards," he said, then turned and winked at his ten-year-old daughter. "You are starting to sound like your mother with your worrying."

Dustin lifted an impatient eyebrow at her husband. "And you are callous in your treatment of your sons. Who ever heard of sending a six-year-old boy to foster?"

"Richard was two months shy of his seventh birthday," Christopher re-explained for the hundredth time. " 'Twas better to send him with Curtis to begin their training together. I wanted to send them to Marcus."

"Marcus already has Peter," Dustin shot back. "I did not want to send him so far north, as you well know. We haven't seen Peter in almost a year."

Christopher shook his head. "Peter is a fully-trained squire and Marcus says he fights better than most of his knights. You should be very proud of your son."

"I *am*," Dustin insisted, avoiding her husband's gaze. "But he is so far away and I miss him terribly."

"Christ, Dustin, he's almost eighteen years old and is as big as I am," Christopher said. "He's not a child any longer and you would do well to remind yourself of that."

Dustin made a face. "He is still a child of six to me. For a man with four sons, your attitude is most heartless."

Christopher shook his head again, after seven children, they still could not agree on the proper form of child-rearing. Dustin would keep them to her bosom until they were thirty if she had her way, while he was quite convinced that early fostering was necessary.

"I am not heartless, sweetheart, I am simply more practical than you," he said, stroking Brielle's long, blond hair affectionately. "But Myles goes to Marcus."

"He does not," she said firmly. "He goes to Canterbury when he is eight and no earlier. I am sure David is doing a fine job with our sons. They do not need to go to Marcus."

"Of course he is doing a fine job, he's my brother," Christopher said, watching as his brother dismounted his warhorse and shook hands with Jeffrey. "But Marcus has done an outstanding job with Peter. I feel David may be too soft on Curtis and Richard because he is their uncle."

Dustin caught sight of David too, and her face lit up. "There's David. But where are my boys?"

Christopher chuckled, patting Myles on the leg. "You shall go to Somerhill, won't you? You want to foster with Peter and Uncle Marcus?"

"Aye, Dada," Myles nodded solemnly, although he did not realize the entire concept of fostering. All he knew was that his brothers had been gone a long time, living with their Uncle David. He was too young to remember Peter. It was just him and his three sisters, one of which was a baby. He had been lonely without Curtis and Richard to play with, although his father had done a fine job of filling in.

"There they are!" Dustin screeched, rushing down the steps. From behind the wall of horses and men, a lovely woman and several children appeared, walking toward them.

Christopher put his hand on his wife. "Do not hug them. Treat them like young men."

She scowled at him. "They are my sons and I shall hug them if I want to."

"Nay, Dustin, you shall embarrass them in front of the soldiers," Christopher admonished. "Let them bow to you here in public. Hug them later in private, if you would."

She furrowed her brow impatiently, knowing his words to be true but, Lord, how she had missed her children.

She resumed her place between Christin and Brielle, waiting impatiently for Emilie and the brood of children to reach them. When finally they were upon them, Dustin could not take her eyes from her two blond-headed boys.

"Greetings, my lord," Emilie politely kissed Christopher on both cheeks. "Thank you for having us for Christmas. The children could hardly wait."

Christopher smiled. "You look lovely, Emilie," he acknowledged the three girls standing next to her. "And I am pleased to see your children look like you and not my dastardly brother. Good Christmas to you, ladies."

The girls curtsied prettily for their Uncle Christopher. Christina, Colleen and Caroline were polite, sweet girls with their mother's disposition and their father's spirit. And they always, always chattered, driving David to the brink of madness, yet at this moment, they were uncharacteristically quiet. They knew their Uncle Christopher to be an important man. He always struck awe into their little hearts every time they met, although he had been nothing but kind and gentle with them. Somehow, his presence enough was imposing.

"Christin, Brielle, take your cousins inside," he instructed his daughters. "Show them where they are to sleep." Giggling, Christin and Brielle eagerly took hold of their cousins and whisked them up the stairs. Christopher watched the girls with pride, never thinking that one day his children and David's would be walking hand-in-hand.

"Where is your son, my lady?" he asked Emilie.

"In the wagon with his nurse," she replied. "At six months, he weighs eighteen pounds. David is most pleased."

"No doubt," Christopher remarked. " 'Tis about time he gave you a son. There are too many women at Canterbury."

Emilie raised her brows in feigned outrage. "And what about Lioncross? You have three daughters of your own, sire, in addition to your wife, your sister, and her two daughters."

Christopher waved at her. "Rebecca is only three months old, but already her temperament is as mine. She is a calm, even-tempered baby, of which I am greatly pleased. Christin and Brielle are too much like their mother and I fear I am losing control over them already," he said, shifting his grip on Myles. "As for Deborah's daughters, they are angels. My daughters could learn lessons on obedience from them."

Emilie laughed, seeking out Dustin. "Is this true?"

Dustin shrugged and gave Emilie a hug. "He thinks any woman who speaks her mind and has half a wit is disobedient. Now, where is your new son? I am anxious to see him."

"David is probably retrieving him himself," Emilie said, glancing back to the huge caravan disassembling in the bailey. "He cannot stay away from Daniel."

Dustin nodded in agreement, her gaze falling on her two sons standing a few feet behind Emilie. Emilie, for her part, made up a discreet excuse and left the family alone.

"Hello," Dustin greeted her sons, repressing a huge urge to gather them against her. Curtis de Lohr and his brother, Richard, displayed a much practiced bow.

"Hello, Mother," Curtis said formally.

Dustin's heart sank. They were so grown up, so stiff with her, that she felt tears sting her eyes. Christopher put Myles down and approached his sons.

"Gentlemen," he said, putting his hands on his hips. "How has the baron been treating you? Well, I hope?"

"Well, Father," Curtis said evenly. "We eat at his table every night and sleep in our own bedchamber."

Christopher's eyes narrowed. This was exactly what he did not want. "Then you do not sleep with the other pages?"

"Nay, Father," Curtis shook his head. "Richie…uh, Richard and I have our own room."

"Hmm, I see," Christopher said, his voice low.

Dustin looked at her husband and could see his displeasure. She, however, was quite happy that her boys were being treated like one of the family.

"I am so glad you have returned," she said quickly. "You have a new sister. Would you like to go and see her?"

They boys nodded eagerly and she bade them go into the castle. She was still smiling when she turned to face her stern husband. Immediately, her look became impatient.

"Now, what's wrong with you?" she demanded.

He raised an eyebrow at her tone. "That is between David and me."

"It is *not*," she said. "They are my sons, too. I would know what you are planning to tell your brother about their treatment."

He looked at her a moment. "They will never learn to become proper pages or squires if they are being coddled, Dustin. I was most specific to David in that regard."

"They are not being coddled," she insisted. "Since when is kindness considered coddling? They are still little boys, for heaven's sake. Why must they be treated like men?"

"You do not understand, Dustin," he said, gazing off across the bailey and seeing his brother approach. "I would speak to David alone."

"Can the man at least wash the dust from his tongue before you lay into him?" Dustin asked annoyed.

"Leave us," Christopher told her, annoyed as well.

She looked at him a moment, at his strong profile and his most beautiful blond hair with streaks of gray. "Do not talk to me like that. I am not a wench to be dismissed at your whim."

He looked at her. "Nay, you are a countess, who is expected to obey her husband," he said. "Leave us, *please*."

She raised her eyebrow, seeing a way around all of this. Immediately, she went to him and threw her arms around his neck, kissing him soundly. He returned her kiss, the sweetness of it filling him as it always had. She pulled back and smiled at him through smoky eyes, pleased to see him reacting.

"You still cannot stay," he whispered huskily.

She slapped him playfully and he laughed low. She turned on her heel in a defiant blur of blond hair and fabric, marching away from him, but not before he planted a plate-sized hand on her behind. She yelped and rubbed the assaulted area, but it was all in fun and she fought off a grin even as she continued on her way.

David came up on his brother and did not even afford him the opportunity to speak. "I know what you are going to say," he exclaimed. "I know that look on your face and I do not like it. Your sons have not been treated any differently than the other pages."

Christopher put his hands on his hips. "Then why did they tell me they take meals with you and sleep in their own bedchamber?"

"Because they do," he snapped, although it was not in anger. "Emilie insisted until they are a year older. She says that they are still babies and...."

"Good Christ, David," Christopher muttered, putting a hand over his face. "She sounds like Dustin. And you allow this?"

"Tell me, brother, when my own son comes to foster here at age six or seven, will you tell Dustin that he cannot eat at the table with the rest of the family?" David shot back, crossing his arms expectantly. "Will you? The first time Dustin catches a glimpse of my little boy eating his supper from his lap in the corner, she will come apart at the seams. Trust me, for I have witnessed it and you, too, will be unable to deny her."

Christopher glared at his brother, not unfriendly, before shaking his head in defeat. "Then I send them to Somerhill. I cannot risk their training due to family ties."

"Oh, hell, you know Gabrielle will treat them the same way. Thank God she has not ruined Peter," David insisted. "And Marcus will go along with her in everything. Nay, they are better off with me."

"They are not," Christopher snapped, agitated on his sons' behalf. "Then I send them to Edward. He will train them to be proper pages."

"You mean the new Earl of Wolverhampton?" David said tauntingly. "Jesus, he has been so involved in John's court, he will not have the time to train the boys."

"Ah, but he has Max with him and Max is as fine a trainer as ever lived, as you well know," Christopher was suddenly relieved and satisfied with his own rapid decision. "Come the New Year, I send Curtis and Richard to Wolverhampton. I might take them there myself."

"You have seen quite a bit of him, haven't you?" David remarked.

Christopher nodded, clapping his brother on the shoulder as they moved for the castle. He truly was glad to see him. "We have been working on a charter for John's signature," he said. "The majority of earls and feudal barons have come together in the matter. Despite any disagreements or hatred, we all seem to have a common bond, we hate John."

"What kind of a charter?" David asked.

Christopher waved his hand carelessly, he did not want to get into the specifics out here in the open, but later when there was more time to talk. "We call it the Magna Carta. Sean de Lara has drafted most of it. You remember Sean, do you not?"

David nodded. "The Shadow Lord? Of course. After he left your service, he went to serve John, or so we thought. I still find it difficult to believe he was a spy for William Marshal. Who would have known?"

Christopher wriggled his eyebrows. "Not me," he replied. "Like you, we were all convinced he was John's strongest supporter. The man was brilliant in his cover. But I shall tell you more about it later."

David nodded, not really caring. He had never involved himself much in politics or scholarly pursuits. He left those things up to his brother, the Earl of Hereford and Worcester.

"I hear your new son is doing well." Christopher changed the subject, talking about John was painful for him. "Emilie was near to bursting to tell us of him."

David swelled with pride and Christopher smiled broadly at his brother. After three girls, this little boy was his pride and joy. "He's incredible, Chris. Biggest damn baby I ever saw, and smart. He's trying to sit up already."

"Wait, little brother, you forget how large Curtis was when he was born," Christopher reminded him, just to pop his bubble a bit. "He was so big we almost lost him and his mother."

Easily the most painful and frightening time of Christopher's life, but he could speak of it now without shuddering. David remembered well the panic and the grief. "Aye, he was as fat as a pig. But Daniel is bigger, see him and tell me if you do not agree."

Christopher looked at him dubiously. "I will judge for myself," he said as they mounted the steps to the keep. The winter sun overhead was bright but offered no heat, only illuminating the countryside brilliantly. Remarkably, there was no snow.

"By the way, Marcus and Gabrielle are joining us for Christmas feast," Christopher said. "They are bringing Peter and should be here by tomorrow."

"Excellent," David said. "I haven't seen Marcus in a year. How are he and his wife faring?"

"Well, he says," Christopher replied. What happened eleven years ago was a faded memory in his mind, another chapter in life, and he had forgiven Marcus a long time ago. They were still, as always, the best of friends, and David went on as if nothing had ever happened. The human character was forgiving that way. "He and Gabrielle are bringing the twins and their young son."

David grinned, scratching at his head as he surveyed the dismantling of his caravan. Christopher crossed his arms, passing a gaze over the workings, as well.

"And Peter; Jesus, he's going to outshine us all, isn't he?" David said. "Marcus swears he has never seen the likes of him."

Christopher nodded faintly. " 'Tis only right that he be greater than his father. Curtis, Richard, and Myles will be just like him. They will all outshine the sun."

"And Daniel," David reminded him. "Between us we have five sons. A grand enough dynasty for the de Lohr name."

"Indeed," Christopher agreed.

"Who knew, Chris," David murmured after a moment.

Christopher glanced at him. "What?"

David was still smiling. "Who knew we would end up like this? Married, with children, and lord of our own keeps. Who in the hell knew?"

Christopher shrugged. The very same idea constantly amazed him. "Sometimes I wonder if I shall awaken from this dream, cold and tired and old and alone. I never thought to achieve this heaven."

"Nor did I," David admitted fully. "Richard only lived to see our eldest children. I wonder what he would say to all of this."

Christopher gazed at brother, his friend. "He would say that we have reached paradise."

Dustin appeared in the doorway, her beautiful face with nary a line in it in spite of her thirty-four years and her body still voluptuous and supple even after birthing six children.

"Are you going to stand out here all day?" she wanted to know. "I have got a house full of children and dogs, and I demand you come in here and control them." Then she eyed David with mock anger. "As for you, baron; you have turned my sweet sons into miniature soldiers."

David made a helpless gesture. Christopher smiled at his wife and she blew a kiss in his general direction before retreating into the castle. "And that, dear brother, is my very private paradise," he said softly.

David watched his massive brother lumber into the keep, pausing a moment before following him. He never thought he would see the day when Christopher de Lohr would be content with his life.

The greatest warrior who ever lived was an earl for nine years, and was, mayhap the mightiest earl in the realm. Certainly he was the most feared. People still called him the Defender, although the title was empty. Men still referred to him as the Lion's Claw, even though they had passed into a new century and onto a new king. But the man's reputation stayed with him, drawing respect from every corner of the civilized world. They knew this man, this Defender.

But the Defender cared naught for the admiration. His life as a warrior was past, the life a husband and father more demanded than he ever imagined, and far more satisfying. This man, this Defender, who had struggled with war and deception and betrayal to persevere and overcome, this man who would pass into legend for his skill, when it was his generosity and forgiveness that was indeed legendary.

The beating heart of the de Lohr dynasty.

☙ THE END ❧

AFTERWORD

2013:
The following "afterword" was the original epilogue.

I hope you were entertained by Dustin and Christopher – they were certainly entertaining to write about.

I made Christopher an unmovable icon, a man groomed for war his entire life until it was his entire existence. He was so devoted to Richard and his profession because it was all he had ever known. Being virtually abandoned at a young age, he had nothing else but his career. He had no idea that he had a human side until he married a little spitfire of a woman named Dustin Barringdon. I do not believe he consciously ignored his human emotions and feelings, but he was merely uncomfortable with them until he understood what his heart was telling him. By the time all was said and done, no one more than he realized what a miraculous change he had gone through, and no one more than he was as pleased.

And then there was Dustin, a young, spoiled, immature girl who grew into a strong-willed, responsible woman. I truly liked Dustin because she was pure of heart, even if she was stubborn as a mule. She did not want a husband, and Christopher did not want a wife, yet somehow, they quickly realized they could not live without one another. They were both searching for something in life; and with each other, they found it.

Marcus and David were interesting characters; one brave and controlled, one reckless and passionate. It was Marcus' misfortune to have allowed himself to rein out of control where Dustin was concerned. But he believed that nothing could ever come between him and Christopher; not even Christopher's wife, and he was proven very wrong. Wiser for it, he was able to move on with his life. As far as David was concerned, seeing how well his brother had responded to marriage quelled his own fears of the union. He too, succumbed to the inevitable.

King Richard died in 1199 A.D. and his brother John inherited the throne; Richard having left no legitimate heirs. There was a rumor that he had fathered a son at one point, but the boy had no claim to the throne. And, as you know, Lord Robin of the Hood continued to make John's life miserable for a time. It would be interesting to know if Robin and Christopher ever met again under different circumstances.

Yet, most importantly, I *liked* these people. They were strong, moralistic (mostly), and fun to create. I hope you think so, too.

Thank you for allowing me to entertain you.

The de Lohr Dynasty Series contains the following novels:

Archangel

Other novels that Christopher de Lohr appears in:

Devil's Dominion

For more information on other series and family groups, as well as a list of all of Kathryn's novels, please visit her website at: www.kathrynleveque.com.

Bonus Chapters of the exciting Medieval Romance **THE WOLFE** to follow.

1231 A.D. – After a nasty skirmish along the England/Scotland border at Bog Wood, a badly wounded knight has crawled off to die. As women from the Clan Scott fan out across the battlefield to collect the spoils of war, one woman breaks off from the pack. She is sickened by the tradition of stealing valuables off the dead and runs off to hide. In her hiding place, however, lingers the badly wounded knight. The young woman is frightened at first but her natural instinct to lend aid takes over. She tends the knight and saves his life. Little does the Lady Jordan Scott know that she has just saved the life of the dreaded English knight known to her people as The Wolf....

Several months later, peace is proposed along the border. An English groom is offered to a Scots bride. The Lady Jordan Scott is that bride and her groom is the aged and powerful Earl of Teviot, John de Longley. When Lord de Longley sends his mighty and hated army to collect his new bride, the captain of the army personally retrieves Lady Jordan. When Jordan looks upon the fearsome English knight, she realizes there is something oddly familiar about his voice. When the man finally reveals himself, she sees that it is none other than the man whose life she saved. Sir William de Wolfe, the scourge of the Scots, makes his presence known.

William has never forgotten about his Scots angel. One look at the Lady Jordan after all of these months and he is stricken with appreciation and adoration. He has thought of nothing else but the lady since the time she tended his injury and now, his infatuation with her takes flight. As he escorts her back to Northwood Castle to wed his liege, each passing minute sees him fall more and more hopelessly in love with her. Jordan comes to know the man beyond The Wolf of legend, and so the love story begins....

Join William and Jordan in a tale of true and utter devotion, of a love that bleeds beyond the boundaries of Scots and English, and where loyalty, friendship, and family bind them all together in this uncertain and political world. These are the dark days of dark times, but in the midst of a treacherous world of secrets and hatred, William and Jordan share a love that is only dreamt of. Come and be a part of the journey of The Wolf and his lady that transcends time.

PART I

THE WILDS OF THE NORTH

There upon a midnight blue
The knights went riding two by two
Out upon the moonlit moors
Death consumed them, brought by war
Into their midst, a phantom came
Known by heart, this gentle rain
A lady's name…
A river, she was called
Loved and cherished, one and all
This lady known to knights so bold
This is now the story told.
~ Prelude to The Wolfe

CHAPTER ONE

The month of December
Year of our Lord 1231
Skirmish of Bog Wood near Blackadder Water, the England/Scotland border

"BY EVERYTHING THAT is holy, I do hate a battle."

A soft female sigh filled the damp and cool air. The reply was harsh. "So help me, Caladora, if ye faint again I shall take a stick to ye."

Five women stood high atop a hill, looking down upon a grisly scene far below in what was once a peaceful and serene valley. Where lavender heather used to wash amidst the lush green there were now broken, bloody corpses, the result of a fight that had lasted for a day and a night. Now, everything was eerily still with only the occasional cries of the dying. No more sounds of swords; only the sounds of death.

The sun was beginning to set over the distant hills, casting the valley in a shadowed light. To the women waiting on the high hill, it looked as if Hell itself was setting in to begin claiming its souls. It was ended, this battle; one battle in a mightier war that had been going on for as long as anyone could remember. The war for the Scots border.

The Lady Jordan Scott waited with her aunts and cousins, waiting for the signal from her father that would send them down into the valley to begin assessing their own wounded and making sure any enemy wounded were sent into the netherworld. She hated it; all of it. She hated seeing good men die, watching their life blood drain away and listening to their pleas for help. She hated the bloody English for causing all of this blessed pain and suffering because they believed themselves the superior race. All Scots were wild men in their eyes, unthinking and unfeeling, and somehow the English felt compelled to act as their cage-keeper.

But Jordan was anything but wild and unthinking. She had a heart and a mind and soul, sometimes softer than her clansmen would have liked. As the sun continued to set she pulled the hood of her woolen cloak closer, staving off the chill and the gloom. Just when the wait seemed excessive, a shout from one of her father's men released the dam of women who now poured down into the valley. As the dusk deepened, the hunt began.

Jordan was one of the last one into the valley, dragging her feet even when her aunts cast her threatening glares. She ignored them. In fact, she moved away from them so they would not watch every move she made, removing her hood and picking her targets among the dead.

Her long, honey-colored hair hung loose about her as she bent over a young man and began to tug on a gold signet ring. It seemed to be securely stuck to his finger and she swallowed hard; her father would expect her to take out her dirk and cut off the finger, throwing the whole thing into her basket.

She wrinkled her nose at that prospect and let the dead hand fall back to the ground. She was not going to cut off the finger no matter what her father said. She didn't have the stomach for it. But the man at her feet suddenly groaned and Jordan startled with fear; without hesitation, she yanked her dirk from its sheath at her forearm plunged the blade deep into his soft neck. The man stilled, silenced forever by the cold steel of her knife.

Gasping with shock, Jordan stared down at the man and could scarcely believe what she had done. She didn't know why she had done it, only that she had been terrified and afraid if she didn't kill the man that he would rise up and kill her. Her breath came in short, horrified pants as she stared down at her kill. *Sweet Jesu'*, had she deteriorated to such a scared rabbit that she would kill before thinking?

In disgust she threw down her dirk and stumbled away from the dead man, wondering if indeed her father's warring ways were claiming her. Already, she had to get away from the destruction and clear her thoughts. She didn't care if her family thought she was weak. They had tried to toughen her up, to make her strong and fearless, but she didn't have it in her. She was sweet and nurturing, kind and gentle. There were those better suited to tend those on the battlefield and cut fingers off for the gold they wore; she was going to find a place to hide and wait until the hunting and killing was over.

Glancing over her shoulder to see if she was being watched, Jordan wandered away from the field of destruction and into a small valley. Nestled at the bottom among a few scrawny trees was a small stream, the water glistening silver in the moonlight.

It was peaceful and calm, and she could feel her composure returning. She knelt by the stream and washed her hands as if cleansing away the confusion and revulsion she felt. She knew she was a disappointment to her father on two accounts: not being born male, and not being able to sufficiently deal with the normal aspects of being a daughter of one of the fiercest war lords on the Scottish border. Although her father loved her dearly and never made her feel anything less, she knew deep down he wished she were stronger. Sometimes she wished it, too.

Her father did not pretend that he always understood his only child, especially where her loves for music and animals were concerned. Jordan could sing like an angel and could dance a Scottish jig like the devil himself, accomplishments for which he was enormously proud, but sometimes he just could not comprehend the female mind. He was a warrior, a baron by title, and his world was one of death and fighting, not the gentle world where his daughter dwelled.

Still, he would not be pleased if he found out she had run off like a scared goat and sought refuge this night. Jordan found a large boulder by the creek and sat on its icy surface, watching the water bubble in the moonlight and wondering why she wasn't like the rest of her female kin, bold and fearless. Above her, a nighthawk rode the drafts, crying out to its mate and she watched it for a moment before returning moodily to the stream.

"If you are thinking of drowning yourself, 'tis a bit shallow."

The voice came from the darkness behind her. Jordan leapt off the rock, terrified as she whirled to face her accoster. She could make out a form of a man lying at the base of one of the bushy trees but could not make out much more in the darkness.

Panic rose in her throat and she realized with deep regret that she had left her dirk back on the battlefield. She could scream, but he appeared to be large and would most likely pounce and slit her throat before she could utter a sound. She froze, unsure of what to do next. She certainly did not want to provoke the man with the decidedly English accent.

"What…what do ye want?" she demanded shakily.

The moon emerged from behind the clouds, revealing the landscape in bright silver light. Jordan could see right away the man was gravely injured, as there was a great deal of dark blood covering his legs and the ground beneath him. It didn't take her long to figure out that he was unable to rise, much less attack her. Her courage surged and she was sure she could run back and retrieve her dirk before he could move upon her, the damnable English devil. She would do to him exactly what he would do to her given half a chance.

But on the heels of that thought came another. Jordan's blood ran cold with abhorrence; she had just killed one man and punished herself endlessly for it. Now she was planning the death of another. More of her father's violent influence was a part of her than she cared to admit. Perhaps this wounded man was innocent of any killing at all, she thought naïvely. Mayhap he was a victim of the situation, forced to fight by the hated English king. Perhaps he didn't want to fight at all and then found himself a casualty.

Jordan forced herself to calm, realizing that the man could not hurt her. She took a step to get a better look at him yet still kept a healthy distance between them.

"Speak up," she told him, feeling braver. "What are ye doing here? What do ye want?"

She heard the man sigh. "What do I want?" he repeated wearily. "I want to return home. But what I want and what will be are two entirely different things all together. What do you intend to do with me?"

Jordan eyed him beneath the silver moonlight. "I intend to do nothing with ye," she replied softly. "I dunna need to. From the looks of that wound, ye will be dead by morn."

The man laid his head back against the tree in a defeated gesture. "Mayhap," he said, eyeing her in the darkness just as she was eyeing him. "Will you tell me something?"

"What?"

"What is your name?"

She saw no harm in giving her name to a dying man. "Jordan."

His head came up from the trunk. "Jordan? A sound name. Yet it is usually a man's name."

Jordan moved a few steps closer. "My mother, being a pious woman, named me for the River Jordan," she replied. "Jordan Mary Joseph is my full name. Moreover, I was intended to be a male child."

The man's eyes grew intense and Jordan felt a shiver run down her spine. It struck her just how handsome he was, English or no, and her cheeks grew warm.

"You are most definitely not a male child, Jordan Mary Joseph," he said, almost seductively. "How old are you?"

"I have seen twenty years," she replied, flattered and disarmed by his statement.

"Then you are married with children," he stated. "Was your husband on the battlefield?"

"I have no husband," Jordan said flatly. At twenty, she was embarrassed that she had not yet wed; it was a sore subject and one she certainly did not wish to discuss with him.

"No husband?" he repeated, evidently shocked. "Why not?"

She frowned. "Ye ask too many questions, English."

He did not reply. He lay back against the tree again, closing his eyes. His strength was draining and Jordan guessed that his death was swiftly approaching.

As she gazed at him, she began to feel pity for the knight. He was perhaps ten years older than her, still a young man. He was very big with enormous hands and big, muscular legs, and his facial features, although surrounded by mail and a helm, were chiseled and handsome. She was coming to feel sorry that his life would soon be over soon from a wound sustained in a senseless, meaningless skirmish.

A thought occurred to her; she knew that she could make his last hours more comfortable with what she carried in her satchel. The healing items were meant for her own people but she simply could not leave the knight and not help him. It was her soft heart tugging at her, concern for another. She hoped her Scot ancestors moldering in the ground would forgive her treasonous act.

"English," she said softly. "Would ye let me tend yer wound?"

One eye opened in mild surprise. She could see suspicion in the mysterious depths.

"Why?" he whispered. "So you may finish what your clansman started?"

"Nay," she answered, although she didn't blame his distrust. "So that I may make yer last hours a bit more bearable." When he did not reply, she frowned at him. "I promise I wunna intentionally hurt ye. Ye can bleed to death or ye can let me help ye; 'tis all the same to me."

After an eternal pause, he reached up with effort and tore the helmet from his head, revealing dark wet hair plastered to his pasty head. Clumsily, he began to remove his armor.

Jordan closed the distance between them with small, rapid steps and knelt beside him. His hands were heavy and unwieldy and she batted them away, finishing the job of the removal herself. She fumbled a bit with his cuisses, or thigh armor, because the wound was along the edge of the armor where it met his breeches. A vulnerable point, she noticed. She felt a little apprehensive being so close to an English warrior and deliberately avoided his gaze. She could feel his eyes on her, watching every move she made. Her palms began to sweat as she stripped off the remainder of the protective gear.

As Jordan bent over her work, her pink tongue between her teeth in concentration, the knight studied the fine porcelain features and the huge round eyes of the most amazing green color. He could see it even in the moonlight. Her eyebrows arched ever-so-delicately and her lashes were long and dense. She had stopped biting her tongue long enough for him to see that her lips were soft and sensuous.

Her hair licked at him as she moved and the scent of lavender was unmistakable. Her hair was dark blond, straight and silky. Every time she threw the satiny mass over her shoulder to keep it out of her way, he was greeted by the perfume of the purple buds and found it utterly captivating. Even as he stared at her, he could not believe this woman was a Scot; she embodied everything he had always believed they were not. In fact, it took him a moment to realize that she was physically perfect. If God himself had come to him and asked him to describe his perfect mate, he would have described Jordan feature for feature. It was an odd realization.

Unaware of the knight's thoughts, Jordan glanced up and met his gaze and was faced with the most fascinating shade of hazel she had ever seen. Yet for his size and his strength, and the fact that the man was obviously a seasoned knight, they were the kindest eyes she had ever encountered. Unnerved, she tore her eyes away and continued her good deed with draining concentration. The man intimidated her in too many ways to comprehend.

The armor off, Jordan could see the wound in his thigh was substantial. He had packed linen rags on it in an attempt to stop the bleeding, but he had quickly become too weak to do much more. It was a deep, long gash that ran nearly the entire length of his long thigh. She tore his breeches away in an attempt to have a clear field to tend the wound, noticing that his legs were as thick as tree trunks.

Jordan picked bits of material and mail from the wound, wiping at the clotted blood and dirt that had invaded the area. The further involved she became, the more she could see that the gash was all the way to the bone.

Jordan retrieved her bag and began to pull out her aids; whisky, silk thread and needle, and strips of boiled linen.

"Here," she said, thrusting the open whisky bottle at him and keeping her eyes on the wound. "Drink this."

He accepted the bottle from her and he took several long swallows. She took it back from him and set it beside her, pausing with a furrowed brow and thinking that even if he survived the wound, he would surely loose the leg. She did not know that he was still watching her face intently, marveling at the incredible beauty of it.

The knight, in fact, did not make it a habit of gawking at women. Outside of an occasional whore, he had never had a remotely serious relationship with a woman, although there had been many a female who had tried to woo him. He had a great deal of respect for the opposite sex, but Northwood Castle was his life and a wife did not fit into his plans.

"Will I live, Lady Jordan?" he asked after a moment. "Or should I prepare my greeting for St. Peter?"

She sighed and picked up the whisky bottle. Reluctantly, she met his eyes for a brief moment to convey a silent apology before dousing the entire length of the wound with the burning alcohol.

The knight's only reaction was to snap his head away from her so that she could not see his face. Not a sound was uttered nor a twitch of the muscle seen. *Remarkable*, she thought. She had never seen anyone take the pain of a whisky burn so well.

Some women preferred to wash the whisky away with water before closing the wound, but not Jordan. The liquor itself did incredibly well in helping heal wounds and preventing infection, so she left it on and took her threaded needle and began to sew up the laceration. She worked quickly, knowing the pain was unbearable and was continually amazed that the soldier had yet to utter one word. She had seen men scream and faint in similar situations.

When she was finally finished, she laid a strip of clean linen the length of the wound and bound him twice about the thigh to hold it in place, once at the top of his leg and once near the knee. She worked so fast that she knew she was not doing a very good job, just wanting to be done with her charitable act hurriedly lest she be discovered. She was increasingly concerned that her aunts and cousins would come looking for her. She knew that jostling him about must be excruciating, yet he had not so much as flinched.

Only when she had stopped completely did he turn his head back to look at her, and she swallowed at the agony she read in his eyes. She found new respect for this Englishman who bore his pain with stoic silence. She began to hope that he would live, although she did not know why. She furthermore wished she had done a better mending job on his leg, taking the time she took with her own wounded.

"I dunna know what good I have done for ye," she said quietly.

He grasped her soft hand tightly in his clammy one. Jordan stiffened, startled by the action and fighting the urge to yank her hand away.

"You are an angel of mercy," he whispered. "I thank you for your efforts, my lady. I shall do my best not to betray them."

His sincerity was gripping. Gently, she removed her hand and put her things away. The half-moon was high above and the scattered clouds had disappeared, bathing the land in a silver glow. Jordan felt as if she had done something good this night, albeit to the enemy and she felt better now than she had earlier when she first descended to the stream. Mayhap fate had led her to the stream purposely to find the soldier and tend him. She suddenly felt like returning to the battlefield to continue with her expected duties.

"I must return, English." She rose and gave him a long look. "I will forget that I saw ye here."

She turned to leave but he stopped her.

"My name is Sir William de Wolfe," he said with quiet authority. "Remember it, for I shall return one day to thank you properly and I do not wish to be cut down while bearing a gift."

It took a moment, but even in the moonlight he saw her face go white and her jaw slacken.

"*Sweet Jesu'*," she gasped. "Surely ye're not the English captain they call The Wolf?"

He looked at her, sensing her surge of fear. He sighed; he did not want her to fear him. This was the one time when he wished his reputation had not preceded him.

"I simply said my name was de Wolfe, not *The Wolf*," he murmured.

She looked extremely dubious. "But ye were in his command?"

He shrugged vaguely. "Now, back to what I said," he said, shifting the subject. "I will return with a proper reward for you. Will you accept it?"

She could not be sure that the knight wasn't, in fact, the hated Wolf, but it was truly of no matter now. It was done. Perhaps she did not want to believe he was the hated and feared devil, so she chose to believe as such. How could she live with herself if it was discovered that she had tended to the man that had killed more kinsmen that she could count? She knew she could not, so she forced herself to believe his words. Furthermore, her aunt had said The Wolf was dark and devilish. This man was uncannily beautiful in a masculine sense.

After a moment's pause, she finally spoke. "English, if ye survive this wound then I will gladly accept yer gift."

He smiled weakly, deep dimples in both cheeks and her heart fluttered strangely in her chest. He was indeed the most handsome man she had ever seen, even if he was English. But she had the most horrible lurking feeling that he was indeed who she feared he was. It made her want to run.

"Luck be with ye," she said as she abruptly turned and trudged back up the hill.

William watched the figure in the billowing cloak, his pain-clouded mind lingering on the silken hair and beautiful face. He had never seen such a fine woman. Angel was certainly an apt term. If she were to be the last person he saw on earth then he would die a contented man.

He suspected that she did not believe his evasive answer but, thankfully, had made no more mention of it. The thought that she feared and hated him brought a curious tightness in his stomach that he quickly attributed to his helpless state. He did not want to admit that it might be regret.

He was growing weaker with each breath. His strength was waning as he leaned back against the tree, wondering if he would again see the light of morning. He closed his eyes for he could not keep them open, and without realizing it, his mind drifted into unconsciousness, safe and warm and dark.

CHAPTER TWO

April, Year of our Lord 1232
Langton Castle, 17.7km northwest of the English border

"WHAT A LOVELY day," Caladora exclaimed softly. "This is the first day the sun has dared show itself in months."

Jordan eyed her cousin from behind her tapestry loom. "Bright the day, I shall give ye, but there is still a chill in my bones."

"Yer always cold, Jordan." The comment came from another cousin, Jemma. The brunette-haired lass stabbed at a pretty piece of embroidery. "Yer hands are like ice even on the warmest days."

"Always," Jordan concurred regretfully.

Caladora Scott, daughter of Nathaniel and Anne Scott, sat back to her needlework. Tall and lovely in a fragile way, she had the luxurious red hair with highlights of gold, a color enhanced on her older brothers Robert and Benjamin.

Jemma Scott, on the other hand, was as short and dark as Caladora was tall and fair, but she well-proportioned and busty. She was a very pretty girl and a possessed the true fire of a Scot; with three older brothers, she had learned to take care of herself. Her father Matthew was forever chiding his daughter on the true qualities of a lady, lest he never marry her off, but her mother Lilith had given up lecturing Jemma a long time ago.

Jemma would marry in due time, her mother knew, but her husband would have to possess the patience of Job and the strength of Samson to handle her. She had been betrothed shortly after birth to a young lad from the McKean clan; however, the lad had died at five years of age and Matthew was reluctant to promise her again due to her wild nature. No man wanted to tame the wild horse.

"Isn't it wonderful that the English have finally come to their senses and have given us a few months of peace?" Caladora sighed, distracting the others from their wandering thoughts.

Jordan shrugged, biting at her lip in concentration. "We shall see how long it lasts. I dunna trust the English."

"And what of the messenger that arrived yesterday?" Jemma wanted to know. "My father said he came from the English king himself."

Jordan scowled. "Pah. He was probably sent here to demand our unconditional surrender."

"Jordi, ye are a cynical soul," Caladora said.

" 'Tis my right to be cynical," Jordan replied. "I have seen war and death by the English for nigh twenty years now. I canna trust them."

There was a knock at the solar door. A soldier in the green and red Scott tartan entered and bowed deeply.

"Ladies, Laird Scott requests Lady Jordan's presence in his hall immediately," he said.

Jordan secured the loom sticks and brushed her hands against her brown brocade surcoat. "Mayhap me Da wishes me to chase off the English messenger," she muttered.

Caladora and Jemma giggled at their cousin's jest and returned to their sewing when the door slammed shut.

Jordan found her father alone in the cavernous great hall of Langton Castle that smelled of smoke and rushes. Generations of Scotts had walked these floors, had spoken within these walls, and it reeked of family and war and the passion that was in every Scotsman. Thomas sat in his large oak chair, his graying brow furrowed. He watched his beautiful daughter sweep gracefully into the room, her surcoat swirling and her long hair flowing.

His heart was breaking. For the sake of his clan, his family and peasants alike, he was being forced into a precarious position and Jordan was to become the sacrificial lamb. He dreaded telling her that her future was to be irrevocably changed. His stomach was twisting in knots of anxiety so that he wished he could die rather than have to tell her what was to come.

His sweet Jordan Margaret, the only child he and his beloved Elinor had been blessed with. With Elinor gone, Jordan had been his life and his salvation, and now he would lose that, too. He wondered if his grief would kill him.

"Greetings, Da," she kissed him.

Thomas forced a smile and grasped her hand. "Sit wi' me, Jordan." He moved to the side and allowed her a corner of the huge chair. "Give the old man a hug."

He put his arms about his daughter and held her tightly for a moment as he collected his thoughts. Jordan could sense something in his manner and she was puzzled. He was usually loud and supremely confident, but not today. He seemed pensive and subdued. She didn't like it.

"What's amiss?" she asked.

Thomas looked at her, memorizing each feature. He knew he had to tell her before he lost his courage. He'd already put it off as long as he could and if he delayed further, he might never tell her at all. With every breath he took, his bravery was waning.

"Yesterday a messenger arrived from King Henry," he began.

"I know, I saw him," she replied.

"He brought a missive," Thomas replied, trying to keep his manner calm and even. Jordan was sharp and would pick up on any apprehension. "Apparently the man is as weary as we are of the border wars and wishes to seal a peace."

Jordan's eyes darkened. "Dunna trust him," she said. "He will strike when yer guard is down."

"I think not," her father said patiently. "We will both be sacrificing a great deal for this peace and neither would do anything to jeopardize it."

His words didn't make much sense but she knew she didn't like them. She was suspicious and forced her father to look at her.

"What sacrifice?" she demanded. "What are the demons demanding from ye? Our land? Money? What then?"

Thomas was riveted to her green eyes, intensely so. He dreaded bringing forth the words but he had to. "Ye," he finally murmured. " 'Tis ye he is demanding, lass."

Jordan stared at him as the news set in. Then her eyes widened enormously until they threatened to pop from their sockets. Thomas tried to anticipate her reaction, wanting so badly to beg forgiveness and plead understanding.

He could not bear it if she hated him forever. He wanted to explain everything to her, to make her understand that he made the best decision he felt he could. He prayed she would grasp his battle-weary reasons. He was so very tired of fighting and dying for a bloody bit of land.

"What?" she gasped, then louder. "He *what?*"

Steady, man, Thomas told himself. *Be strong*. "I promised ye in marriage to a noble of the king's choosing to cement a peace alliance," he said evenly. "This will be a great honor for ye, Jordan. You will be the instrument of peace for our clan and for the generations yet to come. Do ye not understand that, lass?"

"Nay." She shot up from the chair. "I dunna want to marry an Englishman. They are our enemy, men who have killed our kin and our friends. How can ye ask me this?"

Thomas remained strong in the face of her frightened and furious barrage. "I am not asking ye, I am *telling* ye, and ye will do as I say," he said, somewhat coldly. "Jordan, I am Laird of clan Scott. Ye are my only daughter. 'Tis yer duty to do what is asked of ye, whether or not it is agreeable. Do you think that if I had any other options that I wunna take them? I am not doing this to punish ye, lass. I have no choice."

Jordan just stared at him. Then, she had to sit down or fall down. From fury to despondency, her manner swiftly changed as realization settled deep. It was sickening as well as terrifying. All of the dreams and hopes she had ever held for her future had been dashed in a series of brief, brutal statements. She was reeling.

"Do ye realize what ye are asking of me?" she finally whispered. "Ye are asking me to bed with our enemy, to bear his children, to be loyal to his house and hold. That is not a punishment, Da; it is a death sentence."

He approached her. "It will be what ye make of it."

She glared at him. "It will be what my husband makes of it."

Thomas could not lose control of the situation now; he was struggling not to feel pity for her. He had to let her know that there was no room for discussion.

"What I have done to seal a peace is certainly nothing new in the trials of history, Jordan," he said. "Yer new husband, I am sure, is just as distraught over this arrangement as ye are. If ye will show him a quiet and obedient wife, then I am sure that he will treat ye accordingly. The messenger has already been sent on his way with a reply to King Henry, and I am sure we will hear from the man within the month. Ye had better prepare yerself."

It was done. Jordan hung her head miserably and Thomas swore that his heart would break If he had to look at her another minute. But he was not beyond showing compassion for what he had done to her. Moving to his daughter, he gently touched her honey-blond head.

"Jordi-girl, I love you more than anything in this world," he said softly, feeling her pain along with his own. "I dinna want to do this, but I must think of the entire clan's future. Ye are our best hope for peace. Would ye rather that I had pledged Jemma or Caladora in yer stead?"

She sighed in defeat. "Of course not," she murmured. " 'Tis my duty as daughter of laird Scott and I wunna let ye delegate the duty to anyone else simply because I am a-feared to go. But what if my new husband is a horrible man and locks me in the tower to rot? What he beats me or sends me to whore? What if he doesna honor the treaty at all?"

Thomas stroked her hair. "We will have to trust the English, Jordan. I know it is difficult, but we must show faith."

She shook her head slowly. "You ask much," she said. "After all of the pain the English have caused, ye ask a great deal."

Thomas sighed faintly. "That's why I am making the greatest sacrifice of all," he whispered. "I am sending my own flesh into the enemy camp as a show of good faith and I expect the same from them."

She watched her father's expression and began to forget her own fear and anger. At that moment, she started down the path to understanding the extent of her father's love for her.

Jordan had been selfish, of course, for she had only thought of her own feelings as if she were the only one who had any. Thomas was hurting, too. He'd had to make the most difficult decision of his life and she was making it far more difficult by arguing with him. If there had been another way, she knew he would have done it. As much as she loathed the idea of marrying an English lord, she would if her father wanted her to.

"Oh, Dada," she whispered, shaking her head. "I am afraid. I am so afraid. To live out my life with people who hate the very sight of me is a horrible sentence to bear."

Thomas' insides were aching for her. "I know, my sweet lass," he muttered. "It is killing me to know that. But….there was nothing else I could have done. I can only hope that someday ye will find it in yer heart to forgive me."

Her head came up. "For what? For doing as ye must?" she asked. "There is nothing to forgive. I can only hope now that the English king selects a suitable husband for me. At least someone I could grow to tolerate over the years."

Her father cracked a smile. "And someone who can tolerate yer endless singing and fondness for clothes."

She smiled back in feigned outrage. "My singing is not endless and there is nothing wrong with liking pretty things."

He gave her a wry smirk. "You have a coat for every day of the year."

The mood was lightening as he teased her and Jordan rose to the taunt. "Mayhap if I make my new husband go broke, he will send me home," she teased lightly, watching him roll his eyes in agreement. She watched his tired face, glad to see he was smiling somewhat, as she sobered. "I wunna disappoint ye da. I shall be the very model of a Scots lady."

Thomas smiled bravely and hugged her fiercely, drawing strength from her. "I know," he said softly. There was nothing more he could say.

The time would be upon them before they knew it.

Read the rest of **THE WOLFE** in eBook or in paperback.

Now, please enjoy bonus chapters from ARCHANGEL, Gart Forbes' novel. ARCHANGEL is available in eBook, paperback, or in audiobook format.

CHAPTER ONE

Year of Our Lord 1204 A.D.
The Month of May
Dunster Castle, Somerset

HE WAS SEEING ghosts.

It was true that he was weary after having spent the last seven days traveling from Kent to the shadowed edges of the Exmoor Forest. It was also true that the wilds of Somerset and Cornwall were said to breed wraiths and other netherworld creatures, and Dunster was right in the middle of dark and mysterious lands. But being a man of logic, Sir Gart Forbes wasn't one to believe in ghosts or phantoms or fairies. Still, he wasn't quite sure what he had seen.

He was standing in the darkened bailey of Dunster just after sunset. The castle was perched on the top of a hill, fortified and old even in Saxon times, and the battlements were lined with men standing guard, sentries with big dogs and big torches to keep away the night. Gazing up the wooden steps that led into the second floor of the enormous square keep, Gart swore he saw something at the top of the stairs that had just as quickly vanished.

All around him were sounds of the bailey as the men settled in for the night. He had brought one hundred men with him from Denstroude Castle in Kent, seat of Baron Thornden, Sir David de Lohr. Lord de Lohr was in the keep up in the third floor great hall and these wraiths, these wispy creatures, were between Gart and his liege. With a weary sigh, knowing he must have lost his mind somewhere back on the dusty road, Gart slowly mounted the steps.

The stairs were dark and old. Gart's enormous boots tested the weight of each plank as he made his way up and could hear the wood groan. Normally, he would have been focused on the meal awaiting him, but at this moment, he had to admit he was curious to see if the wraiths would make another appearance.

He didn't have long to wait. The moment he stepped inside the great Norman arch that embraced the entry, something small and white jumped into his path.

"Boo!"

Before Gart could open his mouth to speak, the phantom darted off and hid. It wasn't so much a phantom now that he had a closer look – it was a child, completely white from head to toe. Gart watched the child disappear into a darkened room, a solar that was directly off the entry to the right. His brow furrowed and he shook his head, undecided as to whether he was irritated or amused. He settled for amused until two more wraiths jumped out at him with sticks.

Gart was in armor so he didn't feel the blows, but his amusement quickly turned to irritation when one of the sticks landed a blow a little too close to his groin. He reached down to grab one of the children but his hand came away completely white. They were covered in something white and powdery.

Gart grabbed a stick that came flying at his groin again, yanking it out of the child's hand and tossing it out the door. He locked gazes with a boy no more than seven years of age and he would never forget the look of fury on the boy's face.

With a yell, the child charged him and tried to bite him, but all he came away with was mail to the mouth. Gart grabbed the child by the hair and the boy screamed.

"Let me go!" he howled. "I will have you arrested if you do not let me go!"

Gart's hand was bigger than the child's head as he gazed down at him. "Is that so?"

"It is!" The lad tried to kick him, struggling to dislodge the iron grip. "If you do not let me go, I… I will have you boiled! I will have you flogged! I will have you…!"

Gart put up a hand, cutting him off. "I understand your meaning," he said, noticing that the two other white-covered children were beating at his armored legs. He shoved one away by the head and kneed the other one across the floor. It wasn't a kick as much as it was a good push with his kneecap. Then he let go of the child in his grip.

"Let me pass and you can assault the next fool who walks in the door," he told them.

The three boys were not so easily dissuaded. They rushed back at him with their fists and sticks and Gart shoved them all away again, only to have them rush him once more as he tried to mount the stairs to the third level.

Irritation growing, he managed to grab all three of them, carry them over to the dark and empty solar, and shove them inside. Slamming the door closed, he noticed there was no exterior bolt as the boys beat at the door and yelled from the other side. Gart stood there as long as he could, holding the door shut as delicious smells taunted him from the hall above. He didn't have time for this foolishness. Daring to let go of the latch, he made a break for the stairs.

The solar door flew open and the three boys charged out, catching Gart as he was halfway up the spiral stone stairs. They grabbed at his feet and he kicked back, attempting to dislodge them. He didn't want to outright hurt them but they were annoying and beastly, so he finally kicked out and sent one boy crashing into the other two.

The whole lot of them slid down the stairs, leaving a trail of white powder as they went. They hit hard in a group, the older ones falling on the smaller one. The little lad at the bottom of the pile began to wail loudly and rub his head where he had smacked it.

Gart smirked at the screams, thinking now they would finally leave him alone. He hadn't taken two steps before he started to feel some remorse. They were just children, after all. He had been a child once, thirty years ago during times he could hardly remember. These children were just playing games. At least, he hoped so. Maybe they were really murderers in disguise. Taking another step, the cries prevented him from continuing.

With a heavy sigh he turned on the stairwell, peering down at the pile of boys at the bottom. The two older ones were attempting to pick the younger one up and convince him that he wasn't injured. Gart took a couple of steps down, watching the boys who seemed much less aggressive than they had been moments earlier.

"What are you three doing?" he demanded softly.

Three pairs of big blue eyes looked up at him as if startled by the question. He could see the hostility seep back into their expressions but, so far, not one of them had made a move against him. They seemed to be posturing an awful lot.

"Brendt hurt his head," the tallest child said angrily. "You did…."

Gart waved the boy off. "That is not what I meant," he took another step down. "What are you three doing attacking men who enter the keep?"

The tallest boy's brow furrowed. "Robbing them!"

Gart couldn't help it as his features screwed up in confusion. "*Robbing* them?"

"Aye," the boy insisted. "This is our castle. Whoever comes in this door belongs to us."

Gart stared at the lad a moment before finally shaking his head. Truth be told, he was fighting off a grin. The lad was deadly serious.

"Who are you?" he finally asked.

The boy stood tall. "Romney de Moyon," he announced. "These are my brothers, Orin and Brendt. Our father is Julian de Moyon, Baron Buckland, and this is our castle. Who are you?"

Gart came down the rest of the stairs and stood in front of them, massive fists resting on his hips. He avoided the question. "Why do you have white powder all over you?"

Romney looked at his brothers before returning his attention to Gart. "Because we are ghosts. You cannot see ghosts and it makes it easier to rob people."

Gart rubbed his hand over his chin and mouth so the boy would not see his grin. It was really quite dastardly and very humorous, he thought.

"I see you quite clearly," he ran a finger across Romney's chest, peering at the white powder. "What is this?"

"Dust from the stone," Romney told him. "Father is building a house for the soldiers and this is the dust from the white stone."

Gart inspected it a moment longer before wiping it on his tunic. His gaze moved to the youngest, who was no longer crying, but still rubbing his head.

"Had you not attacked me, you would not have hurt your head," he was looking at the smallest boy but lecturing all three. "Does your father know what you are doing?"

Romney lifted his shoulders, for the first time losing some of his confidence. "He does not care," he said. "Will you give me your money or will I have to fight you to the death?"

Gart bit his lip to keep his smile from breaking loose. "Are you sure you want to fight me to the death?"

"I am sure."

"I do not have any money on me."

Romney's fair brow furrowed and he looked to his brothers with uncertainty. "Well," he said reluctantly. "We will wait until you return for it. Come back with your money."

"I will not," Gart said flatly. "Why do you want my money, anyway?"

"Because," Romney said. "We want to buy nice things for my mother and sister."

Gart scratched his head. "Your mother and sister?" he repeated. "Surely they have enough nice things."

Romney shrugged. "It makes them happy. When Mother is crying, it will make her stop."

Gart scratched at his chin again, a little puzzled at the last sentence but he didn't pursue it.

"I see," he said. "I am afraid that I am going to disappoint you, your mother and your sister. You will have to get your ill-gotten gains somewhere else."

Romney didn't like that answer at all. It was clear he wasn't used to having his wishes denied. Gart eyed the children one more time before turning for the stairs and the three were on him in an instant with their fists and sticks. Gart rolled his eyes with frustration as he grabbed Romney by the arm and twisted it behind his back. Romney screamed and the other two lads stopped their onslaught.

"Oww!" Romney howled. "You are hurting me!"

Gart lifted an eyebrow. "I am getting tired of being attacked simply because I walked into this keep," he said in a low voice. "If you promise to cease your assault, I will let you go. Otherwise, I will bind all three of you and toss you into a closet."

Before the boy could reply, they heard a voice from the floor above. It was a female voice, soft and sweet, and soon the swish of a voluminous surcoat could be seen and heard. Great yards of crimson fabric descended the stairs, calling for Romney and Orin. As Gart stood there with Romney's arm twisted behind his back, a vision in red appeared.

"Romney!" the woman gasped. "What has happened? Are you injured?"

Gart stared at the woman in surprise, although his stone-like features did not give him away. He was actually stunned speechless for a moment as a vision from his past made an unexpected appearance. Although it had been years since he had last seen her, there was no mistaking the ethereal beauty. There wasn't anything like it anywhere else in England.

"Emberley?" he asked hesitantly. "Emberley de Russe?"

The Lady Emberley de Russe de Moyon came to a halt when she heard her name, staring at the enormous knight with shock and some fear. He had her son by the arm and the child was in obvious pain, but as she gazed at the man, he began to look vaguely familiar.

From the mists of her memories emerged the face as a very young man, someone her brother had been friends with. She had known that face well, long ago. Now he had grown into a strikingly handsome man. Her deep blue eyes lit up with recognition.

"Gart?" she asked.

Her voice was soft with uncertainty. Gart's green eyes glittered as he nodded his head, realizing he still had Romney by the arm and hastening to release the child. He tried not to feel guilty that this glorious creature had witnessed him roughing up the child.

"It is me." He just stared at her, a rather soft expression coming over his masculine features. "I have not seen you in years."

Emberley smiled broadly, a dimple on her chin and beautiful straight teeth. "It has been some time," she agreed. "I believe the last time I saw you was when I had just returned home from fostering at Chepstow Castle and you and my brother were newly knighted."

He nodded. "I recall," he said. "That was many years ago."

She warmed to the recognition. "Twelve years, at least," she agreed, cocking her head thoughtfully. "I also seem to remember that on the day I returned you and my brother tore through the outer ward on your chargers, slicing up anything that did not have a heartbeat. My mother yelled at you and my brother for an hour after it was over."

Gart was grinning, an unusual occurrence for him. The man had features of stone and cracking a smile was something that did not come easily. He was trying not to appear too embarrassed.

"We could not help ourselves," he admitted. "Erik had a new sword that your father had given him. We wanted to make sure that it worked properly."

Emberley laughed in remembrance. "My mother took it away for a week," she snorted. "Erik and my father were furious."

Gart's smile grew as he stared at the woman. His last memory of her was a slip of a girl barely past womanhood but to see her now, he could hardly believe the change. She was positively magnificent. His eyes moved over her luscious blond hair, arranged into a beautiful style that had it pulled off her face and trailing down her back. She had spectacular dark blue eyes, like sapphires, and ruby lips that were parted in a magnificent smile. The longer he looked at her, the more enamored he became.

"I was banned from visiting Morton Castle for a while," he said, wanting off the subject of his wild youth. "But that was long ago and now I find you at Dunster. Why are you here?"

Emberley lifted her hand as if to embrace the entire structure. "I live here," she replied. "You and my brother were in the Holy Land with Richard when I was betrothed to Julian de Moyon. Did you not hear of it?"

He shook his head. "I will confess, I did not," he said, somewhat regretfully. "My focus was on sand and battles until… well, until Erik was killed. Then I returned home to more battles and more intrigue."

Her smile faded, her dark blue eyes glimmering warmly at him. "I heard that you brought my brother home for burial," she said softly. "I never had the chance to thank you. It meant a great deal to my parents."

"Do they live still?"

She nodded. "Still," she said quietly. "They live at Morton Castle and have never gotten over the death of my brother. The fact that I have sons has eased their grief somewhat."

Gart gazed into her lovely eyes, the same color and shape as her brother's had been. He realized he missed his best friend very much, someone he'd not thought of in almost eight years. It was a sobering realization.

"Erik was a great knight," he said somberly. "He is missed."

Emberley smiled in agreement, in sympathy, knowing that her brother and Gabriel Forbes had been best friends since childhood. In fact, she had practically grown up knowing Forbes, a man known as Gart because he didn't like to be called Gabriel. To see him now brought her a great deal of emotional comfort in a life that knew little.

He was an enormous man, very tall, with a muscular body and long, muscular legs. He had sculpted cheekbones and a square jaw, and murky green eyes that were mysterious and intense. His hair, a dark shade of dark blond, had been practically shaved from his scalp but it did not detract from his virile, male handsomeness. The man was powerfully and painfully handsome.

Truth be told, Emberley had always been fond of Gart. As a young girl, she would dream of marrying him. But those days were long gone, as were her dreams. As she thought on the faded days of her childhood, she glanced at her boys and realized they were covered in white powder. Her brow furrowed.

"Why are my children dusty white?" she pointed at them.

Gart tore his eyes off her to look at the boys. "These are your children?"

She nodded. "Romney is my eldest," she smiled at the boy with pride. "He is an intelligent lad, sweet and loving. Orin is my middle son and Brendt is the youngest. Boys, why are you covered in white powder?"

She addressed her sons, who had a complete change of demeanor since her arrival and were now innocent little angels.

"We were playing, Mama," Orin insisted. "We were ghosts."

Emberley's delicate eyebrows lifted. "Ghosts? Why on earth are you ghosts?"

Romney took charge of the conversation before Orin blew their cover. "Because," he said simply, hoping that would be enough to satisfy his mother. "Mama, can we eat in the hall tonight? I want to see all of the knights!"

Emberley shook her head. "Nay," she told him. "You must eat in your chamber. Your father has business to attend to and does not want you underfoot." She looked at Gart. "Am I to understand that you have met my sons already?"

Gart wasn't sure how to answer. He looked at the boys, who all gazed back at him quite innocently. He didn't believe it for a moment. In fact, he was resisting the urge to scowl at them with disbelief.

"Aye," he said slowly, reluctantly. "I have just arrived and the boys were… that is to say, they were…."

"Mama," Romney latched on to his mother's arm. "We were going to show Sir Gart to the hall. May we do that, Mama? May we, please?"

"Of course, sweetheart," Emberley smiled at her eldest. "That is quite gracious of you."

Gart eyed the boys suspiciously as the youngest one reached out and took his big hand. "We will show you, Sir Gart," he said politely. "Come with us."

Gart didn't want to pull away from the child because he didn't want to offend Emberley. He stood there dumbly as the boy took his hand and Emberley smiled happily.

" 'Tis so good to see you again, Gart," she said sincerely, her dark blue gaze drifting over his handsome features. "It has been a very long time. Much has happened since you and I last saw one another. I would like to know what you have been doing in the twelve years since I last saw you."

Gart could only nod. Realizing she was the baron's wife dampened his enthusiasm at their re-acquaintance and he was coming to think that he had been very, very stupid as a young man not to have realized her potential. True, she'd always been a lovely girl, but had he known she would have grown into such an exquisite creature, he might have vied for her hand. But that thought was tempered by the fact that she had apparently raised three hooligans who had her completely fooled. The woman was raising a pack of wild animals.

Emberley smiled at him and beckoned him to follow her back up the stairs. He did so willingly, gladly, but the moment she turned her back on the boys and headed up the stairs, the youngest one yanked his hand from Gart's fist and began smacking him on the leg.

Romney, too, waited until his mother's back was turned before shaking a fist at Gart, making horrible and threatening faces at him. Orin still had a stick and he whacked Gart on the back with it. Gart grabbed the stick and tossed it away but when Emberley turned around at the sounds coming from behind her, the four of them froze and smiled innocently at her. Emberley grinned and continued up the stairs.

The attack against Gart resumed and continued all the way into the great hall above.

CHAPTER TWO

"FORBES IS THE one they call 'Sach'."

Baron Buckland looked at the man who spoke. "What does that mean?"

Sir David de Lohr, Baron Thornden, wriggled his blond eyebrows, noticing that Forbes was entering the smelly, smoky hall in the company of a very beautiful woman.

De Lohr and Baron Buckland sat at the far end of the long, scrubbed table, enjoying the heat from the enormous hearth and the fine alcohol. Now their focus was on the pair approaching from the darkened entry.

"It is an abbreviated Celtic name," de Lohr told him quietly. "It means 'insane'."

Julian de Moyon, Baron Buckland, lifted his dark eyebrows. "Insane?" he repeated. "The man is mad?"

De Lohr shrugged vaguely, collecting his half-drained cup of tart port wine. "Not in the literal sense," he said, his voice lowering as Forbes drew near. "But there is no one fiercer on the field of battle or in the face of adversity. He is absolutely fearless and skilled beyond compare."

Julian's gaze moved between the enormous knight with the shaved head and chiseled features, and his wife as they approached the table.

"He is a giant," he commented quietly. "Look of the size of his hands."

De Lohr nodded slightly as he lifted his cup. "Those hands can rip a man's head from his body. I have seen it myself. I pity the man who truly enrages Forbes."

Julian looked at him, shocked, as Gart and Emberley reached the table. Emberley's warm smile turned into something forced as she focused on her husband.

"My lord," she addressed him. "This is Sir Gart Forbes, a man who was friends with my brother long ago. Gart and I knew each other when we were very young."

Julian eyed Gart, more focused on his wife. "Get out," he snapped. "The men have business to conduct."

Emberley's smile faded and her cheeks turned red, reflexive reaction to her husband's humiliation. He hadn't even acknowledged her polite introduction, which wasn't unusual. Still, she was embarrassed even though she should have been used to the treatment after all of these years.

"I will bid you gentlemen a good eve," she said politely to the table, turning to Gart one last time. "I hope to see you before you leave so we may finish our conversation."

Before Gart could reply, Julian slammed his fist against the table. "I told you to leave, woman. Go before I take my hand to you."

Gart eyed the baron, looking to Emberley and seeing how ashamed she was. He didn't like the way the man spoke to her. His first impression of the baron was not a good one. He smiled at Emberley, a gesture that those who knew him did not believe he was capable of. Gart Forbes was not a man who smiled, in any case.

"I will not leave before speaking with you, my lady," he said kindly. "Good eve to you."

Emberley's trembling smile turned real as she silently thanked him for his graciousness. Gathering her skirts, she fled the hall as Gart watched. His gaze lingered on the empty doorway a moment, thinking of Emberley and her three wild, beasty boys before returning his attention to the table. Seeing the baron and his crass manners, he was coming to see why the boys behaved as they did. He was coming to not like what he was seeing.

But he was a mere knight and his opinion was not of issue. He did what he was told to do and served whoever his liege directed. Without a word he sat down, collecting his cup and taking a large measure of wine only to realize that Julian was staring at him. Gart stared back, noting the small, dark-haired man with the bushy mustache.

"You are Forbes?" Julian confirmed.

Gart nodded shortly. "Aye, my lord."

"I have heard much of your abilities."

Gart simply nodded and Julian sat forward in his seat. He seemed to be taking a good deal of interest in studying him. The man was enormous, no doubt. Everything about him was big, from the top of his shaved head to the bottom of his massive feet. His voice was so deep that it seemed to bubble up from the ground. But it was his eyes that had Julian's attention – they had a sinister and calculating look about them.

As Julian gazed at the man, he could see why the soldiers had nicknamed him "Sach." From what he could see, it suited him.

"I understand you have been in Normandy for the past year, fighting on the king's behalf," Julian finally said.

Gart regarded the baron, his hand tightening around his cup. "I have, my lord," he replied.

"How did the battles fare?"

"My lord?"

"Were they well supplied and well commanded?"

Gart wasn't sure of the motivation behind the question but he nodded. "They were, my lord."

Julian digested the answer and, satisfied, moved on. "Am I to understand that you know my wife?"

"I do, my lord," Gart answered. "Her brother and I were the best of friends until his death in The Levant."

Julian snorted as he collected his wine cup. "Then you know she has always been a beautiful girl," he took a long drink of wine and smacked his lips. "She has provided me with three fine sons, perhaps the only thing that keeps her useful to me other than her obvious beauty."

Gart didn't react to the statement although he didn't like the way the man said it. Having nothing to say to him, he returned to his drink as Julian turned to the baron seated to his left.

"Does he know that you are sending him back to France?" he asked.

David glanced at Gart. "That has not been decided yet," he said evenly. "I am here to discuss the possibility. You and my brother are allies and he has asked me to come to Dunster to hear of your situation. I was told there was an issue with your lands in France."

Julian shook his head. "Not my lands," he said. "The queen's lands. Even as John fights to regain what he has lost in Normandy, his wife also has lands that are compromised. She needs protection and I have sworn to help her."

De Lohr wasn't too quick to support his claim. "What do you have to do with the queen?"

Julian smiled lazily, toying with his cup. "Have you not heard, my friend?" he flicked a careless wrist. "The queen and I are madly in love. She has my heart and I would do anything for her, including defending her lands against Philip Augustus. The French king envies her properties near Angouleme and I have sworn to keep them safe, which is why I need your assistance."

De Lohr sighed faintly. He had heard from his brother, the powerful Earl of Hereford and Worcester, that Baron Buckland was something of a political player and an opportunist. The man had rich lands, however, and a great deal of money and manpower, and spent a great deal of time in London soliciting the favor of the king. It seemed that he had garnered the favor of the queen instead.

"Surely she has enough troops," David said. "She cannot possibly need more men."

Julian poured himself more wine. "She is afraid," he said. "Afraid of the French king, afraid of her own mother who rules similar lands… the woman needs help and I have sworn to obtain it. Will you not supply me with men and knights for this purpose?"

It was evident that David was resistant. Gart stayed out of the conversation, listening to his liege and Buckland go back and forth on what was, and was not, appropriate support. Gart had served de Lohr for six years and knew the man and his family were rigidly opposed to John. They had been strong supporters of Richard until four years ago when the man was killed in France. Then, they had no choice but to support John as the rightful king. It was something that still left a bad taste in their mouths.

Gart sat at the table for quite some time listening to the arguing and pleading. He ate, he drank, and he generally grew weary of the bickering. Finally excusing himself just after midnight, he intended to return to the stables to collect his bags and then find a warm corner of Dunster to sleep in. He was exhausted and decided to let the barons do their bickering alone. He had no say in it, anyway.

Taking the spiral stairs down to the entry level, he could see remnants of white powder on the floor and steps. He half expected the three little hooligans to come jumping out at him again and knew, reasonably, that they would be in bed and long asleep by now. Quitting the keep, he took the wooden stairs to the bailey and proceeded across the dark, dusty ward.

The moon was full overhead, casting the landscape in an eerie silver glow. Gart glanced up at the sky, seeing a million stars spread across the dark expanse. It was a beautiful night and unseasonably clear.

As he lowered his gaze in search of the stables, he could see the sentries upon the battlements as pinpoints of torch light moved through the darkness. Somewhere, a dog barked. Just as the stables came into view to the northeast section of the castle, his gaze fell upon a small and lone figure near the northeast tower.

He wouldn't have paid any attention except the figure turned and began to walk, and he noticed immediately that it wasn't a soldier. It was too small and too finely wrapped. Drawing closer, he realized he was gazing up at a woman as she walked the battlements.

Not only was it very late for a lone woman to be taking a nightly stroll, it was also unsafe. Only someone very comfortable with her position within the castle would show such confidence walking alone. Curious, he made his way to the northeast turret and took the stairs to the battlements.

The battlements were long and narrow, perched high on the walls of Dunster. There was a thirty-foot drop to the bailey below as he made his way along the narrow walkway. He could see the cloaked figure ahead of him, heading in the direction of the gatehouse. He picked up his pace, passing a couple of sentries, to catch up with her.

"My lady?" he said when he came to within a few feet of her.

Startled, Emberley spun around and nearly lost her balance. Gart quickly reached out to grab her so she wouldn't topple over the side. When he was sure she was steady, he immediately dropped his hands.

"God's Bones," Emberley cursed softly, patting her chest as if to restart her heart. "You frightened me."

He smiled, his strong feature shadowed in the moonlight. "My apologies," he said. "I did not mean to."

Emberley wasn't truly upset and she returned his smile to let him know. "I know you did not," she replied, studying him for a brief moment. Her gaze moved over his features in a warm, comforting manner. "I was lost in thought and did not hear you approach."

"Surely there are safer places to lose oneself in thought. Why are you on the battlements?"

She gazed across the wilds of Somerset beyond the castle walls. "I do not sleep well and walking helps me to relax," she told him. "Many are the nights I have spent upon this wall walk."

His eyes glimmered in understanding. "I know the feeling well," he said quietly. "I do not sleep well, either. Even now, I am exhausted from a week in the saddle but I do not know if I will be able to sleep."

Her smile grew. "Perhaps if you stay here any length of time, you and I will keep each other sorry company on nightly walks."

He flashed his teeth, big and straight and white. "There are worse things I can think of."

She laughed softly, leaning against the battlement wall as a night bird sang overhead. In the still of the night, it was calm and soothing. Emberley seemed to be staring at Gart quite intently. From the expression on her face, there seemed to be more on her mind than sleepless nights.

"May I ask you a question?" she finally asked.

"Of course."

"How much did my children steal from you?"

His smile faded and his eyebrows lifted. "Why would you ask that?"

She sighed heavily. "I know what they were doing in the entry earlier this eve," she said softly. "You do not have to pretend. I know they were robbing you."

He shook his head. "They did not rob me."

She cocked her head as if she didn't believe him. "Gart," she lowered her voice reprovingly. "Do not lie for them. I know what they do. They do it to everyone that enters the keep."

He chewed his lip thoughtfully and averted his gaze, leaning on the battlements just as she was. His eyes moved out over the shadowed land.

"How would you know this?"

She sighed with exasperation. "Because many visitors have told me this," she said. "They give them money simply to keep the peace. But I make the boys give it back. If they have stolen from you, please…."

He put up a hand to stop her, turning to look at her lovely face. She was a positively exquisite creature, made more beautiful by the haunting moonlight. As he gazed into her lovely eyes, her beauty nearly erased every thought in his head. It was a struggle to speak rationally.

"They did not steal from me because I did not have any money on my person," he told her. "Therefore, I am not lying to protect them. They did not rob me."

"But they tried."

He reluctantly nodded. "They did."

She held his gaze a moment longer before looking away and shaking her head. "Their motives are so complex," she said. "Romney believes that money will buy things to make Lacy and I happy."

"Lacy?"

"Their two-year-old sister," she explained softly. Then she started throwing her hands around as she spoke. "They rob anyone who enters the keep or, as Romney explains it, they exact a toll from visitors, and then the boys escape the castle and run off into town to purchase things. One time they purchased perfume for me and another time it was a belt, which I am sure they stole. Unless they robbed the king, they could not have afforded it. It terrifies me that they do this. I am afraid that one of these days, they will fall victim to bandits or wild animals. It is not safe for them outside of these walls."

"Nor is it safe for visitors inside of the walls with those three on the loose."

She looked at him and burst out in giggles. "This is serious," she chided him, although she was grinning. "I am nearly at my wits end with them. I apologize that they tried to rob you, Gart. You must think me horrible for raising such terrible children."

He looked at her, a smile playing on his full lips. "I think your children are bold and clever," he said, although it was not quite the truth. "Why do they feel the need to buy you nice things?"

Her smile faded and he could sense her manner becoming guarded. She looked away, off towards the forests to the east. The silence that followed was heavy as she thought on her answer.

"Things… things are not entirely pleasant here," she said, vaguely. "I suppose they think that gifts can make them better."

He watched her profile in the moonlight, a long and pregnant pause. "You are not happy."

It was a statement and not a question. Emberley shrugged. "I have four beautiful children," she said with feigned enthusiasm. "There is much to be thankful for."

He shifted, inadvertently moving closer to her in the process. "I did not question your gratitude," he said. "I questioned your happiness."

She shrugged again, still not meeting his eye. "It does not matter if I am happy or not. My children are healthy and we have much to be thankful for."

He sighed faintly, knowing he shouldn't involve himself in something that did not concern him, but unable to resist. He had known Emberley since childhood. He had seen her grow up for the most part. With Erik gone, he almost felt compelled to act in the man's place, to perhaps advise or console her. It was a foolish thought but he couldn't help himself.

"Does your husband always speak to you so rudely?" he asked quietly.

She looked at him as if startled by the question. "It is his way," she said rather lamely. "It is his right."

"I know what his rights are," Gart said. "I would suspect by the way he spoke to you that he does it quite regularly."

In the moonlight, Emberley's cheeks flushed dully. "It is his way," she repeated softly.

"Perhaps it is, but I do not like it," Gart said. "Based upon that observation, I will ask another question."

"What question is that?"

"Has he ever struck you?"

She hung her head, refusing to look at him. "Gart, I am sure you are asking out of concern, but it truly is none of your affair."

He watched her lowered head, her lovely profile, seeing tears pooling in her eyes. He suddenly felt very, very angry as he realized the truth. She didn't even have to tell him. He knew.

"So he takes his hands to you," he rumbled. " 'Tis a vile, foul man that would strike a woman."

Emberley took a deep breath and wiped quickly at her eyes before the tears could fall. When she turned to look at him, he could read the anxiety on her face.

"I appreciate your concern," she whispered, laying a soft, white hand on his wrist. "I truly do. But you must not ask me any more questions. You would not like the answers and if Julian found out, he would not like that I have told you."

His jaw flexed. "Your husband was quite eager to announce to the men in the hall that he and the queen were lovers," he said. "Is this true?"

She yanked her hand away from his wrist and he would never forget the expression on her face. It was something between disgust and shame. Turning on her heel, she tried to rush away from him but he was on her in an instant, his colossal hands grasping her slender arms. She tried to shrug him off but he wouldn't budge.

"Leave me alone," she snapped. "I do not see where my husband's affairs are any business of yours."

He cooled, releasing her. She stepped away from him but she didn't run. She faced him defensively and he backed off.

"You are correct," he agreed calmly. "They are not my business. I suppose since your only brother was my best friend, perhaps I was showing interest on his behalf. It is simply that I look at you and see that young girl who used to follow Erik around and…forgive me. I should not have overstepped myself. I was only concerned."

Emberley gazed at the man, cooling significantly at his placating words. Then she sighed heavily as if all of the fight suddenly left her. Her defensive mechanism was always close to the surface, preparing to defend her tender heart from her cruel husband and his cruel words. She realized she need not be defensive with Gart. For as long as she'd known him, she'd never once heard of him showing women any manner of cruelty.

"You need not ask forgiveness," she said, remorseful. "It is I who must ask for your grace. I should not have snapped so. I know you are only asking out of concern."

He gazed steadily at her. "Great concern," he corrected gently. "Erik would ask this of me."

She smiled gratefully. "I know," she whispered. "I miss him very much."

"As do I."

"You are a good friend, Gart," she said. "When you were not upsetting my mother, I know she looked upon you as a son."

He gave her a lopsided grin. "I am thinking that Erik and I were much like your boys – into great mischief and mayhem in our youth."

She laughed softly. "Then perhaps you will not think me such a terrible mother that my boys rob anyone who enters the keep."

He was glad to see she was no longer tense and angry with him, thinking he would try yet again to get at the truth of the matter now that he seemed to have broken her defenses down.

"I never thought you a terrible mother," he said quietly. "But I would like to know the truth of your husband's treatment of you."

Her smile faded as she gazed up at him. "Why?" she lifted her shoulders. "There is nothing you can do. He is my husband and may do as he pleases."

Gart knew that and somehow, it hurt his heart. He knew it would have hurt Erik's. "Is he truly the queen's lover?" he asked quietly.

She nodded without emotion. "They have been lovers for almost a year," she replied. "I do not know what she sees in Julian other than his wealth. He is a terrible character and a horrible…."

She trailed off, embarrassed at divulging more information than she should, and Gart's expression grew serious.

"I am truly sorry," he said in his soft, deep voice. "You do not deserve such disrespect. The man is a fool."

Her smile returned, weakly. "You are very kind."

"Kindness has nothing to do with it. It is true."

Her smile grew, now modest. "I appreciate your concern. It has done my heart good to see you, Gart. You remind me of better days."

Her words, kind and sweet, softened him. His heart began to beat strangely in his chest as he reached out and took her small hand in his, bringing it to his lips for a gentle kiss.

"It has done my heart a world of good to see you," he said softly. "I see Erik in your eyes and it comforts me."

Gart's warm kiss on her hand made Emberley's breathing quicken. She was taken back to the days when he was a handsome, very young man and she was his adoring public. He had grown into such a magnificent man she could hardly believe it. She wondered how different her life would have been had she had not married Julian. If only Gart could have been her husband... *but no*. She chased the thought away as quickly as it came. It would do no good for her to long for a man she could never have. That opportunity was long gone.

"I am glad," she squeezed his hand and let it go. "Perhaps we will have more opportunity to speak in the next few days. Do you know when you are leaving?"

He shook his head, wishing she hadn't let go of his hand. Her touch had been magic.

"I do not," he told her. "My liege and your husband are debating that as we speak."

She pulled her cloak more tightly around her slender body. The evening was growing cool and damp in spite of the bright moonlight.

"Then perhaps tomorrow we may...."

She was cut off when something hit the wall just behind Gart. Startled, he jumped forward and threw his arms around her to protect her. But it was the wrong move. Standing several feet behind him was Julian. The arrow he held in his left hand, the second of two he had collected from the armory after spying his wife and Forbes upon the battlements, went sailing in Gart's direction. Gart put up an armored arm and easily deflected it.

Unwinding his arms from Emberley and turning to face Julian as the man approached, Gart could tell by his face that they were in for a good deal of trouble.

"Whore!" Julian screamed.

Gart remained cool, keeping Emberley protectively behind him. "My lord," he said evenly. "Your wife and I were discussing days past when we knew each other. We were discussing her dead brother."

Julian's thin face was livid. He approached Gart and slugged him in the chest, although with Gart's size and Julian's diminutive stature, Gart hardly felt the blow. Still, the implication was obvious.

"You are alone with my wife," he snarled. "You had your arms around her in a disgraceful embrace. How dare you violate my hospitality by taking my wife and... and wooing her."

Gart shook his head. "I did not violate anything, my lord," he was calm and steady. "Your wife and I knew each other as children and were discussing...."

Julian cut him off by shoving him back and reaching around to grab Emberley by the wrist. He pulled hard and she stumbled, nearly toppling over the side of the wall railing. Gart grabbed her to keep her from going over but Julian was wild with fury – he pounded on Gart's steadying arm even as he yanked at his wife.

Emberley didn't put up a fight but she was trying to keep her balance as he yanked. Sensing her hesitation as resistance, Julian slapped her hard across the face.

"I will deal with you, you treacherous whore," he snarled, lifting his hand to strike her again. "You are a…."

Before he could bring the hand down, Gart reached out and grabbed it. Julian turned to scream at him but was faced with an expression so tense, so deadly, that the words died in his throat.

De Lohr was suddenly on the battlements, as were several other de Lohr soldiers, and they were moving for Gart in a group, trying to pull him away from Buckland. Even Emberley, her right cheek stinging from the slap, reached out and grasped Gart by the arm.

"Gart, no," she whispered, begging. "Please let him go."

Gart heard her, as he also heard his liege behind him, firmly and quietly ordering him to let the baron's arm go. But at the moment, Gart could only see Buckland. From a man he had initially found distasteful and unpleasant, that displeasure had grown into full-blown loathing quickly. All he could see was a weak, bully of a man and he hated him for it.

"You will not strike her ever again," he growled. "Is that clear?"

Julian was torn between fear and outrage. "You cannot make demands of me!" he howled. "I will do as I please with my own wife!"

Emberley's soft voice infiltrated Gart's rage. "Please, Gart," she begged softly. "Please let him go."

Her sweet, pleading voice broke through his haze of rage and he tore his eyes away from Buckland long enough to look at her. She mouthed the world "*please*", her big eyes beseeching him, and he reluctantly let the man's hand go. But Julian wasn't a smart man – he slugged Emberley in the jaw simply to demonstrate his power and Gart went straight for his neck.

Emberley screamed as she fell onto the wall walk, trapped beneath Julian as Gart tried to break the man's neck. But soldiers and knights were swarming over them and someone pulled her free of the fighting. Shaken, she looked up to see that it was de Lohr. His handsome face was taut as he made sure she was secure before diving into the fray.

Terrified for Gart, Emberley positioned herself back against the wall as she watched eight men pull Gart off her husband. He was such a big man and fed by such anger that his strength had been astounding. Julian was unhurt but he was furious, screaming threats at Gart. Knowing his wrath would eventually be turned against her, Emberley wisely fled the wall walk and raced for the keep, hearing the angry voices behind her filling the night with foul language and brutality.

Heart pounding, Emberley mounted the steps into the keep, running up the spiral stairs until she reached her children's chambers on the third floor. Scooping sleeping Lacy out of her bed, she fled into the boys' bower and closed the door, throwing the heavy bolt behind her. It would take an army to break the old door down and all of the pounding and screaming Julian would do could not breach it. She knew she was safe, at least for the moment.

With her daughter still sleeping heavily in her arms, Emberley sank to the floor and wept.

CHAPTER THREE

"THANKS TO YOU, I had to pledge men to Buckland's cause, whether or not I agreed with it." De Lohr was rightfully seething. "What on earth possessed you to touch another man's wife?"

Gart stood in the dark, dusty stables, silently and stoically taking a verbal lashing from his liege. He deserved it, he knew, but he didn't regret his actions. Not one bit. De Lohr knew this, which was why he was so furious.

Gart Forbes was the best knight he had ever seen, and he had seen a lot of good men in his life. Many talented men had passed beneath his command or his brother's command at one time or another. But Forbes was different – they didn't call the man "Sach" without good reason. He was power, strength, cunning and brutality all rolled into one but, more than that, he was grossly unpredictable, as evidenced by the scene on the wall walk.

Gart could have easily snapped Buckland's neck but he hadn't – he just wanted to scare the man. Forbes had bouts of volatile fury but he was as cunning as a fox. He knew exactly what he was doing when he wrapped his hands around Buckland's throat.

"I did not touch her, at least not in the manner you are suggesting," Gart told him. "I swear upon my oath that we were simply talking."

David gazed at him a moment, trying to read the unreadable face, before letting out a heavy sigh.

"I believe you," he said, with less anger than he had been exhibiting earlier. "But Buckland has used this entire circumstance into blackmailing me for support."

"Blackmailing?"

De Lohr nodded with some disgust. "If I provide him with four hundred men, he will not have you thrown in jail," he said, throwing up his hands. "I have no choice. Unless I want to lose my best knight, then I must support him. I hope you liked France because you will be heading back there shortly."

The last sentence was spoken with some irony. Gart stared at de Lohr for a long moment before breaking down into a puzzled, disgusted expression. He just shook his head and turned away, pacing over to his charger. The beast was tethered in a far stall because he was so vicious, but with Gart, the black and white steed was as tame as a kitten. The animal nickered softly as Gart approached and began stroking the big neck, giving it an affectionate slap.

"My apologies, my lord," he finally said. "It was not my intention to put you in an awkward position."

De Lohr sighed with regret. "What were you doing with her alone up on the battlements? Did you not stop to think that it was a compromising position to say the least?"

Gart shook his head. "We were speaking," he reiterated. "I have not seen her in twelve years, this lovely young girl who was the sister of my best friend. Seeing her… it is as if I am seeing him again. I simply wanted to speak with her. Perhaps old memories are clouding my judgment but I do not believe so. We did nothing wrong."

De Lohr nodded his head in resignation. "Even so, you are not the one who will ultimately suffer in all of this. It will be her. Buckland is a vicious fool with a mean streak in him. She will be lucky if he does not beat her senseless for this."

Gart knew that but it didn't help the raging fury he felt, starting in his toes and rising up through his big body. By the time it reached his head, his face was red and he was sweating. De Lohr caught his expression and he put his hands up as if to stop the building tide. He knew that look well.

"There is nothing you can do about it," he told him sternly. "Your interference is what caused all of this in the first place. Had you simply walked away…."

"He struck her," Gart cut him off. "Could you have stood by while he did that?"

David rolled his eyes. "She is the man's wife, Gart. He can do with her as he pleases."

"Even assault her?"

"Aye, even assault her."

"You did not answer my question. Could you have stood by and watched him beat her?"

De Lohr eyed him, finally shaking his head after a moment. "Nay," he admitted, looking away. "But it is different with me. I am a man of rank and you are a mere knight. What you did, in most circles, would land you in the vault for the rest of your life."

Gart's jaw ticked dangerously. His face was still red and sweating, never a good sign. "I will not let him take out his anger on her. I cannot."

De Lohr threw up his hands. "You have no choice," he said. "Gart, I will send you home this night if you cannot control yourself. You are already in enough trouble. Anymore from you and I may not be able to placate Buckland. He would throw you in jail and bury the key."

Gart didn't reply. Anything more out of his mouth would get him in deeper trouble. De Lohr was only trying to help him and he knew it.

There was a big pile of dry hay on the other side of his charger, stacked there by the grooms. He made his way over to the hay and plopped down into it, lying back against the clean, scratchy stuff. Folding his hands over his chest, he closed his eyes.

David watched him a moment, knowing that Gart was doing what he needed to do to calm down and stay on an even keel. Without another word, he quit the stable for his own quarters in the keep, a small room that Buckland had allocated to him.

Even as de Lohr made his way through the cold, bright night towards the distant keep, he knew that this was not the end of it. He could feel it. Gart felt as if he were protecting his best friend's sister and unable to process that the fact she was another man's wife took precedence.

David wondered what horrors awaited them come the dawn.

☙

GART AWOKE TO three little faces staring at him. Startled, he sat up, hay stuck to his back and arms. It was just growing light outside, the sky in shades of pinks and blues as the sun pierced the veil of night. It was cold in the stable as the animals began to stir, hungry for their morning meal. Gart rubbed the sleep from his eyes as Romney, Orin and Brendt gazed back at him.

"What are you doing here?" he asked them, shaking the sleep from his mind.

The boys were not particularly well dressed against the cold and Romney looked particularly pale, which concerned him. They all looked a little lost. Gart also noticed something else – without all of the white powder on him, Romney's ashen face bore a striking resemblance to his long-dead uncle. The mirror image was uncanny.

"We are sorry we tried to rob you yesterday," Romney said somberly.

Gart rested his arms on his up-bent knees. "You did not rob me. I did not have anything for you to steal."

Romney and Orin looked at each other, bewildered. "We tried to rob you," Romney looked back at Gart. "Mother told us to apologize."

Gart thought on that a moment, studying Romney. More and more, he could see Erik in the boy, even down to the expressions on the child's face. He couldn't help but think how thrilled Erik would have been with his three nephews.

"I see," he said. "Then your apology is accepted."

Romney cocked his head. "She said that you and Uncle Erik were friends."

Gart nodded. "We were," he said, eyeing the brown-haired, blue-eyed boy. "In fact, I was just thinking that you look a good deal like him. He was a great knight."

"Mother said he died in the Holy Land for Richard's damn crusade."

Gart fought of a smile. "She said that?"

Romney nodded solemnly. "She said it was damn foolish and damn stupid."

Gart bit his lip to keep from smiling. "Your uncle was a great knight on the crusade," he said. "We fought together for almost two years."

"How did he die?"

Gart didn't feel like smiling anymore and the grin faded from his lips. "A Saracen arrow pierced his helm," he said quietly. "It lodged in his eye and it killed him."

"Oh," Romney looked thoughtful, distressed. "Did it hurt?"

"I would imagine so."

Romney continued to look distressed as Orin and Brendt decided the charger was more worthy of their attention. Gart saw the boys moving towards it.

"Do not touch him," he admonished. "He will stomp you."

The boys drew back in fear, gravitating back towards their eldest brother. Romney was still looking at Gart.

"Since we are sorry that we robbed you, will you give us money anyway?" he asked.

Gart gazed steadily at the boy. "Why?"

"Because Mother needs a present."

"Why?"

"She is unhappy."

Gart's good humor faded completely. "Why is she unhappy?"

Romney seemed to lose some of his confidence. He looked at Orin and Brendt, who gazed back at him with wide eyes. Suddenly, Orin rushed Gart and grabbed the neck of his wrinkled tunic.

"Becausth," Orin had an extremely lazy tongue and a bad lisp. He yanked at Gart's tunic and began hitting him with his little fists. "He did thisth… and thisth… and she cries."

Gart put his hands on the lad to both steady him and pull him off. Even Romney moved forward to pull his violent brother away from the enormous knight. But Gart didn't miss the gist of what the boy said. In fact, he began to feel the familiar fury build in his feet again and start to work its way up. *She will be lucky if he does not beat her senseless for this.* He wondered if de Lohr's prophetic words had come true.

"Who?" he had Orin by the arms but he was looking at Romney. "Who made your mother cry?"

Romney wouldn't look at him. He was more interested in pulling Orin away from the man. "Father," he muttered. "He hits her and she cries."

The slow build of fury began to gain speed. Gart could feel the sweat popping out on his forehead and he struggled to control the brewing anger.

"Did he hit her last night?" he asked quietly.

Romney shook his head. "Nay," he replied, giving Orin a good yank and sending the boy off of Gart and onto his bum. "He did it this morning. She cried and cried."

The rage reached Gart's head and his cheeks began to turn red. "Where is your mother now?"

Romney shrugged, either losing interest with the conversation or afraid to say much more. He fidgeted uncomfortably. "In her bed," he said. "Father is leaving for London. Will you give us money now so we can buy her a present?"

Gart stared at the little boy, feeling a great many emotions in his heart that he was unfamiliar with. He'd spent most of his life allowing only one emotion to infiltrate his mind, and that emotion was fury. It worked well for his purposes. The soldiers didn't call him insane for no reason. They called him that because it was the truth.

But now he was feeling something more than fury. He was feeling great sadness and grief, feeling as if he had failed somehow. When he'd meant to protect Emberley, it seemed as if he'd only gotten her into more trouble. He had no reason to believe that the boys were lying to him and he muttered a silent prayer to Erik, begging the man's forgiveness for what he had done. It was a struggle to keep a rein on what he was feeling.

"Where is your father?" he asked, hoping he didn't sound as angry as he felt.

Romney shrugged. "In the hall," he said. "I heard him tell people that he was leaving for London today to see the queen."

Gart stood up from the hay pile, brushing pieces of hay off his arms and back as he went to the bags that were lodged against the wall next to his charger. The grooms began coming into the barn to feed and water the animals but he ignored them as he began to rummage through his bags. Although he wanted very much to go charging into the keep, he kept his cool. He knew that would only make the situation worse. He had to keep his wits about him. But he noticed as he dug through his bags, his hands were shaking.

As he rummaged through his possessions, he realized he had company. He glanced to either side and noticed that Romney was on one side of him while Orin and Brendt were on the other. They were watching him dig through his satchels with great interest. Surely the knight had many wonderful things in that dark and mysterious bag. Finally, they could stand it no longer.

Romney reached in and grabbed a strip of carefully rolled leather, pulling it out to look at it as Gart took it away. As he was distracted with Romney, Orin reached in and pulled out a very sharp razor. Gart snatched it before the boy could injure himself and told the boys not to stick their hands where they did not belong. As he packed away the razor and rolled up the leather strip, little Brendt literally climbed into the largest of his satchels.

He gleefully tried to bury himself in the clothing that had been carefully rolled up and packed. Gart removed the boy from his satchel but in doing so, it opened up the door for Orin to plunge head-first into another bag. Soon, Gart was occupied removing the boys from his bags rather than searching for clean clothes. He would remove one and another would take his place. He swore there were twelve children and not just three, so fast they moved. Finally, he stood up and spread his big arms.

"Cease," he roared softly, jabbing a finger at Brendt, who was back in his satchel and trying to pull one of Gart's enormous tunics over his head. "You – out. And stay out. All of you stay out."

Brendt started to weep and Romney turned his big, blue eyes to Gart. "He wants the tunic," he told him.

Gart waved his hands impatiently. "Fine," he snapped without force, lifting the boy out of his bag. "He can take the tunic. But you other two – get out and stay out. I do not have time for this foolery."

Dejected and scolded, Romney and Orin actually began to repack one of Gart's bags. He looked at their sad faces and began to feel like an ogre for scolding them. But he didn't apologize. He helped them replace what they had pulled out. With both bags repacked, he removed one carefully rolled-up tunic, removed his dirty tunic, put it back in his bag and then sealed everything up.

Meanwhile, Brendt had managed to pull the tunic he stole from Gart over his little blond head and was trying to walk with it. The tunic was far too long for him and he tripped, laughing as he wallowed in the dirt. Romney and Orin giggled at him and Gart couldn't help but crack a smile as the lad tried to get back to his feet without tripping again. He couldn't quite seem to manage it, which sent Romney and Orin howling with laughter. Even Gart was snorting, his gaze moving over the three boys. They were good boys even if they were mischievous. Erik would have been proud. Gart was starting to realize what Erik's mother and father must have gone through when Erik and Gart were into mayhem. Now, he understood.

Pulling the fresh tunic over his head, he proceeded to reclaim his armor. The boys watched with great interest as he pulled on his mail coat, his hauberk, and proceeded with pieces of plate armor that were still fairly rare. He wore great, well-crafted plate armor on both forearms that bore the crest of de Lohr. He also had a big piece that fit over his chest and back, hung from his shoulders by big leather straps. Romney inspected the piece curiously and even tried to lift it, but Gart discouraged him. It was an expensive piece and too heavy for the boy to play with. Leaving the chest piece in the stable next to his bags, Gart headed out into the dusty courtyard.

Dunster Castle was a massive place built in a long, rectangular configuration which positioned the stables on the far north side, away from the keep but near the kitchens and the well. There were two blocks of stables and as Gart emerged from the block that extended on the northeast wall, he could see that there was great activity from the block lodged against the north wall.

Two chargers and several other horses had been brought out and were being prepared, as well as a big wagon that was being loaded down with goods. The animals were excited and their breath puffed up in great clouds in the cold morning air. Gart's gaze lingered on the group, knowing it must be the baron's escort to London. Just as he passed from the stable yards into the big bailey beyond, he caught sight of de Lohr heading towards him.

Gart was surprisingly in control as he and David came together. Romney, Orin and Brendt were clustered around Gart, following him like puppies, something that didn't go unnoticed by de Lohr. He eyed the boys as he came upon Gart.

"Are you summoning your own army?" he asked.

Gart had no idea what he was talking about until he followed David's gaze and saw the boys standing around him. He grunted.

"Do not let their small size fool you," he told him. "They are brave beyond measure."

David lifted an eyebrow at Romney. "I know," he said. "They were unafraid to rob me yesterday when I entered the keep."

Gart lifted an eyebrow at Romney, who looked both fearful and defiant. "Mother only said we had to apologize to you. She did not say we had to apologize to everyone."

Gart just shook his head, resigned. "What did you steal from the baron?"

Romney's brow furrowed deeply. "Not much."

David fought off a grin. "I gave them a pence each to let me pass," he said. "I was afraid for my life."

Gart's eyes narrowed at Romney. "You will give him back his money. That is not a request."

Romney was deeply displeased. "It is upstairs."

"Go and get it. *Now*."

The boys darted off, scattering like frightened chickens at Gart's deep and growling tone. They weren't used to such commands but the instinct for survival bade them to obey it. David waited until they were well away before looking at Gart with a grin.

"Brave and bold boys," he commented. "I thought it was quite humorous."

"Did they hit you with a stick?"

"They tried. I paid them before they could whack me."

"Yet I did not," Gart wriggled his eyebrows. "They were not afraid to attack me when I would not pay their demands."

David snorted. "I would like to have seen that. The mighty Gart Forbes being set upon by three small bandits. Those children did what grown men are afraid to do."

Gart shrugged, his gaze trailing up to the enormous dark-stoned keep to the right. "Their mother interrupted what would have surely been a bloodbath," he said. "Speaking of their mother, I am told that the earl beat her this morning."

David's smile faded and he sighed heavily. "That is why I have come to find you," he said quietly. "Knowing how you feel, I wanted you to hear the news from me."

"Did he kill her?"

David shook his head sadly. "From what I can gather, she barricaded herself in her children's room last night after the incident on the wall to avoid her husband's wrath," he said quietly. "My chamber is on the floor below theirs and I could hear him banging at the door a good portion of the night. Then it faded away until dawn when, apparently, one of her sons unbolted the door and the earl was lying in wait. He locked the children out of the room, including the crying two-year-old girl, and proceeded to beat his wife. I could hear the woman screaming. By the time I reached the floor, I found four crying children staring back at me. Even the servants were crying. So I took everyone down to the hall, made sure the children were tended, before returning to the chamber. By the time I returned, all was silent and the earl was just emerging. He told me that if I wanted to remain a trusted ally, I would leave well enough alone."

By this time, Gart was the familiar shade of red. The veins on his neck and temple were standing out, throbbing. De Lohr knew that look. It was always the calm before the storm.

"Did you see Lady Emberley?" Gart asked through clenched teeth. "Is someone at least tending to her injuries?"

David shook his head. "The earl will not let anyone near her," he explained, sickened. "He says she must be punished. The servants are too afraid to go against his wishes and I cannot do it because he would not only break his alliance with my brother, but more than likely accuse me the same way he accused you. The man has a warped and dangerous mind."

Gart couldn't stand it any longer. He began to walk towards the keep. David reached out and grabbed him.

"Wait," he snapped softly. "The earl is in the hall and if he sees you …."

Gart turned on him, his face red with rage. "I am going to see to Lady Emberley's health and well-being, and her husband be damned," he snarled. "Her brother was my best friend and I will not…."

De Lohr put up a silencing hand. "Listen to me," he cut him off. "I knew you would not be stopped but I also know that if Buckland sees you, there is no telling how volatile this situation will become. Do you not understand that your actions have brought this about? What do you think will happen if you do not understand your place and continue this behavior? It appears as if you are attempting to come between the baron and his wife."

Gart was so angry that he was sweating, his big hands working much in the same manner they did right before he plunged into battle. He was starting to reach the point that every man feared, the insanity that would soon overtake him. It was at that point that he would start ripping heads from bodies, Buckland's included, and to hell with the consequences.

"I am not trying to come between the baron and his wife," he said in a manner that suggested the whole idea ridiculous.

"It appears that way. Can you swear to me that there is nothing more to this than the concern of an old friend?"

"I can swear it."

De Lohr sighed softly. He wasn't sure if he believed him, given the fact that the man was acting in a way he had never seen before, but he would not dispute him. At least, not yet. "Very well," he said quietly. "But you must show restraint, Gart. This situation is delicate to say the least."

"I am going to see to her," Gart repeated, his jaw gnashing. "I must see what has happened. If you cannot understand that, then I cannot explain it to you any more than I already have."

David just shook his head, tightening his grip on Gart's arm. "I understand," he lowered his voice. "I also understand that whatever I say, you will do as you please."

"That is a fair assessment."

David sighed in resignation. "Then we must act carefully. You and I will enter the keep and I will distract the baron so you can slip to the upper floors to tend the lady. Meanwhile, I am going to tell Buckland that I have sent you away and hopefully that will appease him. But in doing so, you need to make every effort to stay out of the man's way until he leaves for London. If you hear him coming, hide or all will be lost, including his trust in me. Is that clear?"

Gart was agreeable with the plan for the most part. "It is," he replied. "My charger and possessions are still here, however. What if the earl sees them?"

David shook his head. "He would not know your possessions or charger from the next man's. He does not seem particularly bright or observant."

Satisfied, Gart could feel himself calming now that there was a plan, something that would enable him to see to Emberley. Taking a deep breath, he struggled to calm himself. "And once the baron has left Dunster? What then?"

David shrugged. "You can remain here if you wish, at least until I send for you. I suspect we will be mobilizing for France in the next three or four weeks, so be prepared. If you leave Dunster, go back to Denstroude because that is where I shall look for you."

Gart nodded, the dull, red tone of his face fading to a normal healthy color. David eyed the man one last time, just to make sure he was going to do as he was told, before finally nodding his head.

"Very well," he turned for the keep. "Let us make our move."

Gart was right behind him.

Read the rest of **ARCHANGEL** in eBook or in paperback.

About Kathryn Le Veque

Medieval Just Got Real.

KATHRYN LE VEQUE is a USA TODAY Bestselling author, an Amazon All-Star author, and a #1 bestselling, award-winning, multi-published author in Medieval Historical Romance and Historical Fiction. She has been featured in the NEW YORK TIMES and on USA TODAY's HEA blog. In March 2015, Kathryn was the featured cover story for the March issue of InD'Tale Magazine, the premier Indie author magazine. She was also a quadruple nominee (a record!) for the prestigious RONE awards for 2015.

Kathryn's Medieval Romance novels have been called 'detailed', 'highly romantic', and 'character-rich'. She crafts great adventures of love, battles, passion, and romance in the High Middle Ages. More than that, she writes for both women AND men – an unusual crossover for a romance author – and Kathryn has many male readers who enjoy her stories because of the male perspective, the action, and the adventure.

On October 29, 2015, Amazon launched Kathryn's Kindle Worlds Fan Fiction site WORLD OF DE WOLFE PACK. Please visit Kindle Worlds for Kathryn Le Veque's World of de Wolfe Pack and find many action-packed adventures written by some of the top authors in their genre using Kathryn's characters from the de Wolfe Pack series. As Kindle World's FIRST Historical Romance fan fiction world, Kathryn Le Veque's World of de Wolfe Pack will contain all of the great story-telling you have come to expect.

Kathryn loves to hear from her readers. Please find Kathryn on Facebook at Kathryn Le Veque, Author, or join her on Twitter @kathrynleveque, and don't forget to visit her website at www.kathrynleveque.com.

Made in the USA
San Bernardino, CA
20 January 2017